WILBUR SMITH
SMITH WILBUR SM
WILBUR SMITH
SMITH WILBUR SM
WILBUR SMITH
SMITH WILBUR SM
WILBUR SMITH
SMITH WILBUR SM
WILBUR SMITH
SMITH WILBUR SM
WILBUR SMITH
SMITH WILBUR SM

£1.50
161

Wilbur
SMITH

Wilbur SMITH

When the Lion Feeds

The Diamond Hunters

Eagle in the Sky

Gold Mine

Shout at the Devil

Heinemann/Octopus

When the Lion Feeds first published in Great Britain in 1964
The Diamond Hunters first published in Great Britain in 1971
Eagle in the Sky first puplished in Great Britain in 1974
Gold Mine first published in Great Britain in 1970
Shout at the Devil first published in Great Britain in 1968

This edition first published in 1976 by
William Heinemann Limited
15–16 Queen Street, London W.1
in association with
Octopus Books Limited
59 Grosvenor Street, London W.1

ISBN 0 7064 0573 0

Printed in Great Britain by
Jarrold & Sons Ltd., Norwich

CONTENTS

When the Lion Feeds

Wilbur SMITH

WHEN THE LION FEEDS

This book is for

ELFREDA AND HERBERT JONES SMITH

1. NATAL

I

A single wild pheasant flew up the side of the hill almost brushing the tips of the grass in its flight. It drooped its wings and hung its legs as it reached the crest and then dropped into cover. Two boys and a dog followed it up from the valley: the dog led, with his tongue flopping pink from the corner of his mouth, and the twins ran shoulder to shoulder behind him. Both of them were sweating in dark patches through the khaki shirts, for the African sun still had heat although it stood half-mast down the sky.

The dog hit the scent of the bird and it stopped him quivering: for a second he stood sucking it up through his nostrils, and then he started to quarter. He worked fast, back and forth, swinging at the end of each tack, his head down and only his back and his busy tail showing above the dry brown grass. The twins came up behind him. They were gasping for breath, for it had been a hard pull up the curve of the hill.

'Keep out to the side, you'll get in my way,' Sean panted at his brother and Garrick moved to obey. Sean was his senior by four inches in height and twenty pounds in weight: this gave him the right to command. Sean transferred his attention back to the dog.

'Put him up, Tinker. Seek him up, boy.'

Tinker's tail acknowledged Sean's instructions, but he held his nose to the ground. The twins followed him, tensed for the bird to rise. They carried their throwing sticks ready and moved forward a stealthy pace at a time, fighting to control their breathing. Tinker found the bird crouched flat in the grass; he jumped forward giving tongue for the first time, and the bird rose. It came up fast on noisy wings, whirling out of the grass.

Sean threw; his kerrie whipped past it. The pheasant swung away from the stick, clawing at the air with frantic wings, and Garrick threw. His kerrie cartwheeled up, hissing, until it smacked into the pheasant's fat brown body. The bird toppled, feathers flurried from it and it fell. They went after it. The pheasant scurried broken-winged through the grass ahead of them, and they shouted with excitement as they chased it. Sean got a hand to it. He broke its neck and stood laughing, holding the warm brown body in his hands, and waited for Garrick to reach him.

'Ring-a-ding-a-doody, Garry, you sure gave that one a beauty!'

Tinker jumped up to smell the bird, and Sean stooped and held it so he could get his nose against it. Tinker snuffled it, then tried to take it in his mouth, but Sean pushed his head away and tossed the bird to Garrick. Garrick hung it with the others on his belt.

'How far do you reckon that was–fifty feet?' Garrick asked.

'Not as much as that,' Sean gave his opinion. 'More like thirty.'

'I reckon it was at least fifty. I reckon it was farther than any you've hit today.' Success had made Garrick bold. The smile faded from Sean's face.

'Yeah?' he asked.

'Yeah!' said Garrick. Sean pushed the hair off his forehead with the back of his hand, his hair was black and soft and it kept falling into his eyes.

'What about that one down by the river? That was twice as far.'

'Yeah?' asked Garrick.

'Yeah!' said Sean truculently.

'Well, if you're so good, how did you miss this one–hey? You threw first. How come you missed, hey?'

Sean's already flushed faced darkened and Garrick realized suddenly that he had gone too far. He took a step backwards.

'You'd like to bet?' demanded Sean. It was not quite clear to Garrick on what Sean wished to bet, but from past experience he knew that whatever it was the issue would be settled by single combat. Garrick seldom won bets from Sean.

'It's too late. We'd better be getting home. Pa will clobber us if we're late for dinner.' Sean hesitated and Garrick turned, ran back to pick up his kerrie then set off in the direction of home. Sean trotted after him, caught up with him and passed him. Sean always led. Having proved conclusively his superior prowess with the throwing sticks Sean was prepared to be forgiving. Over his shoulder he asked, 'What colour to you reckon Gypsy's foal will be?'

Garrick accepted the peace-offering with relief and they fell into a friendly discussion of this and a dozen other equally important subjects. They kept running: except for an hour, when they had stopped in a shady place by the river to roast and eat a couple of their pheasants, they had run all day.

Up here on the plateau it was grassland that rose and fell beneath them as they climbed the low round hills and dropped into the valleys. The grass around them moved with the wind: waist-high grass, soft dry grass the colour of ripe wheat. Behind them and on each side the grassland rolled away to the full range of the eye, but suddenly in front of them was the escarpment. The land cascaded down into it, steeply at first then gradually levelling out to become the Tugela flats. The Tugela river was twenty miles away across the flats, but today there was a haze in the air so they could not see that far. Beyond the river, stretched far to the north and a hundred miles east to the sea, was Zululand. The river was the border. The steep side of the escarpment was cut by vertical gulleys, and in the gulleys grew dense, olive-green bush.

Below them, two miles out on the flats, was the homestead of Theunis Kraal. The house was a big one, Dutch-gabled and smoothly thatched with combed grass. There were horses in the small paddock: many horses, for the twins' father was a wealthy man. Smoke from the cooking fires blued the air over the servants' quarters and the sound of someone chopping wood carried faintly up to them.

Sean stopped on the rim of the escarpment and sat down in the grass. He took hold of one of his grimy bare feet and twisted it up into his lap. There was a hole in the ball of his heel from which he had pulled a thorn earlier in the day and now it was plugged with dirt. Garrick sat down next to him.

'Man, is that going to hurt when Ma puts iodine on it!' gloated Garrick. 'She'll have to use a needle to get the dirt out. I bet you yell–I bet you yell your head off!'

Sean ignored him. He picked a stalk of grass and started probing it into the wound. Garrick watched with interest. Twins could scarcely have been less alike. Sean was already taking on the shape of a man: his shoulders were thickening, and there was hard muscle forming in his puppy fat. His colouring was vivid: black hair, skin brown from the sun, lips and cheeks that glowed with the fresh young blood beneath their surface, and blue eyes, the dark indigo-blue of cloud shadow on mountain lake.

Garrick was slim, with the wrists and ankles of a girl. His hair was an undecided brown that grew wispy down the back of his neck, his skin was freckled, his nose and the rims of his pale blue eyes were pink with persistent hayfever. He was fast losing interest in Sean's surgery. He reached across and fiddled with one of Tinker's pendulous ears, and this broke the rhythm of the dog's panting; he gulped twice and the saliva dripped from the end of his tongue. Garrick lifted his head and looked down the slope. A little below where they were sitting was the head of one of the bushy gullies. Garrick caught his breath.

'Sean, look there–next to the bush!' His whisper trembled with excitement.

'What's it?' Sean looked up startled. Then he saw it.

'Hold Tinker.' Garrick grabbed the dog's collar and pulled his head around to prevent him seeing and giving chase. 'He's the biggest old inkonka in the world,' breathed Garrick. Sean was too absorbed to answer.

The bushbuck was picking its way warily out of the thick cover. A big ram, black with age; the spots on his haunches were faded like old chalk marks. His ears pricked up and his spiral horns held high, big as a pony, but stepping daintily, he came out into the open. He stopped and swung his head from side to side, searching for danger, then he trotted diagonally down the hill and disappeared into another of the gullies. For a moment after he had gone the twins were still, then they burst out together.

'Did you see him, hey–did you see them horns?'

'So close to the house and we never knew he was there–'

They scrambled to their feet jabbering at each other, and Tinker was infected with their excitement. He barked around them in a circle. After the first few moments of confusion Sean took control simply by raising his voice above the opposition.

'I bet he hides up in the gulley every day. I bet he stays there all day and comes out only at night. Let's go and have a look.'

Sean led the way down the slope.

On the fringe of the bush, in a small cave of vegetation that was dark and cool and carpeted with dead leaves, they found the ram's hiding-place. The ground was trampled by his hooves and scattered with his droppings and there was the mark of his body where he had lain. A few loose hairs, tipped with grey, were left on the bed of leaves. Sean knelt down and picked one up.

'How are we going to get him?'

'We could dig a hole and put sharpened sticks in it,' suggested Garrick eagerly.

'Who's going to dig it–you?' Sean asked.

'You could help.'

'It would have to be a pretty big hole,' said Sean doubtfully. There was silence while both of them considered the amount of labour involved in digging a trap. Neither of them mentioned the idea again.

'We could get the other kids from town and have a drive with kerries,' said Sean.

'How many hunts have we been on with them? Must be hundreds by now, and we haven't even bagged one lousy duiker–let alone a bushbuck.' Garrick hesitated and then went on. 'Besides, remember what that inkonka did to Frank Van Essen, hey? When it finished sticking him they had to push all his guts back into the hole in his stomach!'

'Are you scared?' asked Sean.

'I am not, so!' said Garrick indignantly, then quickly, 'Gee, it's almost dark. We'd better run.'

They went down the valley.

2

Sean lay in the darkness and stared across the room at the grey oblong of the window. There was a slice of moon in the sky outside. Sean could not sleep: he was thinking about the bushbuck. He heard his parents pass the door of the bedroom; his stepmother said something and his father laughed: Waite Courteney had a laugh as deep as distant thunder.

Sean heard the door of their room close and he sat up in bed. 'Garry.' No answer.

'Garry.' He picked up a boot and threw it; there was a grunt. 'Garry.'

'What you want?' Garrick's voice was sleepy and irritable.

'I was just thinking–tomorrow's Friday.'

'So?'

'Ma and Pa will be going into town. They'll be away all day. We could take the shotgun and go lay for that old inkonka.'

Garrick's bed creaked with alarm.

'You're mad!' Garrick could not keep the shock out of his voice. 'Pa would kill us if he caught us with the shotgun.' Even as he said it he knew he would have to find a stronger argument that that to dissuade his brother. Sean avoided punishment if possible, but a chance at a bushbuck ram was worth all his father's right arm could give. Garrick lay rigid in his bed, searching for words.

'Besides, Pa keeps the cartridges locked up.'

It was a good try, but Sean countered it.

'I know where there are two buckshots that he has forgotten about: they're in the big vase in the dining-room. They've been.there over a month.'

Garrick was sweating. He could almost feel the sjambok curling round his buttocks, and hear his father counting the strokes: eight, nine, ten.

'Please, Sean, let's think of something else. . . .'

Across the room Sean settled back comfortably on his pillows. The decision had been made.

3

Waite Courteney handed his wife up into the front seat of the buggy. He patted her arm affectionately then walked around to the driver's side, pausing to fondle the horses and settle his hat down over his bald head. He was a big man, the buggy dipped under his weight as he climbed up into the seat. He gathered up the reins, then he turned and his eyes laughed over his great hooked nose at the twins standing together on the veranda.

'I would esteem it a favour if you two gentlemen could arrange to stay out of trouble for the few hours that your mother and I will be away.'

'Yes, Pa,' in dutiful chorus.

'Sean, if you get the urge to climb the big blue gum tree again then fight it, man, fight it.'

'All right, Pa.'

'Garrick, let us have no more experiments in the manufacture of gunpowder–agreed?'

'Yes, Pa.'

'And don't look so innocent. That really frightens the hell out of me!'

Waite touched the whip to the shiny round rumps in front of him and the buggy started forward, out along the road to Ladyburg.

'He didn't say anything about not taking the shotgun,' whispered Sean virtuously. 'Now you go and see if all the servants are out of the way–if they see us, they'll kick up a fuss. Then come round to the bedroom window and I'll pass it out to you.'

Sean and Garrick argued all the way to the foot of the escarpment. Sean was carrying the shotgun across one shoulder, hanging on to the butt with both hands.

'It was my idea, wasn't it?' he demanded.

'But I saw the inkonka first,' protested Garrick. Garrick was bold again: with every yard put between him and the house his fear of reprisal faded.

'That doesn't count,' Sean informed him. 'I thought of the shotgun, so I do the shooting.'

'How come you always have the fun?' asked Garrick, and Sean was outraged at the question.

'When you found the hawk's nest by the river, I let you climb for it. Didn't I? When you found the baby duiker, I let you feed it. Didn't I?' he demanded.

'All right. So I saw the inkonka first, why don't you let me take the shot?'

Sean was silent in the face of such stubbornness, but his grip on the butt of the shotgun tightened. In order to win the argument Garrick would have to get it away from him–this Garrick knew and he started to sulk. Sean stopped among the trees at the foot of the escarpment and looked over his shoulder at his brother.

'Are you going to help–or must I do it alone?'

Garrick looked down at the ground and kicked at a twig. He sniffed wetly; his hayfever was always bad in the mornings.

'Well?' asked Sean.

'What do you want me to do?'

'Stay here and count to a thousand slowly. I'm going to circle up the slope and wait where the inkonka crossed yesterday. When you finish counting come up the gulley. Start shouting when you are about halfway up. The inkonka will break the same way as yesterday–all right?'

Garrick nodded reluctantly

'Did you bring Tinker's chain?'

Garrick pulled it from his pocket, and at the sight of it the dog backed away. Sean grabbed his collar, and Garrick slipped it on. Tinker laid his ears flat and looked at them reproachfully.

'Don't let him go. That old inkonka will rip him up. Now start counting,' said Sean and began climbing. He kept well out to the left of the gulley. The grass on the slope was slippery under his feet, the gun was heavy and there was sharp lumps of rock in the grass. He stubbed his toe and it started to bleed, but he kept on upwards. There was a dead tree on the edge of the bush that Sean had used to mark the bushbuck's hide. Sean climbed above it and stopped just below the crest of the slope where the moving grass would break up the silhouette of his head on the skyline. He was panting. He found a rock the size of a beer barrel to use as a rest for the gun, and he crouched behind it. He laid the stock of the gun on the rock, aimed back down the hill and traversed the barrels left and right to make sure his field of fire was clear. He imagined the bushbuck running in his sights and he felt excitement shiver along his forearms, across his shoulders and up to the back of his neck.

'I won't lead on him–he'll be moving fairly slowly, trotting most probably. I'll go straight at his shoulders,' he whispered.

He opened the gun, took the two cartridges out of his shirt pocket, slid them into the breeches and snapped the gun closed. It took all the strength of both his hands to pull back the big fancy hammers, but he managed it and the gun was double-loaded and cocked. He laid it on the rock in front of him again and stared down the slope. On his left the gulley was a dark-green smear on the hillside, directly below him was open grass where the bushbuck would cross. He pushed impatiently at the hair of his forehead: it was damp with sweat and stayed up out of his eyes.

The minutes drifted by.

'What the hell is Garry doing? He's so stupid sometimes!' Sean muttered and almost in answer he heard Garrick shout below him. It was a small sound, far down the slope and muffled by the bush. Tinker barked once without enthusiasm; he was also sulking, he didn't like the chain. Sean waited for his forefinger on one trigger, staring down at the edge of the bush. Garrick shouted again–and the bushbuck broke from cover.

It came fast into the open with its nose up and its long horns held flat against its back. Sean moved his body sideways swinging the gun with its run, riding the pip of the foresight on its black shoulder. He fired the left barrel and the recoil threw him off balance; his ears hummed with the shot and the burnt powder smoke blew back into his face. He struggled to his feet still holding the gun. The bushbuck was down in the grass, bleating like a lamb and kicking as it died.

'I got him,' screamed Sean. 'I got him first shot! Garry, Garry! I got him, I got him!'

Tinker came pelting out of the bush dragging Garry behind him by the chain and, still screaming, Sean ran down to join them. A stone rolled under his foot and he fell. The shotgun flew out of his hand and the second barrel fired. The sound of the explosion was very loud.

When Sean scrambled on to his feet again Garrick was sitting in the grass whimpering–whimpering and staring at his leg. The blast of the shotgun had smashed into it and churned the flesh below the knee into tatters–bursting it open so the bone chips showed white in the wood and the blood pumped dark and strong and thick as custard.

'I didn't mean it. . . . Oh God, Garry, I didn't mean it. I slipped. Honest, I slipped.' Sean was staring at the leg also. There was no colour in his face, his eyes were big and dark with horror. The blood pumped out on to the grass.

'Stop it bleeding! Sean, please stop it. Oh, it's sore! Oh! Sean, please stop it!'

Sean stumbled across to him. He wanted to vomit. He unbuckled his belt and strapped it round the leg, and the blood was warm and sticky on his hands. He used his sheathed knife to twist the belt tight. The pumping slowed and he twisted harder.

'Oh, Sean, it's sore! It's sore. . . .' Garrick's face was waxy-white and he was starting to shiver as the cold hand of shock closed on him.

'I'll get Joseph,' Sean stammered. 'We'll come back quickly as we can. Oh, God, I'm sorry!' Sean jumped up and ran. He fell, rolled to his feet and kept running.

They came within an hour. Sean was leading three of the Zulu servants. Joseph, the cook, had brought a blanket. He wrapped Garrick and lifted him and Garrick fainted as his leg swung loosely. As they started back down the hill Sean looked out across the flats: there was a little puff of dust on the Ladyburg road. One of the grooms was riding to fetch Waite Courteney.

They were waiting on the veranda of the homestead when Waite Courteney came back to Theunis Kraal. Garrick was conscious again. He lay on the couch: his face was white and the blood had soaked through the blanket. There was blood on Joseph's uniform and blood had dried black on Sean's hands. Waite Courteney ran up on to the veranda; he stooped over Garrick and drew back the blanket. For a second he stood staring at the leg and then very gently he covered it again.

Waite lifted Garrick and carried him down to the buggy. Joseph went with him and they settled Garrick on the back seat. Joseph held his body and Garrick's stepmother took the leg on her lap to stop it twisting. Waite Courteney climbed quickly into the driver's seat: he picked up the reins, then he turned his head and looked at Sean still standing on the veranda. He didn't speak, but his eyes were terrible–Sean could not meet them. Waite Courteney used the whip on the horses and drove them back along the road to Ladyburg: he drove furiously with the wind streaming his beard back from his face.

Sean watched them go. After they had disappeared among the trees he remained standing alone on the veranda; then suddenly he turned and ran back through the house. He ran out of the kitchen door and across the yard to the saddle-room, snatched a bridle down from the rack and ran to the paddock. He picked a bay mare and worked her into a corner of the fence until he could slip his arm around her neck. He forced the bit into her mouth, buckled the chin strap and swung up on to her bare back.

He kicked her into a run and put her to the gate, swaying back as her body heaved up under him and falling forward on her neck as she landed. He gathered himself and turned her head towards the Ladyburg road.

It was eight miles to town, and the buggy reached it before Sean. He found it outside Doctor Van Rooyen's surgery: the horses were blowing hard, and their bodies were dark with sweat. Sean slid down off the mare's back; he went up the steps to the surgery door and quietly pushed it open. There was the sweet reek of chloroform in the room. Garrick lay on the table, Waite and his wife stood on each side of him, and the doctor was washing his hands in an enamel basin against the far wall. Ada Courteney was crying silently, her face blurred with tears. They all looked at Sean standing in the doorway.

'Come here,' said Waite Courteney, his voice flat and expressionless. 'Come and stand here beside me. They're going to cut off your brother's leg and, by Christ, I'm going to make you watch every second of it!'

4

They brought Garrick back to Theunis Kraal in the night. Waite Courteney drove the buggy very slowly and carefully and Sean trailed a long way behind it. He was cold in his thin khaki shirt, and sick in the stomach with what he had seen. There were bruises on his upper arm where his father had held him and forced him to watch.

The servants had lanterns burning on the veranda. They were standing in the shadows, silent and anxious. As Waite carried the blanket-wrapped body up the front steps one of them called softly in the Zulu tongue. 'The leg?'

'It is gone,' Waite answered gruffly.

They sighed softly all together and the voice called again. 'He is well?'

'He is alive,' said Waite.

He carried Garrick through to the room that was set aside for guests and sickness. He stood in the centre of the floor holding the boy while his wife put fresh sheets on the bed; then he laid him down and covered him.

'Is there anything else we can do?' asked Ada.

'We can wait.'

Ada groped for her husband's hand. 'Please, God, let him live,' she whispered. 'He's so young.'

'It's Sean's fault!' Waite's anger flared up suddenly. 'Garry would never had done it on his own.' He tried to disengage Ada's hand.

'What are you going to do?' she asked.

'I'm going to beat him! I'm going to thrash the skin off him!'

'Don't, please don't.'

'What do you mean?'

'He's had enough. Didn't you see his face?'

Waite's shoulders sagged wearily and he sat down on the armchair beside the bed. Ada touched his cheek.

'I'll stay here with Garry. You go and try to get some sleep, my dear.'

'No,' Waite said. She sat down on the side of the chair and Waite put his arm around her waist. After a long while they slept, huddled together on the chair beside the bed.

5

The days that followed were bad. Garrick's mind escaped from the harness of sanity and ran wild into the hot land of delirium. He panted and twisted his fever-flushed face from side to side; he cried and whimpered in the big bed; the stump of his leg puffed up angrily and the stitches were drawn so tight it seemed they must tear out of the swollen flesh. The infection oozed yellow and foul-smelling on to the sheets.

Ada stayed by him all that time. She swabbed the sweat from his face and changed the dressings on his stump, she held the glass for him to drink and gentled him when he raved. Her eyes sunk darkly into their sockets with fatigue and worry, but she would not leave him. Waite could not bear it. He had the masculine dread of suffering that threatened to suffocate him if he stayed in the room: every half hour or so he came in and stood next to the bed and then he turned away and went back to his restless wandering around the house. Ada could hear his heavy tramp along the corridors.

Sean stayed in the house also: he sat in the kitchen or at the far end of the veranda. No one would speak to him, not even the servants; they chased him when he tried to sneak into the bedroom to see Garrick. He was lonely with the desolate loneliness of the guilty–for Garry was going to die, he knew it by the evil silence that hung over Theunis Kraal. There was no chatter nor pot-clatter from the kitchens, no rich deep laughter from his father: even the dogs were subdued. Death was at Theunis Kraal. He could smell it on the soiled sheets that were brought through to the kitchen from Garrick's room; it was a musky smell, the smell of an animal. Sometimes he could almost see it: even in bright daylight sitting on the veranda he sensed it crouched near him like a shadow on the edge of his vision. It had no form as yet. It was a darkness, a coldness that was gradually building up around the house, gathering its strength until it could take his brother.

On the third day Waite Courteney came roaring out of Garrick's room. He ran through the house and out into the stable yard. 'Karlie. Where are you? Get a saddle on to Rooiberg. Hurry, man, hurry–damn you. He's dying, do you hear me, he's dying.'

Sean did not move from where he sat against the wall next to the back door. His arm tightened around Tinker's neck and the dog touched his cheek with a cold nose; he watched his father jump up on to the stallion's back and ride. The hooves beat away towards Ladyburg and when they were gone he stood up and slipped into the house: he listened outside Garrick's door and then he opened it quietly and went in. Ada turned towards him, her face was tired. She looked much older than her thirty-five years, but her black hair was drawn back behind her head into a neat bun and her dress was fresh and clean. She was still a beautiful woman despite her exhaustion. There was a gentleness about her, a goodness that suffering and worry could not destroy. She held out her hand to Sean and he crossed and stood beside her chair and looked down at Garrick. Then he knew why his father had gone to fetch the doctor. Death was in the room–strong and icy cold hovered over the bed. Garrick lay very ill: his face was yellow, his eyes were closed and his lips were cracked and dry.

All the loneliness and the guilt came swelling up into Sean's throat and choked him into sobs, sobs that forced him to his knees and he put his face into Ada's lap and cried. He cried for the last time in his life, he cried as a man cries–painfully, each sob tearing something inside him.

Waite Courteney came back from Ladyburg with the doctor. Once more Sean was driven out and the door closed. All night he heard them working in Garrick's room, the murmuring of their voices and the scuff of feet on the yellow wood floor. In the morning it was over. The fever was broken and Garrick was alive. Only just alive–his eyes were sunk into dark holes like those of a skull. His body and his mind were never to recover completely from that brutal pruning.

It was slow–a week before he was strong enough to feed himself. His first need was for his brother, before he was able to talk above a whisper it was, 'Where's Sean?'

And Sean, still chastened, sat with him for hours at a time. Then when Garrick slept Sean escaped from the room, and with a fishing-rod or his hunting sticks and Tinker barking behind him went into the veld. It was a measure of Sean's repentance that he allowed himself to be contained within the sick-room for such long periods. It chafed him like ropes on a young colt: no one would ever know what it cost him to sit quietly next to Garrick's bed while his body itched and burned with unexpended energy and his mind raced restlessly.

Then Sean had to go back to school. He left on a Monday morning while it was still dark. Garrick listened to the sounds of departure, the whicker of the horses outside on the driveway and Ada's voice reciting last minute instructions: 'I've put a bottle of cough mixture under your shirts, give it to Fraülein as soon as you unpack. Then she'll see that you take it at the first sign of a cold.'

'Yes, Ma.'

'There are six vests in the small case–use a new one every day.'

'Vests are sissy things.'

'You will do as you're told, young man.' Waite's voice, 'Hurry up with your porridge–we've got to get going if I'm to have you in town by seven o'clock.'

'Can I say goodbye to Garry?'

'You said goodbye last night–he'll still be asleep now.'

Garrick opened his mouth to call out, but he knew his voice would not carry. He lay quietly and listened to the chairs scraping back from the dining-room table, the procession of footsteps out on to the veranda, voices raised in farewells and at last the wheels of the buggy crunching gravel as they moved away down the drive. It was very quiet after Sean had left with his father.

After that the weekends were, for Garrick, the only bright spots in the colourless passage of time. He longed for them to come, and each one was an eternity after the last–time passes slowly for the young and the sick. Ada and Waite knew a little of how he felt. They moved the centre of the household to his room: they brought two of the fat leather armchairs from the lounge and put them on each side of his bed and they spent the evenings there. Waite with his pipe in his mouth and a glass of brandy at his elbow, whittling at the wooden leg he was making and laughing his deep laugh, Ada with her knitting and the two of them trying to reach him. Perhaps it was this conscious effort that was the cause of their failure, or perhaps it is impossible to reach back down the years to a small boy. There is always that reserve, the barrier between the adult and the secret world of youth. Garrick laughed with them and they talked together, but it was not the same as having Sean there. During the day Ada had the running of a large household and there were fifteen thousand acres of land and two thousand head of cattle that needed Waite's attention. That was the loneliest time for Garrick. If it had not been for the books, he might not have been able to bear it. He read everything that Ada brought to him: Stevenson, Swift, Defoe, Dickens and even Shakespeare. Much of it he didn't understand, but he read hungrily and the opium of the printed word helped him through the long days until Sean came home each Friday.

When Sean came home it was like a big wind blowing through the house. Doors slammed, dogs barked, servants scolded and feet clattered up and down the passages. Most of the noise was Sean's, but not all of it. There were Sean's followers: youngsters from his class at the village school. They accepted Sean's authority as willingly as did Garrick, and it was not only Sean's fists that won this acceptance but also the laughter and the sense of excitement that went with him. They came out to Theunis Kraal in droves that summer, sometimes as many as three on one bare-backed pony: sitting like a row of sparrows on a fence rail. They came for the added attraction of Garry's stump. Sean was very proud of it.

'That's where the doc sewed it up,' pointing to the row of stitch marks along the pink fold of scar tissue.

'Can I touch it, man?'

'Not too hard or it'll burst open.' Garrick had never received attention like this in his life before. He beamed round the circle of solemn, wide-eyed faces.

'It feels funny–sort of hot.'

'Was it sore?'

'How did he chop the bone–with an axe?'

'No.' Sean was the only one in a position to answer technical questions of this nature. 'With a saw. Just like a piece of wood.' He made the motions with his open hand.

But even this fascinating subject couldn't hold them for long and presently there would be a restlessness among them.

'Hey, Sean, Karl and I know where there's a nest of squawkers–you wanta have a look?' or 'Let's go and catch frogs,' and Garrick would cut in desperately.

'You can have a look at my stamp collection if you like. It's in the cupboard there.'

'Naw, we saw it last week. Let's go.'

This was when Ada, who had been listening to the conversation through the open kitchen door, brought in the food. Koeksusters fried in honey, chocolate cakes with peppermint icing, watermelon konfyt and half a dozen other delicacies. She knew they wouldn't leave until it was finished and she knew also that there'd be upset stomachs when it was, but that was preferable to Garrick lying alone and listening to the others riding off into the hills.

The weekends were short, gone in a breathless blur. Another long week began for Garrick. There were eight of them, eight dreary weeks before Doctor Van Rooyen agreed to let him sit out on the veranda during the day. Then suddenly the prospect of being well again became a reality for Garrick. The leg that Waite was making was nearly finished: he shaped a leather bucket to take the stump and fitted it to the wood with flat-headed copper nails; he worked carefully, moulding the leather and adjusting the straps that would hold it in place. Meanwhile, Garrick exercised along the veranda, hopping beside Ada with an arm around her shoulder, his jaws clenched with concentration and the freckles very prominent on his face that had been without the sun for so long. Twice a day Ada sat on a cushion in front of Garrick's chair and massaged the stump with methylated spirits to toughen it for its first contact with the stiff leather bucket.

'I bet old Sean'll be surprised, hey? When he sees me walking around.'

'Everyone will,' Ada agreed. She looked up from his leg and smiled.

'Can't I try it now? Then I can go out fishing with him when he comes on Saturday.'

'You mustn't expect too much, Garry, it's not going to be easy at first. You will have to learn to use it. Like riding a horse–you remember how often you fell off before you learned to ride.'

'But can I start now?'

Ada reached for the spirits bottle, poured a little into her cupped hand and spread it on the stump. 'We'll have to wait until Doctor Van Rooyen tells us you're ready. It won't be long now.'

It wasn't. After his next visit Doctor Van Rooyen spoke to Waite as they walked together to the doctor's trap.

'You can try him with the peg-leg–it'll give him something to work for. Don't let him overtire himself and watch the stump doesn't get rubbed raw. We don't want another infection.'

'Peg-leg.' Waite's mind echoed the ugly word as he watched the trap out of sight. 'Peg-leg': he clenched his fists at his sides, not wanting to turn and see the pathetically eager face behind him on the veranda.

6

'Are you sure that's comfortable?' Waite squatted in front of Garrick's chair adjusting the leg, and Ada stood next to him.

'Yes, yes, let me try it now. Gee, old Sean will be surprised, hey? I'll be able to go back with him on Monday, won't I?' Garrick was trembling with eagerness.

'We'll see,' Waite grunted non-committally. He stood up and moved round beside the chair.

'Ada, my dear, take his other arm. Now listen, Garry, I want you to get the feel of it first. We'll help you up and you can just stand on it and get your balance. Do you understand?'

Garrick nodded vigorously.

'All right, then up you come.'

Garrick drew the leg towards him and the tip scraped across the wooden floor. They lifted him and he put his weight on it.

'Look at me–I'm standing on it. Hey, look I'm standing on it.' His face glowed. 'Let me walk, come on! Let me walk.'

Ada glanced at her husband and he nodded. Together they led Garrick forward. He stumbled twice, but they held him. Klunk and klunk again the peg rang on the floor boards. Before they reached the end of the veranda Garrick had learned to lift the leg high as he swung it forward. They turned and he stumbled only once on the way back to the chair.

'That's fine, Garry, you're doing fine,' laughed Ada.

'You'll be on your own in no time,' Waite grinned with relief. He had hardly dared to hope it would be so easy, and Garrick fastened on his words. 'Let me stand on my own now.'

'Not this time, boy, you've done well enough for one day.'

'Oh, gee, Pa. Please. I won't try and walk, I'll just stand. You and Ma can be ready to catch me. Please, Pa, please.'

Waite hesitated and Ada added her entreaty. 'Let him, dear, he's done so well. It'll help build up his confidence.'

'Very well. But don't try to move,' Waite agreed. 'Are you ready, Garry? Let him go!' They took their hands off him cautiously. He teetered slightly and their hands darted back.

'I'm all right–leave me.' He grinned at them confidently and once more they released him. He stood straight and steady for a moment and then he looked down at the ground. The grin froze on his face. He was alone on a high mountain, his stomach turned giddily within him and he was afraid, desperately unreasonably afraid. He lurched violently and the first shriek tore from him before they could hold him. 'I'm falling. Take it off! Take it off!'

They sat him in the chair with one swift movement.

'Take it off! I'm going to fall!' The terrified screams racked Waite as he tore at the straps that held the leg.

'It's off, Garry, you're safe. I'm holding you.' Waite took him to his chest and held him, trying to quieten him with the strength of his arms and the security of his own big body, but Garrick's terrified struggling and his shrieks continued.

'Take him to the bedroom, get him inside.' Ada spoke urgently and Waite ran with him, still holding him against his chest.

Then for the first time Garrick found his hiding-place. At the moment when his terror became too great to bear he felt something move inside his head, fluttering behind his eyes like the wings of a moth. His vision greyed as though he was in a mist bank. The mist thickened and blotted out all sight and sound. It was warm in the mist–warm and safe. No one could touch him here, for it wrapped and protected him. He was safe.

'I think he's asleep,' Waite whispered to his wife, but there was a puzzled expression in his voice. He looked carefully at the boy's face and listened to his breathing.

'It happened so quickly though–it isn't natural. And yet–and yet he looks all right.'

'Do you think we should call the doctor?' Ada asked.

'No.' Waite shook his head. 'I'll just cover him up and stay with him until he wakes.'

He woke in the early evening, sat up and smiled at them as though nothing had happened. Relaxed and shyly cheerful, he ate a big supper and no one mentioned the leg. It was almost as though Garrick had forgotten about it.

7

Sean came home on the following Friday afternoon. He had a black eye–not a fresh one; it was already turning green round the edges of the bruise. Sean was very reticent on the subject of how he had obtained it. He brought with him also a clutch of fly-catchers' eggs which he gave to Garrick, a live red-lipped snake in a cardboard box which Ada immediately condemned to death despite Sean's impassioned speech in its defence, and a bow carved from M'senga wood which was, in Sean's opinion, the best wood for a bow.

His arrival wrought the usual change in the household of Theunis Kraal–more noise, more movement and more laughter.

There was a huge roast for dinner that evening, with potatoes baked in their jackets. These were Sean's favourite foods and he ate like a hungry python.

'Don't put so much in your mouth,' Waite remonstrated from the head of the table, but there was a fondness in his voice. It was hard not to show favouritism with his sons. Sean accepted the rebuke in the spirit it was given. 'Pa, Frikkie Oberholster's bitch had pups this week, six of them.'

'No,' said Ada firmly.

'Gee, Ma, just one.'

'You heard your mother, Sean.' Sean poured gravy over his meat, cut a potato in half and lifted one piece to his mouth. It had been worth a try. He hadn't really expected them to agree.

'What did you learn this week?' Ada asked. This was a nasty question. Sean had learned as much as was necessary to avoid trouble–no more.

'Oh, lots of things,' he replied airily and then to change the subject. 'Have you finished Garry's new leg yet, Pa?'

There was silence. Garrick's face was expressionless and he dropped his eyes to his plate. Sean put the other half of the potato in his mouth and spoke around it.

'If you have, me and Garry can go fishing up at the falls tomorrow.'

'Don't talk with your mouth full,' snapped Waite with unnecessary violence. 'You've got the manners of a pig.'

'Sorry, Pa,' Sean muttered. The rest of the meal passed in uneasy silence, and as soon as it finished, Sean escaped to the bedroom. Garry went with him, hopping along the passage with one hand on the wall to balance himself.

'What's Pa so mad about?' Sean demanded resentfully as soon as they were alone.

'I don't know.' Garrick sat on the bed. 'Sometimes he just gets mad for nothing–you know that.'

Sean pulled his shirt off over his head, screwed it into a ball and threw it against the far wall.

'You'd better pick it up, else there'll be trouble,' Garrick warned mildly. Sean dropped his pants and kicked them after the shirt. This show of defiance put him in a better mood. He walked across and stood naked in front of Garrick.

'Look,' he said with pride. 'Hairs!'

Garrick inspected them. Indisputably they were hairs.

'There aren't very many.' Garrick couldn't disguise the envy in his voice.

'Well, I bet I've got more than you have,' Sean challenged. 'Let's count them.'

But Garrick knew himself to be an outright loser; he slipped off the bed and hopped across the room. Steadying himself against the wall, he stooped and picked up Sean's discarded clothing, he brought it back and dropped it in the soiled-linen basket beside the door. Sean watched him and it reminded him of his unanswered question.

'Has Pa finished your leg yet, Garry?'

Garry turned slowly, he swallowed and nodded once, a quick jerky movement.

'What's it like? Have you tried it yet?'

The fear was on Garrick again. He twisted his face from side to side as though seeking an escape. There were footsteps in the passage outside the door. Sean dived at his bed and snatching up his nightgown pulled it over his head as he slid between the sheets. Garrick was still standing beside the clothes basket when Waite Courteney came into the room. 'Come on, Garry, what's holding you up?'

Garrick hurried across to his bed and Waite looked at Sean. Sean grinned at him with all the charm of his good looks and Waite's face softened into a grin also. 'Nice to have you home again, boy.' It was impossible to be angry with Sean for long.

He reached out and took a handful of Sean's thick black hair. 'Now I don't want to hear any talking in here after the lamp's out–do you understand?'

He tugged Sean's head from side to side gently, embarrassed by the strength of his feeling for his son.

8

The next morning Waite Courteney rode back to the homestead for his breakfast when the sun was high. One of the grooms took his horse and led it away to the paddock and Waite stood in front of the saddle-room and looked around him. He looked at the neat white posts of the paddock, at the well-swept yard, at his house filled with fine furniture. It was a good feeling to be rich–especially when you knew what it was like to be poor. Fifteen thousand acres of good grassland, as many cattle as the land would carry, gold in the bank. Waite smiled and started across the yard.

He heard Ada singing in the dairy.

'How rides the farmer
Sit, sit, so
Sit, sit, so–tra la
The Capetown girls say
Kiss me quick
Kiss me quick–tra la.'

She had a clear sweet voice and Waite's smile broadened–it was a good feeling to be rich and to be in love. He stopped at the door of the dairy; because of the thick stone walls and heavy thatch it was cool and dark in the room. Ada stood with her back to the door, her body moving in time to the song and the turning of the butter churn. Waite watched her for a moment, then he walked up behind her and put his arms around her waist.

Startled, she turned within his arms and he kissed her on the mouth. 'Good morning, my pretty maid.'

She relaxed against him. 'Good morning, sir,' she said.

'What's for breakfast?'

'Ah, what a romantic fool I married!' She sighed. 'Come along, let's go and see.'

She took off her apron, hung it behind the door, patted her hair into place and held her hand out to him. They walked hand-in-hand across the yard and into the kitchen. Waite sniffed loudly.

'Smells all right. Where are the boys?'

Joseph understood English though he could not speak it. He looked up from the stove.

'Nkosi, they are on the front veranda.'

Joseph had the typical moon-round face of the Zulu, when he smiled his teeth were big and white against the black of his skin.

'They are playing with Nkosizana Garry's wooden leg.'

Waite's face flushed. 'How did they find it?'

'Nkosizana Sean asked me where it was and I told him you had put it in the linen cupboard.'

'You bloody fool!' roared Waite. He dropped Ada's hand and ran. As he reached the lounge he heard Sean shout and immediately there was the sound of someone falling heavily on the veranda. He stopped in the middle of the lounge floor; he couldn't bear to go out and face Garrick's terror. He felt sick with dread and with his anger at Sean.

Then he heard Sean laugh. 'Get off me, man, don't just lie there.'

And then, incredibly, Garrick's voice. 'Sorry, it caught in the floor boards.'

Waite walked across to the window and looked out on to the veranda. Sean and Garrick lay in a heap together near the far end. Sean was still laughing and on Garrick's face was a set nervous smile. Sean scrambled up. 'Come on. Get up.'

He gave Garrick his hand and dragged him to his feet. They stood clinging to each other, Garrick balancing precariously on his peg. 'I bet if it was me I could just walk easy as anything,' said Sean.

'I bet you couldn't, it's jolly difficult.'

Sean let go of him and stood back with his arms spread ready to catch him. 'Come on.'

Sean walked backwards in front of him and Garrick followed unsteadily, his arms flapping out sideways as he struggled to keep his balance, his face rigid with concentration. He reached the end of the veranda and caught on to the rail with both hands. This time he joined in Sean's laughter.

Waite became aware that Ada was standing beside him; he glanced sideways at her and her lips formed the words 'come away.' She took his arm.

9

At the end of June 1876 Garrick went back to school with Sean. It was almost four months since the shooting. Waite drove them. The road to Ladyburg was through open forest, two parallel tracks with the grass growing in between–it brushed the bottom of the buggy. The horses trotted in the tracks, their hooves silent on the thick powder dust. At the top of the first rise Waite slowed the horses and turned his seat to look back at the homestead. The early sun gave the whitewashed walls of Theunis Kraal an orange glow and the lawns around the house were brilliant green. Everywhere else the grass was dry in the early winter and the leaves of the trees were dry also. The sun was not yet high enough to rob the veld of its colour and light it only with the flat white glare of midday. The leaves were golden and russet and red-brown, the same red-brown as the bunches of Afrikander cattle that grazed among the trees. Behind it all was the back-drop of the escarpment, striped like a zebra with the green black bush that grew in its gullies.

'Look, there's a hoopoe, Sean.'

'Yeah, I saw it long ago. That's a male.'

The bird flew up from in front of the horses: chocolate and black and white wings, its head crested like an Etruscan helmet.

'How do you know?' challenged Garrick.

''Cause of the white in its wings.'

'They've all got white in their wings.'

'They haven't–only the males.'

'Well, all the ones I've seen got white in their wings,' said Garrick dubiously.

'Perhaps you've never seen a female. They're jolly rare. They don't come out of their nests much.'

Waite Courteney smiled and turned back in his seat. 'Garry's right, Sean, you can't tell the difference by their feathers. The male's a little bigger, that's all.'

'I told you,' said Garrick, brave under his father's protection.

'You know everything,' muttered Sean sarcastically. 'I suppose you read it in all those books, hey?'

Garrick smiled complacently. 'Look, there's the train.'

It was coming down the escarpment, dragging a long grey plume of smoke behind it. Waite started the horses into a trot. They went down to the concrete bridge over the Baboon Stroom.

'I saw a yellow fish.'

'It was a stick, I saw it too.'

The river was the boundary of Waite's land. They crossed the bridge and went up the other side. In front of them was Ladyburg. The train was running into the town past the cattle sale pens; it whistled and shot a puff of steam high into the air.

The town was spread out, each house padded around by its orchard and garden. A thirty-six ox team could turn in any of the wide streets. The houses were burnt brick or whitewashed, thatched or with corrugated-iron roofs painted green or dull red. The square was in the centre and the spire of the church was the hub of Ladyburg. The school was on the far side of town.

Waite trotted the horses along Main Street. There were a few people on the side walks; they moved with early morning stiffness beneath the flamboyant trees that lined the street and every one of them called a greeting to Waite. He waved his whip at the men and lifted his hat to the women, but not high enough to expose the bald dome of his head. In the centre of town the shops were open, and standing on long thin legs in front of his bank was David Pye. He was dressed in black like an undertaker.

'Morning, Waite.'

'Morning, David,' called Waite a little too heartily. It was not six months since he had paid off the last mortgage on Theunis Kraal and the memory of debt was too fresh in his mind; he felt as embarrassed as a newly released prisoner meeting the prison governor on the street.

'Can you come in and see me after you've dropped off your boys?'

'Have the coffee ready,' agreed Waite. It was well known that no one was ever offered coffee when they called on David Pye. They went on down the street, turned left at the far end of Church Square, passed the courthouse and down the dip to the school hostel.

There was half a dozen Scotch carts and four-wheelers standing in the yard. Small boys and girls swarmed over them unloading their luggage. Their fathers stood in a group at one end of the yard–brown-faced men, with carefully brushed beards, uncomfortable in their suits which still showed the creases of long hanging. These men lived too far out for the children to make the daily journey into school. Their land sprawled down to the banks of the Tugela or across the plateau halfway to Pietermaritzburg.

Waite stopped the buggy, climbed down and loosened the harness on his horses and Sean jumped from the outside seat to the ground and ran to the nearest bunch of boys. Waite walked across to the men; their ranks opened for him, they smiled their welcomes and in turn reached for his right hand. Garrick sat alone on the front seat of the buggy, his leg stuck out stiffly in front of him and his shoulders hunched as though he were trying to hide.

After a while Waite glanced back over his shoulder. He saw Garrick sitting alone and he made as if to go to him, but stopped immediately. His eyes quested among the swirl of small bodies until they found Sean. 'Sean.'

Sean paused in the middle of an animated discussion. 'Yes, Pa.'

'Give Garry a hand with the case.'

'Aw, gee, Pa–I'm talking.'

'Sean!' Waite scowled with both face and voice.

'All right, I'm going.' Sean hesitated a moment longer and then went to the buggy.

'Come on, Garry. Pass the cases down.'

Garrick roused himself and climbed awkwardly over the back of the seat. He handed the luggage down to Sean who stacked it beside the wheel, then turned to the group that had followed him across.

'Karl, you carry that. Dennis, take the brown bag. Don't drop it, man, it's got four bottles of jam in it.' Sean issued his instructions.

'Come on, Garry.'

They started off towards the hostel and Garrick climbed down from the buggy and limped quickly after them.

'You know what, Sean?' said Karl loudly. 'Pa let me start using his rifle.'

Sean stopped dead, and then more with hope than conviction, 'He did not!'

'He did,' Karl said happily. Garrick caught up with them and they all stared at Karl.

'How many shots did you have?' asked someone in an awed voice.

Karl nearly said, 'Six' but changed it quickly.

'Oh, lots–as many as I wanted.'

'You'll get gun-shy–my Pa says if you start too soon you'll never be a good shot.'

'I never missed once,' flashed Karl.

'Come on,' said Sean and started off once more–he had never been so jealous in his life. Karl hurried after him.

'I bet you've never shot with a rifle, Sean, I bet you haven't, hey?' Sean smiled mysteriously while he searched for some new topic; he could see that Karl was going to kick the subject to death.

From the veranda of the hostel a girl ran to meet him.

'It's Anna,' said Garrick.

She had long brown legs, skinny; her skirts fussed about them as she ran. Her hair was black, her face was small with a pointed chin. 'Hello, Sean.'

Sean grunted. She fell in beside him, skipping to keep pace with him.

'Did you have a nice holiday?'

Sean ignored her, always coming and trying to talk to him, even when his friends were watching.

'I've got a whole tin of shortbread, Sean. Would you like some?' There was a flash of interest in Sean's eyes; he half turned his head towards her, for Mrs Van Essen's shortbread was rightly famous throughout the district, but he caught himself and kept grimly on towards the hostel.

'Can I sit next to you in class this term, Sean?'

Sean turned furiously on her. 'No, you can't. Now go away–I'm busy.'

He went up the steps. Anna stood at the bottom; she looked as though she was going to cry and Garrick stopped shyly beside her.

'You can sit next to me if you like,' he said softly.

She glanced at him, looking down at his leg. The tears cleared and she giggled. She was pretty. She leaned towards him.

'Peg-leg,' she said and giggled again. Garrick blushed so vividly, and suddenly his eyes watered. Anna put both hands to her mouth and giggled through them, then she turned and ran to join her friends in front of the girls' section of the hostel. Still blushing, Garrick went up the steps after Sean; he steadied himself on the banisters.

Fraülein stood at the door of the boys' dormitory. Her steel-rimmed spectacles and the iron grey of her hair gave her face an exaggerated severity, but this was relieved by the smile with which she recognized Sean.

'Ah, my Sean, you have come.' What she actually said was, 'Ach, mein Sean, you haf gom.'

'Hello, Fraülein,' Sean gave her his number one very best smile.

'Again you have grown,' Fraülein measured him with her eyes. 'All the time you grow, already you are the biggest boy in the school.'

Sean watched her warily, ready to take evasive action if she attempted to embrace him as she did sometimes when she could no longer contain her feelings. Sean's blend of charm, good looks and arrogance had completely captured her Teutonic heart.

'Quickly, you must unpack. School is just now starting.' She turned her attention to her other charges and Sean, with relief, led his men through into the dormitory.

'Pa says that next weekend I can use his rifle for hunting, not just targets,' Karl steered the conversation back.

'Dennis, put Garry's case on his bed.' Sean pretended not to hear.

There were thirty beds arranged along the walls, each with a locker beside it. The room was as neat and cheerless as a prison or a school. At the far end a group of five or six boys sat talking. They looked up as Sean came in but no greetings were exchanged–they were the opposition.

Sean sat down on his bed and bounced experimentally, it was hard as a plank. Garrick's peg thumped as he walked down the dormitory and Ronny Pye, the leader of the opposition, whispered something to his friends and they all laughed, watching Garrick. Garrick blushed again and sat down quickly on his bed to hide his leg.

'I guess I'll shoot duiker first before Pa lets me shoot kudu or bushbuck,' Karl stated and Sean frowned.

'What's the new teacher like?' he asked.

'He looks all right,' one of the others answered. 'Jimmy and I saw him at the station yesterday.'

'He's thin and got a moustache.'

'He doesn't smile much.'

'I suppose next holiday Pa will take me shooting across the Tugela,' Karl said aggressively.

'I hope he's not too keen on spelling and things,' Sean declared. 'I hope he doesn't start all that decimal business again, like old Lizard did.'

There was a round of agreement and then Garrick made his first contribution. 'Decimals are easy.'

There was a silence while they all looked at him.

'I might even shoot a lion,' said Karl.

IO

There was a single schoolroom to accommodate the youngest upwards of both sexes. Double desks; on the walls a few maps, a large set of multiplication tables and a picture of Queen Victoria. From this dais Mr Anthony Clark surveyed his new pupils. There was a hushed anticipation; one of the girls giggled nervously and Mr Clark's eyes sought the sound, but it stopped before he found it.

'It is my unfortunate duty to attempt your education,' he announced. He wasn't joking. Long ago his sense of vocation had been swamped by an intense dislike for the young: now he taught only for the salary.

'It is your no more pleasant duty to submit to this with all the fortitude you can muster,' he went on, looking with distaste at their shining faces.

'What's he saying?' whispered Sean without moving his lips.

'Shh,' said Garrick.

Mr Clark's eyes swivelled quickly and rested on Garrick. He walked slowly down the aisle between the desks and stopped beside him; he took a little of the hair that grew at Garrick's temple between his thumb and his forefinger and jerked it upwards. Garrick squeaked and Mr Clark returned slowly to his dais.

'We will now proceed. Standard Ones kindly open your spelling books at page one. Standard Twos turn to page fifteen. . . .' He went on allocating their work.

'Did he hurt you?' breathed Sean. Garrick nodded almost imperceptibly and Sean conceived an immediate and intense hatred for the man. He stared at him.

Mr Clark was a little over thirty years old–thin, and his tight three-piece suit emphasized this fact. He had a pale face made sad by his drooping moustache, and his nose was upturned to such a degree that his nostrils were exposed; they pointed out of his face like the muzzle of a double-barrelled shotgun. He lifted his head from the list he held in his hand and aimed his nostrils straight at Sean. For a second they stared at each other.

'Trouble,' thought Mr Clark; he could pick them unerringly. 'Break him before he gets out of control.'

'You, boy, what's your name?'

Sean turned elaborately and looked over his shoulder. When he turned back there was a little colour in Mr Clark's cheeks. 'Stand up.'

'Who, me?'

'Yes, you.'

Sean stood.

'What's your name?'

'Courteney.'

'Sir!'

'Courteney, sir.'

They looked at each other. Mr Clark waited for Sean to drop his eyes but he didn't.

'Big trouble, much bigger than I thought,' he decided and said aloud, 'All right, sit down.'

There was an almost audible relaxation of tension in the room. Sean could sense the respect of the others around him; they were proud of the way he had carried it off. He felt a touch on his shoulder. It was Anna, the seat behind him was as close as she could sit to him. Ordinarily her presumption would have annoyed him, but now that small touch on his shoulder added to his glow of self-satisfaction.

An hour passed slowly for Sean. He drew a picture of a rifle in the margin of his spelling book then rubbed it out carefully, he watched Garrick for a while until his brother's absorption with his work irritated him.

'Swot,' he whispered, but Garrick ignored him.

Sean was bored. He shifted restlessly in his seat and looked at the back of Karl's neck–there was a ripe pimple on it. He picked up his ruler to prod it. Before he could do so Karl lifted his hand as if to scratch his shoulder but there was a scrap of paper between his fingers. Sean put down the ruler and surreptitiously reached for the note. He held it on his lap, on it was written one word.

'Mosquitoes.'

Sean grinned. Sean's imitation of a mosquito was one of the many reasons why the previous schoolmaster had resigned. For six months old Lizard had believed that there were mosquitoes in the room–then for the next six months he had known there were not. He had tried every ruse he could think of to catch the culprit, and in the end it had got him. Every time the monotonous hum began the tic in the corner of his mouth became more noticeable.

Now Sean cleared his throat and started to hum. Instantly the room was tense with suppressed laughter. Every head, including Sean's, was bent studiously over a book. Mr Clark's hand hesitated in writing on the blackboard but then went on again evenly.

It was a clever imitation; by lowering and raising the volume Sean gave the effect of an insect moving about the room. A slight trembling at his throat was the only sign that he was responsible.

Mr Clark finished writing and turned to face the room. Sean did not make the mistake of stopping, he allowed the mosquito to fly a little longer before settling.

Mr Clark left his dais and walked down the row of desks furthest from Sean. Once or twice he paused to check the work of one of his pupils. He reached the back of the room and moved across to Sean's row. He stopped at Anna's desk.

'It is unnecessary to loop your L's like that,' he told her. 'Let me show you.' He took her pencil and wrote. 'You see what I mean. To show off when writing is as bad as showing off in your everyday behaviour.'

He handed her back her pencil and then pivoting on one foot he hit Sean a mighty crack across the side of the head with his open hand. Sean's head was knocked sideways and the sound of the blow was very loud in the quiet room.

'There was a mosquito sitting on your ear,' said Mr Clark.

II

In the following two years Sean and Garrick made the change from child to young manhood. It was like riding a strong current, being swept with speed along the river of life.

There were parts of the river that flowed steadily:
Ada was one of these. Always understanding, with the ability to give her understanding expression, unchanging in her love for her husband and the family she had taken as her own.
Waite was another. A little more grey in his hair but big as ever in body, laugh and fortune.

There were parts of the river that ran faster:
Garrick's reliance on Sean. He needed him more strongly each month that passed, for Sean was his shield. If Sean was not there to protect him when he was threatened, then he used his final refuge: he crawled back into himself, into the warm dark mists of his mind.
They went to steal peaches: the twins, Karl, Dennis and two others. There was a thick hedge around Mr Pye's orchard and the peaches that grew on the other side of it were as big as a man's fist. They were sweet as honey but tasted even sweeter when taken on the plunder account. You reached the orchard through a plantation of wattle trees.
'Don't take too many off one tree!' Sean ordered. 'Old Pye will notice it as sure as anything.'
They came to the hedge and Sean found the hole.
'Garry, you stay here and keep cats for us. If anyone comes give a whistle.' Garrick tried not to show his relief, he had no stomach for the expedition.
Sean went on. 'We'll pass the peaches out to you–and don't eat any until we're finished.'
'Why doesn't he come with us?' asked Karl.
''Cause he can't run, that's why. If he gets caught they'll know who the rest of us are for sure and we'll all get it.'
Karl was satisfied. Sean went down on his hands and knees and crawled into the hole in the hedge and one at a time the others followed him until Garrick was left alone.
He stood close to the hedge, drawing comfort from its protecting bulk. The minutes dragged by and Garrick fidgeted nervously–they were taking an awfully long time.
Suddenly there were voices, someone was coming through the plantation towards him. Panic beat up inside him and he shrank back into the hedge, trying to hide; the idea of giving a warning never even entered his head.
The voices were closer and then through the trees he recognized Ronny Pye: with him were two of his friends. Each of them was armed with a slingshot and they walked with their heads thrown back, searching the trees for birds.
For a time it seemed they would not notice Garrick in the hedge; but then, when they had almost passed, Ronny turned his head and saw him. They stared at each other, ten paces apart, Garrick crouched against the hedge and

Ronny's expression of surprise slowly changed to one of cunning. He looked around quickly, to make sure that Sean was not there.

'It's old Hobble-dee-hoy,' he announced and his friends came back and stood on each side of him.

'What're you doing, Peg-leg?'

'Rats got your tongue, Peg-leg?'

'No, termites got his leg!'–laughter aimed to hurt.

'Talk to us, Peg-leg.' Ronny Pye had ears that stood out on each side of his head like a pair of fans. He was small for his age which made him vicious and his hair was ginger.

'Come on. Talk to us, Peg-leg.'

Garrick moistened his lips with his tongue, already there were tears in his eyes.

'Hey, Ronny, make him walk for us, like this.' One of the others gave a graphic imitation of Garrick's limp. Again laughter, louder now, more confident and they closed in on him. 'Show us how you walk.'

Garrick swung his head from side to side searching for an escape.

'Your brother's not here,' crowed Ronny. 'No good looking for him, Peg-leg.'

He caught a hold of Garrick's shirt and pulled him out of the hedge.

'Show us how you walk.'

Garrick plucked ineffectually at Ronny's hand.

'Leave me, I'll tell Sean. I'll tell Sean unless you leave me.'

'All right, I'll leave you,' agreed Ronny with both hands shoved him in the chest. 'Don't come my way–go that way!' Garrick stumbled backwards.

One of the others was ready for him. 'Don't come my way–go that way!' and pushed him in the back. They formed a ring around him and kept him staggering between them.

'Go that way!'

'Go that way!'

The tears were streaked down his cheeks now. 'Please, please stop.'

'Please, please,' they mimicked him.

Then, with a rush of relief, Garrick felt the fluttering start behind his eyes–their faces dimmed, he hardly felt their hands upon him. He fell and and his face hit the ground, but there was no pain. Two of them stooped over him to lift him, and there was dirt mixed with the tears on his cheeks.

Sean came through the hedge behind them; the front of his shirt bulged with peaches. For a second he crouched on his hands and knees while he took in what was happening, then he came out of his crouch at a run. Ronny heard him, dropped Garrick and turned.

'You've been pinching Pa's peaches,' he shouted. 'I'll tell–'

Sean's fist hit him on the nose and he sat down. Sean swung towards the other two but they were already running, he chased them a few paces and then came back for Ronny, but he was too late. Ronny was dodging away between the trees holding his face and his nose was bleeding on to his shirt.

'Are you all right, Garry?' Sean knelt beside him, trying to wipe the dirt off his face with a grubby handkerchief. Sean helped him to his feet, and Garrick stood swaying slightly with his eyes open but a remote and vacant smile on his lips.

There were landmarks along the course of the river. Some of them small as a pile of rocks in shallow water:

Waite Courteney looked at Sean across the breakfast table at Theunis Kraal. The fork-load of egg and grilled gammon stopped on the way to his mouth.

'Turn your face towards the window,' he commanded suspiciously. Sean obeyed. 'What the hell is that on your face?'

'What?' Sean ran his hand over his cheek.

'When did you last bath?'

'Don't be silly, my dear.' Ada touched his leg under the table. 'It isn't dirt–it's whiskers.'

'Whiskers, are they?' Waite peered closely at Sean and started to grin, he opened his mouth to speak and Ada knew instantly that he was going to make a joke–one of those ponderous jokes of his, as subtle as an enraged dinosaur, that would wound Sean deep in his half-formed manhood. Quickly she cut in, 'I think you should buy him a razor, don't you, Waite?'

Waite lost the thread of his joke, he grunted and put the egg into his mouth.

'I don't want to cut them,' said Sean and flushed scarlet.

'They'll grow quicker if you shave them a bit at first,' Ada told him.

Across the table from her Garrick fingered his jowls wistfully.

Some of the landmarks were big as headlands:

Waite fetched them from school at the beginning of the December holidays. In the confusion of loading their cases onto the buggy and shouting farewells to Fraülein and to their friends, some of whom they would not see for another six weeks, the twins did not notice that Waite was acting strangely.

It was only later when the horses were heading for home at twice their normal speed that Sean asked, 'What's the hurry, Pa?'

'You'll see,' said Waite, and both Garrick and Sean looked at him with sudden interest. It had been an idle question of Sean's but Waite's answer had them immediately intrigued. Waite grinned at the bombardment of questions but he kept his answers vague. He was enjoying himself. By the time they reached Theunis Kraal the twins were in a frenzy of curiosity.

Waite pulled the horses up in front of the house and one of the grooms ran to take the reins. Ada was waiting on the veranda and Sean jumped down and ran up the steps to her. He kissed her quickly. 'What's happening?' he pleaded. 'Pa won't tell us but we know it's something.'

Garrick hurried up the steps also. 'Go on, tell us.' He caught hold of her arm and tugged it.

'I don't know what you're talking about,' Ada laughed. 'You'd better ask your father again.'

Waite climbed up after them, put one arm around Ada's waist and squeezed her.

'I don't know where they got this idea from,' said Waite, 'but why not tell them to go and have a look in their bedroom? They might as well have their Christmas presents a bit earlier this year.'

Sean beat Garrick to the lounge and was far in the lead by the time he reached the door of their bedroom.

'Wait for me,' called Garrick desperately. 'Please wait for me.'

Sean stopped in the doorway.

'Jesus Christ,' he whispered–they were the strongest words he knew. Garrick came up behind him and together they started at the pair of leather cases that lay on the table in the middle of the room–long flat cases, heavy polished leather with the corners bound in brass.

'Rifles!' said Sean. He walked slowly to the table as though he were stalking the cases, expecting them at any moment to vanish.

'Look!' Sean reached out to touch with one finger the gold lettering stamped into the lid of the nearest case. 'Our names on them even.'

He sprung the locks and lifted the lid. In a nest of green baize, perfumed with gun oil, glistened a poem in steel and wood.

'Jesus Christ,' said Sean again. Then he looked over his shoulder at Garrick. 'Aren't you going to open yours?'

Garrick limped up to the table trying to hide his disappointment: he had wanted a set of Dickens so badly.

In the river there were whirlpools:

The last week of the Christmas holidays and Garrick was in bed with one of his colds. Waite Courteney had gone to Pietermaritzburg for a meeting of the Beef Growers' Association and there was very little work to do on the farm that day. After Sean had dosed the sick cattle in the sanatorium paddock and ridden an inspection around the south section he returned to the homestead and spent an hour talking to the stableboys, then he drifted up to the house. Garry was asleep and Ada was in the dairy making butter. He asked for and got an early lunch from Joseph and ate it standing in the kitchen. While he ate he thought over the problem of how to fill the afternoon. He weighed the alternatives carefully. Take the rifle and try for duiker along the edge of the escarpment or ride to the pools above the White Falls and fish for eels. He was still undecided after he had finished eating so he crossed the yard and looked into the cool dimness of the dairy.

Ada smiled at him across the churn. 'Hello, Sean, I suppose you want your lunch.'

'Joseph gave it to me already, thanks, Ma.'

'Joseph has already given it to me,' Ada corrected mildly. Sean repeated it after her and sniffed the dairy smell–he liked the cheesy warmth of new butter and the tang of the cow dung smeared on the earth floor.

'What are you going to do this afternoon?'

'I came to ask you if you wanted venison or eels–I don't know if I want to go fishing or shooting.'

'Eels would be nice–we could jelly them and have them for dinner tomorrow when your father comes home.'

'I'll get you a bucket full.'

He saddled the pony, hung his tin of worms on the saddle and with his pole over his shoulder rode towards Ladyburg. He crossed the Baboon Stroom bridge and turned off the road to follow the stream up to the falls. As he skirted the wattle plantation below the Van Essens' place he realized he had made a mistake in picking this route. Anna, with her skirts held up to her knees, came pelting out from among the trees. Sean kicked the pony into a trot and looked straight ahead.

'Sean–hey, Sean.'

She was ahead of him, running to intercept him; there was no chance of evading her so he stopped the pony.

'Hello, Sean.' She was panting and her face was flushed.

'Hello,' he gruffed.

'Where are you going?'

'There and back to see how far it is.'

'You're going fishing–may I come with you?' She smiled appealingly. Her teeth were small and white.

'No, you talk too much; you'll frighten the fish.'

He started the pony.

'Please, I'll be quiet; honest I will.' She was running next to him.

'No.' He flicked the reins and pulled away from her. He rode for a hundred yards then looked round and she was still following with her black hair streaming out behind her. He stopped the pony and she caught up with him.

'I knew you'd stop,' she told him through her gasps.

'Will you go home? I don't want you following me.'

'I'll be quiet as anything–honest I will.'

He knew she'd follow him right up to the top of the escarpment and he gave in. 'All right, but if you say a word, just one single word, I'll send you home.'

'I promise–help me up, please.'

He dragged her on to the pony's rump and she sat sideways with her arms round his waist. They climbed the escarpment. The path ran close beside the White Falls and they could feel the spray blowing off them fine as mist. Anna kept her promise until she was sure they'd gone too far for Sean to send her back alone. She started talking again. When she wanted an answer from him, which wasn't very often, she squeezed his waist and Sean grunted. Sean knee-haltered the pony and left him among the trees above the pools. He hid his saddle and bridle in an ant-bear hold and they walked down through the reeds to the water. Anna ran ahead of him and when he came out on to the sandbank she was throwing pebbles into the pool.

'Hey, stop that!' You'll frighten the fish,' Sean shouted.

'Oh. I'm sorry. I forgot.'

She sat down and wriggled her bare toes into the sand. Sean baited his hook and lobbed it out into the green water–the current drifted his float in a wide circle under the far bank and they both watched it solemnly.

'It doesn't seem as though there are any fish here,' Anna said.

'You've got to be patient–you can't expect to catch one right away.'

Anna drew patterns in the sand with her toes and five minutes passed slowly. 'Sean–'

'Ssh!'

Another five minutes.

'Fishing's a silly old thing.'

'Nobody asked you to come,' Sean told her.

'It's hot here!' Sean didn't answer.

The high reed beds shut out any breeze and the white sand threw the sun's heat back at them. Anna stood up and wandered restlessly across the sand to the edge of the reeds. She picked a handful of the long spear-shaped leaves and plaited them together.

'I'm bored,' she announced.

'Well, go home then.'

'And I'm hot.'

Sean pulled his line in, inspected the worms and cast them out again. Anna stuck her tongue out at his back.

'Let's have a swim,' she suggested.

Sean ignored her. He stuck the butt of his rod into the sand, pulled his hat down to shield his eyes from the glare and leaned back on his elbows with his legs stretched out in front of him. He could hear the sand crunching as she moved and then there was another silence. He started to worry what she was doing, but if he looked around it would be a show of weakness.

'Girls!' he thought bitterly.

There was the sound of running feet just behind him. He sat up quickly and started to turn. Her white body flashed past him and hit the water, with a smack like a rising trout. Sean jumped up. 'Hey, what're you doing?'

'I'm swimming,' laughed Anna, waist-deep in green water, with her hair slicked wetly down her shoulders and over her breasts. Sean looked at those breasts, white as the flesh of an apple and nippled in dark pink, almost red. Anna dropped on to her back and kicked the water white.

'*Voet sak,* little fishes! Scat, little fishes,' she gurgled.

'Hey, you mustn't do that,' Sean said half-heartedly. He wanted her to stand up again, those breasts gave him a strange tight feeling in his stomach, but Anna knelt with the water up to her chin. He could see them through the water. He wanted her to stand up.

'It's lovely! Why don't you come in?' She rolled on her stomach and ducked her head under the water; the twin ovals of her bottom broke the surface and Sean's stomach tightened again.

'Are you coming in?' she demanded, rubbing the water out of her eyes with both hands. Sean stood bewildered–within a few seconds his feelings towards her had undergone a major revolution. He wanted very much to be in the water with all those mysterious white bulges–but he was shy.

'You're scared! Come on, I give you guts to come in.' She teased him. The challenge pricked him.

'I'm not scared.'

'Well, come on then.'

He hesitated a few seconds longer, then he threw off his hat and unbuttoned his shirt. He turned his back on her while he dropped his pants then spun round and dived into the pool, thankful for the cover it gave him. His head came out and Anna pushed it under again. He groped and caught her legs, straightened up and threw her on her back. He dragged her towards the shallows, where the water couldn't cover her. She was thrashing her arms to keep her head out and screaming delightedly. Sean's heels snagged a rock and he fell, letting go of her; before he could recover she had leapt on him and straddled his back. He could have thrown her off, but he liked the feel of her flesh on his–warm through the cool water, slippery with wetness. She picked up a handful of sand and rubbed it into his hair. Sean shrugged gently. She threw her arms round his neck and he could feel the whole length of her body along his back. The tightness of his stomach moved up into his chest and he wanted to hold her. He rolled over and reached for her but she twisted out of his hands and dived back into the deep again. Sean splashed after her but she kept out of his reach, laughing at him.

At last they faced each other, still chin deep, and Sean was getting angry. He wanted to hold her. She saw the change of his mood and she waded to the bank, walked to his clothes and picked up his shirt. She dried her face on it, standing naked and unashamed–she had too many brothers for modesty. Sean watched the way her breasts changed shape as she lifted her arms, he looked at the lines of her body and saw that her once skinny legs had filled out; her thighs touched each other all the way up to the base of her belly and there she wore the dark triangular badge of womanhood. She spread the shirt out on the sand and sat down upon it, then she looked at him.

'Are you coming out?'

He came out awkwardly, covering himself with his hands. Anna moved over on the shirt. 'You can sit down, if you like.'

He sat hurriedly and drew his knees up under his chin. He watched her from the corner of his eye. There were little goose-pimples round her nipples from the cold water. She was aware that he was watching her and she pulled back her shoulders, enjoying it. Sean felt bewildered again–she was so clearly in control now. Before she had been someone to growl at but now she was giving the orders and he was obeying.

'You've got hairs on your chest,' Anna said, turning to look at him. Sparse and silky though they were, Sean was glad that he had them. He straightened out his legs.

'And you're much bigger there than Frikkie.' Sean tried to pull up his knees again but she put her hand on his leg and stopped him.

'Can I touch you?'

Sean tried to speak but his throat had closed and no sound came through it. Anna did not wait for an answer.

'Oh, look! It's getting all cheeky–just like Caribou's.'

Caribou was Mr Van Essen's stallion.

'I always know when Pa is going to let Caribou service a mare, he tells me to go and visit Aunt Lettie. I just hide in the plantation. You can see the paddock jolly well from the plantation.'

Anna's hand was soft and restless, Sean could think of nothing else.

'Do you know that people service, just like horses do?' she asked.

Sean nodded, he had attended the biology classes conducted by Messrs Daffel and Company in the school latrines. They were quiet for a while, then Anna whispered.

'Sean, would you service me?'

'I don't know how,' croaked Sean.

'I bet horses don't either the first time, nor people for that matter,' Anna said. 'We could find out.'

They rode home in the early evening, Anna sitting up behind Sean, her arms tight round his waist and the side of her face pressed between his shoulders. He dropped her at the back of the plantation.

'I'll see you at school on Monday,' she said and turned to go.

'Anna–'

'Yes?'

'Is it still sore?'

'No,' and then, after a moment's thought, 'it feels nice.'

She turned and ran into the wattle trees.

Sean rode slowly home. He was empty inside; it was a sad feeling and it puzzled him.

'Where are the fish?' asked Ada.

'They weren't biting.'

'Not even one?'

Sean shook his head and crossed the kitchen.

'Sean.'

'Yes, Ma.'

'Is something wrong?'

'No'–quick denial–'No, I'm fine.' He slipped into the passage.

Garrick was sitting up in bed. The skin around his nostrils was inflamed and chapped; he lowered the book he was reading and smiled at Sean as he came into the room. Sean went to his own bed and sat on it.

'Where have you been?' Garrick's voice was thick with cold.

'Up at the pools above the falls.'

'Fishing?'

Sean didn't answer, he leaned forward on the bed with his elbows on his knees. 'I met Anna, she came with me.'

Garrick's interest quickened at the mention of her name and he watched Sean's face. Sean still had that slightly puzzled expression.

'Garry,' he hesitated; he had to talk about it. 'Garry, I screwed Anna.'

Garrick drew in his breath with a small hiss. He went very pale, only his nose was still red and sore-looking.

'I mean,' Sean spoke slowly as though he were trying to explain it to himself, 'I mean really screwed her, just like we've talked about. Just like. . . .' He made a helpless gesture with his hands, unable to find the words. Then he lay back on the bed.

'Did she let you?' Garrick's voice was almost a whisper.

'She asked me to,' Sean said. 'It was slippery–sort of warm and slippery.'

And then later, long after the lamp was out and they were both in bed, Sean heard Garrick's soft movements in the darkness. He listened for a while until he was certain.

'Garry!' He accused him loudly.

'I wasn't, I wasn't.'

'You know what Pa told us. Your teeth will fall out and you'll go mad.'

'I wasn't, I wasn't.' Garrick's voice was choked with his cold and his tears.

'I heard you,' said Sean.

'I was just scratching my leg. Honestly, honestly, I was.'

And at the end the river plunged over the last waterfall and swept them into the sea of manhood.

Mr Clark had not been able to break Sean. He had provoked instead a bitter contest in which he knew himself to be slowly losing ground, and now he was afraid of Sean. He no longer made Sean stand, for Sean was as tall as he was. The contest had been on for two years; they had explored each other's weaknesses and knew how to exploit them.

Mr Clark could not bear the sound of anyone sniffing; perhaps subconsciously he took it as mockery of his own deformed nose. Sean had a repertoire that varied from a barely audible connoisseur-testing-the-bouquet-of-brandy sniff to a loud hawking in the back of his throat.

'Sorry, sir, I can't help it. I've got a bit of a cold.'

But then, to even the score, Mr Clark had realized that Sean was vulnerable through Garrick. Hurt Garrick even a little and you were inflicting almost unbearable agony on Sean.

It had been a bad week for Mr Clark. His liver, weakened by persistent bouts of malaria, had been troubling him. He had suffered with a bilious headache for three days now; there had been unpleasantness with the Town Council about the terms on which his contract was to be renewed; Sean had been in good sniffing form the day before and Mr Clark had had about as much as he was prepared to take.

He came into the schoolroom and took his place on the dais; he let his eyes move slowly over his pupils until they came to Sean.

'Just let him start,' thought Mr Clark. 'Just let him start today and I'll kill him.'

The seating had been rearranged in the last two years. Sean and Garrick had been separated and Garrick was now at the front of the room where Mr Clark could reach him easily. Sean was near the back.

'English Readers,' said Mr Clark. 'Standard Ones turn to page five. Standard Twos turn to–'

Garrick sniffed wetly, hayfever again.

Mr Clark shut his book with a snap.

'Damn you!' he said softly, and then, his voice rising, 'Damn you!' Now he was shaking with rage, the edges of his nostrils were white and flared open.

He came down from the dais to Garrick's desk. 'Damn you! Damn you–you bloody little cripple,' he screamed and hit Garrick across the face with his open hand. Garrick cupped both hands over his cheek and stared at him.

'You dirty little swine,' Mr Clark mouthed at him. 'Now you're starting it too.'

He caught a handful of Garrick's hair and pulled his head down so that his forehead hit the top of the desk. 'I'll teach you. By God, I'll teach you.'

'I'll show you.' Bump.

'I'll teach you.' Bump.

It took Sean that long to reach them. He grabbed Mr Clark's arm and pulled him backwards. 'Leave him alone! He didn't do anything!'

Mr Clark saw Sean's face in front of him–he was past all reason–the face that had tormented him for two long years. He bunched his fist and lashed out at it.

Sean staggered back from the blow, the sting of it made his eyes water. For a second he lay sprawled across one of the desks, watching Clark and then he growled.

The sound sobered Clark, he backed away but only two paces before Sean was on him. Hitting with both hands, grunting with each punch, Sean drove him against the blackboard. Clark tried to break away but Sean caught the collar of his shirt and dragged him back–the collar tore half loose in his hand and Sean hit him again. Clark slid down the wall until he was sitting against it and Sean stood panting over him.

'Get out,' said Clark. His teeth were stained pink by the blood in his mouth and a little of it spilled out on to his lips. His collar stood up at a jaunty angle under one ear.

There was no sound in the room except Sean's breathing.

'Get out,' said Clark again and the anger drained out of Sean leaving him trembling with reaction. He walked to the door.

'You too,' Clark pointed at Garrick. 'Get out and don't come back!'

'Come on, Garry,' said Sean.

Garrick stood up from his desk and limped across to Sean and together they went out into the school yard.

'What are we going to do now?' There was a big red lump on Garrick's forehead.

'I suppose we'd better go home.'

'What about our things?' asked Garrick.

'We can't carry all that–we'll have to send for them later. Come on.'

They walked out through the town and along the road to the farm. They had almost reached the bridge on the Baboon Stroom before either of them spoke again.

'What do you reckon Pa will do?' asked Garrick. He was only putting into words the problem that had occupied them both since they left the school.

'Well, whatever he does, it was worth it.' Sean grinned. 'Did you see me clobber him, hey? Smackeroo–right in the chops.'

'You shouldn't have done it, Sean. Pa's going to kill us. Me too and I didn't do anything.'

'You sniffed,' Sean reminded him.

They reached the bridge and leaned over the parapet side by side to watch the water.

'How's your leg?' asked Sean.

'It's sore–I think we should rest a bit.'

'All right, if you say so,' Sean agreed.

There was a long silence, then, 'I wish you hadn't done it, Sean.'

'Well, wishing isn't going to help. Old Nose-Holes is as punched up as he'll ever be and all we can do is think of something to tell Pa.'

'He hit me,' said Garrick. 'He might have killed me.'

'Yes,' agreed Sean righteously, 'and he hit me too.'

They thought about it for a while.

'Perhaps we should just go away,' suggested Garrick.

'You mean without telling Pa?' The idea had attraction.

'Yeah, we could go to sea or something,' Garrick brightened.

'You'd get seasick, you even get sick in a train.'

Once more they applied their minds to the problem. Then Sean looked at Garrick, Garrick looked at Sean and as though by agreement they straightened up and srarted off once more for Theunis Kraal.

Ada was in front of the house. She had on a wide-brimmed straw hat that kept her face in shadow and over one arm she carried a basket of flowers. Busy with her garden, she didn't notice them until they were halfway across the lawn and when she did she stood motionless. She was steeling herself, trying to get her emotions under control; from experience she had learned to expect the worst from her stepsons and be thankful when it wasn't as bad as that.

As they came towards her they lost momentum and finally halted like a pair of clockwork toys running down.

'Hello,' said Ada.

'Hello,' they answered her together.

Garrick fumbled in his pocket, drew out a handkerchief and blew his nose. Sean stared up at the deep Dutch-gabled roof of Theunis Kraal as though he had never seen it before.

'Yes?' Ada kept her voice calm.

'Mr Clark said we were to go home,' announced Garrick.

'Why?'Ada's calm was starting to crack.

'Well–' Garrick glanced at Sean for support. Sean's attention was still riveted on the roof.

'Well . . . You see Sean sort of punched him in the head until he fell down. I didn't do anything.'

Ada moaned softly, 'Oh, no!' She took a deep breath. 'All right. Start at the beginning and give me the whole story.'

They told it in relays, a garbled rush of words, interrupting each other and arguing over the details. When they had finished Ada said, 'You better go to your room. Your father is working in the home section today and he'll be back for his lunch soon. I'll try and prepare him a little.'

The room had the cheery atmosphere of a condemned cell.

'How much do you reckon he'll give us?' asked Garrick.

'I reckon until he gets tired, then he'll rest and give us some more,' Sean answered.

They heard Waite's horse come into the yard. He said something to the stable boy and they heard him laugh; the kitchen door slammed and there was half a minute of suspense before they heard Waite roar. Garrick jumped nervously.

For another ten minutes they could hear Waite and Ada talking in the kitchen, the alternate rumble and soothing murmur. Then the tap of Ada's feet along the passage and she came into the room.

'Your father wants to see you–he's in the study.'

Waite stood in front of the fireplace. His beard was powdered with dust and his forehead as corrugated as a ploughed land with the force of his scowl.

'Come in,' he bellowed when Sean knocked and they filed in and stood in front of him. Waite slapped his riding-whip against his leg and the dust puffed out of his breeches.

'Come here,' he said to Garrick and took a handful of his hair. He twisted Garrick's face up and looked at the bruise on his forehead.

'Hmm,' he said. He let go of Garrick's hair and it stood up in a tuft. He threw the riding-whip on the stinkwood desk.

'Come here,' he said to Sean. 'Hold out your hands–no palms down.'

The skin on both hands was broken and one knuckle was swollen and puffy looking.

'Hmm,' he said again. He turned to the shelf beside the fireplace, took a pipe out of the rack and filled it from the stone jar of tobacco.

'You're a pair of bloody fools,' he said, 'but I'll take a chance and start you on five shillings a week all found. Go and get your lunch . . . we've got work to do this afternoon.'

They stared at him a moment in disbelief and then back towards the door.

'Sean.' Sean stopped, he knew it was too good to be true. 'Where did you hit him?'

'All over, Pa, anywhere I could reach.'

'That's no good,' Waite said. 'You must go for the side of his head–here,' he tapped the point of his jaw with his pipe, 'and keep your fists closed tight or you'll break every finger in your hands before you're much older.'

'Yes, Pa.'

The door closed softly behind him and Waite allowed himself to grin.

'They've had enough book learning anyway,' he said aloud and struck a match to his pipe; when it was drawing evenly he blew out smoke.

'Christ, I wish I could have watched it. That little pen-pusher will know better than to tangle with my boy again.'

12

Now Sean had a course along which to race. He was born to run and Waite Courteney led him out of the stall in which he had fretted and gave him his lead. Sean ran, unsure of the prize, unsure of the distance; yet he ran with joy, he ran with all his strength.

Before dawn, standing with his father and Garrick in the kitchen, drinking coffee with hands cupped around the mug, Sean felt excitement for each coming day.

'Sean, take Zama and N'duti with you and make sure there are no strays in the thick stuff along the river.'

'I'll only take one herdboy, Pa, you'll need N'duti at the dipping tank.'

'All right, then. Try and meet us back at the tank before midday, we've got to push through a thousand head today.'

Sean gulped the remains of his coffee and buttoned his jacket. 'I'll get going then.'

A groom held his horse at the kitchen door. Sean slid his rifle into the scabbard and went up into the saddle without putting his foot into the steel; he lifted a hand and grinned at Waite, then he swung the horse and rode across the yard. The morning was still dark and cold. Waite watched him from the doorway.

'So goddamned sure of himself,' thought Waite. Yet he had the son he had hoped for and he was proud.

'What you want me to do, Pa?' Garrick asked beside him.

'Well, there are those heifers in the sick paddock–'

Waite stopped. 'No. You'd better come with me, Garry.'

Sean worked in the early morning when the sunlight was tinted as a stage effect, all golden and gay, and the shadows were long and black. He worked in the midday sun and sweated in the heat; in the rain; in the mist that swirled down grey and damp from the plateau; in the short African twilight, and came home in the dark. He loved every minute of it.

He learned to know cattle. Not by name, for only the trek oxen were named, but by their size and colour and markings, so that by running his eye over one of the herds he knew which animals were missing.

'Zama, the old cow with the crooked horn. Where is she?'

'Nkosi,' no longer the diminutive Nkosizana–little lord.

'Nkosi, yesterday I took her to the sick paddock, she has the worm in her eye.'

He learned to recognize disease almost before it started. The way a beast moved and held its head. He learned the treatment for them. Screw worm–kerosene poured into the wound until the maggots fell out like a shower of rice. Opthalmia–rinse the eye with permanganate. Anthrax and quarter-evil–a bullet and a bonfire for the carcass.

He delivered his first calf among the acacia trees on the bank of the Tugela; he did it alone with his sleeves rolled up above the elbows and the soapy feel of the slime on his hands. Afterwards, while the mother licked it and it staggered at each stroke of the tongue, Sean felt a choking sensation in his throat.

All this was not enough to burn up his energy. He played while he worked.

Practising his horsemanship: swinging from the saddle and running beside his horse, up again and over the other side, standing on the saddle at full gallop and then opening his legs and smacking down on his backside–his feet finding the stirrups without groping.

Practising with his rifle until he could hit a running jackal at a hundred and fifty paces, cutting the fox-terrier-sized body in half with the heavy bullet.

Then there was much of Garrick's work to do also.

'I don't feel very well, Sean.'

'What's wrong?'

'My leg's sore, you know how it chafes if I ride too much.'

'Why don't you go home, then?'

'Pa says I've got to fix the fence round the Number Three dip tank.' Garrick leaned forward on his horse to rub his leg, giving a brave little smile.

'You fixed it last week,' Sean protested.

'Yes–but the wires sort of came loose again.' There was always a strange impermanency about any repairs that Garrick effected.

'Have you got the wire cutters?' and Garrick produced them with alacrity from his saddle bag.

'I'll do it,' said Sean.

'Hell, man, thanks a lot,' and then a second's hesitation. 'You won't tell Pa, will you?'

'No–you can't help it if your leg's sore,' and Garrick rode home, sneaked through to his bedroom and escaped with Jim Hawkins into the pages of *Treasure Island*.

From this work came a new emotion for Sean. When the rain brought the grass out in green and filled the shallow pans on the plateau with water it was no longer simply a sign that the bird-nesting season had begun and that the fishing in the Baboon Stroom would improve–now it meant that they could take cattle up from the valley, it meant that there would be fat on the herds they drove into the sale pens at Ladyburg, it meant that another winter had ended and again the land was rich with life and the promise of life. This new emotion extended to the cattle also. It was a strong, almost savage feeling of possession.

It was in the late afternoon. Sean was sitting on his horse among trees, looking out across open vleiland at the small herd that was strung out before him. They were feeding, heads down, tails flicking lazily. Between Sean and the main body of cattle was a calf–it was three days old, still pale-beige in colour and unsure of its legs. It was trying them out, running clumsy circles in the short grass. From the herd a cow lowed and the calf stopped dead and stood with its legs splayed awkwardly under it and its ears up. Sean grinned and picked up the reins from his horse's neck; it was time to start back for the homestead.

At that moment he saw the lammergeyer: it had already begun its stoop at the calf, dropping big and dark brown from the sky, wings cocked back and its talons reaching for the strike. The wind rustled against it with the speed of its dive.

Sean sat paralysed and watched. The eagle hit the calf and Sean heard bone break, sharp as the snap of a dry stick, and then the calf was down in the grass struggling feebly with the eagle crouched on top of it.

For a second longer Sean sat, dazed with the speed at which it had happened. Then hatred came on him. It came with a violence and twisted his stomach. He hit his horse with his heels and it jumped forward. He drove it at the eagle and as he rode he screamed at it, a high-pitched formless sound, an animal expression of hate.

The eagle turned its head, looking at him sideways with one eye. It opened its great yellow beak and answered his scream, then it loosed its claws from the calf and launched itself into the air. Its wings flogged heavily and it moved low along the ground, gaining speed, lifting, drawing away from Sean.

Sean pulled his rifle from the scabbard and hauled his horse back on to its haunches. He threw himself out of the saddle and levered open the breech of the rifle.

The eagle was fifty yards ahead of him rising fast now. Sean slipped a cartridge into the breech, closed it and brought the rifle up in one continuous movement.

It was a difficult shot. Moving away from him and rising, the beat of its wings jerking its body. Sean fired. The rifle jumped back into his shoulder and the gunsmoke whipped away on the wind, so he could watch the bullet connect.

The eagle collapsed in the air. It burst like a pillow in a puff of feathers and fell with its six-feet-long wings fluttering limply. Before it hit the ground Sean was running.

It was dead when he reached it, but he reversed his rifle: holding it by the muzzle, he swung the butt down from above his head on to its body. At the third blow the butt of his rifle broke off, but he kept on hitting. He was sobbing with fury.

When he stopped and stood panting the sweat was running down his face and his body was trembling. The eagle was a squashy mess of broken flesh and feathers.

The calf was still alive. The rifle was jammed. Sean knelt beside it with tears of anger burning his eyes and killed it with his hunting-knife.

13

So strong was this new feeling that Sean could hate even Garrick. He did not hate for long, though. Sean's anger and his hatred were quick things, with flames like those of a fire in dry grass: hot and high but soon burnt out and afterwards the ashes dead and no smouldering.

Waite was away when it happened. For three consecutive years Waite Courteney had been nominated for the chairmanship of the Beef Growers' Association and each time he had stood down. He was human enough to want the prestige the office carried with it, but he was also sensible to the fact that his farm would suffer from his frequent absences. Sean and Garrick had been working for two years when the annual election of office bearers came around again.

The night before Waite left for the meeting in Pietermaritzburg he spoke to Ada. 'I had a letter from Bernard last week, my dear,' he was standing before the mirror in their bedroom trimming his beard. 'They insist that I stand for the chair this year.'

'Very wise of them,' said Ada. 'They'd have the best man if you did.'

Waite frowned with concentration as he snipped at his whiskers. She believed so unquestioningly in him that he seldom doubted himself. Now looking at his face in the mirror he wondered how much of his success was owed to Ada's backing.

'You can do it, Waite.' Not a challenge, not a question, but a calm statement of fact. When she said it he believed it.

He laid the scissors down on the chest of drawers and turned to her. She sat cross-legged on the bed in a white nightgown, her hair was down in a dark mass around her shoulders. 'I think Sean can look after things here,' she said, and then quickly, 'and of course Garry.'

'Sean's learning fast,' Waite agreed.

'Are you going to take the job?'

Waite hesitated. 'Yes,' he nodded and Ada smiled.

'Come here,' she held out her hands to him.

Sean drove Waite and Ada to the station at Ladyburg: at the last minute Waite had insisted that she go with him, for he wanted her to be there to share it with him.

Sean put their luggage into the coach and waited while they talked with the small group of cattlemen who were going up to the meeting. The whistle blew and the travellers scattered to their compartments. Ada kissed Sean and climbed up. Waite stayed a second longer on the platform.

'Sean, if you need any help go across to Mr Erasmus at Lion Kop. I'll be back on Thursday.'

'I won't need any help, Pa.'

Waite's mouth hardened. 'Then you must be God, he's the only one who never needs help,' Waite said harshly. 'Don't be a bloody fool–if you run into trouble ask Erasmus.'

He climbed up after Ada. The train jerked, gathered speed and ran out towards the escarpment. Sean watched it dwindle, then he walked back to the buggy. He was master of Theunis Kraal and he liked the feeling. The small crowd on the platform was dispersing and out of it came Anna.

'Hello, Sean.' She had on a green cotton dress that was faded with washing, her feet were bare. She smiled with her small white teeth and watched his face.

'Hello, Anna.'

'Aren't you going up to Pietermaritzburg?'

'No, I've got to look after the farm.'

'Oh!'

They waited in silence, uncomfortable before so many people. Sean coughed and scratched the side of his nose.

'Anna, come on. We've got to get home.' One of her brothers called from in front of the ticket office and Anna leaned towards Sean.

'Will I see you on Sunday?' she whispered.

'I'll come if I can. But I don't know–I've got to look after the farm.'

'Please try, Sean.' Her face was earnest. 'I'll be waiting for you, I'll take some lunch and wait all day. Please come, even if it's only for a little while.'

'All right, I'll come.'

'Promise?'

'Promise.'

She smiled with relief. 'I'll wait for you on the path above the waterfall.'

She turned and ran to join her family and Sean drove back to Theunis Kraal. Garrick was lying on his bed reading.

'I thought Pa told you to get on with the branding of those new cattle we bought on Wednesday.'

Garrick laid down his book and sat up. 'I told Zama to keep them in the kraal until you got back.'

'Pa told you to get on with it. You can't keep them there all day without feed or water.'

'I hate branding,' muttered Garrick. 'I hate it when they moo like that as you burn them, and I hate the stink of burning hair and skin–it gives me a headache.'

'Well someone's got to do it. I can't, I've got to go down and mix new dip into the tanks for tomorrow.' Sean was losing his temper. 'Hell, Garry, why are you always so damn helpless?'

'I can't help it, I can't help it if I've only got one leg.' Garrick was close to tears again. The reference to his leg had the desired effect–Sean's temper steadied instantly.

'I'm sorry,' Sean smiled his irresistible smile. 'I tell you what. I'll do the branding–you fix the tanks. Get the drums of dip loaded on to the Scotch cart, take a couple of the stable boys with you to help. Here are the keys of the storeroom.' He tossed the bunch on to the bed beside Garrick. 'You should be finished before dark.'

At the door he turned.

'Garry, don't forget to do all six tanks–not just the ones near the house.'

So Garrick loaded six drums of dip on to the Scotch cart and went off down the hill. He was home well before dark. The front of his breeches were stained with the dark, tarry chemical and some of it had soaked into the leather of his single riding-boot. As he came out of the kitchen into the passage Sean shouted from the study. 'Hey, Garry, did you finish them?'

Garrick was startled. Waite's study was a sacred place, the inner sanctum of Theunis Kraal. Even Ada knocked before going into it and the twins went there only to receive punishment. Garrick limped along the passage and pushed open the door.

Sean sat with his boots on top of the desk and his ankles neatly crossed. He leaned back in the swivel chair.

'Pa will kill you,' Garrick's voice was shaky.

'Pa's in Pietermaritzburg,' said Sean.

Garrick stood in the doorway and looked around the room. It was the first time he had really seen it. On every previous visit he had been too preoccupied with the violence to come and the only item in the room he had studied closely was the seat of the big leather easy chair as he bent over the arm of it and exposed his backside to the sjambok.

Now he looked at the room. The walls were panelled to the ceiling, the wood was dark yellow and polished. The ceiling was fancy plaster, in a pattern of oak leaves. A single lamp hung from the centre of it on a brass chain. You could walk into the fireplace of brown chipped stone and there were logs laid ready for the match.

Pipes and tobacco jar on the ledge beside the fireplace, guns in a rack along one wall, a bookcase of green and maroon leather bound volumes: encyclopaedias, dictionaries, books on travel and farming, but no fiction. There was an oil painting of Ada on the wall opposite the desk, the artist had captured a little of her serenity: she wore a white dress and carried her hat in her hand. A magnificent set of Cape buffalo horns above the fireplace dominated the room with their great crenellated bosses and wide sweep to the tips.

It was a man's room, with loose dog-hairs on the leopard-skin rugs, and the presence of the man strongly there–it even smelled of Waite. It was as distinctively his as the tweed coat and Terai hat that hung behind the door.

Next to where Sean sat the cabinet was open and bottle of brandy stood on top of it. Sean had a goblet in his hand.

'You're drinking Pa's brandy,' Garrick accused.

'It's not bad.' Sean lifted the glass and inspected the liquid; he took a careful sip and held it in his mouth, preparing himself to swallow. Garrick watched him with awe and Sean tried not to blink as it went down his throat.

'Would you like some?'

Garrick shook his head and the fumes came up Sean's nose and his eyes ran.

'Pa will kill you!' said Garrick again.

'Sit down,' ordered Sean, his voice husky from the brandy. 'I want to work out a plan for the time Pa's away.'

Garrick advanced on the armchair, but before he reached it he changed his mind–the associations were too painful. He went to the sofa instead and sat on the edge.

'Tomorrow,' Sean held up one finger, 'we'll dip all the cattle in the home section. I've told Zama to start bringing them early–you did do the tanks, didn't you?'

Garrick nodded and Sean went on.

'On Saturday,' Sean held up his second finger, 'we'll burn fire breaks along the top of the escarpment. The grass is dry as hell up there. You take one gang and start near the falls, I'll ride down to the other end, near Fredericks Kloof. On Sunday . . .' Sean said and then paused. On Sunday Anna.

'I want to go to church on Sunday,' said Garrick quickly.

'That's fine,' agreed Sean. 'You go to church.'

'Are you going to come?'

'No,' said Sean.

Garrick looked down at the leopard-skin rugs that covered the floor–he didn't try to persuade Sean for Anna would be at the service. Perhaps afterwards, if Sean wasn't there to distract her, he could drive her home in the buggy. He started a day dream and wasn't listening as Sean went on talking.

In the morning it was full daylight by the time Sean reached the dip tank. He pushed a small herd of stragglers before him and they came out through the trees and stirrup high grass into the wide area of trampled earth around the tank. Garrick had started running cattle through the dip and there were about ten head already in the draining kraal at the far end, standing wet and miserable, their bodies dark with drip.

Sean drove his herd through the gates of the entrance kraal into the solid pack of brown bodies that were already there. N'duti slid the bars of the gate back into place to hold them.

'I see you, Nkosi.'

'I see you, N'duti. Plenty of work today!'

'Plenty,' agreed N'duti, 'always plenty of work.'

Sean rode around the kraal and tied his horse beneath one of the trees, then walked across to the tank. Garrick was standing by the parapet and leaning against one of the columns that supported the roof.

'Hello, Garry, how's it going?'

'Fine.'

Sean leaned over the parapet next to Garry. The tank was twenty feet long and eight wide, the surface of the liquid was below ground level. Around the tank was a low wall and over it a roof of thatch to prevent rain diluting the contents.

The herdboys drove the cattle up to the edge and each beast hesitated on the brink.

'E'yapi, E'yapi,' screamed the herdboys and the push of bodies behind it forced it to jump. If one was stubborn, Zama leaned over the railing of the kraal, grabbed its tail and bit it.

Each beast jumped with its nose held high and its forefeet gathered up under its chest; it disappeared completely under the oil black surface and came up again swimming frantically along the tank until its hooves touched the sloping bottom at the far end and it could lumber up into the draining kraal.

'Keep them moving, Zama,' shouted Sean.

Zama grinned at him and bit with big white teeth into a reluctant tail.

The ox was a heavy animal and it splashed a drop up on to Sean's cheek as he leaned over the wall. Sean did not bother to wipe it off, he went on watching.

'Well, if we don't get top prices for this lot at the next sale then the buyers don't know good cattle,' he said to Garry.

'They're all right,' agreed Garry.

'All right? They're the fattest oxen in the district.' Sean was about to enlarge on the theme, but suddenly he was aware of discomfort–the drop of dip was burning his cheek. He wiped it off with his finger and held it to his nose; the smell of it stung his nostrils. For a second he stared at it stupidly and the spot on his cheek burned like fire.

He looked up quickly. The cattle in the draining kraal were milling restlessly and as he looked one of them staggered sideways and bumped against the railing.

'Zama!' shouted Sean, and the Zulu looked up. 'Stop them. For God's sake don't let any more through.'

There was another ox poised on the edge. Sean snatched off his hat and jumped up on to the wall, he beat the ox in the face with his hat trying to drive it back, but it sprang out into the tank. Sean caught hold of the railing and stepped into the space it had left on the edge of the tank.

'Stop them' he shouted. 'Get the bars in, don't let any more through.'

He spread his arms across the entrance, holding on to the railing on each side, kicking at the faces of the cattle in front of him.

'Hurry, damn you, get the bars in,' he shouted. The oxen pressed towards him, a wall of horned heads. Pushed forward by those behind and held back by Sean they started to panic; one of them tried to jump over the railing. As it swung its head its horn raked Sean's chest, up across the ribs, ripping his shirt.

Behind him Sean felt the wooden bars being dropped into place, blocking the entrance to the tank, and then Zama's hands on his arm pulling him up out of the confusion of horns and hooves. Two of the herdboys helped him over the railing and Sean shrugged their hands off as soon as he was on the ground.

'Come on,' he ordered and ran to his horse.

'Nkosi, you are bleeding.'

Blood had splotched in front of Sean's shirt but he felt no pain. The cattle that had been through the dip were now in terrible distress. They charged about the kraal, bellowing pitifully; one of them fell and when it got to its feet again its legs were shaking so that it could barely stand.

'The river,' shouted Sean, 'get them down to the river. Try and wash it off. Zama, open the gate.'

The Baboon Stroom was a mile away. One of the oxen died before they could get them out of the kraal, another ten before they reached the river. They died in convulsions, with their bodies shuddering and their eyes turned back into their heads.

Sean drove those that remained down the bank into the river. The water was clear and as each beast went into it, the dip washed off in a dark brown cloud.

'Stand here, Zama. Don't let them come out.'

Sean swam his horse to the far bank and turned back the oxen that were trying to climb it.

'Nkosi–one is drowning,' called N'duti and Sean looked across the river. A young ox was in convulsions in the shallows: its head was under the water and its feet thrashed the surface.

Sean slid off his horse and waded out to it. The water was up to his armpits. He tried to hold its head out and drag it to the bank.

'Help me, N'duti,' he shouted, and the Zulu came into the river. It was a hopeless task: each time the ox lunged it pulled them both under with it. By the time they got the ox to the bank it was dead.

Sean sat in the mud beside the body of the ox: he was exhausted and his lungs ached with the water he had breathed.

'Bring them out, Zama,' he gasped. The survivors were standing in the shallows or swimming in aimless circles. 'How many?' asked Sean. 'How many are dead?'

'Two more while you were in the water. Altogether thirteen, Nkosi.'

'Where's my horse?'

'It ran, and I let it go. It will be back at the house.'

Sean nodded.

'Bring them up to the sick paddock. We must watch them for a few days.'

Sean stood up and started walking back towards the dip tank. Garrick was gone, and the main herd was still in the kraal. Sean opened the gate and turned them loose. He felt better by then, and as his strength returned with it came his anger and his hatred. He started along the track towards the homestead. His boots squelched as he walked and he hated Garrick more strongly with each step. Garrick had mixed the dip. Garrick had killed his cattle and Sean hated him.

As Sean came up the slope below the house he saw Garrick standing in the yard. Garrick saw him also; he disappeared into the kitchen and Sean started to run. He went in through the kitchen door and nearly knocked down one of the servants.

'Garrick,' shouted Sean. 'Damn it–where are you?'

He searched the house; once quickly and then again thoroughly. Garrick was gone, but the window of the bedroom was open and there was a dusty boot print on the sill. Garrick had gone over it.

'You bloody coward,' howled Sean and scrambled out after him. He stood a second, with his head swinging from side to side and his fists opening and closing.

'I'll find out,' he howled again. 'I'll find you wherever you're hiding.'

He started across the yard towards the stables and halfway there he saw the door of the dairy was closed. When he tried it he found it was locked from inside. Sean backed away from it and then charged it with his shoulder–the lock burst and the door flew open. Sean skidded across the room and came up against the far wall. Garrick was trying to climb out of the window, but it was small and high up. Sean caught him by the seat of his pants and pulled him down.

'Watcha do to the dip, hey? Watcha do to it?' He shouted in Garrick's face.

'I didn't mean to. I didn't know it'd kill them.'

'Tell me what you did.' Sean had hold of the front of his shirt and was dragging him towards the door.

'I didn't do anything. Honest I didn't know.'

'I'm going to hammer you anyway, so you might as well tell me.'

'Please, Sean, I didn't know.'

Sean jammed Garrick against the doorway and held him there with his left hand–his right hand he drew back with the fist bunched.

'No, Sean. Please, no.'

And suddenly the anger was gone from Sean, his hands sank back to his sides.

'All right–just tell me what you did,' he said coldly. His anger was gone but not his hatred.

'I was tired and it was getting late and my leg was hurting,' whispered Garrick, 'and there were still four more tanks to do, and I knew you'd check that all the drums were empty, and it was so late . . . and . . .'

'And?'

'And so I emptied all the dip into the one tank . . . but I didn't know it would kill them, truly I didn't.'

Sean turned away from him and started walking slowly back towards the house. Garrick stumbled after him.

'I'm sorry, Sean, honest I'm sorry. I didn't know that . . .'

Sean walked ahead of him into the kitchen and slammed the door in his face. He went through into Waite's study. From the bookshelf he lifted down the heavy leather-covered stock register and carried it to the desk. He opened the book, picked up a pen and dipped it. For a moment he stared at the page and then in the 'deaths' column he wrote the number *13* and after it the words 'dip poisoning'. He pressed down so hard with the pen that the nib cut the paper.

It took Sean and the herdboys all the rest of that day and the next to bale out the tank, refill it with clean water and mix in fresh dip. He saw Garrick only at meals and they didn't speak.

The next day was Sunday. Garrick went into town early, for the church service started at eight o'clock. When he had gone Sean began his preparations. He shaved–leaning close to the mirror and handling the cut-throat gingerly, shaping his side burns and clearing the hair from the rest of his face until his skin was smooth and fresh-looking. Then he went through to the master-bedroom and helped himself to a generous portion of his father's brilliantine, taking care to screw the lid back on the bottle and replace it exactly as he found it. He rubbed the brilliantine into his hair and sniffed its perfume appreciatively. He combed his hair over his forehead, parted it down the centre and polished it into a gloss with Waite's silver-backed brushes. Then a clean white shirt, breeches worn only once before, boots as shiny as his hair–and Sean was ready.

The clock on the mantelpiece in the lounge assured him that he was well ahead of time. To be exact, he was two hours early. Eight o'clock now: church didn't end until nine and it would be another hour before Anna could escape from under the eyes of her family and reach the rendezvous above the falls. He settled down to wait. He read the latest copy of the *Natal Farmer*. He had read it three times before for it was a month old, and now even the excellent article on 'Stomach parasites in Cattle and Sheep' had lost much of its punch. Sean's attention wandered–he thought about the day ahead and felt the familiar movement within his breeches. This necessitated a rearrangement for the breeches were tight fitting. Then fantasy palled: Sean was a doer not a thinker, and he went through to the kitchen to solicit a cup of coffee from Joseph. When he had finished it, there was still half an hour to go.

'The hell with it,' said Sean and shouted for his horse. He climbed the escarpment, letting his horse move diagonally up the slope and at the top he dismounted and let it blow. Today he could see the course of the Tugela river out across the plain–it was a belt of dark green. He could count the roofs of the houses in Ladyburg and the church spire, copper clad, shone in the sunlight like a beacon fire.

He mounted again and rode along the edge of the plateau until he reached the Baboon Stroom above the falls. He followed it back and forded it at a shallow place, lifting his feet up on the saddle in front of him to keep his boots dry. He off-saddled next to the pools and knee-haltered his horse, then he followed the path until it dropped over the edge of the plateau into the thick forest that surrounded the falls. It was cool and damp in the forest with moss growing on the trees, for the roof of leaves and creepers shut out the sun. There was a bottle-bird in the undergrowth.

'Glug, glug, glug,' it said, like water poured from a bottle, and its call was almost drowned in the ceaseless thunder of the falls.

Sean spread his handkerchief on a rock beside the path, sat down on it and waited. Within five minutes he was fidgeting impatiently–within half an hour he was grumbling aloud.

'I'll count to five hundred. . . . If she hasn't come by then I'm not going to wait.'

He counted and when he reached the promised figure he stopped and peered anxiously down the path. There was no sign of Anna.

'I'm not going to sit here all day,' he announced and made no effort to stand up. A fat yellow caterpillar caught his eye; it was on the trunk of a tree farther down the slope. He picked up a pebble and threw it. It bounced off the tree an inch above the caterpillar.

'Close,' Sean encouraged himself and stopped for another stone. After a while he had exhausted the supply of pebbles around his feet and the caterpillar was still moving leisurely up the trunk. Sean was forced to go out on a foraging expedition for more pebbles. He came back with both hands full and once more took up his position on the rock. He piled the pebbles between his feet and reopened the bombardment. He aimed each throw with the utmost concentration and with his third pebble he hit squarely and the caterpillar popped in a spurt of green juice. Sean felt cheated. He looked around for a new target and instead found Anna standing beside him.

'Hello, Sean.' She had on a pink dress. She carried her shoes in one hand and a small basket in the other. 'I brought some lunch for us.'

'What took you so long?' Sean stood up and wiped his hands on his breeches. 'I thought you weren't coming.'

'I'm sorry–everything went wrong.'

There was an awkward pause and Anna flushed slightly as Sean looked at her. Then she turned and started up the path. 'Come on–I'll race you to the top.'

She ran fast on bare feet, holding her skirts up to her knees and she was out in the sunshine before Sean caught her. He put his arms around her from behind and they fell together into the grass beside the path. They lay holding each other, laughing and panting at the same time.

'The service went on and on–I thought it would never finish,' said Anna, 'and afterwards–'

Before she could finish Sean covered her mouth with his and immediately her arms came up around his neck. They kissed with the tension building up steadily between them until Anna was moaning softly and moving her body against his. Sean released her mouth and moved his lips down across her cheek to her neck.

'Oh, Sean, it's been so long. It's been a whole week.'

'I know.'

'I've missed you so–I thought about you every day.'

Sean had his face pressed into her neck, he didn't answer.

'Did you miss me, Sean?'

'Hmm,' Sean murmured and lifted his mouth to take the lobe of her ear between his teeth.

'Did you think about me while you were working?'

'Hmm.'

'Tell me properly, Sean, say it properly.'

'I missed you, Anna, I thought about you all the time,' lied Sean and kissed her on the mouth. She clung to him and Sean's hand went down, right down to her knee and then up again under her clothes. Anna caught his wrist and held his hand away. 'No, Sean, just kiss me.'

Sean waited until her grip relaxed and then tried again, but this time she twisted away from him and sat up. 'Sometimes I think that's all you want to do.'

Sean felt his temper coming up, but he had the good sense to check it.

'That's not true, Anna. It's just that I haven't seen you for so long and I've missed you so much.'

She softened immediately and reached out to touch his cheek. 'Oh, Sean, I'm sorry. I don't mind really, it's just that–oh, I don't know.' She scrambled to her feet and picked up the basket. 'Come on, let's go on to the pools.'

They had a special place. It was walled in by the reeds and shaded by a big tree that grew on the bank above; the sand was washed clean and white. Sean spread his saddle blanket for them to sit on. They could hear the river, close by but hidden and the reeds rustled and nodded their fluffy heads with each breath of the wind.

'–and I couldn't get rid of him,' Anna chattered as she knelt on the blanket and unpacked the basket. 'He just sat there and every time I said something he blushed and wriggled on his seat. In the end I just told him, "I'm sorry, Garry, I have to go!"'

Sean scowled. The mention of Garrick had reminded him of the dip; he hadn't forgiven him yet.

'And then when I got into the house I found that Pa and Frikkie were fighting. Ma was in tears and the other kids were locked in the bedroom.'

'Who won?' asked Sean with interest.

'They weren't really fighting–they were just shouting at each other. They were both drunk.'

Sean was always slightly shocked at Anna's casual reference to her family's drinking habits. Everybody knew about Mr Van Essen and his two eldest boys but Anna didn't have to talk about it. Once Sean had tried to correct her. 'You shouldn't say things like that about your Pa. You should respect him.'

And Anna had looked at him calmly and asked, 'Why?' which was a difficult question. But now she changed the subject.

'Do you want to eat yet?'

'No,' said Sean and reached for her. She fought back, shrieking demurely until Sean held her down and kissed her. Then she lay quietly, answering his kisses.

'If you stop me now I'm going to get mad,' whispered Sean and deliberately unfastened the top button of her dress. She watched his face with solemn eyes and her hands stayed on his shoulders until he had undone her blouse down to the waist and then with her fingers she traced the bold black curves of his eyebrows.

'No, Sean, I won't stop you. I want to as well, I want to as much as you do.'

There was so much to discover and each thing was strange and wonderful and they were the first to find it. The way the muscles stood out down the side of his chest beneath his arms and yet left a place where she could see the outline of his ribs. The texture of her skin, smooth and white with the faint blue suggestion of veins beneath. The deep hollow down the centre of his back–pressing her fingers into it she could feel his spine. The down on her cheeks, so pale and fine he could see it only in the sunlight. The way their lips felt against each other and the tiny flutter of tongues between. The smell of their bodies, one milky warm and the other musky and vigorous. The hair that covered his chest and grew thicker under his arms, and hers: startlingly dark against white skin, and small silky nest of it. Each time there was something new to find and greet with soft sounds of delight.

Now, kneeling before her as she lay with her head thrown back and her arms half-raised to receive him, Sean suddenly bowed his head and touched her with his mouth. The taste of her was clean as the taste of the sea.

Her eyes flew open. 'Sean, no, you mustn't–oh no, you mustn't.' There were lips within lips and a bud as softly resilient as a tiny green grape. Sean found it with the tip of his tongue.

'Oh, Sean, you can't do that. Please, please, please.' And her hands were in the thick hair at the back of his head holding him there.

'I can't stand it any more, come over me . . . quickly, quickly, Sean.'

Filling like a sail in a hurricane, swollen and hard and tight, stretched beyond its limit until it burst and was blown to shreds in the wind and was gone. Everything gone. The wind and the sail, the tension and the wanting, all gone. There was left only the great nothingness which is peace. Perhaps a kind of death; perhaps death is like that. But, like death, not an ending–for even death contains the seeds of resurrection. So they came back from peace to a new beginning, slowly at first and then faster until they were two people again. Two people on a blanket among reeds with the sunlight white on the sand about them.

'Each time it's better and better–isn't it, Sean?'

'Ah!' Sean stretched, arching his back and spreading his arms.

'Sean, you do love me, don't you?'

'Sure. Sure I love you.'

'I think you must love me to have done'–she hesitated–'to do what you did.'

'I just said so, didn't I?' Sean's attention wandered to the basket. He selected an apple and polished it on the basket.

'Tell me properly. Hold me tight and tell me.'

'Hell, Anna, how many times have I got to say it?' Sean bit into the apple. 'Did you bring any of your Ma's shortbread?'

It was coming on night when Sean got back to Theunis Kraal. He turned his horse over to one of the grooms and went into the house. His body tingled from the sun, and he felt the emptiness and sadness of after-love, but it was a good sadness, like the sadness of old memories.

Garrick was in the dining-room, eating alone. Sean walked into the room and Garrick looked up nervously.

'Hello, Garry.' Sean smiled at him and Garrick was momentarily dazzled by it. Sean sat down in the chair beside him and punched him lightly on the arm.

'Have you left any for me?' His hatred was gone.

'There's plenty,' Garrick nodded eagerly. 'Try some of the potatoes, they're jolly good.'

14

'They say the Governor sent for your Pa while he was in Pietermaritzburg. Had him alone for nearly two hours.' Stephen Erasmus took the pipe out of his mouth and spat down on to the railway lines. In his brown homespun and *veldschoen* he did not look like a rich cattleman. 'Well, we don't need a prophet to tell us what it was about, do we?'

'No, sir,' Sean agreed vaguely. The train was late and Sean wasn't listening. He had an entry in the stock register to explain to his father and he was mentally rehearsing his speech.

'*Ja,* we know what it's about all right.' Old Erasmus put the pipe back between his teeth and spoke around it. 'It's been two weeks now since the British Agent was recalled from Cetewayo's kraal at Gingindhlovu. *Liewe Here!* in the old days we'd have called out the Commando long ago.' He packed his pipe, pushing down on to the glowing tobacco with a calloused forefinger. Sean noticed that the finger was twisted and scarred by the trigger-guards of a hundred heavy rifles.

'You've never been on commando have you, *Jong*?'

'No, sir.'

'About time you did then,' said Erasmus, 'about bledy time.'

Up on the escarpment the train whistled and Sean started guiltily.

'There she is.' Erasmus stood up from the bench on which they were sitting and the station master came out from his office with a rolled red flag in his hand. Sean felt his stomach sink slowly until it stopped somewhere just above his knees.

The train ran in past them, whooshing steam and brake-whining. The single passenger coach stopped precisely opposite the wooden platform. Erasmus came forward and took Waite's hand.

'*Goeie More,* Steff.'

'*More*, Waite. They tell me you're the new chairman now. Well done, man.'

'Thanks. Did you get my telegram?' Waite spoke in Afrikaans.

'*Ja*. I got it. I told the others, we'll all be out at Theunis Kraal tomorrow.'

'Good,' Waite nodded. 'You'll stay for lunch, of course. We've got a lot to talk about.'

'Is it what I think it is?' Erasmus grinned wickedly. The tobacco had stained his beard yellow around his mouth and his face was brown and wrinkled.

'I tell you all about it tomorrow, Steff,' Waite winked at him, 'but in the meantime you'd better get that old muzzle-loader of yours out of moth-balls.'

They laughed, one deep down and the other a rusty old laugh.

'Grab the bags, Sean. Let's get home.' Waite took Ada's arm and they walked with Erasmus to the buggy. Ada had on a new dress, blue with leg o'mutton sleeves and a picture hat; she looked lovely but a little worried as she listened to them talking. It's strange how women can never face the prospect of war with the same boyish enthusiasm as their men.

'Sean!' Waite Courteney's roar carried clearly from his study along the corridor and through the closed door of the sitting-room. Ada dropped her knitting into her lap and her features set into an expression of unnatural calm. Sean stood up from his chair.

'You should have told him earlier,' Garrick said in a small voice. 'You should have told him during lunch.'

'I didn't get a chance.'

'Sean!' Another blast from the study.

'What's happened now?' asked Ada quietly.

'It's nothing, Ma. Don't worry about it.'

Sean crossed to the door.

'Sean,' Garrick's stricken voice, 'Sean, you won't–I mean you don't have to tell–' He stopped and sat hunched in his chair, his eyes full of desperate appeal.

'It's all right, Garry, I'll fix it.'

Waite Courteney stood over the desk. Between his clenched fists the stock register lay open. He looked up as Sean came in and closed the door.

'What's this?' He prodded the page with a huge square-tipped finger. Sean opened his mouth and then closed it again.

'Come on. I'm listening.'

'Well, Pa–'

'Well, Pa–be buggered. Just tell me how you've managed to massacre half the cattle on this farm in a little over a week?'

'It's not half the cattle–it's only thirteen.' Sean was stung by the exaggeration.

'Only thirteen,' bellowed Waite, '*only* thirteen. God Almighty, shall I tell you how much that is in cash? Shall I tell you how much that is in hard work and time and worry?'

'I know, Pa.'

'You know,' Waite was panting. 'Yes, you know everything. There's nothing anyone can tell you, is there? Not even how to kill thirteen head of prime oxen.'

'Pa–'

'Don't Pa me, by Jesus.' Waite slammed the heavy book closed. 'Just explain to me how you managed it. What's "dip poisoning"? What the bloody hell is "dip poisoning"? Did you give it to them to drink? Did you stick it up their arses?'

'The dip was too strong,' said Sean.

'And why was the dip too strong? How much did you put in?'

Sean took a deep breath, 'I put in four drums.'

There was silence and then Waite asked softly, *'How much?'*

'Four drums.'

'Are you mad? Are you raving bloody mad?'

'I didn't think it would harm them.' His carefully rehearsed speech forgotten, Sean unconsciously repeated the words he had heard from Garrick. 'It was getting late and my leg was–' Sean bit the sentence off and Waite stared at him, then the confusion cleared from his face.

'Garry!' he said.

'No,' shouted Sean. 'It wasn't him, I did it.'

'You're lying to me.' Waite came round from behind the desk. There was a note of disbelief in his voice. To his knowledge it was the first time it had ever happened. He stared at Sean and then his anger was back more violently than before. He had forgotten the oxen–it was the lie that concerned him now. 'By Christ, I'll teach you to tell the truth.' He snatched up his sjambok from the desk.

'Don't hit me, Pa,' Sean warned him, backing away. Waite threw up the sjambok and swung it down overarm. It hissed softly and Sean twisted away from it, but the tip of the lash caught his shoulder. Sean gasped at the pain and lifted his hand to it.

'You lying little bastard!' shouted Waite and swung the whip sideways as though he was scything wheat, and this time it curled around Sean's chest under his uplifted arm. It split his shirt like a razor cut and the cloth fell away to expose the red ridged welt across his ribs and around his back.

'Here's some more!' Waite lifted the sjambok again and as he stood with his arm thrown back and his body turned off balance he knew he had made a mistake. Sean was no longer clutching the whip marks; his hands were held low and his fists were bunched. At the corners his eyebrows were lifted, giving an expression of satanical fury to his face. He was pale and his lips were drawn back tight, showing his teeth. His eyes, no longer blue but burning black, were on a level with Waite's.

'He's coming for me.' Waite's surprise slowed his reflexes, he couldn't bring his whip-arm down before Sean was on him. Sean hit him, standing solidly on both feet, bringing the full weight of his body into the punch, hurling it into the middle of Waite's exposed chest.

Heart punched, strength oozing out of him, Waite staggered back against the desk. The sjambok fell out of his hand and Sean went after him. Waite had the sensation of being a beetle in a saucer of treacle: he could see and think but he could barely move. He saw Sean take three quick paces forward, saw his right hand cocked like a loaded rifle, saw it aimed at his defenceless face.

In that instant, while his body moved in slow motion but his mind raced, the scales of paternal blindness dropped from Waite Courteney's eyes and he realized that he was fighting a man who matched him in strength and height, and who was his superior in speed. His only advantage lay in the experience he had gathered in forty years of brawling.

Sean threw his punch: it had all the power of the first one and Waite knew that he could not survive that in his face–and yet he could not move to avoid it.

He dropped his chin on to his chest and took Sean's fist on the top of his head. The force of it flung him backwards over the desk, but as it hit he heard the brittle crackle of Sean's fingers breaking.

Waite dragged himself to his knees, using the corner of the desk as a support, and looking at his son. Sean was doubled up with pain, holding his broken hand against his stomach. Waite pulled himself to his feet and sucked in big breaths of air, he felt his strength coming back.

'All right,' he said, 'if you want to fight–then we fight.' He came round the desk, moving slowly, his hands ready, no longer underestimating his man.

'I am going to knock the daylights out of you,' announced Waite. Sean straightened up and looked at him. There was agony in his face now, but the anger was there also. Something surged up inside Waite when he saw it.

He can fight and he's game. Now we'll see if he can take a beating. Rejoicing silently Waite moved in on him, watching Sean's left hand, disregarding the broken right for he knew what pain was in it. He knew that no man could use a hand in that condition.

He shot out his own left hand, measuring with it, trying to draw Sean. Sean side-stepped, moving in past it. Waite was wide open for Sean's right, his broken right, the hand he could not possibly use–and Sean used it with all his strength into Waite's face.

Waite's brain burst into bright colours and darkness, he spun sideways, falling, hitting the leopard-skin rug with his shoulder and sliding with it across the floor into the fireplace. Then in the darkness he felt Sean's hands on him and heard Sean's voice.

'Pa, oh, my God, Pa. Are you all right?'

The darkness cleared a little and he saw Sean's face, the anger gone from it and in its place worry that was almost panic.

'Pa, oh, my God! Please, Pa.'

Waite tried to sit up, but he could not make it. Sean had to help him. He knelt next to Waite holding him, fumbling helplessly with his face, trying to brush the hair back off his forehead, stroking the rumpled beard into place. 'I'm sorry, Pa, truly I'm sorry. Let me help you to the chair.'

Waite sat in the chair and massaged the side of his jaw. Sean hovered over him, his own hand forgotten.

'What you want to do–kill me?' asked Waite ruefully.

'I didn't mean it. I just lost my temper.'

'I noticed,' said Waite, 'I just happened to notice that.'

'Pa–about Garry. You don't have to say anything to him, do you?'

Waite dropped his hand from his face and looked at Sean steadily.

'I'll make a bargain with you,' he said, 'I'll leave Garry out of it if you'll promise me two things. One: You never lie to me again.'

Sean nodded quickly.

'Two: If anybody ever takes a whip to you again you swear to me you'll give him the same as you just gave me.'

Sean started to smile and Waite went on gruffly. 'Now let's have a look at your hand.'

Sean held it out and Waite examined it, moving each finger in turn. Sean winced.

'Sore?' asked Waite. *He hit me with that. Sweet Jesus, I've bred me a wild one.*

'A little.' Sean was white-faced again.

'It's a mess,' said Waite. 'You'd better get into town right away and let

Doctor Van have a go at it.'

Sean moved towards the door.

'Hold on.' Sean stopped and Waite pulled himself out of his chair. 'I'll come with you.'

'I'll be all right, Pa, you stay and rest.'

Waite ignored this and walked towards him.

'Really, Pa, I'll be all right on my own.'

'I'm coming with you,' Waite said harshly; and then softly, almost inaudibly, 'I want to, dammit.'

He lifted his arm as though to put it around Sean's shoulders, but before it touched him he let it drop back to his side and together they went out into the corridor.

15

With two fingers in splints Sean handled his knife awkwardly at lunch the next day, but his appetite was unimpaired. As was only right and fitting he took no part in the conversation except on the rare occasions that a remark was addressed directly to him. But he listened, his jaws chewing steadily and his eyes moving from speaker to speaker. He and Garry sat side by side in a backwater of the luncheon board while the guests were grouped in order of seniority around Waite.

Stephen Erasmus by age and wealth was in the right-hand seat; opposite him Tim Hope-Brown, just as wealthy but ten years younger; below him Gunther Niewenhuizen, Sam Tingle and Simon Rousseau. If you added it all together you could say that Waite Courteney had about a hundred thousand acres of land and half a million sterling sitting around his table. They were brown men–brown clothing, brown boots and big brown, calloused, hands. Their faces were brown and battered-looking and now that the meal was in its closing stages their usual reserve was gone and there was a tendency among them to talk all at the same time and to perspire profusely. This was not entirely a consequence of the dozen bottles of good Cape Mossel that Waite had provided nor of the piles of food they had eaten–it was more than that. There was a sense of expectancy among them, an eagerness they were finding it difficult to suppress.

'Can I tell the servants to clear away, Waite?' Ada asked from the end of the table.

'Yes, thank you, my dear. We'll have coffee in here, please.'

He stood up and fetched a box of cigars from the sideboard and carried it to each of his guests in turn. When the ends were cut and the tips were glowing, every man leaning back in his chair with a recharged glass and a cup of coffee in front of him, Ada slipped out of the room and Waite cleared his throat for silence.

'Gentlemen.' They were all watching him. 'Last Tuesday I spent two hours with the Governor. We discussed the recent developments across the Tugela.'

Waite lifted his glass and sipped at it, then held it by the stem and rolled it between his fingers as he went on.

'Two weeks ago the British Agent at the Zulu king's kraal was recalled. Recalled is perhaps the wrong word–the king offered to smear him with honey and tie him over an ant-hill, an offer that Her Britannic Majesty's Agent declined with thanks. Shortly thereafter he packed his bags and made for the border.'

There was a small ruffle of laughter.

'Since then Cetewayo has collected all his herds which were grazing near the Tugela and driven them into the north; he has commanded a buffalo hunt for which he has decided he will need *all* his impis–twenty thousand spears. This hunt is to be held along the banks of the Tugela, where the last buffalo was seen ten years ago.' Waite sipped at his glass, watching their faces. 'And he has ordered that all wounded game is to be followed across the border.'

There was a sigh then, a murmur from them. They all knew that this was the traditional Zulu declaration of war.

'So, man, what are we going to do about it? Must we sit here and wait for them to come and burn us out?'

Erasmus leaned forward watching Waite.

'Sir Bartle Frere met Cetewayo's Indunas a week ago. He has given them an ultimatum. They have until January the eleventh to disband the impis and take the Queen's Agent back into Zululand. In the event that Cetewayo disregards the ultimatum, Lord Chelmsford is to command a punitive column of regulars and militia. The force is being assembled now and will leave Pietermaritzburg within the next ten days. He is to cross the Tugela at Rorkes Drift and engage the impis before they break out. It is intended to end this constant threat to our border and break the Zulu nation for ever as a military power.'

'It's about bledy time,' said Erasmus.

'His Excellency has gazetted me full colonel and ordered me to raise a commando from the Ladyburg district. I have promised him at least forty men fully armed, mounted and provisioned who will be ready to join Chelmsford at the Tugela. Unless any of you object I am appointing you gentlemen as my captains and I know I can rely upon you to help me make good my promise to His Excellency.'

Suddenly Waite dropped his stilted manner and grinned at them. 'You will collect your own pay. It will be in cattle, as usual.'

'How far north has Cetewayo driven his herds?' asked Tim Hope-Brown.

'Not far enough, I'll warrant,' cackled Stephen Erasmus.

'A toast,' said Simon Rousseau jumping to his feet and holding up his glass. 'I give you a toast: the Queen, Lord Chelmsford and the Royal Herds of Zululand.'

They all stood and drank it, and then suddenly embarrassed by their display they sat down again, coughing awkwardly and shuffling their feet.

'All right,' said Waite, 'let's get down to details. Steff, you'll be coming and your two eldest boys?'

'*Ja*, three of us and my brother and his son. Put down five, Erasmus.'

'Good. What about you, Gunther?'

They began the planning. Men, horses and wagons were marshalled on paper; each of the captains was allotted a series of tasks. There was question, answer and argument that filled the hours before the guests left Theunis Kraal. They rode in a bunch, trippling their horses, sitting slack and long-legged in the saddles, moving up the far slope along the road to Ladyburg. Waite and his sons stood on the front step and watched them go.

'Pa–' Garry tried tentatively for Waite's attention.

'Yes, boy?' Waite kept his eyes on the group. Steff Erasmus turned in the saddle and waved his hat above his head, Waite waved back.

'Why do we have to fight them, Pa? If the Governor just sent somebody to talk to them, then we wouldn't have to fight.'

Waite glanced at him, frowning slightly.

'Anything worth having is worth fighting for, Garry. Cetewayo has raised twenty thousand spears to take this from us–' Waite swept his arm in a circle that took in the whole of Theunis Kraal. 'I think it's worth fighting for–don't you, Sean?'

'You bet,' Sean nodded eagerly.

'But couldn't we just make a treaty with them?' Garry persisted.

'Another cross on a piece of paper.' Waite spoke with fierce disdain. 'They found one like that on Piet Retrief's body–hell of a lot of good it did him.'

Waite walked back into the house with his sons following him.

He lowered himself into his armchair, stretched his legs out in front of him and smiled at Ada. 'Damn good lunch, my dear.' He clasped his hands over his stomach, belched involuntarily and was immediately contrite. 'I beg your pardon–it just slipped out.'

Ada bent her head over her sewing to hide her smile.

'We've got a lot to do in the next few days.' He turned his attention back to his sons. 'We'll take one mule wagon and a pair of horses each. Now about ammunition. . . .'

'But, Pa, couldn't we just–?' Garry started again.

'Shut up,' said Waite, and Garry subsided miserably into one of the other chairs.

'I've been thinking,' announced Sean.

'Not you as well,' growled Waite. 'Damn it to hell, here's your chance to win your own cattle and. . . .'

'That's just what I've been thinking,' Sean cut in. 'Everybody will have more cattle than they know what to do with. The prices will drop way down.'

'They will at first,' admitted Waite, 'but in a year or two they'll climb back again.'

'Shouldn't we sell now? Sell everything except the bulls and breeding cows, then after the war we'll be able to buy back at half the price.'

For a moment Waite sat stunned and then slowly his expression changed.

'My God, I never thought of that.'

'And Pa,' Sean was twisting his hands together in his enthusiasm, 'we'll need more land. When we bring the herds back across the Tugela there won't be enough grazing to go round. Mr Pye has called the mortgages on Mount Sinai and Mahoba's Kloof. He's not using the land. Couldn't we lease them from him now before everybody starts looking for grazing?'

'We had a lot to do before you started thinking,' said Waite softly, 'but now we've really got to work.'

He searched his pockets, found his pipe and while he filled it with tobacco he looked at Sean. He tried to keep his face neutral but the pride kept showing.

'You keep thinking like that and you'll be a rich man one day.' Waite could not know how true his prophecy would prove–the time was still remote when Sean could drop the purchase price of Theunis Kraal across a gaming table, and laugh at the loss.

16

The Commando was moving out on New Year's Day. New Year's Eve was set down for a double celebration: 'Welcome 1879', and 'God speed the Ladyburg Mounted Rifles'. The whole district was coming into town for the *braaivleis* and dancing that was being held in the square. Feast the warriors–laugh, dance and sing, then form them up and march them out to war.

Sean and Garry rode in early. Ada and Waite were to follow later in the afternoon. It was one of those bright days of a Natal summer: no wind and no clouds, the kind of day when the dust from a wagon hangs heavy in the air. They crossed the Baboon Stroom and from the farther ridge looked down across the town and saw the wagon dust on every road leading into Ladyburg.

'Look at them come,' said Sean; he screwed up his eyes against the glare and stared at the north road. 'That will be the Erasmus wagon. Karl will be with them.'

The wagons looked like beads on a string.

'That's the Petersens',' said Garry, 'or the Niewehuisens'.'

'Come on,' shouted Sean, and slapped the free end of his reins across his horse's neck. They galloped down the road. The horses they rode were big glossy animals, with their manes cropped like English hunters.

They passed a wagon. There were two girls sitting beside mama on the box seat, the Petersen sisters. Dennis Petersen and his father were riding ahead of the wagon.

Sean whooped as he raced past the wagon and the girls laughed and shouted something that was lost in the wind.

'Come on, Dennis,' howled Sean as he swept past the two sedately trotting outriders. Dennis's horse reared and then settled in to run, chasing Sean. Garry trailed them both.

They reached the cross roads, lying flat along their horses' necks, pumping the reins like jockeys. The Erasmus wagon was trundling down to meet them.

'Karl,' Sean called as he held his horse a little to stand in the stirrups. 'Karl. Come on, man, catch a wayo, Cetewayo!'

They rode into Ladyburg in a bunch. They were all flush-faced and laughing, excited and happy at the prospect of dancing and killing.

The town was crowded, its streets congested with wagons and horses and men and women and girls and dogs and servants.

'I've got to stop at Pye's store,' said Karl, 'come with me–it won't take long.'

They hitched their horses and went into the store; Sean, Dennis and Karl walked noisily and talked aloud. They were men, big sun-burned raw-boned men, muscled from hard work, but uncertain of the fact that they were men. Therefore, walk with a swagger and laugh too loud, swear when Pa isn't listening and no one will know you have your doubts.

'What are you going to buy, Karl?'

'Boots.'

'That'll take all day–you'll have to try them on. We'll miss half the fun.'

'There'll be nothing doing for another couple hours,' protested Karl. 'Wait for me, you chaps.'

Karl sitting on the counter, trying boots on his large feet, was not a spectacle that could hold Sean's interest for long. He drifted away among the piles of merchandise that cluttered Pye's store. There were stacks of pick handles, piles of blankets, bins of sugar and salt and flour, shelves of groceries and clothing, overcoats and women's dresses and hurricane-lamps and saddles hanging from the roof, and all of it was permeated by the peculiar smell of a general dealer's store: a mixture of paraffin, soap and new cloth.

Pigeon to its coop, iron to magnet. . . . Sean's feet led him to the rack of rifles against the far wall of the room. He lifted down one of the Lee Metford carbines and worked the action; he stroked the wood with his fingertips, then he weighed it in his hands to feel the balance and finally brought it up to his shoulder.

'Hello, Sean.' His ritual interrupted, Sean looked up at the shy voice.

'It's Strawberry Pie,' he said smiling. 'How's school?'

'I've left school now. I left last term.'

Audrey Pye had the family colouring but with a subtle difference–instead of carrot her hair was smoked copper with glints in it. She was not a pretty girl, her face was too broad and flat, but she had that rare skin that too seldom goes with red hair: creamy unfreckled purity.

'Do you want to buy anything, Sean?'

Sean placed the carbine back in the rack.

'Just looking,' he said. 'Are you working in the store now?'

'Yes.' She dropped her eyes from Sean's scrutiny. It was a year since he'd last seen her. A lot can change in a year; she now had that within her blouse which proved she was no longer a child. Sean eyed it appreciatively and she glanced up and saw the direction of his eyes; the cream of her skin clouded red. She turned quickly towards the trays of fruit.

'Would you like a peach?'

'Thanks,' said Sean and took one.

'How's Anna?' asked Audrey.

'Why ask me?' Sean frowned.

'You're her beau, aren't you?'

'Who told you that?' Sean's frown became a scowl.

'Everybody knows that.'

'Well, everybody's wrong.' Sean was irritated by the suggestion that he was one of Anna's possessions. 'I'm nobody's beau.'

'Oh!' Audrey was silent a moment, then, 'I suppose Anna will be at the dance tonight?'

'Most probably.' Sean bit into the furry golden peach and studied Audrey. 'Are you going, Strawberry Pie?'

'No,' Audrey answered wistfully. 'Pa won't let me.'

How old was she? Sean made a quick calculation . . . three years younger than he was. That made her sixteen. Suddenly Sean was sorry she wouldn't be at the dance.

'That's a pity,' he said. 'We could have had some fun.' Linking them together, with the plural 'we', Sean threw her into confusion again. She said the first words she could think of, 'Do you like the peach?'

'Hmm.'

'It's from our orchard.'

'I thought I recognized the flavour.' Sean grinned and Audrey laughed. Her mouth was wide and friendly when she laughed. 'I knew you used to pinch them. Pa knew it was you. He used to say he'd set a mantrap in that hole in the hedge.'

'I didn't know he'd found that hole–we used to cover it up each time.'

'Oh, yes,' Audrey assured him, 'we knew about it all the time. It's still there. Some nights when I can't sleep I climb out of my bedroom window and go down through the orchard, through the hedge into the wattle plantation. It's so dark and quiet in the plantation at night–scary, but I like it.'

'You know something,' Sean spoke thoughtfully. 'If you couldn't sleep tonight and came down to the hedge at ten o'clock, you might catch me pinching peaches again.'

It took a few seconds for Audrey to realize what he had said. Then the colour flew up her face again and she tried to speak but no words came. She turned with a swirl of skirt and darted away among the shelves. Sean bit the last of the flesh off the peach pip and dropped it on the floor. He was smiling as he walked across to join the others.

'Hell's teeth, Karl, how much longer are you going to be?'

17

There were fifty or more wagons outspanned around the perimeter of the square but the centre was left open, and here the braaivleis pits were burning, the flames already sinking to form glowing beds. Trestle-tables stood in two lines near the fires and the women worked at them cutting meat and boerwors, buttering bread, arranging platoons of pickle bottles, piling the food on trays and sweetening the evening with their voices and laughter.

In a level place a huge buck-sail was spread for dancing and at each corner a lantern hung on a pole. The band was tuning with squeaks from the fiddles and preliminary asthma from the single concertina.

The men gathered in knots among the wagons or squatted beside the braaivleis pits, and here and there a jug pointed its base briefly at the sky.

'I don't like to be difficult, Waite,' Petersen came across to where Waite was standing with his captains, 'but I see you've put Dennis in Gunther's troop.'

'That's right.' Waite offered him the jug and Petersen took it and wiped the neck with his sleeve.

'It's not you, Gunther,' Petersen smiled at Gunther Niewehuisen, 'but I would be much happier if I could have Dennis in the same troop as myself. Keep an eye on him, you know.'

They all looked at Waite to hear what he would say. 'None of the boys are riding with their fathers. We've purposely arranged it that way. Sorry, Dave.'

'Why?'

Waite Courteney looked away, over the wagons at the furious red sunset that hung above the escarpment. 'This isn't going to be a bushbuck shoot, Dave. You may find that you'll be called upon to make decisions that will be easier for you if you're not making them about your own son.'

There was a murmur of agreement and Steff Erasmus took his pipe out of his mouth and spat into the fire. 'There are some things it is not pretty for a man to see. They are too hard for him to forget. He should not see his son kill his first man, also he should not see his son die.'

They were silent then, knowing this truth. They had not spoken of it before because too much talk softens a man's stomach, but they knew death and understood what Steff had said. One by one their heads turned until they were all staring across the square at the gathering of youngsters beyond the fires. Dennis Petersen said something but they could not catch the words and his companions laughed.

'In order to live a man must occasionally kill,' said Waite, 'but when he kills too young, he loses something . . . a respect for life: he makes it cheap. It is the same with a woman, a man should never have his first woman until he understands about it. Otherwise that too becomes cheap.'

'I had my first when I was fifteen,' said Tim Hope-Brown. 'I can't say it made them any cheaper; in fact I've known them to be bloody expensive.'

Waite's big boom led the laughter.

'I know your old man pays you a pound a week but what about us, Sean?' protested Dennis, 'we aren't all millionaires.'

'All right, then,' Sean agreed, 'five shillings in the pool. Winner takes the lot.'

'Five bob is reasonable,' Karl opined, 'but let's get the rules clear so there's no argument afterwards.'

'Kills only, woundings don't count,' said Sean.

'And they have to be witnessed,' insisted Frikkie Van Essen. He was older than the others; his eyes were already a little bloodshot for he had made a start on the evening's drinking.

'All right, dead Zulus only and a witness to each kill. The highest score takes the pool.' Sean looked around the circle of faces for their assent. Garry was hanging back on the fringe. 'Garry will be banker. Come on, Garry, hold out your hat.'

They paid the money into Garrick's hat and he counted it.

'Two pounds–from eight of us. That's correct.'

'Hell, the winner will be able to buy his own farm.'

They laughed.

'I've got a couple of bottles of smoke hidden in my saddle bags,' Frikkie said. 'Let's go and try them.'

The hands of the clock on the church tower showed quarter before ten. There were silver-edged clouds around the moon, and the night had cooled. Rich meaty smelling steam from the cooking pits drifted across the dancers, fiddles sawed and the concertina bawled the beat, dancers danced and the watchers clapped in time and called encouragement to them. Someone whooped like a Highlander in the feverish pattern of movement, in the fever of fun. Damn the dribble of minutes with laughter, hold the hour, lay siege against the dawn!

'Where are you going, Sean?'

'I'll be back just now.'

'But where are you going?'

'Do you want me to tell you, Anna, do you really want to know?'

'Oh, I see, Don't be long. I'll wait for you by the band.'

'Dance with Karl.'

'No, I'll wait for you, Sean. Please don't be long. We've got such a little time left.'

Sean slipped through the circle of wagons, he kept in the tree shadow along the sidewalk, round the side of Pye's store and down the lane, running now, jumped the ditch and through the barbed wire fence. It was dark in the plantation and quiet as she had said; dead leaves rustled and a twig popped under his feet. Something ran in the darkness, scurry of small feet. Sean's stomach flopped over: nerves, only a rabbit. He came to the hedge and searched for the hole, missed it and turned back, found it and through into the orchard. He stood with his back against the wall of vegetation and waited. The trees were moon grey and black below. He could see the roof of the house beyond them. He knew she'd come, of course. He had told her to.

The church clock chimed the hour and then later the single stroke of the quarter hour. Angry now, damn her! He went up through the orchard, cautiously staying in shadow. There was a light in one of the side windows, he could see it spilling out into a yellow square on the lawn. He circled the house softly.

She was at the window with the lamp behind her. Her face was dark but lamplight lit the edges of her hair into a coppery halo. There was something of yearning in her attitude, leaning forward over the sill. He could see the outline of her shoulders through the white cloth of her gown.

Sean whistled, pitching it low to reach her only, and she started at the sound. A second longer she stared out from light into the dark and then she shook her head, slowly and regretfully from side to side. She closed the curtains and through them Sean saw her shadow move away. The lamp went out.

Sean went back through the orchard and the plantation. He was trembling with anger. From the lane he heard the music in the square and he quickened his pace. He turned the corner and saw the lights and movement.

'Silly little fool,' he said out loud, anger still there but something else as well. Affection? Respect?

'Where have you been? I've waited nearly an hour.' Possessive Anna.

'There and back to see how far it is.'

'Funny! Sean Courteney, where have you been?'

'Do you want to dance?'

'No.'

'All right, don't then.'

Karl and some of the others were standing by the cooking pits. Sean started for them.

'Sean, Sean, I'm sorry.' Penitent Anna. 'I'd love to dance, please.'

They danced, jostled by other dancers, but neither of them spoke until the band stopped to wipe their brows and wet dry throats.

'I've got something for you, Sean.'

'What is it?'

'Come, I'll show you.'

She led him from the light among the wagons and stopped by a pile of saddles and blankets. She knelt and opened one of the blankets and stood up again with the coat in her hands.

'I made it for you. I hope you like it.'

Sean took it from her. It was a sheepskin, tanned and polished, stitched with love, the inside wool bleached snowy white.

'It's beautiful,' Sean said. He recognized the labour that had gone into it. It made him feel guilty: gifts always made him feel guilty.

'Thank you very much.'

'Try it on, Sean.'

Warm, snug at the waist, room to move in the shoulders; it enhanced his considerable bulk. Anna stood close to him, arranging the collar.

'You look nice in it,' she said. Smug pleasure of the giver.

He kissed her and the mood changed. She held him tight around the neck.

'Oh, Sean, I wish you weren't going.'

'Let's say goodbye properly.'

'Where?'

'My wagon.'

'What about your parents?'

'They've gone back to the farm. Pa's coming in tomorrow morning. Garry and I are sleeping here.'

'No, Sean, there are too many people. We can't.'

'You don't want to,' Sean whispered. 'It's a pity because it might be the last time ever.'

'What do you mean?' She was suddenly still and small in his arms.

'I'm going away tomorrow. You know what might happen?'

'No. Don't talk like that. Don't even think it.'

'It's true.'

'No, Sean, don't. Please don't.'

Sean smiled in the darkness. So easy, so very easy.

'Let's go to my wagon.' He took her hand.

18

Breakfast in the dark, cooking fires around the square, voices quiet, men standing with their wives, holding the small children in farewell. The horses saddled, rifles in the scabbards and blanket rolls behind, four wagons drawn up in the centre of the square with the mules in the traces.

'Pa should be here any minute. It's nearly five o'clock,' said Garry.

'They're all waiting for him,' agreed Sean. He shrugged at the weight of the bandolier strapped over his shoulder.

'Mr Niewehuizen has made me one of the wagon drivers.'

'I know,' said Sean. 'Can you handle it?'

'I think so.'

Jane Petersen came towards them.

'Hello, Jane. Is your brother ready yet?'

'Nearly. He's just saddling up.'

She stopped in front of Sean and shyly held out a scrap of green-and-yellow silk.

'I've made you a cockade for your hat, Sean.'

'Thanks, Jane. Won't you put it on for me?' She pinned up the brim of Sean's hat; he took it back from her and set it at a jaunty angle on his head.

'I look like a general now,' he said and she laughed at him. 'How about a goodbye kiss, Jane?'

'You're terrible,' said little Jane and went away quickly, blushing. Not so little, Sean noticed. There were so many of them you hardly knew where to start.

'Here's Pa,' announced Garry as Waite Courteney rode into the square.

'Come on,' said Sean and untied his horse. From all around the square men were leading out their horses.

'See you later,' said Garry and limped off towards one of the waiting mule wagons.

Waite rode at the head of the column. Four troops of fifteen men in double file, four wagons behind them, and then the loose horses driven by black servants.

They moved out across the square, through the litter of the night's festivities, and into the main street. The women watched them in silence, standing motionless with the children gathered around them. These women had seen men ride out before against the tribes; they did not cheer for they were wise in the ways of death, they had learned that there is no room for glory in the grave.

Anna waved to Sean. He did not see her for his horse was skittish and he was past her before he had it under control. She let her hand drop back to her side and watched him go. He wore the sheepskin coat.

Sean did see the coppery flash and the swiftly-blown kiss from the upstairs window of Pye's store. He saw it because he was looking for it. He forgot his injured pride sufficiently to grin and wave his hat.

Then they were out of the town, and at last even the small boys and dogs that ran beside them fell back and the column trotted out along the road to Zululand.

The sun came up and dried the dew. The dust rose from under the hooves and drifted out at an angle from the road. The column lost its rigidity as men spurred ahead or dropped back to ride with their friends. They rode in groups and straggles, relaxed and cheerfully chatting, as informal as a party out for a day's shooting. Each man had taken to the field in the clothing he considered most suitable. Steff Erasmus wore his church suit, but he was the most formally attired of the group. They had only one standard item of uniform among them: this was the green-and-yellow cockade. However, even here there was scope for individual taste: some wore them on their hats, some on their sleeves and others on their chests. They were farmers, not fighting men, but their rifle scabbards were battered with use, their bandoliers worn with easy familiarity and the wood of their gun butts was polished from the caress of their hands.

It was middle afternoon before they reached the Tugela.

'My God, look at that!' whistled Sean. 'I've never seen so many people in one place in my life before.'

'They say there are four thousand,' said Karl.

'I know there are four thousand.' Sean ran his eyes over the camp. 'But I didn't know four thousand was that many.'

The column was riding down the last slope to Rorkes Drift. The river was muddy brown and wide, rippling over the shallows of the crossing place. The banks were open and grassy with a cluster of stone-walled buildings on the near side. In a quarter-mile radius around the buildings Lord Chelmsford's army was encamped. The tents were laid out in meticulous lines, row upon row with the horses picketed between them. The wagons were marshalled by the drift, five hundred at least, and the whole area swarmed with men.

The Ladyburg Mounted Rifles, in a solid bunch that overflowed the road behind their Colonel, came down to the perimeter of the camp and found their passage blocked by a sergeant in a dress coat and with a fixed bayonet.

'And who be you, may I ask?'

'Colonel Courteney–and a detachment of the Ladyburg Mounted Rifles.'

'What's that? Didn't catch it.'

Waite Courteney stood in his stirrups and turned to face his men.

'Hold on there, gentlemen. We can't all talk at once.'

The hubbub of conversation and comment behind him faded and this time the sergeant heard him.

'Ho! Beg your pardon, sir. I'll call the orderly officer.'

The orderly officer was an aristocrat and a gentleman. He came and looked at them. 'Colonel Courteney?' There was a note of disbelief in his voice.

'Hello,' said Waite with a friendly smile. 'I hope we are not too late for the fun.'

'No, I don't believe you are.' The officer's eyes fastened on Steff Erasmus. Steff lifted his top hat politely. *'More, Meneer.'* The bandoliers of ammunition looked a little out of place slung across his black frockcoat.

The officer tore his eyes away from him. 'You have your own tents, Colonel?'

'Yes, we've got everything we need.'

'I'll get the sergeant here to show you where to make camp.'

'Thank you,' said Waite.

The officer turned to the sergeant. So carried away was he that he took the man by the arm. 'Put them far away. Put them on the other side of the Engineers–' he whispered frantically. 'If the General sees this lot. . . .' He shuddered, but in a genteel fashion.

19

Garrick first became conscious of the smell. Thinking about it served as a rallying point for his attention and he could start to creep out of the hiding-place in his mind. For Garrick these returns to reality were always accompanied by a feeling of light-headedness and a heightening of the senses. Colours were vivid, skin sensitive to the touch, tastes and smells sharp and clear.

He lay on a straw mattress. The sun was bright, but he was in shade. He lay on the veranda of the stone-walled hospital above Rorkes Drift. He thought about the smell that had brought him back. It was a blending of corruption and sweat and dung, the smell of ripped bowels and congealing blood.

He recognized it as the smell of death. Then his vision came into focus and he saw the dead. They were piled along the wall of the yard where the cross-fire from the store and the hospital had caught them; they were scattered between the buildings, and the burial squads were busy loading them on to the wagons. They were lying down the slope to the drift, they were in the water and on the far bank. Dead Zulus, with their weapons and shields strewn about them. Hundreds of them, Garrick thought with astonishment: no, thousands of them.

Then he was aware that there were two smells; but both of them were the smells of death. There was the stink of the black, balloon-bellied corpses swelling in the sun and there was the smell from his own body and the bodies of the men about him, the same smell of pain and putrefaction but mixed with the heaviness of disinfectant. Death wearing antiseptic–the way an unclean girl tries to cover her menstrual odour.

Garrick looked at the men around him. They lay in a long row down the veranda, each on his own mattress. Some were dying and many were not but on all of them the bandages were stained with blood and iodine. Garrick looked at his own body. His left arm was strapped across his bare chest and he felt the ache start beating within him, slow and steady as a funeral drum. There were bandages around his head. I'm wounded–again he was astonished. How? But how?

'You've come back to us, Cocky,' cheerful Cockney from beside him. 'We thought you'd gone clean bonkers.'

Garrick turned his head and looked at the speaker; he was a small monkey-faced man in a pair of flannel underpants and a mummy suit of bandages.

'Doc said it was shock. He said you'd come out of it soon enough.' The little man raised his voice, 'Hey, Doc, the hero is completely mentos again.' The doctor came quickly, tired-looking, dark under the eyes, old with overwork.

'You'll do,' he said, having groped and prodded. 'Get some rest. They're sending you back home tomorrow.' He moved away for there were many wounded, but then he stopped and looked back. He smiled briefly at Garrick, 'I doubt it will ease the pain at all but you've been recommended for the Victoria Cross. The General endorsed your citation yesterday. I think you'll get it.' Garrick stared at the doctor as memory came back patchily.

'There was fighting,' Garrick said.

'You're bloody well tooting there was!' the little man beside him guffawed.

'Sean!' said Garrick. 'My brother! What happened to my brother?' There was silence then and Garrick saw the quick shadow of regret in the doctor's eyes. Garrick struggled into a sitting position.

'And my Pa. What happened to my father?'

'I'm sorry,' said the doctor with simplicity, 'I'm afraid they were both killed.'

Garrick lay on his mattress and looked down at the Drift. They were clearing the corpses out of the shallows now, splashing as they dragged them to the bank. He remembered the splashing as Chelmsford's army had crossed. Sean and his father had been among the scouts who had led the column, three troops of the Ladyburg Mounted Rifles and sixty men of the Natal Police. Chelmsford had used these men who knew the country over which the initial advance was to be made.

Garrick had watched them go with relief. He could hardly believe the good fortune that had granted him a squirting dysentery the day before the ultimatum expired and the army crossed the Tugela.

'The lucky bastards,' protested one of the other sick as they watched them go. Garrick was without envy: he did not want to go to war, he was content to wait here with thirty other sick men and a garrison of sixty more to hold the Drift while Chelmsford took his army into Zululand.

Garrick had watched the scouts fan out from the Drift and disappear into the rolling grassland, and the main body of men and wagons follow them until they too had crawled like a python into the distance and left a well-worn road behind them through the grass.

He remembered the slow slide of days while they waited at the Drift. He remembered grumbling with the others when they were made to fortify the store and the hospital with bags and biscuit tins filled with sand. He remembered the boredom.

Then, his stomach tightened, he remembered the messenger.

'Horseman coming.' Garrick had seen him first. Recovered from his dysentery he was doing sentry duty above the Drift.

'The General's left his toothbrush behind, sent someone back for it,' said his companion. Neither of them stood up. They watched the speck coming across the plain towards the river.

'Coming fast,' said Garrick. 'You'd better go and call the Captain.'

'I suppose so,' agreed the other sentry. He trotted up the slope to the store and Garrick stood up and walked down to the edge of the river. His peg sank deep into the mud.

'Captain says to send him up to the store when he gets here.' Garrick's companion came back and stood beside him.

'Something funny about the way he's riding,' said Garrick, 'he looks tired.'

'He must be drunk. He's falling about in the saddle like it's Saturday night.'

Garrick gasped suddenly. 'He's bleeding, he's wounded.'

The horse plunged into the Drift and the rider fell forward on to its neck; the side of his shirt was shiny black with blood, his face was pale with pain and dust. They caught his horse as it came out of the water and the rider tried to shout but his voice was a croak. 'In the name of God prepare yourselves. The Column's been surrounded and wiped out. They're coming–the whole black howling pack of them. They'll be here before nightfall.'

'My brother,' said Garrick. 'What happened to my brother?'

'Dead,' said the man. 'Dead, they're all dead.' He slid sideways off his horse.

They came, the impis of Zulu in the formation of the bull, the great black bull whose head and loins filled the plain and whose horns circled left and right across the river to surround them. The bull stamped with twenty thousand feet and sang with ten thousand throats until its voice was the sound of the sea on a stormy day. The sunlight reflected brightly from the spear blades as it came singing to the Tugela.

'Look! Those in front are wearing the helmets of the Hussars,' one of the watchers in the hospital exclaimed. 'They've been looting Chelmsford's dead. There's one wearing a dress coat and some are carrying carbines.'

It was hot in the hospital for the roof was corrugated-iron and the windows were blocked with sandbags. The rifle slits let in little air. The men stood at the slits, some in pyjamas, some stripped to the waist and sweating in the heat.

'It's true then, the Column has been massacred.'

'That's enough talking. Stand to your posts and keep your mouths shut.'

The impis of Zulu crossed the Tugela on a front five hundred yards wide. They churned the surface to white with their crossing.

'My God! Oh, my God!' whispered Garrick as he watched them come. 'We haven't got a chance, there are so many of them.'

'Shut up. Damn you,' snapped the sergeant at the Gatling machine-gun beside him and Garry covered his mouth with his hand.

'–Grabbed O'Riley by the neck
Shoved his head in a pail of water
Rammed that pistol up his–'

sang one of the malaria cases in delirium and somebody else laughed, shrill hysteria in the sound.

'Here they come!'

'Load!'

The metallic clashing of rifle mechanism. 'Hold your fire, men. Fire on command only.'

The voice of the bull changed from a deep sonorous chant to the shrill ululation of the charge–high-pitched frenzy of the blood squeal.

'Steady, men. Steady. Hold it. Hold your fire.'

'Oh, my God!' whispered Garrick softly, watching them come black up the slope. 'Oh, my God!–please don't let me die.'

'Ready!'

The van had reached the wall of the hospital yard. Their plumed head-dresses were the frothy crest of a black wave as they came over the wall.

'Aim!'

Sixty rifles lifted and held, aimed into the press of bodies.

'Fire!'

Thunder, then the strike of bullets into flesh, a sound as though a handful of gravel had been flung into a puddle of mud. The ranks reeled from the blow. The clustered barrels of the Gatling machine-gun jump–jump–jumped as they swung, cutting them down so they fell upon each other, thick along the wall. The stench of burnt black powder was painful to breathe.

'Load!'

The bullet-ravaged ranks were re-forming as those from behind came forward into the gaps.

'Aim!'

They were coming again, solid black and screaming halfway across the yard.

'Fire!'

Garrick sobbed in the shade of the veranda and pressed the fingers of his right hand into his eye sockets to squeeze out the memory.

'What's the trouble, Cocky?' The Cockney rolled painfully on to his side and looked at Garrick.

'Nothing!' said Garrick quickly. 'Nothing!'

'Coming back to you, is it?'

'What happened? I can only remember pieces of it.'

'What happened!' The man echoed his question, 'What didn't happen!'

'The doctor said–' Garrick looked up quickly, 'He said the General had endorsed my citation. That means Chelmsford's alive. My brother and my father–they must be alive as well!'

'No such luck, Cocky. The Doc's taken a fancy to you–you with one leg doing what you did–so he made inquiries about your folk. It's no use.'

'Why?' asked Garrick desperately. 'Surely if Chelmsford's alive they must be too?'

The little man shook his head. 'Chelmsford's made a base camp at a place called Isandhlwana. He left a garrison there with all the wagons and supplies. He took a flying column out to raid, but the Zulus circled around him and attacked the base camp, then they came on here to the Drift. As you know, we held them for two days until Chelmsford's flying column came to help us.'

'My folk–what happened to them?'

'Your father was at the Isandhlwana camp. He didn't escape. Your brother was with Chelmsford's column but he was cut off and killed in one of the skirmishes before the main battle.'

'Sean dead?' Garrick shook his head. 'No, it's not possible. They couldn't have killed him.'

'You'd be surprised how easily they did it,' said the Cockney. 'A few inches of blade in the right place is enough for the best of them.'

'But not Sean–you didn't know him. You couldn't understand.'

'He's dead, Cocky. Him and your Pa and seven hundred others. The wonder is we aren't too.' The man wriggled into a more comfortable position on his mattress. 'The General made a speech about our defence here. Finest feat of arms in the annals of British courage–or something like that.'

He winked at Garrick. 'Fifteen citations for the old V.C.–you's one of them. I ask you, Cocky, isn't that something? What's your girl friend going to do when you come home with a mucking great gong clanking around on your chest, hey?'

He stared at Garrick and saw the tears oozing in oily lines down his cheeks.

'Come on, Cock. You're a bloody hero.' He looked away from Garrick's grief. 'Do you remember that part–do you remember what you did?'

'No,' Garrick's voice was husky. *Sean. You can't leave me alone. What am I going to do, now that you're gone?*

'I was next to you. I saw it all. I'll tell you about it,' said the Cockney.

As he talked so the events came back and fitted into sequence in Garrick's mind.

'It was on the second day, we'd held off twenty-three charges.'

Twenty-three, was it as many as that? Garrick had lost count; it might have been but a single surging horror. Even now he could taste the fear in the back of his throat and smell it rancid in his own sweat.

'Then they piled wood against the hospital wall and set fire to it.' Zulus coming across the yard carrying bundles of faggots, falling to the rifles, others picking up the bundles and bringing them closer until they too died and yet others came to take their place. Then flames pale yellow in the sunlight, a dead Zulu lying on the bonfire, his face charring, and the smell of him mingled with the smoke.

'We knocked a hole in the back wall and started to move the sick and wounded out through it and across to the store.'

The boy with the assegai through his spine had shrieked like a girl as they lifted him.

'Them bloody savages came again as soon as they saw we were pulling out. They came from that side,' he pointed with his bandaged arm, 'where the chaps in the store couldn't reach them, and there was only you and I and a couple of others at the loopholes–everyone else was carrying the wounded.'

There had been a Zulu with the blue heron feathers of an Induna in his head-dress. He had led the charge. His shield was dried oxhide dappled black and white, and at his wrists and ankles were bunches of war rattles. Garrick had fired at the instant the Zulu half-turned to beckon to his warriors–the bullet sliced across the tensed muscles of his belly and unzipped it like a purse. The Zulu went down on his hands and knees with his entrails bulging out in a pink and purple mass.

'They reached the door of the hospital and we couldn't fire on them from the angle of the windows.'

The wounded Zulu started to crawl towards Garrick, his mouth moving and his eyes fastened on Garrick's face. He still had his assegai in his hand. The other Zulus were beating at the door and one of them ran his spear blade through a crack in the woodwork and lifted the bar. The door was open.

Garrick watched the Zulu crawling towards him through the dust with his pink wet bowels swinging like a pendulum under him. The sweat was running down Garrick's cheeks and dripping off the end of his chin, his lips were trembling. He lifted his rifle and aimed into the Zulu's face. He could not fire.

'That's when you moved, Cocky. I saw the bar lifted out of its brackets and I knew that in the next second there'd be a mob of them in through the door and we'd stand no chance against their spears at close range.'

Garrick let go his rifle and it rattled on the concrete floor. He turned away from the window. He could not watch that crippled, crawling thing. He wanted to run, to hide. That was it–to hide. He felt the fluttering start behind his eyes, and his sight began to grey.

'You were nearest to the door. You did the only thing that could have saved us. Though I know I wouldn't have had the guts to do it.'

The floor was covered with cartridge cases–brass cylinders shiny and treacherous under foot. Garrick stumbled; as he fell he put out his arm.

'Christ,' the little Cockney shuddered, 'to put your arm into the brackets like that–I wouldn't have done it.'

Garrick felt his arm snap as the mob of Zulus threw themselves against the door. He hung there staring at his twisted arm, watching the door tremble and shake as they beat against it. There was no pain and after a while everything was grey and warm and safe.

'We fired through the door until we had cleared them away from the other side. Then we were able to get your arm free, but you were out cold. Been that way ever since.'

Garrick stared out across the river. He wondered if they had buried Sean or left him in the grass for the birds.

Lying on his side Garrick drew his legs up against his chest, his body was curled. Once as a brutal small boy he had cracked the shell of a hermit crab. Its soft fat abdomen was so vulnerable that its vitals showed through the transparent skin. It curled its body into the same defensive attitude.

'I'll reckon you'll get your gong,' said the Cockney.

'Yes,' said Garrick. He didn't want it. He wanted Sean back.

20

Doctor van Rooyen gave Ada Courteney his arm as she stepped down from the buggy. In fifty years he had not obtained immunity from other people's sorrow. He had learned only to conceal it: no trace of it in his eyes, or his mouth, or his lined and whiskered face.

'He's well, Ada. They did a good job on his arm: that is, for military surgeons. It will set straight.'

'When did they arrive?' asked Ada.

'About four hours ago. They sent all the Ladyburg wounded back in two wagons.'

Ada nodded, and he looked at her with the professional shield of indifference, hiding the shock he felt at the change in her appearance. Her skin was as dry and lifeless as the petals of a pressed flower, her mouth had set determinedly against her grief and her widow's weeds had doubled her age.

'He's waiting for you inside.' They walked up the steps of the church and the small crowd opened to let them pass. There were subdued greetings for Ada and the usual funereal platitudes. There were other women there wearing black, with swollen eyes.

Ada and the doctor went into the cool gloom of the church. The pews had been pushed against the wall to make room for the mattresses. Women were moving about between them and men lay on them.

'I'm keeping the bad ones here, where I can watch them,' the doctor told her. 'There's Garry.'

Garrick stood up from the bench on which he was sitting. His arm was slung awkwardly across his chest. He limped forward to meet them, his peg tapped loudly on the stone floor.

'Ma, I'm–' he stopped. 'Sean and Pa–'

'I've come to take you home, Garry.' Ada spoke quickly, flinching at the sound of those two names.

'They can't just let them lie out there, they should–'

'Please, Garry. Let's go home,' said Ada. 'We can talk about it later.'

'We are all very proud of Garry,' said the doctor.

'Yes,' said Ada. 'Please, let's go home, Garry.' She could feel it there just below the surface and she held it in: so much sorrow confined in so small a place. She turned back towards the door, she mustn't let them see it. She mustn't cry here in front of them, she must get back to Theunis Kraal.

Willing hands carried Garrick's bags out to the buggy and Ada took the reins. Neither of them spoke again until they crossed the ridge and looked down at the homestead.

'You're the master of Theunis Kraal now, Garry,' said Ada softly and Garrick stirred uneasily on the seat beside her. He didn't want it, he didn't want the medal. He wanted Sean.

21

'I hope you don't mind me coming,' said Anna, 'but I had to talk to you.'

'No. I'm glad you did. Truly I'm glad,' Garrick assured her earnestly. 'It's so good to see you again, Anna. It feels like forever since we left.'

'I know, and so much–so much has happened. My Pa and yours. And–and Sean.' She stopped. 'Oh, Garry, I just can't believe it yet. They've told me and told me but I can't believe it. He was so–so alive.'

'Yes,' said Garrick, 'he was so alive.'

'He talked about dying the night before he left. I hadn't even thought about it until then,' Anna shook her head in disbelief, 'and I never dreamed it could happen to him. Oh Garry, what am I going to do?'

Garrick turned and looked at Anna. The Anna he loved, Sean's Anna. But Sean was dead. He felt an idea move within him, not yet formed in words, but real enough to cause a sick spasm of conscience. He shied away from it.

'Oh, Garry. What can I do?'

She was asking for help, the appeal was apparent in her voice. Her father killed at Isandhlwana, her elder brothers still with Chelmsford at Tugela, her mother and the three small children to feed. How blind of him not to see it!

'Anna, can I help you? Just tell me.'

'No, Garry. I don't think anyone can.'

'If it's money–' He hesitated discreetly. 'I'm a rich man now. Pa left the whole of Theunis Kraal to Sean and I, and Sean isn't–' She looked at him without answering.

'I can lend you some to tide you over–' blushed Garrick, 'as much as you need.'

She went on staring at him while her mind adjusted itself. Garrick master of Theunis Kraal, he was rich, twice as rich as Sean would have been. And Sean was dead.

'Please, Anna. Let me help you. I want to, really I do.'

He loved her, it was pathetically obvious–and Sean was dead.

'You will let me, Anna?'

She thought of hunger and bare feet, dresses washed until you could see through them when you held them to the light, petticoats patched and cobbled. And always the fear, the uncertainty you must live with when you are poor. Garry was rich and alive, Sean was dead.

'Please tell me you will.' Garrick leaned forward and took her arm, he gripped it fiercely in his agitation and she looked into his face. You could see the resemblance, she thought, but Sean had strength where here there was softness and uncertainty. The colour was wrong also, pale sand and paler blue instead of brutal black and indigo. It was as though an artist had taken a portrait and with a few subtle strokes had altered its meaning completely so as to make it into an entirely different picture. She did not want to think about his leg.

'It's sweet of you, Garry,' she said, 'but we've got a little in the bank and the plot is free of debt. We've got the horses; we can sell them if we have to.'

'What is it then? Please tell me.'

She knew then what she was going to do. She could not lie to him–it was too late for that. She would have to tell him, but she knew that the truth would not make any difference to him. Well, perhaps a little–but not enough to prevent her getting what she wanted. She wanted to be rich, and she wanted a father for the child she carried within her.

'Garry, I'm going to have a baby.'

Garrick's chin jerked up and his breathing jammed and then started again.

'A baby?'

'Yes, Garrick. I'm pregnant.'

'Whose? Sean's?'

'Yes, Garry. I'm going to have Sean's baby.'

'How do you know, are you sure?'

'I'm sure.'

Garrick pulled himself out of his chair and limped across the veranda. He stopped against the railing and gripped it with his good hand; the other was still in the sling. His back was turned to Anna and he stared out across the lawns of Theunis Kraal to the lightly-forested slope beyond.

Sean's baby. The idea bewildered him. He knew that Sean and Anna did that together. Sean had told him and Garrick had not resented it. He was jealous, but only a little, for Sean had let him share in it by telling him and so some of it had belonged to him also. But a baby. Sean's baby.

Slowly the full implication came to him. Sean's baby would be a living part of his brother, the part that had not been cut down by the Zulu blades. He had not completely lost Sean. Anna–she must have a father for her child, it was unthinkable that she could go another month without marrying. He could have both of them, everything he loved in one package. Sean and Anna. She must marry him, she had no other choice. Triumph surged up within him and he turned to her.

'What will you do, Anna?' He felt sure of her now. 'Sean's dead. What will you do?'

'I don't know.'

'You can't have the baby. It would be a bastard.' He saw her wince at the word. He felt very certain of her.

'I'll have to go away–to Port Natal.' She spoke without expression in her voice. Looking calmly at him, knowing what he would say, 'I'll leave soon,' she said, 'I'll be all right. I'll find some way out.'

Garrick watched her face as she spoke. Her head was small on shoulders wide for a girl, her chin was pointed, her teeth were slightly crooked but white–she was very pretty despite the catlike set of her eyes.

'I love you, Anna,' he said. 'You know that, don't you?'

She nodded slowly and her hair moved darkly on her shoulders. The cat eyes softened contentedly. 'Yes, I know, Garry.'

'Will you marry me?' He said it breathlessly.

'You don't mind? You don't mind about Sean's baby?' she said, knowing he did not.

'I love you, Anna.' He came towards her clumsily and she looked up at his face. She did not want to think about the leg.

'I love you, nothing else matters.' He reached for her and she let him hold her.

'Will you marry me, Anna?' He was trembling.

'Yes.' Her hands were quiescent on his shoulders. He sobbed softly and her expression changed to one of distaste, she made the beginnings of a movement to push him away but stopped herself.

'My darling, you won't regret it. I swear you won't,' he whispered.

'We must do it quickly, Garry.'

'Yes. I'll go into town this afternoon and speak to Padre–'

'No! Not here in Ladyburg,' Anna cut in sharply. 'People will have too much to say. I couldn't stand it.'

'We'll go up to Pietermaritzburg,' Garrick acquiesced.

'When, Garry?'

'As soon as you like.'

'Tomorrow,' she said. 'We'll go tomorrow.'

22

The Cathedral in Pietermaritzburg stands on Church Street. Grey stone with a bell-tower and iron railings between the street and the lawns. Pigeons strut puff-chested on the grass.

Anna and Garrick went up the paved path and into the semi-dark of the Cathedral. The stained glass window had the sun behind it, making the interior glow weirdly with colour. Because they were both nervous they held hands as they stood in the aisle.

'There's no one here,' whispered Garrick.

'There must be,' Anna whispered back. 'Try through that door there.'

'What shall I say?'

'Just tell him we want to get married.'

Garrick hesitated.

'Go on.' Anna still whispered, pushing him gently towards the door of the vestry.

'You come with me,' said Garrick. 'I don't know what to say.'

The priest was a thin man with steel-rimmed spectacles. He looked over the top of them at the nervous pair in the doorway and shut the book on the desk in front of him.

'We want to get married,' Garrick said and blushed crimson.

'Well,' said the priest drily, 'you have the right address. Come in.'

He was surprised at their haste and they argued a little, then he sent Garrick down to the Magistrates' Court for a special licence. He married them, but the ceremony was hollow and unreal. The drone of the priest's voice was almost lost in the immense cavern of the Cathedral as they stood small and awed before him. Two old ladies who came in to pray stayed on gleefully to witness for them, and afterwards they both kissed Anna and the priest shook Garrick's hand. Then they went out again into the sunlight. The pigeons still strutted on the lawn and a mule wagon rattled down Church Street with the coloured driver singing and cracking his whip. It was as though nothing had happened.

'We're married,' said Garrick doubtfully.

'Yes,' agreed Anna, but she sounded as though she didn't believe it either.

They walked back to the hotel side by side. They didn't talk or touch each other. Their luggage had been taken up to their room and the horses had been stabled. Garrick signed the register and the clerk grinned at him.

'I've put you in Number Twelve, sir, it's our honeymoon suite.' One of the eyelids drooped slightly and Garrick stammered in confusion.

After dinner, an excellent dinner, Anna went up to the room and Garrick sat on in the lounge drinking coffee. It was almost an hour later that he mustered the courage to follow her. He crossed the drawing-room of their suite, hesitated at the bedroom door then went in. Anna was in bed. She had pulled the bedclothes up to her chin and she looked at him with her inscrutable cat's eyes.

'I've put your nightshirt in the bathroom, on the table,' she said.

'Thank you,' said Garrick. He stumbled against a chair as he crossed the room. He closed the door behind him, undressed quickly and leaning naked over the basin splashed water on to his face; then he dried and pulled the nightshirt over his head. He went back into the bedroom: Anna lay with her face turned away from him. Her hair was loose on the pillow, shining in the lamp-light.

Garrick sat on the edge of the chair. He lifted the hem of his nightshirt above his knee and unfastened the straps of his leg, laid the peg carefully beside the chair and massaged the stump with both hands. It felt stiff. He heard the bed creak softly and he looked up. Anna was watching him, staring at his leg. Hurriedly Garrick pulled down his nightshirt to cover the protruding slightly enlarged end with its folded line of scar-tissue. He stood up, balancing, and then hopped one-legged across to the bed. He was blushing again.

He lifted the edge of the blankets and slipped into the bed and Anna jerked violently away from him.

'Don't touch me,' she said hoarsely.

'Anna. Please don't be scared.'

'I'm pregnant, you mustn't touch me.'

'I won't. I swear I won't.'

She was breathing hard, making no attempt to hide her revulsion.

'Do you want me to sleep in the drawing-room, Anna? I will if you say so.'

'Yes,' she said, 'I want you to.'

He gathered his dressing-gown from the chair and stooping picked up his leg. He hopped to the door and turned back to face her. She was watching him still.

'I'm sorry, Anna, I didn't mean to frighten you.' She did not answer him and he went on.

'I love you. I swear I love you more than anything in the world. I wouldn't hurt you, you know that, don't you? You know I wouldn't hurt you?'

Still she did not answer and he made a small gesture of appeal, the wooden leg clutched in his hand and the tears starting to fill his eyes. 'Anna, I'd kill myself rather than frighten you!'

He went quickly through the door and closed it behind him, Anna scrambled out of the bed and with her nightdress flurrying around her legs she ran across the room to the door and turned the key in the lock.

23

In the morning Garrick was bewildered to find Anna in a mood of girlish gaiety. She had a green ribbon in her hair and her green frock was faded but pretty. She chattered happily through breakfast and while they were having their coffee she leaned across the table and touched Garrick's hand. 'What shall we do today, Garry?'

Garrick looked surprised, he hadn't thought that far ahead. 'I suppose we'd better catch the afternoon train back to Ladyburg,' he said.

'Oh, Garry,' Anna pouted effectively. 'Don't you love me enough to give me a honeymoon?'

'I suppose–' Garrick hesitated and then 'of course, I didn't think of it.' He grinned excitedly. 'Where can we go?'

'We could take the mail boat down the coast to Capetown,' Anna suggested.

'Yes!' Garrick adopted the idea immediately. 'It'll be fun.'

'But, Garry–' Anna's eagerness faded. 'I only have two old dresses with me.' She touched her clothes. Garrick sobered also while he grappled with this new problem. Then he found the solution.

'We'll buy you some more!'

'Oh, Garry, could we? Could we really?'

'We'll buy you all you can use, more than you can use. Come on, finish your coffee and we'll go into town and see what they have.'

'I'm finished.' Anna stood up from the table ready to go.

24

They had a stateroom on the *Dunottar Castle* from Port Natal to Capetown. There were other young people aboard. Anna, in her elegant new clothing and sparkling with excitement, formed the centrepiece of a gay little group that played deck games, dined, danced and flirted as the mailboat drove south through the sunny golden days of early autumn.

At first Garrick was content to stay unobtrusively close to Anna. He was there to hold her coat, fetch a book or carry a rug. He watched her fondly, revelling in her success, hardly jealous when she almost disappeared behind a palisade of attentive young men, not resenting the sofa which formed his uncomfortable bed in the drawing-room of their suite.

Then gradually there came a realization among their travelling companions that Garrick was paying for most of the refreshments and other little expenses that came up each day. They became aware of him and of the fact that he appeared to be the richest of the group. From there it needed only a small adjustment to their thinking to admit Garrick to the circle. The men addressed remarks directly at him and some of the other girls flirted with him openly and sent him on small errands. Garrick was at once overjoyed and appalled by these attentions, for he could not cope with the lightning exchange of banter that flickered around him and left him stammering and blushing. Then Garrick found how easy it really was.

'Have a dram, old chap?'

'No, really. I don't, you know.'

'Nonsense, everybody does. Steward, bring my friend here a whisky.'

'Really, no really I won't.'

And of course Garrick did. It tasted foul and he spilt a little on Anna's evening dress; while he wiped it up with his handkerchief she whispered a barbed reprimand and then laughed gaily at a joke from the moustached gentleman on her right. Garrick shrank miserably back in his chair and forced down the rest of the whisky. Then slowly and exquisitely the glow came upon him, starting deep down inside him and spreading out warmly to the very tips of his fingers.

'Have another one, Mr Courteney?'

'Yes, thanks. I'll have the same again, but I think it's my round.' He had the next drink. They were sitting in deck-chairs on the upper deck in the shelter of the superstructure, there was a moon and the night was warm. Someone was talking about Chelmsford's Zulu campaign.

'You're wrong on that point,' Garrick said clearly. There was a small silence.

'I beg your pardon!' the speaker glanced at him with surprise. Garrick leaned forward easily in his chair and began talking. There was a stiffness at first but he made a witticism and two of the women laughed. Garrick's voice strengthened. He gave a quick and deep-sighted résumé of the causes and effects of the war. One of the man asked a question. It was a sharp one but Garrick saw the essence of it and answered neatly. It was all very clear and he found the words without effort.

'You must have been there,' one of the girls hazarded.

'My husband was at Rorkes Drift,' said Anna quietly, looking at him as though he were a stranger. 'Lord Chelmsford has cited him for the award of the Victoria Cross. We are waiting to hear from London.'

The party was silent again, but with new respect.

'I think it's my round, Mr Courteney. Yours is whisky, isn't it?'

'Thank you.'

The dry musty taste of the whisky was less offensive this time; he sipped it thoughtfully and found there was a faint sweetness in the dry.

As they went down to their staterooms later that night Garrick put his arm around Anna's waist.

'What fun you were tonight!' she said.

'Only a reflection of your charm, my darling, I am your mirror.' He kissed her cheek and she pulled away, but not violently.

'You're a tease, Garry Courteney.'

Garrick slept on his back on the sofa with a smile on his face and no dreams, but in the morning his skin felt tight and dry and there was a small ache behind his eyes. He went through to the bathroom and cleaned his teeth; it helped a little but the ache behind his eyes was still there. He went back to the drawing-room and rang for the cabin steward.

'Good morning, sir.'

'Can you bring me a whisky and soda?' Garry asked hesitantly.

'Certainly, sir.'

Garry did not put the soda into it but drank it neat, like medicine. Then afterwards miraculously the glow was there again, warming him. He had hardly dared to hope for it.

He went through to Anna's cabin. She was rosy with sleep, her hair a joyous tangle on the pillow.

'Good morning, my darling.' Garrick stooped over her and kissed her, and his hand moved to cover one of her breasts through the silk of her gown.

'Garry, you naughty boy.' She slapped his wrist, but jokingly.

There was another honeymoon couple aboard returning to their farm near Capetown–seventy-five acres of the finest vines on the whole of the Cape Peninsula, the man's own words. Anna and Garrick were forced by sheer persistence to accept their invitation to stay with them.

Peter and Jane Hugo were a delightful pair. Very much in love, rich enough, popular and in demand with Capetown society. With them Anna and Garrick spent an enchanted six weeks.

They went racing at Milnerton.

They swam at Muizenberg in the warm Indian Ocean. They picknicked at Clifton and ate crayfish, fresh caught and grilled over open coals. They rode to hounds with the Cape Hunt and caught two jackals after a wild day's riding over the Hottentots' Holland. They dined at the Fort and Anna danced with the Governor.

They went shopping in the bazaars that were filled with treasures and curiosities from India and the Orient. Whatever Anna wanted she was given. Garry bought himself something as well–a silver flask, beautifully worked and set with cornelians. It fitted into the inside pocket of his coat without showing a bulge. With its help Garrick was able to keep pace with the rest of the company.

Then the time came for them to leave. The last night there were only the four of them for dinner and it was sad with the regret of present parting, but happy with the memory of shared laughter.

Jane Hugo cried a little when she kissed Anna goodnight. Garry and Peter lingered on downstairs until the bottle was finished and then they walked upstairs together and shook hands outside Garry's bedroom. Peter spoke gruffly. 'Sorry to see you two go. We've got used to having you round. I'll wake you early and we can go out for a last early morning ride before the boat leaves.'

Garry changed quietly in the bathroom and went through to the bedroom.

His peg made no sound on the heavily carpeted floor. He crossed to his own bed and sat down to unstrap his peg.

'Garry,' Anna whispered.

'Hullo, I thought you were asleep.'

There was a stirring and Anna's hand came out from under the bedclothes, held towards him in invitation.

'I was waiting to say goodnight to you.'

Garry crossed to her bed, suddenly awkward again.

'Sit down for a minute,' said Anna and he perched on the edge of her bed. 'Garry, you don't know how much I've enjoyed these last weeks. They've been the happiest days of my whole life. Thank you so much, my husband.'

She reached up and touched his cheek. She looked small and warm curled up in the bed.

'Kiss me goodnight, Garry.'

He leaned forward to touch her forehead with his lips but she moved quickly and took it full on her mouth.

'You can come in, if you like,' she whispered, her mouth still against his. She opened the bedclothes with one hand.

So Garry came to her when the bed was warm, and the wine still sang a little in her head and she was ready in the peculiar passion of early pregnancy. It should have been so wonderfully good.

Impatient now, ready to lead him, she reached down to touch and then stilled into surprised disbelief. Where there should have been hardness, male and arrogant, there was slackness and uncertainty.

Anna started to laugh. Not even the shotgun blast had hurt as deeply as that laugh.

'Get out,' she said through the cruel laughter. 'Go to your own bed.'

25

Anna and Garrick had been married two full months when they came back to Theunis Kraal. Garrick's arm was out of plaster, Peter Hugo's doctor had fixed that for him.

They took the road that by-passed the village and crossed the Baboon Stroom bridge. At the top of the rise Garry pulled the horses to a halt and they looked out across the farm.

'I can't understand why Ma moved into town,' said Garrick. 'She didn't have to do that. There's plenty of room for everybody at Theunis Kraal.'

Anna sat silently and contentedly beside him. She had been relieved when Ada had written to them at Port Natal after they had telegraphed her the news of their marriage. Young as she was Anna was woman enough to recognize the fact that Ada had never liked her. Oh, she was sweet enough when they met, but Anna found those big dark eyes of hers disconcerting. They looked too deep and she knew they found the things she was trying to hide.

'We'll have to go and see her as soon as we can. She must come back to the farm–after all Theunis Kraal is her home too,' Garrick went on. Anna moved slightly in her seat, *let her stay in the house in Ladyburg, let her rot there,* but her voice was mild as she answered, 'Theunis Kraal belongs to you now, Garry, and I'm your wife. Perhaps your stepmother knows what's best.' Anna touched his arm and smiled at him, 'Anyway we'll talk about it some other time. Let's get home now, it's been a long drive and I'm very tired.'

Immediately concerned, Garrick turned to her. 'I'm terribly sorry, my dear. How thoughtless of me.' He touched the horses with the whip and they went down the slope towards the homestead.

The lawns of Theunis Kraal were green and there were cannas in bloom, red and pink and yellow.

It's beautiful, thought Anna, *and it's mine. I'm not poor any more.* She looked at the gabled roof and the heavy yellow wood shutters on the windows as the carriage rolled up the drive.

There was a man standing in the shade of the veranda. Anna and Garrick saw him at the same time. He was tall with shoulders as wide and square as the crosstree of a gallows, he stepped out of the shadow and came down the front steps into the sunlight. He was smiling with white teeth in a brown burnt face; it was the old irresistible smile.

'Sean,' whispered Anna.

26

Sean really noticed him for the first time when they stopped to water the horses. They had left Chelmsford's Column the previous noon to scout towards the north-east. It was a tiny patrol–four mounted white men and half-a-dozen Nongaai, the loyal Native troops from Natal.

He took the reins from Sean's hands. 'I will hold your horse while you drink.' His voice had a resonance to it and Sean's interest quickened. He looked at the man's face and liked it immediately. The whites of the eyes had no yellow in them and the nose was more Arabic than negroid. His colour was dark amber and his skin shone with oil.

Sean nodded. There is no word in the Zulu language for 'thank you', just as there are no words for 'I am sorry'.

Sean knelt beside the stream and drank. The water tasted sweet for he was thirsty; when he stood again there were damp patches on his knees and water dripping from his chin.

He looked at the man who was holding his horse. He wore only a small kilt of civet-cat tails: no rattles nor cloak, no head-dress. His shield was black rawhide and he carried two short stabbing spears.

'How are you called?' Sean asked, noticing the breadth of the man's chest and the way his belly muscles stood out like the static ripples on a windswept beach.

'Mbejane.' Rhinoceros.

'For your horn?' The man chuckled with delight, his masculine vanity tickled.

'How are you called, Nkosi?'

'Sean Courteney.'

Mbejane's lips formed the name silently and then he shook his head.

'It is a difficult name.' He never said Sean's name–not once in all the years that were to follow.

'Mount up,' called Steff Erasmus. 'Let's get moving.'

They swung up on to the horses, gathered the reins and loosened the rifles in the scabbards. The Nongaai who had been stretched out resting on the bank stood up.

'Come on,' said Steff. He splashed through the stream. His horse gathered itself and bounded up the far bank and they followed him. They moved in line abreast across the grassland, sitting loose and relaxed in their saddles, the horses trippling smoothly.

At Sean's right stirrup ran the big Zulu, his long extended stride easily pacing Sean's horse. Once in a while Sean dropped his eyes from the horizon and looked down at Mbejane; it was a strangely comforting feeling to have him there.

They camped that night in a shallow valley of grass. There were no cooking fires; they ate biltong for supper, the black strips of dried salt meat, and washed it down with cold water.

'We're wasting our time. There hasn't been a sign of Zulu in two days' riding,' grumbled Bester Klein, one of the troopers.

'I say we should turn back and rejoin the Column. We're getting farther and farther away from the centre of things–we're going to miss the fun when it starts.'

Steff Erasmus wrapped his blanket more closely about his shoulders: the night's first chill was on them.

'Fun, is it?' He spat expertly into the darkness. 'Let them have the fun, if we find the cattle.'

'Don't you mind missing the fighting?'

'Look, you, I've hunted bushmen in the Karroo and the Kalahari, I've fought Xhosas and Fingoes along the Fish river, I went into the mountains after Moshesh and his Basutos. Matabele, Zulu, Bechuana–I've had fun with all of them. Now four or five hundred head of prime cattle will be payment enough for any fun we miss.' Steff lay back and adjusted his saddle behind his head. 'Anyway what makes you think there won't be guards on the herds when we find them? You'll get your fun–I promise you.'

'How do you know they've got the cattle up here?' insisted Sean.

'They're here,' said Steff, 'and we'll find them.' He turned his head towards Sean. 'You've got the first watch, keep your eyes open.' He tilted his top hat forward over his face, groped with his right hand to make sure his rifle lay beside him and then spoke from under the hat, 'Goodnight.' The others settled down into their blankets: fully-dressed, boots on, guns at hand. Sean moved out into the darkness to check the Nongaai pickets.

There was no moon, but the stars were fat and close to earth; they lit the land so that the four grazing horses were dark blobs against the pale grass. Sean circled the camp and found two of his sentries awake and attentive. He had posted Mbejane on the north side and now he went there. Fifty yards in front of him he picked up the shape of the small bush beside which he had left Mbejane. Suddenly Sean smiled and sank down on to his hands and knees, he cradled his rifle across the crooks of his elbows and began his stalk. Moving flat along the ground silently, slowly he closed in on the bush. Ten paces from it he stopped and lifted his head, careful to keep the movement inchingly slow. He stared, trying to find the shape of the Zulu among the scraggy branches and bunches of leaves. The point of a stabbing spear pricked him below the ear in the soft of his neck behind the jaw bone. Sean froze but his eyes rolled sideways and in the starlight he saw Mbejane kneeling over him holding the spear.

'Does the Nkosi seek me?' asked Mbejane solemnly, but there was laughter deep down in his voice. Sean sat up and rubbed the place where the spear had stung him.

'Only a night ape sees in the dark,' Sean protested.

'And only a fresh caught catfish flops on its belly,' chuckled Mbejane.

'You are Zulu,' Sean stated, recognizing the arrogance, although he had known immediately from the man's face and body that he was not one of the bastard Natal tribes who spoke the Zulu language but were no more Zulu than a tabby-cat is a leopard.

'Of Chaka's blood,' agreed Mbejane, reverence in his voice as he said the old king's name.

'And now you carry the spear against Cetewayo, your king?'

'My king?' The laughter was gone from Mbejane's voice. 'My king?' he repeated scornfully.

There was silence and Sean waited. Out in the darkness a jackal barked twice and one of the horses whickered softly.

'There was another who should have been king, but he died with a sharpened stick thrust up into the secret opening of his body, until it pierced his gut and touched his heart. That man was my father,' said Mbejane. He stood up and went back into the shelter of the bush and Sean followed him. They squatted side by side, silent but watchful. The jackal cried again up above the camp and Mbejane's head turned towards the sound.

'Some jackals have two legs,' he whispered thoughtfully. Sean felt the tingle along his forearms.

'Zulus?' he asked. Mbejane shrugged, a small movement in the darkness.

'Even if it is, they will not come for us in the night. In the dawn, yes, but never in the night.' Mbejane shifted the spear in his lap. 'The old one with the tall hat and grey beard understands this. Years have made him wise, that's why he sleeps so sweetly now but mounts up and moves in the darkness before each dawn.'

Sean relaxed slightly. He glanced sideways at Mbejane.

'The old one thinks that some of the herds are hidden near here.'

'Years have made him wise,' repeated Mbejane. 'Tomorrow we will find the land more broken, there are hills and thick thorn bush. The cattle will be hidden among them.'

'Do you think we'll find them?'

'Cattle are difficult to hide from a man who knows where to look.'

'Will there be many guards with the herds?'

'I hope so,' answered Mbejane, his voice a purr. His hand crept to the shaft of his assegai and caressed it. 'I hope there will be very many.'

'You would kill your own people, your brothers, your cousins?' asked Sean.

'I would kill them as they killed my father.' Mbejane's voice was savage now. 'They are not my people. I have no people. I have no brothers–I have nothing.'

Silence settled between them again, but slowly the ugliness of Mbejane's mood evaporated and in its place came a sense of companionship. Each of them felt comforted by the other's presence. They sat on into the night.

27

Mbejane reminded Sean of Tinker working a bird, he had the same half-crouched gait and the same air of complete absorption. The white men sat their horses in silence watching him. The sun was well up already and Sean unbuttoned his sheepskin coat and pulled it off. He strapped it on to the blanket roll behind him.

Mbejane had moved out about fifty yards from them and now he was working slowly back towards them. He stopped and minutely inspected a wet pat of cow dung.

'Hierdie Kaffir verstaan wat hy doen,' opined Steff Erasmus approvingly, but no one else spoke. Bester Klein fidgeted with the hammer of his carbine; his red face was already sweating in the rising heat.

Mbejane had proved right, they were in hilly country. Not the smoothly rounded hills of Natal but hills with rocky crests, deeply gullied and ravined between. There was thorn forest and euphorbia covering the sides of the hills with a lattice work of reptile grey trunks, and the grass was coarse and tall.

'I could use a drink,' said Frikkie Van Essen and wiped his knuckles across his lips.

'Chee peep, chee peep,' a barbet called stridently in the branches of the kaffir boom tree under which they waited. Sean looked up; the bird was brown and red among the scarlet flowers which covered the tree.

'How many?' asked Steff and Mbejane came to stand at his horse's head.

'Fifty–no more,' he answered.

'When?'

'Yesterday, after the heat of the day they moved slowly down the valley. They were grazing. They cannot be more than half an hour's ride ahead of us.'

Steff nodded. Fifty head only, but there would be more.

'How many men with them?'

Mbejane clucked his tongue disgustedly. 'Two *umfaans.*' He pointed with his spear at a dusty place where the print of a half-grown boy's bare foot showed clearly. 'There are no men.'

'Good,' said Steff. 'Follow them.'

'They told us that if we found anything we must go back and report,' protested Bester Klein quickly. 'They said we shouldn't start anything on our own.'

Steff turned in his saddle. 'Are you frightened of two *umfaans*?' he asked coldly.

'I'm not frightened of anything, it's just what they told us.' Klein flushed redder in his already red face.

'I know what they told us, thank you,' said Steff. 'I'm not going to start anything, we're just going to have a look.'

'I know you,' burst out Klein. 'If you see cattle you'll go mad for them. All of you, you're greedy for cattle like some men are for drink. Once you see them you won't stop.' Klein was a railway ganger.

Steff turned away from him. 'Come on, let's go.'

They rode out of the shade of the kaffir boom tree into the sunlight, Klein muttering softly to himself and Mbejane leading them down the valley.

The floor of the valley sloped gradually and on each side of them the ground rose steep and rocky. They travelled quickly with Mbejane and the other Nongaai thrown out as a screen and the horsemen cantering in a line with their stirrups almost touching.

Sean levered open the breech of his rifle and drew out the cartridge. He changed it for another from the bandolier across his chest.

'Fifty head is only ten apiece,' complained Frikkie.

'That's a hundred quid–as much as you earn in six months.' Sean laughed with excitement and Frikkie laughed with him.

'You two keep your mouths shut and your eyes open.' Steff's voice was phlegmatic, but he couldn't stop the excitement from sparkling in his eyes.

'I knew you were going to raid,' sulked Klein. 'I knew it, sure as fate.'

'You shut up also,' said Steff and grinned at Sean.

They rode for ten minutes; then Steff called softly to the Nongaai and the patrol halted. No one spoke and every man stood with his head alert and his ears straining.

'Nothing,' said Steff at last. 'How close are we?'

'Very close,' Mbejane answered. 'We should have heard them from here.'

Mbejane's exquisitely muscled body was shiny with sweat and the pride of his stance set him apart from the other Nongaai. There was a restrained eagerness about him, for the excitement was infectious.

'All right, follow them,' said Steff. Mbejane settled the rawhide shield securely on his shoulder and started forward again.

Twice more they stopped to listen and each time Sean and Frikkie were more restless and impatient.

'Sit still,' snapped Steff. 'How can we hear anything with you moving about?'

Sean opened his mouth, but before he could answer they all heard an ox low mournfully ahead of them among the trees.

'That's it!'

'We've got them!'

'Come on!'

'No, wait!' Steff ordered. 'Sean, take my farlookers and climb up that tree. Tell me what you can see.'

'We're wasting time,' argued Sean. 'We should–'

'We should learn to do as we're damn well told,' said Steff. 'Get up that tree.'

With the binoculars slung around his neck, Sean clambered upwards until he sat high in a crotch of two branches. He reached out and broke off a twig which obscured his vision, then exclaimed immediately, 'There they are, right ahead of us!'

'How many?' Steff called up to him.

'A small herd–two herdboys with them.'

'Are they among the trees?'

'No,' said Sean, 'they're in the open. Looks like a patch of swamp.'

'Make sure there aren't any other Zulus with them.'

'No–' Sean started to answer but Steff cut him short.

'Use the glasses, dammit. They'll be hiding if they're there.'

Sean brought up the glasses and focused them. The cattle were fat and sleek skinned, big horned and bodies dappled black on white. A cloud of white tick-birds hovered over them. The two herdboys were completely naked, youngsters with the thin legs and the disproportionately large genitals of the Africans. Sean turned the glasses slowly back and forth searching the patch of swamp and the surrounding bush. At last he lowered them.

'Only the two herdboys,' he said.

'Come down then,' Steff told him.

The herdboys fled as soon as the patrol rode out into the open. They disappeared among the fever trees on the far side of the swamp.

'Let them go,' laughed Steff. 'The poor little buggers are going to be in enough trouble as it is.'

He spurred his horse forward into the vivid green patch of swamp grass. It was lush: thick and tall enough to reach his saddle.

The others followed him in with the mud squelching and sucking at the hooves of the horses. They could see the backs of the cattle showing above the grass a hundred yards ahead of them. The tick-birds circled squawking.

'Sean, you and Frikkie cut around to the left–' Steff spoke over his shoulder and before he could finish the grass around them was full of Zulus, at least a hundred of them in full war dress.

'Ambush!' yelled Steff. 'Don't try and fight, too many of them. Get out!' and they dragged him off his horse.

Horses panicked in the mud, whinnying as they reared. The bang of Klein's rifle was almost drowned in the triumphant roar of the warriors. Mbejane jumped to catch the bridle of Sean's horse; he dragged its head around.

'Ride, Nkosi, quickly. Do not wait.'

Klein was dead, an assegai in his throat and the blood bursting brightly from the corners of his mouth as he fell backwards.

'Hold on to my stirrup leather.' Sean felt surprisingly calm. A Zulu came at him from the side; Sean held his rifle across his lap and fired with the muzzle almost in the man's face. It cut the top off his head. Sean ejected the cartridge case and reloaded.

'Ride, Nkosi!' Mbejane shouted again. He had made no effort to obey Sean: his shield held high he barged into two of the attackers and knocked them down into the mud. His assegai rose and fell, rose and fell.

'*Ngi Dhla*,' howled Mbejane. 'I have eaten.' Fighting madness on him, he jumped over the bodies and charged. A man stood to meet him and Mbejane hooked the edge of his shield under his and jerked it aside, exposing the man's left flank to his blade.

'*Ngi Dhla,*' Mbejane howled again.

He had torn an opening in the ring of attackers and Sean rode for it, his horse churning heavily through the mud. A Zulu caught at his reins and Sean fired with his muzzle touching the man's chest. The Zulu screamed.

'Mbejane,' shouted Sean. 'Take my stirrup!'

Frikkie Van Essen was finished; his horse was down and Zulus swarmed over him with red spears.

Leaning out of the saddle Sean circled Mbejane's waist with his arm and plucked him out of the mud. He struggled wildly but Sean held him. The ground firmed under his horse's hooves, they were moving faster. Another Zulu stood in their way with his assegai ready. With Mbejane kicking indignantly under one arm and his empty rifle in his other hand Sean was helpless to defend himself. He shouted an obscenity at the Zulu as he rode down on him. The Zulu dodged to one side and darted in again. Sean felt the sting of the blade across his shin and then the shock as it went on into his horse's chest. They were through, out of the swamp and into the trees.

Sean's horse carried him another mile before it fell. The assegai had gone in deep. It fell heavily but Sean was able to kick his feet out of the irons and jump clear. He and Mbejane stood looking down at the carcass–both of them were panting.

'Can you run in those boots?' asked Mbejane urgently.

'Yes.' They were light *veldschoen*.

'Those breeches will hold your legs.' Mbejane knelt swiftly and with his assegai cut away the cloth until Sean's legs were bare from the thighs down. He stood up again and listened for the first sounds of pursuit. Nothing.

Leave your rifle, it is too heavy. Leave your hat and your bandolier.'

'I must take my rifle,' protested Sean.

'Take it then,' Mbejane flashed impatiently. 'Take it and die. If you carry that they'll catch you before noon.'

Sean hesitated a second longer and then he changed his grip, holding the rifle by the barrel like an axe. He swung it against the trunk of the nearest tree. The butt shattered and he threw it from him.

'Now we must go,' said Mbejane.

Sean glanced quickly across at his dead horse, the leather thongs held his sheepskin coat on to the saddle. All Anna's hard work wasted, he thought wryly. Then following Mbejane he started to run.

The first hour was bad; Sean had difficulty matching his step to that of Mbejane. He ran with his body tensed and soon had a stabbing stitch in his side. Mbejane saw his pain and they stopped for a few minutes while Mbejane showed him how to relax it away. Then they went on with Sean running smoothly. Another hour went by and Sean had found his second wind.

'How long will it take us to get back to the main army?' grunted Sean.

'Two days perhaps . . . don't talk,' answered Mbejane.

The land changed slowly about them as they ran. The hills not so steep and jagged, the forest thinned and again they were into the rolling grassland.

'It seems we are not being followed.' It was half an hour since Sean had last spoken.

'Perhaps,' Mbejane was non-committal. 'It is too soon yet to tell.'

They ran on side by side, in step so their feet slapped in unison on the hard-baked earth.

'Christ, I'm thirsty,' said Sean.

'No water,' said Mbejane, 'but we'll stop to rest a while at the top of the next rise.'

They looked back from the crest. Sean's shirt was soaked with sweat and he was breathing deeply but easily.

'No one following us,' Sean's voice was relieved 'We can slow down a bit now.'

Mbejane did not answer. He also was sweating heavily but the way he moved and held his head showed he was not yet beginning to tire. He carried his shield on his shoulder and the blade of the assegai in his other hand was caked with black, dry blood. He stared out along the way they had come for fully five minutes before he growled angrily and pointed with his assegai.

'There! Close to that clump of trees. Can you see them?'

'Oh, hell!' Sean saw them: about four miles behind, on the edge of the forest where it thinned out, a black pencil line drawn on the brown parchment of grassland. But the line was moving.

'How many of them?' asked Sean.

'Fifty,' hazarded Mbejane. 'Too many.'

'I wish I had brought my rifle,' muttered Sean.

'If you had they would be much closer now–and one gun against fifty–' Mbejane left it unfinished.

'All right, let's get going again,' said Sean.

'We must rest a little longer. This is the last time we can stop before nightfall.'

Their breathing had slowed. Sean took stock of himself: he was aching a little in the legs, but it would be hours yet before he was really tired. He hawked a glob of the thick gummy saliva out of his throat and spat it into the grass. He wanted a drink but knew that would be fatal folly.

'Ah!' exclaimed Mbejane. 'They have seen us.'

'How do you know?' asked Sean.

'Look, they are sending out their chasers.' From the head of the line a trio of specks had detached themselves and were drawing ahead.

'What do you mean?' Sean scratched the side of his nose uneasily. For the first time he was feeling the fear of the hunted–vulnerable, unarmed, with the pack closing in.

'They are sending their best runners ahead to force us beyond our strength. They know that if they push us hard enough–even though they break their own wind while they do it–we will fall easily to the others that follow.'

'Good God,' Sean was now truly alarmed. 'What are we going to do about it?'

'For every trick, there is a trick,' said Mbejane. 'But now we have rested enough, let us go.'

Sean took off down the hill like a startled duiker, but Mbejane pulled him up sharply.

'That is what they want. Run as before.' And once again they fell into the steady lope, swinging long-legged and relaxed.

'They're closer,' said Sean when they reached the top of the next hill. Three specks were now well ahead of the others.

'Yes.' Mbejane's voice was expressionless. They went over the crest and down the other side, the slap-slap-slap of their feet together and their breathing an unaltering rhythm: suck blow, suck blow.

There was a tiny stream in the bottom of the valley, clean water rippling over white sand. Sean jumped it with only a single longing glance and they started up the far slope. They were just short of the crest when behind them they heard a thin distant shout. He and Mbejane looked round. On the top of the hill they had just left, only a half mile away, were the three Zulu runners, and as Sean watched they plunged down the slope towards him with their tall feather head-dresses bobbing and their leopard-tail kilts swirling about their legs. They had thrown aside their shields, but each man carried an assegai.

'Look at their legs,' exulted Mbejane. Sean saw that they ran with the slack, blundering steps of exhaustion.

'They are finished, they have run too hard.' Mbejane laughed. 'Now we must show them how afraid we are: we must run like the wind, run as though a hundred Tokoloshe* breathe on our necks.'

It was only twenty paces to the crest of the slope and they pelted panic-

*A chimera of Zulu mythology.

stricken up and over the top. But the instant they were out of sight Mbejane caught Sean's arm and held him.

'Get down,' he whispered. They sank into the grass and then crawled back on their stomachs until they lay just below the crest.

Mbejane held his assegai pointed forward, his legs were gathered up under him and his lips were drawn back in a half grin.

Sean searched in the grass and found a rock the size of an orange. It fitted neatly into his right hand.

They heard the Zulus coming, their horny bare feet pounding up the hill and then their breathing, hoarse hissing gasps, closer and closer until suddenly they came up over the crest. Their momentum carried them down to where Sean and Mbejane stood up out of the grass to meet them. Their fatigue-grey faces crumbled into expressions of complete disbelief; they had expected to find their quarry half a mile ahead of them. Mbejane killed one with his assegai, the man did not even lift his arms to parry the thrust; the point came out between his shoulders.

Sean hurled the rock into the face of another. It made a sound like a ripe pumpkin dropped on a stone floor; he fell backwards with the assegai spinning from his hand.

The third man turned to run and Mbejane landed heavily on his back, bore him down and then astride his chest, pushed his chin back and cut his throat.

Sean looked down at the man he had hit; he had lost his head-dress and his face had changed shape. His jaw hung lopsided, he was still moving feebly.

I have killed three men today, thought Sean, *and it was so easy*.

Without emotion he watched Mbejane come across to his victim. Mbejane stooped over him and the man made a small gasping sound then lay still. Mbejane straightened up and looked at Sean.

'Now they cannot catch us before dark.'

'And only a night ape can see in the dark,' said Sean. Remembering the joke, Mbejane smiled; the smile made his face younger. He picked up a bunch of dry grass and wiped his hands on it.

The night came only just in time to save them. Sean had run all day and at last his body was stiffening in protest; his breathing wheezed painfully and he had no moisture left to sweat with.

'A little longer, just a little longer.' Mbejane whispered encouragement beside him.

The pack was spread out, the stronger runners pressing a scant mile behind them and the others dwindling back into the distance.

'The sun is going; soon you can rest.' Mbejane reached out and touched his shoulder; strangely, Sean drew strength from that brief physical contact. His legs steadied slightly and he stumbled less frequently as they went down the next slope. Swollen and red, the sun lowered itself below the land and the valleys were full of shadow.

'Soon now, very soon.' Mbejane's voice was almost crooning. He looked back: the figures of the nearest Zulu were indistinct. Sean's ankle twisted under him and he fell heavily; he felt the earth graze the skin from his cheek and he lay on his chest with his head down.

'Get up,' Mbejane's voice was desperate. Sean vomited painfully, a cupful of bitter bile.

'Get up,' Mbejane's hands were on him, dragging him to his knees.

'Stand up or die here,' threatened Mbejane. He took a handful of Sean's hair and twisted it mercilessly. Tears of pain ran into Sean's eyes, and he swore and lashed out at Mbejane.

'Get up,' goaded Mbejane and Sean heaved to his feet.

'Run,' said Mbejane, half-pushing him and Sean's legs began to move mechanically under him. Mbejane looked back once more. The nearest Zulu was very close but almost merged into the fading twilight. They ran on, Mbejane steadying Sean when he staggered, Sean grunting in his throat with each step, his mouth hanging open, sucking air across a swollen tongue.

Then quickly, in the sudden African transition from day to night, all colour was gone from the land and the darkness shut down in a close circle about them. Mbejane's eyes flicked restlessly back and forth, picking up shapes in the gloom, judging the intensity of the light. Sean reeled unseeing beside him.

'We will try now,' decided Mbejane aloud. He checked Sean's run and turned him right at an acute angle on their original track, now they were heading back towards the hunters at a tangent that would take them close past them but out of sight in the darkness.

They slowed to a walk, Mbejane holding Sean's arm across his shoulders to steady him, carrying his assegai ready in his other hand. Sean walked dully, his head hanging.

They heard the leading pursuers passing fifty paces away in the darkness and a voice called in Zulu, 'Can you see them?'

'*Aibo!*' Negative answered another.

'Spread out, they may try to turn in the dark.'

'*Yeh-bo!*' Affirmative.

Then the voices were passed and silence and night closed about them once more. Mbejane made Sean keep walking. A little bit of moon came up and gave them light and they kept going with Mbejane gradually working back on to a course towards the south-east. They came to a stream at last with trees along its bank. Sean drank with difficulty, for his throat was swollen and sore. Afterwards they curled together for warmth on the carpet of leaves beneath the trees and they slept.

28

They found Chelmsford's last camp on the following afternoon: the neat lines of black camp fires and the flattened areas where the tents had stood, the stakes which had held the horse pickets and the piles of empty bully-beef tins and five-pound biscuit tins.

'They left two days ago,' said Mbejane.

Sean nodded, not doubting the correctness of this. 'Which way did they go?'

'Back towards the main camp at Isandhlwana.'

Sean looked puzzled.

'I wonder why they did that.'

Mbejane shrugged. 'They went in haste–the horsemen galloped ahead of the infantry.'

'We'll follow them,' said Sean.

The spoor was a wide road for a thousand men had passed along it and the wagons and gun carriages had left deep ruts.

They slept hungry and cold beside the spoor and the next morning there was frost in the low places when they started out.

A little before noon they saw the granite dome of Isandhlwana standing out against the sky and unconsciously they quickened their pace. Isandhlwana, the Hill of the Little Hand. Sean was limping for his boot had rubbed the skin from one heel. His hair was thick and matted with sweat and his face was plastered with dust.

'Even army bully beef is going to taste good,' said Sean in English, and Mbejane did not answer for he did not understand, but he was looking ahead with a vaguely worried frown on his face.

'Nkosi, we have seen no one for two days' march. It comes to me that we should have met patrols from the camp before now.'

'We might have missed them,' said Sean without much interest, but Mbejane shook his head. In silence they went on. The hill was closer now so they could make out the detail of ledge and fissure that covered the dome in a lace-work pattern.

'No smoke from the camp,' said Mbejane. He lifted his eyes and started visibly.

'What is it?' Sean felt the first tingle of alarm.

'*N'yoni*,' said Mbejane softly and Sean saw them. A dark pall, turning like a wheel slowly, high above the hill of Isandhlwana, still so far off that they could not distinguish the individual birds: only a shadow, a thin dark shadow in the sky. Watching it Sean was suddenly cold in the hot noonday sun. He started to run.

There was movement below them on the plain. The torn canvas of an overturned wagon flapped like a wounded bird, the scurry and scuffle of the jackals and higher up the slope of the kopje the hunch-shouldered trot of a hyena.

'Oh, my God!' whispered Sean. Mbejane leaned on his spear; his face was calm and withdrawn but his eyes moved slowly over the field.

'Are they dead? Are they all dead?' The question required no answer. He could see the dead men in the grass, thick about the wagons and then scattered more thinly back up the slope. They looked very small and inconsequential. Mbejane stood quietly waiting. A big black kolbes vulture planed across their front, the feathers in its wing-tips flated like the fingers of a spread hand. Its legs dropped, touched and it hopped heavily to rest among the dead, a swift transformation from beautiful flight to obscene crouching repose. It bobbed its head, ruffled its feathers and waddled to dip its beak over a corpse that wore the green Hunting Tartan of the Gordons.

'Where is Chelmsford? Was he caught here also?'

Mbejane shook his head. 'He came too late.'

Mbejane pointed with his spear at the wide spoor that skirted the battlefield and crossed the shoulder of Isandhlwana towards the Tugela. 'He has gone back to the river. He has not stopped even to bury his dead.'

Sean and Mbejane walked down towards the field. On the outskirts they picked their way through the debris of Zulu weapons and shields; there was rust forming on the blades of the assegais. The grass was flattened and stained where the dead had lain, but the Zulu dead were gone–sure sign of victory.

They came to the English lines. Sean gagged when he saw what had been done to them. They lay piled upon each other, faces already black, and each one of them had been disembowelled. The flies crawled in their empty stomach cavities.

'Why do they do that?' he asked. 'Why do they have to hack them up like that?'

He walked on heavily past the wagons. Cases of food and drink had been smashed open and scattered in the grass, clothing and paper and cartridge cases lay strewn around the dead, but the rifles were gone. The smell of putrefaction was so thick that it coated his throat and tongue like castor oil.

'I must find Pa,' Sean spoke quietly in almost a conversational tone. Mbejane walked a dozen paces behind him. They came to the lines where the Volunteers had camped. The tents had been slashed to tatters and trampled into the dust. The horses had been stabbed while still tethered to their picket lines; they were massively bloated. Sean recognized Gypsy, his father's mare. He crossed to her.

'Hello, girl,' he said. The birds had taken her eyes out; she lay on her side, her stomach so swollen that it was as high as Sean's waist. He walked around her. The first of the Ladyburg men lay just beyond. He recognized all fifteen of them although the birds had been at them also. They lay in a rough circle, facing outwards. Then he found a sparse trail of corpses leading up towards the shoulder of the mountain. He followed the attempt that the Volunteers had made to fight their way back towards the Tugela and it was like following a paper chase. Along the trail, thick on each side of it, were the marks where the Zulus had fallen.

'At least twenty of them for every one of us,' whispered Sean, with a tiny flicker of pride. He climbed on up and at the top of the shoulder, close under the sheer rock cliff of Isandhlwana, he found his father.

There were four of them, the last four: Waite Courteney, Tim Hope-Brown, Hans and Nile Erasmus. They lay close together. Waite was on his back with his arms spread open, the birds had taken his face away down to the bone, but they had left his beard and it stirred gently on his chest as the wind touched it. The flies, big metallic green flies, crawled thick as swarming bees in the open pit of his belly.

Sean sat down beside his father. He picked up a discarded felt hat that lay beside him and covered his terribly mutilated face. There was a green-and-yellow silk cockade on the hat, strangely gay in the presence of so much death. The flies buzzed sullenly and some came to settle on Sean's face and lips. He brushed them away.

'You know this man?' asked Mbejane.

'My father,' said Sean, without looking up.

'You too.' Compassion and understanding in his voice, Mbejane turned away and left them alone.

'I have nothing,' Mbejane had said. Now Sean also had nothing. There was hollowness: no anger, no sorrow, no ache, no reality even. Staring down at this broken thing, Sean could not make himself believe that this was a man. Meat only; the man had gone.

Later Mbejane came back. He had cut a sheet of canvas from one of the unburned wagons and they wrapped Waite in it. They dug his grave. It was hard work for the soil was thick with rock and shale. They laid Waite in the grave, with his arms still wide-spread in *rigor mortis* beneath the canvas for Sean could not bring himself to break them. They covered him gently and piled rocks upon the place. They stood together at the head of the grave.

'Well, Pa–' Sean's voice sounded unnatural. He could not make himself believe he was talking to his father.

'Well, Pa–' he started again, mumbling self-consciously. 'I'd like to say thanks for everything you've done for me.' He stopped and cleared his throat. 'I reckon you know I'll look after Ma and the farm as best I can–and Garry also.' His voice trailed away once more and he turned to Mbejane.

'There is nothing to say.' Sean's voice was surprised, hurt almost.

'No,' agreed Mbejane. 'There is nothing to say.'

For a few minutes longer Sean stood struggling to grapple with the enormity of death, trying to grasp the utter finality of it, then he turned away and started walking towards the Tugela. Mbejane walked a little to one side and a pace behind him. *It will be dark before we reach the river,* thought Sean. He was very tired and he limped from his blistered heel.

29

'Not much farther,' said Dennis Petersen.

'No,' Sean grunted. He was irritated at statement of the obvious; when you come out of Mahoba's Kloof and have the Baboon Stroom next to the road on your left hand, then it is five miles to Ladyburg. As Dennis had said: not much farther.

Dennis coughed in the dust. 'That first beer is going to turn to steam in my throat.'

'I think we can ride ahead now.' Sean wiped at his face, smearing the dust. 'Mbejane and the other servants can bring them in the rest of the way.'

'I was going to suggest it.' Dennis was obviously relieved. They had almost a thousand head of cattle crowding the road ahead of them and raising dust for them to breathe. It had been two days' drive from Rorkes Drift where the Commando had disbanded.

'We'll hold them in the sale pens tonight and send them out tomorrow morning–I'll tell Mbejane.'

Sean clapped his heels into his horse and swung across to where the big Zulu trotted at the heel of the herd. A few minutes' talk and then Sean signalled to Dennis. They circled out on each side of the herd and met again on the road ahead of it.

'They've lost a bit of condition,' grumbled Dennis looking back.

'Bound to,' said Sean. 'We've pushed them hard for two days.'

A thousand head of cattle, five men's share of Cetewayo's herds–Dennis and his father, Waite, Sean and Garrick–for even dead men drew a full share.

'How far ahead of the others do you reckon we are?' asked Dennis.

'Dunno,' said Sean. It wasn't important and any answer would be only a guess: pointless question is just as irritating as obvious statement. It suddenly occurred to Sean that but a few months previously a question like that would have started a discussion and argument that might have lasted half an hour. What did that mean? It meant that he had changed. Having answered his own question, Sean grinned sardonically.

'What'er you laughing at?' asked Dennis.

'I was just thinking that a lot has changed in the last few months.'

'*Ja,*' said Dennis and then silence except for the broken beat of their hooves. 'It's going to seem funny without Pa,' Dennis said wistfully. Mr Petersen had been at Isandhlwana. 'It's going to seem funny being just Ma, the girls and me on the farm.'

They didn't speak again for a while. They were thinking back across the brief months and the events that had changed their lives.

Neither of them yet twenty years of age, but already head of his family, a holder of land and cattle, initiated into grief and a killer of men. Sean was older now with new lines in his face, and the beard he wore was square and spade-shaped. They had ridden with the Commandos who had burned and plundered to avenge Isandhlwana. At Ulundi they had sat their horses behind the ranks of Chelmsford's infantry in the hot sun, quietly waiting as Cetewayo massed his impis and sent them across open ground to overwhelm the frail square of men. They had waited through the din of the regular, unhurried volleys and watched the great black bull of Zulu tearing itself to shreds against the square. Then at the end the ranks of infantry had opened and they had ridden out, two thousand horsemen strong, to smash for ever the power of the Zulu empire. They had chased and hunted until the darkness had stopped them and they had not kept score of the kill.

'There's the church steeple,' said Dennis.

Sean came back slowly out of the past. They were at Ladyburg.

'Is your stepmother out at Theunis Kraal?' asked Dennis.

'No, she's moved into town–the cottage on Protea Street.'

'I suppose she doesn't want to be in the way now that Anna and Garry are married,' said Dennis.

Sean frowned quickly.

'How do you like old Garry getting Anna?' Dennis chuckled and shook his head. 'I reckon you could have got twenty-to-one odds he didn't have a chance.'

Sean's frown became a scowl. Garry had made him look such a damn fool–Sean hadn't finished with Anna.

'Have you heard from them yet? When are they coming home?'

'The last time we heard was from Pietermaritzburg; they sent a wire to Ma just to say they were married. She got it a couple of days before I arrived home from Isandhlwana. That was two months ago; as far as I know we haven't heard since.'

'I suppose Garry's so firmly settled on the nest they'll have to prise him off with a crowbar.' Dennis chuckled again, lewdly. Sean had a sudden and shockingly vivid mental picture of Garry on top of Anna; her knees were up high, her head was thrown back and her eyes were closed; she was making that little mewing sound.

'Shut up, you dirty bastard,' snarled Sean.

Dennis blinked. 'Sorry, I was only joking.'

'Don't joke about my family, he's my brother.'

'And she was your girl, hey?' murmured Dennis.

'Do you want a punch?'

'Cool down, man, I was joking.'

'I don't like that kind of joke, see?'

'All right. All right. Cool down.'

'It's dirty, that's dirty talk.' Sean was trying desperately to shut out the picture of Anna; she was in wild orgasm, her hands pleading at the small of Garrick's back.

'Jesus, since when have you become a saint?' asked Dennis and, urging his horse into a gallop, drew ahead of Sean; he kept going along the main street towards the hotel. Sean considered calling him back, but finally let him go.

Sean turned right into a shady side street. The cottage was the third house down, Waite had purchased it three years before as an investment. It was a charming little place, set among trees in a small green garden with flowers: thatched, whitewashed and surrounded by a wooden picket fence. Sean hitched his horse at the gate and went up the path.

There were two women in the sitting-room when he pushed the door open. They both stood up, surprise instantly becoming delight as they recognized him. It warmed him inside to see it–it's good to be welcome.

'Oh Sean, we weren't expecting you.' Ada came quickly to him. He kissed her and saw that sorrow had left its marks on her. He felt vaguely guilty that Waite's death had not wrought so obvious a change in him. He held her away at arm's length.

'You're beautiful,' he said. She was thin. Her eyes were too big for her face and the grief was in them like shadows in the forest, but she smiled and laughed at him.

'We thought you'd be back on Friday. I'm so glad you've come earlier.'

Sean looked past Ada.

'Hello, Strawberry Pie.' She was hovering impatiently for his attention.

'Hello, Sean.' She flushed a little with his eyes on her, but she did not drop hers.

'You look older,' she said, hardly noticing the dust that caked his skin, powdered his hair and eyelashes, and reddened his eyes.

'You've just forgotten what I look like,' he said, turning back to Ada.

'No, I'd never do that,' whispered Audrey so softly that neither of them heard her. She felt swollen up inside her chest.

'Sit down, Sean.' Ada led him to the big armchair across from the fireplace. There was a daguerreotype of Waite on the mantel.

'I'll get you a cup of tea.'

'How about a beer, Ma?' Sean sank into the chair.

'Of course–I'll get it.'

'No.' Audrey flew across the room towards the kitchen. 'I'll get it.'

'They're in the pantry, Audrey,' Ada called after her, and then to Sean, 'She's such a sweet child.'

'Look again,' Sean smiled. 'She's no child.'

'I wish Garry–' Ada cut herself short.

'What do you wish?' Sean prompted her. She was quiet for a moment, wishing that Garrick could have found a girl like Audrey instead of–

'Nothing,' she said to Sean and came to sit near him.

'Have you heard from Garry again?' asked Sean.

'No. Not yet, but Mr Pye says he had a cheque come through the bank–cashed in Capetown.'

'Capetown?' Sean raised a dusty eyebrow. 'Our boy's living life to the hilt.'

'Yes,' said Ada, remembering the size of that cheque. 'He is.'

Audrey came back into the room: she had a large bottle and a glass on a tray. She crossed to Sean's chair. Sean touched the bottle; it was cold.

'Quickly, wench,' Sean encouraged her. 'I'm dying of thirst.'

The first glass emptied in three swallows, Audrey poured again and, with the replenished glass in his fist, Sean settled back comfortably in the chair.

'Now,' said Ada, 'tell us all about it.'

In the warmth of their welcome–his muscles aching pleasantly, the glass in his hand–it was good to talk. He had not realized that there was so much to tell. At the first hint of slackening in his flow of speech either Ada or Audrey was ready with a question to keep him going.

'Oh, my goodness,' gasped Audrey at last. 'It's nearly dark outside, I must go.'

'Sean,' Ada stood up. 'Will you see that she gets home safely?'

They walked side by side in the half darkness, under the flamboyants. They walked in silence until Audrey spoke.

'Sean, were you in love with Anna?' She blurted out the question and Sean experienced his standard reaction: quick anger. He opened his mouth to blast her, then checked. It was a nice question. Had he been in love with Anna? He thought about it now for the first time, phrasing the question with care that he might answer it with truth. He felt a sudden rush of relief and he was smiling when he told her.

'No, Strawberry Pie, no, I was never in love with Anna.' The tone of his voice was right, he wasn't lying. She walked on happily beside him.

'Don't bother to come up to the house.' She noticed for the first time his stained and dirty clothing that might embarrass him in front of her parents. She wanted it to be right from the start.

'I'll watch you till you get to the door,' said Sean.

'I suppose you'll be going out to Theunis Kraal tomorrow?' she asked.

'First thing in the morning,' Sean assured her. 'There's a hell of a lot of work to do.'

'But you'll be coming to the store?'

'Yes,' said Sean and the way he looked at her made her blush and hate her redhead's skin which betrayed her so easily. She went quickly up the path and then stopped and looked back.

'Sean, please don't call me Strawberry Pie any more.'

Sean chuckled. 'All right, Audrey, I'll try to remember.'

30

Six weeks had gone since his return from the Zulu Campaign, Sean reflected, six weeks that had passed in a blur of speed. He sipped coffee from a mug the size of a German beer *stein,* sitting in the centre of his bed with his nightshirt hitched up to his waist and his legs crossed in comfortable Buddha fashion. The coffee was hot; he sipped noisily and then exhaled steam from his mouth.

The last six weeks had been full–too full for brooding grief or regret, although in the evenings, when he sat in the study with Waite's memory all about him, the ache was still there.

The days seemed to pass before they had fairly begun. There were three farms now: Theunis Kraal and the other two rented from old man Pye. He had stocked them with the looted cattle and the purchases he had made since his return. The price of prime beef had dropped to a new low, with nearly a hundred thousand cattle brought back from Zululand, and Sean could afford to be selective in his buying. He could also afford to wait while the price climbed up again.

Sean swung his legs off the bed and walked across the room to the washstand. He poured water from the jug into the basin and tested it tentatively with one finger. It was so cold it stung. He stood hesitating in his ridiculously feminine nightshirt, with dark chest hairs curling out above the elaborately embroidered front. Then he mustered his courage and plunged his face into the basin; he scooped water with both hands and poured it over the back of his neck, massaged it into his hair with hooked fingers and emerged at last blowing heavily with water dripping down on to his nightshirt. He towelled, stripped off the damp garment and stood naked peering out of the window. It had lightened enough for him to make out the smoky swirl of drizzle and mist beyond the pane.

'A hell of a day,' he grumbled aloud, but his tone was deceptive. He felt excitement for this day; he was fresh and sharp-edged, hungry for breakfast, ready to go for there was work to do.

He dressed, hopping on one leg as he got into his breeches, stuffing in the tails of his shirt and then sitting on the bed to pull on his boots. Now he was thinking about Audrey–he must try and get into town tomorrow to see her.

Sean had decided on matrimony. He had three good reasons. He had found that it was easier to get into the Bank of England's vaults than to get under Audrey's petticoats without marrying her. When Sean wants something no price was too high to pay.

Living at Theunis Kraal with Garry and Anna, Sean had decided that it would be pleasant to have his own woman to cook for him, mend his clothes and listen to his stories, for Sean was feeling a little left out.

The third consideration, by no means the least significant, was Audrey's connections with the local bank. She was one of the very few weaknesses in old man Pye's armour. He might even weigh in with Mahoba's Kloof Farm as a wedding present, though even the optimist in Sean realized that this hope was extravagant. Pye and his money were not easily parted.

Yes, Sean decided, he would have to find time to get into town and tell Audrey–in Sean's mind it wasn't a question of asking her. Sean brushed his hair, combed his beard, winked at himself in the mirror and went out into the passage. He could smell breakfast cooking and his mouth started to water.

Anna was in the kitchen. Her face was flushed from the heat of the stove.

'What's for breakfast, little sister?'

She turned to him, quickly brushing the hair off her forehead with the back of her hand.

'I'm not your sister,' she said, 'I wish you wouldn't call me that.'

'Where's Garry?' Sean asked as though he had not heard her protest.

'He's not up yet.'

'The poor boy's exhausted, no doubt.' Sean grinned at her and she turned away in confusion. Sean looked at her bottom without desire. Strange that Anna being Garry's wife should kill his appetite for her. Even the memory of what they had done before was vaguely obscene, incestuous.

'You're getting fat,' he said noticing the new heaviness of her body. She ducked her head but did not answer and Sean went on, 'I'll have four eggs, please, and tell Joseph not to dry them out completely.'

Sean went through into the dining-room and Garry came in through the side door at the same moment. His face was still vacant from sleep. Sean got a whiff of his breath; it smelled of stale liquor.

'Good morning, Romeo,' said Sean and Garry grinned sheepishly. His eyes were bloodshot and he hadn't shaved.

'Hello, Sean. How did you sleep?'

'Beautifully, thank you. I take it that you did also.' Sean sat down and spooned porridge from the tureen.

'Have some?' he asked Garry.

'Thanks.' Sean passed him the plate. He noticed how Garry's hand shook. *I'll have to talk to him about letting up on the bottle a trifle.*

'Hell, I'm hungry.' They talked the jerky, disconnected conversation of the breakfast table. Anna came through and joined them. Joseph brought the coffee.

'Have you told Sean yet, Garry?' Anna spoke suddenly, clearly and with decision.

'No.' Garry was taken by surprise, he spluttered his coffee.

'Told me what?' Sean asked. They were silent and Garrick fluttered his hand nervously. This was the moment he had been dreading–what if Sean guessed, what if he knew it was his baby and took them away, Anna and the baby, took them away and left Garry with nothing. Haunted by wild unreasonable fears, Garrick stared fixedly across the table at his brother.

'Tell him, Garry,' commanded Anna.

'Anna's going to have a baby,' he said. He watched Sean's face, saw the surprise change slowly to delight, felt Sean's arm close round his shoulders in a painful hug, almost crushing him.

'That's great,' Sean exulted, 'that's wonderful. We'll have the house full of kids in no time if you keep that up, Garry. I'm proud of you.'

Grinning stupidly with relief Garrick watched Sean hug Anna more gently and kiss her forehead.

'Well done, Anna, make sure it's a boy. We need cheap labour around here.'

He hasn't guessed, thought Garrick, *he doesn't know and it will be mine. No one can take it away from me now.*

That day they worked in the south section. They stayed together, Garry laughing in happy confusion at Sean's banter. It was delightful to have Sean give him so much attention. They finished early; for once Sean was in no mood for work.

'My reproductive brother, every barrel loaded with buck-shot.' Sean leaned across and punched Garry's shoulder. 'Let's knock it off and go into town. We can have a few quick ones to celebrate at the hotel and then go and tell Ada.'

Sean stood up in the stirrup and yelled above the moo and mill of her herd.

'Mbejane, bring those ten sick ones up to the house and don't forget that tomorrow we are going to fetch cattle from the sale pens.'

Mbejane waved in acknowledgement and Sean turned back to Garrick.

'Come on, let's get the hell out of here.'

They rode side by side, globules of moisture covering their oilskins and shining on Sean's beard. It was still cold and the escarpment was hidden in the wet mist.

'It's real brandy-drinking weather,' said Sean and Garrick did not answer. He was frightened again. He didn't want to tell Ada. She would guess. She guessed everything, she would know it was Sean's child. You couldn't lie to her.

The horses' hooves plopped wetly in the mud. They reached the spot where the road forked and climbed over the ridge to Ladyburg.

'Ada's going to love being a grandma,' chuckled Sean, and at that moment his horse stumbled slightly, broke its gait and started favouring its near fore.

Sean dismounted, lifted the hoof and saw the splinter driven deep into the frog.

'Damn it to hell,' he swore. He bent his head, gripped the hilt of the splinter with his teeth and drew it out.

'Well, we can't go into Ladyburg now, that leg will be sore for days.' Garry was relieved; it put off the time when he must tell Ada.

'Your horse isn't lame. Off you go, man, give her my love.' Sean looked up at him.

'We can tell her some other time. Let's get back home,' Garry demurred.

'Go on, Garry, it's your baby. Go and tell her.'

Garrick argued until he saw Sean's temper rising, then with a sigh of resignation he went and Sean led his own horse back to Theunis Kraal. Now that he was walking the oilskin was uncomfortably hot and heavy, Sean took it off and slung it over the saddle.

Anna was standing on the *stoep* as he came up to the homestead.

'Where's Garry?' she called.

'Don't worry. He's gone into town to see Ada. He'll be back by suppertime.'

One of the stable boys came to take Sean's horse. They talked together and then Sean stooped to lift the injured hoof. His breeches tightened across his buttocks and enhanced the long moulded taper of his legs. Anna looked at him. He straightened up and his shoulders were wide beneath the damp white linen of his shirt. He smiled at her as he came up the steps of the *stoep*. The rain had made his beard curl and he looked like a mischievous pirate.

'You must take better care of yourself now.' He put his hand on her upper arm to lead her inside. 'You can't stand around in the cold any more.' They went in through the glass doors. Anna looked up at him, the top of her head on a level with his shoulder.

'You're a damn fine woman, Anna, and I'm sure you're going to make a fine baby.' It was a mistake, for as he said it his eyes softened and his face turned down towards her. He let his arm drop around her shoulders.

'Sean!' She said his name as though it were an exclamation of pain. She moved quickly, fiercely within the circle of his arm, her body flattened itself against his and her hands went up to catch in the thick hair at the back of his head. She pulled his face down and her mouth opened warm and wet across his lips, her back arched and thrust her thighs against his legs. She moaned softly as she kissed him. For startled seconds Sean stood imprisoned in her embrace, then he tore his face away.

'Are you mad?' He tried to push her from him, but she fought her way back through his fending hands. She locked her arms around him and pressed her face against his chest.

'I love you. Please, please. I love you. Just let me hold you, that's all. I just want to hold you.' Her voice was muffled by the damp cloth of his shirt. She was shivering.

'Get away from me.' Roughly Sean broke her hold and almost threw her backwards on to the couch beside the fireplace.

'You're Garry's wife now, and you'll soon be the mother of his child. Keep your hot little body for him.' Sean stood back from her with his anger starting to mount.

'But I love you, Sean. Oh, my God, if I could only make you understand how I've suffered, living here with you and not being able to touch you even.'

Sean strode across to where she sat. 'Listen to me.' His voice was harsh. 'I don't want you. I never loved you, but now I could no more touch you than I could go with my own mother.' She could see the revulsion in his face. 'You're Garry's wife; if ever again you look at another man I'll kill you.'

He lifted his hands holding them with the fingers crooked ready. 'I'll kill you with my bare hands.'

His face was close to hers. She could not bear the expression in his eyes: she lashed out at him. He pulled back in time to save his eyes, but her nails gouged bloody lines across his cheek and down the side of his nose. He caught her wrists and held her while a thin trickle of blood dribbled down into his beard. She twisted in his hands, jerking her body from side to side, and she screamed at him.

'You swine, you dirty, dirty swine. Garry's wife, you say. Garry's baby, you say.' She threw her head back and laughed wildly through her screaming. 'Now I'll tell you the truth. What I have within me you gave me. It's yours! Not Garry's!' Sean let go her wrists and backed away from her.

'It can't be,' he whispered, 'you must be lying.' She followed him.

'Don't you remember how you said goodbye to me before you went to war? Don't you remember that night in the wagon? Don't you remember–don't you? Don't you?' She was talking quietly now, using her words to wound him.

'That was months ago. It can't be true,' Sean stammered, still moving away from her.

'Three and a half months,' she told him. 'Your brother's baby will be a little early, don't you think? But lots of people have premature babies–' Her voice droned on steadily, she was shivering uncontrollably now and her face was ghostly pale. Sean could stand it no longer.

'Leave me, leave me alone. I've got to think. I didn't know.' He brushed past her and went out into the passage. She heard the door of Waite's study slam shut and she stood still in the centre of the floor. Gradually her panting came under control and the storm surf of her anger abated to expose the black reefs of hatred beneath. She crossed the floor, went down the passage and into her own bedroom. She stood in front of the mirror and looked at herself.

'I hate him,' her lips formed the words in the mirror. Her face was still pale. 'There's one thing I can take from him. Garry's mine now, not his.'

She pulled the pins from her hair and let them drop on to the floor; her hair fell down her back. She shook it on to her shoulders then lifted her hands and tangled it into confusion. Her teeth closed on her own lips, she bit until she tasted blood.

'Oh, God, I hate him, I hate him,' she whispered through the pain. Her hands came down on to the front of her dress. She tore it open, then in the mirror looked without interest at the round bosses of her nipples that were already darkening with the promise of fruition. She kicked off her shoes.

'I hate him.' She stooped and her hands went up under her skirts into the petticoats. She loosened her pantaloons and stepped out of them; she held them across her chest to tear them, then threw them next to the bed. She swept her arm across the top of her dressing-table: one of the bowls hit the floor and burst with a splash of face-powder and there was the sudden pungent reek of spilled perfume. She crossed to the bed and dropped on to it. She lifted her knees and her petticoats fell back like petals of a flower: her white legs and lower body were the stamen.

Just before nightfall there was a shy knock on her door.

'What is it?' she asked.

'The Nkosikazi has not told me what I should cook for dinner.' Old Joseph's voice was raised respectfully.

'There will be no dinner tonight. You and all the servants may go.'

'Very well, Nkosikazi.'

Garrick came home in the dark. He had been drinking; she heard him stagger as he crossed the *stoep*, and his voice slur as he called.

'Hallo. Where's everybody? Anna! Anna! I'm back.' Silence for a while as he lit one of the lamps and then the hurried thump, thump of his peg along the passage and his voice again edged with alarm.

'Anna, Anna, where are you?'

He pushed the door open and stood with the lamp in his hand. Anna rolled away from the light, pressing her face into the pillow and hunching her shoulders. She heard him set the lamp down on the dressing-table, felt his hands pulling down her skirts to cover her nakedness, then gently turn her to face him. She looked into his face and saw the uncomprehending horror in it.

'My darling, oh Anna, my darling, what's happened?' He stared at her broken lips and her breasts. Bewildered he turned his head and looked at the bottles on the floor, at her torn pantaloons. His face hardened and came back to her.

'Are you hurt?' She shook her head.

'Who? Tell me who did it.' She turned away from him again, hiding her face.

'My darling, my poor darling. Who was it–one of the servants?'

'No,' her voice stifled with shame.

'Please tell me, Anna. What happened?'

She sat up quickly and threw her arms about him, holding him hard so her lips were near his ear. 'You know, Garry. You know who did it.'

'No, I swear I don't, please tell me.'

Anna drew her breath in deep, held it a second then breathed it out. 'Sean!'

Garrick's body convulsed in her arms, she heard him grunt as though he had been hit. Then he spoke. 'This too. Now this too.'

He loosened her hands from his neck and pushed her gently down on to the pillows. He crossed to the cupboard, opened one of the drawers and took out Waite's service pistol.

He's going to kill Sean, she thought. Garrick went out of the room without looking at her again. She waited with her hands clenched at her sides and her whole body stretched tightly. When the shot came at last it was surprisingly muted and unwarlike. Her body relaxed, her hands opened and she began to cry softly.

31

Garry limped down the passage. The pistol was heavy and the checkered grip rough in his hand. There was light showing under the study door at the end of the passage. It was unlocked. Garrick went in.

Sean sat with his elbows on the desk and his face in his hands but he looked up as Garrick came in through the door. The scratches had already dried black across his cheek, but the flesh around them was red and inflamed. He looked at the pistol in Garrick's hand.

'She has told you.' There was no question or expression in his voice.

'Yes.'

'I hoped that she wouldn't,' said Sean. 'I wanted her to spare you that at least.'

'Spare me?' Garrick asked. 'What about her? Did you think of her?'

Sean did not answer, instead he shrugged and laid back tiredly in his chair.

'I never realized before what a merciless swine you are,' choked Garrick. 'I have come to kill you.'

'Yes.' Sean watched the pistol come up. Garrick was holding it with both hands, his sandy hair hung forward on to his forehead.

'My poor Garry,' Sean said softly and immediately the pistol started to shake. It sank until Garrick held it, still with both hands between his knees. He crouched over it, blubbering–chewing at his lips to stop himself. Sean started out of his chair to go to him, but Garrick recoiled against the door-jamb.

'Keep away from me,' he yelled, 'don't touch me.' He threw the pistol, the sharp edge of the hammer cut across Sean's forehead, jerking his head back. The pistol glanced off and hit the wall behind him. It fired and the bullet splintered the panelled wood-work.

'We're finished,' Garrick screamed. 'We're finished for ever.' He groped wildly for the door and stumbled out into the passage, through the kitchens into the rain. He fell many times as the grass caught his peg, but each time he scrambled up and kept running. He sobbed with each step in the utter darkness of the night.

At last the growl of the rain-engorged Baboon Stroom blocked his way. He stood on the bank with the drizzle blowing into his face.

'Why me, why always me?' He screamed his agony into the darkness. Then with a rush of relief as strong as the torrent in the river-bed below him he felt the moth flutter its wings behind his eyes. The warmth and the greyness closed about him and he sank down on to his knees in the mud.

32

Sean took very little with him: his bedroll, a rifle and a spare horse. Twice in the darkness he lost the path to Mbejane's kraal but each time his horse found it again. Mbejane had built his big grass beehive hut well away from the quarters of the other servants, for he was Zulu of royal blood. When at last Sean came to it there were a few minutes of sleepy stirring and muttering within before Mbejane, with a blanket draped around his shoulders and an old paraffin lamp in his hand, came out to Sean's shouts.

'What is it, Nkosi?'

'I am going, Mbejane.'

'Where to?'

'Wherever the road leads. Will you follow?'

'I will get my spears,' said Mbejane.

Old man Pye was still in his office behind the bank when they reached Ladyburg. He was counting the sovereigns and stacking them in neat golden piles and his hands were as gentle on them as a man's hands on the body of the woman he loves, but he reached quickly for the open drawer at his side as Sean shouldered the door open.

'You don't need that,' said Sean and Pye lifted his hand guiltily off the pistol.

'Good gracious! I didn't recognize you, my boy.'

'How much have I got credited to my account?' Sean cut through the pleasantries.

'This isn't banking hours, you know.'

'Look here, Mr Pye, I'm in a hurry. How much have I got?'

Pye climbed out of his chair and crossed to the big iron safe. Shielding it with his body he tumbled the combination and swung open the door. He brought the ledger across to the desk.

'Carter–Cloete–Courteney,' he muttered as he turned the pages. 'Ah–Ada–Garrick–Sean. Here we are. Twelve hundred and ninety-six pounds eight and eight pence; of course, there are last month's accounts at the store still unpaid.'

'Call it twelve hundred then,' said Sean. 'I want it now and while you are counting it you can give me pen and paper.'

'Help yourself, there on the desk.'

Sean sat at the desk, pushed the piles of gold out of his way, dipped the pen and wrote. When he had finished he looked up at old Pye.

'Witness that, please.'

Pye took the paper and read it through. His face went limp with surprise.

'You're giving your half share of Theunis Kraal and all the cattle to your brother's first born!' he exploded.

'That's right, please witness it.'

'You must be mad,' protested Pye. 'That's a fortune you're giving away. Think what you're doing–think of your future. I had hoped that you and Audrey–' He stopped himself and went on. 'Don't be a fool, man.'

'Please witness it, Mr Pye,' said Sean and, muttering under his breath, Pye signed quickly.

'Thank you.' Sean folded the document, slipped it into an envelope and sealed it. He put it away inside his coat.

'Where's the money?' he asked.

Pye pushed a canvas bag across to him. His expression was one of disgust; he wanted no truck with fools.

'Count it,' he said.

'I'll take your word for it,' said Sean and signed the receipt.

Sean rode out past the sale-pens and up the escarpment along the road to Pietermaritzburg. Mbejane trotted at his stirrup leading the spare horse. They stopped at the top of the escarpment. The wind had blown the clouds open and the starlight came through. They could see the town below them with here and there a lighted window.

I should have said goodbye to Ada, Sean thought. He looked down the valley towards Theunis Kraal. He could see no light. He touched the letter in the inside pocket of his coat.

'I'll post it to Garry from Pietermaritzburg,' he spoke aloud.

'Nkosi?' asked Mbejane.

'I said, "It's a long road, let us begin."'

'Yes,' agreed Mbejane. 'Let us begin.'

2. WITWATERSRAND

I

They turned north from Pietermaritzburg and climbed steadily up across bleak grassland towards the mountains. On the third day they saw the Drakensberg, jagged and black as the teeth of an ancient shark along the skyline.

It was cold; wrapped in his kaross Mbejane trailed far behind Sean. They had exchanged perhaps two dozen words since they left Pietermaritzburg for Sean had his thoughts and they were evil company. Mbejane was keeping discreetly out of his way. Mbejane felt no resentment, for a man who had just left his home and his cattle was entitled to brood. Mbejane was with sadness himself–he had left a fat woman in his bed to follow Sean.

Mbejane unplugged his small gourd snuff-box, picked a pinch and sniffed it delicately. He looked up at the mountains. The snows upon them were turning pink in the sunset and in a little while now they would make camp, and then again perhaps they would not. It made no difference.

Sean rode on after dark. The road crossed another fold in the veld and they saw the lights in the valley below.

'Dundee', Sean thought without interest. He made no effort to hasten his horse but let it amble down towards the town. Now he could smell the smoke from the coal mine, tarry and thick in the back of his throat. They entered the main street. The town seemed deserted in the cold. Sean did not intend stopping–he would camp on the far side; but when he reached the hotel he hesitated. There was warmth in there and laughter and the sound of men's voices and he was suddenly aware that his fingers were stiff with cold.

'Mbejane, take my horse. Find a place to camp beyond the town and make a fire so I won't miss you in the dark.'

Sean climbed down and walked into the bar. The room was full, miners most of them–he could see the grey coal dust etched into their skins. They looked at him incuriously as he crossed to the counter and ordered a brandy. He drank it slowly, making no attempt to join the loud talk around him.

The drunk was a short man built like Table Mountain, low, square and solid. He had to stand on tiptoe to put his arm around Sean's neck.

'Have a drink with me, *Boetie*.' His breath smelt sour and old.

'No thanks.' Sean was in no mood for drunks.

'Come on, come on,' the drunk insisted; he staggered and Sean's drink slopped on to the counter.

'Leave me alone.' Sean shrugged the arm away.

'You've got something against me?'

'No. I just feel like drinking alone.'

'You don't like my face, maybe?' The drunk held it close to Sean's. Sean didn't like it.

'Push off, there's a good fellow.'

The drunk slapped the counter.

'Charlie, give this big ape a drink. Make it a double. If he don't drink it, I ram it down his throat.'

Sean ignored the proffered glass. He swallowed what remained in his own and turned for the door. The drunk threw the brandy in his face. The spirit burned his eyes and he hit the man in the stomach. As his head came down Sean hit him again–in the face. The drunk spun sideways, fell and lay bleeding from his nose.

'What you hit him for?' Another miner was helping the drunk into a sitting position.

'It wouldn't cost you nothing to have a drink with him.' Sean felt the hostility in the room; he was the outsider.

'This boy is looking for trouble.'

'He's a tough monkey. We know how to handle tough monkeys.'

'Come on, let's sort this bastard out.'

Sean had hit the man as a reflex action. He was sorry now, but his guilt evaporated as he saw them gathering against him. Gone too was his mood of depression and in its place was a sense of relief. This was what he needed.

There were six of them moving in on him in a pack. Six was a fairly well-rounded number. One of them had a bottle in his hand and Sean started to smile. They were talking loudly, spreading courage and waiting for one of their fellows to start it.

Sean saw movement out of the side of his eye and jumped back to cover it with his hands ready.

'Steady on there,' a very English voice soothed him. 'I have come to offer my services. It seems to me you have adversaries and to spare.' The speaker had stood up from one of the tables behind Sean. He was tall, with a gauntly ravaged face and an immaculate grey suit.

'I want them all,' said Sean.

'Damned unsporting.' The newcomer shook his head. 'I'll buy the three gentlemen on the left if your price is reasonable.'

'Take two as a gift and consider yourself lucky.' Sean grinned at him and the man grinned back. They had almost forgotten the impending action in the pleasure of meeting.

'Very decent of you. May I introduce myself–Dufford Charleywood.' He shifted the light cane into his left hand and extended his right to Sean.

'Sean Courteney.' Sean accepted the hand.

'Are you bastards going to fight or what?' protested one of the miners impatiently.

'We are, dear boy, we are,' said Duff and moved lightly as a dancer towards him, swinging his cane. Thin as it was it made a noise like a well-hit baseball along the man's head.

'Then there were five,' said Duff. He flicked the cane and, weighted with lead, it made a most satisfactory swish. Like a swordsman he lunged into the throat of the second miner. The man lay on the floor and made a strangling noise.

'The rest are yours, Mr Courteney,' said Duff regretfully.

Sean dived in low, spreading his arms to scoop up all four pairs of legs at once. He sat up in the pile of bodies and started punching and kicking.

'Messy, very messy,' murmured Duff disapprovingly. The yelps and thuds gradually petered into silence and Sean stood up. His lip was bleeding and the lapel was torn off his jacket.

'Drink?' asked Duff.

'Brandy, please.' Sean smiled at the elegant figure against the bar. 'I won't refuse another drink this evening.'

They took the glasses to Duff's table, stepping over the bodies as they went.

'Mud in your eye!'

'Down the old red lane!'

Then they studied each other with frank interest, ignoring the clearing up operations being conducted around them.

'You are travelling?' asked Duff.

'Yes, are you?'

'No such luck. I am in the permanent employ of Dundee Collieries Ltd.'

'You work here?' Sean looked incredulous for Duff was a peacock among pigeons.

'Assistant Engineer,' nodded Duff. 'But not for long; the taste of coal-dust sticks in my craw.'

'May I suggest something to wash it out?'

'A splendid idea,' agreed Duff.

Sean brought the drinks to the table.

'Where are you headed?' asked Duff.

'I was facing north when I started,' shrugged Sean, 'I just kept going that way.'

'Where did you start from?'

'South.' Sean answered abruptly.

'Sorry, I didn't mean to pry.' Duff smiled. 'Yours is brandy, isn't it?'

The barman came round from behind the counter and crossed to their table.

'Hello, Charlie,' Duff greeted him. 'I take it you require compensation for the damage to your fittings and furniture?'

'Don't worry about it, Mr Charleywood. Not often we have a good barney like that. We don't mind the odd table and chair as long as it's worth watching. Have it on the house.'

'That's extremely good of you.'

'That's not what I came across for, Mr Charleywood. I've got something I'd like you to take a look at, you being a mining chap and all. Could you spare a minute, sir?'

'Come on, Sean. Let's see what Charlie's got for us. My guess is it's a beautiful woman.'

'It's not actually, sir,' said Charlie seriously and led the way through into the back room. Charlie reached up and took a lump of rock down from one of the shelves. He held it out to Duff. 'What do you make of that?'

Duff took it and weighed it in his hand, then peered closely at it. It was glassy grey, blotched with white and dark-red and divided by a broad black stripe.

'Some sort of conglomerate.' Duff spoke without enthusiasm. 'What's the mystery?'

'Friend of mine brought it down from Kruger's Republic on the other side of the mountains. He says it's gold bearing. They've made a big strike at a place called Witwatersrand just outside Pretoria. Of course, I don't put much store by these rumours 'cos you hear them all the time: diamonds and gold, gold and diamonds.'

Charlie laughed and wiped his hands on his apron.

'Anyway my friend says the Boers are selling mining licences to them as want to dig for the stuff. Thought I'd just get you to have a look.'

'I'll take this with me, Charlie, and pan it in the morning. Right now my friend and I are drinking.'

2

Sean opened his eyes the next morning to find the sun burning in through the window above his bed. He closed them again hurriedly and tried to remember where he was. There was a pain in his head that distracted him and a noise. The noise was a regular croaking rattle; it sounded as though someone was dying. Sean opened his eyes and turned his head slowly. Someone was in the bed across the room. Sean groped for a boot and threw it; there was a snort and Duff's head came up. For a second he regarded Sean through eyes as red as a winter sunset and then he subsided gently back into the blankets.

'Keep it down to a bellow,' whispered Sean. 'You are in the presence of grave illness.'

A long time later a servant brought coffee.

'Send word to my office that I am sick,' commanded Duff.

'I have done so.' The servant clearly understood his master. He went on, 'There is one outside who seeks the other Nkosi.' He glanced at Sean. 'He is greatly worried.'

'Mbejane. Tell him to wait,' said Sean.

They drank coffee in silence, sitting on the edge of their beds.

'How did I get here?' asked Sean.

'Laddie, if you don't know, then nobody does.' Duff stood up and crossed the room to find fresh clothing. He was naked and Sean saw that although he was slim as a boy his body was finely muscled.

'My God, what does Charlie put in his liquor?' complained Duff as he picked up his jacket.

He found the lump of rock in the pocket, brought it out and tossed it on to the packing-case that served as a table. He regarded it sourly as he finished dressing, then he went to the great pile of bachelor debris that filled one corner of the room. He scratched around and came out with a steel pestle-and-mortar and a battered black gold pan.

'I feel very old this morning,' he said as he started to crush the rock to powder in the mortar. He poured the powder into the pan, carried it out to the corrugated iron water tank beside the front door and filled the pan from the tap.

Sean followed him and they sat together on the front step. Duff worked the pan, using a practised dip and swing that set the contents spinning like a whirlpool and slopped a little over the front lip with each turn. He filled it again with clean water.

Suddenly Sean felt Duff stiffen beside him. He glanced at his face and saw that his hangover had gone; his lips were shut in a thin line and his blood-shot eyes were fastened over the pan.

Sean looked down and saw the gleam through the water, like the flash of a trout's belly as it turns to take the fly. He felt the excitement prickle up his arms and lift the hair on his neck.

Quickly Duff splashed fresh water into the pan; three more turns and he flicked it out again. They sat still, not speaking, staring at the golden tail curved round the bottom of the pan.

'How much money have you got?' Duff asked without looking up.

'Little over a thousand.'

'As much as that. Excellent! I can raise about five hundred but I'll throw in my mining experience. Equal partners–do you agree?'

'Yes.'

'Then why are we sitting here? I'm going down to the bank. Meet me on the edge of town in half an hour.'

'What about your job?' Sean asked.

'I hate the smell of coal–the hell with my job.'

'What about Charlie?'

'Charlie is a poisoner–the hell with Charlie.'

3

They camped the night in the mouth of the pass with the mountains standing up before them. They had pushed the pace all that afternoon and the horses were tired–they turned their tails to the wind and cropped at the dry winter grass.

Mbejane built a fire in the shelter of a red stone outcrop and they huddled beside it brewing coffee, trying to keep out of the snow-cold wind, but it came down off the mountains and blew a plume of sparks from the fire. They ate; then Mbejane curled up beside the fire, pulled his kaross over his head and did not move again until morning.

'How far is it to this place?' Sean asked.

'I don't know,' Duff admitted. 'We'll go up through the pass tomorrow–fifty or sixty miles through the mountains–and then we'll be out into the high veld. Perhaps another week's riding after that.'

'Are we chasing rainbows?' Sean poured more coffee into the mugs.

'I'll tell you when we get there.' Duff picked up his mug and cupped his hands around it. 'One thing's certain–that sample was stinking with gold. If there's much of that stuff somebody's going to get rich.'

'Us, perhaps?'

'I've been on gold stampedes before. The first ones in make the killings. We might find the ground for fifty miles around as thick with claim pegs as quills on a porcupine's back.' Duff sipped noisily at his coffee. 'But we've got money–that's our ace in the hole. If we peg a proposition we've got capital to work it. If we're too late we can buy claims from the brokers. If we can't, well, there're other ways of getting gold than grubbing for it–a store, a saloon, a transport business, take your pick.'

Duff flicked the coffee grounds out of his mug. 'With money in your pocket you're somebody; without it anyone can kick you in the teeth.' He took a long black cheroot out of his top pocket and offered it to Sean. Sean shook his head and Duff bit the tip from the cheroot and spat it into the fire. He picked up a burning twig and lit it, sucking with content.

'Where did you learn mining, Duff?'

'Canada.' The wind whipped the smoke away from his mouth as Duff exhaled.

'You've been around?'

'I have, laddie. It's too damn cold to sleep; we'll talk instead. For a guinea I'll tell you the story of my life.'

'Tell me first, I'll see if it's worth it!' Sean pulled the blanket up around his shoulders and waited.

'Your credit is good,' agreed Duff. He paused dramatically. 'I was born thirty-six years ago, fourth and youngest son to the sixteenth Baron Roxby–that is, not counting the others who never made it to puberty.'

'Blue blood,' said Sean.

'Of course, just look at my nose. But please don't interrupt. Very early in the game my father, the sixteenth Baron, dispelled with a horsewhip any natural affection we may have owed him. Like Henry the Eighth he preferred children in the abstract. We kept out of his way and that suited everybody admirably. A sort of armed truce.

'Dear father had two great passions in life: horses and women. During his sixty-two glorious years he acquired a fine collection of both. My fifteen-year-old cousin, a comely wench as I recall, was his last and unattained ambition. He took her riding every day and fingered her most outrageously as he helped her in and out of the saddle. She told me about it with giggles.

'However father's horse, a commendably moral creature, cut short the pursuit by kicking father on the head, presumably in the middle of one of these touching scenes. Poor father was never the same again. In fact so much was he altered by this experience that two days later, to the doleful clangour of bells and a collective sigh of relief from his sons and his neighbours who owned daughters, they buried him.'

Dufford leaned forward and prodded the fire.

'It was all very sad. I or any of my brothers could have told father that not only was my cousin comely but she had the family sporting instincts developed to a remarkable degree. After all who should know better than we? We were her cousins and you know how cousins will be cousins. Anyway father never found out and to this day I feel guilty–I should have told him. He would have died happier . . . Do I bore you?'

'No, go on. I've had half a guinea's worth already,' Sean laughed.

'Father's untimely decease made no miraculous change in my life. The seventeenth Baron, brother Tom, once he had the title was every bit as tight-fisted and unpleasant as father had been. There I was at nineteen on an allowance too small to enable me to pursue the family hobbies, gathering mould in a grim old castle forty miles from London, with the development of my sensitive soul being inhibited by the undiluted company of my barbaric brothers.

'I left with three months' advance allowance clutched in my sweaty palm and the farewells of my brothers ringing in my ears. The most sentimental of these was "don't bother to write".

'Everybody was going to Canada: it seemed like a good idea so I went too. I made money and spent it. I made women and spent them also, but the cold got to me in the end.'

Duff's cheroot had died; he re-lit it and looked at Sean.

'It was so cold you couldn't urinate without getting frostbite on your equipment, so I began to think of lands tropical, of white beaches and sun, of exotic fruits and even more exotic maidens. The peculiar circumstances that finally decided me to leave are painful to recall and we will not dwell upon them. I left, to say the least, under a cloud. So here you see me freezing slowly to death, with a bearded ruffian for company and not an exotic maiden within a day's ride.'

'A stirring tale–well told,' applauded Sean.

'One story deserves another–let's hear your tale of woe.'

Sean's smile slid off his face. 'Born and bred here in Natal. Left home a week or so ago also in painful circumstances.'

'A woman?' asked Duff with deep compassion.

'A woman,' agreed Sean.

'The sweet bitches,' sighed Duff. 'How I love them.'

4

The pass ran like a twisted gut through the Drakensberg. The mountains stood up sheer and black on each side of them, so they rode in shadow and saw the sun only for a few hours in the middle of the day. Then the mountains dropped away and they were out into the open.

Open was the word for the high veld. It stretched away flat and empty, grass and brown grass dwindling to a distant meeting with the pale empty sky. But the loneliness could not blunt the edge of their excitement: each mile covered, each successive camp along the ribbon road ground it sharper until at last they saw the name in writing for the first time. Forlorn as a scarecrow in a ploughed land the signpost pointed right and said, 'Pretoria', pointed left and said, 'Witwatersrand'.

'The Ridge of White Waters,' whispered Sean. It had a ring to it that name–a ring like a hundred millions in gold.

'We're not the first,' muttered Duff. The left-hand fork of the road was deeply scored by the passage of many wagons.

'No time to worry about that.' Sean had the gold sickness on him now. 'There's a little speed left in these mokes–let's use it.'

It came up on the horizon as a low line above the emptiness, a ridge of hills like a hundred others they had crossed. They went up it and from the top looked down. Two ridges ran side by side, north and south, four miles or so apart. In the shallow valley between they could see the flash of the sun off the swamp pools that gave the hills their name.

'Look at them,' groaned Sean.

The tents and wagons were scattered along the length of the valley and in between them the prospect trenches were raw wounds through the grass. The trenches were concentrated along a line down the centre of the valley.

'That's the strike of the reef,' said Duff, 'and we're too late–it's all pegged!'

'How do you know?' protested Sean.

'Use your eyes, laddie. It's all gone.'

'There might be some they've overlooked.'

'These boys overlook nothing. Let's go down and I'll show you.' Duff prodded his horse and they started down. He spoke over his shoulder to Sean. 'Look up there near that stream–they aren't wasting time. They've got a mill going already. It's a four-stamp rig by the looks of it.'

They rode into one of the larger encampments of tents and wagons; there were women at work around the fires and the smell of food brought saliva jetting from under Sean's tongue. There were men also, sitting among the wagons waiting for their suppers.

'I'm going to ask some of these characters what's going on here,' said Sean. He climbed down off his horse and tossed the reins to Mbejane. Duff watched him with a wry grin as he tried in succession to engage three different men in conversation. Each time Sean's victim avoided his eyes, mumbled vaguely and withdrew. Sean finally gave up and came back to the horses.

'What's wrong with me,' he asked plaintively. 'Have I got a contagious clap?'

Duff chuckled. 'They've got gold sickness,' he said. 'You're a potential rival. You could die of thirst and not one of them would spit on you, lest it gave you strength to crawl out and peg something they hadn't noticed.'

He sobered. 'We're wasting time. There's an hour left before dark, let's go and have a look for ourselves.'

They trotted out towards the area of mauled earth. Men were working pick and shovel in the trenches, some of them lean and tough-looking with a dozen natives working beside them; others far from an office stool, sweating and gritting teeth against the pain of blistered palms, their faces and arms burnt angry red by the sun. All of them greeted Sean and Duff with the same suspicious hostility.

They rode slowly towards the north and every hundred yards with sickening regularity they came across a claim peg with a cairn of stones around its foot and the scrap of canvas nailed to it. Printed in crude capitals on the canvas was the owner's name and his licence number.

Many of the claims were as yet untouched and on these Duff dismounted and searched in the grass, picking up pieces of rock and peering at them before discarding them again. Then once more they moved on with sinking spirits and increasing exhaustion. They camped after dark in the open windy ridge and while the coffee brewed they talked.

'We're too late.' Sean scowled into the fire.

'We've got money, laddie, just remember that. Most of these gentlemen are broke–they are living on hope, not beef and potatoes. Look at their faces and you'll see despair starting to show. It takes capital to work reef gold: you need machinery and money for wages, you have to pipe in water and pile rock, you need wagons and time.'

'Money's no good without a claim to work,' brooded Sean.

'Stay with me, laddie. Have you noticed how many of these claims haven't been touched yet? They belong to speculators and my guess is that they are for sale. In the next few weeks you'll see the men sorted out from the boys–'

'I feel like packing up. This isn't what I expected.'

'You're tired. Sleep well tonight and tomorrow we'll see how far this reef runs–then we'll start some scheming.'

Duff lit one of his cheroots and sucked on it: in the firelight his face was as gaunt as a Red Indian's. They sat on in silence for a while, then Sean spoke.

'What's that noise?' It was a dull tom-tom beat in the darkness.

'You'll get used to that if you stay around here much longer,' said Duff. 'It's the stamps on that mill we saw from the high ground. It's a mile or so farther up the valley; we'll pass it in the morning.'

They were on the move again before the sun was up and they came to the mill in the morning's uncertain light. The mill crouched black and ugly on the smooth curve of the ridge, defiant as a quixotic monster. Its jaws thumped sullenly as it chewed the rock; it snorted steam and screeched metallically.

'I didn't realize it was so big,' said Sean.

'It's big all right,' agreed Duff, 'and they cost money, they don't give them away. Not many men around here can afford a set-up like that.'

There were men moving around the mill, tending its needs, feeding it rock and fussing about the copper tables over which its gold-laden fæces poured. One of the men came forward to offer them the usual hospitality. 'This is private ground. We don't want sightseers around here–keep going.'

He was a dapper little man with a round brown face and a derby hat pulled down to his ears. His moustache bristled like the whiskers of a fox terrier.

'Listen, François, you miserable bloody earthworm, if you talk to me like that I'll push your face around the back of your head,' Duff told him, and the dapper one blinked uncertainly and came closer, peering up at them.

'Who are you? Do I know you?'

Duff pushed his hat back so the man could see his face.

'Duff!' crowed the little man delightedly. 'It's old Duff.' He bounced forward to take Duff's hand as he dismounted. Sean watched the orgy of reunion with amusement. It lasted until Duff managed to bring it under control and lead the little Afrikander across to make the introduction.

'Sean, this is François du Toit. He's an old friend of mine from the Kimberley diamond fields.'

François greeted Sean and then relapsed once more into the excited chorus of '*Gott,* it's good to see you, old Duff.' He pounded Duff's back despite the nimble footwork that Duff was using to spoil his aim. Another few minutes of this passed before François composed himself to make his first coherent statement.

'Listen, old Duff, I'm just in the middle of cleaning the amalgam tables. You and your friend go down to my tent. I'll be with you in half an hour, tell my servant to make you some breakfast. I won't be long, man. *Gott,* man, it's good to see you.'

'An old lover of yours?' asked Sean when they were alone.

Duff laughed. 'We were on the diamond fields together. I did him a favour once–pulled him out of a caving drive when the rock fall had broken his legs. He's a good little guy and meeting him here is the proverbial answer to a prayer. What he can't tell us about the goldfield no one else can.'

François came bustling into the tent well under the promised half hour and during breakfast Sean was an outsider in a conversation where every exchange began, 'Do you remember–?' or 'What happened to old so and so?'

Then, when the plates were empty and the coffee mugs filled, Duff asked, 'So, what are you doing here, Franz? Is this your own outfit?'

'No, I'm still with the Company.'

'Not that whoreson Hradsky?' Duff registered mock alarm. 'That–that that's ta–ta–terrible,' he imitated a stutter.

'Cut it out, Duff.' François looked nervous. 'Don't do that, you want me to lose my job?'

Duff turned to Sean with an explanation. 'Norman Hradsky and God are equals, but in this part of the world God takes his orders from Hradsky.'

'Cut it out, Duff.' François was deeply shocked but Duff went on imperturbably.

'The organization through which Hradsky exercises his divine powers is referred to with reverently bated breath as "The Company". In actual fact its full and resounding title is The South African Mining and Lands Company. Do you get the picture?'

Sean nodded smiling and Duff added as an afterthought, 'Hradsky is a bastard and he stutters.'

It was too much for François. He leaned across and caught Duff's arm. 'Please, man. My servant understands English, cut it out, Duff.'

'So the Company has started on these fields, hey? Well, well, it must be pretty big,' mused Duff and François followed with relief on to safer ground.

'It is! You just wait and see, it's going to make the diamond fields look like a church bazaar!'

'Tell me about it,' said Duff.

'They call it the Rotten Reef or the Banket or the Heidelberg Reef–but in fact there are three reefs, not one. They run side by side like layers in a sandwich cake.'

'All three have pay gold?' Duff shot the question and François shook his head. There was a light in his eyes; he was happy talking gold and mining.

'No–you can forget about the outer reef, just traces there. Then there's the Main Reef. That's a bit better, it's as much as six feet thick in places and giving good values, but it's patchy.'

François leaned eagerly across the table; in his excitement his thick Afrikaans accent was very noticeable.

'The bottom reef is the winner, we call it the Leader Reef. It's only a few inches thick and some places it fades out altogether, but it's rich. There's gold in it like plums in a pudding. It's rich, Duff, I'm telling you that you won't believe it until you see it!'

'I'll believe you,' said Duff. 'Now tell me where I can get some of this Leader Reef for myself.'

François sobered instantly, a shutter dropped over his eyes and hid the light that had shone there a moment before.

'It's gone. It's all gone,' he said defensively. 'It's all been pegged, you've come too late.'

'Well, that's that,' said Duff and a big silence settled on the gathering. François fidgeted on his stool, chewing at the ends of his moustache and scowling into his mug. Duff and Sean waited quietly; it was obvious that François was wrestling with himself, two loyalties tearing him down the middle. Once he opened his mouth and then closed it again; he blew on his coffee to cool it and the heat came off it in steam.

'Have you got any money?' He fired the question with startling violence.

'Yes,' said Duff.

'Mr Hradsky has gone down to Capetown to raise money. He has a list of a hundred and forty claims that he will buy when he gets back.' François paused guiltily. 'I'm only telling you this because of what I owe you.'

'Yes, I know.' Duff spoke softly. François took an audible breath and went on.

'On the top of Mr Hradsky's list is a block of claims that belongs to a woman. She is willing to sell and they are the most likely-looking propositions on the whole field.'

'Yes?' Duff encouraged him.

'This woman has started an eating-house about two miles from here on the banks of the Natal Spruit. Her name is Mrs Rautenbach, she serves good food. You could go and have a meal there.'

'Thanks, François.'

'I owed it to you,' François said gruffly, then his mood changed quickly and he chuckled. 'You'll like her, Duff, she's a lot of woman.'

Sean and Duff went to eat lunch at Mrs Rautenbach's. It was an unpainted corrugated-iron building on a wooden frame and the sign above the veranda said in letters of red and gold 'Candy's Hotel. High-class cuisine. Free toilet facilities. No drunks or horses admitted. Proprietor. Mrs Candella Rautenbach.'

They washed off the dust in the enamel basin which stood on the veranda, dried themselves on the free towel and combed in the free mirror on the wall.

'How do I look?' asked Duff.

'Ravishing,' said Sean, 'but you don't smell so good. When did you last bath?'

They went into the dining-room and found it almost full, but there was an empty table against the far wall. The room was hot and thick with pipe smoke and the smell of cabbage. Dusty bearded men laughed and shouted or ate silently and hungrily. They crossed the room to the table and a coloured waitress came to them.

'Yes?' she asked. Her dress was damp at the armpits.

'May we have the menu?'

The girl looked at Duff with faint amusement. 'Today we got steak and mashed potatoes with pudding afterwards.'

'We'll have it,' Duff agreed.

'You sure as hell won't get nothing else,' the girl assured him and trotted back to the kitchen.

'The service is good,' Duff enthused. 'We can only hope that the food and the proprietress are of the same high standard.'

The meat was tough but well flavoured and the coffee was strong and sweet. They ate with appreciation until Sean who was facing the kitchen stopped his fork on its way to his mouth. A hush was on the room.

'Here she is,' he said.

Candy Rautenbach was a tall and bright, shiny blonde and her skin was Nordic flawlessness as yet unspoiled by the sun. She filled the front of her blouse and the back of her skirt with a pleasant abundance. She was well aware of and yet not disconcerted by the fact that every eye in the room was on one of those areas. She carried a ladle which she twitched threateningly at the first hand that reached out to pinch her rump, the hand withdrew and Candy smiled sweetly and moved on among the tables. She stopped occasionally to chat with her customers and it was clear that many of these lonely men came here not only to eat. They watched her avidly, grinning with pleasure when she spoke to them. She reached their table and Sean and Duff stood up. Candy blinked with surprise.

'Sit down, please.' The small courtesy had touched her. 'You are new here?'

'We got in yesterday,' Duff smiled at her. 'And the way you cook a steak makes me feel as though I were home again.'

'Where are you from?' Candy looked at the two of them with perhaps just a shade more than professional interest.

'We've come up from Natal to have a look around. This is Mr Courteney–he is interested in new investments and he thought that these goldfields might provide an outlet for some of his capital.'

Sean just managed to stop his jaw dropping open and then quickly assumed the slightly superior air of a big financier as Duff went on.

'My name is Charleywood. I am Mr Courteney's mining adviser.'

'Pleased to meet you. I am Candy Rautenbach.' She was impressed.

'Won't you join us for a few minutes, Mrs Rautenbach?' Duff drew back a chair for her and Candy hesitated.

'I have to check up in the kitchen–perhaps later.'

'Do you always lie so smoothly?' Sean spoke with admiration when Candy had gone.

'I spoke no untruths,' Duff defended himself.

'No, but the way you tell the truth! How the hell am I going to play up to the role you have created for me?'

'You'll learn to live with it, don't worry. Just look wise and keep your mouth shut,' Duff advised. 'What do you think of her anyway?'

'Toothsome,' said Sean.

'Decidedly palatable,' agreed Duff.

When Candy came back Duff kept the conversation light and general for a while, but when Candy started asking some sharp questions it was immediately apparent that her knowledge of geology and mining was well above average and Duff remarked on it.

'Yes, my husband was in the game. I picked it up from him.' She reached into one of the pockets of her blue and white checked skirt and brought out a small handful of rock samples. She put them down in front of Duff. 'Can you name those?' she asked. It was the direct test, she was asking him to prove himself.

'Kimberlite. Serpentine. Feldspar.' Duff reeled them off and Candy relaxed visibly.

'As it happens I have a number of claims pegged along the Heidelberg Reef. Perhaps Mr Courteney would care to have a look át them. Actually, I am negotiating at the moment with The South African Mining and Lands Company who are very interested.'

Sean made his solitary but valuable contribution to the conversation. 'Ah yes,' he nodded sagely. 'Good old Norman.'

Candy was shaken–not many men used Hradsky's Christian name. 'Will tomorrow morning be convenient?' she asked.

5

That afternoon they bought a tent from a disillusioned hopeful who had thrown up his job on the Natal Railways to make the pilgrimage to Witwatersrand and now needed money to get home. They pitched it near the Hotel and went down to the Natal Spruit to take a long overdue bath. That night they held a mild celebration on the half bottle of brandy that Duff produced from his saddlebag and the next morning Candy took them out to the claims. She had twenty of them pegged right along the Banket. She led them to a spot where the reef outcropped.

'I'll leave you two to look around. If you're interested we can talk about it when you come to the Hotel. I've got to get back now, there'll be hungry mouths to feed.'

Duff escorted Candy to her horse, giving her his arm across the rough ground and helping her into the saddle in a manner he must have learned from his father. He watched her ride away then came back to Sean. He was elated.

'Tread lightly, Mr Courteney, walk with reverence for beneath your feet lies our fortune.'

They went over the ground, Sean like a friendly bloodhound and Duff cruising with the restless circling of a tiger shark. They inspected the claim notices, paced out the boundaries and filled their pockets with ćhips of rock, then they rode back to their tent and Duff brought out his pestle, mortar and pan. They took them down to the bank of the Natal Spruit and all afternoon crushed the rock and worked the pan. When they had tested the last sample Duff gave his judgement.

'Well, there's gold–and I'd say it's payable gold. It's not nearly as rich as the one we panned at Dundee but that must have been a selected piece of the Leader Reef!' He paused and looked seriously at Sean. 'I think it's worth a try. If the Leader Reef is there we'll find it and in the meantime we won't lose money by working the main reef.'

Sean picked up a pebble and tossed it into the stream in front of him. He was learning for the first time the alternate thrill and depression of gold sickness when one minute you rode the lightning and the next you dropped abruptly into the depths. The yellow tails in the pan had looked pathetically thin and undernourished to him.

'Supposing you're right and supposing we talk Candy into selling her claims, how do we go about it? That four-stamp mill looked a devilishly complicated and expensive bit of machinery to me, not the kind of thing you can buy over the counter in every general dealer's store.'

Duff punched his shoulder and smiled lopsidedly at him. 'You've got your Uncle Duff looking after you. Candy will sell her claims–she trembles when I touch her, a day or two more and she'll be eating out of my hand. As for the mill . . . When I came out to this country I fell in with a rich Cape farmer whose lifelong ambition had been to have his own gold mine. He selected a ridge which in his undisputed wisdom as a grower of grapes he considered to be an ideal place for his mine. He hired me to run it for him, purchased a mill of the latest and most expensive vintage and prepared himself to flood the market with gold. After six months when we had processed vast quantities of assorted quartz, schist and earth and recovered sufficient gold to fit into a mouse's ear without touching the sides my patron's enthusiasm was somewhat dampened and he dispensed with my invaluable services and closed the circus down. I left for the diamond fields and as far as I know the machinery is still lying there waiting for the first buyer with a couple of hundred pounds to come and pick it up.' Duff stood up and they walked back towards the tent. 'However, first things first. Do you agree that I should continue the negotiations with Mrs Rautenbach?'

'I suppose so.' Sean was feeling more cheerful again. 'But are you sure your interest in Mrs Rautenbach is strictly line of duty?'

Duff was shocked. 'Don't you think for a minute that my intentions are anything but to further the interests of our partnersnip. You can't believe that my animal appetite plays any part in what I intend doing?'

'No, of course not,' Sean assured him. 'I hope you can force yourself to go through with it.'

Duff laughed. 'While we are on the subject I think this is as good a time as any for you to develop a stomach ailment and retire to your lonely bed. From now on until we've got the agreement signed your boyish charm will be of no great value in the proceedings. I'll tell Candy that you've given me authority to act on your behalf.'

Duff combed his curls, put on the clothes that Mbejane had washed for him and disappeared in the direction of Candy's Hotel. Time passed slowly for Sean; he sat and chatted with Mbejane, drank a little coffee and when the sun went down returned to his tent. He read one of Duff's books by the light of the hurricane lamp but could not concentrate on it; his mind kept straying to thoughts of blonde hair. When someone scratched on the canvas door he leapt up with a confused hope that Candy had decided to come and deal with him direct. It was the coloured girl from the Hotel, her crinkly black hair at odds with what he had been thinking.

'Madame says she's sorry to hear about your sickness and to tell you to have two spoons of this,' she told him and offered Sean the bottle of castor oil.

'Tell your mistress, thank you very much.'

Sean accepted the medicine and started to close the tent flap again.

'Madame told me to stay and make sure that you took two full spoons–I have to take the bottle back and show her how much you've had.'

Sean's stomach cringed. He looked at the coloured girl standing resolute in the doorway, determined to carry out her instructions. He thought of poor Duff doing his duty like a man–he could do no less. He swallowed down the thick clinging oil with his eyes closed then went back to his book. He slept uneasily starting up occasionally to look at the empty bed across the tent. The medicine drove him out into the cold at half past two in the morning. Mbejane was curled up next to the fire and Sean scowled at him. His regular contented snoring seemed a calculated mockery. A jackal yelped miserably up on the ridge, expressing Sean's feelings exactly, and the night wind fanned his bare buttocks.

Duff came home in the dawning. Sean was wide awake.

'Well, what happened?' he demanded.

Duff yawned. 'At one stage I began to doubt whether I was man enough. However, it worked out to the satisfaction of all concerned. What a woman!' He pulled off his shirt and Sean saw the scratches across his back.

'Did she give you any castor oil?' Sean asked bitterly.

'I'm sorry about that.' Duff smiled at him sympathetically. 'I tried to dissuade her–truly I did. She's a very motherly person. Most concerned about your stomach.'

'You still haven't answered my question. Did you make any progress with the claims?'

'Oh that–' Duff pulled the blankets up under his chin. 'We disposed of that early on in the proceedings. She'll take a down payment of ten pounds each on them and give us an option to buy the lot at any time during the next two years for ten thousand. We arranged that over dinner. The rest of the time was devoted, in a manner of speaking, to shaking hands over the deal. Tomorrow afternoon–or rather this afternoon–you and I'll ride across to Pretoria and get a lawyer to write up an agreement for her to sign. But right now I need some sleep. Wake me at lunch time. Goodnight, laddie.'

Duff and Sean brought the agreement back from Pretoria the following evening. It was an impressive four-page document full of 'in so much as' and 'party of the first part'. Candy led them to her bedroom and they sat around anxiously while she read it through twice.

She looked up at last and said, 'That seems all right–but there is just one other thing.' Sean's heart sank and even Duff's smile was strained. It had all been too easy so far.

Candy hesitated and Sean saw with faint surprise that she was blushing. It was a pleasant thing to see the peach of her cheeks turning to ripe apple and they watched it with interest, their tension lessening perceptibly. 'I want the mine named after me.'

They nearly shouted with relief.

'An excellent idea! How about the Rautenbach Reef Mine?'

Candy shook her head. 'I'd rather not be reminded of him–we'll leave him out of it.'

'Very well–let's call it the Candy Deep. A little premature, I suppose, as we are still at ground level, but pessimism never pays,' suggested Duff.

'Yes, that's lovely,' Candy enthused, flushing again but this time with pleasure. She scrawled her name across the bottom of the document while Sean fired out the cork of the champagne which Duff had bought in Pretoria. They clinked glasses and Duff gave the toast 'To Candy and the Candy Deep–may one grow sweeter and the other deeper with each passing day.'

6

'We'll need labour, about ten natives to start with. That'll be your problem,' Duff told Sean. It was the following morning and they were eating breakfast in front of the tent. Sean nodded but didn't try to answer until he had swallowed his mouthful of bacon.

'I'll get Mbejane on to that right away. He'll be able to get us Zulus, even if he has to drive them here with a spear at their backs.'

'Good–in the meantime you and I'll ride back to Pretoria again to buy the basic equipment. Picks, shovels, dynamite and the like.' Duff wiped his mouth and filled his coffee cup. 'I'll show you how to start moving the overburden and stacking the ore in a dump. We'll pick a site for the mill and then I'll leave you to get on with it while I head south for the Cape to see my farmer friend. God and the weather permitting ours will be the second mill working on these fields.'

They brought their purchases back from Pretoria in a small ox wagon. Mbejane had done his work well. There were a dozen Zulus lined up for Sean's approval next to the tent with Mbejane standing guard over them like a cheerful sheepdog. Sean walked down the line stopping to ask each man his name and joke with him in his own language. He came to the last in the line. 'How are you called?'

'My name is Hlubi, Nkosi.'

Sean pointed at the man's well-rounded paunch bulging out above his loincloth.

'If you come to work for me, we'll soon have you delivered of your child.'

They burst out in delightful laughter and Sean smiled at them affectionately: proud simple people, tall and big-muscled, completely defenceless against a well-timed jest. Through his mind flashed the picture of a hill in Zululand, a battlefield below it and the flies crawling in the pit of an empty stomach. He shut the picture out quickly and shouted above their laughter.

'So be it then–sixpence a day and all the food you can eat. Will you sign on to work for me?'

They chorused their assent and climbed up on to the back of the wagon. Sean and Duff took them out to the Candy Deep and they laughed and chattered like children going on a picnic.

It took another week for Duff to instruct Sean in the use of dynamite, to explain how he wanted the first trenches dug and to mark out the site for the mill and the dump. The moved the tent up to the mine and worked twelve hours every day. At night they rode down to Candy's Hotel to eat a full meal and then Sean rode home alone. He was so tired by evening that he hardly envied Duff the comfort of Candy's bedroom; instead he found himself admiring Duff's stamina. Each morning he looked for signs of fatigue in his partner but, although his face was lean and gaunt as ever, his eyes were just as clear and his lopsided smile just as cheerful.

'How you do it beats me,' Sean told him the day they finished marking out the mill site.

Duff winked at him. 'Years of practice, laddie, but between you and me the ride down to the Cape will be a welcome rest.'

'When are you going?' Sean asked.

'Quite frankly I think that every day I stay on here increases the risk of someone else getting in before us. Mining machinery is going to be a premium from now on. You have got things well in hand now . . . What do you say?'

'I was starting to think along the same lines,' Sean agreed. They walked back to the tent and sat down in the camp chairs, from where they could look down the length of the valley. The week before about two dozen wagons had been outspanned around Candy's Hotel, but now there were at least two hundred and from where they sat they could count another eight or nine encampments, some even larger than the one around Candy's place. Wood and iron buildings were beginning to replace the canvas tents and the whole veld was criss-crossed with rough roads along which mounted men and wagons moved without apparent purpose.

The restless movement, the dust clouds raised by the passage of men and beasts, the occasional deep crump, crump of dynamite firing in the workings along the Banket–all heightened the air of excitement, of almost breathless expectancy that hung over the whole goldfield.

'I'll leave at first light tomorrow,' Duff decided. 'Ten days' riding to the railhead at Colesberg and another four days by train will get me there. With luck I'll be back in under two months.' He wriggled round in his chair and looked directly at Sean. 'After Paying Candy her two hundred pounds and with what I spent in Pretoria I've only got about a hundred and fifty left. Once I get to Paarl I'll have to pay out three or four hundred for the mill, then I'll need to hire twenty or thirty wagons to bring it up here–say eight hundred pounds altogether to be on the safe side.'

Sean looked at him. He had known this man a few short weeks. Eight hundred was the average man's earnings for three years. Africa was a big land, a man could disappear easily. Sean loosened his belt and dropped it on to the table; he unbuttoned the money pouch.

'Give me a hand to count it out,' he told Duff.

'Thanks,' said Duff and he was not talking about the money. With trust asked for so simply and given so spontaneously the last reservations in their friendship shrivelled and died.

7

When Duff had gone Sean drove himself and his men without mercy. They stripped the overburden of the Reef and exposed it across the whole length of the Candy claims, then they broke it up and started stacking it next to the mill site. The dump grew bigger with every twelve-hour day worked. There was still no trace of the Leader Reef but Sean found little time to worry about that. At night he climbed into bed and slept away his fatigue until another morning called him back to the workings. On Sundays he rode across to François's tent and they talked mining and medicines. François had an enormous chest of patent medicines and a book entitled *The Home Physician*. His health was his hobby and he was treating himself for three major ailments simultaneously. Although he was occasionally unfaithful, his true love was sugar diabetes. The page in *The Home Physician* which covered this subject was limp and grubby from the touch of his fingers. He could recite the symptoms from memory and he had all of them. His other favourite was tuberculosis of the bone; this moved around his body with alarming rapidity taking only a week to leave his hip and reach his wrist. Despite his failing health, however, he was an expert on mining and Sean picked his brain shamelessly. François's sugar diabetes did not prevent him from sharing a bottle of brandy with Sean on Sunday evenings. Sean kept away from Candy's Hotel–that shiny blonde hair and peach skin would have been too much temptation. He couldn't trust himself not to wreck his new friendship with Duff by another importunate affair, so instead he sweated away his energy in the trenches of the Candy Deep.

Every morning he set his Zulus a task for the day, always just a little more than the day before. They sang as they worked and it was very seldom that the task was not complete by nightfall. The days blurred into each other and turned to weeks which quadrupled like breeding amœbæ and became months. Sean began to imagine Duff giving the Capetown girls a whirl with his eight hundred pounds. One evening he rode south for miles along the Cape road, stopping to question every traveller he met and when he finally gave up and returned to the goldfields he went straight to one of the canteens to look for a fight. He found a big, yellow-haired German miner to oblige him. They went outside and for an hour they battered each other beneath a crisp Transvaal sky surrounded by a ring of delighted spectators. Then he and the German went back into the canteen, shook each other's bleeding hands, drank a vow of friendship together and Sean returned to the Candy Deep with his devil exorcized for the time being.

The next afternoon Sean was working near the north boundary of the claims; at this point they had burrowed down about fifteen feet to keep contact with the reef. Sean had just finished marking the shot holes for the next blast and the Zulus were standing around him taking snuff and spitting on their hands before attacking the rock once more.

'Mush, you shag-eared villains. What's going on here, a trade union meeting?' The familiar voice came from above their heads, Duff was looking down at them. Sean scrambled straight up the side of the trench and seized him in a bear hug. Duff was thinner, his jowls covered with a pale stubble and his curly hair white with dust. When the fury of greeting had subsided a little Sean demanded, 'Well, where's the present you went to fetch me?'

Duff laughed, 'Not far behind, all twenty-five wagons full of it.'

'You got it then?' Sean roared.

'You're damn right I did! Come with me and I'll show you.'

Duff's convoy was strung out four miles across the veld, most of the wagons double-teamed against the enormous weight of the machinery. Duff pointed to a rust-streaked cylinder that completely filled one of the leading wagons.

'That is my particular cross, seven tons of the most spiteful stubborn and evil boiler in the world. If it's broken the wagon axle once it's broken it a dozen times since we left Colesberg, not to mention the two occasions on which it capsized itself–once right in the middle of a river.'

They rode along the line of wagons.

'Good God! I didn't realize there'd be so much.' Sean shook his head dubiously. 'Are you sure you know how it all fits together?'

'Leave it to your Uncle Duff. Of course, it's going to need a bit of work done on it, after all it's been lying out in the open for a couple of years. Some of it was rusted up solid, but the judicious use of grease, new paint and the Charleywood brain will see the Candy Deep plant breaking rock and spitting out gold within a month.' Duff broke off and waved to a horseman coming towards them. 'This is the transport contractor. Frikke Malan–Mr Courteney, my partner.'

The contractor pulled up next to them and acknowledged the introduction. He wiped the dust off his face with the sleeve of his shirt.

'*Gott,* man, Mr Charleywood, I don't mind telling you that this is the hardest money I've ever worked for. Nothing personal–but I'll be *vragtig* glad to see the last of this load.'

8

Duff was wrong; it took much longer than a month. The rust had eaten deep into parts of the machinery and each bolt they twisted open was red with the scaly cancer. They worked the usual twelve-hour day chipping and scraping, filing and greasing, knuckles knocked raw against steel and palms wet and red where the blisters had burst. Then one day suddenly and miraculously they were finished. Along the ridge of the Candy Deep, neat and sweet smelling in its new paint, thick with yellow grease and waiting only to be fitted together, lay the dismembered mill.

'How long has it taken us so far?' Duff asked.

'It seems like a hundred years.'

'Is that all?' Duff feigned surprise. 'Then I declare a holiday–two days of meditation.'

'You meditate, brother–I'm going to do some carousing.'

'That's an excellent alternative–let's go!'

They started at Candy's place but she threw them out after the third fight so they moved on. There were a dozen places to drink at and they tried them all. Others were celebrating, because the day before old Kruger, the President of the Republic, had given official recognition to the goldfields. This had the sole effect of diverting the payments for mining licenses from the pockets of the farmers who owned the land into the Government coffers. No one worried about that, except possibly the farmers. Rather it was an excuse for a party. The canteens were packed with swearing, sweating men. Duff and Sean drank with them.

The Crown and Anchor boards were doing a steady business in every bar and the men who crowded around them were the new population of the goldfields. Diggers bare to the waist and caked with dirt, salesmen with loud clothes and louder voices selling everything from dynamite to dysentery cure, an evangelist peddling salvation, gamblers mining pockets, gentlemen trying to keep the tobacco juice off their boots, boys new-flown from home and wishing themselves back, Boers bearded and drab-suited, drinking little but watching with inscrutable eyes the invaders of their land. Then there were the others, the clerks and farmers, the rogues and contractors listening greedily to the talk of gold.

The coloured girl, Martha, came to find Sean and Duff on the afternoon of the second day. They were in a mud-brick and thatch hut called The Tavern of the Bright Angels. Duff was doing a solo exhibition of the Dashing White Sergeant partnered by a chair; Sean and the fifty or so other customers were beating the rhythm on the bar counter with glasses and empty bottles.

Martha skittered across to Sean, slapping at the hands that tried to dive up her skirts and squealing sharply every time her bottom was pinched. She arrived at Sean's side flushed and breathless.

'Madame says you must come quickly–there's big trouble,' she gasped and started to run the gauntlet back to the door. Someone flipped up her dress behind and a concerted masculine roar approved the fact that she wore nothing under the petticoats.

Duff was so engrossed in his dancing that Sean had to carry him bodily out of the bar and dip his head in the horse trough outside before he could gain his attention.

'What the hell did you do that for?' spluttered Duff and swung a round-arm punch at Sean's head. Sean ducked under it and caught him about the body to save him falling on his back.

'Candy wants us–she says there's big trouble.'

Duff thought about that for a few seconds, frowning with concentration, then he threw back his head and sang to the tune of 'London's Burning',

'Candy wants us–Candy wants us
We don't want Candy, we want brandy.'

He broke out of Sean's grip and headed back for the bar. Sean caught him again and pointed him in the direction of the Hotel. Candy was in her bedroom. She looked at the two of them as they swayed arm-in-arm in the doorway.

'Did you enjoy your debauch?' she asked sweetly. Duff mumbled and tried to straighten his coat. Sean tried to steady him as his feet danced an involuntary sideways jig.

'What happened to your eye?' she asked Sean and he fingered it tenderly; it was puffed and blue. Candy didn't wait for an answer but went on, still sweetly:

'Well, if you two beauties want to own a mine by tomorrow you'd better sober up.'

They stared at her and Sean spoke deliberately but nevertheless indistinctly.

'Why, what's the matter?'

'They're going to jump the claims, that's the matter. This new proclamation of a State goldfield has given the drifters the excuse they've been waiting for. About a hundred of them have formed a syndicate. They claim that the old titles aren't legal any more; they are going to pull out the pegs and put in their own.'

Duff walked without a stagger across to the washbasin beside Candy's bed; he splashed his face, towelled it vigorously then stooped and kissed her. 'Thanks, my sweet.'

'Duff, please be careful,' Candy called after them.

'Let's see if we can't hire a few mercenaries,' Sean suggested.

'Good idea, we'll try and find a few sober characters–there should be some in Candy's dining-room.'

They made a short detour on their way back to the mine and stopped at François's tent; it was dark by then and François came out in a freshly ironed nightshirt. He raised an eyebrow when he saw the five heavily armed men with Sean and Duff.

'You going hunting?' he asked.

Duff told him quickly and François was hopping with agitation before he had finished.

'Steal my claims, the thunders, the stinking thunders!' He rushed into his tent and came out again with a double-barrelled shotgun.

'We'll see, man, we'll see how they look full of buckshot.'

'François, listen to me,' Sean shouted him down. 'We don't know which claims they'll go to first. Get your men ready and if you hear shooting our way come and give us a hand–we'll do the same for you.'

'*Ja, ja*, we'll come all right–the dirty thunders.' His nightshirt flapping around his legs François trotted off to call his men.

Mbejane and the other Zulus were cooking dinner, squatting round the three-legged pot. Sean rode up to them.

'Get your spears,' he told them. They ran for their huts and almost immediately came crowding back.

'Nkosi, where's the fight?' they pleaded, food forgotten.

'Come on, I'll show you.'

They placed the hired gunmen amongst the mill machinery from where they could cover the track which led up to the mine. The Zulus they hid in one of the prospect trenches. If it developed into a hand-to-hand fight the syndicate was in for a surprise. Duff and Sean walked a little way down the slope to make sure their defenders were all concealed.

'How much dynamite have we got?' Sean asked thoughtfully. Duff stared at him for a second, then he grinned.

'Sufficient, I'd say. You're full of bright ideas this evening.' He led the way back to the shed which they used as a storeroom.

In the middle of the track a few hundred yards down the slope they buried a full case of explosive and placed an old tin can on top of it to mark the spot. They went back to the shed and spent an hour making grenades out of bundles of dynamite sticks, each with a detonator and a very short fuse. Then they settled down huddled into their sheepskin coats, rifles in their laps and waited.

They could see the lights of the encampments straggled down the valley and hear an occasional faint burst of singing from the canteens, but the moonlit road up to the mine remained deserted. Sean and Duff sat side by side with their backs against the newly painted boiler.

'How did Candy find out about this, I wonder?' Sean asked.

'She knows everything. That hotel of hers is the centre of this goldfield and she keeps her ears open.'

They relapsed into silence again while Sean formed his next question.

'She's quite a girl–our Candy.'

'Yes,' agreed Duff.

'Are you going to marry her, Duff?'

'Good God!' Duff straightened up as though someone had stuck a knife into him. 'You going mad, laddie, or else that was a joke in the worst possible taste.'

'She dotes on you and from what I've seen you're fairly well disposed towards her.' Sean was relieved at Duff's quick rejection of the idea. He was jealous, but not of the woman.

'Yes, we've got a common interest, that I won't deny–but marriage!' Duff shivered slightly, not altogether from the cold. 'Only a fool makes the same mistake twice.'

Sean turned to him with surprise. 'You've been married before?' he asked.

'With a vengeance. She was half Spanish and the rest Norwegian, a smoking bubbly mixture of cold fire and hot ice.' Duff's voice went dreamy. 'The memory has cooled sufficiently for me to think of it with a tinge of regret.'

'What happened?'

'I left her.'

'Why?'

'We only did two things well together and one of them was fight. If I close my eyes I can still see the way she used to pout with these lovely lips and bring them close to my ear before she hissed out a particularly foul word, then–hey ho! back to bed for the reconciliation.'

'Perhaps you made the wrong choice. You look around, you'll see millions of happily married people.'

'Name me one,' challenged Duff and the silence lengthened as Sean thought.

Then Duff went on, 'There's only one good reason for marriage, and that's children.'

'And companionship–that's another good reason.'

'Companionship from a woman?' Duff cut in incredulously. 'Like perfume from garlic. They're incapable of it. I suppose it's the training they get from their mothers, who are after all women themselves, but how can you be friends with someone who suspicions every little move you make, who takes your every action and weighs it on the balance of he loves me, he loves me not?' Duff shook his head unhappily. 'How long can a friendship last when it needs an hourly declaration of love to nourish it? The catechism of matrimony, "Do you love me, darling?" "Yes, darling, of course I do, my sweet." It's got to sound convincing every time otherwise tears.'

Sean chuckled.

'All right, it's funny–it's hilarious until you have to live with it,' Duff mourned. 'Have you ever tried to talk to a woman about anything other than love? The same things that interest you leave them cold. It comes as a shock the first time you try talking sense to them and suddenly you realize that their attention is not with you–they get a slightly fixed look in their eyes and you know they are thinking about that new dress or whether to invite Mrs Van der Hum to the party, so you stop talking and that's another mistake. That's a sign; marriage is full of signs that only a wife can read.'

'I hold no brief for matrimony, Duff, but aren't you being a little unfair, judging everything by your own unfortunate experience?'

'Select any woman, slap a ring on her third finger and she becomes a wife. First she takes you into her warm, soft body, which is pleasant, and then she tries to take you into her warm, soft mind, which is not so pleasant. She does not share, she possesses–she clings and she smothers. The relation of man to woman is uninteresting in that it conforms to an inescapable pattern, nature has made it so for the very good reason that it requires us to reproduce; but in order to obtain that result every love, Romeo and Juliet, Bonaparte and Josephine not excepted, must lead up to the co-performance of a simple biological function. It's such a small thing–such a short-lived, trivial little experience. Apart from that man and woman think differently, feel differently and are interested in different things. Would you call that companionship?'

'No, but is that a true picture? Is that all there is between them?' Sean asked.

'You'll find out one day. Nature in her preoccupation with reproduction has planted in the mind of man a barricade; it has sealed him off from the advice and experience of his fellowmen, inoculated him against it. When your time comes you'll go to the gallows with a song on your lips.'

'You frighten me.'

'It's the sameness of it all that depresses me–the goddamn monotony of it.' Duff shifted his seat restlessly then settled back against the boiler. 'The interesting relationships are those in which sex the leveller takes no hand–brothers, enemies, master and servant, father and son, man and man,'

'Homosexuals?'

'No, that's merely sex out of step and you're back to the original trouble. When a man takes a friend he does it not from an uncontrollable compulsion but in his own free choice. Every friendship is different, ends differently or goes on for ever. No chains bind it, no ritual or written contract. There is no question of forsaking all others, no obligation to talk about it–mouth it up and gloat on it the whole time.' Duff stood up stiffly. 'It's one of the good things in life. How late is it?'

Sean pulled out his watch and tilted its face to catch the moonlight. 'After midnight–it doesn't look as if they're coming.'

'They'll come–there's gold here, another uncontrollable compulsion. They'll come. The question is when.'

The lights along the valley faded out one by one, the deep sing-song voices of the Zulus in the prospect trench stilled and a small cold wind came up and moved the grass along the ridge of the Candy Deep. Sitting together, sometimes drowsing, sometimes talking quietly, they waited the night away. The sky paled, them pinked prettily. A dog barked over near Hospital Hill and another joined it. Sean stood up and stretched, he glanced down the valley towards Ferrieras Camp and saw them. A black moving blot of horsemen, overflowing the road, lifting no dust from the dew-damp earth, spreading out to cross the Natal Spruit then bunching together on the near bank before coming on.

'Mr Charleywood, we have company.'

Duff jumped up.

'They might miss us and go on to the Jack and Whistle first.'

'We'll see which road they take when they come to the fork. In the meantime let's get ready. Mbejane,' shouted Sean and the black head popped out of the trench.

'Nkosi?'

'Are you awake? They are coming.'

The blackness parted in a white smile. 'We are awake.'

'Then get down and stay down until I give the word.'

The five mercenaries were lying belly down in the grass, each with a newly-opened packet of cartridges at his elbow. Sean hurried back to Duff and they crouched behind the boiler.

'The tin can shows up clearly from here. Do you think you can hit it?'

'With my eyes closed,' said Sean.

The horsemen reached the fork and turned without hesitation towards the Candy Deep, quickening their paces as they came up the ridge. Sean rested his rifle across the top of the boiler and picked up the speck of silver in his sights.

'What's the legal position, Duff?' he asked out of the corner of his mouth.

'They've just crossed our boundary–they are now officially trespassers,' Duff pronounced solemnly.

One of the leading horses kicked over the tin can and Sean fired at the spot on which it had stood. The shot was indecently loud in the quiet morning and every head in the syndicate lifted with alarm towards the ridge, then the ground beneath them jumped up in a brown cloud to meet the sky. When the dust cleared there was a struggling tangle of downed horses and men. The screams carried clearly up to the crest of the ridge.

'My God,' breathed Sean, appalled at the destruction.

'Shall we let them have it, boss?' called one of the hired men.

'No,' Duff answered him quickly. 'They've had enough.'

The flight started, riderless horses, mounted men and others on foot were scattering back down the valley. Sean was relieved to see that they left only a half a dozen men and a few horses lying in the road.

'Well, that's the easiest fiver you've ever earned,' Duff told one of the mercenaries. 'I think you can go home now and have some breakfast.'

'Wait, Duff.' Sean pointed. The survivors of the explosion had reached the road junction again and there they were being stopped by two men on horseback.

'Those two are trying to rally them.'

'Let's change their minds, they're still within rifle range.'

'They are not on our property any more,' disagreed Sean. 'Do you want to wear a rope?'

They watched while those of the syndicate who had had enough fighting for one day disappeared down the road to the camps and the rest coagulated into a solid mass at the crossroad.

'We should have shot them up properly while we had the chance,' grumbled one of the mercenaries uneasily. 'Now they'll come back–look at that bastard talking to them like a Dutch uncle.'

They left their horses and spread out, then they started moving cautiously back up the slope. They hesitated just below the line of boundary pegs then ran forward, tearing up the pegs as they came.

'All together, gentlemen, if you please,' called Duff politely and the seven rifles fired. The range was long and the thirty or so attackers ran doubled up and dodging. The bullets had little effect at first, but as the distance shortened the men started falling. There was a shallow donga running diagonally down the slope and as each of the attackers reached it he jumped down into it and from its safety started a heated reply to the fire of Sean's men. Bullets spanged off the machinery, leaving bright scars where they struck.

Mbejane's Zulus were adding their voices to the confusion.

'Let us go down to them now, Nkosi.'

'They are close–let us go.'

'Quiet down, you madmen, you'd not go a hundred paces against those rifles,' Sean snarled impatiently.

'Sean, cover me,' whispered Duff. 'I'm going to sneak round the back of the ridge, rush them from the side and lob a few sticks of dynamite into that donga.'

Sean caught his arm, his fingers dug into it so that Duff winced.

'You take one step and I'll break a rifle butt over your head–you're as bad as those Blacks. Now keep shooting and let me think.' Sean peered over the top of the boiler but ducked again as a bullet rang loudly against it, inches from his ear. He stared at the new paint in front of his nose, put his shoulder against it; the boiler rocked slightly. He looked up and Duff was watching him.

'We'll walk down together and lob that dynamite,' Sean told him. 'Mbejane and his boodthirsty heathens will roll the boiler in front of us. These other gentlemen will cover us, we'll do this thing in style.'

Sean called the Zulus out of the trench and explained to them. They chorused their approval of the scheme and jostled each other to find a place to push against the boiler. Sean and Duff filled the front of their shirts with the dynamite grenades and lit a short length of tarred rope each.

Sean nodded to Mbejane.

'Where are the children of Zulu?' sand Mbejane, shrilling his voice in the ancient rhetorical question.

'Here,' answered his warriors braced ready against the boiler.

'Where are the spears of Zulu?'

'Here,'

'How bright are the spears of Zulu?'

'Brighter than the Sun.'

'How hungry are the spears of Zulu?'

'Hungrier than the locust.'

'Then let us take them to the feeding.'

'*Yeh-bo.*' Explosive assent and the boiler revolved slowly to the thrust of the black shoulders.

'*Yeh-bo.*' Another reluctant revolution.

'*Yeh-bo.*' It moved more readily.

'*Yeh-bo.*' Gravity caught it. Ponderously it bumped down the slope and they ran behind it. The fire of the donga doubled its volume, rattling like hail against the huge metal cylinder. The singing of the Zulus changed its tone also; the deep-voiced chanting quickened, climbed excitedly and became the blood trill. That insane, horrible squealing made Sean's skin crawl, tickled his spine with the ghost fingers of memory, but it inflamed him also. His mouth opened and he squealed with them. He touched the first grenade with the burning rope then flung it in a high spluttering sparking arc. It burst in the air above the donga. He threw again. Crump, crump. Duff was using his explosive as well. The boiler crashed over the lip of the donga and came to rest in a cloud of dust; the Zulus followed it in, spreading out, still shrieking, and now their assegais were busy. The white men broke, clawed frantically out of the ravine and fled, the Zulus hacking at them as they ran.

When François arrived with fifty armed diggers following him the fight was over.

'Take your boys down to the camps. Comb them out carefully. We want every one of those that got away,' Duff told him. 'It's about time we had a little law and order on this field.'

'How will we pick out the ones that were in on it?' asked François.

'By their white faces and the sweat on their shirts you will know them,' Duff answered.

François and his men went, leaving Sean and Duff to clean up the battlefield. It was a messy job–the stabbing spears had made it so. They destroyed those horses that the blast had left still half alive and they gleaned more than a dozen corpses from the donga and the slope below it. Two of them were Zulus. The wounded, and there were many, they packed into a wagon and took them down to Candy's Hotel.

It was early afternoon by the time they arrived. They threaded the wagon through the crowd and stopped it in front of the Hotel. It seemed the entire population of the goldfield was there, packed around the small open space in which François was holding his prisoners.

François was almost hysterical with excitement. He was sweeping the shotgun around in dangerous circles as he harangued the crowd. Then he darted back to prod one of the prisoners with the twin muzzles.

'You thunders,' he screamed. 'Steal our claims–hey–steal our claims.'

At that moment he caught sight of Duff and Sean bringing the wagon through the press.

'Duff, Duff. We got them. We got the whole lot of them,' The crowd backed respectfully away from the menace of that circling shotgun and Sean flinched as it pointed directly at him for a second.

'So I see, François,' Duff assured him. 'In fact, I have seldom seen anyone more completely had.'

François's prisoners were swathed in ropes; they could move only their heads and as additional security a digger with a loaded rifle stood over each of them. Duff climbed down off the wagon.

'Don't you think you should slacken those ropes a little?' Duff asked dubiously.

'And have them escape?' François was indignant.

'Do you think they'd get very far?'

'No, I don't suppose so.'

'Well, another half an hour and they'll all have gangrene–look at that one's hand already, a beautiful shade of blue.'

Reluctantly François conceded and told his men to untie them.

Duff pushed his way through the crowd and climbed the steps of the Hotel. From there he held up his hands for silence.

'There have been a lot of men killed today–we don't want it to happen again. One way we can prevent it is to make sure that this lot get what they deserve.' Cheers were led by François.

'But we must do it properly. I suggest we elect a committee to deal with this affair and with any other problems that crop up on these fields. Say ten members and a chairman.'

More cheers.

'Call it the Diggers' Committee,' shouted someone and the crowd took up the name enthusiastically.

'All right, the Diggers' Committee it is. Now we want a chairman, any suggestions?'

'Mr Charleywood,' shouted François.

'Yes, Duff–he'll do.'

'Yes, Duff Charleywood.'

'Any other suggestions?'

'No,' roared the crowd.

'Thank you gentlemen.' Duff smiled at them. 'I am sensible of the honour. Now, ten members.'

'Jock and Trevor Heyns.'

'Karl Lochtkamper.'

'François du Toit.'

'Sean Courteney.'

There were fifty nominations. Duff baulked at counting votes so the committee was elected by applause. He called the names one at a time and judged the strength of the response to each. Sean and François were among those elected. Chairs and a table were brought out to the veranda and Duff took his seat. With a water-jug he hammered for silence, declared the first session of the Diggers' Committee open and then immediately fined three members of the crowd ten pounds each for discharging firearms during a meeting–gross contempt of Committee. The fines were paid and a proper air of solemnity achieved.

'I'll ask Mr Courteney to open the case for the prosecution.'

Sean stood up and gave a brief description of the morning's battle, ending, 'You were there, Your Honour, so you know all about it anyway.'

'So I was,' agreed Duff. 'Thank you, Mr Courteney. I think that was a very fair picture you presented. Now,' he looked at the prisoners, 'who speaks for you?'

There was a minute of shuffling and whispering, then one of them was pushed forward. He pulled off his hat and blushed purple.

'Your Worship,' he began, then stopped, wriggling with embarrassment.

'Your Worship.'

'You've said that already.'

'I don't rightly know where to begin, Mr Charleywood–I mean Your Honour, sir.'

Duff looked at the prisoners again.

'Perhaps you'd like to reconsider your choice.'

The first champion was withdrawn in disgrace and a fresh one sent forward to face the Committee. He had more fire.

'You bastards got no right to do this to us,' he started and Duff promptly fined him ten pounds. His next attempt was more polite.

'Your Honour, you can't do this to us. We had our rights, you know, the new proclamation and all, I mean, them old titles wasn't legal no more now, was they? We just came along as peaceful as you please, the old titles not being legal, we got a right to do what we done. Then you bastards, I mean Your Honour, dynamited us and like we had a right to protect ourselves,

I mean after all, didn't we, sir?'

'A brilliant defence most ably conducted. Your fellows should be grateful to you,' Duff complimented him, then turned to his Committee. 'Well now, how say you merry gentlemen. Guilty or not guilty?'

'Guilty.' They spoke together and François added for emphasis, 'the dirty thunders.'

'We will now consider sentence.'

'String them up,' shouted someone and instantly the mood changed. The mob growled: an ugly sound.

'I'm a carpenter, I'll whip you up a handsome set of gallows in no time at all.'

'Don't waste good wood on them. Use a tree.'

'Get the ropes.'

'String them up.'

The crowd surged in, lynch mad. Sean snatched François's shotgun and jumped up on to the table.

'So help me God, I'll shoot the first one of you that touches them before this court says so.' They checked and Sean pressed his advantage. 'At this range I can't miss. Come on, try me–there's two loads of buckshot in here. Someone will get cut in half.' They fell back still muttering.

'Perhaps you've forgotten, but there's a police force in this country and there's a law against killing. Hang them today and it'll be your turn tomorrow.'

'You're right, Mr Courteney, it'll be cruel heartless murder. That it will,' wailed the spokesman.

'Shut up, you bloody fool,' Duff snarled at him and someone in the crowd laughed. The laughter caught on and Duff sighed silently with relief. That had been very close.

'Give them the old tar-and feathers.'

Duff grinned. 'Now you're talking sense. Who's got a few barrels of tar for sale?' He looked round. 'What, no offers? Then we'll have to think of something else.'

'I've got ten drums of red paint–thirty shillings each, good imported brand.' Duff recognized the speaker as a trader who had opened a general dealer's store down at Ferrieras Camp.

'Mr Tarry suggests paint. What about it?'

'No, it comes off too easily–that's no good.'

'I'll let you have it cheap–twenty-five shillings a drum.'

'No–stick your ruddy paint,' the crowd booed him.

'Give them a twist on Satan's Roulette Wheel,' shouted another voice, and the crowd clamoured agreement.

'That's it–give them the wheel.'

'Round and round and round she goes–where she stops nobody knows,' roared a black-bearded digger from the roof of the shanty across the road. The crowd howled.

Sean watched Duff's expression–the smile had gone. He was weighing it up. If he stopped them again they might lose all patience and risk the shotgun. He couldn't chance it.

'All right. If that's what you want.' He faced the terrified cluster of prisoners. 'The sentence of this court is that you play roulette with the devil for one hour and that you then leave this goldfield–if we catch you back here again you'll get another hour of it. The wounded are excused the first half of the sentence. I think they've had enough. Mr du Toit will supervise the punishment.'

'We'd prefer the paint, Mr Charleywood,' pleaded the spokesman again.

'I bet you would,' said Duff softly, but the crowd was carrying them away already, out towards the open veld beyond the Hotel. Most of them had staked claims of their own and they didn't like claim jumpers. Sean climbed down off the table.

'Let's go and have a drink,' Duff said to him.

'Aren't you going to watch?' asked Sean.

'I've seen it done once before down in the Cape. That was enough.'

'What do they do?'

'Go and have a look, I'll be waiting for you at the Bright Angels. I'll be surprised if you stay the full hour.'

By the time Sean joined the crowd most of the wagons had been gathered from the camps and drawn up in a line. Men swarmed round them fitting jacks under the axles to lift the big back wheels clear of the ground. Then the prisoners were hustled forward–one to each wheel. Eager hands lifted them and held them while their wrists and ankles were lashed to the rim of the wheel with the hub in the middle of their backs and their arms and legs spreadeagled like stranded starfish. François hurried along the line checking the ropes and placing four diggers at each wheel, two to start it and another two to take over when those were tired. He reached the end, came back to the centre again, pulled his watch from his pocket, checked the time, then shouted.

'All right–turn them, *kerels*.'

The wheels started moving, slowly at first then faster as they built up momentum. The bodies strapped to them blurred with the speed.

'Round and round and round she goes–round and round and round she goes,' chanted the crowd gleefully.

Within minutes there was a burst of laughter from the end of the line of wagons. Someone had started vomiting, it sprayed from him like yellow sparks from a catherine wheel. Then another and another joined in, Sean could hear them retching and gasping as the centrifugal force flung the vomit up against the back of their throats and out of their noses. He waited a few more minutes but when their bowels started to empty he turned away gagging and headed for the Bright Angel.

'Did you enjoy it?' asked Duff.

'Give me a brandy,' answered Sean.

9

With the Diggers' Committee dispensing rough justice a semblance of order came to the camps. President Kruger wanted no part in policing the nest of ruffians and cut-throats which was growing up just outside his Capital and he contented himself with placing his spies among them and leaving them to work out their own salvation. After all, the field was far from proved and the chances were that in another year the veld would again be as deserted as it had been nine months before. He could afford to wait; in the meantime the Diggers' Committee had his tacit sanction.

While the ants worked, cutting down into the reef with pick and with dynamite, the grasshoppers waited in the bars and shanties. So far only the Jack and Whistle mill was turning out gold, and only Hradsky and François du Toit knew how much gold was coming out of it. Hradsky was still in Capetown crusading for capital and François spoke to no one, not even to Duff, about the mill's productivity.

The rumours flew like sand in a whirlwind. One day it seemed that the reef had pinched out fifty feet below the surface, and the next the canteens buzzed with the news that the Heyns brothers had gone down a hundred feet and were pulling out nuggets the size of musket balls. Nobody knew but everybody was prepared to guess.

Up at the Candy Deep, Duff and Sean worked on relentlessly. The mill took shape on its concrete platform, its jaws open for the first bite at the rock. The boiler was swung up on to its cradle by twenty sweating, singing Zulus. The copper tables were fitted up ready to be smeared with quicksilver. There was no time to worry about the reef nor the dwindling store of money in Sean's cash belt. They worked and they slept–there was nothing else. Duff took to sharing Sean's tent up on the ridge and Candy had her featherbed to herself again.

On the twentieth of November they fired the boiler for the first time. Tired and horny-handed, their bodies lean and tempered hard with toil, they stood together and watched the needle creep up round the pressure gauge until it touched the red line at the top.

Duff grunted. 'Well, at least we've got power now.' Then he punched Sean's shoulder. 'What the hell are you standing here for–do you think this is a Sunday School picnic? There's work to do, laddie.'

On the second of December they fed the mill its first meal and watched the powdered rock flow across the amalgam tables. Sean threw his arm round Duff's neck in an affectionate half-Nelson, Duff hit him in the stomach and pulled his hat down over his eyes, they drank a glass of brandy each at supper and laughed a little but that was all. They were too tired to celebrate. From now on one of them must be in constant attendance of that iron monster. Duff took the first night shift and when Sean went up to the mill next morning he found him weaving on his feet, his eyes sunk deep in dark sockets. 'By my reckoning we've run ten tons of rock through her. Time to clean the tables and see just how much gold we've picked up.'

'You go and get some sleep,' said Sean and Duff ignored him.

'Mbejane, bring a couple of your savages here, we're going to change the tables.'

'Listen, Duff, it can wait an hour or two. Go and get your head down.'

'Please stop drivelling–you're as bad as a wife.'

Sean shrugged. 'Have it your own way, show me how you do it then.'

They switched the flow of powdered rock on to the second table that was standing ready; then with a broad bladed spatula Duff scraped the mercury off the copper top of the first table, collecting it in a ball the size of a coconut.

'The mercury picks up the tiny particles of gold,' he explained to Sean as he worked, 'and lets the grains of rock wash across the table and fall off into the dump. Of course it doesn't collect it all, some of it goes to waste.'

'How do you get the gold out again?'

'You put the whole lot in a retort and boil off the mercury–the gold stays behind.'

'Hell of a waste of mercury, isn't it?'

'No, you catch it as it condenses and use it again. Come on, I'll show you.'

Duff carried the ball of amalgam down to the shed, placed it in the retort and lit the blow-lamp. With the heat on it the ball dissolved and started to bubble. Silently they stared at it. The level in the retort fell.

'Where's the gold?' Sean asked at last.

'Oh, shut up,' Duff snapped impatiently, and then, repentant, 'Sorry, laddie, I feel a bit jaded this morning.'

The last of the mercury steamed off and there it was, glowing bright, molten yellow. A drop of gold the size of a pea. Duff shut off the blow-lamp and neither of them spoke for a while. Then Sean asked, 'Is that all?'

'That, my friend, is all,' agreed Duff wearily. 'What do you want to do with it–fill a tooth?'

He turned towards the door with a droop to his whole body.

'Keep the mill running, we might as well go down with our colours flying.'

10

It was a miserable Christmas dinner. They ate it at Candy's Hotel. They had credit there. She gave Duff a gold signet ring and Sean a box of cigars. Sean had never smoked before now the sting of it in his lungs gave him a certain masochistic pleasure. The dining-room roared with men's voices and cutlery clatter, the air was thick with the smell of food and tobacco smoke while in one corner–marooned on a little island of gloom–sat Sean, Duff and Candy.

Once Sean lifted his glass at Duff and spoke like an undertaker's clerk 'Happy Christmas.'

Duff's lips twitched back in a dead man's grin. 'And the same to you.'

They drank. Then Duff roused himself to speak. 'Tell me again–how much have we got left? I like to hear you say it; you have a beautiful voice, you should have played Shakespeare.'

'Three pounds and sixteen shillings.'

'Yes, yes, you got it just right that time–three pounds and sixteen shillings–now to really make me feel Christmasy, tell me how much we owe.'

'Have another drink,' Sean changed the subject.

'Yes, I think I will, thank you.'

'Oh please, you two, let's just forget about it for today,' pleaded Candy. 'I planned for it to be such a nice party–look, there's François! Hey, François–over here!'

The dapper du Toit bustled across to their table.

'Happy Christmas, kerels, let me buy you a drink.'

'It's nice to see you.' Candy gave him a kiss. 'How are you? You're looking fine.'

François sobered instantly. 'It's funny you should say that, Candy. As a matter of fact I'm a bit worried.' He tapped his chest and sank down into an empty chair. 'My heart, you know, I've been waiting for it to happen, and then yesterday I was up at the mill, just standing there, you understand, when suddenly it was as though a vice was squeezing my chest. I couldn't breathe–well, not very well anyway. Naturally I hurried back to my tent and looked it up. Page eighty-three. Under "Diseases of the Heart".' He shook his head sadly. 'It's very worrying. You know I wasn't a well man before, but now this.'

'Oh, no,' wailed Candy. 'I can't stand it–not you too.'

'I'm sorry, have I said something wrong?'

'Just in keeping with the festive spirit at this table.' She pointed at Duff and Sean. 'Look at their happy faces–if you'll excuse me I'm going to check up in the kitchen.' She went.

'What's wrong, old Duff?'

Duff flashed his death's head grin across the table at Sean.

'The man wants to know what's wrong–tell him.'

'Three pounds sixteen shillings,' said Sean and François looked puzzled.

'I don't understand.'

'He means we're broke–flat broke.'

'*Gott*, I'm sorry to hear that, Duff, I thought you were going good. I've heard the mill running all this month. I thought you'd be rich by now.'

'The mill's been running all right and we've recovered enough gold to block a flea's backside.'

'But why, man? You are working the Leader Reef aren't you?'

'I'm beginning to think this Leader Reef of yours is a bedtime story.'

François peered into his glass thoughtfully.

'How deep are you?'

'We've got one incline shaft down about fifty feet.'

'No sign of the Leader?' Duff shook his head and François went on.

'You know when I first spoke to you a lot of what I said was just guessing.'

Duff nodded.

'Well, I know a bit more about it now. What I am going to tell you is for you alone–I'll lose my job if it gets out, you understand?'

Duff nodded again.

'So far the Leader Reef has only been found at two places. We've got it on the Jack and Whistle and I know the Heyns brothers have struck it on the Cousin Jock Mine. Let me draw it for you.' He picked up a knife and drew in the gravy on the bottom of Sean's plate. 'This is the Main Reef running fairly straight. Here I am, here is the Cousin Jock and here you are in between us. Both of us have found the Leader and you haven't. My guess is it's there all right–you just don't know where to look.

'At the far end of the Jack and Whistle claims the Main Reef and the Leader are running side by side two feet apart but by the time they reach the boundary nearest to the Candy Deep they've opened up to seventy feet apart. Now on the boundary of the Cousin Jock they're back to fifty feet apart. To me it seems that the two reefs form the shape of a long bow, like this.' He drew it in. 'The Main Reef is the string and the Leader Reef is the wood. I'm telling you, Duff, if you cut a trench at right-angles to the Main Reef you'll find it–and when you do you can buy me a drink.'

They listened gravely and when François finished Duff leaned back in his chair. 'If we'd known this a month ago! Now how are we going to raise the money to cut this new trench and still keep the mill running?'

'We could sell some of our equipment,' suggested Sean.

'We need it, every scrap of it, and besides if we sold one spade the creditors would be on us like a pack of wolves, howling for their money.'

'I'd make you a loan if I had it–but with what Mr Hradsky pays me–' François shrugged. 'You'll need about two hundred pounds. I haven't got it.'

Candy came back to the table in time to hear François's last remark.

'What's this all about?'

'Can I tell her, François?'

'If you think it will do any good.'

Candy listened, then thought for a moment. 'Well, I've just bought ten plots of ground in Johannesburg, this new Government village down the valley, so I'm short myself. But I could let you have fifty pounds if that would help.'

'I've never borrowed money from a lady before–it'll be a new experience. Candy, I love you.'

'I wish you meant that,' said Candy, but luckily for Duff his hearing failed him completely just as Candy spoke. He went on hurriedly.

'We'll need another hundred and fifty or so–let's hear your suggestions, gentlemen.'

There was a long silence, then Duff started to smile and he was looking at Sean.

'Don't tell me, let me guess,' Sean forestalled him. 'You're going to put me out to stud?'

'Close–but not quite right. How are you feeling, laddie?'

'Thank you, I'm all right.'

'Strong?'

'Yes.'

'Brave?'

'Come on, Duff, let's have it. I don't like that look in your eye.'

Duff pulled a notebook out of his pocket and wrote in it with a stump of pencil. Then he tore out the page and handed it to Sean. 'We'll have posters like this put up in every canteen on the goldfields.'

Sean read it:

ON NEW YEAR'S DAY MR SEAN COURTENEY HEAVYWEIGHT CHAMPION OF THE TRANSVAAL REPUBLIC WILL STAND TO MEET ALL COMERS IN FRONT OF CANDY'S HOTEL FOR A PURSE OF FIFTY POUNDS A SIDE.

Spectators' Fee, 2*s*. All Welcome.

Candy was reading it over his shoulder. She squeaked.

'That's wonderful. I'll have to hire extra waiters to serve drinks and I'll run a buffet luncheon. I suppose I could charge two shillings a head?'

'I'll fix the posters,' François was not to be outdone, 'and I'll send a couple of my chaps down to put up a ring.'

'We'll close the mill down until New Year–Sean will have to get a lot of rest. We'll put him on light training only. No drinking, of course, and plenty of sleep,' said Duff.

'It's all arranged then, is it?' asked Sean. 'All I've got to do is go in there and get beaten to a pulp?'

'We're doing this for you, laddie, so that you can be rich and famous.'

'Thank you, thank you very much.'

'You like to fight, don't you?'

'When I'm in the mood.'

'Don't worry, I'll think up some dirty names to call you–get you worked up in no time.'

11

'How are you feeling?' Duff asked for the sixth time that morning.

'No change since five minutes ago,' Sean reassured him.

Duff pulled out his watch, stared at it, held it to his ear and looked surprised that it was still ticking.

'We've got the challengers lined up on the veranda. I've told Candy to serve them free drinks–as much as they want. Every minute we can wait here gives them a little longer to take on a load of alcohol. François is collecting the gate money in my valise; as you win each bout the stakes will go into it as well. I've got Mbejane stationed at the mouth of the alley beside the Hotel. If there's a riot one of us will throw the bag to him and he'll head for the long grass.'

Sean was stretched out on Candy's bed with his hands behind his head. He laughed. 'I can find no fault with your planning. Now for pity's sake calm down, man. You're making me nervous.'

The door burst open and Duff leapt out of his chair at the crash. It was François, he stood in the doorway holding his chest.

'My heart,' he panted. 'This is doing my heart no good.'

'What's happening outside?' Duff demanded.

'We've collected over fifty pounds gate money already. There's a mob up on the roof that haven't paid, but every time I go near them they throw bottles at me.'

François cocked his head on one side. 'Listen to them.' The noise of the crowd was barely softened by the flimsy walls of the Hotel. 'They won't wait much longer–you'd better come out before they start looking for you.'

Sean stood up. 'I'm ready.'

François hesitated.

'Duff, you remember Fernandes, that Portuguese from Kimberley?'

'Oh no!' Duff anticipated him. 'Don't tell me he's here.'

François nodded. 'I didn't want to alarm you but some of the local boys clubbed in and telegraphed south for him. He arrived on the express coach half an hour ago. I had hoped he wasn't going to make it in time, but–' He shrugged.

Duff looked at Sean sadly.

'Bad luck, laddie.'

François tried to soften the blow. 'I told him it was first come first served. He's sixth in the line so Sean will be able to make a couple of hundred quid anyway–then we can always say he's had enough and close the contest.'

Sean was listening with interest. 'This Fernandes is dangerous?'

'They were thinking of him when they invented that word,' Duff told him.

'Let's go and have a look at him.'

Sean led the way out of Candy's room and down the passage.

'Did you get hold of a scale to weigh them with?' Duff asked François as they hurried after Sean.

'No, there's not one on the fields that goes over a hundred and fifty pounds–but I have Gideon Barnard outside.'

'How does that help us?'

'He's a cattle dealer–all his life he's been judging animals on the hoof. He'll give us the weights to within a few pounds.'

Duff chuckled. 'That'll have to do then. Besides I doubt we'll be claiming any world titles.'

Then they were out on the veranda blinking in the brightness of the sun and the thunder of the crowd.

'Which is the Portuguese?' whispered Sean–he needn't have asked. The man stood out like a gorilla in a cage of monkeys. A shaggy coating of hair began on his shoulders and continued down his back and chest, completely hiding his nipples and exaggerating the bulge of his enormous belly.

The crowd opened a path for Sean and Duff and they walked along it to the ring. Hands slapped Sean's back but the well-wishes were drowned in the churning sea of sound. Jock Heyns was the referee–he helped Sean through the ropes and ran his hands over his pockets.

'Just checking,' he apologized. 'We don't want any scrap iron in the ring.' Then he beckoned to a tall, brown-faced fellow who was leaning on the ropes chewing tobacco.

'This is Mr Bernard–our weighing steward. Well, what do you say, Gideon?'

The steward hosed a little juice from the side of his mouth.

'Two hundred and ten.'

'Thank you.' Jock held up his hands and after a few minutes was rewarded with a comparative silence.

'Ladies and Gentlemen.'

'Who you talking to, Guvnor?'

'We are privileged to have with us today–Mr Sean Courteney.'

'Wake up, *Boet*, he's been with us for months.'

'The heavyweight champion of the Republic.'

'Why not make it the world, cock, he's got just as much right to that title.'

'Who will fight six bouts–'

'If it lasts that long.'

'–for his title and a purse of fifty pounds each.'

Sustained cheering.

'The first challenger–at two hundred and ten pounds–Mr Anthony–'

'Hold on,' Sean shouted, 'who says he's first?'

Jock Heyns had taken a deep breath to bellow the name, he let it escape with a hiss. 'It was arranged by Mr du Toit.'

'If I fight them, then I pick them–I want the Port . . .'

Duff's hand whipped over Sean's mouth and his whisper was desperate. 'Don't be a bloody fool–take the easy ones first. Use your head–we aren't doing this for fun, we're trying to finance a mine, remember?'

Sean clawed Duff's hand off his mouth. 'I want the Portuguese,' he shouted.

'He's joking,' Duff assured the crowd, then turned on Sean fiercely. 'Are you mad? That dago's a man-eater, we're fifty pounds poorer before you start.'

'I want the Portuguese,' repeated Sean with all the logic of a small boy picking the most expensive toy in the shop.

'Let him have the dago,' shouted the gentlemen on the hotel roof and Jock Heyns eyed them nervously; it was clear that they were about to add a few more bottles to the argument.

'All right,' he agreed hastily. 'The first challenger, at–' he glanced at Barnard and repeated after him, 'two hundred and fifty-five pounds–Mr Felezardo da Silva Fernandes.'

In a storm of hoots and applause the Portuguese waddled down off the veranda and into the ring. Sean had seen Candy at the dining-room window and he waved to her. She blew him a two-handed kiss and at that instant Trevor Heyns, the timekeeper, hit the bucket which served as a gong and Sean heard Duff's warning shout. Instinctively he started to duck. There was a flash of lightning inside his skull and he found himself sitting in among the legs of the first line of spectators.

'The bastard King hit me,' Sean complained loudly. He shook his head and was surprised to find it still attached to his body. Someone poured a glass of beer over him and it steadied him. He felt his anger flaming up through his body.

'Six,' counted Jock Heyns.

The Portuguese was standing at the ropes. 'Come back, Leetle Sheet, I haf some more for you, not half.'

Sean's anger jumped in his throat.

'Seven, eight.'

Sean gathered his legs under him.

'I kiss your mother.' Fernandes puckered his lips and smacked them. 'I love your sister, like this.' He demonstrated graphically.

Sean charged. With the full weight of his run behind it, his fist thudded into the Portuguese's mouth, then the ropes caught Sean and catapulted him back into the crowd once more.

'You weren't even in the ring, how could you hit him?' protested one of the spectators who had broken Sean's fall. He had money on Fernandes.

'Like this!' Sean demonstrated. The man sat down heavily and had nothing further to say. Sean hurdled the ropes. Jock Heynes was halfway through his second count when Sean interrupted him by lifting the reclining Portuguese to his feet, using the tangled bush of his hair as a handle. He balanced the man on his unsteady legs and hit him again.

'One, two, three . . .' resignedly Jock Heyns began his third count, this time he managed to reach ten.

There was a howl of protest from the crowd and Jock Heyns struggled to make himself heard above it.

'Does anyone want to lodge a formal objection?'

It seemed that there were those who did.

'Very well, please step into the ring. I can't accept shouted comments.' Jock's attitude was understandable–he stood to lose a considerable sum if his decision were reversed. But Sean was patrolling the ropes as hungrily as a lion at feeding time. Jock waited a decent interval, then held up Sean's right arm.

'The winner–ten minutes for refreshments before the next bout. Will the keepers please come and fetch their property.' He gestured towards the Portuguese.

'Nice going, laddie, unorthodox perhaps but beautiful to watch.' Duff took Sean's arm and led him to a chair on the veranda.

'Three more to go, then we can call it a day.' He handed Sean a glass.

'What's this?'

'Orange juice.'

'I'd prefer something a little stronger.'

'Later, laddie.'

Duff collected the Portuguese purse and dropped it into the valise while that gentlemen was being carried from the ring by his straining sponsors and laid to rest at the far end of the veranda.

Mr Anthony Blair was next. His heart was not in the encounter. He moved prettily enough on his feet but always in the direction best calculated to keep him out of reach of Sean's fists.

'The boy's a natural long-distance champ.'

'Watch it, Courteney, he'll run you to death.'

'Last lap, Blair, once more round the ring and you've done five miles.'

The chase ended when Sean, now sweating gently, herded him in a corner and there dispatched him.

The third challenger had by this time developed a pain in his chest.

'It hurts like you wouldn't believe it,' he announced through gritted teeth.

'Does it sort of gurgle in your lungs as you breathe?' asked François.

'Yes, that's it–gurgles like you wouldn't believe it.'

'Pleurisy,' diagnosed du Toit with more than a trace of envy in his voice.

'Is that bad?' the man asked anxiously.

'Yes it is. Page one hundred and sixteen. The treatment is–'

'Then I won't be able to fight. Hell, that's bad luck,' the invalid complained cheerfully.

'It's exceptionally bad luck,' agreed Duff. 'it means you'll have to forfeit your purse money.'

'You wouldn't take advantage of a sick man?'

'Try me,' Duff suggested pleasantly.

The fourth contestant was a German. Big, blond and happy-faced. He stumbled three or four times on his way to the ring, tripped over the ropes and crawled to his corner on hands and knees; once there he was able to regain his feet with a little help from the ring post. Jock went close to him to smell his breath and before he could dodge, the German caught him in a bear hug and led him into the opening steps of a waltz. The crowd loved it and there were no objections when at the end of the dance Jock declared Sean the winner on a technical knockout. More correctly the decison should have gone to Candy who had provided the free drinks.

'We can close down the circus now if you want to, laddie,' Duff told Sean. 'You've made enough to keep the Candy Deep afloat for another couple of months.'

'I haven't had a single good fight out of the lot of them. But I like the looks of this last one. The others were for business; this one I'll have just for the hell of it.'

'You've been magnificent–now you deserve a little fun,' agreed Duff.

'Mr Martin Curtis. Heavyweight champion of Georgia, U.S.A.' Jock introduced him.

Gideon Barnard put his weight at two hundred and ten pounds, the same as Sean's. Sean shook his hand and from the touch of it knew he was not going to be disappointed.

'Glad to know you.' The American's voice was as soft as his grip was hard.

'Your servant, sir,' said Sean and hit the air where the man's head had been an instant before. He grunted as a fist slogged into his chest under his raised right arm and backed away warily. A soft sigh blew through the crowd and they settled down contentedly. This was what they had come to see.

The red wine was served early; it flew in tiny drops every time a punch was thrown or received. The fight flowed smoothly around the square of trampled grass. The sound of bone on flesh was followed immediately by the growl of the crowd and the seconds between were filled with the hoarse breathing of the two men and the slither, slither of their feet.

'Yaaaa!' Through the tense half silence ripped a roar like that of a mortally wounded foghorn. Sean and the American jumped apart startled, and turned with everyone else to face Candy's Hotel. Fernandes was with them again; his mountain-wide hairiness seemed to fill the whole veranda. He picked up one of Candy's best tables and holding it across his chest tore off two of its legs as though they were the wings of a roasted chicken.

'François, the bag!' shouted Sean. François snatched it up and threw it high over the heads of the crowd. Sean held his breath as he followed its slow trajectory, then he blew out again with relief as he saw Mbejane field the pass and vanish around the corner of the Hotel.

'Yaaaa!' Fernandes gave tongue again. With a table leg in each hand he charged the crowd that stood between him and Sean; it scattered before him.

'Do you mind if we finish this some other time?' Sean asked the American.

'Of course not. Any time at all. I was just about to leave myself.'

Duff reached through the ropes and caught Sean's arm.

'There's someone looking for you–or had you noticed?'

'It might just be his way of showing friendliness.'

'I wouldn't bet on it–are you coming?'

Fernandes rumbled to a halt, braced himself and threw. The table leg whirred like a rising pheasant an inch over Sean's head, ruffling his hair with the wind of its passage.

'Lead on, Duff.' Sean was uncomfortably conscious of the fact that Fernandes was again in motion towards him, still armed with a long oak, and that three very thin ropes were all that stood between them. The speed that Sean and Duff turned on then made Mr Blair's earlier exhibition seem like that of a man with both legs in plaster. Fernandes, carrying top weight as he was, never looked like catching them.

François came up to the Candy Deep just after midday with the news that the Portuguese, after beating three of his sponsors into insensibility, had left on the noon coach back to Kimberley.

Duff uncocked his rifle.'Thanks, Franz, we were waiting lunch for him. I thought he might call on us.'

'Have you counted the takings?'

'Yes, your commission is in that paper bag on the table.'

'Thanks, man, let's go down and celebrate.'

'You go and have one for us.'

'Hey, Duff, you promised–' Sean started.

'I said later–in three or four weeks' time. Now we've got a little work to do, like digging a trench fifty feet deep and three hundred yards long.'

'We could start first thing tomorrow.'

'You want to be rich, don't you?' asked Duff.

'Sure, but–'

'You want nice things, like English suits, French champagne and–'

'Yes, but–'

'Well, stop arguing, get off your fat arse and come with me.'

12

The Chinese use firecrackers to keep the demons away. Duff and Sean applied the same principle. They kept the mill running; as long as its clunking carried across the valley to the ears of their creditors all was well. Everyone accepted the fact that they were working a payable reef and left them alone, but the money they fed into the front of the mill had halved its value by the time it came out of the other side in those pathetic little yellow pellets.

In the meantime they cut their trench, tearing into the earth in a race against Settlement Day. They fired dynamite and as the last stones dropped back out of the sky they were in again, coughing with the fumes, to clear the loosened rock and start drilling the next set of holes. It was summer, the days were long and while it was light they worked. Some evenings they lit the last fuses by lantern light.

Sand fell through the hour-glass faster than they had bargained for, the money dribbled away and on the fifteenth of February Duff shaved himself, changed his shirt and went to see Candy about another loan. Sean watched him walk away down the slope. They had sold the horses a week before, and he said a small prayer–the first for many years.

Duff came back in the late morning. He stood on the edge of the trench and watched Sean tamping in the charges for the next cut. Sean's back was shiny with sweat; each individual muscle standing out in relief, swelling and subsiding as he moved.

'That's the stuff, laddie, keep at it.'

Sean looked up with dust-reddened eyes. 'How much?' he asked.

'Another fifty, and this is the last–or so she threatens.'

Sean's eyes fastened on the package Duff held under his arm.

'What's that?'

He could see the stains seeping through the brown paper and the saliva flooded out from under his tongue.

'Prime beef chops–no mealie meal porridge for lunch today.' Duff grinned at him.

'Meat.' Sean caressed the word. 'Underdone–bleeding a little as you bite it, a trace of garlic, just enough salt.'

'And you beside me, singing in the wilderness,' agreed Duff. 'Cut out the poetry, light those fuses and let's go and eat.'

An hour later they walked side by side along the bottom of their trench, Mbejane and his Zulus crowding behind them. Sean belched. 'Ah, pleasant memory, I'll never be able to look another plate of mealie meal in the face again.'

They reached the end, where the freshly broken earth and rock lay piled. Sean felt the thrill start in his hands, tingle up his arms and squeeze his lungs. Then Duff's fingers were biting into his shoulder; he could feel them trembling.

It looked like a snake, a fat grey python crawling down one wall of the trench, disappearing under the heap of new rubble and out the other side.

Duff moved first, he knelt and picked up a piece of the reef, a big grey mottled lump of it and kissed it.

'It must be it, hey, Duff? It must be the Leader?'

'It's the end of the rainbow.'

'No more mealie meal,' Sean said softly and Duff laughed. Then Sean laughed. Wildly, crazily, together they howled their triumph.

13

'Let me hold it again,' said Sean.

Duff passed it across to him.

'Hell, it's heavy.'

'There's nothing heavier,' agreed Duff.

'Must be all of fifty pounds.'

Sean held the bar in two hands, it was the size of a cigar box. 'More!'

'We've retrieved all our losses in two days' working.'

'And some to spare, I'd say.'

Sean placed the gold bar on the table between them. It shone with little yellow smiles in the lantern light and Duff leaned forward and stroked it; its surface felt knobbly from the rough casting.

'I can't keep my hands off it,' he confessed sheepishly.

'I can't either!' Sean reached out to touch it. 'We'll be able to pay Candy out for the claims in another week or two.'

Duff started. 'What did you say?'

'I said we'd be able to pay Candy out.'

'I thought I wasn't hearing things.' Duff patted his arm indulgently. 'Listen to me, laddie, I'll try and put it simply. How long have we got the option on these claims for?'

'Three years.'

'Correct–now the next question. How many people on these fields have any money?'

Sean looked mystified. 'Well, we have now and–and . . .'

'No one else, that is until Hradsky gets back,' Duff finished for him.

'What about the Heyns brothers? They've cut open the Leader Reef.'

'Certainly, but it won't do them any good, not until their machinery arrives from England.'

'Go on!' Sean wasn't quite sure where Duff was leading.

'Instead of paying Candy out now we are going to use this'–he patted the gold bar–'and all its little brothers to buy every likely claim we can lay our hands on. For a start there are Doc Sutherland's claims between us and the Jack and Whistle. Then we are going to order a couple of big ten-stamp mills and when those are spilling out gold we'll use it to buy land, finance brick works, engineering shops, transport companies and the rest. I've told you before there are more ways of making gold than digging for it.'

Sean was staring at him silently.

'Have you got a head for heights?' asked Duff.

Sean nodded.

'You're going to need it, because we are going up where the eagles fly–you are about to be a party to the biggest financial killing this country has ever seen.'

Sean lit one of Candy's cigars; his hand was a little unsteady.

'Don't you think it would be best to–well–not try and go too quickly. Hell, Duff, we've only been working the Leader for two days–'

'And we've made a thousand pounds,' Duff interrupted him. 'Listen to me, Sean, all my life I've been waiting for an opportunity like this. We're the first in on this field, it's as wide open as the legs of a whore. We're going to go in and take it.'

The next morning Duff had the good fortune to find Doc Sutherland early enough to talk business with him, before he began the day's drinking. Another hour would have been too late. As it was Doc knocked over his glass and fell out of his chair before he finally signed away twenty-five claims to Sean and Duff. The ink was hardly dry on the agreement before Duff was riding down to Ferrieras Camp to look for Ted Reynecke who held the claims on the other side of the Cousin Jack. Up on the Candy Deep Sean nursed the mill and bit his nails. Within seven days Duff had bought over one hundred claims and committed them to forty thousand pounds in debts.

'Duff, you're going mad.' Sean pleaded with him. 'We'll lose everything again.'

'How much have we pulled out of the Candy Deep so far?'

'Four thousand.'

'Ten per cent of what we owe in ten days–and with a miserable little four-stamp mill at that. Hold on to your hat, laddie, tomorrow I'm going to sign up for the forty claims on the other side of the Jack and Whistle. I would have had them today but that damned Greek is holding out for a thousand pounds apiece. I'll have to give it to him, I suppose.'

Sean clutched his temples.

'Duff–please, man, we're in over our necks already.'

'Stand back, laddie, and watch the wizard work.'

'I'm going to bed–I suppose I'll have to take your shift again in the morning if you're determined to spend tomorrow ruining us.'

'That's not necessary, I've hired that Yankee–Curtis. You know, your sparring partner. It turns out he's a miner and he's willing to work for thirty a month. So you can come to town with me and watch me make you rich. I'm meeting the Greek at Candy's Hotel at nine o'clock.'

14

At nine o'clock Duff was talking and Sean sat silently on the edge of his chair; at ten the Greek had still not put in an appearance, Duff was moody and Sean was garrulous with relief. At eleven Sean wanted to go back to the mine.

'It's an omen, Duff, God looked down and he saw us sitting here all ready to make a terrible mistake. "No," he said, "I can't let them do it–I'll have the Greek break a leg–I can't let it happen to such nice boys."'

'Why don't you go and join a Trappist monastery?' Duff checked his watch. 'Come on, let's go!'

'Yes, sir!' Sean stood up with alacrity. 'We'll get back in plenty of time to clean the tables before lunch.'

'We're not going home, we're going to look for the Greek.'

'Now listen, Duff.'

'I'll listen later–come on.'

They rode across to the Bright Angels, left the horses outside and walked in together. It was dark in the canteen after the sunshine outside, but even in the gloom a group at one of the tables caught their attention immediately. The Greek sat with his back to them; the line of his parting seemed to be drawn with white chalk and a ruler through the oily black waves of his hair. Sean's eyes switched from him to the two men that sat across the table from him. Jews, there was no mistaking it, but there any similarity ended. The younger one was thin with smooth olive skin drawn tight across the bold bones of his cheeks; his lips were very red and his eyes, fringed with girl's lashes, were coffee-brown and melting. In the chair beside him was a man with a body that had been shaped in wax then held near a hot flame. Shoulders rounded to the verge of deformity drooped down over a pear-shaped body; with difficulty they supported the great Taj Mahal domed head. His hair was styled in the fashion of Friar Tuck, thick only around the ears. But the eyes–flickering yellow eyes–there was nothing comical about them.

'Hradsky,' hissed Duff, then his expression changed. He smiled as he walked across to the table.

'Hello, Nikky, I thought we had an appointment.'

The Greek twisted quickly in his chair.

'Mr Charleywood, I'm sorry, I was held up.'

'So I see, the woods are full of highwaymen.'

Sean saw the flush start to come out of Hradsky's collar then sink back again.

'Have you sold?' Duff asked.

The Greek nodded nervously.

'I'm sorry, Mr Charleywood, but Mr Hradsky paid my price and no haggling–cash money, too!'

Duff let his eyes wander across the table.

'Hello, Norman. How's your daughter?'

This time the flush escaped from Hradsky's shirt and flooded over his face. He opened his mouth, his tongue clucked twice, then he closed it again.

Duff smiled, he looked at the younger Jew. 'Say it for him, Max.'

The toffee eyes dropped to the table top. 'Mr Hradsky's daughter is very well.'

'I believe she married soon after my involuntary departure from Kimberley.'

'That is correct.'

'Wise move, Norman, much wiser than having your bully boys run me out of town. That wasn't very nice of you.'

No one spoke.

'We must get together some time and have a chat about old times. Until then, fa–fa–fare ye we–we–well.'

On the way back to the mine Sean asked, 'He's got a daughter? If she looks like him you were lucky to escape.'

'She didn't–she was like a bunch of ripe grapes with the bloom on them.'

'I can hardly credit it.'

'Neither could I. The only conclusion I could reach was that Max did that job for him as well.'

'What's the story about Max?'

'He's the Court Jester. Rumour has it that after Hradsky has finished hanging it out, Max shakes it for him.'

Sean laughed and Duff went on, 'But don't underestimate Hradsky. His stutter is his only weakness and with Max to talk for him he's overcome that. Beneath that monumental skull is a brain as quick and merciless as a guillotine. Now that he's arrived on this goldfield there's going to be some action; we'll have to gallop to keep up with him.'

Sean thought for a few seconds, then, 'Talking about action, Duff, now that we've lost the Greek's claims and won't have to use all our ready money satisfying him, let's give some thought to ordering new machinery to work the claims we have got.'

Duff grinned at him.

'I sent a telegram to London last week. There'll be a pair of brand new ten-stamp mills on the water to us before the end of the month.'

'Good God, why didn't you tell me?'

'You were worried enough as it was–I didn't want to break your heart.'

Sean opened his mouth to blast Duff out of the saddle, Duff winked at him before he could talk and Sean's lips trembled. He felt the laughter in his throat, he tried to stop it but it swamped him.

'How much is it going to cost us?' he howled through his mirth.

'If you ask that question once more, I'll strangle you.' Duff laughed back at him. 'Rest content in the knowledge that if we're going to have enough to honour the bills of lading when those mills arrive at Port Natal, we'll have to run a mountain of Leader Reef through our little rig during the next few weeks.'

'What about the payments on the new claims?'

'That's my department–I'll worry about that.'

And so their partnership crystallized; their relationship was established over the weeks that followed. Duff with his magic tongue and his charming, lopsided grin was the one who negotiated, who poured the oil on the storm waters churned up by impatient creditors. He was the storehouse of mining knowledge which Sean tapped daily, he was the conceiver of schemes, some wild, others brilliant. But his fleeting nervous energy was not designed to bring them to fruition. He lost interest quickly and it was Sean who finally rejected the least likely Charleywood brain children and adopted the others that were more deserving; once he had made himself stepfather to them, he reared as though they were his own. Duff was the theorist, Sean the practician. Sean could see why Duff had never found success before, but at the same time he recognized that without him he would be helpless. He watched with profound admiration the way that Duff used the barely sufficient flow of gold from the Candy Deep to keep the mill running, pay the tradesmen, meet the claim monies as they fell due and still save enough for the new machinery. He was a man juggling with live coals: hold one too long and it burns, let one fall and all fall. And Duff, deep-down-uncertain Duff, had a wall to put his back against. His speech never showed it but his eyes did when he looked at Sean. Sometimes he felt small next to Sean's big body and bigger determination, but it was a good feeling: like being on a friendly mountain.

They put up the new buildings around the mill: storerooms, a smelting house and cabins for Sean and Curtis. Duff was sleeping at the Hotel again. The location for the Natives sprawled haphazard down the back slope of the ridge, retreating a little each week as the white mountain of the mine dump grew and pushed it back. The whole valley was changing. Hradsky's new mills arrived and stood up along the ridge, tall and proud until their own dumps dwarfed them. Johannesburg, at first a mere pattern of surveyors' pegs, sucked the scattered encampments on to her grassy chequer-board and arranged them in a semblance of order along her streets.

The Diggers' Committee, its members tired of having to scrape their boots every time they went indoors, decreed public latrines be erected. Then, flushed with their own audacity, they built a bridge across the Natal Spruit, purchased a water cart to lay the dust on the streets of Johannesburg and passed a law prohibiting burials within half a mile of the city centre. Sean and Duff as members of the Committee felt it their duty to demonstrate their faith in the goldfield, so they bought twenty-five plots of ground in Johannesburg, five pounds each to be paid within six months. Candy recruited all her customers and in one weekend of frantic effort they razed her Hotel to the ground, packed every plank and sheet of iron on to their wagons, carried it a mile down the valley and re-erected it on her own land in the centre of the township. During the party she gave them on that Sunday night they nearly succeeded in dismantling it for the second time. Each day the roads from Natal and the Cape fed more wagons, more men into the Witwatersrand goldfield. Duff's suggestion that the Diggers' Committee levy a guinea a head from all newcomers to help finance the public works was reluctantly rejected, the general feeling being that if it led to civil rebellion there were more newcomers than Committee members and no one fancied being on the losing side.

One morning, when he came out to the mine, Duff brought a telegram with him. He handed it to Sean without comment. Sean read it. The machinery had arrived.

'Good God, it's three weeks early.'

'They must have had a downhill sea, or a following wind or whatever it is that makes ships go faster,' muttered Duff.

'Have we got enough to pay the bill?' asked Sean.

'No.'

'What are we going to do?'

'I'll go and see the little man at the bank.'

'He'll throw you out in the street.'

'I'll get him to give us a loan on the claims.'

'How the hell are you going to do that–we haven't paid for them yet.'

'That's what you call financial genius. I'll simply point out to him that they're worth five times what we bought them for.' Duff grinned. 'Can you and Curtis carry on here without me for today while I go and arrange it?'

'You arrange it and I'll happily give you a month's holiday.'

When Duff came back that afternoon he carried a paper with him. It had a red wax seal in the bottom corner, across the top it said 'Letter of Credit' and in the middle, standing out boldly from the mass of small print, was a figure that ended in an impressive string of noughts.

'You're a bloody marvel,' said Sean.

'Yes, I am rather, aren't I?' agreed Duff.

15

The Heyns brothers' machinery was on the same ship. Jock and Duff rode down to Port Natal together, hired a hundred wagons and brought it all back in one load.

'I'll tell you what I'll do with you, Jock, I'll wager you that we get our mills producing before you do. Loser pays for the transport on the whole shipment,' Duff challenged him when they reached Johannesburg where, in Candy's new bar-room, they were washing the dust out of their throats.

'You're on!'

'I'll go further, I'll put up a side bet of five hundred.'

Sean prodded Duff in the ribs.

'Gently, Duff–we can't afford it.' But Jock had already snapped up the bet.

'What do you mean we can't afford it?' whispered Duff. 'We've got nearly fifteen hundred pounds left on the letter of credit.'

Sean shook his head. 'No, we haven't.'

Duff pulled the paper from his inside pocket and tapped Sean's nose with it. 'There–read for yourself.'

Sean took it out of Duff's hand.

'Thanks, old chap. I'll go and pay the man now.'

'What man?'

'The man with the wagons.'

'What wagons?'

'The wagons that you and Jock hired in Port Natal. I've bought them.'

'The hell you say!'

'It was your idea to start a transport business. Just as soon as they've off loaded they'll be on their way again to pick up a shipment of coal from Dundee.'

Duff grinned at him. 'Don't you ever forget an idea? All right, laddie, off you go–we'll just have to win the bet, that's all.'

One of the mills they placed on the Candy Deep, the other on the new claims beyond the Cousin Jock Mine. They hired two gangs from among the unemployed in Johannesburg. Curtis supervised one of them and Sean the other, while Duff darted back and forth keeping an eye on both. Each time he passed the Cousin Jock he spent a few minutes checking Trevor and Jock's progress.

'They've got the edge on us, Sean; their boilers are up and holding pressure already,' he reported fretfully, but the next day he was smiling again.

'They didn't mix enough cement in the platform–it started to crumble as soon as they put the crusher on it. They'll have to cast it again. That set them back three or four days.'

The betting down in the canteens fluctuated sharply with each change of fortune. François came up to the Candy Deep one Saturday afternoon. He watched them work, made a suggestion or two, then remarked, 'They're giving three-to-one against you at the Bright Angels; they reckon the Heynses will be finished by next weekend.'

'Go down and put another five hundred pounds on for me,' Duff told him, and Sean shook his head despairingly.

'Don't worry, laddie, we can't lose–that amateur mining engineer, Jock Heyns, has assembled his crusher jaws all arse-about-face. I only noticed it this morning–he's in for a surprise when he tries to start up. He'll have to strip the whole damn rig.'

Duff was right–they brought both their mills into production a comfortable fifteen hours before the Heyns brothers. Jock rode over to see them with his jaw on his chest. 'Congratulations.'

'Thanks, Jock, did you bring your cheque book?'

'That's what I came to talk about. Can you give me a little time?'

'Your credit's good,' Sean assured him, 'come and have a drink and let me sell you some coal.'

'Ah, yes, I heard your wagons arrived back this morning. What price are you charging?'

'Fifteen pounds a hundredweight.'

'Good God. You bloody bandit, I bet it cost you less than five shillings a hundredweight.'

'A man's entitled to a reasonable profit,' protested Sean.

It had been a long hard pull up to the top of the hill but Sean and Duff had arrived at last and from there it was downhill all the way. The money poured in.

The geological freak that had bowed the Leader Reef away from the Main across the Candy Deep claims had, at the same time, enriched it–injected it full of the metal. François was there one evening when they put the ball of amalgam into the retort. His eyes bulged as the mercury boiled away; he stared at the gold the way a man watches a naked woman.

'*Gott!* I'm going to have to call you two thunders "Mister" from now on.'

'Have you ever seen richer reef, François?' Duff gloated.

François shook his head slowly. 'You know my theory about the reef being the bed of an old lake–well this bears it out. The kink in your reef must have been a deep trench along the bottom of the lake. It would have acted as a natural gold trap. Hell, man, what luck. With your eyes closed you have picked the plum out of the pudding. The Jock and Whistle is half as rich as this.'

Their overdraft at the bank dropped like a barometer in a hurricane; the tradesmen started greeting them with a smile; they gave Doc Sutherland a cheque which would have kept even him in whisky for a hundred years. Candy kissed them both when they paid her out in full, plus interest at seven per cent. Then she built herself a new Hotel, double storied, with a crystal chandelier in the dining-room and a magnificent bedroom suite on the second floor done out in maroon and gold. Duff and Sean rented it immediately but with the express understanding that if ever the Queen visited Johannesburg they would allow her to use it. In anticipation Candy called it the Victoria Rooms.

François, with a little persuasion, agreed to take over the running of the Candy Deep. He moved his possessions, one chest of clothes and four chests of patent medicines, across from the Jack and Whistle. Martin Curtis was the manager of the mill on the new claims; they named it the Little Sister Mine. Although not nearly as rich as the Candy Deep it was producing a sweet fortune each month, for Curtis worked as well as he fought.

By the end of August Sean and Duff had no more creditors: the claims were theirs, the mills were theirs and they had money to invest.

'We need an office of our own here in town. We can't run this show from our bedrooms,' complained Sean.

'You're right,' agreed Duff, 'we'll build on that corner plot nearest the market square.' The plan was for a modest little four-room building, but it finally expanded to two stories, stinkwood floors, oak panelling and twenty rooms. What they couldn't use they rented.

'The price of land has trebled in three months,' said Sean, 'and it's still moving.'

'You're right–now's the time to buy,' Duff agreed. 'You're starting to think along the right lines.'

'It was your idea.'

'Was it?' Duff looked surprised.

'Don't you remember your "up where the eagles fly" speech?'

'Don't you forget anything?' asked Duff.

They bought land: one thousand acres at Orange Grove and another thousand around Hospital Hill. Their transport wagons, now almost four hundred strong, plied in daily from Port Natal and Lourenço Marques. Their brickfields worked twenty-four hours a day, seven days a week, to try to meet the demand for building materials.

It took Sean almost a week to dissuade Duff from building an Opera House but he succeeded and instead they joined most of the other members of the Diggers' Committee in financing a different type of pleasure palace. At Duff's suggestion they called it the Opera House. They recruited performers not from the great companies of Europe but from the dock areas of Capetown and Port Natal and chose as the conductor a Frenchwoman of vast experience named Blue Bessie after the colour of her hair. The Opera House provided entertainment on two levels. For the members of the Committee and the other emergent rich there was a discreet side entrance, a lavishly furnished lounge where one could buy the finest champagne and discuss the prices on the Kimberley Stock Exchange, and beyond the lounge were a series of tastefully decorated retiring-rooms. For the workers there was a bare corridor to queue in, no choice for your money and a five-minute time limit. In one month the Opera House produced more gold than the Jack and Whistle mine.

By December there were millionaires in Johannesburg: Hradsky, the Heyns brothers, Karl Lochtkamper, Duff Charleywood, Sean Courteney and a dozen others. They owned the mines, the land, the buildings and the city: the aristocracy of the Witwatersrand, knighted with money and crowned with gold.

A week before Christmas, Hradsky, their unacknowledged but undoubted king, called them all to a meeting in one of the private lounges of Candy's Hotel.

'Who the hell does he think he is,' complained Jock Heyns, 'ordering us round like a bunch of kaffirs.'

'*Verdammt Juden!*' agreed Lochtkamper.

But they went, every last man of them, for whatever Hradsky did had the smell of money about it and they could no more resist it than a dog can resist the smell of a bitch in season.

Duff and Sean were the last to arrive and the room was already hazed with cigar smoke and tense with expectation. Hradsky sagged in one of the polished leather armchairs with Max sitting quietly beside him; his eyes flickered when Duff walked in but his expression never changed. When Duff and Sean had found chairs Max stood up. 'Gentlemen, Mr Hradsky has invited you here to consider a proposition.'

They leaned forward slightly in their chairs and there was a glitter in their eyes like hounds close upon the fox.

'From time to time it is necessary for men in your position to find capital to finance further ventures and to consolidate past gains; on the other hand those of us who have money lying idle will be seeking avenues for investment.' Max cleared his throat and looked at them with his sad brown eyes.

'Up to the present there has been no meeting-place for these mutual needs such as exists in the other centres of the financial world. Our nearest approach to it is the Stock Exchange at Kimberley which, I'm sure you will agree, is too far removed to be of practical use to us here at Johannesburg. Mr Hradsky has invited you here to consider the possibility of forming our own Exchange and, if you accept the idea, to elect a chairman and governing body.'

Max sat down and in the silence that followed they took up the idea, each one fitting it into his scheme of thinking, testing it with the question 'How will I benefit?'

'*Ja*, it's dom fine idea.' Lochtkamper spoke first.

'Yes, it's what we need.'

'Count me in.'

While they schemed and bargained, setting the fees, the place and the rules, Sean watched their faces. The faces of bitter men, happy men, quiet ones and big bull-roarers but all with one common feature–that greedy glitter in the eyes. It was midnight before they finished.

Max stood up again.

'Gentlemen, Mr Hradsky would like you to join him in a glass of champagne to celebrate the formation of our new enterprise.'

'This I can't believe; the last time he paid for drinks was back in 'sixty,' declared Duff. 'Quickly somebody–find a waiter before he changes his mind.'

Hradsky hooded his eyes to hide the hatred in them.

16

With its own Stock Exchange and bordel Johannesburg became a city. Even Kruger recognized it; he deposed the Diggers' Committee and sent in his own police force, sold monopolies for essential mining supplies to members of his family and Government, and set about revising his tax laws with special attention to mining profits. Despite Kruger's efforts to behead the gold-laying goose, the city grew, overflowed the original Government plots and spread bawling and blustering out into the surrounding veld.

Sean and Duff grew with it. Their way of life changed swiftly; their visits to the mines fell to a weekly inspection and they left it to their hired men. A steady river of gold poured down from the ridge to their offices on Eloff Street, for the men they hired were the best that money could find.

Their horizons closed in to encompass only the two panelled offices, the Victoria Rooms and the Exchange. Yet within that world Sean found a thrill that he had never dreamed existed. He had been oblivious to it during the first feverish months; he had been so absorbed in laying the foundations that he could spare no energy for enjoying or even noticing it.

Then one day he felt the first voluptuous tickle of it. He had sent to the bank for a land title document he needed, expecting it to be delivered by a junior clerk–but instead the sub-manager and a senior clerk filed it respectfully into his office. It was an exquisite physical shock and it gave him a new awareness. He noticed the way men looked at him as he passed them on the street. He realized suddenly that over fifteen hundred human beings depended on him for their livelihood.

There was satisfaction in the way a path cleared for him and Duff as they crossed the floor of the Exchange each morning to take their places in the reserved leather armchairs of the members' lounge. When Duff and he leaned together and talked quietly before the trading began, even the other big fish watched them. Hradsky with his fierce eyes hooded by sleepy lids, Jock and Trevor Heyns, Karl Lochtkamper–any of them would have given a day's production from their mines to overhear those conversations.

'Buy!' said Sean.

'Buy! Buy! Buy!' clamoured the pack and the prices jumped as they hit them, then slumped back as they sucked their money away and put it to work elsewhere.

Then one March morning in 1886 the thrill became so acute it was almost an orgasm. Max left the chair at Norman Hradsky's side and crossed the lounge towards them. He stopped in front of them, lifted his sad eyes off the patterned carpet and almost apologetically proffered a loose sheaf of papers.

'Good morning, Mr Courteney. Good morning, Mr Charleywood. Mr Hradsky has asked me to bring this new share issue to your attention. Perhaps you would be interested in these reports, which are, of course, confidential, but he feels they are worthy of your support.'

You have power when you can force a man who hates you to ask for your favours. After the first advance by Hradsky they worked together often. Hradsky never acknowledged their existence by word or look. Each morning Duff called a cheerful greeting across the full width of the lounge, 'Hello, chatterbox,' or 'Sing for us, Norman.'

Hradsky's eyes would flicker and he would sag a little lower into his chair, but before the bell started the day's trading Max would stand up and come across to them, leaving his master staring into the empty fireplace. A few soft sentences exchanged and Max would walk back to Hradsky's side.

Their combined fortunes were irresistible: in one wild morning's trading alone they added another fifty thousand to their store of pounds.

An untaught boy handles his first rifle like a toy. Sean was twenty-two. The power he held was a more deadly weapon than any rifle, and much sweeter, more satisfying to use. It was a game at first with the Witwatersrand as a chessboard, men and gold for pieces. A word or a signature on a slip of paper would set the gold jingling and the men scampering. The consequences were remote and all that mattered was the score, the score chalked up in black figures on a bank statement. Then in that same March he was made to realize that a man wiped off the board could not be laid back in the box with as much compassion as a carved wooden knight.

Karl Lochtkamper, the German with a big laugh and a happy face, laid himself open. He needed money to develop a new property on the east end of the Rand; he borrowed and signed short-term notes on his loans, certain that he could extend them if necessary. He borrowed secretly from the men he thought he could trust. He was vulnerable and the sharks smelt him out.

'Where is Lochtkamper getting his money?' asked Max.

'Do you know?' asked Sean.

'No, but I can guess.'

Then the next day Max came back to them again.

'He has eight notes out. Here is the list,' he whispered sadly. 'Mr Hradsky will buy the ones that have a cross against them. Can you handle the rest?'

'Yes,' said Sean.

They closed on Karl on the last day of the quarter; they called the loans and gave him twenty-four hours to meet them. Karl went to each of the three banks in turn.

'I'm sorry, Mr Lochtkamper, we have loaned over our budget for this quarter.'

'Mr Hradsky is holding your notes–I'm sorry.'

'I'm sorry, Mr Lochtkamper, Mr Charleywood is one of our directors.'

Karl Lochtkamper rode back to the Exchange. He walked across the floor and into the lounge for the last time. He stood in the centre of the big room, his face grey, his voice bitter and broken.

'Let Jesus have this much mercy on you when your time comes. Friends! My friends! Sean, how many times have we drunk together? And you, Duff, was it yesterday you shook my hand?'

Then he went back across the floor, out through the doors. His suite in the Great North Hotel wasn't fifty yards from the Exchange. In the members' lounge they heard the pistol shot quite clearly.

That night Duff and Sean got drunk together in the Victoria rooms.

'Why did he have to do it? Why did he have to kill himself?'

'He didn't,' answered Duff. 'He was a quitter.'

'If I'd known he was going to do that–my God, if only I'd known.'

'Damn it, man, he took a chance and lost–it's not our fault. He would have done the same to us.'

'I don't like this–it's dirty. Let's get out, Duff.'

'Someone gets knocked down in the rush and you want to cry "enough!"'

'It's different now somehow, it wasn't like this at the start.'

'Yes, and it'll be different in the morning. Come on, laddie, I know what you need.'

'Where are we going?'

'To the Opera House.'

'What will Candy say?'

'Candy doesn't have to know.'

Duff was right; it was different in the morning. There was the usual hurly-burly of work at the office and some tense action at the Exchange. He thought about Karl only once during the day and somehow it didn't seem to matter so much. They sent him a nice wreath.

He had faced the reality of the game he was playing. He had considered the alternative which was to get out with the fortune he had already made; but to do that would mean giving up the power he held. The addiction was already seated too deeply, he could not deny it. So his subconscious opened, sucked in his conscience and swallowed it deep down into its gut. He could feel it struggling there sometimes, but the longer it stayed swallowed the more feeble those struggles became. Duff comforted him: Duff's words were like a gastric juice that helped to digest that lump in the gut and he had not yet learned that what Duff said and what Duff did were not necessarily what Duff believed.

Play the game without mercy, play to win.

17

Duff stood with his back to the fireplace in Sean's office smoking a cheroot while they waited for the carriage to take them up to the Exchange. The fire behind him silhouetted his slimly tapered legs with the calves encased in polished black leather. He still wore his top coat, for the winter morning was cold. It fell open at his throat to show a diamond that sparkled and glowed in his cravat.

'. . . you get used to a woman somehow,' he was saying. 'I've known Candy four years now and yet it seems I've been with her all my life.'

'She's a fine girl,' Sean agreed absently as he dipped his pen and scribbled his signature on the document in front of him.

'I'm thirty-five now,' Duff went on. 'If I'm ever to have a son of my own . . .'

Sean laid down the pen deliberately and looked up at him; he was starting to grin.

'The man said to me once "They take you into their soft little minds" and again he said "They don't share, they possess". Is this a new tune I hear?'

Duff shifted uneasily from one foot to the other.

'Things change,' he defended himself. 'I'm thirty five . . .'

'You're repeating yourself,' Sean accused and Duff smiled weakly.

'Well, the truth is . . .'

He never finished the sentence; hooves beat urgently in the street outside and both their faces swung in the direction of the window.

'Big hurry!' said Sean coming quickly to his feet. 'Big trouble!' He crossed to the window. 'It's Curtis, and by his face it's not good news he brings.'

There were voices outside the door raised in agitation and the quick rush of feet, then Martin Curtis burst into the room without knocking. He wore a miner's overall and splattered gumboots. 'We've hit a mud rush on the ninth level.'

'How bad?' Duff snapped.

'Bad enough–it's flooded right back to number eight.'

'Jesus, that will take two months at least to clear,' Sean exclaimed. 'Does anyone else in town know–have you told anyone?'

'I came straight here–Cronje and five men were up at the face when it blew.'

'Get back there immediately,' ordered Sean, 'but ride quietly, we don't want the whole world to know there's trouble. Don't let a soul off the property. We must have time to sell out.'

'Yes, Mr Courteney.' Curtis hesitated. 'Cronje and five others were hit by the rush. Shall I send word to their wives?'

'Can't you understand English? I don't want a whisper of this to get out before ten o'clock. We're got to have time.'

'But, Mr Courteney–' Curtis was appalled. He stood staring at Sean and Sean felt the sick little stirring of guilt. Six men drowned in treacle-thick mud . . . He made an irresolute gesture with his hands.

'We can't–' He stopped and Duff cut in.

'They're dead now, and they'll be just as dead when we tell their wives at ten o'clock. Get going, Curtis.'

They sold their shares in the Little Sister within an hour of the start of trading and a week later they bought them back at half the price. Two months later the Little Sister was back on full production again.

18

They split their land at Orange Grove into plots and sold them, all but a hundred acres and on that they started building a house. Into the designing of it they poured their combined energy and imagination. With money Duff seduced the horticulturist of the Cape Town Botanical Gardens and brought him up by express coach. They showed him the land.

'Make me a garden,' said Duff.

'The whole hundred acres?'

'Yes.'

'It'll cost a pretty penny.'

'That is no problem.'

The carpets came from Persia, the wood from the Knysna forests and the marble from Italy. On the gates at the entrance to the main drive they engraved the words 'At Xanadu did Kublai Khan a stately pleasure dome decree'. As the gardener had predicted, it all cost a pretty penny. Each afternoon when the Exchange closed they would drive up together and watch the builders at work. One day Candy came with them and they showed it off to her like two small boys.

'This will be the ballroom.' Sean bowed to her. 'May I have the pleasure of this dance?'

'Thank you, sir.' She curtsied, then swept away on his arm across the unsanded boards.

'This will be the staircase,' Duff told her, 'marble–black and white marble–and there on the main landing in a glass case will be Hradsky's head, beautifully mounted with an apple in his mouth.'

They climbed laughing up the rough concrete ramp.

'This is Sean's room–the bed is being made of oak, thick oak to withstand punishment.' They trooped with linked arms down the passage.

'And this is my room–I was thinking of a solid gold bath but the builders says it's too heavy and Sean says it's too vulgar. Look at that view; from here you can see out across the whole valley. I could lie in bed in the mornings and read the prices in the Exchange floor with a telescope.'

'It's lovely,' Candy said dreamily.

'You like it?'

'Oh yes.'

'It could be your room too.'

Candy started to blush and then her face tightened with annoyance. 'He was right–you are vulgar.'

She started for the door and Sean fumbled for his cigars to cover his embarrassment. With two quick steps Duff caught her and turned her to face him. 'You sweet idiot, that was a proposal.'

'Let me go.' Near to tears she twisted in his hands. 'I don't think you're funny.'

'Candy–I'm serious. Will you marry me?'

The cigar dropped out of Sean's mouth but he caught it before it hit the ground. Candy was standing very still, her eyes fastened on Duff's face.

'Yes or no–will you marry me?'

She nodded once slowly and then twice very fast.

Duff looked at Sean over his shoulder. 'Leave us, laddie.'

On the way back to town Candy had regained her voice. She chattered happily and Duff answered her with his lopsided grin. Sean hunched morosely in one corner of the carriage. His cigar was burning unevenly and he threw it out of the window.

'You'll let me keep the Victoria rooms, I hope, Candy.'

There was a silence.

'What do you mean?' asked Duff.

'Two's company,' Sean answered.

'Oh, no,' Candy exclaimed.

'It's your house as well.' Duff spoke sharply.

'I give it to you–a wedding present.'

'Oh shut up,' Duff grinned, 'it's big enough for all of us.'

Candy crossed quickly to Sean's seat and put her hand on his shoulder.

'Please–we've been together a long time. We'd be lonely without you.'

Sean grunted.

'Please!'

'He'll come,' said Duff.

'Please.'

'Oh, well–' Sean frowned ungraciously.

19

They went racing at Milnerton. Candy with a hat full of ostrich feathers, Sean and Duff with pearl grey toppers and gold beads on their canes.

'You can pay for your wedding gown by putting fifty guineas on Trade Wind! She can't lose–' Duff told Candy.

'What about Mr Hradsky's new filly? I've heard she's a good bet,' Candy asked and Duff frowned.

'You want to go over to the enemy?'

'I thought you and Hradsky were almost partners.' Candy twirled her parasol. 'From the rumours I've heard you work with him all the time.'

Mbejane slowed the carriage as they ran into the crush of pedestrians and coaches outside the Turf Club gates.

'Well you've heard wrong both times. His Sun Dancer will never hold Trade Wind over the distance, she's bred too light in the legs. Frenchified with Huguenot blood; she'll fade within the mile. And as far as Hradsky being our partner, we throw him an occasional bone. Isn't that right, Sean?'

Sean was watching Mbejane's back. The Zulu, in loin cloths only and his spears laid carefully on the boards at his feet, was handling the horses with an easy familiarity. They cocked their ears back to catch his voice, deep and soft, as he talked to them.

'Isn't that right, Sean?' Duff repeated.

'Of course,' agreed Sean vaguely. 'You know–I think I'll get Mbejane a livery. He looks out of place in those skins.'

'Well, some of the other horses from the same stud were stayers. Sun Honey won the Cape Derby twice and Eclipse showed up the English stock in the Metropolitan Handicap last year,' Candy argued.

'Huh,' Duff smiled his superiority, 'well, you can take my word for it that Trade Wind will walk the main race today and he'll be back in his stable before Sun Dancer sees the finishing post.'

'Maroon and gold–the same as our racing colours,' Sean muttered thoughtfully. 'That would go very well with his black skin, perhaps a turban with an ostrich feather in it.'

'What the hell are you talking about?' complained Duff.

'Mbejane's livery.'

They left the carriage in the reserved area and went through to the members' grandstand, Candy sailing prettily between her escorts.

'Well, Duff, we've got the nicest looking woman here today.'

'Thank you.' Candy smiled up at Sean.

'Is that why you keep trying to look down the front of her dress?' challenged Duff.

'You filthy-minded beast.' Sean was shocked.

'Don't deny it,' Candy teased, 'but I find it very flattering–you're welcome.'

They moved through the throng of butterfly-coloured dresses and stiffly-suited men. A ripple of greetings moved with them.

'Morning, Mr Courteney.' The accent was on the 'Mister'. 'How's your Trade Wind for the big race?'

'Put your pants on him.'

'Hello, Duff, congratulations on your engagement.'

'Thanks, Jock, it's time you took the plunge as well.'

They were rich, they were young, they were handsome and all the world admired them. Sean felt good, with a pretty girl on his arm and a friend walking beside him.

'There's Hradsky–let's go across and engage in a little hog-baiting,' Duff suggested.

'Why do you hate him so much?' Candy asked softly.

'Look at him and answer your own question. Have you ever seen anything more pompous, joyless and unlovable?'

'Oh, leave him alone, Duff, don't spoil the day. Let's go down to the paddock.'

'Come on!' Duff steered them across to where Hradsky and Max were standing alone by the rail of the track.

'Salome, Norman, and peace to you also, Maximilian.'

Hradsky nodded and Max murmured sadly; his lashes touched his cheeks as he blinked.

'I noticed you two chatting away and thought I would come across and listen to your stimulating repartee.'

He received no answer and went on. 'I saw your new filly exercising on the practice track yesterday evening and I said to myself, Norman's got a girl friend–that's what it is–he's bought a hack for his lady. But now they tell me you are going to race her. Oh, Norman, I wish you'd consult me before you do these silly things. You're an impetuous little devil at times.'

'Mr Hradsky is confident that Sun Dancer will make a reasonable showing today,' Max murmured.

'I was about to offer you a side bet, but being a naturally kind-hearted person, I feel it would be taking an unfair advantage.'

A small crowd had gathered round them listening with anticipation. Candy tugged gently at Duff's elbow trying to lead him away.

'I thought five hundred guineas would be acceptable to Norman.' Duff shrugged. 'But let's forget it.'

Hradsky made a fierce little sign with his hands and Max interpreted smoothly. 'Mr Hradsky suggests a thousand.'

'Rash, Norman, extremely rash.' Duff sighed. 'But I suppose I must accommodate you.'

They walked down to the refreshment pavilion. Candy was quiet awhile, then she said, 'An enemy like Mr Hradsky is a luxury that even you two gods can't afford. Why don't you leave him alone?'

'It's a hobby of Duff's,' explained Sean as they found seats at one of the tables. 'Waiter–bring us a bottle of Pol Roger.'

Before the big race they went down to the paddock. A steward opened the wicket gate for them and they passed into the ring of circling horses. A gnome in silk of maroon and gold came to meet them and touched his cap then stood awkwardly fingering his whip.

'He looks good this morning sir.' The little man nodded at Trade Wind. There was a dark patch of sweat on the horse's shoulder and he mouthed the snaffle, lifting his feet delicately. Once he snorted and rolled his eyes in mock terror.

'He's got an edge on him, sir, eager kind of–if you follow me.'

'I want you to win, Harry,' said Duff.

'So do I, sir, I'll do my best.'

'There's a thousand guineas for you if you do.'

'A thousand–' the jockey repeated on an outgoing breath.

Duff looked across to where Hradsky and Max were standing talking to their trainer. He caught Hradsky's eye, glanced significantly at Hradsky's honey-coloured filly and shook his head sympathetically.

'Win for me, Harry,' he said softly.

'That I will, sir!'

The groom led the big stallion across to them and Sean flicked the jockey up into the saddle.

'Good luck.'

Harry settled his cap and gathered up the reins; he winked at Sean, his hobgoblin face wrinkling in a grin.

'There's no better luck than a thousand guineas, sir, if you follow me.'

'Come on.' Duff caught Candy's arm. 'Let's get a place at the rail.'

They hustled her out of the paddock and across the members' enclosure. The rail was crowded but a place opened for them respectfully and no one jostled them.

'I can't understand you two,' Candy laughed breathlessly. 'You make an extravagant bet, then you fix it so you can get nothing even if you win.'

'Money's not the problem,' Duff assured her.

'He won that much from me at Klabejas last night,' Sean commented. 'If Trade Wind beats the filly his prize will be the look on Hradsky's face–the loss of a thousand guineas will hurt him like a kick between the legs.'

The horses came parading past, stepping high next to the grooms who held them, then they turned free and cantered back, dancing sideways, throwing their heads, shining in the sunlight like the bright silk upon their backs. They moved away round the curve of the track.

The crowd rustled with excitement, a bookmaker's voice carried over the buzz.

'Twenty-to-one bar two. Sun Dancer at fives. Trade Wind even money.'

Duff showed his teeth as he smiled. 'That's right, you tell the people.'

Candy twisted her gloves nervously and looked up at Sean.

'You there in the grandstand–can you see what they're doing?'

'They're in line now, moving up together–it looks as though they'll get away first time,' Sean told her without taking his binoculars from his eyes. 'Yes, there they go–they're away!'

'Tell me, tell me,' commanded Candy, pounding Sean's shoulder.

'Harry's showing in front already–can you see the filly, Duff?'

'I saw a flash of green in the pack–yes, there she is lying sixth or seventh.'

'What horse is that next to Trade Wind?'

'That's Hamilton's gelding, don't worry about him, he won't last to the turn.'

The frieze of horses, their heads going like hammers and the dust lifting pale and thin behind them, were framed by the guide rail and the white mine dumps beyond them. Like a string of dark beads they moved up the back stretch and then bunched in the straight.

'Trade Wind's still there–I think he's making ground–the gelding's finished and no sign of the filly yet.'

'Yes! There she is, Duff, wide on the outside. She's moving up.'

'Come on, my darling–' Duff half whispered. 'Let's see you foot it now.'

'She's clear of the pack–she's coming up, Duff, she's coming up fast,' Sean warned.

'Come on, Trade Wind, hold her off,' Duff pleaded. 'Keep her there, boy.'

The pounding of the hooves reached them now, a sound like distant surf, but rising sharply. The colours showed, emerald green above a honey skin and maroon and gold leading on the bay.

'Trade Wind–come on Trade Wind,' shrieked Candy. Her hat flopped over her eyes as she hopped; she ripped it off impatiently and her hair tumbled to her shoulders.

'She's catching him, Duff!'

'Give him the whip, Harry, for Christ's sake–the whip, man.'

The hoof beats crescendoed, thundered up to them, then passed. The filly's nose was at Harry's boot, creeping steadily forward, now level with Trade Wind's heaving shoulder.

'The whip, God damn you,' screamed Duff, 'give him the whip.'

Harry's right arm moved, fast as a mamba–crack, crack; they heard the whip above the howling crowd, above the drumming of hooves and the bay jumped at its sting. Like a pair in harness the two horses swept over the finishing line.

'Who won?' Candy asked as though she were in pain.

'I couldn't see, damn it,' Duff answered.

'Nor could I–' Sean took out his handkerchief and wiped his forehead. 'That didn't do my heart any good–as François would say. Have a cigar, Duff.'

'Thanks–I need one.'

Everyone in the crowd turned to face the board above the judges' box and an uneasy silence held them.

'Why do they take such a long time to make up their minds?' complained Candy. 'I'm so upset that I can only last a minute before I visit the Ladies' Room.'

'The numbers are going up,' shouted Sean.

'Who is it?' Candy jumped to try and see over the heads of the crowd then stopped hurriedly with an expression of alarm on her face.

'Number Sixteen,' bellowed Duff and Sean together, 'it's Trade Wind!'

Sean punched Duff in the chest and Duff leaned over and snapped Sean's cigar in half. Then they caught Candy between them and hugged her. She let out a careful shriek and fought her way out of their arms. 'Excuse me,' she said and fled.

'Let me buy you a drink.' Sean lit the mutilated stump of his cigar.

'No, it's my honour, I insist.' Duff took his arm and they walked with big satisfied grins towards the pavilion. Hradsky was sitting at one of the tables with Max. Duff walked up behind him, lifted his top hat off his head with one hand and with the other ruffled Hradsky's few remaining hairs.

'Never mind, Norman, you can't win all the time.'

Hradsky turned slowly. He retrieved his hat and smoothed back his hair, his eyes glittered yellow.

'He's going to talk,' whispered Duff excitedly.

'I agree with you, Mr Charleywood, you can't win all the time,' said Norman Hradsky. It came out quite clearly with only a small catch on the 'c's'–they were always difficult letters for him. He stood up, put his hat back on his head and walked away.

'I will have a cheque delivered to your office early on Monday morning,' Max told them quietly without taking his eyes off the table. Then he stood up and followed Hradsky.

20

Sean came through from the bathroom, his beard in wild disorder and a bath-towel around his wait.

> 'The famous Duke of York
> He had ten thousand men
> He marched them up to the top of the hill
> And he marched them down again.'

He sang as he poured bay rum from a cut-glass bottle into his cupped hands and rubbed it into his hair. Duff sat in one of the gilt chairs watching him. Sean combed his hair carefully then smiled at himself in the mirror.

'You magnificent creature,' Sean told his reflection.

'You're getting fat,' Duff grunted.

Sean looked hurt. 'It's muscle.'

'You've got a backside on you like a hippopotamus.'

Sean removed his towel and turned his back to the mirror; he surveyed it over his shoulder.

'I need a heavy hammer to drive a long nail,' he protested.

'Oh, no,' groaned Duff. 'Your wit at this time of the morning is like pork for breakfast, heavy on the stomach.'

Sean took a silk shirt out of his drawer, held it like a toreador's cape, made two passes and swirled it on to his back with a half veronica.

'*Olé!*' applauded Duff wryly. Sean pulled on his trousers and sat to fit his boots.

'You're in a nice mood this morning,' he told Duff.

'I've just come through an emotional hurricane!'

'What's the trouble?'

'Candy wants a church wedding.'

'Is that bad?'

'Well, it's not good.'

'Why?'

'Is your memory so short?'

'Oh, you mean your other wife.'

'That's right, my other wife.'

'Have you told Candy about her?'

'Good God, no.' Duff looked horrified.

'Yes, I see your problem–what about Candy's husband? Doesn't that even the score between you?'

'No, he has gone to his reward.'

'Well, that's convenient. Does anyone else know you're married already?' Duff shook his head.

'What about François?'

'No, I never told him.'

'Well, what's your problem–take her down to the church and marry her.'

Duff looked uncomfortable.

'I don't mind marrying a second time in a magistrate's court, it would only be a couple of old Dutchmen I'd be cheating, but to go into a church–' Duff shook his head.

'I'd be the only one who'd know,' said Sean.

'You and the headman.'

'Duff,' Sean beamed at him. 'Duff, my boy, you have scruples–this is amazing!'

Duff squirmed a little in his chair.

'Let me think.' Sean held his forehead dramatically. 'Yes, yes, it's coming to me–that's it.'

'Come on, tell me.' Duff sat on the edge of his chair.

'Go to Candy and tell her it's all fixed, not only are you prepared to marry her in a church but you're even going to build your own church.'

'That's wonderful,' Duff murmured sarcastically, 'that's the way out of my difficulties all right.'

'Let me finish.' Sean started filling his silver cigar case. 'You also tell her that you want a civil ceremony as well–I believe that's what royalty do. Tell her that, it should win her over.'

'I still don't follow you.'

'Then you build your own chapel at Xanadu–we can find a distinguished-looking character, dress him up in a dog collar and teach him the right words. That keeps Candy happy. Immediately after the service the priest takes the coach for Capetown. You take Candy down to the magistrate's office and that keeps you happy.'

Duff looked stunned then slowly his face broke into a great happy smile. 'Genius–pure inspired genius.'

Sean buttoned his waistcoat. 'Think nothing of it. And now if you'll excuse me I'll go and do some work–one of us has to make sufficient to allow you to indulge these strange fancies of yours.'

Sean shrugged on his coat, picked up his cane and swung it. The gold head gave it a balance like a hand-made shotgun. The silk next to his skin and the halo of bay rum round his head made him feel good.

He went down the stairs. Mbejane had the carriage waiting for him in the hotel yard. The body tilted slightly at Sean's weight and the leather upholstery welcomed him with a yielding softness. He lit his first cigar of the day and Mbejane smiled at him.

'I see you, Nkosi.'

'I see you also, Mbejane, what is that lump on the side of your head?'

'Nkosi, I was a little drunk, otherwise that ape of Basuto would never have touched me with his fighting stick.'

Mbejane rolled the carriage smoothly out of the yard and into the street.

'What were you fighting about?'

Mbejane shrugged. 'Must a man have a reason to fight?'

'It is usual.'

'It is in my memory that there was a woman,' said Mbejane.

'That is also usual–who won this fight?'

'The man bled a little, his friends took him away. The woman, when I left, was smiling in her sleep.'

Sean laughed, then ran his eyes over the undulating plain of Mbejane's bare back. It was definitely not in keeping. He hoped his secretary had remembered to speak to the tailor. They pulled up in front of his offices. One of his clerks hurried down off the veranda and opened the door of the carriage.

'Good morning, Mr Courteney.'

Sean went up the stairs with his clerk running ahead of him like a hunting dog.

'Good morning, Mr Courteney,' another polite chorus from the row of desks in the main office. Sean waved his cane at them and went through into his own office. His portrait leered at him from above the fireplace and he winked at it.

'What have we this morning, Johnson?'

'These requisitions, sir, and the pay cheques, sir, and development reports from the engineers, sir, and . . .'

Johnson was a greasy-haired little man in a greasy-looking alpaca coat; with each 'sir' he made a greasy little bow. He was efficient so Sean hired him, but that didn't mean he liked him.

'You got a stomach ache, Johnson?'

'No, sir.'

'Well, for God's sake, stand up straight, man.'

Johnson shot to attention.

'Now let's have them one at a time.'

Sean dropped into his chair. At this time of the day came the grind. He hated the paper work and so he tackled it with grim concentration, making random checks on the long rows of figures, trying to associate names with faces and querying requisitions that appeared exorbitant until finally he wrote his signature between the last of Johnson's carefully pencilled crosses and threw his pen on to the desk.

'What else is there?'

'Meeting with Mr Maxwell from the Bank at twelve-thirty, sir.'

'And then?'

'The agent for Brooke Bros. at one, and immediately after that Mr MacDougal, sir, then you're expected up at the Candy Deep mine.'

'Thank you, Johnson, I'll be at the Exchange as usual this morning if anything out of the ordinary comes up.'

'Very good, Mr Courteney. Just one other thing.' Johnson pointed at the brown paper parcel on the couch across the room. 'From your tailor.'

'Ah!' Sean smiled. 'Send my servant in here.' He walked across and opened the parcel. Within a few minutes Mbejane filled the doorway.

'Nkosi?'

'Mbejane–your new uniform.' Sean pointed at the clothes laid out on the couch. Mbejane's eyes switched to the gold and maroon finery, his expression suddenly dead.

'Put it on–come on, let's see how you look.'

Mbejane crossed to the couch and picked up the jacket. 'These are for me?'

'Yes, come on, put it on.' Sean laughed.

Mbejane hesitated, then slowly he loosened his loin cloth and let it drop. Sean watched him impatiently as he buttoned on the jacket and pantaloons, then he walked in a critical circle around the Zulu.

'Not bad,' he muttered and then in Zulu, 'Is it not beautiful?'

Mbejane wriggled his shoulders against the unfamiliar feel of the cloth and said nothing.

'Well, Mbejane, do you like it?'

'When I was a child I went with my father to trade cattle at Port Natal. There was a man who went about the town with a monkey on a chain, the monkey danced and the people laughed and threw money to it. That monkey had such a suit as this. Nkosi, I do not think he was a very happy monkey.'

The smile slipped off Sean's face. 'You would rather wear your skins?'

'What I wear is the dress of a warrior of Zululand.'

There was still no expression on Mbejane's face. Sean opened his mouth to argue with him but before he could speak he lost his temper.

'You'll wear that uniform,' he shouted. 'You'll wear what I tell you to wear and you'll do it with a smile, do you hear me?'

'Nkosi, I hear you.' Mbejane picked up his loin cloth of leopard tails and left the office. When Sean went out to the carriage Mbejane was sitting on the driver's seat in his new livery. All the way to the Exchange his back was stiff with protest and neither of them spoke. Sean glared at the doorman of the Exchange, drank four brandies during the morning, rode back to his office again at noon scowling at Mbejane's still protesting back, shouted at Johnson, snapped at the bank manager, routed the representative from Brooke Bros. and drove out to the Candy Deep in a high old rage. But Mbejane's silence was impenetrable and Sean couldn't re-open the argument without sacrifice of pride. He burst into the new administrative building of the Candy Deep and threw the staff into confusion.

'Where's Mr du Toit?' he roared.

'He's down the Number Three shaft, Mr Courteney.'

'What the hell is he doing down there? He's supposed to be waiting for me here.'

'He didn't expect you for another hour, sir.'

'Well, get me some overalls and a mining helmet, don't just stand there.'

He clapped the tin hat on his head and stamped his heavy gum-boots across to the Number Three shaft. The skip dropped him smoothly five hundred feet into the earth and he climbed out at the tenth level.

'Where's Mr du Toit?' he demanded of the shift boss at the lift station.

'He's up at the face, sir.'

The floor of the drive was rough and muddy; his gumboots squelched as he set off down the tunnel. His carbide lamp lit the uneven rock walls with a flat white light and he felt himself starting to sweat. Two natives pushing a cocopan back along the railway lines forced him to flatten himself against one wall to allow them to pass and while he waited he felt inside his overalls for his cigar case. As he pulled it out it slipped from his hand and plunked into the mud. The cocopan was gone by that time so he stooped to pick up the case. His ear came within an inch of the wall and a puzzled expression replaced his frown of annoyance. The rock was squeaking. He laid his ear against it. It sounded like someone grinding his teeth. He listened to it for a while trying to guess the cause; it wasn't the echo of shovels or drills, it wasn't water. He walked another thirty yards or so down the drive and listened again. Not so loud here but now the grinding noise was punctuated with an occasional metallic snap like the breaking of a knife blade. Strange, very strange; he had never heard anything like it before. He walked on down the drive, his bad mood lost in his preoccupation with this new problem. Before he reached the face he met François.

'Hello, Mr Courteney.' Sean had long since given up trying to stop François calling him that. '*Gott*, I'm sorry I wasn't there to meet you. I thought you were coming at three.'

'That's all right, François, how are you?'

'My rheumatism's been giving me blazes, Mr Courteney, but otherwise I'm all right. How's Mr Charleywood?'

'He's fine.' Sean couldn't restrain his curiosity any longer. 'Tell me something, Franz, just now I put my ear against the wall of the drive and I heard an odd noise, I couldn't make out what it was.'

'What kind of noise?'

'A sort of grinding, like–like . . .' Sean searched for words to describe it, 'like two pieces of glass being rubbed together.'

François's eyes flew wide open and then began to bulge, the colour of his face changed to grey and he caught Sean's arm.

'Where?'

'Back along the drive.'

The breath jammed in François's throat and he struggled to speak through it, shaking Sean's arm desperately.

'Cave-in!' he croaked. 'Cave-in, man!'

He started to run but Sean grabbed him. François struggled wildly.

'François, how many men up at the face?'

'Cave-in.' François's voice was now hysterically shrill. 'Cave-in.' He broke Sean's grip and raced away towards the lift station, the mud flying from his gumboots. His terror infected Sean and he ran a dozen paces after François before he stopped himself. For precious seconds he wavered with fear slithering round like a reptile in his stomach; go back to call the others and perhaps die with them or follow François and live. Then the fear in his belly found a mate, a thing just as slimy and cold; its name was shame, and shame it was that drove him back towards the face. There were five blacks and a white man there, bare-chested and shiny with sweat in the heat. Sean shouted those two words at them and they reacted the way bathers do when someone on the beach shouts 'shark'. The same moment of paralysed horror, then the panic. They came stampeding back along the tunnel. Sean ran with them, the mud sucked at his heavy boots and his legs were weak with easy living and riding in carriages. One by one the others passed him.

'Wait for me,' he wanted to scream. 'Wait for me.' He slipped on the greasy footing, scraping his shoulder on the rough wall as he fell, and dragged himself up again, mud plastered in his beard, the blood humming in his ears. Alone now he blundered on down the tunnel. With a crack like a rifle shot one of the thick shoring timbers broke under the pressure of the moving rock and dust smoked from the roof of the tunnel in front of him. He staggered on and all around him the earth was talking, groaning, protesting with little muffled shrieks. The timbers joined in again, crackling and snapping, and as slowly as a theatre curtain the rock sagged down from above him. The tunnel was thick with dust that smothered the beam of his lamp and rasped his throat. He knew then that he wasn't going to make it but he ran on with the loose rock starting to fall about him. A lump hit his mining helmet and jarred him so that he nearly fell. Blinded by the swirling dust fog he crashed at full run into the abandoned cocopan that blocked the tunnel, he sprawled over the metal body of the trolley with his thigh bruised from the collision.

'Now I'm finished,' he thought, but instinctively he pulled himself up and started to grope his way around the cocopan to continue his flight. With a roar the tunnel in front of him collapsed. He dropped on his knees and crawled between the wheels of the cocopan, wriggling under the sturdy steel body just an instant before the roof above him collapsed also. The noise of the fall around him seemed to last for ever, but then it was over and the rustling and grating of the rock as it settled down was almost silence in comparison. His lamp was lost and the darkness pressed as heavily on him as the earth squeezed down on his tiny shelter. The air was solid with dust and he coughed; he coughed until his chest ached and he tasted salty blood in his mouth. There was hardly room to move, the steel body of the trolley was six inches above him, but he struggled until he managed to open the front of his overalls and tear a piece off the tail of his shirt. He held the silk like a surgical mask across his mouth and nose. It strained the dust out of the air so he could breathe. The dust settled; his coughing slowed and finally stopped. He felt surprised that he was still alive and cautiously be started exploring. He tried to straighten out his legs but his feet touched rock. He felt with his hands, six inches of head room and perhaps twelve inches on either side, warm mud underneath him and rock and steel all round. He took off his helmet and used it as a pillow. He was in a steel coffin buried five hundred feet deep. He felt the first flutter of panic. 'Keep your mind busy, think of something, think of anything but the rock around you, count your assets,' he told himself. He started to search his pockets, moving with difficulty in the cramped space.

'One silver cigar case with two Havanas.' He laid it down next to him.

'One box of matches, wet.' He placed it on top of the case.

'One pocket watch.'

'One handkerchief, Irish linen, monogrammed.'

'One comb, tortoiseshell–a man is judged by his appearance.' He started to comb his beard but found immediately that though this occupied his hands it left his mind free. He put the comb down next to his matches.

'Twenty-five pounds in gold sovereigns–' He counted them carefully, 'yes, twenty-five. I shall order a bottle of good champagne.' The dust was chalky in his mouth so he went on hurriedly, 'and a Malay girl from the Opera. No, why be mean–ten Malay girls. I'll have them dance for me, that'll pass the time. I'll promise them a sovereign each to bolster their enthusiasm.'

He continued the search, but there was nothing else. 'Gumboots, socks, well-cut trousers, shirt torn I'm afraid, overalls, a tin hat and that's all.'

With his possessions laid out carefully beside him and his cell explored he had to start thinking. First he thought about his thirst. The mud in which he lay was too thick to yield water. He tried straining it through his shirt without success, and then he thought about air. It seemed quite fresh and he decided that sufficient was filtering in from the loosely packed rock around him to keep him alive.

To keep him alive–alive until the thirst killed. Until he died curled up like a foetus in the warm womb of the earth. He laughed, a worm in a dark warm womb. He laughed again and recognized it as the beginnings of panic, he thrust his fist into his mouth to stop himself, biting down hard on his knuckles. It was very quiet, the rock had stopped moving.

'How long will it take? Tell me, Doctor. How long have I got?'

'Well, you are sweating. You'll lose moisture quite rapidly. I'd say about four days,' he answered himself.

'What about hunger, Doctor?'

'Oh, no, don't worry about that, you'll be hungry, of course, but the thirst will kill you.'

'And typhoid, or is it typhus, I can never remember. What about that, Doctor?'

'If there were dead men trapped in here with you there'd be a good chance, but you're alone, you know.'

'Do you think I'll go mad, Doctor, not immediately, of course, but in a few days?'

'Yes, you'll go mad.'

'I've never been mad before, not that I know of anyway, but I think it will help to go mad now, don't you?'

'If you mean, will it make it easier, well, I don't know.'

'Ah! now you're being obscure–but I follow you. You mean in that sleep of madness what dreams will come? You mean, will madness be more real than reality? You mean, will dying mad be worse than dying thirsty? But then I may beat the madness. This cocopan might buckle under the strain, after all there must be thousands of tons of rock bearing down on it. That's quite clever, you know, Doctor; as a medical man you should appreciate it. Mother Earth was saved but, alas, the child was stillborn, she bore down too hard.' Sean had spoken aloud, and now he felt foolish. He picked up a piece of stone and tapped the cocopan with it.

'It sounds firm enough. A most pleasing noise, really.' He beat harder on the metal body–one, two, three, one two, three–then dropped the stone. Soft as an echo, distant as the moon, he heard his taps repeated. His whole body stiffened at the sound, and he started to shiver with excitement. He snatched up the stone: three times he rapped, and three times the answer came back to him.

'They heard me, sweet merciful Christ, they heard me.' He laughed breathlessly. 'Dear Mother Earth, don't bear down, please don't bear down. Just be patient. Wait a few days and by Caesarian they'll take this child out of your womb.'

Mbejane waited until Sean disappeared down the Number Three shaft before he took off his new jacket. He folded it carefully on the driver's seat next to him. He sat and enjoyed the feel of the sun on his skin for a while, then he climbed off the carriage and went to the horses. He took them one at a time to the trough for water then returned them to their harnesses, buckling them in loosely. He picked up his spears from the footboard and moved across to a patch of short grass next to the administrative building. He sat down and went to work on the blade, humming softly to himself as he honed. At last he ran an expert thumb along each edge, grunted, shaved a few hairs off his forearm, smiled contentedly and laid his spears beside him in the grass. He lay back and the sun warmed him to sleep.

The shouting woke him. He sat up and automatically checked the height of the sun. He had slept an hour or more. Duff was shouting and François, mud-splattered and frightened-looking, was answering him. They were standing together in front of the administrative building. Duff's horse was sweating. Mbejane stood up and went across to them; he listened closely, trying to understand their staccato voices. They went too fast for him, but something was wrong, that much he knew.

'It's caved in almost to the Number Ten lift station,' François said.

'You left him in there,' accused Duff.

'I thought he was following me, but he turned back.'

'What for–why did he turn back?'

'To call the others–'

'Have you started clearing the drive?'

'No, I was waiting for you.'

'You stupid bloody idiot, he might be alive in there . . . every minute is vital.'

'But he hasn't a chance, Mr Charleywood, he must be dead.'

'Shut up, damn you.'

Duff swung away from him and started running towards the shaft. There was a crowd gathered beneath the high steel structure of the head gear, and suddenly Mbejane knew it was Sean. He caught up with Duff before he reached the shaft.

'Is it the Nkosi?'

'Yes.'

'What has happened?'

'The rock has fallen on him.'

Mbejane pushed his way into the skip next to Duff and neither of them spoke again until they reached the tenth level. They went down the drive, only a short way before they reached the end. There were men there with crowbars and shovels standing undecided, waiting for orders, and Mbejane shouldered a path through them. He and Duff stood together in front of the new wall of broken rock that sealed the tunnel, and the silence went on and on. Then Duff turned on the white shift-boss.

'Were you at the face?'

'Yes.'

'He went back to call you, didn't he?'

'Yes.'

'And you left him there?'

The man couldn't look at Duff.

'I thought he was following us,' he muttered.

'You thought only for your own miserable skin,' Duff told him, 'you filthy little coward, you slimy yellow bastard, you . . .'

Mbejane caught Duff's arm and Duff stopped his tirade. They all heard it then–clink, clink, clink.

'It's him–it must be him,' whispered Duff, 'he's alive!' He snatched a crowbar from one of the natives and knocked against the side of the tunnel. They waited, their breathing the only sound, until the answer came back to them louder and sharper than before. Mbejane took the crowbar out of Duff's hands. He thrust it into a crack in the rock jam and his back muscles bunched as he heaved. The bar bent like a liquorice stick, he threw it away and went at the stone with his bare hands.

'You!' Duff snapped at the shift-boss. 'We'll need timber to shore up as we clear the fall–get it.' He turned to the natives. 'Four of you working on the face at one time–the rest of you carry the stone away as we loosen it.'

'Do you want any dynamite?' asked the shift-boss.

'And bring the rock down a second time? Use your brains, man. Go and get that timber and call Mr du Toit while you're at the surface.'

In four hours they cleared fifteen feet of tunnel, breaking the larger slabs of stone with sledge hammers and prising the pieces out of the jam. Duff's body ached and his hands were raw. He had to rest. He walked slowly back to the lift station and there he found blankets and a huge dish of soup.

'Where did this come from?'

'Candy's Hotel, sir. Half Johannesburg is waiting at the head of the shaft.'

Duff huddled into a blanket and drank a little of the soup. 'Where's du Toit?'

'I couldn't find him, sir.'

Up at the face Mbejane worked on. The first four natives came back to rest and fresh men took their place. Mbejane led them, grunting an order occasionally but otherwise reserving his strength for the assault on the rock. For an hour Duff rested and when he returned to the head of the tunnel Mbejane was still there. Duff watched him curl his arms round a piece of stone the size of a beer keg, brace his legs and tear the stone out of the jam. Earth and loose rock followed it burying Mbejane's legs to the knees and Duff jumped forward to help him.

Another two hours and Duff had to rest again. This time he led Mbejane back with him, gave him a blanket and made him drink a little soup. They sat next to each other with their backs against the wall of the tunnel and blankets over their shoulders. The shift-boss came to Duff.

'Mrs Rautenbach sent this down for you, sir.'

It was a half-bottle of brandy.

'Tell her, thank you.' Duff pulled the cork with his teeth and swallowed twice. It brought the tears into his eyes–he offered the bottle to Mbejane.

'It is not fitting,' Mbejane demurred.

'Drink.'

Mbejane drank, wiped the mouth of the bottle carefully on his blanket and handed it back. Duff took another swallow and offered it again but Mbejane shook his head.

'A little of that is strength, too much is weakness. There is work to do now.'

Duff corked the bottle.

'How long before we reach him?' asked Mbejane.

'Another day, maybe two.'

'A man can die in two days,' mused the Zulu.

'Not one with a body like a bull and a temper like a devil,' Duff assured him. Mbejane smiled and Duff went on groping for his words in Zulu.

'You love him, Mbejane?'

'Love is a woman's word.'

Mbejane inspected one of his thumbs; the nail was torn loose, standing up like a tombstone; he took it between his teeth, pulled it off and spat it on to the floor of the drive. Duff shuddered as he watched.

'Those baboons will not work unless they are driven.' Mbejane stood up. 'Are you rested?'

'Yes,' lied Duff, and they went back to the face.

Sean lay in the mud with his head on the hard pillow of the helmet. The darkness was as solid as the rock around him. He tried to imagine where the one ended and the other began–by doing that he could stop himself feeling his thirst so strongly. He could hear the ring of hammer on stone and the rattle of rock falling free but it never seemed to come any closer. The whole side of his body was stiff and sore but he could not turn over, his knees caught on the cocopan every time he tried and the air in his little cave was starting to taste stale–his head ached. He moved again, restlessly, and his hand brushed the small pile of sovereigns. He struck at them, scattering them into the mud. They were the bait that had led him into this trap. Now he would give them, and all the millions of others, for just the feel of the wind in his beard and the sun in his face. The darkness clung to him, thick and cloying as black treacle; it seemed to fill his nose, his throat and eyes, smothering him. He groped and found the matchbox. For a few seconds of light he would burn up most of the precious oxygen in his cave and call it fair exchange–but the box was sodden. He struck match after match but the wet heads crumbled without a spark and he threw them away and clenched his eyelids to keep the darkness out. Bright colours formed in front of his closed eyes, moving and rearranging themselves until suddenly and very clearly they formed a picture of Garrick's face. He hadn't thought about his family for months, he had been too busy reaping the golden harvest, but now memories crowded back. There were so many things he had forgotten. Everything else had become unimportant when compared with power and gold–even lives, men's lives, had meant nothing. But now it was his own life, teetering on the edge of the black cliff.

The sound of the sledge-hammers broke into his thoughts again. There were men on the other side of the blocked tunnel trying to save him, working their way into the treacherous rock pile which might collapse again at any minute. People were more valuable than the poisonous metal, the little gold discs that lay smugly beside him in the mud while men struggled to save him.

He thought of Garry, crippled by his careless shotgun, father to the bastard he had sired, of Ada whom he had left without a word of goodbye, of Karl Lochtkamper with the pistol in his hand and half his head splattered across the floor of his bedroom, or other nameless men dead or broken because of him.

Sean ran his tongue across his lips and listened to the hammers; he was certain they were nearer now.

'If I get out of here, it'll be different. I swear it.'

Mbejane rested for four hours in the next thirty-six. Duff watched the flesh melt off him in sweat. He was killing himself. Duff was worn out; he could no longer work with his hands but he was directing the teams who were shoring up the reclaimed tunnel. By the second evening they had cleared a hundred feet of the drive. Duff paced it out and when he reached the face he spoke to Mbejane.

'How long since you last signalled to him?'

Mbejane stepped back with a sledge-hammer in his tattered hands; its shaft was sticky and brown with blood.

'An hour ago and even then it sounded as though there were but the length of a spear between us.'

Duff took a crowbar from one of the other natives and tapped the rock. The answer came immediately.

'He's hitting something made of iron,' Duff said. 'It sounds as though he's only a few feet away. Mbejane, let these other men take over. If you wish you can stay and watch but you must rest again now.'

For answer Mbejane lifted the hammer and swung it against the face. The rock he hit cracked and two of the natives stepped up and levered it loose with their crowbars. At the back of the hole it left in the wall they could see the corner of the cocopan. Everyone stared at it, then Duff shouted.

'Sean, Sean, can you hear me?'

'Stop talking and get me out of here.' Sean's voice was hoarse with thirst and dust, and muffled by the rock.

'He's under the cocopan.'

'It's him.'

'Nkosi, are you all right?'

'We've found him.'

The shouts were picked up by the men behind them in the drive and passed back to those waiting at the lift station.

'They've found him–he's all right–they've found him.'

Duff and Mbejane jumped forward together, their exhaustion completely forgotten. They cleared the last few lumps of rock and with their shoulders touching knelt and peered under the cocopan.

'Nkosi, I see you.'

'I see you also, Mbejane, what took you so long?'

'Nkosi, there were a few small stones in the way.'

Mbejane reached under the cocopan and with his hands under Sean's armpits pulled him out.

'What a hell of a place you choose to go to ground in, laddie. How are you feeling?'

'Give me some water and I'll be all right.'

'Water–bring water,' shouted Duff.

Sean gulped it, trying to drink the whole mug in one mouthful. He coughed and it shot out of his nose.

'Easy, laddie, easy.' Duff thumped his back. Sean drank the next mugful more slowly and finished panting from the effort.

'That was good.'

'Come on, we've got a doctor waiting up on top.' Duff draped a blanket over his shoulders. Mbejane picked Sean up across his chest.

'Put me down, damn you, I haven't forgotten how to walk.'

Mbejane set him down gently, but his legs buckled like those of a man just out of bed from a long illness and he clutched at Mbejane's arm. Mbejane picked him up again and carried him down to the lift station. They rode up in the skip into the open.

'The moon's shining. And the stars–my God, they're beautiful.' There was wonder in Sean's voice; he sucked the night air into his lungs but it was too rich for him and he started coughing again. There were people waiting at the head of the shaft and they crowded round them as they stepped out of the skip.

'How is he?'

'Are you all right, Sean?'

'Doc Symmonds is waiting in the office.'

'Quickly, Mbejane,' said Duff, 'get him out of the cold.'

One on either side of him they hurried Sean across to the administrative building and laid him on the couch in François's office. Symmonds checked him over, looked down his throat and felt his pulse.

'Have you got a closed carriage here?'

'Yes,' Duff answered.

'Well, wrap him up warmly and get him home to bed. With the dust and bad air he's been breathing there's serious danger of pneumonia. I'll come down with you and give him a sedative.'

'I won't need one, Doc,' Sean grinned at him.

'I think I know what's best for you, Mr Courteney.' Doctor Symmonds was a young man. He was the fashionable doctor among the rich of Johannesburg and he took it very seriously.

'Now if you please, we'll get you to your hotel.' He started to pack his instruments back into his valise.

'You're the doctor,' Sean agreed, 'but before we go will you have a look at my servant's hands, they're in a hell of a mess. There's hardly any meat left on them.'

Doctor Symmonds did not look up from what he was doing. 'I have no Kaffir practice, Mr Courteney, I'm sure you'll find some other doctor to attend to him when we get back to town.'

Sean sat up slowly, he let the blankets slip off his shoulders. He walked across to Doctor Symmonds and held him by the throat against the wall. The doctor had a fine pair of waxed moustaches and Sean took one of them between the thumb and forefinger of his free hand: he plucked it out like feathers from the carcass of a dead fowl and Doctor Symmonds squealed.

'Starting now, Doctor, you have a Kaffir practice,' Sean told him. He pulled the handkerchief out of Symmonds' top pocket and dabbed at the little drops of blood on the doctor's bare upper lip.

'Be a good fellow–see to my servant.'

21

When Sean woke the next morning the hands of the grandfather clock across the bedroom pointed at the top of their dial. Candy was in the room opening the curtains and with her were two waiters, each with a loaded tray.

'Good morning, how is our hero this morning?' the waiters put down their trays and went out as she came across to Sean's bed.

Sean blinked the sleep out of his eyes. 'My throat feels as though I've just finished a meal of broken glass.'

'That's the dust,' Candy told him and laid her hands on his forehead. Sean's hand sneaked round behind her and she squeaked as he pinched her. Standing well away from the bed she rubbed her bottom and made a face at him.

'There's nothing wrong with you!'

'Good, then I'll get up.' Sean started to pull back the bedclothes.

'Not until the doctor's had a look at you, you won't.'

'Candy, if that bastard puts one foot in this room I'll punch him so hard in the mouth his teeth will march out of his backside like soldiers.'

Candy turned to the breakfast trays to cover her smile. 'That's no way to talk in front of a lady. But don't worry, it isn't Symmonds.'

'Where's Duff?' Sean asked.

'He's having a bath, then he's coming to eat breakfast with you.'

'I'll wait for him, but give me a cup of coffee in the meantime, there's a sweetheart.'

She brought the coffee to him. 'Your savage has been camping on my trail all morning, he wants to see you. I've just about had to put an armed guard on this room to keep him out.'

Sean laughed. 'Will you send him in, Candy?'

She went to the door and stopped with a hand on the latch.

'It's nice to have you back, Sean, don't do anything silly like that again, will you?'

'That's a promise,' Sean assured her.

Mbejane came quickly and stood in the doorway. 'Nkosi, is it well with you?'

Sean looked at the iodine-stained bandages on his hands and the maroon and gold livery without answering. Then he rolled on his back and stared at the ceiling. 'I sent for my servant and instead there comes a monkey on a chain.'

Mbejane stood still, his face expressionless but for the hurt in his eyes.

'Go–find my servant. You will know him by his dress which is that of a warrior of Zululand.'

It took a few seconds for the laughter to start rolling around in Mbejane's belly; it shook his shoulders and creased the corners of his mouth. He closed the door very softly behind him and when he came back in his loin cloth Sean grinned at him.

'Ah! I see you, Mbejane.'

'And I see you also.'

He stood by the bed and they talked. They spoke little of the cave-in and not at all of Mbejane's part in the rescue. Between them it was understood, words could only damage it. Perhaps they would talk of it later, but not now.

'Tomorrow, will you need the carriage?' Mbejane asked at last.

'Yes–go now. Eat and sleep.' Sean reached out and touched Mbejane's arm. Just that small physical contact–that almost guilty touching–and Mbejane left him.

Then Duff came in in a silk dressing -gown and they ate eggs and steak from the trays and Duff sent down for a bottle of wine just to rinse the dust out of their throats once more.

'They tell me François is still down at the Bright Angels–he's been on the drink ever since he got out of that shaft. When he sobers up he can come to the office and collect his pay packet.'

Sean sat up. 'You're going to fire him?'

'I'm going to fire him so high he'll only touch the ground when he reaches Capetown.'

'What the hell for?' demanded Sean.

'What for?' Duff echoed. 'What for? For running–that's what for.'

'Duff, he was in a cave-in at Kimberley, wasn't he?'

'Yes.'

'Broke his legs, didn't you say?'

'Yes.'

'Shall I tell you something? If it were to happen to me a second time I'd run as well.'

Duff filled his wine glass without answering.

'Send down to the Bright Angels, tell him alcohol is bad for the liver–that should sober him–tell him unless he's back at work by tomorrow morning we'll dock it off his pay,' Sean said. Duff looked at him with a puzzled expression. 'What is this?'

'I had some time to think while I was down in that hole. I decided that to get to the top you don't have to stamp on everyone you meet.'

'Ah, I understand.' Duff gave his lopsided grin. 'A good resolution–New Year in August. Well, that's all right, you had me worried there, I thought a rock had fallen on your head. I also make good resolutions.'

'Duff, I don't want François fired.'

'All right, all right–he stays on. If you like we can open a soup kitchen at the office and turn Xanadu into a home for the aged.'

'Oh, go and burst. I just don't think it's necessary to fire François, that's all.'

'Who's arguing? I agreed with you, didn't I? I have deep respect for good resolutions. I make them all the time.'

Duff pulled his chair up to the bed. 'Quite by chance I happen to have a pack of cards with me.' He took them out of his dressing-gown pocket. 'Would you care for a game of Klabejas?'

Sean lost fifty pounds before he was saved by the arrival of the new doctor. The doctor tapped his chest and tut-tutted, looked down his throat and tut-tutted, wrote out a prescription and confined him to bed for the rest of the day. He was just leaving when Jock and Trevor Heyns arrived. Jock had a bunch of flowers which he presented to Sean in an embarrassed fashion.

Then the room began to fill in earnest: the rest of the crowd from the Exchange arrived, someone had brought a case of champagne, a poker game started in one corner and a political meeting in another.

'Who does this Kruger think he is, anyway–God or something? You know what he said last time we went to see him about getting the vote, he said "Protest, protest–I have the guns and you have not!"'

'Three Kings wins–you *are* holding cards!'

'–you wait and see. Consolidated Wits. will hit thirty shillings by the end of the month.'

'–and the taxes–they're putting another twenty per cent on dynamite.'

'–a new piece at the Opera, Jock's got a season ticket on her–no one else has had a look in yet.'

'All right, you two–stop that. If you want to fight go outside–this is a sick room.'

'This bottle's empty–break open a new one, Duff.'

Sean lost another hundred to Duff and then a little after five Candy came in. She was horrified. 'Out, all of you, out!'

The room emptied as quickly as it had filled and Candy wandered around picking up cigar butts and empty glasses.

'The vandals! Someone's burnt a hole in the carpet and look at this–champagne spilt all over the table.'

Duff coughed and started pouring himself another drink.

'Don't you think you've had enough of that, Dufford?'

Duff put down his glass. 'And it's time you went and changed for dinner.' Duff winked sheepishly at Sean, but he went.

Duff and Candy came back to his room after supper and had a liqueur with him.

'Now to sleep,' Candy commanded and went across to draw the curtains.

'It's still early,' protested Duff with no effect. Candy blew the lamp out.

Sean was not tired, he had lain in bed all day and now his brain was overactive. He lit a cigar and smoked, listening to the street noises below his window and it was past midnight before he finally drifted off. When he awoke, he woke screaming, for the darkness was on him again and the blankets pressed down on him suffocating him. He fought them off and stumbled blindly across the room. He had to have air and light. He ran into the thick velvet curtains and they closed around his face; he tore himself free and hit the french windows with his shoulder; they burst open and he was out on the balcony, out in the cold air with the moon fat and yellow in the sky above him. His gasping slowed until he was breathing normally again. He went back inside and lit the lamp, then he went through to Duff's empty bedroom. There was a copy of *Twelfth Night* on the bedside table and he took it back to his own room. He sat with the lamp at his elbow and forced his eyes to follow the printed words even though they made no sense. He read until the dawn showed grey through the open windows, then he put down the book. He shaved, dressed and went down the back stairs into the hotel yard. He found Mbejane in the stables.

'Put a saddle on the grey.'

'Where are you going, Nkosi?'

'To kill a devil.'

'Then I will come with you.'

'No, I will be back before midday.'

He rode up to the Candy Deep and tied his horse outside the administration buildings. There was a sleepy clerk in the front offices.

'Good morning, Mr Courteney. Can I help you?'

'Yes. Get me overalls and a helmet.'

Sean went to the Number Three Shaft. There was a frost on the ground that crunched as he walked on it and the sun had just cleared the eastern ridge of the Witwatersrand. Sean stopped at the hoist shed and spoke to the driver.

'Has the new shift gone on yet?'

'Half an hour ago, sir.' The man was obviously surprised to see him. 'The night shift finished blasting at five o'clock.'

'Good–drop me down to the fourteenth level.'

'The fourteenth is abandoned now, Mr Courteney, there's no one working there.'

'Yes, I know.'

Sean walked across to the head of the shaft. He lit his carbide lamp and while he waited for the skip he looked out across the valley. The air was clear and the sun threw long shadows. Everything stood out in sharp relief. He had not been up this early in the morning for many months and he had almost forgotten how fresh and delicately coloured a new day was. The skip stopped in front of him. He took a deep breath and stepped into it. When he reached the fourteenth level he got out and pushed the recall signal for the skip and he was alone in the earth again. He walked up the tunnel and the echo of his footsteps went with him. He was sweating and a muscle in his cheek started to jerk; he reached the face and set the carbide lamp down on a ledge of rock. He checked to make sure his matches were in his pocket, then he blew out the lamp. The darkness came squeezing down on him. The first half hour was the worst. Twice he had the matches in his hand ready to strike but he stopped himself. The sweat formed cold wet patches under his arms and the darkness filled his open mouth and choked him. He had to fight for each lungful of air, suck in, hold it, breathe out. First he regulated his breathing and then slowly, slowly his mind came under control and he knew he had won. He waited another ten minutes breathing easily and sitting relaxed with his back against the side of the tunnel, then he lit the lamp. He was smiling as he went back to the lift station and signalled for the skip. When he reached the surface he stepped out and lit a cigar; he flicked the match into the square black opening of the shaft.

'So much for you, little hole.'

He walked back towards the administration building. What he could not know was that the Number Three shaft of the Candy Deep was to take something from him just as valuable as his courage and that, next time, what it took it would not give back. But that was many years ahead.

22

By October Xanadu was nearly finished. The three of them drove out to it as usual one Saturday afternoon.

'The builder is only six months behind schedule–now he says he'll be finished by Christmas and I haven't found the courage yet to ask him which Christmas,' Sean remarked.

'It's all the alterations Candy has thought up,' Duff said. 'She's got the poor man so confused he doesn't know whether he's a boy or a girl.'

'Well, if you'd consulted me in the first place it would have saved a lot of trouble,' Candy told them.

The carriage turned in through the marble gates and they looked around them. Already the lawns were smooth and green and the jacaranda trees lining the drive were shoulder high.

'I think it's going to live up to its name–that gardener's doing a good job,' Sean spoke with satisfaction.

'Don't you call him a gardener to his face or we'll have a strike on our hands. He's a horticulturist,' Duff smiled across at him.

'Talking about names,' Candy interrupted, 'don't you think Xanadu is–well, a bit outlandish?'

'No, I do not,' Sean said. 'I picked it myself. I think it's a damn good name.'

'It's not dignified–why don't we call it Fair Oaks?'

'Firstly, because there isn't an oak tree within fifty miles and secondly because it's already called Xanadu.'

'Don't get cross, it was just a suggestion.'

The builder met them at the top of the drive and they began the tour of the house. That took an hour, then they left the builder and went out into the garden. They found the gardener with a gang of natives near the north boundary.

'How's it going, Joubert?' Duff greeted him.

'Not bad, Mr Charleywood, but it takes time you know.'

'You've done a damn fine job so far.'

'It's kind of you to say so, sir.'

'When are you going to start laying out my maze?'

The gardener looked surprised; he glanced at Candy, opened his mouth, closed it again and looked once more at Candy.

'Oh, I told Joubert not to worry about the maze.'

'Why did you do that? I wanted a maze–ever since I visited Hampton Court as a child I've wanted my own maze.'

'They're silly things,' Candy told him. 'They just take up a lot of space and they're not even nice to look at.'

Sean thought Duff was going to argue, but he didn't. They talked to the gardener a little longer, then they walked back across the lawns in front of the house towards the chapel.

'Dufford, I've left my parasol in the carriage, would you mind getting it for me?' Candy asked.

When Duff was gone Candy took Sean's arm.

'It's going to be a lovely home. We're going to be very happy here.'

'Have you two decided on a date yet?' Sean asked.

'We want the house finished first so we can move straight in. I think we'll make it some time in February next year.'

They reached the chapel and stopped in front of it.

'It's a sweet little church.' Candy spoke dreamily. 'And such a nice idea of Dufford's–a special church of our own.'

Sean shuffled uncomfortably. 'Yes,' he agreed, 'it's a very romantic idea.' He glanced over his shoulder and saw Duff coming back with the parasol.

'Candy–it's none of my business. I don't know anything about marriage, but I know about training horses–you break them to the halter before you put the saddle on their backs.'

'I don't follow you.' Candy looked puzzled. 'What are you trying to say?'

'Nothing–just forget it. Here comes Duff.'

When they got back to the hotel there was a note at the reception desk for Sean. They went through into the main lounge and Candy went off to check the menu for dinner. Sean opened the envelope and read the note.

I should like to meet you and Mr Charleywood to discuss a matter of some importance. I will be at my hotel after dinner this evening and hope that it will be convenient for you to call on me then. N. Hradsky.

Sean passed the note across to Duff.

'What do you suppose he wants?'

'He has heard of your deadly skill as a Klabejas player. He wants to take lessons,' Duff answered.

'Shall we go?'

'Of course. You know I can't resist Norman's exhilarating company.'

It was a superb dinner. The crayfish, packed in ice, had come up from Capetown by express coach.

'Candy–Sean and I are going across to see Hradsky. We might be back a little late,' Duff told her when they were finished.

'As long as it's Hradsky,' Candy smiled at him. 'Don't get lost–I have my spies at the Opera House you know.'

'Shall we take the carriage?' Duff asked Sean, and Sean noticed that he hadn't laughed at Candy's joke.

'It's only two blocks, we might as well walk.'

They walked in silence. Sean felt his dinner settling down comfortably inside him, he belched softly and took another puff from his cigar. When they had almost reached the Grand National Hotel Duff spoke.

'Sean . . .' He stopped.

'Yes?' Sean prompted him.

'About Candy . . .' He stopped again.

'She's a fine girl,' Sean prompted again.

'Yes, she's a fine girl.'

Is that all you wanted to say?'

'Well–oh! never mind. Let's go and see what Saul and David want.'

Max met them at the door of Hradsky's suite.

'Good evening, gentlemen, I am so pleased you could come.'

'Hello, Max.' Duff went past him to where Hradsky was standing in front of the fireplace.

'Norman, my dear fellow, how are you?'

Hradsky nodded in acknowledgement and Duff took hold of the lapels of Hradsky's coat and adjusted them carefully; then he picked an imaginary piece of fluff off his shoulder.

'You have a way with clothes, Norman. Don't you agree that Norman has a way with clothes, Sean? I know of no one else who can put on a twenty-guinea suit and make it look like a half-filled bag of oranges.' He patted Hradsky's arm affectionately. 'Yes, thank you–I will have a drink.' He went across to the liquor cabinet and poured one for himself. 'Now, what can you gentlemen do for me?'

Max glanced at Hradsky and Hradsky nodded.

'I will come to the point immediately,' said Max. 'Our two groups of companies are the largest on the Witwatersrand.'

Duff put his glass back on top of the cabinet and dropped his grin. Sean sat down in one of the armchairs, his expression also serious; both of them could guess what was coming.

'In the past,' continued Max, 'we have worked together on numerous occasions and we have both benefited from it. The next logical step, of course, is to combine our strength, pool our resources and go on together to new greatness.'

'I take it that you are proposing a merger?'

'Precisely, Mr Courteney, a merger of these two vast financial ventures.'

Sean leaned back in his chair and started to whistle softly. Duff picked up his glass again and took a sip.

'Well, gentlemen, what are your feelings on the subject?' asked Max.

'Have you got a proposal worked out, Max, something definite for us to think about?'

'Yes, Mr Courteney, I have.' Max went to the stinkwood desk which filled one corner of the room and picked up a sheaf of papers. He carried it across to Sean. Sean scanned through it.

'You've done quite a bit of work here, Max. It's going to take us a day or two to work out exactly what you are offering.'

'I appreciate that, Mr Courteney. Take as long as you wish. We have worked for a month to draw up that scheme and I hope our labours have not been in vain. I think you will find our offer very generous.'

Sean stood up.

'We'll contact you again in the next few days, Max. Shall we go, Duff?'

Duff finished his drink.

'Goodnight, Max, look after Norman. He's very precious to us, you know.'

They went to their building on Eloff Street. Sean let them in through one of the side doors, lit the lamps in his office and Duff pulled up an extra chair to the desk. By two o'clock the following morning they understood the essentials of Hradsky's offer. Sean stood up and went to open one of the windows, for the room was thick with cigar smoke. He came back and flopped on to the couch, arranged a cushion behind his head and looked at Duff.

'Let's hear what you've got to say.'

Duff tapped his teeth with a pencil while he arranged his words.

'Let's decide first if we want to join with him.'

'If he makes it worth our while, we do,' Sean answered.

'I agree with you–but only if he makes it worth our while.' Duff laid back in his chair. 'Now the next point. Tell me, laddie, what is the first thing that strikes you about this scheme of Norman's?'

'We get nice-sounding titles and fat cash payments and Hradsky gets control,' Sean answered.

'You have laid your finger on the heart of it–Norman wants control. More than money, Norman wants control, so that he can sit at the top of the pile, look down on everyone else and say, "All right, you bastards, what if I do stutter?"'

Duff stood up, he walked round the desk and stopped in front of Sean's couch.

'Now for my next question. Do we give him control?'

'If he pays our price, then we give him control,' Sean answered. Duff turned away and went across to the open window.

'You know I rather like the feeling of being top man myself,' he said thoughtfully.

'Listen, Duff, we came here to make money. If we go in with Hradsky we'll make more,' Sean said.

'Laddie, we've got so much now that we could fill this room waist deep in sovereigns. We've got more than we'll ever be able to spend and I like being top man.'

'Hradsky's more powerful than we are–let's face up to that. He's got his diamond interests as well, so you're not top man even now. If we join him you still won't be top man and you'll be a damn sight richer.'

'Unassailable logic,' Duff nodded. 'I agree with you then. Hradsky gets control but he pays for it; we'll put him through the wringer until he's dry.'

Sean swung his legs off the couch. 'Agreed–now let's take this scheme of his by the throat, tear it to pieces and build it up again to suit ourselves.'

Duff looked at his watch. 'It's after two o'clock. We'll leave it now and start on it when we're fresh in the morning.'

They had their lunch brought down to the office the next day and ate it at the desk. Johnson, who had been sent up to the Stock Exchange with instructions to keep an eye on prices and call them immediately anything out of the ordinary happened, reported back after high change.

'It's been as quiet as a graveyard all day, sir, there's all sorts of rumours flying about. Seems someone saw the lights burning in this office at two o'clock this morning. Then when you didn't come to the Exchange but sent me instead–well, I can tell you, sir, there were a lot of questions asked.' Johnson hesitated, then his curiosity got the better of him.

'Can I help you at all, sir?' He started sidling across towards the desk.

'I think we can manage on our own, Johnson. Shut the door as you go out, please.'

At half-past seven they decided it was enough for one day and they went back to the hotel. As they walked into the lobby Sean saw Trevor Heyns disappear into the lounge and heard his voice.

'Here they are!'

Almost immediately Trevor appeared again with his brother.

'Hello, boys,' Jock appeared surprised to see them. 'What are you doing here?'

'We live here,' said Duff.

'Oh, yes, of course. Well, come and have a drink with us.' Jock smiled expansively.

'And then you can pump us and find out what we've been doing all day,' Duff suggested.

Jock looked embarrassed. 'I don't know what you mean, I just thought we'd have a drink together, that's all.'

'Thanks all the same, Jock, we've had a hard day. I think we'll just go on up to bed,' Duff said. They were halfway across the lobby before Duff turned back to where the two brothers were standing.

'I'll tell you boys something,' he said in a stage whisper. 'This is really big–it's so big it takes a while for the mind to grasp it. When you two realize that it's been right there under your noses all the time, you're going to kick yourselves.'

They left the Heyns brothers in the lobby staring after them and went up the stairs.

'That wasn't very kind,' Sean laughed. 'They won't sleep for a week.'

23

When neither Sean nor Duff put in an appearance at the Exchange the next morning, the rumours surged round the members' lounge and the prices started running amok. Reliable information that Sean and Duff had struck a rich new goldfield across the vaal sent the prices up like rocketing snipe; then twenty minutes later the denial came in and clipped fifteen shillings a share off the Courteney–Charleywood stock. Johnson ran backwards and forwards between the office and the Exchange all morning. By eleven he was so tired he could hardly talk.

'Don't worry any more, Johnson,' Sean told him. 'Here's a sovereign–go down to the Grand National and buy yourself a drink, you've had a hard morning.'

One of Jock Heyns's men, who had been detailed off to watch the Courteney–Charleywood offices, followed Johnson down to the Grand National and heard him place his order with the barman. He raced back to the Exchange and reported to Jock.

'Their head clerk has just gone and ordered himself a bottle of French champagne,' he panted.

'Good God!' Jock nearly jumped out of his chair and beside him Trevor signalled frantically for his clerk.

'Buy,' he whispered in the man's ear. 'Buy every scrap of their script you can lay your hands on.'

Across the lounge Hradsky settled down a little further in his chair; he clasped his hands contentedly over the front of his stomach and he very nearly smiled.

By midnight Sean and Duff had completed their counter-proposal to Hradsky's offer.

'How do you think Norman will react to it?' asked Sean.

'I hope his heart is strong enough to stand the shock,' Duff grinned. 'The only reason that his jaw won't hit the floor is that his great gut will be in the way.'

'Shall we go down to his hotel now and show him?' suggested Sean.

'Laddie, laddie.' Duff shook his head sorrowfully. 'After all the time I've spent on your education, and you still haven't learned.'

'What do we do then?'

'We send for him, laddie, we make him come to us. We play him on the home ground.'

'How does that help?' Sean asked.

'It gives us an advantage immediately–it makes him remember that he's the one doing the asking.'

Hradsky came down to their office at ten o'clock the next morning; he came in state driven behind a four-in-hand and attended by Max and two secretaries. Johnson met them at the front door and ushered them into Sean's office.

'Norman, dear old Norman, I'm delighted to see you,' Duff greeted him and, fully aware of the fact that Hradsky never smoked, Duff thrust a cheroot between his lips. When everyone was seated Sean opened the meeting.

'Gentlemen, we have spent some time examining your proposition and in the main we find it just, fair and equitable.'

'Hear, hear,' Duff agreed politely.

'At the outset I want to make it quite clear,' Sean went on, 'that Mr Charleywood and myself feel strongly that the union of our two ventures is desirable–nay! essential. If you will forgive the quotation, "*ex unitate vires*".'

'Hear, hear–hear, hear.' Duff lit his cigar.

'As I was saying, we have examined your proposition and we accept it readily and happily, with the exception of a few minor details which we have listed.' Sean picked up the thick pile of paper. 'Perhaps you would care to glance through it and then we can proceed to the drawing-up of a formal agreement.'

Max accepted the sheaf gingerly. 'If you want privacy, Mr Charleywood's office which adjoins this room is at your disposal.'

Hradsky took his band next door and an hour later when he led them back again they looked like a party of pallbearers. Max was on the verge of tears, he cleared the lump from his throat.

'I think we should examine each item separately,' he said sadly, and three days later they shook hands on the deal.

Duff poured the drinks and gave each man a glass. 'To the new company, Central Rand Consolidated. It has been a long confinement, gentlemen, but I think we have given birth to a child of which we can be proud.'

Hradsky had control, but it had cost him dearly.

Central Rand Consolidated had its christening party on the main floor of the Johannesburg Stock Exchange; ten per cent of the shares were put out for sale to the public. Before the day's dealing began the crowd had overflowed the

Stock Exchange building and jammed in the street for a block in each direction. The President of the Exchange read the prospectus of Central Rand Consolidated; in the cathedral hush his every word carried clearly to the members' lounge. The bell rang and still the hush persisted. Hradsky's authorized clerk broke the silence timidly. 'I sell C.R.C.'s.'

It was nearly a massacre; two hundred men were trying to buy shares from him simultaneously. First his jacket and then his shirt disintegrated beneath the clutching hands; he lost his spectacles, crushed to powdered glass beneath the trampling feet. Ten minutes later he managed to fight his way out of the crowd and reported to his masters, 'I was able to sell them, gentlemen.'

Sean and Duff laughed. They had reason to laugh, for in those ten minutes their thirty per cent holding in C.R.C. had appreciated in value by half a million pounds.

24

That year Christmas dinner at Candy's Hotel was considerably better than it had been five years previously. Seventy-five people sat down to it at one table and by three o'clock, when it ended, only half of them were able to stand up. Sean used the banisters to get up the stairs and at the top he told Candy and Duff solemnly, 'I love you–I love you both desperately–but now I must sleep.' He left them and set off down the corridor bouncing against the walls like a trick billiard shot until he ricocheted through the door into his suite.

'You'd better make sure he's all right, Dufford.'

'A case of the blind drunk leading the blind drunk,' said Duff indistinctly, and also employing the wall to wall route followed Sean down the corridor. Sean was sitting on the edge of his bed wrestling with one of his boots.

'What you trying to do, laddie, break your ankle?'

Sean looked up and smiled beatifically. 'Come in, come in–all four of you. Have a drink.'

'Thanks, I brought my own.'

Duff closed the door behind him like a conspirator and produced a bottle from under his coat. 'She didn't see me–she didn't know her little Dufford had a big beautiful bottle in his inside pocket.'

'Would you mind helping me with this damn boot?' Sean asked.

'That's a very good question,' said Duff seriously as he set a course across the room for one of the armchairs. 'I'm glad you asked it.' He reached the chair and dropped into it. 'The answer, of course, is, Yes! I would mind.'

Sean let his foot drop and lay back on the bed.

'Laddie, I want to talk to you,' Duff said.

'Talk's free–help yourself.'

'Sean, what do you think of Candy?'

'Lovely pair of titties,' Sean opined.

'Sure, but a man cannot live by titties alone.'

'No, but I suppose she's also got the other basic equipment,' Sean said drowsily.

'Laddie, I'm being serious now–I want your help. Do you think I am doing the right thing–this marriage business, I mean.'

'Don't know much about marriage.' Sean rolled over on his face.

'She's calling me Dufford already–did you notice that, laddie? That's an omen, that's an omen of the most frightful portent. Did you notice, hey?' Duff waited a second for an answer which he didn't receive. 'That's what the other one used to call me. "Dufford," she'd say–I can hear it now–"Dufford, you're a pig".'

Duff looked hard at the bed. 'Are you still with me?'

No answer.

'Sean, laddie, I need your help.'

Sean snored softly.

'Oh, you drunken oaf,' said Duff miserably.

25

Xanadu was finished by the end of the January and the wedding was set for the twentieth of February. Duff sent the Commandant and the entire police force of Johannesburg an invitation: in return they put a twenty-four hour a day guard on the ballroom of Xanadu where the wedding gifts were laid out on long trestle tables. Sean drove up with Duff and Candy on the afternoon of the tenth, as Duff put it, to make the latest count of the booty. Sean gave the constable on duty a cigar and then they went through into the ballroom.

'Look, oh look,' squealed Candy. 'There's a whole lot of new presents!'

'This one's from Jock and Trevor,' Sean read the card.

'Open quickly, please, Dufford, let's see what they've given us.'

Duff prised the lid off the case and Sean whistled softly.

'A solid gold dinner service,' gasped Candy. She picked up one of the plates and hugged it to her chest. 'Oh, I just don't know what to say.'

Sean examined the other boxes. 'Hey, Duff, this one will make you specially happy–"Best wishes, N. Hradsky".'

'This I must see,' said Duff with the first enthusiasm he had shown in a month. He unwrapped the parcel.

'A dozen of them!' Duff hooted gleefully. 'Norman, you priceless little Israelite, a whole dozen dish towels.'

'It's the thought that counts,' laughed Sean.

'Dear old Norman, how it must have hurt him to shell out for them! I'll have him autograph them and I'll frame them and hang them in the front hall.'

They left Candy to arrange the presents and they went out into the garden.

'Have you got this mock priest organized?' asked Duff.

'Yes, he's at a hotel in Pretoria. He's in training now–he'll be able to rattle through the service like an old hand when the time comes.'

'You don't think that faking it is just as bad as doing it properly?' asked Duff dubiously.

'It's a hell of a time to think of that now,' said Sean.

'Yes, I suppose it is.'

'Where are you going for the honeymoon?' Sean asked.

'We'll coach down to Capetown and take the mail boat to London, then a month or so on the Continent. Be back here about June.'

'You should have a good time.'

'Why don't you get married as well?'

'What for?' Sean looked surprised.

'Well, don't you feel as though you're letting the old firm down a bit–me going into this alone?'

'No,' said Sean. 'Anyway, who is there to marry?'

'What about that lass you brought to the races last Saturday; she's a lovely piece of work.'

Sean raised an eyebrow. 'Did you hear her giggle?'

'Yes, I did,' admitted Duff. 'You couldn't very well miss it.'

'Can you imagine that giggle coming at you across the breakfast table?' Sean asked.

Duff shuddered. 'Yes, I see your point. But as soon as we get back I'll have Candy start picking you out a suitable female.'

'I've got a better idea, you let Candy run your life and I'll run my own.'

'That, laddie, is what I'm very much afraid is going to happen.'

Hradsky reluctantly agreed that the activities of the group–the mines, the workshops, the transport companies, all of them–should be suspended on the twentieth to allow their employees to attend Duff's nuptials. This meant that half the business on the Witwatersrand would shut down for the day. Consequently, most of the independent companies decided to close as well. On the eighteenth the wagons carrying the food and liquor started caravanning up the hill to Xanadu. Sean in a burst of benevolence that night invited the entire company from the Opera House to the wedding. He remembered it vaguely the next morning and went down to cancel the invitation but Blue Bessie told him that most of the girls had already gone into town to buy new dresses.

'The hell with it then–let them come. I just hope Candy doesn't guess who they are, that's all.'

On the night of the nineteenth Candy gave them the use of the dining-room and all the downstairs lounges of the Hotel for Duff's bachelor party. François arrived with a masterpiece made up in the mine workshops–an enormous ball and chain. This was formally locked on to Duff's leg and the party began.

Afterwards there was a school of thought that maintained that the building contractor commissioned to repair the damage to the Hotel was a bandit and that the bill for just under a thousand pounds that he presented was nothing short of robbery. However, none of them could deny that the Bok-Bok game in the dining-room, played by a hundred men, had done a certain amount of damage to the furniture and fittings; nor that the chandelier had not been able to support Mr Courteney's weight and on the third swing had come adrift from the ceiling and knocked a moderately large hole through the floor. Neither did anyone dispute the fact that after Jock Heyns had tried unsuccessfully for half an hour to shoot a glass off the top of his brother's head with champagne corks, the resulting ankle-deep lake of wine in the one lounge made it necessary for the floor to be relaid. Nevertheless they felt that a thousand was a little bit steep. On one point, however, everyone agreed–it was a memorable party.

At the beginning Sean was worried that Duff's heart wasn't in it for Duff stood by the bar with the metal ball under one arm listening to the lewd comment, with a lopsided grin fixed on his face. After seven or eight drinks Sean stopped worrying about him and went off to have his way with the chandelier. At midnight Duff talked François into releasing him from his chains and he slipped out of the room. No one–least of all Sean–noticed him go.

Sean could never remember how he got to bed that night but next morning he was tactfully awakened by a waiter with a coffee tray and a note.

'What time is it?' asked Sean as he unfolded the note.

'Eight o'clock, baas.'

'No need to shout,' muttered Sean. His eyes focused with difficulty for the pain in his head was pushing them out of their sockets.

Dear Best Man,

This serves as a reminder that you and Duff have an appointment at eleven o'clock. I am relying on you to get him there, whole or in pieces. Love Candy.

The brandy fumes in the back of his throat tasted like chloroform, he washed them out with coffee and lit a cigar which started him coughing, and every cough nearly took the top off his head. He stubbed out the cigar and went to the bathroom. Half an hour later he felt strong enough to wake Duff. He went across the sitting-room and pushed open Duff's door; the curtains in the room were still drawn. He pulled them open and was nearly blinded by the sunlight that poured in through them. He turned to the bed and frowned with surprise. He walked slowly across and sat on the edge of it.

'He must have slept in Candy's room,' Sean muttered as he looked at the unused pillows and neatly tucked blankets. It took a few seconds for him to find the fault in his reasoning.

'Then why did she write that note?' He stood up, feeling the first twinge of alarm. A picture of Duff, drunk and helpless lying out in the yard or knocked over the head by one of the busy Johannesburg footpads, came very clear to mind. He ran across the bedroom and into the sitting-room. Halfway to the door he saw the envelope propped up on the mantelpiece and he took it down.

'What is this, a meeting of the authors' guild?' he muttered. 'The place is thick with letters.'

The paper crackled as he opened it and he recognized Duff's back sloping hand.

The first the worst, the second the same. I'm not going through with it. You're the best man so make my excuses to all the nice people. I'll be back when the dust has settled a little. D.

Sean sat down in one of the armchairs, he read through it twice more. Then he exploded.

'Damn you, Charleywood–"make my excuses". You craven bastard. Walk out and leave me to sweep up the mess.'

He rushed across the room with his dressing-gown flapping furiously round his legs. 'You'll make your own damned excuses–even if I have to drag you back on the end of a rope.'

Sean ran down the back stairs. Mbejane was in the stable yard talking to three of the grooms.

'Where is Nkosi Duff?' Sean roared.

They stared at him blankly.

'Where is he?' Sean's beard bristled.

'The baas took a horse and went for a ride,' answered one of the grooms nervously.

'When?' bellowed Sean.

'In the night–perhaps seven, eight hours ago. He should be back soon.'

Sean stared at the groom, breathing heavily. 'Which way did he go?'

'Baas, he did not say.'

Eight hours ago–he could be fifty miles away by now. Sean turned and went back to his room. He threw himself on the bed and poured another cup of coffee.

'This is going to break her up badly–' He imagined the tears and the chaos of undisciplined grief.

'Oh, hell–damn you to hell, Charleywood.' He sipped the coffee and thought about going as well–taking a horse and getting as far away as possible. 'It's no mess of my making–I want no part of it.' He finished the coffee and started dressing. He looked in the mirror to comb his hair and saw Candy standing alone in the chapel, waiting while the silence turned to murmuring and then to laughter.

'Charleywood, you pig,' Sean scowled. 'I can't let her go up there–it'll be bad enough without that. I'll have to tell her.'

He picked up his watch from the dressing-table, it was past nine.

'Damn you, Charleywood.'

He went down the passage and stopped outside Candy's door. He could hear women's voices inside and he knocked before he went in. There were two of Candy's friends and the coloured girl Martha. They stared at him.

'Where's Candy?'

'In the bedroom–but you mustn't go in. It's bad luck.'

'It's the worst bloody luck in the world,' agreed Sean. He knocked on the bedroom door.

'Who is it?'

'Sean.'

'You can't come in–what do you want?'

'Are you decent?'

'Yes, but you mustn't come in.'

He opened the door and looked in on a confusion of squealing females.

'Get out of here'–he said harshly–'I have to speak to Candy alone.'

They fled and Sean closed the door behind them. Candy was in a dressing-gown. Her face was quick with anticipation; her hair was pulled back and hung shiny and soft. She was beautiful, Sean realized. He looked at the frothy pile of her wedding-dress on the bed.

'Candy, bad news–I'm afraid. Can you take it?' He spoke almost roughly–hating it, hating every second of it.

He saw the bloom on her face wither until her expression was dead–blank and dead as a statue.

'He's gone,' said Sean. 'He's run out on you.'

Candy picked up a brush from her dressing-table and started stroking it listlessly through her hair. It was very quiet in the room.

'I'm sorry, Candy.'

She nodded without looking at him; instead she was looking down the lonely corridor of the future. It was worse than tears would have been, that silent acceptance. Sean scratched the side of his nose–hating it.

'I'm sorry–I wish I could do something about it.' He turned to the door.

'Sean, thank you for coming and telling me.' There was no emotion in her voice; like her face it was dead.

'That's all right,' Sean said gruffly.

He rode up to Xanadu. There were people clustered about the marquees on the lawn; by the quality of their laughter he could tell they were drinking already. The sun was bright and as yet not too hot, the band was playing from the wide veranda of the mansion, the women's dresses were gay against the green of the lawns. 'Gala day' fluttered the flags above the tents. 'Gala day' shouted the laughter.

Sean rode up the drive, lifting his hand in brief acknowledgement of the greetings that were shouted to him. From the vantage point of his horse's back he spotted François and Martin Curtis, glasses in hand, standing near the house talking to two of the Opera girls. He gave his horse to one of the native grooms and strode across towards them.

'Hello, boss,' called Curtis. 'Why so glum–you're not the one getting married.' They all laughed.

'François, Martin, come with me please.'

'What's the trouble, Mr Courteney?' François asked as he led them aside.

'The party's over,' Sean said grimly. 'There'll be no wedding.'

They gaped at him.

'Go around and tell everybody. Tell them they'll get their presents back.'

He turned to leave them.

'What's happened, boss?' Curtis asked.

'Just tell them that Candy and Duff changed their minds.'

'Do you want us to send them home?'

Sean hesitated. 'Oh, the hell with it–let them stay–let them all get sick drunk. Just tell them there'll be no wedding.'

He went up to the house. He found the pseudo-priest waiting nervously in the downstairs study. The man's adam's apple had been rubbed raw by the starch-stiff dog collar.

'We won't need you,' Sean told him.

He took out his cheque book, sat down at the desk and filled in a cheque form.

'That's for your trouble. Now get out of town.'

'Thank you, Mr Courteney, thank you very much.' The man looked mightily relieved; he started for the door.

'My friend,' Sean stopped him. 'If you ever breathe a word about what we planned to do today, I'll kill you. Do I make myself clear?'

Sean went through to the ballroom, he slipped a small stack of sovereigns into the constable's hand.

'Get all these people out of here.' He gestured with his head at the crowds that were wandering among the tables looking at the gifts. 'Then lock the doors.'

He found the chef in the kitchen. 'Take all this food outside–give it to them now. Then lock up the kitchens.'

He went round the house closing the doors and drawing the curtains. When he walked into the study there was a couple on the big leather couch and the man's hand was under the girl's skirts; she was giggling.

'This isn't a whore house,' Sean shouted at them and they left hurriedly. He sank into one of the chairs. He could hear the voices and the laughter from outside on the lawn, the band was playing a Strauss waltz. It irritated him and he scowled at the marble fireplace. His head was aching again and the skin of his face felt dry and tight from the night's debauch.

'What a mess–what a bloody mess,' he said aloud. After an hour he went out and found his horse. He rode out along the Pretoria Road until he had passed the last houses, then he turned off into the veld. He cantered into the sea of grass with his hat pushed back on his head so the sun and the wind could find his face. He sat relaxed and loose in the saddle and let his horse pick its own way. In the late afternoon he came back to Johannesburg and left his horse with Mbejane in the stable yard. He felt better; the exercise and the fresh air had cleared his head and helped him to see things in truer perspective. He ran himself a deep hot bath, climbed into it and while he soaked the last of his anger at Duff smoothed out. He had control of himself again. He got out of the bath and towelled, then he slipped on his gown and went through to the bedroom. Candy was sitting on his bed.

'Hello, Sean.' She smiled at him, a brittle smile. Her hair was a little tangled now, her face was pale and unrouged. She had not changed from the dressing-gown he had seen her in that morning.

'Hello, Candy.' He picked up the cut-glass bottle of bay rum and rubbed some into his hair and beard.

'You don't mind me coming to see you, do you?'

'No, of course not.' He started combing his hair. 'I was about to come and see you myself.'

She drew her legs up under her in the double-jointed manner of women that is impossible for a man to copy.

'Can I have a drink, please?'

'I'm sorry–I thought you never touched the stuff.'

'Oh, today is special.' She laughed too gaily. 'It's my wedding day, you know.'

He poured the brandy without looking at her. He hated this suffering and he felt his anger at Duff coming back strongly. Candy took the drink and sipped it. She pulled a face. 'It tastes awful.'

'It'll do you good.'

'To the bride,' she said and drank it down quickly.

'Another one?' asked Sean.

'No thanks.' She stood up and went across to the window. 'It's getting dark now–I hate the darkness. Darkness distorts things so; what is bad in the daylight is unbearable at night.'

'I'm sorry, Candy, I wish I could help you.'

She whirled and came to him, her arms circled tight round his neck and her face pale and frightened pressed to his chest.

'Oh, Sean, please hold me–I'm so afraid.'

He held her awkwardly.

'I don't want to think about it. Not now, not now in the darkness,' she whispered. 'Please help me. Please help me not to think about it.'

'I'll stay with you. Don't get yourself upset. Come and sit down. I'll get you another drink.'

'No, no,' she clung to him desperately. 'I don't want to be alone. I don't want to think. Please help me.'

'I can't help you–I'll stay with you but that's all I can do.' Anger and pity mixed together in Sean like charcoal and saltpetre; his fingers tightened hard on her shoulders, digging into the flesh until they met bone.

'Yes, hurt me. That way I'll forget for a while. Take me to the bed and hurt me, Sean, hurt me deep.'

Sean caught his breath. 'You don't know what you're saying, that's crazy talk.'

'It's what I want–to forget for a little. Please, Sean, please.'

'I can't do that, Candy, Duff's my friend.'

'He's finished with me and I with him. I'm your friend too. Oh, God, I'm so alone. Don't you leave me too. Help me, Sean, please help me.'

Sean felt his anger slide down from his chest and flare up, cobra-headed, from his thighs. She felt it also.

'Yes, oh please, yes.'

He picked her up and carried her to the bed. He stood over her while he tore off his gown. She moved on the bed shedding her clothing and spreading herself to meet him, to take him in and let him fill the emptiness. He covered her quickly bayoneting through the soft veil and into the warmth of her body. There was no desire in it, it was cruel and hard drawn out to the frontiers of endurance. For him an expression of anger and pity; for her an act of renunciation. Once was not enough. Again and yet again he took her, until there were brown smudges on the bedclothes from his bleeding back, until her body ached and they lay entwined, wet and tired from the fury of it. In the quiescence of after-passion Sean spoke softly. 'It didn't help, did it?'

'Yes, it did.' Physical exhaustion had weakened the barriers that held back her grief. Still holding on to him, she started to cry.

A street lamp outside the room threw a silver square of light on the ceiling. Sean laid on his back and watched it, listening to Candy's sobs. He recognized the moment they reached their climax and followed their decline into silence. They slept then and later before the day woke together as if by arrangement.

'You are the only one who can help him now,' Candy said.

'Help him do what?' asked Sean.

'Find what he is looking for. Peace, himself–whatever you want to call it. He's lost, you know, Sean. He's lost and lonely, almost as lonely as I am. I could have helped him, I'm sure I could.'

'Duff lost?' Sean asked cynically. 'You must be mad!'

'Don't be so blind, Sean, don't be misled by the big talk and the grand manner. Look at the other things.'

'Like what?' asked Sean.

She didn't answer for a while. 'He hated his father, you know.'

'I guessed as much from the little he told me.'

'The way he revolts at any discipline. His attitude to Hradsky, to women, to life. Think about it, Sean, and then tell me if he acts like a happy man.'

'Hradsky did him a disservice once–he just doesn't like him,' Sean defended Duff.

'Oh, no–it's much deeper than that. In a way Hradsky is an image of his father. He's so broken up inside, Sean, that's why he clings to you. You can help him.'

Sean laughed outright. 'Candy, my dear, we like each other, that's all, there are no deep and dark motives in our friendship. Don't you start getting jealous of me now.'

Candy sat up and the blankets slipped down to her waist. She leaned towards Sean and her breasts swung forward, heavy, round and silver-white in the half light.

'There's a strength in you, Sean, a kind of solid sureness in you that you haven't discovered yet. Duff has recognised it and so will other unhappy people. He needs you, he needs you very badly. Look after him for me, help him to find what he seeks.'

'Nonsense, Candy,' Sean muttered with embarrassment.

'Promise me you'll help him.'

'It's time you went back to your room,' Sean told her. 'People will start talking.'

'Promise me, Sean.'

'All right, I promise.'

Candy slipped out of the bed. She dressed quickly. 'Thank you, Sean, goodnight.'

26

For Sean Johannesburg was poorer without Duff: the streets were not so busy, the Rand Club was drearier and the thrills at the Stock Exchange not so intense. However, there was work to do; his share and Duff's as well.

It was late every evening when the conferences with Hradsky and Max ended and he went back to the Hotel. In the reaction from the day's tension, when his brain was numb and his eyes burned, there was little energy to spare for regret. Yet he was lonely. He went to the Opera House and drank champagne with the crowd there. One of the girls did the Can-Can on the big table in the centre of the room and when she stopped in front of Sean and Trevor Heyns, with her forehead touching her knees and her petticoats hanging over her shoulders, Sean let Trevor whip her pants down–a week before he would have punched Trevor in the nose rather than concede the honour. It wasn't so much fun any more. He went home early.

The following Saturday noon Curtis and François came into the office for the weekly progress meeting. When they had finished and Hradsky had left, Sean suggested, 'Come along with me, we'll go and have a pot or twelve at the Grand National Bar, baptize the weekend so to speak.'

Curtis and François fidgeted in their chairs.

'We had arranged to meet some of the other boys down at the Bright Angels, boss.'

'That's fine, I'll come along with you,' said Sean eagerly, the prospect of being with ordinary men again was suddenly very attractive to him. He felt sickened of the company of those who shook his hand and smiled at him while they waited for a chance to wipe him off the board. It would be good to go along with these two and talk mining and not stocks and shares, to laugh with men who didn't give a damn if C.R.C.'s hit sixty shillings on Monday. He'd get a little drunk with François and Martin; later on perhaps he'd have a fight–an honest, snorting, stand-up fight. God, yes, it would be good to be with men who were clean inside–even if there was dirt under their nails and the armpits of their shirts were stained with sweat.

Curtis glanced quickly at François. 'There'll be just a crowd of roughnecks down there, boss, all the diggers come in on a Saturday.'

'That's fine,' said Sean. 'Let's go.'

He stood up and buttoned his dove-grey coat; the lapels were edged in black watered silk and matched the black pearl pin in his tie. He picked up his cane from the desk.

'Come on–let's get moving.'

They ran into the noise from the Bright Angels a block before they reached the building. Sean grinned and quickened his step like an old gun dog with the scent of the bird in its nostrils again. François and Curtis hurried along on either side of him. There was a big digger standing on the bar counter. Sean recognized him as one of his men from the Little Sister Mine; the man's body was tilted back to balance the weight of the demi-john he held to his lips and his throat jerked regularly as he swallowed. The crowd around his feet were chanting:

'Drink it, down, down, down, down, down.'

The digger finished, he threw the bottle against the far wall and belched like an air-locked geyser. He bowed to acknowledge the applause and then he caught sight of Sean standing in the doorway. He wiped his mouth guiltily with the back of his hand and jumped down off the counter. The other men in the crowd turned and saw Sean and the noise tapered off. They spread out along the bar in silence. Sean led François and Curtis into the room. He placed a pile of sovereigns on the counter.

'Set them up, barman, take the orders. Today is Saturday and it's time to tie the dog loose.'

'Cheers, Mr Courteney.'

'Good luck, sir.'

'*Gezondheid,* Mr Courteney.'

Their voices were subdued with respect.

'Drink up, man, there's plenty more where that came from.'

Sean stood with François and Martin at the bar. They laughed at his jokes. His voice was loud with good fellowship and his face flushed with happiness. He bought more drinks. After a while his bladder started making its presence felt and he went through the back door into the washrooms. There were men talking in there; he stopped before he rounded the edge of the screen into the room. '. . . what's he want to come here for, hey? This isn't the mucking Rand Club.'

'Shh! He'll hear you, man, do you want to lose your job?'

'I don't give a damn. Who does he think he is–"Drink up, boys, there's plenty more where that came from–I'm the boss, boys, do as you're told, boys, kiss my arse, boys."' Sean stood paralysed.

'Pipe down, Frank, he'll go just now.'

'The sooner the better, say I, the big dandy bastard with his ten-guinea boots and gold cane. Let him go back where he belongs.'

'You're drunk, man, don't talk so loud.'

'Sure I'm drunk, drunk enough to go in there and tell him to his face . . .'

Sean backed out through the door and walked slowly across the bar to François and Curtis.

'I hope you'll excuse me; I've just remembered there's something I've got to do this afternoon.'

'That's too bad, boss.' Curtis looked relieved. 'Perhaps some other time, hey?'

They were pleased to see him when he went up to the Rand Club. Three men nearly fought one another to buy him a drink.

27

He had dinner with Candy that night and over the liqueurs he told her about it. She listened without interruption until he finished.

'They didn't want me there. I don't see what I've done to them that they should dislike me that way.'

'And it worries you?' she asked.

'Yes, it worries me. I've never had people feel like that towards me before.'

'I'm glad it worries you.' She smiled gently at him. 'One day you're going to grow into quite a nice person.'

'But why do they hate me?' Sean followed his original line of thought.

'They're jealous of you–you say this man said, "ten-guinea boots and gold cane"–that is what's behind it. You're different from them now, you're rich. You can't expect them to accept that.'

'But I've never done anything to them,' he protested.

'You don't have to. One thing I've found in this life–for everything you get you have to pay a price. This is part of the payment you have to make for success.'

'Hell, I wish Duff was here,' said Sean.

'Then Duff would explain to you that it doesn't matter, wouldn't he?' said Candy. '"Who gives a damn for them, laddie, the unwashed herd? We can do without them,"' she mimicked. Sean scratched the side of his nose and looked down at the table.

'Please, Sean, don't ever let Duff teach you that people don't matter. He doesn't believe it himself–but he's so convincing. People are important. They are more important than gold or places or–or anything.'

Sean looked up at her. 'I realized that once; when I was trapped in the Candy Deep. I saw it very clear then in the darkness and the mud. I made a resolution.' He grinned sheepishly. 'I told myself I'd never hurt anyone again if I could help it. I really meant it, Candy. I felt it so strongly at the time–but, but . . .'

'Yes, I think I understand. That's a big resolution to make and a much bigger one to keep. I don't think any single experience is enough to change a person's way of thinking. It's like building a wall brick by brick. You add to it a little at a time until at last it's finished. I've told you before, Sean, that you have a strength in you. I think one day you'll finish building your wall–and when you do, it will have no weak spots.'

28

The next Tuesday Sean rode up to Xanadu for the first time since Duff had left. Johnson and four of the clerks from the office were at work in the ballroom, packing and labelling the presents.

'Nearly finished, Johnson?'

'Just about, Mr Courteney, I'll send a couple of wagons up tomorrow morning to fetch this lot.'

'Yes, do that. I don't want them lying around here any longer.'

He went up the marble staircase and stood on the top landing. The house had a dead feeling to it: new and sterile, it was waiting for people to come into it and bring it to life. He went down the corridor, stopping to look at the paintings that Candy had chosen. They were oils in soft pastels, woman's colours.

'We can do without these–I'll get some fire in them, scarlets and blacks and bright blues.'

He pushed open the door to his own bedroom. This was better: vivid Persian rugs on the floor, walls panelled in dark satiny wood and a bed like a polo field. He lay on the bed and looked up at the scrolled ornate plaster ceiling.

'I wish Duff were back–we can do some real living in this house.' He went downstairs again.

Johnson was waiting at the foot of the stairs. 'All finished, sir.'

'Good man! Off you go, then.'

He went through into the study and walked across to the gun rack. He took down a Purdey shotgun, carried it to the french windows and looked at it in the light. His nostrils flared a little at the nostalgic smell of gun oil. He brought the gun up to his shoulder, felt the true exciting balance of it and enjoyed it. He swung the barrels in an arc across the room, following the flight of an imaginary bird, and suddenly Duff's face was in his sights. Sean was taken so by surprise that he stood with the gun trained at Duff's head.

'Don't shoot, I'll come quietly,' said Duff solemnly.

Sean lowered the shotgun and carried it back to the rack.

'Hello.'

'Hello,' Duff answered, still standing in the doorway. Sean made a pretence of fitting the gun into the rack with his back to Duff.

'How are you, laddie?'

'Fine! Fine!'

'How's everybody else?'

'To whom do you refer, in particular?' Sean asked.

'Candy, for one.'

Sean considered the question. 'Well, you could have damaged her more by feeding her into a stamp mill.'

'Bad, hey?'

'Bad,' agreed Sean.

They stood in silence for a while.

'I take it that you are not very well disposed towards me either,' Duff said at last.

Sean shrugged his shoulders and moved across to the fireplace.

'Dufford, you're a pig,' he said conversationally.

Duff winced. 'Well, it was nice knowing you, laddie. I suppose from here on our paths diverge?'

'Don't drivel, Duff, you're wasting time. Pour the drinks and then you can tell me what it feels like being a pig. Also I want to discuss with you those paintings Candy has plastered along the upstairs corridor. I don't know whether to give them away or burn them.'

Duff straightened up from leaning against the door jamb; he tried to stop the relief showing on his face but Sean went on quickly, 'Before we close the lid on the subject and bury it, I want to tell you this. I don't like what you did. I can see why you did it, but I don't like it. That's my piece said. Have you got anything to add to it?'

'No,' said Duff.

'All right then. I think you'll find a bottle of Courvoisier right at the back of the cabinet behind the whisky decanter.'

Sean went down to Candy's Hotel that evening and found Candy in her office.

'He's back, Candy.'

'Oh!' Candy caught her breath. 'How is he, Sean?'

'A little chastened, but not much.'

'I didn't mean that–I meant is he well?'

'The same as ever. He had the grace to ask how you were,' said Sean.

'What did you tell him?' asked Candy.

Sean shrugged and sat down in the chair next to her desk. He looked at the tall stacks of sovereigns that Candy was counting.

'Is that last night's bar takings?' he asked, avoiding her question.

'Yes,' she answered absently.

'You're rich–will you marry me?' he smiled.

Candy stood up and walked across to the window.

'I suppose you two will be moving up to Xanadu now,' she said. Sean grunted and she went on quickly. 'The Heyns brothers will take over the Victoria rooms–they've spoken to me about it already, so don't worry about that. You'll have fun up there, it will be marvellous for you. I bet you'll have parties every night and crowds of people. I don't mind, I've gotten used to the idea now.'

Sean stood up and went to her, he took her gently by the elbow and turned her to face him. He gave her the silk handkerchief out of his top pocket to blow her nose.

'Do you want to see him again, Candy?'

She shook her head, not trusting her voice.

'I'll look after him like I promised.' He gave her a hug and turned to go.

'Sean,' she called after him. He looked back. 'You'll come to see me sometimes. We could have dinner and talk a little. You'll still be my friend, won't you?'

'Of course, Candy, of course, my dear.'

She smiled damply. 'If you pack your things and Duff's I'll have them sent up to Xanadu for you.'

29

Sean looked across the boardroom table at Duff, seeking his support. Duff blew a thick ring of cigar smoke. It spun and expanded like a ripple in a pond before it hit the table top and disintegrated. Duff wasn't going to back him up, Sean realized bitterly. They had argued half the previous night. He had hoped that Duff might still change his mind. Now he knew he wouldn't. He made one last appeal.

'They have asked for a ten per cent wage increase. I believe they need it–prices have soared in this town, but wages have remained the same. These men have wives and children, gentlemen, can't we take that into account?'

Duff blew another smoke ring and Hradsky pulled his watch from his pocket and looked at it pointedly. Max coughed and interrupted. 'I think we've been over that before, Mr Courteney. Could we put it to the vote now?'

Sean watched Hradsky's hand go up against him. He didn't want to look at Duff. He didn't want to see him vote with Hradsky, but he forced himself to turn his head. Duff's hands were on the table in front of him. He blew another smoke ring and watched it hit the table top.

'Those in favour of the motion?' asked Max, and Duff and Sean raised their right hands together. Sean realized then how much it would have meant if Duff had voted against him. Duff winked at him and he couldn't help grinning.

'That is thirty votes for, and sixty against,' declared Max. 'Therefore Mr Courteney's motion falls to the ground. I will inform the Mineworkers' Union of the decision. Now is there any other business before we close the meeting?'

Sean walked with Duff back to his own office.

'The only reason I supported you was because I knew Hradsky would win anyway,' said Duff pleasantly. Sean snorted.

'He's right, of course,' Duff went on unperturbed as he held open the door to Sean's office. 'A ten per cent wage increase would jump the group working costs up ten thousand a month.'

Sean kicked the door closed behind them and didn't answer.

'For God's sake, Sean, don't carry this goodwill-towards-men attitude to absurdity. Hradsky's right–Kruger is likely to slap another one of his taxes on us at any moment and we've got to finance all that new development on the East Rand. We can't let production costs creep up now.'

'All right,' gruffed Sean. 'It's all settled. I just hope we don't have a strike on our hands.'

'There are ways of dealing with strikes. Hradsky has got the police on our side and we can have a couple of hundred men up from Kimberley in no time at all,' Duff told him.

'Damn it, Duff, it's wrong. You know it's wrong. That grotesque Buddha with the little eyes knows it's wrong. But what can I do? Damn it, what can I do?' Sean exploded. 'I feel so bloody helpless.'

'Well, you're the one who wanted to give him control.' Duff laughed at him. 'Stop trying to change the world and let's go home.'

Max was waiting for them in the outer office. He looked nervous. 'Excuse me, gentlemen, could I have a word with you?'

'Who's talking,' Sean asked abruptly, 'you or Hradsky?'

'It's a private matter, Mr Courteney.' Max dropped his voice.

'Can't it wait until tomorrow?' Sean pushed past him and kept going for the door.

'Please, Mr Courteney, it's of the utmost importance.'

Max plucked desperately at Sean's arm.

'What is it, Max?' Duff asked.

'I have to speak to you alone.' Max dropped his voice again and glanced unhappily at the street door.

'Well, speak then,' Duff encouraged him. 'We're alone now.'

'Not here. Can you meet me later?'

Duff raised an eyebrow. 'What is this, Maximilian, don't tell me you are selling dirty pictures.'

'Mr Hradsky is waiting for me at the hotel. I told him I was coming to find some papers, he'll get suspicious if I don't go back immediately.' Max was nearly in tears; his Adam's apple played hide-and-seek behind his high collar, bobbing out and disappearing again. Duff was suddenly very interested in what Max had to say.

'You don't want Norman to know about this?' he asked.

'My goodness, no.' Max came closer to tears.

'When do you want to meet us?'

'Tonight, after ten o'clock when Mr Hradsky has retired.'

'Where?' asked Duff.

'There's a side road round the east end of the Little Sister Mine dump. It's not used any more.'

'I know it,' said Duff. 'We'll ride along there about half past ten.'

'Thank you, Mr Charleywood, you won't regret it.' Max scampered for the door and disappeared.

Duff adjusted his beaver at the correct angle, then he prodded Sean in the belly with the point of his cane.

'Smell it–suck it in.' Duff sniffed appreciatively and Sean did the same.

'I don't smell a thing,' Sean declared.

'The air is thick with it,' Duff told him. 'The sweet smell of treachery.'

They left Xanadu just after half past nine. Duff insisted on wearing a black opera cloak.

'Atmosphere is vital, laddie, you can't go to a rendezvous like this dressed in dirty khaki pants and *veldschoen*. It would ruin the whole thing.'

'Well, I'm damned if I'm going to get into fancy dress. This is a very good suit. It will have to do.'

'Can't I persuade you to wear a pistol in your belt?' asked Duff wistfully.

'No,' laughed Sean.

'No?' Duff shook his head. 'You're a barbarian, laddie. No taste, that's your trouble.'

They avoided the main streets on their way through Johannesburg and met the Cape road half a mile beyond the town. There was only a minute slice of moon left in the dark bowl of the sky. The stars, however, were big and by their light the white mine dumps, each the size of a large hill, stood out like pustules on the earth's face.

Despite himself, Sean felt a little breathless with excitement–Duff's zest was always infectious. They cantered with their stirrups almost touching. Duff's cloak billowing out behind him and the breeze of their passage fanning the tip of Sean's cigar to a fierce red spark.

'Slow down, Duff, the turning's just about here somewhere. It's overgrown, we'll miss it.'

They reined to a walk.

'What's the time?' asked Duff.

Sean drew on his cigar and held his watch close to the glow. 'A quarter after ten. We're early.'

'My bet is Maximilian will be there before us–here's the road.' Duff turned his horse on to it and Sean followed him. The Little Sister Mine dump rose up next to them, steep and white in the starlight. They skirted it but its bulk threw a shadow over them. Duff's horse snorted and shied and Sean gripped with his knees as his own horse danced sideways. Max had stepped out from a scraggy cluster of bushes next to the road.

'Well met by moonlight, Maximilian,' Duff greeted him.

'Please bring your horses off the road, gentlemen.' Max was still showing signs of the afternoon's agitation. They tied their horses next to Max's among the bushes and walked across to join him.

'Well, Max, what's new? How are the folks?' Duff asked.

'Before we go any further in this matter, I want you gentlemen to give me your word of honour that, whether anything comes of it or not, you will never say a word to anybody of what I tell you tonight.' Max was very pale, Sean thought, or perhaps it was just the starlight.

'I agree to that,' said Sean.

'Cross my heart,' said Duff.

Max opened the front of his coat and brought out a long envelope. 'I think if I show you these first it will make it easier to explain my proposition.'

Sean took the envelope from him. 'What are they, Max?'

'The latest statements from all four banks at which Mr Hradsky deals.'

'Matches, Sean, give us a light, laddie,' said Duff eagerly.

'I have a lantern with me,' Max said and he squatted down to light it. Sean and Duff squatted with him and spread the bank statements in the circle of yellow light. They examined them in silence until at last Sean rocked back on his heels and lit another cigar.

'Well, I am glad I don't owe that much money,' Sean announced. Sean folded up the sheets and put them back in the envelope. He slapped the envelope into the palm of his free hand and started chuckling. Max reached across, took it from him and placed it carefully back inside his coat.

'All right, Max, spell it out for us,' said Sean. Max leaned forward and blew out the lantern. What he had to say was easier said in darkness.

'The large cash payment that Mr Hradsky had to make to you gentlemen and the limitation of output from his diamond mines in terms of the new cartel agreements in the diamond industry have forced him to borrow heavily on all his banks.' Max stopped and cleared his throat. 'The extent of this borrowing you have seen. Of course, the banks demanded security for the loans and Mr Hradsky has given them his entire holding of C.R.C. shares. The banks have set a limit on the shares of thirty-five shillings each. As you know C.R.C.'s are currently quoted at ninety shillings, which leaves a wide margin of safety. However, if the shares were to suffer a set-back and fall in price to thirty-five shillings the banks would sell. They would dump every single share that Mr Hradsky owns in C.R.C.'s on to the market.'

'Go on, Max,' said Duff. 'I'm beginning to like the sound of your voice.'

'It occurred to me that if Mr Hradsky was temporarily absent from Johannesburg–say if he went on a trip to England to buy new machinery or something of that nature–it would be possible for you gentlemen to force the price of C.R.C.'s down to thirty five shillings. Done correctly it would only take three or four days to accomplish. You could sell short and start rumours that the Leader Reef had pinched out at depth. Mr Hradsky would not be here to defend his interests and as soon as C.R.C.'s hit thirty-five shillings the banks would off-load his shares. The price would crash and you, with ready cash available, would be in a position to buy up C.R.C. shares at a fraction of their actual value. There is no reason why you shouldn't gain control of the group and make a couple of million to boot.'

There was another silence. It lasted a long time before Sean asked, 'What do you get out of it, Max?'

'Your cheque for one hundred thousand pounds, Mr Courteney.'

'Wages are going up,' remarked Sean. 'I thought the standard pay for this type of work was thirty pieces of silver. The rate, I believe, was set by a countryman of yours.'

'Shut up,' snapped Duff, then more pleasantly to Max, 'Mr Courteney likes his little jokes. Tell me, Max, is that all you want–just the money? I'll be frank with you–it doesn't ring true. You must be a moderately rich man as it is.'

Max stood up quickly and started towards the horses. He hadn't reached them before he swung around. His face was in darkness but his voice was naked as he screamed at them.

'Do you think I don't know what they call me–"The Court Jester", "Hradsky's tongue", "Lick-arse". Do you think I like it? Do you think I enjoy crawling to him every minute of every day? I want to be free again. I want to be a man again.' His voice choked off and his hands came up and covered his face. He was sobbing. Sean couldn't watch him and even Duff looked down at the ground in embarrassment. When Max spoke again it was in his usual soft and sad voice.

'Mr Courteney, if you wear your yellow waistcoat to the office tomorrow, I will take it as a sign that you intend to follow my suggestion and that my terms are acceptable to you. I will then make the necessary arrangements to ensure Mr Hradsky's absence from the country.' He untied his horse, mounted and rode away down the track towards the Cape Road. Neither Sean nor Duff moved to stand up. They listened to the hoof-beats of Max's horse fade into the darkness, before Duff spoke. 'Those bank statements were genuine–I had a good look at the seals.'

'And even more genuine was Max's emotion.' Sean flicked his cigar away into the bushes. 'No one could act that well. It made me feel quite sick listening to him. Hell, how can a man so cold-bloodedly betray his trust?'

'Laddie, let's not turn this into a discussion of Max's morals. Let's concern ourselves with the facts. Norman has been delivered into our hands, neatly trussed, spiced with garlic and with a sprig of parsley behind each ear. I say let's cook him and eat him.'

Sean smiled at him. 'Give me a few good reasons. I want you to convince me. The way I feel towards him after that meeting this afternoon, I shouldn't be surprised if I convince easily.'

'One,' Duff held up a finger. 'Norman deserves it.'

Sean nodded.

'Two,' another of Duff's fingers came up. 'If we gain control we can run things the way we want. You can indulge your good resolution and give everybody a pay rise and I'll be top man again.'

'Yes!' Sean tugged at his moustache thoughtfully.

'Three. We came here to make money, we'll never get another opportunity like this. And my last reason, but the most potent–you look so beautiful in that yellow waistcoat, laddie, I wouldn't miss seeing you in it tomorrow morning, not for a thousand C.R.C. shares.'

'It is rather natty,' admitted Sean. 'But listen, Duff, I don't want another Lochtkamper business. Messy, you know.'

Duff stood up.

'Norman's a big boy, he wouldn't do that. Anyway, he'll still be rich–he's got his diamond mines. We'll only be relieving him of his responsibilities on the Witwatersrand.'

They walked across to the horses. Sean had his foot in the stirrup when he stiffened and exclaimed, 'My God, I can't do it. It's all off.'

'Why?' Duff was alarmed.

'I spilt gravy on that waistcoat–I can't possibly wear it tomorrow. My tailor would murder me.'

30

There was no problem in arranging Hradsky's absence–someone had to go to London. There was machinery to buy for the new areas on the East Rand and they had to select two engineers from the hundred or so applicants waiting in England. Not ungraciously, Hradsky allowed himself to be elected for the job.

'We'll give him a farewell party,' Duff suggested to Sean during dinner that night. 'Well, not really a farewell party–but a wake.'

Sean started whistling the 'Dead March' and Duff tapped it out on the table with the handle of his knife.

'We'll have it at Candy's Hot–' Duff cut himself short. 'We'll have it here. We'll really lay it on for poor old Norman so afterwards he'll be able to say, "the bastards may have cleaned me out, but they certainly gave me a grand party".'

'He doesn't like parties,' said Sean.

'That's an excellent reason why we should give him one,' agreed Duff.

A week later when Hradsky and Max left on the morning coach for Port Natal there were fifty members of the Johannesburg Stock Exchange still in full evening dress from the night's party to wave him goodbye. Duff made a touching, if somewhat slurred, little speech and presented Hradsky with a bouquet of roses. Nervous of the crowd that milled about them, the horses bolted when the driver cracked his whip and Max and Hradsky were thrown together in an undignified heap on the rear seat of the coach. The crowd cheered them out of sight. With an arm around his shoulder Sean led Duff across the street to the office and deposited him in one of the deep leather armchairs.

'Are you sober enough to talk sense?' Sean asked dubiously.

'Sure. Always at your service as the lady said to the customer.'

'I managed to have a word with Max last night,' Sean told him. 'He will send us a telegram from Port Natal when he and Hradsky are safely on the mailboat. We won't start anything until we receive it.'

'Very wise–you're the wisest chap I know,' Duff grinned happily.

'You'd better go to bed,' Sean told him.

'Too far,' said Duff. 'I'll sleep here.'

It was another ten days before Max's telegram arrived. Sean and Duff were eating lunch in the Rand Club when it was delivered to their table. Sean slit open the envelope and read the message to Duff.

'Sailing four o'clock this afternoon. Good luck. Max.'

'I'll drink to that,' Duff lifted his wine glass.

'Tomorrow,' said Sean, 'I'll go up to the Candy Deep and tell François to pull all the men out of the bottom levels of the mine. No one's to be allowed in.'

'Put a guard at the fourteenth level,' suggested Duff. 'That'll make it more impressive.'

'Good idea,' agreed Sean. He looked up as someone passed their table and suddenly he started to smile. 'Duff, do you know who that is?'

'Who are you talking about?' Duff looked bewildered.

'That chap who's just gone out into the lounge–there he is, going into the lavatories.'

'Isn't that Elliott, the newspaper fellow?'

'Editor of the *Rand Mail*,' nodded Sean. 'Come with me, Duff.'

'Where are we going?'

'To get a bit of cheap publicity.'

Duff followed Sean out of the dining-room, across the lounge and into the men's lavatories. The door of one of the closets was closed and as they walked in someone farted softly behind it. Sean winked at Duff and went across to the urinal. As he addressed himself to it he said, 'Well, all we can hope for now, Duff, is that Norman will be able to work a miracle in England. Otherwise–' He shrugged his shoulder. Duff picked up his cue.

'We're taking a hell of a chance relying on that. I still say we should sell out now. C.R.C.'s were at ninety-one shillings this morning so it's obvious that the story hasn't leaked out yet. But when it does you won't be able to give the bloody shares away. I say we should get out while the going's good.'

'No,' Sean disagreed. 'Let's wait until we hear from Norman. It's taking a bit of a chance, I know, but we have a responsibility to the men working for us.' Sean took Duff's arm and led him out of the lavatory again; at the door he added the cherry to the top of the pie. 'If and when C.R.C. collapses there are going to be thousands of men out of work–do you realize that?'

Sean closed the door behind them and they grinned delightedly at each other.

'You're a genius, laddie,' whispered Duff.

'I'm happy to say I agree with you,' Sean whispered back.

The next morning Sean woke with the knowledge that something exciting was going to happen that day. He lay and savoured the feeling before he sent his mind out to hunt for the reason. Then he sat up suddenly and reached for the newspaper that lay folded on the coffee tray beside his bed. He shook it open and found what he was looking for on the front page, big headlines: *Is all well with the Central Rand Consolidated? Norman Hradsky's mystery journey.* The story itself was a masterpiece of journalistic evasion. Seldom had Sean seen anyone write so fluently or convincingly on a subject about which he knew nothing. 'It is suggested', Usually reliable sources report' and 'There is reason to believe'–all the old phrases of no significance. Sean groped for his slippers and padded down the corridor to Duff's room.

Duff had all the blankets and most of the bed; the girl was curled up like a pink anchovy on the outskirts. Duff was snoring and the girl whimpered a little in her sleep. Sean tickled Duff's lips with the tassel of his dressing-gown cord. Duff's nose twitched and his snores gurgled into silence. The girl sat up and looked at Sean with eyes wide but vacant from sleep.

'Quickly, run,' Sean shouted at her, 'the rebels are coming.'

She leapt straight into the air and landed three feet from the bed quivering with panic. Sean ran a critical eye of her. A pretty filly, he decided, and made a mental note to take her for a trot just as soon as Duff put her out to grass.

'All right,' he reassured her, 'they've gone away now.'

She became aware of her nakedness and Sean's frank appraisal of it. She tried to cover it with hands too small for the task. Sean picked up Duff's gown from the foot of the bed and handed it to her.

'Go and have a bath or something, sweetheart, I want to talk to Mr Charleywood.'

With the gown on she recovered her composure and told him severely, 'I didn't have any clothes on, Mr Courteney.'

'I would never have guessed,' said Sean politely.

'It's not nice.'

'You are too modest–I thought it was better than average. Off you go now, there's a good girl.' With a saucy flick of her head she disappeared into the bathroom and Sean transferred his attention to Duff. Duff had held grimly on to the threads of sleep throughout the exchange but he let go when Sean whacked him across the backside with the folded newspaper. Like a tortoise coming out of its shell his head emerged from the blankets. Sean handed him the paper and sat down on the edge of the bed. He watched Duff's face crease into laughter lines before he spoke.

'You better get down to the Editor's office and shout at him a little–just to confirm his suspicions. I'll go up to the Candy Deep and close all the bottom levels. I'll meet you back at the Exchange at opening time and don't forget to clean that grin off your face before you show it round town. Try to look haggard, it shouldn't be difficult for you.'

When Sean arrived at the Stock Exchange building the crowd had filled the street outside. Mbejane eased the landau into it and it opened to give them a passage. Sean scowled straight ahead and ignored the questions which were shouted at him from all around. Mbejane stopped the carriage outside the main entrance and four police constables held back the mob while Sean hurried across the pavement and through the double doors. Duff was there ahead of him, the centre of a turbulent circle of members and brokers. He saw Sean and waved frantically over the heads of his inquisitors. That was sufficient to switch their attention from Duff to Sean and they flocked to him, ringing him in with anxious angry faces. Sean's hat was knocked forward over his eyes and a button popped off his coat as one of them caught hold of his lapels.

'Is it true?' the man shouted, spittle flying from his lips into Sean's face. 'We've got a right to know if it's true.'

Sean swung his cane in a full overarm stroke on to the man's head and sent him tottering backwards into the arms of those behind him.

'Back, you bastards,' he roared at them using both the point and the edge of his cane to beat them away, scattering them across the floor until he stood alone, glowering at them with the cane still twitching restlessly in his hand.

'I'll make a statement later on. Until then, behave yourselves.' He adjusted his hat, picked the loose thread where the button had been from his coat and stalked across to join Duff. He could see Duff's grin starting to lift the corner of his mouth and he cautioned him silently with his eyes. Grim-faced they walked through into the members' lounge.

'How's it going your end?' Duff kept his voice low.

'Couldn't be better.' Sean contrived a worried expression. 'I've got an armed guard on the fourteenth level. When this bunch hear about that, they'll really start frothing at the mouth.'

'When you make your statement, let it ring with obvious false confidence,' Duff instructed. 'If it goes on like this we'll have the shares down to thirty-five shillings within an hour of opening.'

Five minutes before opening time Sean stood in the President's box and made his address to his fellow members, Duff listened to him with mounting admiration. Sean's hearty reassurances and verbal side-stepping were enough to strike despair into the souls of the most hardened optimists. Sean finished his speech and climbed down from the box amid a gloomy lack of applause. The bell rang and the brokers stood singly or in small disconsolate groups about the floor. The first tentative offer was made. 'I sell C.R.C.'

But there was no rush to buy. Ten minutes later there was a sale recorded at eighty-five shillings, six shillings lower than the previous day's closing price. Duff leaned across to Sean. 'We'll have to start selling some of our own shares to get things moving, otherwise everybody's going to keep sitting on the fence.'

'That's all right,' Sean nodded, 'we'll buy them back later at a quarter of the price. But wait until the news about the Candy Deep gets out.'

It was just before ten o'clock when that happened. The reaction was sharp. In one quick burst of selling C.R.C.'s dropped to sixty shillings. But there they hung, fluctuating nervously in the chaos of hope and doubt.

'We'll have to sell now,' whispered Duff, 'they are short of script. We'll have to give it to them otherwise the price will stick here.'

Sean felt his hands trembling and he clenched them in his pockets. Duff was showing signs of the strain as well, there was a nerve jumping in his cheek and his eyes had receded into their sockets a little. This was a game with high stakes.

'Don't overdo it–sell thirty thousand.'

The price of C.R.C.'s sagged under the weight but levelled out at forty-five shillings. There was still another hour until high change and Sean's whole body was screwed up tight with tension. He felt the cold patches of sweat under his arms.

'Sell another thirty thousand,' he ordered his clerk and even to himself his voice sounded wheezy. He stubbed out his cigar in the copper ashtray next to his chair; it was already half full of butts. It was no longer necessary for either of them to act worried. This time the price stuck at forty shillings and the sale of sixty thousand more of their shares failed to move it down more than a few shillings.

'Someone's buying up,' muttered Sean uneasily.

'It looks like it,' agreed Duff. 'I'll lay odds it's that bloody Greek Efthyvoulos. It looks as if we'll have to sell enough to glut him before they'll drop any further.'

By high change Duff and Sean had sold three-quarters of their holdings in C.R.C.'s and the price still stood stubbornly at thirty-seven and sixpence. So tantalizingly close to the magic figure that would release a flood of Hradsky's shares on to the unprepared market, but now they were nearing the stage when they would no longer have any shares with which to force the price down that last two and sixpence.

The market closed and left Duff and Sean sitting limply in their armchairs, shaken and tired as prizefighters at the end of the fifteenth round. Slowly the lounge emptied but still they sat on. Sean leaned across and put his hand on Duff's shoulder. 'It's going to be all right,' he said. 'Tomorrow it will be all right.'

They looked at each other and they exchanged strength, each of them drawing it from the other until they were both smiling. Sean stood up. 'Come on, let's go home.'

Sean went to bed early and alone. Although he felt drained of energy, sleep was a long time coming to him and when it did it was full of confused dreams and punctuated with sharp jerks back into wakefulness. It was almost a relief to see the dawn define the windows as grey squares and to be released from his unrewarding rest. At breakfast he drank a cup of coffee and found that his stomach was unable to accept the plateful of steak and eggs that was offered it for it was already screwing up tight in anticipation of the day ahead. Duff was edgy and tired-looking as well; they spoke only a little during the meal and not at all in the carriage when Mbejane drove them down to the Exchange.

The crowd was outside the Stock Exchange again. They forced their way through it and into the building; they took their seats in the lounge and Sean looked round at the faces of his fellow members. In each of them were the marks of worry, the same darkness round the eyes and the jerkiness in movement. He watched Jock Heyns yawn extravagantly and had to do the same; he lifted his hand to cover his mouth and found it was trembling again. He laid the hand on the arm of his chair and kept it still. Across the lounge Bonzo Barnes caught Sean's eye and looked away quickly, then he also gaped into a cavernous yawn. It was the tension. In the years ahead Sean would see men yawn like that while they waited for the dawn to send them against the Boer guns. Duff leaned across to him and broke his line of thought.

'As soon as the trading starts, we'll sell. Try and panic them. Do you agree?'

'Sudden death,' Sean nodded. He couldn't face another morning of that mental agony. 'Couldn't we offer shares at thirty-two shillings and sixpence and get it over with?' he asked.

Duff grinned at him. 'We can't do that, it's too obvious–we'll just have to go on suffering to sell at best and let the price fall on its own.'

'I suppose you're right–but we'll play our high cards now and dump the rest of our shares as soon as the market opens. I don't see how the price can possibly hold after that.'

Duff nodded. He beckoned to their authorized clerk who was waiting patiently at the door of the lounge and when the man came up to them he told them, 'Sell one hundred thousand C.R.C.'s at best.'

The clerk blinked but he jotted the order down on his pad and went out on to the main floor where the other brokers were gathering. It was a few minutes from the bell.

'What if it doesn't work?' Sean asked. The tightness in his belly was nauseating him.

'It must work–it's got to work,' Duff whispered as much to himself as to Sean. He was twisting his fingers round the head of his cane and chewing against clenched teeth. They sat and waited for the bell and when it rang Sean jumped then reached sheepishly for his cigar case. He heard their clerk's voice, raised sharply, 'I sell C.R.C.'s,' and then the confused mumble of voices as the trading started. Through the lounge door he saw the recorder chalk up the first sale. 'Thirty-seven shillings.'

He drew hard on his cigar and lay back in his chair forcing himself to relax, ignoring the restless tapping of Duff's fingers on the arm of the chair next to him. The recorder wiped out the figures and wrote again. 'Thirty-six shillings.'

Sean blew out cigar smoke in a long jet. 'It's moving,' he whispered and Duff's hand clenched on the arm of the chair, his knuckles paling from the pressure of his grip.

'Thirty-five.' The elusive number at last. Sean heard Duff sigh next to him and his voice, 'Now! watch it go, laddie, now the banks will come on. Get ready, laddie, get ready now.'

'Thirty-four and six,' wrote the recorder.

'They must come in now,' said Duff again. 'Get ready to get rich, laddie.'

Their clerk was coming back across the floor and into the lounge. He stopped in front of their chairs. 'I managed to sell them, sir.'

Sean straightened up quickly. 'So soon?' he asked.

'Yes, sir, three big sales and I got rid of them all. I'm afraid the last was only at thirty-four and sixpence.'

Sean stared back at the board. The figure was still at thirty-four and sixpence.

'Duff, something's going on here. Why haven't the banks come in yet?'

'We'll force them to off-load.' Duff's voice was unnaturally hoarse. 'We'll force the bastards.' He pulled himself half out of his chair and snarled at the clerk.

'Sell another one hundred thousand at thirty shillings.' The man's face went slack with surprise. 'Hurry, man, do you hear me? What are you waiting for?' The clerk backed away from Duff, then he turned and scurried out of the lounge.

'Duff, for God's sake.' Sean grabbed his arm. 'Have you gone mad?'

'We'll force them,' muttered Duff. 'They'll have to sell.'

'We haven't got another hundred thousand shares.' Sean jumped up. 'I'm going to stop him.' He ran across the lounge but before he reached the door he saw the sale being chalked up on the board at thirty shillings. He pushed his way across the crowded floor until he reached his clerk. 'Don't sell any more,' he whispered.

The man looked surprised. 'I've sold them already, sir.'

'The whole hundred thousand?' There was horrified disbelief in Sean's voice.

'Yes, sir, someone took the lot in one batch.'

Sean walked back across the floor in a daze. He sank into the chair beside Duff.

'They're sold already.' He spoke as though he didn't believe himself.

'We'll force them, we'll force them to sell,' muttered Duff again and Sean turned to him with alarm. Duff was sweating in little dewdrops across his forehead and his eyes were very bright.

'Duff, for God's sake,' Sean whispered to him, 'steady man.' Sean knew that they were watched by everybody in the lounge. The watching faces seemed as large as those seen through a telescope and the buzz of their voices echoed strangely in his ears. Sean felt confused: everything seemed to be in slow motion like a bad dream. He looked through into the trading floor and saw the crude number thirty still chalked accusingly against C.R.C. Where are the banks? Why weren't they selling?

'We'll force them, we'll force the bastards,' Duff said again. Sean tried to answer him but the words wouldn't come. He looked back across the trading floor and now he knew it was a bad dream for Hradsky and Max were there, walking across the floor towards the members' lounge. Men were crowding around them and Hradsky was smiling and holding up his hands as if to fend off their questions. They came through into the lounge and Hradsky went to his chair by the fireplace. He lowered himself into it with his shoulder sagging forward and his waistcoat wrinkled tightly around the full bag of his belly. He was still smiling and Sean thought that his smile was one of the most unnerving things he had ever seen. He watched it with flesh-crawling fascination and beside him Duff was just as still and stricken. Max spoke quietly to Hradsky and then he stood up and walked across to Sean and Duff. He stopped in front of them.

'The clerk informs us that you have contracted to sell to Mr Hradsky five hundred thousand shares in C.R.C.'s at an average price of thirty-six shillings.' Max's lashes drooped sadly on to his cheeks. 'The total issue of C.R.C.'s, as you know, is one million shares. During the last two days Mr Hradsky was able to purchase another seventy-five thousand shares apart from the ones you sold to him. This makes his total holdings of C.R.C.'s almost six hundred thousand shares. It seems therefore that you have sold shares that don't exist. Mr Hradsky foresees that you will have some difficulty fulfilling your contract.'

Sean and Duff went on staring at him. He turned to leave them and Duff blurted out, 'But the banks–why didn't the banks sell?'

Max smiled a mournful little smile. 'The day he reached Port Natal Mr Hradsky transferred sufficient funds from his accounts there to liquidate his overdrafts in Johannesburg. He sent you that telegram and returned here immediately. We only arrived an hour ago.'

'But–but, you lied to us. You tricked us!'

Max inclined his head. 'Mr Charleywood, I will not discuss honesty with a man who does not understand the meaning of the word.' He went back to Hradsky's side. Everyone in the lounge had heard him and while Duff and Sean went on sitting among the ruins of their fortune the struggle to buy C.R.C. shares started on the main floor. In five minutes the price was over ninety shillings and still climbing. When it reached one hundred shillings, Sean touched Duff's arm.

'Let's go.' They stood up together and started for the door of the members' lounge. As they passed Hradsky's chair he spoke.

'Yes, Mr Charleywood, you can't win all the time.' It came out quite clearly with only a slight catch on the 'c's'–they were always difficult letters for Norman Hradsky.

Duff stopped, he turned to face Hradsky, his mouth opened as he struggled to find a reply. His lips moved, groping, groping for words–but there were none. His shoulders drooped, he shook his head and turned away. He stumbled once at the edge of the floor. Sean held his arm and guided him through the excited jabber of brokers. No one took any notice of the two of them. They were bumped and jostled before they were through the crush and out on to the pavement. Sean signalled Mbejane to bring the carriage. They climbed into it and Mbejane drove them to Xanadu.

They went through into the drawing-room.

'Get me a drink, please, Sean.' Duff's face was grey and crumpled-looking. Sean poured two tumblers half full of brandy and carried one across to Duff. Duff drank and then sat staring into the empty glass.

'I'm sorry–I lost my head. I thought we'd be able to buy those shares for dirt, when the banks started selling.'

'It doesn't matter,' Sean's voice was tired. 'We were smashed before that happened. Christ! What a well-laid trap it was!'

'We couldn't have known. It was so damn cunning, we couldn't have guessed, could we, Sean?' Duff was trying to excuse himself.

Sean kicked off his boots and loosened his collar. 'That night up at the mine dump–I would have staked my life Max wasn't lying.' He lay back in the chair and stirred his brandy with a circular movement of his hand. 'Christ, how they must have laughed to see us stampede into the pitfall!'

'But we aren't finished, Sean, we aren't completely finished, are we?' Duff was pleading with him, begging for a peg to hang his hope on. 'We'll come out of this all right, you know we will, don't you? We'll save enough out of the wreckage to start again. We'll build it all up again, won't we, Sean?'

'Sure,' Sean laughed brutally. 'You can get a job down at the Bright Angels cleaning out the spittoons and I'll get one at the Opera House playing the piano.'

'But–but–there'll be something left. A couple of thousand even. We could sell this house.'

'Don't dream, Duff, this house belongs to Hradsky. Everything belongs to him.' Sean flicked the brandy that was left in his glass into his mouth and swallowed it. He stood up quickly and went across to the liquor cabinet. 'I'll explain it to you. We owe Hradsky a hundred thousand shares that don't exist. The only way we can deliver them is to buy them from him first and he can set his own price on them. We're finished, Duff, do you know what that means? Smashed! Broken!' Sean poured brandy into his glass, slopping a little on the sideboard. 'Have another drink on Hradsky, it's his brandy now.' Sean swept his arm round the room, pointing at the rich furniture and heavy curtains. 'Take a last look at this lot. Tomorrow the Sheriff will be here to attach it; then through the due processes of the law it will be handed to its rightful owner–Mr Norman Hradsky.' Sean started back towards his chair and then he stopped.

'The due processes of the law,' he repeated softly. 'I wonder–it might just work.'

Duff sat up eagerly in his chair. 'You've got an idea?'

Sean nodded. 'Well, half an idea anyway. Listen, Duff, if I can save a couple of thousand out of this do you agree that we get out of here?'

'Where to–where will we go?'

'We were facing north when we started. It's as good a direction as any. They say there's gold and ivory beyond the Limpopo for those who want it.'

'But, why can't we stay here? We could play the stock market.' Duff looked uncertain, almost afraid.

'Damn it, Duff, we're finished here. It's a different story playing the market when you are paying the fiddler and calling the tune, but with a mere thousand or so we'd be among the dogs fighting for the scraps under Hradsky's table. Let's get out and start again. We'll go north, hunt ivory and prospect for a new reef. We'll take a couple of wagons and find another fortune. I bet you've forgotten how it feels to sit on a horse and handle a rifle, to have the wind in your face and not a whore or a stockbroker within five hundred miles.'

'But it means leaving everything we've worked for,' Duff groaned.

'Sweet merciful heavens, man, are you blind or just plain stupid? Sean stormed at him. 'You don't own anything, so how the hell can you leave something you haven't got? I'm going down to see Hradsky and try to make a deal with him. Are you coming?'

Duff looked at him without seeing him, his lips were trembling and he was shaking his head. At last he was realizing the position they were in and the impact of it had dazed him. The higher you ride the further there is to fall.

'All right,' said Sean. 'Wait for me here.'

Hradsky's suite was full of talking, laughing men. Sean recognized most of them as the courtiers who used to cluster round the throne on which he and Duff had sat. The King is dead, long live the King! They saw him standing in the doorway and the laughter and loud voices fizzled out. He saw Max take two quick steps to the stinkwood desk in the corner, pull open the top drawer and drop his hand into it. He stood like that watching Sean. One by one the courtiers picked up their hats and canes and hurried out of the room. Some of them mumbled embarrassed greetings as they brushed past Sean. Then there were only the three of them left: Sean standing quietly in the doorway, Max behind the desk with his hand on the pistol and Hradsky in the chair by the fireplace watching through the yellow, half-hooded eyes.

'Aren't you going to invite me in, Max?' Sean asked and Max glanced quickly at Hradsky, saw his barely perceptible nod and looked back at Sean. 'Come in, please, Mr Courteney.'

Sean pushed the door shut behind him. 'You won't need the gun, Max, the game is over.'

'And the score is in our favour, is it not, Mr Courteney?'

Sean nodded. 'Yes, you've won. We are prepared to make over to you all the C.R.C. shares we hold.'

Max shook his head unhappily. 'I'm afraid it's not quite so easy as that. You have undertaken to sell us a certain number of shares and we must insist upon delivery in full.'

'Just where do you suggest we get them?' Sean asked.

'You could buy them on the Stock Exchange.'

'From you?'

Max shrugged but made no reply.

'So you are going to twist the knife, are you?'

'You put it very poetically, Mr Courteney,' agreed Max.

'Have you considered the consequences of forcing us into bankruptcy?'

'I will admit freely that the consequences to you do not concern us.'

Sean smiled. 'That was not very nice, Max, but I was talking about it from your point of view. Sequestration orders, creditors' meetings–you can rest assured that the liquidator appointed will be a member of the *Volksraad* or a relative of one. There will be court actions and counter actions, enforced sale of the shares in the estate and costs to pay. A liquidator with any sense at all could string it out for three or four years, all the time drawing a handsome commission. Have you thought about that, Max?'

The narrowing of Max's eyes showed that he hadn't. He looked at Hradsky with a trace of helplessness in his face, and Sean took a little comfort from that look.

'Now what I suggest is this–you let us draw ten thousand, take our horses and personal belongings. We in exchange will give you the rest. Shares, bank accounts, property, everything. You cannot possibly get more out of it if you force us into bankruptcy.'

Hradsky gave Max a message in their private facial code and Max interpreted it to Sean.

'Would you mind waiting outside, please, while we discuss this offer of yours.'

'I'll go down and have a drink at the bar,' said Sean. He pulled his watch from his waistcoat pocket and checked the time. 'Will twenty minutes be enough?'

'Ample, thank you, Mr Courteney.'

Sean had his drink by himself although the bar was nowhere near empty. This was not an arrangement of his own choosing, but he was flying the fever flag of failure and so he had to take an isolation berth at one end of the bar while all the other ships steered wide of him. No one looked in his direction and the conversation that went on round him was carefully arranged so as to exclude him. While he waited out the twenty minutes he amused himself by imagining the reactions of these his friends if he were to ask them for a loan. This helped to take the sting out of their snubs but still he felt it rankling. He looked at his watch again. The twenty minutes were up. Sean walked along the counter towards the door. Jock and Trevor Heyns saw him coming, they turned away abruptly and immediately became absorbed in staring at the bottle-lined shelves behind the bar counter. Sean stopped level with Jock and cleared his throat deferentially. 'Jock, could you spare a minute?'

Jock turned slowly. 'Ah, Sean. Yes, what is it?'

'Duff and I are leaving the Rand. I have something for you, just something to remember us by. I know Duff would want you to have it too.'

Jock reddened with embarrassment. 'That's not necessary,' he said and started to turn back to his drink.

'Please, Jock.'

'Oh, all right,' Jock's voice was irritable. 'What is it?'

'This,' Sean said and stepped forward, moving his weight behind the fist. Jock's large and whisky-flushed nose was a target to dream about. It was not one of Sean's best punches, he was out of training, but it was good enough to send Jock in a spectacular back-somersault over the counter. Dreamily Sean picked up Jock's glass and emptied it over Trevor's head.

'Next time you meet me smile and say "Hello",' he told Trevor. 'Until then–stay out of mischief.'

He went up the stairs to Hradsky's suite in much better spirits. They were waiting for him.

'Give me the word, Max,' Sean could even grin at him.

'Mr Hradsky has very generously–'

'How much?' Sean cut him short.

'Mr Hradsky will allow you to take fifteen hundred and your personal effects. As part of the agreement you will give an undertaking not to embark on any business venture on the Witwatersrand for a period of three years.'

'That will be too soon,' said Sean. 'Make it two thousand and you've got a deal.'

'The offer is not open to discussion.'

Sean could see they meant it. They didn't have to bargain; it was a statement.

'All right, I accept.'

'Mr Hradsky has sent for his lawyer to draw up the agreement. Would you mind waiting, Mr Courteney?'

'Not at all, Max, you forget I am a gentleman of leisure now.'

31

Sean found Duff still sitting in the chair where he had left him in the drawing-room of Xanadu. The bottle clutched in his hand was empty and he was unconscious. He had spilt brandy down the front of his waistcoat and three of the buttons were undone. Huddled in the big chair, his body seemed to have shrunk and the curly hair hanging on to his forehead softened the gaunt lines of his face. Sean loosened his fingers from the neck of the bottle and Duff moved restlessly, muttering and twisting his head.

'Bedtime for small boys,' said Sean. He lifted him out of the chair and hung him over one shoulder.

Duff sicked up copiously.

'That's the way, show Hradsky what you think of his bloody carpet,' Sean encouraged him. 'Give him another one for luck, but not on my boots.'

Duff did as he was bid and, chuckling, Sean carried him up the stairs. At the top he stopped and with Duff still bundled over one shoulder tried to analyse his own feelings. Damn it, he felt happy. It was ridiculous to feel so happy in the midst of disaster. He went on down the passage still wondering at himself and into Duff's room. He dropped Duff on the bed and stripped his clothes off, then he rolled him under the blankets. He brought the enamel wash basin from the bathroom and placed it next to the bed.

'You may need this–sleep well. There's a long ride ahead of us tomorrow.'

He stopped again at the top of the stairs and looked down their marble slope into the splendour of the lobby. He was leaving all of it and that was nothing to feel happy about. He laughed aloud. Perhaps it was because he had faced complete annihilation and at the last instant had changed it into something less; by avoiding the worst he had made defeat into a victory. A pathetic little victory to be sure, but at least they were no worse off now than they had been when they had arrived on the Rand. Was that the reason? Sean thought about it and found that it wasn't the whole truth. There was also a feeling of release. That was another part of it. To go on his way: north to a new land. He felt the tingle of anticipation.

'Not a whore or a stockbroker within five hundred miles,' he said aloud and grinned. He gave up trying to find words for his feeling. Emotion was so damned elusive: as soon as you cornered it, it changed its shape and the net of words which you had ready to throw over it was no longer suitable. He let it go free to range through his body, accepting and enjoying it. He ran down the stairs, out through the kitchens and into the stable yard.

'Mbejane!' he shouted, 'where the hell are you?'

The clatter of a stool overturning in the servants' quarters and the door of one of the rooms burst open.

'Nkosi–what is it?' The urgency of Sean's voice had alarmed Mbejane.

'Which are the best six horses we have?'

Mbejane named them, making no attempt to hide his curiosity.

'Are they all salted against the Nagana?'*

'All of them, Nkosi.'

*Sleeping sickness. Salting involved deliberate exposure to the sting of the tsetse fly. Animals that recovered were then immune.

'Good–have them ready before tomorrow's light. Two with saddles, the others to carry the packs.'

Mbejane turned on his smile. 'Could it be we are going hunting, Nkosi?'

'It could easily be,' Sean agreed.

'How long will we be gone, Nkosi?'

'How long is for ever? Take leave of all your women, bring your kaross and your spears and we will see where the road leads.'

Sean went back to his bedroom. It took him half an hour to pack. The pile of discarded clothing in the centre of the room grew steadily and what he kept made only half a horseload. He crammed it into two leather valises. He found his sheepskin coat in the back of one of the closets and threw it over a chair with his leather breeches and slouch hat, ready to wear in the morning. He went down to the study and made his selection from the gun rack, ignoring the fancy doubles and obscure calibres. He took down a pair of shotguns and four Mannlichers.

Then he went to tell Candy goodbye. She was in her suite but she opened quickly to his knock.

'Have you heard?' he asked her.

'Yes, the whole town knows. Oh! Sean, I'm so sorry–please come in.' She held the door open for him. 'How is Duff?'

'He'll be all right–right now he's both drunk and asleep.'

'I'll go to him,' she said quickly. 'He'll need me now.'

For answer Sean raised an eyebrow and looked at her until she dropped her eyes.

'No, you're right. I suppose. Perhaps later, when he's got over the first shock.' She looked up at Sean and smiled. 'I suppose you need a drink. It must have been hell for you as well.' She went across to the cabinet. She had on a blue gown and it clung to the womanish thrust of her hips and did not go high enough to cover the cleft of her breasts. Sean watched her pour his drink and bring it to him. She was lovely, he thought.

'Till we meet again, Candy,' Sean lifted his glass.

Her eyes wide and very blue. 'I don't understand. Why do you say that?'

'We're going, Candy, first thing tomorrow.'

'No, Sean–you're joking.' But she knew he wasn't. There wasn't much to say after that. He finished his drink and they talked for a while, then he kissed her.

'Be happy, please,' he ordered her.

'I'll try. Come back one day soon.'

'Only if you promise to marry me,' he smiled at her and she caught hold of his beard and tugged his head from side to side.

'Get away with you–before I hold you to that.' He left her then because he knew she was going to weep and he didn't want to watch it.

The next morning Duff packed his gear under Sean's direction. He followed each instruction with a dazed obedience, answering when Sean spoke but otherwise withdrawn in a protective shell of silence. When he had finished Sean made him pick up his bags and marched him down to where the horses waited in the chill gloom of not-yet day. With the horses were men, four shapes in the darkness. Sean hesitated before going out into the yard.

'Mbejane,' he called. 'Who are these with you?'

They came forward into the light that poured through the doorway and Sean chuckled.

'Hlubi, of the noble belly! Nonga! and is it you, Kandhla?' Men who had worked beside him in the trenches of the Candy Deep, had plied the spades that had uncovered his fortune, had plied the spears that protected it from the first predators. Happy at his recognition of them, for it had been many years, they crowded forward smiling as widely and whitely as only a Zulu can.

'What brings you three rogues together so early in the day?' Sean asked, and Hlubi answered for them.

'Nkosi, we heard talk of a trek and our feet burned, we heard talk of hunting and we could not sleep.'

'There is no money for wages,' Sean spoke gruffly to cover the sudden rush of affection he felt for them.

'We made no talk of wages,' Hlubi answered with dignity. Sean nodded, it was the reply he had expected. He cleared his throat and went on.

'You would come with me when you know that I have the Tagathi on me?' He used the Zulu word for witchcraft. 'You would follow me knowing that behind me I leave a spoor of dead men and sorrow?'

'Nkosi,' Hlubi was grave as he answered. 'Something always dies when the lion feeds–and yet there is meat for those that follow him.'

'I hear the chatter of old women at a beer drink,' Mbejane observed drily. 'There is no more to say and the horses grow restless.'

They rode down the driveway of Xanadu between the jacaranda trees and the smooth wide lawns. Behind them the mansion was grey and unlighted in the half darkness. They took the Pretoria road, climbed to the ridge and checked their horses at the crest. Sean and Duff looked back across the valley. The valley was filled with early morning mist, and the mine headgears probed up out of it. They watched the mists turn to gold as the low sun touched them and a mine hooter howled dismally.

'Couldn't we stay for just a week longer–perhaps we could work something out?' Duff asked softly.

Sean sat silently staring at the golden mist. It was beautiful. It hid the scarred earth and it hid the mills–it was a most appropriate cloak for that evil, greedy city. Sean turned his horse away towards Pretoria and slapped the loose end of his reins across its neck.

3. THE WILDERNESS

I

They stayed five days in Pretoria, just long enough to buy the wagons and commission them, and when they left on the morning of the sixth day they went north on the Hunters Road. The wagons moved in column urged on by the Zulus and a dozen new servants that Sean had hired. They were followed by a mixed bag of black and white urchins and stray dogs; men called good luck after them and women waved from the verandas of the houses which lined the road. Then the town was behind them and they were out into the veld with only a dozen of the more adventurous mongrels still following them.

They made fifteen miles the first day and when they camped that night beside the ford of a small stream, Sean's back and legs ached from his first full day in the saddle in over five years. They drank a little brandy and ate steaks grilled over wood embers, then they let the fire die and sat and looked at the night. The sky was a curtain at which a barrel of grape-shot had been fired, riddling it with the holes through which the stars shone. The voices of the servants made a hive murmur as a background to the wailing of a jackal in the darkness beyond the firelight. They went to their living wagon early and for Sean the feel of rough blankets instead of silk sheets and the hardness of a straw mattress were not sufficient to keep him long from sleep.

From an early start the following morning they put another twenty miles behind them before outspan that night and twenty more the next day. The push and urgent drive were habits Sean had acquired on the Rand when every minute was vital and the loss of a day was a disaster. They were habits that stuck, and he pushed the caravan northward as impatiently as he would have chivvied the men on the Candy Deep who were cutting a drive to intersect the Reef. Then one morning, when they were inspanning the oxen at the usual hour of dawn, Mbejane asked him, 'Do we go to meet someone, Nkosi?'

'No. Why do you ask?'

'When a man moves fast there is usually a reason. I was seeking the reason for our haste.'

'The reason is–' Sean stopped. He looked around him quickly as if to find it, then he cleared his throat and scratched the side of his nose, '–outspan an hour before high sun,' he finished abruptly and went to his horse. He and Duff rode out a mile or two ahead of the wagons that day, then instead of keeping to the track or hurrying back to chase up the caravan Sean suggested, 'Let's ride across to the kopje over there. We'll leave the horses at the bottom and climb up to the top.'

'What for?' asked Duff.

'For the hell of it–come on.'

They hobbled the horses and set off up the steep side of the kopje, picking their way over the tumbled boulders and through the tangle of tree trunks. They were sweating and blowing hard when they came out on the summit and found a place with a shade and a flat rock ledge on which to sit. Sean gave Duff a cheroot and they smoked and looked out across the land that was spread like a map below them.

Here the grasslands of the high veld were starting to blend into the forests and hilly country of the bushveld. There were vleis open as wheatfields, ending suddenly against a hill or bounded by haphazard plantations of tall trees. From the height at which they sat they could trace the courses of underground rivers by the dark green and superior height of the trees that grew above them. Everything else was the colour of Africa–brown, a thousand different shades of brown. Pale brown grass on red brown soil, with twisted, chocolate-brown tree trunks reaching up to the moving masses of brown leaves at their tips. Flickering indefinite brown were the herds of springbok that fed among the trees and on the slopes of the bare bulging brown hills, and the brown land reached away vast and unhurried into immeasurable distance, unmarred by the scratchings of man: tranquil and dignified in its immensity.

'It makes me feel small, but sort of safe–as though no one will notice me here,' said Duff, then laughed self-consciously.

'I know what you mean,' Sean answered him. He saw that for the first time since they had left the Rand the strain was gone from Duff's face. They smiled at each other and leaned back against the rock face behind them. They watched their wagons, far below them, coil into the tight circle of the laager and the cattle turned free move out to graze. The sun sank and the shadows stretched out longer and longer across the land. At last they went down the hill and found their horses. That night they stayed later than usual next to the fire and though they talked little there was the old feeling between them again. They had discovered a new reef that was rich with the precious elements of space and time. Out here there was more of those two treasures than a man could use in a dozen life-times. Space to move, to ride or to fire a rifle; space spread with sunlight and wind, grass and trees, but not filled with them. There was also time. This was where time began: it was a quiet river, moving but not changed by movement; draw on it as much as you would and still it was always full. It was measured by the seasons but not restricted by them, for the summer that was now standing back to let autumn pass was the same summer that had flamed a thousand years before and would flame again a thousand years hence. In the presence of so much space and time all striving was futile.

From then on their lives took their tempo from the leisurely turning of wagon wheels. Sean's eyes which had been pointing straight ahead along the line of travel now turned aside to look about him. Each morning he and Duff would leave the wagons and wander out into the bush. Sometimes they would spend the day panning for gold in the sands of a stream, another day they would search for the first signs of elephant, but mostly they just rode and talked or lay hidden and watched the herds of game that daily became more numerous. They killed just enough to feed themselves, their servants and the pack of dogs that had followed them when they left Pretoria. They passed the little Boer settlement at Pietersburg and then the Zoutspansberg climbed up over the horizon, its sheer sides dark with rain forest and high rock cliffs. Here under the mountains they spent a week at Louis Trichardt, the most northerly permanent habitation of white men.

In the town they spoke with men who had hunted to the north of the mountains, across the Limpopo. These were taciturn brown-faced Boers with tobacco-stained beards–big men with the peace of the bush in their eyes. In their courteous, unhurried speech Sean sensed a fierce possessive love of the animals that they hunted and the land through which they moved so freely. They were a different breed from the Natal Afrikanders and those he had met on the Witwatersrand, and he conceived the respect for them that would grow stronger in the years ahead when he would have to fight them.

There was no way through the mountains, they told him, but wagons could pass around them. The western passage skirted the edge of the Kalahari desert and this was bad country where the wagon wheels sank into the sandy soil and the marches between water became successively longer. To the east there was good rich forest land, well watered and stocked with game; low country, hotter the nearer one went to the coast, but the true bushveld where a man could find elephant.

So Dean and Duff turned east and, holding the mountains always in sight at their left hand, they went down into the wilderness.

2

Within a week's trek they saw elephant sign: trees broken and stripped of their bark. Although it was months old–the trees already dried out–nevertheless Sean felt the thrill of it and that night spent an hour cleaning and oiling his rifles. The forest thickened until the wagons had to weave continually between the trunks of the trees. But there were clearings in the forest–open vleis filled with grass where buffalo grazed like herds of domestic cattle and white tick birds squawked about them. This country was well watered with streams as clear and merry as a Scottish trout stream, but the water was blood-warm and the banks thick with bush. Along the rivers, in the forest and in the open were the herds of game: impala twisting and leaping away at the first approach with their crumpled horns laid back, kudu with big ears and soft eyes, black sable antelope with white bellies and horns curved like a naval cutlass, zebra trotting with the dignity of fat ponies, while about them frolicked their companions, the gnu, waterbuck, nyala, roan antelope and–at last–elephant.

Sean and Mbejane were ranging a mile ahead of the wagons when they found the spoor. It was fresh, so fresh that sap still oozed from the mahobahoba tree where the bark had been prised loose with the tip of a tusk and then stripped off. The wood beneath was naked and white.

'Three bulls,' said Mbejane. 'One very big.'

'Wait here,' Sam spun his horse and galloped back to the column. Duff lay on the driver's seat of the first wagon rocking gently to its motion, his hat covering his face and his hands behind his head.

'Elephant! Duff,' Sean yelled. 'Not an hour ahead of us. Get saddled up, man!'

Duff was ready in five minutes. Mbejane was waiting for them; he had already worked the spoor a short distance and picked up the run of it and now he went away on it. They followed him, riding slowly side by side.

'You've hunted elephant before, laddie?' asked Duff.

'Never,' said Sean.

'Good grief!' Duff looked alarmed. 'I thought you were an expert. I think I'll go back and finish my sleep, you can call me when you've had a little more experience.'

'Don't worry,' Sean laughed with excitement. 'I know all about it; I was raised on elephant stories.'

'That sets my heart at ease,' Duff murmured sarcastically and Mbejane glanced over his shoulder at them, not trying to conceal his irritation.

'Nkosi, it is not wise to talk now for we will soon come up with them.'

So they went on in silence: passing a knee-high pile of yellow dung that looked like the contents of a coir mattress, following the oval pad marks in the dust and the trail of torn branches.

It was a good hunt, this first one. The small breeze held steadily into their faces and the spoor ran straight and hot. They closed in, each minute strengthening the certainty of the kill. Sean sat stiff and eager in the saddle with his rifle across his lap, his eyes restlessly moving over the frieze of bush ahead of him. Mbejane stopped suddenly and came back to Sean's stirrup.

'Here they halted for the first time. The sun is hot and they will rest but this place was not to their liking and they have moved on. We will find them soon now.'

'The bush becomes too thick,' Sean grunted; he eyed the untidy tangle of catbush into which the spoor had led them. 'We will leave the horses here with Hlubi and go in on foot.'

'Laddie,' Duff demurred. 'I can run much faster on horseback.'

'Off!' said Sean and nodded to Mbejane to lead. They moved forward again. Sean was sweating and the drops clung heavily to his eyebrows and trickled down his cheeks; he brushed them away. The excitement was an indigestible ball in his stomach and a dryness in his throat.

Duff sauntered casually next to Sean with that small half-smile on his face, but there was a quickness in his breathing. Mbejane cautioned them with a gesture of his hand and they stopped. Minutes passed slowly and then Mbejane's hand moved again, pink-palmed eloquence.

'It was nothing,' said the hand. 'Follow me.'

They went on again. There were Mopani flies swarming at the corners of Sean's eyes, drinking the moisture, and he blinked them away. Their buzzing was so loud in his ears that he thought it must carry to their quarry. His every sense was tuned to its limit: hearing magnified, vision sharp and even his sense of smell so clear that he could pick up the taint of dust, the scent of a wild flower and Mbejane's faintly musky body-smell.

Suddenly in front of him Mbejane was still; his hand moved again gently, unmistakable.

'They are here,' said the hand.

Sean and Duff crouched behind him, searching with eyes that could see only brown bush and grey shadows. The tension coarsened their breathing and Duff was no longer smiling. Mbejane's hand came up slowly and pointed at the wall of vegetation in front of them. The seconds strung together like beads on the string of time and still they searched.

An ear flapped lazily and instantly the picture jumped into focus. Bull elephant, big and very close, grey among grey shadow. Sean touched Mbejane's arm. 'I had seen it,' said that touch.

Slowly Mbejane's hand swivelled and pointed again. Another wait, another searching and then a belly rumbled, a great grey belly filled with half-digested leaves. It was a sound so ridiculous in the silence that Sean wanted to laugh–a gurgling sloshy sound–and Sean saw the other bull. It was standing in shadow also, with long yellow ivory and small eyes tight-closed. Sean put his lips to Duff's ear.

'This one is yours,' he whispered. 'Wait until I get into position for the other,' and he began moving out to the side, each step exposing a little more of the second bull's flank until the shoulder was open to him and he could see the point of the elbow beneath the baggy, wrinkled skin. The angle was right; from here he could reach the heart. He nodded at Duff, brought his rifle up–leaning forward against the recoil, aiming close behind the massive shoulder–and he fired.

The gunfire was shockingly loud in the confined thorn bush; dust flew in a spurt from the bull's shoulder and it staggered from the strike of the bullet. Beyond it the third elephant burst from sleep into flight and Sean's hands moved neatly on his weapon, ejecting and reloading, swinging up and firing again. He saw the bullet hit and he knew it was a mortal wound. The two bulls ran together and the bush opened to them and swallowed them: they were gone, crashing away wounded, trumpeting in pain. Sean ran after them, dodging through the catbush, oblivious to the sting of the thorns that snatched at him as he passed.

'This way, Nkosi,' Mbejane shouted beside him. 'Quickly or we will lose them.' They sprinted after the sounds of flight–a hundred yards, two hundred, panting now and sweating in the heat. Suddenly the catbush ended and in front of them was a wide river-bed with steep banks. The river sand was blindingly white and in the middle was a sluggish trickle of water. One of the bulls was dead, lying in the stream with the blood washing off him in a pale brown stain. The other bull was trying to climb the far bank; it was too steep for him and he slid back wearily. The blood dripped from the tip of his trunk, and he swung his head to look at Sean and Mbejane. His ears cocked back defiantly and he began his charge, blundering towards them through the soft river sand.

Sean watched him come and there was sadness in him as he brought up his rifle, but it was the proud regret that a man feels when he watches hopeless courage. Sean killed with a brain shot, quickly.

They climbed down the bank into the river-bed and went to the elephant; it knelt with its legs folded under it and its tusks driven deep into the sand with the force of its fall. The flies were already clustering at the little red mouths of the bullet wounds. Mbejane touched one of the tusks and then he looked up at Sean.

'It is a good elephant,' He said no more, for this was not the time to talk. Sean leaned his rifle against the bull's shoulder; he felt in his top pocket for a cheroot and stood with it unlit between his teeth. He would kill more elephant, he knew, but always this would be the one he would remember. He stroked his hand over the rough skin and the bristles were stiff and sharp.

'Where is Nkosi Duff?' Sean remembered him suddenly. 'Did he also kill?'

'He did not shoot,' answered Mbejane.

'What!' Sean turned quickly to Mbejane. 'Why not?'

Mbejane sniffed a pinch of snuff and sneezed, then he shrugged his shoulders.

'It is a good elephant,' he said again, looking down at it.

'We must go back and find him.' Sean snatched up his rifle and Mbejane followed him. They found Duff sitting alone in the catbush with his rifle propped beside him and a water-bottle to his lips. He lowered the bottle as Sean came up and saluted him with it.

'Hail! the conquering hero comes.' There was something in his eyes that Sean could not read.

'Did you miss yours?' Sean asked.

'Yes,' said Duff, 'I missed mine.' He lifted the bottle and drank again. Suddenly and sickenly Sean was ashamed for him. He dropped his eyes, not wanting to acknowledge Duff's cowardice.

'Let's get back to the wagons,' he said. 'Mbejane can come with packhorses for the tusks.'

They did not ride together on the way home.

3

It was almost dark when they arrived back at the laager. They gave their horses to one of the servants and washed in the basin that Kandhla had ready for them, then they went to sit by the fire. Sean poured the drinks, fussing over the glasses to avoid looking at Duff. He felt awkward. They'd have to talk about it and he searched his brain for a way to bring it into the open. Duff had shown craven and Sean started to find excuses for him–he may have had a misfire or he may have been unsighted by Sean's shot. At all events Sean determined not to let it stay like this, sour and brooding between them. They'd talk it out then forget it. He carried Duff's glass to him and smiled at him.

'That's right, try to cover it with a grin,' Duff lifted his glass. 'To our big brave hunter. Dammit, laddie, how could you do it?'

Sean stared at Duff. 'What do you mean?'

'You know what I mean, you're so damned guilty you can't even look me in the face. How could you kill those bloody great animals–but even worse how could you *enjoy* doing it?'

Sean subsided weakly into his chair. He couldn't tell which of his emotions were uppermost–relief or surprise. Duff went on quickly.

'I know what you're going to say, I've heard the arguments before–from my dear father. He explained it to me one evening after we'd ridden down a fox. When I say "we", I mean twenty horsemen and forty hounds.'

Sean had not yet rallied from the shock of finding himself in the dock after preparing himself to play the role of prosecutor.

'Don't you like hunting?' he asked incredulously. The way he might have asked, 'don't you like eating?'

'I'd forgotten what it was like. I was carried away by your excitement, but when you started to kill them it all came back to me.' Duff sipped his brandy and stared into the fire. 'They never had a chance. One minute they were sleeping and the next you were ripping them with bullets the way the hounds ripped that fox. They didn't have a chance.'

'But, Duff, it wasn't meant to be a contest.'

'Yes, I know, my father explained that to me. It's a ritual–a sacred rite to Diana. He should have explained it to the fox as well.'

Sean was getting angry now. 'We came out here to hunt ivory–and that's what I'm doing.'

'Tell me that you killed those elephant only for their teeth, laddie, and I'll call you a liar. You loved it. Christ! You should have seen your face and the face of your damned heathen.'

'All right! I like hunting and the only other man I ever met who didn't was a coward,' Sean shouted at him.

Duff's face paled and he looked up at Sean. 'What are you trying to say?' he whispered. They stared at each other and in the silence Sean had to choose between letting his temper run or keeping Duff's friendship, for the words that would spoil it for ever were crowding into his mouth. He made his hands relax their grip on the arms of his chair.

'I didn't mean that,' he said.

'I hoped you didn't,' Duff's grin came precariously back on to his face. 'Tell me why you like hunting, laddie. I'll try and understand but don't expect me to hunt with you again.'

It was like explaining colour to a blind man, describing the lust of the hunter to someone who was born without it. Duff listened in agonized silence as Sean tried to find the words for the excitement that makes a man's blood sing through his body, that heightens his senses and allows him to lose himself in an emotion as old as the urge to mate. Sean tried to show him how the nobler and more beautiful was the quarry, the stronger was the compulsion to hunt and kill it, that it had no conscious cruelty in it but was rather an expression of love: a fierce possessive love. A devouring love that needed the complete and irrevocable act of death for its consummation. By destroying something, a man could have it always as his own: selfish perhaps, but then instinct knows no ethics. It was all very clear to Sean, so much a part of him that he had never tried to voice it before and now he stumbled over the words, gesticulating in helpless inarticulateness, repeating himself, coming at last to the end and knowing by the look on Duff's face that he had failed to show it to him.

'And you were the gentleman who fought Hradsky for the rights of man,' Duff said softly, 'the one who always talked about not hurting people.'

Sean opened his mouth to protest but Duff went on. 'You get ivory for us and I'll look for gold–each of us to what he is best suited. I'll forgive you your elephants as you forgave me my Candy–still equal partners. Agreed?'

Sean nodded and Duff held up his glass.

'It's empty,' he said. 'Do me a favour, laddie.'

4

There was never any aftertaste to their disputes, no rankling of unspoken words or lingering of doubt. What they had in common they enjoyed, where there were differences they accepted them. So when after each hunt the packhorses brought the tusks into the camp there was no trace of censure in Duff's face or voice; there was only the genuine pleasure of having Sean back from the bush. Sometimes it was a good day and Sean would cut the spoor, follow, kill and be back in the laager the same night. But more often, when the herd was moving fast or the ground was hard or he could not kill at the first approach, he would be gone for a week or more. Each time he returned they celebrated, drinking and laughing far into the night, lying late in bed the next morning, playing Klabejas on the floor of the wagon between their cots or reading aloud out of the books that Duff had brought with him from Pretoria.

Then a day or two later Sean would be gone again, with his dogs and his gunboys trotting behind him.

This was a different Sean from the one who had whored it up at the Opera House and presided over the panelled offices in Eloff Street. His beard, no longer groomed and shaped by a barber, curled on to his chest. The doughy colour of his face and arms had been turned by the sun to the rich brown of a newly-baked loaf. The seat of his pants that had been stretched to danger point across his rump now hung loosely; his arms were thicker and the soft swell of fat had given way to the flatness and bulge of hard muscle. He walked straighter, moved quicker and laughed more easily.

In Duff the change was less noticeable. He was lean and gaunt-faced as ever, but now there was less of the restlessness in his eyes. His speech and movements were slower and the golden beard he was growing had the strange effect of making him appear younger. Each morning he left the wagons, taking one of the servants with him, and spent the days wandering in the bush, tapping with his prospecting hammer at the occasional outcrops of rock or squatting beside a stream and spinning the gravel in his pan. Every evening he came back to camp and analysed the bag of rock samples he had collected during the day; then he threw them away, bathed and set out a bottle and two glasses on the table beside the fire. While he ate his supper he listened and waited for the dogs to bark, for the sound of horses in the darkness and Sean's voice. If the night remained silent he put the bottle away and climbed up into his wagon. He was lonely then, not with a deep loneliness but just enough to add relish to Sean's return.

Always they moved east, until gradually the silhouette of the Zoutpansberg softened as the mountains became less steep and began to fade into the tail of the range. Scouting along their edge Sean found a pass and they took the wagons up and over and down into the Limpopo valley beyond. Here the country changed character again; it became flat, the monotony of thorn scrub relieved only by the baobab trees with their great, swollen trunks crowned in a little halo of branches. Water was scarce and Sean rode ahead from each camp to find the next waterhole before they moved. However, the hunting was good for the game was concentrated on the isolated drinking places, and before they were halfway from the mountains to the Limpopo Sean had filled another wagon with ivory.

'We'll be coming back this way, I suppose?' Duff asked.

'I suppose so,' agreed Sean.

'Well then, I don't see any point in carrying a ton of ivory with us. Let's bury it and we can pick up on our way back.'

Sean looked at him thoughtfully. 'About once in every year you come up with a good idea–we'll do exactly that.'

The next camp was a good one. There was water–an acre of muddy liquid not as heavily salted with elephant urine as some of the previous ones had been; there was a shade provided by a grove of wild fig trees and the grazing was of a quality that promised to restore the condition that the oxen had lost since crossing the mountains. They decided to make it a rest camp: bury the ivory, do some repairs and maintenance on the wagons and let the servants and animals fatten up a little. The first task was to dig a hole large enough to contain all the hundred-odd tusks they had accumulated and it was evening on the third day before they finished.

5

Sean and Duff sat together inside the laager and watched the sun go down, bleeding below the land, and after it had gone the clouds were oyster and lilac-coloured in the brief twilight. Kandhla threw wood on the fire and it burnt up fiercely. They ate grilled kudu liver, and thick steaks with a rind of yellow fat on them, and they drank brandy with their coffee. The conversation lagged into contented silence for they were both tired. They sat staring into the fire, too lazy to make the effort required for bed. Sean watched the fire pictures form in the coals, the faces and the phantoms flickering and fading. He saw a tiny temple have its columns pulled out from under it by a fiery Samson and collapse in a shower of sparks–a burning horse changed magically into a dragon of blue flame. He looked away to rest his eyes and when he turned back there was a small black scorpion scuttling out from under the loose bark on one of the logs. It lifted its tail like the arm of a flamenco dancer and the flames that ringed it shone on its glossy body armour. Duff was also watching it, leaning forward with his elbows on his knees.

'Will he sting himself to death before the flames reach him?' he asked softly. 'I have heard that they do.'

'No,' said Sean.

'Why not?'

'Only man has the intelligence to end the inevitable; in all other creatures the instinct of survival is too strong,' Sean answered him, and the scorpion crabbed sideways from the nearest flames and stopped again with its raised sting jerking slightly. 'Besides he's immune to his own poison so he has no choice.'

'He could jump down into the fire and get it over with,' murmured Duff, subdued by the little tragedy.

The scorpion started its last desperate circuit of the closing ring. Its tail drooped and the grip of its claws was unsteady on the rough bark; it was shrivelling with the heat, its legs curling up and its tail subsiding. The flames caressed it with swift yellow hands and smeared its shiny body with the dullness of death. The log tipped sideways and the speck was gone.

'Would you?' asked Sean. 'Would you have jumped?'

Duff sighed softly. 'I don't know,' he said and stood up. 'I'm going to pump out my bilges and crawl into bed.' He walked away and went to stand at the edge of the circle of firelight.

Since they had left Pretoria the small voices of the jackals had yapped discreetly around each outspan–they were so much a part of the African night that they went unnoticed–but now suddenly there was a difference. Only one jackal spoke, and with a voice that stammered shrilly–a sound of pain, a crazy hysterical shrieking that made Sean's skin prickle. He scrambled to his feet and stood staring undecided into the darkness. The jackal was coming towards the camp, coming fast–and suddenly Sean knew what was happening.

'Duff!' he called. 'Come back here! Run, man, run!'

Duff looked back at Sean helplessly, his hands held low in front of him and his water arcing down, curving silver in the firelight from his body to the ground.

'Duff!' Sean's voice was a shout. 'It's a rabid jackal. Run, damn you, run!' The jackal was close now, very close, but at last Duff started to move. He was halfway back to the fire before he tripped. He fell and rolled over and brought his feet up and under his body to rise. His head turned to face the darkness from which it would come. Then Sean saw it. It flitted out of the shadows like a grey moth in the bad light and went straight for where Duff knelt. Sean saw him try to cover his face with his hands as the jackal sprang at him. One of the dogs twisted out of Mbejane's hand and brushed past Sean's legs. Sean snatched up a piece of firewood and sprinted after it, but already Duff was on his back, his arms flailing frantically as he tried to push away the terrier-sized animal that was slashing at his face and hands. The dog caught it and dragged it off, worrying it, growling through locked jaws. Sean hit the jackal with the club–breaking its back. He swung again and again, beating its body into shapelessness before he turned to Duff. Duff was on his feet now. He had unwound the scarf from his neck and was mopping with it at his face but the blood dribbled down his chin and blotched the front of his shirt. His hands were trembling. Sean led him close to the fire, pulled Duff's hands down and examined the bites. His nose was torn and the flesh of one cheek hung open in a flap.

'Sit down!'

Duff obeyed, holding the scarf to his face again. Sean went quickly to the fire: with a stick he raked embers into a pile, then he drew his hunting-knife and thrust the blade into the coals.

'Mbejane,' he called, without taking his eyes off the knife. 'Throw the jackal on to the fire. Put on plenty of wood. Do not touch its body with your hands. When you have done that tie up that dog and keep the others away from it.' Sean turned the knife in the fire. 'Duff, drink as much of that brandy as you can.'

'What are you going to do?'

'You know what I've got to do.'

'He bit my wrist as well.' Duff held up his hand for Sean to see the punctures, black holes from which the blood oozed watery and slow.

'Drink.' Sean pointed at the brandy bottle. For a second they looked at each other and Sean saw the horror moving in Duff's eyes: horror of the hot knife and horror of the germs which had been injected into him. The germs that must burn out before they escaped into his blood, to breed and ferment there until they ate into his brain and rode him to a screaming, gibbering death.

'Drink,' said Sean again. Duff took up the bottle and lifted it to his mouth. Sean stooped and pulled the knife out of the fire. He held the blade an inch from the back of his hand. It was not hot enough. He thrust it back into the coals.

'Mbejane, Hlubi, stand on each side of the Nkosi's chair. Be ready to hold him.' Sean loosened his belt, doubled the thick leather and handed it to Duff. 'Bite on this.'

He turned back to the fire and this time when he drew the knife its blade was pale pink. 'Are you ready?'

'The work you are about to do will break the hearts of a million maids.' A last hoarse attempt at humour from Duff.

'Hold him,' said Sean.

Duff gasped at the touch of the knife–a great shuddering gasp–and his back arched, but the two Zulus held him down remorselessly. The edges of the wound blackened and hissed as Sean ran the blade in deeper. The stink of burning brought the vomit into his throat. He clenched his teeth. When he stepped back Duff hung slackly in the Zulu's hands, sweat had soaked his shirt and wet his hair. Sean heated the knife again and cleaned the bites in Duff's wrist while Duff moaned and writhed weakly in the chair. He smeared axle grease over the burns and bandaged the wrist loosely with strips torn from a clean shirt. They lifted Duff into the wagon and laid him on the cot. Sean went out to where Mbejane had tied the dog. He found scratches beneath the hair on its shoulder. They put a sack over its head to stop it biting and Sean cauterized its wounds also.

'Tie it to the far wagon, do not let the other dogs near it, see it has food and water,' he told Mbejane.

Then he went back to Duff. Delirious with pain and brandy Duff did not sleep at all that night and Sean stayed by his cot until the morning.

6

About fifty yards from the laager under one of the wild fig trees the servants built Duff a hut. The framework was of poles and over it they stretched a tarpaulin. They made a bed for him and brought his mattress and blankets from the wagon. Sean joined four trek-chains together, forging new links and hammering them closed. He passed one end of the chain round the base of the fig tree and riveted it back up on itself. Duff sat in the shade of a wagon and watched them work. His hurt hand was in a sling and his face was swollen, the wound crusty-looking and edged in angry red. When he was finished with the chain, Sean walked across to him.

'I'm sorry, Duff, we have to do it.'

'They abolished the slave trade some time ago–just in case you didn't know.' Duff tried to grin with his distorted face. He stood up and followed Sean to the hut. Sean looped the loose end of the chain round Duff's waist. He locked it with a bolt through two of the kinks then flattened the end of the bolt with a dozen strokes of the hammer.

'That should hold you.'

'An excellent fit,' Duff commended him. 'Now let us inspect my new quarters.'

Sean followed him into the hut. Duff lay down on the bed. He looked very tired and sick.

'How long will it take before we know?' he asked quietly.

Sean shook his head. 'I'm not sure. I think you should stay here at least a month–after that we'll allow you back into society.'

'A month–it's going to be fun. Lying here expecting any minute to start barking like a dog and lifting my leg against the nearest tree.'

Sean didn't laugh. 'I did a thorough job with the knife. It's a thousand to one you'll be all right. This is just a precaution.'

'The odds are attractive–I'll put a fiver on it.' Duff crossed his ankles and stared up at the roof. Sean sat down on the edge of the bed. It was a long time before Duff ended the silence.

'What will it be like, Sean, have you ever seen someone with rabies?'

'No.'

'But you've heard about it, haven't you? Tell me what you've heard about it,' Duff persisted.

'For Chrisake, Duff, you're not going to get it.'

'Tell me, Sean, tell me what you know about it.' Duff sat up and caught hold of Sean's arm.

Sean looked steadily at him for a moment before he answered. 'You saw that jackal, didn't you?'

Duff sank back on to his pillows. 'Oh, my God!' he whispered.

Together they started the long wait. They used another tarpaulin to make an open shelter next to the hut and under it they spent the days that followed.

In the beginning it was very bad. Sean tried to pull Duff out of the black despair into which he had slumped, but Duff sat for hours at a time gazing out into the bush, fingering the scabs on his face and only occasionally smiling at the banquet of choice stories that Sean spread for him. But at last Sean's efforts were rewarded–Duff began to talk. He spoke of things he had never mentioned before and listening to him Sean learned more about him than he had in the previous five years. Sometimes Duff paced up and down in front of Sean's chair with the chain hanging down behind him like a tail; at other times he sat quietly, his voice filled with longing for the mother he had never known.

'–there was a portrait of her in the upper gallery, I used to spend whole afternoons in front of it. It was the kindest face I had ever seen–'

Then it hardened again as he remembered his father, 'that old bastard'.

He talked of his daughter. '–she had a fat chuckle that would break your heart. The snow on her grave made it look like a big sugar-iced cake, she would have liked that–'

At other times his voice was puzzled as he examined some past action of his, angry as he remembered a mistake or a missed opportunity. Then he would break off and grin self-consciously. 'I say, I am talking a lot of drivel.'

The scabs on his face began to dry up and come away, and more often now his old gaiety bubbled to the surface.

On one of the poles that supported the tarpaulin roof he started a calendar, cutting a notch for each day. It became a daily ceremony. He cut each notch with the concentration of a sculptor carving marble and when he had finished he would stand back and count them aloud as if by doing so he could force them to add up to thirty, the number that would allow him to shed his chain.

There were eighteen notches on the pole when the dog went mad. It was in the afternoon. They were playing klabejas. Sean had just dealt the cards when the dog started screaming from among the wagons. Sean knocked over his chair as he jumped up. He snatched his rifle from where it leant against the wall and ran down to the laager. He disappeared behind the wagon to which the dog was tied and almost immediately Duff heard the shot. In the abrupt and complete stillness that followed, Duff slowly lowered his face into his hands.

It was nearly an hour before Sean came back. He picked up his chair, set it to the table and sat down.

'It's you to call–are you going to take on?' he asked as he picked up his cards. They played with grim intensity, fixing their attention on the cards, but both of them knew that there was a third person at the table now.

'Promise you'll never do that to me,' Duff blurted out at last.

Sean looked up at him. 'That I'll never do what to you?'

'What you did to that dog.'

The dog! The bloody dog. He should never have taken a chance with it, he should have destroyed it that first night.

'Just because the dog got it doesn't mean that you–'

'Swear to me,' Duff interrupted fiercely, 'swear you won't bring the rifle to me.'

'Duff, you don't know what you're asking. Once you've got it–' Sean stopped; anything he said would make it worse.

'Promise me,' Duff repeated.

'All right, I swear it then.'

7

It was worse now than it had been in the beginning. Duff abandoned his calendar and with it the hope that had been slowly growing stronger. If the days were bad then the nights were hell, for Duff had a dream. It came to him every night–sometimes two or three times. He tried to keep awake after Sean had left, reading by the light of a lantern; or he lay and listened to the night noises, the splash and snort of buffalo drinking down at the waterhole, the liquid half-warble of night birds or the deep drumming of a lion. But in the end he would have to sleep and then he dreamed.

He was on horseback riding across a flat brown plain: no hills, no trees, nothing but lawnlike grass stretching away on all sides to the horizon. His horse threw no shadow–he always looked for a shadow and it worried him that there never was one. Then he would find the pool–clear water, blue and strangely shiny. The pool frightened him but he would not stop himself going to it. He would kneel beside it and look into the water; the reflection of his own face looked up at him–animal-snouted, shaggy-brown with wolf teeth, white and long. He would wake then and the horror of that face would last until morning.

Nearly desperate with his own utter helplessness, Sean tried to help him. Because of the accord they had established over the years and because they were so close to each other, Sean had to suffer with him. He tried to shut himself off from it; sometimes he succeeded for an hour or even half a morning, but then it came back with a stomach-swooping shock. Duff was going to die–Duff was going to die an unspeakable death. Was it a mistake to let someone get too deep inside you, so that you must share his agony in every excruciating detail? Didn't a man have enough of his own that he must share the full measure of another's suffering?

By then the October winds had started, the heralds of the rain: hot winds full of dust, winds that dried the sweat on a man's body before it had time to cool him, thirsty winds, that during daylight brought the game to the waterhole in full view of the camp.

Sean had half a case of wine hoarded under his cot. That last evening he cooled four bottles, wrapping them in wet sacking. He took them up to Duff's shelter just before supper and set them on the table. Duff watched him. The scars on his face were almost completely healed now, glass red marks on his pale skin.

'Chateau Olivier,' said Sean and Duff nodded.

'It's a good wine–most probably travel-sick.'

'Well, if you don't want it, I'll take it away again,' said Sean.

'I'm sorry, laddie,' Duff spoke quickly. 'I didn't mean to be ungrateful. This wine suits my mood tonight. Did you know that wine is a sad drink?'

'Nonsense!' Sean disagreed as he twisted the corkscrew into the first cork. 'Wine is gay.' He poured a little into Duff's glass and Duff picked it up and held it towards the fire so the light shone through it.

'You see only the surface, Sean. A good wine has the elements of tragedy within it. The better the wine the more sad it is.'

Sean snorted. 'Explain yourself,' he invited.

Duff put his glass down on the table again and stared at it. 'How long do you suppose this wine has taken to reach its present perfection?'

'Ten or fifteen years, I suppose,' Sean answered.

Duff nodded. 'And now all that remains is to drink it–the work of years destroyed in an instant. Don't you think that is sad?' Duff asked softly.

'My God, Duff, don't be so damned morbid.'

But Duff wasn't listening to him. 'Wine and mankind have this in common. They can find perfection only in age, in a lifetime of seeking. Yet in the finding they find also their own destruction.'

'So you think that if a man lives long enough he will reach perfection?' Sean challenged him, and Duff answered him still staring at the glass.

'Some grapes grew in the wrong soil, some were diseased before they went to the press and some were spoiled by a careless vintner–not all grapes make good wine.' Duff picked up his glass and tasted from it, then he went on. 'A man takes longer and he must find it not within the quiet confines of the cask but in the cauldron of life; therefore his is the greater tragedy.'

'Yes, but no one can live for ever,' Sean protested.

'So you think that makes it less sad?' Duff shook his head. 'You're wrong, of course. It does not detract from it, it enhances it. If only there were some escape, some way of ensuring that what is good could endure instead of this complete hopelessness.'

Duff lay back in his chair, his face pale and gaunt-looking. 'Even that I could accept, if only they had given me more time.'

'I've had enough of this talk. Let's discuss something else. I don't know what you're worrying about. You're not fit to drink yet, you've got another twenty or thirty years to go,' Sean said gruffly and Duff looked up at him for the first time.

'Have I, Sean?'

Sean couldn't meet his eyes. He knew Duff was going to die. Duff grinned his lopsided grin and looked down again at his glass. Slowly the grin disappeared and he spoke again.

'If only I had more time, I could have done it. I could have found the weak places and fortified them. I could have seen the answers.' His voice rose higher. 'I could have! I know I could have! Oh God, I'm not ready yet. I need more time.' His voice was shrill and his eyes wild and haunted. 'It's too soon–it's too soon!'

Sean couldn't stand it, he jumped up and caught Duff's shoulders and shook him.

'Shut up, God damn you, shut up,' he shouted at him. Duff was panting, his lips were parted and quivering. He touched them with the tips of his fingers as though to stop them.

'I'm sorry, laddie, I didn't mean to let go like that.' Sean dropped his hands from Duff's shoulders.

'Both of us are too damned edgy,' he said. 'It's going to be all right, you wait and see.'

'Yes–it will be all right.' Duff ran his fingers through his hair, combing it back from his eyes. 'Open another bottle, laddie.'

8

That night after Sean had gone to bed, Duff had his dream again. The wine he had drunk slowed him down and prevented him from waking. He was trapped in his fancy, struggling to escape into wakefulness but only reaching the surface before he sank back to dream that dream again.

Sean went up to Duff's shelter the next morning early. Although the night's coolness still lingered under the spreading branches of the wild figs the rising day promised to blow dry and burn hot. The animals could sense it. The trek oxen were clustered among the trees and a small herd of eland was moving from the waterhole. The bull, with his short thick horns and the dark tuft on his forehead, was leading his cows away to find shade. Sean stood in the doorway of the hut and waited while his eyes adjusted themselves to its gloom. Duff was awake.

'Get out of bed or you'll have bed sores to add to your happiness.'

Duff swung his feet off the litter and groaned.

'What did you put in that wine last night?' He massaged his temples gently. 'I've got a hundred hobgoblins doing a Cossack dance around the roof of my skull.'

Sean felt the first twinge of alarm. He put his hand on Duff's shoulder feeling for the heat of fever, but Duff was quite cool. He relaxed.

'Breakfast's ready,' said Sean. Duff played with his porridge and barely tasted the grilled eland liver. He kept screwing his eyes up against the glare of the sun and when they had finished their coffee he pushed back his chair.

'I'm going to take my tender head to bed.'

'All right.' Sean stood up as well. 'We're a bit short of meat. I'll go and see if I can get a buck.'

'No, stay and talk to me,' Duff said quickly. 'We can have a few hands of cards.'

They hadn't played in days and Sean agreed readily. He sat on the end of Duff's bed and within half an hour he had won thirty-two pounds from him.

'You must let me teach you this game sometime,' he gloated.

Petulantly, Duff threw his hand in. 'I don't feel like playing any more.' He pressed his fingers to his closed eyelids. 'I can't concentrate with this headache.'

'Do you want to sleep?' Sean gathered up the cards and put them in their box.

'No. Why don't you read to me?'

Duff picked up a leather-bound copy of *Bleak House* from the table beside the bed and tossed it into Sean's lap.

'Where shall I start?' Sean asked.

'It doesn't matter, I know it almost by heart.' Duff lay back and closed his eyes. 'Start anywhere.'

Sean read aloud. He stumbled on for half an hour with his tongue never quite catching the rhythm of the words. Once or twice he glanced up at Duff, but Duff lay still with a faint sheen of sweat on his face and the scars very noticeable. He was breathing easily. Dickens is a powerful sleeping-draught for a hot morning and Sean's eyelids sagged down and his voice slowed and finally stopped. The book slid off his lap.

The small tinkle of Duff's chain disturbed him; he awoke and looked at the bed. Duff crouched apelike. The madness was a fire in his eyes and his cheeks twitched. A yellowish froth coated his teeth and formed a thin line of scum along his lips.

'Duff–' Sean said, and Duff lunged at him with fingers hooked and a noise in his throat that was not human nor yet animal. It was a sound that jellied Sean's stomach and took the strength from his legs.

'Don't!' screamed Sean, and the chain caught on one of the posts of the bed, jerking Duff back sprawling on to the bed before he could sink his teeth into Sean's paralysed body.

Sean ran. He ran out of the hut and into the bush. He ran with terror trembling in his legs and choking his breath. He ran with his heart taking its beat from his racing feet and his lungs pumping in disordered panic. A branch ripped across his cheek and the sting of it served to steady him. His feet slowed–he stopped and stood gasping, staring back towards the camp. He waited while his body settled and he forced his terror down until it was only a sickening sensation in his stomach. Then he circled through the thorn bush and approached the laager from the side farthest away from Duff's shelter. The camp was empty, the servants had fled in the same terror that had driven Sean. He remembered that his rifle was still in the hut beside Duff's bed. He slipped into his wagon and quickly opened the case of unused rifles. His hands were unsteady again as he fumbled with the locks, for the chain might have parted and at every second he expected to hear that inhuman sound behind him. He found his bandolier hanging on the end of his cot and he took cartridges from it. He loaded the rifle and cocked it. The weight of steel and wood in his hands gave him comfort. It made him a man again.

He jumped down out of the wagon and with the rifle held ready he went cautiously out of the circle of wagons. The chain had held. Duff stood in the shade of the wild fig plucking at it. He was making a sound like a new-born puppy. His back was turned to Sean and he was naked, his torn clothing scattered about him. Sean walked slowly towards him. He stopped outside the reach of the chain.

'Duff!' Sean called uncertainly. Duff spun and crouched, the froth was thick in his golden beard; he looked at Sean and his teeth bared. Then he charged screaming until the chain caught him and threw him on to his back once more. He scrambled to his feet and fought the chain, his eyes fastened hungrily on Sean. Sean backed away. He brought up the rifle and aimed between Duff's eyes.

Swear to me. Swear to me you won't bring the rifle to me.

Sean's aim wavered. He kept moving backwards. Duff was bleeding now. The steel links had smeared the skin off his hips, but still he pulled against them fighting to get at Sean–and Sean was shackled just as effectively by his promise. He could not end it. He lowered the rifle and watched in impotent pity.

Mbejane came to him at last.

'Come away, Nkosi. If you will not end it, come away. He no longer has need of you. The sight of you inflames him.'

Duff still struggled and screamed against his chain. From his torn waist the blood trickled down and clung in the hair of his legs with the stickiness of molten chocolate. With each jerk of his head the froth sprayed from his mouth and splattered his chest and arms.

Mbejane led Sean back into the laager. The other servants were there and Sean roused himself to give orders.

'I want everyone away from here. Take blankets and food–go camp on the far side of the water. I will send for you when it is over.' He waited until they had gathered their belongings and as they were leaving he called Mbejane back. 'What must I do?' he asked.

'If a horse breaks a leg?' Mbejane answered him with a question.

'I gave him my word,' Sean shook his head desperately, still facing towards the sound of Duff's raving.

'Only a rogue and a brave man can break an oath,' Mbejane answered simply. 'We will wait for you.' He turned and followed the others. When they were gone Sean hid in one of the wagons and through a tear in the canvas he watched Duff. He saw the idiotic shaking of his head, the curious shambling gait as he moved around the circle of the chain. He watched when the pain made him roll on the ground and claw at his head, tearing out tufts of hair and leaving long scratches down his face. He listened to the sounds of insanity: the bewildered bellows of pain, the senseless giggling and that growl, that terrible growl.

A dozen times he sighted along the rifle barrel, holding his aim until the sweat ran into his eyes and blurred them and he had to take the butt from his shoulder and turn away.

Out there on the end of the chain, its exposed flesh reddening in the sun, a piece of Sean was dying. Some of his youth, some of his laughter, some of his carefree love of life–so he had to creep back to the hole in the canvas and watch.

The sun reached its peak and started down again and the thing on the chain grew weaker. It fell and was a long time crawling on its hands and knees before it regained its feet again.

An hour before sunset Duff had his first convulsion. He was standing facing Sean's wagon, swinging his head from side to side, his mouth working silently. The convulsion took him and he stiffened; his lips pulled up grinning, showing his teeth, his eyes rolled back and disappeared leaving only the whites, and his body started to bend backwards. That beautiful body, still slim as a boy's with the long moulded legs, bending tighter and tighter until with a brittle crack the spine snapped and he fell. He lay wriggling, moaning softly and his trunk was twisted at an impossible angle from the broken spine.

Sean jumped from the wagon and ran to him: standing over him he shot Duff in the head and turned away. He flung his rifle from him and heard it clatter on the hard earth. He walked back to his wagon and took a blanket off Duff's cot. He came back and wrapped Duff in it, averting his eyes from the mutilated head. He carried him to the shelter and laid him on the bed. The blood soaked through the blanket, spreading on the cloth, like ink spilled on blotting-paper. Sean sank down on the chair beside the bed.

Outside the darkness gathered and became complete. Once in the night a hyena came and snuffled at the blood outside on the earth, then it moved away. There was a pride of lions hunting in the bush beyond the waterhole; they killed two hours before dawn and Sean sat in the darkness and listened to their jubilant roaring.

In the morning, Sean stood up stiffly from his chair and went down to the wagons. Mbejane was waiting beside the fire in the laager.

'Where are the others?' Sean asked.

Mbejane stood up. 'They wait where you sent them. I came alone–knowing you would need me.'

'Yes,' said Sean. 'Get two axes from the wagon.'

They gathered wood, a mountain of dry wood, and packed it around Duff's bed–then Sean put fire to it. Mbejane saddled a horse for Sean and he mounted up and looked down at the Zulu.

'Bring the wagons on to the next waterhole. I will meet you there.'

Sean rode out of the laager. He looked back only once and saw that the breeze had spread the smoke from the pyre in a mile-long smudge across the tops of the thorn trees.

9

Like a bag of pus at the root of an infected tooth the guilt and grief rotted in Sean's mind. His guilt was double-edged. He had betrayed Duff's trust, and he had lacked the courage to make the betrayal worthwhile. He had waited too long. He should have done it at the beginning, cleanly and quickly, or he should not have done it at all. He longed with every fibre of his body to be given the chance to do it again, but this time the right way. He would gladly have lived once more through all that horror to clear his conscience and clean the stain from the memory of their friendship.

His grief was a thing of emptiness, an aching void–so immense that he was lost in it. Where before there had been Duff's laughter, his twisted grin and infectious zest there was now only a grey nothingness. No glimmer of sun penetrated it and there were no solid shapes in it.

The next waterhole was shallow soup in the centre of a flat expanse of dry mud the size of a polo field. The mud was cracked in an irregular chequered pattern forming small brickettes, each the size of a hand. A man could have jumped across the water without wetting his feet. Scattered thickly round its circumference were the droppings of animals that had drunk there. Back and forth across its surface, changing direction as the wind veered, a few loose feathers sailed. The water was brackish and dirty. It was a bad camp. On the third day Mbejane went to Sean's wagon. Sean lay in his cot. He had not changed his clothes since leaving Duff. His beard was beginning to mat, sticky with sweat for it was hot as an oven under the wagon canvas.

'Nkosi, will you come and look at the water. I do not think we should stay here.'

'What is wrong with it?' Sean asked without interest.

'It is dirty, I think we should go on towards the big river.'

'Do whatever you think is right.' Sean rolled away from him, his face towards the side of the wagon.

So Mbejane took the wagon train down towards the Limpopo. It was two days later that they found the ribbon of dark green trees that lined the banks. Sean stayed in his cot throughout the trek, jolting over the rough ground, sweating in the heat but oblivious to all discomfort. Mbejane put the wagons into laager on the bank above the river-bed, then he and all the other servants waited for Sean to come to life again. Their talk round the fire at nights was baited with worry and they looked often towards Sean's living wagon, where it stood unlit by lantern, dark as the mood of the man that lay within.

Like a bear coming out of its cave at the end of winter, Sean came out of the wagon at last. His clothes were filthy. The dogs hurried to meet him, crowding round his knees, begging for attention and he did not notice them. Vaguely he answered the greeting of his servants. He wandered down the bank into the river-bed.

The summer had shrunk the Limpopo into a sparse line of pools strung out down the centre of the watercourse. The pools were dark olive green. The sand around them was white, glaring snowfield white, and the boulders that choked the barely moving river were black and polished smooth. The banks were steep, half a mile apart and walled in with trees. Sean walked through the sand, sinking to his ankles with each step. He reached the water and sat down at the edge, he dabbled his hand in it and found it warm as blood. In the sand next to him was the long slither mark of a crocodile, and a troop of monkeys were shaking the branches of a tree on the far bank and chattering at him. A pair of Sean's dogs splashed across the narrow neck between two pools and went off to chase the monkeys. They went half-heartedly with their tongues flapping at the corners of their mouths for it was very hot in the whiteness of the river-bed. Sean stared into the green water. It was lonely without Duff; he had only his guilt and his sorrow for company. One of the dogs that had stayed with him touched his cheek with its cold nose. Sean put his arm round its neck and the dog leaned against him. He heard footsteps in the sand behind him, he turned and looked up. It was Mbejane.

'Nkosi, Hlubi has found elephant not an hour's march up stream. He has counted twenty who show good ivory.'

Sean looked back at the water. 'Go away,' he said.

Mbejane squatted down beside him with his elbows on his knees. 'For whom do you mourn?' he asked.

'Go away, Mbejane, leave me alone.'

'Nkosi Duff does not need your sorrow–therefore I think that you mourn for yourself.' Mbejane picked up a pebble and tossed it into the pool.

'When a traveller gets a thorn in his foot,' Mbejane went on softly, 'and he is wise he plucks it out–and he is a fool who leaves it and says "I will keep this thorn to prick me so that I will always remember the road upon which I have travelled." Nkosi, it is better to remember with pleasure than with pain.' Mbejane lobbed another pebble into the pool, then he stood up and walked back to the camp. When Sean followed him ten minutes later he found a saddle on his horse, his rifle in the scabbard and Mbejane and Hlubi waiting with their spears. Kandhla handed him his hat, he held it by the brim, turning it in his hands. Then he clapped it on to his head and swung up on to the horse.

'Lead,' he ordered.

During the next weeks Sean hunted with a single-mindedness that left no time for brooding. His returns to the wagons were short and intermittent; his only reasons for returning at all were to bring in the ivory and change his horse. At the end of one of these brief visits to camp and as Sean was about to mount up for another hunt, even Mbejane complained. 'Nkosi, there are better ways to die than working too hard.'

'You look well enough,' Sean assured him, although Mbejane was now as lean as a greyhound and his skin shone like washed anthracite.

'Perhaps all men look healthy to a man on horseback,' Mbejane suggested and Sean stopped with one foot in the stirrup. He looked at Mbejane thoughtfully, then he lowered his leg again. 'We hunt on foot now, Mbejane, and the first to ask for mercy earns the right to be called "woman" by the other.'

Mbejane grinned; the challenge was to his liking. They crossed the river and found spoor before midday–a small herd of young bulls. They followed it until nightfall and slept huddled together under one blanket, then they went on again next morning. On the third day they lost the spoor in rocky ground and they cast back towards the river. They picked up another herd within ten miles of the wagons, went after them and killed that evening–three fine bulls, not a tusk between them under fifty pounds weight. A night march back to the wagons, four hours' sleep and they were away again. Sean was limping a little now and on the second day out, during one of their infrequent halts, he pulled off his boot. The blister on his heel had burst and his sock was stiff with dried blood. Mbejane looked at him expressionlessly. 'How far are we from the wagons?' asked Sean.

'We can be back before dark, Nkosi.' Mbejane carried Sean's rifle for him on the return. Not once did his mask of solemnity slip. Back in camp Kandhla brought a basin of hot water and set it in front of Sean's chair. While Sean soaked his feet in it his entire following squatted in a circle about him. Every face wore an expression of studied concern and the silence was broken only by the clucking sounds of Bantu sympathy. They were loving every minute of it and Mbejane with the timing of a natural actor was building up the effect, playing to his audience. Sean puffed at a cheroot, scowling to stop himself laughing. Mbejane cleared his throat and spat into the fire. Every eye was on him; they waited breathlessly.

'Nkosi,' said Mbejane, 'I would set fifty head of oxen as your marriage price–if you were my daughter.'

One instant more of silence, then a shout of laughter. Sean laughed with them at first, but after a while when Hlubi had nearly staggered into the fire and Nonga was sobbing loudly on Mbejane's shoulder with tears of mirth streaming down his cheeks, Sean's own laughter stopped. It wasn't *that* funny.

He looked at them sourly–at their wide open pink mouths and their white teeth, at their shaking shoulders and heaving chests and suddenly it came to him very clearly that they were no longer laughing at him. They were laughing for the joy of it. They were laughing because they were alive. A chuckle rattled up Sean's throat and escaped before he could stop it, another one bounced around inside his chest and he lay back in his chair, opened his mouth and let it come. The hell with it, he was alive, too.

In the morning when he climbed out of his wagon and limped across to see what Kandhla was cooking for breakfast, there was a faint excitement in him again, the excitement of a new day. He felt good. Duff's memory was still with him, it always would be, but now it was not a sickening ache. He had plucked out the thorn.

10

They moved camp three times in November, keeping to the south bank of the river, following it back towards the west. Slowly the wagons which they had emptied of ivory beside the waterhole began to fill again, for the game was concentrated along the river. The rest of the land was dry but now each day there was promise of relief.

The clouds that had been scattered across the sky began to crowd together, gathering into rounded dark-edged masses or rearing proudly into thunderheads. All of nature seemed impressed by their growing importance. In the evenings the sun dressed them in royal purple and during the day the whirlwinds did dervish dances for their entertainment. The rains were coming. Sean had to make a decision, cross the Limpopo and cut himself off from the south when the river flooded, or stay where he was and leave the land beyond undisturbed. It wasn't a difficult decision. They found a place where the banks flattened out a little on both sides of the river. They unloaded the first wagon and double-teamed it; then with everybody shouting encouragement the oxen galloped down the steep slope into the river-bed. The wagon bounced behind them until it hit the sand where it came to a halt, tilted at an abandoned angle, with its wheels sunk axle-deep into the sand.

'On to the spokes,' shouted Sean. They flung themselves on the wheels and strained to keep them turning, but half the oxen were down on their knees, powerless in the loose footing.

'Damn it to hell.' Sean glared at the wagon. 'Outspan the oxen and take them back. Get out the axes.'

It took them three days to lay a bridge of corduroyed branches across the river and another two to get all the wagons and ivory to the far bank. Sean declared a holiday when the last wagon was manhandled into the laager and the whole camp slept late the next morning. The sun was high by the time Sean descended from his wagon. He was still muzzy and a little liverish from lying abed. He yawned wide and stretched like a crucifix. He ran his tongue round his mouth and grimaced at the taste, then he scratched his chest and the hair rasped under his fingers.

'Kandhla, where's the coffee? Don't you care that I am near dead from thirst?'

'Nkosi, the water will boil very soon.'

Sean grunted and walked across to where Mbejane squatted with the other servants by the fire watching Kandhla.

'This is a good camp, Mbejane.' Sean looked up at the roof of leaves above them. It was a place of green shade, cool in the late morning heat. Christmas beetles were squealing in the wide stretched branches.

'There is good grazing for the cattle,' Mbejane agreed; he stretched out his hand towards Sean.

'I found this in the grass–someone else has camped here.' Sean took it from him and examined it, a piece of broken china with a blue fig-leaf pattern. It was a shock to Sean, that little fragment of civilization in the wilderness; he turned it in his fingers and Mbejane went on. 'There are the ashes of an old fire there against the shuma tree and I found the ruts where wagons climbed the bank at the same place as ours.'

'How long ago?'

Mbejane shrugged. 'A year perhaps. Grass has grown in the wagon tracks.'

Sean sat down in his chair, he felt disturbed. He thought about it and grinned as he realized he was jealous; there were strangers here in the land he was coming to regard as his own, those year-old tracks gave him a feeling of being in a crowd. Also there was the opposite feeling, that of longing for the company of his own kind. The sneaking desire to see a white face again. It was strange that he could resent something and yet wish for it simultaneously.

'Kandhla, am I to have coffee now or at supper tonight?'

'Nkosi, it is done.' Kandhla poured a little brown sugar into the mug, stirred it with a stick and handed it to him. Sean held the mug in both hands, blowing to cool it, then sipping and sighing with each mouthful. The talk of his Zulus passed back and forth about the circle and the snuff-boxes followed it, each remark of worth being greeted with a solemn chorus of 'It is true, it is true,' and the taking of snuff. Small arguments jumped up and fell back again into the leisurely stream of conversation. Sean listened to them, occasionally joining in or contributing a story until his stomach told him it was time to eat. Kandhla started to cook, under the critical supervision and with the helpful suggestions of those whom idleness had made garrulous. He had almost succeeded in grilling the carcass of a guinea-fowl to the satisfaction of the entire company, although Mbejane felt that he should have added a pinch more salt, when Nonga sitting across the fire from him jumped to his feet and pointed towards the north. Sean shaded his eyes and looked.

'For Chrissake,' said Sean.

'Ah! ah! ah!' said his servants.

A white man rode towards them from the trees; he cantered with long stirrups, slouched comfortably, close enough already for Sean to make out the great ginger beard that masked the bottom half of his face. He was a big man; the sleeves of his shirt rolled high around thick arms.

'Hello,' shouted Sean and went eagerly to meet him. The rider reined in at the edge of the laager. He climbed stiffly out of the saddle and grabbed Sean's outstretched hand. Sean felt his fingerbones creak in the grip.

'Hello, man! How goes it?' He spoke in Afrikaans. His voice matched the size of his body and his eyes were on a level with Sean's. They pumped each other's arms mercilessly, laughing, putting sincerity into the usual inanities of greeting.

'Kandhla–get out the brandy bottle,' Sean called over his shoulder, then to the Boer, 'Come in, you're just in time for lunch. We'll have a dram to celebrate. Hell, it's good to see a white man again!'

'You're on your own, then?'

'Yes–come in, man, sit down.'

Sean poured drinks and the Boer took one up.

'What's your name?' he asked.

'Courteney–Sean Courteney.'

'I'm Jan Paulus Leroux–glad to meet you, meneer.'

'Good health, meneer,' Sean answered him and they drank. Jan Paulus wiped his whiskers on the palm of his hand and breathed out heavily, blowing the taste of the brandy back into his mouth.

'That was good,' he said and held out his mug. They talked excitedly, tongues loose from loneliness, trying to say everything and ask all the questions at once–meetings in the bush are always like this. Meanwhile the tide was going out in the bottle and the level dropped quickly.

'Tell me, where are your wagons?' Sean asked.

'An hour or two behind. I came ahead to find the river.'

'How many in your party?' Sean watched his face, talking just for the sound of it.

'Ma and Pa, my little sister and my wife–which reminds me–you had better move your wagons.'

'What?' Sean looked puzzled.

'This is my outspan place,' the Boer explained to him. 'See, there are the marks of my fire–this is my camp.'

The smile went out of Sean's voice. 'Look around you, Boer, there is the whole of Africa. Take your pick–anywhere except where I am sitting.'

'But this is my place.' Jan Paulus flushed a little. 'I always camp at the same place when I return along a spoor.'

The whole temper of their meeting had changed in a few seconds. Jan Paulus stood abruptly and went to his horse. He stooped and tightened the girth, hauling so savagely on the strap that the animal staggered off balance. He flung himself on to its back and looked down at Sean.

'Move your wagons,' he said, 'I camp here tonight.'

'Would you like to bet on that?' Sean asked grimly.

'We'll see!' Jan Paulus flashed back.

'We certainly shall,' agreed Sean.

The Boer wheeled his horse and rode away. Sean watched his back disappear among the trees and only then did he let his anger slip. He rampaged through the laager working himself into a fury, pacing out frustrated circles, stopping now and then to glare out in the direction from which the Boer's wagons would come–but under all the external signs of indignation was his unholy anticipation of a fight. Kandhla brought him food, hurrying along behind him with the plate. Sean waved him away impatiently and continued his pugnacious patrol. At last a trek whip popped in the distance and an ox lowed faintly, to be answered immediately by Sean's cattle. The dogs started barking and Sean crossed to one of the wagons on the north side of the laager and leaned against it with assumed nonchalance. The long line of wagons wound out of the trees towards him. There were bright blobs of colour on the high box seat of the lead wagon. Women's dresses! Ordinarily they would have made Sean's nostrils flare like those of a stud stallion, but now his whole attention was concentrated on the larger of the two outriders. Jan Paulus cantered ahead of his father, and Sean, with his fists clenched into bony hammers at his sides, watched him come. Jan Paulus sat straight in the saddle; he stopped his horse a dozen paces from Sean and shoved his hat on to the back of his head with a thumb as thick and as brown as a fried sausage; he tickled his horse a little with his spurs to make it dance and he asked with mock surprise, 'What, *Rooi Nek*, still here?'

Sean's dogs had rushed forward to meet the other pack and now they milled about in a restrained frenzy of mutual bottom-smelling, stiff-limbed with tension, backs abristle and legs cocking in the formal act of urination.

'Why don't you go and climb a tree? You'll feel more at home there,' Sean suggested mildly.

'Ah! so?' Jan Paulus reared in his stirrups. He kicked loose his right foot, swung it back over his horse's rump to dismount and Sean jumped at him. The horse skittered nervously, throwing the Boer off balance and he clutched at the saddle. Sean reached up, took a double handful of his ginger beard and leaned back on it with all his weight. Jan Paulus came over backward with his arms windmilling, his foot caught in the stirrup and he hung suspended like a hammock, held at one end to the plunging horse and at the other by his chin to Sean's hands. Sean dug his heels in, revelling in the Boer's bellows.

Galvanised into action by Sean's example, the dogs cut short the ceremony and went at each other in a snarling, snapping shambles; the fur flew like sand in a Kalahari dust-storm.

The stirrup-leather snapped; Sean fell backwards and rolled to his feet just in time to meet Jan Paulus's charge. He smothered the punch that the Boer bowled overarm at him, but the power behind it shocked him; then they were chest to chest and Sean felt his own strength matched. They strained silently with their beards touching and their eyes inches apart. Sean shifted his weight quickly and tried for a fall, but smoothly as a dancer Jan Paulus met and held him. Then it was his turn; he twisted in Sean's arms and Sean sobbed with the effort required to stop him. Oupa Leroux joined in by driving his horse at them, scattering the dogs, his hippo-hide sjambok hissing as he swung it. 'Let it stand! you thunders, give over–hey! Enough, let it stand!'

Sean shouted with pain as the lash cut across his back and at the next stroke Jan Paulus howled as loudly. They let go of each other and massaging their whip-weals retreated before the skinny old white-beard on the horse.

The first of the wagons had come up now and two hundred pounds of woman, all in one package, called out from the box seat, 'Why did you stop them, Oupa?'

'No sense in letting them kill each other.'

'Shame on you–so you must spoil the boys' fun. Don't you remember how you loved to fight? Or are you now so old you forget the pleasures of your youth? Leave them alone!'

Oupa hesitated, swinging the sjambok and looking from Sean to Jan Paulus.

'Come away from there, you old busybody,' his wife ordered him. She was solid as a granite kopje, her blouse packed full of bosom and her bare arms brown and thick as a man's. The wide brim of her bonnet shaded her face but Sean could see it was pink and pudding-shaped, the kind of face that smiles more easily than it frowns. There were two girls on the seat beside her but there was no time to look at them. Oupa had pulled his horse out of the way and Jan Paulus was moving down on him. Sean went up on his toes, crouching a little, preoccupied with the taste he had just had of the other's strength, watching Jan Paulus close in for the main course and not too certain he was going to be able to chew this mouthful.

Jan Paulus tested Sean with a long right-hander but Sean rolled his head with it and the thick pad of his beard cushioned the blow; he hooked Jan Paulus in the ribs under his raised arm and Jan Paulus grunted and circled away.

Forgetting his scruples, Oupa Leroux watched them with rising delight. It was going to be a good fight. They were well matched–both big men, under thirty, quick and smooth on their feet. Both had fought before and that often; you could tell it by the way they felt each other out, turning just out of reach, moving in to offer an opening that a less experienced man might have attempted and regretted, then dropping back.

The fluid, almost leisurely pattern of movement exploded. Jan Paulus jumped in, moving left, changed direction like the recoil of a whip lash and used his right hand again; Sean ducked under it and laid himself open to Jan Paulus's left. He staggered back from its kick, bleeding where it had split the flesh across his cheek-bone, and Jan Paulus followed him eagerly, his hands held ready, searching for the opening. Sean kept clear, instinct moving his feet until the blackness faded inside his head and he felt the strength in his arms again. He saw Jan Paulus following him and he let his legs stay rubbery; he dropped his hands and waited for Jan Paulus to commit himself. Too late Jan Paulus caught the cunning in Sean's eyes and tried to break from the trap, but clenched bone raked his face. He staggered away and now he was bleeding also.

They fought through the wagons with the advantage changing hands a dozen times. They came together and used their heads and their knees, they broke and used their fists again. Then locked chest to chest once more they rolled down the steep bank into the river-bed of the Limpopo. They fought in the soft sand and it held their legs, it filled their mouths when they fell and clung like white icing-sugar to their hair and beards. They splashed into one of the pools and they fought in the water, coughing with the agony of it in their lungs, floundering like a pair of bull hippos, their movements slowing down until they knelt facing each other, no longer able to rise, the water running from them and the only sound their gasping for air.

Not sure whether the darkness was actuality or a fantasy of fatigue, for the sun had set by the time they were finished, Sean watched Jan Paulus starting to puke, retching with a tearing noise to bring up a small splash of yellow bile. Sean crawled to the edge of the pool and lay with his face in the sand. There were voices echoing in his ears and the light of a lantern–the light was red–filtered through the blood that had trickled into his eyes. His servants lifted him and he hardly felt them. The light and the voices faded into blackness as he slipped over the edge of consciousness.

The sting of iodine woke him and he struggled to sit up but hands pushed him down.

'Gently, gently, the fight is over.' Sean focused his one eye to find the voice. The pinkness of Ouma Leroux hung over him. Her hands touched his face and the antiseptic stung him again. He exclaimed through puffed lips.

'So! Just like a man,' Ouma chuckled. 'Your head nearly knocked off without a murmur but one touch of medicine and you cry like a baby.'

Sean rang his tongue round inside his mouth; one tooth loose but all the others miraculously present. He started to lift his hand to touch his closed eye but Ouma slapped it down impatiently and went on working over him.

'Glory, what a fight!' She shook her head happily. 'You were good, *kerel*, you were very good.'

Sean looked beyond her and saw the girl. She was standing in shadow, a silhouette against the pale canvas. She was holding a basin. Ouma turned and dipped the cloth in it, washing out the blood before she came back to his face. The wagon rocked under her weight and the lantern that hung from the roof swung, lighting the girl's face from the side. Sean's legs straightened on his cot and he moved his head slightly to see her better.

'Be still, *jong*,' Ouma commanded. Sean looked past her at the girl–at the full serene line of her lips and the curve of her cheek. He saw the pile of her hair fluff up in happy disarray and then, suddenly penitent, slide down behind her neck, curl over her shoulder and hang to her waist in a plait as thick as his wrist.

'Katrina, do you expect me to reach right across to the basin each time? Stand closer, girl.'

She stepped into the light and looked at Sean. Green, laughing, almost bubbling green was the colour of her eyes. Then she dropped them to the basin. Sean stared at her, not wanting to miss the moment when she would look up again.

'My big bear,' Ouma spoke with grudging approval. 'Steal our camp site, fight my son and ogle my daughter. If you go on like this I might have to knock the thunder out of you myself. Glory, but you are a dangerous one! Katrina, you had better go back to our wagons and help Henrietta see to your brother. Leave the basin on the chest there.'

She looked at Sean once more before she left. There were secret shadows in the green–she didn't have to smile with her mouth.

11

Sean woke to the realization that something was wrong. He started to sit up but the pain checked him: the stiffness of bruised muscle and the catch of half-dried scab. He groaned and the movement hurt his lips. Slowly he swung his legs off the cot and roused himself to take stock of the damage. Dark through the hair of his chest showed a heel imprint of Jan Paulus's boot. Sean prodded round it gently, feeling for the give of a broken rib; then, satisfied with that area, he went on to inspect the raw graze that wrapped round on to his back, holding his left arm high and peering closely at the broken skin. He picked a bit of blanket fluff from the scab. He stood up, only to freeze as a torn muscle in his shoulder knifed him. He started to swear then softly monotonously, and he kept it up all through the painful business of climbing down out of the wagon.

His entire following watched his descent–even the dogs looked worried. Sean reached the ground and started to shout.

'What the hell–' He stopped hurriedly as he felt his lip crack open again and start to bleed.

'What the hell'–he said again, keeping his lips still–'are you doing standing round like a bunch of women at a beer drink–is there no work here? Hlubi, I thought I sent you out to look for elephant.' Hlubi went. 'Kandhla, where's breakfast? Mbejane, get me a basin of water and my shaving-mirror.' Sean sat in his chair and morosely inspected his face in the mirror.

'If a herd of buffalo had stampeded across it they would have done less damage.'

'Nkosi, it is nothing compared to his face,' Mbejane assured him.

'Is he bad?' Sean looked up.

'I have spoken to one of his servants. He has not left his bed yet and he lies there, growling like a wounded lion in a thicket; but his eyes are as tightly closed as those of a new cub.'

'Tell me more, Mbejane. Say truly, was it a good fight?'

Mbejane squatted down next to Sean's chair. He was silent a moment as he gathered his words.

'When the sky sends its cloud impis against the peaks of the Drakensberg, with thunder and the spears of lightning, it is a thing to thrill a man. When two bull elephants fight unto death there is no braver show in all the veld. Is this not so?'

Sean nodded, his eyes twinkling.

'Nkosi, hear me when I tell you these things were as the play of little children beside this fight.'

Sean listened to the praises. Mbejane was well versed in the oldest art of Zululand and when he had finished he looked at Sean's face. It was happy. Mbejane smiled and took a fold of paper out of his loin cloth. 'A servant from the other camp brought this while you slept.'

Sean read the note. It was written in a big round schoolgirl hand and worded in High Dutch. He liked that writing. It was an invitation to dinner.

'Kandhla, get out my suit and my number one boots.' He picked up the mirror again. There wasn't very much he could do about his face–trim the beard, perhaps, but that was all. He laid the mirror down and looked upstream to where the Leroux wagons were half hidden among the trees.

Mbejane carried a lantern in front of Sean. They walked slowly to enable Sean to limp with dignity. When they reached the other laager, Jan Paulus climbed stiffly out of his chair and nodded an equally stiff greeting. Mbejane had lied–except for a missing tooth there was little to choose between their faces. Oupa slapped Sean's back and pressed a tumbler of brandy into his hand. He was a tall man, but twenty thousand suns had burnt away his flesh and left only stringy muscle, had faded his eyes to a pale green and toughened his skin to the texture of a turkey's neck. His beard was yellowish-white with still a touch of ginger round the mouth. He asked Sean three questions without giving him time to answer the first, then he led him to a chair.

Oupa talked, Sean listened and Jan Paulus sulked. Oupa talked of cattle and hunting and the land to the north. After a few minutes Sean realized that he was not expected to take part in the conversation: his few tentative efforts were crushed under Oupa's verbal avalanche. So Sean listened half to him and half to the whisper of women's voices from the cooking fires behind the laager. Once he heard her laugh. He knew it was her for it was the rich sound of the thing that he had seen in her eyes. At last the women's business with food and pots was finished and Ouma led the girls to where the men sat. Sean stood up and saw that Katrina was tall, with shoulders like a boy. As she walked towards him the movement pressed her skirt against her legs–they were long but her feet was small. Her hair was red-black and tied behind her head in an enormous bun.

'Ah, my battling bear,' Ouma took Sean's arm, 'let me present my daughter-in-law, Henrietta–here is the man that nearly killed your husband.' Jan Paulus snorted from his chair and Ouma laughed, her bosom wobbling merrily. Henrietta was a small dark-eyed girl. *She doesn't like me,* Sean guessed instantly. He bowed slightly and took her hand. She pulled it away.

'This is my youngest daughter, Katrina. You met her last night.'

She does like me. Her fingers were long and square-tipped in his. Sean risked his lips with a smile.

'Without her ministrations I might have bled to death,' he said. She smiled straight back at him but not with her mouth.

'You wear your wounds well, meneer, the blue eye has an air of distinction.'

'That will be enough from you, girl,' Oupa spoke sharply. 'Go and sit by your mother.' He turned to Sean. 'I was telling you about this horse–well, I said to the fellow, "He's not worth five pounds let alone fifteen, look at those hocks, thin as sticks." So he says to me, trying to get me away, you follow, he says, "Come and look at the saddle." But I can see he's worried–'

The thin cotton of the girl's blouse could hardly contain the impatient push of her breasts, Sean thought that he had never seen anything so wonderful.

There was a trestle-table next to the cooking fire; they went to it at last. Oupa said grace. Sean watched him through his lashes. Oupa's beard waggled as he spoke and at one point he thumped the table to emphasize the point he was making to the Almighty. His 'amen' had such an impressive resonance that Sean had to make an effort to stop himself applauding and Oupa fell back spent.

'Amen,' said Ouma and ladled stew from a pot the size of a bucket. Henrietta added pumpkin fritters and Katrina stacked slices of fresh mealie bread on each plate. A silence fell on the table, spoiled only by the clank of metal on china and the sound of Oupa breathing through his nose.

'Mevrouw Leroux, I have waited a long time to taste food like this again.' Sean mopped up the last bit of gravy with a piece of mealie bread. Ouma beamed.

'There's plenty more, meneer. I love to see a man eat. Oupa used to be a great trencherman. My father made him take me away for he could not afford to feed him every time he came courting.' She took Sean's plate and filled it. 'You look to me like a man who can eat.'

'I think I'll hold my own in most company,' Sean agreed.

'So?' Jan Paulus spoke for the first time. He passed his plate to Ouma. 'Fill it up, please, Mother, tonight I am hungry.'

Sean's eyes narrowed, he waited until Jan Paulus had his plate back in front of him, then he took up his fork deliberately. Jan Paulus did the same.

'Glory,' said Ouma happily. 'Here we go again. Oupa, you may have to go out and shoot a couple of buffalo before dinner is finished tonight.'

'I will bet one sovereign on Jan Paulus,' Oupa challenged his wife. 'He is like an army of termites. I swear that if there was nothing else he'd eat the canvas off the wagons.'

'All right,' agreed Ouma. 'I've never seen the Bear eat before, but it seems to me he has plenty of room to put it.'

'Your woollen shawl against my green bonnet that Jan Paulus gives up first,' Katrina whispered to her sister-in-law.

'When Jannie has finished the stew he'll eat the Englishman,' Henrietta giggled. 'But it's a pretty bonnet–I'll take the wager.'

Plateful for plateful, Ouma measuring out each ladle with scrupulous fairness, they ate against each other. The talk round the table dwindled and halted.

'More?' asked Ouma each time the plates were clean, and each time they looked at each other and nodded. At last the ladle scraped the bottom of the pot.

'That's the end of it, my children, we will have to call it another draw.'

The silence went on after she had spoken. Sean and Jan Paulus sat very still looking at their respective plates. Jan Paulus hiccupped, his expression changed. He stood up and went into the darkness.

'Ah! listen! listen!' crowed Ouma. They waited and then she exploded into laughter. 'The ungrateful wretch, is that what he thinks of my food? Where's your sovereign, Oupa?'

'Wait, you greedy old woman, the game's not finished yet.' He turned and stared at Sean. 'To me it looks as though your horse is nearly blown.'

Sean closed his eyes. The sounds of Jan Paulus's distress came to him very clearly.

'Thank you for a–' He didn't have time to finish. He wanted to get far away so the girl couldn't hear him.

12

The following morning during breakfast Sean thought about his next move. He would write an invitation to dinner and then he would deliver it himself. They would have to ask him to stay for coffee and then, if he waited, there would be a chance. Even Oupa would have to stop talking sometime and Ouma might relax her vigilance. He was sure there'd be a chance to talk to the girl. He didn't know what he would say to her but he'd worry about that when the time came. He climbed into the wagon and found pencil and paper in his chest. He went back to the table and spread the paper in front of him. He chewed the end of the pencil and stared out into the bush. Something moved against the trees. Sean put the pencil down and stood up. The dogs barked then stopped as they recognized Hlubi. He was coming at a trot–he was coming with news. Sean waited for him.

'A big herd, Hkosi, with many showing ivory. I saw them drink at the river and then go back into the bush, feeding quietly.'

'When?' asked Sean to gain time. He was searching for a plausible excuse to stay in camp–it would have to be good to satisfy Mbejane who was already saddling one of the horses.

'Before the sun this morning,' answered Hlubi and Sean was trying to remember which was his sore shoulder–he couldn't hunt with a sore shoulder. Mbejane led the horse into the laager. Sean scratched the side of his nose and coughed.

'The tracker from the other camp follows close behind me, Nkosi, he too has seen the herd and brings the news to his master. But I, being as swift as a springbok when I run, have outdistanced him,' Hlubi ended modestly.

'Is that so?' For Sean it changed the whole problem, he couldn't leave the herd to that red-bearded Dutchman. He ran across to the wagon and snatched his bandolier from the foot of the cot. His rifle was already in the scabbard.

'Are you tired, Hlubi?' Sean buckled the heavy ammunition belt across his chest. The sweat had run in oily streaks down the Zulu's body; his breathing was deep and quick.

'No, Nkosi.'

'Well, then, lead us to these elephants of yours, my fleet-footed springbok.' Sean swung up on to his horse. He looked over his shoulder at the other camp. She would still be there when he came back.

Sean was limited to the speed of Hlubi's feet while the two Leroux had only to gallop along the easy spoor left by Sean's party and they caught up with him before he had gone two miles.

'Good morning to you,' Oupa greeted him as he drew level and pulled his horse in to a trot. 'Out for a morning's ride, I see.'

Sean made the best of it with a grin. 'If we are all to hunt then we must hunt together. Do you agree?'

'Of course, meneer.'

'And we must share the bag equally, one third to each man.'

'That is always the way.' Oupa nodded.

'Do you agree?' Sean turned in his saddle towards Jan Paulus. Jan Paulus grunted. He showed little inclination to open his mouth since he had lost his tooth.

They found the spoor within an hour. The herd had wrecked a road through the thick bush along the river. They had stripped the bark from the saplings and left them naked and bleeding. They had knocked down bigger trees to reach the tender top leaves and they had dropped their great piles of dung in the grass.

'We need no trackers to follow this.' Jan Paulus had the first excitement on him. Sean looked at him and wondered how many elephant had died in front of his rifle. A thousand perhaps, and yet the excitement was on him again now.

'Tell your servants to follow us. We'll go ahead. We'll catch them within an hour.' He smiled at Sean, gap-toothed, and Sean felt the excitement lift the hair on his own forearms. He smiled back.

They cantered in rough line abreast, slack-reined to let the horses pick their own way among the fallen trees. The river bush thinned out as they moved north and soon they were into parkland. The grass brushed their stirrups and the ground beneath it was firm and smooth.

They rode without talking, leaning forward in their saddles, looking ahead. The rhythmic beat of hooves was a war drum. Sean ran his fingers along the row of bullets strapped across his chest, then he drew his rifle, checked the load and thrust it back into its scabbard.

'There!' said Oupa and Sean saw the herd. It was massed among a grove of fever trees a quarter of a mile ahead.

'Name of a name,' Paulus whistled. 'There must be two hundred at least.'

Sean heard the first pig-squeal of alarm, saw ears fan out and trunks lift. Then the herd bunched together and ran with their backs humped, a thin screen of dust trailing behind them.

'Paulus take the right flank. You, meneer, in the middle and I'll ride left,' shouted Oupa.

Sean jammed his hat down over his ears and his horse jumped under him as he hit it with his heels. Like a thrown trident the three horsemen hurled themselves at the herd. Sean rode into the dust. He picked an old cow elephant from the moving mountain range in front of him and pressed his horse so close upon her that he could see the bristles in her tail tuft and the erosion of her skin, wrinkled as an old man's scrotum. He touched his hand to his horse's neck and it plunged–from full gallop to standstill in half a dozen strides. Sean threw his feet free of the stirrups and hit the ground, loose-kneed to ride the shock. The cow's spine was a line of lumps beneath the grey skin–Sean broke it with his first bullet and she dropped, sliding on her hindquarters like a dog with worms. His horse started to run again before he was properly in the saddle and everything became movement and noise, dust and the smell of burnt powder. Chase them, coughing in the dust. Close with them. Off the horse and shoot. Wet blood on grey skin. Slam, slam of the rifle–its barrel hot, recoiling savagely. Sweat in the eyes, stinging. Ride. Shoot again. Two more down, screaming, anchored by paralysed legs. Blood-red as a flag. Load, cramming cartridges into the rifle. Ride. Chase them, shoot again and again. The bullets striking on flesh with a hollow sound, then up and ride again. Ride–until the horse could no longer keep up with them and he had to let them go. He stood holding his horse's head, the dust and the thirst closed his throat. He could not swallow. His hands trembled in reaction. His shoulder was aching again. He untied his silk scarf, wiped his face with it and blew the mud out of his nose, then he drank from his water-bottle. The water tasted sweet.

The hunt had led from parkland into mopani bush. It was very thick, shiny green leaves hanging to the ground and pressing close around him. The air was still and warm to breathe. He turned back along the line of the chase. He found them by their squealing. When they saw him they tried to charge, dragging themselves towards him–using the front legs only and groping with their trunks. They sagged into stillness after the head shot. This was the bad part. Sean worked quickly. He could hear the other rifles in the mopani forest around him and when he came to one of the long clearings among the trees he saw Jan Paulus walking towards him, leading his horse.

'How many?' called Sean.

'*Gott*, man, I didn't count. What a killing, hey? Have you got a drink for me? I dropped my water-bottle somewhere.'

Jan Paulus's rifle was in its saddle scabbard. The reins were slung over his shoulder and his horse followed him with its head drooping from exhaustion. The clearing was walled in with the dense mopani trees and a wounded elephant broke into the open. It was lung shot–the side of its chest painted with froth–and when it squealed the blood sprayed in a pink spout from the end of its trunk. It went for Jan Paulus, streaming the black battle ensigns of its ears. His horse reared, the reins snapped, it turned free and galloped away, leaving him full in the path of the charge. Sean went up on to his horse's back without touching stirrups. His horse threw its head, dancing in a tight circle, but he dragged it around and drove it to intercept the charge.

'Don't run, for God's sake, don't run!' he shouted as he cleared his rifle from the scabbard. Jan Paulus heard him. He stood with his hands at his sides, his feet apart and his body braced. The elephant heard Sean shout also and it swung its head and Sean saw the first hesitation in its run. He fired, not trying to pick his shot, hoping only to hurt it, to bring it away from Jan Paulus. The bullet slapped into it with the sound of a wet towel flicked against a wall. The elephant turned, clumsy with the weakness of its shattered lungs. Sean gathered his horse beneath him and wheeled it away and the elephant followed him.

Sean fumbled as he reloaded, his hands were slippery with sweat. One of the brass shells slipped through his fingers, tapped against his knee and dropped into the grass under his horse's hooves. The elephant gained on him. He loosened his bed-roll from the saddle and let it fall–they would sometimes stop to savage even a fallen hat, but not this one. He turned in the saddle and fired into it. It squealed again so close upon him that the brown blood splattered into his face. His horse was almost finished; he could feel its legs flopping with every stride and they were nearly at the end of the clearing racing towards the solid wall of green mopani. He pushed another round into the breech of his rifle and swung his body across the saddle. He slid down until his feet touched the ground and he was running next to his horse. He let go and was flung forward, but he fought to keep his balance, his body jarring with the force of his run. Then, still on his feet, he turned for his first steady shot. The elephant was coming in fast, almost on top of him, hanging over him like a cliff. Its trunk coiled on its chest and the curves of its ivory were lifted high.

It's too close, much too close. I can't hit the brain from here.

He aimed at the hollow in its forehead just above the level of its eyes. He fired and the elephant's legs folded up; its brain burst like an overripe tomato within the bone castle of its skull.

Sean tried to jump aside as the massive body came skidding down upon him, but one of its legs hit him and threw him face down into the grass. He lay there. He felt sick, for his stomach was still full of warm oily fear.

After a while he sat up and looked at the elephant. One of its tusks had snapped off flush with the lip. Jan Paulus came, panting from his run. He stopped next to the elephant and touched the wound in its forehead, then he wiped his fingers on his shirt.

'Are you all right, man?'

He took Sean's arm and helped him to his feet; then he picked up Sean's hat and dusted it carefully before handing it to him.

13

In the three-sided shelter formed by the belly and out-thrust legs of one of the dead elephants they made their camp that night. They drank coffee together and Sean sat between the two Leroux with his back against the rough skin of the elephant's belly. The silhouettes of the tree against the night sky were deformed by the shapes of the vultures that clustered in them and the darkness was ugly with the giggling of hyena. They had set a feast for the scavengers. They spoke little for they were tired, but Sean could feel the gratitude of the men who sat beside him and before they rolled into their blankets Jan Paulus said gruffly, 'Thank you, *kerel.*'

'You might be able to do the same for me one day.'

'I hope so, *ja*! I hope so.'

In the morning Oupa said, 'It's going to take us three or four days to cut out all this ivory.' He looked up at the sky. 'I don't like these clouds. One of us had better ride back to camp to fetch more men and wagons to carry the ivory.'

'I'll go.' Sean stood up quickly.

'I was thinking of going myself.' But Sean was already calling to Mbejane to saddle his horse and Oupa couldn't really argue with him, not after yesterday.

'Tell Ouma to take the wagons across the river,' he acquiesced. 'We don't want to be caught on this side when the river floods. Perhaps you wouldn't mind helping her.'

'No,' Sean assured him. 'I don't mind at all.'

His horse was still tired from the previous day's hunt and it was three hours before he reached the river.

He tied his horse on the bank and went down to one of the pools. He stripped off his clothes and lowered himself into the water. He scrubbed himself with handfuls of the coarse sand and when he waded out of the pool and dried on his shirt his skin was tingling. He rode along the bank and the temptation to gallop his horse was almost unbearable. He laughed to himself a little.

'The field's almost clear, though I wouldn't put it past that suspicious old Dutchman to follow me.'

He laughed again and thought about the colour of her eyes, green as *crème-de-menthe* in a crystal glass, and the shape of her bosom. The muscles in his legs tightened and the horse lengthened its stride in response to the pressure of his knees. 'All right, run then,' Sean encouraged it, 'I don't insist on it, but I would be grateful.'

He went to his own wagons first and changed his sweaty shirt for a fresh one, his leather breeches for clean calico and his scuffed boots for soft polished leather. He scrubbed his teeth with salt and dragged a comb through his hair and beard. He saw in the mirror that the battle damage to his face was fading and he winked at his image' 'How can she resist you?' He gave his moustache one more twirl, climbed out of the wagon and was immediately aware of a most uncomfortable feeling in his stomach. He walked towards the Leroux' laager thinking about it, and he recognized it as the same feeling he used to have when Waite Courteney called him to the study to do penance for his boyhood sins.

'That's odd,' he muttered. 'Why should I feel like that?' His confidence faded and he stopped. 'I wonder if my breath smells–I think I'd better go back and get some cloves.' He turned with relief, knew it as cowardice and stopped again. 'Get a grip on yourself. She's only a girl, an uneducated little Dutch girl. You've had fifty finer women.'

'Name me two,' he shot back at himself.

'Well, there was–Oh! for Chrissake, come on.' Resolutely he set off for the Leroux' laager again.

She was sitting in the sun within the circle of wagons. She was leaning forward on the stool and her newly-washed hair fell thickly over her face almost to the ground. With each stroke of the brush it leapt like a live thing and the sun sparkled the red lights in it. Sean wanted to touch it–he wanted to twist fistfuls of it round his hands and he wanted to smell it, it would smell warm and slightly milky like a puppy's fur. He stepped softly towards her but before he reached her she took the shiny mass with both hands and threw it back over her shoulders–a startled flash of green eyes, one despairing wail, 'Oh, no! not with my hair like this.' A swirl of skirts that sent the stool flying and she was gone into her wagon. Sean scratched the side of his nose and stood awkwardly.

'Why are you back so soon, meneer?' she called through the canvas. 'Where are the others? Is everything all right?'

'Yes, they're both fine. I left them and came to fetch wagons to carry the ivory.'

'Oh, that's good.' Sean tried to interpret the inflexion of her voice: was it good that they were fine, or good that he had left them? So far the indications were favourable; her confusion at seeing him boded well.

'What's wrong?' Ouma bellowed from one of the other wagons. 'It's not Oupa, don't tell me something has happened to him?' The wagon rocked wildly and her pink face, puckered with sleep, popped out of the opening. Sean's reassurances were smothered by her voice.

'Oh, I knew this would happen. I had a feeling. I shouldn't have let him go.'

'Paulus, oh, Jan Paulus–I must go to him. Where is he?'

Henrietta came running from the cooking fire behind the wagons and then the dogs started barking and the servants added their chatter to the confusion. Sean tried to shout them all down and watch Katrina emerging from her wagon at the same time. She had disciplined her hair now–it had a green ribbon in it and hung down her back. She was laughing and she helped him to quieten Ouma and Henrietta.

They brought him coffee, then they sat round him and listened to the story of the hunt. Sean went into detail on the rescue of Jan Paulus and was rewarded by a softening of the dislike in Henrietta's eyes. By the time Sean had finished talking it was too late to start moving the wagons across the river. So he talked some more, it was most agreeable to have three women as an attentive audience, and then they ate supper.

With ostentatious tact Ouma and Henrietta retired early to their respective living wagons and left Sean and Katrina sitting by the fire. At carefully-spaced intervals there was a stage cough from Ouma's wagon, a reminder that they were not entirely alone. Sean lit a cheroot and frowned into the fire searching desperately for something intelligent to say, but all his brain could dredge up was, 'Thank God, Oupa isn't here.' He sneaked a glance at Katrina: she was staring into the fire as well and she was blushing. Instantly Sean felt his own cheeks starting to heat up. He opened his mouth to talk and made a squawking noise. He shut it again.

'We can speak in English if you like, meneer.'

'You speak English?' Sean's surprise brought his voice back.

'I practise every night–I read aloud out of my books.'

Sean grinned at her delightedly–it was suddenly very important that she could speak his language. The dam, holding back all the questions that there were to ask and all the things there were to say, burst and the words came pouring out over each other. Katrina fluttered her hands when she couldn't find the word she wanted and then lapsed back into Afrikaans. They killed the short taut silences with a simultaneous rush of words, then laughed together in confusion. They sat on the edges of their chairs and watched each other's faces as they talked. The moon came up, a red rain moon, and the fire faded into a puddle of ashes.

'Katrina, it's long past the time decent people were asleep. I'm sure Meneer Courteney is tired.'

They dropped their voices to a whisper, drawing out the last minutes.

'In just one minute, girl, I'm coming out to fetch you to bed.'

They walked to her wagon and with each step her skirts brushed against his leg. She stopped with one hand on the wagon step. She wasn't as tall as he'd imagined, the top of her head came to his chin. The seconds slid by as he hesitated, reluctant to touch, strangely frightened to test the delicate thread they had spun together lest he destroy it before it became strong. Slowly he swayed towards her and something surged up inside him as he saw her chin lift slightly and the lashes fall over her eyes.

'Goodnight, Meneer Courteney.' Ouma's voice again, loud and with an edge to it. Sean started guiltily.

'Goodnight, mevrouw.'

Katrina touched his arm just above the elbow, her fingers were warm.

'Goodnight, meneer, I shall see you in the morning.'

She rustled up the steps and slipped through the opening of the canvas. Sean scowled at Ouma's wagon.

'Thanks very much–and if there is ever anything I can do for you, please don't hesitate to ask.'

14

They started moving the wagons early next morning. There was no time to talk to Katrina in the bustle of inspanning and working the wagons across the corduroy bridge. Sean spent most of the morning in the river-bed and the white sand bounced the heat up at him. He threw off his shirt and sweated like a wrestler. He trotted beside Katrina's wagon when they ran it through the river-bed. She looked once at his naked chest and arms; her cheeks darkened in the shadow of her bonnet and she dropped her eyes and didn't look at him again. With only the two wagons that were going back to fetch the ivory still on the north bank and the rest safely across, Sean could relax. He washed in one of the pools, put on his shirt and went across to the south bank looking forward to a long afternoon of Katrina's company.

Ouma met him. 'Thank you, my bear, the girls have made you a parcel of cold meat and a bottle of coffee to eat on your way.' Sean's face went slack. He had forgotten all about that stinking ivory; as far as he was concerned Oupa and Paulus could keep the lot of it.

'Don't worry about us any more now, meneer. I know how it is with a man who is a man. When there's work to do everything else comes after.'

Katrina put the food in his hands. Sean looked for a sign from her. One sign and he'd defy even Ouma.

'Don't be too long,' she whispered. The thought that he might shirk work had obviously not even occurred to her. Sean was glad he hadn't suggested it.

It was a long ride back to the elephant.

'You've taken your time, haven't you?' Oupa greeted him with sour suspicion. 'You'd better get to work if you don't want to lose some of your share.'

Taking out the tusks was a delicate task: a slip of the axe would scar the ivory and halve its value. They worked in the heat with a blue haze of flies around their faces, settling on their lips and crawling into their nostrils and eyes. The carcases had started to rot and the gases ballooned their bellies and escaped in posthumous belches. They sweated as they worked and the blood caked their arms to the elbows, but each hour the wagons filled higher until on the third day they loaded the last tusk. Sean reckoned his share at twelve hundred pounds, the equivalent of a satisfactory day on the Stock Exchange.

He was in a good mood on the morning that they started back to the camp, but it deteriorated as the day wore on and they struggled with the heavily-loaded wagons. The rain seemed to have made up its mind at last and now the sky's belly hung down as heavily as that of a pregnant sow. The clouds trapped the heat beneath them and the men panted and the oxen complained mournfully. At mid-afternoon they heard the first far thunder.

'It will be on us before we pass the river,' fretted Oupa. 'See if you can't get some pace out of those oxen.'

They reached Sean's camp an hour after dark and threw his share of the ivory out of the wagons almost without stopping; then they went down to the river and across the bridge to the south bank.

'My mother will have food ready,' Jan Paulus called back to Sean. 'When you have washed come across and eat with us.'

Sean had supper with the Leroux, but his attempts to get Katrina by herself were neatly countered by Oupa whose suspicions were now confirmed. The old man played his trump card immediately after supper and ordered Katrina to bed. Sean could only shrug helplessly in reply to Katrina's appealing little glance. When she had gone Sean went back to his own camp. He was dizzy with fatigue and he fell on to his cot without bothering to undress.

The rains opened their annual offensive with a midnight broadside of thunder. It startled Sean to his feet before he was awake. He pulled open the front of the wagon and heard the wind coming.

'Mbejane, get the cattle into the laager. Make sure all the canvas is secure.'

'It is done already, Nkosi, I have lashed the wagons together so the oxen cannot stampede and I have——' Then the wind whipped his voice away.

It came out of the east and it frightened the trees so they thrashed their branches in panic; it drummed on the wagon canvas and filled the air with dust and dry leaves. The oxen turned restlessly within the laager. Then came the rain: stinging like hail, drowning the wind and turning the air to water. It swamped the sloping ground that could not drain it fast enough, it blinded and it deafened. Sean went back to his cot and listened to its fury. It made him feel drowsy. He pulled the blankets up to his chin and slept.

In the morning he found his oilskins in the chest at the foot of his cot. They crackled as he pulled them on. He climbed out of the wagon. The cattle had churned the inside of the laager to calf-deep mud and there was no chance of a fire for breakfast. Although the rain was still falling the noise was out of proportion to its strength. Sean paused in his inspection of the camp; he thought about it and suddenly he knew that it was the flood voice of the Limpopo that he heard. Sliding in the mud, he ran out of the laager and stood on the bank of the river. He stared at the mad water. It was so thick with mud it looked solid and it raced so fast it appeared to be standing still. It humped up over piles of submerged rock, gullied through the deeps and hissed in static waves through the shallows. The branches and tree trunks in it whisked past so swiftly that they did little to dispel the illusion that the river was frozen in this brown convulsion.

Reluctantly Sean lifted his eyes to the far bank. The Leroux' wagons were gone.

'Katrina,' he said with the sadness of the might-have-been, then again, 'Katrina,' with the sense of his loss melting in the flame of his anger; and he knew that his wanting was not just the itch that is easily scratched and forgotten, but that it was the true ache, the one that gets into your hands and your head and your heart as well as your loins. He couldn't let her go. He ran back to his wagon and threw his clothes on to the cot.

'I'll marry her,' he said and the words startled him. He stood naked, with an awed expression on his face.

'I'll marry her,' he said again; it was an original thought and it frightened him a little. He took a pair of shorts out of his chest and put his legs into them; he pulled them up and buttoned the fly.

'I'll marry her!' He grinned at his own daring. 'I'm damned if I won't!' He buckled his belt on and tied a pair of *veldschoen* to it by their laces. He jumped down into the mud. The rain was cold on his bare back and he shivered briefly. Then he saw Mbejane coming out of one of the other wagons and he ran.

'Nkosi, Nkosi, what are you doing?' Sean put his head down and ran faster with Mbejane chasing him out on to the bank of the river.

'It's madness . . . let us talk about it first,' Mbejane shouted. 'Please, Nkosi, please.' Sean slipped in the mud and slithered down the bank. Mbejane jumped down after and caught him at the edge of the water, but the mud had coated Sean's body like grease and Mbejane couldn't hold him. Sean twisted out of his hands and sprang far out. He hit the water flat and swam on his back trying to avoid the undertow. The river swept him away. A wave slapped into his mouth and he doubled up to cough; immediately the river caught him by the heels and pulled him under the surface. It let him go again, just long enough to snatch air then it stirred him in a whirlpool and sucked him under once more. He came up beating at the water with his arms, then it tumbled him over a cascade and he knew by the pain in his chest that he was drowning. He swooped down a shute of swift water between rocks and it didn't matter any more. He was too tired. Something scraped against his chest and he put out his hand to protect himself; his fingers closed round a branch and his head lifted out of the water. He drank air and then he was clinging to the branch, still alive and wanting to live. He started kicking, edging across the current, riding the river with his arms around the log.

One of the eddies beneath the south bank swung the log in, under the branches of a tree. He reached up, caught them and dragged himself out. He knelt in the mud and water came gushing up out of him, half through his mouth and half through his nose. He had lost his *veldschoen*. He belched painfully and looked at the river. How fast was it moving, how long had he been in the water? He must be fifteen miles below the wagons. He wiped his face with his hand. It was still raining. He stood shakily and faced upstream.

It took him three hours to reach the spot opposite his wagons. Mbejane and the others waved in wild relief when they saw him, but their shouts could not carry across the river. Sean was cold now and his feet were sore. The tracks of the Leroux' wagons were dissolving in the rain. He followed them and at last the pain in his feet healed as he saw the flash of canvas in the rain mist ahead of him.

'Name of a name,' shouted Jan Paulus. 'How did you cross the river?'

'I flew, how else?' said Sean. 'Where's Katrina?'

Paulus started to laugh, leaning back in the saddle. 'So that's it then, you haven't come all this way to say goodbye to me.'

Sean flushed. 'All right, laughing boy. That's enough merriment for today . . . Where is she?'

Oupa came galloping back towards them. He asked his first question when he was fifty yards away and his fifth as he arrived. From experience Sean knew there was no point in trying to answer them. He looked beyond the two Leroux and saw her coming. She was running back from the lead wagon, her bonnet hanging from its ribbon around her throat and her hair bouncing loosely with each step. She held her skirts out of the mud, her cheeks flushed darker than the brown of her face and her eyes were very green. Sean ducked under the neck of Oupa's horse and went wet, muddy and eager to meet her.

Then the shyness stopped them and they stood paces apart. 'Katrina, will you marry me?'

She went pale. She stared at him then turned away, she was crying and Sean felt the bottom drop out of his stomach.

'No,' shouted Oupa furiously. 'She won't marry you. Leave her alone, you big baboon. You've made her cry. Get out of here. She's only a baby. Get out of here.' He forced his horse between them.

'You hold your mouth, you old busybody.' Ouma came panting back to join the discussion. 'What do you know about it anyway? Just because she's crying doesn't mean she doesn't want him.'

'I thought he was going to let me go,' sobbed Katrina, 'I thought he didn't care.'

Sean whooped and tried to dodge around Oupa's horse.

'You leave her alone,' shouted Oupa desperately, manœuvring his horse to cut Sean off. 'You made her cry. I tell you she's crying.'

Katrina was undoubtedly crying. She was also trying to get around Oupa's horse.

'*Vat haar*,' shouted Jan Paulus. 'Get her, man, go and get her!'

Ouma caught the horse by the reins and dragged it away; she was a powerful woman. Sean and Katrina collided and held tight.

'Hey, that's it, man,' Jan Paulus jumped off his horse and pounded Sean's back from behind. Unable to protect himself Sean was driven forward a pace with each blow.

Much later Oupa muttered sulkily. 'She can have two wagons for her dowry.'

'Three!' said Katrina.

'Four!' said Ouma.

'Very well, four. Take your hands off him, girl. Haven't you any shame?' Hastily Katrina dropped her arm from Sean's waist. Sean had borrowed a suit of clothing from Paulus and they were all standing round the fire. It had stopped raining but the low clouds were prematurely bringing on the night.

'And four of the horses,' Ouma prompted her husband.

'Do you want to beggar me, woman?'

'Four horses,' repeated Ouma.

'All right, all right . . . four horses.' Oupa looked at Katrina, his eyes were stricken. 'She's only a baby, man, she's only fifteen years.'

'Sixteen,' said Ouma.

'Nearly seventeen,' said Katrina, 'and anyway you've promised, Pa, you can't go back on your word now.'

Oupa sighed; then he looked at Sean and his face hardened.

'Paulus, get the Bible out of my wagon. This big baboon is going to swear an oath.'

Jan Paulus put the Bible on the tailboard of the wagon. It was thick and the cover was of black leather, dull with use.

'Come here,' Oupa said to Sean. 'Put your hand on the book . . . don't look at me. Look up, man, look up. Now say after me, "I do most solemnly swear to look after this woman"–don't gobble, speak slower–"until I can find a priest to say the proper words. Should I fail in this then I ask you, God, to blast me with lightning, sting me with serpents, burn me in eternal fire–"' Oupa completed the list of atrocities, then he grunted with satisfaction and tucked the Bible under his arm. 'He won't have a chance to do all that to you . . . I'll get you first.'

Sean shared Jan Paulus's wagon that night; he wasn't in a mood for sleep and anyway Jan Paulus snored. It was raining again in the morning, depressing weather for farewells. Jan Paulus laughed, Henrietta cried and Ouma did both. Oupa kissed his daughter.

'Be a woman like your mother,' he said, then he scowled at Sean.

'Remember, just you remember!'

Sean and Katrina stood together and watched the trees and the curtain of rain hide the wagon train. Sean held Katrina's hand. He could feel the sadness on her; he put his arm round her and her dress was damp and cold. The last wagon disappeared and they were alone in a land as vast as solitude. Katrina shivered and looked up at the man beside her. He was so big and overpoweringly male; he was a stranger. Suddenly she was frightened. She wanted to hear her mother's laugh and see her brother and father riding ahead of her wagon, the way it had always been.

'Oh, please, I want . . .' she pulled out from his arm. She never finished that sentence, for she looked at his mouth and his lips were full and burnt dark by the sun–they were smiling. Then she looked at his eyes and her panic smoothed away. With those eyes watching over her she was never to feel frightened again, not until the very end and that was a long time away. Going into his love was like going into a castle, a thick-walled place. A safe place where no one else could enter. The first feeling of it was so strong that she could only stand quietly and let the warmth wrap her.

15

That evening they outspanned Katrina's wagons back at the south bank of the river. It was still raining. Sean's servants waved and signalled to them, but the brown water bellowed down between them cutting off all sound and hope of passage. Katrina looked at the water. 'Did you really swim that, meneer?'

'So fast that I hardly got wet.'

'Thank you,' she said.

Despite the rain and smoky fire Katrina served up a meal as good as one of Ouma's. They ate it in the shelter of the tarpaulin beside her wagon. The wind guttered the hurricane lamp, flogged the canvas and blew a fine haze of rain in on them. It was so uncomfortable that when Sean suggested that they go into the wagon Katrina barely hesitated before agreeing. She sat on the edge of her cot and Sean sat on the chest opposite her. From an awkward start their conversation was soon running as fast as the river outside the wagon.

'My hair is still wet,' Katrina exclaimed at last. 'Do you mind if I dry it while we talk?'

'Of course not.'

'Then let me get my towel out of the chest.'

They stood up at the same time. There was very little space in the wagon. They touched. They were on the cot. The movement of his mouth on hers, the warm taste of it, the strong pleading of his fingers at the nape of her neck and along her spine–all these things were strangely confusing. She responded slowly at first, then faster with bewildered movements of her own body and little graspings at his arms and shoulders. She did not understand and she did not care. The confusion spread through her whole body and she could not stop it, she did not want to. She reached up and her fingers went into his hair. She pulled his face down on hers. His teeth crushed her lips–sweet, exciting pain. His hand came round from her back and enclosed a fat round breast. Through the thin cotton he found the erectness of her nipple and rolled it gently between his fingers. She reacted like a filly feeling the whip for the first time. One instant she lay under the shock of his touch and then her convulsive heave caught him by surprise. He went backwards off the cot and his head cracked against the wooden chest. He sat on the floor and stared up at her, too surprised even to rub the lump on his head. Her face was flushed and she pushed the hair back from her forehead with both hands. She was shaking her head wildly in her effort to speak through her gasping. 'You must go now, meneer–the servants have made a bed for you in one of the other wagons.'

Sean scrambled to his feet. 'But, I thought . . . surely we are . . . well, I mean.'

'Keep away from me,' she warned anxiously. 'If you touch me again tonight, I'll . . . I'll bite you.'

'But, Katrina, please, I can't sleep in the other wagon.' The thought appalled him.

'I'll cook your food, mend your clothes . . . everything! But until you find a priest . . .' She didn't go on, but Sean got the idea. He started to argue. It was his introduction to Boer immovability and at last he went to find his own bed. One of Katrina's dogs was there before him–a three-quarters-grown brindle hound. Sean's attempts to persuade it to leave were as ill-fated as had been his previous arguments with its mistress. They shared the bed. During the night a difference of opinion arose between them as to what constituted a half-share of the blankets. From it the dog earned its name–Thief.

16

Sean determined to show Katrina just how strongly he resented her attitude. He would be polite but distant. Five minutes after they had sat down to breakfast the next morning this demonstration of disapproval had deteriorated to the stage where he was unable to take his eyes off her face and he was talking so much that breakfast lasted an hour.

The rain held steadily for three more days and then it stopped. The sun came back, as welcome as an old friend, but it was another ten days before the river regained its sanity. Time, rain or river meant very little to the two of them. They wandered out into the bush together to pick mushrooms; they sat in camp and when Katrina was working Sean followed her around. Then, of course, they talked. She listened to him. She laughed at the right places and gasped with wonder when she was meant to. She was a good listener. As for Sean, if she had repeated the same word over and over the sound of her voice alone would have held him entranced. The evenings were difficult. Sean would start getting restless and make excuses to touch her. She wanted him to, but she was frightened of the confusion that had so nearly trapped her the first night. So she drew up a set of rules and put them to him. 'Do you promise not to do anything more than kiss me?'

'Not unless you say I can,' Sean agreed readily.

'No.' She saw the catch in that.

'You mean, I must never do anything but kiss you even if you say I can?'

She started to blush. 'If I say so in the daytime, that's different . . . but anything I say at night doesn't count, and if you break your promise I'll never let you touch me again.'

Katrina's rules stood unchanged by the time the river had dropped enough for the wagons to be taken across to the north bank. The rains were resting, gathering their strength, but soon they would set in once more. The river was full but no longer murderous. Now was the time to cross. Sean took the oxen across first, swimming them in a herd. Holding on to one of their tails he had a Nantucket sleigh-ride across the river and when he reached the north bank there was a joyous welcome awaiting him.

They took six thick coils of unused rope from the stores wagon and joined them together. With the end of the rope round his waist Sean made one of his horses tow him back across the river, Mbejane paying out the line to him as he went. Then Sean supervised Katrina's servants as they emptied all the water barrels and lashed them to the sides of the first wagon to serve as floats. They ran the wagon into the water, tied on the rope and adjusted the barrels so that the wagon floated level. Sean signalled to Mbejane and waited until he had made the other end of the rope fast to a tree on the north bank. Then they pushed the wagon into the current and watched anxiously as it swung across the river like a pendulum, the current driving it but the tree anchoring it. It hit the north bank a distance the exact width of the river downstream of the tree, and Sean's party cheered as Mbejane and the other servants ran down the bank to retrieve it. Mbejane had a team of oxen standing ready and they dragged it out. Sean's horse towed him across the river again to fetch the rope.

Sean, Katrina and all her servants rode across on the last wagon. Sean stood behind Katrina with his arms round her waist, ostensibly to steady her, and the servants shouted and chattered like children on a picnic.

The water piled up brown against the side of the wagon, tilting it and making it roll, and with an exhilarating swoop they shot across the river and crashed into the far bank. The impact tumbled them overboard, throwing them into the knee-deep water beside the bank. They scrambled ashore. The water streamed out of Katrina's dress, her hair melted wetly over her face; she had mud on one cheek and she was gasping with laughter. Her sodden petticoats clung to her legs, tripping her, and Sean picked her up and carried her to his own laager. His servants shouted loud encouragement after him and Katrina shrieked genteelly to be put down, but held tight round his neck with both arms.

17

Now that the rains had changed every irregularity in the land into a waterhole and sowed new green grass where before had been dust and dry earth, the game scattered away from the river. Every few days Sean's trackers came into camp to report that there were no elephant. Sean condoled with them and sent them out again. He was well satisfied; there was a new quarry now, more elusive and therefore more satisfying than an old bull elephant with a hundred and fifty pounds of ivory on each side of his face. Yet to call Katrina his quarry was a lie. She was much more than that.

She was a new world–a place of endless mysteries and unexpected delights, an enchanting mixture of woman and child. She supervised the domestic routine with deceptive lack of fuss. With her there, suddenly his clothes were clean and had their full complement of buttons; the stew of boots and books and unwashed socks in his wagon vanished. There were fresh bread and fruit preserves on the table; Kandhla's eternal grilled steaks gave way to a variety of dishes. Each day she showed a new accomplishment. She could ride astride, though Sean had to turn his back when she mounted and dismounted. She cut Sean's hair and made as good a job of it as his barber in Johannesburg. She had a medicine chest in her wagon from which she produced remedies for every ailing man or beast in the company. She handled a rifle like a man and could strip and clean Sean's Mannlicher. She helped him load cartridges, measuring the charges with a practised eye. She could discuss birth and procreation with a clinical objectivity and a minute later blush all over when he looked at her that way. She was as stubborn as a mule, haughty when it suited her, serene and inscrutable at times and at others a little girl. She would push a handful of grass down the back of his shirt and run for him to chase her, giggle for minutes at a secret thought, play long imaginative games in which the dogs were her children and she talked to them and answered for them. Sometimes she was so naïve that Sean thought she was joking until he remembered how young she was. She could drive him from happiness to spitting anger and back again within the space of an hour. But, once he had won her confidence and she knew that he would play to the rules, she responded to his caresses with a violence that startled them both. Sean was completely absorbed in her. She was the most wonderful thing he had ever found and, best of all, he could talk to her. He told her about Duff. She saw the extra cot in his wagon and found clothing that was obviously too small for him. She asked about it and he told her all of it and she understood.

The days became weeks. The cattle grew fat, their skins sleek and tight. Katrina planted a small vegetable garden and reaped a crop from it. Christmas came and Katrina baked a cake. Sean gave her a kaross of monkey skins that Mbejane had worked on in secret. Katrina gave Sean hand-sewn shirts, each with his initials embroidered on the top pocket, and she relaxed the rules a fraction.

Then when the new year had begun and Sean hadn't killed an elephant in six weeks, Mbejane headed a deputation from the gunboys. The question he had to ask, though tactfully disguised, was simply, 'Did we come here to hunt, or what?'

They broke camp and moved north again and the strain was showing on Sean at last. He tried to sweat it out by long days of hunting but this didn't help for conditions were so bad that they added to his irritability. The grass in most places was higher than a mounted man's head, its sharp edges cut as he passed through it. But the grass seeds were the worst: half an inch long and barbed like an arrow they worked their way quickly through clothing and into the skin. In the humid heat the small wounds they made festered within hours. Then there were the flies. Hippo-flies, green-headed flies, sand-flies and with one thing in common–they stung. The soft skin behind the ears was their favourite place. They'd creep upon him, settle so lightly he wouldn't feel it–then, ping with the red-hot needle. Always wet, sometimes with sweat, other times with rain, Sean would close with a herd of elephant. He would hear them moving in the long grass around him and see the white canopy of egrets fluttering over them, but it was seldom he could get a shot at them. If he did he had to stand in the centre of a storm of blundering bodies. Often they would be following a herd, almost upon them, when Sean would lose interest and they'd all go back to camp. He couldn't keep away.

He was miserable, his servants were miserable, and Katrina was happy as a bird at daybreak. She had a man, she was mistress of a household which she ran with confidence and, because her senses were not yet as seasoned as Sean's, she was physically content. Even with Sean's strict adherence to the rules, their evenings in her wagon would end for her with a sigh and a shudder and she would go dreamy-eyed to bed and leave Sean with a burning devil inside of him. The only person Sean could complain to was Thief. He would lie with his snout buried in Sean's armpit, with at least his share of the blankets over him, and listen quietly.

The Zulus could see what the trouble was but they didn't understand it. They didn't discuss it, of course, but if one of them spread his hands expressively or coughed in a certain way the others knew what he meant. Mbejane came closest to actually putting it into words. Sean had just thrown a tantrum. It was a matter of a lost axe and who was responsible. Sean lined them up and expressed doubts as to their ancestry, present worth and future prospects, then he stormed off to his wagon. There was a long silence and Hlubi offered his snuff-box to Mbejane.

Mbejane took a pinch and said, 'It's a stupid stallion that doesn't know how to kick down a fence.'

'It is true, it is true,' they agreed, and there the matter rested.

18

A week later they reached the Sabi river. The mountains on the far side were blue-grey with distance and the river was full–brown and full.

The next morning was fresh and cool from the night's rain. The camp smelt of wood-smoke, cattle and wild mimosa. From one of the ostrich eggs that Mbejane had found the day before, Katrina made an omelette the size of a soup-plate. It was flavoured with nutmeg and chunks of mushroom, yellow and rich. Afterwards there were scones and wild honey, coffee and a cheroot for Sean.

'Are you going out today?' Katrina asked.

'Uh huh.'

'Oh!'

'Don't you want me to?'

'You haven't stayed in camp for a week.'

'Don't you want me to go?'

She stood up quickly and started clearing the table. 'Anyway you won't find any elephant . . . you haven't found anything for ages.'

'Do you want me to stay?'

'It's such a lovely day.' She signed to Kandhla to take the plates away.

'If you want me to stay, ask me properly.'

'We could look for mushrooms.'

'Say it,' said Sean.

'All right then, please!'

'Mbejane! Take the saddle off that horse, I won't be using him.'

Katrina laughed. She ran to her wagon, skirts swirling around her legs, calling to the dogs. She came back with her bonnet on and a basket in her hand. The dogs crowded round them, jumping up and barking.

'Go on . . . seek up then,' Sean told them and they raced ahead, circling back barking, chasing one another. Sean and Katrina walked holding hands. The brim of Katrina's bonnet kept her face in shadow, but even then her eyes when she looked at him were bright green. They picked the new mushrooms, round and hard, brown and slightly sticky on top, fluted underneath delicately as a lady's fan. In an hour they had filled the basket and they stopped under a marula tree. Sean lay on his back. Katrina broke off a blade of grass and tickled his face with it until he caught her wrist and pulled her down on to his chest. The dogs watched them, sitting around them in a circle, their tongues hanging out pink and wet.

'There's a place in the Cape, just outside Paarl. The mountains stand over it and there's a river . . . the water's very clear, you can see the fish lying on the bottom,' said Katrina. Her ear was against his chest and she was listening to his heart. 'Will you buy me a farm there one day?'

'Yes,' said Sean.

'We'll build a house with a wide veranda and on Sundays we'll drive to church with the girls and the little ones in the back and the bigger boys riding next to the buggy.'

'How many will there be?' asked Sean. He lifted the side of her bonnet and looked at her ear. It was a very pretty ear, in the sunlight he could see the fine fur on the lobe.

'Oh lots . . . boys mostly, but a few girls.'

'Ten?' suggested Sean.

'More than that.'

'Fifteen?'

'Yes, fifteen.'

They lay and thought about it. To Sean it seemed a fairly well-rounded number.

'And I'll keep chickens, I want lots of chickens.'

'All right,' said Sean.

'You don't mind?'

'Should I?'

'Some people mind chickens, some people don't like them at all,' said Katrina. 'I'm glad you don't mind them. I've always wanted them.'

Stealthily Sean advanced his mouth towards her ear but she felt him move and sat up.

'What are you doing?'

'This,' said Sean and his arm shot out.

'No, Sean, they're watching us.' She waved her hand at the dogs.

'They'll understand,' said Sean and then they were both quiet for a long time.

The dogs burst out together in full hunting chorus. Katrina sat up and Sean turned his head and saw the leopard. It stood fifty yards away on the edge of the thick bush along the river bank watching them, poised elegantly in tights of black and gold, long and small-bellied. It moved then, blurring with speed, touching the ground as lightly as a swallow touches the water when it drinks in flight. The dogs went after it in a pack, Thief leading them, his voice cracking with excitement.

'Back, come back,' shouted Sean. 'Leave it, damn you, come back.'

'Stop them, Sean, go after them. We'll lose them all.'

'Wait here,' Sean told her.

He ran after the sound of the pack. Not shouting, saving his wind. He knew what would happen and he listened for it. He heard the tone of the hunt change–sharper now. Sean stopped and stood panting, peering ahead. The dogs were not moving. The sound of their barking was steady in volume.

'The swine has stopped; he's going to take them.'

He started running again and almost immediately heard the first dog scream. He kept running. He found the dog lying where the leopard had flung it–the old bitch with white ears, her stomach was stripped out. Sean went on. The tan ridgeback next, disembowelled, still alive and crawling to meet him. He ran on; always the hunt was out of sight ahead of him but he kept after it. He no longer stopped to help the dogs that had been mauled. Most of them were dead before he reached them. The saliva thickened in his mouth, his heart jumped against his ribs and he reeled as he ran.

Suddenly he was in the open and the hunt was spread out before him. There were three dogs left. One of them was Thief. They were circling the leopard, belling him, darting in at his back legs, snapping, then jumping back as the leopard spun snarling. The grass was short and green in the clearing. The sun was directly overhead: it threw no shadow, it lit everything with a flat, even light. Sean tried to shout but his throat wouldn't let the sound out. The leopard dropped on to its back and lay with the sprawled grace of a sleeping cat, its legs open and its belly exposed. The dogs hung back, hesitating. Sean shouted again but his voice still would not carry. That creamy yellow belly, soft and fluffy, was too much temptation. One of the dogs went for it, dipping its head, its mouth open. The leopard closed on it like a spring trap. It caught and held the dog with its front paws and its back legs worked quickly. The dog yammered at the swift surgeon strokes and then it was thrown aside, its bowels hanging out. The leopard relaxed again to show the yellow bait of its belly. Sean was close now and this time the two dogs heard his shout. The leopard heard it also. It flashed to its feet and tried to break, but the instant it turned Thief was at it, slashing at its back legs forcing it to swing and crouch.

'Here, boy, leave him! Here, Thief, come here!'

Thief took Sean's shout as encouragement. He danced just out of reach of the flicking paws, shrilly taunting the leopard. The hunt was finely balanced now. Sean knew if he could get the dogs to slacken their attack the leopard would run. He went forward a pace, stooped to pick up a stone to throw at Thief and his movement tipped the balance. When he straightened up the leopard was watching him and he felt the eel of fear move in his stomach. It was going to come for him. He knew it by the way its ears flattened against its head and its shoulders bunched like loaded springs. Sean dropped the stone and reached for the knife on his belt.

The leopard's lips peeled back. Its teeth were yellow, its head with the ears flattened was like a snake's. It came fast and low against the ground, brushing the dogs aside. Its run was long-reaching, smoothly beautiful. It snaked towards him, fast over the short grass. It came into the air, lifting high, very fast and very smoothly. Sean felt the shock and the pain together. The shock threw him backwards and the pain sucked the breath from his lungs. Its claws hooked into his chest, he felt them scrape his ribs. He held its mouth from his face, his forearm against its throat and he smelt the overripe grave smell of its breath. They rolled together in the grass, its front claws still holding in the flesh of his chest, and he felt its back legs coming up to rake his stomach. He twisted desperately to keep clear of them, using his knife at the same time, slipping the blade into its back. The leopard screamed, its back legs came up again, he felt the claws go into his hip and tear down his thigh. The pain was deep and strong and he knew he was badly hurt. The legs came up again. This time they would kill him.

Thief locked his teeth in the leopard's leg before the claws could catch in Sean's flesh, he dragged back, digging in with his front feet, holding the leopard stretched out across Sean's body. Sean's vision was dissolving into blackness and bright lights. He pushed the knife into the leopard's back, close to the spine and pulled it down between the ribs the way a butcher cuts a chop. The leopard screamed again with its body shuddering and its claws curling in Sean's flesh. Sean cut again, deep and long–and again, then again. Tearing at it, mad with the pain, its blood gushed out and mixed with his and he rolled away from it. The dogs were worrying it, growling. It was dead. Sean let the knife slip out of his hand and touched the tears in his leg. The blood was dark red, pouring with the thickness of treacle, much blood. He was looking down a funnel of darkness. The leg was far away, not his–not his leg.

'Garry,' he whispered, 'Garry, oh God! I'm sorry. I slipped, I didn't mean it, I slipped.' The funnel closed and there was no leg–only darkness. Time was a liquid thing, all the world was liquid, moving in darkness. The sun was dark and only the pain was steady, steady as a rock in the dark moving sea. He saw Katrina's face indistinct in the darkness. He tried to tell her how sorry he was. He tried to tell her it was an accident, but the pain stopped him. She was crying. He knew she would understand so he went back into the dark sea. Then the surface of the sea boiled and he choked in the heat, but always the pain was there like a rock to hold on to. The steam from the sea coiled up around him and it hardened into the shape of a woman and he thought it was Katrina, then he saw its head was a leopard's head and its breath stank like the rotting of a gangrenous leg.

'I don't want you–I know who you are,' he shouted at it. 'I don't want you. It's not my child,' and the thing broke into steam, twisting grey steam, and came back gibbering at him on a chain that tinkled, frothing yellow from the grey misty mouth, and terror came with it. He twisted and covered his face, holding on to the pain for the pain was real and steady.

Then after a thousand years the sea froze and he walked on it and the white ice stretched away wherever he looked. It was cold and lonely on the ice. There was a small wind, a cold small wind, the wind whispered across the ice and its whispering was a sad sound, and Sean held his pain, hugging it close to him for he was lonely and only the pain was real. Then there were other figures moving around him on the ice, dark figures all hurrying one way, crowding him, pushing him along with them and he lost his pain, lost it in the desperate hurrying press. And though they had no faces, some of the figures wept and others laughed and they hurried forward until they came to the place where the crevasse split across the ice in front of them. The crevasse was wide and deep and its sides were white, then pale-green shading to blue and at last to infinite blackness, and some of the figures threw themselves joyfully into it singing as they fell. Others clung to edges, their formless faces full of fear, and still others stepped off into the void, tiredly, like travellers at the end of a long journey. When Sean saw the crevasse he began to fight, throwing himself back against the crowd that bore him forward, carrying him to the edge of the pit, and his feet slid over the edge. He clawed with his fingers at the slippery edge of the ice. He fought and he shouted as he fought for the dark drop sucked at his legs. Then he lay quietly and the crevasse had closed and he was alone. He was tired–wasted and terribly tired. He closed his eyes and the pain came back to him, throbbing softly in his leg.

He opened his eyes and he saw Katrina's face. She was pale and her eyes were big and heavily underscored in blue. He tried to lift his hand to touch her face but he couldn't move.

'Katrina,' he said. He saw her eyes go green with surprise and happiness.

'You've come back. Oh, thank God. You've come back.'

Sean rolled his head and looked at the canvas of the wagon tent.

'How long?' he asked. His voice was a whisper.

'Five days . . . Don't talk–please, don't talk.'

Sean closed his eyes. He was very tired so he slept.

19

Katrina washed him when he woke. Mbejane helped her lift and turn him, his big pink-palmed hands very gentle as he handled the leg. They washed the smell of fever off him and changed the dressings. Sean watched Katrina as she worked and every time she looked up they smiled at each other. Once he used a little of his strength to ask Mbejane, 'Where were you when I needed you?'

'I slept in the sun, Nkosi, like an old woman,' Mbejane half-laughed, half-apologized. Katrina brought him food and when he smelt it he was hungry. He ate it all and then he slept again.

Mbejane built a shelter with open sides and a roof of thatch. He sited it in the shade on the bank of the Sabi. Then he made a bed of poles and laced leather thongs. They carried Sean from the wagon, Katrina fussing around them until they had laid him in the shelter. Katrina went back to the wagon for pillows and when she returned she found Thief and Sean settling down comfortably.

'Sean, get that monster out of there–those blankets have just been washed.'

Thief flattened his body and hid his head in Sean's armpit.

'It's all right, he's quite clean,' Sean protected him.

'He smells.'

'He does not.' Sean sniffed at Thief. 'Well, not much anyway.'

'You two!' She put the pillows under Sean's head and went round to his leg. 'How does it feel?'

'It's fine,' said Sean. Thief inched himself up the bed until he reached the pillows.

In the slow slide of days Sean's body healed and the well of his strength filled. The moving air under the shelter dried the scabs off his chest and leg, but there would be scars. In the mornings, after breakfast, Sean held court from his couch. Katrina sat on the end of the bed and his servants squatted around him. First they talked over domestic matters–the health of the oxen, mentioning them by name, discussing their eyes, hooves and stomachs. There was a tear in the canvas of one wagon. The single remaining bitch was in season–was Thief man enough for the job yet? There was meat to kill–perhaps the Nkosikaze would take the rifle later today. Hlubi had caught four barbel of medium size in his fish trap, and here the talk turned to the bush around them. A lion had killed a buffalo below the first bend in the river–there you could see the vultures. During the night a herd of cow elephant had drunk a mile upstream. Each item was considered by the meeting. Everyone felt free to comment or argue against any view which conflicted with his own. When everything had been said Sean gave them their tasks for the day and sent them away. Then he and Katrina could be alone.

From the shelter they could see the full sweep of the river, with the crocodiles lying on the white sandbars and the kingfishers plopping into the shallows. They sat close to each other and they talked of the farm they would have. Sean would grow grapes and breed horses and Katrina would keep chickens. By the next rainy season they would have filled all the wagons; one more trip after that and they would have enough to buy the farm.

Katrina kept him in bed long after he was strong enough to leave it. She mothered him and he loved it. Shamelessly, in the fashion of the male, he accepted her attentions and even exaggerated his injuries a little. Finally but reluctantly Katrina let him up. He stayed in camp a week more, until his legs stopped wobbling, then one evening he took his rifle and went with Mbejane to shoot fresh meat. They went slowly, Sean favouring his leg, and he shot a young eland not far from the laager. Sean sat against a msasa tree and smoked a cheroot while Mbejane went back to fetch servants to carry the meat. Sean watched them butcher the carcase; there were slabs of white fat on the meat. They slung it on poles and carried it between them, two men to a pole, and when they got back to camp Sean found Katrina in one of her inscrutable moods. When he talked to her at supper she answered him from far away and afterwards by the fire she sat detached from him. She was very lovely and Sean was puzzled and a little resentful. At last he stood up.

'It's time for bed–I'll see you to your wagon.'

'You go. I'll sit a little longer.'

Sean hesitated. 'Is there something wrong? Have I done something wrong?'

'No,' she said quickly. 'No. I'm all right. You go to bed.'

He kissed her cheek. 'If you need me I'll be close. Goodnight, sleep sweet.'

He straightened up. 'Come on, Thief,' he said. 'Time for bed.'

'Leave Thief with me, please.' Katrina caught the skin at the back of the dog's neck and restrained him.

'Why?'

'I just feel like company.'

'Then I'll stay as well,' Sean moved to sit down again.

'No, you go to bed.' She sounded desperate and Sean looked hard at her.

'Are you sure you're all right?'

'Yes, please go.'

He went to his wagon and looked back at her. She was sitting very straight, holding the dog. He climbed into the wagon. The lamp was lit and he stopped in surprise when he saw his cot. There were sheets on it, not just the rough blankets. He ran his hand over the smooth fabric; it was crisp from new ironing. He sat on the cot and pulled off his boots. He undid his shirt and threw it on to the chest, then he lay back and looked up at the lamp.

'There's something bloody funny going on here,' he said.

'Sean'–her voice just outside the wagon. Sean jumped up and opened the flap. 'Can I come in?'

'Yes, of course.' He gave her his hand and lifted her into the wagon. He looked at her face. She was frightened.

'There *is* something wrong,' he said.

'No, don't touch me. There's something I've got to tell you. Sit down on the cot.'

Sean watched her face. He was worried.

'I thought I loved you when I came away with you. I thought we had for ever to be together.' She swallowed painfully. 'Then I found you there in the grass–torn and dead. Before our life together had begun you were dead.'

Sean saw the pain come back into her eyes; she was living it again. He put out his hand to her but she held his wrist.

'No, wait . . . please let me finish. I have to explain to you. It's very important.'

Sean dropped his hand and she went on speaking quickly.

'You were dead and I, too, was dying inside. I felt empty. There was nothing left. Nothing . . . just the hollowness inside and the dry dead feeling on the outside. I touched your face and you looked at me. I prayed then, Sean, and I prayed through the days when you fought the rotting of your body.'

She knelt in front of him and held him around the waist.

'Now we are alive and together again, but I know that it cannot be for ever. A day more, a year, if we are lucky, twenty. But not for ever. I see how small I have been to us. I want to be your wife.'

He bent to her quickly but she pulled away and stood up. She slipped the buttons and her clothing fell away. She loosed her hair and let it drop shiny bright down the whiteness of her body.

'Look at me, Sean, I want you to look at me. This and my love I can give you . . . is it enough?'

There was smoothness, hollow and swell, hair like black fire and soft light on soft skin. He saw the flush from her cheeks spread on to her breasts until they glowed, pink and shy but proud in their perfection. He looked no further. He took her to him and covered her nakedness with his big body. She was trembling and he put her between the sheets and gentled her with his voice until the trembling stopped and she lay with her face pressed up under his beard into his neck.

'Show me how . . . I want to give everything to you. Please show me how,' she whispered.

So they married each other and their marriage was a comingling of many things. There was the softness of the wind in it and wanting, the way the baked earth wants the rain. There was pain sharp and swift, movement like running horses, sound low as voices in the night but glad as a greeting, joy climbing on eagles' wings, the triumphant surge and burst of wild water on a rock shore and then there was stillness and warmth within and the snuggling of drowsy puppies, and sleep. Yet it did not end in the sleep, it went on to another seeking and finding, another union and a stranger mystery in the secret depths of her body.

20

In the morning she brought her Bible to him.

'Hey, hey,' protested Sean, 'I've already sworn one oath.' Katrina laughed at him, the memory of the night still warm and happy inside her. She opened the book at its fly leaf.

'You've got to write your name in it . . . here, next to mine.'

She watched him, standing next to his chair with her hip touching his shoulder.

'And your date of birth,' she said.

Sean wrote: 'Ninth Jan. 1862.' Then he said: 'What's this "date of death" . . . do you want me to fill that in as well?'

'Don't talk like that,' she said quickly and touched the wooden table.

Sean was sorry he'd said it. He tried to cover up. 'There's only space for six children.'

'We can write the others in the margin. That's what Ma did . . . hers even go over on to the first page of Genesis. Do you think we'll get that far, Sean?'

Sean smiled at her. 'The way I feel now we should reach the New Testament without much trouble.'

They had made a good start. By June the rains were over and Katrina walked with her shoulders back to balance her load. There was a good feeling in the camp. Katrina was more woman than child now. She was big and radiant, pleased with the awe her condition inspired in Sean. She sang to herself often and sometimes in the night she would let him share in it. She would let him pull the nightdress back from the mound of her stomach and lay his ear against the tight-stretched, blue-veined skin. He listened to the suck and gurgle and felt the movement against his cheek. When he sat up his eyes would be full of the wonder of it and she would smile proudly at him and take his head on her shoulder and they would lie together quietly. In the daytime things were right as well. Sean laughed with the servants and hunted without the intensity of before.

They moved north along the Sabi river. Sometimes they camped for a month at one place. The game came back to the rivers as the veld dried out and once more the ivory started piling up in the wagons.

One afternoon in September Sean and Katrina left the camp and walked along the bank. The land was brown again and smelt of dry grass. The river was pools and white sand.

'Hell, it's hot.' Sean took off his hat and wiped the sweat off his forehead. 'You must be cooking under all those clothes.'

'No, I'm all right.' Katrina was holding his arm.

'Let's have a swim.'

'You mean with no clothes on?' Katrina looked shocked.

'Yes, why not?'

'It's rude.'

'Come on.' He took her down the bank protesting every step and at a place where boulders screened the water he prised her out of her dress. She was laughing and gasping and blushing all at the same time. He carried her into the pool and she sat down thankfully with the water up to her chin.

'How's that feel?' Sean asked.

She let her hair down and it floated out round her, she wriggled her toes in the sand and her stomach showed through the water like the back of a white whale.

'It's nice,' she admitted. 'It feels like silk underwear against my skin.'

Sean stood over her with only his hat on. She looked at him.

'Sit down,' she said uncomfortably and looked away from him.

'Why?' he asked.

'You know why . . . you're rude, that's why.'

Sean sat down beside her.

'You should be used to me by now.'

'Well, I'm not.'

Sean put his arm around her under the water.

'You're lovely,' he said. 'You're my fancy.'

She let him kiss her ear.

'What's it going to be?' He touched the ripe swelling. 'Boy or girl?' This was currently the favourite topic of conversation.

'Boy.' She was very definite.

'What shall we call him?'

'Well, if you don't find a *predikant* soon we'll have to call him the name you're always giving to the servants.'

Sean stared at her. 'What do you mean?'

'You know what you call them when you're cross.'

'Bastard,' said Sean, then really concerned, 'Hell, I hadn't thought of that! We'll have to find a priest. No child of mine will be a bastard. We'll have to go back to Louis Trichardt.'

'You've got about a month,' Katrina warned him.

'My God, we'll never make it. We've left it too late.' Sean's face was ghastly. 'Wait, I've got it. There are Portuguese settlements across the mountains on the coast.'

'Oh, Sean, but they're Roman Catholics.'

'They all work for the same boss.'

'How long will it take to cross the mountains?' Katrina asked doubtfully.

'I don't know. Perhaps two weeks to reach the coast on horseback.'

'On horseback?' Katrina looked still more doubtfully.

'Oh hell . . . you can't ride.' Sean scratched the side of his nose. 'I'll have to go and fetch one. Will you stay on your own? I'll leave Mbejane to look after you.'

'Yes, I'll be all right.'

'I won't go if you don't want me to. It's not that important.'

'It is important, you know it is. I'll be all right, truly I will.'

Before he left the next morning Sean took Mbejane aside. 'You know why you're not coming with me, don't you?'

Mbejane nodded, but Sean answered his own question. 'Because there is more important work for you to do here.'

'At night,' said Mbejane, 'I will sleep beneath the Nkosikazi's wagon.'

'You'll sleep?' asked Sean threateningly.

'Only once in a while and then very lightly,' Mbejane grinned.

'That's better,' said Sean.

21

Sean said goodbye to Katrina. There were no tears, she understood necessity and helped him to a quiet acceptance of it. They stood a long while beside their wagon, holding each other, their lips almost touching as they whispered together and then Sean called for his horse. Hlubi followed him leading the packhorse when he crossed the Sabi and when Sean reached the far bank he turned and looked back. Katrina was still standing by their wagon and behind her hovered Mbejane. In her bonnet and green dress she looked very young. Sean waved his hat over his head and then set off towards the mountains.

The forest dwindled into grassland as they climbed and each night was colder than the last. Then, in its turn the grassland conceded to the sheer bluffs and misty gorges of the mountain back. Sean and Hlubi struggled upwards, following the game trails, losing them, turning back from impassable cliffs, scouting for a pass, leading the horses over the steep pitches and at night sitting close to the fire and listening to the baboons barking in the kranses around them. Then suddenly, in the middle of a morning that was bright as a cut diamond, they were at the top. To the west the land lay spread out like a map and the distance they had travelled in a week was pathetically small. By straining his eyes and his imagination Sean could make out the dark-green belt of the Sabi watercourse. To the east the land merged with a blueness that was not the sky and for a while he failed to recognize it. Then–'the sea,' he shouted and Hlubi laughed with him for it was a godlike feeling to stand above the world. They found an easier route down the eastern slopes and followed it on to the coastal plain. At the bottom of the mountains they came to a native village. To see cultivated lands and human dwellings again was a small shock to Sean. He had come to accept the fact he and his retinue were the only people left on earth.

The entire population of the village fled when they saw him. Mothers snatched up a child in each hand and ran as fast as their menfolk–memories of the slave-traders still persisted in this part of Africa. Within two minutes of his arrival Sean again had the feeling that he was the only person left on earth. With the contempt of the Zulu for every other tribe in Africa, Hlubi shook his head sadly.

'Monkeys,' he said.

They dismounted and tied their horses under the big tree that was the centre of the village. They sat in the shade and waited. The huts were grass beehives, their roofs blackened with smoke, and a few chickens picked and scratched at the bare earth between them. Half an hour later Sean saw a black face watching him from the edge of the bush and he ignored it. Slowly the face emerged, followed closely by a reluctant body. With a twig, Sean went on drawing patterns in the dust between his feet. Out of the corner of his eye he watched the hesitant approach. It was an old man with stork thin legs and one eye glazed into a white jelly by tropical ophthalmia. Sean concluded that his fellows had picked him to act as ambassador on the grounds that all their number he would be the least loss.

Sean looked up and gave him a radiant smile. The old man froze and then his lips twitched into a sickly grin of relief. Sean stood up, dusted his hands on the sides of his breeches and went to shake the old man's hand. Immediately the bush around them swarmed with people, they poured back into the village jabbering and laughing: they crowded round Sean and felt his clothing, peered into his face and exclaimed delightedly. It was obvious that most of them had never seen a white man before. Sean was trying to shake off One-Eye, who still had a possessive hold on Sean's right hand, and Hlubi leaned disdainfully against the tree, taking no part in the welcome. One-Eye ended the confusion by screeching at them in a voice rusty with age. The courage he had displayed earlier now earned its reward. At his command a dozen of the younger women scampered off and came back with a carved wooden stool and six earthenware pots of native beer. By the hand, on which he had not for an instant relaxed his grip, One-Eye led Sean to the stool and made him sit; the rest of the villagers squatted in a circle round him and one of the girls brought the biggest beer-pot to Sean. The beer was yellow and it bubbled sullenly. Sean's stomach shied at the sight of it. He glanced at One-Eye who was watching him anxiously, he lifted the pot and sipped. Then he smiled with surprise; it was creamy and pleasantly tart.

'Good,' he said.

'Goot,' chorused the villagers.

'Your health,' said Sean.

''ealt,' said the village as one man, and Sean drank deep. One of the girls took another beer-pot to Hlubi. She knelt in front of him and shyly offered it. She had a plaited-grass string around her waist from which a small kilt hung down in front, but her stern was completely exposed and her bosoms were the size and shape of ripe melons. Hlubi looked at them until the girl hung her head, then he lifted the beer-pot.

Sean wanted a guide to the nearest Portuguese settlement. He looked at One-Eye and said, 'Town? Portagee?'

One-Eye was almost overcome by Sean's attention. He grabbed Sean's hand again before he could pull it away and shook it vigorously.

'Stop that, you bloody fool,' said Sean irritably and One-Eye grinned and nodded, then without releasing Sean's hand he began an impassioned speech to the other villagers. Sean meanwhile was searching his memory for the name of one of the Portuguese ports on this coast.

'Nova Sofala,' he shouted as he got it.

One-Eye broke off his speech abruptly and stared at Sean.

'Nova Sofala,' said Sean again pointing vaguely towards the east and One-Eye showed his gums in his biggest grin yet.

'Nova Sofala,' he agreed pointing with authority and then it was only a matter of minutes before it was understood between them that he would act as guide. Hlubi saddled the horses, One-Eye fetched a grass sleeping mat and a battle-axe from one of the huts. Sean mounted and looked at Hlubi to do the same but Hlubi was acting strangely.

'Yes?' Sean asked with resignation. 'What is it?'

'Nkosi.' Hlubi was looking at the branches of the tree above them. 'The Old One could lead the packhorse.'

'You can take it in turns,' said Sean.

Hlubi coughed and transferred his eyes to the fingernails of his left hand.

'Nkosi, is it possible that you will return to this village on the way back from the sea?'

'Yes, of course,' said Sean, 'we'll have to leave the Old One here. Why do you ask?'

'I have a thorn in my foot, Nkosi, it gives me pain. If you do not require me I will wait here for you. Perhaps the torn wound will have healed by then.' Hlubi looked up at the tree again and shuffled his feet with embarrassment. Sean had not noticed him limping and he was puzzled as to why Hlubi should start malingering now. Then Hlubi could not stop himself from glancing at where the girl stood in the circle of villagers. Her kilt was very small and from the sides gave her no cover at all. Understanding came to Sean and he chuckled.

'The thorn you have is painful, but it's not in your foot.' Hlubi shuffled his feet again. 'You said they were monkeys . . . have you changed your mind?' Sean asked.

'Nkosi, they are indeed monkeys,' Hlubi sighed. 'But very friendly monkeys.'

'Stay then . . . but do not weaken yourself too much. We have mountains to cross on the way home.'

22

One-Eye led the packhorse–this made him very proud. Through tall grass, mangrove swamp and thick hot jungle, then through white coral sand and the curving stems of palm trees, they came at last to the sea. Nova Sofala was a fort with brass cannon and thick walls. The sea beyond it was muddy brown from the estuary that flowed into it.

The sentry at the gates said, '*Madre de Dio*' when he saw Sean, and took him to the Commandant. The Commandant was a small man with fever-yellowed face and a tired, sweat-darkened tunic. The Commandant said, '*Madre de Dio,*' and shot his chair back from his desk. It took some time for him to realize that contrary to appearance this dirty, bearded giant was not dangerous. The Commandant could speak English and Sean laid his problem before him.

For a certainty he could be of assistance. There were three Jesuit missionaries in the fort, freshly arrived from Portugal and eager for employment. Sean could take his pick but first he must bath, eat dinner with the Commandant and help him sample the wines that had arrived on the same boat as the missionaries. Sean thought that was a good idea.

At dinner he met the missionaries. They were young men, pinkfaced still, for Africa had not yet had a chance to mark them. All three of them were willing to go with him and Sean selected the youngest–not for his appearance but rather for his name. 'Father Alphonso' had a heroic ring to it. The Jesuits went early to bed and left the Commandant, the four junior officers and Sean to the port. They drank toasts to Queen Victoria and her family and to the King of Portugal and his family. This made them thirsty so they drank to absent friends, then to each other. The Commandant and Sean swore a mutual oath of friendship and loyalty and this made the Commandant very sad, he cried and Sean patted his shoulder and offered to dance the Dashing White Sergeant for him. The Commandant said that he would esteem it as a very great honour and furthermore he would be delighted. He himself did not know this dance but perhaps Sean would instruct him. They danced on the table. The Commandant was doing very well until in his enthusiasm he misjudged the size of the table. Sean helped the junior officers put him to bed and in the morning Sean, Father Alphonso and One-Eye started back towards the mountains.

Sean was impatient of any delay now; he wanted to get back to Katrina. Father Alphonso's English was on a par with Sean's Portuguese. This made conversation difficult, so Alphonso solved the problem by doing all the talking. At first Sean listened but when he decided that the good father was trying to convert him he no longer bothered. Alphonso did not seem put out–he just went on talking and clinging to the horse with both hands while his cassock flapped about his legs and his face sweated in the shade of his wide-brimmed hat. One-Eye followed them like an ancient stork.

It took them two days back to One-Eye's village and their entry was a triumphal procession. Father Alphonso's face lit up when he saw so many prospective converts. Sean could see him mentally rubbing his hands together, and he decided to keep going before Alphonso forgot the main object of the expedition. He gave One-Eye a hunting-knife in payment for his services. One-Eye sat down under the big tree in the centre of the village, his own thin legs no longer able to support his weight and the knife clutched to his chest.

'Hlubi, you've had enough of that . . . come on now!' Sean had not dismounted and was restlessly waiting for Hlubi to say his farewells to three of the village girls. Hlubi had displayed traditional Zulu taste–all three of them were big-breasted, big-bottomed and young. They were also crying.

'Come on, Hlubi . . . what's the trouble?'

'Nkosi, they believe that I have taken them for my wives.'

'What made them think that?'

'Nkosi, I do not know.' Hlubi broke the armhold that the plumpest and youngest had around his neck, he snatched up his spears and fled. Sean and Alphonso galloped after him. The villagers shouted farewells and Sean looked back and saw One-Eye still sitting at the base of the big tree.

The pace which Sean set was at last telling on Alphonso. His verbal spring-tides slackened and he showed a measure of reluctance to let his backside touch the saddle; he rode crouched forward on his horse's neck with his buttocks in the air. They crossed the mountains and went down the other side; the ground levelled out into the Sabi Valley and they rode into the forest. On the ninth day out from Nova Sofala they reached the Sabi river. It was late afternoon. Flocks of guinea-fowl were drinking in the river-bed, they went up in a blue haze of whirling wings as Sean led his party down the bank. While the horses watered Sean spoke with Hlubi.

'Do you recognize this part of the river?'

'Yes, Nkosi, we are two hours' march upstream from the wagons . . . we held too far to the north coming through the forest.'

Sean looked at the sun, it was on the tree-tops.

'Half an hour's light left . . . and there's no moon tonight.'

'We could wait until morning,' Hlubi suggested hopefully. Sean ignored him and motioned to Alphonso to mount up. Alphonso was prepared to debate the advisability of moving on. Sean took a handful of his cassock and helped him into the saddle.

23

In the darkness the lantern burning in Katrina's wagon glowed through the canvas and guided them the last half mile into camp. Thief bayed them welcome and Mbejane ran out at the head of the other servants to take Sean's horse. His voice was loud with worry and relief.

'Nkosi, there is little time . . . it has begun.'

Sean jumped off his horse and ran to the wagon. He tore open the canvas flap.

'Sean.' She sat up. Her eyes were very green in the lantern light, but they were dark-ringed. 'Thank God, you've come.'

Sean knelt beside her cot and held her. He said certain things to her and she clung to him and moved her lips across his face. The world receded and left one wagon standing in darkness, lit by a single lamp and the love of two people.

Suddenly she stiffened in his arms and gasped. Sean held her, his face suddenly helpless and his big hands timid and uncertain on her shoulders.

'What can I do, my fancy? How can I help you?'

Her body relaxed slowly and she whispered, 'Did you find a priest?'

'The priest!' Sean had forgotten about him. Still holding on to her he turned his head and bellowed, 'Alphonso . . . Alphonso. Hurry, man.'

Father Alphonso's face in the opening of the wagon was pale with fatigue and grimy with dust.

'Marry us,' said Sean. 'Quickly, man, che-cha, chop-chop . . . you savvy?'

Alphonso climbed into the wagon. The skirts of his cassock were torn and his knees were white and bony through the holes. He stood over them and opened his book. 'Ring?' he asked in Portuguese.

'I do,' said Sean.

'No! No! Ring?' Alphonso held up a finger and made an encircling gesture. 'Ring?'

'I think he wants a wedding ring,' whispered Katrina.

'Oh, my God,' said Sean. 'I'd forgotten about that.' He looked round desperately. 'What can we use? Haven't you got one in your chest or something?'

Katrina shook her head, opened her lips to answer but closed them again as another pain took her. Sean held her while it lasted and when she relaxed he looked up angrily at Alphonso.

'Marry us . . . damn you. Don't you see there's not time for all the trimmings?'

'Ring?' said Alphonso again. He looked very unhappy.

'All right, I'll get you a ring.' Sean leapt out of the wagon and shouted at Mbejane.

'Bring my rifle, quickly.'

If Sean wanted to shoot the Portuguese that was his business and Mbejane's duty was to help him. He brought Sean the rifle. Sean found a gold sovereign in the pouch of his belt, he threw it on the ground and held the muzzle of the rifle on it. The bullet punched a ragged hole through it. He tossed the rifle back to Mbejane, picked up the small gold circle and scrambled back into the wagon.

Three times during the service the pains made Katrina gasp and each time Sean held her tight and Alphonso increased the speed of his delivery. Sean put the punctured sovereign on Katrina's finger and kissed her. Alphonso gabbled out the last line of Latin and Katrina said, 'Oh, Sean, it's coming.'

'Get out,' Sean told Alphonso and made an expressive gesture towards the door–thankfully Alphonso went.

It did not take long then, but to Sean it was an eternity like that time when they had taken Garrick's leg. Then in a slippery rush it was finished. Katrina lay very quiet and pale, while on the cot below her, still linked to her, purple-blotched and bloody lay the child that they had made.

'It's dead,' croaked Sean. He was sweating and he had backed away against the far wall of the wagon.

'No,' Katrina struggled up fiercely. 'No, it's not . . . Sean, you must help me.'

She told him what to do and at last the child cried.

'It's a boy,' said Katrina softly. 'Oh, Sean . . . it's a boy.' She was more beautiful than he had ever seen her before; pale and tired and beautiful.

24

Sean's protests were in vain–Katrina left her bed the next morning and squeezed into one of her old dresses. Sean hovered between her and the child on the cot.

'I'm still so *fat*,' she lamented.

'Fancy, please stay in bed another day or two.'

She pulled a face at him and went on struggling with the lacing of her bodice.

'Who's going to look after the baby?'

'I will!' said Sean earnestly. 'You can tell me what to do.'

Arguing with Katrina was like trying to pick up quicksilver with your fingers, not worth the effort. She finished dressing and took up the child.

'You can help me down the steps.' She smiled at him. Sean and Alphonso set a chair for her in the shade of one of the big shuma trees and the servants came to see the child. Katrina held him in her lap and Sean stood over them in uncertain possession. For Sean it seemed unreal yet . . . too much for his mind to digest in so short a time. He grinned dazedly at the steady stream of comment from his servants and his arm was limp when Alphonso shook his hand for the twentieth time that morning.

'Hold your child . . . Nkosi. Let us see you with him on your arm,' called Mbejane and the other Zulus took up the cry. Sean's expression changed slowly to one of apprehension.

'Pick him up, Nkosi.'

Katrina proffered the bundle and a hunted look came into Sean's eyes.

'Have no fear, Nkosi, he has no teeth, he cannot harm you,' Hlubi encouraged him. Sean held his first-born awkwardly and assumed the hunchbacked posture of the new father. The Zulus cheered him and slowly Sean's face relaxed and his smile was a glow of pride.

'Mbejane, is he not beautiful?'

'As beautiful as his father,' Mbejane agreed.

'Your words are a blade with two edges,' laughed Sean. He looked at the child closely. It wore a cap of dark hair, its nose was flat as a bulldog's, its eyes were milky-grey and its legs were long, skinny and red.

'How will you name him?' asked Hlubi. Sean looked at Katrina.

'Tell them,' he said.

'He shall be called Dirk,' she said in Zulu.

'What is the meaning?' asked Hlubi, and Sean answered him.

'It means a dagger . . . a sharp knife.'

There was immediate nodded approval from all the servants. Hlubi produced his snuff-box and passed it among them and Mbejane took a pinch.

'That,' he said, 'is a good name.'

25

Paternity, the subtle alchemist, transformed Sean's attitude to life within twelve hours. Never before had anything been so utterly dependent upon him, so completely vulnerable. That first evening in their wagon he watched Katrina sitting cross-legged on her cot, stooping forward over the child to give it her breast. Her hair hung in a soft wing across one cheek, her face was fuller, more matronly and the child in her lap fed with a red face and small wheezings. She looked up at him and smiled and the child tugged her breast with its tiny fists and hunting mouth.

Sean crossed to the cot, sat beside them and put his arm around them. Katrina rubbed her cheek against his chest and her hair smelt warm and clean. The boy went on feeding noisily. Sean felt vaguely excited as though he were on the threshold of a new adventure.

A week later, when the first rain clouds built up in the sky, Sean took the wagon across the Sabi and on to the slopes of the mountains to escape the heat of the plains. There was a valley he had noticed when he and Hlubi had made their journey to the coast. The valley bottom was covered with short sweet grass and cedar trees grew along a stream of clear water. Sean took them to this place.

Here they would wait out the rainy season and when it was finished and the baby was strong enough to travel they could take the ivory south and sell it in Pretoria. It was a happy camp. The oxen spread out along the valley, filling it with movement and the contented sound of their lowing; there was laughter among the wagons and at night when the mist slumped down off the mountains the camp fire was bright and friendly. Father Alphonso stayed with them for nearly two weeks. He was a pleasant young man and although he and Sean never understood what the other was saying yet they managed well enough with sign language. He left at last with Hlubi and one of the other servants to escort him back over the mountains, but before he did he managed to embarrass Sean by kissing him goodbye. Sean and Katrina were sorry to see him go. They had grown to like him and Katrina had almost forgiven him his religion.

The rains came with the usual flourish and fury. Weeks drifted into months. Happy months, with life centring around Dirk's cot. Mbejane had made the cot for him out of cedarwood and one of Katrina's chests produced the sheets and blankets for it. The child grew quickly: each day he seemed to occupy more of his cot, his legs filled out, his skin lost its blotchy-purple look and his eyes were no longer a vague milky-blue. There was green in them now–they would be the same colour as his mother's.

To fill the long lazy days Sean started to build a cabin beside the stream. The servants joined in and from a modest first plan it grew into a thing of sturdy plastered walls and neatly thatched roof with a stone fireplace at one end. When it was finished Sean and Katrina moved into it. After their wagon with its thin canvas walls, the cabin gave a feeling of permanence to their love. One night, when the rain hissed down in darkness outside and the wind whined at the door like a dog wanting to be let in, they spread a mattress in front of the fireplace and there in the moving firelight they started another baby.

Christmas came, and after it the New Year. The rains stuttered and stopped and still they stayed on in their valley. Then at last they had to go, for their supplies of basic stores–powder, salt, medicines, cloth–were nearly finished. They loaded the wagons, inspanned and left in the early morning. As the line of wagons wound down the valley towards the plains Katrina sat on the box seat of the lead wagon holding Dirk on her lap and Sean rode beside her. She looked back–the roof of their cabin showed brown through the branches of the cedar trees. It seemed forlorn and lonely.

'We must come back one day, we've been so happy here,' she said softly. Sean leaned out of the saddle towards her and touched her arm.

'Happiness isn't a place, my fancy, we aren't leaving it here, we're taking it with us.'

She smiled at him. The second baby was starting to show already.

26

They reached the Limpopo river at the end of July and found a place to cross. It took three days to unload the wagons, work them through the soft sand and then carry the ivory and stores across. They finished in the late afternoon of the third day and by then everyone was exhausted. They ate an early supper and an hour after sunset the Zulus were rolled in their blankets, and Sean and Katrina were sleeping arms-around and head-on-chest in the wagon. In the morning Katrina was quiet and a little pale. Sean didn't notice it until she told him that she felt tired and was going to lie down–immediately he was all attentive. He helped her into the wagon and settled the pillows under her head.

'Are you sure you're all right?' he kept asking.

'Yes . . . it's nothing, I'm just a bit tired. I'll be all right,' she assured him. She appreciated his concern but was relieved when finally he went to see the business of reloading the wagons, for Sean's ministrations were always a little clumsy. She wanted to be left alone, she felt tired and cold.

By midday the wagons were loaded to Sean's satisfaction. He went to Katrina's wagon, lifted the canvas and peeped in. He expected her to be asleep. She was lying on the cot with her eyes open and two of the thick grey blankets wrapped around her. Her face was as pale as a two-day corpse. Sean felt the first leap of alarm, he scrambled into the wagon.

'My dear, you look ghastly. Are you sick?' He put his hand on her shoulder and she was shivering. She didn't answer him, instead her eyes moved from his face to the floor near the foot of the bed and Sean's eyes followed hers. Katrina's luxury was her chamber-pot; it was a massive china thing with red roses hand-painted on it. She loved it dearly and Sean used to tease her when she was perched on top of it. Now the pot stood near the foot of the bed and when Sean saw what was in it his breathing stopped. It was half full of a liquid the colour of milk stout. 'Oh, my God,' he whispered. He went on staring at it, standing very still while a gruesome snatch of doggerel he remembered hearing sung in the canteens of the Witwatersrand began trotting through his brain like an undertaker's hack.

Black as the Angel,
Black as disgrace
When the fever waters flow
They're as black as the ace.

Roll him in a blanket
Feed him on quinine
But all of us we know
It's the end of the line.

Black as the Angel
Black as disgrace
Soon we'll lay him down below
And chuck dirt in his face.

He raised his head and looked steadily at her, scarching for the signs of fear. But just as steadily she looked back at him.

'Sean, it's blackwater.'

'Yes . . . I know,' Sean said, for there was nothing to be gained by denial, no room for extravagant hope. It was blackwater fever: malaria in its most malignant form, attacking the kidneys and turning them to fragile sacks of black blood that the slightest movement could rupture. Sean knelt by her cot. 'You must lie very still.' He touched her forehead lightly with the tips of his fingers and felt the heat of her skin.

'Yes,' she answered him, but already the expression in her eyes was blurring and she made the first restless movement of delirium. Sean put his arm across her chest to hold her from struggling.

By nightfall Katrina was deep in the nightmare of malaria. She laughed, she screamed in senseless terror, she shook her head and fought him when he tried to make her drink. But she had to drink, it was her one chance, to flush out her kidneys that she might live. Sean held her head and forced her.

Dirk started crying, hungry and frightened by the sight of his mother.

'Mbejane!' shouted Sean, his voice pitched high with desperation. Mbejane had waited all afternoon at the entrance of the wagon.

'Nkosi, what can I do?'

'The child . . . can you care for him?'

Mbejane picked up the cot with Dirk still in it. 'Do not worry about him again. I will take him to the other wagon.'

Sean turned his whole attention back to Katrina. The fever built up steadily within her. Her body was a furnace, her skin was dry and with every hour she was wilder and her movements more difficult to control.

An hour after dark Kandhla came to the wagon with a pot of steaming liquid and a cup. Sean's nose wrinkled as he caught the smell of it.

'What the hell is that?'

'I have stewed the bark from a maiden's breast tree . . . the Nkosikazi must drink it.'

It had the same musty smell as boiling hops and Sean hesitated. He knew the tree. It grew on high ground, it had a diseased-looking lumpy bark and each lump was the size and shape of a breast surmounted by a thorn.

'Where did you get it? I have seen none of these trees near the river.' Sean was marking time while he decided whether to make Katrina drink the brew. He knew these Zulu remedies, what they didn't kill they sometimes cured.

'Hlubi went back to the hills where we camped four days ago . . . he brought the bark into the camp an hour ago.'

A thirty-mile round journey in something under six hours–even in his distress Sean could smile.

'Tell Hlubi the Nkosikazi will drink his medicine.'

Kandhla held her head and Sean forced the evil-smelling liquid between her lips–he made her finish the whole potful. The juice of the bark seemed to relieve the congestion of her kidneys; four times before morning she passed frothy black water. Each time Sean held her gently, cushioning her body from any movement that might have killed her. Gradually her delirium became coma; she lay huddled and still in the cot, shaken only by the brief fits of shivering. When the morning sun hit the wagon canvas and lit the interior, Sean saw her face, and he knew that she was dying. Her skin was an opaque yellowish white, her hair had lost its glow and was lifeless as dry grass. Kandhla brought another pot of the medicine and they fed it to her. When the pot was empty Kandhla said, 'Nkosi, let me lay a mattress on the floor beside the Nkosikazi's bed. You must sleep and I will stay here with you and wake you if the Nkosikazi stirs.'

Sean looked at him with haunted eyes. 'There will be time to sleep later, my friend.' He looked down at Katrina and went on softly. 'Perhaps, very soon there will be time.'

Suddenly Katrina's body stiffened and Sean dropped on his knees beside her cot. Kandhla hovered anxiously behind him. It took Sean a while to understand what was happening and then he looked up at Kandhla.

'Go! go quickly!' he said and the suffering in his voice sent Kandhla stumbling blindly from the wagon. Sean's second son was born that morning and while Kandhla watched over Katrina Sean wrapped the child in a blanket, took him into the veld and buried him. Then he went back to Katrina and stayed with her while days and nights blended together into a hopeless muddle of grief. As near as Katrina was to death, that near was Sean to insanity. He never moved out of the wagon, he squatted on the mattress next to her cot, wiping the perspiration from her face, holding a cup to her lips or just sitting and watching her. He had lost his child and before his eyes Katrina was turning into a wasted yellow skeleton. Dirk saved him. Mbejane brought the boy to him and he romped on the mattress, crawling into Sean's lap and pulling his beard. It was the one small glimmer of light in the darkness.

27

Katrina survived. She came back slowly from the motionless coma that precedes death and with her hesitant return Sean's despair changed to hope and then to a wonderful relief. Her water was no longer black but dark pink and thick with sediment. She was aware of him now and, although she was so weak that she could not lift her head off the pillow, her eyes followed him as he moved about the wagon. It was another week before she learned about the baby. She asked him, her voice a tired whisper, and Sean told her with all the gentleness of which he was capable. She did not have the strength for any great show of emotion; she laid quietly staring up at the canvas above her head and her tears slid down across her yellow cheeks.

The damage that the fever had done to her body was hardly credible. Her limbs were so thin that Sean could completely encircle her thigh with one hand. Her skin hung in loose yellow folds from her face and body and pink blood still stained her water. This was not all: the fever had sucked all the strength from her mind. She had nothing left to resist the sorrow of her baby's death, and the sorrow encased her in a shell through which neither Sean nor

Dirk could reach her. Sean struggled to bring her back to life, to repair the terrible damage to her mind and body. Every minute of his time he employed in her service.

He and the servants scoured the veld for thirty miles around the laager to find delicacies to tempt her appetite, wild fruits, honey, giraffe marrows, the flesh of a dozen animals: kabobs of elephant heart and duiker liver, roasted iguana lizard as white and tender as a plump pullet, golden fillets of the yellow-mouthed bream from the river. Katrina picked at them listlessly then turned away and lay staring at the canvas wall of the cot.

Sean sat beside her and talked about the farm they would buy, trying vainly to draw her into a discussion of the house they would build. He read to her from Duff's books and the only reaction he received was a small quivering of her lips when he read the words 'death' or 'child'. He talked about the days on the Witwatersrand, searching his mind for stories that might amuse her. He brought Dirk to her and let him play about the wagon. Dirk was walking now, his dark hair had started to curl and his eyes were green. Dirk, however, could not be too long confined in the wagon. There was too much to do, too much to explore. Before long he would stagger to the entrance and issue the imperial summons: 'Bejaan! Bejaan!'

Almost immediately Mbejane's head would appear in the opening and he would glance at Sean for permission.

'All right, take him out then . . . but tell Kandhla not to stuff him full of food.'

Quickly, before Sean changed his mind, Mbejane would lift Dirk down and lead him away. Dirk had nearly two dozen Zulus to spoil him. They competed hotly for his affections, no effort was too much–dignified Mbejane down on his hands and knees being ridden mercilessly in and out among the wagons, Hlubi scratching himself under the arms and gibbering insanely in his celebrated imitation of a baboon while Dirk squealed with delight, fat Kandhla raiding Katrina's store of fruit preserves to make sure Dirk was properly fed and the others keeping in the background, anxious to join the worship but fearful of incurring the jealously of Mbejane and Hlubi. Sean knew what was happening but he was powerless to prevent it. His time was completely devoted to Katrina.

For the first time in his life Sean was giving more than just a superficial part of himself to another human being. It was an isolated sacrifice: it went on throughout the months it took for Katrina to regain sufficient of her strength to enable her to sit up in bed without assistance; it continued through the months that she needed before Sean judged it safe to resume the trek towards the south. They built a litter for her–Sean would not risk the jarring of the wagon–and the first day's trek lasted two hours. Four of the servants carried the litter and Katrina lay in it, protected from the sun by a strip of canvas spread above her head. Despite the gentleness with which the Zulus handled her, at the end of the two hours Katrina was exhausted. Her back ached and she was sweating in small beads from her yellow skin. The next week they travelled two hours daily and then gradually increased the time until they were making a full day's journey.

They were halfway to the Magaliesberg, camped at a muddy waterhole in the thorn flats, when Mbejane came to Sean.

'There is still one wagon empty of ivory, Nkosi.'

'The others are full,' Sean pointed out.

'Four hours' march from this place there is enough ivory buried to fill those wagons.'

Sean's mouth twisted with pain. He looked away towards the south-east and he spoke softly. 'Mbejane, I am still a young man and yet already I have stored up enough ugly memories to make my old age sad. Would you have me steal from a friend not only his life but his share of ivory also?'

Mbejane shook his head. 'I asked, that is all.'

'And I have answered, Mbejane. It is his . . . let it lie.'

28

They crossed the Magaliesberg and turned west along the mountain range. Then, two months after they had left the Limpopo river, they reached the Boer settlement at Louis Trichardt. Sean left Mbejane to outspan the wagons on the open square in front of the church and he went to search for a doctor. There was only one in the district, Sean found him in his surgery above the general dealer's store and took him to the wagons. Sean carried his bag for him and the doctor, a greybeard and unused to such hardships, trotted to keep up with Sean. He was panting and pouring sweat by the time they arrived. Sean waited outside while the doctor completed his examination and when he finally made his descent from the wagon Sean fell on him impatiently. 'What do you think, man?'

'I think, meneer, that you should give hourly thanks to your Maker.' The doctor shook his head in amazement. 'It seems hardly possible that your wife could have survived both the fever and the loss of the child.'

'She is safe then, there's no chance of a relapse?' Sean asked.

'She is safe now . . . but she is still a very sick woman. It may take a year before her body is fully mended. There is no medicine I can give you. She must be kept quiet, feed her well and wait for time to cure her.' The doctor hesitated. 'There is other damage–' he tapped his forehead with his forefinger. 'Grief is a terrible destroyer. She will need love and gentleness and after another six months she will need a baby to fill the emptiness left by the one she lost. Give her those three things, meneer, but most of all give her love.' The doctor hauled his watch from his waistcoat and looked at it. 'Time! there is so little time. I must go, there are others who need me.' He held out his hand to Sean. 'Go with God, meneer.'

Sean shook his hand. 'How much do I owe you?'

The doctor smiled, he had a brown face and his eyes were pale blue; when he smiled he looked like a boy. 'I make no charge for words. I wish I could have done more.' He hurried away across the square and when he walked you could see that his smile lied, he was an old man.

'Mbejane,' said Sean. 'Get a big tusk out of the wagon and take it to the doctor's room above the store.'

Katrina and Sean went to the morning service in the church next day. Katrina could not stand through the hymns. She sat quietly in her pew, watching the altar, her lips forming the words of the hymn and her eyes full of her sorrow.

They stayed on for three more days in Louis Trichardt and they were made welcome. Men came to drink coffee with them and see the ivory and the women brought them eggs and fresh vegetables, but Sean was anxious to move south. So on the third day they started the last stage of their trek.

Katrina regained her strength rapidly now. She took over the management of Dirk from the servants, to their ill-concealed disappointment, and soon she left her litter and rode on the box seat of the lead wagon again. Her body filled out and there was colour showing once more through the yellow skin of her cheeks. Despite the improvement to her body the depression of her mind still persisted and there was nothing that Sean could do to lift it.

A month before the Christmas of 1895 Sean's wagon train climbed the low range of hills above the city and they looked down into Pretoria. The jacaranda trees that filled every garden were in bloom–masses of purple–and the busy streets spoke well of the prosperity of the Transvaal Republic. Sean outspanned on the outskirts of the city, simply pulling the wagons off the road and camping beside it, and once the camp was established and Sean had made certain that Katrina no longer needed his help he put on his one good suit and called for his horse. His suit had been cut to the fashion of four years previously and had been made to encompass the belly he had acquired on the Witwatersrand. Now it hung loosely down his body but bunched tightly around his thickened arms. His face was burnt black by the sun and his beard bushed down on to his chest and concealed the fact that the stiff collar of his shirt could no longer close around his neck. His boots were scuffed almost through the uppers, there was not a suspicion of polish on them and they had completely lost their shape. Sweat had soaked through his hat around the level of the band and left dark greasy marks; the brim drooped down over his eyes so he had to wear it pushed on to the back of his head. There was, therefore, some excuse for the curious glances that followed him that afternoon as he rode down Church Street with a great muscular savage trotting at his one stirrup and an overgrown brindle hound at the other. They pushed their way between the wagons that cluttered the wide street; they passed the Raadsaal of the Republican Parliament, passed the houses standing back from the road in their spacious purple and green gardens and came at last to the business area of the city that crowded round the railway station. Sean and Duff had bought their supplies at a certain general dealer's stores and now Sean went back to it. It was hardly changed–the signboard in front had faded a little but still declared that I. Goldberg, Importer & Exporter, Dealer in Mining Machinery, Merchant & Wholesaler, was prepared to consider the purchase of gold, precious stone, hides and skins, ivory and other natural produce. Sean swung down from the saddle and tossed his reins to Mbejane. 'Unsaddle, Mbejane. This may take time.'

Sean stepped up on to the sidewalk, lifted his hat to two passing ladies and went through into the building where Mr Goldberg conducted his diverse activities. One of the assistants hurried to meet him, but Sean shook his head and the man went back behind the counter. He had seen Mr Goldberg with two customers at the far end of the store. He was content to wait. He browsed around among the loaded shelves of merchandise, feeling the quality of a shirt, sniffing at a box of cigars, examining an axe, lifting a rifle down off the rack and sighting at a spot on the wall, until Mr Goldberg bowed his customers through the door and turned to Sean. Mr Goldberg was short and fat. His hair was cropped short and his neck bulged over the top of his collar. He looked at Sean and his eyes were expressionless while he rifled through the index cards of his memory for the name. Then he beamed like a brilliant burst of sunlight. 'Mr Courteney, isn't it?'

Sean grinned. 'That's right. How are you, Izzy?' They shook hands. 'How's business?'

Mr Goldberg's face fell. 'Terrible, terrible, Mr Courteney. I'm a worried man.'

'You look well enough on it,' Sean prodded his stomach. 'You've put on weight.'

'You can joke, Mr Courteney, but I'm telling you it's terrible. Taxes and worry, taxes and worry,' Mr Goldberg sighed, 'and now there's talk of war.'

'What's this?' Sean frowned.

'War, Mr Courteney, war between Britain and the Republic.'

Sean's frown dissolved and he laughed. 'Nonsense, man, not even Kruger could be such a bloody fool! Get me a cup of coffee and a cigar and we'll go through to your office and talk business.'

Mr Goldberg's face went blank and his eyelids drooped almost sleepily.

'Business, Mr Courteney?'

'That's right, Izzy, this time I'm selling and you're buying.'

'What are you selling, Mr Courteney?'

'Ivory!'

'Ivory?'

'Twelve wagon loads of it.'

Mr Goldberg sighed sadly. 'Ivory's no good now, the bottom's fallen out of it. You can hardly give it away.' It was very well done; if Sean had not been told the ruling prices two days before he might have been convinced.

'I'm sorry to hear that,' he said. 'If you're not interested, I'll see if I can find someone else.'

'Come along to my office anyway,' said Mr Goldberg. 'We can talk about it. Talk costs nothing.'

Two days later they were still talking about it. Sean had fetched his wagons and had off-loaded the ivory in the back yard of the store. Mr Goldberg had personally weighed each tusk and written the weights down on a sheet of paper. He and Sean had added the columns of figures and agreed on the total. Now they were in the last stages of agreeing the price.

'Come on, Izzy, we've wasted two days already. That's a fair price and you know it . . . let's get it over with,' Sean growled.

'I'll lose money on this,' protested Mr Goldberg. 'I've got to make a living, every man's got to live.'

'Come on,' Sean held out his right hand. 'Let's call it a deal.'

Mr Goldberg hesitated a second longer, then he put his pudgy hand in Sean's fist and they grinned at each other, both well satisfied. One of Mr Goldberg's assistants counted out the sovereigns, stacking them in piles of fifty along the counter, then Sean and Mr Goldberg checked them and agreed once more. Sean filled two canvas bags with the gold, slapped Mr Goldberg's back, helped himself to another cigar and headed heavily laden for the bank.

'When are you going into the veld again?' Mr Goldberg called after him.

'Soon!' said Sean.

'Don't forget to get your supplies here.'

'I'll be back,' Sean assured him.

Mbejane carried one of the bags and Sean the other. Sean was smiling and streamers of cigar smoke swirled back from his head as he strode along the sidewalk. There's something in the weight of a sack of gold that makes the man who holds it stand eight feet tall.

That night as they lay together in the darkness of the wagon Katrina asked him.

'Have we enough money to buy the farm yet, Sean?'

'Yes,' said Sean. 'We've got enough for the finest farm in the whole Cape peninsula . . . and, after one more trip, we'll have enough to build the house and the barns, buy the cattle, lay out the vineyard and still have some left over.'

Katrina was silent for a moment then, 'So we are going back into the bushveld again?'

'One more trip,' said Sean. 'Another two years and then we'll go down to the Cape.' He gave her a hug. 'You don't mind, do you?'

'No,' she said. 'I think I'd like that. When will we leave?'

'Not just yet awhile,' Sean laughed. 'First we're going to have some fun.' He hugged her again, her body was still painfully thin; he could feel the bones of her hips pressed against him.

'Some pretty clothes for you, my fancy, and a suit for me that doesn't look like a fancy dress. Then we'll go out and see what this burg has to offer in the way of entertainment–' He stopped as the idea swelled up in his mind. 'Damn it! I know what we'll do. We'll hire a carriage and go across to Jo'burg. We'll take a suite at the Grand National Hotel and do some living. Bath in a china bath, sleep in a real bed; you can have your hair prettied-up and I'll have my beard trimmed by a barber. We'll eat crayfish and penguin eggs . . . I can't remember when I last tasted pork or mutton . . . we'll wash it down with the old bubbling wine and waltz to a good band–' Sean raced on and when he stopped for breath Katrina asked softly, 'Isn't the waltz a very sinful dance, Sean?'

Sean smiled in the darkness. 'It certainly is!'

'I'd like to be sinful just once . . . not too much, just a little with you to see what it's like.'

'We will be'–said Sean–'as wicked as hell.'

29

The next day Sean took Katrina to the most exclusive ladies' shop in Pretoria. He chose the material of half a dozen dresses. One of them was to be a ball gown in canary-yellow silk. It was extravagance and he knew it, but he didn't care once he saw the flash of guilty delight in Katrina's cheeks and the old green sparkle in her eyes. For the first time since the fever she was living again. He spilled out his sovereigns with thankful abandon. The sales girls were delighted with him, they crowded round him with trays of feminine accessories.

'A dozen of those,' said Sean and, 'yes, those will do.' Then a flash of green on the racks across the room caught his eye–it was Katrina's green.

'What's that?' He pointed and two sales girls nearly knocked each other down in the rush to get it for him. The winner carried the shawl back to him and Sean took it and placed it around Katrina's shoulders. It was a beautiful thing.

'We'll take it,' said Sean and Katrina's lips quivered–then suddenly she was crying, sobbing brokenly. The excitement had been too much. There was immediate consternation among the shop assistants, they flapped around Sean like hens at feeding time while he picked Katrina up and carried her out to the hired carriage. At the door he paused and spoke over his shoulder.

'I want those dresses finished by tomorrow evening. Can you do it?'

'They'll be ready, Mr Courteney, even if my girls have to work all night on them.'

He took Katrina back to the wagons and laid her on her cot.

'Please forgive me, Sean, I've never done that in my life before.'

'It's all right, my fancy, I understand. Now you just go to sleep.'

The following day Katrina stayed at the camp resting, while Sean went to see Mr Goldberg again and buy from him the stores they would need for the next expedition. It took another day to load the wagons and by then Katrina seemed well enough to make the trip to Johannesburg.

They left in the early afternoon. Mbejane driving, Sean and Katrina sitting close together on the back seat holding hands under the travelling rug and Dirk bouncing round the interior of the carriage, pausing now and then to flatten his face against a window and keeping up a flow of comment in the peculiar mixture of English, Dutch and Zulu that Sean called Dirkese. They reached Johannesburg long before Sean expected to. In four years the town had doubled its size and had spread out into the veld to meet them. They followed the main road through the new areas and came to the centre. There were changes here as well but it was, in the main, the way he remembered it. They threaded their way through the babble of Eloff Street, and around them, mingling with the crowds on the sidewalks, were the ghosts of the past. He heard Duff laugh and twisted quickly in his seat to place the sound; a dandy in a boater hat with gold fillings in his teeth laughed again from a passing carriage and Sean heard that it was not Duff's laugh. Very close, but not the same. All of it was like that–similar but subtly changed, nostalgic but sad with the knowledge of loss. The past was lost–and he knew then that you can never go back. Nothing is the same, for reality can exist at one time only and in one place only. Then it dies and you have lost it and you must go on to find it at another time and in another place.

They took a suite at the Grand National, with a sitting-room and two bedrooms, a private bathroom and a balcony that looked out over the street–over the rooftops to where the headgears and white dumps stood along the ridge. Katrina was exhausted. They had supper sent up to the room early and when they had eaten Katrina went to bed and Sean went down alone to drink a nightcap at the bar. The bar-room was crowded. Sean found a seat in the corner and sat silently in the jabber of conversation. In it, but no longer a part of it.

They had changed the picture above the bar–it used to be a hunting print; but now it was a red-coated general, impressively splattered with blood, taking leave of his staff in the middle of a battlefield. The staff looked bored. Sean let his eyes wander on along the dark panelled walls. He remembered–there was so much to remember! Suddenly he blinked. Near the side door was a star-shaped crack in the wooden panelling. Sean started to grin and put down his glass and massaged the knuckles of his right hand. If Oakie Henderson hadn't ducked under that punch it would have taken his head off.

Sean signalled to the barman. 'Another brandy, please.' While the man was pouring, Sean asked, 'What happened to that panel near the door?'

The man glanced up and then back at the bottle. 'Some fellow put his fist through it in the old days. Boss left it like that, sort of souvenir, you know.'

'He must have been quite a fellow . . . that wood's an inch thick. Who was he?' Sean asked expectantly.

The man shrugged. 'One of the drifters. They come and they go. Make a few pounds, piss it against the wall and then go back where they came from.' He looked at Sean with bored eyes. 'That'll be half a dollar, mate.' Sean drank the brandy slowly, turning the glass in his hands between sips and watching the liquor cling to its sides like thin oil. By a cracked panel in a bar-room they shall remember you.

And now I shall go to bed, he decided, this is no longer my world. My world is upstairs sleeping–I hope! He smiled a little to himself and finished the brandy in his glass.

'Sean'–a voice at his ear and a hand on his shoulder as he turned to leave. 'My God, Sean, is it really you?'

Sean stared at the man beside him. He did not recognize the neatly clipped beard and the big sun-burned nose with the skin peeling off the tip, but suddenly he knew the eyes.

'Denis, you old rogue. Denis Petersen from Ladyburg. That's right, isn't it?'

'You didn't recognize me!' laughed Denis. 'So much for our friendship–you disappear without a word and ten years later you don't even know me!'

Now they were both laughing.

'I thought they would have hanged you long ago–' Sean defended himself. 'What on earth are you doing in Johannesburg?'

'Selling beef–I'm on the committee of the Beef Growers' Association.' There was pride in Denis's voice. 'I have been up here negotiating the renewal of our contracts.'

'When are you going back?'

'My train leaves in an hour.'

'Well, there's time for a drink before you go–what will it be?'

'I'll have a small brandy, thanks.'

Sean ordered the drinks and they took them up and stood, suddenly awkward in the awareness that ten years were between their once complete accord.

'So, what have you been doing with yourself?' Denis ended the pause.

'This and that, you know–a bit of mining, just come back from the bushveld. Nothing very exciting.'

'Well, it's good to see you again anyway. Your health.'

'And yours,' said Sean, and then suddenly he realized that here was news of his family–news he had been without for many years.

'How's everyone at Ladyburg–your sisters?'

'Both married–so am I, with four sons,' and the pride was in Denis's voice again.

'Anyone I know?' asked Sean.

'Audrey–you know old Pye's daughter.'

'No!' Sean ripped out the word, and then quickly, 'That's wonderful, Denis. I'm pleased for you–she was a lovely girl.'

'The best,' agreed Denis complacently. He had the sleek well-fed, well-cared for look of a married man, fatter in the face and his stomach starting to show. I wonder if I have it yet, Sean thought. 'Of course, old man Pye's dead now–that's one creditor he couldn't buy off. Ronnie's taken over the bank and the store.'

'The bat-eared bush rat,' said Sean and knew immediately that he had said the wrong thing. Denis frowned slightly. 'He's family now, Sean. A very decent chap really–and a clever business man.'

'I'm sorry, I was joking. How's my mother?' Sean changed the subject by asking the question that had been in the forefront of his mind and he had picked the right topic. Denis's expression softened immediately–you could see the warmth in his eyes.

'The same as ever. She's got a dress shop now, next door to Ronnie's store. It's a gold mine–no one would think of buying anywhere else but at Aunt Ada's. She's godmother to my two eldest. I guess she's godmother to half the kids in the district,' and then his expression hardened again. 'The least you could have done was write to her sometime, Sean. You can't imagine the pain you have caused her.'

'There were circumstances.' Sean dropped his eyes to his glass.

'That's no excuse–you have a duty which you neglected. There is no excuse for it.'

You little man, Sean lifted his head and looked at him without trying to disguise his annoyance. You pompous, preaching little man peering out at the world one-eyed through the keyhole of your own self-importance. Denis had not noticed Sean's reaction and he continued. 'That's a lesson a man must learn before he grows up–we all have our responsibilities and our duties. A man grows up when he faces those duties, when he accepts the burdens that society places on him. Take my own case: despite the vast amount of work I have on the farms–I now own Mahoba's Kloof as well–and despite the demands made on me by my family, yet I have time to represent the district on the committee of the Beef Growers' Association, I am a member of the Church Council and the village management board, and I have every reason to believe that next month I will be asked to accept the office of mayor.' Then he looked steadily at Sean. 'What have *you* done with your life so far?'

'I've lived it,' Sean answered, and Denis looked a little perplexed–then he gathered himself.

'Are you married yet?'

'I was–but I sold her to the Arab slavers up north.'

'You did what?'

'Well,' grinned Sean, 'she was an old wife and the price was good.'

'That's a joke, hey? Ha, ha!' You couldn't fool good old Denis–Sean laughed out loud. This unbelievable little man!

'Have a drink, Denis,' he suggested.

'Two is my limit, thanks Sean.' Denis pulled the gold hunter from his waistcoat pocket and inspected it. 'Time to go–I'm afraid. Nice seeing you again.'

'Wait,' Sean stopped him. 'My brother–how's Garry?'

'Poor old Garry.' Denis shook his head solemnly.

'What's wrong with him?' Sean's voice was sharp with his sense of dread.

'Nothing–' Denis reassured him quickly. 'Well, I mean nothing more than ever was.'

'Why did you say "poor old Garry" then?'

'I don't really know–except that everybody says it. It's habit, I suppose–he's just one of those people you say *poor old* in front of.'

Sean suppressed his irritation, he wanted to know. He had to know.

'You haven't answered me–how is he?'

Denis made a significant gesture with his right hand. 'Looking into the bottle quite a bit these days–not that I blame him with that woman he married. You were well out of it there if I may say so, Sean.'

'You may,' Sean acquiesced, 'but is he well? How are things at Theunis Kraal?'

'We all took a bit of a beating with the rindepest* but Garry–well, he lost over half of his herds. Poor old Garry, everything happens to him.'

'My God–fifty per cent!'

'Yes–but, of course, Ronnie helped him out. Gave him a mortgage on the farm to tide him over.'

'Theunis Kraal bonded again,' groaned Sean. 'Oh Garry, Garry.'

'Yes–well,' Denis coughed uneasily. 'Well, I think I'd better be going. *Totsiens*, Sean.' He held out his hand. 'Shall I tell them I saw you?'

'No,' said Sean quickly. 'Just leave it stand.'

'Very well then.' Denis hesitated. 'Are you all right, Sean? I mean'–he coughed again–'are you all right for money?'

Sean felt his unhappiness dissolve a little; this pompous little man was going to offer him a loan. 'That's very good of you, Denis. But I've got a couple of pounds saved up–enough to eat on for a few days,' he spoke seriously.

'All right then.' Denis looked mightily relieved. 'All right then–*totsiens*, Sean,' and he turned and walked quickly out of the bar. As he left the room so he went out of Sean's mind, and Sean was thinking of his brother again.

Then suddenly Sean decided. I will go back to Ladyburg when this next trip is over. The dream farm outside Paarl would not lose anything in being transplanted to Natal–and he suddenly longed to sit in the panelled study at Theunis Kraal again, and to feel the mist come cold down the escarpment in the mornings, and see the spray blowing off the white falls in the wind. He wanted to hear Ada's voice again and to explain to her, knowing she would understand and forgive.

But more, much more it was Garry–poor old Garry. I must go back to him–ten years is a long time and he will have lost the bitterness. I must go back to him–for his sake and for Theunis Kraal. With the decision made, Sean finished his drink and went up the stairs to his suite.

Katrina was breathing softly in her sleep, the dark mass of her hair spread out on the pillow. While he undressed he watched her and slowly the melancholy dissolved. Gently he pulled back the blankets on his side of the bed and just then Dirk whimpered from the next room. Sean went through to him. 'All right, what's the trouble?'

Dirk blinked owlishly and searched for an excuse, then the relief flooded into his face and he produced the one that creaked with age. 'I want a drink a water.'

The delay while Sean went through to the bathroom gave Dirk an opportunity to rally his forces and when Sean came back he opened the offensive in earnest.

'Tell me a story, Daddy.' He was sitting up now, bright-eyed.

'I'll tell you a story about Jack and a Nory–' said Sean.

'Not that one–' protested Dirk. The saga of Jack and his brother lasted five seconds and Dirk knew it. Sean sat down on the edge of the bed and held the glass for him.

'How about this one? There once a king who had everything in the world . . .

* An epidemic cattle disease.

but when he lost it he found out that he had never had anything and that he now had more than he ever had before.'

Dirk looked stunned.

'That's not a very good one,' he gave his opinion at last.

'No,' said Sean. 'It isn't . . . is it? But I think we should be charitable and admit that it's not too bad for this time of night.'

30

Sean woke feeling happy. Katrina was sitting up in bed filling cups from a pewter coffee pot and Dirk was hammering at the door to be let in. Katrina smiled at him. 'Good morning, meneer.'

Sean sat up and kissed her. 'How did you sleep, fancy?'

'Well, thank you,' but there were dark rings under her eyes. Sean went across to the bedroom door.

'Prepare to receive cavalry,' he said and swung it open, Dirk's charge carried him on to the bed and Sean dived after him. When two men are evenly matched, weight will usually decide and within seconds Dirk had straddled Sean's chest, pinning him helplessly and Sean was pleading for quarter.

After breakfast Mbejane brought the carriage round to the front of the hotel. When the three of them were settled in it, Sean opened the small window behind the driver's seat and told Mbejane, 'To the office first. Then we have to be at the Exchange by ten o'clock.'

Mbejane grinned at him. 'Yes, Nkosi, then lunch at the Big House.' Mbejane had never been able to master the word Xanadu.

They went to all the old places. Sean and Mbejane laughing and reminiscing at each other through the window. There was a panic at the Exchange, crowds on the pavement outside. The offices on Eloff Street had been refaced and a brass plate beside the front door carried the roll of the subsidiaries of Central Rand Consolidated. Mbejane stopped the carriage outside and Sean boasted to Katrina. She sat silently and listened to him, suddenly feeling inadequate for a man who had done so much. She misinterpreted Sean's enthusiasm and thought he regretted the past and wished he were back.

'Mbejane, take us up to the Candy Deep,' Sean called at last. 'Let's see what's happening there.'

The last five hundred yards of the road was overgrown and pitted with disuse. The administration block had been demolished and grass grew thick over the foundations. There were new buildings and headgears half a mile farther along the bridge, but here the reef had been worked out and abandoned. Mbejane pulled up the horses in the circular drive in front of where the offices had stood. He jumped down and held their heads while Sean helped Katrina out of the carriage. Sean lifted Dirk and sat him on his shoulder and they picked their way through the waist-high grass and piles of bricks and rubbish towards the Candy Deep Number Three Shaft.

The bare white concrete blocks that had held the machinery formed a neat geometrical pattern in the grass. Beyond them reared the white mine dump; some mineral in the powdered rock had leaked out in long yellow stains down its sides. Duff had once had the mineral identified. It was of little commercial value, used occasionally in the ceramics industry. Sean had forgotten the name of it; it sounded like the name of a star–Uranus perhaps.

They came to the shaft. The edges of it had crumbled and the grass hung into it, the way an unkempt moustache hangs into an old man's mouth. The headgear was gone and only a rusty barbed-wire fence ringed the shaft. Sean bent his knees: keeping his back straight for Dirk still sat on his shoulder, he picked up a lump of rock the size of a man's fist and tossed it over the fence. They stood quietly and listened to it clatter against the sides as it fell. It fell for a long time and when at last it hit the bottom the echo rang faintly up from a thousand feet below.

'Throw more!' commanded Dirk, but Katrina stopped him.

'No, Sean, let's go. It's an evil place.' She shuddered slightly. 'It looks like a grave.'

'It very nearly was,' said Sean softly, remembering the darkness and the rock pressing down upon him.

'Let's go,' she said again, and they went back to where Mbejane waited with the carriage.

Sean was gay at lunch, he drank a small bottle of wine, but Katrina was tired and more miserable than she had been since they left Louis Trichardt. She had begun to realize the type of life he had led before she met him and she was frightened that now he wanted to return to it. She had only known the bush and the life of the Trek-Boer, she knew she could never learn to live like this. She watched as he laughed and joked during the meal, she watched the easy assurance with which he commanded the white head waiter, the way he picked his way through the maze of cutlery that was spread out on the table before them and at last she could hold it in no longer.

'Let's go away, let's go back into the bush.'

Sean stopped with a loaded fork halfway to his mouth. 'What?'

'Please, Sean, the sooner we go the sooner we'll be able to buy the farm.'

Sean chuckled. 'A day or two more won't make any difference. We're starting to have fun. Tonight I'll take you dancing–we were going to be sinful, remember?'

'Who will look after Dirk?' she asked weakly.

'Mbejane will–' Sean looked at her closely. 'You have a good sleep this afternoon and tonight we'll go out and tie the dog loose.' He grinned at the memories that expression invoked.

When Katrina woke from her rest that evening she found the other part of the reason for her depression. For the first time since the baby her periodic bleeding had started again, the tides of her body and mind were at their lowest ebb. She said nothing to Sean, but bathed and put on the yellow gown. She brushed her hair furiously, dragging the brush through it until her scalp tingled, but still it hung dull and lifeless–as dull as the eyes that looked back at her out of the yellow face in the mirror.

Sean came up behind her and leaned over her to kiss her cheek. 'You look,' said he, 'like a stack of gold bars five-and-a-half feet high.' But he realized that the yellow gown had been a mistake: it matched too closely the fever colour of her skin. Mbejane was waiting in the sitting-room when they went through.

'It may be late before we return,' Sean told him.

'That is of no account, Nkosi,' Mbejane's face was as impassive as ever, but Sean caught a sparkle of anticipation in his eyes and realized that Mbejane could hardly wait to get Dirk to himself.

'You are not to go into his room,' Sean warned.

'What if he cries, Nkosi?'

'He won't . . . but if he does see what he wants, give it to him then leave him to sleep.'

Mbejane's face registered his protest.

'I'm warning you, Mbejane, if I come home at midnight and find him riding you round the room I'll have both your hides for a kaross.'

'His sleep shall be unspoiled, Nkosi,' lied Mbejane.

In the hotel lobby Sean spoke to the receptionist. 'Where can we find the best food in this town?' he asked.

'Two blocks down, sir, the Golden Guinea. You can't miss it.'

'It sounds like a gin palace,' Sean was dubious.

'I assure you, sir, that you'll have no complaint when you get there. Everyone goes there. Mr Rhodes dines there when he's in town, Mr Barnato, Mr Hradsky–'

'Dick Turpin, Cesare Borgia, Benedict Arnold,' Sean continued for him. 'All right, you have convinced me. I'll take a chance on having my throat cut.'

Sean went out through the front entrance with Katrina on his arm. The splendour of the Golden Guinea subdued even Sean a little. A waiter with a uniform like a major-general's led them down a marble staircase, across the wide meadow of carpet between the group of elegant men and women to a table that even in the soft light dazzled with its bright silver and snowy linen. Chandeliers of crystal hung from the vaulted ceiling, the band was good, and the air was rich with the fragrance of perfume and expensive cigars.

Katrina stared helplessly at the menu until Sean came to her rescue and ordered the meal in a French accent that impressed her but not the waiter. The wine came and with it Sean's high spirits returned. Katrina sat quietly opposite him and listened. She tried to think of something witty to answer him with; in their wagon or alone in the veld they could talk for hours at a time but here she was dumb.

'Shall we dance?' Sean leaned across the table and squeezed her hand. She shook her head.

'Sean, I couldn't. Not with all these people watching. I'd only make a fool of myself.'

'Come on, I'll show you how . . . it's easy.'

'No, I couldn't, truly I couldn't.'

And to himself Sean had to admit that the dance floor of the Golden Guinea on a Saturday night was not the best place for a waltz lesson. The waiter brought the food, great steaming dishes of it. Sean addressed himself to it and the one-sided conversation wilted. Katrina watched him, picking at the too rich food herself, acutely conscious of the laughter and voices around them, feeling out of place and desperately miserable.

'Come on, Katrina,' Sean smiled at her. 'You've hardly touched your glass. Be a devil and get a little of that in you to warm you up.'

Obediently she sipped the champagne. She didn't like the taste. Sean finished the last of his crayfish thermidor and leaning back in his chair glowing with wine and good food said, 'Man . . . I only pray the chef can keep the rest of the meal up to that standard.' He belched softly behind his fingers and ran his eyes contentedly round the room. 'Duff used to say that a well-cooked crayfish was proof that–'

Sean stopped abruptly. He was staring at the head of the marble staircase–a party of three had appeared there. Two men in evening dress hovering attentively on each side of a woman. The woman was Candy Rautenbach. Candy with her blonde hair piled on top of her head. Candy with diamonds in her ears and at her throat, her bosom overflowing her gown as white as the frothy head on a beer tankard. Candy with bright blue eyes above a red mouth, Candy poised and lovely. Laughing, she glanced towards him and her eyes met his across the room. She stared in open disbelief, the laughter frozen on her lips, then suddenly her pose was gone and she was running down the stairs towards him, holding her skirts up to her knees, her escorts cantering after her in alarm, waiters scattering out of her path and every head in the room turning to watch her. Sean pushed back his chair, stood up to meet her and Candy reached him and jumped up to throw her arms around his neck. There was a long incoherent exchange of greetings and at last Sean prised her loose from his neck and turned her to face Katrina. Candy was flushed and panting with excitement; with every breath her bosom threatened to spring out of her bodice, and she was still holding on to Sean's arm.

'Candy, I want you to meet my wife, Katrina. My dear, this is Candy Rautenbach.'

'How do you do.' Katrina smiled uncertainly and Candy said the wrong thing.

'Sean, you're joking! You married?'

Katrina's smile faded. Candy noticed the change and went on quickly, 'But I must applaud your choice. I am so pleased to meet you, Katrina. We must get together sometime and I'll tell you all about Sean's terrible past.'

Candy was still holding Sean's arm and Katrina was watching her hand–the long tapered fingers against the dark cloth of Sean's suit. Sean saw the direction of Katrina's eyes and tried tactfully to disengage himself but Candy held on. 'Sean, these are my two current beaux.' They were standing to heel behind her like well-trained gundogs. 'They are both so nice I can't make up my mind about them. Harry Lategaan and Derek Goodman. Boys, this is Sean Courteney. You've heard lots about him.'

They shook hands all round.

'Do you mind if we join you?' asked Derek Goodman.

'I'd be upset if you didn't!' said Sean. The men spread out to find chairs while Candy and Katrina studied each other. 'Is this your first visit to Johannesburg, Mrs Courteney?' Candy smiled sweetly. *I wonder where Sean found her, she's thin as a stick and that complexion!–that accent! he could have done better for himself–he could have had his pick.*

'Yes, we won't be here very long though.' *She's a harlot. She must be–her breasts half-naked and the paint on her face and the way she touches Sean. She must have been his mistress. If she touches him again I'll–I'll kill her.*

Sean came back to the table carrying a chair and set it down for Candy. 'Candy's one of my old friends, my dear, I'm sure you two will like each other.'

'I'm sure we will,' said Candy but Katrina didn't answer and Candy turned back to him. 'Sean, how wonderful it is to see you again. You look so well . . . as sunburnt and handsome as the first time I met you. Do you remember that day you and Duff came to eat at the Hotel?

A shadow fell across Sean's face at the mention of Duff's name. 'Yes, I remember.' He looked round and snapped his fingers for the waiter. 'Let's have some more champagne.'

'I'll get it,' Candy's escorts cut in simultaneously and then started wrangling good-naturedly as to whose turn it was.

'Is Duff with you tonight, Sean?' Candy asked.

'Candy, didn't Derek get the drinks last time? It's my turn now.' Harry sought her support. Candy ignored them and looked at Sean for a reply but he turned and went round the table to the seat beside Katrina.

'I say, old girl, can I have the first dance?' asked Derek.

'I'll spin you for it, Derek, winner pays but gets first dance,' Harry suggested.

'You're on.'

'Sean, I said is Duff here tonight?' Candy looked at him across the table.

'No, he's not. Listen, you two, how about letting me in on this.' Sean avoided her eyes and joined in the haggle with Harry and Derek. Candy bit her lip–she wanted to press Sean further. She wanted to know about Duff–then suddenly she turned on her smile again. She wasn't going to plead with him.

'What is this?' She tapped Harry's shoulder with her fan. 'Am I going to be the prize in a game of chance? Derek will pay for the wine and Sean gets first dance.'

'I say, old girl, that's a bit rough, you know.' But Candy was already standing up.

'Come on, Sean, let's see if you can still tread a stately measure.'

Sean glanced at Katrina. 'You don't mind, do you . . . just one dance?'

Katrina shook her head.

I hate her. She's a harlot. Katrina had never in her life spoken the word out loud, she had seen it only in her Bible, but now it gave her a fierce pleasure to think it. She watched Sean and Candy walk arm-in-arm to the dance floor.

'Would you care to dance, Mrs Courteney?' said Derek. Katrina shook her head again without looking at him. She was staring at Sean and Candy. She saw Sean take her in his arms and a cold lump settled in her stomach. Candy was looking up into Sean's face, laughing at him, her arm on his shoulder, her hand in his.

She's a harlot. Katrina felt her tears very near the surface and thinking that word held them back. Sean swirled Candy into a turn–Katrina stiffened in her chair, her hands clenching in her lap–their legs were touching, she saw Candy arch her back slightly and press her thighs against Sean. Katrina felt as though she were suffocating, jealousy had spread up cold and tight through her chest.

I could go and pull him away, she thought. *I could stop him doing that. He has no right. It's as though the two of them are doing–doing it together. I know they have before, I know it now–Oh God, make them stop it. Please make them stop.*

At last Sean and Candy came back to the table. They were laughing together and when he reached her chair Sean dropped his hand on Katrina's shoulder. She moved away from it but Sean seemed not to notice. Everybody was having a good time. Everybody except Katrina. Harry and Derek were jostling for position. Sean's big laugh kept booming out and Candy was sparkling like the diamonds she wore. Every few minutes Sean turned to Katrina and tried to draw her into the conversation but Katrina stubbornly refused to be drawn. She sat there hating them all. Hating even Sean–for the first time she was unsure of him, jealous and frightened for him. She stared down at her hands on the tablecloth in front of her and saw how bony they were, chapped and reddened by the sun and wind, ugly compared to Candy's. She pulled them quickly into her lap and leaned across towards Sean. 'Please, I want to go back to the hotel. I don't feel well.'

Sean stopped in the middle of a story and looked at her with a mixture of concern and dismay. He didn't want to leave and yet he knew she was still sick. He hesitated one second and then he said, 'Of course, my fancy, I'm sorry. I didn't realize–' He turned to the others. 'We'll have to be going . . . my wife's not too strong . . . she's just had one hell of a go of blackwater.'

'Oh, Sean, must you?' Candy couldn't hide her disappointment. 'There's still so much to talk about.'

'I'm afraid so. We'll get together another night.'

'Yes,' agreed Katrina quickly, 'next time we come to Johannesburg we'll see you.'

'Oh, I don't know . . . perhaps before we go,' Sean demurred. 'Some night next week. How about Monday?'

Before Candy could answer Katrina interrupted. 'Please, Sean, can we go now. I'm very tired.' She started towards the stairs but looked back to see Candy jump up and take Sean's arm, hold her lips close to his ear and whisper a question. Sean answered her tersely and Candy turned back to the table and sat down. When they were out on the street Katrina asked, 'What did she say to you?'

'She just said goodbye,' muttered Sean and Katrina knew he was lying. They didn't talk again on the way back to the hotel. Katrina was preoccupied with her jealousy and Sean was thinking about what Candy had asked and what he had answered.

'Sean, where's Duff? You must tell me.'

'He's dead, Candy.'

The second before she turned back to the table Sean had seen her eyes.

31

Sean woke with a headache and Dirk's jumping on his chest did not help to ease it at all. Sean had to bribe him off with the promise of sweets. Dirk, sensing his advantage, raised his price to a packet of bull's eyes and two lollipops, the kind with red stripes, before he allowed Katrina to lead him away to the bathroom. Sean sighed and settled back under the blankets. The pain moved up and crouched just behind his eyes. He could taste stale champagne on his own breath and his skin smelt of cigar smoke. He drowsed back in half sleep and the ache faded a little.

'Sean, it's Sunday you know. Are you coming to church with us?' Katrina asked coldly from the bedroom door. Sean squeezed his eyelids tighter closed.

'Sean!' No answer.

'Sean!' He opened one eye.

'Are you going to get up?'

'I don't feel very well,' he croaked. 'I think I have a touch of malaria.'

'Are you coming?' Katrina demanded remorselessly. Her feelings towards him had not softened during the night.

'I don't feel up to it this morning, truly I don't. I'm sure the Good Lord will understand.'

'Thou shalt not take the Lord's name in vain,' Katrina warned him with ice in her voice.

'I'm sorry.' Sean pulled the blankets up to his chin defensively. 'But truly, fancy, I can't get up for another couple of hours. My head would burst.'

Katrina turned back into the sitting-room and Sean heard her speak to Dirk in a voice purposely pitched to reach him.

'Your father's not coming with us. We will have to go down to breakfast by ourselves. Then we will have to go to church on our own.'

'But,' Dirk pointed out, 'he's going to buy me a packet of bull's eyes and *two* lollipops with red stripes.' In Dirk's opinion that levelled the score. Sean heard the door of the suite close and Dirk's voice receded down the passage. Sean relaxed slowly and waited for the ache behind his eyes to diminish. After a while he became aware of the coffee tray on the table beside the bed and he weighed the additional pain that the effort of sitting up would involve against the beneficial effect of a large cup of coffee. It was a difficult decision but in the end he carefully raised his body to a sitting position and poured a cupful. There was a small jug of fresh cream on the tray, he took it in his right hand and was just about to add a little to the cup when there was a knock on the sitting-room door.

'Come in!' called Sean. He supposed it was the waiter coming to collect the tray. Sean searched his mind for a really scathing remark to send him on his way. He heard the sitting-room door open.

'Who is it?' he asked. There were quick footsteps and then Sean started so violently that the cream slopped out of the jug on to his sheets and his new nightshirt.

'Good God, Candy, you shouldn't have come here.' Sean was in a frenzy of agitation. He put the jug back on the tray with nervous haste and wiped ineffectually at the mess on his nightshirt with his hands. 'If my wife . . . Did anyone see you? You mustn't stay. If Katrina knows you've been here she'll . . . well I mean, she won't understand.'

Candy's eyes were puffy and rimmed with red. She looked as though she hadn't slept. 'It's all right, Sean, I waited across the street until I saw your wife leave. One of my servants followed her, she went to the Dutch church on Commissioner Street and there the service lasts about fifty years.' She came into the room and sat down on the edge of his bed.

'I had to talk to you alone. I couldn't let you go without knowing about Duff. I want you to tell me about it . . . everything about it. I promise not to cry, I know how you hate it.'

'Candy, let's not torture ourselves with it. He's dead. Let's remember him alive.' Sean had forgotten his headache for its place had been taken by pity for her and worry at the position in which she had placed him.

'Tell me, please. I must know. I'd never rest again if I didn't,' she said quietly.

'Candy, don't you see that it doesn't matter? The way in which he went is not important. All that you need to know is he's gone.' Sean's voice faded but went on softly, almost to himself, 'He's gone, that is the only thing that matters, he's gone and left us richer for knowing him and a little poorer for having lost him.'

'Tell me,' she said again and they looked at each other, their emotions locked behind expressionless faces. Then Sean told her, his words limping at first, then faster and stronger as the horror of it came back to him. When he had finished she said nothing. She sat on the edge of the bed staring down at the patterned carpet. Sean moved closer to her and put his arm around her.

'There is nothing we can do. That's the thing about death, there is nothing you can do to make it change its mind.'

She leaned against him, against the comfort of his big body and they sat silently until suddenly Candy pulled away from him and smiled her gay brittle smile.

'And now tell me about you. Are you happy? Was that your son with Katrina? He's a lovely child.'

With relief Sean followed her away from the memory of Duff. They talked about each other, filling in the blanks from the time they had last met until suddenly Sean returned to reality.

'Good God, Candy, we've been talking for ages. Katrina will be back at any moment. You had better run.'

At the door she turned, buried her fingers in his beard and tugged his head from side to side. 'If she ever throws you out, you magnificent brute, here's somebody who'll have a place for you.'

She stood up on her toes and kissed him. 'Be happy,' she commanded and the door closed softly behind her.

Sean rubbed his chin, then he pulled off his nightshirt, screwed it into a ball, tossed it through the open door of the bedroom and went to the bathroom. He was towelling himself and whistling the waltz that the band had played the night before, sweating a little in the steamy warmth of the bathroom when he heard the front door open. 'Is that you, Fancy?'

'Daddy! Daddy! Mummy got sweets for me.' Dirk hammered on the bathroom door, and Sean wrapped the towel round his waist before opening it.

'Look! Look at all my sweets,' gloated Dirk. 'Do you want one, Pa?'

'Thank you, Dirk,' Sean put one of the huge striped humbugs in his mouth, moved it to one side and spoke around it.

'Where's your Mummy?'

'There.' Dirk pointed at the bedroom. He closed the sweet packet carefully. 'I'll keep some for Bejaan,' he announced.

'He'll like that,' Sean said and went across to the bedroom. Katrina lay on the bed; as soon as he saw her he knew something was desperately wrong. She lay staring up at the ceiling, her eyes unseeing, her face as yellow and set as that of a corpse. Two quick strides carried him to her. He touched her cheek with his fingers and the sense of dread settled on him again, heavily, darkly.

'Katrina?' There was no response. She lay still without a flicker of life in her eyes. Sean swung round and ran out of the suite, down the corridor to the head of the stairs. There were people in the lobby below him and he yelled over their heads to the clerk behind the desk.

'Get a doctor, man, as fast as you can . . . my wife's dying.'

The man stared up at him blankly. He had a neck too thin for his high stiff collar and his black hair was parted down the centre and polished with grease.

'Hurry, you stupid bastard, get moving,' roared Sean. Everybody in the lobby was looking at him. He still wore only a small towel around his waist and, heavy with water, his hair hung down over his forehead.

'Move, man! Move!' Sean was dancing with impatience. There was a heavy stone vase on the banister at Sean's side, he picked it up threateningly and the clerk jerked out of his trance and scuttled for the front door. Sean ran back to the suite.

Dirk was standing by Katrina's bed, his face distorted by the humbug it contained and his eyes large with curiosity. Sean snatched him up, carried him through to the other bedroom and locked the door on his outraged howls. Dirk was unused to being handled in that manner. Sean went back to Katrina and knelt beside her bed. He was still kneeling there when the doctor arrived. Tersely Sean explained about the blackwater, and the doctor listened then sent him to wait in the sitting-room. It was a long wait before the doctor came through to him and Sean sensed that behind his professional poker face the man was puzzled.

'Is it a relapse?' Sean demanded.

'No, I don't think so. I've given her a sedative.'

'What's wrong with her? What is it?' Sean pursued him and the doctor hedged.

'Has your wife had some sort of shock . . . some bad news, something that could have alarmed her? Has she been under nervous strain?'

'No . . . she's just come back from church. Why? What's wrong?' Sean caught the doctor's lapels and shook him in his agitation.

'It appears to be some sort of paralytic hysteria. I've given her laudanum. She'll sleep now and I'll come back to see her this evening.'

The doctor was trying to loosen Sean's hands from his jacket. Sean let him go and pushed past him to the bedroom.

The doctor called again just before dark, Sean had undressed Katrina and put her into the bed, but apart from that she had not moved. Her breathing was shallow and fast despite the drug she had been given. The doctor was baffled.

'I can't understand it, Mr Courteney. There is nothing I can find wrong with her apart from her general run-down condition. I think we'll just have to wait and see, I don't want to give her any more drugs.'

Sean knew the man could be of no more help to him and he hardly noticed when he left with a promise to come again in the morning. Mbejane gave Dirk his bath, fed him and put him to bed and then he slipped quietly out of the suite and left Sean alone with Katrina. The afternoon of worry had tired Sean. He left the gas burning in the sitting-room and stretched out on his own bed. After a while he slept.

When the rhythm of his breathing changed Katrina looked across at him. Sean lay fully clothed on top of his blankets, one thickly-muscled arm thrown above his head and his tension betrayed by the twitching of his lips and the frown that puckered his face. Katrina stood up and moved across to stand over him, lonely as she had never been in the solitude of the bush, hurt beyond the limits of physical pain and with everything that she believed in destroyed in those few minutes that it had taken for her to discover the truth.

She looked down at Sean and with surprise realized that she still loved him, but now the security that she had found with him was gone. The walls of her castle had proved paper. She had felt the first cold draughts blowing in through them as she watched him reliving his past and regretting it. She had felt the walls tremble and the wind howl stronger outside when he danced with that woman–then, they had collapsed into ruin around her. Standing in the half-darkened room, watching the man she trusted so completely and who just as completely had betrayed her, she went carefully over the ground again to make sure there was no mistake.

That morning, she and Dirk had stopped at the sweet shop on the way back from church. It was almost opposite the hotel. It had taken Dirk a long time to select his tuppenny worth. The profusion of wares on display unmanned him and reduced him to a state of dithering indecision. Finally, with the assistance of the proprietor and a little prompting from Katrina his purchases were made and packed into a brown paper bag. They were just about to go when Katrina looked out through the large front window of the shop and saw Candy Rautenbach leaving the hotel. She came quickly down the front steps, glanced about her, crossed the street to a waiting carriage and her coachman whisked her away. Katrina had stopped the instant she caught sight of her. A pang of last night's jealousy returned, for Candy looked very lovely even in the morning sunlight. It was not until Candy's carriage disappeared that Katrina began to question her presence at their hotel at eleven o'clock on a Sunday morning. Her jealousy was a bayonet thrust up under her ribs: it made her catch her breath. Vividly she remembered Candy's whispered question as they left the Golden Guinea the previous night. She remembered the way Sean had answered and the way he had lied about it afterwards. Sean knew that Katrina would go to church that morning. How simple it all was! Sean had arranged to meet her, he had refused to accompany Katrina and while Katrina was out of the way that harlot had gone to him.

'Mummy, you're hurting me.' Unconsciously she had tightened her grip on Dirk's hand. She hurried out of the shop, dragging Dirk with her. She almost ran across the hotel lobby, up the stairs and along the passage. The door was closed. She opened it and the smell of Candy's perfume met her. Her nostrils flared at it. There was no mistaking it, she remembered it from the previous evening–the smell of fresh violets. She heard Sean call from the bathroom, Dirk ran across the room and hammered on the door.

'Daddy! Daddy! Mummy got sweets for me.'

She put her Bible down on top of the writing desk and moved across the thick carpet with the smell of violets all around her. She stood in the doorway of the bedroom. Sean's nightshirt lay on the floor, there were still damp stains on it. She felt her legs begin to tremble. She looked up and saw the stains on the bed, grey on the white sheets. She felt giddy, her cheeks burned; she only just managed to reach her own bed.

32

She knew there was no mistake. Sean had taken that woman in such a casually blatant manner–in their own bedroom, almost before her eyes, that his rejection of her could hardly have been more final if he had slapped her face and thrown her into the street. Weakened by fever, depressed by the loss of her child and the phase of her cycle, she had not the resilience to fight against it. She had loved him but she had proved insufficient for him. She could not stay with him: the stubborn pride of her race would not allow it. There was only one alternative.

Timidly she bent over him and as she kissed him she smelt the warm man-smell of his body and felt his beard brush her cheek. Her determination wavered; she wanted to throw herself across his chest, lock her arms around his neck and plead with him. She wanted to ask for another chance. If he could tell her how she had failed him she could try to change, if only he could show her what she had done wrong. Perhaps if they went back into the bush again–She dragged herself away from his bed. She pressed her knuckles hard against her lips. It was no use. He had decided and even if she begged him to take her back there would always be this thing between them. She had lived in a castle and she would not change it now for a mud hut. Driven by the trek whip of her pride she moved quickly across to the wardrobe. She put on a coat and buttoned it–it reached to her ankles and covered her nightdress; she spread the green shawl over her head, winding the loose end around her throat. Once more she looked across at Sean. He slept with his big body sprawled and the frown still on his face.

In the sitting-room she stopped beside the writing desk. Her Bible lay where she had left it. She opened the front cover, dipped the pen and wrote. She closed the book and went to the door. There she hesitated once more and looked back at Dirk's bedroom. She could not trust herself to see him again. She lifted an end of the shawl to cover her mouth, then she went out into the passage and closed the door softly behind her.

33

Sean was surprised to find himself fully dressed and lying on top of his bed when he woke next morning. It was still half dark outside the hotel windows and the room was cold. He propped himself up one elbow and rubbed at his eyes with the back of a clenched fist. Then he remembered and he swung his legs off the bed and looked at Katrina's bed. The blankets were thrown back and it was empty. Sean's first feeling was relief, she had recovered enough to get up on her own. He went through to the bathroom, stumbling a little from the stiffness of uneasy sleep. He tapped on the closed door.

'Katrina?' he questioned and then again louder. 'Katrina, are you in there?'

The handle turned when he tried it and the door swung open without resistance. He blinked at the empty room, white tiles reflecting the uncertain light, a towel thrown across a chair where he had left it. He felt the first twinge of alarm. Dirk's room–the door was still locked, the key on the outside. He flung it open. Dirk sat up in bed, his face flushed, his curls standing up like the leaves of a sisal bush. Sean ran out into the passage, along it and looked down into the lobby. There was a light burning behind the reception desk. The clerk slept with his head on his arms, sitting forward on his chair snoring. Sean went down the stairs three at a time. He shook the clerk.

'Has anybody been out through here during the night?' Sean demanded.

'I . . . I don't know.'

'Is that door locked?' Sean pointed at the front door.

'No, sir, there's a night latch on it. You can get out but not in.'

Sean ran out on to the pavement. Which way, which way to search for her? Which way had she gone? Back to Pretoria to the wagons? Sean thought not. She would need transport and she had no money to hire it. Why should she leave without waking him, leave Dirk, leave her clothing and disappear into the night. She must have been unbalanced by the drugs the doctor had given her. Perhaps there was something in his theory that she had suffered a shock, perhaps she was wandering in her nightdress through the streets with no memory, perhaps–Sean stood in the cold grey Transvaal morning, the city starting to murmur into wakefulness around him, the questions crowding into his head and finding there no answers with which to mate.

He turned and ran back through the hotel, out of the rear door into the stable yard.

'Mbejane,' he shouted, 'Mbejane, where the hell are you?'

Mbejane appeared quickly from the stall where he was currying one of the hired horses.

'Nkosi.'

'Have you seen the Nkosikazi?'

Mbejane's face creased into a puzzled frown. 'Yesterday–'

'No, man,' shouted Sean. 'Today, last night . . . have you seen her?'

Mbejane's expression was sufficient reply.

Sean brushed impatiently past him and ran into the stable. He snatched a saddle off the rack and threw it on to the back of the nearest horse. While he clinched the girth and forced a bit between its teeth he spoke to Mbejane.

'The Nkosikazi is sick. She has left during the night. It is possible that she walks as one who still sleeps. Go quickly among your friends and tell them to search for her, tell them that there's ten pounds in gold for the one who finds her. Then come back here and care for Dirk until I return.'

Sean led the horse from the stable and Mbejane hurried off to spread the word. Sean knew that within minutes half the Zulus in Johannesburg would be looking for Katrina–tribal loyalty and ten pounds in gold were strong incentives. He swung up on to the horse and galloped out of the yard. He tried the Pretoria road first. Three miles out of town a native herd boy grazing sheep beside the road convinced him that Katrina had not passed that way. He turned back. He paid a visit to the police station at Marshal Square. The Kommandant remembered him from the old days; Sean could rely on his co-operation. Sean left him and rode fast through the streets that were starting to fill with the bustle of a working day. He hitched his horse outside the hotel and took the front steps three at a time. The clerk had no news for him. He ran up the stairs and along the passage to his suite. Mbejane was feeding Dirk his breakfast. Dirk beamed at Sean through a faceful of egg and spread his arms to be picked up but Sean had no time for him.

'Has she come back?'

Mbejane shook his head. 'They will find her, Nkosi. Fifty men are searching for her now.'

'Stay with the child,' said Sean and went down to his horse. He stood beside it ready to mount but not knowing which way to go. 'Where the hell has she got to?' he demanded aloud. In her night clothes with no money, where the hell had she gone?

He mounted and rode with aimless urgency through the streets, searching the faces of the people along the sidewalks, turning down the sanitary lanes and peering into backyards and vacant plots. By midday he had tired his horse and worked himself into a ferment of worry and bad temper. He had searched every street in Johannesburg, made a nuisance of himself at the police station and sworn at the hotel clerk, but there was still no sign of Katrina. He was riding down Jeppe Street for the fifth time when the imposing double-storey of Candy's Hotel registered through his preoccupation.

'Candy,' he whispered. 'She can help.'

He found her in her office among Persian rugs and gilt furniture, walls covered with pink and blue patterned wallpaper, a mirrored ceiling hung with six crystal waterfalls of chandeliers and a desk with an Indian mosaic top. Sean pushed aside the little man in the black alpaca coat who tried to stop him entering and burst into the room. Candy looked up and her small frown of annoyance smoothed as she saw who it was.

'Sean . . . oh, how nice to see you.' She came round from behind the desk, the bell tent of her skirts covering the movement of her legs so she seemed to float. Her skin was smooth white and her eyes were happy blue. She held out her hand to him, but hesitated as she saw his face. 'What is it, Sean?'

He told her in a rush and she listened and when he had finished she rang the bell on her desk.

'There's brandy in the cabinet by the fireplace,' she said, 'I expect you are in need of one.'

The little man in the alpaca coat came quickly to the bell. Sean poured himself a large brandy and listened to Candy giving orders.

'Check the railway station. Telegraph the coach stages on each of the main roads. Send someone up to the hospital. Check the registers of every hotel and boarding-house in town.'

'Very well, madame.' The little man bobbed his head as he acknowledged each instruction and then he was gone.

Candy turned back to Sean.

'You can pour a drink for me also and then sit down and simmer down. You're behaving just the way she wanted you to.'

'What do you mean?' demanded Sean.

'You are being given a little bit of wifely discipline, my dear. Surely you have been married long enough to recognize that?'

Sean carried the glass across to her and Candy patted the sofa next to her.

'Sit down,' she said. 'We'll find your little Cinderella for you.'

'What do you mean . . . wifely discipline?' he demanded again.

'Punishment for bad behaviour. You may have eaten with your mouth open, answered back, taken more than your share of the blankets, not said good morning with the right inflection or committed one of the other mortal sins of matrimony, but–' Candy sipped her drink and gasped slightly, 'I see that time has not given you a lighter hand with the brandy bottle. One Courteney tot always did equal an imperial gallon . . . but, as I was saying, my guess is that little Katy is having an acute attack of jealousy. Probably her first, seeing that the two of you have spent your whole married life out in the deep sticks and she has never had an opportunity of watching the Courteney charm work on any other female before.'

'Nonsense,' said Sean. 'Who's she got to be jealous of?'

'Me,' said Candy. 'Every time she looked at me the other night I felt as though I'd been hit in the chest with an axe.' Candy touched her magnificent bosom with her fingertips, skilfully drawing Sean's attention to it. Sean looked at it. It was deeply cleft and smelt of fresh violets. He shifted restlessly and looked away.

'Nonsense,' he said again. 'We're just old friends, almost like–' he hesitated.

'I hope, my dear, that you weren't going to say "brother and sister" . . . I'll not be party to any incestuous relationship . . . or had you forgotten about that?'

Sean had not forgotten. Every detail of it was still clear. He blushed and stood up.

'I'd better be going,' he said. 'I'm going to keep looking for her. Thanks for your help, Candy, and for the drink.'

'Whatever I have is yours, m'sieur,' she murmured, lifting an eyebrow at him, enjoying the way he blushed. 'I'll let you know as soon as we hear anything.'

The assurance that Candy had given him wore thinner as the afternoon went by with no news of Katrina. By nightfall Sean was again wild with worry, it had completely swamped his bad temper and even anæsthetized his fatigue. One by one Mbejane's tribesmen came in to report a blank score, one by one the avenues Candy's men were exploring proved empty and long before midnight Sean was the only hunter left. He rode hunched in the saddle, a lantern in his hand, riding the ground that had already been covered a dozen times, visiting the mining camps along the ridge, stopping to question late travellers he met along the network of roads between the mines. But the answer was always the same. Some thought he was joking: they laughed until they saw that his face was haunted and dark-eyed in the lantern light, then they stopped laughing and moved hurriedly on. Others had heard about the missing woman; they started to question him, but as soon as Sean realized they could not help him, he pushed past them and went on searching. At dawn he was back at the hotel. Mbejane was waiting for him.

'Nkosi, I have had food ready for you since last night. Eat now and sleep a little. I will send the men out to search again today, they will find her.'

'Tell them, I will give one hundred pounds to the one who finds her.' Sean passed his hand wearily across his face. 'Tell them to hunt the open veld beyond the ridges, she may not have followed a road.'

'I will tell them . . . but now you must eat.'

Sean blinked his eyes, they were red-veined and each had a little lump of yellow mucus in the corner.

'Dirk?' he asked.

'He is well, Nkosi, I have stayed with him all the while.'

Mbejane took Sean firmly by the arm. 'There is food ready. You must eat.'

'Saddle me another horse,' said Sean. 'I will eat while you do it.'

Without sleep, unsteady in the saddle as the day wore on, Sean widened the circle of his search until he was out into the treeless veld and the mine headgears were small spidery triangles on the horizon.

A dozen times he met Zulus from the city, big black men in loin cloths, moving at their businesslike trot, hunting the ground like hounds. There was a concealed sympathy behind their greetings.

'Mbejane has told us, Nkosi. We will find her.' And Sean left them and rode on alone, more alone that he had ever been in his life before. After dark he rode back into Johannesburg, the faint flutter of hope inside him stilled as he limped stiffly into the gas-lit lobby of the hotel and saw the pity in the reception clerk's face.

'No word, I'm afraid, Mr Courteney.'

Sean nodded. 'Thanks anyway. Is my son all right?'

'Your servant has taken good care of him, sir. I sent dinner up to him an hour ago.'

The stairs seemed endless as he climbed them. By God, he was tired–sick-tired and sick with worry. He pushed open the door of his suite and Candy stood up from a chair across the room. The hope flared up in him again.

'Have you–' he started eagerly.

'No,' she said quickly. 'No, Sean, I'm sorry.' He flopped into one of the chairs and Candy poured a drink for him from a decanter that was waiting on the writing desk. He smiled his thanks and took a big gulp at the glass. Candy lifted his legs one at a time and pulled off his boots, ignoring his faint protest. Then she took up her own glass and went to sit across the room from him.

'I'm sorry I joked yesterday,' she apologized softly. 'I don't think I realized how much you love her.' She lifted her glass to him. 'Here's a speedy end to the search.'

Sean drank again, half a glass at a swallow.

'You do love her, don't you?' Candy asked.

Sean answered her sharply. 'She's my wife.'

'But it's not only that,' Candy went on recklessly, knowing his anger was just below the surface of his fatigue.

'Yes, I love her. I'm just learning how much, I love her as I'll never be able to love again.' He drained his glass and stared at it, his face grey under the brown and his eyes dark with unhappiness. 'Love,' he said. 'Love,' mouthing the word, weighing it. 'They've dirtied that word . . . they sell love at the Opera House . . . they have used that word so much that now when I want to say "I love Katrina" it doesn't sound what I mean.' Sean hurled the glass against the far wall, it shattered with a crack and a tingle and Dirk stirred in the bedroom. Sean dropped his voice to a fierce whisper. 'I love her so it screws my gut, I love her so that to think of losing her now is like thinking of dying.'

He clenched his fists and leaned forward in his chair. 'I'll not lose her now, by Christ, I'll find her and when I do I'll tell her this. I'll tell her just like I'm telling you.' He stopped and frowned. 'I don't think I've ever said to her "I love you." I've never liked using that word. I've said "Marry me" and "You're my fancy," but I've never said it straight before.'

'Perhaps that's part of the reason she ran away, Sean, perhaps because you never said it she thought you never felt it.' Candy was watching him with a strange expression–pity and understanding and a little yearning.

'I'll find her,' said Sean, 'and this time I'll tell her . . . if it's not too late.'

'You'll find her and it won't be too late. The earth can't have swallowed her, and she'll be glad to hear you say it.' Candy stood up. 'You must rest now, you have a hard day ahead of you.'

Sean slept fully dressed in the chair in the sitting-room. He slept brokenly, his mind struggling and kicking him back to half wakefulness every few minutes. Candy had turned the gas low before she left and its light fell in a soft pool on to the writing desk beneath it. Katrina's Bible lay where she had left it and each time Sean started awake the fat, leather-covered book caught his eye. Some time before dawn he woke for the last time and knew he could not sleep again.

He stood up and his body still ached and his eyes felt gritty. He moved across to the gas lamp and turned it up high, he let his hand drop from the lamp on to the Bible. Its leather was cool and softly polished beneath his fingers. He opened the front cover and caught his breath with a hiss.

Beneath Katrina's name, in her carefully rounded writing, the ink still freshly blue, *she had filled in the date of death.*

The page magnified slowly in front of his eyes until it filled the whole field of his vision. There was a rushing sound in his ears, the sound of a river in flood, but above it he heard voices, different voices.

'Let's go, Sean, it looks like a grave.'

'But more than anything she needs love.'

'The earth can't have swallowed her.'

And his own voice, 'If it's not too late, if it's not too late.'

The morning light was gathering strength as he reached the ruins of the old Candy Deep office block. He left his horse and ran through the grass towards the mine dump. The wind was small and cold, it moved the tops of the grass and went on to where Katrina's green shawl was caught on the barbed wire fence that ringed the shaft. In the wind the shawl flapped its wings like a big green bird of prey.

Sean reached the fence and looked down into the mouth of the shaft. At one place the grass had been torn away from the edge as though someone had snatched at it as they fell.

Sean loosed the shawl from the spikes of the barbed wire, he balled the heavy material in his fists, then he held it out over the shaft and let it drop. It spread out as it floated down into the blackness, and it was the bright green of Katrina's eyes.

'Why?' whispered Sean. 'Why have you done this to us, my fancy?' He turned away and walked back to his horse, stumbling carelessly in the rough footing.

Mbejane was waiting for him in the hotel suite.

'Get the carriage,' Sean told him.

'The Nkosikazi–?'

'Get the carriage,' Sean repeated.

Sean carried Dirk downstairs. He paid his bill at the reception desk and went out to where Mbejane had the carriage ready. He climbed up into it and held Dirk on his lap.

'Drive back to Pretoria,' Sean said.

'Where's Mummy?' Dirk demanded.

'She's not coming with us.'

'Are we going alone?' Dirk insisted and Sean nodded wearily.

'Yes, Dirk, we are going alone.'

'Is Mummy coming just now?'

'No, Dirk. No, she's not.'

It was finished, Sean thought. It was all over–all the dreams and the laughter and the love. He was too numbed to feel the pain yet–it would come later.

'Why are you squeezing me so hard, Daddy?'

Sean slackened his grip and looked down at the child on his lap. It was not finished, he realized; it was only a new beginning.

But first I must have time for this to heal: time–and a quiet place to lie up with this wound. The wagons are waiting and I must go back into the wilderness.

Perhaps after another year I will have healed sufficiently to start again, to go back to Ladyburg with my son, back to Ladyburg, and to Ada and to Garry–he thought. Then suddenly and sickeningly he felt the pain again, and the deep raw ache of it frightened him.

Please God, prayed Sean who had never prayed before, *please God, give me the strength to endure it.*

'Are you going to cry, Daddy? You look like you're going to cry.' Dirk was watching Sean's face with solemn curiosity. Sean pulled the child's head gently against his shoulder and held it there.

If tears could pay both our debts, thought Sean, if with my tears I could buy for you an indulgence from all pain, if by weeping now I could do all your weeping for you–then I would cry until my eyes were washed away.

'No, Dirk,' he answered. 'I am not going to cry–crying never helps very much.'

And Mbejane took them to where the wagons waited at Pretoria.

The Diamond Hunters

His flight had been delayed for three hours at Nairobi, and despite four large whiskies he slept only fitfully until the intercontinental Boeing touched down at Heathrow. Johnny Lance felt as though someone had thrown a handful of grit in each eye, and his mood was ugly as he came through the indignity of Customs and Immigration into the main hall of the international terminus.

The Van Der Byl Diamond Company's London agent was there to meet him.

'Pleasant trip, Johnny?'

'Like the one to hell,' Johnny grunted.

'Good practice for you.' The agent grinned. The two of them had seen some riotous times together.

Reluctantly Johnny grinned back at him.

'You got me a room and a car?'

'Dorchester–and Jag.' The agent handed over the car keys. 'And I've got two first-class seats reserved on tomorrow's nine o'clock flight back to Cape Town. Tickets at the hotel reception desk.'

'Good boy.' Johnny dropped the keys into the pocket of his cashmere overcoat and they started for the exit. 'Now where is Tracey van der Byl?'

The agent shrugged. 'Since I wrote to you she has dropped out of sight. I don't know where you can start looking.'

'Great, just great!' said Johnny bitterly as they came out into the car park. 'I'll start with Benedict.'

'Does the Old Man know about Tracey?'

Johnny shook his head. 'He's a sick man. I didn't tell him.'

'Here's your car.' The agent stopped by the pearl-grey Jaguar. 'Any chance of a drink together?'

'Not this trip, sorry.' Johnny slipped in behind the wheel. 'Next time.'

'I'll hold you to that,' said the agent and walked away.

It was almost dark by the time Johnny crossed the Hammersmith flyover in the moist smoky grey of the evening, and he lost himself twice in the maze of Belgravia before he found the narrow mews behind Belgrave Square and parked the Jaguar.

The exterior of the flat had been lavishly redecorated since his last visit, and Johnny's mouth twisted. He might not be so hot at earning the stuff–but our boy Benedict certainly was a dab hand at spending it.

There were lights burning and Johnny hit the door knocker half a dozen lusty cracks. It echoed hollowly about the mews, and in the silence that followed Johnny heard the whisper of voices from behind the curtains, and a shadow passed quickly across the window.

Johnny waited three minutes in the cold, then he stepped back into the middle of the mews.

'Benedict van der Byl,' he bellowed. 'I'll give you a count of ten to get this door open. Then I'll kick the bloody thing down.'

He drew breath and bellowed again.

'This is Johnny Lance–and you know I mean it.'

The door opened almost immediately. Johnny pushed his way through it, not glancing at the man who held it, and started for the lounge.

'Dammit, Lance. You can't go in there.' Benedict van der Byl started after him.

'Why not?' Johnny glanced back at him. 'It is a Company flat–and I'm the General Manager.'

Before Benedict could reply, Johnny was through the door.

One of the girls picked up her clothing from the floor and ran naked into the bedroom passage. The other pulled a full-length caftan over her head and glared at Johnny sulkily. Her hair was in wild disorder, fluffed out into a grotesque halo of stiff curls.

'Nice party,' said Johnny. He glanced at the movie projector on the side table, and then at the screen across the room. 'Films and all.'

'Are you the fuzz?' demanded the girl.

'You've got an infernal cheek, Lance.' Benedict van der Byl was beside him, tying the belt of his silk dressing-gown.

'Is he fuzz?' the girl demanded again.

'No,' Benedict assured her. 'He works for my father.' With the statement he seemed to gather self-assurance, drawing himself up to his full height and smoothing his long dark hair with one hand. His voice regained its polish and lazy inflection. 'Actually, he is Daddy's messenger boy.'

Johnny turned to him, but he addressed the girl without looking at her.

'Beat it, girlie. Follow your friend.'

She hesitated.

'Beat it!' Johnny's voice crackled like a bush fire, and she went.

The two men stood facing each other. They were the same age, in their early thirties–both tall, both dark-haired–different in every other way.

Johnny was big in the shoulders and lean across the hips and belly, his skin polished and browned by the desert sun. The line of his heavy jawbone stood out clearly, and his eyes seemed still to seek far horizons. His voice clipped and twanged with the accents of the other land.

'Where is Tracey?' he asked.

Benedict lifted one eyebrow in a pantomime of arrogant surprise. His skin was pale olive, unstained by sunlight for it was months since he had last visited Africa. His lips were very red, as though they had been painted, the classical lines of his features were blurred by flesh. There were soft little pouches under his eyes, and a plumpness beneath the silk dressing-gown that suggested he ate and drank often and exercised infrequently.

'My dear chap, what on earth makes you think I know where my sister is? I haven't seen her for weeks.'

Johnny turned away and crossed to one of the paintings on the far wall. The room was hung with good original South African artists–Alexis Preller, Irma Stern and Tretchikoff–an unusual mixture of techniques and styles, but someone had convinced the Old Man they were sound investments.

Johnny turned back to face Benedict van der Byl. He studied him as he had the paintings, comparing him with the clean young athlete he had been a few years before. A clear mental image in his mind pictured Benedict moving with leopard grace across the green field of play under the packed grandstands, turning smoothly beneath the high floating arc of the ball to gather it neatly, head high, and break back in field to open the line for the return kick.

'You're getting fat, Laddy Buck,' he said softly, and Benedict's anger stained his cheeks dull red.

'Get out of here,' he snapped.

'In a minute–tell me about Tracey first.'

'I've told you–I don't know where she is. Whoring it up around Chelsea, I expect.'

Johnny felt his own anger surge fiercely, but his voice remained level.

'Where is she getting the money, Benedict?'

'I don't know–the Old Man–'

Johnny cut him short. 'The Old Man is keeping her on an allowance of ten pounds a week. From what I hear she's throwing more than that around.'

'Christ, Johnny,' Benedict's tone became conciliatory, 'I don't know. It's not my business. Perhaps Kenny Hartford is–'

Again Johnny interrupted impatiently. 'Kenny Hartford is giving her nothing. That was part of the divorce agreement when they split up. Now I want to know who is subsidizing her trip to oblivion. How about it, big brother?'

'Me?' Benedict was indignant. 'You know there is no love wasted between us.'

'Must I spell it out?' Johnny asked. 'All right, then. The Old Man is dying–without losing his horror of all weakness and sin. If Tracey turns into a drug-soaked little tramp–then there's a good chance that our boy Benedict will come back into full favour. It would be a good gamble on your part to lay out a few thousand now, to send Tracey to hell. Cut her off completely from her father–and all those nice fat millions.'

'Who said anything about drugs?' Benedict blustered.

'I did.' Johnny stepped up to him. 'You and I have a little unfinished business. It would give me intense pleasure to take you to pieces and see what makes you work.'

He held Benedict's eyes for long seconds, then Benedict looked down and fiddled with the cord of his dressing-gown.

'Where is she, Benedict?'

'I don't know, damn you!'

Johnny moved softly across to the movie projector and picked up a reel of film from the table beside it. He peeled off a few feet of celluloid from the reel and held it up to the light.

'Pretty!' he said, but the line of his mouth tightened with disgust.

'Put that down,' snapped Benedict.

'You know what the Old Man thinks about this sort of thing, don't you, Benedict?'

Suddenly Benedict went pale.

'He wouldn't believe you.'

'Yes, he would.' Johnny tossed the reel on the table and turned back to Benedict. 'He believes me because I've never lied to him.'

Benedict hesitated, wiped his lips nervously with the back of his hand.

'I haven't seen her for two weeks. She was renting a place in Chelsea. Stark Street. No. 23. She came to see me.'

'What for?'

'I lent her a couple of pounds,' Benedict muttered sulkily.

'A couple of pounds?' Johnny asked.

'All right, a couple of hundred. After all, she is my sister.'

'Damn decent of you,' Johnny lauded him. 'Write down the address.'

Benedict crossed to the leather-topped writing desk and scribbled on a card. He came back and handed the card to Johnny.

'You like to think you're big and dangerous, Lance.' His voice was pitched low but it shook with fury. 'Well, I'm dangerous too–in a different sort of way. The Old Man can't live for ever, Lance. When he's gone I'm coming after you.'

'You frighten the hell out of me.' Johnny grinned at him, and went down to the car.

The traffic was solid in Sloane Square as Johnny eased the Jaguar slowly down towards Chelsea. There was plenty of time to think; to remember how close they had been–the three of them. He and Tracey and Benedict.

Running together as wild young things with the endless beaches and mountains and sun-washed plains of Namaqualand as their playground. That was before the Old Man made the big strike on the Slang river, before there was money for shoes. When Tracey wore dresses made from flour sacks sewn together, and they rode to school each day, all three of them bare-back on a single pony like a row of bedraggled little brown sparrows on a fence.

He remembered how the long sun-drenched weeks while the Old Man was away were spent in laughter and secret games. How they climbed the *kopje* behind the mud-walled shack each evening and looked towards the north across the limitless land, flesh-coloured and purple in the sunset, searching for the wisp of dust in the distance that would mean the Old Man was coming home.

Then the almost painful excitement when the dusty, rackety Ford truck with its mudguards tied on with wire was suddenly there in the yard, and the Old Man was climbing down from the cab, a sweat-stained hat on the back of his head and the dust thick in the stubble of his beard, swinging Tracey squealing above his head. Then turning to Benedict, and lastly to Johnny. Always in that order–Tracey, Benedict, Johnny.

Johnny had never wondered why sometimes he was not first. It was always that way. Tracey, Benedict, Johnny. The same way as he had never wondered why his name was Lance and not van der Byl. Then it had come to an end suddenly, the whole brightly sunlit dream of childhood was gone and lost.

'Johnny, I'm not your real father. Your father and mother died when you were very young.' And Johnny had stared at the Old Man in disbelief.

'Do you understand, Johnny?'

'Yes, Pa.'

Tracey's hand groped for his beneath the table top like a little warm animal. He jerked his own hand away from it.

'I think you'd better not call me that any more, Johnny.' He could remember the exact tone of the Old Man's voice, neutral, matter of fact, as it splintered the fragile crystal of his childhood to fragments. The loneliness had begun.

Johnny accelerated the Jaguar forward and swung into the King's Road. He was surprised that the memory hurt so intensely–time should have mellowed and softened it.

His life from then on had become a ceaseless contest to win the Old Man's approval–he dare not hope for his love.

Soon there were other changes, for a week later the old Ford had come roaring unexpectedly out of the desert in the night, and the barking of the dogs and the Old Man's shouted laughter had brought them, sleepy-eyed, tumbling from their bunks.

The Old Man had lit the Petromax lamp and sat them on the kitchen chairs about the scrubbed deal table. Then with the air of a conjurer he had laid something that looked like a big lump of broken glass on the table.

The three sleepy children had stared at it solemnly, not understanding. The harsh glare of the Petromax was captured within the crystal, captured, repeated, magnified and thrown back at them in fire and blue lightning.

'Twelve carats–' gloated the Old Man. 'Blue-white and perfect, and there is a cartload where that came from.'

After that there were new clothes and motor cars, the move to Cape Town, the new school and the big house on Wynberg Hill–but always the contest. The contest that did not earn the Old Man's approval as it was designed to do, but earned instead Benedict van der Byl's jealousy and hatred. Without his drive and purpose, Benedict could not hope to match Johnny's achievements in the classroom and on the sports field. He fell far behind the pace that Johnny set–and hated him for it.

The Old Man did not notice for he was seldom with them now. They lived alone in the big house with the thin silent woman who was their housekeeper, and the Old Man came infrequently and for short periods. Always he seemed tired and distracted. Sometimes he brought presents for them from London and Amsterdam and Kimberley, but the presents meant very little to them. They would have liked it better had it stayed the way it was in the desert.

In the void left by the Old Man the hostility and rivalry between Johnny and Benedict flourished to such proportions that Tracey was forced to choose between them. She chose Johnny.

In their loneliness they clung to each other.

The grave little girl and the big gangling boy built together a castle against the loneliness. It was a bright secure place where the sadness could not reach them–and Benedict was excluded from it.

Johnny swung the Jaguar out of the line of traffic into old Church Street, down towards the river in Chelsea. He drove automatically and the memories came crowding back.

He tried to recapture and hold the castle of warmth and love that he and Tracey had built so long ago, but instantly his mind leapt to the night on which it had collapsed.

One night in the old house on Wynberg Hill Johnny had come awake to the sound of distant weeping. He had gone barefooted in his pyjamas, following that heart-rending whisper of grief. He was afraid, fourteen years old and afraid in the dark house.

Tracey was weeping into her pillow and he had stooped over her.

'Tracey. What is it? Why are you crying?'

She had jumped up, kneeling on the bed, and flung both arms about his neck.

'Oh, Johnny. I had a dream, a terrible dream. Hold me, please. Don't go away, don't leave me.' Her whisper was still thick and muffled with tears. He had gone into her bed and held her until at last she slept.

Every night after that he had gone to her room. It was innocent and completely childlike, the twelve-year-old girl and the boy who was her brother, in fact if not in name. They held each other in the bed, and whispered and laughed secretly until sleep carried them both away.

Then suddenly the castle was blasted by the bright electric glare of the overhead light. The Old Man was standing in the door of the bedroom, and Benedict was behind him in his pyjamas dancing with excitement and chanting triumphantly.

'I told you, Pa! I told you so!'

The Old Man was shaking with rage, the bush of grey hair standing erect like the mane of a wounded lion. He had dragged Johnny from the bed, and struck away Tracey's clinging hands.

'You little whore,' he bellowed, holding the terrified boy easily with one hand and leaning forward to strike his daughter in the face with his open hand. Leaving her sobbing, face down on the bed, he dragged Johnny down the passages to the study on the ground floor. He threw him into the room with a violence that sent him staggering against the desk.

The Old Man had gone to the rack and taken out a light Malacca cane. He came to Johnny and, taking a handful of his hair, threw him face down over the desk.

The Old Man had beaten him before, but never like this. Mad with rage the Old Man's blows had been unaimed, some fell across Johnny's back.

Yet in the agony it was deadly important to the boy that he should not cry out. He bit through his lip so the taste of blood was salt and copper in his mouth. He must not hear me cry! And he choked back the moans feeling his pyjama trousers hanging heavy and sodden with blood.

His silence served only as a goad to the Old Man's fury. Flinging the cane aside, he pulled the boy upright and attacked him with his hands. Slamming Johnny's head from side to side with full, open-handed blows that burst in Johnny's skull with blinding flashes of light.

Still Johnny kept on his feet, clinging to the edge of the desk. His lips broken and swollen and his face bloated and darkening with bruises, until at last the Old Man was driven far beyond the borders of sanity. He bunched his fist and drove it into Johnny's face–and with a wonderful sense of relief Johnny felt the pain go out in a warm flood of darkness.

Johnny heard voices first. A strange voice:

'–As though he's been savaged by a a wild beast. I'll have to inform the police.'

Then a voice he recognized. It took him a little time to place it. He tried to open his eyes but they seemed locked tight, his face felt enormous, swollen and hot. He forced the fat lids of his eyes back and recognized Michael Shapiro, the Old Man's secretary. He was talking quietly to the other man.

There was the smell of antiseptic and the doctor's bag lay open on the table beside the bed.

'Listen, Doctor. I know it looks bad–but hadn't you better talk to the boy before you stir up the police?'

They both looked towards the bed.

'He's conscious.' The doctor came to him quickly. 'What happened to you, Johnny? Tell us what happened. Whoever did this to you will be punished–I promise you.'

The words were wrong. Nobody must ever punish the Old Man.

Johnny tried to speak but his lips were stiff and swollen. He tried again.

'I fell,' he said. 'I fell. Nobody! Nobody! I fell down.'

When the doctor had gone Mike Shapiro came and stood over him. His Jewish eyes were dark with pity, and something else–anger perhaps, or admiration. 'I'm taking you to my house, Johnny. You will be all right now.'

He stayed two weeks under the care of Michael Shapiro's wife, Helen. The scabs came away, the bruises faded to a dirty yellow, but his nose stayed crooked with a lump at the bridge. He studied his new nose in the mirror, and liked it. It made him look like a boxer, he thought or a pirate, but it was many months before the tenderness passed and he could finger it freely.

'Listen, Johnny, you are going to a new school. A fine boarding-school in Grahamstown.' Michael Shapiro tried to sound enthusiastic. Grahamstown was five hundred miles away. 'In the holidays you'll be going to work in Namaqualand–learning all about diamonds and how to mine them. You'll enjoy that, won't you?'

Johnny had thought about it for a minute, watching Michael's face and reading in it his shame.

'I won't be going home again then?' By home he meant the house on Wynberg Hill. Michael shook his head.

'When will I see–' Johnny hesitated as he tried to find the right words, '–when will I see them again?'

'I don't know, Johnny,' Michael answered him honestly.

As Michael had promised it was a fine school.

On his first Sunday after the church service, he had followed the other boys back to their classroom for the session of compulsory letter-writing. The others had immediately began dashing off hasty scribbles to their parents. Johnny sat miserably until the master in charge stopped at his desk.

'Aren't you going to write home, Lance?' he asked kindly. 'I'm sure they'll all want to hear how you are.'

Johnny picked up his pen obediently, and puzzled over the blank writing-pad.

He wrote at last:

Dear Sir,

I hope you will be pleased to hear that I am now at school. The food is good, but the beds are very hard.

We go to church every day and play rugby football.

Yours faithfully,
Johnny.

From then until he left school and went up to university three years later, he wrote every week to the Old Man. Every letter began with the same salutation and went on, 'I hope you will be pleased to hear–' There was never a reply to any of these letters.

Once each term he received a typewritten letter from Michael Shapiro setting out the arrangements that had been made for the school holidays. Usually these involved a train journey hundreds of miles across the Karroo to some remote village in the vast dry wasteland, where a light aircraft belonging to Van Der Byl Diamonds was waiting to fly him still deeper into the desert to one of the Company's concession areas. Again as Michael Shapiro had promised he learned about diamonds and how to mine them.

When the time to move on to university arrived, it was completely natural that he chose to take a degree in Geology.

During all that time he was an outcast from the van der Byl family. He had seen none of them–not the Old Man, nor Tracey, nor even Benedict.

Then, in one long eventful afternoon, he saw all three of them. It was his final year at university. His degree was a certainty. He had headed the lists at every examination from his first year onwards. He had been elected the senior student of Stellenbosch University, but now there was a further honour almost within his grasp.

In ten days' time the national selectors would announce the rugby team to meet the New Zealand All Black touring team–and Johnny's place at flank forward was as certain as his degree in Geology.

The sporting press had nicknamed Johnny 'Jag Hond' after that ferocious predator of the African wilds, the Cape hunting dog; an animal of incredible stamina and determination that savages its prey on the run. The nickname had stuck fast, and Johnny was a favourite of the crowds.

In the line-up of the team from Cape Town University was another crowd-pleaser whose place in the national side to meet the All Blacks seemed equally assured. From his position at full back Benedict van der Byl dominated the field of play with a grace and artistry that was almost godlike. He had grown tall and wide-shouldered, with long powerful legs and dark brooding good looks.

Johnny led the visiting team out onto the smooth green velvet field, and while he jogged and flexed his back and shoulders he looked up at the packed stands seeking assurance that the high priests of rugby football were all there. He saw Doctor Danie Craven sitting with the other selectors in the privileged position below the Press enclosure. While in front of the Doctor, leaning back to exchange a few words with him, sat the Prime Minister.

This meeting between the two universities was one of the high spots of the rugby season, and the *aficionados* travelled thousands of miles to watch it.

The Prime Minister smiled and nodded, then leaned forward to touch the shoulder of the big white-headed figure that sat in the row below him.

Johnny felt an electric tingle run up his spine as the white head lifted and looked directly at him. It was the first time he had seen the Old Man in the seven years since that terrible night.

Johnny lifted his arm in salute, and the Old Man stared at him for long seconds before he turned away to speak with the Prime Minister.

Now the drum majorettes came out in ranks onto the field. White-booted, dressed in Cape Town University colours with short swinging skirts and tall hats, they high-stepped and paraded, lovely young girls flushed with excitement and exertion.

The roar of the crowd drummed with the blood in Johnny's ears, for Tracey van der Byl was leading the first rank. He knew her instantly, despite the passage of years in which she had grown to young womanhood. Her legs and arms were sun-bronzed and her dark hair hung glossily to her shoulders. She cavorted and kicked and stamped, shouting the traditional cheers, jiggling her firm young bottom with innocent abandon while the crowds screamed and writhed, beginning already to work themselves into an hysterical frenzy. Johnny watched Tracey. He stood completely still in the thunderous uproar. She was the most beautiful woman he had ever seen.

Then the show was over, the drum majorettes retreating back through the stadium entrance, and the home team trotted onto the field.

The presence of the Old Man and Tracey added intensity to the glare of hatred that Johnny turned on the tall white-clad figure that fell back to take control of the Cape Town back field.

Benedict van der Byl reached his position and turned. From inside his calf-length sock he took a comb and ran it through his dark hair. The crowd bellowed and whistled, loving this little theatrical gesture. Benedict returned the comb to his sock and posed with one hand on his hip, his chin lifted arrogantly as he surveyed the opposition.

Suddenly he intercepted Johnny's glare, and the pose altered as he dropped his eyes and shuffled his feet a little.

The whistle fluted, and play began. It was everything the crowds had hoped for, a match that would long be remembered and gloated over. Massive panzer offensives by the forwards, long probing raids by the backs with the oval ball flickering from hand to hand, until a bone-jarring tackle smashed the carrier to the turf. Hard and fast and clean play swung from side to side, a hundred times the crowd came up on its feet as one, eyes and mouths wide in screaming unbearable tension, to sink back with a groan as the ball was held by a desperate defence within inches of the goal line.

No score and three minutes of play left, Cape Town attacking from a set scrummage, driving through a gap in the defence and then putting the ball in the air with a long raking pass, taken cleanly by the Cape Town wing without a break in his stride. His feet twinkled across the green turf, and again the crowd came up with a gasp.

Johnny hit him low, just above the knee, with his shoulder. The two of them rolled together out of the field of play lifting a puff of white lime from the line and the crowd groaned and sank back.

While they waited to receive the throw, Johnny whispered hoarse orders. His gold and maroon jersey was soaked with sweat, and blood from a grazed hip stained his white shorts.

'Get it back fast. Don't run with it. Give it to Dawie. Kick high and deep, Dawie.'

Johnny leaped high to the flight of the thrown ball, with a bunched fist he punched it back accurately into Dawie's hands, at the same moment twisting his body to block the attackers.

Dawie fell back two paces and kicked. The power of the kick swung his right foot above his head, and the impetus flung him forward to put his forwards 'on side'.

The ball climbed slowly, flying like a dart with no wobble or roll in the air, reaching the zenith of its trajectory high over mid-field, then floating back to earth.

Twenty thousand heads followed its flight, a hush had fallen over the field–and in the unnatural silence Benedict van der Byl was drifting back deep into his own territory, anticipating the drop of the ball with deceptively unhurried strides, yet timing it with the precision of the gifted athlete.

The ball slotted neatly into his arms, and he began moving lazily infield to open his angle for the return kick. Still a tense throbbing mesmeric hush hung over the field, Benedict van der Byl was at the focus of attention.

'Jag Hond!' A single voice in the crowd alerted them, and twenty thousand heads swung downfield.

'Jag Hond!' A roar now. Johnny was well clear of the pack, arms pumping and legs churning as he bore down on Benedict. It was a futile effort, he could not hope to intercept a player of Benedict's calibre from such long range, yet Johnny was burning the last of the physical reserves in that charge. His face was a sweat-shining mask of determination, and clods of torn grass flew from under his savagely driving boots.

Then something happened which was unaccountable, almost past belief. Benedict van der Byl glanced round and saw Johnny. He broke his stride, two clumsy shuffling paces, and tried to pivot away deeper into his own ground. All the assurance had gone from his body, all the skill and grace. He tripped and stumbled, almost fell and the ball popped out of his hands, bouncing awkwardly.

Benedict scrambled after it, groping blindly, looking back over his shoulder. Now on his face was an expression of naked terror. Johnny was very close. Grunting at each stride like a gut-shot lion, massive shoulders already bunching for the strike, his lips drawn back into a murderous parody of a grin.

Benedict van der Byl dropped to his knees and covered his head with both arms, cringing down on to the green turf.

Johnny swept past him without a check, stooping easily in his run to gather the bouncing ball.

When Benedict uncovered his head and, still kneeling, looked up, Johnny stood ten yards away between the goal posts watching him. Then deliberately Johnny placed the ball between his feet to complete the formality of the touchdown.

Now, as if by agreement, both Johnny and Benedict looked towards the main grandstand. They saw the Old Man rise from his seat and make his way slowly through the ecstatic crowds towards the exit.

The day after the match, Johnny went back into the desert.

He was down in the bottom of a fifteen-foot prospect trench that had been dug across the grain of the country rock. It was oppressively hot in the confines of the trench and Johnny was stripped to a skimpy pair of khaki shorts, his sun-browned muscles oily with sweat, but he worked steadily at his sampling. He was establishing the contours and profile of an ancient marine terrace that the ages had buried beneath the sand. It was here on the bedrock that he expected to find the thin layer of diamond-bearing gravel.

He heard the jeep pull up at ground level above him, and the crunch of footsteps. Johnny straightened up and held his aching back muscles.

The Old Man stood at the edge of the trench and looked down at him. He held a folded newspaper in his hand. This was the first time Johnny had seen him at close range in all the years, and he was shocked at the change. The mass of bushy hair was so white, and his features were folded and creased like those of a mastiff, leaving the big hooked nose standing like a hillock from his face. But there was no wasting or deterioration in his body, and his eyes were still that chilling enigmatic blue.

He dropped the newspaper into the trench and Johnny caught it, still staring up at the Old Man.

'Read it!' said the Old Man. The paper was folded to the sports page, and the headline was thick and bold.

JAG HOND IN. VAN DER BYL OUT.

The shock was as delicious as the plunge into a mountain stream. He was in–he would carry the gold and green, and wear the leaping springbok on his blazer pocket.

He looked up, proud and happy, standing bare-headed in the sun waiting for the Old Man to speak.

'Make up your mind,' said the Old Man softly. 'do you want to play ball–or work for Van Der Byl Diamonds? You can't do both.' And he walked back to the jeep and drove away.

Johnny cabled his withdrawal from the team to the Doctor personally. The storm of outraged protest and abuse in the national Press, and the hundreds of viperous letters Johnny received accusing him of cowardice and treachery and worse made him thankful for the sanctuary of the desert.

Neither Johnny nor Benedict had ever played the game again. Thinking about it, even at this remove of time, Johnny felt the sting of disappointment. He had wanted that green and gold badge of honour so very deeply. Brusquely he pulled the Jaguar off the road and scanned the street map of London and found Stark Street tucked away off the King's Road. He drove on remembering how it had been after the Old Man had taken it from him. The agony of mind had been scarcely endurable.

His companions in the desert were Ovambo tribesmen from the north, and a few of those taciturn white men that the desert produces, as hardy and uncompromising as her vegetation or her mountain ranges.

The deserts of the Namib and the Kalahari are amongst the loneliest places on earth, and the desert nights are long. Not even the day's unremitting physical labour could tire Johnny sufficiently to drug his dreams of a lovely girl in a short white skirt and high boots–or an old white-headed man with a face like a granite cliff.

Out of those long days and longer nights came solid achievements to stand like milestones marking the road of his career. He brought in a new diamond field, small but rich, in country which no one else had believed would yield diamonds. He pegged a uranium lode which Van Der Byl Diamonds sold for two and a half millions, and there were other fruits from his efforts almost as valuable if not as spectacular.

At twenty-five, Johnny Lance's name was whispered in the closed and forbidding walls of the diamond industry as one of the bright young comers.

There were approaches–a junior partnership in a firm of consulting geologists, field manager for one of the struggling little companies working marginal ground in the Murderers' Karroo. Johnny turned them down. They were good offers, but he stayed on with the Old Man.

Then the big Company noticed him. A century ago the first payable pipe of 'blue ground' in Southern Africa was discovered on a hard scrabble farm owned by a Boer named De Beer. Old De Beer sold his farm for £6,000, never dreaming that a treasure worth £300,000,000 lay beneath the bleak dry earth. The strike was named De Beers New Rush, and a horde of miners, small businessmen, drifters, chancers, rogues and scoundrels moved in to purchase and work minute claims, each the size of a large room.

From this pretty company of fortune's soldiers two men rose high above the others, until between them they owned most of the claims in De Beers New Rush. When these two, Cecil John Rhodes and Barney Barnato, at last combined their resources, a formidable financial enterprise was born. From such humble beginnings the company has grown to awesome respectability and dignity. Its wealth is fabled, its influence immeasurable, its income is astronomical. It controls the diamond supply to the world. It controls also mineral concessions over areas of Central and Southern Africa which total hundreds of thousands of square miles, and its reserves of unmined precious and base minerals cannot be calculated. Small diamond companies are allowed to co-exist with the giant until they reach a certain size–then suddenly they become part of it, gobbled up as a tiger shark might swallow any of its pilot fish who become too large and daring. The big Company can afford to buy the best prospects, equipment–and men. It reached out one of its myriad tentacles to draw in Johnny Lance. The price they set on him was twice his present salary, and three times his future prospects.

Johnny turned it down flat. Perhaps the Old Man did not notice, perhaps it was mere coincidence that a week later Johnny was promoted Field Manager of Beach Operation. The nickname that went with the job was 'King Canute'.

Van Der Byl Diamonds had thirty-seven miles of beach concession. The tiny ribbon of shoreline, one hundred and twenty feet above high-water mark, and one hundred and twenty feet below low-water mark. Inland the concession belonged to the big Company. It had purchased the land, a dozen vast ranches, simply to obtain the mineral rights. The sea concession, territorial up to waters twelve miles off shore, belonged to them also. Granted to them by Government charter twenty years before. But Van Der Byl Diamonds had the Admiralty strip–and it was 'King Canute's' job to work it.

The sea-mist came smoking in like ground pearl dust off the cold waters of the Benguela current. From out of the mist bank the high unhurried swells marched in towards the bright yellow sands and the tall wave-cut cliffs of Namaqualand.

The swells peaked up sharply as they felt the land. Their crests trembled and turned luminous green, began to dissolve in plumes of wind-blown spray, arched over and slid down upon themselves in the roar and rumble of white water.

Johnny stood on the driver's seat of the open Land-Rover. He wore a sheepskin jacket against the chill of the dawn mist, but his head was bare and his dark hair fluttered nervously against his forehead in the wind.

His heavy jaw was thrust forward, and his hands in the pockets of the sheepskin jacket were balled into fists. He scowled aggressively as he measured the height and push of the surf. With his crooked nose he looked like a boxer waiting for the gong.

Suddenly with an awkward angry movement he jerked his left hand from his pocket and looked down at the dial of his wrist watch. Two hours and three minutes to low tide. He pushed his fist back into his pocket, and swivelled quickly to look at his bulldozers.

There were eleven of them, big bright yellow D8 Caterpillars, lined up along the high-water mark. The operators sat goggled and tense in their high stern seats. They were all watching him anxiously.

Beyond them, standing well back, were the earth-loaders. They were ungainly, pregnant-looking machines with swollen bellies, and heavily lugged tyres that stood taller than a man. When the time came they would rush in at thirty miles an hour, drop a steel blade beneath their bellies and scrape up a fifteen-ton load of sand or gravel, race back inland and drop their load, turn and rush back for another gargantuan bite cut of the earth.

Johnny was steeling himself, judging the exact moment in which to hurl a quarter of a million pounds' worth of machinery into the Atlantic Ocean, in the hope of recovering a handful of bright pebbles.

The moment came, and Johnny spent half a minute of precious time in scrutinizing his preparations before committing himself to action.

Then 'GO!' he shouted into his loudhailer and windmilled his right arm in the unmistakable command to advance.

'Go!' he shouted again, but his voice was lost. Even the sound of the wild surf was lost in the bull bellow of the diesels. Lowering their massive steel blades, a chorus line of steel monsters, they crawled forward.

Now the golden sand curled before the scooped blades, like butter from the knife. It built up before the monstrous machines, becoming a pile and then a high wall. Thrusting, pulling back, butting, worrying, the bulldozers swept the wall of sand forward. The arms of the operators pumping the handles of the controls like mad barmen drawing a thousand pints of beer, the diesels roaring and muttering and roaring again.

The wall of sand met the first low push of sea water up the beach and smothered it. In seeming astonishment and uncertainty the sea pulled back, swirling and creaming before the advancing dyke of sand.

The bulldozers were performing a complicated but smoothly practised ballet now. Weaving and crossing, blades lifting and falling, backing and advancing, all under the supervision of the master choreographer, Johnny Lance.

The Land-Rover darted back and forward along the edge of the huge pit that was forming, with Johnny roaring orders and instructions through the electric loud-hailer.

Gradually a sickle-shaped dyke of sand was thrown out into the sea, while behind it the bulldozer blades cut down, six, ten, fifteen feet through the loose yellow sand.

Then suddenly they hit the oyster line, that thin layer of fossilized oyster shell that so often covers the diamond gravels of South West Africa.

Johnny saw the change in the character of his pit, saw the shell curling from the blades of the bulldozers.

With half a dozen orders and hand signals he had his 'dozers flatten a ramp at each end of his pit, to give the earthloaders access. Then he ordered them away to hold the dyke against the sea.

He glanced at his watch. 'One hour thirteen minutes,' he muttered. 'We're running tight!'

Quickly he checked his pit. Two hundred yards long, fifteen feet deep, the overburden of sand stripped away, the oyster line showing clean and white in the sun, the bulldozers clear of the pit bottom–fighting back the sea.

'Right,' he grunted. 'Let's see what we've got.'

He turned to face the two earthloaders waiting expectantly above the high-water mark.

'Go in and get it!' he shouted, and gave the windmill arm signal.

Nose to tail the earthloaders roared forward, swinging wide at the head of the pit, then swooping down the ramp and dashing along the bottom. They scooped up a load of shell and gravel without checking their speed and went bellowing up the far ramp, swinging again to race up and deposit their load below the cliff, but above the high-water mark.

Round they went, and round again, chasing their tails, while the bulldozers held back the sea which was now becoming angry–sending its cohorts to skirmish along the dyke, seeking a weak place to attack.

Johnny glanced at his watch.

'Three minutes to low water,' he spoke aloud, and grinned. 'We're going to make it–I think!'

He lit a cigarette, relaxing a little now. He dropped into the driving seat and swung the Land-Rover up the beach, parking it beyond the mountain of gravel that the earth loaders were building.

He climbed out and took up a handful of the gravel.

'Lovely!' he whispered. 'Oh sweet! Sweet!'

It was right. All the signs were good. In the single handful he identified a small garnet, and a larger lump of agate.

He scooped another handful.

'Jasper,' he gloated. 'And banded ironstone!'

All these stones were the team-mates of the diamond, you found them together.

The shape was right also, the stones polished round and shiny as marbles, not flattened like coins which would mean they had washed in only one direction. Round stones meant a wave action zone–a diamond trap!

'We've hit a jewel box–I'll take Lysol on that!'

From thirty-seven miles of beach Johnny had picked a two-hundred yard stretch, and hit it right on the nose. A choice not by luck, but by careful study of the configuration of the coastline, aerial photographs of the wave patterns and bottom contours of the sea, an analysis of the beach sands, and finally by that indefinable 'feel' for ground that a good diamond man has.

Johnny Lance was mightily delighted with himself as he climbed back into the Land-Rover. The earthloaders had scraped the gravel down to bed-rock. Their job was finished, and they pulled out of the pit and stood with panting exhausts beside the enormous pile of gravel they had recovered.

'Bottom boys!' roared Johnny, and the patient army of Ovambo tribesmen who had been squatting about the beach came swarming down into the pit. Their job was to sweep and clean the pit bottom, for a high proportion of the diamonds would have worked their way down through the gravel into the crevices and irregularities of the bed-rock.

The sea changed its mood, furious at the brutal rape of its beaches it came hissing and tearing at the sand dyke. The tide was making now, and the bulldozers had to redouble their efforts to keep it out.

In the pit the Ovambos worked in a frenzy of activity, sparing only an occasional apprehensive glance for the wall of sand that held the Atlantic at bay.

Now Johnny was tensing up again. If he pulled them out early he would be leaving diamonds down there, if he left them in too late he might drown machinery–and men.

He cut it fine, just a fraction too fine. He pulled the bottom boys out with the sea beginning to break over the dyke, and to seep through under it.

Then he began to pull out his bulldozers, ten of them out–one still coming infinitely slowly, waddling across the wide bottom of the empty pit.

The sea broke through, it broke simultaneously in two places and came boiling into the pit in a waist-high wave.

The bulldozer operator saw it, hesitated one second, then his spirit failed him and he jumped down from his machine; abandoning it to the sea he sprinted ahead of the wave, making for the steep nearest side of the pit.

'Bastard!' swore Johnny as he watched the operator scramble to safety. 'He could have made it.' But his anger was against himself also. His decision to withdraw had been too long delayed, that was £20,000 worth of machinery he had sacrificed to the sea.

He slammed the Land-Rover into gear, and put her to the pit. She went off the edge like a ski jump, falling fifteen feet before she hit the bottom, but her fall was cushioned by the slope of sand and she sprang forward bravely to meet the rush of sea water.

It broke over the bonnet, slewing the vehicle viciously, but Johnny fought her head round and kept her going towards the stranded bulldozer.

The engine of the Land-Rover had been sealed and waterproofed against just such an emergency, and now she ploughed forward throwing a sheet of water to each side. But her forward rush faltered as the green water poured over her.

Now suddenly the entire sand dyke collapsed under the white surf and the Atlantic took control. The tall wave of green water that raced across the pit hit the Land-Rover, upending her, throwing Johnny into the jubilant frothing water, while the Land-Rover rolled over on her back, pointing all four wheels to the sky in surrender.

Johnny went under but came up immediately. Half swimming, half wading, battered by the boisterous sea, he struggled on towards the yellow island of steel.

The sea struck him down, and he went under again. Found his feet for a moment, then had them cut from under him once more.

Then suddenly he had reached the bulldozer and was dragging himself up over the tracks to the driver's seat. He was coughing and vomiting sea water, as he reached the controls.

The bulldozer sat immovable, held down by her own twenty-six tons of dead weight on to the hard bed-rock of the pit. Although the sea burst over her, and swirled through her tracks, it could not move her.

Through eyes blurred and swimming with salt water and his own tears, Johnny briefly checked the gauges on the instrument panels. She had oil pressure and engine revs, and high above his head the exhaust pipe chugged blue smoke.

Johnny coughed again. Vomit and sea water shot up his throat in a scalding jet, but he pushed the throttle wide and threw in both clutch levers.

Ponderously the great machine ground forward, almost contemptuously shouldering the sea aside, her tracks solidly gripping the bed-rock.

Johnny looked about him quickly. The sand ramps at each end of the pit were washed away. The sides were sheer now, and behind him the sea was rushing unimpeded into the pit

A wave broke over his head, and Johnny shook the water from his hair like a spaniel and looked around with mounting desperation for an avenue of escape.

With a shock of surprise he saw the Old Man. He had thought him to be four hundred miles away in Cape Town, but here he was on the edge of the pit. The white hair shone like a beacon.

Instinctively Johnny swung the bulldozer towards him, crawling through the turbulent waters towards him.

The Old Man was directing two of the other bulldozers, reversing them as close as he dared to the lip of the bank of sand, while from the service truck parked below the cliff a line of Ovambos came staggering down the beach with the heavy tractor tow chain over their shoulders. They shuffled bow-legged under the tremendous weight of the chain, sinking ankle deep into the sand with each step.

The Old Man roared at them, urging them on, but the words were lost in the thunder of diesel engines and the ranting of the wind and the sea. Now he turned back to Johnny.

'Get her in close,' the Old Man yelled through cupped hands. 'I'll bring the end of the chain down to you!'

Johnny waved an acknowledgement, then grabbed at the controls as the force of the next wave pushed even the giant tractor off its line, and Johnny felt the diesel falter for the first time–the water had found its way through the seals at last.

Then he was under the high bank of yellow sand that towered twenty feet above him and he scrambled forward over the engine bonnet to meet the Old Man.

The Old Man was poised on the lip of the pit with the end of the chain draped in a loop over both shoulders. He was stooped beneath its weight, and when he stepped forward the sand crumpled away beneath him and he came sliding and slipping down the steep incline, buried waist deep, the great chain snaking after him.

Judging the rush of the sea, Johnny jumped down to help him. Together, battered by the sea, they dragged the chain to the bulldozer.

'Fix it on to the blade arm,' grunted the Old Man, and they got a double turn of chain around the thick steel arm.

'Shackle!' Johnny snapped at him, and while the Old Man untied the length of rope which secured the steel shackle around his waist, Johnny looked up at the cliff of sand that hung over them.

'Christ!' he said softly, the sea was attacking it–and now it was soft and trembling above them, ready to collapse and smother them.

The Old Man passed him the huge shackle, and Johnny began with numbed hands to secure the end of the chain. He must pass the thick case-hardened pin through two links and then screw it closed. It was a herculean task under these conditions, with the surf bursting over his head, the drag of the sea on the chain, and the cliff of sand threatening to fall on them at any moment. From twenty feet above them Johnny's foreman was watching anxiously, ready to pass the word to the two waiting bulldozers to throw their combined weights on the chain.

The thread of the pin caught, half a dozen turns would secure it, he would have finished the job by the time the word was passed to the 'dozer operators.

'Okay,' he nodded and gasped at the Old Man. 'Pull!'

The Old Man lifted his head and bellowed up the bank.

'Pull!'

The foreman acknowledged with a wave.

'Okay.' And his head disappeared behind the bank as he ran back to the bulldozers, and at that moment the surf swung the chain. A movement of a few inches, but enough to catch Johnny's left index finger between two of the links.

The Old Man saw his face, saw his struggling to free himself.

'What is it?'

Then the water sucked back, for a moment, and he saw what had happened. He waded forward to help–but from above them came the throaty roar of the diesels and the chain began running away, snaking and twisting up the bank like a python.

The Old Man reached Johnny and caught him about the shoulders to steady him. They braced themselves in horror, staring at the captive hand.

The chain jerked taut, severing the finger cleanly in a bright burst of scarlet, and Johnny reeled back into the Old Man's arms. The great yellow bulk of the bulldozer was dragged relentlessly down on top of them, threatening to crush them both, but using the next break and push of the sea the Old Man dragged Johnny clear–and they were carried sideways along the bank, tumbled helplessly by the strength of the water out of the bulldozer's path.

Johnny clutched his injured hand to his chest, but it hosed a bright stream of blood that discoloured the water about them. His head went under and salt water shot down his throat into his lungs. He felt himself drowning, the strength oozing out of him.

He surfaced again, and through bleary eyes saw the glistening wet bulldozer half-way up the sand bank. He felt the Old Man's arms about his chest and he went under again relaxing as the darkness closed over his eyes and brain.

When the darkness cleared from his eyes, he was lying on the dry sand of the beach and the first thing he saw was the Old Man's face above him, furrowed and pouched, his silver white hair plastered across his forehead.

'Did we get her out?' Johnny asked quickly.

'Ja,' the Old Man answered. 'We got her out.' And he stood up, walked to the jeep, and drove away, leaving the foreman to tend to Johnny.

Johnny grinned at the memory, and lifting his left hand off the driving-wheel of the Jaguar he licked the shiny stump of his index finger.

'It was worth a finger,' he murmured aloud, and still searching for road signs he drove on slowly.

He smiled again comfortably, shaking his head with amusement as he remembered his hurt and disappointment when the Old Man had walked away and left him lying on the beach. He had not expected the Old Man to fall on his shoulders sobbing his gratitude and begging forgiveness for all the years of misery and loneliness–but he had expected something more than that.

After a two-hundred mile round jeep-journey through the desert night to the nearest hospital where they had trimmed and bound the stump, Johnny was back at the workings the next day in time to watch the first run of gravel from the beach.

In his absence, the gravel had been screened to sieve off all the over-size rock and stone, then it had been puddled through a tank of silicon mud to float off all the material with a specific gravity less than 2·5, then finally what was left had been run through a ball mill–a long steel cylinder containing steel balls the size of a baseball. The cylinder revolved continually and the steel balls crushed to powder all substance softer than 4 on Mohs hardness scale.

Now there was a residue, a thousandth part of the gravel they had won from the sea. In this remainder would be the diamonds–if diamonds there were.

When Johnny arrived back at the shed of galvanized iron and wood on the cliff above the beach that housed his separation plant, he was still half groggy from the anaesthetic and lack of sleep.

His hand throbbed with the persistence of a lighthouse, his eyes were reddened and a thick black stubble covered his jaws.

He went to stand beside the grease table that filled half the shed. He was swaying a little on his feet, as he looked around at the preparations. The massive bin at the head of the table was filled with the concentrated diamond gravels, the plates greased down, and his crew was standing ready.

'Let's go!' Johnny nodded at his foreman, who immediately threw in the lever that set the table shaking like an old man with palsy.

The table was a series of steel plates, each slightly inclined and thickly coated with dirty yellow grease. From the bin at the head of the shuddering table a mixture of gravel and water begun to dribble, its consistency and rate of flow carefully regulated by the foreman. It spread all over the greased table like spilled treacle, dropping from one plate to the next, and finally into the waste bin at the end of the table.

A diamond is unwettable, immerse it in water, scrub it–but it comes out dry. A coat of grease on a steel plate is also unwettable, so wet gravel and sea shell will slide over it and keep moving across the agitating, sloping table.

But a diamond when it hits grease sticks like a half-sucked toffee to a woollen blanket.

In the excitement and anxiety of the moment Johnny felt his weariness recede, even the pain in his stump was muted by it. His eyes and whole attention were fastened on that glistening yellow sheet of grease.

The little stuff under a carat in weight, or the industrial black diamond and boart would not be visible on the table; the agitation was too rapid–blurring with speed, and the flow of loose material would disguise them.

So complete was his absorption that it was some seconds before he was aware of a presence beside him. He glanced up quickly.

The Old Man was there, standing with the wide stance and tension-charged attitude that was his own special way.

Johnny was acutely conscious of the Old Man's bulk beside him–and he felt the first flicker of alarm. What if this was a barren run? He needed diamonds now–as he had never needed anything in his life. He scanned the blurring plates of yellow grease, seeking the purchase price that could buy back the Old Man's esteem. The speckled gravel flowed imperturbably across the plates, and Johnny felt a flutter of panic.

Then from across the table the foreman let out a whoop, and pointed.

'Thar she blows!'

Johnny's eyes darted to the head of the table. There beneath the outlet from the bin, half buried in the thick grease by its own weight, anchored solidly while the worthless gravel washed past it, was a diamond.

A big fat five-carat thing, that glowed sulky and yellow, like a wild animal resenting its captivity.

Johnny sighed softly and darted a sideways glance at the Old Man. The Old Man was watching the table without expression, and though he must have been conscious of Johnny's scrutiny, he did not look up. Johnny's eyes were dragged irresistibly back to the table.

By some freakish chance, the next diamond fell from the bin directly onto the one already anchored in the grease.

When diamond strikes diamond it bounces like a golf ball off a tarmac road.

The second diamond, a white beauty the size of a peach pip, clicked loudly as it struck the other then spun head high in the air.

Both Johnny and the foreman laughed involuntarily with delight at the beauty of that twinkling drop of solid sunlight.

Johnny reached across the table with his good hand, and snatched it out of the air. He rubbed it between his fingers–revelling in the soapy feel of it, then turned and offered it to the Old Man.

The Old Man looked at the diamond, nodded in acknowledgement. Then he pulled back the cuff of his coat and checked his wrist watch.

'It's late. I must get back to Cape Town.'

'Won't you stay for the rest of the run, sir?' Johnny realized his tone was too eager. 'We could have a drink together afterwards.' He remembered after he had spoken, that the Old Man abhorred alcohol.

'No.' The Old Man shook his head. 'I have to get back by this evening.' Now he looked steadily into Johnny's eyes. 'You see, Tracey is getting married tomorrow afternoon and I must be there.'

Then he smiled, watching Johnny's face, but nobody could ever guess the meaning of a smile on the Old Man's lips–for it never showed in his eyes.

'Didn't you know?' he asked, still smiling. 'I thought you had received an invitation.' And he went out of the shed to where his jeep stood in the bright sunshine waiting to take him out to the aircraft landing-strip among the sand dunes.

The pain in his injured hand, and the Old Man's words denied Johnny the sleep he so desperately needed, but it was two o'clock in the morning before he threw back his blankets and lit the lamp beside his camp bed.

'He said I had been invited–and, by God, I'll be there.'

He drove through the night, and the next morning. The first two hundred miles were on desert tracks of sand and stone, then he reached the metalled highway in the dawn and turned south across the great plains and over the mountains. It was noon before he saw the squat blue silhouette of Table Mountain on the skyline dwarfing the city that huddled beneath it.

He checked in at the Vineyard Hotel, and hurried to his room to bath and shave and change into a suit.

The grounds of the old house were crowded with expensive automobiles, and the overflow was parked along both sides of the street outside, but he found a space for the dusty Land-Rover. He walked up through the white gates and across the green lawns.

There was a band playing in the house, and a hubbub of voices and laughter drifted out through the windows of the ballroom.

He went in through the side door. The passages were thronged with guests, and he made his way amongst them seeking a familiar face in the groups of loud-voiced gesticulating men and giggling women. At last he found one.

'Michael.' And Michael Shapiro looked round, recognized him and letting the conflicting emotions of pleasure, surprise and alarm show clearly on his face.

'Johnny. It's good to see you.'

'Is the ceremony over?'

'Yes, and the speeches also–thank God.' He took Johnny's arm and led him aside. 'Let me get you a glass of champagne.' Michael hailed a waiter and put a crystal glass into Johnny's hand.

'Here's to the bride,' Johnny murmured and drank.

'Does the Old Man know you are here?' Michael came out with the question that was burning his mouth, and when Johnny shook his head, Michael's expression became thoughtful.

'What's he like, Michael, Tracey's husband?'

'Kenny Hartford?' Michael considered the question. 'He's all right, I suppose. Nice-looking boy, plenty of money.'

'What's he do for a crust of bread?'

'His daddy left him the whole loaf–but to fill in the time he does fashion photography.' And Johnny pulled down the corners of his mouth.

Michael frowned. 'He's all. right, Johnny. The Old Man picked him carefully.'

'The Old Man?' Johnny's jaw thrust out.

'Of course, you know him–he wouldn't leave an important decision like that to anybody else.'

Johnny finished his champagne in silence, and Michael watched his face anxiously.

'Where is she? Have they left yet?'

'No.' Michael shook his head. 'They're still in the ballroom.'

'Thanks, Michael. I think I'll go and wish luck to the bride.'

'Johnny.' Michael caught hold of his elbow. 'Don't do anything stupid–will you?'

Johnny stood at the head of the marble staircase that led down into the ballroom. The floor was crowded with dancing couples and the music was loud and merry. The bridal party sat at a raised table across the floor.

Benedict van der Byl saw Johnny first. His face flushed and he leaned quickly to whisper to the Old Man, then began to rise from his seat. The Old Man placed a restraining hand on Benedict's shoulder, and smiled across the room at Johnny.

Johnny went down the stairs and made his way through the dancers. Tracey had not seen him. She was talking to the silky-faced young man who sat beside her. He had wavy blond hair.

'Hello, Tracey.' She looked up at Johnny and caught her breath. She was more beautiful than he remembered.

'Hello, Johnny.' Her voice was almost a whisper.

'May I dance with you?' She was pale now, and her eyes went to the Old Man, not to her new husband. The gleaming white bush of hair nodded slightly, and Tracey stood up.

They made one circuit of the dance floor before the band stoppped playing. Johnny had planned a hundred different things to say to her, but he was dumb until the music ended and the opportunity was passing.

Hurriedly now in the few seconds that were left Johnny told her:

'I hope you will be happy, Tracey. But if you ever need help–ever–I will come, I promise you that.'

'Thank you.' Her voice was husky, and for a moment she looked like the little girl who had cried in the night. Then he took her back to her husband.

The promise had been made five years ago, and now he had come to London to honour it.

Number 23 Stark Street was a neat double-storied cottage with a narrow front. He parked outside it. It was dark now and lights burned on both floors. He sat in the parked Jaguar, suddenly reluctant to go farther. Somehow he knew that Tracey was here, and he knew it would not be pretty. For a moment he recaptured the image of her as a lovely young woman in a wedding dress of white satin, then he climbed out of the Jaguar and went up the steps to the front door. He reached for the bell before he noticed with surprise that the door was ajar. He pushed it open and walked into a small sitting-room furnished with feminine taste.

The room had been hastily ransacked, one of the curtains was spread on the floor and on it were piled books and ornaments. Pictures had been taken down from the walls and stacked ready for removal.

Johnny picked up one of the books, and opened the cover. On the fly leaf was a handwritten name. 'Tracey van der Byl'. He dropped it back on the pile as he heard footsteps on the stairs from the floor above.

A man came down the stairs. He was dressed in soiled green velvet trousers, sheepskin boots, and shabby frock coat of military cut frogged with tarnished gold braid. He was carrying an armful of women's dresses.

He saw Johnny and stopped nervously, his pink lips opened in vacant surprise but his eyes were beady and bright under the thatch of lank blond hair.

'Hello,' Johnny smiled pleasantly. 'Are you moving out?' And he drifted quietly closer to the man on the stairs and stood looking up at him.

Suddenly from the floor above a low wail echoed down the stairs. It was an eerie sound, without passion or pain, as though steam were escaping from a jet, only just recognizable as human. Johnny went rigid at the sound, and the man on the stairs glanced nervously over his shoulder.

'What have you done to her?' Johnny asked softly, without menace.

'No. Nothing! She's on a trip. A bad trip.' The man's denial was frantic. 'It's her first time on acid.'

'So you're cleaning the place out, are you?' Johnny asked mildly.

'She owes me plenty. She can't pay. She promised–and she can't pay.'

'Oh,' said Johnny. 'That's different. I thought you were hitting the place.' He reached into his overcoat and brought out his wallet, riffling the wad of banknotes. 'I'm a friend of hers. How much does she owe you?'

'Fifty nicker.' The man's eyes sparkled when he saw the wallet. 'I gave her credit.'

Johnny counted off ten fivers, and held them out. The man dropped the bundle of clothing over the banisters and came eagerly down the last few stairs.

'Did you sell her the stuff–the acid?' Johnny asked, and the man stopped a pace from him, his expression stiffening with suspicion.

'Oh, for God's sake.' Johnny grinned. 'We are not children–I know the score.' He offered the banknotes. 'Did you get the stuff for her?'

The man grinned back at him weakly, and nodded as he reached for the money. Johnny's free hand snapped closed on the thin wrist and he swung him off his feet, forcing his wrist up between his shoulder-blades.

Johnny stuffed the money into his pocket, and marched him up the stairs.

'Let's go and have a look, shall we?'

There was a mattress on the iron bedstead covered with a grey Army blanket. Tracey sat cross-legged on the blanket. She wore only a thin cotton slip and her hair hung lank and lustreless to her waist. Her arms crossed over her chest were thin and white as sticks of chalk. Her face also was pale, the skin translucent in the light of the electric bulb. She was rocking gently back and forth and wailing softly, her breath steaming in the icy cold room.

It was her eyes that shocked Johnny the most. They seemed to have expanded to an enormous size, and beneath each was a dark bruised-looking smear. The pupils of the eyes were distended and glittery with the same adamant sheen as uncut diamonds.

The big glittery green eyes fastened on Johnny and the man in the doorway, and the wail rose abruptly to a shriek. The shriek died away, and she bowed forward and buried her face in her hands covering her eyes.

'Tracey,' said Johnny softly. 'Oh God, Tracey!'

'She'll be all right,' the man whimpered and twisted in his grip. 'It's the first time–she'll be all right.'

'Come.' Johnny dragged him out of the room, and pushed the door closed with his foot. He held him against the wall, and his face was set and pale, his eyes merciless–but he spoke quietly, patiently as though he was explaining to a child.

'I'm going to hurt you now. I'm going to hurt you very badly. Just as badly as I can without killing you. Not because I enjoy it, but because that girl is a very special person to me. In the future when you think about giving poison to another girl–I want you to remember what I did to you tonight.'

Johnny held him with his left hand against the wall and he used his right hand, punching up under the ribs at an angle to tear the stomach muscles. With three or four blows he was too high, and he felt ribs crack and snap under his fist.

When he stepped back the man sagged slowly face forward, and Johnny caught him cleanly in the mouth snapping his teeth off at the gums, splitting his lips open like the petals of a rose. The man had made a lot of noise. Johnny looked into Tracey's room to make sure she had not been disturbed, but she was still bowed forward, rocking rhythmically on her haunches.

He found the bathroom and dampened his handkerchief to wipe the blood off his hands and the front of his overcoat. He came out into the passage again and stooped over the unconscious body to check the pulse. It was strong and regular, and he felt a lift of relief as he dragged the man's face out of the puddle of his own vomit and blood to prevent him drowning.

He went through to Tracey and, despite her frantic struggles, wrapped her in the greasy Army blanket and carried her down to the Jaguar.

She quietened down and lay like a sleeping child in the back seat while he tucked the blanket round her, then he went back into the house and phoned 999, giving the address and hanging up immediately.

He left Tracey in the car outside the Dorchester, while he went in to speak to the reception clerk. Within minutes Tracey was in a wheelchair on her way up to the two-bedroom suite on the second floor. The doctor was there fifteen minutes later.

After the doctor had gone Johnny bathed, and carrying a tumbler of Chivas Regal in one hand he went into Tracey's room and stood by her bed. Whatever the doctor had given her had put her out cleanly. She lay gaunt and pale–yet with a strangely fragile beauty that seemed enhanced by the bruised discoloration of her eye sockets.

He stooped to brush the hair from her cheek, and her breath was light and warm on his hand. He felt such an infinity of tenderness for her then as he had never known for any other person, he was amazed by the strength of it.

He stooped over her and gently brushed her lips with his own. Her lips were dry and flaky white, and their touch was harsh as sandpaper.

Johnny straightened up and went to the armchair across the room. He sank into it wearily, and sipped the whisky, feeling its warmth spread from his belly and untie the knots in his muscles. He watched the pale ruined face on the pillows.

'We are in a hell of a mess, you and I,' he spoke aloud, and felt anger again. For long minutes it was undirected, but slowly it jelled and found an object to focus on.

For the first time in his life he was angry with the Old Man.

'He has brought you to this,' he said to the girl on the bed. 'And me–'

The reaction was swift, his loyalty was a thing grown part of his existence. Always he had trained himself to believe that the Old Man's machinations were just and wise–even if at times the justice and wisdom were hidden from him. Mortal man does not doubt the omnipotence of his gods.

Sickened by his own treachery, he began to examine the Old Man's motives and actions under the bright light of reason.

Why had the Old Man sent Michael Shapiro to fetch him out of the desert?

'He wants you in Cape Town, Johnny. Benedict didn't measure up. The Old Man has given him the London Office, it's a form of exile. He's picked you to take over the Company,' Michael explained. 'Tracey is out of the way. She and her husband are in London also. I guess the Old Man thinks it's safe to have you back in Cape Town now.'

Michael watched Johnny's undisguised joy and went on slowly.

'I'm speaking out of turn, perhaps. Mr van der Byl is a strange man. He's not like other people. I know how you feel about him, I've watched it all, you know–but listen, Johnny, you can go anywhere on your own now. There are a lot of other companies that want you–' But he had seen the expression on Johnny's face, and stopped '–okay, Johnny. Forget I ever said it. I only spoke because I like you.'

Thinking on it now, there had been substance in Michael's warning. Certainly he was General Manager of Van Der Byl Diamonds, but he was no nearer to the Old Man than he had ever been. He lived under the mountain but the mountain was remote and he had not been able to scale the lowest slopes.

He had found the city as lonely as the desert, and he was ripe for the first attractive woman who set her snares for him.

Ruby Grange was tall and slim with hair the colour they call 'Second Cape' in a diamond, like sunlight through a crystal glass of champagne.

He wondered now at his own naïvety. That he should be so easily misled, and should have rushed so headlong into her web. After the wedding she had revealed herself, exposing the deeply calculating greed, the driving hunger for flattery and material possessions which was her main-spring, and her complete absorption with herself–Johnny had not been able to believe it. For months he fought off the growing certainty until it could be denied no longer, and he looked with chilled dismay on the shallow selfish little creature he had married.

He had withdrawn from her and flung all his energies into the Company.

This, then, was his life and he saw that it was an empty thing, hollowed out by the Old Man's hand.

For the first time his mind skirted the idea that it was a carefully calculated and sadistic revenge for the innocent action of a half-grown boy.

As though it were an escape from thoughts too dreadful to be borne, he fell asleep in the chair and the glass fell from his hand.

Jacobus Isaac van der Byl sat in a leather chair before the X-ray viewer. Fear had blasted the granite of his features, leaving them cracked and sagging, recognizable but subtly altered below the gleaming white mane.

Fear was in his eyes also, moving below the surface like slimy water creatures in the pale blue pools. With the fear chilling and numbing his limbs he watched the cloudy and swirling images on the screen.

The specialist was talking softly, impersonally as though he were lecturing one of this classes.

'–enveloping the thymus here, and extending beyond the trachea.'

The point of his gold pencil followed the ghostly outline on the screen. The Old Man swallowed with an effort. it seemed to be swelling in his throat as he listened, and his voice was hoarse and blurred to his own ears.

'You will operate?' he asked, and the specialist paused in his explanation. He glanced at the surgeon across the desk. The exchange was as guilty as that of conspirators.

The Old Man swivelled his chair and faced the surgeon.

'Well?' he demanded harshly.

'No.' The surgeon shook his head apologetically. 'It's too late. If only you had–'

'How long?' The Old Man overrode his explanation.

'Six months, not more.'

'You are certain?'

'Yes.'

The Old Man's chin sank onto his chest and he closed his eyes. There was complete silence in the room, they watched him with professional pity and interest as he reached his own personal acceptance of death.

At last the Old Man opened his eyes and stood up slowly. He tried to smile but his lips would not hold the shape.

'Thank you, gentlemen,' he croaked in this new rough voice. 'Will you excuse me, please. There are many things to arrange now.'

He went down to where the Rolls waited at the entrance. He walked slowly, shuffling his feet and the chauffeur came to him quickly, but the Old Man shrugged away his helping hands and climbed into the back seat of the car.

Michael Shapiro was waiting for him in the study of the big house. He saw the change in him immediately and jumped up from his chair. The Old Man stood in the doorway, his body seemed to have shrunk.

'Six months,' he said. 'They gave me six months.' He went to his desk and sat in the chair behind it.

'After all the money they've taken from me.' He said it as though he had expected to buy off death, and they had tricked him. He closed his eyes again, and when he opened them there was a glint of cunning in them, even his face had a pinched foxy look to it.

'Where is he? Is he back yet?'

'Yes, the Boeing got in at nine this morning. He's at the office now.' Michael was shocked, it was the first time he had seen the Old Man without the mask.

'And the girl?' He had not called her 'daughter' since the divorce.

'Johnny has her in a private nursing-home.'

'Worthless slut,' said the Old Man softly, and Michael stilled the protest before it reached his lips. 'Get your pad. I want you to take something down.' The Old Man chuckled hoarsely. 'We'll see!' he said, making it sound like a threat. 'We'll see!'

Johnny's doctor was waiting at Cape Town airport.

'Take her, Robin. Dry her out, and fatten her up. She's up to her gills with drugs and she probably hasn't eaten for a month.'

Tracey showed her first spark of spirit.

'Where do you think–'

'Into a nursing-home.' Johnny anticipated her questions. 'For as long as is necessary.'

'I'm not–'

'Oh, yes, you bloody well are.' He took her arm, and Robin grabbed the other. They walked her, still protesting weakly to the car park.

'Thanks, Robin, Old Soldier, give her the full workout.'

'I'll send her back to you like new,' Robin promised and drove away. Johnny took a few moments to look at the massive squat silhouette of the mountain–his own private home-coming ceremony. Then he fetched the Mercedes from the airport garage, and hesitated between home or the office, decided he was not up to an interrogation from Ruby and chose the office. He kept a clean shirt and shaving tackle in his private bathroom there.

They descended on him like a tribe of man-eating Amazons as he came in through the glass doors into the lusciously furnished and carpeted reception area of Van Der Byl Diamonds head office.

The two pretty little receptionists began yipping joyfully in chorus.

'Oh, Mr Lance, I have a whole sheaf of messages–'

'Oh, Mr Lance, your wife–'

Trying not to run he made it to within ten feet of his own door, when the Old Man's secretary popped out of ambush from behind the frosted-glass panel.

'Mr Lance, where on earth have you been? Mr van der Byl has been asking–'

Which alerted Lettie Pienaar, his own secretary.

'Mr Lance, thank goodness you're back.'

Johnny stopped and held up his hands in an attitude of surrender.

'One at a time, ladies. There is enough to go round–don't panic.'

Which broke the reception team into a quivering jelly of giggles, and sent the Old Man's watchdog back behind her panel sniffing disgustedly.

'Which is the most important, Lettie?' he asked as he went to his desk and flipped through his mail, shrugged out of his coat and began stripping tie and shirt as he headed for his bathroom.

They shouted at each other through the open door of the bathroom, as Johnny shaved quickly and showered, Lettie bringing him up to date on every aspect of Company and domestic business.

'Mrs Lance has phoned regularly. She called me a liar when I told her you were at Cartridge Bay.' Lettie was silent a moment, then as Johnny came out of the bathroom she asked, 'By the way, where have you been?'

'Don't *you* start that.' Johnny stood over the desk, and began flipping through the accumulated papers. 'Get my wife on the phone, please–no, hold it. Tell her I'll be home at seven.'

Lettie saw she had lost his attention, and she stood and went out. Johnny settled down behind his desk.

Van Der Byl Diamonds was a sick company. Despite Johnny's protests the Old Man had been drawing off its reserves and feeding them into his other ventures–the property-developing company, the clothing factory, Van Der Byl fisheries, the big irrigation scheme on the Orange river–and now the cupboard was almost bare.

The beach concessions were reaching the end of a short but glorious life. They were starting to work break-even ground. The Old Man had sold the Huib Hoch concession to the big Company for a quick profit–but the profit had been just as quickly transferred out of Johnny's control.

There was only one really fat goose left in his pen, and it wasn't laying eggs yet.

Eighteen months earlier Johnny had purchased two offshore diamond grounds from a company which had died in attempting to work them. It had been strangled by its own inefficiency.

Taking diamonds from the sea is about eight times more expensive than working them from a dry open-cast. One must dredge the gravel from the wild and unpredictable waters of the Skeleton Coast, load it into dumb barges, tow the barges to a safe base, off-load it and then begin the recovery process–or rather, that was the method the defunct company had attempted.

Johnny had dreamed up, and then ordered a vessel which was completely self-contained. It could lie out at sea, suck up the gravel and process it, spilling the waste gravel back into the sea as rapidly as it was sucked aboard. It was fitted with a sophisticated recovery plant that was completely computerized and contained within the ocean-going hull. It needed only a small crew, and it could work in all weather conditions short of a full tornado.

The *Kingfisher* was lying at Portsmouth dockyards rapidly nearing completion. Her trials were scheduled for early August.

Financing the building of this vessel had been a nightmare for Johnny. The Old Man had been unhelpful, when he wasn't being downright obstructive. He never discussed the venture without that little smile twitching at his lips. He had restricted Van Der Byl Diamonds' monetary involvement in the project so severely that Johnny had been forced to raise two millions outside the Company.

He had found the money, and the Old Man had smiled again.

Kingfisher should have been lying on the grounds three months ago, sucking up diamonds. The whole financial structure of the scheme was based on her completion on schedule, but *Kingfisher* was running six months behind and now the foundations were shivering.

Sitting at his desk Johnny was working out how to shore up the whole edifice and keep it from collapsing before he could get *Kingfisher* working. The creditors were rumbling and creaking, and Johnny had only his own enthusiasm and reputation left to keep them quiet.

Now he must ask them to defer their interest payments for another three months. He picked up the telephone.

'Get me Mr Larsen at Credit Finance,' he said, steeling himself as he did so, jutting out his jaw and thrusting one bunched fist into his coat pocket.

At five o'clock he stood up from his desk and went to the cabinet. He poured three fingers of whisky and went back to lower himself wearily into his swivel chair. He felt no elation at having won another reprieve, he was too tired.

The unlisted telephone on his desk rang and he picked it up.

'Lance,' he said.

'How was London?' he recognized the voice instantly, feeling no surprise that the Old Man knew about his journey. The Old Man knew everything. Before he could answer the hoarse croak came again, 'Come up to the house–now!' And the receiver clicked dead.

Johnny looked at the whisky in his hand regretfully and set it down untouched. The Old Man would smell it and smile.

Cloud was blowing over the mountain, and the setting sun turned it to the colour of tangerine and peaches. The Old Man stood at the window and watched the cloud cascade down into the valley, dispersing as it fell.

He turned from the window as Johnny entered the study and instantly Johnny was aware that something momentous had taken place in his absence.

He glanced quickly at Michael Shapiro for a cue, but Michael's grey-streaked head was bowed over the papers he held on his lap.

'Good evening,' Johnny addressed the Old Man.

'Sit there.' The Old Man indicated the Spanish leather chair opposite his desk.

'Read it,' the Old Man ordered Michael, and Michael cleared his throat and patted the papers into a neat square before he began.

The Old Man sat with his eyes on Johnny's face. It was a candid, intimate scrutiny, but Johnny felt no discomfort under it. It was almost as though the Old Man's eyes were caressing him.

Mike Shapiro read intelligently, bringing out the meaning of the involved and convoluted legal phrases. The document was the Old Man's Last Will and Testament, and it took twenty minutes for Mike to complete the reading of it. When he had finished there was silence in the room, and the Old Man broke it at last.

'Do you understand?' he asked. There was a gentleness about him that there had never been before. He seemed to have shrunk, the flesh withering on his bones and leaving them dry and light–like the sun-dried bones of a long dead seabird.

'Yes, I understand.' Johnny nodded.

'Explain it to us simply, not in your lawyer's gobbledy-gook, just to be certain,' the Old Man insisted, and Mike began to speak.

'Mr van der Byl's private estate, with the exception of his shares in Van Der Byl Diamond Co Ltd, after taxes and expenses, is placed in Trust for his two children, Tracey–'

The Old Man interrupted impatiently, swatting Mike's words out of the air as though they were flies.

'Not that. The Company. Tell him about the shares in the Company.'

'Mr van der Byl's shares in the Company are to be divided equally between you and the two van der Byl children, Tracey–'

Again the Old Man interrupted.

'He knows their names, dammit.'

It was the first time ever that either of them had heard him swear. Mike grinned ruefully at Johnny, as though asking for his sympathy, but Johnny was intent on the Old Man, studying his face, feeling the deep satisfying thrill swelling within his chest.

A third share in Van Der Byl Diamonds was no great fortune–nobody knew that better than Johnny.

However, by placing Johnny's name on the list with Tracey and Benedict–he had made him his own. This was what he had worked for all these years. The declaration was public, an acknowledgement to the world.

Johnny Lance had a father at last. He wanted to reach out and touch the Old Man. His chest felt swollen, tight with emotion. Behind his eyelids was a slow soft burning. Johnny blinked.

'This is–' His voice was ragged, and he coughed. 'I just don't know how to tell you–'

The Old Man interrupted him impatiently, silencing him with an imperious gesture, and he croaked at Mike.

'Now read him the codicil to the Will. No, don't read it. Explain it to him.'

Michael's expression changed; he looked down at his papers as he spoke, as though reluctant to meet Johnny's eyes. He cleared his throat unnecessarily and shifted in his seat.

'"By the codicil to the Will, dated the same date, and duly signed by Mr van der Byl the bequest of shares in Van Der Byl Diamond Co Ltd to JOHN RIGBY

LANCE, is made conditional on the issue by the said JOHN RIGBY LANCE of a personal guarantee for the debts of the company, including the present loan account and amounts outstanding to tributary companies for royalties and options."'

'Christ,' said Johnny, stiffening in his chair and turning to stare incredulously at the Old Man. The tightness in his chest was gone. 'What are you trying to do to me?'

The Old Man dismissed Mike Shapiro quietly, without even looking at him. 'I'll call you when I want you.' And when he had gone he repeated Johnny's question.

'What am I trying to do to you?' he asked. 'I am trying to make you responsible for debts totalling about two and a half million Rand.'

'No creditor would come to me for half a million, I would be hard pressed to raise ten thousand on my personal account.' Johnny shook his head irritably, the whole thing was nonsensical.

'There is one creditor who could come to you, and subject you to the full process of law. Not to receive payment in cash–but in personal satisfaction. He would smash you–and delight in doing so.'

Johnny's eyes narrowed disbelievingly. 'Benedict?'

The Old Man nodded. 'For once Benedict will hold the top cards. He won't be able to dislodge you from the management of the Company, because Tracey will support you as she always has done–but he will be able to watch every move you make from his seat on the Board of Directors. He will be able to hound you, bring you and the Company down without suffering financial loss himself. And when you fall–you know better than to expect mercy from him. You will be devoured by the ogre you have created.'

'Created?' Johnny's voice was shocked. 'What do you mean?'

'You turned him into what he is now. You broke his heart, made him weak and useless–'

'You are crazy.' Johnny came to his feet. 'I have never done anything to Benedict. It was he who–'

But the Old Man's husky croak brushed aside Johnny's protests. 'He tried to run with you–but could not. He gave up, became small and vicious. Oh, I know about the way he is–how you made him.'

'Please, listen to me. I did not–'

But the Old Man went on remorselessly. 'Tracey also, you have ruined her life. You enslaved her, in your sin–'

'That night!' Johnny shouted at him. 'You never let me explain. We never–'

Now the Old Man's voice was a whiplash.

'Silence!' And Johnny could not defy him, the habit was too deeply engrained. The Old Man was trembling, his eyes glittering with passion. 'Both my children! You have plagued me and my family. My son is a weak-willed drifter, trying to hide his hurt in a hunt for pleasure. I have given him the instruments to destroy you, and when he does so perhaps he will become a man.'

The Old Man's voice was strained now, rusty and painracked. He swallowed with an effort, his throat convulsing–but there was no softening of the glitter in his eyes.

'My daughter also, tortured by her lust. A lust which you awakened–she also seeks an escape from her guilty passion. Your destruction will be her release.'

'You're wrong,' Johnny cried out, half in protest, half in entreaty. 'Please let me explain–'

'This is how it will work. I have made you vulnerable, linking you to a crippled and foundering enterprise. This time we will be rid of you.' He stopped to pant quickly, like a running dog. His breathing was strangled, harsh-sounding. 'Benedict will cut you down, and Tracey will have to watch you go. She cannot help you, her inheritance is carefully tied up, she has no control of the capital. Your only hope is the *Kingfisher*. The *Kingfisher* will turn into a vampire and suck your life blood! You asked why I was systematically transferring the assets of Van Der Byl Diamonds to my other companies? Well, now you know the answer.'

Johnny's lips moved. He was very pale. His voice came out small and whispery.

'I could refuse to sign the guarantee.'

The Old Man smiled bleakly, a drawing back of the lips that was without warmth or humour.

'You will sign it.' His voice was wheezy. 'Your pride and conceit will not let you do otherwise. You see, I know you. I've studied you all these years. But if you refuse to sign the guarantee, I will still have smashed you. Your shares will go to Benedict. You will be out. Out! Gone! We will be finished with you at last.' Then his voice dropped, 'But you will sign, I know it.'

Involuntarily Johnny lifted his hands towards the Old Man, a gesture of supplication. 'In all this time. When I stayed with you, when I–' His voice went husky and dried up. 'Did you never feel anything for me–anything at all?'

The Old Man sat up in his chair. He seemed to regain his bulk and he began to smile. He spoke quietly now, he did not have to shout.

'Get out of my nest, cuckoo. Get out and fly!' he said.

Slowly Johnny's expression changed, the line of his jaw hardened, thrusting out aggressively. His shoulders went back. He pushed his hands into his pockets, balling his fists into bony hammers.

He nodded once in understanding.

'I see.' He nodded again, and then he started to grin. It was an unconvincing grin, that twisted his mouth out of shape, and left his eyes dark and haunted.

'All right, you mean old bastard, I'll show you.'

He turned and walked from the room without looking back.

The Old Man's expression lit in deep satisfaction. He chuckled, then his breath caught. He began to cough, and the pain ripped his throat with a violence that left him clinging weakly to the edge of his desk.

He felt the crab of death move within his flesh, sinking its claws more deeply into his throat and lungs–and he was afraid.

He called out in his pain and fear, but there was nobody in the old house to hear him.

Kingfisher was launched in August and ran her trials in the North Sea. Benedict was aboard, by the Old Man's express command. With a vessel of such complexity, and of such revolutionary design, it would have been a miracle had she functioned perfectly. August that year was not the month for miracles. At the end of the trials Johnny had compiled a list of twenty-three modifications that were necessary.

'How long?' he asked the representative of the shipyard.

'A month.' The reply was hesitant.

'You mean two,' said Benedict and laughed out loud. Johnny looked at him thoughtfully, he guessed that the Old Man had spoken to him.

'I'll tell you something, Johnny.' Benedict was still laughing. 'I'm glad this cow isn't my dream of paradise.'

Johnny froze. Those words were the Old Man's, repeated parrot fashion. It was all the confirmation he needed.

Johnny flew back to Cape Town to find his creditors on the verge of mutiny. They wanted to sell out, and take the loss.

Johnny spent two whole precious days on Larsen's wine farm at Stellenbosch calming his fears. When Fifi Larsen twenty years younger than her husband, squeezed Johnny's thigh under the lunch table he knew it would be all right–for another two months.

During the next hectic, strength-sapping week of arguments and negotiations, Johnny made time to see Tracey.

She had been out of the nursing-home for a month now, staying with friends on a small farm near Somerset West.

When Johnny climbed out of the Mercedes, and Tracey came down from the stoep to greet him, he had his first real lift of pleasure in a long time.

'God,' he said. 'You look great.'

She was dressed in a cotton summer dress with open sandals on her feet. Her friends were away for the day, so they walked through the orchards. He studied her openly, noticing how her cheeks and arms had filled out and the colour had come back into them. Her hair was bright and springing with lights in the sun, but there were still the dark smears under her eyes, and she smiled only once when he picked a sprig of peach blossoms for her. She seemed to be afraid of him, and unsure of herself.

At last he faced her and placed his hands on her shoulders. 'All right. What's eating you?'

It came out in a quick staccato rush of words.

'I want to thank you for coming to find me. I want to explain why I was–like that. In that state. I don't want you to believe–well, bad things about me.'

'Tracey, you don't have to explain to me.'

'I want to. I must.' And she told him, not looking at his face, twisting and tearing the blossoms in her hands.

'You see, I didn't understand, I thought all men were like that. Not wanting, I mean not doing it–' She broke off and started again. 'He was kind, you understand. And there were lots of parties and friends around all the time, every night. Then he wanted to go to London–for his career. There was not enough scope here. Even then I didn't know. Well, I knew he had lots of men friends and that some of them were different–but . . . Then I went to his studio and found them, and they laughed. Kenny and the boy twined together like snakes. "But you must have known," he said. Something just snapped in my head, I felt spoiled, dirty and horrible and I wanted to die. There was nobody to go to and I didn't want anybody–I just wanted to die.' She stopped and stood waiting for him to speak.

'Do you still want to die?' he asked gently, and she looked up startled and shook her shining hair.

'I don't want you to die either.' And suddenly they were both laughing. After that it was good between them and they talked with all the strangeness gone until it was almost dark.

'I must go,' Johnny said.

'Your wife?' she asked, the laughter fading.

'Yes. My wife.'

It was dark when Johnny went through the front door of the new split-level ranch type in Bishopscourt which was his house but not his home; the telephone was ringing. He picked up the receiver.

'Johnny?'

'Hello Michael.' He recognized the voice.

'Johnny, get up here to the old house right away.' Michael Shapiro's voice was strained.

'Is it the Old Man?' Johnny asked anxiously.

'No talk–just come, quickly!'

The curtains were drawn, and a log fire roared on the stone hearth. But the Old Man was cold. The coldness was deep inside him where the flames could not warm it. His hands shook as he picked sheets of paper from the open document box, glanced at them and then dropped them into the fire. They exploded into orange flame, then curled and blackened to ash. At last the box was empty but for a thick wad of multi-coloured envelopes bound together with a ribbon. He loosened the knot, picked out the first envelope, and slipped from it a single sheet of writing paper.

Dear Sir.

I hope you will be pleased to hear that I am now at school. The food is good but the beds are very hard–

He dropped both envelope and letter on the fire and selected another. One at a time he read and then burned them

–that I have been selected to play for the first fifteen–

Sometimes he smiled, once he chuckled.

–I was top in all subjects except history and religious teaching. I hope to do better next–

When there was one envelope left he held it a long time in his blue-veined bony hands. Then with an impatient flick of his wrist he threw it onto the fire and reached up to the mantelpiece to pull himself to his feet. As he stood he looked into the gilt-framed mirror above the fireplace.

He stared at his reflection, mildly surprised by the change that the last few weeks had wrought in his appearance. His eyes had lost the sparkle of life, fading to a pale dirty brownish blue–the colour of putrefaction. They bulged from the sockets, in the glassy startled stare which is peculiar to the later stages of terminal cancer.

The watery feeling of limb, and the coldness were not the result of the pain-killing drugs, he knew. Nor was the shuffling feet-dragging gait with which he crossed the thick Bokhara carpet to the stinkwood desk.

He looked down at the oblong leather case with its brass-bound corners, and he coughed, a single flesh-tearing bark. He caught at the desk to steady himself, waiting for the pain to pass before he sprang the catch on the case and laid the lid back.

His hands were quite steady as he took the barrel and butt section of the Purdey Royal twelve-bore shotgun from the case and fitted them together.

He died the way he had lived–alone.

'God, how I hate black.' Ruby Lance stood in the centre of the bedroom floor, staring at the clothing laid out on the double bed. 'It makes me look so washed out.'

She swung her head from side to side, setting the champagne-coloured cascade of her hair swinging. She turned and moved lazily across the room to the tall mirrors. She smiled at herself, a languid slanting of the eyes, and then she spoke over the shoulder of her own image.

'You say that Benedict van der Byl has arrived from England?'

'Yes,' Johnny nodded. He sat slumped in the chair beside his dressing-room door, pressing his fingers into his eyes.

Ruby came up on her toes, pulling in her stomach and pushing forward her small hard breasts.

'Who else will be there?' she asked, cupping her hands under her breasts and squeezing out the nipples between thumb and forefinger, inspecting them critically. Johnny took his hand from his eyes.

'Did you hear me?' Ruby's voice took on a sharp admonishing note. 'I'm not talking to myself you know.'

She turned away from the mirror to face him. Standing long and slim and golden as a leopard, even her eyes had the yellow intentness of a leopard's stare. She gave the impression that at any moment she would draw her lips back in a snarl.

'It's a funeral,' he said quietly. 'Not a cocktail party.'

'Well, you can't expect me to die of sorrow. I couldn't stand him.' She crossed to the bed and picked up the pair of peach-coloured panties and rubbed the glossy material against her cheek. Then she stepped into them with two long-legged strides.

'At least I can wear something pretty under the weeds.' She snapped the elastic against her sun-gilt belly, and the almost colourless blonde curls were flattened beneath the sheer silk.

Johnny stood up slowly, and went into his dressing-room. Scornfully she called after him. 'Oh for God's sake, Johnny Lance, stop dragging that long face around as though it's the end of the world. Nobody owes that old devil a thing–he collected all his debts long before they fell due.'

They were a few minutes early, and they stood together beneath the pine trees outside the entrance to the chapel.

When the pearl-grey Rolls drew up at the gate and brother and sister stepped down and came up the paved path, Ruby could not contain her interest.

'Is that Benedict van der Byl?'

Johnny nodded.

'He's very good-looking.'

But Johnny was looking at Tracey. The change in her appearance since he had last seen her was startling. She walked like a desert girl again, straight and proud. She came directly to Johnny and stopped in front of him. She removed her dark glasses, and he could see she had been weeping, for her eyes were slightly puffy. She wore no make-up, and with dark scarf framing her face she looked like a nun. The marks that sorrow had left gave her face maturity.

'I did not think this day would ever come,' she said softly.

'No,' Johnny agreed. 'It was as though he would live for ever.'

Tracey moved a step closer to him, she reached out as if to touch Johnny's arm but her fingers stopped within inches of his sleeve. Johnny understood the gesture, it was a sharing of sorrow, an understanding of mutual loss, and an unstated offer of comfort.

'I don't think we have met.' Ruby used her sugar and arsenic tone. 'It is Miss van der Byl, isn't it?'

Tracey turned her head and her expression went flat and neutral. She replaced the dark glasses, masking her eyes.

'Mrs Hartford,' she said. 'How do you do.'

Mike Shapiro stood beside Johnny in the pew. He spoke without moving his lips, just loud enough for Johnny to catch the words.

'Benedict knows the conditions of the Will. You can expect his first move immediately.'

'Thanks, Mike.'

Johnny kept his eyes on the massive black coffin. The candlelight glinted and sparkled on the elaborate silver handles.

As yet he could find no interest for the conflict that lay ahead. That would come. Now he was too deeply involved in the passing of an era, his life had reached another point of major departure. He knew it would change, had already changed.

He looked across the aisle suddenly, his gaze drawn intuitively.

Benedict van der Byl was watching him, and at that moment the priest asked for the pallbearers.

They went to stand beside the coffin, Benedict and Johnny on opposite sides of the polished black casket among the massed display of arum lilies. They watched each other warily. It seemed to Johnny that the whole scene was significant. The two of them standing over the Old Man's corpse, facing each other, with Tracey looking on anxiously.

Johnny glanced back into the body of the church, looking for Tracey. Instead he found Ruby. She was watching them both, and Johnny knew suddenly that the board had changed more than he realized. A new piece had been added to the game.

He felt Mike Shapiro nudge him, and he stepped forward and grasped the silver handle. Between them they carried the Old Man out into the sunshine.

The handle had cut into his palm with the weight of the coffin. He went on massaging it, even after the coffin had gone down into the pit. The crude mounds of fresh earth were covered with blankets of bright green artificial grass. The mourners began to drift away, but Johnny went on standing there bareheaded. Until Ruby came to touch his arm.

'Come on.' Her voice pitched low, but stinging. 'You're making a fool of yourself.'

Benedict and Tracey were waiting under the pine trees by the churchyard gate, shaking hands and talking quietly to the departing mourners.

'You are Ruby, of course.' Benedict took her hand, smiling a little, urbane and charming. 'The flattering reports I've had of you hardly do you justice.' And Ruby glowed, seeming like a butterfly to spread her wings to the sun.

'Johnny.' Benedict turned to him, and Johnny was taken off balance by the friendly warmth of his smile and the grip of his hand. 'Michael Shapiro tells me that you have accepted my father's legacy and the conditions attached to it–you have signed the guarantee. It's wonderful news. I don't know what we would have done without you in Van Der Byl Diamonds. You are the only one that can pull the Company through this difficult period. I want you to know I am behind you all the way, Johnny. I intend becoming much more involved with the Company now, giving you all the help you need.'

'I knew I could depend on you, Benedict.' Johnny accepted the challenge as smoothly as it was thrown down. 'I think everything is going to turn out all right.'

'We have a meeting on Monday, then I must return to London on Thursday–but I hope you can have dinner with me before then–you and your lovely wife, of course.'

'Thank you.' Ruby, seeing the refusal on Johnny's lips, interrupted quickly. 'We'd enjoy that.'

'You were going to refuse, weren't you?' She sat with her legs curled up sideways under her, watching him from the passenger seat of the Mercedes with the slanting eyes of a Persian cat.

'You're damn right.' Johnny nodded grimly.

'Why?'

'Benedict van der Byl is poison.'

'You say so.'

'Yes, I say so.'

'Could be you're jealous of him.' Ruby lit one of her gold-tipped cigarettes, pouting the smoke through her lips.

'Good God!' Johnny gave one harsh snort of laughter, then they were silent, both staring ahead.

'I think he's pretty dreamy.'

'You can have him.' Johnny's tone was disinterested, but her retort was shrill.

'I could too–if I wanted to. Anyway you and that Tracey creature mooning–'

'Cut it out, Ruby.'

'Oh my, I've said the wrong thing. The precious Mrs Hartford–'

'Cut it out, I said.' Johnny's tone was sharp.

'Little Miss Fancy Pants–God! She almost had them down for you in the bloody graveyard–'

'Shut up, damn you.'

'Don't you swear at me.' And she lashed out at him flat-handed, leaning forward across the seat to strike him in the mouth. His lower lip smeared against his teeth, and the taste of blood seeped into his mouth. He took the handkerchief from his breast pocket and held it to his mouth, steering the Mercedes with one hand.

Ruby sat curled in her corner of the seat, puffing quickly at the cigarette. Neither of them spoke again until he drew up in front of the double garage. Then Ruby slipped out of the Mercedes and ran across the lawns to the front door. She slammed it behind her, with a force that rattled the full-length glass panel.

Johnny parked the Mercedes, closed the garage door and followed her slowly into the house. She had kicked off her shoes on the wall-to-wall carpet in the lounge, and run through onto the patio beside the swimming pool. She stood barefooted staring down into the clear water, hugging herself about the shoulders.

'Ruby.' He came up behind her, forcing the anger out of his voice with an effort, trying to keep it conciliatory. 'Listen to me–'

She spun around to face him, eyes blazing like a cornered leopard.

'Don't try and gentle talk me, you bastard. What do you think I am–your damned servant? When did I last get to do anything I wanted?'

With Ruby he had long ago realized that placation was the short cut to peace, so he was roused by the implication.

'I've never stopped you from–'

'Good! That's just fine! then you won't stop me going away.'

'What do you mean?' He was caught between shock and a sneaking sense of hope. 'Are you talking about divorce–'

'Divorce? Are you out of your little mind! I know all about the big bagful of goodies the Old Man left you in his Will. Well, little Ruby is getting her pinkies into that bag–starting right now.'

'What do you want exactly?' His voice was cold and flat.

'A new wardrobe, and a quick whip around all those nice places you go to all the time–London, Paris and the rest. That will do for a start.'

He thought for a moment, assessing how far he could stretch his overdraft; since his marriage his bank statement had seldom been typed in black. It was worth it, he decided. He could afford no distraction over the next few months. He could move faster and think quicker without having Ruby Lance sitting between his shoulder-blades–much better she should go.

'All right,' he nodded. 'If that's what you want.'

Her eyes narrowed slightly and her mouth pinched in as she studied his face.

'That was too easy,' she said. 'You want to get rid of me? Don't get any ideas, Johnny boy, you put one finger–or anything else–out of line and I'll chop it off.'

'There is a Mrs Hartford to see you, sir.' Lettie Pienaar's voice whispered through on the intercom, then just audibly she added, 'Lucky you!'

Johnny grinned. 'You're fired for insolence–but send her in before you go.'

He stood up as Tracey came in, and went around his desk to meet her. She wore a no-nonsense grey suit, with her hair scraped back from her face. She should have looked like a school marm–but she didn't.

'You've got your times mixed up, Tracey. The Directors' meeting is at two this afternoon.'

'That's a sweet greeting.' She sat down in an egg-shaped swivel chair, crossing long legs which Johnny dragged his eyes off with an effort. 'I've come looking for a job.'

'A job?' He stared at her blankly.

'Yes, a job. You know–work? Employment?'

'What on earth for?'

'Well, now that you've dragged me back from the bright lights with all the finesse of a caveman–you don't expect me to sit around until I drop dead of boredom. Besides, your tame doctor feels that good healthy employment is essential to the completion of my–ah–cure.'

'I see.' He sank back into his own chair. 'Well–what can you do?'

'Mr Lance.' Tracey widened her eyes suggestively, but made her voice prim. '–Really!'

'All right,' Johnny chuckled. 'What are your qualifications?'

'You may or may not know that I have a law degree from the University of Cape Town.'

'I didn't.'

'Also, it occurred to me that during the next few months you might need someone around whom you can trust.' She was serious now, and Johnny's smile faded also. 'Like the old days,' she added quietly. They were silent for a few seconds.

'It just so happens that we are looking for a personal assistant in our legal department.' Johnny murmured, and then softly, 'Thanks, Tracey.'

The Board Room of Van Der Byl Diamonds was furnished in soft forest colours, browns and greens. A long luxurious room that reflected the opulence of the days when the Company had been glutted with capital. But now the air was charged with a tension that crackled in the air like static electricity.

The subject of debate was the diamond recovery vessel, *Kingfisher*. The Company's last hope. Her only substantial asset, and Johnny's personal cross.

'This vessel should have been in operation nine months ago. All the estimates were based on that assumption–yet, she is still lying awaiting completion on the slips at Portsmouth.' Benedict was speaking with unconcealed relish. 'In consequence, the interest charges that are accruing put us in a position–'

'The shipyard was out on strike for a total of four months during construction–in addition they were working to rule for–' Johnny's jaw was thrust out, he was ready to fight.

'Ah! I don't think we are particularily interested in the unpredictability of the British workman–the contract should have gone to the Japanese company. Their tender was lower–'

'It would have,' grated Johnny, 'if your father had not insisted–'

'Please, let us not attempt to lay the blame at the door of a dead man.' Benedict's tone was sanctimonious. 'Let us rather try and rectify a grievous situation. When will *Kingfisher* be ready for sea?'

'On the thirteenth of September.'

'It had better be.' Benedict dropped his eyes to his notes. 'Now, this man whom you have engaged to captain the vessel–Sergio Caporetti–let us hear a little about him, please.'

'Fifteen years' experience on offshore oil-drilling vessels in the Red Sea. Three years as Captain of Atlantis Diamonds' offshore dredger operating off the West Coast. He's one of the best, no doubt about it.'

'All right.' Almost reluctantly Benedict accepted this, and consulted his notes. 'Now, we have two sea-concession areas. No 1 area off Cartridge Bay; No 2 some twenty miles north of that. Judging by your prospecting results you will elect to work No 1 area first.'

Johnny nodded, waiting for the next attack to develop. Benedict sat back in his chair.

'Atlantis Diamonds Ltd went broke working our No 1 area–what makes you think you can succeed where they failed?'

'We've been over this before,' Johnny snapped.

'I wasn't there, remember? Humour me, please. Go over it again.'

Quickly Johnny explained that Atlantis Diamonds' costs had been inflated by their method of operation. Their dredgers were not self-propelled but had to be towed by tugs. The gravel they recovered had been stored, taken into Cartridge Bay in bulk, transhipped ashore to be processed at a land-based plant. *Kingfisher* was a self-propelled and self-contained vessel. She would suck up the gravel, process it through the most sophisticated system of cyclone and X-ray equipment and dump the waste overboard.

'Our costs will be one quarter those of Atlantis Diamonds,' he finished.

'And our loan account is a mere two millions,' Benedict murmured dryly. Then he looked towards Mike Shapiro at the bottom of the table. 'Mr Secretary, please note the following motion–"That this Company proceed to sell the vessel *Kingfisher* presently building at Portsmouth. That it sells all diamond concessions at the most advantageous terms negotiable, and goes into voluntary liquidation forthwith." Have you got that?'

It was a direct frontal attack. Clearly if the motion succeeded the Company was worthless. They could not recover the price of the *Kingfisher* on a forced sale. There would be a shortfall–and Johnny had signed the guarantee. It was a straight test that Benedict was making. A setting of the lines of battle. Tracey held the balance between Johnny and Benedict. He was forcing her to declare herself.

Benedict watched her while the motion was put to the vote. He leaned forward in the padded leather chair, a slightly amused smile on the full red lips. Beautifully groomed and tailored, with the grace that wealth and position gave to a man and which cannot be counterfeited. But the clean athletic lines of his body were fractionally blurred by indulgence, and there was a little too much flesh along the line of his jaw that gave him the petulant look of a spoilt child.

Tracey voted with Johnny Lance, not hesitating a second before lifting her hand. Returning Benedict's smile levelly, and watching her brother's smile alter subtly–become wolfish, for Benedict did not like to lose.

'Very well, my darling sister. Now we know how we stand at least.' He turned easily to Johnny. 'I presume you wish me to continue with my duties in London.'

For years now Benedict had handled the London sales of the Company's stones. It was an unexacting task, which the Old Man had judged within his capabilities.

'Thank you, Benedict,' Johnny nodded. 'Now, I have a proposal to put to the meeting–"That the Directors of this Company, as a gesture of solidarity, agree to waive their rights to Directors' fees until such time as the Company's financial position is on a more sound footing."'

It was a puny counter attack, but the best he could mount at the moment.

Take-off was in the first light from Youngsfield, and Johnny swung the twin-engined Beechcraft on to a northerly heading, leaving the blue massif of Table Mountain on the left hand.

Tracey wore an anorak over her rose-coloured shirt, and the bottoms of her denim pants were tucked into soft leather boots, her dark hair caught at the nape of her neck with a leather thong.

She sat very still, looking ahead through the aircraft's windshield at the dawn-touched contours of the land ahead. At the bleak lilac and purple mountains and the great lion-coloured plains spreading down to meet the mists that hung over the cold Atlantic.

In her stillness Johnny sensed her excitement and found it infectious.

The sun exploded over the horizon, washing golden and bright over the plains, and tipping the mountains with flame.

'Namaqualand.' Johnny pointed ahead.

She laughed with excitement, like a child at Christmas, turning in the seat to face him.

'Do you remember–' She began, then stopped in confusion.

'Yes,' said Johnny. 'I remember.'

They landed before noon on a rough air-strip bulldozed out of the wilderness. There was a Land-Rover waiting to take them down to the beach to inspect the progress of the workings.

There was little remaining along the thirty-seven-mile Admiralty strip worth working. It was a clean-up and shut-down operation.

When the reigning 'King Canute' handed over the parcel of diamonds that made up the month's recovery, he was apologetic.

'You took out all the plums, Johnny. It's not like the old days.'

Johnny prodded the pathetic pile of small, low-grade stones with his forefinger.

'No, it's not,' he agreed. 'But every little bit helps.'

They climbed back into the Beechcraft and flew on northwards.

Now they passed over areas where the desert had been scratched and torn over wide areas.

The tractors had left centipede tracks in the soft earth.

'Ours?' asked Tracey.

'I wish they were. We'd have no worries then. No, all this belongs to the big Company.'

Johnny checked his watch, automatically comparing the progress of the flight to his estimates. Then he lifted the microphone from the R/T set.

'Alexandra Bay Control. This is Zulu Sugar Peter Tango Baker.'

He knew that they had him on the radar plot, and were watching him–not because they were worried about his safety, but because he was now over the Proclaimed Diamond Area of South West Africa–that vast jealously guarded tract of nothingness.

The radio crackled back at him instantly, demanding his permit number, his flight plan, querying his intentions and his destination.

Having convinced Control of his innocence, and received their permission to continue his flight, he switched off his R/T set, and grimaced at Tracey.

He felt ruffled by this small brush with Olympus. He knew that most of it was professional jealousy. He smarted under the knowledge that he was working ground that the big Company would despise as not sufficiently lucrative to bother about.

Sometimes Johnny dreamed about discovering a fault in a land title, or an error in a survey that had been casually performed seventy years previously before the value of this parched denuded earth had been realized. He imagined himself being able to claim the mineral rights to a few square miles plumb in the middle of the big Company's richest field. He shivered voluptuously at the thought, and Tracey looked at him inquiringly.

He shook his head, then this line of thought took him on to a further destination.

'Tracey, I am going to show you something.'

He banked the aircraft, crossing the coastline with its creamy lines of surf running in on the freezing white sands of the beach.

'What?' She was expectant, receptive to the new tone in his voice.

'Thunderbolt and Suicide,' he said, and she made a small grimace of incomprehension.

'There.' He pointed ahead, and through the light smoke of the sea mist she saw them show bare–white and shiny, like a pair of albino whales.

'Islands?' she asked. 'What's so special about them?'

'Their shape,' he answered. 'See how they lie like the mouth of a funnel, with a small opening between them.'

She nodded. The two islands were almost identical twins, two narrow wedges of smooth granite, each about three miles long, lying in a chevron pattern to each other–but not quite meeting at the peak. The mighty Atlantic swells bore up from the south and ran into the mouth of the funnel. Finding themselves trapped in this granite corral, the swells reared up wildly and hurled themselves on the cliffs in massive bomb-bursts of spray before streaming out in white foam through the narrow opening between the two islands.

'I can see how Thunderbolt gets its name.' Tracey eyed the wild booming surf with awe. 'But how about Suicide?'

'The old guano collectors must have called it that, after they tried landing on it.'

'Guano,' Tracey nodded. 'That accounts for the colour.'

Johnny put the Beechcraft into a shallow dive, hurtling in low over the green water. Ahead of them the seabirds rose in alarm, streaming in a long black smear into the sky, the cormorants and gannets whose excreta through the ages had painted the rocks that glaring white.

As they flashed through the gap below the level of the cliffs, Tracey exclaimed, 'There's some sort of tower there–look! In the back of the island.'

'Yes,' Johnny agreed. 'It's an old wooden gantry they used for loading the guano into the longboats.'

He pulled the Beechcraft up in a climbing turn, gaining height to look down on the two islands.

'Do you see where the surf comes through the gap? Now look beneath the surface, can you see the reefs under the water?'

They lay like long dark shadows through the green water, at right angles to the drift of white foam.

'Well, you are looking at the most beautifully designed natural diamond trap in the world.'

'Explain,' Tracey invited.

'Down there,' he pointed south, 'are the big rivers. Some of them dried up a million years ago, but not before they had spat the diamonds they carried into the sea. The tide and the wind has been working them up towards the north for all these ages. Throwing some of them back on the beach but carrying others up this way.'

He levelled the Beechcraft out and resumed their interrupted flight northwards.

'Then suddenly they run up against Thunderbolt and Suicide. They are concentrated and squeezed through the gap, then they are confronted by a series of sharp reefs across their path. They cannot cross them–they just settle down in the gullies and wait for someone to come and suck them out.'

He sighed like a man crossed in love.

'My God, Tracey. The smell of those diamonds reeks in my nostrils. I can almost see the shine of them through a hundred and sixty feet of water.'

He shook himself as though awakening from a dream.

'I've been in the game all my life, Tracey. I've got the "feel", the same as a water-diviner has. I tell you with absolute certainty there are millions of carats of diamonds lying in the crotch of Thunderbolt and Suicide.'

'What's the snag?' Tracey asked.

'The concession was granted twenty years ago to the big Company.'

'By whom?'

'The Government of South West Africa.'

'Why aren't they mining it?'

'They will–sometime in the next twenty years. They aren't in any hurry.'

They lapsed into silence, staring ahead, though once Johnny clucked his tongue irritably and shook his head–still thinking about Thunderbolt and Suicide.

To distract him Tracey asked, 'Where do they come from in the first place–the diamonds?'

'Volcanic pipes,' Johnny answered. 'There are more than a hundred known pipes in Southern Africa. Not all yield stones, but then some do. New Rush–Finsch–Dutoitspan–Bulfontein–Premier–Mwadui. Great oval-shaped treasure chests, filled with the legendary "Blue Ground"–the mother lode of the diamond.'

'There are no pipes here–surely?' Tracey turned towards him in her seat.

'No,' Johnny agreed. 'We are after the alluvial stones. Some of the ancient pipes exploded with the force of a hydrogen bomb, spraying diamonds over hundreds of square miles. Others were submarine pipes that discharged their treasure into the restless sea. Others of the more passive volcanic pipes were simply eroded away by wind and water and the diamonds were exposed.'

'Then they were washed down into the sea?' she guessed.

Johnny nodded. 'That's right. Over millions of years they were moved infinitely slowly by landslides, floods, rivers and rainwater. Where all the other pebbles and stones were abraded and worn away to nothingness–the diamonds, four hundred times harder than any other natural substance on earth, were unmarked. So at last they reached the sea and mingled with the others from the submarine pipes, to be laid down by wave action on the beaches, or finally to come up against a place like Thunderbolt and Suicide.'

Tracy opened her mouth to ask another question, but Johnny interrupted.

'Here we are. There is Cartridge Bay.' And he pushed the nose of the aircraft down slightly. It was more a lagoon than a bay. Separated from the sea by a narrow sandspit, it spread away into the treeless waste, an enormous extent of quite shallow water in tranquil contrast to the unchecked surf that burst on the sandpit. There was a deep water entrance through the sandspit, and a channel that was clearly defined in darker green from the air. The channel meandered across the lagoon to where a cluster of lonely whitewashed buildings sprang up on the edge of the desert.

Johnny banked steeply towards the buildings, and below them flocks of black and white pelican and pink flamingo rose in panic from the shadows.

Johnny landed and taxied across to the waiting Land-Rover with the white lightning insignia of Van Der Byl Diamonds painted on its side.

Lugging the cool box that contained their lunch, Johnny led Tracey to the vehicle and introduced her to his foreman. Then they climbed in and went bumping down to the buildings of the lagoon. Johnny received from his foreman a report on the progress of the work. The buildings had been abandoned by the defunct Atlantis Diamond Company. Johnny was renovating them to serve as a base for the *Kingfisher*; a rest and recreation centre for the crew, a radio centre, a refuelling depot and a workshop to handle running maintenance and repairs. In addition he was putting a jetty out into the lagoon for the converted seventy-foot pilchard trawler that would be *Kingfisher*'s service boat–acting as tender and ferry.

They ran an extensive inspection of the base. Johnny was pleased with the interest Tracey showed, and he enjoyed answering her questions for his own enthusiasm was high. It was nearly two o'clock before they had finished.

'How are the watchtowers coming?' Johnny asked.

'All up, ready and waiting.'

And suddenly Johnny had a two-edged inspiration.

'Might as well go and have a look.' He made it casual.

'Okay, I'll fetch the Land-Rover,' the foreman agreed.

'I know the way.' Johnny put him off. 'You go and get your lunch.'

'It's no trouble–' the foreman began, caught Johnny's frown, cut himself short, then glanced at Tracey. 'Yeah! Sure! Fine! Okay–here are the keys.' He handed Johnny the Land-Rover keys, and disappeared into his own quarters.

Johnny checked the grub box, and they climbed into the open Land-Rover.

'Where are we going?' Tracey asked.

'Inspect the watchtowers along the sandspit.'

'Watchtowers?'

'We've put up a line of fifty-foot wooden towers along the beach. From them we will take continual bearings on *Kingfisher* when she is working offshore. By radio we will be able at any time to give her the exact position over the bottom to within a few feet, as a check to the computer.'

'My, you are clever.' Tracey fluttered her eyelashes at him in mock admiration.

'Silly wench,' said Johnny, and let out the clutch. He swung down past the radio shack onto the hard wet sand at the edge of the lagoon; accelerating he hit second then third and they went away around the curve of the lagoon, headed towards the great yellow wind-carved dunes that lined the coast.

Tracey stood up on her seat, clutching the edge of the windscreen, and the wind snatched at her hair. She pulled the retaining thong from it, and shook it out into a shiny black flag that snapped and snaked behind her.

'Look! Look!' she cried as the flocks of startled flamingoes lurched into flight, streaming white and pink and black over the glossy silver water.

Johnny laughed with her, and swung the Land-Rover towards the dunes.

'Hold on!' he shouted, and she clung to the windscreen, shrieking in delicious terror as they flew up the steep side of a dune, spinning a cloud of sand from the rear wheels and then dropped over the crest in a stomach-churning swoop. They crossed the sandspit and hit the beach, racing along it, playing tag with the waves that shot up the sand.

Five miles up the beach Johnny parked above the high watermark and they ate cold chicken and drank a bottle of chilled white wine sitting side by side in the sand, leaning against the seat cushions from the Land-Rover. Then they went down to the edge of the sea to wash the chicken grease from their fingers.

'Yipes! It's cold.' Tracey scooped a double handful of seawater. Then she looked at Johnny and her expression became devilish.

He backed away, but not quickly enough. The icy water hit him in the chest, and he gasped.

'War!' It was their childhood cry.

Tracey whirled and went off long-legged along the beach, with Johnny pounding after her. She sensed him gaining on her, and shouted.

'It was a mistake! I didn't mean it! I'm sorry!'

At the last moment as he reached out to grip her shoulder, she jinked and ran knee-deep into the sea. Turning at bay to face him, she kicked a spray of water at him, shouting defiance and laughter.

'All right, come on then!'

Braving the flying spray, he reached her and picked her up kicking and struggling and waded out waist deep.

'No, no–please. Johnny. I give in–I'll do anything.'

At that moment a freak wave, bigger and stronger than the others, knocked Johnny's legs out from under him. They went under, and were rolled up the beach, to stagger out, completely soaked, clinging together, helpless with laughter.

They stood beside the Land-Rover trying to wring the water out of their clothing.

'Oh, you beast!' sobbed Tracey through her laughter. Her hair was a sodden mass, and drops of sea water clung in her eyelashes like dew.

Johnny took her in his arms and kissed her, and they stopped laughing.

She went loose against his chest, her eyes tightly closed and her lips, salty with sea water, opened against his.

The radio telephone in the Land-Rover beside them began to bleat fretfully, flashing its little red warning light.

They drew apart slowly, reluctantly, and stared at each other with dazed, bemused eyes.

Johnny reached into the Land-Rover, unhooked the microphone and lifted it to his lips.

'Yes?' his voice cracked. He cleared his throat and repeated, 'Yes?'

The foreman's voice was distorted and scratchy through the speaker.

'Mr Lance, I'm sorry to have–' he was clearly about to finish '–interrupted you.' But he stopped abruptly, and began again. 'It's just that I think you should know we've had a gale warning. Northerly gale building up quickly. If you want to get back to Cape Town you had better get airborne before it hits us–otherwise you could be shut in for days.'

'Thanks. We'll be back right away.' He hung up, and Tracey smiled shakily. Her voice was also husky and unnatural-sounding.

'And a damn good thing, too!'

Tracey's hair was still damp, and the borrowed polo-neck jersey swamped her. The grey trousers were also borrowed, rolled up to show her bare feet.

She sat very quietly and thoughtfully in the passenger seat of the Beechcraft. Far below them a small fishing vessel lay with a white cloud of seabirds hovering over it, and she watched it with exaggerated attention. There was a heavy feeling of restraint between them now, they could no longer meet each other's eyes.

'Pilchard trawler.' Johnny noticed her gaze.

'Yes,' said Tracey, and they were silent again.

'Nothing happened.' Johnny spoke again gruffly.

'No,' she agreed. 'Nothing happened.' Then shyly she reached out and took his hand. Lightly she rubbed the stump of his missing finger.

'Still friends?' she asked.

'Still friends.' He grinned at her with relief, and they flew on towards Cape Town.

Hugo Kramer watched the aircraft through his binoculars, balancing easily against the roll and pitch of the bridge.

'Police patrol?' asked the man at the helm beside him.

'No,' Hugo replied without lowering the glasses. 'Red and white twin Beechcraft. Registration ZA–PTB. Private aircraft, probably one of the diamond companies.'

He lowered the glasses, and crossed to the wing of the bridge. 'Anyway, we are well outside territorial waters.'

The drone of the aircraft engine faded away, and Hugo transferred his attention to the frantic activity on the deck below him.

The trawler, *Wild Goose,* lay heeled over under the weight of fish that filled her purse seine-net; at least a hundred tons of seething silver pilchards bulging the net out alongside the trawler into a round bag fifty feet across. While above it a shrieking canopy of sea birds swirled and wheeled and dived, frantic with greed.

Three of the crew on a scoop-net which hung from the overhead derrick were dipping the fish out of the net, swinging a ton of fish at each scoop over the side, and dropping them like a silver cloudburst into the trawler's hold. The donkey engine on the winch clattered harshly in time to their movements.

Hugo watched with satisfaction. He had a good crew, and although the fishing was only a cover for the *Wild Goose*–yet Hugo took pride in his Teutonic thoroughness which dictated that the cover should be as solid as possible. In any case, all profits from fishing were for his personal account. It was part of the agreement with the Ring.

He packed the binoculars carefully into their leather case, and hung them behind the chartroom door. Then he clambered swiftly down the steel ladder to deck level, moving with catlike grace despite the heavy rubber hip boots he wore.

'I'll take her for a while,' he told the man at the winch controls. He spoke in Afrikaans, but his accent was shaded with the German of South West Africa.

Wide-shouldered under the blue fisherman's jersey, he worked with smooth economic movements. His hands on the winch controls were rough and reddened by wind and sun, for his skin was too fair to weather. The skin of his face also was red, and half-boiled, peeling so there were pinky raw places on his cheeks and black scabs on his lips.

The hair that hung out under his cap was white as bleached sisal, and his eyelashes were thick and colourless, giving him a mild near-sighted look. His eyes were the palest cornflower blue, yet without being weak and watery as those of most albinos; they were slitted now, as he judged the roll and dip of the boat–engaging the clutch to meet the movement, or pulling on the drum brake.

'Skipper!' A shout from the bridge above him.

'Ja.' Hugo did not allow his attention to waver as he replied. 'What is it?'

'Gale warning! There is a northerly bluster building up.'

And Hugo grinned, pulled on the brake and shut the throttle.

'All right, clean up. Cut the purse rope, let the fish go free.'

He turned and swarmed up the ladder to the bridge, and went to his chart table.

'It will take us three hours to get in position,' he muttered aloud, leaning over the chart, then he barged out onto the wing of the bridge again to chase up his crew.

They had cut the purse rope on the net, allowing the net to fall open like a woman's skirt, and the fish were pouring out, a dark spreading stain through the gap. Two men had the pressure hose on, washing loose fish from the deck into the sea, others were slamming the hatch-covers closed.

Within forty minutes *Wild Goose* was running south under full throttle to take up her waiting station.

The diamond coast of South Western Africa lies in the belt of the Trades. The prevailing wind is the south-easter, but periodically the wind system is completely reversed and a gale comes out of the north, off the land.

It is a Sirocco-type wind like the 'Khamsin' of the Libyan desert, or the 'Simoom' of Tripoli.

It was the same searing dry wind out of the desert, filling the sky with brooding dust and sand clouds, smothering everything beneath a hellish pall like the smoke from a great battlefield.

The dust clouds were part of the design, the Ring had taken account of them when they planned the system–for the north wind lifted into the sky such a quantity of mica dust that the radar screens of the diamond security police were cluttered and confused, throwing up phantom echoes and making it impossible to pick up the presence of a small airborne object.

Turn Back Point was three miles inland, and sixty miles north of the Orange river. The name was given by the first travellers, and expressed their views on continuing a journey northwards. Those old travellers had not known that they stood in the centre of an elevated marine terrace, an ancient beach now lifted above the level of the sea, and that it was the richest prospect of an area so diamond-rich that it was to be ring-fenced, patrolled by jeep and dog and aircraft, guarded by gun and radar, a laager so secure that a man leaving it would have to submit to X-ray, and take nothing out with him but the clothes he wore.

At Turn Back Point was one of the four big separation plants where all the gravel from the big Company's working from miles around was processed. The settlement was comparatively large, with plant, workshops and stores, and accommodation for five hundred men and their families. Yet not all the Company's efforts to make it attractive and livable could alter the fact that Turn Back Point was a hell-hole in a savage and forbidding desert.

Now with the north wind blowing, what had been unpleasant before was almost unbearable. The buildings were tightly sealed, even the joints around the windows and doors were plugged with cloth or paper–and yet the red dust seeped in to powder the furniture, the desks, the bed linen, even the interior of the refrigerators, with a thin gritty film. It settled in the hair, was sugary between the teeth, clogged the nostrils–and with it came that searing heat that seemed to dry the moisture from the eyeballs.

Outside the dust was a red glittering fog which reduced visibility to a dozen yards. Men who were forced out into that choking dry soup wore dust goggles to protect their eyes, and the mica dust covered their clothing with a shiny coating that glittered even in that dun light.

Beyond the settlement a man moved now through the fog, carrying a small cylindrical object. He leaned forward into the wind, moving slowly away into the desert. He reached a shallow depression and went down into it. Setting his burden on the sand, he rested a moment. Then he knelt over the cylinder. He appeared monstrous under his leather jacket and cap, his face covered by goggles and a scarf.

The fibre-glass cylinder was painted with yellow fluorescent paint. At one end was a transparent plastic bubble which housed an electric globe, at the other end was a folded envelope of rubberized nylon material attached to the cylinder by a stainless steel coupling, and linked to the coupling was a small steel bottle of hydrogen gas. The whole assembly was eighteen inches long, and three inches in diameter. It weighed a few ounces more than fifteen pounds.

Within the cylinder were two separate compartments. The larger contained a highly sophisticated piece of transistorized electronic equipment which would transmit a homing signal, light or extinguish its lamp on long-distance radio signal command, and also at command it would control the inflow of hydrogen gas into the nylon balloon through the connecting coupling.

The smaller compartment held simply a sealed plastic container into which were packed twenty-seven diamonds. The smallest of these stones weighed fourteen carats, the largest a formidable fifty-six carats. Each of these stones had been selected by experts for colour, brilliance, and perfection. These were all first-water diamonds, and once they were cut they would fetch in the open market between seven hundred thousand and a million pounds–depending on the skill of the cutting.

There were four members of the Ring at Turn Back Point. Two of them were long service and trusted diamond sorters employed behind the guarded walls of the processing plant. They worked together, to check each other, for the Company operated a system of employee double check–which was completely useless when there was collusion. These men selected the finest stones and got them out of the plant.

The third member of the Ring was a diesel mechanic in the Company workshops. It was his job to receive and assemble the equipment which arrived concealed in a marked drum of tractor grease. He also packed the stones into the cylinder and passed it on to the man who was now kneeling out in the desert, preparing to launch the cylinder into the swirling dust fog.

His final check completed, the man stood up and went to the lip of the depression and peered out into the dust storm. At last he seemed satisfied, and hurried back to the yellow cylinder. With an incisive twist of the bevelled release ring he opened the valve on the bottle of hydrogen gas. There was a snakelike hiss, and the nylon balloon began to inflate. The folds of material crackled as they filled. The balloon lifted, eager to be gone, but the man restrained it with difficulty until the balloon was smooth and tight. He let go, and the balloon with its dangling cylinder leapt into the sky, and almost instantly was gone into the dust clouds.

The man stood with his face lifted to the dark furnace-red sky. His goggles glinted blindly, but his attitude was one of triumph, and when he turned away he walked lightly with the step of a man freshly released from danger.

'One more package,' he promised himself. 'Just one more, and I'll pull out. Buy that farm on the Olifants river, do a bit of fishing, take a shooting trip every year–'

He was still dreaming when he reached the parked Land-Rover and climbed into the driver's seat. He started the engine, switched on the headlights, and drove slowly down the track towards the settlement.

The sign on the rear of the departing Land-Rover was in white paint so that it showed clearly through the haze of red dust.

'SECURITY PATROL', it read.

Wild Goose lay on station, with her diesels throbbing softly ticking over to hold her head into the wind. Even twenty miles out at sea the wind was searing hot and the occasional splatter of spray on Hugo's face was refreshing.

He stood in the corner of the bridge where he could watch the sea and the helmsman, but he was anxious. *Wild Goose* had been lying on station for fifteen hours now, during ten of which the norther had howled dismally through her rigging.

He was always anxious at the beginning of a pick-up. There was so much that could have gone wrong, anything from a police sweep to a tiny electrical fault in the equipment.

'What time is it, Hansie?' he shouted and the helmsman glanced up at the chronometer above his head.

'Three minutes after six, skipper.'

'Dark in half an hour,' Hugo grunted disgustedly, slitted those pale-lashed eyes into the wind once more, then shrugged and ambled back into the bridge house.

He stopped at the console beside his chart table. Even to an experienced eye the machine was an ordinary 'Fish-Finder', an adaptation of the old wartime anti-submarine device, the ASDIC, to the more prosaic business of plotting the depth and position of the pilchard shoals beneath the surface.

However, this model had undergone a costly and specialized conversion. The Ring had flown an expert out from Japan to do the work.

Now the set hummed softly, its control panel lit soft green by internal light, but the sound was neutral, and the circular glass screen was blank.

'You want some coffee, Hansie?' Hugo asked the old coloured man at the wheel. His crew were handpicked, loyal and trusted. They had to be–one loud mouth could blow a multi-million pound business.

'Ja dankie, skipper.' The old man creased his weather-battered face in appreciation, and Hugo shouted down the companionway to the galley.

'Cooky, how's it for a pot of coffee?'

But the reply was lost, for at that moment the console came to life dramatically. A row of lights blinked on above the control panel, the muted hum changed to a rapid beep-beep signal, and the screen glowed ghostly green.

'She's up!' Hugo shouted his relief, and ran to the set. His first mate rushed through from his cabin behind the bridge, tucking his shirt into unbuttoned trousers, his face puckered with sleep.

'About bloody time,' he blurted, groggily.

'Take over from Hansie,' Hugo told him, and he settled into the padded seat in front of the ASDIC set.

'Right, bring her round two points to port and open her up.'

The *Wild Goose* swung her head into the sea, and her motion changed from easy swoop and glide to a crabbing butting lunge, and the spray burst over the glass of the bridge.

Sitting before the console Hugo was tracking the flight of the balloon and keeping *Wild Goose* on an interception course.

Driven by the forty-knot norther the balloon crossed the coastline, climbing swiftly to three thousand feet. Hugo manipulated the knob on the console which sent the balloon a command to release gas and maintain altitude. Her response was recorded immediately on the screen.

'Good,' Hugo whispered. 'Good girl.' Then louder. 'Bring her around a bit, Oscar–the balloon is drifting to the south.'

For twenty minutes more they butted through the swells.

'Okay,' Hugo broke the silence. 'I'm going to ditch her.' He twisted the knob clockwise slowly, expelling all the gas from the nylon balloon.

'Ja. That's it. She's down now.' He looked out of the window above the set. The dust-laden clouds had brought the night on prematurely. It was dark outside, with a low black ceiling through which no star showed.

Hugo turned his attention back to the set.

'That's it, Oscar. You're right on course. Hold her there.'

Then he glanced across at old Hansie and another younger crewman. They were sitting patiently on the bench against the far bulkhead. Both of them were clad in full oilskins, shiny yellow plastic from head to ankle, with gumboots below that.

'Okay, Hansie,' Hugo nodded. 'You can get up into the bows. We are only a mile or so away now.'

They climbed down onto the wave-swept deck, and Hugo watched them scuttling forward between each green burst of water and crouching in the bows, both of them ducking each time another swell poured over the top of them, their yellow plastic suits showing clearly in the murky deck lights.

'I'm going to switch on now,' Hugo warned the helm. 'We should have her visual.'

'Right.' Oscar peered ahead, and Hugo flicked a switch on the panel, commanding the balloon to turn on her guide light.

Almost immediately there was a shout from Oscar.

'There she is. Dead ahead!'

Hugo jumped up and ran forward. It took a few seconds for his eyes to adjust, then he made out the tiny red firefly of light ahead of them in the vast blackness of sea and sky. It showed for a second, then was gone in the trough of the next wave.

'I'll take her.' Hugo replaced Oscar at the wheel. 'You get on the spotlight.'

The beam of the spotlight was a solid white shaft through the darkness. The fluorescent yellow paint of the cylinder glowed in the circle of the spot.

Hugo laid *Wild Goose* up wind of the cylinder, and then allowed her to drift down gently on it. Hansie and his assistant were ready with the twenty-foot boat-hook.

Delicately Hugo manœuvred down over the bobbing yellow cylinder, and grunted with satisfaction as the boat-hook slipped through the recovery ring and the cylinder was hauled in over the bows.

He watched while the two dripping oilskin-clad figures clambered back up the ladder into the wheelhouse, and laid the cylinder on the chart table.

'Good! Good!' Hugo slapped their backs heartily. 'Now go and get dry–both of you.' They climbed down the companionway, and Hugo handed the wheel over to Oscar.

'Home!' he instructed him. 'As quick as you like.' And he carried the cylinder through into his cabin.

Sitting at the fold-down table in his cabin Hugo unscrewed the lower section of the cylinder and took out the plastic container. He opened it and spilled the contents out on the table-top.

He whistled softly, and picked up the biggest stone. Although he was no expert he knew instinctively that it was a brilliant of exceptional quality. Even the roughness of its exterior could not mask the fire in its depths.

To him it was worthless, there was nowhere he could market a stone like that. There was no temptation to take it out of the Ring–all it would mean for him was fifteen years at hard labour.

The Ring was based on this mutual reliance, no one part of it could function without all the others–yet each part was self-contained and watertight. Only one man knew all its parts, and nobody knew who that one man was.

From the drawer beside him Hugo took out his tools and set them on the table. He lit the spirit stove and set the pot of paraffin wax on the gimbal above it to heat.

Then he poured the diamonds into a shiny metal can. It was the type of ordinary commercial can used for packing and preserving foodstuffs.

Balancing easily against the ship's motion, he lifted the pot from the stove, and poured the steaming liquid wax over the diamonds, filling the can to rim level.

The wax was cooled and solidified quickly, turning opaque and white. The stones were now incorporated in a cake of wax that would prevent them rattling, and would give the sealed can authentic weight.

Hugo lit a cigarette and crossed the cabin to look out into the wheelhouse. The helmsman winked at him and Hugo smiled.

He went back to the table, the can was cool enough to handle. He placed the circular lid over it, and moved to the portable Jenny bolted to a chest of drawers. Carefully he clinched the lid into place, his eyes squinting at the smoke from the cigarette that dangled from his lips.

Satisfied at last he set the sealed can on the table, while he went to where his jacket hung on the door. From the inside pocket he pulled out a manilla envelope, then from the envelope he drew a printed, colour-screened label. He came back to the bench and meticulously pasted the label around the can. On the label was a highly glamorized artist's conception of a leaping pilchard, making it look like a Scottish salmon.

'Pilchards in Tomato Sauce.' Hugo read the label aloud, as he leaned back to admire his work. 'A product of South West Africa.' He smiled with satisfaction and began packing his equipment away.

'How much?' The foreman of the fish pump called across the narrowing gap between *Wild Goose* and the jetty.

'About fifty tons,' Hugo shouted back. 'Then the norther chased us home.'

'Ja. None of the boats stayed out.' The foreman watched his gang secure the mooring ropes, and swing the hose of the vacuum pump over *Wild Goose*'s hold to begin pumping out the pilchards.

'Take over, Oscar.' Hugo picked up his jacket and cap. 'I'll be back tomorrow.' He jumped down onto the jetty and strode down towards the canning factory with its awesome stink of pilchard oil. His jacket was slung over his shoulder, one finger hooked through the tag.

He went down the alley between the boiler rooms and the fish-drying plant, across a wide yard where the bags of fish meal were piled to the height of a double-storey building. He turned in through the double doors of the cavernous warehouse filled to roof height with cardboard cartons, each stencilled with the words:

1 gross cans.	Pilchards in tomato sauce.
Consign to:	Vee Dee Bee Agencies Ltd, 32 Bermondsey Street, London SE1.

He went to the cubicle that served the warehouse storeman as an office.

'Hello, Hugo. Good trip?' The storeman was Hugo's brother-in-law.

'Fifty ton.' Hugo hung his coat casually on the hook behind the door. 'I've got to take a leak,' he said, and went to the latrine across the floor of the warehouse.

He came back, and drank a cup of tea with his brother-in-law. Then he stood and said, 'Jeannie will be waiting.'

'Give her my love.'

'She don't need yours. She's going to get plenty of mine!' Hugo winked, and took his coat from the hook. It was lighter now, the can was gone from the pocket.

He went through the main gates of the harbour, exchanging a casual greeting with the customs officer, and went to the battered early model convertible in the car park.

He kissed the girl at the driving-wheel, threw his coat on the back seat and climbed in over the door.

'You drive,' he told her, grinning. 'I want both hands free.'

She squeaked and pulled his hand out of her skirts.

'Can't you wait till we get home?'

'I've been at sea five days and I'm hungry as hell.'

'You're a caution, you are.' She laughed at him and started the car.

This was Sergio Caporetti, the man Johnny had chosen to captain the *Kingfisher*. He was a round man, the same shape as a snowman. He filled the doorway of Johnny's office, and his great belly bulged into the room ahead of him. His face was round also, like a baby's–but he had beautiful dark Italian eyes fringed with thick lashes like a girl's.

'Come in, Sergio,' Johnny greeted him. 'Nice to see you.'

The Italian crossed the room deceptively quickly, and Johnny's hand was completely engulfed by the enormous hairy paw.

'So, at last we are ready,' Sergio grunted. 'Three months I sit on bum–do nothing. Look at me–' He slapped his belly with a sound like a pistol shot. '–fat! No good.'

'Well, not quite ready.' Johnny qualified the statement. He was flying Sergio and his crew over to England well ahead of time. He wanted the big Italian to have plenty of opportunity to study and get to know the revolutionary new equipment with which *Kingfisher* was fitted. Then when the vessel was ready for sea, Sergio would sail her out to Africa.

'Sit down, Sergio. Let's go over the crew list–'

When Sergio left an hour later, Johnny went as far as the lift with him.

'If you have any problems phone me, Sergio.'

'Si.' Sergio shook hands. 'Don't worry–Caporetti is in charge. All is well.'

On his way back Johnny stopped at the reception desk.

'Is Mrs Hartford in today?' he asked one of the little receptionists, and both of them replied in chorus like Tweedledum and Tweedledee.

'No, Mr Lance.'

'Has she phoned at all to say where she is?'

'No, Mr Lance.'

Tracey had disappeared. Five days now there had been no sign of her, her new office was deserted and unused. Johnny was worried and angry. He was worried that she had gone on another binge, and he was angry because he missed her.

He was scowling ferociously as he went back into his office.

'Goodness me.' Lettie Pienaar stood beside his desk with a batch of mail in her hand. 'We do look happy. Here's something to cheer you.'

She handed him a postcard with a colour picture of the Eiffel Tower. It was the first word from Ruby since she had left. Johnny read it quickly.

'Paris–' he said, '–is fun, it seems.' He tossed the card onto the desk and plunged back into the day's work.

He worked late, stopped at the steakhouse to eat, then drove back to the silent house in Bishopscourt.

The crunch of tyres on the gravel drive and headlights flashing across the bedroom wall woke him. He sat up in bed as the front-doorbell began a series of urgent peals and he switched on the bedside light. Two o'clock–Christ!

He pulled a dressing gown over his nudity and tottered down the passage, switching on lights as he went. The doorbell kept ringing.

He turned the front-door key. The door flew open and Tracey came in like a strong wind, clutching a briefcase to her chest.

'Where the hell have you been?' Johnny was suddenly fully awake, angry and relieved.

'Johnny! Johnny!' She was dancing with excitement, incoherent, her cheeks flaming and eyes shining. 'I've got them–at least, it, both of them.'

'Where have you been?' Johnny was not to be so easily sidetracked, and with an obvious effort Tracey brought her excitement under control, but she was still smiling and gave the impression of humming like an electric motor.

'Come.' She took his hand and dragged him into the lounge. 'Get yourself a large whisky and sit down,' she ordered, imperious as a queen.

'I don't want a whisky, and I don't–'

'You'll need one,' she interrupted, and went to the open liquor cabinet, poured a massive whisky into a crystal glass, squirted soda into it, and brought it back to Johnny.

'Tracey, what the hell is going on?'

'Please, Johnny. It's so wonderful, don't spoil it for me. Just sit there, please!'

Johnny sank reluctantly into the chair, and Tracey slipped the catch on her briefcase and drew out a sheaf of documents. She stood in the centre of the floor, and took up the pose of a Victorian actress.

'This–' she explained, '–is a translation from the original German of a proclamation by Governor in Council dated May 3rd 1899 and issued at Windhoek. I will leave out the preamble and go straight to the meat.'

She cleared her throat and began reading:

'In consideration of the sum of 10,000 marks which is hereby paid and received, the rights to mine, win, recover, collect or carry away all metals, whether base or precious, stones whether base, semi-precious or precious, minerals, guano, vegetation and other substances organic or inorganic for a period of Nine Hundred and Ninety-Nine years is granted to Messrs Farben, Hendryck and Mosenthal SA, Guano Merchants of 14 Bergenstrasse, Windhoek, in respect of a circular area ten kilometres in radius whose centre shall be a point situate at the highest elevation of the island lying on latitude 23° 15′ South and longitude 15° 12′ East.'

Tracey paused and looked at Johnny. He was frozen, stony-faced, staring at her with all his attention. She went on quickly, gabbling it out.

'All the old German mineral concessions and rights were ratified by the Union Parliament when the Union of South Africa took over the mandate after the Great War.'

He nodded, unable to speak. Tracey's smile kept breaking out.

'That concession still has all the force of law behind it. The grant of any subsequent rights is invalid, and although the original grant was mainly for the recovery of guano–yet it covers precious stones also.'

Again Johnny nodded, and Tracey put the document at the bottom of the sheaf of papers in her hand.

'The concession Company, Farben, Hendryck and Mosenthal SA, is still in existence. The Company's only remaining asset, apart from any long-forgotten concessions, is an old building at 14 Bergenstrasse, Windhoek.'

Tracey seemed to change the subject suddenly.

'You asked me where I have been, Johnny. Well I've been to Windhoek, and over most of the worst roads in South West Africa.

'The Farben, Hendryck and Mosenthal Company is owned by the brothers Hendryck, a couple of karakul fur farmers. They are a pair of horrible old men, and when I saw them slitting the throats of those poor little Persian lambs just to prevent the fur uncurling, well–' Tracey paused, and gulped. 'Well, I didn't explain to them about the concession. I just offered to buy the Company, and they asked twenty thousand and I said "sign", and they signed and I left them chuckling with glee. They thought they'd been terribly clever. There! It's all yours!'

Tracey handed the Agreement to Johnny and while he read it she went on.

'I made the Agreement in the name of Van Der Byl Diamonds, I signed it as a Director–I hope you don't mind.'

'Christ!' Johnny took a long deep swallow of whisky, then set the glass down and stood up.

'Mind?' he repeated. 'You bring me the concession to Thunderbolt and Suicide–and ask me if I mind.'

He reached for her, and eagerly she went to him.

'Tracey, you're wonderful.' They hugged each other ecstatically, and Johnny swung her off her feet. Without either of them planning it they were suddenly lying, still in each other's arms, on the couch. Then they were kissing, and the laughter dwindled into small murmurs and incoherent sounds.

Tracey pulled away from him at last, and slipped off the couch. She stood in the centre of the floor. Her breathing was ragged. Her hair was a dark tangle.

'Whoa! That's enough.'

'Tracey.' He started up from the couch, wild for her, but she held him at the full stretch of her arms, her hands flat on his chest, backing away in front of him.

'No, Johnny, no!' She shook her head urgently. 'Listen to me.'

He stopped. The wild look faded from his eyes.

'Look, Johnny, God knows I'm no saint, but–well, I don't want us to–well, not on a couch in some other woman's house. That's not how I want it to be.'

Benedict eased the big honey-coloured Bentley out of the traffic stream that clogged Bermondsey Street and turned into the gates of the warehouse. He parked beside the loading bank and climbed out.

As he pulled off his gloves, he glanced along the bank. Mountains of goods were stacked ready for distribution. Cases of Cape wine and spirits, canned fruit in brown cartons, canned fish, forty-gallon drums of fish oil, bundles of raw hides stiff as boards, and cases of indefinable goods–all of it the produce of Southern Africa.

Vee Dee Bee Agencies had grown out of all recognition in the ten years since Benedict had launched it.

Benedict climbed the steps to the bank three at a time, and strode down between the towering stacks of goods that reached up into the murk of the high ceiling. He walked with the assurance of a man on his own ground, the skirts of his overcoat swirling about his knees, broad-shouldered and tall. The storeman and porters greeted him deferentially as he passed, and when he entered the main office there was a stirring and whispering among the ranks of typists as though a wind had blown through a forest.

The Managing Director hurried out of his office to greet Benedict and usher him in.

'How are you, Mr van der Byl? There's tea coming now.' And he stood behind Benedict to take his coat.

The meeting lasted half an hour, Benedict reading through the weekly sales and cost reports, querying an item here, remarking on a figure with pleasure or displeasure as it deserved. Many people watching him work would have been startled. This was not the indolent playboy they thought they knew, this was a hard-eyed businessman coldly and unemotionally milking the maximum profit from his enterprise.

There would have been others who wondered where Benedict had found the capital to finance a business of this magnitude, especially if they had known that he owned the premises, and that Vee Dee Bee Agencies was by no means his only stake in the world of business. He had not received money from his father–the Old Man had not believed Benedict capable of successfully negotiating the purchase of a pound of butter.

The meeting ended, and Benedict stood up and shrugged on his overcoat, while his Managing Director went to the grey steel safe in the corner, tumbled the combination and swung the heavy door open.

'The shipment arrived yesterday,' he explained as he reached into the safe and brought out the can. 'On the SS *Loch Elsinore* from Walvis Bay.'

He handed the can to Benedict, who examined it briefly, smiling a little at the painting of the leaping fish and the lettering 'Pilchards in Tomato Sauce'.

'Thank you.' He slipped the can into his briefcase, and the Managing Director walked with him back to the Bentley.

Benedict left the Bentley in a garage in Broadwick Street, and walked through the jostle of Soho until he reached the grimy brick building behind the square. He pressed the bell opposite the card that read Aaron Cohen, Manufacturing Jeweller, and when the door opened he climbed the stairs to the top and fourth floor. Again he rang, and after a while an eye peered at him through the peephole–but the door opened almost immediately.

'Hello, Mr van der Byl. Come in! Come in!' The young doorman welcomed him in and locked the door behind him. 'Papa is expecting you!' he went on as they both looked up at the eye of the closed-circuit TV camera above the wrought-iron grille that barred the passage.

Whoever was viewing the screen was satisfied, for there was an electrical buzz and the grille swung open. The doorman led Benedict down the passage.

'You know the way. Papa is in his office.'

Benedict was in a shabby little reception room, with a threadbare carpet and a pair of chairs that looked like Ministry of Works rejects. He turned to the right-hand door and went through it into a long room that clearly occupied most of the top floor of the building.

Along one side of the room ran a narrow bench, to which were bolted twenty small lathes. Each machine ran off a belt from a central drive below the bench. The man tending the machines wore a white dust jacket, and he grinned at Benedict. 'Hello, Mr van der Byl, Papa is expecting you.' But Benedict delayed a moment to watch the operation of the saws. In the jaw of each lathe was set a diamond, and spinning against the diamond was a circular blade of phosphor bronze. As Benedict watched, the man turned back to the task of spreading a fine paste of olive oil and diamond dust onto the cutting edge of each blade–for it was not the bronze that cut. Only a diamond will cut a diamond.

'Some nice stones, Larry,' Benedict remarked, and Larry Cohen nodded.

'All of them between four and five carats.'

Benedict leaned close and examined one of the diamonds. The line of the cut was marked with Indian ink on the stone. Benedict knew what heart-searching and discussion, what examination and drawing upon the rich storehouses of experience had preceded the positioning of that ink line. It might take two days to saw through each diamond, so Benedict left the bench and moved on.

In a row down the other side of the room sat the other Cohen brothers. Eight of them. Old Aaron was a great breeder of boys. They ranged in age from nearly forty to nineteen years and there were a couple who were still in school and hadn't yet come into the business.

'How do you like this one, Mr van der Byl?' Michael Cohen looked up as Benedict approached. Michael was shaping a fine diamond, cutting it into a round using a lesser stone as a blade. A small tray beneath the lathe caught the dust from the two stones. This dust would be used later for sawing and polishing.

'A beauty,' said Benedict. These men were of the brotherhood, working with diamonds all their lives and loving them as other men love women or horses or fine paintings.

He moved on down the room, greeting each of the brothers, stopping to watch for a minute the loving care with which the elder boys, master craftsmen each of them, were cutting the precisely-angled facets that make up the perfect round brilliant. The fifty-eight facets–table, stars, pavilions and the others which endow a cut stone with its mystic 'life' and 'fire'.

Leaving them crouched over their wheels, so similar to those of a potter, he went through the door at the end of the room.

'Benedict, my friend.' Aaron Cohen came from his desk to embrace him. He was a tall thin man in his late sixties with a thick silvery-grey mane of hair, round-shouldered from years of crouching over a diamond wheel. 'I did not know you were in London, they told me you were in Cape Town. Yesterday was Ruth's birthday. If we had known–'

Benedict took the envelope from his pocket and shook twenty-seven diamonds onto the blotter of the desk.

'What do you think of those, Papa?'

'Shu! Shu!' Papa patted his own cheeks with delight, and he reached instinctively for the biggest stone.

'I should live to see such a stone!' He screwed a jeweller's *loupe* into his eye, turning to catch the natural light from the high windows, and scrutinized the diamond through the eyepiece.

'Ah, yes. There is a feather,* but small. V.V.S.I.† But we will cut through it. Yes, we will take two gems from this stone. Two perfect diamonds of ten or twelve carats each, and perhaps five smaller ones.' More than half a diamond's bulk is lost in the cutting.

'Yes! Yes! From this stone we will sell a hundred thousand pounds' worth of polished diamonds!'

Aaron crossed to the door. 'Boys! Come see! I will show you a prince among diamonds.' And his sons crowded into the office. Michael took it first and gave his opinion. 'A good stone, yes. But not of the same water as the stone we had in the last batch. You remember that octahedron crystal–'

'What you talking!' his father interrupted. 'You wouldn't know a diamond from a piece of gorgonzola cheese already!'

'He is right, Papa.' Larry joined in the discussion. 'The other stone was better.'

'So the Big Lover argues with his father! Little shiksas with skirts up around their tochis you know all about. Dancing the Watusi and the Cha-Cha. Yes! But diamonds you know from nothing.' This declaration precipitated a full-scale, family argument in which each of the brothers joined with gusto.

'Shuddup! Shuddup! Back to work all of you! Out! out!' Aaron broke up the meeting, driving his sons from the office and slamming the door behind them.

'Shu!' He looked to heaven. 'What a business! Now we can weigh the stones.'

When they had weighed and tallied the stones, and Aaron had locked them into the safe, Benedict told him:

'I am thinking of breaking up the Ring.'

Aaron froze and looked across the desk at Benedict. Between them there was always a pretence that their relationship was legitimate. They never spoke about the Ring, or where the unregistered stones came from, or how the finished gems were sent to Switzerland.

'Why?' Aaron asked carefully.

'I am a rich man now. With my father's money, and what I have made from the Ring and invested. A very rich man. I no longer need to take the risks.'

'Such problems I wish I had. But perhaps you are wise–I would not think to argue with you.'

'There will be one or two more packages. Then it will be finished.'

Aaron nodded. 'I understand,' he said. 'Like all good things it must end.'

It was a little after noon when Benedict parked the Bentley outside the mews flat off Belgrave Square. He went to shower immediately he was home. In all the years he had lived here he had never grown accustomed to London's grime-laden atmosphere, and he bathed or showered at least three times a day.

He sang in the shower, and then enveloped in a huge bath towel he left a

*Semi-transparent veinlike flaw.
†Very very slight imperfection.

string of damp footprints through to the lounge where he mixed a Martini, and screwed up his eyes at the first stinging taste of the drink.

The phone rang.

'Van der Byl,' he said into the mouthpiece, and then his expression changed as he listened. Quickly he put down the glass and used both hands to hold the telephone receiver.

'What on earth are you doing here?' His tone of astonishment was not faked.

'What a wonderful surprise. When can I see you? How about right now–for lunch? That's great! No, nothing I can't put off–this is a pretty special occasion, you know. Where are you staying? The Lancaster. Fine. Look, give me forty-five minutes, and I'll meet you in the Looking-Glass Room on the top floor. Yes, ten past one. God, what a delightful–I've said that already. See you in three-quarters of an hour.'

He replaced the receiver, swallowed the remains of his Martini and headed for the bedroom suite. This would make a good day into a truly memorable one, he thought, as he quickly selected a silk shirt. He looked at his reflection in the mirror and grinned.

'The ball has really started bouncing your way, Benedict,' he whispered.

She was not at the bar, nor in the Looking-Glass Room. Benedict crossed to the tall picture windows for a glimpse of one of London's finest views across Hyde Park and the Serpentine. It was a smoky blue day, and the pale sun added bronze to the autumn shades of gold and red in the park.

He turned from the windows, and she was crossing the room towards him. His stomach swooped with delight for she also was pale gold with the coppery sheen of sun on her long legs and bare arms. The grace of her carriage was as he remembered it, the precise lifting and laying down of narrow feet on the thick pile of the carpet.

He stood quite still, letting her come to him. Heads turned all across the room, for she was a splendid golden creature. Benedict knew suddenly and clearly that he wanted this woman for himself.

'Hello, Benedict,' she said, and he stepped forward to take her hand in both of his.

'Ruby Lance!' He squeezed her long fingers gently. 'It's so good to see you again.'

The use of her surname was the clue to the strength of his reaction. She belonged to the one man in the world that Benedict most envied and hated. For this reason she was infinitely desirable.

'Let us celebrate with a little drink. I think the occasion deserves at the very least a champagne cocktail.'

She sat with those long slim legs neatly crossed, leaning back in her chair, holding the stemmed glass with tapering fingers. Her hair hung straight to her shoulders, like some rare silken tapestry in white gold, and her eyes watched him with a catlike candour, a calm feline intentness that seemed to look into his soul.

'I should not have bothered you,' she said. 'But I know so few people here.'

'How long can you stay?' He brushed aside the disclaimer. 'I must cancel my other arrangements.'

'A week.' She made it sound like an offer that was subject to negotiation.

'Oh, no!' His voice was mock distressed. 'You can do better than that–we won't be able to do half what I had planned in so short a time. You can stay longer, surely?'

'Perhaps,' she agreed, and lifted the glass an inch. 'It's good to see you.'

'And you.' Benedict agreed with emphasis. They sipped the sparkling wine watching each other's eyes.

Where others must wait weeks and months Benedict went in immediately as though it were his right. A smile and a murmured word, and theatre tickets were his or the doors of fashionable restaurants opened magically.

That first night he took her to the National Theatre, then for dinner at Le Coeur de France where a very famous movie actor stopped at their table.

'Hello, Benedict. We are all going on to the yacht later for a bit of a party. Join us, won't you?' And those legendary eyes turned to Ruby. 'And bring your beautiful friend with you.'

They ate breakfast under the awning on the afterdeck of the yacht, eggs and bacon and Veuve Cliquot champagne, and watched the hubbub of dawn traffic on the wondrously smelly old Thames. Ruby was the only girl in the party without a fur to cheat the chill of the river dawn. Benedict made a mental note of the fact.

On the way home she sat with those long legs curled under her in the seat of the Bentley, still sleek and golden despite the night's exertions, but with the lightest touching of blue beneath her eyes.

'I can't remember having enjoyed an evening so much, Benedict.' She patted a tiny pink-lipped yawn. 'You're a wonderful companion.'

'Tonight again?' he asked.

'Yes, please,' she murmured.

She sensed an urgency in him, when she came down into the lobby of the Lancaster that evening. He came quickly to meet her as she stepped out of the lift, and the quiet assurance with which he kissed her cheek and took her arm surprised her.

They were silent as he snaked the Bentley through the evening traffic. Ruby realized that at the tips of her long tapered fingers, within touching distance, was a fortune such as she had never before allowed herself to dream about. She was deadly afraid. A wrong move, even a wrong word might drive that fortune beyond her grasp for ever. She would never have a chance like this again, and she was afraid to move, almost paralysed with fear. The decision she knew she would have to make very soon would be fateful. Must she counter his advance with withdrawal, or must she meet it as frankly as it was made?

She was so deeply involved with her thoughts that when the Bentley came to a standstill she looked up with surprise. They were parked in a mews outside an expensive-looking flat.

Benedict came round and opened her door, and led her without protest into the flat.

She looked about her curiously, recognizing some of the art works on display in the entrance hall. Benedict took her through into the long lounge and settled her solicitously into the tapestry-covered chair which dominated the room like a throne, and suddenly her fear was gone. She felt queenlike in her control. She knew with certainty that this would all be hers.

Benedict stood in the centre of the room, almost a petitioner in his attitude, and he began to speak. She listened quietly, her expression showing no hint of the triumphant surge of her spirits, and when he stopped to wait for her reply she did not hesitate.

'Yes,' she said.

'I will be with you when you tell him,' Benedict promised.

'It won't be necessary,' Ruby assured him. 'I can handle Johnny Lance.'

'No.' Swiftly Benedict crossed to her chair and took her hands, drawing her to her feet. 'I must be there with you. Promise me that.'

Then it came suddenly evident to Ruby that the strength of her position was unassailable. Benedict needed her not for any physical reasons–but merely because she belonged to Johnny Lance.

Looking steadily into Benedict's eyes she determined to test her intuition.

'He does not have to know about you,' she said. 'I could arrange a divorce with him.'

'He *must* know about me. That's what I want, don't you see?'

'Yes, I see.' She was secure.

'It is agreed?' He could barely conceal his anxiety.

'Yes,' she nodded. 'It's agreed.' And they smiled at each other–each completely satisfied.

'Come.' He led her almost reverently into his bedroom, and Ruby stopped in the doorway with a little cry of delight.

The double bed was a mountain of glowing fur in a score of shades ranging from soft pinkish cream, through beige and oyster, pale smoky blue to midnight and jet glossy black.

'Choose one!' he ordered her. 'To seal our bargain.'

She moved like a sleepwalker towards the bed, but as she reached the centre of the Khedive carpet Benedict called out softly.

'Wait.'

She stopped obediently and he came up behind her. She felt his hands on the back of her neck, and she lowered her chin, shaking her hair forward so that he could unhook the clasp and draw down the fastening of her dress.

She stepped out of the dress as it dropped around her ankles, then waited passively as he carefully removed her brassiere.

'Now,' he said. 'Try them on.'

In her stockings and high-heeled shoes she went to the bed, subtly emphasizing the lilt of her movements, and took up the first fur.

Benedict was sprawled in the wingback chair across the room as she glanced back at him. His face was gloating and flushed, so that his features seemed swollen and coarsened as he stared at her. She understood now that this was a form of ritual in which they were engaged. Like a victorious Roman general, Benedict was conducting his own personal triumph, reviewing the spoils and the plunder. It had no basis in sexual or physical desire, but was rather a service of worship to Benedict himself. She was the priestess of this rite.

Yet, knowing this, Ruby felt no resentment. Rather she found herself excited by the cold perversity of the pageant. As she paraded and postured, turned and swirled, and flared the skirts of a wild mink, she was very conscious of his eyes upon her body. She knew it was perfect, and his scrutiny stirred her physically for the first time in her life. She felt her blood quicken and pound, felt her heart flutter within its cage of ribs like a captive bird, and her loins tighten like a clenching fist. For her also the ritual was narcissistic–satisfying her own deep emotional need.

As she discarded each of the coats she dropped it in the centre of the floor, until there was a knee-high pile of precious fur.

At last she faced him, hugging the soft creamy cloud tightly about her body.

Then she opened her arms, and the coat also, standing on tip-toe to tighten and highlight the hard muscle in her legs and flanks.

'This one,' she whispered, and he came out of the chair, picked her up in his arms and laid her, still wrapped in mink, on the great pile of mink.

Ruby woke in the double bed to a feeling of excitement and enormous well-being such as she had not experienced since she was a schoolgirl on the first morning of a holiday.

The morning was far advanced, pale sunshine in a square shaft poured through the open window like a stage effect.

Benedict in a yellow silk dressing-gown stood beside the bed watching her with an unfathomable expression which changed immediately he realized that she was awake.

'My man has collected your luggage from the Lancaster. Your toilet things are in the bathroom, your clothing in the dressing-room.'

He sat down carefully on the edge of the bed, and leaned forward to kiss her forehead and then each cheek.

'We will breakfast when you are ready.' He sat back and watched her eyes; clearly he was waiting for her to say something important. Immediately she was on guard, wary of making a mistake, seeking a clue in his expression.

'Last night,' he asked. 'Was it as good for you, as it was for me?'

Understanding washed over her in a warm wave. He wanted assurance, a comparison between himself and Johnny Lance.

'I have never in my life–' She placed the emphasis carefully, '–experienced anything like it.'

He nodded, relieved, pleased–and stood up.

'After breakfast we will go to town.'

This morning, Edmund, Benedict's man, chauffeured the Bentley. When they alighted at the north end of Bond Street and walked arm in arm along the pavement, Edmund tailed them at a dignified crawl, steadfastly ignoring the abuse of other drivers.

The morning was cool enough for Ruby to wear her new cream mink, and the looks of admiration and envy she drew drom the other strollers delighted Benedict. He wanted to impress her, he wanted to flaunt his wealth.

'The wife of a diamond man must have diamonds.' He spoke on impulse as they came up to an expensive-looking jewellers. Ruby squeezed his arm and turned to look into the window.

'Good Lord,' Benedict laughed. 'Not here!' And Ruby looked at him with surprise.

Mockingly Benedict began reading the signs in the window

'Paradise Jewellers. A large selection of blue-white gems. Certificate of flawlessness with every diamond. Perfect flawless stones at bargain prices as advertised on TV and in the national Press. Small deposit secures your ring now. A diamond is for ever–show her you really care.'

'But they are such a well-known firm. They have branches all over the world–even in South Africa!' Ruby protested, and bridled a little as Benedict smiled patronizingly.

'Let me explain about diamonds. They are bought for two reasons by two different types of people. Firstly by rich men as investments that will not erode and can only increase in value. These men buy notable stones on the advice of experts, the best of the gem diamond production goes to them. So when

Richard Burton buys Liz a £300,000 diamond he is not being extravagant–on the contrary he is being ultra-conservative and thrifty with his money.'

'That's the kind of meanness I like,' Ruby laughed, and Benedict smiled at her honesty.

'You may find me as thrifty,' he promised.

'Go on,' she said, 'tell me more about diamonds.'

'Well, there is another type who buys diamonds. Usually just one in his life, luckily for him–and he very seldom tries to resell it again or he would get a nasty shock. This type is Joe Everybody–who wants to get married. He usually goes to somebody like Paradise Jewellers.' Benedict poked a derisive finger at the sign in the window. 'Because he has seen it on telly and can get a ring on the instalment plan. In many cases the deposit covers the dealer for the cost of the stone–the rest goes on advertising, finance charges and, of course, profit.'

'How do you know Paradise Jewellers are that type?' Ruby's attention was wide-eyes and girlish.

'You recognize them firstly by the big advertising splurge, then by their language.' Again he studied the notices in the window. '"A large Selection of blue-white gems"–of every thousand stones of jewellery quality produced only one is fine enough in colour to be termed blue-white. It is unlikely they have a large selection. "Gem" is a special term reserved for a diamond which is in every way superb. "Flawless stones at bargain prices"–the lack of flaws in a diamond is only one of many factors governing its value. As for bargain prices–there ain't no such animal. Prices are maintained at the lowest level by fierce competition among expert and canny dealers, and there are no "sales" or special prices for anyone.'

'But where should a person buy a diamond?' Ruby was impressed and dismayed despite herself.

'Not here.' Benedict chuckled. 'Come, I will show you.' And before she could protest he had taken her arm and swept her into the shop, to be greeted with enthusiasm by the manager who must have noticed Ruby's mink and the attendant Bentley, which was causing a small traffic jam outside the shop.

'Good morning, madam and sir. May I be of service to you?'

'Yes,' Benedict nodded. 'A selection of your blue-white gems. The best you have.'

'This way, please.' The manager backed away in front of them, snapping his fingers like a flamenco dancer to summon his assistants.

'Now.' Benedict turned to Ruby, as they settled down in the manager's office with a tray of diamond rings in front of them. 'You cannot examine a diamond properly in its setting.'

He selected the biggest diamond, took from his pocket a gold-plated penknife fitted with a special tool and prised open the claws of the setting to a chorus of horrified squeals from the staff.

'I will make good any damage,' he snapped, and they subsided as Benedict took the loose stone and laid it on the velvet-covered tray.

'Firstly, size. This stone is about one carat.' He looked for confirmation to the manager who nodded. 'Let us say the value of this stone is £500. Ten similar stones will be worth £5,000, right? However, a ten-carat stone may be worth as much as £75,000. So the price per carat rises sharply as the total weight of the stone increases. If I were investing I would not touch a stone under three carats.'

The staff were listening now with as much attention as Ruby.

'Next, colour,' said Benedict, and glanced at the manager. 'A sheet of clean white paper, please.'

The manager scratched in his drawer and laid a sheet of paper in front of Benedict who placed the stone upon it, bottom upwards.

'We compare the colour it "draws" from white paper in good natural light.' He looked up at the manager. 'Switch off the fluorescent lights, and open those curtains, please,'

The manager obeyed with alacrity.

'This is a matter of experience. The colour is judged by a standard. We forget about the fancy rare colours like blue and red and green, and take our top standard as blue-white. A stone so white as to appear slightly blue, after which the distinctions drop to "fine white", and "white". Then stones which "draw" a yellowish tinge which we call "Cape"–in different shades, then finally stones which "draw" a brown colour–which will reduce the value of a stone by up to eighty per cent.'

Benedict fished in his fob pocket and pulled out a guinea case which he opened.

'Every expert carries a special diamond which he uses as a gauge for colour by which to judge all other stones. This is mine.'

The staff exchanged apprehensive looks as Benedict placed a small diamond beside the other. He studied them a moment then replaced his gauge in the case.

'Second Silver Cape, I'd say,' he grunted, and the staff looked suitably abashed. 'Now we consider the stone's perfection.' He looked at the manager. 'Please lend me your *loupe.*'

'Loupe?' The manager was mystified.

'Yes, your jeweller's glass.'

'I–' the manager was deeply embarrassed.

'You sell diamonds–yet you do not own a *loupe.*' Benedict shook his head in disapproval. 'No matter, I have my own.'

Benedict took the glass from his inner pocket and placed it in his eye.

'Imperfections can be almost negligible–a "natural" at the girdle, or a bubble or pinpoint of carbon in the stone, on the other hand they can be gross "cracks", "clouds", "ice", or "feathers" which will ruin the value of the stone. But this one is flawless–so when the certificate of flawlessness is issued there will be no misrepresentation.' Benedict closed the glass and tucked it back into his pocket. 'However, in order to produce a flawless stone, the cut has been squeezed.'

He held up the stone between thumb and forefinger.

'The cut or "make" of a stone is the fourth and final decider in its value. The "make" should conform closely to the "ideal". This stone had been cut to exclude a flaw, and in consequence it is badly proportioned–heavy and out of round. I would prefer to see a graceful stone which includes a slight imperfection rather than a grotesque little cripple like this.'

He put the diamond down on the desk.

'The asking price by Paradise Jewellers for this stone is £500–which would be fair and correct for a gem. However, the colour is poor and although it is flawless it is of ungainly make. Its true value would be about–ah, let's see–£185 approximately.'

There was another chorus of protest from the assembled staff, led by the manager.

'I assure you sir, that all our stones have been most carefully appraised.'

'How long have you been with Paradise Jewellers?' Benedict demanded brusquely. 'Four months, isn't it?'

The manager gaped at him.

'Before that you were a salesman in the showroom of a large firm of embalmers and undertakers.'

'I, well–I mean.' The manager fluttered his hands weakly. 'How did you know that?'

'I like to know about all my employees.'

'Employees?' The manager looked stunned.

'That's correct. My name is Benedict van der Byl. I own Paradise Jewellers.'

Ruby clapped her hands and cooed her applause.

'What a bundle of surprises you are!' she exclaimed.

Benedict smiled in acknowledgement and inclined his head.

'Now,' he said, as he rose and helped Ruby to her feet. 'We will go and buy some real diamonds.'

Aaron Cohen sold them two fine white twin marquise-cut brilliants, and Ruby chose the mounting for a pair of white-gold earrings from a leather-bound catalogue.

Benedict gave Aaron his cheque for twenty thousand pounds, then turned to Ruby.

'Now,' he said. 'We'll have lunch at the Celeste Grill-room. The food is bloody awful–but the décor is stupendous. We had best phone and reserve a table–it isn't really necessary but they get terribly hurt if you don't.'

As they settled back in the lush upholstery of the Bentley, Benedict instructed the chauffeur.

'Go past Trafalgar Square, Edmund. I want to pick up the newspapers from South Africa House.'

Edmund double-parked outside the Ambassador's entrance, and the doorman recognized the car and hurried inside to fetch the bundle of newspapers.

As they pulled away around the square towards Haymarket, Benedict selected a copy of the *Cape Argus*.

'Let's see what's happening at home.' He glanced at the front page, and stiffened perceptibly.

'What is it?' Ruby leaned towards him anxiously, but he ignored her. His eyes were darting across the page like the shuttle of a loom. She saw the colour fade from his face, leaving it white and intent. He finished reading, and pushed the paper towards her. She spread the page.

VAN DER BYL DIAMONDS WIN VALUABLE CONCESSION.

APPEAL COURT SUPPORTS KAISER'S MINERAL GRANT.

LANCE GETS THUNDERBOLT AND SUICIDE.

Bloemfontein, Thursday.

In an urgent application by the Central Diamond Mines Ltd to prevent Van Der Byl Diamonds Ltd prospecting and mining a concession area off the South West African Coast, Mr Justice Tromp today dismissed the application with costs stating in his judgement: 'The original concession granted by German Imperial Decree in 1899, and subsequently ratified by Act of the Union Parliament in Act 24 of 1920 must hold good in law, and will take precedence over any subsequent grant or concession purporting to have been made by the Minister of Mines to any other party.'

The area in dispute covers 100 square kilometres surrounding two small islands lying some fifteen miles south of Cartridge Bay and five miles offshore. The islands are known as Thunderbolt Island and Suicide Island, and at the turn of the century were the site of considerable exploitation by a German Guano Company. Mr John Rigby Lance the General Manager of Van Der Byl Diamond Co Ltd, acquired the rights to the concession when he took over the inoperative guano company.

In Cape Town today Mr Lance stated: 'It's the opportunity I have waited for all my life. All indications are that Thunderbolt and Suicide will prove to be one of the richest marine diamonds fields in the world.'

Van der Byl Diamond Co has a diamond-dredging vessel nearing completion in the United Kingdom, and Mr Lance stated that he hoped to begin recovery operations off Thunderbolt and Suicide Islands before the end of the year.

Ruby lowered the paper and looked at Benedict. What she saw was an intense physical shock.

Benedict had crumpled down in the seat. Gone was all the assurance and *savoir faire*. His face was still deathly pale, but now his lips trembled and with disgust she saw that his eyes were swimming with tears. He hunched forward over his hands, shaking his head gently and hopelessly.

'The bastard,' he whispered, and his voice was soggy and muffled. 'He does it every time. I thought that I had him at last, but–Oh God, I hate him.'

He looked at her, his face soft with self-pity. 'He does it every time. Often I've thought I had him, but he just–'

She was mystified by his reaction.

'Aren't you pleased? Van Der Byl Diamonds will make millions–'

'No! No!' he cut in savagely, and then the years of hatred and frustration and humiliation began pouring out. Ruby listened quietly, slowly beginning to understand it all, marvelling at the accumulation of pain and hatred that he exposed for her. He remembered conversations from twenty years ago. Small childhood episodes, innocent remarks that had festered and rankled for a decade.

'You don't want him to succeed, is that it?' she asked.

'I want to crush him, break him, humiliate him.'

For ten seconds Ruby was silent.

'Well, what are we going to do about it?' she asked flatly.

'Nothing, I suppose.' Benedict's tone irritated her. 'He always comes out on top, you just can't–'

'Nonsense,' Ruby snapped. She was angry now. 'Let's go over it carefully, and see how we can stop him. He is only human, and you have shown me enough to prove you are a brilliant and successful businessman.'

Benedict's expression changed, becoming trusting and animated. He turned to her almost eagerly. He blinked his eyes. 'Do you really believe that?'

The bunk was too narrow, Sergio Caporetti decided, much too narrow. He would have one of the carpenters alter it today.

He lay on his back, wedged in firmly, with the blanket-covered mound of his belly blocking his view southwards. He lay and assessed his physical condition. It was surprisingly good. There was but a small blurred pain behind his eyes and the taste of stale cigars and rank wine in the back of his throat was bearable. The leaden feeling in his lower limbs alarmed him until he realized that he was still wearing his heavy fisherman's boots. He remembered one of the girls complaining about that.

He hoisted himself on one elbow, and looked at the girls. One on each side of him, jamming him solidly into the bunk, with magnificent hillocks of pink flesh. Big strong girls both of them, he had chosen them with care, neither of them an ounce under twelve stone. Sergio sighed happily–it had been a wonderful weekend. The girls were snoring, in such harmony that it might have been a rehearsed stage act. He listened to them with mild admiration for a few minutes, then crawled over the outside girl and stood in the centre of the cabin, clad only in his heavy boots. He yawned extravagantly, scratching the thick black wiry curls that covered his chest and belly, and cocked an eye at the bulkhead clock. Four o'clock on a Monday morning, but it had been a truly memorable weekend.

The table was hidden under a forest of empty wine bottles, and dirty plates. There was a congealed mass of cold spaghetti bolognaise in a dish and he picked it up. As he climbed out of the cabin on to *Kingfisher*'s bridge he was scooping up spaghetti with his fingers and cramming it into his mouth.

He stood at the rail of the bridge, a naked hairy figure in tall black boots clutching a dish of spaghetti to his chest, and looked around the dockyard.

Kingfisher was in stocks undergoing the modifications that Johnny Lance had ordered. She was standing high above the level she would attain when she was launched. Although she was a vessel of a mere 3,000 ton displacement, she appeared black and monstrous in the floodlights that illuminated the shipbuilders' yard. It was obvious from her unusual silhouette that she was designed for a special purpose. Her superstructure was situated well aft like that of an oil tanker, while her foredeck was crowded by the huge gantry which would control the dredge, and by the massive storage tanks for the compressed air.

At this hour of the morning the shipyard was deserted, and wisps and tendrils of sea mist drifted about *Kingfisher*'s bulk.

Standing fifty feet above the dry dock, still wolfing cold spaghetti, Sergio urinated over the rail–deriving a simple honest pleasure from the long arching stream and the tinkle of liquid striking the concrete far below.

He clumped back into his cabin, and looked down fondly on his two sleeping Valkyries while he finished the last of the spaghetti. Then he wiped his fingers carefully on his chest hair and called to them gently.

'Come, my kittens, my little doves, the time for play she has passed–the time for work she commences.'

With Latin gallantry he bundled them into a taxi at the dockyard gates, pressing onto each of them a lusty buss, a bank-note, a bottle of Chianti, protestations of deep affection, and the promise of another party next Friday night.

He picked his way through the dockyard jungle of machinery and buildings, lighting a long black cigar and inhaling smoke pleasurably until he came in sight of *Kingfisher* and halted with surprise and annoyance. There was a big honey-coloured Bentley parked near the gangway that led up to *Kingfisher*'s deck. He resented visits from the Company bosses, especially this one, and especially at this ridiculous hour on a Monday morning.

The hose spiralled down into greenness, and they followed it down holding hands. Tracey was still a little nervous. This was not like the Mediterranean, a warm blue friendly embrace of waters to welcome the diver–it was the wild Atlantic, coldly menacing, green and untamed. It frightened her, and Johnny's hand gave her comfort.

Their Draeger demand valves repeated their breathing in a singing metallic wheeze, and icy leaks and rivulets kept finding their way into the cuffs and neck of Tracey's rubber suit.

Sixty feet below the surface Johnny paused, and peered into the glass window of her mask. He grinned at her, his mouth distorted by the bulky mouthpiece, and she gave him a thumbs-up sign. They both looked upwards. The surface was silvered like an imperfect mirror, and the black cigar shape of the boat was lapped in strange light. The hose and anchor chain pierced the silver ceiling and hung down into the shady green depths.

Johnny pointed downwards, and she nodded. They put their heads down, pointed their flippers to the surface, and still hand in hand they paddled steadily towards the sea bed.

Tracey was aware of a crackling hissing sound now, and from out of the greenery blackness below them scudded clouds of silver bubbles twisting and writhing towards the surface. She strained her eyes downwards, following the line of the hose, and slowly out of the murk materialized the black rubber-clad forms of the two men working at the end of the hose; they appeared weird and mystical like black priests performing a satanical mass.

She and Johnny reached the sea and hung just above it, a little way off from the two men on the hose. Johnny indicated the depth gauge that he wore like a wrist watch. It showed a depth of 120 feet. Then he turned and by a hand signal showed her the direction of the reefs.

They were in a valley between these long peaked underwater ridges of black rocks, the same reefs that Tracey had seen from the air. There was a distinct pull of water as the current drifted at right angles to the direction of the reefs.

Johnny squeezed her hand, and then pulled her down. They lay on their bellies on the floor of the sea, and Johnny scooped a handful of the white sand, washed it quickly so that the smaller particles were carried away in a cloud on the current, then he showed her the coarse gravel which remained. Again he grinned, and she returned his smile.

Still leading her by the hand, he swam slowly towards the two men working on the hose, and stopped to watch them.

Attached to the end of the hose was a rigid steel pipe two inches in diameter, and twenty feet long–although now only half its length was visible above the sand bottom. The two divers were forcing it down through sand and gravel to reach bed-rock. The hose itself was attached to a compressor on the deck of the boat which was generating a vacuum in the hose and sucking up the sand and gravel as the steel pipe was forced downwards.

They were prospecting the Thunderbolt and Suicide field. Taking these two-inch samples at five-hundred-foot intervals to ascertain the depth of the water, the thickness of the overburden, and the content of the gravel beds. They were also mapping and plotting the reefs, so that by the time *Kingfisher* arrived they would have a fairly clear picture of the topography and aspect of the field. They would know where to begin dredging, and roughly what to expect when they did.

So far the results had endorsed Johnny's most optimistic expectations. There was a good thick catchment of gravel in all the gullies between the reefs. As he had expected, the heavier gravels had been laid down in the gullies closest to the gap between Thunderbolt and Suicide, and the smaller and lighter gravels had been carried farther. In some of the gullies the gravel beds were fifteen feet deep, and the types of stone present were all highly promising. He had isolated garnet, jasper, ironstone, beryl chips and titanium dust.

However, the conclusive and definite proof had also come up through that two-inch hose out of the depths. They had already pulled the first diamonds from the Thunderbolt and Suicide fields. When you considered the odds against finding a stone in a two-inch sample at five-hundred-foot centres and that payable gravel contained one part diamond in fifty million, it was exciting and encouraging that they had already recovered four diamonds. Small stones, to be sure, not one of them more than half a carat, but diamonds for all that, and some of them of excellent quality.

One of the men on the hose turned and gave Johnny a flat-handed cut-out sign. The pipe was on bed-rock. Johnny nodded and jerked a thumb upwards, and drawing Tracey with him started for the surface.

They climbed the ladder over the survey boat's counter moving clumsily under the weight of the air bottles strapped to their backs, but there were willing hands to help them aboard and strip off the heavy equipment, and unzip the clinging rubber suits.

Tracey accepted a towel gratefully from one of the crew, and while she tilted her head to dry her sodden mane of hair, she looked across half a mile of green sea to the two white whale-backed islands with their attendant clouds of sea birds. The wave bursts on the cliffs sounded like distant artillery, or far thunder.

'God, this is a wild and exciting place.' Her voice bubbled with excitement as she scrubbed at her hair. 'It makes one come alive.'

Johnny understood her feelings, it was the forbidding restless sea and the harsh land that promised danger and adventure. He was about to reply, but the two hose men came aboard at that moment, the taller of them spitting out his mouthpiece and letting it fall to his chest.

'We'll move up to the next point, if it's okay by you, Mr Lance?' The man pulled off his mask and hood, exposing white-blond hair and a sun-broiled face.

'Fine, Hugo,' Johnny agreed, and watched approvingly as Hugo Kramer gave the order to get the anchor and the hose up before taking *Wild Goose* seawards to her next prospecting point. Johnny had been reluctant to charter *Wild Goose* as the prospecting vessel and as the service boat for *Kingfisher*. He did not know Hugo Kramer, and Benedict van der Byl's insistence on the man had made his suspicious.

However, it was natural that they should use a skipper from the van der Byl fleet and Johnny was now prepared to admit he had been wrong. Kramer was an intelligent and willing worker, resourceful and trustworthy, a fine seaman who handled *Wild Goose* with all the skill it would need to bring her alongside *Kingfisher* in a heavy sea. His unfortunate physical appearance Johnny hardly noticed any more, although the original shock of that pink face, white hair and those blind-looking eyes had been considerable.

Tracey was not so charitable. The man made her uneasy. There was a wild-animal ferocity about him, a barely controlled violence. The way he looked at her sometimes made her skin prickle. He did it now; turning back from issuing his order he ran his eyes over her body. In the black silk costume her good round breasts showed at their best, and Hugo Kramer looked at them with those white-fringed bland eyes. Instinctively she covered them with the towel, and it seemed as though his lips twitched with amusement as he turned to Johnny.

'They tell me this dredger of yours is something special, Mr Lance?'

'She is, Hugo. Not like the other half-baked barges and bastardized conversions that have been tried by other companies. She's the first diamond recovery vessel designed expressly for the job.'

'What's different about her?'

'Nearly everything. Her hose is operated off a gantry on the foredeck, it goes through a well pierced through her hull.'

'What kind of hose?'

'Eighteen-inch armoured woven steel with rubber liner. We can get it down to a hundred fathoms, and it has a compensating section in it to stop it plunging with the wave action of the hull.'

'Eighteen inches is pretty big. How will you build up vacuum?'

'That's the point, Hugo. We don't suck–we blow! We evacuate water from the hose by purging it with compressed air, the inrush of water into the opening of the hose sucks in the gravel.'

'Hey, that's neat. So the deeper you work the more effective it will be!'

'Right.'

'What about the actual recovery? Are you going to have the usual screening, ball mill, and grease table arrangement?'

'That's what killed the other companies–trying to separate by the old methods. No. We've got a cyclone to start with.'

'Cyclone?'

'You know a cream separator?'

'Yeah.'

'Same principle. Just spin the gravel in a circular tank and float off everything with a specific gravity of less than 2·5. Take what is left, dry it, spread it on a conveyor belt and run it under an X-ray machine which pinpoints every single diamond. As you know, diamonds fluoresce under X-rays and they show up crisply. The X-ray machine reports the diamond to the central computer–' Johnny's voice and whole attitude was charged with enthusiasm which was impossible for his listeners to resist. Tracey was carried along with him, watching his eyes and his mouth as he talked, smiling when he smiled, her lips following his faithfully.

'This is the cyclone room,' Benedict van der Byl explained as, with a hand on her elbow, he helped Ruby Lance down off the last rung of the ladder. 'I explained to you how it worked.'

'Yes.' Ruby nodded, and looked around the room with interest. The roughly riveted and grey painted plating of *Kingfisher*'s hull formed a square metal box, in the centre of which stood the cyclone. It was also painted battleship grey, a ten-foot-high cone shaped circular tower.

'The gravel is blown in through here.' Benedict indicated the eighteen-inch pipe which entered the cyclone room through the forward bulkhead, then connected to the bottom of the cyclone. 'Up it goes.' Benedict flung his hand upwards. 'And round it goes.' He made a stirring motion. 'The heavy stuff is thrown off and led away through that.' A smaller pipe emerged from the shoulder of the cyclone and disappeared through the farther bulkhead. 'While the lighter stuff shoots out through the top and is sprayed overboard again.'

'I understand. Now, where is the weak spot?' Ruby asked.

'Come.' Benedict led her across the room, picking their way among the litter left by the workmen who still swarmed through *Kingfisher*. They reached a steel door in the bulkhead.

'Watch your head.' They ducked into a long passageway with doors at both ends. On their right hand was an enclosed tunnel that ran the length of the room.

'This is the conveyor room,' Benedict explained. 'The concentrated gravels fall through a hot air draught from an electric furnace to dry them. They are gathered on a conveyor belt, concealed in that tunnel, and carried through into the X-ray room.'

'This is where you will fit it?' Ruby asked.

'Yes. In the conveyor tunnel. It will mean moving that inspection hatch back twelve feet to give us the space.'

Ruby nodded. 'The man who will do the work–can you trust him?'

'Yes. He has worked for me before.' Benedict did not add that the same man had designed the electronic equipment for the balloons used by the Ring, and had flown out from Japan to convert the ASDIC equipment on *Wild Goose*.

'All right.' Ruby seemed satisfied. More and more she was becoming the driving force in the alliance, bolstering Benedict's resolution when he showed timidity or when he tried to evade the actions which must, in time, lead to a confrontation with Johnny Lance.

'Let's see the X-ray room.'

It was a tiny cupboard-like compartment. The floor, roof and all four walls were clad with thick sheet lead. Suspended from the roof was the X-ray machine, and under it a circular table whose surface was covered with a honeycomb-patterned stainless steel sheet.

'The concentrated gravel spills onto the table, and the table revolves under the X-ray machine which fluoresces each diamond and the computer picks it up and reports its size and exact position on the table. The computer then commands one of those–' Benedict pointed to a forest of hard plastic tubes, each attached to a metal arm, '–to swing out over the table exactly above the diamond and suck it up. The computer selects the correct diameter of tube for the size of the diamond–and, after the tube has obeyed the computer the table passes under a second X-ray machine which confirms that the diamond has been collected. If, by chance, the tube fails to suck up the stone, then the computer automatically sends the table on another circuit. If, however, the diamond is safely gathered then the waste material is scraped from the table and it swings round to pick up more gravel from the cyclone room–and repeat the whole process. The system is 100 per cent effective. Every single diamond is recovered by it. Even stones as small as sugar grains.'

'Where is the computer?' Ruby asked.

'There.' Benedict pointed through the small leaded glass window which overlooked the X-ray table. Beyond it was another small compartment. Ruby flattened her nose against the glass, and peered in. The computer occupied most of the room, a huge glossy enamelled cabinet not unlike a refrigerator despite the switches and dials. Benedict peered in beside her.

'The computer runs the entire operation. It controls the flow of compressed air into the dredger pipe, it regulates the cyclone, runs the X-ray machine and the table, it weighs and counts the diamonds recovered before depositing them in a safe, and it even navigates the *Kingfisher* and reports to the bridge her exact position over the sea bed, it checks the lubrication and temperature of the engines and power plant and on request will make a complete and immediate report of the whole or any part of the operation.'

Ruby was still peering into the computer room.

'What happens to the diamonds once they have been picked off the revolving table?' she asked.

'They are sucked through an electronic scale which weighs each stone, then they are carried through into the computer room and deposited in that safe.' Benedict pointed out the steel door set in the bulkhead. 'The safe has a time and combination lock. So the system works without a diamond being touched by human hands.'

'Let's go and talk to the Italian peasant,' suggested Ruby, and as she turned from the window Benedict slippped his arm about her shoulders and hugged her possessively.

'Not now,' snapped Ruby irritably, shrugging off his arm, and she led the way out of the X-ray compartment, passing the locked door of the computer control room opposite the door to the conveyor room. She was impressed with the ingenuity of the system–but the fact that it had been constructed by Johnny Lance made her angry.

Her loyalties had changed completely, going to the highest bidder.

Sergio Caporetti felt a small twinge of pity when he looked at Ruby Lance. So thin, and with a backside like a boy. She would be little comfort to a man on a cold night. Sergio worked the cheroot from one corner of his mouth to the other, anointing the stub with saliva in the process. Also she was cold-blooded, he decided. Sergio had a very sensitive intuition when it came to judging the temperature of a woman's passion. Cold like a snake, he decided, his pity giving way to revulsion. He repressed a small shudder as he watched her settle onto the day couch in his cabin, and cross her long golden legs precisely. Just like a snake, she would eat a man as though he were a little hopping frog. Sergio had admiration for Johnny Lance, but–he decided–not even he would be safe with a woman like this.

'You like my ship?' he asked, an attempt at friendliness. 'She is *very* fine ship.'

Sergio actually used a more forceful adjective than *very*, one that suggested *Kingfisher* was capable of procreation, and Ruby's lips curled with disgust. She ignored the question and lit a cigarette, swinging one leg impatiently, and turned her head to stare through the porthole.

Sergio was hurt by the rebuff, but he had no time to brood on it for Benedict van der Byl came to stand in the centre of the cabin with his hands clasped behind his back.

'Mr Caporetti–' he asked quietly. 'How much do you like money?'

Sergio grinned, and pushed the grubby maritime cap to the back of his head. 'I like it pretty good, I like it better than my mother–and I love my mother like my life,' he said.

'Would you like to become a rich man?' Benedict asked, and Sergio sighed wistfully.

'Si!' he nodded. 'But it is the impossible thing. There is too much *vino*, too much lovely girls, and the cards they are cruel like –' Sergio paused to find a suitable simile and glanced at Ruby, '–like a thin woman. No. Money she does not stay long, she comes and she goes.'

'What would you do for twenty-five thousand pounds?' Benedict asked.

'For twenty-five thousand–' Sergio's eyes were dark liquid and lovely as those of a dying gazelle or a woman in love '–there is nothing I will not do.'

Kingfisher sailed for Africa on October 4th. As the representative of the owners, Benedict van der Byl drove down from London to bid her *bon voyage*, and he spent an hour behind locked doors with Sergio Caporetti before the departure of the vessel.

Kingfisher made good time southwards on her first leg of the voyage, but the unscheduled delay of ten days at the islands of Las Palmas infuriated Johnny. His urgently cabled inquiries from Cape Town elicited the reply that there were teething troubles in *Kingfisher*'s engine room which were being attended to in the Las Palmas dockyards. The voyage would be resumed as soon as the repairs had been effected.

The Japanese gentleman who welcomed *Kingfisher* to Las Palmas was named Kaminikoto. This was too much for Sergio's tongue, so he called him 'Kammy'.

Sergio's crew was sent ashore with the excuse that the work on *Kingfisher* was dangerous. They were installed in the best tourist hotel and liberally supplied with intoxicating liquor. Sergio did not see them for the next ten days that he and Kammy were busy on the modifications to *Kingfisher*'s computer, and recovery equipment.

During those ten days Sergio and Kammy discovered that despite physical appearances they were brothers.

Kammy had mysterious packing-cases brought on board and they worked like furies from dawn until after dark each day. Then they relaxed.

Kammy was half Sergio's size with a face like a mischievous monkey. At all times he wore a Homburg hat. On the one occasion that Sergio saw him in his bath without his headgear he discovered that Kammy was as bald as St Peter's dome.

Kammy's abundant tastes in women were identical to Sergio's. This made the hiring of partners an easy matter, for what suited the one suited the other. Sergio took south with him fond memories of the little Japanese clad only in his Homburg hat, uttering birdlike cries of encouragement and excitement, while perched like a jockey on top of a percheron mare.

When at last Sergio shepherded his debauched crew back aboard *Kingfisher* the only obvious sign of their labours was that the inspection hatch on the conveyor tunnel had been moved back twelve feet.

'It is my best work,' Kammy told Sergio. Already he was sad at the prospect of parting. They were brothers. 'I signed my name. You will remember me when you see it.'

'You good guy, Kammy. The best!' Sergio embraced him, lifting him off his feet and kissing him heartily on each cheek while Kammy clutched desperately at his Homburg.

They left him standing on the wharf, a forlorn and solitary figure, while *Kingfisher* butted out into the Atlantic and swung away southwards.

Ruefully Johnny Lance glanced over at the mountain of empty champagne bottles beyond the barbecue pits. The bill for this little party would be in the thousands, but it was not an extravagance. The guest list included all Van Der Byl Diamond Company's major creditors and their wives, Johnny Lance was showing them all what they were getting for their money. To appear prosperous was almost as reassuring to a creditor as being prosperous. He was going to stuff them full of food and champagne, show them over the *Kingfisher* and fly them back home, hoping sincerely that they would be sufficiently impressed to stop badgering him for a while–and let him get on with the business of taking the Company out into the clear.

Tracey caught his eye. Her humorous roll of the eyes was a plea for sympathy, for she was surrounded by a pack of middle-aged bankers and financiers whom champagne had made susceptible to her charms. Johnny winked at her in reply, then glanced around guiltily to find Ruby, and was relieved that she was in deep conversation with Benedict van der Byl in a far corner of the marquee.

He made his way out of the crowd to the edge of the dune, and lit a cigarette while he looked back across Cartridge Bay.

The chartered Dakotas that had flown the guests and caterers up from Cape Town were standing on the airstrip beyond the buildings.

The marquee was situated on the crest of a sand-dune overlooking the narrow entrance to the bay. The dune had been bulldozed to accommodate the tent, the laden tables, and the barbecue pits around which white-clad servants were busy, and the spitted carcasses of three sheep and a young ox were already browning crisply and emitting a cloud of fragrant steam.

Tracey watched Johnny standing out on the edge of the dune. He looked tired, she thought. The strain of the last few months had worn him. Looking back on it now she realized that every few days had thrust a crisis upon him. The terrible worry of the court case that had won them Thunderbolt and Suicide had barely ended before Johnny had faced the delays in the construction of *Kingfisher*, the bullying of creditors, the sniping of Benedict and a hundred other worries and frustrations.

He was like a prize-fighter coming out to the bell of the last round, she thought tenderly, as she studied the profile of his face now staring out to sea. His stance was still aggressive, the big jaw pushed out and the hand with the missing finger that held the cigarette balled into a fist, but there were blue shadows under his eyes and lines of tension at the corners of his mouth.

Suddenly, there was an alertness in Johnny's attitude, he shaded his eyes with a hand before turning back towards the marquee.

'All right, everyone!' he called, stilling the babble of their voices. 'Here she comes.'

Immediately the uproar was redoubled and the whole party trooped out into the sunlight, their excitement and the shrillness of their voices enhanced by the Pommery they had been walloping back since mid-morning.

'Look! There she is!'

'Where? Where?'

'I can't see her.'

'Just to the left of that cloud on the horizon.'

'Oh yes! Look! Look!'

Tracey took a second glass of champagne from one of the waiters, and carried it across to Johnny.

'Thanks.' He smiled at her with the ease that now existed between them.

'It's taken her long enough to get here.' Tracey picked out the faraway speck on the green ocean that was *Kingfisher*. 'When will she begin working?'

'Tomorrow.'

'How long will it be before we know–well, if it has come off?'

'A week.' Johnny turned to her. 'A week to be certain, but we'll know in a day or two how it's shaping up.'

They were silent then, staring out at the gradually approaching speck. The crowd lost interest quickly and drifted back to the liquor, and the fragrant steaming platters of golden-brown meat that were coming from the barbecue pits.

Tracey broke the long friendly silence at last. She spoke hesitantly, as though reluctant to bring up a painful subject.

'How long has Ruby been back now–ten days?'

'About that,' Johnny agreed, glancing at her quickly. 'I haven't seen much of her,' he admitted. 'But she seems to be a lot more relaxed–at least she's off my back.'

'She and Benedict seem to have become very pally.' Tracey glanced across to where the other couple were now included in a boisterous circle of revellers.

'She bumped into him in London.' Johnny agreed, sounding offhand. 'She tells me they had lunch a couple of times.'

She waited for him to continue, to express some suspicion or reservation, but he seemed to have no further interest in the subject; instead he began running over the day's further arrangements with her.

'I'm relying on you to take charge of the wives when we go aboard. Keep an eye on Mrs Larsen particularly–she's up to her gills in bubbly.'

For the next two hours that it took *Kingfisher* to make her approach and enter the channel of Cartridge Bay, Johnny hardly took his eyes from her unusual silhouette. She was not a pretty vessel but the white lightning insignia of Van Der Byl Diamonds on her funnel gave her a special beauty in his eyes. As she passed below them and entered the bay, Larsen proposed a toast to her successful career, then they all descended the dune and climbed into the waiting Land-Rovers and drove round the bay to meet her. By the time they arrived *Kingfisher* had made fast alongside the jetty, and Captain Sergio Caporetti was waiting to welcome them aboard.

He stood at the head of the gangway, and sensible to the importance of the moment he was decked in his finest and best; a double-breasted suit with a cream and lilac pinstripe set off the tomato-red silk tie, but his two-tone black and white crocodile skin shoes drew attention to his large feet and his gait was that of an emperor penguin. A liberal application of a hair pomade with a penetrating smell of violets had flattened his black hair into a shiny slick, bisected by the ruler-straight line of white scalp which was his parting. However, the aroma of the pomade was at odds with the particularly stinky cheroot of a brand which Sergio reserved for weddings, funerals and other special occasions.

His beautiful gazelle eyes became passionate and dark as they lit on Fifi Larsen. Mrs Larsen's tight-fitting slacks moved as though they were full of live rabbits and her pink sweater was straining its seams. Her eyes were sparling with champagne and she giggled without apparent reason, flushing under Sergio's scrutiny.

The tour of *Kingfisher* began, Sergio Caporetti taking up an escort position directly behind Mrs Larsen. They had hardly descended the first ladder when Mrs Larsen let out a small squeak and shot about eighteen inches into the air, before coming back to earth with all her plentiful womanhood aquiver.

'My dear Fifi, whatever is wrong?' Her husband was all solicitude, while behind her Sergio Caporetti wore an expression of cherubic innocence. Johnny felt dizzy with alarm, for he had seen Sergio's great hairy paw settling comfortably onto those majestic buttocks. Mrs Fifi Larsen had been thoroughly goosed.

In relieved disbelief Johnny heard her reply, which was preceded by another giggle.

'I seem to have twisted my ankle. Perhaps there is somewhere I could sit down.'

Johnny looked around frantically for Tracey to get Mrs Larsen out of Sergio's clutching range, but before he could signal her, Fifi was limping away on Sergio Caporetti's arm, bravely declining all offers of help.

'Please don't let me spoil your fun. I'll just sit in the Captain's cabin for a few minutes.'

Quickly Johnny moved up beside the silver-haired Larsen and resolved to stay close beside him. Even if he could not prevent Fifi visiting Sergio's quarters, he was going to make good and sure that her husband didn't join the party.

'This is the explosives locker.' Johnny took Larsen's arm and led him away. 'We keep a store of plastique explosives for underwater blasting–'

Larsen's concern at his wife's injury dissolved and he became immersed in the tour of *Kingfisher*. Johnny followed the line of production for him from the moment the gravel was sucked in through the dredge.

As they left the cyclone room Johnny preceded him, holding the steel door open for Larsen.

'From the cyclone the concentrates pass through here into–' He stopped with surprise as they entered the narrow compartment beyond the cyclone.

'What's wrong, Lance?' Larsen demanded.

'No. It's nothing,' Johnny assured him. After the surprise of finding that the inspection plate in the conveyor tunnel had been moved he realized that it was as well from a security angle. Probably the marine architects had ordered the modification. 'The concentrates are carried through into the next compartment to the X-ray room. This way, please.'

As Johnny led the way to the next door he resolved to check with the architects. Larsen asked a question and he replied and the conveyor tunnel was forgotten. They went through into the X-ray room.

'He noticed it.' Benedict puffed quickly and nervously at the cigarette cupped in his hand. 'He doesn't miss a thing. The bastard.'

'He noticed it, yes. But he accepted it.' Ruby was definite. 'I know him. I was watching him. He was disturbed for a second then he rationalized it. I could almost see his mind work. He accepted it.'

They stood together on the exposed angle of *Kingfisher*'s bridge. Suddenly Ruby laughed.

'Don't look so worried,' she warned him merrily. 'We are being watched by your sister again. She's down on the foredeck. Come.'

Still smiling she led him around the angle of the bridge house, and out of sight she was immediately deadly serious again.

'That sister of yours is getting suspicious. We must keep away from each other until you tell Johnny.'

Benedict nodded.

'When are you going to tell him?' she demanded.

'Soon.'

'How soon?' Ruby would not be able to rest until it was out in the open, until Benedict had committed himself, yet she must not push him too hard.

'As soon as *Kingfisher* runs the Company under. I will pick the moment that he is beaten financially, then I will tell him. I want it to be the *coup de grâce*.'

'When will it be, Benedict darling? I am so anxious to be with you–without all this subterfuge.'

Benedict opened his mouth to reply and froze like that, his expression changing slowly into that of a man who doubts the evidence of his own eyes. He was staring over Ruby's shoulder.

Ruby turned quickly. The curtain across the Captain's porthole behind her was open a chink. She looked in upon a spectacle of such whole-hearted rubicund magnitude that it should have occurred only on Olympus between Jupiter and Juno.

In the cabin Fifi Larsen was receiving treatment for her sprained ankle.

'Well, you've got your toy now. Let's hope for all our sakes you can do something with it,' Benedict smiled pleasantly as he came across to where Johnny stood with Larsen under the great gallows-shaped gantry on the foredeck of *Kingfisher* that would raise and lower the dredging head.

'Toy, Mr van der Byl?' Larsen's white eyebrows bristled. 'Surely you have no doubts? I mean, now that you've got this Thunderbolt and Suicide concession?'

'Oh, I wouldn't say doubts, Mr Larsen. Reservations perhaps, but not really doubts. Mr Lance has been the champion of this venture. His enthusiasm has carried it–in the face of all opposition. Even that of my late father.' Benedict turned to Larsen smoothly.

'Your father opposed the scheme? I didn't know that!' Larsen was perturbed.

'Not opposed it, Mr Larsen.' Benedict smiled reassuringly. 'Not really opposed it. But you will notice that he was prepared to risk your money–not his own. That will give you some idea of how he felt.'

There was a chilled silence, before Larsen turned to Johnny.

'Well, Lance, thank you for an interesting day. Very interesting. I'll be watching your progress with attention–close attention.' And he turned away and strode to where a subdued and demure Fifi was waiting with a group of other wives.

'Thanks.' Johnny gave Benedict a bleak grin.

'Don't mention it.' Benedict smiled that charming boyish smile.

'At the end of this week I'll take that little speech of yours, roll it into a ball and ram it down your throat,' Johnny promised him softly, and Benedict's expression changed. His eyes slitted and his grin showed his teeth and tightened the soft line of his jaw.

'You're pretty slick with your mouth, Lance.'

They glared at each other, the antagonism so apparent, as elemental as a pair of rutting stags, that they were suddenly the centre of all attention. The guests stared curiously, aware of the drama but not understanding it.

Ruby started forward quickly to intervene, taking Johnny's elbow, her voice sugary.

'Oh, Benedict, do you mind if I talk to Johnny a moment? I have to know if he's returning to Cape Town with me this evening.'

She led him away, and the tension dissolved. The disappointed guests began drifting to the gangplank and filing down onto the jetty.

In the confusion of embarkation aboard the two Dakotas, Johnny managed to exchange a last word with Tracey.

'You'll stay here until you know?' she asked. He nodded.

'Good luck, Johnny. I'll pray for you,' she whispered, then followed Ruby Lance up into the fuselage of the Dakota.

Johnny watched the two big aircraft taxi down to the end of the strip, turn in succession and roar away into the purple and red sky of evening.

After they had gone it was very still, and the silence of the desert was complete. Johnny sat in the open Land-Rover and smoked a cigarette while the night came down around him.

He was uneasy, aware of a deep-down tickle of apprehension and foreboding which he could not pin down.

The last glow of sunset faded from the Western sky, and the desert stars were bright and hard and close to the earth, silvering the dome of space with the splendour that the city-dweller would never guess at.

Still Johnny hunched in the seat of the open Land-Rover trying to explore the source of his uneasiness, but with so little success that at last he must attribute it to the strain and fatigue of the last few months, his involvement with Tracey, his steadily worsening relationship with Ruby–and the latest clash with Benedict.

He flicked the stub of his cigarette away, watching morosely the explosion of red sparks as it struck the earth, then he started the Land-Rover and drove slowly down towards the jetty.

Kingfisher's lights were smeared in paths of yellow and silver across the still waters of the bay. Every porthole was lit brightly, giving her the festive air of a cruise ship.

Johnny left the Land-Rover at the head of the jetty, and walked out to her. The muted throb of her engines cheered him a little, the knowledge that the vessel was preparing for the morrow.

On deck he paused beside the gigantic compressed air tanks, each the size of a steam locomotive, and checked the pressure gauges. The needles were moving perceptibly around the dials, and his mood lightened a little.

He went up the ladder to the bridge, and into the chartroom where Sergio and Hugo were drinking coffee.

'Not my fault, Mr Lance,' Sergio began defensively. 'I am a gentleman–I cannot refuse a lady.'

'You'll dig your own grave with that spade of yours one day,' Johnny warned him grimly, as he went to the chart table and hung over it.

'Now let's get cracking.' Johnny's sense of dread lifted completely as he looked down at the large-scale Admiralty chart. The twin humps of Thunderbolt and Suicide were clearly marked. 'Hugo, have you got the prospecting schedules?'

'There, on the table.' Hugo and Sergio came to stand on each side of Johnny while he opened the bound file of typewritten sheets.

'The soundings we made differ from the Admiralty chart. We'll put in our figures, before we plot the dredging pattern.'

The three of them settled over the chart with dividers and parallel to begin marking in the path that *Kingfisher* would follow through the maze of reefs and gullies.

It was long after midnight before Johnny made his way wearily to the guest cabin below the bridge. He kicked off his shoes, lay on the bunk to rest a moment before undressing and fell into a deathlike sleep of exhaustion.

He was awakened by one of the crew with a mug of coffee and he pulled on a windbreaker before hurrying onto the bridge.

Kingfisher was just passing out through the channel of Cartridge Bay into the open sea, and Sergio grinned at him from where he stood beside the helm.

Dawn was only a lemon-coloured promise over the desert behind them, and the sea was black as washed anthracite, kicked into a chop by the small morning wind. They stood on the darkened bridge and sipped steaming coffee, cupping their hands around the enamel mugs.

Then they turned and ran south, parallel to the desert which was now touched with hot orange and violet. The sea birds were up, a flight of malgas turned to glowing darts of fire by the early sun as they winged swiftly across the bows.

With dramatic suddenness the sun came up over the horizon, and highlighted the chalk-white cliffs of Thunderbolt and Suicide far ahead so that they shone like beacons on the cold green sea. The curtains of spray that burst on the islands flashed and faded as they shot into the sky and fell again.

Wild Goose was waiting for them lying under the lee of the islands, but she came out to meet them, staggering and plunging theatrically over the short uneasy sea that hooked around the islands or boiled through the gap between them.

The radio telephone began crackling and squawking as the sighting reports from Johnny's watch towers on the shore started coming in, cross referencing to give *Kingfisher* her position over the ground. There were short exchanges between Sergio and Hugo on *Wild Goose* as they came together, and the little trawler worked in close, ready to give assistance with the laying of the cables if she were needed.

But standing in the angle of the bridge, Sergio Caporetti had the situation under his control. The grubby marine cap pushed to the back of his head and a long black cheroot stuck in the side of his mouth, he stood balanced on the balls of his feet, his eyes darting from judging the set of the sea surf to the repeater of the computer which was feeding him from his soundings and position–yet attentive to the R T reports from shore and from *Wild Goose*.

Johnny was contented with his choice of man as he watched Sergio at work. *Kingfisher* crept slowly up into the lee of Suicide Island, half a mile from the pearly white cliffs, then she hung there a moment before Sergio punched one of the buttons on her control panel.

From forward there was the harsh metallic roar of an anchor cable running out, and as *Kingfisher* backed away leaving a yellow painted buoy the size of a barrage balloon bobbing under the cliffs of Suicide so one of the massive deck winches began automatically paying out its six-inch steel cable.

Kingfisher backed and crept forward, drifted down on the current or butted up against it while she went through the laborious but delicate operation of laying her four anchors at each point of the compass. Chained above each anchor floated the huge yellow buoys, and from each buoy the steel cables led to the winches on *Kingfisher*'s deck. On instruction from the computer the winches on each quarter would pay out or reel in the cable to hold *Kingfisher* steady over the ground while she worked.

It was mid afternoon before *Kingfisher* was ready, pinned down like an insect to a board, and the computer reported that she was directly over the gully that Johnny had selected as the starting point. She had twenty-five fathoms of water under her–and then the thick bank of gravel.

'All is ready.' Sergio turned to Johnny, who had stood by quietly all this time–not interfering in the task of positioning. 'You will begin the programme now?'

'Yes.' Johnny stirred himself.

'I would like to watch,' Sergio suggested, and Johnny nodded.

'All right, come.' Sergio handed over the bridge to the helmsman and they went down to the armoured door of the computer room.

Johnny opened the lock. There were only two keys to this compartment. Johnny had one and Benedict van der Byl had the other. He had insisted on having the duplicate, and Johnny had reluctantly agreed not knowing that the key would be used in Las Palmas.

The heavy steel door swung back, and Johnny stepped over the coaming and seated himself before the console of the computer. Covered in cellophane and suspended on a clip above the keyboard of the computer were the cards containing the various programme codes.

Johnny selected the sheet headed: PRIMARY OPERATION: DREDGING AND RECOVERY, and began feeding the code into the computer, punching it on the keyboard.

'Beta, stroke, oh, oh, seven, alpha.'

And within the enamelled console, a change of sound heralded the beginning of the new programme, the hum of her reels and the click of the selectors, while on her control panel the lights blinked and flashed.

Now the computer's screen began to answer the instruction, spelling out her response like a typewriter.

> New programme.
> Primary Operation. Dredging and Recovery.
> Phase One.
> Initiate safety procedure:–
> a) Report air pressure . . . 1
> b) Report air pressure . . . 2

Johnny leaned back in the padded stool and watched the exhaustive check that the computer now made of *Kingfisher*'s equipment, typing out the results on the screen.

'What she do now?' Sergio asked curiously, as though he had never spent ten days in this compartment assisting his Japanese friend. Johnny explained the procedure briefly.

'How come you know this so good?' Sergio inquired.

'I spent a month at the Computer Company's head office in America last year while they designed this machine.'

'You the only one in the Company who can work it?'

'Mr Benedict van der Byl has done the course as well as I,' Johnny told him, then he leaned forward again. 'Now she is set.'

The screen on the computer reported itself satisfied.

> Phase One Completed.
> Initiate Phase Two.
> Lowering and siting of dredge head.

Johnny stood up. 'Okay, let's get upstairs.'

He locked the door of the computer room and followed Sergio up to the bridge.

Johnny went to stand beside the repeater screen on the bridge, which was relaying the computer's signals exactly as they were printed on the main screen in the compartment below. He could see out through the windows of the wheelhouse, and he watched the automatic response of the heavy equipment on the foredeck.

The gantry swung forward, and the steel arms picked the dredge head from its chocks, and lifted it with the armoured suction hose dangling behind it. Then the gantry swung back, and with a jerky mechanical movement lowered the head through the square opening in the deck. This well pierced the hull, and through it the hose began to snake–a monstrous black python sliding into its hole. The huge reels that held the hose revolved smoothly, as the dredge was lowered to the sea bed.

'Head on bottom.'

The computer screen reported, and the hose reels stopped abruptly.

Phase Two Completed.
Initiate Phase Three.
Cyclone Revolutions 300.
Vent dredge pump.

There was a rising high-pitched whine now, like the approach of a jet aircraft. The sound reached a peak, and steadied–and immediately another sound overlaid it. The dull bubbling roar of high-pressure air through water, a sound of such power and excitement that Johnny felt the hair on his forearms prickle erect. He stood still as a statue, his expression rapt and his lips set in a small secret smile. That sound was the culmination of two years of planning and endeavour, the sweet reward of the driving dedication that had made a dream into reality.

Suddenly he wished that Tracey were with him to share this moment, and then he knew instinctively that she had deliberately left him alone to savour his moment of triumph.

He grinned then, as he watched the thick black hose engorge and pulse with internal life, like a great artery–pumping, pumping, pumping.

In his imagination Johnny could see the rich porridgy mixture of sea water and mud and gravel that shot up the hose into the spinning cyclone, he could imagine the steel dredge head on the sea bed below the hull surging rhythmically to stir the sand and pound loose any gravel that pressure had welded into a conglomerate.

From the waste pipe over *Kingfisher*'s stern poured a solid stream of dirty yellow water mixed with the sand and gravel that had been rejected and spun out of the cyclone. It stained the green sea with a cloudy fecal discharge, like the effluent from a sewage outlet.

For three days and two nights *Kingfisher*'s pumps roared, and she inched forward along the marine gully like a fussy housewife vacuuming every speck of dust from her floor. As the third evening spread its dark cloak over her, Johnny Lance sat on the padded seat in front of the computer console. He sat forward on the stool with his elbows on his knees and his face in his hands for a full hour. He sat like that in the attitude of despair.

When he lifted his head, his face was haggard and the lines of defeat were clearly cut into his features with the cold chisel of failure.

From the meagre recovery of small diamonds that *Kingfisher* had made in the last three days it was clear beyond reasonable doubt that despite all the indications of Thunderbolt and Suicide field would not support the running costs of the vessel let alone cover the overheads, or the interest charges and capital repayments on the loan account.

Van Der Byl Diamond Company was finished–and Johnny Lance was financially ruined beyond any possibility of ever finding redemption.

It remained only for the jackals to assemble and squabble over the carcass. Sergio Caporetti leaned over the railing of the bridge, blowing long streamers of blue cheroot smoke from mouth and nostrils to help foul a morning which was already thick and grey with sea-fret. The islands of Thunderbolt and Suicide were blanketed by the mist, but the surf broke against their hidden cliffs like distant artillery and the sea birds' voices were plaintive and small as lost souls in the void.

Wild Goose came bustling up out of the mist, swinging in under *Kingfisher*'s side to hover there under power with two of her crew fending off.

Hugo Kramer stuck his white blond head out of the wheelhouse window, and shouted up at the deck.

'Okay, boss. Come on!'

Sergio watched the tall figure on *Kingfisher*'s deck rise and look around like a man walking from sleep. Johnny Lance lifted his head and looked up at the bridge, and Sergio noticed that he was unshaven, a new beard darkened his jaw and emphasized its prominence. He looked as though he had not slept, and he hunched into the wind-breaker with the collar turned up against the mist. He did not smile, but lifted one hand in farewell salute to Sergio–who noticed incongruously that the index finger was missing from the hand. Somehow, that pathetic little detail struck Sergio. He was sorry, truly sorry. But there is always a loser in every game, and twenty-five thousand pounds is a lot of money.

'Good luck, Johnny.'

'Thanks, Sergio.' Johnny went to the rail lugging his briefcase and swung it; he dropped swiftly down the steel rungs set in *Kingfisher*'s hull and jumped the narrow gap of surging water to *Wild Goose*'s deck.

The trawler's engine bellowed, and she pulled away, rounding on to a course for Cartridge Bay. Johnny Lance stood on her open deck looking back at *Kingfisher*.

'He's a good guy.' Sergio shook his head with regret.

'He's a boss,' the helmsman grunted. 'No boss is any good.'

'Hey, you! I am also a boss,' Sergio challenged him.

'Like I said.' The helmsman suppressed a grin.

'I kiss your mother,' Sergio insulted him with dignity, then changed the subject. 'I go below now, take over.'

Sergio opened the door to the control room with the duplicate key. He closed the door behind him, seated himself at the console and took from his pocket a sheet of paper headed: KAMINIKOTO SECONDARY RECOVERY PROGRAMME.

Ten minutes later he came out of the control room and locked the door.

'Kammy, I love you,' he chuckled as he closed off the water-tight doors that isolated this deck from the one above. He wound the locking bars into position to ensure that he was not interrupted by one of his own crew.

From the tool cupboard on the bulkhead he selected a pair of set spanners and went through into the conveyor room. It took him twenty minutes to unscrew the heavy, deeply threaded bolts that secured the hatch. It had been designed to resist easy entry–a deterrent to casual investigation, but at least

Sergio could lift the steel plate off its seating.

He eyed the small square opening with distaste, and reflexively sucked in his pendulous belly. The hatch had not been designed to afford passage to a man of his dimensions.

He took off his cap and jacket and hung them on the cock of one of the pipes, then he ground out his cheroot under his heel and brushed back the hair from his forehead with both hands, checked that his flashlight was in his pocket, and committed himself to the hatch.

He wriggled and kicked, and grunted and built up a heavy sweat for five minutes before he had squeezed through into the conveyor belt tunnel. He squatted on his haunches, panting heavily and flashed his torch along the tunnel. Above his head the conveyor belt carrying the gravel ran smoothly, but the residual heat from the driers made it unbearably hot. He began to crawl rapidly to the end of the tunnel.

From the inside it was impossible to tell, without measuring, that the conveyor belt tunnel was shorter by twelve feet than the external length.

The end of the tunnel was false, and beyond it was a secret cubicle only just large enough to house Kaminikoto's equipment through which all the gravel passed on its journey to the X-ray room.

The Japanese genius for miniaturization was demonstrated by the equipment in this secret cubicle. It was an almost exact copy of the sorting equipment in the main X-ray compartment–except that it had been scaled down to one tenth of the size without affecting its efficiency; in addition, this miniature plant could discriminate in the diamonds it selected. It would not allow a stone over four carats to pass through, and it screened out fixed percentages of the smaller stones–allowing only a proportion of the smaller and less valuable diamonds to proceed through into the main X-ray room.

It was an amazing piece of electrical engineering, but Sergio was unimpressed as he lay on his side in the cramped hot tunnel and began laboriously to unscrew another smaller plate in the false bulkhead.

At last it was open, and he reached through the opening; after a few seconds of fiddling and groping and heavy breathing he brought out a stainless steel cup with a capacity of about two pints. There were clamps on the cup to hold it in position below the chute under Kaminikoto's machine.

The metal cup was heavy, and Sergio placed it carefully on the deck beside him before propping himself on an elbow and shining the flashlight into the cup. His expression changed, and he groped in the cup and took something out of it, stared at it a moment then dropped it back.

'By the blood of all the martyrs!' he gasped with shock, and then immediately contrite for his blasphemy he crossed himself awkwardly with the hand holding the flashlight. Then again he shone the torch into the cup, and shook his head in disbelief. Quickly he pulled a canvas drawstring bag from his pocket, and lying on his side he carefully poured the contents of the cup into the bag, drew the string tight and stuffed it back into his pocket where it made a big hard bulge on his hip like a paper sack of rock-candy. He clamped the stainless steel cup back into position, screwed the cover plate over the opening, and backed away down the tunnel on hands and knees.

He very badly needed a cheroot.

Four hours later Hugo Kramer shinned up the ladder onto *Kingfisher*'s deck while his helmsman took the trawler down to leeward to wait for him.

Sergio shouted down from the bridge.

'Johnny he has gone?'

'Ja!' Hugo shouted back. 'He should almost be in Cape Town by now. That Beechcraft is a fast plane.'

'Good.'

'How did it go with you?' Hugo countered.

'Come up–I'll show you.'

Sergio led him into his cabin behind the bridge and locked the door carefully. Then he went to each of the portholes and drew the curtains across them, before crossing to his desk and switching on the reading lamp.

'Sit down.' Sergio indicated the chair opposite the desk. 'You want a drink, or something?'

'Come on,' Hugo grated impatiently. 'Stop mucking around, let's have a look.'

'Ah!' Sergio looked at him sadly. 'You Germans, you are always in too much hurry. You cannot rest, enjoy life–'

'Cut the crap!' Hugo's pale eyes were on his face, and Sergio was suddenly aware that this man was dangerous, like a tiger-shark. Coldly dangerous, without malice or passion. Sergio was surprised he had not noticed it before. I must be careful with this one, he thought, and he unlocked the drawer of his desk and took out the canvas bag.

He loosened the drawstring and poured the diamonds onto the blotter. The smallest was the size of a match head–perhaps point one of a carat, and the poorest quality was black and granular-looking, ugly little industrial stones, for Kammy had been careful not to take out only the best and so distort the *Kingfisher*'s recovery as to arouse suspicion. There were hundreds of these tiny crystals and chips which would fetch a few pounds in the industrial market; but there were other stones in the full range of quality and shapes and sizes–as big as green peas, or as marbles, and a few bigger than that. Some of them were perfect octahedron crystals, others water-worn, chipped or amorphous in shape.

They formed a dully glittering pile in the centre of the blotter, in all perhaps five hundred diamonds, yet all of these were dwarfed by one single stone that lay in the centre of the pile, rising out of it the way Mount Everest rises from her foothills.

There are freak diamonds so large or unusual that they become legend. Diamonds who have their own names and whose histories are recorded and invested with romance. The great 'paragons'–stones of the first water whose cut and finish weight exceed one hundred metric carats.

Africa has produced many of them: the *Jonker Diamond*, a 726-carat rough cut to a brilliant of 125 carats that hangs about the throat of the Queen of Nepal; the *Jubilee Diamond*, a superb 245-carat cushion of unearthly fire fashioned out of 650-carat rough–then the biggest of them all, a monstrous rough stone of 3,106 carats, the *Cullinan* which yielded not one, but two paragons. The *Great Star of Africa* at 530 carats and the *Cullinan II* at 317 carats. Both these stones grace the Crown Jewels of England.

Now on Sergio Caporetti's desk lay a rough stone which would add yet another paragon to the list.

'Have you weighed it?' asked Hugo, and Sergio nodded.

'How much?'

'Three hundred and twenty carats,' Sergio said softly.

'Jesus!' whispered Hugo, and Sergio crossed himself quickly to dissociate from the use of names.

Reverently Hugo Kramer leaned forward and picked up the big diamond. It filled the palm of his hand, the cleavage plane that formed its base was smooth and clean as an axe-stroke. There were bigger diamonds in history, but this diamond had a special feature which would set it in a niche of its own and endow it with peculiar value.

Its colour was the serene blue of a high summer sky.

This stone could pay half the total bill for *Kingfisher*'s construction–if it were ever used for that purpose.

Hugo replaced the blue diamond on the desk and lit a cigarette without taking his eyes from it.

'This field–it is bigger–richer, far richer than we had guessed.'

Sergio nodded.

'In three days we have taken diamonds that I hoped to see once in five years,' Hugo went on as he began picking out the larger diamonds from the pile and laying them in a line across the desk-top in approximate order of size, while Sergio opened his desk drawer and took out a box of his special occasion cheroots.

'We must tell the boss,' Hugo decided. He began arranging the diamonds in a neat circle about the big Blue, thinking deeply. 'He must know how rich it is before he talks to Lance. He must make arrangements. He will know what to do–he's a clever one.'

'What about these?' Sergio indicated the treasure on the desk. 'Are you going to take them off?'

Hugo hesitated. 'No,' he decided. 'We could never get rid of this big Blue through the usual channel, it is too big, too distinctive. We will keep it aboard. When the boss takes over the Company again–then we will just declare it all nice and legal. No trouble.' He stood up. 'Look after them. I must hurry if I am to get a message to Cape Town in time.'

'The Company bears my father's name, Mr Larsen. It's as simple as that.' Benedict's voice was husky with emotion, and he looked down at his hands. 'I have a duty to my father's memory.'

'My boy, well–' Larsen came to lay his hand on Benedict's arm. 'Well, I just don't know what to say. Honour is a rare and precious thing these days.' With his free hand he was groping almost frantically for the bell on the desk behind him. He must get this signed up solid before the youngster changed his mind.

'I tried to warn you, Mr Larsen. My father and I never had any faith in this marine recovery scheme. Lance pushed it through–'

'Yes, quite so,' Larsen agreed, and turned to his assistant who came into the office at the trot in response to the bell. 'Ah, Simon. The Van Der Byl Diamond loan. Will you have an agreement made out immediately–Mr van der Byl will take over the capital amounts, and the out-standing interest as well.' By rolling his eyes Larsen tried to convey to his assistant the deadly urgency of the situation. The young man understood and fifteen minutes later laid the Agreement on Larsen's desk. Larsen unscrewed the cap of his pen and handed it to Benedict.

Larsen and three of his young men ushered Benedict out through the glass doors of the bank and across the pavement to where the Rolls stood in the reserved parking bay in Adderley Street.

Benedict settled into the back seat, acknowledged the bank official's farewells, and tapped on the chauffeur's window. As they pulled away, Ruby Lance slipped her hand through his arm and squeezed it.

'Did you get it?' she asked.

Benedict grinned happily. 'I frightened five years' growth out of old Larsen. He almost broke his neck in the hurry to give it to me.'

'Now you've got it all.' Ruby snuggled a little closer to him on the soft leather upholstery. Benedict nodded, and checked his watch.

'The meeting is set for fifteen minutes' time. I'll go up the front way, but I want you to go up in the private lift from the basement garage, and wait in my office. We will be in the Board Room. I will ring you at the right moment.'

The Rolls picked its way slowly down around the Heerengracht and double-parked outside the building. The chauffeur came to open the door, but before he alighted Benedict smiled into Ruby's face.

'This will be one of the high moments of my life,' he said softly. 'This time I've got the bastard cold.'

'I'll be waiting for you,' Ruby said, and he climbed out of the Rolls. He waited until it had turned into the entrance ramp of the basement garage, then he crossed the pavement into the main lobby of the skyscraper. He strode to the elevator with long eager strides, and his mouth kept pulling into a small excited smile.

The Board Room was set high, and the picture windows looked up at the great squat mountain, whose sheer cliffs dropped directly to the wooded slopes up which the first buildings of the city straggled.

Johnny Lance stood at the head of the table. He had lost weight in the last few days, so that his shoulders appeared bony and gaunt under the white silk shirt. He had discarded his jacket, and pulled the knot of his tie down an inch. The bones of his cheeks and jaw made harsh angles that were accentuated and not softened by the deep shades of fatigue that darkened his eyes. His hands were thrust deep into his pockets, and he spoke without reference to the sheaf of paper that lay on the table before him.

'Our working costs are as close as dammit to a hundred pounds an hour; right Mike?' And Michael Shapiro nodded. 'Well, we worked the Suicide main gully for sixty-six hours, and we recovered a princely 200 carats of the lousiest pile of junk I've ever seen. If we get a thousand quid for the lot we'll be doing well. This for an expenditure of six and a half thousand.'

Johnny paused, and looked around the table. Michael Shapiro was doodling on his note pad with fierce concentration, Tracey van der Byl was pale, her eyes never left Johnny's face and her expression ached with pity and helpless compassion; Benedict van der Byl was looking out of the window at the mountain, he was slumped comfortably in his chair, smiling a little and listening politely.

'The Suicide main gully is one of the five most likely parts of the entire concession. It's no good, so the rest of the field may be useless. We have the two other concessions, the original fields, to try. However, it will take three or four days to get *Kingfisher* moved up the coast.' Johnny paused, and Benedict swivelled his chair, still with the small smile on his lips.

'The interest payments fall due on the 30th–three days' time. Where are you going to find one hundred and fifty thousand Rand?'

'Yes,' Johnny nodded. 'I think I can persuade Larsen to extend for a few weeks; he will bloody well have to if he wants to protect his–'

'Hold on,' Benedict murmured. 'Larsen has got nothing to do with it.'

Johnny was silent, watching him warily. 'Explain,' he invited.

'I've taken over the loan from Larsen,' Benedict told him. 'I'm not interested in extending.'

'Larsen wouldn't have negotiated without warning me.' Johnny was stricken, his disclaimer was wrung from him in pain.

'Shapiro?' Benedict turned to Michael Shapiro for confirmation.

'Sure, Johnny. It's true. I've seen the documents.'

'Thanks, Michael.' Johnny's voice was bitter with accusation. 'Thanks for letting me know.'

'He showed me a few minutes before the meeting, Johnny. I swear I didn't know.' Michael's expression was distressed.

'Right.' Benedict straightened up in his chair, his voice was brisk. 'Let's get down to first principles. You've ruined my father's Company, Lance–but, thank God, I may be able to retrieve the situation. Call it sentiment or what you like, but I want your shares–and yours.' He turned to Tracey and nodded at her.

'No,' said Tracey sharply.

'Right.' Benedict smiled at her. 'Then I'm going to hammer Johnny Lance for his full obligations. That way I get the Company anyway, but I'll make damn sure he remains an unrehabilitated bankrupt for the rest of his life.'

Tracey lifted her hand to her throat, and turned her eyes to Johnny. Waiting for him to set a lead. There was a long stark silence, then Johnny Lance dropped his eyes.

'I've still got three days.' His voice was gruff and tired.

'Three days you have.' Benedict grinned coldly. 'And you're welcome to them.'

Johnny picked up his papers and put them under one arm; he took his jacket off the back of the chair and swung it over his shoulder.

'Wait,' ordered Benedict.

'What for?' Johnny's grin was twisted. 'You've had your fun.'

Benedict lifted the receiver of the telephone on the table and dialled swiftly.

'Come through, please, darling.' He spoke into the mouthpiece and smiled at Johnny as he hung up. Then as the door opened he went to meet Ruby Lance, and kissed her on the mouth. The two of them stood, arm in arm, and looked at Johnny.

'The Company is not the only thing I've taken from you,' Benedict said softly.

'I want a divorce.' Ruby looked steadily into Johnny's face. 'Benedict and I are going to get married.'

They were all watching Johnny, and they saw him flinch. He looked from one face to the other, then his mouth tightened and his forehead furrowed.

Tracey saw his anger mounting, and her eyes flicked to Benedict's face. He was leaning forward expectantly, his lips quivering with expectation, his eyes alight with triumph. Tracey wanted to scream out a warning to Johnny, stop him falling into the trap that Benedict had set so carefully.

Johnny took a pace forward, coming up onto the balls of his feet. He was about to make his defeat total and ineradicable. Then Benedict spoiled it for himself, he goaded once more.

'Game, set and match, Johnny Lance,' he crowed.

The effort of will that Johnny made to recover his reason was not shown on his face, he made the step forward seem natural and he continued towards the door.

'The house is in your name, of course, Ruby, so would you please send my things down to the Tulbagh Hotel,' he asked quietly.

He stopped in front of the couple and spoke to Ruby.

'You'll want to protect your reputation, of course, so I'll not sue for aldultery. We'll call it desertion.'

'You're eating your guts out,' jeered Benedict. 'Lance can't keep his woman. Van der Byl took her away from him. Go on, sue for adultery–let the world hear it.'

'As you wish,' Johnny agreed.

And he walked out of the Board Room to the elevators.

Johnny flopped onto the bed fully dressed, and rubbed his closed eyes with his finger-tips. He felt confused and off-balance, the edge of his mind which usually slashed quickly and incisively through a problem was dulled. This problem was so multiplied and tangled that he felt like a man in a thicket of African ebony trying to cut his way out with a blunt machete.

Without opening his eyes he groped for the telephone, and the girl on the hotel switchboard downstairs answered. He gave her a number in Kimberley.

'Person to person, Mr Ralph Ellison.'

'Fifteen minutes' delay, Mr Lance,' the girl told him.

'Okay,' Johnny replied. 'Ask room service to send me up a Chivas Regal and soda.' He suddenly needed liquor, something to dull the pain. 'Make that a double, honey–no, make it two doubles.'

He had drained both glasses by the time his Kimberley call came through.

'Ralph?' Johnny spoke into the receiver.

'Johnny, how nice of you to call.' There was an echo like distant laughter beneath those cool ambassadorial tones in Ralph Ellison's voice and Johnny knew instantly that the word was out. Damn it, he was slow–of course Benedict would have blocked him.

'Are you still interested in a deal on the Thunderbolt and Suicide Concession?' Johnny loosed a despairing long-range shot.

'Of course, you know we are always interested,' Ralph replied.

'The price is two million.' Johnny lost interest and lay back on the bed, closing his eyes again. He knew Ralph was having his revenge–you didn't take this boy to court and win without sowing yourself a minefield to retreat over.

'Two million,' Ralph murmured. 'Now that's a little high–for a field that's yielding 200 carats of small industrial diamonds per 10,000 loads, that's definitely on the high side. Of course we wouldn't want that battleship of yours either–we are not starting our own navy.' Ralph chuckled juicily. 'We could talk around fifty to a hundred grand–no more than that, Johnny.'

'Okay, Ralph.' Johnny spoke wearily. 'Thanks all the same. We'll have a drink together sometime.'

'Any time, Johnny,' Ralph agreed. 'Any time at all. You call me.'

Johnny dropped the receiver back on its hook and looked at the ceiling. He had heard that a gunshot wound was numb at first–he felt numb now. All the energy had seeped out of him, he had lost direction.

The telephone shrilled and he picked it up. The girl on the switchboard asked politely:

'Are you finished, Mr Lance?'

'Yes,' said Johnny. 'You might say that.'

'Is there anything else you require?' The girl sounded puzzled.

'Yes, honey, send up the hemlock.'

'I beg your pardon?'

'Two more big fat whiskies, please.'

He drank them in the bath, and while he dried himself the doorbell tinkled. He wound the bath towel round his waist and went through to open the door.

Tracey stepped into the bedroom and closed the door behind her. They stood looking at each other for a long moment. Her eyes were big and dark, reflecting his agony faithfully.

'Johnny–' Her voice was husky, and she reached out and laid the palm of her hand on his chest. His shoulders sagged, and he moved close to her, his forehead sinking onto her shoulder. He sighed, a ragged broken exhalation of breath.

'Come,' she said, and led him to the bed. Leaving him there she went to the windows and closed the curtains.

It was warm and safe in the half dark of the curtained room, and they held each other as they had done long years before. Clinging together, so their breathing mingled, and it was not necessary to speak.

When they became lovers it seemed that they had waited all their lives for that moment.

Afterwards he lay with her in his arms and he felt strength flowing back into him, drawing it from her. When he sat up in the bed the bemused, almost dazed expression had gone. His jaw was out and his eyes were bright.

'We've still got three days,' he said.

'Yes.' She sat up beside him. 'Go, Johnny. Go quickly, don't waste another moment.'

'I'll pull *Kingfisher* out of the main gully. I'll find those diamonds. They are there. I *know* they are there. I'll take her right down into the jaws of Thunderbolt and Suicide, I'll find those bloody diamonds–damned if I won't.' He swung his legs off the bed, reached for his clothes, glancing at his wristwatch as he did so. 'Four o'clock. I can get to Cartridge Bay a few minutes after dark. Will you call the communications office, ask them to radio Cartridge Bay and have a flare set for me, and *Wild Goose* standing by to run me out?'

'I'll phone them from here. Then I'll take a bath–you go on. Don't waste time.' Tracey nodded eagerly, and Johnny let his eyes drop down over her body. He reached out and touched one big white breast almost diffidently.

'You are beautiful–I hate to go.'

'It will all be here, waiting for you, when you get back.'

'It wasn't the way I'd planned it. It wasn't good the way I'd dreamed about it.' Benedict paced angrily over the floor of the Old Man's study, swinging towards the windows and pausing to stare at the mountain across the valley.

'You hurt him. You crushed him.' Ruby moved restlessly in her chair across the room from him, curling her long golden legs defensively under her, sitting like a cat in the big chair. She was worried, and it showed in the tiny crows' feet at the corners of her eyes and the way she held her lips pursed. She should have anticipated this reaction from him, she should have known that his moment of triumph could never match his anticipation of it–and that revenge must always be followed by sour distaste and a feeling of disappointment. She realized that her safest course was to leave him alone now, she should never have returned with him to the old house on Wynberg Hill. She stood up.

'Darling.' She crossed to him. 'I'm going home now. I want to pack his clothes and get rid of them. I want to wipe out every memory of him. From now on it's you and I–together.'

She stretched up to kiss him, but Benedict turned his face away.

'Oh! So you're going, are you?' His expresssion was petulant, his lips pouting spitefully.

'We're both tired, darling. Let us both rest a while– and I'll come back later this evening.'

'So now you're giving the orders, are you?' He laughed nastily.

'Darling–'

'And cut out all the darlings. We pulled a deal and it didn't work out. You were meant to be a club to break his skull–and do you know something? He didn't give a damn. I was watching him, he was pleased–yes! He was bloody well delighted to get rid of you.'

'Benedict–' She stepped back.

'Listen.' He stepped close to her, and pushed his face towards hers. 'If you're so bloody anxious to go, why don't you bloody well go–and keep going. If he doesn't want you–then I sure as hell don't want you either.'

'Benedict,' she whispered. The colour faded from her face, leaving it washed white as beach sand. She stared at him in horror, as her dreams began to fall into ruins around her. 'You don't mean that.'

'I don't? Is that so?' He threw back his head and laughed again. 'Listen, you got some nice diamonds and a mink coat. You got a big house in Bishopscourt–now, that's pretty good pay for a whore.'

'Benedict–' She gasped at the insult, but he wasn't listening.

'I proved I could have you, didn't I? I proved I could take you away from him–and that's what it was all about. Now, why don't you go on home like a good girl.'

'The machine. I know about that thing in *Kingfisher*.' It was a mistake. Until then she still had a chance. His face changed shape and the blood flooded into it. His voice when he spoke was unsteady, thick with rage for his lips seemed to have swollen.

'Try it,' he whispered back at her. 'Go on, try it. They'll give you fifteen years. You're in it as deep as I am. Think about it–fifteen years in a woman's prison, my beauty. And think about this also–' He showed her his hand, holding it like a blade before her eyes. 'I'll kill you. I swear before God, I'll kill you with my bare hands. You know I'll do it–you know enough about me now.'

She backed away from him, and he followed her still holding his hand at her throat.

'You've been paid. Now get out.'

A few seconds longer she stood before him, and he was not too far gone in rage to see the fear in her eyes mingle with something else that made her eyes slit and drew her lips back to show the little white teeth.

'All right,' she said. 'I'll go.' And she walked from the room, stepping daintily, the long yellow hair swinging against her shoulders.

Ruby drove slowly for her vision was blurred with her tears. Twice other drivers hooted at her but she kept both hands clenched on the wheel and stared ahead, following the De Waal Drive around the lower slopes of the mountain.

Before she reached the University she swung off the road and drove up through the pine forests until she reached the car park behind the Cecil Rhodes Memorial. She left the car and walked down onto the wide paved terrace below the Greek columns and stone steps where the mounted statue eternally searched the horizon with one hand lifted to shade his eyes.

She went to the parapet and looked across to the far blue mountains of the Helderberg. She hugged herself about the shoulders for the wind through her silk summer dress was as cold as her misery.

Now the tears broke over her lids and slid down her cheeks to fall unheeded onto the silken front of her dress. They were the tears of self-pity, but also the tears of an anger as searing cold as dry ice.

'The swine,' she whispered through lips that trembled. Near her two young students sitting on the parapet, kicking their legs over the drop beneath them and hugging each other in the abandon of first love, turned to glance at her.

The boy whispered to the girl, and she giggled in unthinking cruelty–but looked away as Ruby directed a long venomous glare at her. Then in embarrassment the couple scrambled off the parapet and moved away, leaving her alone.

Never for one moment did she consider standing aside, Benedict's threats meant nothing–her only concern was to take the action which would injure him most severely. The consequences to herself were not part of her calculations. She wanted only to select the swiftest and most terrible vehicle of retribution. As the dark clouds that fogged her reason slowly cleared, the means came to her readily.

Johnny was staying at the Tulbagh Hotel.

She turned and ran back to her car, the long yellow banner of her hair floating behind her like the pennant at the tip of a cavalry lance. She drove fast until she hit the downtown rush-hour crowds. The tears dried on her face as she crawled, fuming with impatience, along the slow river of traffic.

It was after five when she parked in a loading zone outside the entrance to the Tulbagh and ran into the lobby.

'What room is Mr Lance in?' she demanded of the girl at the desk.

'Mr Lance checked out an hour ago.' Curiously the girl examined Ruby's ruined make-up.

'Did he say where he was going?' Ruby snapped at her, feeling the sickening slide of disappointment within her.

'No, madam.' The girl shook her head. 'But he was in a hurry.'

'Damn! Damn!' Ruby swore bitterly. She turned from the desk undecided where next to look. Perhaps Johnny had gone back to the office.

Across the lobby the elevator doors slid open and Tracey Hartford stepped out. Even in her impatience Ruby recognized in the glow that seemed to emanate from her that Tracey was a girl freshly risen from the bed of the man she loved. There was not a vestige of doubt in Ruby's mind as to the identity of that man.

The shock of it paralysed her for a moment. Then she felt the urge to cross the floor and claw that smug smile from Tracey's face. She fought it down, and instead, she stepped into her path as Tracey started for the glass outer doors.

'Where is Johnny?' she demanded, and Tracey came up short. Her little gasp of guilt confirmed Ruby's suspicion.

'Where is he, damn you!' Ruby's voice was pitched low but brittle with emotion.

'He's not here.' Tracey recovered herself, quickly masking her expression.

'Where has he gone? I must see him.'

'He's flown up to Cartridge Bay.'

'When did he leave? It's important–terribly important.'

'An hour ago. He'll be airborne already.'

'Can you get a message to him?' In her impatience Ruby caught Tracey's wrist, holding her in a grip that marked the skin.

'I can radio him–' Tracey pulled her hand free.

'No,' Ruby cut in quickly. She could not have her message shouted across the ether for all to hear. 'Can you follow him–charter a plane?'

Tracey shook her head. 'They won't fly to an unscheduled airfield after dark.'

'Then you must follow him–by car. You must drive up there.'

'Why?' Tracey stared at her, puzzled by this strange insistence, noticing the dried tears and the wild look in Ruby's eyes. 'It's an eight-hour drive.'

'I'll tell you. Can we use Johnny's room?'

Tracey hesitated, remembering the unmade bed. Then the hotel manager came into the lobby and Tracey turned to him with relief.

The Beechcraft bucked suddenly and dropped a wing, instinctively Johnny corrected the lunge with stick and rudder then glanced quickly at his instrument panel for an explanation. There was none to be found there, so he looked over the wing and for the first time noticed the dust on the great plains below him; it was moving low against the earth in long streamers like mist, and the setting sun turned it to mauve and old gold. With a prickle of alarm he scanned the horizon ahead, and saw it coming down from the north like a great moving range of blue mountains. Even as he watched it, it rolled across the low sun, turning it into a sullen red orb. The light in the cockpit changed to a weird glow as though the door to a furnace had been thrown open.

Again the Beechcraft crabbed awkwardly as another gust of high wind hit her, and at the same moment the radio crackled and came alive.

'Zulu Sugar Peter Tango Baker this is Alexandra Bay Control, come in please.'

The voice of the controller was almost unintelligible with storm static. Johnny reached for the transmit switch of the radio, then stopped his hand. He thought quickly. He could guess they were trying to reach him to cancel his flight approval. That was a big norther boiling down out of the desert. They would abort his flight, and divert him out of the path of the storm.

He checked his wrist watch. Twenty minutes' flying time to Cartridge Bay. No–he was flying full into the eye of the wind, say twenty-five or thirty minutes. Quickly he searched the coast on his port side and saw the long white lines of surf stretched ahead into the thickening purple gloom. The coast was still clear, it might stay that way for another thirty minutes.

'Zulu Sugar Peter Tango Baker this is Alexandra Bay. I say again–come in. Come in. Zulu Sugar Peter Tango Baker.' The agitation in the controller's voice came through over the static.

There was a fair chance of getting in to Cartridge Bay, racing the storm and winning. He could edge out to the westward and come in from the sea, pick up *Kingfisher*'s riding lights as a beacon and sneak in under the leading edge of the dust clouds. If he missed he could turn and run with the wind for home. The radio was hissing and crackling angrily now, the controller's voice sometimes lost in the interference, sometimes coming through strongly.

'–Cancelled. I say again: your flight approval is cancelled. Do you read me, Zulu Sugar Peter Tango Baker. Come in, please.–Beaufort force seven.–visibility in the storm area–I say again, there is nil visibility in–'

The norther would roar for days now and with it would blow away his last chance of working the gap at Thunderbolt and Suicide.

Johnny switched off the radio, cut off contact with Control and immediately it was strangely quiet in the cockpit. He settled himself down into the bucket seat, and eased open the throttles, watching the needles creep up around the dials of the rev counters.

Now he was down to an altitude of three hundred feet and the Beechcraft was leaping about like a hooked marlin. He was flying her on instruments for outside the cockpit it was completely dark. He could not see his own wing-tips, but above him the stars still showed. He was riding the vanguard of the storm, and the dust clouds were ahead, racing to meet him and blanket the flare path at Cartridge Bay.

Every few seconds he darted a quick glance ahead, hoping to pick up the lights, then his eyes flew back to the instrument panel.

'Now,' he thought grimly. 'It should be now. I should be over the grounds. Thirty seconds more and I'll know I've missed her.'

He looked up again, and there was *Kingfisher* dead ahead. All her lights were ablaze, a burning beacon of hope in the darkness. She appeared to be riding easily, for the wind had not yet had time to thrash the sea into a frenzy.

He flashed over her, seeming to graze her superstructure in passing, and now he was searching anxiously for the glow of the flare path on the land beyond.

It came up as a patch of lesser darkness in the absolute blackness of the night. He steadied on course towards it, watching it change to a long double line of oil-burning flares that smoked and fluttered in the wind.

He flew her in fast, high above the stall and the shock of touchdown threatened to tear the undercarriage off her. Then he was jolting and trundling down the earthen runway with the flares flashing past his wingtips.

'Lance, old man,' he murmured thankfully, 'that was a very shaky do!'

The wind hum against the body of the car, and the snarl of rubber on tarmac as the Mercedes snaked through the bends of the twisting mountain road were sounds to match the racing of Tracey's blood and the hammer of her heart.

She drove with an inspired abandon, watching the bends leap at her out of the darkness, sensing the massive crags and cliffs that hung over the road and blotted out half the night sky.

The silver sheet of Clanwilliam Lake reflected the stars, and then was left behind. Down from the mountains she went and over the Olifants River to make a brief fuel stop at Vanrynsdorp and scan the road map anxiously in the light of the gasoline pumps. She read with a sinking feeling the mileage figures printed along the little red ribbon of the road, and knew that for her each mile would be multiplied by her own urgency.

Then once more behind the wheel she faced the vast emptiness of Namaqualand–and sent the Mercedes flying across it.

'–There is some type of machine, I don't know how it works, but it filters out the diamonds. Benedict had it installed at Las Palmas–'

The headlights were puny little white shafts, and the road a long blue smear that went on endlessly. Tracey lit a cigarette with one hand, hearing Ruby's voice again in her ears.

–There is one diamond amongst them. He called it "The Big Blue". Benedict says it's worth a million–'

Tracey was not sure she believed it. It was the enormity of the treachery and deceit that she could not accept.

'–The Italian, the Captain, be careful of him. He works for Benedict. The other one also–Hugo–they are all in it. Warn Johnny.'

Benedict! Weak, spoilt Benedict, the playboy, the spendthrift. Could he have planned and carried this through?

A gust of wind hit the car from the side, taking her unawares, pushing the Mercedes off the tar onto the gravel. Tracey fought to hold the skid. Dust and gravel roared out in a cloud from under the wheels. Then she was back on the road, hurtling northwards.

'Warn Johnny! Warn Johnny!'

Benedict van der Byl sat in his father's chair, in his father's house, and he was alone. His loneliness ate deep into the fibres of his whole being.

Before him on the stinkwood desk stood a crystal glass and a decanter. The brandy was no comfort, its warmth in his throat and belly seemed only to accentuate the icy cold of his loneliness. His fantasy showed him as a hollow man. He thought of himself as a husk, filled only with the cold of melancholia.

He looked about the room with its dark panelled wood-work and he smelled the musty dead smell. He wondered how many times his father had sat in this chair alone and lonely. Lonely and afraid as the cancer ate him alive.

He stood up and moved listlessly about the room, touching the furniture as if he were trying to communicate with the man who lived and died here. He moved across and stood in front of the curtained windows. The rug was new. It replaced the other that they had been unable to clean.

'The Old Man had the right idea.' He spoke aloud, his voice sounding strange in his own ears.

Then on an impulse he crossed quickly to the cupboard that flanked the massive stone fireplace, and tried the door. It was locked.

Without passion he stood back and kicked in the panel. The wood splintered and he kicked again, smashing the door from its hinges.

The oblong leather case was on the top shelf, and he took it down and carried it to the desk. He sprang the catches and laid back the lid.

He lifted out the blue metalled double barrels of the Purdey Royal, and the gun oil was greasy on his hands.

'Jacobus Isaac van der Byl.' He read aloud the name in gold inlay set into the steel among the engraved pheasants and gundogs.

He smiled then.

'The old devil.' He shook his head smiling as though at some private joke, and began slowly to assemble the shotgun. He weighed it in his hands, feeling the sweet pure balance of the weapon.

'The old bastard made his own decisions.' And still smiling he carried the gun across to the new carpet. He placed it butt down between his feet with the barrels pointed at the ceiling and leaning slowly forward he opened his mouth and placed the muzzles between his lips, then reaching farther down he placed a thumb on each trigger and pushed them simultaneously.

'Click! Click!'

The firing pins fell on the empty chambers, and Benedict straightened up and wiped the taste of gun oil from his lips. He grinned again.

'That's the way he did it. Both barrels in the back of the throat. What a cure for tonsils?' he chuckled, and glanced across at the shattered cupboard door. The square packets of cartridges were on the second shelf.

He tucked the gun under his arm and went to the cupboard again, moving more purposefully now. He snatched down a packet of SSG and broke it open. Suddenly his hands were shaking and the fat red cartridges spilled onto the floor. He stooped and picked up two of them.

With mounting excitement and dread he broke open the shotgun and slipped the cartridges into the blank eyes of the breeches. They slid home against the seating with a solid double thunk, and he hurried back to the spot in front of the window.

His eyes were bright and his breathing quick as he pushed the safety catch onto 'Fire' and placed the butt between his feet once more.

He took the muzzles in his mouth again, in an obscene soul kiss and reached down for the triggers. They were cold and oily. He caressed them lightly, feeling the fine grooving in the curves of metal, thrilling to the touch and feel of them as he had never thrilled to the feel of a woman's body.

Then abruptly he stood up again. He was gasping for breath.

Unsteadily he carried the weapon back to the desk and laid it on the dark polished wood.

As he poured brandy into the crystal glass his eyes were fastened with perverse fascination on the beautiful glistening weapon.

The steam had fogged the mirrored walls of the bathroom, so her image was dewed and misty. Ruby Lance dried herself slowly with one of the thick fluffy towels. She was in no hurry; she wanted Tracey to have a start of at least four hours on her journey to Cartridge Bay. With a deep narcissistic pleasure she noticed in the mirror how her whole body glowed with soft pink highlights from the hot water of the bath.

Wrapping herself in the towel she went through into the dressing-room and picked up one of the silver-backed brushes began stroking it through her hair, moving across to the open wardrobe to select a dress for the occasion. It must be something special, perhaps the unworn full-length Louis Feraud of daffodil satin.

Still undecided she went back to seat herself at the dressing-table and began the complicated ritual of applying her make up. She worked with meticulous care until at last she smiled at her reflection with satisfaction.

She dropped the towel, went back to the wardrobe, and stood slim and naked before it. Pouting slightly with concentration she decided against the Feraud. Then suddenly she smiled, and reached for Benedict's mink.

She wrapped herself in the pale cloud of fur, fluffing up the collar to frame her face. It was perfect. Just the fur and a pair of golden slippers, pale gold, a perfect match for her hair.

Now suddenly she was eager to go. She ran from the house to where her car was parked in the driveway.

She switched off the headlights as she turned into the driveway that curved up to where the old house crouched on the top of Wynberg Hill. The whisper of the engine was unobtrusive and blended with the whimper of the night breeze in the chestnut trees that flanked the driveway.

She parked in the courtyard, and saw that Benedict's Rolls was still in the garage and a light burned in the window of the study, a yellow oblong behind the curtains. The front door was open. Her slippered feet made no sound along the gloomy passages, and when she tried the door to the study it swung open readily. She stepped into the room, and closed the door behind her. She stood with her back to the dark panelled wood. A single shaded lamp lit the room dimly.

Benedict sat behind the desk. The room was heavy with the smell of cigar smoke and brandy fumes. He had been drinking. His face was flushed, and the top button of his shirt was undone. On the desk in front of him lay a shot-gun. Ruby was surprised at the presence of the weapon, it disconcerted her and the words she had prepared were forgotten.

Benedict looked up at her. His eyes were slightly unfocused; and he blinked slowly. Then he grinned; it twisted his mouth and his voice when he spoke was slurred.

'So you've come back.'

Instantly her hatred returned in full flood. But she kept her face impassive. 'Yes,' she agreed. 'I've come back.'

'Come here.' He swivelled his chair to the side of the desk. Ruby did not move, she leaned back against the door.

'Come here.' Benedict's voice was stronger now, and suddenly Ruby smiled and obeyed.

She stood in front of him, huddled in the fur.

'Kneel down,' commanded Benedict, and she hesitated.

'Down!' his voice crackled. 'Down, damn you!'

Ruby sank to her knees in front of him, and he straightened up in the chair. She knelt in front of him in the attitude of submission, with her head forward so the golden hair hung like a curtain over her face.

'Say it,' he gloated. 'Ask me to forgive you.'

Slowly she lifted her face and looked up at him. She spoke softly.

'Tracey left for Cartridge Bay at five-thirty this evening.'

Benedict's expression changed.

'She has a start of four hours–she is halfway there already.'

He stared at her with his lips parting, soft and red and slack.

'She is going to Johnny,' Ruby went on. 'She knows about the thing in *Kingfisher*. She knows about the big blue diamond.'

He began to shake his head in disbelief.

'By dawn tomorrow Johnny will know also. So you see, my darling, you have lost again–haven't you? You can never beat him, can you, Benedict? Can you, my darling?'

Her voice was rising, ringing with triumph.

'You?' he croaked. 'You?'

And she laughed, nodding her head in agreement, unable to speak through her laughter.

Benedict lunged clumsily out of the chair, his hands going for her throat. She went over backwards with him on top of her. Her laughter died gurgling in her throat.

They rolled together on the floor. Benedict's hands locked on her neck, his voice rising in a scream of fury and despair. Her long legs kicking and thrashing, clawing at his face and hands, she fought him with the strength of a cornered animal.

They rolled back suddenly and Benedict's head struck the solid leg of the desk with a crack that jarred his whole body. His grip on her throat loosened and she tore herself free with fresh breath hissing into her open mouth. She rolled away from him and in one fluid movement gained her feet, reeling back from him with the front of the mink torn open and her hair tangled across her face.

Benedict dragged himself up the desk onto his knees. He was still screaming, a high keening note without form or coherence, as Ruby spun away from him and stumbled to the door.

Blinded by her own hair, fighting for strangled breath, she fumbled for the door handle with her back turned to him

Benedict reached up and lifted the shotgun off the desk. Still kneeling beside the desk he held the weapon across his hip. The recoil was a liquid pulsing jolt in his hands and the muzzle blast was thunderous in the confines of the room, the long yellow flame lighting the scene like a photographer's flash-bulb.

The heavy charge caught Ruby in the small of her back. At that range there was no spread of shot and it went through spine and pelvis in a solid shattering ball. It tore out through the front of her belly, spinning her sideways along the wall. She slid down into a sitting position, facing him with the mink flared open about her.

On his knees Benedict swung the gun to follow her fall and he fired the second barrel; again the brief thunder and flame of the muzzle blast flashed across the room.

At even closer range than the first charge it struck her full in her beautiful golden face.

Benedict stood in the garage with his forehead pressed against the cold metal of the Rolls-Royce. The shotgun was still in his hands, and his pockets were crammed with cartridges that he had picked up from the floor before leaving the study.

He was shivering violently, like a man in high fever.

'No!' he moaned to himself, repeating the single negative over and over again, leaning against the big car.

Abruptly he gagged, remembering the carnage he had created. Then he retched, still leaning against the Rolls, bringing up the brandy mingled with his horror.

It left him pale and weak, but steadier. Through the open window he threw the gun onto the back seat of the Rolls, and climbed shakily into the driver's seat.

He sat there bowed over the steering-wheel, and now his instinct of self-preservation took hold of him.

It seemed to him there was but one avenue of escape still open to him. *Wild Goose* had the range to take him across an ocean–South America perhaps, and there was money in Switzerland.

He started the Rolls and reversed out of the garage, the spin of tyres against concrete burning blue smoke into the beams of the headlights.

The Mercedes crawled through the thick sand, the headlights probing ineffectually into the bright orange fog of dust that whipped endlessly over the track ahead. The hot gritty wind buffeted the car, rocking it on its suspension.

Tracey sat forward in the driver's seat peering ahead through eyes that felt raw and swollen with fatigue and mica dust.

From the main road to the coast this jeep track was the only land access to Cartridge Bay. It was a hundred miles of tortuous trail, made up of deep sandy ruts and broken stone where it crossed one of the many rocky ridges.

The radiator of the Mercedes was boiling furiously, over-heating in the searing wind and the slogging low-gear grind through thick sand. In places Tracey followed the track only by driving through gaps in the stunted knee-high growth of desert bush. Every few minutes a tumbleweed, driven by the wind, would blow across the track like a frightened furry animal.

At times she was sure she had missed a turning and was now grinding aimlessly out into the desert, then reassuringly the twin ruts would show up in the lights ahead of her. Once she did drive off the road, and immediately the Mercedes came to a gentle standstill with its rear wheels spinning helplessly in the soft sand. She had to climb out of the cab and, with her bare hands, scoop away the sand from behind the wheels and stuff bundles of tumbleweed into the depressions to give the wheels purchase. She almost wept with relief when the Mercedes pulled back sluggishly onto the trail again.

The slow dawn broke through the dustclouds and Tracey switched off the headlights and drove on until suddenly, and quite unexpectedly, she reached Cartridge Bay. The depot buildings loomed suddenly before her, and she left the Mercedes and ran to the living quarters. The foreman opened the door to her insistent hammering, and stared at her in astonishment before ushering her in. Tracey cut off his questions with her own.

'Where is *Wild Goose*?'

'She took Mr Lance out to *Kingfisher*, but she's back now lying at the jetty.'

'Hugo Kramer–the Captain?'

'He's aboard, holed up in his cabin.'

'Thanks.' Tracey left him, pushed the door open against the wind and ran out into the storm.

Wild Goose lay at her moorings, secured by heavy lines to the bollards, but fidgeting and fretting at the push of the wind. There was a gangplank laid to her deck, and lights showed at her portholes. Tracey went aboard.

Hugo Kramer came to the doorway of his cabin in a suit of rumpled striped pyjamas. Tracey pushed past him.

'You took Lance out to *Kingfisher*?' she accused him, her voice sharp and anxious.

'Yes.'

'You idiot, didn't you realise there was something up? Good God, why otherwise would he fly in through this weather?'

Hugo stared at her, and instinctively she knew that what Ruby had told her was true.

'I don't know what you're talking about,' he blurted.

'You'll know all right when we are all sitting behind bars–we'll have fifteen long years to think about it. Lance has tumbled to it, you fool, I've got to stop him. Take me out to *Kingfisher*.'

He was confused–and afraid.

'I know nothing about–' Hugo started again.

'You're wasting time.' Brusquely Tracey brushed his protests aside. 'Take me out to *Kingfisher*.'

'Your brother–where is he? Why didn't he come?'

Tracey had anticipated the question. 'Lance beat him up–badly. He's in hospital. He sent me.'

Suddenly Hugo was convinced.

'*Gott!*' he swore. 'What are we going to do? This storm–I may be able to get you out there, but I won't be able to leave *Wild Goose*. My crew can't handle her in this sea. What can you do on your own?'

'Get me out there,' said Tracey. 'Get me aboard *Kingfisher* and you can come back. The Italian, Caporetti, he and I will take care of Lance. In this storm a man can be washed overboard very easily.'

'Ja.' Hugo's face lit with relief.'That's it. The Italian!' And he reached for his oilskins hanging on the bulkhead. As he pulled them on over his pyjamas he looked at Tracey with new respect.

'You,' he said. 'I didn't know you were in it.'

'Did you think my brother and I would stand by and let a stranger take our birthright from us?'

Hugo grinned. 'You're a cool one, I'll say that for you. You had me fooled.' And he went out onto the bridge.

Johnny Lance and Sergio Caporetti stood shoulder to shoulder on *Kingfisher*'s bridge. The ship was taking the big green seas over the bows, solid walls of water, and the wind whipped spray that spattered the armoured glass windows of the bridge house.

Kingfisher had slipped her moorings the previous evening, leaving the big yellow buoys floating on their anchor cables and she was working free of her fetters. She was on computer navigation, holding her position over the ground against the swells and the wind by use of her engine and rudder.

'She is no good.' Sergio spoke morosely. 'We come too close to the rocks. I get sick in my heart looking at them.'

The dust clouds did not carry this far out to sea despite the vicious screeching of the wind. The visibility was a mile or more, quite enough to show the brooding twin hulks of Thunderbolt and Suicide. The storm-crazed swells burst against them, throwing white spray two hundred feet into the gloomy sky, then surging back to expose the gleaming white rock.

'Hold her,' growled Johnny. Twice during the night they had changed position, each time edging down closer on the gap between the two islands. *Kingfisher* was battling gamely to hold her ground against the insidious sucking current that added its pull to that of the swell and the wind.

Johnny was not attempting to work any one of the gullies extensively, he wanted only to sample as much of the field as possible in the time that was left to him. The storm would not stop him–for *Kingfisher* was constructed to work in worse weather than this. Her compensating hose section was keeping the dredge-head on the bottom despite the lift and fall of her hull.

'Calm down, Sergio.' Johnny relented a little. 'The computer is foolproof.'

'The goddamned computer she no got eyes to see those rocks. Me, I got eyes–and it gives me a sick heart.'

Twice during the night Johnny had gone down into the control room and ordered the computer to report its recovery of diamonds. Each time the reply had been consistent–not a single stone over four carats, and precious few of any others.

'I'm going through to the plot. Watch her,' Johnny told Sergio, and staggering against the pitch and roll he went through the door behind the bridge.

He paused beside the repeater screen of the computer, and at a glance saw that *Kingfisher* was holding her primary operation and all departments were running normally. He passed the screen and leaned over the chart table.

The large scale chart of the South West African coast between Luderizt and Walvis Bay was pinned down on the board. The *Wild Goose* soundings were pencilled in, and the pattern of *Kingfisher*'s sweeps were carefully plotted around the islands of Thunderbolt and Suicide.

Johnny picked up a pair of dividers and stared moodily at the chart. Suddenly a surge of anger rose in him against those two names. They had promised so much and delivered so little.

He stared at the names Thunderbolt and Suicide printed in italics among the maze of soundings, and his anger turned to blind red hatred.

With the points of the dividers he slashed at the chart, ripping the thick linen paper once, and twice, in a ragged cross-shaped tear.

This small act of violence dissipated his anger. He felt embarrassed, it had been a petty childish gesture. He tried to smooth the edges of the tear, and through the gap he felt another loose scrap of paper which someone had slipped under the chart. He probed a finger through the tear in the chart and wormed the scrap out. He glanced at the scribbled title and the lines of figures and numbers that followed.

The sheet was headed: 'KAMINIKOTO SECONDARY RECOVERY PROGRAMME.'

He studied it, puzzled by the title but recognizing the numbers as a computer programme. The writing was in Sergio Caporetti's pointed continental style. The easiest way to resolve the mystery was to ask Sergio. Johnny started back for the bridge.

'Boss,' Sergio called anxiously, as Johnny stepped through the door. 'Look!'

He was pointing ahead into the eye of the wind. Johnny hurried to his side, the paper crumpled and forgotten in his hand

'*Wild Goose*.' Sergio identified the small craft that was staggering and plunging towards them out of the gloom.

'What the hell is he doing here?' Johnny wondered aloud. *Wild Goose* was lost for long seconds behind the walls of green sea, then again she was lifted high into unnatural prominence, showing the red lead of her bottom as she rode the crests; water poured from her scuppers, before she shot down the steep slope of the next wave to bury her nose deep in frothing water. She came down swiftly on the wind, rounding to and beginning to edge in under *Kingfisher*'s counter.

'What the hell is he playing at?' Johnny protested, and then in disbelief he saw a slim figure dart from *Wild Goose*'s wheelhouse and run to the side nearest *Kingfisher*.

'It's Tracey,' shouted Johnny.

She reached the rail just as another swell burst over the bows and smothered her. Johnny expected to see her washed away, but she was still there clinging to the rail.

Thrusting the page of paper into his pocket, Johnny went out through the wing of the bridge and swarmed down the steel ladder to the deck, jumping the last ten feet and running the instant he landed.'

He reached the side and looked down on the drowned-kitten figure of Tracey.

'Go back,' he yelled. 'Go back. Don't try it.'

She shouted something that was lost in the next smother of spray, and when it cleared he saw her poising herself to jump the gap of surging water between the two vessels.

He flung himself over *Kingfisher*'s side and climbed swiftly down the steel rungs.

He was still ten feet above her as she gathered herself for the leap.

'Go back,' he shouted desperately.

She jumped, missed her hold and fell into the murderous stretch of water between the hulls. Her head bobbed below Johnny, and he was aware of the next swell bearing down on them. It would throw *Wild Goose* against the steel cliff of *Kingfisher*, crushing Tracey between them.

Johnny went down those last ten feet and hanging outwards by one arm he got his other arm around her, and with a heave that crackled in his muscles and joints he plucked her from the water just as the two vessels dashed together with a crunching impact that tore splinters from *Wild Goose*'s planking, and left a smear of alien paint on *Kingfisher*'s steel plating.

Wild Goose swung away, and with her diesels bellowing went bucking off into the wind.

With puddles of sea water forming around her feet from her sodden clothing, Tracey stood in the centre of *Kingfisher*'s guest cabin. Her dark hair was plastered down her face and neck, and she was shivering so violently from shock and the icy water that she could not talk. Her teeth chattered together, and her lips were blue with cold.

Desperately she was trying to form words, her eyes never leaving Johnny's face.

Quickly he stripped off her clothing and throwing one towel around her shoulders he began roughly to chafe warmth back into her with another.

'You little idiot,' he berated her. 'Are you stark staring bloody mad?'

'Johnny,' she gasped through her chattering teeth.

'Christ–that was so close,' he snarled at her as he knelt to rub her legs.

'Johnny, listen.'

'Shut up and dry your hair.'

Humbly she obeyed him, her shivers became controllable as he crossed to the locker and found a thick jersey which he pulled over her head. It hung almost to her knees.

'Now,' he said, taking her roughly by the shoulders. 'What the hell is this all about?'

And she told him in a rush of words that poured out like water from a broken dam. Then she burst into tears and stood there forlornly in the voluminous jersey with her damp hair dangling about her shoulders, sobbing as though her heart was breaking.

Johnny took her in his arms.

For a long minute Tracey revelled in his warmth and strength, but she was the first to pull away.

'Do something, Johnny,' she implored him, her voice still thick with tears. 'Stop them. You mustn't let them get away with it.'

He went back to the locker, and while he ransacked it for clothing that might fit her, Johnny's mind was racing over the story she had told him.

He watched her pull on a pair of blue serge trousers and tie them at the waist with a length of cord. She folded back the cuffs and tucked them into thick woollen socks, before thrusting her feet into a pair of seaboots that were only a few sizes too large for her.

'Where do we start?' she asked, and he remembered the sheet of paper. He fished it out of his pocket and flattened it on the table beside the bunk. Quickly he ran his eyes over the columns of figures. His first guess was right–it *was* a computer programme.

'Stay here,' he ordered Tracey.

'No.' Her response was immediate, and he grinned.

'Listen, I'm just going up onto the bridge to keep them busy there. I'll come back for you, I promise. You won't miss anything.'

'How is she, boss?' Sergio Caporetti's concern was genuine. Johnny realised that he must be worrying himself into a frenzy trying to guess the reason for Tracey's arrival.

'She is pretty shaken up,' Johnny answered.

'What she want–that was big chance she takes. Nearly fish food.'

'I don't know,' Johnny said. 'I want you to take over up here. Keep *Kingfisher* working. I'm going to get her to bed–I'll let you know what it's all about as soon as I find out.'

'Okay, boss.'

'Oh, and Sergio–keep an eye on those rocks. Don't let her drift down any closer.'

Johnny chose a powerful incentive to keep Sergio up on the bridge.

Johnny left him and went below, stopping only at the guest cabin.

'Come on.'

Tracey followed him, lurching unsteadily with *Kingfisher*'s antics in the high sea.

Two decks down they reached the computer control room and Johnny unlocked the heavy steel door, then locked it again behind them.

Tracey wedged herself against the bulkhead and watched as Johnny seated himself at the console and clipped the rumpled sheet into the board.

Reading from the sheet he typed the first line of figures on the keyboard. Immediately the computer registered a protest.

'Operator error,' it typed back. Johnny ignored its denial and typed the second line. This time it was more emphatic.

'No procedure. Operator error.'

And Johnny typed the next line of figures. He guessed that whoever had stored this programme in the computer's memory would have placed a series of blocks to prevent accidental discovery. Again the denial flashed back at him.

'Operator error.'

And Johnny muttered, 'Thrice before the cock crows,' striking an incongruously biblical note in the tense atmosphere of the control room.

He typed the last line of figures and the denial faded from the screen. The console clicked like a monstrous crab, then suddenly it started to print again.

'Kaminikoto Secondary Recovery Programme.
Installed October 1969. At Las Palmas by
Hideki Kaminikoto. Doctor Of Science.
Tokyo University.

The little Japanese had been unable to resist autographing his masterpiece. Tracey and Johnny crouched over the screen, staring at it with awful fascination as the computer began spelling out its report. It began with the number of hours worked, and the weight of gravel processed during that time.

Next it reported the weight of concentrates recovered from the cyclone and finally, in a series of columns, it printed out the weights and sizes of all the diamonds won from the sea. The Big Blue showed up in the place of honour, and wordlessly Tracey touched the figure 320 with a forefinger. Johnny nodded grimly.

The computer ended by giving a grand total of carats recovered, and Johnny spoke for the first time.

'It's true,' he said softly. 'It doesn't seem possible–but it is.'

The click and hum of the computer ceased, and the screen went blank.

Johnny straightened up in the chair.

'Where would they put it?' he asked himself, as he ran quickly over the line of recovery. He stood up from the chair and peered through the leaded glass peephole into the X-ray room. 'It must be this side of the cyclone, this side of the drier–' He was speaking aloud. '–Between the drier and the X-ray room.'

Then there bobbed to the surface of memory the modification in design which he had meant to query, but which he had forgotten.

'The inspection plate on the conveyor tunnel!' He punched his fist into his palm. 'They moved the inspection plate! That's it! It's in the conveyor tunnel.'

His hands were frantic with haste as he unlocked the steel door of the control room.

Sergio Caporetti paced his bridge like a captive bear, puffing so furiously on his cheroot that sparks flew from its tip. The wind howled hungrily around the wheelhouse, and the swells still marched in from the north.

Suddenly he reached a decision and turned to the helmsman.

'Watch those goddamn rocks–watch them good.'

The helmsman nodded and Sergio shambled through the chartroom to his own cabin. He locked the door behind him, and crossed to his desk. Fumbling with his keys he opened the bottom drawer of his desk and reaching under the pile of cheroot packets he brought out the canvas bag.

Weighing it thoughtfully in his hand, he looked about the cabin for a more secure hiding-place. Through the canvas he could feel the nutty irregular shape of the stones.

'That Johnny, he is a clever bastard,' he muttered. 'It better be a good place.'

Then he reached a decision. 'Best place where I can watch them all a time.'

He opened his jacket and stuffed the bag into his inside pocket. He buttoned the jacket and patted the bulge over his heart

'Fine!' he said. 'Good!' And stood up from the desk. He hurried back, unlocking the door into the chartroom, and headed for the bridge. He stopped in the middle of the chartroom and his head swung towards the repeater screen of the computer. The buzzer was going like a rattlesnake, and the red bulb that warned of a new procedure was blinking softly.

Fearfully Sergio approached the screen and stooped over it. A single glance was enough, and he rushed from it to the chart table. He saw the cross-shaped tear in the chart.

'Mary Mother!'

He ripped back the thick crackling paper and searched under it. He stepped back from the table and hit himself across the chest.

'Fool!' he said. 'Idiot!' He spent ten seconds in self-castigation, then he looked about for a weapon. The locking handle of the cabin was a twelve-inch steel bar with a heavy head. He pulled out the pin and worked it loose. He slipped it into the waistband of his trousers.

'I'm going below,' he told the helmsman curtly, and clambered down the companionway. Swiftly he moved through the ship, balancing easily to her roll and pitch.

When he reached the lowest deck he became more stealthy, creeping silently forward. Now he carried the steel bar in his right hand. Every few paces he stopped to listen, but *Kingfisher*'s hull was groaning and popping as she worked in the swells.

He could hear no other sound. He crept up to the door of the control room and cautiously peered through the small armoured glass window. The control room was empty. He tried the handle, and found it locked.

Then he heard voices–from the open doorway of the conveyor room behind him. Quickly he crossed to it and flattened himself against the jamb.

Johnny's voice came muffled and indistinct:

'There's another hatch in here. Get me a half-inch spanner from the tool cupboard.'

'What's a half-inch spanner look like?'

'It's a big one. The size is stamped on it.'

Sergio glanced one-eyed around the door jamb. The cover was off the inspection hatch in the conveyor tunnel, and Tracey's head was thrust into the opening. It was clear that Johnny Lance was in there, and that he had found the secret compartment.

Tracey drew her head out of the hatch, and Sergio ducked back and looked down the passageway. The tool cupboard was bolted to the bulkhead under the stairs from the deck above. He turned and darted around the corner of the passageway.

Tracey came out of the conveyor room, and went to the cupboard. She opened the doors on the glittering array of tools, each clipped securely into its rack.

While she stood before the cupboard, completely absorbed in her search for a half-inch spanner, Sergio came from around the corner and crept up silently behind her.

He lifted the steel bar over his shoulder and came up on his toes, poised to strike.

Tracey was muttering softly to herself, head bowed slightly, handling the spanners–and Sergio knew the blow would crush her skull.

He closed his mind to the thought, and aimed carefully at the base of her skull. He started the blow, and then checked it. For a second that seemed to last for a long time he remained frozen. He couldn't do it.

With an exclamation of satisfaction Tracey found what she was searching for. As she turned away from the cupboard Sergio shrank back behind the angle of the bulk-head, and Tracey hurried back into the conveyor room.

'I've got it, Johnny,' she shouted into the hatch.

'Bring it to me. Hurry, Tracey. Sergio will be getting suspicious,' he shouted back, and Tracey hitched up her voluminous trousers and wriggled into the hatch.

On hands and knees she crawled up beside him. It was cramped and hot in the narrow tunnel. He took the spanner from her.

'Hold the flashlight.' She took it from him, holding the beam on the panel while he unscrewed the retaining bolts and lifted off the cover.

Lying on his side he peered into the opening.

'There's a container of sorts,' he grunted, and reached in. For a minute he struggled with the clamps, then slowly he lifted out the stainless steel cup.

At that moment *Kingfisher* reared and plunged to a freak wave and the cup slipped from Johnny's fingers, and from it spilled the diamonds. They cascaded over both of them, a glittering shower of stones of all sizes and colours. some lodged in Tracey's damp hair, the rest rolled and bounced and scattered about them, catching the light from the torch and throwing it back in splinters of sunshine.

'Yipes!' gasped Tracey and laughed at Johnny's whoop of triumph.

Lying side by side they scrabbled and snatched at the treasure scattered around them.

'Look at this one,' exulted Tracey.

'And this.' They were crazy with excitement, hands filled with diamonds. They hugged each other and kissed ecstatically, laughing into each other's mouths.

Johnny sobered first, 'Come on. Let's get out of here.'

'What about the diamonds?'

'Leave them. There'll be plenty of time later.'

They crawled backwards down the tunnel, still laughing and exclaiming, and one after the other emerged into the conveyor room. while they straightened their clothing, and regained their breath, Tracey asked, 'What now?'

'First thing is to get young Sergio safely under lock and key, his crew also.' Johnny's face hardened. 'The bloody bastards,' he added angrily.

'Then?' Tracey asked.

'Then we'll pull up the hose, and sail *Kingfisher* back into Cartridge Bay. Then we'll call up the police on the radio. There's going to be an accounting with the whole gang of the bastards–your darling brother included.'

Johnny started for the door, asking as he crossed the deck:

'Why did you close the door, Tracey?'

'I didn't,' she replied as she hurried after him, and Johnny's expression changed. He ran to the heavy steel door and threw his weight on it. It did not move, and he swung round to face the door that led into the cyclone room.

It was closed also. He charged across the room and grabbed the handle, heaving at it with all his strength.

He stood back at last, and looked wildly about the long narrow cabin. There was no other opening, no hatch or porthole–nothing except the tiny square peephole in the centre of the steel door that led into the cyclone room beyond. The peephole was covered with three-inch armoured glass that was as strong as the steel that surrounded it. He looked through it.

The tall cyclone reached from floor to roof, dominating the room. Beyond it the steel pipe that carried the gravel from the sea bed pierced the roof from the deck above, but the cyclone room was deserted.

Johnny sobered first. 'Come on. Let's get out of here.'

'We've got problems,' he said.

After closing and locking both the doors that led into the conveyor room, Sergio climbed quickly back to his bridge. The helmsman looked at him curiously.

'How's the lady?'

'Fine,' Sergio snapped at him. 'She's safe.' And then with unnecessary violence, 'Why you no mind your own business, hey? You think you Captain for this ship?'

Startled, the helmsman quickly transferred his attention back to the storm which still raged lustily about them. Sergio began to pace up and down the bridge, balancing easily and instinctively to her exaggerated motion. His smooth baby face was crumpled into a massive scowl, and he puffed on one of his cheroots. With all his soul Sergio Caporetti was lamenting his involvement in this business. He wished that he had never heard of *Kingfisher*. He would have traded his hopes of a life hereafter to be sitting on the seafront at Ostia, sipping *grappa* and watching the girls go by.

Impulsively he pulled open the storm doors at the angle of the bridge and went out onto the exposed wing. The wind buffeted him and set his soft hair dancing and flickering.

From inside his jacket he pulled the canvas bag.

'This is the trouble,' he muttered, looking at the bag in his hand. 'Bloody little stones.'

He threw back his arm like a baseball pitcher, set to hurl the bag out into that hissing green sea below him, but again he could not make the gesture. Swearing quietly to himself, he stuffed the stones back into his jacket, and went back into the wheelhouse.

'Call the radio operator,' he ordered, and the helmsman reached quickly for the voice tube.

The radio operator reached the bridge still owl-eyed with sleep and buttoning his clothing.

'Get on to *Wild Goose*,' Sergio told him.

'I won't be able to raise her in this,' the man protested, glancing out at the storm.

'Call her.' Sergio stepped towards him threateningly. 'Keep calling until you get her.'

Wild Goose staggered and wallowed through the turbulence at the entrance to Cartridge Bay, then fought her way into the sanctuary of the channel.

Hugo relaxed perceptibly. It had been a long hard run back from Thunderbolt and Suicide. Yet there was an uneasy feeling that still persisted. He hoped that the girl was able to handle Lance. He was a tough cooky that Lance, he wished that he had been able to go along with her and make sure of the business. Fifteen years was one hell of a long time–he would be almost fifty years old at the end of it.

Hugo followed the channel markers that appeared like milestones out of the dust clouds, until ahead he made out the loom of the jetty and the depot buildings.

There was a figure on the jetty, crouched beside the mountain of dieseline drums. With a prickle of alarm, Hugo strained his eyes in the bad visibility.

'Who the hell is it?' He puzzled aloud. The figure straightened and came forward to stand on the edge of the jetty. Bareheaded, dressed in rumpled dark business suit, the man carried a shotgun in one hand–and it was another few seconds before Hugo recognized him.

'Christ! It's the boss!' Hugo felt alarm flare in his stomach and chest, it tightened his breathing.

Benedict van der Byl jumped down onto the deck of *Wild Goose* at the moment she touched the jetty.

'What happened?' Benedict demanded as he barged into the wheelhouse.

'I thought you were in hospital,' Hugo countered.

'Who told you that?'

'Your sister.'

'You've seen her? Where is she?'

'I took her out to *Kingfisher*. Like you said. She went out to deal with Lance.'

'Deal with Lance! She's with him, you idiot, she's not with us. She knows the whole deal. Everything!'

'She told me–' Hugo was appalled. But Benedict cut him short.

'The whole thing's blown up. We've got to clear out. Get your crew to load those drums of dieseline into the hold. How are your water tanks?'

'Full.'

'Food?'

'We are stocked up.'

'For how long?'

'Three weeks–at a push, four.'

'Thank God for that.' Benedict looked relieved. 'This storm will blow another three days–we'll have that much start. They'll never find us in this. By the time it clears we'll be well on our way.'

'Where to–Angola?'

'God no! We have to get well clear. South America.'

'South America!'

'Yes–we can do it, carrying extra fuel.'

Hugo was silent a moment, becoming accustomed to the idea.

'We can do it,' Benedict repeated.

'Yes.' Hugo nodded. 'We can do it,' he agreed thoughtfully. For the first time he examined Benedict closely. He saw that he was in an emotional and physical mess, his bloodshot eyes were sunk into deep plum-coloured hollows, dark new beard covered his jowls, and there was a gaunt hunted look to him–like some fugitive animal.

He was filthy with dust, and there was a streak of something that could have been dried vomit down the front of his jacket.

'But, what do we do when we get there?' For the first time since he had known Benedict he felt in control. This was the time to deal, to make bargains.

'We'll get ashore on some deserted spot, and then we split up and disappear.'

'What about money?' Hugo spoke carefully. He glanced down at the shotgun. Benedict's hands were fidgety and restless on the weapon.

'I've got money.'

'How much?' Hugo asked.

'Enough.' Benedict blinked cautiously.

'For me also?' Hugo prodded him, and Benedict nodded.

'How much for me?' Hugo went on.

'Ten thousand.'

'Pounds?'

'Pounds,' Benedict agreed.

'That's not enough.' Hugo shook his head. 'I'll need more than that.'

'Twenty.' Benedict increased his bid, but he knew he was playing from weakness into strength. Ruby was lying mutilated in his study, the net was probably being spread for him already.

'Fifty,' said Hugo decisively.

'I haven't that much.'

'Who are you kidding, Buster!' Hugo snorted. 'You've been stacking it away for years.'

Benedict let the barrels of the shotgun swing towards Hugo's belly suggestively.

'Go ahead,' Hugo grinned at him, screwing up his pale albino eyes. 'That'll leave you to paddle this canoe–you want to try it? You'd pile her up on the bar at the entrance–that's how far you'd get.'

Benedict swung the barrels aside.

'Fifty,' he agreed.

'Right!' Hugo spoke briskly. 'Let's get the hell out of here.'

Wild Goose was clear of the land, and of the towering blinding dust clouds. The following seas came sweeping up under her stern urging her on her westward flight, while the high-pitched shriek of the wind in her rigging cried to her to hasten.

'Why don't you get down below and grab some sleep?' Hugo said. He found Benedict's restless haunting presence in the crowded wheelhouse disconcerting.

Benedict ignored the suggestion. 'Switch on the radio,' he said.

'What for? You'll get nothing on the set.'

'We are out of the dust,' Benedict replied. 'We might pick up a police message.'

The image of Ruby was so clear in his mind. He wanted to know if they'd found her yet. He felt his gorge rising again. That head–oh God–that head! He crossed quickly to the radio set and switched it on.

'They won't be in on us yet,' said Hugo, but Benedict was manipulating the dials–searching the tortured radio waves. The static wailed and gibbered and shrieked like a maniac.

'Turn it off,' snapped Hugo, and at that moment a voice cut in on them.

'–*Wild Goose*,' said the voice from the loudspeaker quite clearly. Benedict crouched eagerly over the set, his hands were busy on the dials, and Hugo came up beside him.

'–Come in, *Wild Goose*. This is *Kingfisher*. I repeat, come in *Wild Goose*–'

Benedict and Hugo looked at each other. 'Don't answer,' said Hugo, but he made no move to intervene as Benedict lifted the microphone off its hook.

'*Kingfisher*, this is *Wild Goose*.'

'Stand by, *Wild Goose*.' The answer came back immediately. 'Stand by for Captain Caporetti.'

'*Wild Goose* standing by.'

Hugo caught Benedict's shoulder and his voice was angrily uncertain:

'Leave it, don't be a fool.'

Benedict shrugged off the hand, and Sergio's voice boomed out of the speaker.

'This is Caporetti–who dat?'

'No names,' Benedict cautioned him.'Where are your guests?'

'They safe–battened down nicely.'

'Safe? Are you certain? Both of them safe?'

'Si. I have them safe and sure.'

'Stand by.' Benedict crouched over the set, and his mind was racing. Johnny Lance was in his power. This was the last chance he would ever have. Plans began to form, gelling quickly in his mind.

'The diamonds. Caporetti has the diamonds. That big Blue is worth a million on its own,' said Hugo. 'If Caporetti has taken care of the others–it would be worth the risk.'

'Yes.' Benedict turned to him, he had been puzzling how he could make Hugo turn back. He had forgotten the diamonds. 'It would be worth it,' he agreed.

'Just a quick pass alongside *Kingfisher*–pick up Caporetti with the diamonds and we'd be on our way.'

'I have to go aboard.' Benedict qualified the suggestion.

'Why?' Hugo asked.

'Wipe out the reel on the computer that carries the programme–it's got the Jap's name on it. They could trace him. I paid him on my Swiss bank. They'll find the account.'

Hugo hesitated. 'No killing–or anything like that. We've got enough trouble without that.'

'You think I'm crazy?' Benedict demanded.

'Okay, then,' Hugo agreed.

'*Kingfisher*.' Benedict spoke into the microphone. 'We are coming to you. I'll be coming on board to finalize matters.'

'Fine.' Through the static they could hear the relief in Sergio's voice. 'I'll be standing by.'

It took nearly two hours for *Wild Goose* to slug her way back to where *Kingfisher* lay beneath the ghostly white shapes of Thunderbolt and Suicide, and it was after midday before Hugo began manœuvring *Wild Goose* into the big ship's lee.

'Don't waste time,' Hugo cautioned Benedict. 'The sooner we get on our way–the better for all of us.'

'I'll be about half an hour,' Benedict answered. 'You lay off and wait for us.'

'Are you taking that bloody shotgun?' Benedict nodded.

'What for?' But Benedict did not reply, he looked up at the sky. The sun was merely a luminous patch of silver light through the ceiling of sea-fret and wind-driven mist, and still the storm hunted hungrily across the sea.

'It will slow you up on the ladder.' Hugo harped on the shotgun. He wanted very much to part Benedict from it, he wanted it over the side–for its presence aboard would prejudice the plans that Hugo had been forming during the last few hours–plans that took into account the ready market for diamonds in South America, and the undesirability of sharing the proceeds with two partners.

'I'll take it.' Benedict tightened his grip on the stock of the weapon. Without it he would feel naked and vulnerable–and it was part of his own private plans for the future. Benedict's brain had also been busy during the last two hours.

'Suit yourself.' Hugo resigned himself to Benedict's refusal; there would be an opportunity later, during the long passage across the Southern Atlantic. 'You better get up for'ard.'

This time Hugo's approach was neatly executed; in a lull between the colossal swells he touched *Wild Goose*'s bows to the steel side of the factory ship. Benedict stepped across the gap and was up the landing ladder and standing at *Kingfisher*'s rail before the next wave came marching down on them.

He waved Hugo off, then hanging onto the rail, made his way aft to *Kingfisher*'s bridge works.

'Where is Lance?' he demanded of Sergio the moment he stepped onto the bridge, but Sergio glanced significantly at the inquisitively listening helmsman and led Benedict through into his cabin.

'Where is Lance?' Benedict repeated the moment the door was locked.

'He and your sister they are in the conveyor room.'

'The conveyor room?' Benedict was incredulous.

'Si. They find out about Kammy's machine. They open the hatch and go inside. I close both doors. Lock them good.'

'They are in there now?' Benedict asked to gain time to reconstruct his plans.

'Si. Still there.'

'All right.' Benedict reached his decision. 'Now listen, Caporetti, this is what we are going to do. The whole thing has blown up on us. We are going to wipe out as much of the evidence against us as possible, then we are clearing out. We are going to run for South America in *Wild Goose*. You have got the diamonds–haven't you?'

'Si.' Sergio patted the breast of his jacket.

'Give them to me.' Benedict held out his hand, and Sergio grinned.

'I tink I look after them. They keep my heart warm.'

A frown of annoyance narrowed Benedict's eyes, but he let the moment pass.

'All right.' His tone was still friendly. 'Now, what you have to do is get down to the control room and wipe out Kaminikoto's programme. Get his name off that reel. He showed you how to do that?'

'Si.' Sergio nodded.

'How long will it take?'

'Half an hour, not longer,' Sergio answered, and Benedict checked his wrist watch that this would give him time enough to do what he had to do.

'Good! Get cracking.'

'Boss.' Sergio hesitated at the cabin door. 'What about my boys, my crew? They good boys, no trouble for them?'

'They're clean,' Benedict pointed out irritably. 'I'll get them together now, and explain that you have to go ashore. They can keep *Kingfisher* hove to waiting for you to come back. After the storm blows out they are bound to radio base and find out we have disappeared. They'll be all right.'

Sergio nodded his satisfaction.

'I'll call them all to the bridge now. You talk to them.'

The five crew members were gathered on *Kingfisher*'s bridge, and Sergio had disappeared down below.

'Any of you speak English?' Benedict demanded, and two of them affirmed that they did.

'Right,' Benedict addressed them. 'You will have been wondering about all the coming and going in this weather. I want you all to be ready to leave the ship. I want you to get all your valuables–now!'

Quickly they translated to the others, who looked apprchensively at Benedict. He was a strange wide-eyed figure with the shotgun tucked under his arm.

'Right–let's go.' And there was no dissent from any of them as they trooped to the companionway.

Benedict followed them along the passage-way towards the crew quarters, and glanced quickly at his wrist watch. Seven minutes had elapsed. He looked at the men ahead of him.

The backs of their heads formed a solid target. He had shot guineafowl like that in Namaqualand when they were on the ground running away from him in a thick file, down on one knee and aim for the thickest of heads, knocking down half the flock with both barrels.

He knew he could take all five of these men with two shots. Just let them get a little farther ahead so the shot could be spread. But he remembered Ruby and his stomach heaved. The other was just as sure.

'Stop!' he commanded as the five men came level with the paint store. They obeyed and turned back to face him. Now he held the shotgun so that there was no mistaking its menace. They stared at the gun fearfully.

'Open that door.' He pointed at the paint store. Nobody moved.

'You.' Benedict picked on one of those who spoke English. Like a man in a trance he went to the steel door and spun the locking handle. He pulled the door open.

'In!' Eloquently Benedict gestured with the shotgun. Reluctantly the five of them filed into the small windowless cubicle, and Benedict slammed the door on them. He spun the lock, throwing all his weight on the handle to set it.

Now he had a clear field, and his wrist watch gave him another twenty minutes. He hurried for'ard, he wanted to keep well clear of the control room and Sergio Caporetti.

Using the forward companionway he dropped down to the working deck, fumbling out his duplicate set of keys.

WARNING. EXPLOSIVES. NO UNAUTHORIZED ENTRY.

He unlocked the door, and lying the shotgun flat on the deck he lifted a twenty-five pound drum of plastique down from its rack.

In his haste he tore a fingernail on the lid of the drum, but hardly felt the pain. He uncoiled a six-foot length of the soft dark toffee-coloured material and slung it around his neck. Next he selected a cardboard box of pencil time fuses. He read the label.

'Fourteen-minute delay. That's about right.'

Blood from his torn nail left brown blotches on the cardboard as he took four of the pencils from the box, picked up the shotgun and hurried aft. The jet engine whine of the cyclone mounted deafeningly as he came closer to it.

Tracey was curled on the bare steel plating of the deck with Johnny's jacket folded under her head. She was in a fatigue-drugged sleep, so deep as to be almost deathlike.

Every few minutes Johnny interrupted his restless patrol of the conveyor room to stand over her and look down on her unconscious form. His worried expression softened a little each time he studied her pale lovely face. Once he stooped over her and tenderly lifted a strand of dark hair from her cheek, before resuming his pacing up and down the narrow cabin.

Each time he reached the door of the conveyor room he glanced through the tiny windows. The glass had resisted his attempts to smash it with one of the spanners. He wanted to open the window to call for help, but his efforts had not marked the thick armoured glass.

There was no way out of the cabin. Johnny had tried every possible outlet. The apertures for the conveyor system were guarded at one end by the furnace, and at the other by moving machinery which would ferociously chew to tatters anyone who became entangled in it. They were caged securely, and Johnny paced his cage.

Again he stopped before the peephole, but this time he flung himself at the door with clenched fists. The steel plate smeared the skin from his knuckles as he hammered on it and the pain sobered him. He pressed his face to the glass and through it watched Benedict van der Byl enter the conveyor room and, without glancing at the window, cross to the cyclone.

Benedict laid aside the shotgun he carried and for a moment stood looking up at the thick steel pipe that carried the gravel down from the deck pumps above. As he lifted the thick rope of plastique from around his neck, Johnny knew exactly what he was going to do.

He watched him in fascination as Benedict mounted the steel ladder up the side of the cyclone. Hanging with one hand to the ladder, Benedict reached out with the other and clumsily tied the rope of plastique around the gravel pipe. It hung there like a necklace about the throat of some obscene prehistoric monster.

'You bastard! You murdering bloody swine!' Johnny shouted, and again he beat on the steel door with his fists. But the thickness of the door and the whine of the cyclone drowned his voice. Benedict showed no sign of hearing him–but Tracey sat up and looked about her blearily. Then she came to her feet and staggering to the roll and pitch of the ship she went to Johnny and pressed her face to the window beside her.

Benedict was sticking the time pencils into the soft dark explosive. He used all four fuses, taking no chances on a misfire

'What's he doing?' Tracey asked after she had recovered from the surprise of recognizing her brother.

'He's going to cut the pipe, and let *Kingfisher* pump herself full of gravel.'

'Sink her?' Tracey's voice was sharp with alarm.

'She'll pump water and gravel into herself at pressures that will tear away all the inner bulkheads.'

'This one?' Tracey patted the steel plate.

'It'll pop like a paper bag. God, you have no idea of the power in those pumps.'

'No.' Tracey shook her head. 'He's my brother. He won't do it, Johnny. He couldn't murder us.'

'By the time he's finished–' Johnny contradicted her grimly, '–*Kingfisher* will by lying in 200 feet of water. Her hull will be packed so tightly with gravel that it will be like a block of cement. We, and everything in her, including his little machine, will be so flattened as to be unrecognizable. It would cost millions to salvage *Kingfisher*–and no one will care that much.'

'No, not Benedict.' Tracey was almost pleading. 'He's not that bad.'

Johnny interrupted her brusquely. 'He could get away with it. It's a good try–his best chance. Encase all the evidence against him in concrete, and bury it deep.'

'No, Benedict.' Tracey was watching her brother as he climbed down the cyclone ladder and picked up the shotgun. 'Please, Benedict, don't do it.'

Almost as if he had heard her, Benedict turned suddenly and saw the two faces at the window. The shock of guilt held him rigid for a moment, as he stared at them–Tracey's pale lips forming words he could not hear, Johnny's eyes burning with accusation.

Benedict dropped his eyes, he made a gesture that was indecisive, almost pathetic. He looked up at the fused and charged rope of explosive–and then he grinned. a sardonic twitching of the lips, and he stumbled out of the cyclone room and was gone.

'He'll come back,' whispered Tracey. 'He won't let it happen.'

'I wouldn't bet on that–if I were you,' said Johnny.

Benedict reached *Kingfisher*'s rail and clung to it. He looked out to where *Wild Goose* bobbed and hung on the swells. He saw Hugo's face as a white blob behind the wheelhouse window, but as the little trawler began closing in for the pick-up Benedict waved it away. He glanced at his watch again, then looked back anxiously at the bridge.

The long minutes dragged by. Where the hell was the Italian? Benedict could not leave him–not while he still had that diamond; not while he could stop the dredge pumps and release the prisoners locked below.

Again Benedict checked his watch, twelve minutes since he had set the time pencils. He must go back and find Caporetti. He started back along the rail, and at that moment Sergio appeared on the wing of the bridge. He shouted a question at Benedict that was lost in the wind.

'Come on!' Frantically Benedict beckoned to him. 'Come on! Hurry!'

With another last look about the bridge, Sergio ran to the ladder and climbed down to deck level.

'Where my boys?' he shouted at Benedict. 'Why nobody at the con? What you do with them?'

'They are all right,' Benedict assured him. He had turned to the rail and was signalling *Wild Goose* to come alongside.

'Where they?' Sergio demanded. 'Where my boys?'

'I sent them to–' Benedict's reply was cut off as *Kingfisher*'s deck jarred under their feet. The explosion was a dull concussion in her belly, and Sergio's jaw hung open. Benedict backed away from him along the rail.

'Filth!' Sergio's jaw snapped closed, his whole body appeared to swell with anger.

'You kill them, dirty pig. You kill my boys. You kill Johnny–the girl.'

'Keep away from me.' Benedict braced himself against the rail, leaving both hands free to use the gun.

Not even Sergio would advance into the deadly blank eyes of those muzzles. He paused uncertainly.

'I'll blow your guts all over the deck,' Benedict warned him, and his forefinger was hooked around the trigger.

They stared at each other, and the wind fluttered their hair and tore at their clothing.

'Give me those diamonds,' Benedict commanded, and when Sergio stood unmoving, he went on urgently, 'Don't be a hero, Caporetti. I can gun you down and take them anyway. Give them to me–and our deal is still on. You'll come with us. I'll get you out of here. I swear it.'

Sergio's expression of outrage faded. A moment longer he hesitated.

'Come on Caporetti. We haven't got much time.' It may have been his imagination, but to Benedict it seemed that *Kingfisher*'s action in the water had altered, she was sluggish to meet the swells and her roll was more pronounced.

'Okay,' said Sergio, and began unbuttoning his jacket. 'You win. I give you.'

Benedict relaxed with relief, and Sergio thrust his hand into his jacket and stepped towards him. He grasped the canvas bag by its neck, and brought it out held like a cosh.

Sergio was close to him, too close for Benedict to swing the shotgun onto him. Sergio's expression became savage, his intentions blazed in his dark eyes as he lifted the canvas bag and poised himself to deliver a blow at Benedict's head, but he had not reckoned with the extraordinary reflexes of the natural athlete he was facing.

As Sergio launched the blow, Benedict rolled his shoulders and head away from it, lifting the butt of the shotgun as a guard. Sergio's wrist struck the seasoned walnut, and he grunted with the pain. His fingers opened nervelessly and the canvas bag flew from his grip, glanced off Benedict's temple and flew on down the deck, sliding to stop against one of the compressed air tanks thirty feet away.

Benedict danced back, dropping the barrels of the shotgun until Sergio looked into the muzzles.

'Hold it, you bastard,' Benedict snarled at him. 'You've made your choice. Now let's see what your guts look like.'

Sergio was hugging his injured wrist to his belly, crouching over it. Benedict was backing away to where the bag lay against the tank. His face was flushed and hectic with anger, but he kept darting side glances at the canvas bag.

At that moment *Kingfisher* took another wave over her bows, and the water came swooshing down the deck, picking up the bag and washing it towards the scuppers.

'Look out!' Sergio shouted. 'The bag! It's going.'

Benedict lunged for it, sprawling full length. With his free hand he grabbed the sodden canvas as it was disappearing over the side. But he was thirty feet away from Sergio, and he still held the shotgun in his other fist. Sergio could not hope to reach him without getting both charges of the buckshot in his belly.

Instead Sergio spun round and sprinted back along the deck towards the bridge.

Benedict was on his knees frantically stuffing the bag of diamonds into the side pocket of his jacket and shouting after Sergio.

'Stop! Stop or I'll shoot!'

Sergio did not look back nor check his run, and Benedict had the bag in his pocket and now both hands were free. He lifted the shotgun, and tried to balance himself against *Kingfisher*'s wallowing motion as he aimed.

At the shot, Sergio stumbled slightly but kept on running. He reached the ladder and went up it.

Again Benedict aimed, and the shotgun clapped dully in the wind. This time a spasm of pain shuddered through Sergio's big body, and he froze on the ladder.

Benedict fumbled in his pocket for fresh shells, but before he could reload Sergio had begun climbing again. Benedict broke the gun and thrust the shells into the breech. He snapped the gun closed and looked up just as Sergio disappeared through the storm doors–and the two shots that Benedict loosed after him merely pockmarked the paintwork and starred the glass of the wheelhouse. 'The stupid bastard.' Hugo watched from the wheelhouse of *Wild Goose*. 'He's gone berserk.'

Hugo had heard the explosion and seen the shooting.

'Fifteen years is enough–but not the rope as well.'

He swung the wheel and *Wild Goose* sheered in towards *Kingfisher*'s side. Peering through the spray and salt-smattered windows, he saw Benedict drag himself to his feet and start after Sergio along the deck.

Hugo snatched the electric loudhailer from its bracket and pulled open the side window of the wheelhouse, holding the hailer to his lips.

'Hey! You stupid bastard, have you gone mad? What the hell you doing?'

Benedict glanced down at the trawler, then ignored it to give all his attention to reloading the gun. He kept going back along the deck, following Sergio to finish him off.

'You'll get us all strung up, you fool,' Hugo called through the loudhailer. 'Leave him. Let's get out of here.'

Benedict kept scrambling and slipping towards *Kingfisher*'s bridge.

'I'm leaving–now! Do you hear me? You can stew in your own pot. I'm getting out.'

Benedict checked and looked down at the trawler. He shouted and pointed at the bridge. Hugo caught one word: 'Diamonds.'

'All right, friend! Do what you like–I'll see you around,' Hugo hailed, and hit the trawler's throttle wide open. The roar of the diesels and the churning of her propeller convinced Benedict.

'Hugo! Wait! Wait for me, I'm coming.' He scampered back to the ladder and started down it.

Hugo throttled back and brought *Wild Goose* in neatly under the ladder.

'Jump!' he shouted through the hailer, and obediently Benedict jumped to hit the foredeck heavily. The shotgun flew from his hands to fall into the water alongside. Benedict cast one longing glance after the gun, then crawled to his feet and limped back to the wheelhouse.

Already *Wild Goose* was plunging away into the wind, but as Benedict entered the wheelhouse Hugo turned on him with his pink albino face set in a snarl of rage.

'What the hell have you done, you bastard? You lied to me. What was that explosion?'

'Explosion–I don't know. What explosion?'

Hugo hit him a stinging open-handed blow across the cheek.

'We agreed no killing–and you put us all on the spot.' Hugo's attention was focused completely on Benedict who had backed into the farthest corner of the wheelhouse. He massaged the dark red finger marks that stained his cheek.

'You set scuttling charges in *Kingfisher*–didn't you, you dirty son of a bitch? God, I hate to think what you've done with Lance and the girl.'

Outside the storm was nearing its climax. A rain squall swept down on *Wild Goose*–sure sign that the wind must soon drop.

Automatically Hugo switched on the rotating wipers to clear the rain from the screen, as he continued to harangue Benedict.

'I saw you trying to murder the Italian. Christ! What for? He's one of us! Am I next on your list?'

'He had the diamonds,' mumbled Benedict. 'I was trying to get them from him.'

And Hugo's expression changed; he turned away from the wheel and stared at Benedict.

'You haven't got the diamonds? Is that what you're saying?' His tone was almost hurt.

'I tried–he wouldn't–'

And Hugo left the wheel and was across the wheelhouse like a white leopard. He grabbed the front of Benedict's coat, and screamed into his face.

'You left the diamonds! You stick my head in a noose–and I get nothing out of it.'

He was trembling with rage and his pale eyes bulged from their sockets.

Looking into those eyes Benedict realized his own danger. In the time it had taken him to leave *Kingfisher*'s deck and reach the wheelhouse of the trawler he had decided to let Hugo think that Sergio still had the diamonds. Squeamish as Hugo appeared to be about drowning Johnny and Tracey, despite his repeated demands for 'No Killing', Benedict knew intuitively that Hugo had no intention of splitting a million pounds' worth of diamonds with him.

Once Hugo was certain that Benedict had the stones on board, Benedict knew there was no chance that he would reach South America alive.

The crossing might take weeks, the crew of the trawler were in Hugo's pay and loyal only to him. Benedict must sleep, and they would take him in the night.

On the other hand, of course, Benedict had no intention of splitting a million pounds' worth of diamonds with Hugo Kramer. He let his voice whine as he cringed in Hugo's grip.

'I tried. Sergio had them. He wouldn't–that's why I shot him.'

Hugo drew back his hand to slap Benedict again. Benedict twisted slightly, and drove his knee into Hugo's crutch, sending him staggering back across the wheelhouse, clutching himself between the legs and whimpering with the pain.

'Right, Kramer,' Benedict spoke softly. 'That's a little lesson for you. Behave yourself, and you'll get your fifty grand on the other side of the Atlantic.'

They stared at each other. Hugo Kramer weak and pale with agony, Benedict standing tall and arrogant again.

'Treat me gently, Kramer. I'm your meal-ticket. Remember it.'

Hugo gaped at him. The positions had reversed so swiftly. He pulled himself upright and his voice was thick with agony, but humble.

'I'm sorry, Mr van der Byl, I lost my temper. It's been a hell of a –'

'Skipper! Ahead!' The warning was shouted by the coloured crewman, Hansie.

Hugo stumbled to the untended wheel, and peered out into the storm.

Wild Goose was shooting down another slope of green water, and just ahead of her bows Hugo saw one of the huge yellow buoys that *Kingfisher* had laid down and then abandoned. It was held captive in the trough of the swells by the anchor cable. The cable was drawn as tight as a rod of steel across the trawler's bows, lifted just above the surface of the water; shivering drops of water flew from it under the tension of the buoy's drag.

'Oh God!' Hugo spun the wheel and threw *Wild Goose*'s engine into reverse–but she was racing down the swell, and her speed was unchecked as the cable scraped harshly along her keel.

Then came the harsh banging and clattering of the drive shaft as the cable fouled the propeller–followed by a crack as the shaft snapped. *Wild Goose*'s engine screamed into overrev as the load was lifted from it.

Hugo shut the throttle, and there was silence in the wheelhouse. *Wild Goose* swung beam on to the seas which came boiling in over her deck. Without her propeller she was transformed from a husky little sea creature to a piece of driftwood at the mercy of each current and the whim of the wind.

Hugo's head swung slowly until he was looking down-wind to where the massive shapes of Thunderbolt and Suicide just showed through the rain squall.

'Cover your ears–tight!' Johnny Lance pressed Tracey against the bulkhead as far from the cyclone room as they could get. 'There are twenty-five pounds of plastique in there–it will blow like a volcano. He will have used a short fuse, fourteen minutes. We won't have long to wait.'

Johnny set Tracey's shoulders squarely against the steel plating, and crouched over her–trying to shield her with his own body.

They stared into each other's eyes, teeth clenched, the heels of their palms jammed hard over their ears and they cowered away from the blast that must come.

The minutes passed, the longest minutes of Tracey's life. She could not have borne them without screaming hysteria except for that big hard body covering her–even with it she felt her fear mounting steadily during the molasses drip of time.

Suddenly the air lunged at her, driving the breath from her lungs. Johnny was thrown heavily against her. The blast sucked at her eardrums, and burst in her head so that bright lights flashed across her vision and she felt the steel plates heave under her shoulders.

Then her head cleared, and although her eardrums buzzed and sang, she found with a leaping relief that she was still alive.

She reached out for Johnny, but he was gone. In panic she groped, then opened her eyes. He was lurching down the long conveyor room, and when he reached the locked door at the far end he pressed his face to the peephole.

The fumes of the explosion still filled the cyclone room, a swirling bluish fog, but through them Johnny could make out the shambles that was the aftermath.

The huge cyclone had been torn from its mountings, and now sagged against the far bulkhead crushed. It was worth only a single glance before Johnny froze into rigidity at the true horror.

The gravel pipe had been severed cleanly just below its junction with the upper deck. It protruded for six feet, but now the force of the jet through it was flickering and whipping it about as though it were not steel but a rubber garden hose.

The jet was a solid eighteen-inch column, a pillar of brown mud and yellow gravel and sea water that beat against the steel plates of the hull with a hollow drumming roar.

In the few seconds since the explosion the cyclone room was already half-filled with a slimy shifting porridge that rushed from wall to wall with the movement of the ship. If was like some monstrous jelly fish which each second gathered weight and srength.

Tracey reached Johnny's side and he placed his arm around her shoulders. She looked through the armoured glass and he felt her body stiffen.

At that moment the yellowish monster spread over the window, obscuring it completely. Johnny felt the first straining of the steel plates under his hands. They fluttered and bulged, then began to protest aloud at the intolerable pressure. A seam started, and a fine jet of fithy water hissed from the gap and soaked icily through Johnny's jersey.

'Get back.' Johnny dragged Tracey away from the squeaking, groaning bulkhead. Back along the narrow conveyor room they stumbled, moving with difficulty for the deck beneath their feet was slanting as *Kingfisher* began to lean under the increasing weight in her belly.

Still holding Tracey, he reached the locked door and resisted the futile desire to attack it with his bare hands. Instead he forced his brain to work, tried to anticipate the sequence of events that would lead to the final destruction of *Kingfisher*–and all those aboard her.

Benedict had left the other entrance to the cyclone room wide open. Already that viscous mass of mud and water must be spreading rapidly through the lower levels of the hull, following always the avenue of least resistance–finding the weak spots and bursting through them.

If the walls of the conveyor room held against the pressure, the rest of the hull would be filled and they would be enfolded in the tentacles of that great yellow monster–a small bubble of air trapped within it and taken down with it when it returned to the depths from which it had come.

Would the bulkheads of the conveyor room hold? The answer came almost immediately in the squeal of metal against metal, and the crackle of springing rivets.

The monster had found the weak spot, the aperture through the drying furnace into the conveyor, ripping away the fragile baffles, bursting through the furnace in a cloud of steam, it gushed into the conveyor room bringing with it the sewage stench of deep-sea mud.

Kingfisher made another sluggish roll, so different from her usual spry action, and the mud came racing down the tunnel in a solid knee-high wall.

It slammed both of them back against the steel door with a shocking strength, and the feel of it was cold and loathsome as something long dead and putrefied.

Kingfisher rolled back and the mud slithered away, bunched itself against the far bulkhead then charged at them again.

Waist-deep it struck them, and tried to suck them back with the next roll.

Tracey was screaming now, nerves and muscles reaching their breaking-point. She was clinging to Johnny, coated to the waist in stinking ooze, her eyes and mouth wide open in terror as she watched the mud building up for its next assault.

Johnny groped for some hold to anchor them. They must keep on their feet to survive that next rush of mud. He found the locking handle of the door and braced himself against it, holding Tracey with all his strength.

The mud came again, silently, murderously. It burst over their heads and punched them with stunning force against the plating.

Then it sucked back once more, and left them down on their knees, anchored only by Johnny's grip on the locking handle.

Tracey was vomiting the foul mud and it filled her ears and eyes and nostrils, clogging them so that it bubbled at her breathing.

Johnny could feel her weakening in his arms, her struggles becoming more feeble as she tried to regain her feet.

His own strength was going. It needed his last reserve to drag them both upright.

The locking handle turned in his fingers, spinning open. The steel door against which he was braced fell away, so that he staggered backwards without support but still clutching Tracey.

There was just a moment to recognize the big, reassuring bulk of Sergio Caporetti beside him and feel an arm like the trunk of a pine tree steady him before the rush of mud down the conveyor room hit them and knocked all three of them down, sending them swirling and rolling end over end before its strength dissipated in the new space beyond the conveyor room door.

Johnny pulled himself up the bulkhead. He had lost Tracey. Dazed but desperate he looked for her, mumbling her name.

He found her swilling aimlessly in the waist-deep mud, floating on her face. He took a handful of muddy-hair and lifted her face out, but the mud had hold of his legs, pulling him off balance as it surged back and forth.

'Sergio. Help!' he croaked. 'For God's sake, Sergio.'

And Sergio was there, lifting her like a child in his arms and wading to the ladder that led to the deck above. The mud knocked Johnny down again, and when he surfaced Sergio was climbing steadily up the ladder.

Despite the mud and water that blurred Johnny's eyesight, he could see that Sergio's wide back, from shoulders to hips, was speckled with dozens of punctures as though he had been stabbed repeatedly with a knitting needle. From each tiny wound oozed droplets of blood that spread like brown ink on the blotting-paper of his sodden jacket.

At the head of the companionway Sergio turned, still holding Tracey in his arms; he stood like a Colossus looking down at Johnny wallowing and slipping in the mud below.

'Hey, Lance–go switch off your bloody machine. She drown my ship. I sail her myself now–the right way. No bloody fancy machine.'

Johnny steadied himself against the bulkhead and called up at him:

'Sergio, what happened to Benedict van der Byl, where is he?'

'I think he go with *Wild Goose*–but first he shoot the hell out of me, not half. Fix your machine, no time for talk.'

And he was gone, still carrying Tracey.

Another rush of mud carried Johnny down the flooded passage and threw him against the door to the control room. Already his body seemed to be one aching bruise, and still the battering continued as he tried to unlock and open the control room door.

At last, using the suck of the mud to help him, he yanked it open and went in with a burst of yellow slime following him and flooding the compartment shoulder deep.

Clinging to the console of the computer he reached up and punched the master control buttons.

'Dredge Stop.'

'Dredge engines Stop.'

'Main engines manual.'

'Navigation system manual.'

'All programme abort.'

Instantly the roar from the severed dredge pipe, which had echoed through the ship during all their strivings, dwindled as though some vast waterfall had dried. Then there was silence. Though only comparative silence, for the hull still groaned and squeaked at the heart-breaking burden it now carried and the mud slopped and thudded against the plating.

Weak and sick, Johnny clung to the console. He was shivering with cold, and every muscle in his body felt bruised and strained.

Suddenly the ship changed her motion, heaving under his feet like a harpooned whale as she swung broadside to the storm. Johnny roused himself with alarm.

The journey back through the flooded passages to the companionway was an agony of mind and body–for *Kingfisher* was now behaving in a strange and unnatural way.

The scene that awaited Johnny as he dragged himself onto the bridge chilled his soul as the icy mud had chilled his body.

Thunderbolt and Suicide lay less than a furlong off *Kingfisher*'s starboard quarter. Both islands were wreathed in sheets of spray that fumed from the surf that was breaking like cannon-fire on the cliffs.

The maniacal flute of the wind joined with the drum of the surf to produce a symphony fit for the halls of Hell, but above this devil's music Sergio Caporetti bellowed, 'We got no power on port main engine.'

Johnny turned to him. Sergio was hunched over the wheel, and Tracey lay on the deck at his feet like a discarded doll.

'The water she kill port main.' Sergio was pumping the engine telegraph. Then abandoning the effort, he looked over the side.

The reeking white cliffs were closer now, much closer–as though you could reach out a hand to them. The ship was drifting down rapidly on the wind.

Sergio spun the wheel to full port lock, trying to bring *Kingfisher*'s head round to meet the sea and the wind. She was rolling as no ship was ever meant to roll, hanging over at the limit of each swing, so that the wheelhouse windows seemed but a few feet from the crests of the green waves. She hung like that as though she meant never to come upright again. Then sluggishly, reluctantly, she swung back, speeding up as she reached the perpendicular and the great mass of mud and water in her hull shifted and slammed her over on her other side, pinning her like that for eternal seconds before she could struggle upright again for the cycle to be repeated.

Sergio held the wheel at full lock, but still *Kingfisher* wallowed down towards the cliffs of Thunderbolt and Suicide. The wind had her the way a dog carries a bone in its teeth. Under half power and with her decks awash *Kingfisher* could not break that grip.

Johnny was a helpless spectator, held awe-bound so he could not break away even to succour Tracey who was still lying on the deck. He saw everything with a super-natural clarity–from the dribbling little shot holes in Sergio's back, to the ponderous irresistible rush of the white water up the cliffs that loomed so close alongside.

'She no answer helm. She too sick.' Sergio spoke now in conversational tones which carried with surprising clarity through the uproar of the elements. 'All right then. We go the other way. We take the gap.'

For a moment Johnny did not understand, then he saw it. *Kingfisher*'s bows were coming up to the narrow opening between the two islands.

A passage less than a hundred yards wide at its narrowest point, where the vicious cross currents met head on and leapt fifty feet into the air as they collided. Here the surface was obscured by a thick froth of spindrift that heaved and humped up as though the ocean were fighting for breath under the thick cream-coloured blanket.

'No.' Johnny shook his head, staring at that hideous passage. 'We won't make it, Sergio. We won't do it.'

But already Sergio was spinning the wheel from lock to lock, and unbelievably *Kingfisher* was responding. Helped now by the wind she came around slowly, seeming to brush her bows across the white cliff of Thunderbolt, and she steadied her swing and aimed at the gap. It was then Johnny saw it for the first time.

'Christ, there's a boat dead ahead!'

The steep swells had hidden it up to that moment, but now she bobbed up on a crest. It was a tiny trawler, flying in a dirty scrap of canvas as a staysail at her stubby mast, and struggling piteously in the granite jaws of Thunderbolt and Suicide.

'*Wild Goose!*' roared Sergio, and he reached for the handle of the foghorn that hung above his head.

'Now we have some fun.' And he yanked the handle. The croaking bellow of the foghorn echoed off the cliffs that were closing on either side of them.

'Kill my boys–hey? Shoot me–hey? Trick me–hey? Now I trick you– but good!' Sergio punctuated his triumphant yells with blasts on the foghorn.

'Christ, no! You can't do it!' Johnny caught ungently at the big Italian's shoulder, but Sergio struck his hand away and steered directly for the trawler as it lay full in the narrow passage.

'I give him plenty warning.' Sergio sent another blast echoing off the cliffs. 'He no give me warning when he shoot me–the bastard.'

There was a group of men on the trawler's foredeck. Johnny could see that they were manhandling an inflatable escape raft, a thick mattress of black rubber, towards the nearest side of the trawler. But now they were frozen by the bellow of *Kingfisher*'s foghorn. They stood looking up at the tall cliff of steel that bore down on them. Their faces were pale blobs in the gloom.

'Sergio. It's murder. Turn away, damn you, you can miss them. Turn away!' Again Johnny lunged across the wheelhouse and grabbed at the wheel.

Sergio swung a backhanded blow that cracked against Johnny's temple and sent him reeling half-stunned against the storm doors.

'*Who* Captain for this bloody ship!' There was blood on Sergio's lips, the shout had torn something inside him.

Kingfisher's bows were lifting and swinging down like an executioner's axe over the trawler. They were close enough now for Johnny to recognize the men on the trawler's deck– but only one of them held his full attention.

Benedict van der Byl cowered against the trawler's rail, gripping it with both hands. His hair fluttered, soft and dark, in the wind. His eyes were big dark holes like those of a skull in the bone-white face, and his lips a pink circle of terror.

Then suddenly the trawler disappeared under *Kingfisher*'s massive bows, and immediately after that came the splintering crunching sound of her timbers shattering. *Kingfisher* bore down on the passage between the cliffs without a check in her speed.

Johnny fumbled with the catch of the storm doors, and the wind tore it open. He staggered out onto the exposed wing of the bridge and reached the rail.

He stood there with the storm clawing at his clothing and looked down at the wreckage that dragged slowly along *Kingfisher*'s hull, and then was left behind.

There were human heads bobbing among the wreckage, and the wash from

Kingfisher's propeller pushed them towards the cliffs of Suicide.

A wave picked up one of the men and carried him swiftly onto the cliff, sweeping him high and then swirling back to leave the body stranded on that smooth white slope of granite.

The man was still alive, Johnny saw him clawing at the smooth rock with his bare fingers, trying to drag himself above the reach of the sea.

It was Hugo Kramer; even through the fog of spray there was no mistaking that head of pale hair and the lithe twisted body.

The next wave reached up and dragged him back over the rock, tearing the nails from his hooked fingers as he tried to find a hold.

He was swirled and flung about in the turbulence below the cliff before another wave lifted him and hurled him onto the granite. One of his legs was broken at the knee by the force of the impact and the lower part of the leg spun loosely like the blade of a windmill as the water tugged at it.

Once again Hugo was left stranded but now he made no movement. His arms were flung wide, and his leg stuck out at a grossly unnatural angle from the knee.

Then from among these mighty waves there rose up a mass of green water which dwarfed all the others.

It reared up with slow majesty and hung poised over the granite cliff before it fell on Hugo's broken body with a boom that seemed to shake the very rock.

When the giant wave drew back, the cliff was washed clean. Hugo was gone.

The same wave that destroyed him came down the passage between the cliffs and, in contrast to its treatment of Hugo Kramer, it was tender as a mother as it lifted *Kingfisher* and carried her out into the open sea beyond the reach of those cruel cliffs.

Looking back into the gap between the islands, the last trace that Johnny saw of the *Wild Goose* was the black rubber escape raft tossing and leaping high on the turmoil of broken water and creamy spindrift.

'They'll have no use for that,' he said aloud. He searched for a sight of any survivors, but there was none. They were chewed to pulp in the jaws of Thunderbold and Suicide, and swallowed down into the cold green maw of the sea.

Johnny turned away and went back into the wheelhouse. He lifted Tracey from the deck and carried her through to Sergio's cabin.

As he laid her on the bunk he whispered to her, 'I'm glad. I'm glad you didn't see it, my darling.'

At midnight the wind still howled about the ship, hurling sheets of solid rain against the windows of the bridge. Forty minutes later the wind had veered through a hundred and eighty degrees and become a light south-easterly air. The black sky opened like a theatre curtain, and the full moonlight burst through so brightly as to pale the stars. Though the tall black swells still marched in martial ranks from the north, the gentle wind was soothing and lulling them.

'Sergio, you must rest now. I will take the con. Let Tracey dress your back.'

'You take the con!' Sergio snorted scornfully. 'I save the ship–and you sink her for me. Not bloody likely.'

'Listen, Sergio. We don't know how badly you are hurt. You are killing yourself.'

The same argument spluttered and flared intermittently during the long night hours while Sergio clung stubbornly to the helm and coaxed the labouring vessel back towards Cartridge Bay. He insisted on detouring far out to sea to avoid the islands, so that when the bright dawn broke, the land was only a low brown line on the horizon and the mountains of the interior were a distant blue.

An hour after dawn Johnny made radio contact with the very agitated operator at Cartridge Bay.

'Mr Lance, we've been trying to raise you since yesterday evening.'

'I've been busy.' Despite his fatigue Johnny grinned at his own understatement. 'Now, listen to me. We are coming into Cartridge Bay. We'll be there in a couple of hours. I want you to have a doctor, Doctor Robin Sutherland, flown up from Cape Town–also I want you to have the police standing by. I want somebody from both the Diamond police and the Robbery and Murder squad–have you got that?'

'The police are here already, Mr Lance. They are looking for Mr Benedict van der Byl. They found his car here–they have a warrant . . .' The operator's voice broke off and Johnny heard the mumble of background voices, then–'Mr Lance, are you there? Stand by to speak to Inspector Stander of the CID.'

'Negative!' Johnny cut in on the transmission. 'I'm not talking to anybody. He can wait until we get into the Bay. Just you have Doctor Sutherland ready. I've got a badly wounded man on board.'

Johnny leaned over the radio set and shut off the main switch, then he stood and made his way slowly back to the bridge. Every muscle in his body felt stiff and bruised, and he was groggy with tiredness, but he took up the argument with Sergio where they had left off.

'Now listen to me, Sergio. You must lie down, You can take us in over the bar; but now you must get an hour or two's rest.'

Still Sergio would not relinquish the wheel, but he consented to strip to the waist and let Tracey examine his back.

In the expanse of white muscle were little black holes each set in its own purple bruise. Some of the holes had sealed themselves with black clotted blood, from others fluid still oozed–clear or pink in colour–and there was a faint sweetish smell from the wounds.

Johnny and Tracey exchanged worried looks before Tracey reached into the first aid box and set to work.

'How she look, Johnny?' Sergio's jovial tone was belied by his face which was a lump of bread dough touched with greenish blue hues.

'Depends if you like your meat rare.' Johnny matched his tone, and Sergio chuckled but cut it short with a wince.

Johnny put a cheroot between Sergio's lips and held a match for him. As Sergio puffed the tip into a glow, Johnny asked casually, 'What made you change your mind?' And Sergio looked up at him quickly, guiltily, through the cloud of cheroot smoke.

'You had us cold. You could have got away with it–perhaps,' Johnny persisted quietly. 'What made you come back?'

'Listen, Johnny. Me, I've done some damned awful bloody things–but I never killed a man or a woman–ever. He said no killing. Fine, I go alone. Then I hear the plastique blow. I know you two in conveyor room. I think the hell with it. Now, I climb off the wagon–but she's going too fast. I get bum full of buckshot.'

They were silent for a while. Tracey was absorbed in patching the shot-wounds with adhesive tape.

Johnny broke the silence. 'Was there a big diamond, Sergio? A big blue diamond?'

'Si.' Sergio sighed. 'Such a diamond as you will never see again.'

'Benedict had it?'

'Si. Benedict had it.'

'Did he have it on him?'

'In his coat. He put it in his coat pocket.'

Tracey stepped back. 'That's all we can do for now,' she murmured and caught Johnny's eye, shaking her head slightly and frowning with worry. 'The sooner we get him to a doctor the happier I'll be.'

A little before noon Sergio took *Kingfisher* in through the entrance to Cartridge Bay, handling the mud-filled ship with all the aplomb of the master mariner, but as they approached the first turning in the channel he sagged gently to the deck and the wheel spun out of his hands.

Before Johnny could reach the helm, *Kingfisher* had yawned wearily across the channel. She had so little way on her that when she went up on the sandbank there was only a small jolt and she listed over a few degrees.

Johnny pulled the engine telegraph to 'STOP'.

'Help me, Tracey.' He stooped over Sergio and took him under the armpits. Tracey grasped his ankles. Half dragging, half carrying, they got him through to his cabin and laid him on his bunk.

'Hey, Johnny. Sorry, Johnny.' Sergio was mumbling. 'First time I put ship on bank–ever! Idiot! So close– then *wap*! Sorry, hey, Johnny.'

The motor launch left the jetty and came down the channel towards the sandbank on which *Kingfisher* lay stranded. The launch was crowded, and the whine of the outboard engine raised a storm of water fowl into a whirlwind of frightened wings.

As it drew closer Johnny recognized some of the occupants. Mike Shapiro and with him Robin Sutherland, but there were also two uniformed policemen and another person in civilian clothes who stood up in the launch as it came within hail and cupped his hands about his mouth.

'I am a police officer. I have a warrant for the arrest of Benedict–'

Mike Shapiro touched the man's arm, and spoke softly to him. The officer hesitated and glanced up at Johnny again, before nodding agreement and settling back onto his seat.

'Robin, get up here as quick as you can,' Johnny shouted down at the launch, and when Robin came over the side Johnny hustled him towards the bridge, but Mike Shapiro hurried after them.

'Johnny, I must talk to you.'

'It can wait.'

'No, it can't.' Mike Shapiro turned to Tracey. 'Won't you take care of the doctor, please? I must speak to Johnny before the police do.'

Mike led Johnny down the deck and offered him a cigarette, while the three policemen hovered at a discreet distance.

'Johnny, I have some dreadful news. I want to break it to you myself.'

Johnny visibly braced himself. 'Yes?'

–'It's about Ruby–'

Johnny made his statement to the police inspector in *Kingfisher*'s guest cabin. It took two hours for him to relate the full story, and during that time one of the uniformed policemen discovered the crew locked in the paint store below decks. They were half poisoned with paint fumes but able to make their statements to the police.

The inspector kept them waiting in the next-door cabin while he finished his interrogation of Johnny.

'Two more questions for now, Mr Lance. In your opinion was the collision between the two ships accidental or deliberate?'

Jonny looked into the steel-grey eyes and lied for the first time.

'It was unavoidable.'

The inspector nodded and made a note on his pad.

'Last question. The survivors from the trawler, what were their chances?'

'In that storm they had none. There was no hope of effecting a rescue with *Kingfisher* almost disabled, and considering the condition of the surf in the passage between the islands.'

'I understand.' The inspector nodded. 'Thank you, Mr Lance. That is all for the present.'

Johnny left the cabin and went quickly to the upper deck. Tracey and Robin were still working over Sergio's bunk, but Robin looked up and came immediately to Johnny as he stood in the doorway.

'How is he, Robin?'

'He hasn't a chance,' Robin replied, keeping his voice low. 'One lung has collapsed, and there appear to be perforations of the bowel and intestine. I suspect a massive peritonitis. I can't move him without risking a secondary haemorrhage.'

'Is he conscious?'

Robin shook his head. 'He's going fast. God knows how he has lasted this long.'

Johnny moved across to the bunk and placed his arm about Tracey's shoulders. She moved closer to him and they stood looking down at Sergio.

His eyes were closed, and a dark pelt of new beard covered the lower part of his face. His breathing sawed and hissed loudly in the quiet cabin, and the fever lit bright spots of colour in his cheeks.

'You magnificent old rogue.' Johnny spoke softly, and Sergio's eyed blinked open.

Quickly Johnny stooped to him.

'Sergio. Your crew–your boys are safe.'

Sergio smiled. He closed those dark gazelle eyes, then opened them again and whispered painfully, 'Johnny, you give me a job when I come out of prison?'

'They won't have you in prison–you'd lower the tone of the place.'

Sergio tried to laugh. He managed one strangled chuckle, then he came up on his elbows in the bunk with his eyes bulging, his mouth gaping for breath. He coughed once, a harsh tearing sound, and the blood burst from his lips in thick black clots and a bright red spray of droplets.

He fell back on the pillows, and was dead before Robin reached his side.

Tracey was asleep in the bedroom next door. Robin had sedated her heavily enough to keep her that way for the next twelve hours.

Johnny lay naked on the narrow bunk in the second guest room of the Cartridge Bay depot, and when he switched on the bedside lamp his wrist watch showed the time as 2.46 in the morning.

He looked down at his own body. The bruises were dark purple and hot angry red across his ribs and flanks from where the mud had battered him against rough steel plating. He wished now that he had accepted the sleeping pills Robin had offered him, for the ache of his body and the whirl of his thoughts had kept him from sleep all that night.

His mind was trapped on a nightmare roundabout, revolving endlessly the two deaths which Benedict van der Byl must answer for in the dark places to which he had surely gone.

Ruby and Sergio. One he had seen die, the other he could imagine in all its gruesome detail.

Johnny sat up and lit a cigarette, seeking a distraction from the tortured images with which his over-excited brain bombarded him.

He tried to concentrate on reviewing the practical steps that would be necessary to clear up the aftermath of these last disastrous days.

He had spoken that evening by radio to Larsen, and received from him a promise of complete financial support during the time it would take to clear the mud from *Kingfisher*'s hull and recover the diamonds in the conveyor tunnel, and to tide over the period of salvage and repair before the dredger was ready to begin once more harvesting the rich fields of Thunderbolt and Suicide.

A salvage team would fly in tomorrow to begin the work on *Kingfisher*. He had cabled IBM requesting engineers to check out the computer for water damage.

Six weeks, Johnny estimated, before *Kingfisher* was ready for sea.

Then his unruly imagination leapt suddenly ahead to Ruby's funeral. It was set for Tuesday next week. Johnny rolled restlessly on his bunk, trying to shut his mind against the thoughts that assaulted it–but they crowded forward in a dark host.

Ruby, Benedict, Sergio, the big blue diamond.

He sat up again, stubbed out his cigarette and reached across to switch out the bedside lamp.

He froze like that, as a new thought pressed in on him. He heard Sergio's voice in his memory.

'Such a diamond as you will never see again.'

Now he felt the idea come ghosting along his spine so that the hair at the nape of his neck and on his forearms prickled with excitement.

'The Red Gods!' he exclaimed, almost shouting the name. And again Sergio's voice spoke.

'In his coat. He put it in his coat pocket.'

Johnny swung his legs off the bunk, and reached for his clothes. He felt the pounding of his heart beneath his fingers as he buttoned his shirt. He pulled on slacks and sweater, tied the laces of his shoes and snatched up a sheepskin jacket as he ran from the room.

He was shrugging on the jacket as he entered the deserted radio room and switched on the lights. He crossed quickly to the chart table and pored over it.

He found the name on the map, and repeated it aloud. 'The Red Gods.'

North of Cartridge Bay the coast ran straight and featureless for thirty miles, then abruptly the line of it was broken by the out-thrust of red rock, poking into the sea like an accuser's finger.

Johnny knew it well. It was his job to find and examine any such natural feature that might act as a barrier to the prevailing inshore currents. At such a place diamonds and other seaborne objects would be thrown ashore.

He remembered the red rock cliffs carved by wind and sea into the grotesque natural statues which gave the place its name, but more important he remembered the litter of ocean debris on the beaches beneath the cliff. Driftwood, waterlogged planking, empty bottles, plastic containers, scraps of nylon fishing-net corks–all of it cast overboard and carried up by the current to be deposited on this promontory.

He ran his finger down the chart and held it on the dots of Thunderbolt and Suicide. He read the laconic notation over the tiny arrows that flew from the islands towards the stark outline of the Red Gods.

'Current sets South South-West. 5 knots.'

Above the chart table the depot keys hung on their little cuphooks, each labelled and numbered.

Johnny selected the two of them marked GARAGE and LAND-ROVER.

The moon was full and high. The night was still and without a trace of wind. Johnny swung the double doors of the garage open and switched on the parking lights of the Land-Rover. By their glow he checked out the vehicle; petrol tank full, the spare five-gallon cans in their brackets full, the can of drinking-water full. He dipped his finger into the neck of the water containers and tasted it. It was clean and sweet. He lifted the passenger seat and checked the compartment beneath it. Jack and tyre spanner, first aid kit, flashlight, signal rockets and smoke flares, water bottle, canvas groundsheet, two cans of survival rations, tow-rope, tool kit, knapsack, knife and compass. The Land-Rover was equipped to meet any of the emergencies of desert travel.

Johnny climbed behind the wheel and started the engine. He drove quietly and slowly past the depot building, not wanting to awaken those sleeping inside, but when he hit the firm sand at the edge of the lagoon he switched on the headlights and gunned the engine.

He cut across the sand dunes at the entrance to the bay, and swung northwards onto the beach. The headlights threw solid white beams into the sea mist, and startled sea birds rose on flapping ghost wings before the rush of the Land-Rover.

The tide was out and the exposed beach was hard and shiny wet, smooth as a tarmac road. He drove fast, and the white crabs were blinded by the headlights and crunched crisply beneath the tyres.

The dawn came early, silhouetting the mystic shapes of the dunes against the red sky.

Once he startled a strand wolf, one of the brown hyenas which scavenged this bleak littoral. It galloped, hunch-shouldered, in hideous panic for the safety of the dunes. Even in his urgency Johnny felt a stir of revulsion for the loathsome creature.

The cold damp rush of the wind into his face refreshed Johnny. It cooled the gritty feeling of his eyes, and eased the throb of sleeplessness in his temples.

The sun burst over the horizon, and lit the Red Gods five miles ahead with all the drama of stage lighting. They glowed golden red in the dawn, a procession of huge half-human shapes that marched into the sea.

As Johnny drove towards them the light and shadow played over the cliffs and he saw a hundred-foot tall figure of Neptune stooping to dip his flowing red beard into the sea, while a monstrous hunchback with the head of a wolf pranced beside him. Ranks of Vestal Virgins in long robes of red rock jostled with the throng of weird and fantastic shapes. It was eerie and disquieting.

Johnny curbed his fancy and turned his attention to the beaches at the foot of the cliffs.

What he saw started his skin tingling again, and he pressed the accelerator flat against the floor-boards, racing across the wet sand to where a white cloud of sea birds circled and dived and hopped about something that lay at the water's edge.

As he drove towards them a gull flew across the front of the Land-Rover. A long ribbon of something wet and fleshy dangled from its beak, and the gull gulped at it greedily in flight. Its crop was distended and engorged with food.

The sea birds scattered raucously and indignantly as the Land-Rover approached, leaving a human body lying in the centre of an area of sand that was dappled by the prints of their webbed feet, and fouled with dropped feathers and excreta.

Johnny braked the Land-Rover and jumped out. He took one long look at the body, then turned away and braced himself against the side of the vehicle.

His gorge rose in a hot flood of nausea, and he gagged it back.

The body was nude but for a few sodden tatters of clothing and a sea boot still laced onto one foot. The birds had attacked every inch of exposed flesh–except for the scalp. The face was unrecognizable. The nose was gone, the eye sockets were empty black holes. There were no lips to cover the grinning teeth.

Above this ruined face the shock of colourless albino hair looked like a wig placed there as an obscene and tasteless joke.

Hugo Kramer had made the long voyage from Thunderbolt and Suicide to the Red Gods.

Johnny took the canvas groundsheet from under the passenger seat of the Land-Rover. Averting his eyes from the task, he wrapped the corpse carefully, tied the whole bundle with lengths of rope cut from the tow line, then laboriously dragged it up the beach well above the high-water mark.

The thick canvas would keep off the birds, but to make doubly certain Johnny collected the driftwood and planking that was scattered thickly along the high-water line and piled it over the corpse.

Some of the planking was freshly broken and the paint on it was still bright and new. Johnny guessed this was part of the wreckage of *Wild Goose*.

He went back to the Land-Rover, and drove on towards the Red Gods which lay only a mile ahead.

The sun was well up by now, and already its heat was uncomfortable. As he drove he struggled out of the sheepskin jacket without interrupting his search of the beach ahead.

He was looking for another gathering of seagulls, but instead he saw a large black object stranded in the angle formed by the red stone cliffs.

He was fifty yards from if before he realized what it was.

He felt his stomach jar violently and then clench at the shock.

It was a black rubber inflatable life raft–and it had been dragged up the beach *above the high-water line*.

As he climbed out of the Land-Rover Johnny felt his legs trembling beneath him, as though he had just climbed a mountain. The hard knotted sensation in his chest shortened his breathing.

He went slowly towards the raft, and there was a story to read in the soft sand.

The smooth drag mark of the raft, and the two sets of footprints. One set made by bare feet, broad, stubby-toed and with flattened arches, the prints of a man who habitually went barefooted.

These tracks had been made by one of the coloured crew of *Wild Goose*, Johnny decided, dismissed them and turned his whole attention to the other set of footprints.

Shod feet, long and narrow, smooth leather soles; the imprints were sharp edged suggesting new shoes little worn, the length of the stride and the depth of prints were those of a tall heavily-built man.

Johnny realized with mild surprise that his hands were shaking now, and even his lips quivered. He was like a man in high fever; light-headed, weak and shaking. It was Benedict van der Byl. He knew it with complete and utter certainty. Benedict had survived the maelstrom of Thunderbolt and Suicide.

Johnny balled his fists, squeezing hard and he thrust out his jaw, tightening his lips. Still the hatred washed over his mind in dark hot waves.

'Thank God,' he whispered. 'Thank God. Now I can kill him myself.'

The footprints had churned the sand all about the raft. Beside them lay a thick piece of planking which had been used as a lever to rip the emergency water container and the food locker from the floor-boards of the raft.

The food locker had been ransacked and abandoned. They would be carrying the packets of iron rations in their pockets to save weight, but the water container was gone.

The two sets of prints struck out straight for the dunes. Johnny followed them at a run and lost them immediately in the shifting wind-blown sands of the first dune.

Johnny was undismayed. The dunes persisted for only a thousand yards or so, then gave way inland to the plains and salt flats of the interior.

He ran back to the Land-Rover. He had his emotions under control again. His hatred was reduced to a hard indigestible lump below his ribs, and he contemplated for a few seconds lifting the microphone of the Land-Rover's R/T set and calling Cartridge Bay.

Inspector Stander had the police helicopter parked on the landing-strip behind the depot buildings. He could be here in thirty minutes. An hour later they would have Benedict van der Byl.

Johnny dismissed the idea. Officially Benedict was dead, drowned. No one would look for him in a shallow grave in the wastes of the Namib desert.

The crewman with him would be a complication; but he could be bribed and frightened or threatened. Nothing must stand in the path of his vengeance. Nothing.

Johnny opened the Land-Rover's locker and found the knife. He went back to the raft and stabbed the blade through the thick material at a dozen places. The air hissed from the holes, and the raft collapsed slowly.

Johnny bundled it into the back of the Land-Rover. He would bury it in the desert; there must be no evidence that Benedict had come ashore.

He started the engine, engaged the four-wheel drive, and followed the spoor to the foot of the dunes.

He picked his way through the valleys and across the knife-backed ridges of sand.

As he descended the last slope of the dunes he felt the oppressive silence and immensity of the land enfold him. Here, only a mile from the sea, the moderating influence of the cold Benguela did not reach.

The heat was appalling. Johnny felt the sweat pricking from the pores of his skin and drying instantly in the lethal desiccating air.

He swung the Land-Rover parallel to the line of the dunes and crawled along at walking speed, hanging over the side of the vehicle and searching the ground. The bright specks of mica in the sand bounced the heat of the sun into his face.

He cut the spoor again where it came down off the dunes and went away on it, headed arrow straight at the far line of mountains which were already receding into the blue haze as the heat built up towards noon.

Johnny's progress was a series of rushes where the spoor ran true, broken by halts and painstaking casts on the rocky ridges and areas of broken ground. Twice he left the Land-Rover to work the spoor through difficult terrain, but across one of the flat white salt pans he covered four miles in as many minutes. The prints were strung like the beads of a necklace, cut clearly through the glistening crust of salt.

Beyond the pan they ran into a maze of black rocks, riven by gullies, and guarded by the tall misshapen monoliths.

In one of the gullies he found Hansie, the little old coloured crewman from Wild Goose. His skull had been battered in with the blood-caked rock that lay beside him. The blood had dried slick and shiny, and Hansie stared with dry eyeballs at the merciless sky. His expression was of mild surprise.

The story of this new tragedy was written in the sandy bottom of the gully. In an area of milling, confused prints the two men had argued. Johnny could guess that Hansie had wanted to turn back for the coast. He must have known that the road lay beyond the mountains, a hundred miles away. He wanted to abandon the attempt, try for the coast and Cartridge Bay.

The argument ended when he turned his back on Benedict, and returned on his old tracks.

There was a depression in the sand from which Benedict had picked up the rock and followed him.

Standing over Hansie, and looking down at that pathetic crushed head, Johnny realized for the first time that he was following a maniac.

Benedict van der Byl was insane. He was no longer a man, but a raging demented animal.

'I will kill him,' Johnny promised the old white woolly head at his feet. There was no need for subterfuge now.

If he caught up with Benedict and did it, no court in the world would question but that it was self-defence. Benedict had placed himself beyond the laws of man.

Johnny took the deflated rubber raft and spread it over Hansie. He anchored the edges of the rubber sheet with rocks.

He drove on into the dancing, shimmering wall of heat with a new mood on him; murderous, elated expectation. He knew that at this moment in time he was part animal also, corrupted by the savagery of the man he was hunting. He wanted payment in full from Benedict van der Byl in his own coin. Life for life, and blood for blood.

A mile farther on he found the water container. It had been flung aside violently, skidding across the sand with the force of its rejection; the water had poured from its open mouth, leaving a dried hollow in the thirsty earth.

Johnny stared at it in disbelief. Not even a maniac would condemn himself to such a horrible ending.

Johnny went across to where the five-gallon brass drum lay on its side. He picked it up and shook it, there was the sloshy sound of a pint or so of liquid in it.

'God!' he whispered, awed and feeling a twinge of pity despite himself. 'He won't last long now.'

He lifted the container to his lips and sucked a mouthful. Immediately his nostrils flared with disgust, and he spat violently, dropping the can and wiping at his lips with the back of his hand.

'Sea water!' he mumbled. He hurried to the Land-Rover and washed out his mouth with sweet water.

How the contamination had occured he would never know. The raft might have lain for years in *Wild Goose* without its stores being checked or renewed.

From that point onwards Benedict must have known he was doomed. His despair was easy to read in the blundering footsteps. He had started running, with panic driving him. Five hundred yards farther on he had fallen heavily into the bed of a dry ravine, and lain for a while before dragging himself up the bank.

Now he had lost direction. The spoor began a long curve to the northwards, running again. It came round full circle, and where it crossed itself, Benedict had sat down. The marks of his buttocks were unmistakable. He must have controlled his panic here because once more the spoor struck out with determination towards the mountains.

However, within half a mile he had tripped and fallen. Now he was staggering off course again, drifting southwards. Once more he had fallen, but there he had lost a shoe.

Johnny picked it up and read the printed gold lettering on the inner sole. 'BALLY OF SWITZERLAND. SPECIALLY MADE FOR HARRODS. That's our boy Benedict, all right. Forty-guinea black kid,' he muttered grimly, and climbed back into the Land-Rover. His excitement was climaxing now. It would be soon, very soon.

Farther on Benedict had wandered down into the bed of an ancient watercourse, and turned to follow it. His right foot was lacerated by razor flints in the river bed, and at each pace he had left a little dab of brown crumbly blood. He was staggering like a drunkard.

Johnny zigzagged the Land-Rover through the boulders that choked the watercourse. The gully deepened, and spiky cockscomb ridges of black rock hedged it in on either hand. The air in the watercourse was a heavy blanket of heat. It seared the throat, and dried the mucus in Johnny's nostrils brick hard. A small noon breeze came off the mountains, a sluggish stirring of the heavy air, that provided no relief but seemed only to heighten the bite of the sun and the suffocating oppression of the air.

Scattered along the river bed were bushes of stunted scrub. Grotesque little plants, crippled and malformed by the drought of years.

From one of the bushes ahead of the Land-Rover a monstrous black bird flapped its wings lethargically. Johnny screwed up his eyes, uncertain if it was reality or a mirage of the heat and the tortured air.

Suddenly the bird resolved itself into the jacket of a dark blue suit. It hung in the thorny bushes, the breeze stirring the folds of expensive cloth.

'In his coat. He put it in his coat pocket.'

With eyes only for the jacket, recklessly he pressed down the accelerator and the Land-Rover surged forward. Johnny did not see the knee-high boulder of ironstone in his path. He hit it at twenty miles an hour, and the Land-Rover stopped dead with the squeal of tearing metal. Johnny was flung forward against the steering-wheel, the impact driving the breath from his lungs.

He was still doubled up with the pain of it, wheezing for breath, as he hobbled to the jacket and snatched it out of the bush.

He felt the heavy drag of the weighted pocket.

Then the fat canvas bag was in his hands, the contents crunched nuttily as he tore at the drawstring. Nothing else in the world felt like that.

'Such a diamond as you will never see again.'

The drawstring was knotted tightly. Johnny ran back to the Land-Rover. Frantically he scrabbled in the seat locker and found the knife. He cut the drawstring and dumped the contents of the bag onto the bonnet of the Land-Rover.

'Oh God! Oh sweet God!' he whispered through cracked lips. His eyesight blurred, and the big blue diamond glowed mistily, distorted by the tears that flooded his vision.

It was a full minute before he could bring himself to touch it. Then he did so reverently–as though it were a sacred relic.

Johnny Lance had worked all his life to take a stone such as this.

He held it in both hands and sank down into the scrap of shade beside the body of the Land-Rover.

It was another five minutes before the hot cloying smell of engine oil reached the conscious level of his mind.

He turned his head and saw the slowly spreading pool of it beneath the Land-Rover chassis. Quickly he rolled onto his stomach and, still clutching the diamond, crawled under the vehicle. The ironstone boulder had shattered the engine sump. The Land-Rover had belched its lifeblood into the hot sand of the river bed.

He wriggled out from under the body of the Land-Rover and leaned against the front tyre. He looked at his wrist watch and was surprised to see it was already a few minutes after two o'clock in the afternoon.

He was surprised also at the conscious effort it required to focus his eyes on the dial of the watch. Two days and two nights without sleep, the unremitting emotional strain of those days and nights, the battering his body had taken, the long hours in the heat and the soul-corroding desolation of this lunar landscape–all these had taken their toll. He knew he was as light-headed as in the first stages of inebriation, he was beginning to act irrationally. That sudden reckless charge down the boulder-strewn river bed, which had wrecked the Land-Rover, was a symptom of his present instability.

He fondled the great diamond, touching the warm smooth surface to his lips, rubbing it softly between thumb and forefinger, changing it from hand to hand, while every fibre of his muscles and the very marrow of his bones cried out for rest.

A soft and treacherous lethargy spread through his body and reached out to numb his brain. He closed his eyes for a moment to shut out the glare, and when he opened them again with an effort the time was four o'clock. He scrambled to his feet. The shadows in the gully were longer, the breeze had dropped.

Although he moved with the stiffness of an old man, the sleep had cleared his mind and while he wolfed a packet of biscuits spread with meat paste and washed it down with a mugful of lukewarm water he made his decision.

He buried the canvas bag of rough diamonds in the sand beneath the Land-Rover, but he could not bring himself to part with the big Blue. He buttoned it securely into the back pocket of his slacks. Into the light knapsack from the seat locker he packed the two-pint water bottle, the first aid kit, a small hand-bearing compass, two of the smoke flares and the knife. He checked his pockets for his cigarette-lighter and case.

Then without another glance at the radio set on the dashboard of the Land-Rover he turned away and hobbled up the gully on the spoor of Benedict van der Byl.

Within half a mile he had walked the stiffness out of his body, and he lengthened his stride, going well now. The hatred and hunger for vengeance which had died to smouldering ash since he had found the diamonds, now flared up again strongly. It gave power to his legs and sharpened his senses.

The spoor turned abruptly up the side of the gully and he lost it on the black rock of the ridge, but found it again on his first cast.

He was closing fast now. The spoor was running across the grain of the land, and Benedict was clearly weakening rapidly. He had fallen repeatedly, crawled on bloody knees over cruel gravel and rock, he had blundered into the scrub bushes and left threads of his clothing on the hooked red-tipped thorns.

Then the spoor led out of the ridges and scrub into another area of low orange-coloured sandhills and Johnny broke into a trot. The sun was sliding down the sky, throwing blue shades in the hollows of the dunes and the heat abated so that Johnny's sweat was able to cool him before drying.

Johnny was intent on the staggering footprints, beginning to worry now that he would find Benedict already dead. The signs were those of a man in extreme distress, and still he was driving himself on.

Johnny did not notice the other prints that angled in from the dunes and ran parallel to those of Benedict, until they closed in again and began overlaying the human prints.

Johnny stopped and went down on one knee to examine the broad dog-like pug marks.

'Hyena!' He felt the sick little flutter of revulsion in his stomach as he spoke. He glanced around quickly and saw the other sets of prints out on the left.

'A pair of them! They've smelt the blood.'

Johnny began to run on the spoor now. His skin crawled with what he knew could happen when they caught up with a helpless man. The filthiest and most cowardly animals in Africa, but with jaws that could crunch to splinters the thigh bone of a full-grown buffalo, and their thick stubby fangs were coated with such a slime of bacteria from a diet of putrid carrion that their bite was as deadly as that of a black mamba.

'Let me be in time; please God, let me find him in time.'

He heard it then. From beyond the crest of the next dune. The horror of the sound stopped him in mid-stride. It was a shrill giggling gibbering cry that sobbed into silence.

Johnny stood listening, panting wildly from his run.

It came again. The laughter of demons, excited, blood-crazy.

'They've got him.'

Johnny flung himself at the soft slope of sand. He reached the crest and looked down into the saucer-shaped arena formed by the crescent of the dune.

Benedict lay on his back. His white shirt was open to the waist. The blue trousers of his suit were ripped and shredded, exposing his knees. One foot was a bloody lump of sock and congealed dirt.

The pair of hyenas had trampled a path in the sand around his body. They had been circling him for hours, while greed overcame their cowardice.

One hyena sat ten feet from him, squatting obscenely with its flat snakelike head lowered between humped shoulders. Brown and shaggy, spotted with darker brown, its round ears pricked forward, its black eyes sparkling with greed and excitement as it watched its mate.

The other hyena stood with its front paws on Benedict's chest. Its head lowered, and its jaws were locked into Benedict's face. It was leaning back, bracing its paws on his chest, tugging viciously as it sought to tear off a mouthful of flesh. Benedict's head was jerking and twitching as the hyena worried it. His legs were kicking weakly, and his hands fluttered on the sand like maimed white birds.

The flesh of his face tore. Johnny heard it distinctly in the utter silence of the desert evening. It tore with the soft sound of silk–and Johnny screamed.

Both hyenas bolted at the scream, scrambling over the far crest of the dune in horrible clownish panic, leaving Benedict lying with a bloody mask for a face. Looking down at that face Johnny knew he could not kill him now, perhaps could never have killed him. He could not revenge himself on this broken thing with its ruined face and twisted mind.

He dropped onto his knees beside him, and loosened the flap of the knapsack with clumsy fingers.

Benedict's one ear and cheek were hanging over his mouth in a thick flap of torn flesh. The teeth in the side of his jaw were exposed and the blood dribbled and spurted in fine needle jets.

Johnny tore the paper packaging off an absorbent dressing and with it pressed the flap back into place, holding it there with the full pressure of his spread fingers. The blood soaked through the dressing, but it was slowing at the pressure.

'It's all right, Benedict. 'I'm here now. You'll be all right,' he whispered hoarsely as he worked. With his free hand he stripped the packaging off another dressing, and substituted it neatly for the sodden one. He maintained the pressure on the clean dressing while he lifted Benedict's head and cradled it in his lap.

'We'll just dry this bleeding up, then we'll give you a drink.' He reached into the first aid kit for a piece of cotton wool and tenderly began to clean the blood and sand from Benedict's nostrils and lips. Benedict's strangled breathing eased a little but still whistled through the black lips. His tongue was swollen, filling his mouth like a fat purple sponge.

'That's better,' Johnny muttered. Still without relaxing pressure on the compress dressing, he got the screw top off the water bottle. Holding his thumb over the opening to regulate the flow, he let a drop of water fall into the dark dry pit of a mouth.

After another ten drops he propped the water bottle in the sand, and massaged Benedict's throat gently to stimulate the swallowing reflex. The unconscious man gulped painfully.

'That's my boy,' Johnny encouraged him, and began again feeding him a drop at a time, crooning softly as he did it.

'You're going to be all right. That's it, swallow it down.'

It took him twenty minutes to administer half a pint of the warm sweet water, and by then the bleeding was negligible. Johnny reached into the kit again and selected two salt and two glucose tablets. He placed them in his own mouth and chewed them to a smooth thin paste, then he bent over the mutilated face of the man he had sworn to kill and pressed his own lips against Benedict's swollen dry lips. He injected the solution of salt and glucose into Benedict's mouth, then straightened up and began again dripping the water.

When he had given Benedict another four tablets and half the contents of the water bottle, he stoppered it and returned it to the knapsack. He soaked the compress with bright yellow acriflavine solution, and bandaged it firmly into place. This was a more difficult task than he had anticipated and after a few abortive attempts he passed the bandage under the jaw and over the eyes, swathing Benedict's head completely except for the nose and mouth.

By this time the sun was on the horizon. Johnny stood up and stretched his back and shoulders as he watched the splendid gold and red death of another desert day.

He knew he was delaying his next decision. He reckoned it was five miles to where he had abandoned the Land-Rover in the gully. Five miles of hard going, a round trip of four hours–probably five in the dark. Could he leave Benedict here, get back to the vehicle, radio Cartridge Bay, and return to him?

Johnny swung round and looked up at the dunes. There was his answer. One of the hyenas was squatting on the top of a dune watching him intently. Hunger and the approach of night had made it unnaturally bold.

Johnny shouted an obscenity and made a threatening gesture towards it. The hyena jumped up and loped over the back of the ridge.

'Moon rise at eight tonight. I'll rest then–and we'll go in the cool,' he decided and lay down on the sand beside Benedict. The lump in his back pocket prodded him, and he took the diamond out and held it in his hand.

In the darkness the hyenas began to cackle and shriek, and when the moon rose it silhouetted their evil shapes on the ridge above the saucer.

'Come on Benedict. We're going home. There are a couple of nice policemen who want to talk to you.' Johnny lifted him into a sitting position, draped Benedict's arm over his shoulder and came up under him in a fireman's lift.

Johnny stood like that a moment, sinking ankle deep into the soft sand, dismayed at the dead weight of his burden.

'We'll rest every thousand paces,' he promised himself, and began plodding up the dune, counting softly to himself, but knowing that he would not be able to perform that lift again without a rock shelf or some support, against which to brace himself. He had to make it out of the sandhills in one go.

'–Nine hundred and ninety nine. One thousand.' He was counting in his mind only. Husbanding his strength, bowed under the weight, his shoulders and back locked in straining agony, the sand hampering each pace. 'Another five hundred. We'll go another five hundred.'

Behind him padded the two hyenas. They had gobbled the bloody dressing that Johnny had left in the saucer, and the taste of blood was driving them hysterical.

'Right. Just another five hundred.' And Johnny began the third count, and then the fourth, and the fifth.

Johnny felt the drip, drip on the back of his legs. Benedict's head-down position had restarted the bleeding, and the hyenas warbled and wailed at the smell.

'Nearly there, Benedict. Stick it out. Nearly there.'

The first cluster of moon-silver rocks floated towards them and Johnny reeled in amongst them and collapsed face forward. It was a long time before he had regained enough strength to shift Benedict's weight off his shoulders.

He readjusted Benedict's bandages, and fed him a mouthful of water which he swallowed readily. Then Johnny washed down a handful of salt and glucose tablets with two carefully rationed swallows from the water bottle. He rested for twenty minutes by his watch, then using one of the rocks as an anchor he got Benedict across his shoulder again and they went on.

Johnny rested every hour for ten minutes. At one o'clock in the morning they finished the last of the water, and at two o'clock Johnny knew beyond all possibility of doubt that he had missed the watercourse and that he was lost.

He lay against a slab of ironstone, numb with fatigue and despair, and listened to the cackling chorus of death among the rocks nearby. He tried to decide where he had gone wrong. Perhaps the watercourse curved away and he was now moving parallel to it, perhaps he had already crossed it without having recognized it. That was possible, he had heard of others stumbling blindly across a tarmac road without realizing it.

How many ridges had they climbed and descended? He could not remember. There was a place where he had stumbled into a shrub thorn and ripped his legs. Perhaps that was the watercourse.

He crawled across to Benedict.

'Brace up, bucko. We're going back.'

Johnny fell for the last time a little before dawn. When he rolled his head and squinted sideways at his wrist watch it was light enough to read the dial. The time was five o'clock.

He closed his eyes and lay for a long time, he had given up. It had been a good try–but it hadn't worked. In an hour the sun would be up. Then it was finished.

Something was moving near him, soft and stealthy-footed. It was of no interest, he decided. He just wanted to lie here quietly, now that it was finished.

Then he heard the sniffing, the harsh sniffing of a hungry dog. He opened his eyes. The hyena was ten feet away, watching him. Its bottom jaw hung open, and the pink tongue lolled loosely from the side of its mouth. He could smell it, a stink like an animal cage at the zoo, dung and offal and rotting carrion.

Johnny tried to scream, but no sound came from his mouth. His throat was closed, and his tongue filled his mouth. He struggled onto his elbows. The hyena drew back, but without the ludicrous panic of before. Leisurely it trotted away, and then turned to face him again from a distance of twenty yards. It grinned at him, slurping the pink tongue into its mouth as it gulped saliva.

Johnny dragged himself to where Benedict lay, and looked down at him.

Slowly the blind bandaged head turned towards him, the black lips moved.

'Who's there?' A dry husky whisper. Johnny tried to answer but his voice failed him again. He hawked and chewed painfully, working a trace of moisture into his mouth. Now that Benedict was conscious Johnny's hatred flared again.

'Johnny,' he croaked. 'It's Johnny.'

'Johnny?' Benedict's hand came up and he touched the bandages over his eyes.

'What?'

Johnny reached across, lying on his side, and untied the knot at Benedict's temple. He peeled the bandages from his eyes, and Benedict blinked at him. The light of dawn was stronger now.

'Water?' Benedict asked.

Johnny shook his head.

'Please.'

'None.'

Benedict closed his eyes and then opened them, staring in terror at Johnny.

'Ruby!' Johnny whispered. 'Sergio! Hansie!'

A spasm of guilt twisted Benedict's face, and Johnny leaned closer to him to hiss a single word into his ear.

'Bastard!'

Johnny rested on his elbows, swallowing thickly, then he spoke again.

'Up!' He crawled behind Benedict and pushed and dragged him into a sitting position.

'Look.'

Twenty yards away the two hyenas sat expectantly, leering idiotically and bright-eyed with impatience.

Benedict began to tremble. He made a mewing whimpering sound. Johnny worked him slowly backwards until he had him propped against a rock.

He rested again, leaning on the rock beside Benedict.

'I'm going,' he whispered. 'You stay.'

Benedict made that mewing sound again, shaking his head weakly, staring at the two slobbering animals ahead of him.

Johnny slung the knapsack about his neck. He closed his eyes and called upon the last reserves of his strength. With a heave he got to his knees. Darkness and bright lights obscured his vision. They cleared and he heaved again and he was on his feet. His knees buckled and he grabbed at the rock to steady himself.

'Cheerio!' he whispered. 'Have fun!' And he went lurching and staggering away into the wilderness of black rock.

Behind him the mewing whimper rose to a bubbling scream.

'Johnny. Please, Johnny.'

Johnny closed his mind to that cry, and staggered on.

'Murder!' screamed Benedict. The accusation checked Johnny. He leaned against another rock for support, and looked back.

Benedict's face was convulsed, and a thin line of bloody froth rimmed his lips. The tears were pouring unashamedly down his cheeks to soak into the blood and antiseptic-stained bandages.

'Johnny. My brother. Don't leave me.'

Johnny pushed himself away from the rock. He swayed and almost fell. Then he staggered back to Benedict and slipped down into a sitting position beside him.

From the knapsack he took out the knife and laid it on his lap. Benedict was sobbing and moaning.

'Shut up. Damn you!' whispered Johnny.

The sun was well up now. It was burning directly into Johnny's face. He could feel the skin of his cheeks stretching to bursting-point. The veils of darkness kept passing over his vision, but he blinked them away. The flutter of his eyelids was the only movement he had made in the last hour.

The hyenas closed in. They were pacing nervously back and forth in front of where Johnny and Benedict sat. Now one of them stopped and stretched its neck out, sniffing eagerly at Benedict's blood-clotted foot, creeping inch by inch closer.

Johnny stirred and the creature jumped back, bobbing its head ingratiatingly, grinning as if in apology.

The time had come to fall back on their last line of defence. Johnny hoped he had not left it too late. He was very weak. His eyes and ears were tricking him, his vision jumped and blurred and there was a humming sound in the silence as though the desert was an orchard filled with bees. He spun the cog-wheel of his cigarette lighter and the flame lit. Carefully he applied it to the fuse of the smoke flare, and it spluttered and caught.

Johnny lobbed the flare towards the hyenas, and as the clouds of pink smoke spewed out, they fled in shrieking terror.

An hour later they were back. Slinking out of the rocks, cautious again. Johnny saw them only in flashes, between the bursts of darkness in his head. The insect drone in his ears was louder, it was confusing, making it difficult for him to think clearly.

It took him ten minutes to light the second flare. His throw was so weak that the flare pitched only a few inches beyond his own feet. The pink smoke spread over them.

Johnny felt the blood humming in his ears as the swirling pink clouds engulfed him. The sulphurous bite of the smoke in his throat choked him. The sound in his ears became a drumming roar, a rushing clattering hissing bellow. Then there was a wild wind in the stillness of the desert. Miraculously the smoke cloud was ripped away by the wind.

Johnny looked up into the sky from which the great wind came. Twenty feet above him, hanging on the glistening dragon-fly wing of its rotor, was the police helicopter.

Tracey's face was framed in the cabin window of the helicopter. He saw her lips form his name before he fainted.

Eagle in the Sky

EAGLE IN THE SKY

While writing this story I had valuable help from a number of people. Major Dick Lord and Lieutenant Peter Cooke gave me advice on the technique and technicalities of modern fighter combat. Dr Robin Sandell and Dr David Davies provided me with the medical details. A brother angler, the Rev. Bob Redrup, helped with the choice of the title. To them all I am sincerely grateful. While in Israel many of the citizens of that state gave help and hospitality in generous measure. It grieves me that I may not mention their names.
As always my faithful research assistant gave comfort, encouragement and criticism when it was most needed. This book is dedicated to her son – my stepson – Dieter Schmidt.

There was snow on the mountains of the Hottentots' Holland and the wind came off it, whimpering like a lost animal. The instructor stood in the doorway of his tiny office and hunched down into his flight jacket, thrusting his fists deeply into the fleece-lined pockets.

He watched the black chauffeur-driven Cadillac coming down between the cavernous iron-clad hangars, and he frowned sourly. For the trappings of wealth Barney Venter had a deeply aching gut-envy.

The Cadillac swung in and parked in a visitors' slot against the hangar wall, and a boy sprang from the rear door with boyish enthusiasm, spoke briefly with the coloured chauffeur, then hurried towards Barney.

He moved with a lightness that was strange for an adolescent. There was no stumbling over feet too big for his body, and he carried himself tall. Barney's envy curdled as he watched the young princeling approach. He hated these pampered darlings, and it was his particular fate that he must spend so much of his working day in their company. Only the very rich could afford to instruct their children in the mysteries of flight.

He was reduced to this by the gradual running down of his body, the natural attrition of time. Two years previously, at the age of forty-five, he had failed the strict medical on which his position of senior airline captain depended, and now he was going down the other side of the hill, probably to end as a typical fly-bum, steering tired and beaten-up heaps on unscheduled and shady routes for unlicensed and unprincipled charter companies.

The knowledge made him growl at the child who stood before him. 'Master Morgan, I presume?'

'Yes, sir, but you may call me David.' The boy offered his hand and instinctively Barney took it–immediately wishing he had not. The hand was slim and dry, but with a hard grip of bone and sinew.

'Thank you, David.' Barney was heavy on irony. 'And you may continue to call me "sir".'

He knew the boy was fourteen years old, but he stood almost level with Barney's five-foot-seven. David smiled at him and Barney was struck almost as by a physical force by the boy's beauty. It seemed as though each detail of his features had been wrought with infinite care by a supreme artist. The total effect was almost unreal, theatrical. It seemed indecent that hair should curl and glow so darkly, that skin should be so satiny and delicately tinted, or that eyes possess such depth and fire.

Barney became aware that he was staring at the boy, that he was falling under the spell that the child seemed so readily to weave–and he turned away abruptly.

'Come on.' He led the way through his office with its flyblown nude calendars and handwritten notices carrying terse admonitions against asking for credit, or making right-hand circuits.

'What do you know about flying?' he asked the boy as they passed through the cool gloom of the hangar where gaudily coloured aircraft stood in long rows, and out again through the wide doors into the bright mild winter sunshine.

'Nothing, sir.' The admission was refreshing, and Barney felt his mood sweeten slightly.

'But you want to learn?'

'Oh, yes sir!' The reply was emphatic and Barney glanced at him. The boy's eyes were so dark as to be almost black, only in the sunlight did they turn deep indigo blue.

'All right then–let's begin.' The aircraft was waiting on the concrete apron.

'This is a Cessna 150 high-wing monoplane.' Barney began the walk-around check with David following attentively, but when he started a brief explanation of the control surfaces and the principle of lift and wing-loading, he became aware that the boy knew more than he had owned up to. His replies to Barney's rhetorical questions were precise and accurate.

'You've been reading,' Barney accused.

'Yes, sir,' David admitted, grinning. His teeth were of peculiar whiteness and symmetry and the smile was irresistible. Despite himself, Barney realized he was beginning to like the boy.

'Right, jump in.'

Strapped into the cramped cockpit shoulder to shoulder, Barney explained the controls and instruments, then led into the starting procedure.

'Master switch on.' He flipped the red button. 'Right, turn that key–same as in a car.'

David leaned forward and obeyed. The prop spun and the engine fired and kicked, surged, then settled into a satisfying healthy growl. They taxied down the apron with David quickly developing his touch on the rudders, and paused for the final checks and radio procedure before swinging wide on to the runway.

'Right, pick an object at the end of the runway. Aim for it and open the throttle gently.'

Around them the machine became urgent, and it buzzed busily towards the far-off fence markers.

'Ease back on the wheel.'

And they were airborne, climbing swiftly away from earth.

'Gently,' said Barney. 'Don't freeze on to the controls. Treat her like–' he broke off. He had been about to liken the aircraft to a woman, but realized the unsuitability of the simile. 'Treat her like a horse. Ride her light.'

Instantly he felt David's death-grip on the wheel relax, the touch repeated through his own controls.

'That's it, David.' He glanced sideways at the boy, and felt a flare of disappointment. He had felt deep down in his being that this one might be bird, one of the very rare ones like himself whose natural element was the blue. Yet here in the first few moments of flight the child was wearing an expression of frozen terror. His lips and nostrils were trimmed with marble white and there were shadows in the dark blue eyes like the shape of sharks moving beneath the surface of a summer sea.

'Left wing up,' he snapped, disappointed, trying to shock him out of it. The wing came up and held rock steady, with no trace of over-correction.

'Level her out.' His own hands were off the controls as the nose sank to find the horizon.

'Throttle back.' The boy's right hand went unerringly to the throttle. Once more Barney glanced at him. His expression had not altered, and then with a sudden revelation Barney recognized it not as fear, but as ecstasy.

'He is bird.' The thought gave him a vast satisfaction, and while they flew on through the basic instruction in trim and attitude, Barney's mind went back thirty years to a battered old yellow Tiger Moth and another child in his first raptures of flight.

They skirted the harsh blue mountains, wearing their mantles of sun-blazing snow, and rode the tail of the wild winds that came down off them.

'Wind is like the sea, David. It breaks and swirls around high ground. Watch for it.' David nodded as he listened to his first fragment of flying lore, but his eyes were fixed ahead savouring each instant of the experience.

They turned north over the bleak bare land, the earth naked pink and smoky brown, stripped by the harvest of its robes of golden wheat.

'Wheel and rudder together, David,' Barney told him. 'Let's try a steep turn now.' Down went the wing and boldly the nose swept around holding its attitude to the horizon.

Ahead of them the sea broke in long lines of cream on the white beaches. The Atlantic was cold green and ruffled by the wind, flecked with dancing white.

South again, following the coastline where small figures on the white sand paused to look up at them from under shading hands, south towards the great flat mountain that marked the limit of the land, its shape unfamiliar from this approach. The shipping lay thick in the bay and the winter sunshine flashed from the windows of the white buildings huddling below the steep wooded sides of the mountain.

Another turn, confident and sure, Barney sitting with his hands in his lap, and his feet off the rudder bars, and they ran in over the Tygerberg towards the airfield.

'Okay,' said Barney. 'I've got her. And he took them in for the touch-down and taxied back to the concrete apron beside the hangars. He pulled the mixture control fully lean and let the engine starve and die.

They sat silent for a moment, neither of them moving or speaking, both of them unwinding but still aware that something important and significant had happened and that they had shared it.

'Okay?' Barney asked at last.

'Yes, sir,' David nodded, and they unstrapped and climbed down on to the concrete stiffly. Without speaking they walked side by side through the hangar and office. At the door they paused.

'Next Wednesday?' Barney asked.

'Yes, sir.' David left him and started towards the waiting Cadillac, but after a dozen steps he stopped, hesitated, then turned back.

'That was the most beautiful thing that has ever happened to me,' he said shyly. 'Thank you, sir.' And he hurried away leaving Barney staring after him.

The Cadillac pulled off, gathering speed, and disappeared round a bend amongst the trees beyond the last buildings. Barney chuckled, shook his head ruefully and turned back into his office. He dropped into the ancient swivel chair and crossed his ankles on the desk. He fished a crumpled cigarette from the pack, straightened and lit it.

'Beautiful?' he grunted, grinning. 'Crap!' He flicked the match at the waste bin and missed it.

The telephone woke Mitzi Morgan and she crept out from under her pillows groping blindly for it.

''Lo.'

'Mitzi?'

'Hi, Dad, are you coming up?' She came half-awake at her father's voice, remembering that this was the day he would fly up to join the family at their holiday home.

'Sorry, baby. Something has broken here. I won't be up until next week.'

'Oh, Dad!' Mitzi expressed her disappointment.

'Where's Davey?' her father went on quickly to forestall any recriminations.

'You want him to call you back?'

'No, I'll hold on. Call him, please, baby.'

Mitzi stumbled out of bed to the mirror, and with her fingers tried to comb some order into her hair. It was off-blonde and wiry, and fuzzed at the first touch of sun or salt or wind. The freckles were even more humiliating, she decided, looking at herself disapprovingly.

'You look like a Pekinese,' she spoke aloud, 'a fat little Pekinese–with freckles,' and gave up the effort of trying to change it. David had seen her like this a zillion times. She pulled a silk gown over her nudity and went into the passage, pass the door to her parents' suite where her mother slept alone, and into the living area of the house.

The house was stacked in a series of open planes and galleries, glass and steel and white pine, climbing out of the dunes along the beach, part of sea and sky, only glass separating it from the elements, and now the dawn filled it with a strange glowing light and made a feature of the massive headland of the Robberg that thrust out into the sea across the bay.

The Playroom was scattered with the litter of last night's party, twenty house guests and as many others from the big holiday homes along the dunes had left their mark–spilled beer, choked ashtrays and records thrown carelessly from their covers.

Mitzi picked her way through the debris and climbed the circular staircase to the guest rooms. She checked David's door, found it open, and went in. The bed was untouched, but his denims and sweat shirt were thrown across the chair and his shoes had been kicked off carelessly.

Mitzi grinned, and went through on to the balcony. It hung high above the beach, level with the gulls which were already dawn-winging for the scraps that the sea had thrown up during the night.

Quickly Mitzi hoisted her gown up around her waist, climbed up on to the rail of the balcony and stepped over the drop to the rail of the next balcony in line. She jumped down, drew the curtains aside and went into Marion's bedroom.

Marion was her best friend. Secretly she knew that this happy state of affairs existed chiefly because she, Mitzi, provided a foil for Marion's petite little body and wide-eyed doll-like beauty–and was a source of never-ending gifts and parties, free holidays and other good things.

She looked so pretty now in sleep, her hair golden and soft as it fanned out across David's chest. Mitzi transferred all her attention to her cousin, and felt that sliding sensation in her breast as she looked at him. He was seventeen years old now, but already he had the body of a grown man.

He was her most favourite person in all the world, she thought. He's so beautiful, so tall and straight and beautiful, and his eyes can break your heart.

The couple on the bed had thrown aside their covering in the warmth of the night, and there was hair on David's chest now, thick and dark and curly, there was muscle in arm and leg, and breadth across the shoulders.

'David,' she called softly, and touched his shoulder. 'Wake up.'

His eyes opened, and he was awake instantly, his gaze focused and aware.

'Mitz? What is it?'

'Get your pants on, warrior. My papa's on the line.'

'God.' David sat up, dropping Marion's head on to the pillow. 'What time is it?'

'Late,' Mitzi told him. 'You should set the alarm when you go visiting.'

Marion mumbled a protest and groped for the sheets as David jumped from the bed.

'Where's the phone?'

'In my room–but you can take it on the extension in yours.'

She followed him across the balcony railing, and curled up on David's bed while he picked up the receiver and with the extension cord trailing behind him began pacing the thick carpet restlessly.

'Uncle Paul?' David spoke. 'How are you?'

Mitzi groped in the pocket of her gown and found a Gauloise. She lit it with her gold Dunhill, but at the third puff David turned aside from his pacing, grinned at her, took the cigarette from between her lips and drew deeply upon it.

Mitzi pulled a face at him to disguise the turmoil that his nakedness stirred within her, and selected another cigarette for herself.

'He'd die if he knew what I was thinking,' she told herself, and derived a little comfort from the thought.

David finished his conversation and cradled the receiver before turning to her.

'He's not coming.'

'I know.'

'But he is sending Barney up in the Lear to fetch me. Big pow-wow.'

'It figures,' Mitzi nodded, then began a convincing imitation of her father. 'We have to start thinking about your future now, my boy. We have to train you to meet the responsibilities with which destiny has entrusted you.'

David chuckled and rummaged for his running shorts in the drawer of his bureau.

'I suppose I'll have to tell him now.'

'Yes,' Mitzi agreed. 'You sure will have to do that.'

David pulled up his shorts and turned for the door.

'Pray for me, doll.'

'You'll need more than prayer, warrior,' said Mitzi comfortably.

The tide had swept the beach smooth and firm, and no other feet had marked it this early. David ran smoothly, long strides leaving damp footsteps in a chain behind him.

The sun came up casting a soft pink sheen on the sea, and touching the Outeniqua mountains with flame–but David ran unseeing. His thoughts were on the impending interview with his guardian.

It was a time of crisis in his life, high school completed and many roads open. He knew the one he had chosen would draw violent opposition, and he used these last few hours of solitude to gather and strengthen his resolve.

A conclave of gulls, gathered about the body of a stranded fish, rose in cloud as he ran towards them, their wings catching the low sun as they hovered then dropped again when he passed.

He saw the Lear coming before he heard it. It was low against the dawn, rising and dropping over the towering bulk of the Robberg. Then swiftly, coming in on a muted shriek, it streaked low along the beach towards him.

David stopped, breathing lightly even after the long run, and raised both arms above his head in salute. He saw Barney's head through the Perspex canopy turned towards him, the flash of his teeth as he grinned and the hand raised, returning his salute as he went by.

The Lear turned out to sea, one wingtip almost touching the wave crests, and it came back to him. David stood on the exposed beach and steeled himself as the long sleek nose dropped lower and lower, aimed like a javelin at him.

Like some fearsome predatory bird it swooped at him and at the last possible instant David's nerve broke and he flung himself on the wet sand. The jet blast lashed him as the Lear rose and turned inland for the airfield.

'Son of a bitch,' muttered David as he stood up brushing damp sand from his bare chest, and imagined Barney's amused chuckle.

'I taught him good,' thought Barney, sprawled in the co-pilot's seat of the Lear as he watched David ride the delicate line of altitude where skill gave way to chance.

Barney had put on weight since he had been eating Morgan bread, and his paunch peeked shyly over his belt. The beginning of jowls bracketed the wide down-turned mouth that gave him the air of a disgruntled toad, and the cap of hair that covered his skull was sparser and speckled with salt.

Watching David fly, he felt the small warmth of his affection for him that his sour expression belied. Three years he had been chief pilot of the Morgan group and he knew well to whose intervention he owed the post. It was security he had now, and prestige. He flew great men in the most luxuriously fitted machines, and when the time came for him to go out to pasture he knew the grazing would be lush. The Morgan group looked after its own.

This knowledge sat comfortably on his stomach as he watched his protégé handle the jet.

Extended low flying like this required enormous concentration, and Barney watched in vain for any relaxation of it in his pupil.

The long golden beaches of Africa streamed steadily beneath them, punctuated by rock promontories and tiny resorts and fishing villages. Delicately the Lear followed the contours of the coastine, for they had spurned the direct route for the exhilaration of this flight.

Ahead of them stretched another strip of beach but as they howled low along it they saw that this one was occupied.

A pair of tiny feminine figures left the frothy surf and ran panic-stricken to where towels and discarded bikinis lay above the high-water mark. White buttocks constrasted sharply with a coffee-brown tan, and they laughed delightedly.

'Nice change for you to see them running away, David,' Barney grinned as they left the tiny figures far behind and bore onwards into the south.

From Cape Agulhas they turned inland, climbing steeply over the mountain ranges, then David eased back on the throttles and they sank down beyond the crests towards the city, nestling under its mountain.

As they walked side by side towards the hangar, Barney looked up at David who now topped him by six inches.

'Don't let him stampede you, boy,' he warned. 'You've made your decision. See you stick to it.'

David took his British racing green M.G. over De Waal Drive, and from the lower slopes of the mountains looked down to where the Morgan building stood four-square amongst the other tall monuments to power and wealth.

David enjoyed its appearance, clean and functional like an aircraft's wing–but he knew that the soaring freedom of its lines was deceptive. It was a prison and fortress.

He swung off the freeway at an interchange and rode down to the foreshore, glancing up at the towering bulk of the Morgan building again before entering the ramp that led to the underground garages beneath it.

When he entered the executive apartments on the top floor, he passed along the row of desks where the secretaries, hand-picked for their looks as well as their skill with a typewriter, sat in a long row. Their lovely faces opened into smiles like a garden of exotic blooms as David greeted each of them. Within the Morgan building he was treated with the respect due the heir apparent.

Martha Goodrich, in her own office that guarded the inner sanctum, looked up from her typewriter, severe and business-like.

'Good morning, Mister David. Your uncle is waiting–and I do think you could have worn a suit.'

'You're looking good, Martha. You've lost weight and I like your hair like that.' It worked, as it always did. Her expression softened.

'Don't you try buttering me up,' she warned him primly. 'I'm not one of your floozies.'

Paul Morgan was at the picture window looking down over the city spread below him like a map, but he turned quickly to greet David.

'Hello, Uncle Paul. I'm sorry I didn't have time to change. I thought it best to come directly.'

'That's fine, David.' Paul Morgan flicked his eyes over David's floral shirt open to the navel, the wide tooled leather belt, white slacks and open sandals. On him they looked good, Paul admitted reluctantly. The boy wore even the most outlandish modern clothes with a furious grace.

'It's good to see you.' Paul smoothed the lapels of his own dark conservatively-cut suit and looked up at his nephew. 'Come in. Sit down, there, the chair by the fireplace.' As always, he found that David standing emphasized his own lack of stature. Paul was short and heavily built in the shoulders, thick muscular neck and square thrusting head. Like his daughter, his hair was coarse and wiry and his features squashed and puglike.

All the Morgans were built that way. It was proper course of things, and David's exotic appearance was outside the natural order. It was from his mother's side, of course. All that dark hair and flashing eyes, and the temperament that went with it.

'Well, David. First off, I want to congratulate you on your final results. I was most gratified,' Paul Morgan told him gravely, and he could have added–'I was also mightily relieved.' David Morgan's scholastic career had been a tempestuous affair. Pinnacles of achievement followed immediately by depths of disgrace from which only the Morgan name and wealth had rescued him.

There had been the business with the games master's young wife. Paul never did find out the truth of the matter, but had thought it sufficient to smooth it over by donating a new organ to the school chapel and arranging a teaching scholarship for the games master to a foreign university. Immediately thereafter David had won the coveted Wessels prize for mathematics, and all was forgiven–until he decided to test his housemaster's new sports car, without that gentleman's knowledge, and took it into a tight bend at ninety miles an hour. The car was unequal to the test, and David picked himself up out of the wreckage and limped away with a nasty scratch on his calf. It had taken all Paul Morgan's weight to have the housemaster agree not to cancel David's appointment as head of house. His prejudices had finally been overcome by the replacement of his wrecked car with a more expensive model, and the Morgan group had made a grant to rebuild the ablution block of East House.

The boy was wild, Paul knew it well, but he knew also that he could tame him. Once he had done that he would have forged a razor-edged tool. He possessed all the attributes that Paul Morgan wanted in his successor. The verve and confidence, the bright quick mind and adventurous spirit–but above all he possessed the aggressive attitude, the urge to compete that Paul defined as the killer instinct.

'Thank you, Uncle Paul,' David accepted his uncle's congratulations warily. They were silent, each assessing the other. They had never been easy in the other's company, they were too different in many ways–and yet in others too much alike. Always it seemed that their interests were in conflict.

Paul Morgan moved across to the picture windows, so that the daylight back-lit him. It was an old trick of his to put the other person at a disadvantage.

'Not that we expected less of you, of course,' he laughed, and David smiled to acknowledge the fact that his uncle had come close to levity.

'And now we must consider your future.' David was silent.

'The choice open to you is wide,' said Paul Morgan, and then went on swiftly to narrow it. 'Though I do feel business science and law at an American University is what it should be. With this obvious goal in mind I have used my influence to have you enrolled in my old college–'

'Uncle Paul, I want to fly,' said David softly, and Paul Morgan paused. His expression changed fractionally.

'We are making a career decision, my boy, not expressing preferences for different types of recreation.'

'No, sir. I mean I want to fly–as a way of life.'

'Your life is here, with the Morgan group. It is not something in which you have freedom of action.'

'I don't agree with you, sir.'

Paul Morgan left the window and crossed to the fireplace. He selected a cigar from the humidor on the mantel, and while he prepared it he spoke softly, without looking at David.

'Your father was a romantic, David. He got it out of his system by charging around the desert in a tank. It seems you have inherited this romanticism from him.' He made it sound like some disgusting disease. He came back to where David sat.

'Tell me what you propose.'

'I have enlisted in the air force, sir.'

'You've done it? You've signed?'

'Yes, sir.'

'How long?'

'Five years. Short service commission.'

'Five years–' Paul Morgan whispered, 'well, David, I don't know what to say. You know that you are the last of the Morgans. I have no son. It will be sad to see this vast enterprise without one of us at the helm. I wonder what your father would have thought of this–'

'That's hitting low, Uncle Paul.'

'I don't think so, David. I think you are the one who is cheating. Your trust fund is a huge block of Morgan shares, and other assets given to you, on the unstated understanding that you assume your duties and responsibilities–'

'If only he would bawl me out,' thought David fiercely, knowing that he was being stampeded as Barney had warned him. 'If only he would order me to do it–so I could tell him to shove it.' But he knew he was being manipulated by a man skilled in the art, a man whose whole life was the manipulation of men and money, in whose hands a seventeen-year-old boy was as soft as dough.

'You see, David, you are born to it. Anything else is cowardice, self indulgence–' the Morgan group reached out its tentacles, like some grotesque flesh-eating plant, to suck him in and digest him, '–we can have your enlistment papers annulled. It will be the matter of a single phone call–'

'Uncle Paul,' David almost shouted, trying to shut out the all-pervasive flow of words. 'My father. He did it. He joined the army.'

'Yes, David. But it was different at that time. One of us had to go. He was the younger–and, of course there were other personal considerations. Your mother–' he let the rest of it hang for a moment then went on, '–and when it was over he came back and took his rightful place here. We miss him now, David. No one else has been able to fill the gap he left. I have always hoped that you might be the one.'

'But I don't want to.' David shook his head. 'I don't want to spend my life in here.' He gestured at the mammoth structure of glass and concrete that surrounded them. 'I don't want to spend each day poring over piles of paper–'

'It's not like that, David. It's exciting, challenging, endlessly variable–'

'Uncle Paul.' David raised his voice again. 'What do you call a man who fills his belly with rich food–and then goes on eating?'

'Come now, David.' The first edge of irritation showed in Paul Morgan's voice, and he brushed the question aside impatiently.

'What do you call him?' David insisted.

'I expect that you would call him a glutton,' Paul Morgan answered.

'And what do you call a man with many millions–who spends his life trying to make more?'

Paul Morgan froze into stillness. He stared at his ward for long seconds before he spoke.

'You become insolent,' he said at last.

'No, sir. I did not mean it so. You are not the glutton–but I would be.'

Paul Morgan turned away and went to his desk. He sat in the high-backed leather chair and lit the cigar at last. They were silent again for a long time until at last Paul Morgan sighed.

'You'll have to get it out of your system, the way your father did. But how I grudge you five wasted years.'

'Not wasted, Uncle Paul. I will come out with a Bachelor of Science degree in aeronautical engineering.'

'I suppose we'll just have to be thankful for little things like that.'

David went and stood beside his chair.

'Thank you. This is very important to me.'

'Five years, David. After that I want you,' then he smiled slightly to signal a witticism, 'at least they will make you cut your hair.'

Four miles above the warm flesh-coloured earth, David Morgan rode the high heavens like a young god. The sun visor of his helmet was closed, masking with its dark cyclops eye the rapt, almost mystic expression with which he flew. Five years had not dulled the edge of his appetite for the sensation of power and isolation that flight in a Mirage interceptor awoke in him.

The unfiltered sunlight blazed ferociously upon the metal of his craft, clothing him in splendour–while far below the very clouds were insignificant against the earth, scattered and flying like a sheep flock before the wolf of the wind.

Today's flight was tempered by a melancholy, a sense of impending loss. The morrow was the last day of his enlistment. At noon his commission expired and if Paul Morgan prevailed he would become Mister David–new boy at Morgan Group.

He thrust the thought aside, and concentrated on the enjoyment of these last precious minutes; but too soon the spell was broken.

'Zulu Striker One, this is Range Control. Report your position.'

'Range Control, this is Zulu Striker One holding up range fifty miles.'

'Striker One, the range is clear. Your target-markers are figures eight and twelve. Commence your run.'

The horizon revolved abruptly across the nose of the Mirage, as the wing came over and he went down under power, falling from the heights, a controlled plunge, purposeful and precise as the stoop of a falcon.

David's right hand moved swiftly across the weapon selector panel, locking in the rocket circuit.

The earth flattened out ahead, immense and featureless, speckled with a low bush that blurred past his wing-tips as he let the Mirage sink lower. At this height the awareness of speed was breathtaking, and as the first marker came up ahead it seemed at the same instant to flash away below the silvery nose.

Five, six, seven–the black numerals on their glaring white grounds flickered by.

A touch of left rudder and stick, both adjustments made without conscious effort–and ahead was the circular layout of the rocket range, the concentric rings shrinking in size around the central mound–the 'coke' of flight jargon, which was the bull's-eye of the target.

David brought the deadly machine in fast and low, his mach meter recording a speed that was barely sub-sonic. He was runningoff the direct line of track, judging his moment with frowning concentration. When it came he pulled the Mirage's nose in to the 'pitch up' and went over on to the target with his gloved right finger curled about the trigger lever.

The shrieking silver machine achieved her correct slightly nose-down attitude for rocket launch at the precise instant of time that the white blob of 'coke' was centred in the diamond patterns of the reflector sight.

It was an evolution executed with subtle mastery of many diverse skills, and David pressed against the spring-loaded resistance of the trigger. There was no change in the feel of the aircraft, and the hiss of the rocket launch was almost lost beneath the howl of the great jet, but from beneath his wings the brief smoke lines reached out ahead towards the target, and in certainty of a fair strike David pushed his throttle to the gate and waited for the rumbling ignition of his after-burners, giving him power for the climb out of range of enemy flak.

'What a way to go,' he grinned to himself as he lay on his back with the Mirage's nose pointed into the bright blue, and gravity pressing him into the padding of his seat.

'Hello, Striker One. This is Range Control. That was right on the nose. Give the man a coke. Nice shooting. Sorry to lose you, Davey.' The break in hallowed range discipline touched David. He was going to miss them–all of them. He pressed the transmit button on the moulded head of his joystick, and spoke into the microphone of his helmet, 'From Striker One, thanks and farewell,' David said. 'Over and out.'

His ground crew were waiting for him also. He shook hands with each of them, the awkward handshakes and rough jokes masking the genuine affection that the years had built between them. Then he left them and went down the vast metal-skinned cavern, redolent with the smell of grease and oil along which the gleaming rows of needle-nosed interceptors stood, even in repose their forward lines giving them speed and thrust.

David paused to pat the cold metal of one of them, and the orderly found him there peering up at the emblem of the Flying Cobra upon the towering tailplane.

'C.O.'s compliments, sir, and will you report to him right away.'

Colonel 'Rastus' Naude was a dried-out stick of a man, with a wizened monkey face, who wore his uniform and medal ribbons with a casually distracted air. He had flow Hurricanes in the Battle of Britain, Mustangs in Italy, Spitfires and Messerschmitt 109's in Palestine and Sabres in Korea–and he was too old for his present command–but nobody could muster the courage to tell him that, especially as he could out-fly and out-gun most of the young bucks on the squadron.

'So we are getting rid of you at last, Morgan,' he greeted David.

'Not until after the mess party, sir.'

'Ja,' Rastus nodded. 'You've given me enough hardship these last five years. You owe me a bucket of whisky.' He gestured to the hard-backed chair beside his desk. 'Sit down, David.'

It was the first ime he had used David's given name, and David placed his flying helmet on the corner of the desk and lowered himself into the chair, clumsy in the constricting grip of his G-suit.

Rastus took his time filling his pipe with the evil black Magaliesberg shag and he studied the young man opposite him intently. He recognized the same qualities in him that Paul Morgan had prized, the aggressive and competitive drive that gave him a unique value as an interceptor pilot.

He lit the pipe at last, puffing thick rank clouds of blue smoke as he slid a sheath of documents across the desk to David.

'Read and sign,' he said. 'That's an order.' David glanced rapidly through the papers, then he looked up and grinned.

'You don't give in easily, sir,' he admitted.

One document was a renewal of his short service contract for an additional five years, the other was a warrant of promotion–from captain to major.

'We have spent a great deal of time and money in making you what you are. You have been given an exceptional talent, and we have developed it until now you are–I'll not mince words–one hell of a pilot.'

'I'm sorry, sir,' David told him sincerely.

'Damn it,' said Rastus angrily. 'Why the hell did you have to be born a Morgan. All that money–they'll clip your wings, and chain you to a desk.'

'It's not the money.' David denied it swiftly. He felt his own anger stir at the accusation.

Rastus nodded cynically. 'Ja!' he said. 'I hate the stuff also.' He picked up the documents David had rejected, and grunted. 'Not enough to tempt you, hey?'

'Colonel, it's hard to explain. I just feel that there is more to do, something important that I have to find out about–and it's not here. I have to go look for it.'

Rastus nodded heavily. 'All right then,' he said. 'I had a good try. Now you can take your long-suffering commanding officer down to the mess and spend some of the Morgan millions on filling him up with whisky.' He stood up and clapped his uniform hat at a rakish angle over his cropped grey head. 'You and I will get drunk together this night–for both of us are losing something, I perhaps more than you.'

It seemed that David had inherited his love of beautiful and powerful machines from his father. Clive Morgan had driven himself, his wife, and his brand new Ferrari sports car into the side of a moving goods train at an unlit level crossing. The traffic police estimated that the Ferrari was travelling at one hundred and fifty miles an hour at the moment of impact.

Clive Morgan's provision for his eleven-year-old son was detailed and elaborate. The child became a ward of his uncle Paul Morgan, and his inheritance was arranged in a series of trust funds.

On his majority he was given access to the first of the funds which provided an income equivalent to that of, say, a highly successful surgeon. On that day the old green M.G. had given way to a powder-blue Maserati, in true Morgan tradition.

On his twenty-third birthday, control of the sheep ranches in the Karroo, the cattle ranch in South West Africa and Jubulani, the sprawling game ranch in the Sabi-Sand block, passed to him, their management handled smoothly by his trustees.

On his twenty-fifth birthday the number two fund interest would divert to him, in addition to a large block of negotiable paper and title in two massive urban holdings–office and supermarket complexes, and a high-rise housing project.

At age thirty the next fund opened for him, as large as the previous two combined, and transfer to him of the first of five blocks of Morgan stock would begin.

From then onwards, every five years until age fifty further funds opened, further blocks of Morgan stock would be transferred. It was a numbing procession of wealth that stretched ahead of him, daunting in its sheer magnitude; like a display of too much rich food, it seemed to depress appetite.

David drove fast southwards, with the Michelin metallics hissing savagely on the tarmac, and he thought about all that wealth, the great golden cage, the insatiable maw of Morgan Group yawning open to swallow him so that, like the cell of a jelly fish, he would become part of the whole, a prisoner of his own abundance.

The prospect appalled him, adding a hollow sensation in his belly to the pulse of pain that beat steadily behind his eyes–testimony to the foolhardiness of trying to drink level with Colonel Rastus Naude.

He pushed the Maserati harder, seeking the twin opiates of power and speed, finding comfort and escape in the rhythms and precision of driving very fast, and the hours flew past as swiftly as the miles so it was still daylight when he let himself into Mitzi's apartment on the cliffs that overlooked Clifton beach and the clear green Atlantic.

Mitzi's apartment was chaos, that much had not changed. She kept open house for a string of transitory guests who drank her liquor, ate her food and vied with each other as to who could create the most spectacular shambles.

In the first bedroom that David tried there was a strange girl with dark hair curled on the bed in boys' pyjamas, sucking her thumb in sleep.

With the second room he was luckier, and he found it deserted, although the bed was unmade and someone had left breakfast dishes smeared with congealed egg upon the side table.

David slung his bag on the bed and fished out his bathing costume. He changed quickly and went out by the side stairs that spiralled down to the beach and began to run–a trot at first, and then suddenly he sprinted away, racing blindly as though from some terrible monster that pursued him. At the end of Fourth beach where the rocks began, he plunged into the icy surf and swam out to the edge of the kelp at Bakoven point, driving overarm through the water and the cold lanced him to the bone, so that when he came out he was blue and shuddering. But the hunted feeling was gone and he warmed a little as he jogged back to Mitzi's apartment.

He had to remove the forest of pantihose and feminine underwear that festooned the bathroom before he could draw himself a bath. He filled it to the overflow, and as he settled into it the front door burst open and Mitzi came in like the north wind.

'Where are you, warrior?' She was banging the doors. 'I saw your car in the garage–so I know you're here!'

'In here, doll,' he called, and she stood in the doorway and they grinned at each other. She had put on weight again, he saw, straining the seam of her skirt, and her bosom was bulky and amorphous under the scarlet sweater. She had finally given up her struggle with myopia and the metal framed spectacles sat on the end of her little nose, while her hair fuzzed out at unexpected angles.

'You're beautiful,' she cried, coming to kiss him and getting soap down her sweater as she hugged him.

'Drink or coffee?' she asked, and David winced at the thought of alcohol.

'Coffee will be great, doll.'

She brought it to him in a mug, then perched on the toilet seat.

'Tell all!' she commanded and while they chatted the pretty dark-haired girl wandered in, still in her pyjamas and bug-eyed from sleep.

'This is my coz, David. Isn't he beautiful?' Mitzi introduced them. 'And this is Liz.'

The girl sat on the dirty linen basket in the corner and fixed David with such an awed and penetrating gaze that Mitzi warned her. 'Cool it, darling. Even from here I can hear your ovaries bouncing around like ping-pong balls.'

But she was such a silent, ethereal little thing that they soon forgot her and talked as if they were alone. It was Mitzi who said suddenly, without preliminaries, 'Papa is waiting for you, licking his lips like an ivy-league ogre. I ate with them Saturday night–he must have brought your name up one zillion times. It's going to be strange to have you sitting up there on Top Floor, in a charcoal suit, being bright at Monday morning conference–'

David stood up suddenly in the bath, cascading suds and steaming water, and began soaping his crotch vigorously. They watched him with interest, the dark-haired girl's eyes widening until they seemed to fill her face.

David sat down again, slopping water over the edge.

'I'm not going!' he said, and there was a long heavy silence.

'What do you mean–you're not going?' Mitzi asked timorously.

'Just that,' said David. 'I'm not going to Morgan Group.'

'But you have to!'

'Why?' asked David.

'Well, I mean it's decided–you promised Daddy that when you finished with the airforce.'

'No,' David said, 'I made no promise. He just took it. When you said a moment ago–being bright at Monday morning conference–I knew I couldn't do it. I guess I've known all along.'

'What you going to do, then?' Mitzi had recovered from the first shock, and her plump cheeks were tinged with excitement.

'I don't know. I just know I am not going to be a caretaker for other men's achievements. Morgan Group isn't me. It's something that Gramps, and Dad and Uncle Paul made. It's too big and cold–'

Mitzi was flushed, bright-eyes, nodding her agreement, enchanted by this prospect of rebellion and open defiance.

David was warming to it also. 'I'll find my own road to go. There's more to it. There has to be something more than this.'

'Yes,' Mitzi nodded so that she almost shook her spectacles from her nose. 'You're not like them. You would shrivel and die up there on executive suite.'

'I've got to find it, Mitzi. It's got to be out there somewhere.'

David came out of the bath, his body glowing dull red-brown from the scalding water and steam rising from him in light tendrils. He pulled on a Terry robe as he talked and the two girls followed him through to the bedroom and sat side by side on the edge of the bed, eagerly nodding their encouragement as David Morgan made his formal declaration of independence. Mitzi spoiled it, however.

'What are you going to tell Daddy?' she asked. The question halted David's flow of rhetoric, and he scratched the hair on his chest as he considered it. The girls waited attentively.

'He's not going to let you get away again,' Mitzi warned. 'Not without a stand-up, knock-down, drag-em-out fight.'

In this moment of crisis David's courage deserted him. 'I've told him once, I don't have to tell him again.'

'You just going to cut and run?'Mitzi asked.

'I'm not running,' David replied with frosty dignity as he picked up the pigskin folder which held his thick sheaf of credit cards from the bedside table. 'I am merely reserving the right to determine my own future.' He crossed to the telephone and began dialling.

'Who are you calling?'

'The airline.'

'Where are you heading?'

'The same place as their first flight out.'

'I'll cover for you,' declared Mitzi loyally, 'you're doing the right thing, warrior.'

'You bet I am,' David agreed. 'My way–and screw the rest of them.'

'Do you have time for that?' Mitzi giggled, and the dark-haired girl spoke for the first time in a husky intense voice without once taking her eyes off David. 'I don't know about the rest of them, but may I be first, please?'

With the telephone receiver to his ear David glanced at her, and realized with only mild surprise that she was in deadly earnest.

David came out into the impersonal concrete and glass arrivals hall of Schipol Airport, and he paused to gloat on his escape and to revel at this sense of anonymity in the uncaring crowd. There was a touch at his elbow, and he turned to find a tall, smiling Dutchman quizzing him through rimless spectacles.

'Mr David Morgan, I think?' and David gaped at him.

'I am Frederick Van Gent of Holland and Indonesian Stevedoring. We have the honour to act on behalf of Morgan Shipping Lines in Holland. It is a great pleasure to make your acquaintance.'

'God, no!' David whispered wearily.

'Please?'

'No. I'm sorry. It's nice to meet you.' David shook the hand with resignation.

'I have two urgent telex messages for you, Mr Morgan.' Van Gent produced them with a flourish. 'I have driven out from Amsterdam especially to deliver same.'

The first was from Mitzi who had sworn to cover for him.

'Abject apologies your whereabouts extracted with rack and thumbscrew stop be brave as a lion stop be ferocious as an eagle Love Mitzi.'

David said, 'Traitorous bitch!' and opened the second envelope.

'Your doubts understood, your action condoned stop confident your good sense will lead you eventually on to path of duty stop your place here always open affectionately Paul Morgan.'

David said, 'Crafty old bastard,' and stuffed both messages into his pocket.

'Is there a reply?' Van Gent asked.

'Thank you, no. It was good of you to take this trouble.'

'No trouble, Mr Morgan. Can I help you in any way? Is there anything you require?'

'Nothing, but thanks again.' They shook hands and Van Gent bowed and left him. David went to the Avis counter and the girl smiled brightly at him.

'Good evening, sir.'

David slipped his Avis card across the desk. 'I want something with a little jump to it, please.'

'Let me see, we have a Mustang Mach I?' She was pure blonde with a cream and pink unlined face.

'That will do admirably,' David assured her, and as he began filling the form in, she asked, 'Your first visit to Amsterdam, sir?'

'They tell me it's the city with the most action in Europe, is that right?'

'If you know where to go,' she murmured.

'You could show me?' David asked and she looked up at him with calculating eyes behind a neutral expression, made a decision and resumed her writings.

'Please sign here, sir. Your account will be charged,' then she dropped her voice. 'If you have any queries on this contract, you can contact me at this number–after hours. My name is Gilda.'

Gilda shared a walk-up over the outer canal with three other girls who showed no surprise, and made no objection when David carried his single Samsonite case up the steep staircase. However, the action that Gilda provided was in a series of discotheques and coffee bars where lost little people gathered to talk revolution and guru babble. In two days David discovered that pot tasted terrible and made him nauseous, and that Gilda's mind was as bland and unmarked as her exterior. He felt the stirrings of uneasiness when he studied the others that had been drawn to this city by the news that it was wide open, with the most understanding police force in the world. In them he saw symptoms of his own restlessness, and he recognized them as fellow seekers. Then the damp chill of the lowlands seemed to rise up out of the canals like the spirits of the dead on doomsday, and when you have been born under the sun of Africa the wintry effusions of the north are a pale substitute.

Gilda showed no visible emotion when she said goodbye, and with the heaters blasting hot air into the cab of the Mustang, David sent it booming southwards. On the outskirts of Namur there was a girl standing beside the road. In the cold her legs were bare and brown, protruding sweetly from the short faded blue denim pants she wore. She tilted her golden head and cocked a thumb.

David hit the stick down, and braked with the rubber squealing protest. He reversed back to where she stood. She had flat-planed slavic features and her hair was white blonde and hung in a thick plait down her back. He guessed her age at nineteen.

'You speak English?' he asked through the window. The cold was making her nipples stand out like marbles through the thin fabric of her shirt.

'No,' she said. 'But I speak American–will that do?'

'Right on!' David opened the passenger door, and she threw her pack and rolled sleeping bag into the back seat.

'I'm Philly,' she said.

'David.'

'You in show biz?'

'God, no–what makes you ask?'

'The car–the face–the clothes.'

'The car is hired, the clothes are stolen and I'm wearing a mask.'

'Funny man,' she said and curled up on the seat like a kitten and went to sleep.

He stopped in a village where the forests of the Ardennes begin and bought a long roll of crisp bread, a slab of smoked wild boar meat and a bottle of Möet Chandon. When he got back to the car Philly was awake.

'You hungry?' he asked.

'Sure.' She stretched and yawned.

He found a loggers' track going off into the forest and they followed it to a clearing where a long golden shaft of sunlight penetrated the green cathedral gloom.

Philly climbed out and looked around her. 'Keen, Davey, keen!' she said.

David poured the champagne into paper cups and sliced the meat with a penknife while Philly broke the bread into hunks. They sat side by side on a fallen log and ate.

'It's so quiet and peaceful–not at all like a killing ground. This is where the Germans made their last big effort–did you know that?'

Philly's mouth was full of bread and meat which didn't stop her reply. 'I saw the movie, Henry Fonda, Robert Ryan–it was a complete crock.'

'All that death and ugliness, we should do something beautiful in this place,' David said dreamily, and she swallowed the bread, took a sip of wine, before she stood up languidly and went to the Mustang. She fetched her sleeping bag and spread it on the soft bed of leaf mould.

'Some things are for talking about–others are for doing,' she told him.

For a while in Paris it looked as though it might be significant, as though they might have something for each other of importance. They found a room with a shower in a clean and pleasant little pension near the Gare St Lazare, and they walked through the streets all that day, from Concorde to Etoile, then across to the Eiffel Tower and back to Notre Dame. They ate supper at a sidewalk café on the 'Boul Mich', but half-way through the meal they reached an emotional dead end. Suddenly they ran out of conversation, they sensed it at the same time, each aware that they were strangers in all but the flesh and the knowledge chilled them both. Still they stayed together that night, even going through the mechanical and empty motions of love, but in the morning, when David came out of the shower, she sat up in the bed and said, 'You are splitting.'

It was a statement and not a question, and it needed no reply.

'Are you all right for bread?' he asked, and she shook her head. He peeled off a pair of thousand-franc notes and put them on the side table.

'I'll pay the bill downstairs.' He picked up his bag. 'Stay loose,' he said.

Paris was spoiled for him now, so he took the road south again towards the sun for the sky was filled with swollen black cloud and it rained before he passed the turn-off to Fontainebleau. It rained as he believed was only possible in the tropics, a solid deluge that flooded the concrete of the highway and blurred his windscreen so that the flogging of the wipers could not clear it swiftly enough for safe vision.

David was alone and discomforted by his inability to sustain communication with another human being. Although the other traffic had moderated its pace in the rain, he drove fast, feeling the drift and skate of his tyres on the slick surface. This time the calming effect of speed was ineffective and when he ran out of the rain south of Beaune it seemed that the wolf pack of loneliness ran close behind him.

However, the first outpouring of sunshine lightened his mood, and then far over the stone walls and rigid green lines of the vineyards he saw a wind-sock floating like a soft white sausage from its pole. He found the exit from the highway half a mile farther on, and the sign 'Club Aeronautique de Provence'. He followed it to a neat little airfield set among the vineyards, and one of the aircraft on the hard-stand was a Marchetti Aerobatic type F260. David climbed out of the Mustang and stared at it like a drunkard contemplating his first whisky of the day.

The Frenchman in the club office looked like an unsuccessful undertaker, and even when David showed him his logbook and sheafs of licences, he resisted the temptation of hiring him the Marchetti. David could take his pick from the others–but the Marchetti was not for hire. David added a 500-franc note to the pile of documents, and it disappeared miraculously into the Frenchman's pocket. Still he would not let David take the Marchetti solo, and he insisted on joining him in the instructor's seat.

David executed a slow and stately four-point roll before they had crossed the boundary fence. It was an act of defiance, and he made the stops crisp and exaggerated. The Frenchman cried 'Sacré bleu!' with great feeling and froze in his seat, but he had the good sense not to interfere with the controls. David completed the manœuvre and then immediately rolled in the opposite direction with the wing-tip a mere fifty feet above the tips of the vines. The Frenchman relaxed visibly, recognizing the masterly touch, and when David landed an hour later he grinned mournfully at him.

'Formidable!' he said, and shared his lunch with David–garlic polony, bread and a bottle of rank red wine. The good feeling of flight and the aroma of garlic lasted David all the way to Madrid.

In Madrid suddenly it began to happen, almost as though it had been arranged long before, as though his frantic flight across half of Europe was a pre-knowledge that something of importance awaited him in Madrid.

He reached the city in the evening, hurrying the last day's journey to be in time for the first running of the bulls that season. He had read Hemingway and Conrad and much of the other romantic literature of the bullring. He wondered if there might not be something for him in this way of life. It read so well in the books–the beauty, the glamour and excitement–the courage and trial and the final moment of truth. He wanted to evaluate it, to see it here in the great Plaza Des Torros, and then, if it still intrigued him, go on to the festival at Pamplona later in the season.

David checked in at the Gran Via with its elegance faded to mere comfort, and the porter arranged tickets for the following day. He was tired from the long drive and he went to bed early, waking refreshed and eager for the day. He found his way out to the ring and parked the Mustang amongst the tourist buses that already crowded the parking lot so early in the season.

The exterior of the ring was a surprise, sinister as the temple of some pagan and barbaric religion, unrelieved by the fluted tiers of balconies and encrustations of ceramic tiles–but the interior was as he knew it would be from film and photograph. The sanded ring smooth and clean, the flags against the cloud-flecked sky, the orchestra pouring out its jerky, rousing refrain–and the excitement.

The excitement amongst the crowd was more intense than he had known at prize fights or football internationals, they hummed and swarmed, rank upon rank of white eager faces and the music goaded them on.

David was sitting amongst a group of young Australians who wore souvenir sombreros and passed goat-skins of bad wine about, the girls squealing and chittering like sparrows. One of them picked on David, leaning forward to tug his shoulder and offer him the wine-skin. She was pretty enough in a kittenish way and her eyes made it clear that the offer was for more than cheap wine, but he refused both invitations brusquely and went to fetch a can of beer from one of the vendors. His chilly experience with the girl in Paris was still too fresh. When he returned to his seat the Aussie girl eyed the beer he carried reproachfully and then turned brightly and smiling to her companions.

The late arrivals were finding their seats now and the excitement was escalating sharply. Two of them climbed the stairs of the aisle towards where David sat. A striking young couple in their early twenties, but what first drew

David's attention was the good feeling of companionship and love that glowed around them, like an aura setting them apart.

They climbed arm in arm, passed where David sat, and took seats a row behind and across the aisle. The girl was tall with long legs clad in short black boots and dark pants over which she wore an apple-green suède jacket that was not expensive but of good cut and taste. In the sun her hair glittered like coal newly cut from the face and it hung to her shoulders in a sleek soft fall. Her face was broad and sun-browned, not beautiful for her mouth was too big and her eyes too widely spaced, but those eyes were the colour of wild honey, dark brown and flecked with gold. Like her, her companion was tall and straight, dark and strong-looking. He guided her to her seat with a brown muscled arm and David felt a sharp stab of anger and envy for him.

'Big cocky son of a gun,' he thought. They leaned their heads together and spoke secretly, and David looked away, his own loneliness accentuated by their closeness.

The parade of the toreadors began, and they came out with the sunlight glittering on the sequins and embroidery of their suits, as though they were the scales of some flamboyant reptile. The orchestra blared, and the keys to the bull pens were thrown down on to the sand. The toreadors' capes were spread on the *barrera* below their favourites and they retired from the ring.

In the pause that followed David glanced at the couple again. He was startled to find that they were both watching him and the girl was discussing him. She was leaning on her companion's shoulder, her lips almost touching his ear as she spoke and David felt his stomach clench under the impact of those honey golden eyes. For an instant they stared at each other and then the girl jerked away guiltily and dropped her gaze–but her companion held David's eyes openly, smiling easily, and it was David who looked away.

Below them in the ring the bull came out at full charge, head high, and hooves skidding in the sand.

He was beautiful and black and glossy, muscle in the neck and shoulder bunching as he swung his head from side to side and the crowd roared as he spun and burst into a gallop, pursuing an elusive flutter of pink across the ring. They took him on a circuit, passing him smoothly from cape to cape, letting him show off his bulk and high-stepping style, and the perfect sickle of his horns with their creamy points, before they brought in the horse.

The trumpets ushered in the horse, and they were a mockery–a brave greeting for the wretched nag, with scrawny neck and starting coat, one rheumy old eye blinkered so he could not see the fearsome creature he was going to meet.

Clownish in his padding, seeming too frail to carry the big armoured man on his back, they led him out and placed him in the path of the bull–and here any semblance of beauty ended.

The bull went into him head down, sending the gawky animal reeling against the *barrera* and the man leaned over the broad black back and ripped and tore into the hump with the lance, worrying the flesh, working in the steel with all his weight until the blood poured out in a slick tide, black as crude oil, and dripped from the bull's legs into the sand.

Raging at the agony of the steel, the bull hooked and butted at the protective pads that covered the horse's flanks. They came up as readily as a theatre curtain and the bull was into the scrawny roan body, hacking with the terrible horns, and the horse screamed as its belly split open and the purple and pink entrails spilled out and dangled into the sand.

David was dry-mouthed with horror as around him the crowd blood-roared, and the horse went down in a welter of equipment and its own guts.

They drew the bull away and flogged the fallen horse, twisting its tail and prodding its testicles, forcing it to rise at last and stand quivering and forlorn. Then beating it to make it move again they led it from the ring stumbling over its own entrails.

Then they went to work on the bull, slowly, torturously, reducing it from a magnificent beast to a blundering hunk of sweating and bleeding flesh, splattered with the creamy froth blown from its agonized lungs.

David wanted to scream at them to stop it, but sick to the stomach, frozen by guilt for his own part in this obscene ritual, he sat through it in silence until the bull stood in the centre of the ring, the sand about him ploughed and riven by his dreadful struggles. He stood with his head down, muzzle almost touching the sand and the blood and froth dripped from his nostrils and gaping mouth. The hoarse sawing of his breathing carried to David even above the crazed roaring crowd. The bull's legs shuddered and he passed a dribble of loose liquid yellow dung that fouled his back legs. It seemed to David that this was the final humiliation, and he found he was whispering aloud.

'No! No! Stop it! Please, stop it!'

Then the man in the glittering suit and ballet shoes came to end it, and the point of the sword struck bone and the blade arced then spun away in the sunlight, and the bull heaved and threw back thick droplets of blood, before he stood again.

They picked up the sword from the sand and gave it to the man and he sighted over the quiescent, dying beast and again the thrust was deflected by bone and David found that at last he had power in his voice, and he screamed:

'Stop it! You filthy bastards.'

Twelve times the man in the centre tried with sword, and each time the sword flicked out of his hand, and then at last the bull fell of its own accord, weak from the slow loss of much blood and with its heart broken by the torture and the striving. It tried to rise, lunging weakly, but the strength was not there and they killed it where it lay, with a dagger in the back of the neck, and they dragged it out with a team of mules–its legs waggling ridiculously in the air and its blood leaving a long brown smudge across the sand.

Stunned with the monstrous cruelty of it, David turned slowly to look at the girl. Her companion was leaning over her solicitously, whispering to her, trying to comfort her.

She was shaking her head slowly, in a gesture of incomprehension, and her honey-coloured eyes were blinded with weeping. Her lips were apart, quivering with grief, and her cheeks were awash, shiny with her tears.

Her companion helped her to her feet, and gently took her down the steps, leading her away blindly like a new widow from her husband's grave.

Around him the crowd was laughing and exhilarated, high on the blood and the pain–and David felt himself rejected, cut off from them. His heart went out to the weeping girl, she of all of them was the only one who seemed real to him. He had seen enough also, and he knew he would never get to Pamplona. He stood up and followed the girl out of the ring, he wanted to speak to her, to tell her that he shared her desolation, but when he reached the parking lot they were already climbing into a battered old Citroen CV.100, and although he broke into a run, the car pulled away–blowing blue smoke and clattering like a lawn-mower, and turned into the traffic leading east.

David watched it go with a sense of loss that effectively washed away the good feeling of the last few days, but he saw the old Citroen again two days later, when he had abandoned all idea of the Pamplona Festival and headed south. The Citroen looked even sicker than before, under a layer of pale dust and with the canvas showing on a rear tyre. The suspension seemed to have sagged on the one side, giving it a rakishly drunken aspect.

It was parked at a filling station on the outskirts of Zaragoza on the road to Barcelona, and David pulled off the road and park beyond the gasoline pumps. An attendant in greasy overalls was filling the tank of the Citroen under the supervision of the muscular young man from the bullring. David looked quickly for the girl–but she was not in the car. Then he saw her.

She was in a *cantina* across the street, haggling with the elderly woman behind the counter. Her back was turned towards him, but David recognized the mass of dark hair now piled on top of her head. He crossed the road quickly and went into the shop behind her. He was not certain what he was going to do, acting only on impulse.

The girl wore a short floral dress which left her back and shoulders bare, and her feet were thrust into open sandals. But in concession to the ice in the air she wore a shawl over her shoulders. Close to, her skin had a plastic smoothness and elasticity, as though it had been lightly oiled and polished, and down the back of her naked neck the hair was fine and soft, growing in a whorl in the nape.

David moved closer to her as she completed her purchase of dried figs and counted her change. He smelt her, a light summery perfume that seemed to come from her hair. He resisted the temptation to press his face into the dense pile of it.

She turned smiling and saw him standing close behind her. She recognized him instantly, his was not a face a girl would readily forget. She was startled. The smile flickered out on her face and she stood very still looking at him, her expression completely neutral, but her lips slightly parted and her eyes soft and glowing golden. This peculiar stillness of hers was a quality he would come to know so well in the time ahead.

'I saw you in Madrid,' he said, 'at the bulls.'

'Yes,' she nodded, her voice neither welcoming nor forbidding.

'You were crying.'

'So were you.' Her voice was low and clear, her enunciation flawless, too perfect not to be foreign.

'No,' David denied it.

'You were crying,' she insisted softly. 'You were crying inside.' And he inclined his head in agreement. Suddenly she proffered the paper bag of figs.

'Try one,' she said and smiled. It was a warm friendly smile. He took one of the fruits and bit into the sweet flesh as she moved towards the door, somehow conveying an invitation for him to join her. He walked with her and they looked across the street at the Citroen. The attendant had finished filling the tank, and the girl's companion was waiting for her, leaning against the bonnet of the weary old car. He was lighting a cigarette, but he looked up and saw them. He evidently recognized David also, and he straightened up quickly and flicked away the burning match.

There was a soft whooshing sound and the heavy thump of concussion in the air, as fire flashed low across the concrete from a puddle of spilled gasoline. In an instant the flames had closed over the rear of the Citroen, and were drumming hungrily at the coachwork.

David left the girl and sprinted across the road.

'Get it away from the pumps, you idiot,' he shouted, and the driver started out of frozen shock.

It was happy fifth of November, a spectacular pyrotechnic display–but David got the handbrake off and the gearbox into neutral, and he and the driver pushed it into an open parking area alongside the filling station while a crowd materialized, seeming to appear out of the very earth, to scream hysterical encouragement and suggestions while keeping at a discreet distance.

They even managed to rescue the baggage from the rear seat before the flames engulfed it entirely–and belatedly the petrol attendant arrived with an enormous scarlet fire extinguisher. To the delighted applause of the crowd, he drenched the pathetic little vehicle in a great cloud of foam, and the excitement was over. The crowd drifted away, still laughing and chattering and congratulating the amateur firefighter on his virtuoso performance with the extinguisher–while the three of them regarded the scorched and blackened shell of the Citroen ruefully.

'I suppose it was a kindness really–the poor old thing was very tired,' the girl said at last. 'It was like shooting a horse with a broken leg.'

'Are you insured?' David asked, and the girl's companion laughed.

'You're joking–who would insure that? I only paid a hundred U.S. dollars for her.'

They assembled the small pile of rescued possessions, and she spoke quickly to her companion in foreign, slightly guttural language which touched a deep chord in David's memory. He understood what she was saying, so it was no surprise when she looked at him.

'We've got to meet somebody in Barcelona this evening. It's important.'

'Let's go,' said David.

They piled the luggage into the Mustang and the girl's companion folded up his long legs and piled into the back seat. His name was Joseph–but David was advised by the girl to call him Joe. She was Debra, and surnames didn't seem important at that stage. She sat in the seat beside David, with her knees pressed together primly and her hands in her lap. With one sweeping glance, she assessed the Mustang and its contents. David watched her check the expensive luggage, the Nikon camera and Zeiss binoculars in the glove compartment and the cashmere jacket thrown over the seat. Then she glanced sideways at him, seeming to notice for the first time the raw silk shirt with the slim gold Piaget under the cuff.

'Blessed are the poor,' she murmured, 'but still it must be pleasant to be rich.'

David enjoyed that. He wanted her to be impressed, he wanted her to make a few comparisons between himself and the big muscular buck in the back seat.

'Let's go to Barcelona,' he laughed.

David drove quietly through the outskirts of the town, and Debra looked over her shoulder at Joe.

'Are you comfortable?' she asked in the guttural language she had used before.

'If he's not–he can run behind,' David told her in the same language, and she gawked at him a moment in surprise before she let out a small exclamation of pleasure.

'Hey! You speak Hebrew!'

'Not very well,' David admitted. 'I've forgotten most of it,' and he had a vivid picture of himself as a ten-year-old, wrestling unhappily with a strange and mysterious language with back-to-front writing, an alphabet that was squiggly tadpoles and in which most sounds were made in the back of the throat, like gargling.

'Are you Jewish?' she asked, turning in the seat to confront him. She was no longer smiling; the question was clearly of significance to her.

David shook his head. 'No,' he laughed at the notion. 'I'm a half-convinced non-practising monotheist, raised and reared in the Protestant Christian tradition.'

'Then why did you learn Hebrew?'

'My mother wanted it,' David explained, and felt again the stab of an old guilt. 'She was killed when I was a kid. I just let it drop. It didn't seem important after she had gone.'

'Your mother–' Debra insisted, leaning towards him, '–she was Jewish?'

'Yeah. Sure,' David agreed. 'But my father was a Protestant. There was all sorts of hell when Dad married her. Everyone was against it–but they went ahead and did it anyway.'

Debra turned in the seat to Joe. 'Did you hear that–he's one of us.'

'Oh, come on!' David protested, still laughing.

'Mazaltov,' said Joe. 'Come and see us in Jerusalem some time.'

'You're Israeli?' David asked, with new interest.

'Sabras, both of us,' said Debra, with a note of pride and deep satisfaction. 'We are only on holiday here.'

'It must be an interesting country,' David hazarded.

'Like Joe just said, why don't you come and find out some time,' she suggested offhandedly. 'You have the right of return.' Then she changed the subject. 'Is this the fastest this machine will go? We have to be in Barcelona by seven.'

There was a relaxed feeling between them now, as though some invisible barrier had been lowered, as though she had made some weighty judgement. They were out of the city and ahead the open road wound down into the valley of the Ebro towards the sea.

'Kindly extinguish cigarettes and fasten your seat belts,' David said, and let the Mustang go.

She sat very still beside him with her hands folded in her lap and she stared ahead when the bends leapt at them, and the straights streamed in a soft blue blur beneath the body of the Mustang. There was a small rapturous smile on her mouth and the golden lights danced in her eyes, and David was moved to know that speed affected her the way it did him.

He forgot everything else but the girl in the seat beside him and the need to keep the mighty roaring machine on the ribbon of tarmac.

Once when they went twisting down into a dry dusty valley in a series of tight curves and David snaked the Mustang down into it with his hands darting from wheel to gear lever, and his feet dancing heel and toe on the foot pedals–she laughed aloud with the thrill of it.

They bought cheese and bread and a bottle of white wine at a village *cantina* and ate lunch sitting on the parapet of a stone bridge while the water swirled below them, milky with snow melt from the mountains.

David's thigh touched Debra's, as they sat side by side. He could feel the warmth and resilience of her flesh through the stuff of their clothing and she made no move to pull away. Her cheeks were flushed a little brighter than seemed natural, even in the chill little wind that nagged at them.

David was puzzled by Joe's attitude. He seemed to be completely oblivious of David's bird dogging his girl, and he was deriving a childlike pleasure out of tossing pebbles at the trout in the waters below them. Suddenly David wished he would put up a better resistance, it would make his conquest a lot more enjoyable–for conquest was what David had decided on.

He leaned across Debra for another chunk of the white, tangy cheese and he let his arm brush lightly against the tantalizing double bulge of her bosom. Joe seemed not to notice.

'Come on you big ape,' David thought scornfully. 'Fight for it. Don't just sit there.'

He wanted to test himself against this buck. He was big, and strong, and David could tell from the way he moved and held himself that he was well co-ordinated and self-assured. His face was chunky and half ugly, but he knew that some women liked them that way, and he was not fooled by Joe's slow and lazy grin–the eyes were quick and sharp.

'You want to drive, Joe?' he asked suddenly, and the slow grin spread like a puddle of spilled oil on Joe's face–but the eyes glittered with anticipation.

'Don't mind if I do,' said Joe, and David regretted the gesture as he found himself hunched in the narrow back seat. For the first five minutes Joe drive sedately, touching the brakes to test for grab and pull, flicking through the gears to feel the travel and bite of the stick, taking a burst of power through a bend to establish stability and detect any tendency for the tail to break out.

'Don't be scared of her,' David told him, and Joe grunted with a little frown of concentration creasing his broad forehead. Then he nodded to himself and his hands settled firmly, taking a fresh grip, and Debra whooped as he changed down to get the revs peaking. He slid the car through the first bend and David's right foot stabbed instinctively at a non-existent brake pedal and he felt his breathing jam in his throat.

When Joe parked them in the lot outside the airport at Barcelona and switched off the engine, all of them were silent for a few seconds and then David said softly,

'Son of a gun!'

Then they were all laughing. David felt a tinge of regret that he was going to have to take the girl away from him, for he was beginning to like him, despite himself, beginning to enjoy the slow deliberation of his speech and movements that was so clearly a put on and finding pleasure in the big slow smile that took so long to reach its full bloom. David had to harden his resolve.

They were an hour early for the plane they were meeting and they found a table in the restaurant overlooking the runways. David ordered an earthenware jug of Sangria, and Debra sat next to Joe and put her hand on his arm while she chatted, a gesture that tempered David's new-found liking for him.

A private flight landed as the waiter brought the Sangria, and Joe looked up.

'One of the new executive Gulfstreams. They tell me she is a little beauty.' And he went on to list the aircraft's specifications in technical language that Debra seemed to follow intelligently.

'You know anything about aircraft?' David challenged him.

'Some,' admitted Joe, but Debra took the question.

'Joe is in the airforce,' she said proudly, and David stared at them.

'So is Debs,' Joe laughed, and David switched his attention to her. 'She's a lieutenant in signals.'

'Only the reserve,' Debra demurred, 'but Joe is a flier. A fighter pilot.'

'A flier,' David repeated stupidly. He should have known from Joe's clear and steady gaze that was the peculiar mark of the fighter pilot. He should have known by the way he handled the Mustang. If he was an Israeli flier–then he would have flown a formidable number of operations. Hell, every time they took off, they were operational. He felt a vast tide of respect rising within him.

'What squadron are you on–Phantoms?'

'Phantoms!' Joe curled his lip. 'That isn't flying. That's operating a computer. No, we really fly. You ever heard of a Mirage?'

David blinked, and then nodded.

'Yeah,' said David, 'I've heard of them.'

'Well, I fly a Mirage.'

David began to laugh, shaking his head.

'What's wrong?' Joe demanded, his smile fading. 'What's funny about that?'

'I do too,' said David. 'I fly a Mirage.' It was no use trying to get hot against this buck, he decided. 'I've got over a thousand hours on Mirages.' And it was Joe's turn to stare, then suddenly they were both talking at once–Debra's head turning quickly from one to the other.

David ordered another jug of Sangria, but Joe would not let him pay. He repeated for the fiftieth time, 'Well, that beats all,' and punched David's shoulder. 'How about that, Debs?'

Half-way through the second jug, David interrupted the talk which had been exclusively on aviation.

'Who are we meeting, anyway? We've driven across half of Spain and I don't even know who the guy is.'

'This guy is a girl,' Joe laughed, and Debra filled in.

'Hannah,' and she grinned at Joe, 'his fiancée. She is a nursing sister at Hadassah Hospital, and she could only get away for a week.'

'Your fiancée?' David whispered.

'They are getting married in June.' Debra turned to Joe. 'It's taken him two years to make up his mind.'

Joe chuckled with embarrassment, and Debra squeezed his arm.

'Your fiancée?' asked David again.

'Why do you keep saying that?' Debra demanded. David pointed at Joe, and then at Debra.

'What,' he started, 'I mean, who–what the hell?'

Debra realized suddenly and gasped. She covered her mouth with both hands, her eyes sparkling. 'You mean–you thought–? Oh, no,' she giggled. She pointed at Joe and then at herself. 'Is that what you thought?' David nodded.

'He is my brother,' Debra hooted. 'Joe is my brother, you idiot! Joseph Israel Mordecai and Debra Ruth Mordecai–brother and sister.'

Hannah was a rangy girl with bright copper hair and freckles like sovereigns. She was only an inch or two shorter than Joe but he lifted her as she came through the customs gate, swung her off her feet and then engulfed her in an enormous embrace.

It seemed completely natural that the four of them should stay together. By a miracle of packing they got all their luggage and themselves into the Mustang with Hannah perched on Joe's lap in the rear.

'We've got a week,' said Debra. 'A whole week! What are we going to do with it?'

They agreed that Torremolinos was out. It was far south, and since Michener had written *The Drifters*, it had become a hangout for all the bums and freaks.

'I was talking to someone on the plane. There is a place called Colera up the coast. Near the border.'

They reached it in the middle of the next morning and it was still so early in the season that they had no trouble finding pleasant rooms at a small hotel off the winding main street.

The girls shared, and David insisted on a room of his own. He had certain plans for Debra that made privacy desirable.

Debra's bikini was blue and brief, hardly sufficient to restrain a bosom that was more exuberant than David had guessed. Her skin was satiny and tanned to a deep mahogany, although a strip of startling white peeped over the back of her costume when she stooped to pick up her towel. She was long in the waist, and leg, and a strong swimmer–pacing David steadily through the cool blue water when they set out for a rocky islet half a mile off shore.

They had the tiny island to themselves and they found a pitch of flat smooth rock out of the wind and full in the sun. They lay side by side with their fingers entwined and the salt water had sleeked Debra's hair to her shoulders, like the coat of an otter.

They lay in the sun and they talked away the afternoon. There was so much they had to learn about each other.

Her father had been one of the youngest colonels in the American Airforce during World War II, but afterwards he had gone on to Israel. He had been there ever since, and was now a Major-General. They lived in a house in an old part of Jerusalem which was five hundred years old, but was a lot of fun.

She was a senior lecturer in English at the Hebrew University in Jerusalem and, this shyly as though it were a rather special secret, she wanted to write. A small volume of her poetry had already been published. That impressed David, and he came up on one elbow and looked at her with new respect, and a twinge of envy, for someone who saw the way ahead clearly.

She lay with her eyes closed against the sun, and droplets of water sparkling like gems on her thick dark eyelashes. She wasn't beautiful, he decided carefully, but very handsome and very, very sexy. He was going to have her, of course. There was no doubt in David's mind about this, but there seemed little urgency in it now. He was enjoying listening to her talk, she had a quaint way of expressing herself, once she was in full flight, and her accent was strangely neutral–although there were faint echoes of her American background now he knew to look for them. She told him that the poetry was merely a beginning. She was going to write a novel about being young and living in Israel. She had the outline worked out, and it seemed like a pretty interesting story to David. Then she started to talk about her land and the people who lived in it. David felt something move within him as he listened–a nostalgia, a deep race memory. Again his envy stirred. She was so certain where she was from and where she was going–she knew where she belonged, and what her destiny was, and this made her strong. Beside her he felt suddenly insignificant and without purpose.

She opened her eyes suddenly, squinting a little in the sunlight and looked up at him.

'Oh dear,' she smiled. 'We are so sad, David. Do I talk too much?' He shook his head but did not answer her smile, and she became solemn also.

She studied his face carefully, with minute attention. The sun had dried his hair and fluffed it out, and it was soft and fine and very dark. The bone of his cheek and jaw was sculptured and finely balanced, the eyes very clear and slightly Asiatic in cast, the lips full and firm, and the nose delicately fluted with wide nostrils and a straight graceful line.

She reached up and touched his cheek.

'You are very beautiful, David. You are the most beautiful human being I have ever seen.'

He did not move, she ran the finger down his neck on to his chest, twirling it slowly in the dark body hair.

Slowly he leaned forward and placed his mouth over hers. Her lips were warm and soft and tasted of sea salt. Her arms came up around the back of his head and folded around him. They kissed until he reached behind her and unfastened the clasp of her costume between the smooth brown shoulder blades. She stiffened immediately and tried to pull away from him.

David held her gently but firm, murmuring little soothing noises as he kissed her again. Slowly she relaxed and he went on gentling her until her hands went to the back of his neck again, and she sighed and shuddered.

His hands were skilled and expert, masterful enough to prevent rebellion, not rough enough to panic her. He pushed up the thin material of her costume top and was surprised and enchanted with the firm rubbery weight of her breasts and the big husky rose-brown nipples which were pebble hard to his touch.

It was shocking, completely foreign to his experience, for David was not accustomed to check or denial, but Debra placed her hands on his shoulders and shoved him with such force that he lost his balance and slid down the rock, grazing his elbow and ending in a heap at the water's edge.

He scrambled angrily to his feet as Debra came up with a fluid explosive movement, fastening her costume as she did so. A single bound of her long brown legs carried her to the edge of the rocks and she dived outwards, hitting the water flat and surfacing to call back to him.

'I'll race you to the beach.'

David would not accept the challenge and followed her at his own dignified pace. When he emerged unsmilingly from the low surf, she studied his face a moment and then grinned.

'When you sulk you look about ten years old,' she told him, which was no great exercise of tact and David stalked back to his room.

He was still being extremely dignified and aloof that evening when they discovered a discotheque named '2001 A.D.' run by a couple of English boys down on the sea-front. They crowded round a table at which there were already two B.E.A. hostesses and a couple of raggedy-looking beards. The music was loud enough and the rhythm hard enough to jar the spine and loosen the bowels, and when the two hostesses gazed at David with almost religious awe Debra forsook her attitude of cool amusement and suggested to David that they dance. Mollified by this little feminine by-play, David dropped his impersonation of the Ice King.

They moved well together, sharing the gut rhythms of the harsh music, executing the primeval movements that reeked of Africa with a grace that drew the attention of the other dancers.

When the music changed Debra came to him and lay her body against his. David felt some force flowing from her that seemed to charge every nerve of his body–and he knew that no relationship he had with this woman would ever run calmly. It was too deeply felt for that, too volatile and triggered for momentary explosion.

When the record ended they left Joe and Hannah huddled over a carafe of red wine and they went out into the silent street and down to the beach.

There was a moon in the sky that lit the dark cliffs crowding in above the beach, and reflected off the sea in multiple yellow images. The low surf hissed and coughed on the pebble beach and they took off their shoes and walked along it, letting the water wash around their ankles.

In an angle of the cliff, they found a hidden place amongst the rocks and they stopped to kiss again, and David mistakenly took her new soft mood as an invitation to continue from where he had left off that afternoon.

Debra pulled away again, but this time with determination and said angrily, 'Damn you! Don't you ever learn? I don't want to do that. Do we have to go through this every time we are alone?'

'What's the matter?' David was immediately stung by her tone, and furious with this fresh check. 'This is the twentieth century, darling. The simpering virgin is out of style this season–hadn't you heard?'

'And spoilt little boys should grow up before they come out on their own,' she flashed back at him.

'Thanks!' he snarled. 'I don't have to stay around taking insults from any professional virgin.'

'Well, why don't you move out then?' she challenged him.

'Hey, that's a great idea!' He turned his back on her and walked away up the beach. She had not expected that, and she started to run after him–but her pride checked her. She stopped and leaned against the rock.

He shouldn't have rushed me, she thought miserably. I want him, I want him very much, but he will be the first since Dudu. If he will just give me time it will be all right, but he mustn't rush me. If he could only go at my speed, help me to do it right.

It is funny, she thought, how little I remember about Dudu now. It's only three years, but his memory is fading so swiftly, I wonder if I really did love him. Even his face is hazy in my mind, while I know every detail of David's–every plane and line of it.

Perhaps I should go after him and tell him about Dudu, and ask him to be patient and to help me a little. Perhaps I should do that, she thought, but she did not and slowly she walked up the beach, through the silent town to the hotel.

Hannah's bed across the room was empty. She would be with Joe, lying with him, loving with him. I should be with David also, she thought. Dudu is dead, and I'm alive, and I want David and I should be with him–but she undressed slowly and climbed into the bed and lay without sleeping.

David stood in the doorway of '2001 A.D.' and peered through the weirdly flashing lights and the smog, the warm palpable emanation from a hundred straining bodies. The B.E.A. hostesses were still at the table, but Joe and Hannah had gone.

David made his way through the dancers. The one hostess was tall and blonde, with high English colour and china-doll eyes. She looked up and saw David, glanced around for Debra, made sure she was missing before she smiled.

They danced one cut of the record without touching each other and then David leaned close to her and placed both hands on her hips. She strained towards him with her lips parting.

'Have you got a room?' he asked, and she nodded, running the tip of her tongue lewdly around her lips.

'Let's go,' said David.

It was light when David got back to his own room. He shaved and packed his bag, surprised at the strength of his residual anger. He lugged the bag down to the proprietor's office and paid his bill with his Diners Club card.

Debra came out of the breakfast room with Joe and Hannah. They were all dressed for the beach with Terry robes over their bathing gear, and they were gay and laughing–until they saw David.

'Hey!' Joe challenged him. 'Where are you going?'

'I've had enough of Spain,' David told them. 'I'm taking some good advice, and I'm moving out,' and he felt a flare of savage triumph as he saw the quick shadow of pain in Debra's eyes. Both Joe and Hannah glanced at her, and quickly she controlled the quiver of her lips. She smiled then, a little too brightly and stepped forward, holding out her hand.

'Thank you for all your help, David. I'm sorry you have to go. It was fun.' Then her voice dropped slightly and there was a tiny quaver in it. 'I hope you find what you are looking for. Good luck.'

She turned quickly and hurried away to her room. Hannah's expression was steely, and she gave David a curt nod before following Debra.

'So long, Joe.'

'I'll carry your bag.'

'Don't bother.' David tried to stop him.

'No trouble.' Joe took it out of his hand and carried it out to the Mustang. He dumped it on the rear seat.

'I'll ride up to the top of the hills with you and walk back.' He climbed into the passenger seat and settled comfortably. 'I need the exercise.'

David drove swiftly, and they were silent as Joe deliberately lit a cigarette and flicked the match out the window.

'I don't know what went wrong, Davey, but I can guess.'

David didn't reply, he concentrated on the road.

'She's had a bad time. These last few days she has been different. Happy, I guess, and I thought it was going to work out.'

Still David was silent, not giving him any help. Why didn't the big bonehead mind his own business.

'She's a pretty special sort of person, Davey, not because she's my sister. She really is, and I think you should know about her–just so you don't think too badly about her.'

They had reached the top of the hills above the town and the bay. David pulled on to the verge but kept the engine running. He looked down on the brilliant blue of the sea, where it met the cliffs and the pine-covered headlands.

'She was going to be married,' said Joe softly. 'He was a nice guy, older than she was, they worked together at the University. He was a tank driver in the reserve and he took a hit in the Sinai and burned with his tank.'

David turned and looked at him, his expression softening a little.

'She took it badly,' Joe went on doggedly. 'These last few days were the first time I've seen her truly happy and relaxed.' He shrugged, and grinned like a big St Bernard dog. 'Sorry to give you the family history, Davey. Just thought it might help.' He held out a huge brown hand. 'Come and see us. It's your country also, you know. I'd like to show it to you.'

David took the hand. 'I might do that,' he said.

'Shalom.'

'Shalom, Joe. Good luck.' Joe climbed out of the car and when David pulled away he watched him standing on the side of the road with his hands on his hips. He waved and the first bend in the road hid him.

There was a school for aspiring Formula I racing drivers on a neglected concrete circuit near Ostia, on the road from Rome. The course lasted three weeks and cost $500 U.S.

David stayed at the Excelsio in the Via Veneto, and commuted each day to the track. He completed the full course, but after the first week knew it was not what he wanted. The physical limitation of the track was constricting after flying the high heavens, and even the crackling snarling power of a Tyrell Ford could not match the thrust from the engine of a jet interceptor. Although he lacked the dedication and motivation of others in his class his natural talent for speed and his co-ordination brought him out high in the finishing order–and he had an offer to drive on the works team of a new and struggling company that was building and fielding a production team of Formula I racing machines. Of course, the salary was starvation, and it was a measure of his desperation that he came close to signing a contract for the season, but at the last moment he changed his mind and went on.

In Athens he spent a week hanging around the yacht basins of Piraeus and Glyfada. He was investigating the prospects of buying a motor yacht and running it out on charter to the islands. The prospect of sun and sea and pretty girls seemed appealing and the craft themselves were beautiful in their snowy paint and varnished teakwork. In one week he learned that charter work was merely running a sea-going boarding house for a bunch of bored, sunburned and seasick tourists.

On the seventh day the American Sixth Fleet dropped anchor in the bay of Athens. David sat at a table of one of the beach-front cafés and drank *ouzo* in the sun, while he studied the anchored aircraft carriers through his binoculars. On the great flat tops the rows of Crusaders and Phantoms were grouped with their wings folded. Watching them he felt a consuming hunger, a need that was almost spiritual. He had searched the earth, it seemed, and there was nothing for him upon its face. He laid the binoculars aside, and he looked up into the sky. The clouds were high, a brilliant silver against the blue.

He picked up the glass of milky *ouzo* that the sun had warmed and rolled its sweet liquorice taste about his tongue.

'East, west, home is best.'

He spoke aloud, and had a mental image of Paul Morgan sitting in his high office of glass and steel. Like a patient fisherman he tended his lines laid across the world. Right now the one to Athens was beginning to twitch. He could imagine the quiet satisfaction as he began to reel it in, drawing David struggling feebly back to the centre. What the hell, I could still fly Impalas as a reserve officer, he thought, and there was always the Lear–if he could get it away from Barney.

David drained the glass and stood up abruptly, feeling the fading glow of his defiance. He flagged a cab and was driven back to his room at the Grande Bretagne on Syndagma Square.

His defiance was dying so swiftly that one of his companions for dinner that night was John Dinopoulos, Morgan Group's agent for Greece, a slim elegant sophisticate with an unlined sun-tanned face, silver wings in his hair and an elegantly casual way of dressing.

John had selected for David's table companion the female star of a number of Italian spaghetti westerns. A young lady of ample bosom and dark flashing eye whose breathing and bosom had become agitated when John introduced David as a diamond millionaire from Africa.

Diamonds were the most glamorous, although not the most significant of Morgan Group's interests.

They sat upon the terrace of Dionysius, for the evening was mild. The restaurant was carved into the living rock of the hill-top of Lycabettus, under the church of St Paul.

Down the zig-zag path from the church, the Easter procession of worshippers unwound in a flickering stream of candle flames through the pine forest below them, and the singing carried sweetly on the still night air. On its far hill-top the stately columns of the Acropolis were flood-lit so that they glowed as creamily as ancient ivory, and beyond that again on the midnight waters of the bay the American fleet wore gay garlands of fairy lights.

'The glory that was Greece–' murmured the star of Italian westerns, as though she voiced the wisdom of the ages, and placed one heavily jewelled hand on David's thigh while with the other she raised a glass of red Samos wine to him and cast him a look under thick eyelashes that was fraught with significance.

Her restraint was impressive, and it was only after they had eaten the main course of savoury meats wrapped in vine leaves and swimming in creamy lemon sauce that she suggested that David might like to finance her next movie.

'Let's find some place where we can talk about it–' she murmured, and what better place than her suite?

John Dinopoulos waved them away with a grin and a knowing wink, a gesture that annoyed David for it made him see the whole episode for the emptiness that it was.

The star's suite was pretentious, with thick white carpets and bulky black leather furniture. David poured himself a drink while she went to change into clothing more suitable for a discussion of high finance. David tasted the drink, realized that he did not want it and left it on the bar counter.

The star came out of the bedroom in a bedrobe of white satin which was cut back from arm and bosom, and was so sheer that her flesh gleamed with a pearly pink sheen through the material. Her hair was loose, a great wild mane of swirling curls–and suddenly David was sick of the whole business.

'I'm sorry,' he said. 'John was joking–I'm not a millionaire, and I really prefer boys.'

He heard his untouched glass shatter against the door of the suite as he closed it behind him.

Back at his own hotel he ordered coffee from room service, and then on an impulse he picked up the telephone again and placed a Cape Town call. It came through with surprising speed, and the girl's voice on the other end was thickened with sleep.

'Mitzi,' he laughed. 'How's the girl?'

'Where are you, warrior? Are you home?'

'I'm in Athens, doll.'

'Athens–God! How's the action?'

'It's a drag.'

'Yeah! I bet,' she scoffed. 'The Greek girls are never going to be the same again.'

'How are you, Mitzi?'

'I'm in love, Davey. I mean really in love, it's far out. We are going to be married. Isn't that just something else?' David felt a spur of anger, jealous of the happiness in her voice.

'That's great, doll. Do I know him?'

'Cecil Lawley, you know him. He's one of Daddy's accountants.' David recalled a large, pale-faced, bespectacled man with a serious manner.

'Congratulations,' said David. He felt very much alone again. Far from home, and aware that life there flowed on without his presence.

'You want to talk to him?' Mitzi asked. 'I'll wake him up.' There was murmur and mutter on the other end, then Cecil came on.

'Nice work,' David told him, and it really was. Mitzi's share of Morgan Group would be considerably larger than David's. Cecil had drilled himself an oil well in a most unconventional manner.

'Thanks, Davey.' Cecil's embarrassment at being caught tending his oil well carried clearly over five thousand miles of telephone cable.

'Listen, lover. You do anything to hurt that girl, I'll personally tear out your liver and stuff it down your throat, okay?'

'Okay,' said Cecil, and his alarm was brittle in his tone. 'I'll put you back to Mitzi.'

She prattled on for another fifty dollars' worth before hanging up. David lay on the bed with his hands behind his head and thought about his dumpy soft-hearted cousin and her new happiness. Then quite suddenly he made the decision which had been lurking at the edge of his consciousness all these weeks since leaving Spain. He picked up the phone again and asked for the porter's desk.

'I'm sorry to trouble you at this time of the morning,' he said, 'but I should like to get on a flight to Israel as soon as possible, will you please arrange that.'

The sky was filled with a soft golden haze that came off the desert. The gigantic T.W.A. 747 came down through it, and David had a glimpse of dark green citrus orchards before the solid jolt of the touch-down. Lod was like any other airport in the world but beyond its doors was a land like no other he had ever known. The crowd who fought him for a seat in one of the big black sheruts, communal taxis plastered with stickers and hung with gew-gaws, made even the Italians seem shining towers of restrained good manners.

Once aboard, however, it was as though they were on a family outing–and he a member of that family. On one side of him a paratrooper in beret and blouse with his winged insignia on the breast and an Uzzi submachine-gun slung about his neck offered him a cigarette, on the other a big strapping lass also in khaki uniform and with the dark gazelle eyes of an Israeli, which became even darker and more soulful when she looked at David, which was often, shared a sandwich of unleavened bread and balls of fried chick-peas, the ubiquitous pita and falafel, with him and practised her English upon him. All the occupants of the front seat turned around to join the conversation, and this included the driver who nevertheless did not allow his speed to diminish in the slightest and who punctuated his remarks with fierce blasts of his horn and cries of outrage at pedestrians and other drivers.

The perfume of orange blossom lay as heavily as sea mist upon the coastal lowlands, and always afterwards it would be for David the smell of Israel.

Then they climbed into the Judaean hills, and David felt a sense of nostalgia as they followed the winding highway through pine forests and across the pale shining slopes where the white stone gleamed like bone in the sunlight and the silver olive trees twisted their trunks in graceful agony upon the terraces which were the monuments to six thousand years of man's patient labour.

It was so familiar and yet subtly different from those fair and well-beloved hills of the southern cape he called home. There were flowers he did not recognize, crimson blooms like spilled blood, and bursts of sunshine-yellow blossoms upon the slopes–then suddenly a pang that was like a physical pain as he glimpsed the bright flight of chocolate and white wings amongst the trees, and he recognized the crested head of an African hoopoe–a bird which was a symbol of home.

He felt a sense of excitement building within him, unformed and undirected as yet but growing, as he drew closer to the women he had come to see–and to something else of which he was as yet uncertain.

There was, at last, a sense of belonging. He felt in sympathy with the young persons who crowded close to him in the cab.

'See,' cried the girl, touching his arm and pointing to the wreckage of war still strewn along the roadside, the burned-out carapaces of trucks and armoured vehicles, preserved as a memorial to the men who died on the road to Jerusalem. 'There was fighting here.'

David turned in the seat to study her face, and he saw again the strength and certainty that he had so admired in Debra. These were a people who lived each day to its limit, and only at its close did they consider the next.

'Will there be more fighting?' he asked.

'Yes,' she answered him without hesitation.

'Why?'

'Because–if it is good–you must fight for it,' and she made a wide gesture that seemed to embrace the land and all its people, 'and this is ours, and it is good,' she said.

'Right on, doll,' David agreed with her, and they grinned at each other.

So they came to Jerusalem with its tall, severe apartment blocks of custard-yellow stone, standing like monuments upon the hills, grouped about the massive walled citadel that was its heart.

T.W.A. had reserved a room at the Intercontinental Hotel for David while on board the inward flight. From his window he looked across the garden of Gethsemane at the old city, at its turrets and spires and the blazing golden Dome of the Rock–centre of Christianity and Judaism, holy place of the Moslems, battleground for two thousand years, ancient land reborn–and David felt a sense of awe. For the first time in his life, he recognized and examined that portion of himself that was Jewish, and he thought it was right that he should have come to this city.

'Perhaps,' he said aloud, 'it's just possible that this is where it's all at.'

It was early evening when David paid off the cab in the car park of the University and submitted to a perfunctory search by a guard at the main gate. Here body search was a routine that would soon become so familiar as to pass unnoticed. He was surprised to find the campus almost deserted, until he remembered it was Friday–and that the whole tempo was slowing for the Sabbath.

The red-bud trees were in full bloom around the main plaza and the ornamental pool, as David crossed to the admin block and asked for her at the inquiries desk where the porter was on the point of leaving his post.

'Miss Mordecai–' the porter checked his list. 'Yes. English Department. On the second floor of the Lauterman building.' He pointed out through the glass doors. 'Third building on your right. Go right on in.'

Debra was in a students' tutorial, and while he waited for her, he found a seat on the terrace in the warmth of the sun. It was as well, for suddenly he felt a breath of uncertainty cooling his spine. For the first time since leaving Athens, he wondered if he had much cause to expect a hearty welcome from Debra Mordecai. Even at this remove in time, David had difficulty in judging his own behaviour towards her. Self-criticism was an art which David had never seriously practised; with a face and fortune such as his, it was seldom necessary. In this time of waiting he found it novel and uncomfortable to admit that it was just possible that his behaviour may have been, as Debra had told him, that of a spoiled child. He was still exploring this thought, when a burst of voices and the clatter of heels upon the flags distracted him and a group of students came out on to the terrace, hugging their books to their chests, and most of the girls glanced at him with quick speculative attention as they passed.

There was a pause then before Debra came. She carried books under her arm and a sling bag over one shoulder, and her hair was pulled back severely at the nape of her neck; she wore no make-up, but her skirt was brightly coloured in big summery whorls of orange. Her legs were bare and her feet were thrust into leather sandals. She was in deep conversation with the two students who flanked her, and she did not see David until he stood up from the parapet. Then she froze into that special stillness he had first noticed in the *cantina* at Zaragoza.

David was surprised to find how awkward he felt, as though his feet and hands had grown a dozen sizes. He grinned and made a shrugging, self-deprecatory gesture.

'Hello, Debs.' His voice sounded gruff in his own ears, and Debra stirred and made a panicky attempt to brush back the wisps of hair at her temples, but the books hampered her.

'David–' She started towards him, a pace before she hesitated and stopped, glancing at her students. They sensed her confusion and melted, and she swung back at him.

'David–' she repeated, and then her expression crumbled into utter desolation. 'Oh God, and I haven't even a shred of lipstick on.'

David laughed with relief and went towards her, spreading his arms, and she flew at him and it was all confusion with books and sling bag muddled, and Debra making breathless exclamations of frustration before she could divest herself of them. Then at last they embraced.

'David,' she murmured with both arms wound tightly around his neck. 'You beast–what on earth took you so long? I had almost given you up.'

Debra had a motor scooter which she drove with such murderous abandon that she frightened even the Jerusalem taxi-drivers who crossed her path–men with a reputation for steel nerves and disregard for danger.

Perched on the pillion David clung to her waist and remonstrated with her gently as she overtook a solid line of traffic and then cut smartly across a stream coming in the opposite direction with her exhaust popping merrily.

'I'm happy,' she explained over her shoulder.

'Fine! Then let's live to enjoy it.'

'Joe will be surprised to see you.'

'If we ever get there.'

'What's happened to your nerve?'

'I've just this minute lost it.'

She went down the twisting road into the valley of Ein Karem, as though she was driving a Mirage, and called a travelogue back to him as she went.

'That's the Monastery of Mary's Well where she met the mother of John the Baptist–according to the Christian tradition in which you are a professed expert.'

'Hold the history,' pleaded David. 'There's a bus around that bend.'

The village was timeless amongst the olive trees, dug into the slope with its churches and monasteries and high-walled gardens, an oasis of the picturesque, while the skyline above it was cluttered with the high-rise apartments of modern Jerusalem.

From the main street Debra scooted into the mouth of a narrow lane, where high walls of time-worn stone rose on each hand, and braked to a halt outside a forbidding iron gate.

'Home,' she said, and wheeled the scooter into the gatehouse and locked it away before letting them in through a side gate hidden in a corner of the wall.

They came out into a large garden court enclosed by the high rough plastered walls which were lime-washed to glaring white. There were olive trees growing in the court with thick twisted trunks. Vines climbed the walls and spread their boughs overhead; already there were bunches of green grapes forming upon them.

'The Brig is a crazy keen amateur archaeologist,' Debra indicated the Roman and Greek statues that stood amongst the olive trees, the exhibits of pottery amphorae arranged around the walls, and the ancient mosaic tiles which paved the pathway to the house. 'It's strictly against the law, of course, but he spends all his spare time digging around in the old sites.'

The kitchen was cavernous with an enormous open fireplace in which a modern electric stove looked out of place, but the copper pots were burnished until they glowed and the tiled floor was polished and sweet-smelling.

Debra's mother was a tall slim woman with a quiet manner, who looked like Debra's older sister. The family resemblance was striking and, as she greeted them, David thought with pleasure that this was how Debra would look at the same age. Debra introduced them and announced that David was a guest for dinner, a fact of which he had been unaware until that moment.

'Please,' he protested quickly, 'I don't want to intrude.' He knew that Friday was a special night in the Jewish home.

'You don't intrude. We will be honoured,' she brushed aside his protest. 'This house is home for most of the boys on Joe's squadron, we enjoy it.'

Debra fetched David a Goldstar beer and they were sitting on the terrace together when her father arrived. He came in through the wicket gate, stooping his tall frame under the stone lintel and taking off his uniform cap as he entered the garden.

He wore uniform casually cut, and open at the throat with cloth insignia of rank and wings at the breast pocket. He was slightly round-shouldered, probably from cramming his lanky body into the cramped cockpits of fighter aircraft, and his head was brown and bald with a monk's fringe of hair and a fierce spiky moustache through which a gold tooth gleamed richly. His nose was big and hooked, the nose of a biblical warrior, and his eyes were dark and snapping with the same golden lights as Debra's. He was a man of such presence that he commanded David's instant respect. He stood to shake the General's hand and called him 'sir' completely naturally.

The Brig subjected David to a rapid, raking scrutiny and reserved his judgement, showing neither pleasure nor disdain.

Later David would learn that the nickname 'The Brig' was a shortened version of 'The Brigand', a name the British had given him before 1948 when he was smuggling warplanes and arms into Palestine for the *Haganah*. Everyone, even his children called him that and only his wife used his given name, Joshua.

'David is sharing the Sabbath meal with us tonight,' Debra explained to him.

'You are welcome,' said the Brig, and turned to embrace his women with love and laughter, for he had seen neither of them since the previous Sabbath, his duties keeping him at air bases and control rooms scattered widely across the land.

When Joe arrived, he was also in uniform, the casual open-necked khaki of summer, and when he saw David he dropped his slow manner and hurried to him, laughing, and enfolded him in a bear hug, speaking over his shoulder to Debra.

'Was I right?'

'Joe said you would come,' Debra explained.

'It looks like I was the only one who didn't know,' David protested.

There were fifteen at dinner, and the candlelight gleamed on the polished wood of the huge refectory table and the silver Sabbath goblets. The Brig said a short prayer, the satin and gold embroidered *yamulka* looking slightly out of place on his wicked bald head, then he filled the wine goblets with his own hand murmuring a greeting to each of his guests. Hannah was with Joe, her copper hair glowing handsomely in the candlelight, and she greeted David with reserve. There were two of the Brig's brothers with their wives and children and grandchildren, and the talk was loud and confusing as the children vied with their elders for a hearing and the language changed at random from Hebrew to English. The food was exotic and spicy, although the wine was too sweet for David's taste. He was content to sit quietly beside Debra and enjoy the sense of belonging in this happy group. He was startled then when one of Debra's cousins leaned across her to speak to him.

'This must be very confusing for you–your first day in such an unusual country as Israel, and not understanding Hebrew, you not being Jewish–'

The words were not meant unkindly, but all conversation stopped abruptly and the Brig looked up, frowning swiftly, quick to sense an unkindness to a guest at his board.

David was aware of Debra staring at him intently, as if to will words from him, and suddenly he thought how three denials finalized any issue–in the New Testament, in Mohammedan law, and perhaps in that of Moses as well. He did not want to be excluded from this household, from these people. He didn't want to be alone again. It was good here.

He smiled at the cousin and shook his head. 'It's strange, yes–but not as bad as you think. I understand Hebrew, though I don't speak it very well. You see, I am Jewish also.'

Beside him Debra gave a soft gasp of pleasure and exchanged quick glances with Joe.

'Jewish?' the Brig demanded. 'You don't look it,' and David explained, and when he was through the Brig nodded. It seemed that his manner had thawed a little.

'Not only that, but he is a flier also,' Debra boasted, and the Brig's moustache twitched like a living thing so that he had to soothe it with his napkin while he reappraised David carefully.

'What experience?' he demanded brusquely.

'Twelve hundred hours, sir, almost a thousand on jets.'

'Jets?'

'Mirages.'

'Mirages!' The Brig's gold tooth gleamed secretly.

'What squadron?'

'Cobra Squadron.'

'Rastus Naude's bunch?' The Brig stared at David as he asked.

'Do you know Rastus?' David was startled.

'We flew in the first Spitfires from Czechoslovakia together–back in '48. We used to call him Butch Ben Yok–Son of a Gentile–in those days. How is he, he must be getting on now? He was no spring chick even then.'

'He's as spry as ever, sir,' David answered tactfully.

'Well, if Rastus taught you to fly–you must be half good,' the Brig conceded.

As a general rule the Israeli Airforce would not refuse foreign pilots, but here was a Jew with all the marks of a first-class fighter pilot. The Brig had noticed the marvellous *élan* and thrust which that other consummate judge of young men, Paul Morgan, had recognized also and valued so highly. Unless he had read the signs wrongly, something he seldom did, then here was a rare one. Once more he appraised the young man in the candlelight and noticed that clear and steady gaze that seemed to seek a distant horizon. It was the eye of the gunfighter, and all his pilots were gunfighters.

To train an interceptor pilot took many years and nearly a million dollars. Time and money were matters of survival in his country's time of trial–and rules could be bent.

He picked up the wine bottle and carefully refilled David's goblet. 'I will place a telephone call to Rastus Naude,' he decided silently, 'and find out a bit more about this youngster.'

Debra watched her father as he began to question David searchingly on his reasons, or lack of them, for coming to Israel–and on his future plans.

She knew precisely how the Brig's mind was working, for she had anticipated it. Her reasons for inviting David to dinner and for exposing him to the Brig were devious and calculated.

She switched her attention back to David, feeling the tense warm sensation in the pit of her stomach and the electric prickle of the skin upon her forearms as she looked at him.

'Yes, you big cocky stallion,' she thought comfortably, 'you aren't going to find it easy to escape again. This time I'm playing for keeps, and I've got the Brig on to you also.'

She lifted her goblet to him, smiling sweetly at him over the rim.

'You're going to get exactly what you're after, but in trumps and with bells on,' she threatened silently, and aloud she said, '*Lechaim!* To life!' and David echoed the toast.

'This time I'm not going to be put off so easily,' he promised himself firmly as he watched the candlelight explode in tiny golden sparks in her eyes. 'I'm going to have you, my raven-haired beauty, no matter how long it takes or what it costs.'

The telephone beside his bed woke David in the dawn, and the Brig's voice was crisp and alert, as though he had already completed a day's work.

'If you have no urgent plans for today, I'm taking you to see something,' he said.

'Of course, sir.' David was taken off balance.

'I will fetch you from your hotel in forty-five minutes, that will give you time to breakfast. Please wait for me in the lobby.'

The Brig drove a small nondescript compact with civilian plates, and he drove it fast and efficiently. David was impressed with his reaction time and co-ordination–after all the Brig must be well into his fifties, and David allowed himself to contemplate such immense age with awe.

They took the main highway west towards Tel Aviv, and the Brig broke a long silence.

'I spoke with your old C.O. last night. He was surprised to hear where you were. He tells me that you were offered promotion to staff rank before you left–'

'It was a bribe,' said David, and the Brig nodded and began to talk. David listened to him quietly while he watched with pleasure the quickly changing landscape as they came down out of the hills and turned southwards through the low rolling plains towards Beersheba and the desert.

'I am taking you to an airforce base, and I might add that I am flouting all sorts of security regulations to do so. Rastus assured me that you can fly, and I want to see if he was telling me the truth.'

David looked at him quickly.

'We are going to fly?' and he felt a deep and pleasurable excitement when the Brig nodded.

'We are at war here, so you will be flying a combat sortie, and breaking just about every regulation in the book. But you'll find we don't go by the book very much.'

He went on quietly, explaining his own particular view of Israel, its struggle and its chances of success, and David remembered odd phrases he used.

'–We are building a nation, and the blood we have been forced to mix into the foundations has strengthened them–'

'–We don't want to make this merely a sanctuary for all the beaten-up Jews of the world. We want the strong bright Jews also–'

'–There are three million of us, and one hundred and fifty million enemies, sworn to our total annihilation–'

'–If they lose a battle, they lose a few miles of desert, if we lose one we cease to exist–'

–We'll have to give them one more beating. They won't accept the others. They believe their ammunition was faulty in 1948, after Suez the lines were restored so they lost nothing, and in '67 they think they were cheated. We'll have to beat them one more time before they'll leave us alone–'

He talked as to a friend or an ally and David was warmed by his trust, and enlivened by the prospect of flying again.

A plantation of eucalyptus trees grew as a heavy screen alongside the road, and the Brig slowed to a gate in the barbed wire fence and a sign that proclaimed in both languages: 'Chaim Weissmann Agricultural Experimental Centre.'

They turned on to the side road through the plantation, and there was a secondary fence and a guard post amongst the trees.

A guard at the gate checked the Brig's papers briefly, they clearly knew him well. Then they drove on, emerging from the plantation into neatly laid-out blocks of different cereal crops. David recognized oats, barley, wheat and maize–all of it flourishing in the warm spring sunshine. The roads between each field were surveyed long and straight and paved with concrete that had been tinted to the colour of the surrounding earth. There was something unnatural in these smooth two-mile-long fairways bisecting each other at right angles, and to David they were familiar. The Brig saw his interest and nodded, 'Yes,' he said, 'runways. We are digging in–not to be taken by the same tactics we used in '67.'

David pondered it while they drove rapidly towards a giant concrete grain silo that stood tall in the distance. In the fields, scarlet tractors were at work, and overhead irrigation equipment threw graceful glittering ostrich feathers of spray into the air.

They reached the concrete silo and the Brig drove the compact through the wide doors of the barn-like building that abutted it. David was startled to see the lines of buses and automobiles parked in neat lines along the length of the barn. There was transport here for many hundreds of men–and yet he had noticed less than a score of tractor-drivers.

There were guards here again, in paratrooper uniform, and when the Brig led David to the rounded bulk of the silo, he realized suddenly that it was a dummy. A massive bomb-proof structure of solid concrete, housing all the sophisticated communications and radar equipment of a modern fighter base. It was combined control tower and plot for four full squadrons of Mirage fighters, the Brig explained briefly as they entered an elevator and sank below the earth.

They emerged into a reception area where again the Brig's papers were examined, and a paratrooper major was called to pass David through, a duty he performed reluctantly and at the Brig's insistence. Then the Brig led David along a carpeted and air-conditioned underground tunnel to the pilots' dressing-room. It was tiled and spotless, with showers and toilets and lockers like a country club changing-room.

The Brig had ordered clothing for David, guessing his size and doing so accurately. The orderly corporal had no trouble fitting him out in overalls, boots, G-suit, gloves and helmet.

The Brig dressed from his own locker and both of them went through into the ready room, moving stiffly in the constricting grip of the G-suits and carrying their helmets under their arms.

The duty pilots looked up from chess games and magazines as they entered, recognized the general and stood to greet him, but the atmosphere was easy and informal. The Brig made a small witticism and they all laughed and relaxed, while he led David through into the briefing-room.

Swiftly, but without overlooking a detail, he outlined the patrol that they would fly, and checked David out on radio procedure, aircraft identification, and other parochial details.

'All clear?' he asked at last, and when David nodded, he went on, 'Remember what I told you, we are at war. Anything we find that doesn't belong to us we hit it, hard! All right?'

'Yes, sir.'

'It's been nice and quiet the last few weeks, but yesterday we had a little trouble down near Ein Yahav, a bit of nastiness with one of our border patrols. So things are a little sensitive at the moment.' He picked up his helmet and map case then turned to face David, leaning close to him and fixing him with those fierce brown and golden eyes.

'It will be clear up there today, and when we get to forty thousand, you will be able to see it all, every inch of it from Rosh Hanikra to Suez, from Mount Hermon to Eilat, and you will see how small it is and how vulnerable to the enemies that surround us. You said you were looking for something worthwhile–I want you to decide whether guarding the fate of three million people might not be a worthwhile job for a man.'

They rode on a small electric personnel carrier down one of the long underground passages, and they entered the concrete bunker dispersed at one point of a great star whose centre was the concrete silo, and they climbed down from the cart.

The Mirages stood in a row, six of them, sleek and needle-nosed, crouching like leashed and impatient animals, so well remembered in outline, but vaguely unfamiliar in their desert brown and drab green camouflage with the blue Star of David insignia on the fuselage.

The Brig signed for two machines, grinning as he wrote 'Butch Ben Yok' under David's numeral.

'As good a name as any to fly under,' he grunted. 'This is the land of the pseudonym and alias.'

David settled into the tiny cockpit with a sense of homecoming. In here it was all completely familiar and his hands moved over the massed array of switches, instruments and controls like those of a lover as he began his pre-flight check.

In the confined space of the bunkers the jet thunder assaulted the eardrums, their din only made bearable by the perforated steel baffles set into the rear of the structure.

The Brig looked across at David, his head enclosed in the garishly painted helmet, and gave him the high sign. David returned it and reached up to pull the Perspex canopy closed. Ahead of them, the steel blast doors rolled swiftly upwards, and the ready lamps above them switched from red to green.

There was no taxiing to take-off areas; no needless ground exposure. Wing-tip to wing-tip they came up the ramp out of the bunker into the sunlight. Ahead of them stretched one of the long brown runways, and David pushed open his throttle to the gate, and then ignited his afterburners, feeling the thrust of the mighty jet through the cushioning of his seat. Down between the fields of green corn they tore, and then up, with the swooping sensation in the guts and the rapier nose of the Mirage pointed at the sapphire of the sky that arched unbroken and unsullied above them, and once again David experienced the euphoria of jet-powered flight.

They levelled out a little under forty thousand feet avoiding even altitudes or orderly flight patterns, and David placed his machine under the Brig's tail and eased back on the throttles to cruising power, his hands delighting in the familiar rituals of flight which his helmeted head revolved restlessly in the search routine, sweeping every quarter of the sky about him, weaving the Mirage to clear the blind spot behind his own tail.

The air had an unreal quality of purity, a crystalline clarity that made even the most distant mountain ranges stand out in crisp silhouette, hardly shaded with the blue of distance. In the north the Mediterranean blazed like a pool of molten silver in the sunlight, while the sea of Galilee was soft cool green, and farther south the Dead Sea was darker, forbidding in its sunken bed of tortured desert.

They flew north over the ridge of Carmel and the flecked white buildings of Haifa with its orange gold beaches on which the sea broke in soft ripples of creamy lacework. Then they turned together easing back on the power and sinking slowly to patrol altitude at twenty thousand feet as they passed the peak of Mount Hermon where the last snows still lingered in the gullies and upon the high places, streaking the great rounded mountain like an old man's pate.

The softly dreaming greens and pastels delighted David who was accustomed to the sepia monochromes of Africa. The villages clung to the hill-tops, their white walls shining like diamonds above the terraced slopes and the darker areas of cultivated land.

They turned south again, booming down the valley of the Jordan, over the Sea of Galilee with its tranquil green waters enclosed by the thickets of date palm and the neatly tended fields of the Kibbutzim, losing altitude as the land forsook its gentle aspect and the hills were riven and tortured, rent by the wadis as though by the claws of a dreadful predator.

On the left hand rose the mountains of Edom, hostile and implacable, and beneath them Jericho was a green oasis in the wilderness. Ahead lay the shimmering surface of the Dead Sea. The Brig dropped down, and they thundered so low across the salt-thickened water that the jet blast ruffled the surface behind them.

The Brig's voice chuckled in David's earphones, 'That's the lowest you are ever going to fly–twelve hundred feet below sea level.'

They were climbing again as they crossed the mineral works at the southern end of the sea, and faced the blasted and mountainous deserts of the south.

'Hello, Cactus One, this is Desert Flower,' again the radio silence was broken, but this time David recognized the call sign of command net. They were being called directly from the Operation Centre of Airforce Command, situated in some secret underground bunker at a location that David would never learn. On the command plot their position being accurately relayed by the radar repeaters.

'Hello, Desert Flower,' the Brig acked, and immediately the exchange became as informal as two old friends chatting, which was precisely what it was.

'Brig, this is Motti. We've just had a ground support request in your area,' he gave the co-ordinates quickly, 'a motorized patrol of border police is under sneak low-level attack by an unidentified aircraft. See to it, will you.'

'Beseder, Motti, okay.' The Brig switched to flight frequency. 'Cactus Two, I'm going to interception power, confirm to me,' he told David, and they turned together on to the new heading.

'No point in trying a radar scan,' the Brig grumbled aloud. 'He'll be down in the ground clutter. We'll not pick the swine off amongst those mountains. Just keep your eyes open.'

'Beseder.' David had already picked up the word. The favourite Hebrew word in a land where very little was really 'okay'.

David spotted it first, a slim black column of smoke beginning to rise like a pencil line drawn slowly against the windless and dazzling cobalt blue of the horizon.

'Ground smoke,' he said into his helmet microphone. 'Eleven o'clock low.'

The Brig squinted ahead silently, searching for it, and then saw it on the extreme limit of his vision range. He grunted, Rastus had been right in one thing at least. The youngster had eyes like a hawk.

'Going to attack speed now,' he said and David acked and lit his afterburners. The upholstery of the seat smacked into his back under the mighty increase in thrust and David felt the drastic alteration in trim as the Mirage went shooting through the sonic barrier.

Near the base of the smoke column, something flashed briefly against the drab brown earth, and David narrowed his eyes and made out the tiny shape, flitting as a sunbird, its camouflage blending naturally into the backdrop of desert, so it was ethereal as a shadow.

'Bandit turning to port of the smoke,' he called the sighting.

'I have him,' said the Brig, and switched to command net.

'Hello, Desert Flower, I'm on an intruder. Call strike, please.' The decision to engage must be made to command level, and the answering voice was laconic, and flat.

'Brig, this is Motti. Hit him!'

While they spoke they were rushing down so swiftly that the details of the little drama being played out below sprang into comprehension.

Along a dusty border track three patrol vehicles of the border police were halted. They were camouflaged half tracks, tiny as children's toys in the vastness of the desert.

One of the half tracks was burning. The smoke was greasy black and rose straight into the air, the beacon that had drawn them. Lying spread-eagled in the road was a human body, flung down carelessly in death, and the sight of it stirred in David a deeply bitter feeling of resentment such as he had last felt in the bullring at Madrid.

The other vehicles were pulled off the track at abandoned angles, and David could see their crews crouching amongst the scrub and rock. Some of them were firing with small arms at their attacker who was circling for his next run down upon them.

David had never seen the type before, but knew it instantly from the recognition charts that he had studied so often. It was a Russian MIG 17 of the Syrian airforce. The high tailplane was unmistakable. The dappled brown desert camouflage was brightened by the red, white and black roundels with their starred green centres on the fuselage and the stubby swept wings.

The MIG completed its turn, settling swiftly down and levelling off for its next strafing run upon the parked vehicles. The pilot's attention was concentrated on the helpless men cowering amongst the rocks and he was unaware of the terrible vengeance that was bearing down upon him from on high.

The Brig lined up for his pass, turning slightly to bring himself down on the Syrian's tail, attacking in classic style from behind and above, and David dropped back to weave across his rear, covering him and backing up to press in a supporting attack if the first failed.

The Syrian opened fire again and the cannon bursts twinkled like fairy lights amongst the men and trucks. Another truck exploded in a dragon's breath of smoke and flame.

'You bastard,' David whispered as he levelled out behind the Brig, and saw the havoc that was being wrought amongst his people. It was the first time he had thought of them as that, his people, and he felt the cold anger of the shepherd whose flock is under attack.

A line of poetry popped up in his mind 'The Assyrian came down like a wolf on the fold,' and his hands went purposefully to the chore of locking in his cannons-selectors and flicking the trigger forward out of its recess in the moulded grip of the joystick. The soft green glow lit his gunsight as it came alive and he squinted through it.

The Brig was pressing his attack in to close range, rapidly overhauling the slower clumsy-looking MIG, and at that moment that he knew he would open fire David saw the Syrian's wing-shape alter. At the fatal instant he had become aware of his predicament, and he had done what was best in the circumstances. He had pulled on full flap and while his speed fell sharply he dropped one wing in a slide towards the earth a hundred feet below.

The Brig was committed and he loosed his salvo of cannon fire at the instant that the Syrian dropped, ducking under it like a boxer avoiding a heavy punch. David saw the blaze of shot pass high, rending the air above the sand-coloured aircraft. Then the Brig was through, missing with every shell, spiralling up and around in a great flashing circle, raging internally at his failure.

At the instant that David recognized the MIG's manœuvre, he reacted with a rapidity that was purely reflexive. He closed down his power, and hit his air brakes to punch a little of the speed off the Mirage.

The MIG turned steeply away to port, standing on one wing-tip that seemed to be pegged into the bleak desert earth. David released his air brakes, to give his wings lift for the next evolution, and then he dropped his own wing-tip and went sweeping round to follow the Syrian's desperate twists with the Mirage hovering on the edge of the stall.

The Syrian was turning inside him, slower and more manœuvrable; David could not bring his sights to bear, his right forefinger was curled around the trigger but always the dark shape of the MIG was out of centre in the illuminated circle of the sight as the aiming pipper dipped and rose to the pull of gravity.

Ahead of the two circling aircraft rose a steep and forbidding line of cliffs, rent by deep defiles and gullies.

The MIG made no attempt to climb above them, but selected a narrow pass through the hills and went into it like a ferret into its run, a desperate attempt to shake off the pursuit.

The Mirage was not designed for this type of flying, and David felt the urge to hit his afterburners and ride up over the jagged fangs of rock–but to do so was to let the MIG escape, and his anger was still strong upon him.

He followed the Syrian into the rock pass, and the walls of stone on either hand seemed to brush his wing-tips, the gully turned sharply to starboard and David dropped his wing and followed its course. Back upon itself the rock turned, and David swung the needle nose from maximum rate turn starboard to port, and the stall warning device winked amber and red at him as he abused the Mirage's delicate flying capabilities.

Ahead of him the MIG clawed its way through the tunnel of rock. The pilot looked back over his shoulder and he saw the Mirage following him, creeping slowly up on him, and he turned back to his controls and forced his machine lower still, hugging the rugged walls of stone.

The air in the hills was hot and turbulent, and the Mirage bucked and fought against restraint wanting to be free and high, while ahead of it the Syrian drifted tantalizingly off-centre in David's gunsight.

Now the valley turned again and narrowed, before climbing and ending abruptly against a solid dark purple wall of smooth rock.

The Syrian was trapped, he levelled out and climbed steeply upwards, his flight path dictated by the rocks on each side and ahead.

David pushed his throttle to the gate and lit his afterburners, and the mighty engine rumbled, thrusting him powerfully forward, up under the Syrian's stern.

The eternal micro-seconds of mortal combat dragged by, as the Syrian floated lazily into the circle of the gunsight, expanding it to fill it as the Mirage's nose seemed to touch the other's tailplane and David felt the buffeting of the Syrian's slip-stream.

He pressed the cannon trigger and the Mirage lurched as she hurled her deadly load into the other machine in a clattering double stream of cannon fire and an eruption of incendiary shells.

The Syrian disintegrated, evaporating in a gush of silvery smoke, rent through with bright white lightning, and the ejecting pilot's body was blown clear of the fuselage. For an instant it was outlined ahead of David's screen, cruciform in shape with arms and legs thrown wide, the helmet still on the head, and the clothing ballooning in the rush of air. Then it flickered past the Mirage's canopy as David climbed swiftly up out of the valley and into the open sky.

The soldiers were moving about amongst their vehicles, tending their wounded and covering their dead, but they all looked up as David flew back low along the road. He passed so close that he could see their faces clearly. They were sun-browned, some with beards or moustaches, strong young faces, their mouths open as they cheered him, waving their thanks.

My people, he thought. He was still high on the adrenalin that had poured into his blood, and he felt a fierce elation. He grinned wolfishly at the men below him and lifted one gloved hand in salute before climbing up to where the Brig was circling, waiting for him.

The artificial lights of the bunkers were dim after the brilliance of the sun. An engineer helped David from the cockpit as his mates swarmed over the Mirage to refuel and rearm it. This was one of the vital skills of this tiny airforce, the ability to ready a warplane for combat in a fraction of the time usually required for the task. Thus in emergency the machine could return to the battle long before its adversary.

Moving stiffly from the confines of the cockpit, David crossed to where the Brig was already in conversation with the flight controller.

He stood with the gaudy helmet tucked under one arm as he stripped off his gloves, but as David came up he turned to him and his wintry smile exposed the gold tooth in its nest of fur.

Lightly he punched David's arm 'Ken! Yes!' said Major-General Joshua Mordecai. 'You'll do.'

David was late to fetch Debra for dinner that evening, but she had already learned the reason from her father.

They went to the Select behind David's Tower, inside the Jaffa Gate of the old city. Its unpretentious interior, decorated with patterns of rope upon the walls, did not fully prepare David for the excellent meal that the Arab proprietor served them with the minimum of delay–mousakha chicken, with nuts and spices on a bed of kouskous.

They ate almost in silence, Debra quickly recognizing and respecting David's mood. He was in the grip of post-combat *tristesse,* the adrenalin hangover of stress and excitement, but slowly the good food in his belly and the heavy Carmel wine relaxed him, until over the thimble-sized cups of Turkish coffee, black and powerfully reeking of cardamom seed, Debra could ask, 'What happened today, David?'

He sipped the coffee before replying.

'I killed a man.' She set down her cup and studied his face solemnly, and he began to speak, telling her the details of it, the chase and the kill, until he ended lamely, 'I felt only satisfaction at the time. A sense of achievement. I knew I had done what was right.'

'And now?' she prompted him.

'Now I am sad,' he shrugged. 'I am saddened that I had to do it.'

'My father, who has always been a soldier, says that only those who do the actual fighting can truly know what it is to hate war.'

David nodded. 'Yes, I understand that now. I love to fly, but I hate to destroy.'

They were silent again, both of them considering their own personal vision of war, both of them trying to find words to express it.

'And yet it is necessary,' Debra broke the silence. 'We must fight–there is no other way.'

'There is no other way–with the sea at our backs and the Arabs at our throats.'

'You speak like an Israeli,' Debra challenged him softly.

'I made a decision today–or rather I was press-ganged by your father. He has given me three weeks to brush up my Hebrew, and complete the immigration formalities.'

'And then?' Debra leaned towards him.

'A commission in the airforce. That was the only point I scored on, I had just enough strength to hold out for the equivalent rank I would have had back home. He haggled like a secondhand clothes dealer, but I had him, and he knew it. So he gave in at last. Acting major, with confirmation of rank at the end of twelve months.'

'That's wonderful, Davey, you'll be one of the youngest majors in the service.'

'Yeah,' David agreed, 'and after I've paid my taxes I'll have a salary a little less than a bus-driver back home.'

'Never mind,' Debra smiled for the first time. 'I'll help you with your Hebrew.'

'I was going to talk to you about that,' he answered her smile. 'Come on, let's get out of here. I'm restless tonight–and I want to walk.'

They strolled through the Christian quarter. The open stalls on each side were loaded with garish and exotic clothes, and leather work and jewellery, and the smell of spices and food and drains and stale humanity was almost solid in the narrow lanes where the arches met overhead.

Debra drew him into one of the antique stores in the Via Dolorosa, and the proprietor came to them, almost wriggling with pleasure.

'Ah, Miss Mordecai–and how is your dearly esteemed father?' Then he rushed into the back room to brew more coffee for them.

'He's one of the half-honest ones, and he lives in mortal fear of the Brig.'

Debra selected an antique solid gold Star of David on a slim golden neck chain, and though he had never before worn personal jewellery, David bowed his head and let her place it about his neck. The golden star lay against the coarse dark curls of his chest.

'That's the only decoration you'll ever get–we don't usually give medals,' she told him laughingly. 'But welcome to Israel anyway.'

'It's beautiful,' David was touched and embarrassed by the gift, 'thank you.' And he buttoned his shirt over it and then reached awkwardly to kiss her–but she drew away and warned him.

'Not in here. He's a Moslem, and he'd be very offended.'

'All right,' said David. 'Let's go and find some place where we won't hurt anybody's sensibilities.'

They went out through the Lion Gate in the great wall and found a stone bench in a quiet place amongst the olive trees of the Moslem cemetery. There was half a moon in the sky, silver and mysterious, and the night was warm and waiting, seemingly as expectant as a new bride.

'You can't stay on at the Intercontinental,' Debra told him, and they both looked up at its arched and lighted silhouette across the valley.

'Why not?'

'Well, first of all it's too expensive. On your salary you just can't afford it.'

'You don't really expect me to live on my salary?' David protested, but Debra ignored him and went on.

'And what is more important, you aren't a tourist any more. So you can't live like one.'

'What do you suggest?'

'We could find you an apartment.'

'Who would do the housework, and the laundry, and the cooking?' he protested vehemently. 'I haven't had much practice at that sort of thing.'

'I would,' said Debra, and he froze for an instant and then turned slowly on the seat to look at her.

'What did you say?'

'I said, I would,' she repeated firmly, and then her voice quavered. 'That's if you want me to.' He was silent for a long moment.

'See here, Debs. And you talking about living together? I mean, playing house-house on a full-time basis–the whole bit?'

'That's precisely what I am talking about.'

'But–' He could think of nothing further to say. The idea was novel, breathtaking, and alive with enchanting possibilities. All David's previous experiences with the opposite sex had been profuse rather than deep, and he found himself on the frontiers of unexplored territory.

'Well?' Debra asked at last.

'Do you want to get married?' his voice cracked on the word, and he cleared his throat.

'I'm not sure that you are the finest marriage material in the market, my darling David. You are as beautiful as the dawn, and fun to be with–but you are also selfish, immature and spoiled stupid.'

'Thank you kindly.'

'Well, there is no point in me mincing words now, David, not when I am about to throw all caution aside and become your mistress.'

'Wow!' he exclaimed, with all the frost thawing from his voice. 'When you say it straight out like that–it almost blows my mind.'

'Me too,' Debra confessed. 'But one condition is that we wait until we have our own special place, you may recall that I'm not so high on public beaches or rocky islands.'

'I'll never forget,' David agreed. 'Does this mean that you *don't* want to marry me?' He found his mortal terror of matrimony fading under this slur on his potential marriage worth.

'I didn't say that either,' Debra demurred. 'But let's make that decision when both of us are ready for it.'

'Right on, doll,' said David, with an almost idiot grin of happiness spreading over his face.

'And now, Major Morgan, you may kiss me,' she said. 'But do try and help me remember the conditions.'

A long while later, they drew a little apart to breathe and a sudden thought made David frown with worry.

'My God,' he exclaimed, 'what will the Brig say!'

'He won't be joining us,' she told him, and they both laughed together, excited by their own wickedness.

'Seriously, what will you tell your parents?'

'I'll lie to them graciously, and they'll pretend to believe me. Let me worry about that.'

'Beseder,' he agreed readily.

'You are learning,' she applauded. 'Let's just try that kiss again–but this time in Hebrew, please.'

'I love you,' he said in that language.

'Good boy,' she murmured. 'You are going to make a prize pupil.'

There was one more doubt to be set at rest, and Debra voiced it at the iron gate to the garden, when at last he took her home.

'Do you know what the Bris, the Covenant, is?'

'Sure,' he grinned, and made scissors out of his fist and second finger. It seemed in the uncertain light that she blushed, and her voice was only just audible.

'Well, what about you?'

'That,' David told her severely, 'is a highly personal question, the answer to which little girls should find out for themselves,' and his expression became lascivious, 'the hard way.'

'All knowledge is precious as gold,' she said in a small voice, 'and be sure that I will seek the answer diligently.'

David discovered that the acquisition of an apartment in Jerusalem was a task much like the quest for the Holy Grail. Although the high-rise blocks were being thrown up with almost reckless energy, the demand for accommodation far outweighed the supply.

The father of one of Debra's students was an estate agent and the poor man took their problem to his heart; the waiting-list for the new blocks was endless, but an occassional apartment in one of the older buildings fell vacant, and he used all his influence for them.

At unexpected moments of the day, Debra would send out an urgent signal, and David would fetch her in a taxi at the University and they would hell across town, urging on the driver, to inspect the latest offering.

The last of these reminded David of a movie set from *Lawrence of Arabia* complete with a dispirited palm tree out front, a spectacular display of bright laundry hanging from every balcony and window, and all the sounds and smells of an Arab camel market and a nursery-school playground at recess from the courtyard.

There were two rooms and an alleged bathroom. The roses and wreaths of the wallpaper had faded, except in patches where hangings had protected their original pristine virulent colouring.

David pushed open the door of the bathroom and, without entering, inspected the raggedy linoleum floor-covering and the stained and chipped bath tub; then pushing the door further he discovered the toilet bowl festering quietly in the gloom with its seat at a rakish angle like the halo of a drunken angel.

'You and Joe could work on it,' Debra suggested uncertainly. 'It's not really *that* bad.'

David shuddered, and closed the door as though it were the lid of a coffin.

'You're joking–of course,' he said, and Debra's determinedly bright smile cracked and her lip quivered.

'Oh, David, we are never going to find a place.'

'And I can't wait much longer.'

'Nor can I,' admitted Debra.

'Right,' David rubbed his hands together briskly' 'It's time to send in the first team.'

He was not sure what form the presence of Morgan Group would take in Jerusalem, but he found it listed in the business directory under 'Morgan Industrial Finance' and the Managing Director was a large mournful-looking gentleman named Aaron Cohen who had a suite of offices in the Leumi Bank building opposite the main post office. He was overcome with emotion to discover that one of the Morgan family had been ten days in Jerusalem without his knowledge

David told him what he wanted, and in twenty hours he had it signed and paid for. Paul Morgan picked his executives with care, and Cohen was an example of this attention. The price David must pay for this service was that Paul Morgan would have a full report of David's transaction, present whereabouts and future plans on his desk the next morning–but it was worth it.

Above the Hinnom canyon, facing Mount Zion with its impressive array of spires, the Montefiore quarter was being rebuilt as an integrated whole by some entrepreneur. All of it was clad in the lovely golden Jerusalem stone, and the designs of the houses were traditional and ageless. However, the interiors were lavishly modernized with tall cool rooms, mosaic-tiled bathrooms, and ceilings arched like those of a crusader church. Most of them had their own walled and private terraces. The one that Aaron Cohen procured for David was the pick of those that fronted Malik Street. The price was astronomical. That was the first question that Debra asked, once she had recovered her voice. She stood stunned upon the terrace beneath the single olive tree. The stone of the terrace had been cut and polished until it resembled old ivory, and she ran her fingers lightly over the carved front door. Her voice was hushed and her expression bemused.

'David! David! How much is this going to cost?'

'That's not important. What is important is whether you like it.'

'It's too beautiful. It's too much, David. We can't afford this.'

'It's paid for already.'

'Paid for?' She stared at him. 'How much, David?'

'If I said half a million Israeli pounds or a million, what difference would it make? It's only money.'

She clapped her hands over her ears. 'No!' she cried. 'Don't tell me! I'd feel so guilty I wouldn't be able to live in it.'

'Oh, so! You are actually consenting to live in it.'

'Try me,' she said with emphasis. 'You just try me, lover!'

They stood in the central room that opened on to the terrace, and although it was light and airy enough for the savage heat of summer that was coming, it smelled of new paint and varnished woodwork.

'What are we going to do about furniture?' David asked.

'Furniture?' Debra repeated. 'I hadn't thought that far ahead.'

'For what I have in mind, we'll need at least one king-size bed.'

'Sex maniac,' she said, and kissed him.

No modern furniture looked at home under the domed roof, or upon the stone-flagged doors. So they began to furnish from the bazaars and antique shops.

Debra solved the main problem with the discovery in a junk yard of an enormous brass bedstead from which they scraped the accumulated dirt; they polished it until it glowed, fitting it with a new inner-spring mattress, and covered it with a cream-coloured lace bedspread from Debra's bottom drawer.

They purchased *kelim* and woven woollen rugs by the bale from the Arab dealers in the old city, and scattered them thickly upon the stone floors, with leather cushions to sit upon and a low olive-wood table, inlaid with ebony and mother of pearl, to eat off. The rest of the furniture would come when they could find it for sale, or, failing that, have it custom-made by an Arab cabinet-maker that Debra knew of. Both the bed and the table were enormously heavy, and they needed muscle to move them, so they called for Joe. He and Hannah arrived in his tiny Japanese compact, and after they had recovered from the impact of the Morgan palace they fell to work enthusiastically with David supervising. Joe grunted and heaved, while Hannah disappeared with Debra into the modern American kitchen to exclaim with envy and admiration over the washing-machine, dryer, dish-washer and all the other appliances that went with the house. She helped to cook the first meal.

David had laid in a case of Goldstar beer, and after their labours they all gathered about the olive-wood table to warm the house and wet the roof.

David had expected Joe to be a little reserved, after all it was his baby sister who was being set up in a fancy house; but Joe was as natural as ever and enjoyed the beer and the company so well that Hannah had to intervene at last.

'It's late,' she said firmly.

'Late?' asked Joe. 'It's only nine o'clock.'

'On a night like tonight, that's late.'

'What do you mean?' Joe looked puzzled.

'Joseph Mordecai, diplomat extraordinary,' Hannah said with heavy sarcasm, and suddenly Joe's expression changed as he glanced from Debra to David guiltily, swallowed his beer in a single gulp, and hoisted Hannah to her feet by one arm.

'Come on,' he said. 'What are we sitting here for?'

David left the terrace lights burning, and they shone through the slats of the shuttered windows, so the room was softly lit, and the sounds from the outside world were so muted by distance and stone walls as to be a mere murmur that drifted from afar, and seemed rather to accentuate their aloneness than to spoil it.

The brass of the bedstead gleamed softly in the gloom, and the ivory lacework of the bedspread smelled of lavender and moth balls.

He lay upon the bed and watched her undress slowly, conscious of his eyes upon her and shy now as she had never been before.

Her body was slim and with a flowing line of waist and leg, young and tender-looking, with a child's awkward grace, and yet with womanly thrust of hip and bosom.

She came to sit upon the edge of the bed, and he marvelled once again at the lustre and plasticity of her skin, at the subtlety of colouring where the sun had darkened it from soft cream to burned honey, and at the contrast of her dusky rose-tipped breasts and the dark thick bush of curls at the base of her softly curving stomach.

She leaned over him, still shyly, and touched his cheek with one finger, running down his throat on to his chest where the gold star lay upon the hard muscle.

'You are beautiful,' she whispered, and she saw it was true. For he was tall and straight with muscled shoulders and lean flanks and belly. The planes of his face were pure and perfect, perhaps its only fault lying in its very perfection. It was almost unreal, as though she were lying with some angel or god from out of mythology.

She twisted her legs up on to the bed, stretching out beside him upon the lace cover, and they lay on their sides facing each other, not touching but so close that she could feel the warmth of his belly upon her own like a soft desert wind, and his breath stirred the dark soft hair upon her cheek.

She sighed then, with happiness and contentment, like a traveller reaching the end of a long lonely journey.

'I love you,' she said for the first time, and reaching out she took his head, her fingers twining in the thick springing hair at the nape of his neck, and drew it tenderly to her breast.

Long afterwards the chill of night oozed into the room, and they came half-awake and crept together beneath the covers.

As they began drifting back into sleep she murmured sleepily, 'I'm so glad that surgery won't be necessary, after all,' and he chuckled softly.

'Wasn't it better finding out for yourself?'

'Much better, lover. Much, much better,' she admitted.

Debra spent one entire evening explaining to David that a high-performance sports car was not a necessity for travel between his base and the house on Malik Street, for she knew her man's tastes by then. She pointed out that this was a country of young pioneers, and that extravagance and ostentation were out of place. David agreed vehemently, secure in the knowledge that Aaron Cohen and his minions were scouring the country for him.

Debra suggested a Japanese compact similiar to Joe's, and David told her that he would certainly give that his serious consideration.

Aaron Cohen's henchman tracked down a Mercedes Benz 350 SL belonging to the German Chargé d'Affaires in Tel Aviv. This gentleman was returning to

Berlin and wished to dispose of his auto, for a suitable consideration in negotiable cash. A single phone call was sufficient to arrange payment through the Crédit Suisse in Zurich.

It was golden bronze in colour, with a little under twenty thousand kilometres on the clock, and it had clearly been maintained with the loving care of an enthusiast.

Debra, returning on her motor scooter from the University, found this glorious machine parked at the top end of Malik Street, where a heavy chain denied access by all motor-driven vehicles to the village.

She took one look at it, and knew beyond all reasonable doubt who it belonged to. She was really quite angry when she stormed on to the terrace, but she pretended to be angrier than that.

'David Morgan, you really are absolutely impossible.'

'You catch on fast,' David agreed amiably; he was sun-bathing on the terrace.

'How much did you pay for it?'

'Ask me another question, doll. That one is becoming monotonous.'

'You are really–' Debra paused and searched frantically for a word of sufficient force. She found it and delivered it with relish, 'decadent!'

'You don't know the meaning of the word,' David told her gently as he rose from the cushions in the sun and drifted lazily in her direction. Though she had been his lover for only a mere three days she recognized the look in his eye and she began backing away.

'I will teach you the meaning,' he said. 'I am about to give you a practical demonstration of decadence in such a sensitive spot that you are likely to remember it for a long time.'

She ducked behind the olive tree as he lunged, and her books spilled across the terrace.

'Leave me! Hands off, you beast.'

He feinted right, and caught her as she fell for it. He picked her up easily across his chest.

'David Morgan, I warn you, I shall scream if you don't put me down this instant.'

'Let's hear it. Go ahead!' and she did, but in a ladylike fashion so as not to alarm the neighbours.

Joe, on the other hand, was delighted with the 350. The four of them took it on a trial run down the twisting road through the Wilderness of Judaea to the shores of the Dead Sea. The road challenged the car's suspension and David's driving skill, and they whooped with excitement through the bends. Even Debra was able to overcome her initial disapproval, and finally admitted it was beautiful–but still decadent.

They swam in the cool green waters of the oasis of Ein Gedi where they formed a deep rock pool before overflowing and running down into the thick saline water of the sea itself.

Hannah had brought her camera and she photographed Debra and David sitting together on the rocks beside the pool.

They were in their bathing costumes, Debra's brief bikini showing off her fine young body as she half-turned to laugh into David's face. He smiled back at her, his face in profile and the dark sweep of his hair falling on to his forehead. The desert light picked out the pure features and the boldly stated facets of his beauty.

Hannah had a print of the photograph made for each of them, and later those squares of glossy photographic paper were all they had left of it, all that remained of the joy and the laughter of those days, like a lovely flower taken from the growing tree of life and pressed and dried, flattened and desiccated, deprived of its colour and perfume.

But the future threw no shadow over their happiness on that bright day, and with Joe driving this time they ran back for Jerusalem. Debra insisted that they stop for a group of tank corps boys hitch-hiking home on leave, and although David protested it was impossible, they squeezed three of them into the small cab. It was Debra's sop to her feelings of guilt, and she sat in the back seat with her arms around David's neck and they all sang the song that was that year a favourite with the young people of Israel, 'Let there be peace'.

In the last few days while David waited to enter the airforce, he loafed shamelessly, frittering the time away in small chores like having his uniforms tailored. He resisted Debra's suggestion that if regulation issue were good enough for her father, a general officer, then they might be good enough for David. Aaron Cohen supplied him with an introduction to his own tailor. Aaron was beginning to develop a fine respect for David's style.

Debra had arranged membership for David at the University Athletic Club, and he worked out in the first-class modern gym every day, and finished with twenty lengths of the Olympic-size swimming pool to keep himself in shape.

However, at other times, David merely lay sunbathing on the terrace, or fiddled with electrical plugs or other small tasks Debra had asked him to see to about the house.

As he moved through the cool and pleasant rooms, he would find an item belonging to Debra, a book or a brooch perhaps, and he would pick it up and fondle it briefly. Once a robe of hers thrown carelessly across the foot of the bed and redolent of her particular perfume gave him a physical pang as it reminded him sharply of her, and he held the silkiness to his face and breathed the scent of her, and grudged the hours until her return.

However, it was amongst her books that he discovered more about her than years of study would have revealed. She had crates of these piled in the unfurnished second bedroom which they were using as a temporary store-room until they could find shelves and cupboards. One afternoon David began digging around in the crates. It was a literary mixed grill–Gibbon and Vidal, Shakespeare and Mailer, Solzhenitsyn and Mary Stewart, among other strange bedfellows. There was fiction and biography, history and poetry, Hebrew and English, softbacks and leather-bound editions–and a thin green-jacketed volume which he almost discarded before the author's name caught his attention. It was by D. Mordecai and with a feeling of discovery he turned to the flyleaf. *This year, in Jerusalem,* a collection of poems, by Debra Mordecai.

He carried the book through to the bedroom, remembering to kick off his shoes before lying on the lace cover–she was very strict about that–and he turned to the first page.

There were five poems. The first was the title piece, the two-thousand-year promise of Jewry 'Next year in Jerusalem' had become reality. It was a patriotic tribute to her land and even David, whose taste in writing ran to Maclean and Robbins, recognized that it had a superior quality. There were lines of startling beauty, evocative phrasing and penetrative glimpses. It was good, really good, and David felt a strange proprietary pride–and a sense of awe. He had not guessed at these depths within her, these hidden areas of the mind.

When he came to the last poem, he found it was the shortest of the five, and it was a love poem–or rather it was a poem to someone dearly loved who was gone–and suddenly David was aware of the difference between that which was good and that which was magic.

He found himself shivering to the music of her words, felt the hair on his forearms standing erect with the haunting beauty of it, and then at last he felt himself choking on the sadness of it, the devastation of total loss, and the words swam as his eyes flooded, and he had to blink rapidly as the last terrible cry of the poem pierced him to the heart.

He lowered the book on to his chest, remembering what Joe had told him about the soldier who had died in the desert. A movement attracted his attention and he made a guilty effort to hide the book as he sat up. It was such a private thing, this poetry, that he felt like a thief.

Debra stood in the doorway of the bedroom watching him, leaning against the jamb with her hands clasped in front of her, studying him quietly.

He sat up on the bed and weighed the book in his hands. 'It's lovely,' he said at last, his voice was gruff with the emotions that her words had evoked.

'I'm glad you like it,' she said, and he realized that she was shy.

'Why did you not show it to me before?'

'I was afraid you might not like it.'

'You must have loved him very much?' he asked softly.

'Yes, I did,' she said, 'but now I love you.'

Then, finally, his posting came through and the Brig's hand was evident in it all, though Joe admitted that he had used his own family connections to influence the orders.

He was ordered to report to Mirage squadron 'Lance' which was a crack interceptor outfit based at the same hidden airfield from which he had first flown. Joe Mordecai was on the same squadron, and when he called at Malik Street to tell David the news, he showed no resentment that David would outrank him, but instead he was confident that they would be able to fly together as a regular team. He spent the evening briefing David on squadron personnel, from 'Le Dauphin' the commanding officer, a French immigrant, down to the lowest mechanic. In the weeks ahead David would find Joe's advice and help invaluable, as he settled into his niche amongst this tightly-knit team of fliers.

The following day the tailor delivered his uniforms, and he wore one to surprise Debra when she backed in through the kitchen door, laden with books and groceries, using her bottom as a door buffer, her hair down behind and her dark glasses pushed up on top of her head.

She dropped her load by the sink, and circled him with her hands on her hips, her head cocked at a critical angle.

'I should like you to wear that, and come to pick me up at the University tomorrow afternoon, please,' she said at last.

'Why?'

'Because there are a few little bitches that lurk around the Lauterman Building. Some of them my students and some my colleagues. I want them to get a good look at you–and eat their tiny hearts out.'

He laughed. 'So you aren't ashamed of me?'

'Morgan, you are too beautiful for one person, you should have been born twins.'

It was their last day together, so he indulged her whimsy and wore his uniform to fetch her at the English Literature Department, and he was surprised to find how the dress affected the strangers he passed on the street–the girls smiled at him, the old ladies called *shalom,* even the guard at the University gates waved him through with a grin and a joke. To them he was a guardian angel, one of those that had swept death from the very sky above them.

Debra hurried to meet and kiss him, and then walked beside him, her hand tucked proudly and possessively into the crook of his elbow. She took him to eat an early dinner at the staff dining-room in the rounded glass Belgium building.

While they ate, a casual question of his revealed the subterfuge she had used to protect her reputation.

'I'll probably not get off the base for the first few weeks, but I'll write to you at Malik Street–'

'No,' she said quickly, 'I won't be staying there. It would be too lonely without you in that huge bed.'

'Where then? At your parents' home?'

'That would be a dead give-away. Every time you arrive back in town, I leave home! No, they think I am staying at the hostel here at the University. I told them I wanted to be closer to the department–'

'You've got a room here?' He stared at her.

'Of course, Davey. I have to be a little discreet. I couldn't tell my relatives, friends and employers to contact me care of Major David Morgan. This may be the twentieth century, and modern Israel, but I am still a Jewess, with a tradition of chastity and modesty behind me.'

For the first time David began to appreciate the magnitude of Debra's decision to come to him. He had taken it lightly compared to her.

'I'm going to miss you,' he said.

'And I you,' she replied.

'Let's go home.'

'Yes,' she agreed, laying aside her knife and fork. 'I can eat any old time.'

However, as they left Belgium House she exclaimed with exasperation: 'Damn, I have to have these books back by today. Can we go by the library? I'm sorry, Davey, it won't take a minute.'

So they climbed again to the main terrace and passed the brightly-lit plate-glass windows of the Students' Union Restaurant, and went on towards the solid square tower of the library whose windows were lighted already against the swiftly falling darkness. They had climbed the library steps and reached the glass doors when a party of students came pouring out, and they were forced to stand aside.

They were facing back the way they had come, across the plaza with its terraces and red-bud trees, towards the restaurant.

Suddenly the dusk of evening was lit by the searing white furnace glare of an explosion, and the glass windows of the restaurant were blown out in a glittering cloud of flying glass. It was as though a storm surf had burst upon a rock cliff, flinging out its shining droplets of spray, but this was a lethal spray that scythed down two girl students who were passing the windows at that moment.

Immediately after the flash of the explosion the blast swept across the terrace, a draught of violence that shook the red-bud trees and sent David and Debra reeling against the pillars of the library veranda. The air was driven in upon them so that their eardrums ached with the blow, and the breath was sucked from their lungs.

David caught her to him and held her for the moments of dreadful silence that followed the blast. As they stared so, a soft white fog of phosphorus smoke billowed from the gutted windows of the restaurant and began to roll and drift across the terrace.

Then the sounds reached them through their ringing eardrums, the small tinkle and crunch of glass, the patter and crack of falling plaster and shattered furniture. A woman began to scream, and it broke the spell of horror.

There were shouts and running feet. One of the students near them began in a high hysterical voice, 'A bomb. They've bombed the café.'

One of the girls who had fallen under the storm of glass fragments staggered up and began running in small aimless circles, screaming in a thin passionless tone. She was white with plaster dust through which the blood poured in dark rivulets, drenching her skirt.

In David's arms Debra began to tremble. 'The swine,' she whispered, 'oh, the filthy murdering swine.'

From the smoking destruction of the shattered building another figure shambled with slow deliberation. The blast had torn his clothing from his body, and it hung from him in tatters, making him a strange scarecrow figure. He reached the terrace and sat down slowly, removed from his face the spectacles that were miraculously still in place and began fumbling to clean them on the rags of his shirt. Blood dripped from his chin.

'Come on,' grated David, 'we must help.' And they ran down the steps together.

The explosion had brought down part of the roof, trapping and crushing twenty-three of the students who had come here to eat and talk over the evening meal.

Others had been hurled about the large low hall, like the toys of a child in tantrum, and their blood turned the interior into a reeking charnel house. Some of them were crawling, creeping, or moving spasmodically amongst the tumbled furniture, broken crockery and spilled food. Some lay contorted as though in silent laughter at death's crude joke.

Afterwards they would learn that two young female members of El Fatah had enrolled in the university under false papers, and they had daily smuggled small quantities of explosive on to the campus until they had accumulated sufficient for this outrage. A suitcase with a timing device had been left under a table and two terrorists had walked out and got clean away. A week later they were on Damascus television, gloating over their success.

Now, however, there was no reason nor explanation for this sudden burst of violence. It was as undirected, and yet as dreadfully effective as some natural cataclysm. Chilling in its insensate enormity, so that they, the living, worked in a kind of terrified frenzy, to save the injured and to carry from the shambles the broken bodies of the dead.

They laid them upon the lawns beneath the red-bud trees and covered them with sheets brought hurriedly from the nearest hostel. The long white bundles in a neat row upon the green grass was a memory David knew he would have for ever.

The ambulances came, with their sirens pulsing and roof-lights flashing, to carry away death's harvest and the police cordoned off the site of the blast before David and Debra left and walked slowly down to where the Mercedes was parked in the lot. Both of them were filthy with dust and blood, and wearied with the sights and sounds of pain and mutilation. They drove in silence to Malik Street and showered off the smell and the dirt. Debra soaked David's uniform in cold water to remove the blood. Then she made coffee for them and they drank it, sitting side by side in the brass bed.

'So much that was good and strong died there tonight,' Debra said.

'Death is not the worst of it. Death is natural, it's the logical conclusion to all things. It was the torn and broken flesh that still lived which appalled me. Death has a sort of dignity, but the maimed are obscene.'

She looked at him with almost fear in her eyes. 'That's cruel, David.'

'In Africa there is a beautiful and fierce animal called the sable antelope. They run together in herds of up to a hundred, but when one of them is hurt–wounded by a hunter or mauled by a lion–the lead bulls turn upon him and drive him from the herd. I remember my father telling me about that, he would say that if you want to be a winner then you must avoid the company of the losers for their despair is contagious.'

'God, David, that's a terribly hard way to look at life.'

'Perhaps,' David agreed, 'but then, you see, life *is* hard.'

When they made love, there was for the first time a quality of desperation in it, for it was the eve of parting and they had been reminded of their mortality.

In the morning David went to join his squadron and Debra locked the house on Malik Street.

Each day for seventeen days David flew two, and sometimes three, sorties. In the evenings, if they were not flying night interceptions, there were lectures and training films, and after that not much desire for anything but a quick meal and then sleep.

The Colonel, le Dauphin, had flown one sortie with David. He was a small man with a relaxed manner and quick, shrewd eyes. He had made his judgement quickly.

After that first day, David and Joe flew together, and David moved his gear into the locker across from Joe in the underground quarters that the crews on standby used.

In those seventeen days the last links in an iron friendship were forged. David's flare and dash balanced perfectly with Joe's rock-solid dependability.

David would always be the star while Joe seemed destined to be the accompanist, the straight guy who was a perfect foil, the wingman without personal ambition for glory whose talent was to put his number one into the position for the strike.

Quickly they developed into a truly formidable team, so perfectly in accord that communication in the air was almost extra-sensory, similar to the instantaneous reaction of the bird flock or the shoal of fish.

Joe sitting out there behind him was for David like a million dollars in insurance. His tail was secure and he could concentrate on the special task that his superior eyesight and lightning reactions were so suited to. David was the gunfighter, in a service where the gunfighter was supreme.

The I.A.F. had been the first to appreciate the shortcomings of the air-to-air missile, and to revert to the classic type of air combat. A missile could be induced to 'run stupid'. It was possible to make its computer think in a set pattern and then sucker it with a break in the pattern. For every three hundred missile launches in air-to-air combat, a single strike could be expected.

However, if you had a gunfighter coming up into your six o'clock position with his finger on the trigger of twin 30-mm. cannons, capable of pouring twelve thousand shells a minute into you, then your chances were considerably lighter than three hundred to one.

Joe also had his own special talent. The forward scanning radar of the Mirage was a complicated and sophisticated body of electronics, that required firstly a high degree of manual dexterity. The mechanism was operated entirely by the left hand, and the fingers of that hand had to move like those of a concert pianist. However, more important was the 'feel' for the instrument, a lover's touch to draw the optimum results from it. Joe had the 'feel', David did not.

They flew training interceptions, day and night, against high-flying and low-altitude practice targets. They flew low-level training strikes, and at other times they went out high over the Mediterranean and engaged each other in plane-to-plane dog-fights.

However, Desert Flower steered them tactfully away from any actual or potential combat situation. They were watching David.

At the end of the period, David's service dossier passed over Major-General Mordecai's desk. Personnel was the Brig's special responsibility and although each officer's dossier was reviewed by him regularly, he had asked particularly to see David's.

The dossier was still slim, compared to the bulky tomes of some of the old salts and the Brig flicked quickly over his own initial recommendation and the documents of David's acting commission. Then he stopped to read the later reports and results. He grinned wolfishly as he saw the gunnery report. He could pick them out of a crowd, he thought with satisfaction.

At last he came to le Dauphin's personal appraisal:

'Morgan is a pilot of exceptional ability. Recommended that acting rank be confirmed and that he be placed on fully operational basis forthwith.'

The Brig picked up the red pen that was his own special prerogative and scrawled 'I agree' at the foot of the report.

That took care of Morgan, the pilot. He could now consider Morgan, the man. His expression became bleak and severe. Debra's sudden desire to leave home almost immediately David arrived in Jerusalem had been too much of a coincidence for a man who was trained to search for underlying motives and meanings.

It had taken him two days and a few phone calls to learn that Debra was merely using the hostel room at the University as an accommodation address, and that her real domestic arrangements were more comfortable.

The Brig did not approve, very definitely not. Yet he knew that it was beyond his jurisdiction. He had learned that his daughter had inherited his own iron will. Confrontations between them were cataclysmic events, that shook the family to its foundations and seldom ended in satisfactory results.

Although he spent much of his time with young people, still he found the new values hard to live with–let alone accept. He remembered the physical agony of his long and chaste engagement to Ruth with pride, like a veteran reviewing an old campaign.

'Well, at the least she has the sense not to flout it, not to bring shame on us all. She has spared her mother that.' The Brig closed the dossier firmly.

Le Dauphin called David into his office and told him of his change in status. He would go on regular 'green' standby, which meant four nights a week on base.

David would now have to undergo his paratrooper training in unarmed combat and weapons. A downed pilot in Arab territory had a much better chance of survival if he was proficient in this type of fighting.

David went straight from le Dauphin's office to the telephone in the crew-room. He caught Debra before she left the Lauterman Building for lunch.

'Warm the bed, wench,' he told her, 'I'll be home tomorrow night.'

He and Joe drove up to Jerusalem in the Mercedes, and he wasn't listening to Joe's low rumbling voice until a thumb like an oar prodded his ribs.

'Sorry, Joe, I was thinking.'

'Well, stop it. Your thoughts are misting up the windows.'

'What did you say?'

'I was talking about the wedding–Hannah and me.'

David realized it was only a month away now, and he expected the excitement amongst the women was heavy as static on a summer's day before the rain. Debra's letters had been filled with news of the arrangements.

'I would be happy if you will stand up with me, and be my witness. You fly as wingman for a change, and I'll take on the target.'

David realized that he was being honoured by the request and he accepted with proper solemnity. Secretly he was amused. Like most young Israelis David had spoken to, both Debra and Joe claimed not to be religious. He had learned that this was a pose. All of them were very conscious of their religious heritage, and well versed in the history and practice of Judaism. They followed all the laws of living that were not oppressive, and which accorded with a modern and busy existence.

To them 'religious' meant dressing in the black robes and wide-brimmed hats of the ultra-orthodox Mea Shearim, or in following a routine for daily living that was crippling in its restrictions.

The wedding would be a traditional affair, complete with all the ceremony and the rich symbolism, complicated only by the security precautions which would have to be most rigorously enforced.

The ceremony was to take place in the Brig's garden, for Hannah was an orphan. Also the secluded garden and fortress-like walls about it, were easier to protect.

Amongst the guests would be many prominent figures in the government and the military.

'At the last count we have five generals and eighteen colonels on the list,' Joe told him, 'to which add most of the cabinet, even Golda has promised to try and be there. So you see, it's going to make a nice juicy target for our friends in Black September.' Joe scowled and lit two cigarettes, passing one to David. 'If it wasn't for Hannah, you know how women feel about weddings, I would just as soon go down to a registry office.'

'You are fooling nobody,' David grinned. 'You are looking forward to it.'

'Sure,' Joe's scowl cleared. 'It's going to be good to have our own place, like you and Debs. I wish Hannah had been sensible. A year of pretending,' he shook his head. 'Thank God it's nearly over.'

He dropped Joe in the lane outside the Brig's house in Ein Karem.

'I won't bother to invite you in,' Joe said. 'I guess you've got plans.'

'Good guess,' David smiled. 'Will we see you and Hannah? Come to dinner tomorrow night.'

Joe shook his head again. 'I'm taking Hannah down to Ashkelon to visit her parents' graves. It's traditional before a wedding. Perhaps we'll see you Saturday.'

'Right then, I'll try and make it. Debra will want to see you. *Shalom*, Joe,'

'*Shalom, shalom*,' said Joe and David pulled away, flicking the gears in a racing change as he put the Mercedes at the hill. Suddenly he was in a hurry.

The terrace door stood open in welcome, and she was waiting for him. Debra was vibrant and tense with expectation, sitting in one of the new leather chairs with her legs curled under her. Her hair was freshly washed and shimmering like a starling's wing. She was dressed in a billowing kaftan of light silk and subtle honey colours that picked out the gold in her eyes.

She came out of the chair in a swirl of silk, and ran bare-footed across the rugs to meet him.

'David! David!' she cried and he caught her up and spun on his heels, laughing with her.

Afterwards she led him proudly about the rooms and showed him the changes and additions that had turned it into a real home during his absence. David had convinced her that cost was not fundamental and they had chosen the designs for the furniture together. These had been made and delivered by Debra's tame Arab and she had arranged them as they had planned it. It was all in soft leather and dark wood, lustrous copper and brass, set off by the bright rugs. However, there was one article he had never seen before–a large oil-painting on canvas, and Debra had hung it unframed on the freshly painted white wall facing the terrace. It was the only decoration upon the wall, and any other would have been insignificant beside it. It was a harsh dominant landscape, a desert scene which captured the soul of the wilderness; the colours were hot and fierce and seemed to pour through the room like the rays of the desert sun itself.

Debra held his hand and watched David's face anxiously for a reaction as he studied it.

'Wow!' he said at last.

'You like it?' She was relieved.

'It's terrific. Where did you get it?'

'A gift from the artist. She's an old friend.'

'She?'

'That's right. We are driving up to Tiberias tomorrow to have lunch with her. I've told her all about you, and she wants to meet you.'

'What's she like?'

'She's one of our leading artists, and her name is Ella Kadesh, but apart from that I can't begin to describe her. All I can do is promise you an entertaining day.'

Debra had prepared a special dish of lamb and olives and they ate it on the terrace under the olive tree. Again the talk turned to Joe's wedding, and in the midst of it David asked abruptly, 'What made you decide to come with me–without marrying?'

She replied after a moment. 'I discovered that I loved you, and I knew that you were too impatient to play the waiting game. I knew that if I didn't, I might lose you again.'

'Until recently, I didn't realize what a big decision it was,' he mused, and she sipped her wine without replying.

'Let's get married, Debs,' he broke the silence.

'Yes,' she nodded. 'That's a splendid idea.'

'Soon,' he said. 'Soon as possible.'

'Not before Hannah. I don't want to steal her day from her.'

'Right,' David agreed, 'but immediately afterwards.'

'Morgan, you have got yourself a date,' she told him.

It was a three-hour drive to Tiberias so they rose as soon as the sun came through the shutters and tiger-striped the wall above the brass bed. To save time, they shared one bath, sitting facing each other, waist-deep in suds.

'Ella is the rudest person you'll ever meet,' Debra warned him. She looked like a little girl this morning with her hair piled on top of her head and secured with a pink ribbon. 'The greater the impression you make on her, the ruder she will be, and you are expected to retaliate in kind. So please, David, don't lose your temper.'

David scooped up a dab of suds with a finger and smeared it on the tip of her nose.

'I promise,' he said.

They drove down to Jericho, and then turned north along the valley of the Jordan, following the high barbed-wire fence of the border with its warning notice boards for the minefields, and the regular motorized patrols grinding deliberately along the winding road.

It was hot in the valley and they drove with the windows open and Debra pulled her skirts high around her waist to cool her long brown legs.

'Better not do that if you want to be in time for lunch,' David warned her, and she smoothed them down hurriedly.

'Nothing is safe with you around,' she protested.

They came at last out of the barren land into the fertile basin of the Kibbutzim below Galilee, and again the smell of orange blossom was so strong on the warm air that it was difficult to breathe.

At last they saw the waters of the lake flashing amongst the date palms and Debra touched his arm.

'Slow down, Davey. Ella's place is a few miles this side of Tiberias. That's the turn-off, up ahead.'

It was a track that led down to the lake shore and it ended against a wall of ancient stone blocks. Five other cars were parked there already.

'Ella's having one of her lunch parties,' Debra remarked and led him to a gate in the wall. Beyond was a small ruined castle. The tumbled walls formed weird shapes and the stone was black with age; over them grew flamboyant creepers of bougainvillaea and the tall palms clattered their fronds in the light breeze that came off the lake. Other exotic flowering shrubs grew upon the green lawns.

Part of the ruins had been restored and renovated into a picturesque and unusual lakeside home, with a wide patio and a stone jetty against which a motor-boat was moored. Across the green waters of the lake rose the dark smooth whale-back of the Golan Heights.

'It was a crusader fortress,' Debra explained. 'One of the guard posts for traffic across the lake and part of the series leading up to the great castle on the Horns of Hittem that the Moslems destroyed when they drove the crusaders out of the Holy Land. Ella's grandfather purchased it during the Allenby administration, but it was a ruin until she did it up after the war of independence.'

The care with which the alterations had been made so as not to spoil the romantic beauty of the site was a tribute to Ella Kadesh's artistic vision, which was completely at odds with the woman herself.

She was enormous; not simply fat or tall, but big. Her hands and feet were huge, her fingers clustered with rings and semi-precious stones and her toenails through the open sandals were painted a glaring crimson, as if to flaunt their size. She stood as tall as David, but the tent-like dress that billowed about her was covered with great explosive designs that enhanced her bulk until she seemed to make up for two of him. She wore a wig of tiered curls, flaming red in colour and dangling earrings. It seemed she must have applied her eye make-up with a spade, and her rouge with a spray gun. She removed the thin black cheroot from her mouth and kissed Debra before she turned to study David. Her voice was gravelly, hoarse with cheroot smoke and brandy.

'I had not expected you to be so beautiful,' she said, and Debra quailed at the expression in David's eyes. 'I do not like beauty. It is so often deceptive, or inconsequential. It usually hides something deadly–like the glittering beauty of the cobra–or like the pretty wrapper of a candy bar, it contains cloying sweetness and a soft centre.' She shook the stiffly lacquered curls of her wig, and fixed David with her shrewd little eyes. 'No, I prefer ugliness to beauty.'

David smiled at her with all his charm upon display. 'Yes,' he agreed, 'having met you, and seen some of your work, I can understand that.'

She let out a cackle of raucous laughter, and clapped the cheroot back in her mouth. 'Well now, at the very least we are not dealing with a chocolate soldier.' She placed a huge masculine arm about David's shoulders and led him to meet the company.

They were a mixed dozen, all intellectuals–artists, writers, teachers, journalists–and David was content to sit beside Debra in the mild sunshine and enjoy the beer and the amusing conversation. However, Ella would not let him relax for long and when they sat down to the gargantuan *alfresco* meal of cold fish and poultry, she attacked him again.

'Your martial airs and affectations, your pomp and finery. A plague on it I say, a pox on your patriotism, and courage–on your fearlessness and your orders of chivalry. It is all sham and pretence, an excuse for you to stink up the earth with piles of carrion.'

'I wonder if you will feel the same when a platoon of Syrian infantry break in here to rape you,' David challenged her.

'My boy, I find it difficult to get laid these days that I should pray for such a heaven-sent opportunity.' She let out a mighty hoot of laughter and her wig slipped forward at an abandoned angle. Nothing was safe from her, and she pushed the wig back into place and streamed straight into the attack again.

'Your male bombast, your selfish arrogance. To you this woman–' and she indicated Debra with a turkey leg, '–to you she is merely a receptacle of your seething careless sperm. It matters not to you that she is a promise for the future, that within her are the seeds of a great writing talent. No, to you she is a rubbing block, a convenient means to a–'

Debra interrupted her. 'That definitely is enough, I will not allow a public debate on my bedroom,' and Ella turned towards her with the battle lust lighting her eyes.

'Your gift is not yours to use as you wish. You hold it in trust for all mankind, and you have a duty to them. That duty is to exercise your gift, to allow it to grow and blossom and give forth fruit.' She used the turkey leg like a judge's gavel, banging the edge of her plate with it, to silence Debra's protests.

'Have you written a word since you took young Mars to your heart? What of the novel we discussed on this very terrace a year ago? Have your animal passions swamped all else? Has the screeching of your ovaries–'

'Stop it, Ella!' Debra was angry now, her cheeks flushed and her brown eyes snapping.

'Yes! Yes!' Ella tossed the bone aside and sucked her fingers noisily. 'Ashamed you should be, angry with yourself–'

'Damn you,' Debra flared at her.

'Damn me if you will–but you are damned yourself if you do not write! Write, woman, write!' She sat back and the wicker chair protested at the movement of her vast body. 'All right, now we will all go for a swim. David has not seen me in a bikini yet–much he will care for that skinny little wench when he does!'

They drove back to Jerusalem in the night, flushed with the sun, and although the Mercedes seats had not been designed for lovers, Debra managed to sit close up against him.

'She's right, you know,' David broke a long contented silence. 'You must write, Debs.'

'Oh, I will,' she answered lightly.

'When?' he persisted, and to distract him she snuggled a little closer.

'One of these days,' she whispered as she made her dark head comfortable on his shoulder.

'One of these days,' he mimicked her.

'Don't bug me, Morgan.' She was already half-asleep.

'Stop being evasive.' He stroked her hair with his free hand. 'And don't go to sleep while I'm talking to you.'

'David, my darling, we have a lifetime–and more,' she murmured. 'You have made me immortal. You and I shall live for a thousand years, and there will be time for everything.'

Perhaps the dark gods heard her boast, and they chuckled sardonically and nudged each other.

On Saturday Joe and Hannah came to the house on Malik Street, and after lunch they decided on a tourist excursion for David and the four of them climbed Mount Zion across the valley. They entered the labyrinth of corridors that led to David's tomb, covered with splendid embroidered cloth and silver crowns and Torah covers. From there it was a few steps to the room of Christ's last supper in the same building, so closely interwoven were the traditions of Judaism and Christianity in this citadel.

Afterwards they entered the old city through the Zion gate and followed the wall around to the centre of Judaism, the tall cliff of massive stone blocks, bevelled in the fashion of Herodian times, which was all that remained of the fabulous second temple of Herod, destroyed two thousand years before by the Romans.

They were searched at the gate and then joined the stream of worshippers flocking down towards the wall. At the barrier they stood for a long time in silence. David felt again the stirring of a deep race memory, a hollow feeling of the soul which longed to be filled.

The men prayed facing the wall, many of them in the long black coats of the

Orthodox Jew with the ringlets dangling against their cheeks as they rocked and swayed in religious ecstasy. Within the enclosure on the right-hand side, the women seemed more reserved in their devotions.

Joe spoke at last, a little embarrassed and in a gruff tone. 'I think I'll just go say a *sh'ma*.'

'Yes,' Hannah agreed. 'Are you coming with me, Debra?'

'A moment.' Debra turned to David, and took something from her handbag. 'I made it for you for the wedding,' she said. 'But wear it now.'

It was a *yamulka*, an embroidered prayer cap of black satin.

'Go with Joe,' she said. 'He will show you what to do.'

The girls moved off to the women's enclosure and David placed the cap upon his head and followed Joe down to the wall.

A *shamash* came to them, an old man with a long silver beard, and he helped David bind upon his right arm a tiny leather box containing a portion of the Torah.

'So you shall lay these words upon your heart and your soul, and you shall bind them upon your right arm–'

Then he spread a *tallit* across David's shoulders, a tasselled shawl of woven wool, and he led him to the wall, and he began to repeat after the *shamash*:

'Hear, O Israel, the Lord our God, the Lord is one–'

His voice grew surer as he remembered the words from long ago, and he looked up at the wall of massive stone blocks that towered high above him. Thousands of previous worshippers had written down their prayers on scraps of paper and wedged them into the joints between the blocks, and around him rose the plaintive voices of spoken prayer. It seemed to David that in his imagination a golden beam of prayer rose from this holy place towards the heavens.

Afterwards they left the enclosure and climbed the stairs into the Jewish quarter, and the good feeling remained with David, glowing warmly in his belly.

That evening they sat together on the terrace drinking Goldstar beer and splitting sunflower seeds for the nutty kernels, and naturally the talk turned to God and religion.

Joe said, 'I'm an Israeli and then a Jew. First my country, and a long way behind that comes my religion.'

But David remembered the expression on his face as he prayed against the wailing wall.

The talk lasted until late, and David glimpsed the vast body of his religious heritage.

'I would like to learn a little more about it all,' he admitted, and Debra said nothing but when she packed for him to go on base that night she placed a copy of Herman Wouk's *This is my God* on top of his clean uniforms.

He read it and when next he returned to Malik Street, he asked for more. She picked them for him, English works at first but then Hebrew, as his grip upon the language became stronger. They were not religious works only, but histories and historical novels that excited his interest on this ancient centre of civilization which for three thousand years had been a crossroads and a battle ground.

He read anything and everything that she put into his case, from Josephus Flavius to Leon Uris.

This led to a desire to see and inspect the ground. It became so that much of the time they were free together was spent in these explorations. They began with the hill-top fortress of Herod at Masada where the zealots had killed each other rather than submit to Rome, and from there they moved off the tourist beat to the lesser-known historical sites.

In those long sunlit days they might eat their basket lunch sitting on the ruins of a Roman aqueduct and watching a falcon working the thermals that rose off the floor of the desert, after they had searched the bed of a dry wadi for coins and arrowheads brought down by the last ruins.

Around them rose the tall cliffs of orange and golden stone, and the light was so clean and stark that it seemed they could see for ever, and the silence so vast that they were the only living things in the world.

They were the happiest days that David had ever known, and they gave point and meaning to the weary hours of squadron standby, and when the day had ended there was always the house on Malik Street with its warmth and laughter and love.

Joe and David arranged leave of absence from the base for the wedding. It was a time of quiet, and le Dauphin let them go without protest, for he would be a guest.

They drove up to Jerusalem the day before and were immediately conscripted to assist with arrangements. David laboured mightily as a taxi-driver and trucker. The Mercedes transported everything from flowers to musical instruments and distant relatives.

The Brig's garden was decorated with palm leaves and coloured bunting. In the centre stood the *huppah*, a canopy worked with religious symbols in blue and gold, the Star of David and the grapes and ears of wheat, the pomegranates and all the other symbols of fertility. Beneath it, the marriage ceremony would take place. Trestle tables covered with gay cloths set with bowls of flowers and dishes of fruit were arranged beneath the olive trees. There were places for three hundred guests, an open space for the dancing, a raised timber stand hung with flags for the band.

The catering was contracted out to a professional firm and the menu had been carefully decided upon by the chef and the women. It would have two high points–an enormous stuffed tuna, again a symbol of fertility, and a lamb dish in the bedouin style served upon enormous copper salvers.

On the Sunday of the wedding, David drove Debra to the home of the chief surgeon of Hadassah Hospital. Hannah was one of his theatre sisters and he had insisted that she use his home to prepare for the wedding. Debra was to assist her, and David left them and drove on to Ein Karem. The lane leading to the house was cordoned off and thick with secret service men and paratroopers.

While he watched Joe dressing, losing and finding the ring, and sweating with nerves, David lay on Joe's bed and gave him bad advice. They could hear the guests gathering on the garden below, and David stood up and went to the window. He watched an airforce colonel being carefully scrutinized and searched at the gates, but taking it all in good part.

'They are being pretty thorough,' David remarked.

'Hannah has asked to have as few as possible of the guards in the garden. So they are being damned careful about who they let in.' Joe had at last completed dressing and already he was beginning to sweat through the armpits of his uniform.

'How do I look?' he asked anxiously.

'God, you handsome beast,' David told him.

'Piss off, Morgan,' Joe grinned at him, crammed his cap on to his head and glanced at his watch. 'Let's go,' he said.

The Chief Rabbi of the army was waiting with the Brig and the others in the Brig's study. The Rabbi was the mild-mannered man who had personally liberated the Tomb of the Patriarchs in the war of '67. During the advance on Hebron, he had driven a jeep through the disintegrating Arab lines, shot open the door to the tomb with a submachine-gun and chased the Arab guards screaming over the rear wall.

Joe sat at the Brig's desk and signed the *ketubbah*, the marriage contract, then the Rabbi handed him a silken cloth which Joe lifted in a formal act of acquisition to a chorus of congratulatory '*Mazal tovs*' from the witnesses.

The bridegroom's party trooped out into the crowded garden now to await the arrival of the bride, and she came accompanied by the chief surgeon standing in for her dead father, and a party of festively dressed women, including Debra and her mother. They all carried lighted candles.

To David, Hannah had never been particularly attractive, she was too tall and severe in body and expression; however, in her white bridal dress and veil she was transformed.

She seemed to float cloudlike upon the billowing white skirts, and her face was softened by the veil and by the inner happiness that seemed to glow through her green eyes. Red-gold hair framed her cheeks, and the freckles were disguised under make-up applied by Debra's cunning hand. She had used it to mute the rather harsh lines of Hannah's bony nose, and the result was as near to beautiful as she would ever come.

Joe, looking big and handsome in his airforce tans, went forward eagerly to meet her at the gate to the garden and to lower the veil over her face in the ceremony of *bedeken dikalle*.

Joe moved to the *chuppah* canopy where the Rabbi waited with a *tallit* over his shoulders. After Joe the women led Hannah, each of them still carrying a burning candle, and the Rabbi chanted a blessing as the women and the bride circled Joe seven times in a magical circle which in olden times would serve to ward off evil spirits. At last bride and groom stood side by side, facing towards the site of the Temple with the guests and witnesses pressed closely about them and the ceremony proper began.

The Rabbi spoke the benediction over a goblet of wine from which bride and groom both drank. Then Joe turned to Hannah, her face still veiled, and he placed the plain gold ring upon her right forefinger.

'Behold you are consecrated unto me by this ring, according to the law of Moses and Israel.'

Then Joe broke the glass under his heel and the sharp crunch was a signal for an outburst of music and song and gaiety. David left Joe's side and worked his way through the joyous crowd of guests to where Debra waited for him.

She wore a gown of yellow and she had fresh flowers in the dark sheen of her hair. David smelled their perfume as he hugged her surreptitiously about the waist and whispered in her ear, 'You next, my beauty!' and she whispered back, 'Yes, please!'

Joe took Hannah on his arm, and they went to the improvised dance floor. The band began with a light bouncy tune and all the younger ones flocked to join them–while the elders spread out at the tables beneath the palm-decked trellis.

Yet amongst all the laughter and the gaiety, the uniforms added a sombre touch; almost every second man was adorned with the trappings of war, and at the golden gate and the entrance to the kitchens were uniformed paratrooper guards each with a Uzzi submachine-gun slung at his shoulder. It was easy to pick out the secret service men. They were the ones in civilian clothes who moved without smiling, alert and vigilant, amongst the guests.

David and Debra danced together, and she was so light and warm and strong in his arms that when the band paused for breath he resented it. He led her to a quiet corner, and they stood together, discussing the other guests in the most disrespectful terms until Debra giggled at some particularly outrageous remark and struck his arm lightly.

'You are terrible.' She leaned against him. 'I'm dying of thirst, won't you get me something to drink?'

'A glass of cold white wine?' he suggested.

'Lovely,' she said, smiling up into his face. For a moment they studied each other, and suddenly David felt something dark welling up from within him, a terrible despair, a premonition of impending loss. It was a physical thing and he could feel the chill of it enclose his chest and squeeze out all the happiness and the joy.

'What is it, David?' Her own expression altered in sympathy with his, and she tightened her grip on his arm.

'Nothing.' Abruptly he pulled away from her, trying to fight off the feeling. 'It's nothing,' he repeated, but it was still strong in his belly, and he felt a wave of nausea from it. 'I'll get you the wine,' he said and turned away.

He made his way towards the bar, pushing gently through the throng. The Brig caught his eye and smiled bleakly across the garden at him. Joe was with his father and he called to David, laughing, with one arm around his bride. Hannah had her veil pushed up and her freckles were beginning to emerge from under the make-up, glowing vividly against the snow-white lace. David waved at them but went towards the open-air bar at the end of the garden, the mood of sadness was still on him and he didn't want to talk to Joe now.

So he was cut off from Debra at the moment when, with a flourish, a procession of white-jacketed waiters came in through the iron gate of the garden. Each of them carried a huge copper salver from which, even in the warm sun, rose tendrils of steam, and the odour of meat and fish and spices filled the garden. There were gasps and cries of appreciation from the guests.

A way opened for them towards the high table on the raised terrace which led to the kitchen doors and the house.

The procession of waiters passed close to David, and suddenly his attention was drawn from the display of fine food to the face of the second waiter in line. He was a man of medium height and dark complexion, a mahogany face with a thickly drooping moustache.

He was sweating. That was what had drawn David's attention, his face was shiny with sweat. Droplets clung in his moustache and slid down his cheeks. The white jacket was sodden at the armpits as he lifted the gigantic platter on high.

At the moment that he drew level with David their eyes met for an instant. David realized that the man was in the grip of some deep emotion–fear, perhaps, or exhilaration. Then the waiter seemed to become aware of David's scrutiny and his eyes slid nervously away.

David felt suspicion begin to chill his arms as the three figures climbed the stone stairs, and filed behind the table.

The waiter glanced again at David, saw that his gaze was still locked upon his face, and then he said something out of the corner of his mouth to one of his companions. He also glanced at David, and caught his stare, and his expression was sufficient to send alarm flaring urgently through David's chest and brain. Something was happening, something dangerous and ugly, he was certain of it.

Wildly he looked about for the guards. There were two of them on the terrace behind the line of waiters, and one near David beside the gate.

David shoved his way desperately towards him, mindless of the outraged comments of those in his way. He was watching the three waiters and so he saw it begin to happen.

It had obviously been carefully rehearsed for as the three waiters placed the salvers upon the table to the laughter and applause of the guests crowded in the garden below them, so they drew the sheets of plastic on which a thin display of food had been arranged to cover the deadly load that each copper salver carried.

The brown-faced waiter lifted a machine pistol from under the plastic sheet, and turned swiftly to fire a traversing burst into the two paratroopers behind him at point-blank range. The clattering thunder of automatic fire was deafening in the walled garden, and the stream of bullets slashed through the bellies of the two guards like a monstrous cleaver, almost cutting them in half.

The waiter on David's left was a wizened monkey-faced man, with bright black berries for eyes. He, too, lifted a machine pistol from his salver, and he crouched over it and fired a burst at the paratrooper by the gate.

They were going for the guards, taking them first. The pistol shook and roared in his fists, and the bullets socked into human flesh with a rubbery thumping sound.

The guard had cleared his Uzzi, and was trying to aim as a bullet hit him in the mouth and snapped his head back, his paratrooper beret spinning high into the air. The machine-gun flew from his arms as he fell, and it slid across the tiles towards David. David dropped flat below the stone steps of the terrace as the Arab gunner turned their pistols on the wedding crowd, hosing the courtyard with a triple stream of bullets, and unleashing a hurricane of screams and shouts and desperate cries to join the roar of the guns.

Across the yard, a security agent had the pistol out of his shoulder holster and he dropped into the marksman crouch, holding the pistol with both arms extended as he aimed. He fired twice and hit the monkey-faced gunman, sending him reeling back against the wall, but he stayed on his feet and returned the agent's fire with the machine pistol, knocking him down and rolling him across the paving stones.

The yard was filled with a panic-stricken mob, a struggling mass of humanity, that screamed and fell and crawled and died beneath the flail of the guns.

Two bullets caught Hannah in the chest, smashing her backwards over a table of glasses and bottles that shattered about her. The bright blood spurted from the wounds, drenching the front of her white wedding gown.

The centre gunman dropped his pistol as it emptied, and he stooped quickly over the copper salver and came up with a grenade in each hand. He hurled them into the struggling, screaming throng and the double blast was devastating, twin bursts of brightest white flame and the terrible sweep of shrapnel. The screams of the women rose louder, seeming as deafening as the gunfire–and the gunman stooped once more and his hands held another load of grenades.

All this had taken only seconds, but a fleeting moment of time to turn festivity into shocking carnage and torn flesh.

David left the shelter of the stone steps. He rolled swiftly across the flags towards the abandoned Uzzi, and he came up on his knees, holding it at the hip. His paratrooper training made his actions automatic.

The wounded gunman saw him, and turned towards him, staggering slightly, pushing himself weakly away from the wall. His one arm was shattered and hung loosely in the tattered, blood-soaked sleeve of his jacket, but he lifted the machine pistol and aimed at David.

David fired first, the bullets struck bursts of plaster from the wall behind the Arab and David corrected his aim. The bullets drove the gunman backwards, pinning him to the wall, while his body jumped and shook and twitched. He slumped down leaving a glistening wet smear of blood down the white plaster.

David swivelled the gun on to the Arab beside the kitchen door. He was poised to throw his next grenade, right arm extended behind him, both fists filled with the deadly steel balls. He was shouting something, a challenge or a war cry, a harsh triumphant screech that carried clearly above the screams of his victims.

Before he could release the grenade, David hit him with a full burst, a dozen bullets that smashed into his chest and belly, and the Arab dropped both grenades at his feet and doubled over clutching at his broken body, trying to stem the flood of his blood with his bare hands.

The grenades were short fused and they exploded almost immediately, engulfing the dying man in a net of fire and shredding his body from the waist down. The same explosion knocked down the third assassin at the end of the terrace, and David came to his feet and charged up the steps.

The third and last Arab was mortally wounded, his head and chest torn by grenade fragments, but he was still alive, thrashing about weakly as he groped for the machine pistol that lay beside him in a puddle of his own blood.

David was consumed by a terrible rage. He found that he was screaming and raging like a maniac, and he crouched at the head of the stairs and aimed at the dying Arab.

The Arab had the machine pistol and was lifting it with the grim concentration of a drunken man. David fired, a single shot that slapped into the Arab's body without apparent effect, and then suddenly the Uzzi in David's hands was empty, the pin falling with a hollow click on an empty chamber.

Across the terrace, beyond range of a quick rush, the Arab's face was streaked with sweat and blood as he frowned heavily, trying to aim the machine pistol as it wavered. He was dying swiftly, the flame fluttering towards extinction, but he was using the last of his strength.

David stood frozen with the empty weapon in his hand, and the blank eye of the pistol sought him out, and fastened upon him. He watched the Arab's eyes narrow, and his sudden murderous grin of achievement as he saw David in his sights, and his finger tightening on the trigger.

At that range the bullets would hit like the solid stream of a fire hose. He began to move, to throw himself down the stairs, but he knew it was too late. The Arab was at the instant of firing, and at the same instant a revolver shot crashed out at David's side.

Half the Arab's head was cut away by the heavy lead slug, and he was flung backwards with the yellow custard contents of his skull splattering the white-washed wall behind him, and his death grip on the trigger emptied the machine pistol with a shattering roar harmlessly into the grape vines above him.

Dazedly David turned to find the Brig beside him, the dead security guard's pistol in his fist. For a moment they stared at each other, and then the Brig stepped past him and walked to the fallen bodies of the other two Arabs. Standing over each in turn he fired a single pistol shot into their heads.

David turned away and let the Uzzi drop from his hands. He went down the stairs into the garden.

The dead and the wounded lay singly and in piles, pitiful fragments of humanity. The soft cries and the groans of the wounded, the bitter weeping of a child, the voice of a mother, were sounds more chilling than the screaming and the shouting.

The garden was drenched and painted with blood. There were splashes and gouts of it upon the white walls, there were puddles and snakes of it spreading and crawling across the paving, dark slicks of it sinking into the dust, ropes of it dribbling and pattering like rain from the body of a musician as he hung over the rail of the bandstand. The sickly sweetish reek of it mingled with the smell of spice food and spilled wine, with the floury taste of plaster dust and the bitter stench of burned explosive.

The veils of smoke and dust that still drifted across the garden could not hide the terrible carnage. The bark of the olive trees was torn in slabs from the trunks by flying steel, exposing the white wet wood. The wounded and dazed survivors crawled over a field of broken glass and shattered crockery. They swore and prayed, and whispered and groaned and called for succour.

David went down the steps, his feet moving without his bidding; his muscles were numb, his body senseless and only his finger-tips tingled with life.

Joe was standing below one of the torn olive trees. He stood like a colossus, with his thick powerful legs astride, his head thrown back and his face turned to the sky, but his eyes were tight-closed and his mouth formed a silent cry of agony–for he held Hannah's body in his arms.

Her bridal veil had fallen from her head, and the bright copper mane of her hair hung back–almost to the ground. Her legs and one arm hung loosely, also, slack and lifeless. The golden freckles stood out clearly on the milky-white skin of her face–and the bloody wounds bloomed like the petals of the poinsettia tree upon the bosom of her wedding-gown.

David averted his eyes. He could not watch Joe in his anguish, and he walked on slowly across the garden, in terrible dread of what he would find.

'Debra!' he tried to raise his voice, but it was a hoarse raven's croak. His feet slipped in a puddle of thick dark blood, and he stepped over the unconscious body of a woman who lay, face down, in a floral dress, with her arms thrown wide. He did not recognize her as Debra's mother.

'Debra!' He tried to hurry, but his legs would not respond. He saw her then, at the corner of the wall where he had left her.

'Debra!' He felt his heart soar. She seemed unhurt, kneeling below one of the marble Grecian statues, with the flowers in her hair and the yellow silk dress gay and festive.

She knelt, facing the wall, and her head was bowed as though in prayer. The dark wind of her hair hung forward screening her and she held her cupped hands to her face.

'Debra.' He dropped to his knees beside her, and timidly he touched her shoulder.

'Are you all right, my darling?' And she lowered her hands slowly, but still holding them cupped together. A great coldness closed around David's chest as he saw that her cupped hands were filled with blood. Rich red blood, bright as wine in a crystal glass.

'David,' she whispered, turning her face towards him. 'Is that you, darling?'

David gave a small breathless moan of agony as he saw her blood-glutted eye sockets, the dark gelatinous mess that congealed in the thick dark eyelashes and turned the lovely face into a gory mask.

'Is that you, David?' she asked again, her head cocked at a blind listening angle.

'Oh God, Debra.' He stared into her face.

'I can't see, David.' She groped for him. 'Oh David–I can't see.'

And he took her sticky wet hands in his, and he thought that his heart would break.

The stark modern silhouette of Hadassah Hospital stood upon the skyline above the village of Ein Karem. The speed with which the ambulances arrived saved many of the victims whose lives were critically balanced, and the hospital was geared to sudden influxes of war casualties.

The three men–the Brig, Joe and David–kept their vigil together all that night upon the hard wooden benches of the hospital waiting-room. When more was learned of the planning behind the attack, a security agent would come to whisper a report to the Brig.

One of the assassins was a long-term and trusted employee of the catering firm, and the other two were his 'cousins' who had been employed as temporary staff on his recommendation. It was certain that their papers were forged.

The Prime Minister and her cabinet had been delayed by an emergency session, but had been on their way to the wedding when the attack was made. A fortunate chance had saved them, and she sent her personal condolences to the relatives of the victims.

At ten o'clock, Damascus radio gave a report in which El Fatah claimed responsibility for the attack by members of a suicide squad.

A little before midnight, the chief surgeon came from the main theatre, still in his theatre greens and boots, with his mask pulled down to his throat. Ruth Mordecai was out of danger, he told the Brig. They had removed a bullet that had passed through her lung and lodged under her shoulder blade. They had saved the lung.

'Thank God,' murmured the Brig and closed his eyes for a moment, imagining life without his woman of twenty-five years. Then he looked up. 'My daughter?'

The surgeon shook his head. 'They are still working on her in the small casualty theatre.' He hesitated. 'Colonel Halman died in theatre a few minutes ago.'

The toll of the dead was eleven so far, with four others on the critical list.

In the early morning the undertakers arrived for the bodies with their long wicker baskets and black limousines. David gave Joe the keys of the Mercedes, that he might follow the hearse bearing Hannah's body and arrange the details of the funeral.

David and the Brig sat side by side, haggard and with sleepless bruised eyes, drinking coffee from paper cups.

In the late morning the eye surgeon came out to them. He was a smooth-faced, young-looking man in his forties, the greying of his hair seeming incongruous against the unlined skin and clear blue eyes.

'General Mordecai?'

The Brig rose stiffly. He seemed to have aged ten years during the night.

'I am Doctor Edelman. Will you come with me please?'

David rose to follow them, but the doctor paused and looked to the Brig.

'I am her fiancé,' said David.

'It might be best if we spoke alone first, General.' Edelman was clearly trying to pass a warning with his eyes, and the Brig nodded.

'Please, David.'

'But–' David began, and the Brig squeezed his shoulder briefly, the first gesture of affection that had ever passed between them.

'Please, my boy,' and David turned back to the hard bench.

In the tiny cubicle of his office Edelman hitched himself on to the corner of the desk and lit a cigarette. His hands were long and slim as a girl's, and he used the lighter with a surgeon's neat economical movements.

'You don't want it with a sugar coating, I imagine?' He had appraised the Brig carefully, and went on without waiting for a reply. 'Neither of your daughter's eyes are damaged,' but he held up a hand to forestall the rising expression of relief on the Brig's lips, and turned to the scanner on which hung a set of X-ray plates. He switched on the back light.

'The eyes were untouched, there is almost no damage to her facial features–however, the damage is here–' he touched a hard frosty outline in the smoky grey swirls and patterns of the X-ray plates, '–that is a steel fragment, a tiny steel fragment, almost certainly from a grenade. It is no larger than the tip of a lead pencil. It entered the skull through the outer edge of the right temple, severing the large vein which accounted for the profuse haemorrhage, and it travelled obliquely behind the eye-balls without touching them or any other vital tissue. Then, however, it pierced the bony surrounds of the optic chiasma,' he traced the path of the fragment through Debra's head,'and it seems to have cut through the canal and severed the chiasma, before lodging in the bone sponge beyond.' Edelman drew heavily on the cigarette while he looked for a reaction from the Brig. There was none.

'Do you understand the implications of this, General?' he asked, and the Brig shook his head wearily. The surgeon switched off the light of the X-ray scanner, and returned to the desk. He pulled a scrap pad towards the Brig and took a propelling pencil from his top pocket. Boldly he sketched an optical chart, eyeballs, brain, and optical nerves, as seen from above.

'The optical nerves, one from each eye, run back into this narrow tunnel of bone where they fuse, and then branch again to opposite lobes of the brain.'

The Brig nodded, and Edelman slashed the point of his pencil through the point where the nerves fused. Understanding began to show on the Brig's strained and tired features.

'Blind?' he asked, and Edelman nodded.

'Both eyes?'

'I'm afraid so.'

The Brig bowed his head and gently massaged his own eyes with thumb and forefinger. He spoke again without looking at Edelman.

'Permanently?' he asked.

'She has no recognition of shape, or colour, of light or darkness. The track of the fragment is through the optic chiasma. All indications are that the nerve is severed. There is no technique known to medical science which will restore that.' Edelman paused to draw breath, before going on. 'In a word then, your daughter is permanently and totally blinded in both eyes.'

The Brig sighed, and looked up slowly. 'Have you told her?' and Edelman could not hold his gaze.

'I was rather hoping that you would do that?'

'Yes,' the Brig nodded, 'it would be best that way. Can I see her now? Is she awake?'

'She is under light sedation. No pain, only a small amount of discomfort, the external wound is insignificant–and we shall not attempt to remove the metal fragment. That would entail major neurosurgery.' He stood up and indicated to the door. 'Yes, you may see her now. I will take you to her.'

The corridor outside the row of emergency theatres was lined along each wall with stretchers, and the Brig recognized many of his guests laid out upon them. He stopped briefly to speak with one or two of them, before following Edelman to the recovery room at the end of the corridor.

Debra lay on the tall bed below the window. She was very pale, dry blood was still clotted in her hair and a thick cotton wool and bandage covered her eyes.

'Your father is here, Miss Mordecai,' Edelman told her, and she rolled her head swiftly towards them.

'Daddy?'

'I am here, my child.'

The Brig took the hand she held out, and stooped to kiss her. Her lips were cold, and she smelled strongly of disinfectant and anaesthetic.

'Mama?' she asked anxiously.

'She is out of danger,' the Brig assured her, 'but Hannah–'

'Yes. They told me,' Debra stopped him, her voice choking. 'Is Joe all right?'

'He is strong,' the Brig said. 'He will be all right.'

'David?' she asked.

'He is here.'

Eagerly she struggled up on to one elbow, her face lighting with expectation, the heavily bound eyes turned blindly seeking.

'David,' she called, 'where are you? Damn this bandage. Don't worry, David it's just to rest my eyes.'

'No,' the Brig restrained her with a hand on her arm. 'He is outside, waiting,' and she slumped with disappointment.

'Ask him to come to me, please,' she whispered.

'Yes,' said the Brig, 'in a while, but first there is something we must talk about–something I have to tell you.'

She must have guessed what it was, she must have been warned by the tone of his voice for she went very still. That peculiar stillness of hers, like a frightened animal of the veld.

He was a soldier, with a soldier's blunt ways, and although he tried to soften it, yet even his tone was roughened with his own sorrow, so that it came out brutally. Her hand in his was the only indication that she had heard him, it spasmed convulsively like a wounded thing and then lay still, a small tense hand in the circle of his big bony fist.

She asked no questions and when he had done they sat quietly together for a long time. He spoke first.

'I will send David to you now,' he said, and her response was swift and vehement.

'No.' She gripped his hand hard. 'No, I can't meet him now. I have to think about this first.'

The Brig went back to the waiting-room and David stood up expectantly, the pure lines of his face seemingly carved from pale polished marble, and the dark blue of his eyes in deep contrast.

The Brig forestalled him harshly. 'No visitors.' He took David's arm. 'You will not be allowed to see her until tomorrow.'

'Is something wrong? What is it?' David tried to pull away, but the Brig held him and steered him towards the door.

'Nothing is wrong. She will be all right–but she must have no excitement now. You'll be able to see her tomorrow.'

They buried Hannah that evening in the family plot on the Mountain of Olives. It was a small funeral party attended by the three men and a mere handful of relatives, many of who, had others to mourn from the previous day's slaughter.

There was an official car waiting to take the Brig to a meeting of the high command, where retaliatory measures would certainly be discussed, another revolution in the relentless wheel of violence that rolled across the troubled land.

Joe and David climbed into the Mercedes and sat silently, David making no effort to start the engine, Joe lit cigarettes for them, and they both felt drained of purpose and direction.

'What are you going to do now?' David asked him.

'We had two weeks,' Joe answered him. 'We were going down to Ashkelon–' his voice trailed off. 'I don't know. There isn't anything to do now, is there?'

'Shall we go and have a drink somewhere?'

Joe shook his head. 'I don't feel like drinking,' he said. 'I think I'll go back to the base. They are flying night interceptions tonight.'

'Yes,' David agreed quickly, 'I'll come with you.' He could not see Debra until tomorrow, and the house on Malik Street would be lonely and cold. Suddenly he longed for the peace of the night heavens.

The moon was a brightly curved Saracen blade against the soft darkness of the sky, and the stars were fat and silver and gemlike in their clarity.

They flew high above the earth, remote from its grief and sorrow, wrapped in the isolation of flight and lost in the ritual and concentration of night interception.

The target was a Mirage of their own squadron, and they picked it up on the scanner far out over the Negev. Joe locked on to it and called the track and range while David searched for and at last spotted the moving star of the target's jet blast, burning redly against the velvety blackness of the night.

He took them in on a clean interception creeping up under the target's belly and then pulling steeply up past its wing-tip, the way a barracuda goes for the lure from below and explodes out through the surface of the sea. They shot past so close that the target Mirage broke wildly away to port, unaware of their presence until that moment.

Joe slept that night, exhausted with grief, but David lay in the bunk beneath him and listened to him. In the dawn he rose and showered and left Joe still asleep. He drove into Jerusalem and reached the hospital just as the sun came up and lit the hills with its rays of soft gold and pearly pink.

The night sister at the desk was brusque and preoccupied. 'You shouldn't be here until visiting hours this afternoon,' but David smiled at her with all the charm he could muster.

'I just wanted to know if she was doing well. I have to rejoin my squadron this morning.'

The sister was not immune either to his smile or the airforce uniform, and she went to consult her lists.

'You must be mistaken,' she said at last. 'The only Mordecai we have is Mrs Ruth Mordecai.'

'That's her mother,' David told her, and the sister flipped the sheet on her clipboard.

'No wonder I couldn't find it,' she muttered irritably. 'She was discharged last night.'

'Discharged?' David stared at her uncomprehendingly.

'Yes, she went home last night. I remember her now. Her father came to fetch her just as I came on duty. Pretty girl with eye bandages–'

'Yes,' David nodded. 'Thank you. Thank you very much,' and he ran down the steps to the Mercedes, his feet light with relief, freed at last from the gnawing doubt and dread.

Debra had gone home. Debra was safe and well.

The Brig opened the door to him, and let him into the silent house. He was still in his uniform, and it was wilted and rumpled. The Brig's face was fine-drawn, the lines crudely chiselled around his mouth, and his eyes were swollen and bloodshot from worry and sorrow and lack of sleep.

'Where is Debra?' David demanded eagerly, and the Brig sighed and stood aside for him to enter.

'Where is she?' David repeated, and the Brig led him to his study and waved him to a chair.

'Why don't you answer me?' David was becoming angry, and the Brig slumped into a chair across the large bare room, with its severe monastic furnishings of books and archaeological relics.

'I couldn't tell you yesterday, David, she asked me not to. I'm sorry.'

'What is it?' David was fully alarmed now.

'She had to have time to think–to make up her mind.' The Brig stood up again and began to pace, his footsteps echoing hollowly on the bare wooden floor, pausing every now and then to touch one of the pieces of ancient statuary, caressing it absently as he talked, as though to draw comfort from it.

David listened quietly, occasionally shaking his head, as though to deny that what he was hearing was the truth.

'So you see it is permanent, final, without hope. She is blind, David, totally blind. She has gone into a dark world of her own where nobody else can follow her.'

'Where is she? I want to go to her,' David whispered, but the Brig ignored the request and went on steadily.

'She wanted time to make her decision–and I gave it to her. Last night, after the funeral, I went back to her and she was ready. She had faced it, come to terms with it, and she had decided how it must be.'

'I want to see her,' David repeated. 'I want to talk to her.'

Now the Brig looked at him and the bleakness in his eyes faded, his voice dropped, becoming gruff with compassion.

'No, David. That was her decision. You will not see her again. For you she is dead. Those were her words. Tell him I am dead, but he must only remember me when I was alive–'

David interrupted him, jumping to his feet. 'Where is she, damn you?' His voice was shaking. 'I want to see her now.' He crossed swiftly to the door and jerked it open, but the Brig went on.

'She is not here.'

'Where is she?' David turned back.

'I cannot tell you, I swore a solemn oath to her.'

'I'll find her–'

'You might, if you search carefully–but you will forfeit any respect or love she may have for you,' the Brig went on remorselessly. 'Again I will give you her exact words. "Tell him that I charge him on our love, on all we have ever been to each other, that he will let me be, that he will not come looking for me."'

'Why, but why?' David demanded desperately. 'Why does she reject me?'

'She knows that she is altered beyond all hope or promise. She knows that what was before can never be again. She knows that she can never be to you again what you have a right to expect–' he stopped David's protest with an angry chopping gesture of his hand. 'Listen to me, she knows that it cannot endure. She can never be your wife now. You are too young, too vital, too arrogant–' David stared at him. '–she knows that it will begin to spoil. In a week, a month, a year perhaps, it will have died. You will be trapped, tied to a blind woman. She doesn't want that. She wants it to die now, swiftly–mercifully, not to drag on–'

'Stop it,' David shouted. 'Stop it, damn you. That's enough.' He stumbled to the chair and fell into it. They were silent for a while, David crouched in the chair with his face buried in his hands. The Brig standing before the narrow window casement, the early morning light catching the fierce old warrior's face.

'She asked me to make you promise–' he hesitated, and David looked up at him, '–to promise that you would not try to find her.'

'No.' David shook his head stubbornly.

The Brig sighed. 'If you refused, I was to tell you this–she said you would understand, although I don't–she said that in Africa there is a fierce and beautiful animal called the sable antelope, and sometimes one of them is wounded by a hunter or mauled by a lion.'

The words were as painful as the cut of a whiplash, and David remembered himself saying them to her once when they were both young and strong and invulnerable.

'Very well,' he murmured at last, 'if that's what she wants–then I promise not to try and find her, though I don't promise not to try and convince her she is wrong.'

'Perhaps it would be best if you left Israel,' the Brig told him. 'Perhaps you should go back to where you came from and forget all of this ever happened.'

David paused, considering this a moment, before he answered, 'No, all I have is here. I will stay here.'

'Good.' The Brig accepted the decision. 'You are always welcome in this house.'

'Thank you, sir,' said David and went out to where the Mercedes was parked. He let himself into the house on Malik Street, and saw instantly that someone had been there before him.

He walked slowly into the living-room; the books were gone from the olive-wood table, the Kadesh painting no longer hung over the leather couch. In the bathroom he opened the wall cabinet and all her toilet articles had been removed, the rows of exotic bottles, the tubes and pots, even the slot for her toothbrush beside his was empty.

Her cupboard was bare, the dresses gone, the shelves blank, every trace of her swept away, except the lingering scent of her perfume on the air, and the ivory lace cover upon the bed.

He went to the bed and sat upon it, stroking the fine lacework, remembering how it had been.

There was the hard outline of something thin and square upon the pillow, beneath the cover. He turned back the lace and picked up the thin green book.

This year, in Jerusalem. It had been left there as a parting gift.

The title swam and went misty before his eyes. It was all he had left of her.

It seemed as though the slaughter at Ein Karem was the signal for a fresh upsurge of hostility and violence throughout the Middle East. A planned escalation of international tensions, as the Arab nations rattled their impressive, oil-purchased, array of weaponry and swore once more to leave not a single Jew in the land they still called Palestine.

There were savage and merciless attacks on soft targets, ill-protected embassies and consulates around the world, letter bombs, and night ambushes on school buses in isolated areas.

Then the provocations grew bolder, more directly aimed at the heart of Israel. Border infringements, commando-style raids, violations of air space, shellings and a threatening gathering and massing of armed might along the long, vulnerable frontiers of the wedge-shaped territories of the tiny land.

The Israelis waited, praying for peace–but girt for war.

Day after day, month after month, David and Joe flew to maintain that degree of expertise, where instinct and instantaneous reaction superseded conscious thought and reasoned action.

At those searing speeds beyond sound, it was only this training that swung the advantage from one combat to another. Even the superior reaction times of these carefully hand-picked young men were unequal to the tasks of bringing their mighty machines into effective action, where latitudes of error were measured in hundredths of a second, until they had attained this extra-sensory perfection.

To seek out, to recognize, to close, to destroy, and to disengage–it was a total preoccupation that blessedly left little time for brooding and sorrow.

Yet the sorrow and anger, that David and Joe shared, seemed doubly to arm them. Their vengeance was all-consuming.

Soon they joined that select half-dozen strike teams that Desert Flower called to undertake the most delicate of sorties. Again and again they were ordered into combat, and each time the confidence that Command had in them was strengthened.

As David sat in his cockpit, dressed from head to foot in the stiff constricting embrace of a full-pressure suit, breathing oxygen from his closed face mask, although the Mirage still crouched upon the ground, there were four black, red and white miniature roundels painted on the fuselage below his cockpit. The scalps of the enemy.

It was a mark of Desert Flower's trust that Bright Lance flight had been selected for high altitude 'Red' standby. With the starter lines plugged ready to blow compressed air into the compressors and whirl the great engines into life, and the ground crew lounging beside the motors, the Mirages were ready to be hurled aloft in a manner of seconds. Both David and Joe were suited to survive the almost pressureless altitudes above sixty thousand feet where an unprotected man's blood would fizzle like champagne.

David had lost count of the weary uncomfortable days and hours he had sat cramped in his cockpit on 'Red' standby with only the regular fifteen-minute checks to break the monotony.

'Checking 11.15 hours–fifteen minutes to stand-down,' David said into the microphone, and heard Joe's breathing in his ears before the reply.

'Two standing by. Beseder.'

Immediately after stand-down, when another crew would assume the arduous waiting of standby, David would change into a track suit and run for five or six miles to get the stiffness out of his body and to have his sweat wash away the staleness. He was looking forward to that, afterwards he would–

There was a sharp crackle in his earphones and a new voice.

'Red standby–Go! Go!'

The command was repeated over loudspeakers in the underground bunker, and the ground crew boiled into action. With all his pre-flight checks and routine long ago completed, David merely pushed his throttle to starting position, and the whine of the starters showed immediate results. The engine caught and he ran up his power to one hundred per cent.

Ahead of him the blast doors were lifting.

'Bright Lance Two, this is leader going to take off power.'

'Two conforming,' said Joe and they went screaming up the ramp and hurled themselves at the sky.

'Hallo, Desert Flower, this is Bright Lance airborne and climbing.'

'Bright Lance, this is the Brig,' David was not surprised to find that he was in charge of command plot. Distinctive voices and the use of personal names would prevent any chance of the enemy confusing the net with false messages. 'David, we have an intruder approach at high level that should enter our air space in four minutes, if it continues on its present course. We are tracking him at seventy-five thousand feet which means it is either an American U.2, which is highly unlikely, or that it is a Russian spy plane coming over to have a look at our latest dispersals.'

'Beseder, sir,' David acked.

'We are going to try for a storm-climb to intercept as soon as the target becomes hostile in our air space.'

'Beseder, sir.'

'Level at twenty thousand feet, turn to 186 and go to maximum speed for storm-climb.'

At twenty thousand, David went to straight and level flight and glanced into his mirror to see Joe's Mirage hanging out on his tail.

'Bright Lance Two, this is leader. Commencing run now.'

'Two conforming.'

David lit his tail and pushed the throttle open to maximum afterburn position. The Mirage jumped away, and David let the nose drop slightly to allow the speed to build up quickly. They went blazing through the sound barrier without a check, and David retrimmed for supersonic flight, thumbing the little top-hat on the end of his stick.

Their speed rocketed swiftly through mach 1·2, mach 1·5.

Their Mirages were stripped of all their essentials, there were no missiles dangling beneath them, no auxiliary fuel tanks to create drag, the only weapons they carried were their two 30 mm. cannons.

Flying lightly, they drove on up the mach scale, streaking from Beersheba to Eilat in the time it would take a man to walk a city block. Their speed stabilized at mach 1·9, just short of the heat barrier.

'David, this is the Brig. We are tracking you. You are on correct course and speed for interception. Prepare to commence climb in sixteen seconds.'

'Beseder, sir.'

'Counting now. Eight, seven, six . . . two, one. Go! Go!'

David tensed his body and as he pulled up the nose of the Mirage, he opened his mouth and screamed to fight off the effects of gravity. But despite these precautions and the constricting grip of his pressure suit, the abrupt change of direction crammed him down into his seat and the blood drained out of his head so that his vision went grey and then black.

The Mirage was standing on her tail flying at very nearly twice the speed of sound and, as his vision returned, David glanced at the G-meter and saw that he had subjected his body to nearly nine times the force of gravity to achieve this attitude of climb without loss of speed.

Now he lay on his back and stared up at the empty sky while the needle of his altimeter raced upwards, and his speed gradually eroded away.

A quick sweep showed Joe's Mirage rock steady in position below him, climbing in concert with him, and his voice came through calm and reassuring.

'Leader, this is Two. I have contact with target.'

Even under the stress of storm-climb, Joe was busy manipulating his beloved radar, and he had picked up the spy plane high above them.

In this manœuvre they were trading speed for height, and as one increased so the other drained away.

They were like a pair of arrows aimed directly upwards. The bowstring could throw them just so far and then they would hang there in space for a few moments, until they were drawn irresistibly back to earth. In those few moments they must find and kill the enemy.

David lay back in his seat and watched with fresh wonder as the sky turned darker blue and then slowly became the midnight black of space, shot through with the fiery prickings of the stars.

They were at the top edge of the stratosphere, high above the highest clouds or signs of weather as known to earth. Outside the cockpit the air was thin and weak, insufficient for life, hardly sufficient to keep the jets of the Mirage's engines burning–and the cold was a fearsome sixty degrees of frost.

The two aircraft slowly ran out of energy, and they came out together at the top of a mighty parabola. The sensation of flight was gone, they swam through the dark forbidding oceans of space and far below them the earth glowed strangely, with a weird unnatural light.

There was no time to admire the view, the Mirage was wallowing in the thin and treacherous air, her control surfaces skidding and sliding without bite.

Joe was on the target, tracking quietly and steadily and they came round carefully on to the heading, with the aircraft staggering mushily and beginning to fall away from these inhospitable heights.

David stared ahead, holding the Mirage's nose up for sustained altitude but already the stall warning device was flicking amber and red at him. He was running out of time and height.

Then suddenly he saw it, seeming startlingly close in the rare air, ghosting along on its immense wings, like a black manta-ray through the sable and silent sea of space–ahead and slightly below them–calmly and silently, it drifted along, its height giving it a false sense of invulnerability.

'Desert Flower, this is Bright Lance visual on the intruder and requesting permission for strike.' David's cool tone hid the sudden gust of his anger and hatred that the sighting had released.

'Report your target,' the Brig was hedging, it was a dangerous decision to call the strike on an unknown target.

'Desert Flower, it's an Ilyushin Mark 17-11. No apparent markings.'

It needed no markings, it could only belong to one nation. David was closing fast, he could fly no slower than this, and he was rapidly overhauling the other machine. Those huge wings were designed to float upon the feeble air of the stratosphere.

'Closing fast,' he warned Desert Flower. 'Opportunity for strike will pass in approximately ten seconds.'

The silence in his headphones hummed quickly, and he readied his cannons and watched the spy plane blowing up rapidly in size as he dropped down upon it.

Suddenly the Brig made the decision, perhaps committing his country to heavy retaliation, but knowing that the spy plane's cameras were steadily recording vital details of their ability to resist aggression, information that would be passed quickly to their enemies.

'David,' his voice was curt and harsh, 'this is the Brig. Hit him!'

'Beseder.' David let the Mirage's nose drop a fraction, and she responded gratefully.

'Two, this is leader attacking.'

'Two conforming.'

He went down on the Ilyushin so fast, that as she came into his sights he knew he had time for only a few seconds of fire.

He pressed the trigger with the aiming pipper on the spy plane's wing roots, and he saw her rear up like a great fish struck by the steel of the harpoon.

For three seconds he poured his cannon shells into her, and watched them flash and twinkle against the massive black silhouette. Then he was through, falling away below the giant's belly, with his power spent, dropping away like the burned-out shell of a rocket.

Joe came down astern of him, backing up the attack, and in his sights the spy plane hung helplessly on its wide wings, its long rounded nose pointing to the black sky with its cold uncaring stars.

He pressed the trigger and the plane broke up amidst the bright flashes of exploding cannon shells. One wing snapped off at its root and the carcass began its long slow tumble down the heavens.

'Hello, Desert Flower, this is Bright Lance leader. Target destroyed.' David tried to keep his voice level, but he found his hands were trembling and his guts were aching cold from the spill-over of his hatred that not even the enemy's death could expunge.

Again he pressed the button to open the flight net. 'Joe, that's one more for

Hannah,' he said, but for once there was no reply, and after he had listened in vain to the throb of the carrier beam for a few seconds he closed it, and activated his doppler gear for a homing signal, and silently Joe followed him back to base.

Debra had been a steadying and maturing influence, but now David reacted so wildly to her going that Joe had to continue his role of wing man, even when they were off base.

They spent much of their leisure time together, for although they seldom mentioned their loss, yet the sharing of it drew them closer.

Often Joe slept over at Malik Street, for his own home was a sad and depressing place now. The Brig was seldom there in these troubled times, Debra gone and his mother was so altered by her terrible experience that she was grey and broken, aged beyond her years. The bullet wound in her body had closed, but there was other damage that would never heal.

David's wildness was a craving for the forgetfulness of constant action. He was only truly at peace when he was in the air, and on the ground he was restless and mercurial. Joe moved, big and calm beside him, steering him tactfully out of trouble with a slow grin and an easy word.

As a consequence of the downed spy plane, the Syrians began a policy of provocative patrols, calculated infringement of Israeli air space, which was discontinued as soon as retaliation was drawn. As the interceptors raced to engage they would swing away, declining combat, and move back within their own borders.

Twice David saw the greenish luminous blur of these hostile patrols on the screen of his scanning radar, and each time he had surprised himself with the icy feeling of anger and hatred that had lain heavy as a rock upon his heart and lungs as he led Joe in on the interception. Each time, however, the Syrians had been warned by their own radar and they had turned away, increasing speed, and withdrawn discreetly and mockingly.

'Bright Lance, this is Desert Flower. Target is no longer hostile. Discontinue attack pattern.' The Syrian MIG21's had crossed their own frontier, and each time David had answered quietly, 'Two, this is leader. Discontinuing attack pattern and resuming scan.'

The tactics were designed to wear on the nerves of the defenders, and in all the interceptor squadrons the tension was becoming explosive. The provocation was pushing them to the edge of restraint. Incidents were only narrowly being averted, as the hot-bloods crowded their interceptions to the very frontiers of war. Finally, however, there had to come intervention from above as Desert Flower tried to hold them on a tighter leash. They sent the Brig to talk to his crews and as he stood on the dais and looked about the crowded briefing room, he realized that it was unfair to train the hawk and then keep the hood over his eyes and the thong upon his leg, to hold him upon the wrist, when the wild duck were flighting overhead.

He started at a philosophical level, taking advantage of the regard that he knew his young pilots had for him.

'–the object of war is peace, the ultimate strategy of any commander is peace–' There was no response from his audience. The Brig caught the level scrutiny of his own son. How could he talk of placation to a trained warrior who had just buried the mutilated body of his bride? The Brig ploughed on manfully.

'Only a fool allows himself to be drawn on to a field of the enemy's choosing,' he was reaching them now, 'I won't have one of you young pups pushing us into something we are not ready for. I don't want to give them an excuse. That is what they want–' They were thawing now, he saw a head nod thoughtfully and heard a murmur of agreement.

'Any of you looking for big trouble, you don't have to go to Damascus, you know my address,' he tried for his first laugh, and got it. They were chuckling now. 'All right, then. We don't want trouble. We are going to lean right over backwards to prevent it–but we are not going to fall on our arses. When the time comes, I'll give you the word and it won't be the soft word, or the other cheek–' they growled then, a fierce little sound, and he ended it, '–but you wait for that word.'

Le Dauphin stood up and took over from the Brig.

'All right, while I've got you all together, I've a little news for you that may help to cool the hot-heads who want to follow the MIGS over the border.' He motioned to the projection box at the end of the briefing-room, the lights went down and there was a shuffling of feet, and an outburst of coughing. A voice protested resignedly.

'Not *another* film show!'

'Yes,' the colonel took it up. '*Another* film show.' Then as the images began to flash upon the screen he went on, 'This is a military intelligence film, and the subject is a new ground-to-air missile system that has been delivered by the Soviet Army to the armies of the Arab Union. The code name for the system is "Serpent" and it updates the existing "Sam III" system. As far as we know, the system has been installed and is operative in the Syrian defensive perimeter, and will shortly be installed by the Egyptians. It is manned at present by Russian instructors.' As the colonel went on talking, the Brig sat back in his chair and watched their faces in the silver reflection from the screen. They were intent and serious, men looking for the first time on the terrible machines that might be the instrument of their own deaths.

'The missile is fired from a tracked vehicle. Here you see aerial reconnaissance shots of a mobile column. Notice that each vehicle carries a pair of missiles, and you will realize that they constitute an enormous threat–'

The Brig picked out the marvellously pure profile of David Morgan as he leaned forward to study the screen, and he felt a pang of sympathy and sorrow for him–and yet this was underlined by a new respect, a realignment of judgement. The boy had proved himself to be constant, capable of embracing an ideal and remaining loyal to it.

'The improvements in design of the "Serpent" are not certain, but it is believed that the missile is capable of greater speeds, probably in the order of mach 2·5, and that the guidance system is a combination of both infra-red heat seeker and computerized radar control.'

Watching the handsome young face, he wondered if Debra had not misjudged his reserves. It was possible that he would have been capable of–no, the Brig shook his head and groped for a cigarette. He was too young, too greedy for life, spoiled by good looks and riches. He would not be capable of it. Debra was right, as so often was the case. She had chosen the correct course. She could never hold him, she must set him free.

'It is expected that the "Serpent" is capable of engaging targets at altitudes between 1,500 ft. and 75,000 ft.'

There was a stir amongst the listeners, as they assessed the threat of this new weapon.

'The warhead delivers a quarter of a ton of explosive and it is armed with a proximity fuse which is set to fire if the target is passed at range less than 150 feet. Within these limits the "Serpent" is lethal.'

The Brig was still watching David. Ruth and he had not seen the boy at their home for many months. He had come with Joe to spend the Sabbath evening with them twice after the outrage. However, the atmosphere had been stiff and artificial, everybody carefully avoiding mention of Debra's name. He had not come again after the second time, nearly six months ago.

'Evasive tactics at this stage will be the same as for "Sam III".'

'Prayer and good luck!' Someone interjected and that raised a laugh.

'–a maximum-rate turn towards the missile, to screen the radiation from your jet blasts, and attempt to force the "Serpent" to overshoot. In the event that the missile continues to track, you should climb into the sun and then make another maximum-rate turn. The missile may then accept the sun's infra-red radiation as a more tempting target–'

'And if that doesn't work?' a voice called, and another answered flippantly, 'Repeat the following: "Hear O Israel, the Lord our God, the Lord is one."' But this time nobody laughed at the old blasphemy.

The Brig timed his departure from the briefing room to fall in beside David.

'When are we going to see you, David? It's been a long time.'

'I'm sorry, sir. I hope Joe made my apologies.'

'Yes, of course. But why don't you come with Joe this evening? God knows, there will be enough food.'

'I'll be very busy tonight, sir,' David declined lamely.

'I understand.' And as they reached the door of the O.C.'s office the Brig paused, 'Remember you are always welcome,' and he turned away.

'Sir!' the Brig stopped and looked back at him. David spoke rapidly–almost guiltily.

'How is she, sir?' and then again, 'how is Debra? Have you seen her–I mean, recently?'

'She is well,' the Brig answered heavily. 'As well as she can be.'

'Will you tell her I asked?'

'No,' answered the Brig, ignoring the pleading in the dark blue eyes. 'No. You know I can't do that.'

David nodded and turned away. For a moment the Brig looked after him and then with a frown he went on into the colonel's office.

David dropped Joe in Ein Karem, at the entrance to the lane, and then he drove on into the main shopping area of East Jerusalem and parked outside the big new supermarket in Melech George V to do his shopping for the weekend ahead.

He was hanging over the freezer tray pondering the delicate choice between lamb cutlets and steak, when he became aware that he was being watched.

David looked up quickly and saw that she was a statuesque woman with a thick mane of blonde curls. She stood beside the shelves farther down the aisle. Her hair was dyed, he could see the dark shadow of the roots, and she was older than he was, with a womanly heaviness in her hips and bosom and tiny lines at the corners of her eyes. She was eyeing him, a steady appraisal so unashamedly sensual that he felt the check in his breathing and the quick stirring of his loins. He looked back at the meat in the freezer, guilty and angry with the treachery of his body. It had been so long, so very long since he had experienced sexual awareness. He had believed that he never would again. He wanted to throw the pack of steak back into the freezer and leave, but he stood rooted with the breathless feeling squeezing his lungs, and he was aware of the woman's presence at his side. He could feel the warmth of her on his arm, and smell her–the flowery perfume mingled with the natural musky odour of the sexually aroused female.

'The steak is very good,' she said. She had a light sweet voice and he recognized the same breathless quality as his own. He looked at her. Her eyes were green, and her teeth were a little crooked but white. She was even older than he had thought, almost forty. She wore her dress low in front, he could see the crêpe effect of the skin between her breasts. The breasts were big and motherly, and suddenly David wanted to lay his head against them. They looked so soft and warm and safe.

'You should cook it rare, with mushrooms and garlic and red wine,' she said. 'It's very good that way.'

'Is it?' he asked hoarsely.

'Yes,' she nodded, smiling. 'Who will cook it for you? Your wife? Your mother?'

'No,' said David. 'I will cook it myself. I live alone,' and she leaned a little closer to him, her breast touching his arm.

David was dizzy and hot with the brandy. He had bought a bottle of it at the supermarket, and he had drunk it mixed with ginger ale to mask the spiritous taste. He had drunk it fast, and now he leaned over the basin in the bathroom and felt the house rock and sway about him. He steadied himself, gripping the edge of the basin.

He splashed cold water on to his face and shook off the drops, then he grinned stupidly at himself in the mirror above the basin. His hair was damp and hung on to his forehead; he closed one eye and the wavering image in the mirror hardened and squinted back at him.

'Hi there, boy,' he muttered and reached for the towel. He had dripped water down his tunic and this annoyed him. He threw the towel over the toilet seat and went back into the living-room.

The woman was gone. The leather couch still carried the indentation of her backside, and the dirty plates were on the olive-wood table. The air was thick with cigarette smoke and her perfume.

'Where are you?' he called thickly, swaying slightly in the doorway.

'Here, big boy.' He went to the bedroom. She lay on the bed, naked, plump and white with huge soft breasts and swelling belly. He stared at her.

'Come on, Davey.' Her clothing was thrown across the dressing-table, and he saw that her corsets were grey and unwashed. Her hair was yellow against the soft ivory lacework.

'Come to Mama,' she whispered hoarsely, opening her limbs languidly in invitation. She was spread upon the brass bed, upon the lace cover which had been Debra's–and David felt his anger surge within him.

'Get up,' he said, slurring the words.

'Come on, baby.'

'Get off that bed,' his voice tightened and she heard the tone and sat up with mild alarm.

'What is it, Davey?'

'Get out of here,' his voice was rising sharply. 'Get out, you bitch. Get out of here!' He was shaking now, his face pale and his eyes savage blue.

Quivering with panic, she climbed hurriedly from the bed, the great white breasts and buttocks wobbling with ridiculous haste as she stuffed them into the grey corset.

When she had gone, David went through into the bedroom and vomited into the toilet bowl. Then he cleaned the house, scouring pans and plates, polishing the glasses until they shone, emptying the ashtrays, opening the shutters to blow out the stench of cigarette and perfume–and finally, going through into the bedroom, he stripped and remade the bed with fresh sheets and smoothed the lace cover carefully until not a crease or wrinkle showed.

He put on a clean tunic and his uniform cap, and drove to the Jaffa gate. He parked the car in the lot outside the gate and walked through the old city to the reconstructed sephardic synagogue in the Jewish quarter.

It was very quiet and peaceful in the high-domed hall and he sat a long time on the hard wooden bench.

Joe sat opposite David with a worried expression creasing his deep forehead as he studied the board. Three or four of the other pilots had hiked their chairs up and were concentrating on the game also. These chessboard conflicts between David and Joe were usually epics and attracted a partisan audience.

David had been stalking Joe's rook for half a dozen moves and now he had it trapped. Two more moves would shatter the kingsize defence, and the third must force a resignation. David grinned smugly as Joe reached a decision and moved a knight out.

'That's not going to save you, dear boy,' David hardly glanced at the knight, and he hit the rook with a white bishop. 'Mate in five,' he predicted, as he dropped the castle into the box, and then–too late–he realized that Joe's theatrical expression of anguish had slowly faded into a beatific grin. Joseph Mordecai used any deception to bait his traps, and David looked with alarm at the innocuous-seeming knight, suddenly seeing the devious plotting in which the castle was merely bait.

'Oh, you bastard,' David moaned. 'you sneaky bastard.'

'Check!' Joe gloated as he put the knight into a forked attack, and David had to leave his queen exposed to the horseman.

'Check,' said Joe again with an ecstatic little sigh as he lifted the white queen off the board, and again the harassed king took the only escape route open to him.

'And mate,' sighed Joe again as his own queen left the back file to join the attack. 'Not in five, as you predicted, but in three.' There was a loud outburst of congratulation and applause from the onlookers and Joe cocked an eye at David.

'Again?' he said, and David shook his head.

'Take on one of these other patsies,' he said. 'I'm going to sulk for an hour.' He vacated his seat and it was filled by another eager victim as Joe reset the board. David crossed to the coffee machine, moving awkwardly in the grip of his G-suit, and drew a mug of the thick black liquid, stirred in four spoons of sugar and found another seat in a quieter corner of the crewroom beside a slim curly-headed young kibbutznik, with whom David had become friendly. He was reading a thick novel.

'*Shalom*, Robert. How you been?'

Robert grunted without looking up from his book, and David sipped the sweet hot coffee. Beside him, Robert moved restlessly in his seat and coughed softly, David was lost in his own thoughts, for the first time in months thinking of home, wondering about Mitzi and Barney Venter, wondering if the yellowtail were running hot in False Bay this season, and remembering how the proteas looked upon the mountains of the Helderberg.

Again Robert stirred in his chair and cleared his throat. David glanced at him, realizing that he was in the grip of a deep emotion as he read, his lips quivering, and his eyes too bright.

'What you reading?' David was amused, and he leaned forward to read the title. The picture on the dust jacket of the book was instantly familiar. It was a deeply felt desert landscape of fierce colours and great space. Two distant figures, man and woman, walked hand in hand through the desert and the effect was mystic and haunting. David realized that only one person could have painted that–Ella Kadesh.

Robert lowered the book. 'This is uncanny,' his voice was muffled with emotion. 'I tell you, Davey, it's beautiful. It must be one of the most beautiful books ever written.'

With a strange feeling of pre-knowledge, with a sense of complete certainty, of what it would be, David took the book out of his hands and turned it to read the title, *A Place of Our Own*.

Robert was still talking. 'My sister made me read it. She works for the publisher. She cried all night when she read it. It is very new, only published last week, but it's got to be the biggest book ever written about this country.'

David hardly heard him, he was staring at the writer's name in small print below the title.

'Debra Mordecai.'

He ran his fingers lightly over the glossy paper of the jacket, stroking the name.

'I want to read it,' he said softly.

'I'll let you have it when I'm finished,' Robert promised.

'I want to read it now!'

'No way!' Robert exclaimed with evident alarm, and almost snatched the book out of David's hands.

'You wait your turn, comrade!'

David looked up. Joe was watching him from across the room, and David glared at him accusingly. Joe dropped his eyes quickly to the chessboard again, and David realized that he had known of the publication. He started up to go to him, to challenge him, but at that moment the tannoy echoed through the bunker.

'All flights Lance Squadron to "Red" standby,' and on the readiness board the red lamps lit beside the flight designations.

'Bright Lance.'

'Red Lance.'

'Fire Lance.'

David snatched up his flying helmet and joined the lumbering rush of G-suited bodies for the electric personnel carrier in the concrete tunnel outside the crew-room door. He forced a place for himself beside Joe.

'Why didn't you tell me?' he demanded.

'I was going to, Davey. I really was.'

'Yeah, I bet,' David snapped sarcastically. 'Have you read it?'

Joe nodded, and David went on, 'What's it about?'

'I couldn't begin to tell you. You'd have to read it yourself.'

'Don't worry about that,' David muttered grimly, 'I will,' and he jumped down as they reached their hangar and strode across to his Mirage.

Twenty minutes later they were airborne and Desert Flower sent them hastening out over the Mediterranean at interception speed to answer a Mayday call from an El Al Caravelle who reported that she was being buzzed by an Egyptian MIG 21 J.

The Egyptian sheered off and raced for the coast and the protection of his own missile batteries as the Mirages approached. They let him go and picked up the airliner. They escorted her into the circuit over Lod before returning to base.

Still in his G-suit and overalls, David stopped off at le Dauphin's office and got himself a twenty-four-hour pass.

Ten minutes before closing time he ran into one of the bookstores in Jaffa Road.

There was a pyramid display of *A Place of Our Own* on the table in the centre of the store.

'It's a beautiful book,' said the salesgirl as she wrapped it.

He opened a Goldstar, and he kicked off his shoes before stretching out on the lace cover of the bed.

He began to read, and paused only once to switch on the overhead lights and fetch another beer. It was a thick book, and he read slowly–savouring every word, sometimes going back to re-read a paragraph.

It was their story, his and Debra's, woven into the plot she had described to him that day on the island off the Costa Brava, and it was rich with the feeling of the land and its people. He recognized many of the secondary characters, and he laughed aloud with the pleasure and the joy of it. Then at the end, he choked on the sadness as the girl of the story lies dying in Hadassah Hospital, with half her face torn away by a terrorist's bomb, and she will not let the boy come to her. Wanting to spare him that, wanting him to remember her as she was.

It was dawn then, and David had not noticed the passage of the night. He rose from the bed, light-headed from lack of sleep, and filled with a sense of wonder that Debra had captured so clearly the way it had been–that she had seen so deeply into his soul, had described emotions for which he had believed there were no words.

He bathed and shaved and dressed in casual clothes and went back to where the book lay upon the bed. He studied the jacket again, and then turned to the flyleaf for confirmation. It was there. 'Jacket design by Ella Kadesh.'

So early in the morning he had the road almost to himself and he drove fast, into the rising morning sun. At Jericho he turned north along the frontier road, and he remembered her sitting in the seat beside him with her skirts drawn high around her long brown legs and her thick dark hair shaking in the wind.

The whisper of the wind against the body of the Mercedes seemed to urge him, 'Hurry, hurry.' And the urgent drumming of the tyres carried him up towards the lake.

He parked the Mercedes beside the ancient crusader wall and went through into the garden on the lake shore.

Ella sat upon the wide patio before her easel. She wore a huge straw hat the size of a wagon wheel adorned with plastic cherries and ostrich feathers, her vast overalls covered her like a circus tent and they were stiff with dried paint in all her typically vivid colours.

Calmly she looked up from her painting with her brush poised.

'Hail, young Mars!' she greeted him. 'Well met indeed, and why do you bring such honour on my humble little home?'

'Piss on it, Ella, you know damn well why I'm here.'

'So sweetly phrased,' she was shifty, he could see it on her bright little eyes. 'Shame on it that such vulgar words pass such fair lips. Would you like a beer, Davey?'

'No, I don't want a beer. I want to know where she is?'

'Just who are we discussing?'

'Come on, I read the book. I saw the cover. You know, damn you, you know.'

She was silent then staring at him. Then slowly the ornate head-dress dipped in acquiescence.

'Yes,' she agreed. 'I know.'

'Tell me where she is.'

'I can't do that, Davey. You and I both made a promise. Yes, I know of yours, you see.'

She watched the bluster go out of him. The fine young body with the arrogant set of shoulders seemed to sag, and he stood uncertainly in the sunlight.

'How about that beer now, Davey?' She heaved herself up from her stool and crossed the terrace with her stately tread. She came back and gave him a tall glass with a head of froth and they took a seat together at the end of the terrace out of the wind, in the mild winter sunlight.

'I've been expecting you for a week now,' she told him. 'Ever since the book was published. I knew it would set you on fire. It's just too damned explosive–even I wept like a leaky faucet for a couple of days,' she giggled shyly. 'You'd hardly believe it possible, would you?'

'That book was us–Debra and me,' David told her. 'She was writing about us.'

'Yes,' Ella agreed, 'but it does not alter the decision she has made. A decision which I think is correct, by the way.'

'She described exactly how I felt, Ella. All the things I felt and still feel–but which I could never have put into words.'

'It's beautiful and it's true, but don't you see that it confirms her position.'

'But I love her, Ella–and she loves me,' he cried out violently.

'She wants it to stay that way. She doesn't want it to die, she doesn't want it to sicken.' He began to protest, but she gripped his arm in a surprisingly powerful grip to silence him. 'She knows that she can never keep pace with you now. Look at you, David, you are beautiful and vital and swift–she must drag you back, and in time you must as certainly resent it.'

Again he tried to interrupt, but she shook his arm in her huge fist. 'You would be shackled, you could never leave her, she is helpless, she would be your charge for all your life–think on it, David.'

'I want her,' he muttered stubbornly. 'I had nothing before I met her, and I have nothing now.'

'That will change. Perhaps she has taught you something and young emotions heal as swiftly as young flesh. She wants happiness for you, David. She loves you so much that her gift to you is freedom. She loves you so much that for your sake she will deny that love.'

'Oh, God,' he groaned. 'If only I could see her, if I could touch her and talk to her for a few minutes.'

She shook her massive head, and her jowls wobbled dolefully.

'She would not agree to that.'

'Why, Ella, tell me why?' His voice was rising again, desperate with his anguish.

'She is not strong enough, she knows that if you came near her, she would waver and bring even greater disaster upon you both.'

They sat silently together then and looked out across the lake. High mountains of cloud rose up beyond the heights of Golan, brilliant white in the winter sunlight, shaded with blue and bruised grey, and range upon range they bore down upon the lake. David shivered as an icy little wind came ferreting across the terrace and sought them out.

He drank the rest of his beer, and then revolved the glass slowly through his fingers.

'Will you give her a message from me, then?' he asked.

'I don't think–'

'Please, Ella. Just one message.'

She nodded.

'Tell her that what she wrote in the book is exactly how much I love her. Tell her that it is big enough to rise above this thing. Tell her that I want the chance to try.'

She listened quietly, and David made a groping gesture with his hands as though to pluck words from the air that might convince her.

'Tell her–' he paused, then shook his head. 'No, that's all. Just tell her that I love her, and want to be with her.'

'All right, David. I'll tell her.'

'And you will give me her answer?'

'Where can I reach you?'

He gave her the number of the telephone in the crew ready room at the base.

'You'll ring me soon, Ella? Don't keep me waiting.'

'Tomorrow,' she promised. 'In the morning.'

'Before ten o'clock. It must be before ten.'

He stood up, and then suddenly he leaned forward and kissed her sagging and raddled cheek.

'Thank you,' he said. 'You are not a bad old bag.'

'Away with you, you and your blarney. You'd have the sirens of the Odyssey themselves come arunning to your bidding.' She sniffed moistly. 'Get away with you now, I think I'm going to cry, and I want to be alone to enjoy it.'

She watched him go up across the lawns under the date palms and at the gate in the wall he paused and looked back. For a second they stared at each other and then he stepped through the gate.

She heard the engine of the Mercedes whirr and pull away slowly up the track, then the note of it rose as it hit the highway and went racing away southwards. Ella rose heavily and crossed the terrace, went down the steps towards the jetty and its stone boathouses screened from the house by part of the ancient wall.

Her speedboat rode at its mooring, restless in the wind and the chop of the lake. She went on down to the farthest and largest of the boathouses and stood in the open doorway.

The interior had been stripped and repainted with clean white. The furniture was simple and functional. The rugs on the stone floor were for warmth, plain woven wool, thick and rough. The large bed was built into a curtained alcove in the wall beside the fireplace.

On the opposite wall was a gas stove with a double cooking ring above which a nunber of copper cooking pots hung. A door beyond led through to a bathroom and toilet which Ella had added very recently.

The only decoration was the Ella Kadesh painting from the house on Malik Street, which hung on the bare white wall, facing the door. It seemed to lighten and warm the whole room; below it the girl sat at a working table. She was listening intently to her own voice speaking in Hebrew from the tape recorder. Her expression was rapt and intent, and she stared at the blank wall before her.

Then she nodded her head, smiling at what she had just heard. She switched off the recorder and turned in the swivel chair to the second recorder and punched the transmit button. She held the microphone close to her lips as she began to translate the Hebrew into English.

Ella stood in the doorway and watched her work. An American publisher had purchased the English-language rights of *A Place of Our Own*. They had paid Debra an advance of thirty thousand American dollars for the book, and an additional five thousand for her services as translator. She had almost completed the task now.

From where she stood, Ella could see the scar on Debra's temple. It was glazed pinkish white against the deeply tanned skin of her face, a dimple like a child's drawing of a seagull in flight; V-shaped and no bigger than a snowflake, it seemed to enhance her fine looks, almost like a beauty spot, a tiny blemish that gave a focus point for her strong regular features.

She had made no attempt to conceal it for her dark hair was drawn back to the nape of her neck and secured there with a leather thong. She wore no make-up, and her skin looked clean and glowing, tanned and smooth.

Despite the bulky fisherman's jersey and woollen slacks her body appeared firm and slim for she swam each day, even when the snow winds came down from the north.

Ella left the doorway and moved silently closer to the desk, studying Debra's eyes as she so often did. One day she would paint that expression. There was no hint of the damage that lay behind, no hint that the eyes could not see. Rather their calm level gaze seemed to penetrate deeper, to see all. They had a serenity that was almost mystic, a depth and understanding that Ella found strangely disquieting.

Debra pressed the switch of the microphone, ending the recording, and then she spoke again without turning her head.

'Is that you, Ella?'

'How do you do it?' Ella demanded with astonishment.

'I felt the air move when you walked in, and then I smelt you.'

'I'm big enough to blow up a storm, but do I smell so bad?' Ella protested, chuckling.

'You smell of turpentine, and garlic and beer,' Debra sniffed, and laughed with her.

'I've been painting, and I was chopping garlic for the roast, and I was drinking beer with a friend.' Ella dropped into one of the chairs. 'How does it go with the book?'

'Nearly finished. It can go to the typist tomorrow. Do you want some coffee?' Debra stood up and crossed to the gas stove. Ella knew better than to offer her help, even though she gritted her teeth every time she watched Debra working with fire and boiling water. The girl was fiercely independent, utterly determined to live her life without other people's pity or assistance.

The room was laid out precisely, each item in its place where Debra could put her hand to it without hesitation. She could move confidently through her little world, doing her own house-work, preparing her own food and drink, working steadily, and paying her own way.

Once a week, a driver came up from her publisher's office in Jerusalem to collect her tapes and her writing was typed out along with her other correspondence.

Weekly also she would go with Ella in the speedboat up the lake to Tiberias to do their shopping together, and each day she swam for an hour from the stone jetty. Often an old fisherman with whom she had become friendly would row down the lake to fetch her and she would go out with him, baiting her own lines and taking her turn at the oars.

Across the lawns from the jetty, in the crusader castle, there was always Ella's companionship and intelligent conversation–and here in her little cottage there was quietness and safety and work to fill the long hours. And in the night there was the chill of terrible aloneness and silent bitter tears into her solitary pillow, tears which only she knew about.

Debra placed a mug of coffee beside Ella's chair and carried her own back to her work bench.

'Now,' she said, 'you can tell me what is keeping you fidgeting around in your seat, and drumming your fingers on the arm of the chair,' she smiled towards Ella, sensing the surprise. 'You have got something to tell me, and it's killing you.'

'Yes,' Ella spoke after a moment. 'Yes, you are right, my dear.' She took a deep breath and then went on. 'He came, Debra. He came to see me, as we knew he must.'

Debra set the mug down on the table, her hand was steady and her face expressionless.

'I didn't tell him where you were.'

'How is he, Ella? How does he look?'

'He is thinner, a little thinner, I think, and paler than when I last saw him, but it suits him. He is still the most beautiful man I have ever seen.'

'His hair,' Debra asked, 'has he let it grow a little?'

'Yes, I think so. It's soft and dark and thick around his ears and curly down the back.'

Debra nodded, smiling. 'I'm glad he didn't cut it.' They were silent again, and then almost timidly Debra asked, 'What did he say? What did he want?'

'He had a message for you.'

'What was it?'

And Ella repeated it faithfully in his exact words. When she had finished, Debra turned away to face the wall above her desk.

'Please go away now, Ella. I want to be alone.'

'He asked me to give him your reply. I promised to speak to him tomorrow morning.'

'I will come to you later–but please leave me now.' And Ella saw the drop of bright liquid that slid down the smooth brown curve of her cheek.

Mountainously Ella came to her feet and moved towards the door. Behind her she heard the girl sob, but she did not turn back. She went across the stone jetty and up to the terrace. She sat before her canvas and picked up her brush and began to paint. Her strokes were broad and crude and angry.

David was sweating in the stiff shiny skin of his full pressure suit and he waited anxiously beside the telephone, glancing every few minutes at the crew-room clock.

He and Joe would go on high-altitude 'Red' standby at ten o'clock, in seven minutes' time, and Ella had not called him.

David's depression was thunderous and there was black anger and despair in his heart. She had promised to call before ten o'clock.

'Come on, Davey,' Joe called from the doorway and he stood up heavily and followed Joe to the electric carrier. As he took his seat beside Joe he heard it ring in the crew-room.

'Hold it,' he told the driver, and he saw Robert answer the telephone and wave through the glass panel at him.

'It's for you, Davey,' and he ran back into the crew-room.

'I'm sorry, David,' Ella's voice was scratchy and far away. 'I tried earlier but the exchange here–'

'Sure, sure,' David cut her short, his anger was still strong. 'Did you speak to her?'

'Yes, Davey. Yes, I did. I gave her your message.'

'What was her reply?' he demanded.

'There was no reply.'

'What the hell, Ella. She must have said something.'

'She said–' Ella hesitated, '–and these are her exact words–"the dead cannot speak with the living. For David, I died a year ago."'

He held the receiver with both hands but still it shook. After a while she spoke again.

'Are you still there?'

'Yes,' he whispered, 'I'm still here.'

They were silent again, but David broke it at last.

'That's it, then,' he said.

'Yes. I'm afraid that's it, Davey.'

Joe stuck his head around the door.

'Hey, Davey. Cut it short, will you. Time to go.'

'I have to go now, Ella. Thanks for everything.'

'Goodbye, David,' she said, and even over the scratchy connection he could hear the compassion in her tone. It heightened the black anger that gripped him as he rode beside Joe to the Mirage bunker.

For the first time ever, David felt uncomfortable in the cockpit of a Mirage. He felt trapped and restless, sweating and angry, and it seemed hours between each of the fifteen-minute readiness checks.

His ground crew were playing back-gammon on the concrete floor below him, and he could see them laughing and joshing each other. It made him angrier than ever to see others happy.

'Tubby!' he barked in to the microphone, and his voice was repeated by the overhead loudspeakers. The plump, serious young man, who was chief engineer for Lance squadron, climbed quickly up beside his cockpit and peered anxiously through the canopy at him.

'There is dirt on my screen,' David snapped at him. 'How the hell do you expect me to pick up a MIG, when I'm looking through a screen you ate your bloody breakfast off?'

The cause of David's distress was a speck of carbon that marred the glistening perfection of his canopy. Tubby himself had supervised the polishing and buffing of it, and the carbon speck was wind-carried since then. Carefully he removed the offending spot, and lovingly he polished the place where it had been with a chamois leather.

The reprimand had been public and unfair, very unlike their top boy Davey. However, they all made allowances for 'Red' standby nerves–and spots on a canopy played hell with a pilot's nerves. Every time it caught his eye it looked exactly like a pouncing MIG.

'That's better,' David gruffed at him, fully aware that he had been grossly unfair. Tubby grinned and gave a high sign as he climbed down.

At that moment there was a click and throb in his earphones and the distinctive voice of the Brig.

'"Red" standby–Go! Go!'

Under full reheat and with the driving thrust of the after-burners hurling him aloft David called, 'Hello, Desert Flower, Bright Lance airborne and climbing.'

'Hello, David, this is the Brig. We have a contact shaping up for intrusion on our air space. It looks like another teaser from the Syrians. They are closing our border at twenty-six thousand and should be hostile in approximately three minutes. We are going to initiate attack plan Gideon. Your new heading is 42° and I want you right down on the deck.'

David acked and immediately rotated the Mirage's nose downwards. Plan Gideon called for a low-level stalk so that the ground clutter would obscure the enemy radar and conceal their approach until such time as they were in position to storm-climb up into an attack vector above and behind the target.

They dropped to within feet of the ground, lifting and falling over the undulating hills, so low that the herds of black Persian sheep scattered beneath them as they shrieked eastwards towards the Jordan.

'Hello, Bright Lance, this is Desert Flower–we are not tracking you.' Good, thought David, then neither is the enemy. 'Target is now hostile in sector'–the Brig gave the co-ordinates–'Scan for your own contact.'

Almost immediately Joe's voice came in. 'Leader, this is Two. I have a contact.'

David dropped his eyes to his own radar screen and manipulated his scan as Joe called range and bearing. It was a dangerous distraction when flying in the sticky phase of high subsonic drag at zero feet, and his own screen was clear of contact.

They raced onwards for many more seconds before David picked up the faint luminous fuzz at the extreme range of his set.

'Contact firming. Range figures nine six nautical miles. Parallel heading and track. Altitude 25,500 feet.'

David felt the first familiar tingle and slither of his anger and hatred, like the cold of a great snake uncoiling in his belly.

'Beseder, Two. Lock to target and go to interception speed.'

They went supersonic and David looked up ahead at the crests of the thunderheads that reared up from the solid banks of cumulo nimbus lower down. These mountainous upthrusts of silver and pale blue were sculptured into wonderful shapes that teased the imagination–towers and turrets embattled and emblazoned, heroic human shapes standing proud or hunched in the attitude of mourning, the rearing horsemen of the chess-board, a great fleecy pack of wolves, and other animal shapes of fantasy–with the deep crevasses between them bridged in splendour by the rainbows. There were hundreds of these, great blazes of colour, that turned and followed their progress across the sky, keeping majestic station upon them. Above them, the sky was a dark unnatural blue, dappled like a Windsor grey by the thin striation of the cirro cumulus, and the sunlight poured down to shimmer upon the two speeding warplanes. As yet there was no sight of the target. It was up there somewhere amongst the cloud mountains. He looked back at his radar screen. He had taken his radar out of scan and locked it into the target, and now as they closed rapidly he could appraise their relative positions.

The target was flying parallel to them, twenty miles out on their starboard side, and it was high above them and moving at a little more than half their speed. The sun was beyond the target, just short of its zenith, and David calculated his approach path to bring him into an attack vector from above and into the target's starboard quarter.

'Turning to starboard now,' he warned Joe, and they came around together, crossing the target's rear to put themselves in the sun. Joe was calling the range and bearing, it showed a leisurely patrol pattern. There was no indication as yet that the target was aware of the hunters behind and far below.

'Two, this is leader. Arm your circuits.'

Without taking his eyes from the radar screen, David pressed the master switch on his weapon console. He activated the two air-to-air sidewinder missiles that hung under each wing-tip, and immediately heard the soft electronic tone cycling in his earphones. That tone indicated that the missiles were dormant, they had not yet detected an infra-red source to excite them. When they did they would increase the volume and rate of cycle, growling with anticipation, clamouring like hunting dogs on the leash. He tuned them down so he could no longer hear them.

Now he selected his cannon switch, readying the twin 30-mm. weapons in their pods just below his seat. The trigger flicked forward out of its recess in the head of the joystick and he curled his forefinger about it to familiarize himself with the feel of it.

'Two, this is leader. I am commencing visual.' It was a warning to Joe to concentrate all his attention on the screen and feed David with directional data.

'Target is now ten o'clock high, range figures two seven nautical miles.'

David searched carefully, raking the billowing walls of blinding white, breaking off the search to look away at a ground point or a pinnacle of cloud to prevent his eyes focusing short, and to sweep the blind spot behind them, lest the hunters become the hunted.

Then he saw them. There were five of them, and they appeared suddenly out of cloud high above and were immediately outlined against it like tiny black fleas on a newly ironed bedsheet. Just then Joe called the range again.

'Figures one three nautical miles,' but the targets were outlined so crisply against their background that David could make out the delta-winged dart shape, and the high tailplane that identified them beyond all doubt as MIG 21 J.

'I have target visual,' he told Joe. 'Five MIG 21's J.' His tone was flat and neutral, but it was a lie, for now at last his anger had something on which to fasten, and it changed its shape and colour, it was no longer black and aching but cold and bright and keen as a rapier's blade.

'Target is still hostile,' Joe confirmed that they were within Israeli territory, but his tone was not as well guarded as David's. David could detect the huskiness in it, and knew that Joe was feeling that anger also.

It would be another fifteen seconds before they had completed their turn across the enemy's stern, and David assessed the relative positions and saw that so far it had been a perfect approach. The formation sailed on serenely, unaware of the enemy beneath their tail, creeping up in the blind spot where the forward scanning radar could not discover them and rapidly moving into a position up sun. Once there, David would go to attack speed and climb steeply up into a position of superior height and tactical advantage over the enemy formation. Looking ahead now, he realized that chance had given him an added bonus; one of the huge tower blocks of cloud was perfectly placed to screen his climb into the sun. He would use it to cover his stalk, the way the Boer huntsman of Africa stalked wild buffalo from behind a herd of domestic oxen.

'Target is altering course to starboard,' Joe warned him. The MIGS were turning away, edging back towards the Syrian border. They had completed their taunting gesture, they had flaunted the colours of Islam in the face of the infidel, and were making for safety.

David felt the blade of anger in his guts burn colder, sting sharper, and with an effort of restraint he waited out the last few seconds before making his climb. The moment came and his voice was still flat and without passion as he called to Joe, 'Two, this is leader, commencing storm-climb.'

'Two conforming.'

David eased back on the controls and they went up in a climb so vicious that it seemed to tear their bowels from their bellies.

Almost immediately, Desert Flower picked up the radar images as they emerged from the ground clutter.

'Hullo both units Bright Lance. We are now tracking you. Show friend or foe.'

Both David and Joe were lying on their backs in the thrust of storm-climb, but at the order they punched in the I.F.F. systems. Identification Friend or Foe would show a distinctive pattern, a bright halo, around their radar images on command plot identifying them positively even while they were locked with the enemy in the close proximity of the dogfight.

'Beseder–we are tracking you in I.F.F.,' said the Brig, and they went plunging into the pillar of cloud and raked upwards through it. David's eyes darted between the boulé that contained his blind-flying instruments and the radar screen on which the enemy images shone bright and with hard outline, so close now that the individual aircraft in the enemy formation stood out clearly.

'Target is increasing speed and tightening starboard turn,' Joe intoned and David compensated for the enemy's manœuvre.

David was certain that they had not detected his approach, the turn away was coincidental. Another glance at the screen showed that he had achieved his height advantage. He was now two miles off their quarter above them, with the sun at his back. It was the ideal approach.

'Turning now into final leg of attack pattern,' he alerted Joe to his intention and they began the pitch in. The last-second strike which would send their speed rocketing as they closed.

The target centred dead ahead, and the gunsight lit up, glowing softly on the screen ahead of him. The sidewinder missiles caught the first faint emanations of infra-red rays from their victims, and they began to growl softly in David's earphones.

Still blinded by thick grey cloud they raced in, and suddenly they burst out into the clear. Ahead and below them opened a deep trough of space, a valley between cloud ranges and close below them the five MIGS sparkled silvery in the sunlight, pretty and toylike, their red, white and green markings festive and gay, the clean geometrical sweeps of wing and tail nicely balanced and the shark-like mouths of the jet intakes gaping, as they sucked in air.

They were in loose V-formation, two stacked back on each flank of the leader and in the fleeting seconds that David had to study them, he had assessed them. The four wingmen were Syrians, there was an indefinable sloppiness in their flying, a looseness of control. They flew with that lack of polish and confidence of the pupil. They were soft targets, easy pickings.

However, it did not need the three red rings about the leader's fuselage to identify him as a Russian instructor. Some leery old veteran with hawk's blood in his veins, tough and canny, and dangerous as an angry black mamba.

'Engage two port targets,' David ordered Joe, reserving the MIG leader and the starboard echelon for his attack. In David's headphones the missiles were growling their anxiety, they had sniffed out the massed jet blasts below them and already they were tracking, howling their eagerness to kill.

David switched to command net. 'Hello, Desert Flower, this is Bright Lance on target and requesting strike.'

Almost instantly the voice came back. 'David, this is the Brig–' he was speaking rapidly, urgently, '–discontinue attack pattern. I repeat, disengage target. They are no longer hostile. Break off attack.'

Shocked by the command, David glanced down the deep valley of cloud and saw the long brown valley of the Jordan falling away behind them. They had crossed over a line on the earth and immediately their roles had changed from defender to aggressor. But they were closing the target rapidly. It was a fair bounce, they were still unaware.

'We are going to hit them,' David made the decision through the cold bright thing that burned within him and he closed command net and spoke to Joe.

'Two, this is leader attacking.'

'Negative! I say again negative!' Joe called urgently. 'Target is no longer hostile!'

'Remember Hannah!' David shouted into his mask. 'Conform to me!' and he curled his finger about the trigger and touched left rudder, yawing fractionally to bring the nearest MIG into the field of his sights. It seemed to balloon in size as he shrieked towards it.

There was a heart-beat of silence from Joe, and then his voice strangled and rough.

'Two conforming.'

'Kill them, Joe,' David yelled and pressed against the spring-loaded tension of the trigger. There was a soft double hiss, hardly discernible above the jet din, and from under each wing-tip the missiles unleashed, they skidded and twisted as they aligned themselves on the targets, leaving darkly etched trails of vapour across David's front, and at that moment the MIGS became aware.

At a shouted warning from their leader, the entire formation burst into its five separate parts, splintering silvery swift like a shoal of sardines before the driving charge of the barracuda.

The rearmost Syrian was slow, he had only just begun to turn away when one of the sidewinders flicked its tail, followed his turn and united with him in an embrace of death.

The shock wave of the explosion jarred David's machine, but the sound of it was muted as the MIG was enveloped in the greenish-tinted cloud of the strike and it shattered into fragments. A wing snapped off and went whirling high and the brief blooming flower of smoke blew swiftly past David's head.

The second missile had chosen the machine with the red rings, the formation leader, but the Russian had reacted so swiftly and pulled his turn so tight that the missile slid past him in an overshoot, and it lost the scent, unable to follow the MIG around. As David hauled the Mirage round after the Russian, he saw the missile destroy itself in a burst of greenish smoke, far out across the valley of clouds.

The Russian was in a hard right-hand turn, and David followed him. Staring across the imaginary circle that separated them, he could see every detail of the enemy machine; the scarlet helmet of the pilot, the gaudy colours of its roundels, the squiggle of Arabic script that was its identification markings–even the individual rivets that stitched the polished metal skin of the MIG.

David pulled back with all his strength against his joystick, for gravity was tightening the loading of his controls, opposing his efforts to place additional stress on the Mirage lest he tear its wings off the fuselage.

Gravity had hold of David also, its insidious force sucked the blood away from his brain so that his vision dimmed, the colour of the enemy's pilot's helmet faded to dull brown, and David felt himself crushed down into his seat.

About his waist and legs his G-suit tightened its coils squeezing brutally like a hungry python, attempting to prevent the drainage of blood from his upper torso.

David tensed every muscle in his body, straining to resist the loss of blood, and he took the Mirage up in a sliding, soaring yo-yo, up the side of an imaginary barrel. Like a motor-cyclist on a wall of death he whirled aloft, trying once more for the advantage of height.

His vision narrowed, greyed out, until his field was reduced to the limits of his cockpit, and he was pinned heavily to his seat, his mouth sagging open, his eyelids dragging downwards; the effort of holding his right hand on the control column was Herculean.

In the corner of his vision the stall indicator blinked its little eye at him, changing from amber to red, warning him that he was on the verge of catastrophe, courting the disaster of supersonic stall.

David filled his lungs and screamed with all his strength, his own voice echoing through the grey mist. The effort forced a little blood back to his brain and his vision cleared briefly, enough to let him see that the MIG had anticipated his yo-yo and had come up under him, sliding up the wall of death towards his unprotected flank and belly.

David had no alternative but to break out of the turn before the MIG's cannons could bear. He rolled the Mirage out, and went instantly into a tight climbing left-hander, his afterburners still thundering at full power, consuming fuel at a prodigious rate and placing a limit upon these desperate manœuvres.

Neatly and gracefully as a ballet dancer, the Russian followed him out of the turn and locked into his next manœuvre. David saw him coming up into an attack position in his rear-view mirror and he rolled out again and went up and right, blacking out with the rate of turn.

Roll and turn, turn for life, David had judged the Russian fairly. He was a deadly opponent, quick and hard, anticipating each of David's turns and twists, riding always within an ace of strike. Turn, and turn again, in great winging parabolas, climbing always, turning always, vapour trails spinning out from their wing-tips in silky arabesque patterns against the hard blue of the sky.

David's arms and shoulders ached as he fought the control dampers and the weight of gravity, sickened by the drainage of blood and the adrenalin in his system. His cold battle rage turned gradually to icy despair as each of his efforts to dislodge the Russian were met and countered, and always the gaping shark's maw of the MIG hung and twisted a point off his shoulder or belly. All David's expertise, all the brilliance of his natural flying gifts were slowly being discounted by the store of combat experience upon which his enemy could draw.

At one stage, when for an instant they flew wing-tip to wing-tip, David glanced across the gap and saw the man's face. Just the eyes and forehead above the oxygen mask; the skin was pale as bone and the eyes were deep socketed like those of a skull–and then David was turning again, turning and screaming and straining against gravity, screaming also against the first enfolding coils of fear.

He rolled half out of the turn and then without conscious thought, reversed the roll. The Mirage shuddered with protest and his speed bled off. The Russian saw it and came down on him from high on his starboard quarter. As David pushed the stick fully forward and left he kicked on full left rudder, ducking under the blast of cannon fire, and the Mirage went down in a spiralling dive. The blood which gravity had sucked from his head was now flung upwards through his body, filling his head and his vision with bright redness, the red-out of inverted gravitational force. A vein in his nose popped under the pressure and suddenly his oxygen mask was filled with a flood of warm choking blood.

The Russian was after him, following him into the dive, lining him up for his second burst.

David screamed with the metallic salty taste of blood in his mouth and hauled back on the stick with all his strength, the nose came up and over, climbing out of the dive, and again the blood drained from his head–going from red-out to black-out in the fraction of a second and he saw the Russian following him up, drawn by the ploy. At the top David kicked it out in a breakaway roll. It caught the Russian, he was one-hundredth of a second slow in countering and he swung giddily through David's gunsight, an almost impossible deflection shot that sluiced cannon fire wildly across the sky, spraying it like water from a garden hose. The MIG was in David's sights for perhaps one-tenth of a second, but in that time David saw a flash of light, a bright wink of it below the pilot's canopy, and then David rolled and turned out, coming around hard and finding the Russian still hanging in the circuit, but losing air space, swaying out with a feather of white vapour streaming back from below his cockpit canopy.

'I've hit him, David exulted, and his fear was gone, become anger again, a fierce triumphant anger. He took the Mirage up in another soaring yo-yo and this time the MIG could not hold station on him and David flick-rolled off the top and came out with the Russian centred in his gunsight.

He fired a one-second burst and saw the incendiary shells lace in and burst in quick little stabbing stars in the silver fuselage of the MIG.

The Russian came out of his turn, in a gentle dive, flying straight, no longer taking evasive action, probably dead at his controls, and David sat on his tail, and settled the pipper of his gunsight.

He fired another one-second burst and the MIG began to break up. Small unidentifiable pieces of wreckage flew back at David, but the Russian stayed with his machine.

Again David hit him with a two-second burst, and now the MIG's nose sank until she was in a vertical dive still under full power and she went down like a silver javelin. David could not follow her without tearing off his own wings. He pulled out and watched the Russian fly into the earth at a speed that must have exceeded mach 2. He burst like a bomb in a tall tower of dust and smoke that stood for long seconds on the brown plains of Syria.

David shut down his afterburner and looked to his fuel gauges. They were all showing only a narrow strip above the empty notch, and David realized that the last screaming dive after the MIG had taken him down to an altitude of five thousand, he was over enemy territory and too low–much too low.

Expending precious fuel he came around on a westerly heading and went to interception speed, climbing swiftly out of range of flak and searching the heavens above him for sign of either Joe or the other MIGs–although he guessed that the Syrians were either with Allah in the garden of the Houris, or back home with mother by this time.

'Bright Lance Two, this is leader. Do you read me?'

'Leader, this is Two,' Joe's voice answered him immediately. 'I have you visual. In the name of God, get out of there!'

'What is my position?'

'We are fifty miles within Syrian territory, our course for base is 250°.'

'How did you go?'

'I took out one of mine. The other one ran for it, after that I was too busy keeping an eye on you–'

David blinked his eyes and was surprised to find that sweat was pouring down his forehead from under his helmet and his mask was slick and sticky with blood from his nose-bleed. His arms and shoulders still ached, and he felt drunken and light-headed from the effects of gravity and combat and his hands on the control column were shaky and weak.

'I got two,' he said, 'two of the swines–one for Debra, and one for Hannah.'

'Shut up, Davey,' Joe's voice was stiff with tension. 'Concentrate on getting out of here. You are within range of both flak and ground missiles. Light your tail–and let's go.'

'Negative,' David answered him. 'I'm low on fuel. Where are you?'

'Six o'clock high at 25,000.' As he answered, Joe sat up in his seat, leaning forward against his shoulder straps to watch the tiny wedge shape of David's machine far below. It was climbing slowly to meet him, slowly–too slowly, and low–too low. David was vulnerable and Joe was afraid for him, frowning heavily into his face mask and searching restlessly, sweeping heaven and earth for the first hint of danger. Two minutes would see them clear, but they would be two long, slow minutes.

He almost missed the first missile. The ground crew must have allowed David to overfly their launch pad before they put it up in pursuit–for Joe picked up its vapour trail as it streaked in from behind David, closing rapidly with him.

'Missile, break left,' Joe yelled into his mask. 'Go! Go! Go!' and he saw David begin his turn instantly, steeply, side-stepping the sizzling attack of the missile.

'It's lost you!' Joe called, as the missile continued its crazy career through space, beginning to yaw from side to side as it hunted for a target and at last bursting in self-destruction.

'Keep going, Davey,' Joe encouraged him, 'but keep awake, there will be more.'

They both saw the next one leave the ground from its camouflaged vehicle. There was a nest of them on a rocky ridge above a sun-blasted plain. The Serpent slid off the rock and lifted into the sky, climbed rapidly towards David's little machine.

'Light your tail,' Joe told him, 'and wait for it!' He watched the missile boring in, converging with dazzling speed on David's Mirage.

'Break right! Go! Go! Go!' Joe yelled and David twisted violently aside. Again the Serpent slid past him, over-shooting, but this time not losing contact and coming around to attack again, its seekers locked on David's machine.

'He's still on you,' Joe was screaming now. 'Go for the sun, Davey. Try for the sun,' and the Mirage pointed its nose at the great blazing orb that burned above the mountain ranges of dark cloud. The Serpent followed him upwards, hunting him with the dreadful single-mindedness of the automaton.

'He's on to you, Davey. Flip out now! Go! Go! Go!'

David flicked the Mirage out of her vertical climb, and fell like a stone–while the Serpent fastened its attention upon the vast infra-red output from the sun and streaked on towards it, losing the Mirage.

'You've lost it. Get out, Davey, get out!' Joe pleaded with him, but for the moment the Mirage was helpless. In her desperate climb for the sun she had lost manœuvring speed and was wallowing clumsily now. It would be many seconds before she became agile and lithe once more–and by then it would be too late–for Joe saw the third missile become airborne and dart upwards on its feather of flame and smoke aiming at David's Mirage.

Joe did not consciously realize what he was going to do until he had winged over and commenced his dive under full power. He came down with his mach meter indicating twice the speed of sound, and he levelled across David's tail, cutting obliquely across his track under the nose of the oncoming Serpent.

The Serpent saw him with its little cyclops radar eye, and it sensed the heat of his exhausts–fresher, more tantalizing than David's, and it accepted him as an alternative target and swung away after him, leaving David to fly on unscathed.

David saw Joe's aircraft flash past his wing-tip at searing speed, and but an instant behind him followed the Serpent. It took him only a second to realize that Joe had deliberately pulled the missile off him, had accepted the attack that must surely have destroyed David.

He watched with fascinated horror as Joe pulled out of his dive, and used his speed to climb into the sun. The missile followed him smoothly, angling upwards, overhauling Joe's Mirage with effortless ease. Joe was watching the missile in his mirror, and at the last instant he flipped out of the climb–but this time the Serpent was not deceived; as Joe dropped so it swivelled also, and as earlier David had wallowed helplessly now Joe was in the same predicament. He had taken his chance and it had not worked for him. The missile found him, and in a brusque burst of flame, Joe and his Mirage died together.

David flew on alone, his Mirage once more at manœuvring speed and his throat dry with horror and fear and grief. He found himself talking aloud.

'Joe, no, Joe. Oh God no! You shouldn't have done it.'

Ahead of him through the gaps in the massive cloud bases he saw the Jordan.

'It should be you that's going home, Joe,' he said. 'It should be you, Joe,' and felt the hard ball of sorrow in his throat.

But the instinct of survival was still strong and David yawed and glanced back to clear his blind spot–and he saw the last missile coming in on him. It was just a small black speck far behind, with a little frill of dark smoke around it, but it was watching him hungrily with its wicked little eye.

As he saw it, he knew beyond doubt that this one was his, the one that the fates had reserved for him. The attacks he had evaded so far had worn his nerves and strained his judgement, he felt a sense of fatalistic dismay as he watched the attacking missile gaining on him, nevertheless he gathered his scattered reserves for one more supreme effort.

His eyes narrowed to slits, the sweat sliding down his face and drenching his mask, his left hand holding the throttle fully open and his right gripping the control column with the strength, of despair, he judged his moment.

The missile was almost upon him and he screamed with all his might and hurled the Mirage into the turn, but he had misjudged it by the smallest part of a second. As he turned away the missile slid past him and it was close enough to pick up the shadow of the Mirage in the photo-electric eye of its fusing device. The eye winked at him and the missile exploded.

The Mirage was in the critical attitude of its turn, and the cockpit canopy was exposed entirely to the centre of the blast. It hit the plane with a blow that sent it tumbling; like a running man tripping it went over, and it lost lift and flying capability.

The canopy was penetrated by flying steel. A piece struck David's armoured seat with a clang and then it glanced off and struck his left arm above the elbow, snapping the bone cleanly so that the arm dropped uselessly and hung into his lap.

An icy wind raged through the torn canopy as the Mirage hurled itself through space with suicidal force, whipping its nose through the vicious motions and flat plane of high-speed spin. David was thrown against his straps, his ribs bruised and his skin seared from his shoulders, and the broken arm flailing agonizingly.

He tried to hold himself upright in his seat as he reached up over his head, caught hold of the handle of the ejector mechanism and hauled the blind down over his face. He expected to have the charge explode beneath his seat and hurl him free of the doomed Mirage–but nothing happened.

Desperately he released the handle and strained forward to reach the secondary firing mechanism under his seat between his feet. He wrenched it and felt despair as there was no response. The seat was not working, the blast had damaged some vital part of it. He had to fly the Mirage out of it, with one arm and very little altitude left to him. He fastened his right fist on to the moulded grip of the stick, and in the crazy fall and flutter and whirl, David began to fight for control, flying now by instinct alone, for he was badly hurt, and sky and horizon, earth and cloud spun giddily across his vision.

He was aware that he was losing height rapidly, for every time the earth swayed through his line of vision it was closer and more menacing, but doggedly he continued his attempts to roll against the direction of spin.

The earth was very close before he felt the first hint of response, and the ferocity of her gyrations abated slightly. Stick and rudder together, he tried again and the Mirage showed herself willing at last. Gently, with the touch of a lover, he wooed her and suddenly she came out and he was flying straight and level, but she was hard hit. The blast of the missile had done mortal damage, and she was heavy and sick in his hands. He could feel the rough vibration of the engine shaking her, and he guessed that the compressor had thrown a blade and was now out of balance. Within minutes or seconds she would begin to tear herself to pieces. He could not try for climbing power on her.

David looked quickly about him and realized with a shock how far he had fallen in that terrible tumble down the sky. He was only two or three hundred feet above the earth. He was not sure of his direction, but when he glanced at his doppler compass, he found with mild surprise that he was still heading in the general direction of home.

The engine vibration increased, and he could hear the shrill screech of rending metal. He wasn't going to make it home–that was certain, and there was insufficient height to jettison the canopy, release his straps and attempt to scramble out of the cockpit. There was only one course still remaining, he must fly the Mirage in.

Even as he made the decision his one good hand was busy implementing it. Holding the stick between his knees, he let down his landing gear; the nose wheel might hold him up long enough to take some of the speed off her and prevent her cartwheeling.

He looked ahead, and saw a low ridge of rocky ground and sparse green vegetation. Disaster lurked for him there–but beyond it were open fields, ploughed land, orderly blocks of orchard, neatly laid-out buildings. That in itself was cheering. Such order and industry could only mean that he had returned across the border to Israel.

David skimmed over the ridge of broken rocks, sucking in his own belly as though to lift the Mirage bodily over the hungry teeth of granite, and ahead of him lay the fields. He could see women working in one of the orchards, stopping and turning to look at him. So close that he could clearly see the expression of surprise and apprehension on their faces.

There was a man on a blue tractor and he jumped from his seat and fell to the earth as David passed only feet above his head.

All fuel cocks closed, all switches off, master switch off–David went into the final ritual for crash-landing.

Ahead of him lay the smooth brown field, open and clear. He might just be lucky enough, it might just come off.

The Mirage was losing flying speed, her nose coming up, the airspeed needle sinking back, 200 miles per hour, 190, 180, dropping back to her stalling speed of 150.

Then suddenly David realized that the field ahead of him was latticed with deep concrete irrigation channels. They were twenty feet wide, and ten deep, a deadly hazard–enough to destroy a Centurion tank.

There was nothing David could do now to avoid their gaping jaws. He flew the Mirage in, touching down smoothly.

'Smooth as a tomcat pissing on a sheet of velvet,' he thought bitterly, aware that all his skill was unavailing now. 'Even Barney would have been proud of me.' The field was rough, but the Mirage settled to it, pitching and lurching, shaking David ruthlessly about the cockpit, but she was up on all three wheels, losing speed handily, her undercart taking the strain. However, she was still travelling at ninety miles an hour when she went into the irrigation ditch.

It snapped her undercart off like pretzel sticks and she nosed in, struck the far bank of concrete that sheered through metal like a scythe, and sent the fuselage cartwheeling across the field with David still strapped within it. The wings broke away and the body slid on across the soft earth to come to rest at last, right way up like a stranded whale.

The whole of David's left side was numb, no feeling in his arm or leg, the straps had mauled him with their rude grasp, and he was stunned and bewildered in the sudden engrossing silence.

For many seconds he sat still, unable to move or think. Then he smelled it, the pervasive reek of Avtur jet fuel from the ruptured tanks and lines. The smell of it galvanized him with the pilot's deadly fear of fire.

With his right hand he grabbed the canopy release lever and heaved at it. He wasted ten precious seconds with it, for it was jammed solid. Then he turned his attention to the steel canopy breaker in its niche below the lever. This was a tool specially designed for this type of emergency. He lifted it, lay back in his seat and attacked the Perspex dome above his head. The stink of jet fuel was overpowering, filling the cockpit, and he could hear the little pinging and tinkling sound made by white-hot metal.

His left arm hampered him, he had no feeling or use in it. The straps bound him tightly to his seat and he had to pause in his assault upon the canopy to loosen them.

Then he began again. He tore an opening in the Perspex, the size of a hand, and as he worked to enlarge it, a ruptured fuel pressure line somewhere in the shattered fuselage sprayed a jet of Avtur high in the air. it fell in a heavy drizzle upon the canopy like a garden sprinkler, poured down the curved sides and dribbled through the hole David was cutting. It fell into his face, icy cold on his cheeks and stinging his eyes, it drenched his shoulders and the front of his pressure suit, and David began to pray. For the first time ever in his life the words took on meaning and he felt his terror receding.

'Hear O Israel, the Lord our God, the Lord is one.'

He prayed aloud, striking up at the softly yielding Perspex and feeling the soft rain of death in his face. He tore at the opening with his hands, bringing away slabs of transparent material, but ripping his gloves and leaving his blood smearing the jagged edges of the opening.

'Blessed be His name, whose glorious kingdom is for ever–'

The opening was large enough. He hauled himself up in the seat, and found himself caught by the oxygen and radio lines attached to his helmet. He could not reach them with his crippled left arm. He stared down at the offending limb, and saw the blood welling out of the torn sleeve of the suit. There was no pain but it was twisted at a comical angle from the elbow.

'You shall love the Lord your God with all your heart–' he whispered, and with his right hand he tore loose the chin strap and let his helmet drop to the floor-boards. The Avtur soaked into the soft dark mop of his hair and ran down his neck behind his ears, and he thought about the flames of hell.

Painfully he dragged himself out through the opening in the canopy, and now not even prayer could hold off the dark hordes of terror that assaulted his soul.

'–For the anger of God will kindle against you–'

Laboriously he crawled across the slippery sleek metal of the wing root and fell to the ground. He fell face-down and lay for a moment, exhausted by fear and effort.

'–remember all the commands of God–'

He heard voices then as he lay with his face against the dusty earth, and he lifted his head and saw the women from the orchard running towards him across the open field. The voices were shrill but faint and the words were in Hebrew. He knew that he was home.

Steadying himself against the shattered body of the Mirage, he came to his feet with the broken arm dangling at his side, and he tried to shout to them.

'Go back! Beware!' but his voice was a throaty croak, and they ran on towards him. Their dresses and aprons were gay spots of colour against the dry brown earth.

He pushed himself away from the aircraft and staggered to meet the running women.

'Go back!' he croaked in his own terrible distress, with the grip of his G-suit strangling his movements and the evaporating fuel cold as ice in his hair and down his face.

Within the battered hull of the Mirage a puddle of Avtur had been heated by the white-hot shell of the jet compressor. Its low volatility at last was raised to flash point and a dying spark from the electronic equipment was enough to ignite it.

With a dull but awful roar, the Mirage bloomed with dark crimson flame and sooty black smoke, the wind ripped the flames outwards in great streamers and pennants that engulfed all around them, and David staggered onwards in the midst of the roaring furnace that seemed to consume the very air.

He held his breath–if he had not, the flame would have scorched his lungs. He closed his eyes tightly against the agony and ran on blindly. His body and his limbs were protected by the fireproof pressure suit and boots and gloves–but his head was bare and soaked with fuel.

As he ran his head burned like a torch. His hair frizzled off, in a stinking puff of flame and the skin of his scalp and neck and face was exposed. The flames burnt his ears off and most of his nose, they flayed off his skin in a blistering sheet and then they ate into the raw flesh, they burnt away his lips and exposed his teeth and part of the bone of his jaw. They ate through his eyelids and stripped the living meat from his cheeks.

David ran on through the burning air and smoke, and he did not believe that such pain was possible. It exceeded all his imaginings and swamped all the senses of his body and mind–but he knew he must not scream. The pain was a blackness and the vivid colours of flame in his tightly closed eyes, it was a roaring in his ears like all the winds of the world, and in his flesh it was the goads and whips and burning hooks of hell itself. But he knew he could not let this terrible fire enter his body and he ran on without screaming.

The women from the orchard were brought up short by the sudden forest of flame and black smoke that rose up in front of them, engulfing the squashed-insect body of the aircraft, and closing around the running figure of the pilot.

It was a solid impenetrable wall of heat and smoke that blotted out all ahead of them, and forced them to draw back, awed and horrified, before its raging hot breath. They stood in a small group, panting and wild-eyed.

Then abruptly a freak gust of wind opened the heavy oily curtains of smoke, and out of them stumbled a dreadful thing with a scorched and smoking body and a head of flame.

Blindly it came out of the smoke, one arm hanging and its feet dragging and staggering in the soft earth. They stared at this thing in horror, frozen in silence, and it came towards them.

Then a strapping girl, with a strong brown body and a mane of dark hair, uttered a cry of compassion–and raced to meet him.

As she ran, she stripped off her heavy voluminous skirt of thick wool, leaving her strong brown legs bare. She reached David and she swirled the skirt over his head, smothering the flames that still ate into his flesh. The other women followed her, using their clothing to wrap him as he fell and rolled on the earth.

Only then did David begin to scream, from that lipless mouth with the exposed teeth. It was a sound that none of them would ever forget. As he screamed the eyes were open, with the lashes and brow and most of the lids burned away. The eyes were dark indigo blue in the glistening mask of wet scorched meat, and the little blood vessels, sealed by the heat, popped open and dribbled and spurted. As he screamed, the blood and lymph bubbled from the nostril holes where his nose had been, and his body writhed and heaved and convulsed as spasm after spasm of unbearable agony hit him.

The women had to hold him down to control his struggles, and to prevent him tearing with clawed fingers at the ruins of his face.

He was still screaming when the doctor from the kibbutz slashed open the sleeve of his pressure suit with a scalpel and pressed the morphine needle into the twitching jumping muscles of his arm.

The Brig saw the last bright radar image fade from the plot and heard the young radar officer report formally. 'No further contact.' And a great silence fell on the command bunker.

They were all watching him. He stood hunched over the plot and his big bony fists were clasped at his sides. His face was stiff and expressionless, but his eyes were terrible.

It seemed that the frantic voices of his two pilots still echoed from the speakers above his head, as they called to each other in the extremes of mortal conflict.

They had all heard David's voice, hoarse with sorrow and fear.

'Joe! No, Joe! Oh God, no!' and they knew what that meant. They had lost them both, and the Brig was still stunned by the sudden incalculable turn that the sortie had taken.

At the moment he had lost control of his fighters he had known that disaster was unavoidable–and now his son was dead. He wanted to cry out aloud, to protest against the futility of it. He closed his eyes tightly for a few seconds, and when he opened them, he was in control again.

'General alert,' he snapped. 'All squadrons to "Red" standby–' he knew they faced an international crisis. 'I want air cover over the area they went down. They may have ejected. Put up two Phantom flights and keep an umbrella over them. I want helicopters sent in immediately, with paratrooper guards and medical teams–'

Command bunker moved swiftly into general alert procedure.

'Get me the Prime Minister,' he said, he was going to have to do a lot of explaining, and he spared a few vital seconds to damn David Morgan roundly and bitterly.

The airforce doctor took one look at David's charred and scorched head and he swore softly.

'We'll be lucky to save this one.'

Loosely he swathed the head in Vaseline bandages and they hurried with David's blanket-wrapped body on the stretcher to the Bell 205 helicopter waiting in the orchard.

The Bell touched down on the helipad at Hadassah Hospital and a medical team was ready for him. One hour and fifty-three minutes after the Mirage hit the irrigation canal David had passed through the sterile lock into the special burns unit on the third floor of the hospital–into a quiet and secluded little world where everybody wore masks and long green sterile robes and the only contact with the outside world was through the double-glazed windows and even the air he breathed was scrubbed and cleaned and filtered.

However, David was enfolded in the soft dark clouds of morphine and he did not hear the quiet voices of the masked figures as they worked over him.

'It's third degree over the entire area–'

'No attempt to clean it or touch it, sister, not until it stabilizes. I am going to spray with Epigard, and we'll go to intra-muscular Tetracycline four-hourly against infection–'

'It will be two weeks before we dare touch it.'

'Very well, doctor.'

'Oh, and sister, fifteen milligrams of morphine six-hourly. We are going to have a lot of pain with this one.'

Pain was infinity, an endless ocean across which the wave-patterns marched relentlessly to burst up the beaches of his soul. There were times when the surf of pain ran high and each burst of it threatened to shatter his reason. Again there were times when it was low, almost gentle in its throbbing rhythm and he drifted far out upon the ocean of pain to where the morphine mists enfolded him. Then the mists parted and a brazen sun beat down upon his head, and he squirmed and writhed and cried out. His skull seemed to bloat and swell until it must burst, and the open nerve-ends screamed for surcease.

Then suddenly there was the sharply beloved sting of the needle in his flesh, and the mists closed about him once more.

'I don't like the look of this at all. Have we taken a culture, sister?'

'Yes, doctor.'

'What are we growing?'

'I'm afraid it's strep.'

'Yes. I thought so. I think we'll have to change to Cloxacillin–see if we get a better response with that.'

With the pain, David became aware of a smell. It was the smell of carrion and things long dead, the smell of vermin in dirty blankets, of vomit and excreta, and the odour of wet garbage festering in dark alleys–and at last he came to know that the smell was the rotting of his own flesh as the bacteria of Streptococcus infection attacked the exposed tissue.

They fought it with the drugs, but now the pain was underlined with the fevers of infection and the terrible burning thirsts which no amount of liquids could slake.

With the fever came the nightmares and the fantasies to plague and goad him even further beyond the limits of his endurance.

'Joe–' he cried out in his agony, 'try for the sun, Joe. Break left now–Go! Go!' And then he was sobbing from the ruined and broken mouth. 'Oh, Joe! Oh God, no! Joe.'

Until the night-sister could no longer bear it and she came hurrying with the syringe, and his screams turned to babbling and then into the low whimper and moan of the drug sleep.

'We'll start with the acriflavin dressings now, sister.'

When they changed the dressings every forty-eight hours it was under general anaesthetic for the entire head was of raw flesh, a bland expressionless head, a head like a child's drawing, crude lines and harsh colours, hairless, earless, streaked and mottled with yellow runs and patches of soft pus and corruption.

'We are getting a response from the Cloxacillin, it's looking a lot healthier, sister.'

The naked flesh of his eyelids had contracted, pulling back like the glistening petals of a pink rose, exposing the eyeballs to the air without respite. They had filled the eyes' sockets with a yellow ointment to soothe and moisten them, to keep out the loathsome infection that covered his head. The ointment prevented vision.

'I think we'll go for an abdominal pedicel now. Will you prep for afternoon theatre, please, sister?'

Now it was time for the knife, and David was to learn that the pain and the knife lived together in terrible sin. They lifted a long flap of skin and flesh from his belly, leaving it still attached at one end, and they rolled it into a fat sausage, then they strapped his good arm, the one without the plaster cast, to his side and they stitched the free end of the sausage to his forearm, training it to draw its blood supply from there. Then they brought him back from theatre and left him trussed and helpless and blind with the pedicel fastened to his arm, like a remora to the belly of a shark.

'Well, we have saved both eyes,' the voice was proud, fond almost, and David looked up and saw them for the first time. They were gathered around his cot, a circle of craning heads, mouths and noses covered by surgical masks, but his vision was still smeary with ointment and distorted by the drip irrigation that had replaced it.

'Now we will go for the eyelids.'

It was the knife again, the contracted and bunched-up eyelids split and re-shaped and stitched, the knife and pain and the familiar sickly tissue taste and stink of anaesthetic that saturated his body and seemed to exude from the very pores of his skin.

'Beautiful, really lovely–we have cleaned up the infection nicely. Now we can begin.'

The head was cleansed of its running rivers of pus, and now it was glistening and wet, bald and bright red, the colour of a cocktail cherry as granulation tissue formed. There were two gnarled and twisted flaps for ears, the double row of teeth startlingly white and perfect where the lips had been eaten away, a long white blade of exposed bone outlined the point of the jaw, the nose was a stump with the nostrils like the double muzzles of a shotgun, and only the eyes were still beautiful–dark indigo and flawlessly white between the lids of shocking crimson and neatly laid black stitches.

'We'll begin at the back of the neck. Will you prep for this afternoon's theatre, please, sister?'

It was a variation on the theme of the knife. They planed sheets of live skin from his thighs and meshed them to allow a wider spread, then they laid them over the exposed flesh, covering a little at each session, and evaluating each attempt while David lay in his cot and rode the long swells of pain.

'That one is no good. I'm afraid we will have to scrap it and try again.'

While his thighs grew a new crop of skin, they planed fresh sheets from his calves, so that each donor-site became a new source of pain.

'Lovely! An edge-to-edge take with that graft.'

Slowly the cap of skin extended up across the nape of his neck and over his scalp. The meshing of the skin grafts gave them a patterned effect, regular as the scales of a fish, and the new grafts were hard-looking and raised.

'We can move the pedicel up now.'

'This afternoon's theatre, doctor?'

'Yes, please, sister.'

David came to know that they operated every Thursday in the burns unit. He came to dread the Thursday morning rounds when the consultant and his staff crowded around his cot and touched and prodded and discussed the restructuring of his flesh with an impersonal candour that chilled him.

They freed the fat sausage of flesh from his belly and it dangled from his arm like some grotesque white leech, seeming to have a life of its own, drawing blood and sustenance from its grip upon his forearm.

They lifted his arm and strapped it across his chest, and the raw end of the pedicel they split and stitched to his jaw and to the stump of his nose.

'It's taken very nicely. We will begin shaping it this afternoon. We'll have him at the head of the theatre list. Will you see to that please, sister?'

With the living flesh that they had stolen from his belly they fashioned a crude lump of a nose, taut, narrow lips and a new covering for his jaw-bone.

'The oedema has settled. This afternoon I will go for the bone-graft on the jaw.'

They opened his chest and split his fourth rib laterally, robbing it of a long sliver of bone and they grafted this to the damaged jaw-bone, then they spread the flesh of the pedicel over it and stitched it all into place.

On Thursdays it was the knife and the stink of anaesthetic, and for the days between it was the ache and pain of abused and healing flesh.

They fined down the new nose, piercing it with nostrils, they finished the reconstruction of his eyelids. They laid the last grafts behind his ears, they cut a double zig-zag incision around the base of his jaw where the contracting scar tissue was trying to draw his chin down on to his chest. The new lips took firm hold on the existing muscles and David gained control of them so he could form his words again and speak clearly.

The last area of raw flesh was closed beneath the patchwork of skin grafts, flesh grafts and stitches. David was no longer a high-infection risk and he was moved from a sterile environment. Once again he saw human faces, not merely eyes peering over white surgical masks. The faces were friendly, cheerful faces. Men and women proud of their achievement in saving him from death and refleshing his ravaged head.

'You'll be allowed visitors now, I expect you'll welcome that,' said the consultant. He was a distinguished-looking young surgeon who had left a highly paid post at a Swiss Clinic to head this burns and plastic surgery unit.

'I don't think I will be having any visitors,' David had lost contact with the reality of the outside world during the nine months in the burns unit.

'Oh, yes, you will,' the surgeon told him. 'We've had regular inquiries on your progress from a number of people. Isn't that correct, sister?'

'That's right, doctor.'

'You can let them know that he is allowed visitors now.'

The consultant and his group began to move on.

'Doctor,' David called him back. 'I want a look at a mirror,' and they were silent, immediately embarrassed. This request of his had been denied many times over the last months.

'Damn it,' David became angry. 'You can't protect me from it for ever.'

The consultant gestured for the others to leave and they filed out of the ward, while he came back to David's bed.

'All right, David,' he agreed gently. 'We'll find you a mirror–though we don't have much use for them around here.' For the first time in the many months he had known him, David glimpsed the depths of his compassion, and he wondered at it. That a man who lived constantly amongst great pain and terrible disfigurement could still be moved by it.

'You must understand that how you are now is not how you will always be. All I have been able to do, so far, is heal your exposed flesh and make you functional again. You are once more a viable human being. You have not experienced the loss of any of your faculties–but I will not pretend that you are beautiful. However, there remains much that I can still do to change that. Your ears, for example, can be reconstructed with the material I have reserved for that purpose–' He indicated the stump of the pedicel that still hung from David's forearm '–There is much fine work still to be done about the nose and mouth and eyes.' He paced slowly the length of the ward and looked out into the sunlight for a moment before turning back again and coming forward to face David.

'But let me be truthful with you. There are limitations to what I can do. The muscles of expression, those delicate little muscles around the eyes and mouth have been destroyed. I cannot replace those. The hair follicles of your lashes and brows and scalp have been burned away. You will be able to wear a wig, but–'

David turned to his bedside locker and took from the drawer his wallet. He opened it and drew out a photograph. It was the one which Hannah had taken so long ago of Debra and David sitting at the rock-pool in the oasis of Ein Gedi and smiling at each other. He handed it to the surgeon.

'Is that what you looked like, David? I never knew.' The regret showed like a quick shadow in his eyes.

'Can you make me look like that again?'

The surgeon studied the photograph a moment longer, the young god's face with the dark mop of hair and the clean pure lines of the profile.

'No,' he said. 'I could not even come close.'

'That's all I wanted to know.' David took the photograph back from him. 'You say I'm functional now. Let's leave it at that, shall we?'

'You don't want further cosmetic surgery? We can still do a lot–'

'Doctor, I've lived under the knife for nine months. I've had the taste of antibiotics and anaesthetics in my mouth, and the stink of it in my nostrils for all that time. Now all I want is a little escape from pain–a little peace and the taste of clean air.'

'Very well,' the surgeon agreed readily. 'It is not important that we do it now. You could come back at any time in the future.' He walked to the door of the ward. 'Come on. Let's go find a mirror.'

There was one in the nurses' room beyond the double doors at the end of the passage. The room itself was empty and the mirror was set into the wall above the wash basin.

The surgeon stood in the doorway and leaned against the jamb. He lit a cigarette and watched as David crossed towards the mirror and then halted abruptly as he saw his own image.

He wore the blue hospital dressing-gown over his pyjamas. He was tall and finely proportioned. His shoulders were wide, his hips narrow, and he had the same lithe and beautiful man's body.

However, the head that topped it was something from a nightmare. Involuntarily he gasped out loud and the gash of a mouth parted in sympathy. It was a tight lipless mouth, like that of a cobra, white-rimmed and harsh.

Drawn by the awful fascination of horror, David drew closer to the mirror. The thick mane of his dark hair had concealed the peculiar elongation of his skull. He had never realized that it jutted out behind like that, for now the hair was gone and the bald curve was covered with meshed skin, thickened and raised.

The skin and flesh of his face was a patchwork, joined by seams of scar tissue drawn tightly over his cheekbones, giving him a vaguely Asiatic appearance, but the eyes were round and startled, with clumsy lids and puffed dead-looking flesh beneath.

His nose was a shapeless blob, out of balance with his other coarsened features and his ears were gnarled excrescences, seemingly fastened haphazardly to the sides of his head. The whole of it was bland and bald and boiled-looking.

The gash of a mouth twisted briefly in a horrid rictus, and then regained its frozen shape.

'I can't smile, said David.

'No,' agreed the surgeon. 'You will have no control of your expressions.'

That was the truly horrifying aspect of it. It was not the twisted and tortured flesh, with the scarring and stitch marks still so evident–it was the expressionlessness of this mask. The frozen features seemed long dead, incapable of human warmth or feeling.

'Yeah! But you should have seen the other guy!' David said softly, and the surgeon chuckled without mirth.

'We'll have those last few stitches behind your ears out tomorrow–I shall remove what remains of the pedicel from your arm–and then you can be discharged. Come back to us when you are ready.'

David ran his hand gingerly over the bald patterned skull.

'I'm going to save a fortune in haircuts and razor blades,' he said, and the surgeon turned quickly away and walked down the passage, leaving David to get to know his new head.

The clothes that they had found for him were cheap and ill-fitting–slacks and open-neck shirt, a light jacket and sandals–and he asked for some head covering, anything to conceal the weird new shape of his scalp. One of the nurses found him a cloth cap, and then told him that a visitor was waiting for him in the hospital superintendent's department.

He was a major from the military provost marshal's office, a lean grey-haired man with cold grey eyes and a tight hard mouth. He introduced himself without offering to shake hands and then opened the file on the desk in front of him.

'I have been instructed by my office to ask for the formal resignation of your commission in the Israeli Air Force,' he started, and David stared at him. In the long pain-filled, fever-hot nights, the thought of flying once more had seemed like a prospect of paradise.

'I don't understand,' he mumbled, and reached for a cigarette, breaking the first match and then puffing quickly as the second flared. 'You want my resignation–and if I refuse?'

'Then we shall have no alternative other than to convene a court martial and to try for dereliction of duty, and refusing in the face of the enemy to obey the lawful orders of your superior officer.'

'I see,' David nodded heavily, and drew on the cigarette. The smoke stung his eyes.

'It doesn't seem I have any choice.'

'I have prepared the necessary documents. Please sign here, and here, and I shall sign as witness.'

David bowed over the papers and signed. The pen scratched loudly in the silent room.

'Thank you.' The major gathered his papers, and placed them in his briefcase. He nodded at David and started for the door.

'So now I am an outcast,' said David softly, and the man stopped. They stared at each other for a moment, and then the major's expression altered slightly, and the cold grey eyes became ferocious.

'You are responsible for the destruction of two warplanes that are irreplaceable and whose loss has caused us incalculable harm. You are responsible for the death of a brother officer, and for bringing our country to the very brink of open war which would have cost many thousands more of our young people's lives–and possibly our very existence. You have embarrassed our international friends–and given strength to our enemies.' He paused and drew a deep breath. 'The recommendation of my office was that you be brought to trial and that the prosecution be instructed to ask for the death penalty. It was only the personal intervention of the Prime Minister and of Major-General Mordecai that saved you from that. In my view, instead of bemoaning your fate, you should consider yourself highly fortunate.'

He turned away and his footsteps cracked on the stone floor as he strode from the room.

In the bleak impersonal lobby of the hospital, David was suddenly struck by a reluctance to walk on out into the spring sunshine through the glass swing doors. He had heard that long-term prisoners felt this way when the time came for their release.

Before he reached the doors he turned aside and went down to the hospital synagogue. In a corner of the quiet square hall he sat for a long time. The stained-glass windows, set high in the nave, filled the air with shafts of coloured light when the sun came through, and a little of the peace and beauty of that place stayed with him and gave him courage when at last he walked out into the square and boarded a bus for Jerusalem.

He found a seat at the rear, and beside a window. The bus pulled away and ground slowly up the hill towards the city.

He became aware that he was being watched, and he lifted his head to find that a woman with two young children had taken the seat in front of him. She was a poorly dressed, harassed-looking woman, prematurely aged and she held the grubby younger infant on her lap and fed it from a plastic bottle. However, the second child was an angelic little girl of four or five years. She had huge dark eyes and a head of thick curls. She stood on the seat facing backwards, with one thumb thrust deeply into her mouth. She was watching David steadily over the back of the seat, studying his face with that total absorption and candour of the child. David felt a sudden warmth of emotion for the child, a longing for the comfort of human contact, of which he had been deprived all these months.

He leaned forward in his seat, trying to smile, reaching out a gentle hand to touch the child's arm.

She removed her thumb from her mouth and shrank away from him, turning to her mother and clinging to her arm, hiding her face in the woman's blouse.

At the next stop David stepped down from the bus and left the road to climb the stony hillside.

The day was warm and drowsy, with the bee murmur and the smell of the blossoms from the peach orchards. He climbed the terraces and rested at the crest, for he found he was breathless and shaky. Months in hospital had left him unaccustomed to walking far, but it was not that alone. The episode with the child had distressed him terribly.

He looked longingly towards the sky. It was clear and brilliant blue, with high silver cloud in the north. he wished he could ascend beyond those clouds. He knew he would find peace up there.

A taxi dropped him off at the top of Malik Street. The front door was unlocked, swinging open before he could fit his key to the lock.

Puzzled and alarmed he stepped into the living-room. It was as he had left it so many months before, but somebody had cleaned and swept, and there were fresh flowers in a vase upon the olive-wood table–a huge bouquet of gaily coloured dahlias, yellow and scarlet.

David smelled food, hot and spicy and tantalizing after the bland hospital fare.

'Hello,' he called. 'Who is there?'

'Welcome home!' There was a familiar bellow from behind the closed bathroom door. 'I didn't expect you so soon–and you've caught me with my skirts up and pants down.'

There was a scuffling sound and then the toilet flushed thunderously and the door was flung open. Ella Kadesh appeared majestically through it. She wore one of her huge kaftans, it was a blaze of primary colours. Her hat was apple-green in colour, the brim pinned up at the side like an Australian bush hat by an enormous jade brooch and a bunch of ostrich feathers.

Her heavy arms were flung wide in a gesture of welcome, and the face was split in a huge grin of anticipation. She came towards him, and the grin persisted long after the horror had dawned in her bright little eyes. Her steps slowed.

'David?' Her voice was uncertain. 'It is you, David?'

'Hello, Ella.'

'Oh God. Oh, sweet holy name of God. What have they done to you, my beautiful young Mars–'

'Listen, you old bag,' he said harshly, 'if you start blubbering I'm going to throw you down the steps.'

She made a huge effort to control it, fighting back the tears that flooded into her eyes, but her jowls wobbled and her voice was thick and nasal as she enfolded him in her huge arms and hugged him to her bosom.

'I've got a case of cold beers in the refrigerator–and I made a pot of curry for us. You'll love my curry, it's the thing I do best–'

David ate with enormous appetite, washing down the fiery food with cold beer, and he listened to Ella talk. She spouted words like a fountain, using their flow to cover her pity and embarrassment.

'They would not let me visit you, but I telephoned every week and kept in touch that way. The sister and I got very friendly, she let me know you were coming today. So I drove up to make sure you had a welcome–'

She tried to avoid looking directly at his face, but when she did the shadows appeared in her eyes, even though she made a convincing effort at gaiety. When he finished eating at last, she asked, 'What will you do now, David?'

'I would have liked to go back and fly. It's the thing I like to do best–but they have forced me to resign my commission. I disobeyed orders, Joe and I followed them across the border, and they don't want me any more.'

'There was nearly open war, David. It was a crazy thing that you and Joe did.'

David nodded. 'I was mad. I wasn't thinking straight that day–after Debra–'

Ella interrupted quickly. 'Yes, I know. Share another beer?'

David nodded distractedly. 'How is she, Ella?' It was the question he had wanted to ask all along.

'She is just fine, Davey. She has begun the new book, and if anything it's better than the first. I think she will become a very important writer–'

'Her eyes? Is there any improvement?'

Ella shook her head. 'She has come to terms with that now. It doesn't seem to bother her any longer, just as you will come to accept what has happened–'

David was not listening. 'Ella, in all that time, when I was in hospital, every day I hoped–I knew it was useless, but I hoped to hear from her. A card, a word–'

'She didn't know, Davey.'

'Didn't know?' David demanded and leaned across the table to grip Ella's wrist. 'What do you mean?'

'After Joe–was killed, Debra's father was very angry. He believed that you were responsible.'

David nodded, the blank mask of his face concealing his guilt.

'Well, he told Debra that you had left Israel, and gone back to your home. We were all sworn to silence–and that's what Debra believes now.'

David released Ella's wrist, picked up his beer glass and sipped at the head of froth.

'You still haven't answered my question, David. What are you going to do now?'

'I don't know, Ella. I guess I'll have to think about that.'

A harsh warm wind came off the hills and ruffled the surface of the lake, darkening it to black and flecking it with white crests. The fishing boats along the curve of the shore tugged restlessly at their mooring ropes, and the fishing nets upon their drying racks billowed like bridal veils.

The wind caught Debra's hair and shook it out in a loose cloud. It pressed the silk dress she wore against her body, emphasizing the heavy roundness of her breasts and the length of her legs.

She stood on the battlements of the crusader castle, leaning both hands lightly on the head of her cane and she stared out across the water, almost as though she could see beyond it.

Ella sat near her, on a fallen block of masonry out of the wind, but she pinned her hat down with one hand as he spoke, watching Debra's face intently to judge her reactions.

'At the time it seemed the kindest thing to do. I agreed to keep the truth from you, because I did not want you to torture yourself–'

Debra spoke sharply. 'Don't ever do that again.'

Ella made a moue of resignation and went on. 'I had no way of knowing how bad he was, they would not let me see him, and so I suppose I was a coward and I let it drift.'

Debra shook her head angrily, but she remained silent. Ella wondered again that sightless eyes could contain so much expression, for Debra's emotions blazed clearly in the honey-coloured sparks as she turned her head towards Ella.

'It was not the time to distract you. Don't you see, my dear? You were adjusting so nicely–working so well on your book. I did not see that we could gain anything by telling you. I decided to co-operate with your father–and see how things turned out later.'

'Then why are you telling me all this now?' Debra demanded. 'What has happened to change your mind–what has happened to David'

'Yesterday at noon David was discharged from Hadassah Hospital.'

'Hospital?' Debra was puzzled. 'You don't mean he has been in hospital all this time, Ella. Nine months–it's impossible!'

'It's the truth.'

'He must have been terribly hurt,' Debra's anger had changed to concern. 'How is he, Ella? What happened? Is he healed now?'

Ella was silent a moment, and Debra took a pace towards her. 'Well?' she asked.

'David's plane flamed out and he was very badly burned above the head. He has recovered completely now. His burns have healed–but–'

Ella hesitated again, and Debra groped for her hand and found it. 'Go on, Ella! But–?'

'David is no longer the most beautiful man I have ever seen.'

'I don't understand?'

'He is no longer swift and vital and–any woman who sees him now will find it difficult to be near him, let alone love him.'

Debra was listening intently, her expression rapt and her eyes soft-focused.

'He is very conscious of the way he looks now. He is searching for some place to hide, I think. He talks of wanting to fly as though it is some form of escape. He knows he is alone now, cut off from the world by the mask he wears–'

Debra's eyes had misted, and Ella made her gravelly voice gentler and she went on.

'But there is somebody who will never see that mask.' Ella drew the girl closer to her. 'Somebody who remembers only the way he was before.' Debra's grip tightened on Ella's hand, and she began to smile–it was an expression that seemed to radiate from deep within her.

'He needs you now, Debra,' Ella said softly. 'That is all there is left for him.

Will you change your decision now?'

'Fetch him to me, Ella,' Debra's voice shook. 'Fetch him to me as soon as you can.'

David climbed the long line of steps towards Ella's studio. It was a day of bright sunlight and he wore open sandals and light silk slacks of a bronze colour and a short-sleeved shirt with a wide V-neck. His arms were pale from lack of sun, the dark hair of his chest contrasting strongly against the soft cream–and upon his head he wore a wide-brimmed white straw hat to guard the cicatrice from the sun and to soften his face with shadow.

He paused, and he could feel the break of sweat under the shirt and the pumping of his lungs. He despised the weakness of his body and the quivering of his legs as he came out on the terrace. It was deserted, and he crossed to the shuttered doors and went into the gloom.

Ella Kadesh sitting on a Samarkand carpet in the centre of the paved floor was an astonishing sight. For she was dressed in a brief bikini costume adorned with pink roses that almost disappeared under the rolls of ponderous flesh that hung over it from belly and breast. She was in the yoga position of Padmasana, the sitting lotus, and her massive legs were twisted and entwined like mating pythons. Her hands were held before her palm to palm and her eyes were closed in meditation; upon her head her ginger wig was set four square like that of a judge.

David leaned in the doorway and before he could recover his breath he began to laugh. It began as a wheezy little chuckle, and then suddenly he was really laughing, from deep down–great gusts of it that shook his helpless body, and flogged his lungs. It was not mirth but a catharsis of the last dregs of suffering, it was the moment of accepting life again, a taking up once more of the challenge of living.

Ella must have recognized it as such, for she did not move, squatting like some cheerful buddha on the brilliant carpet, and she opened one little eye. The effect was even more startlingly comic, and David reeled away from the door, and fell into one of the chairs.

'Your soul is a desert, David Morgan,' said Ella. 'You have no recognition of beauty, all loveliness would wither on the dung heap which–' But the rest of it was lost as she also began to giggle and the yoga pose broke down, melting like a jelly on a hot day, and she traded him hoot for hoot and bellow for bellow of laughter.

'I'm stuck,' she gasped at last. 'Help me, Davey, you oaf–' And he staggered to her, knelt and struggled to help her unlock her interwoven legs. They came apart with little creaking and popping sounds and Ella collapsed face down on the carpet groaning and giggling at the same time.

'Get out of here,' she moaned. 'Leave me to die in peace. Go and find your woman, she is down on the jetty.'

She watched him go quickly, and then she dragged herself up and went to the door. The laughter dried up and she whispered aloud, 'My two poor little crippled kittens–I wonder if I have done the right thing.' The shadows of doubt crossed her face, and then faded. 'Well, it's too damn late for worry now, Kadesh, you interfering old bag, you should have thought about that before.'

A gaudily coloured towel and beach jacket were spread upon the jetty and a transistor radio, with its volume turned high, blared out a heavy rock tune. Far out in the bay Debra was swimming alone, a steady powerful overarm crawl. Her brown arms flashed wetly in the sun at each stroke and the water churned to froth at the beat of her legs.

She stopped to tread water. Her bathing cap was plain white, and he could see that she was listening for the sound of the radio for she began to swim again, heading directly in towards the jetty.

She came out of the water, pulling off the cap and shaking out her hair. Her body was dark, sun-browned and bejewelled with drops, the muscles looked firm and hard and her tread was confident and sure as she came up the stone steps and picked up her towel.

As she dried herself David stood near and watched her avidly, seeming to devour her with his eyes, trying to make up in that first minute for all those many months. He had pictured her so clearly, and yet there was much he had forgotten. Her hair was softer, cloudier than he remembered. He had forgotten the plasticity and lustre of her skin, it was darker also than it had been before–almost the colour of her eyes–she must have spent many hours each day in the sun. Suddenly and unaffectedly she threw her towel down and adjusted the top of her brief costume, pulling open the thin fabric and cupping one fat breast in her hand to settle it more comfortably, David felt his need of her so strongly that it seemed he could not contain it all within the physical bounds of his chest. He moved slightly and the gravel crunched softly under his shoes.

Instantly the lovely head turned towards him and froze in the attitude of listening. The eyes were wide open, intelligent and expressive, they seemed to look slightly to one side of him–and David had a powerful impulse to turn and glance behind him, following their steady gaze.

'David?' she asked softly. 'Is that you, David?'

He tried to answer her, but his voice failed him and his reply was a small choking sound. She ran to him, swiftly and long-legged as a roused foal, with her arms reaching out and her face lighting with joy.

He caught her up, and she clung to him fiercely, almost angrily–as though she had been too long denied.

'I've missed you, David.' Her voice was fierce also. 'Oh, God, you'll never know how I have missed you,' and she pressed her mouth to the stark gash in his mask of flesh.

This was the first human being who had treated him without reserve–without pity or revulsion–in all those months, and David felt his heart swell harder and his embrace was as fierce as hers.

She broke at last, leaning back to press her hips unashamedly against his, exulting in the hard thrustingness of his arousal, proud to have evoked it–and quickly, questioningly she ran her hands over his face, feeling the new contours and the unexpected planes and angles.

She felt him begin to pull away, but she stopped him and continued her examination.

'My fingers tell me that you are still beautiful–'

'You have lying fingers,' he whispered, but she ignored his words, and pushed forward teasingly with her hips.

'And I'm getting another very powerful message from further south.' She gave a breathless little laugh. 'Come with me, please, sir.'

Holding his hand, she ran lightly up the steps, dragging him after her. He was amazed at the agility and confidence with which she negotiated the climb.

She drew him into the cottage and as he looked about him, quickly taking it all in, she closed and bolted the door. Immediately the room was cool and dim and intimate.

On the bed her body was still damp and cold from the lake, but her lips were hot as she strained against him urgently. The two beautiful young bodies meshed hungrily, almost as if they were attempting to find sanctuary within each other, desperately flesh sought haven within flesh, within each other's encircling arms and legs they searched for and found surcease from the loneliness and the darkness.

The physical act of love, no matter how often repeated, was insufficient for their needs; even in the intervals between they clung desperately to each other; sleeping pressed together, they groped drowsily but anxiously for each other if the movements of sleep separated them for even an instant. They talked holding hands, she reaching up to touch his face at intervals, he staring into her golden eyes. Even when she prepared their simple meals, he stood close beside or behind her so that she could sway against him and feel him there. It was as though they lived in momentary dread of being once more separated.

It was two days before they left the sanctuary of the cottage and walked together along the lake shore or swam from the jetty and lay in the warm sun. But even when Ella looked down at them from the terrace and waved, David asked, 'Shall we go up to her?'

'No,' Debra answered quickly. 'Not yet. I'm not ready to share you with anybody else yet. Just a little while more, please, David.'

And it was another three days before they climbed the path to the studio. Ella had laid on one of her gargantuan lunches, but she had invited no other guests and they were grateful to her for that.

'I thought I'd have to send down a party of stretcher-bearers to carry you up, Davey,' Ella greeted him, with a lecherous chuckle.

'Don't be crude, Ella,' Debra told her primly, flushing to a dark rose brown, and Ella let fly with one of her explosive bursts of mirth that was so contagious they must follow it.

They sat beneath the palm trees and drank wine from the earthenware jugs, and ate hugely, laughing and talking without restraint, David and Debra so involved with each other that they were not aware of Ella's shrewdly veiled appraisal.

The change in Debra was dramatic, all the coolness and reserve were gone now, the armour in which she had clad her emotions was stripped away. She was vital and eager and blooming with love.

She sat close beside David, laughing with delight at his sallies, and leaning to touch and caress him, as though to reassure herself of his presence.

Ella glanced again at David, trying to smile naturally at him, but guiltily aware of the sneaking sensation of repulsion she still felt–repulsion and aching pity–when she looked at that monstrous head. She knew that if she saw it every day for twenty years, it would still disturb her.

Debra laughed again at something David had said and turned her face to him, offering her mouth with a touching innocence.

'What a terrible thing to say,' she laughed. 'I think a gesture of contrition is called for,' and responded eagerly as the great ravaged head bent to her and the thin slit of a mouth touched hers.

It was disquieting to see the lovely dark face against that mask of ruined flesh, and yet it was also strangely moving.

'It was the right thing. For once I did the right thing,' Ella decided, watching them, and feeling a vague envy. These two were bound together completely, made strong by their separate afflictions. Before it had been a mutual itching of the flesh, a chance spark struck from two minds meeting, but now it was something that transcended that.

Ella recalled regretfully a long line of lovers stretching back to the shadowy edges of her memory, receding images which seemed unreal now. If only there had been something to bind her to one of those, if only she had been left something more valuable than half-remembered words and faded memories of brief mountings and furtive couplings. She sighed, and they looked to her questioningly.

'A sad sound, Ella, darling,' Debra said. 'We are selfish, please forgive us.'

'Not sad, my children,' Ella denied hotly, scattering the old phantoms of her memory. 'I am happy for you. You have something very wonderful–strong and bright and wonderful. Protect it as you would your life.'

She took up her wine glass. 'I give you a toast. I give you David and Debra–and a love made invincible by suffering.' And they were serious for a moment while they drank the toast together in golden yellow wine, sitting in golden yellow sunlight, then the mood resumed and they were gay once more.

Once the first desperate demands of their bodies had been met, once they had drawn as close together as physical limits would allow, then they began a coupling of the spirit. They had never really spoken before, even when they had shared the house on Malik Street, they had used only the superficial word symbols.

Now they began learning really to talk. Some nights they did not sleep but spent the fleeting hours of darkness in exploring each other's minds and bodies, and they delighted to realize that this exploration would never be completed–for the area of their minds were boundless.

During the day the blind girl taught David to see. He found that he had never truly used his eyes before, and now that he must see for both of them he had to learn to make the fullest use of his sight. He must learn to describe colour and shape and movement accurately and incisively, for Debra's demands were insatiable.

In turn, David, whose own confidence had been shattered by his disfigurement, taught confidence to the girl. She learned to trust him implicitly as he grew to anticipate her needs. She learned to step out boldly beside him, knowing that he would guide or caution her with a light touch or a word. Her world had shrunk to the small area about the cottage and jetty within which she could find her way surely. Now with David beside her, her frontiers fell back and she was free to move wherever she chose.

Yet they ventured out together only cautiously at first, wandering along the lakeside together or climbing the hills towards Nazareth, and each day they swam in the green lake waters and each night they made love in the curtained alcove.

David grew hard and lean and sun-tanned again, and it seemed they were complete for when Ella asked, 'Debra, when are you going to make a start on the new book?' she laughed and answered lightly.

'Sometime within the next hundred years.'

A week later she asked of David this time:

'Have you decided what you are going to do yet, Davey?'

'Just what I'm doing now,' he said, and Debra backed him up quickly. 'For ever!' she said. 'Just like this for ever.'

Then without thinking about it, without really steeling themselves to it, they went to where they would meet other people in the mass.

David borrowed the speedboat, picked up a shopping list from Ella, and they planed down along the lake shore to Tiberias, with the white wake churning out behind them and the wind and drops of spray in their faces.

They moored in the tiny harbour of the marina at Lido Beach and walked up into the town. David was so engrossed with Debra that the crowds about him were unreal, and although he noticed a few curious glances they meant very little to him.

Although it was early in the season, the town was filled with visitors, and the buses were parked in the square at the foot of the hill and along the lake front, for this was full on the tourist route.

David carried a plastic bag that grew steadily heavier until it was ready to overflow.

'Bread, and that's the lot,' Debra mentally ticked off the list.

They went down the hill under the eucalyptus trees and found a table on the harbour wall, beneath a gaily coloured umbrella.

They sat touching each other and drank cold beer and ate pistachio nuts, oblivious of everything and everybody about them even though the other tables were crowded with tourists. The lake sparkled and the softly rounded hills seemed very close in the bright light. Once a flight of Phantoms went booming down the valley, flying low on some mysterious errand, and David watched them dwindle southward without regrets.

When the sun was low they went to where the speedboat was moored, and David handed Debra down into it. On the wall above them sat a party of tourists, probably on some package-deal pilgrimage, and they were talking animately–their accents were Limehouse, Golders Green and Merseyside, although the subtleties of pronunciation were lost on David.

He started the motor and pushed off from the wall, steering for the harbour mouth with Debra sitting close beside him and the motor burbling softly.

A big red-faced tourist looked down from the wall and, supposing that the motor covered his voice, nudged his wife.

'Get a look at those two, Mavis. Beauty and the beast, isn't it?'

'Cork it, Bert. They might understand.'

'Go on, luv! They only talk Yiddish or whatever.'

Debra felt David's arm go rigid under her hand, felt him begin to pull away, sensing his outrage and anger–but she gripped his forearm tightly and restrained him.

'Let's go, Davey, darling. Leave them, please.'

Even when they were alone on the safety of the cottage, David was silent and she could feel the tension in his body and the air was charged with it.

They ate the evening meal of bread and cheese and fish and figs in the same strained silence. Debra could think of nothing to say to distract him for the careless words had wounded her as deeply. Afterwards she lay unsleeping beside him. He lay on his back, not touching her, with his arms at his sides and his fists clenched. When at last she could bear it no longer, she turned to him and stroked his face, still not knowing what to say. It was David who broke the silence at last.

'I want to go away from people. We don't need people–do we?'

'No,' she whispered. 'We don't need them.'

'There is a place called Jabulani. It is deep in the African bushveld, far from the nearest town. My father bought it as a hunting lodge thirty years ago–and now it belongs to me.'

'Tell me about it.' Debra laid her head on his chest, and he began stroking her hair, relaxing as he talked.

'There is a wide plain on which grow open forests of mopani and mohobahoba, with some big fat old baobabs and a few ivory palms. In the open glades the grass is yellow gold and the fronds of the ilala palms look like beggars' fingers. At the end of the plain is a line of hills, they turn blue at a distance and the peaks are shaped like the turrets of a fairy castle with tumbled blocks of granite. Between the hills rises a spring of water, a strong spring that has never dried and the water is very clear and sweet–'

'What does Jabulani mean?' Debra asked when he had described it to her.

'It means the "place of rejoicing",' David told her.

'I want to go there with you,' she said.

'What about Israel?' he asked. 'Will you not miss it?'

'No,' she shook her head. 'You see, I will take it with me–in my heart.'

Ella went up to Jerusalem with them, filling the back seat of the Mercedes. She would help Debra select the furniture they would take with them from the house and have it crated and shipped. The rest of it she would sell for them. Aaron Cohen would negotiate the sale of the house, and both David and Debra felt a chill of sadness at the thought of other people living in their home.

David left the women at it and he drove out to Ein Karem and parked the Mercedes beside the iron gate in the garden wall.

The Brig was waiting for him in that bleak and forbidding room above the courtyard. When David greeted him from the doorway he looked up coldly, and there was no relaxation of the iron features, no warmth or pity in the fierce warrior eyes.

'You come to me with the blood of my son upon your hands,' he said, and David froze at the words and held his gaze. After a few moments the Brig indicated the tall-backed chair against the far wall, and David crossed stiffly to it and sat down.

'If you had suffered less, I would have made you answer for more,' said the Brig. 'But vengeance and hatred are barren things–as you have discovered.'

David dropped his eyes to the floor.

'I will not pursue them further, despite the dictates of my heart, for that is what I am condemning in you. You are a violent young man, and violence is the pleasure of fools and only the last resort of wise men. The only excuse for it is to protect what is rightfully yours–any other display of violence is abuse. You abused the power I gave you–and in doing it you killed my son, and brought my country to the verge of war.'

The Brig stood up from his desk, and he crossed to the window and looked down into the garden. They were both silent while he stroked his moustache and remembered his son.

At last the Brig sighed heavily and turned back into the room.

'Why do you come to me?' he asked.

'I wish to marry your daughter, sir.'

'You are asking me–or telling me?' the Brig demanded, and then without waiting for an answer returned to his desk and sat down. 'If you abuse this also–if you bring her pain or unhappiness, I will seek you out. Depend upon it.'

David stood up and settled the cloth cap over his gross head, pulling the brim well down.

'We would like you to be at the wedding. Debra asked that particularly–for you and her mother.'

The Brig nodded. 'You may tell her that we will be there.'

The synagogue at Jerusalem University is a gleaming white structure, shaped like the tent of a desert wanderer, with the same billowing lines.

The red-bud trees were in full bloom and the wedding party was larger than they had planned, for apart from the immediate family there were Debra's colleagues from the university, Robert and some of the other boys from the squadron, Ella Kadesh, Doctor Edelman the baby-faced eye surgeon who had worked on Debra, Aaron Cohen and a dozen others.

After the simple ceremony, they walked through the university grounds to one of the reception rooms that David had hired. It was a quiet gathering with little laughter or joking. The young pilots from David's old squadron had to leave early to return to base, and with them went any pretence of jollity.

Debra's mother was still not yet fully recovered, and the prospect of Debra's departure reduced her to quiet grey weeping. Debra tried without success to comfort her.

Before he left, Dr Edelman drew David aside.

'Watch for any sign of atrophy in her eyes, any cloudiness, excessive redness–any complaints of pain, headaches–'

'I will watch for it.'

'Any indications, no matter how trivial–if you have any doubts, you must write to me.'

'Thank you, doctor.'

They shook hands. 'Good luck in your new life,' said Edelman.

Through it all Debra showed iron control, but even she at last succumbed and she, her mother, and Ella Kadesh all broke down simultaneously at the departure barrier of Lod Airport and hung round each other's necks, weeping bitterly.

The Brig and David stood by, stiff and awkward, trying to look as though they were not associated with the weeping trio, until the first warning broadcast gave them an excuse for a brief handshake and David took Debra's arm and drew her gently away.

They climbed the boarding ladder into the waiting Boeing without looking back. The giant aircraft took off and turned away southwards, and as always the sensation of flight soothed David; all the cares and tensions of these last few days left on the earth behind and below, he felt a new lightness of the spirit–excitement for what lay ahead.

He reached across and squeezed Debra's arm.

'Hello there, Morgan,' he said, and she turned towards him and smiled happily–blindly.

It was necessary to spend some time in Cape Town before they could escape to the sanctuary of Jabulani in the north.

David took a suite at the Mount Nelson Hotel, and from there he was able to settle the numerous issues that had piled up in his absence.

The accountants who managed his trust funds demanded ten days of his time and they spent it in the sitting-room of the suite, poring over trust documents and accounts.

In two years his income had grossly exceeded his spending, and the unused portion of his income had to be re-invested. In addition the third trust fund would soon pass to him and there were formalities to be completed.

Debra was hugely impressed by the extent of David's wealth.

'You must be almost a millionaire,' she said in a truly awed voice, for that was as rich as Debra could imagine.

'I'm not just a pretty face,' David agreed, and she was relieved that he could talk so lightly about his appearance.

Mitzi and her new husband came to visit them in their suite. However, the evening was not a success. Although Mitzi tried to act as though nothing had changed, and though she still called him 'warrior', yet it was apparent that she and her feelings had altered.

She was heavily pregnant and more shapeless than David would have thought possible. It was half-way through the evening before David realized the true reason for all the reserve. At first he thought that his disfigurement was worrying them, but after Mitzi had given a half-hour eulogy of the strides that Cecil was making at Morgan Group and the immense trust that Paul Morgan had placed in him, Cecil had asked innocently, 'Are you thinking of joining us at the Group? I'm sure we could find something useful for you to do–ha, ha!'

David could assure them quietly.

'No, thank you. You won't have to worrry about me, Cecil, old boy. You take over from Uncle Paul with my blessing.'

'Good Lord, I didn't mean that.' Cecil was shocked, but Mitzi was less devious.

'He really will be very good, warrior, and you never were interested, were you?'

After that evening they did not see the couple again, and Paul Morgan was in Europe, so David fulfilled his family obligations without much pain or suffering and he could concentrate on the preparations for the move to Jabulani.

Barney Venter spent a week with them in choosing a suitable aircraft to handle the bush airstrip and yet give David the type of performance he enjoyed. At last they decided on a twin-engined Piper Navajo, a six-seater with two big 300-h.p. Lycoming engines and a tricycle undercart, and Barney walked around it with his hands on his hips.

'Well, she's no Mirage.' He kicked the landing-wheel and then checked himself and glanced quickly at David's face.

'I've had enough of Mirages,' David told him. 'They bite!'

On the last day David drove out with Debra to a farm near Paarl. The owner's wife was a dog breeder and when they went down to the kennels one of her labrador pups walked directly to Debra and placed a cold nose on her leg as he inhaled her scent. Debra squatted and groped for his head and after fondling for a few moments she in her turn leaned forward and sniffed the pup's fur.

'He smells like old leather,' she said. 'What colour is he?'

'Black,' said David. 'Black as a Zulu.'

'That's what we'll call him,' said Debra. 'Zulu.'

'You want to choose this one?' David asked.

'No,' Debra laughed. 'He chose us.'

When they flew northwards the next morning the pup was indignant at being placed in the back seat and with a flying scrambling leap he came over Debra's shoulder and took up position in her lap, which seemed to suit them both very well.

'It looks like I have competition,' David muttered ruefully.

From the brown plateau of the high veld, the land dropped away steeply down the escarpment to the bush veld of southern Africa.

David picked up his landmark on the little village of Bush Buck Ridge and the long slim snake of the Sabi River as it twisted through the open forests of the plain. He altered course slightly northwards and within ten minutes he saw the low line of blue hills which rose abruptly out of the flat land.

'There it is, ahead of us,' David told Debra and his tone was infectious. She hugged the dog closer to her and leaned towards David.

'What does it look like?'

The hills were forested with big timber, and turreted with grey rock. At their base the bush was thick and dark. The pools glinted softly through the dark foliage. He described them to her.

'My father named them "The String of Pearls", and that's what they look like. They rise out of the run-off of rain water from the sloping ground beyond the hills. They disappear just as suddenly again into the sandy earth of the plain,' David explained as he circled the hills, slowly losing height. 'They are what give Jabulani its special character, for they provide water for all the wild life of the plain. Birds and animals are drawn from hundreds of miles to the Pearls.' He levelled out and throttled back, letting the aircraft sink lower. 'There is the homestead, white walls and thatch to keep it cool in the hot weather, deep shaded verandas and high rooms–you will love it.'

The airstrip seemed clear and safe, although the windsock hung in dirty tatters from its pole. David circled it carefully before lining up for the landing, and they taxied towards the small brick hangar set amongst the trees. David kicked on the wheel brakes and cut the engines.

'This is it,' he said.

Jabulani was one of a block of estates that bounded the Kruger National Park–the most spectacular nature reserve on earth. These estates were not productive, in that they were unsuitable for the growth of crops and few of them were used for grazing of domestic animals; their immense value lay in the unspoiled bush veld and the wild life–in the peace and space upon which wealthy men placed such a premium that they would pay large fortunes for a piece of this *Lebensraum*.

When David's grandfather had purchased Jabulani he had paid a few shillings an acre, for in those days the wilderness was still intact.

It had been used as a family hunting estate down the years, and as Paul Morgan had never shown interest in the veld, it had passed to David's father and so to David.

Now the eighteen thousand acres of African bush and plain, held as freehold land, was a possession beyond price.

Yet the Morgan family had made little use of it these last fifteen years. David's father had been an enthusiastic huntsman, and with him most of David's school holidays had been spent here. However, after his father's death, the visits to Jabulani had become shorter and further apart.

It was seven years since the last visit, when he had brought up a party of brother officers from Cobra Squadron.

Then it had been immaculately run by Sam, the black overseer, butler and game ranger.

Under Sam's management there had always been fresh crisp linen on the beds, highly polished floors, the exterior walls of the buildings had been snowy white and the thatch neat and well-tended. The deep-freeze had been well stocked with steak and the liquor cupboard filled–with every bottle accounted for.

Sam ran a tight camp, with half a dozen willing and cheerful helpers.

'Where is Sam?' was the first question David asked of the two servants who hurried down from the homestead to meet the aircraft.

'Sam gone.'

'Where to?' And the answer was the eloquent shrug of Africa. Their uniforms were dirty and needed mending, and their manners disinterested.

'Where is the Land-Rover?'

'She is dead.'

They walked up to the homestead and there David had another series of unpleasant surprises.

The buildings were dilapidated, looking forlorn and neglected under their rotting black thatch. The walls were dingy, grey-brown with the plaster falling away in patches.

The interiors were filthy with dust, and sprinkled with the droppings of the birds and reptiles that made their homes in the thatch.

The mosquito gauze, that was intended to keep the wide verandas insect-free, was rusted through and breaking away in tatters.

The vegetable gardens were overgrown, the fences about them falling to pieces. The grounds of the homestead itself were thick with rank weed, and not only the Land-Rover had died. No single piece of machinery on the estate–water pump, toilet cistern, electricity generator, motor vehicle–was in working order.

'It's a mess, a frightful mess,' David told Debra as they sat on the front step and drank mugs of sweet tea. Fortunately David had thought to bring emergency supplies with them.

'Oh, Davey. I am so sorry, because I like it here. It's peaceful, so quiet. I can just feel my nerves untying themselves.'

'Don't be sorry. I'm not. Those old huts were built by Gramps back in the twenties–and they weren't very well built even then.' David's voice was full of a new purpose, a determination that she had not heard for so long. 'It's a fine excuse to tear the whole lot down, and build again.'

'A place of our own?' she asked.

'Yes,' said David delightedly. That's it. That's just it!'

They flew into Nelspruit, the nearest large town, the following day. In the week of bustle and planning that followed they forgot their greater problems. With an architect they planned the new homestead with care, taking into consideration all their special requirements–a large airy study for Debra, workshop and office for David, a kitchen laid out to make it safe and easy for a blind cook, rooms without dangerous split levels and with regular easily learned shapes, and finally a nursery section. When David described this addition Debra asked cautiously, 'You making some plans that I should know about?'

'You'll know about it, all right,' he assured her.

The guest house was to be separate and self-contained and well away from the main homestead, and the small hutment for the servants was a quarter of a mile beyond that, screened by trees and the shoulder of the rocky kopje that rose behind the homestead.

David bribed a building contractor from Nelspruit to postpone all his other work, load his workmen on four heavy trucks and bring them out to Jabulani.

They began on the main house, and while they worked David was busy resurfacing the airstrip, repairing the water pumps and such other machinery as still had life left in it. However, the Land-Rover and the electricity generator had to be replaced.

Within two months the new homestead was habitable, and they could move. Debra set up her tape recorders beneath the big windows overlooking the shaded front garden, where the afternoon breeze could cool the room and waft in the perfume of the frangipani and poinsettia blooms.

While David was completely absorbed in making Jabulani into a comfortable home, Debra made her own arrangements.

Swiftly she explored and mapped in her mind all her immediate surroundings. Within weeks she could move about the new house with all the confidence of a person with normal sight and she had trained the servants to replace each item of furniture in its exact position. Always Zulu, the labrador pup, moved like a glossy black shadow beside her. Early on he had decided that Debra needed his constant care, and had made her his life's work.

Quickly he learned that it was useless staring at her or wagging his tail, to attract her attention he must whine or pant. In other respects she was also slightly feeble-minded, the only way to prevent her doing stupid things like falling down the front steps or tripping over a bucket left in the passage by a careless servant was to bump her with his shoulder, or with his nose.

She had fallen readily into a pattern of work that kept her in her workroom until noon each day, with Zulu curled at her feet.

David set up a large bird bath under the trees outside her window, so the tapes she made had as a background the chatter and warble of half a dozen varieties of wild birds. She had discovered a typist in Nelspruit who could speak Hebrew, and David took the tapes in to her whenever he flew to town for supplies and to collect the mail, and he brought each batch of typing back with him for checking.

They worked together on this task, David reading each batch of writing or correspondence aloud to her and making the alterations she asked for. He made it a habit of reading almost everything, from newspapers to novels, aloud.

'Who needs braille with you around,' Debra remarked, but it was more than just the written word she needed to hear from him. It was each facet and dimension of her new surroundings. She had never seen any of the myriad birds that flocked to drink and bathe below her window, though she soon recognized each individual call and would pick out a stranger immediately.

'David, there's a new one, what is it? What does he look like?'

And he must describe not only its plumage, but its mannerisms and its habits. At other times he must describe to her exactly how the new buildings fitted into their surroundings, the antics of Zulu the labrador, and supply accurate descriptions of the servants, the view from the window of her workroom–and a hundred other aspects of her new life.

In time the building was completed and the strangers left Jabulani, but it was not until the crates from Israel containing their furniture and other possessions from Malik Street arrived that Jabulani started truly to become their home.

The olive-wood table was placed under the window in the workroom.

'I haven't been able to work properly, there was something missing–' Debra ran her fingers caressingly across the inlaid ivory and ebony top '–until now.'

Her books were in shelves on the wall beside the table, and the leather suite in the new lounge looked very well with the animal-skin rugs and woven wool carpets.

David hung the Ella Kadesh painting above the fireplace, Debra determining the precise position for him by sense of touch.

'Are you sure it shouldn't be a sixteenth of an inch higher?' David asked seriously.

'Let's have no more lip from you, Morgan, I have to know exactly where it is.'

Then the great brass bedstead was set up in the bedroom, and covered with the ivory-coloured bedspread. Debra bounced up and down on it happily.

'Now, there is only one thing more that is missing,' she declared.

'What's that?' he asked with mock anxiety. 'Is it something important?'

'Come here.' She crooked a finger in his general direction. 'And I'll show you just how important it is.'

During the months of preparation they had not left the immediate neighbourhood of the homestead, but now quite suddenly the rush and bustle was over.

'We have eighteen thousand acres and plenty of four-footed neighbours–let's go check it all out,' David suggested.

They packed a cold lunch and the three of them climbed into the new Land-Rover with Zulu relegated to the back seat. The road let naturally down to the String of Pearls for this was the focal point of all life upon the estate.

They left the Land-Rover amongst the fever trees and went down to the ruins of the thatched summer house on the bank of the main pool.

The water aroused all Zulu's instincts and he plunged into it, paddling out into the centre with obvious enjoyment. The water was clear as air, but shaded to black in the depths.

David scratched in the muddy bank and turned out a thick pink earthworm. He threw it into the shallows and a dark shape half as long as his arm rushed silently out of the depths and swirled the surface.

'Wow!' David laughed. 'There are still a few fat ones around. We will have to bring down the rods. I used to spend days down here when I was a kid.'

The forest was filled with memories and as they wandered along the edge of the reed banks he reminisced about his childhood, until gradually he fell into silence, and she asked:

'Is something wrong, David?' She had grown that sensitive to his moods.

'There are no animals.' His tone was puzzled. 'Birds, yes. But we haven't seen a single animal, not even a duiker, since we left the homestead.' He stopped at a place that was clear of reeds, where the bank shelved gently. 'This used to be a favourite drinking place. It was busy day and night–the herds virtually lining up for a chance to drink.' He left Debra and went down to the edge, stooping to examine the ground carefully. 'No spoor even, just a few kudu and a small troop of baboon. There has not been a herd here for months, or possibly years.'

When he came back to her she asked gently, 'You are upset?'

'Jabulani without its animals is nothing,' he muttered. 'Come on, let's go and see the rest of it. There is something very odd here.'

The leisurely outing became a desperate hunt, as David scoured the thickets and the open glades, followed the dried water courses and stopped the Land-Rover to examine the sand beds for signs of wild life.

'Not even an impala,' he was worried and anxious. 'There used to be thousands of them. I remember herds of them, silky brown and graceful as ballet dancers, under nearly every tree.'

He turned the Land-Rover northwards, following an overgrown track through the trees.

'There is grazing here that hasn't been touched. It's lush as a cultivated garden.'

A little before noon they reached the dusty, corrugated public road that ran along the north boundary of Jabulani. The fence that followed the edge of the road was ruinous, with sagging and broken wire and many of the uprights snapped off at ground level.

'Hell, it's a mess,' David told her, as he turned through a gap in the wire on to the road, and followed the boundary for two miles until they reached the turn-off to the Jabulani homestead.

Even the signboard hanging above the stone pillars of the gateway, which David's father had fashioned in bronze and of which he had been so proud, was now dilapidated and hung askew.

'Well, there's plenty of work to keep us going,' said David with a certain relish.

Half a mile beyond the gates the road turned sharply, hedged on each side by tall grass, and standing full in the sandy track was a magnificent kudu bull, ghostly grey and striped with pale chalky lines across the deep powerful body. His head was held high, armed with the long corkscrew black horns, and his huge ears were spread in an intent listening attitude.

For only part of a second he posed like that, then, although the Land-Rover was still two hundred yards off, he exploded into a smoky blur of frantic flight. His great horns laid along his back as he fled through the open bush in a series of long, lithe bounds, disappearing so swiftly it seemed he had been only a fantasy, and David described it to Debra.

'He took off the very instant he spotted us. I remember when they were so tame around here that we had to chase them out of the vegetable garden with sticks.'

Again he swung off the main track and on to another overgrown path, on which the new growth of saplings was already thick and tall. He drove straight over them in the tough little vehicle.

'What on earth are you doing?' Debra shouted above the crash and swish of branches.

'In this country when you run out of road, you just make your own.'

Four miles farther on, they emerged abruptly on to the fire-break track that marked the eastern boundary of Jabulani, the dividing line between them and the National Park which was larger than the entire land area of the state of Israel, five million acres of virgin wilderness, three hundred and eighty-five kilometres long and eighty wide, home of more than a million wild animals, the most important reservoir of wild life left in Africa.

David stopped the Land-Rover, cut the engine and jumped down. After a moment of shocked and angry silence he began to swear.

'What's made you so happy?' Debra demanded.

'Look at that–just look at that!' David ranted.

'I wish I could.'

'Sorry, Debs. It's a fence. A game fence!'

It stood eight feet high and the uprights were hardwood poles thick as a man's thigh, while the mesh of the fence was heavy gauge wire. 'They have fenced us off. The National Park's people have cut us off! No wonder there are no animals.'

As they drove back to the homestead David explained to her how there had always been an open boundary with the Kruger National Park. It had suited everybody well enough, for Jabulani's sweet grazing and the perennial water of the pools helped to carry the herds through times of drought and scarcity.

'It's becoming very important to you, this business of the wild animals.' Debra had listened silently, fondling the labrador's head, as David spoke.

'Yes, suddenly it's important. When they were here, I guess I just took them for granted–but now they are gone, well, now they are very important,' he laughed abruptly and bitterly. 'I wonder how often that's been said in Africa–now they are gone it's suddenly important.'

They drove on for a mile or two without speaking and then David said with determination, 'I'm going to get them to pull that fence out. They can't cut us off like that. I'm going to get hold of the head warden, now, right away.'

David remembered Conrad Berg from his childhood when he had been the warden in charge of the southern portion of the park, but not yet the chief. There was a body of legend about the man that had been built up over the years, and two of these stories showed clearly the type of man he was.

Caught out in a lonely area of the reserve after dark with a broken-down truck, he was walking home when he was attacked by a full-grown male lion. In the struggle he had been terribly mauled, half the flesh torn from his back and the bone of his shoulder and arm bitten through. Yet he had managed to kill the animal with a small sheath knife, stabbing it repeatedly in the throat until he hit the jugular. He had then stood up and walked five miles through the night with the hyena pack following him expectantly, waiting for him to drop.

On another occasion one of the estate owners bounding the park had poached one of Berg's lions, shooting it down half a mile inside the boundary. The poacher was a man high in government, wielding massive influence, and he had laughed at Conrad Berg.

'What are you going to do about it, my friend? Don't you like your job?'

Doggedly, ignoring the pressure from above, Berg had collected his evidence and issued a summons. The pressure had become less subtle as the court date approached, but he had never wavered. The important personage finally stood in the dock, and was convicted. He was sentenced to a thousand pounds' fine or six months at hard labour.

Afterwards he had shaken Berg's hand and said to him, 'Thank you for a lesson in courage,' and perhaps this was one of the reasons Berg was now chief warden.

He stood beside his game fence where he had arranged over the telephone to meet David. He was a big man, broad and tall and beefy, with thick heavily muscled arms still scarred from the lion attack, and a red sunburned face.

He wore the suntans and slouch hat of the Park's service, with the green cloth badges on his epaulets.

Behind him was parked his brown Chevy truck with the Park Board's emblem on the door, and two of his black game rangers seated in the back. One of them was holding a heavy rifle.

Berg stood with his clenced fists on his hips, his hat pushed back and a forbidding expression on his face. He so epitomized the truculent male animal guarding its territory that David muttered to Debra, 'Here comes trouble.'

He parked close beside the fence and he and Debra climbed down and went to the wire.

'Mr Berg. I am David Morgan. I remember you from when my father owned Jabulani. I'd like you to meet my wife.'

Berg's expression wavered. Naturally he had heard all the rumours about the new owner of Jabulani; it was a lonely isolated area and it was his job to know about these things. Yet he was unprepared for this dreadfully mutilated young man, and his blind but beautiful wife.

With an awkward gallantry Berg doffed his hat, then realized she would not see the gesture. He murmured a greeting and when David thrust his hand through the fence he shook it cautiously.

Debra and David were working as a team and they turned their combined charm upon Berg, who was a simple and direct man. Slowly his defences softened as they chatted. He admired Zulu, he also kept labradors and it served as a talking-point while Debra unpacked a Thermos of coffee and David filled mugs for all of them.

'Isn't that Sam?' David pointed to the game ranger in the truck who held Berg's rifle.

'Ja.' Berg was guarded.

'He used to work on Jabulani.'

'He came to me of his own accord,' Berg explained, turning aside any implied rebuke.

'He wouldn't remember me, of course, not the way I look now. But he was a fine ranger, and the place certainly went to the bad without him to look after it,' David admitted before he went into a frontal assault. 'The other thing which has ruined us is this fence of yours.' David kicked one of the uprights.

'You don't say?' Berg swished the grounds of his coffee around the mug and flicked it out.

'Why did you do it?'

'For good reason.'

'My father had a gentleman's agreement with the Board, the boundary was open at all times. We have got water and grazing that you need.'

'With all respects to the late Mr Morgan,' Conrad Berg spoke heavily, 'I was never in favour of the open boundary.'

'Why not?'

'Your daddy was a *sportsman*.' He spat the word out, as though it were a mouthful of rotten meat. 'When my lions got to know him and learned to stay this side of the line–then he used to bring down a couple of donkeys and parade them along the boundary–to tempt them out.'

David opened his mouth to protest, and then closed it slowly. He felt the seamed scars of his face mottling and staining with a flush of shame. It was true, he remembered the donkeys and the soft wet lion skins being pegged out to dry behind the homestead.

'He never poached,' David defended him. 'He had an owner's licence and they were all shot on our land.'

'No, he never poached,' Berg admitted. 'He was too damned clever for that. He knew I would have put a rocket up him that would have made him the first man on the moon.'

'So that's why you put up the fence.'

'No.'

'Why then?'

'Because for fourteen years Jabulani has been under the care of an absentee landlord who didn't give a good damn what happened to it. Old Sam here–' he motioned at the game ranger in the truck '–did his best, but still it became a poacher's paradise. As fast as the grazing and water you boast of pulled my game out of the Park, so they were cut down by every sportsman with an itchy trigger finger. When Sam tried to do something about it, he got badly beaten up, and when that didn't stop him somebody put fire into his hut at night. They burned two of his kids to death–'

Daved felt his very soul quail at the thought of the flames on flesh, his cheeks itched at the memory.

'I didn't know,' he said gruffly.

'No, you were too busy making money or whatever is your particular form of pleasure,' Berg was angry. 'So at last Sam came to me and I gave him a job. Then I strung this fence.'

'There is nothing left on Jabulani–a few kudu, and a duiker or two–but otherwise it's all gone.'

'You are so right. It didn't take them long to clean it out.'

'I want it back.'

'Why?' Berg scoffed. 'So you can be a sportsman like your daddy? So you can fly your pals down from Jo'burg for the weekend to shoot the shit out of my lions?' Berg glanced at Debra, and immediately his red face flushed a deep port-wine colour. 'I'm sorry, Mrs Morgan, I did not mean to say that.'

'That's perfectly all right, Mr Berg. I think it was very expressive.'

'Thank you, ma'm.' Then he turned furiously back to David. 'Morgan's Private Safari Service, is that what you are after?'

'I would not allow a shot fired on Jabulani,' said David.

'I bet–except for the pot. That's the usual story. Except for the pot, and you've got the battle of Waterloo being fought all over again.'

'No,' said David. 'Not even for the pot.'

'You'd eat butcher's beef?' Berg asked incredulously.

'Look here, Mr Berg. If you pull your fence out, I'll have Jabulani declared a private nature reserve–'

Berg had been about to say something, but David's declaration dried the words, and his mouth remained hanging open. He closed it slowly.

'You know what that means?' he asked at last. 'You place yourself under our jurisdiction, completely. We'd tie you up properly with a lawyer's paper and all that stuff: no owner's licence, no shooting lions because they are in cattle area.'

'Yes. I know. I've studied the act. But there is something more. I'd undertake to fence the other three boundaries to your satisfaction, and maintain a force of private game rangers that you considered adequate–all at my own expense.'

Conrad Berg lifted his hat and scratched pensively at the long sparse grey hairs that covered his pate.

'Man,' he said mournfully, 'how can I say no to that?' Then he began to smile, the first smile of the meeting. 'It looks like you are really serious about this then.'

'My wife and I are going to be living here permanently. We don't want to live in a desert.'

'Ja,' he nodded, understanding completely that a man should feel that way. The strong revulsion that he had originally felt for the fantastic face before him was fading.

'I think the first thing we should work on is these poachers you tell me about. Let's snatch a couple of those and make a few examples,' David went on.

Berg's big red face split into a happy grin.

'I think I'm going to enjoy having you as a neighbour,' he said, and again he thrust his hand through the fence. David winced as he felt his knuckles cracking in the huge fist.

'Won't you come to dinner with us tomorrow night? You and your wife?' Debra asked with relief.

'It will be a mighty great pleasure, ma'm.'

'I'll get out the whisky bottle,' said David.

'That's kind of you–' said Conrad Berg seriously, 'but the missus and I only drink Old Buck dry gin, with a little water.'

'I'll see to it,' said David just as seriously.

Jane Berg was a slim woman of about Conrad's age. She had a dried-out face, lined and browned by the sun. Her hair was sunbleached and streaked with grey, and, as Debra remarked, she was probably the only thing in the world that Conrad was afraid of.

'I'm talking, Connie,' was enough to halt any flow of eloquence from her huge spouse, or a significant glance at her empty glass sent him with elephantine haste for a refill. Conrad had a great deal of trouble finishing any story or statement, for Jane had to correct the details during the telling, while he waited patiently for an opportunity to resume.

Debra chose the main course with care so as not to give offence, beefsteaks from the deep freeze, and Conrad ate four of them with unreserved pleasure although he spurned the wine that David served.

'That stuff is poison. Killed one of my uncles,' and stayed with Old Buck gin, even through the dessert.

Afterwards they sat about the cavernous fireplace with its logs blazing cheerfully and Conrad explained, with Jane's assistance, the problems that David would face on Jabulani.

'You get a few of the blacks from the tribal areas coming in from the north–'

'Or across the river,' Jane added.

'Or across the river, but they are no big sweat. They set wire snares mostly, and they don't kill that much–'

'But it's a terribly cruel way, the poor animals linger on for days with the wire cutting down to the bone,' Jane elaborated.

'As I was saying, once we have a few rangers busy that will stop almost immediately. It's the white poachers with modern rifles and hunting lamps–'

'Killing lamps,' Jane corrected.

'–killing lamps, they do the real damage. They finished off all your game on Jabulani in a couple of seasons.'

'Where do they come from?' David asked, his anger was rising again, the same protective anger of the shepherd that he had felt as he flew the skies of Israel.

'There is a big copper mine fifty miles north of here at Phalabora, hundreds of bored miners with a taste for venison. They would come down here and blaze away at every living thing–but now it's not worth the trip for them. Anyway they were just the amateurs, the weekend poachers.'

'Who are the professionals?'

'Where the dirt road from Jabulani meets the big national highway, about thirty miles from here–'

'At a place called Bandolier Hill,' Jane supplied the name.

'–there is a general dealer's store. It's just one of those trading posts that gets a little of the passing trade from the main road, but relies on the natives from the tribal areas. The person who owns and runs it has been there eight years now, and I have been after him all that time, but he's the craftiest bastard–I'm sorry, Mrs Morgan–I have ever run into.'

'He's the one?' David asked.

'He's the one,' Conrad nodded. 'Catch him, and half your worries are over.'

'What's his name?'

'Akkers. Johan Akkers,' Jane gave her assistance, the Old Buck was making her slightly owl-eyed, and she was having a little difficulty with her enunciation.

'How are we going to get him?' David mused. 'There isn't anything left on Jabulani to tempt him–the few kudu we have got are so wild, it wouldn't be worth the effort.'

'No, you haven't got anything to tempt him right now, but about the middle of September–'

'More like the first week in September,' Jane said firmly with strings of hair starting to hang down her temples.

'–the first week in September the marula trees down by your pools will come into fruit, and my elephants are going to visit you. The one thing they just can't resist is marula berries, and they are going to flatten my fence to get at them. Before I can repair it a lot of other game are going to follow the jumbo over to your side. You can lay any type of odds you like that our friend Akkers is oiling his guns and drooling at the mouth right this minute. He will know within an hour when the fence goes.'

'This time he may get a surprise.'

'Let's hope so.'

'I think–' David said softly '–that we might run down to Bandolier Hill tomorrow to have a look at this gentleman.'

'One thing is for sure–' said Jane Berg indistinctly, '–a gentleman, he is not.'

The road down to Bandolier Hill was heavily corrugated and thick with white dust that rose in a banner behind the Land-Rover and hung in the air long after they had passed. The hill was rounded and thickly timbered and stood over the mean metalled highway.

The trading post was four or five hundred yards from the road junction, set back amidst a grove of mango trees with their deep green and glistening foliage. It was a type found all over Africa–an unlovely building of mud brick with a naked corrugated iron roof, the walls plastered thickly with posters advertising goods from tea to flashlight batteries.

David parked the Land-Rover in the dusty yard beneath the raised stoop. There was a faded sign above the front steps:

'Bandolier Hill General Dealers'.

At the side of the building was parked an old green Ford one-ton truck with local licence plates. In the shade of the stoop squatted a dozen or so potential customers, African women from the tribal area, dressed in long cotton print dresses, timeless in their patience and their expressions showing no curiosity about the occupants of the Land-Rover. One of the women was suckling her infant with an enormously elongated breast that allowed the child to stand beside her and watch the newcomers without removing the puckered black nipple from his mouth.

Set in the centre of the yard was a thick straight pole, fifteen feet tall, and on top of the pole was a wooden structure like a dog kennel. David exclaimed as from the kennel emerged a big brown furry animal. It descended the pole in one swift falling action, seemingly as lightly as a bird, and the chain that was fastened to the pole at one end was, at the other, buckled about the animal's waist by a thick leather strap.

'It's one of the biggest old bull baboons I've ever seen.' Quickly he described it to Debra, as the baboon moved out to the chain's limit, and knuckled the ground as he made a lesiurely circle about his pole, the chain clinking as it swung behind him. It was an arrogant display, and he ruffled out the thick mane of hair upon his shoulders. When he had completed the circle, he sat down facing the Land-Rover, in a repellently humanoid attitude, and thrust out his lower jaw as he regarded them through small brown, close-set eyes.

'A nasty beast,' David told Debra. He would weigh ninety pounds, with a long dog-like muzzle and a jaw full of yellow fangs. After the hyena, he was the most hated animal of the veld–cunning, cruel and avaricious, all the vices of man and none of his graces. His stare was unblinking and, every few seconds, he ducked his head in a quick aggressive gesture.

While all David's attention was on the baboon, a man had come out of the store and now leaned on one of the pillars of the veranda.

'What can I do for you, Mr Morgan?' he asked in a thick accent. He was tall and spare, dressed in slightly rumpled and not entirely clean khaki slacks and open-neck shirt, with heavy boots on his feet and braces hooked into his pants, crossing his shoulders.

'How did you know my name?' David looked up at him, and he was of middle age with close-cropped greying hair over a domed skull. His teeth were badly fitting with bright pink plastic gums and his skin was drawn over the bones of the cheeks, and his deep-set eyes gave him a skull-like look. He grinned at David's question.

'Could only be you, scarred face and blind wife–you the new owner of Jabulani. Heard you built a new house and all set to live there now.'

The man's hands were huge, out of proportion to the rest of his rangy body, they were clearly very powerful and the lean muscles of his forearms were as tough as rope.

He slouched easily against the pillar and took from his pocket a clasp knife and a stick of black wind-dried meat–the jerky of North America, boucan of the Caribbean, or the biltong of Africa–and he cut a slice as though it were a plug of tobacco, popping it into his mouth.

'Like I asked–what can we do for you?' he chewed noisily, his teeth squelching at each bite.

'I need nails and paint.' David climbed out of the Land-Rover.

'Heard you did all your buying in Nelspruit.' Akkers looked him over with a calculated insolence, studying David's ruined face with attention. David saw that his deep-set eyes were a muddy green in colour.

'I thought there was a law against caging or chaining wild animals.' Akkers had roused David's resentment almost immediately, and the needle showed in his tone. Akkers began to grin again easily, still chewing.

'You a lawyer–are you?'

'Just asking.'

'I got a permit–you want to see it?'

David shook his head, and turned to speak to Debra in Hebrew. Quickly he described the man.

'I think he can guess why we are here, and he's looking for trouble.'

'I'll stay by the car,' said Debra.

'Good.' David climbed the steps to the veranda.

'What about the nails and paint?' he asked Akkers.

'Go on in,' he was still grinning. 'I got a nigger helper behind the counter. He will look after you.'

David hesitated and then walked on into the building. It smelled of carbolic soap and kerosene and maize meal. The shelves were loaded with cheap groceries, patent medicines, blankets and bolts of printed cotton cloth. From the roof hung bunches of army surplus boots and greatcoats, axe-heads and storm lanterns. The floor was stacked with tin trunks, pick handles, bins of flour and maize meal and the hundreds of other items that traditionally make up the stock of the country dealer. David found the African assistant and began his purchase.

Outside in the sunlight Debra climbed from the Land-Rover and leaned lightly against the door. The labrador scrambled down after her and began sniffing the concrete pillars of the veranda with interest where other dogs before him had spurted jets of yellow urine against the white-washed plaster.

'Nice dog,' said Akkers.

'Thank you.' Debra nodded politely.

Akkers glanced quickly across at his pet baboon, and his expression was suddenly cunning. A flash of understanding passed between man and animal. The baboon ducked its head again in that nervous gesture, then it rose from its haunches and drifted back to the pole. With a leap and bound it shot up the pole and disappeared into the opening of its kennel.

Akkers grinned and carefully cut another slice of the black biltong.

'You like it out at Jabulani?' he asked Debra, and at the same time he offered the scrap of dried meat to the dog.

'We are very happy there,' Debra replied stiffly, not wanting to be drawn. Zulu sniffed the proffered titbit, and his tail beat like a metronome. No dog can resist the concentrated meat smell and taste of biltong. He gulped it eagerly. Twice more Akkers fed him the scraps, and Zulu's eyes glistened and his soft silky muzzle was damp with saliva.

The waiting women in the shade of the veranda were watching with lively interest now. They had seen this happen before with a dog, and they waited expectantly. David was in the building, out of sight. Debra stood blind and unsuspecting.

Akkers cut a larger piece of the dried meat and offered it to Zulu, but when he reached for it he pulled his hand away, teasing the dog. With his taste for biltong now firmly established, Zulu tried again for the meat as it was offered. Again it was pulled away at the last moment. Zulu's black wet nose quivered with anxiety, and the soft ears were cocked.

Akkers walked down the steps with Zulu following him eagerly, and at the bottom he showed the dog the biltong once more, letting him sniff it. Then he spoke softly but urgently, 'Get it, boy,' and threw the scrap of biltong at the base of the baboon's pole. Zulu bounded forward, still slightly clumsy on his big puppy paws, into the circle of the chain where the baboon's paws had beaten the earth hard. He ran on under the pole and grubbed hungrily for the biltong in the dust.

The bull baboon came out of his kennel like a tawny grey blur and dropped the fifteen feet through the air; his limbs were spread and his jaws were open in a snarl like a great red trap, and the fangs were vicious, long and yellow and spiked. He hit the ground silently, and his muscles bunched as they absorbed the shock and hurled the long lithe body feet first at the unsuspecting pup. The baboon crashed into him, taking him on the shoulder with all the weight of his ninety pounds.

Zulu went down and over, rolling on his back with a startled yelp, but before he could find his feet or his wits, the baboon was after him.

Debra heard the pup cry, and started forward, surprised but not yet alarmed.

As he lay on his back, Zulu's belly was unprotected, sparsely covered with the silken black hair, the immature penis protruding pathetically, and the baboon went on to him in a crouching leap, pinning him with powerful furry legs as he bowed his head and buried the long yellow fangs deep into the pup's belly.

Zulu screamed in dreadful agony, and Debra screamed in sympathy and ran forward.

Akkers shot out a foot as she passed him and tripped her, sending her sprawling on her hands and knees.

'Leave it, lady,' he warned her, still grinning. 'You'll get hurt if you interfere.'

The baboon locked its long curved eye teeth into the tender belly, and then hurled the pup away from it with all the fierce strength of its four limbs. The thin wall of the stomach was ripped through, and the purple ropes of the entrails came out, hanging festooned in the baboon's jaws.

Again the disembowelled pup screamed, and Debra rolled blindly to her feet.

'David!' she cried wildly. 'David–help me!'

David came out of the building running; pausing in the doorway he took in the scene at a glance and snatched up a pick handle from the pile by the door. He jumped off the veranda, and in three quick strides he had reached the pup.

The baboon saw him coming and released Zulu. With uncanny speed, he whirled and leapt for the pole, racing upwards to perch on the roof of the kennel, his jowls red with blood, as he shrieked and jabbered, bouncing up and down with excitement and triumph.

David dropped the pick and gently lifted the crawling crippled black body. He carried Zulu to the Land-Rover and ripped his bush jacket into strips as he tried to bind up the torn belly, pushing the hanging entrails back into the hole with his fist.

'David, what is it?' Debra pleaded with him, and as he worked he explained it in a few terse Hebrew sentences.

'Get in,' he told her and she clambered into the passenger seat of the Land-Rover. He laid the injured labrador in her lap, and ran around to the driver's seat.

Akkers was back at the doorway of his shop, standing with thumbs hooked into his braces, and he was laughing. The false teeth clucked in the open mouth as he laughed, rocking back and forth on his heels.

On its kennel the baboon shrieked and cavorted, sharing its master's mirth.

'Hey, Mr Morgan,' Akkers giggled, 'don't forget your nails!'

David swung round to face him, his face felt tight and hot, the cicatrice that covered his cheeks and forehead was inflamed and the dark blue eyes blazed with a terrible anger. He started up the steps. His mouth was a pale hard slit, and his fists were clenched at his sides.

Akkers stepped backwards swiftly and reached behind the shop counter. He lifted out an old double-barrelled shotgun, and cocked both hammers with a sweep of his thick bony thumb.

'Self defence, Mr Morgan, with witnesses,' he giggled with sadistic relish. 'Come one step closer and we will get a look at your guts also.'

David paused at the top of the steps, and the gun–held in one huge fist–pointed at his belly.

'David hurry–oh, please hurry,' Debra called anxiously from the Land-Rover, with the weakly squirming body of the pup in her lap.

'We'll meet again.' David's anger had thickened his tongue.

'That will be fun,' said Akkers, and David turned away and ran down the steps.

Akkers watched the Land-Rover pull away and swing into the road in a cloud of dust, before he set the shotgun aside. He went out into the sunlight, and the baboon scrambled down from its pole and rushed to meet him. It jumped up on to his hip and clung to him like a child.

Akkers took a boiled sweet from his pocket and placed it tenderly between the terrible yellow fangs.

'You lovely old thing,' he chuckled, scratching the high cranium with its thick cap of grey fur and the baboon squinted up at his face with narrow brown eyes, chattering softly.

Despite the rough road surface, David covered the thirty miles back to Jabulani in twenty-five minutes. He skidded the vehicle to a halt beside the hangar, and ran with the pup in his arms to the aircraft.

During the flight Debra nursed him gently in her lap, and her skirts were sodden with his dark blood. The pup had quieted, and except for an occasional whimper now lay still. Over the W/T David arranged for a car to meet them at Nelspruit airfield and forty-five minutes after take-off they had Zulu on the theatre table in the veterinary surgeon's clinic.

The veterinary surgeon worked with complete concentration for over two hours at repairing the torn entrails and suturing the layers of abdominal muscle.

The pup was so critically injured, and infection was such a real danger, that they dared not return to Jabulani until it had passed. Five days later when they flew home with Zulu still weak and heavily strapped but out of danger, David altered his flight path to bring them in over the trading store at Bandolier Hill.

The iron roof shone like a mirror in the sun, and David felt his anger very cold and hard and determined.

'The man is a threat to us,' he said aloud. 'A real threat to each of us, and to what we are trying to build at Jabulani.'

Debra nodded her agreement, stroking the pup's head and not trusting herself to speak. Her own anger was as fierce as David's.

'I'm going to get him,' he said softly, and he heard the Brig's voice in his memory.

'The only excuse for violence is to protect that which belongs to you.'

He banked steeply away and lined up for his approach to the the landing-strip at Jabulani.

Conrad Berg called again to sample the Old Buck gin, and to tell David that his application to have Jabulani declared a private nature reserve had been approved by the Board and that the necessary documentation would soon be ready for signature.

'Do you want me to pull the fence out now?'

'No,' David answered grimly. 'Let it stand. I don't want Akkers frightened off.'

'Ja,' Conrad agreed heavily. 'We have got to get him.' He called Zulu to him and examined the scar that was ridged and shaped like forked lightning across the pup's belly. 'The bastard,' he muttered, and then glanced guiltily at Debra. 'Sorry, Mrs Morgan.'

'I couldn't agree more, Mr Berg,' she said softly, and Zulu watched her lips attentively when she spoke–his head cocked to one side.

Like all young things, he had healed cleanly and quickly.

The marula grove that ran thickly along the base of the hills about the String of Pearls came into flower.

The boles were straight and sturdy, each crowned with a fully rounded, many-branched head of dense foliage, and the red flowers made a royal show.

Almost daily David and Debra would wander together through the groves, down the rude track to the pools, and Zulu regained his strength on these leisurely strolls which always culminated in a swim and a lusty shaking off of water droplets, usually on to the nearest bystander.

Then the green plum-shaped fruits that covered the female marulas thickly began to turn yellow as they ripened, and their yeasty smell was heavy on the warm evening breeze.

The herd came up from the Sabi, forsaking the lush reed beds for the promise of the marula harvest. They were led by two old bulls, who for forty years had made the annual pilgrimage to the String of Pearls, and there were fifteen breeding cows with calves running at heel and as many adolescents.

They moved up slowly from the south, feeding spread out, sailing like ghostly grey galleons through the open bush, overloaded bellies rumbling. Occasionally a tall tree would catch the attention of one of the bulls and he would place his forehead upon the thick trunk and, swaying rhythmically as he built up momentum, he would strain suddenly and bring it crackling and crashing down. A few mouthfuls of the tender tip leaves would satisfy him, or he might strip the bark and stuff it untidily into his mouth before moving on northwards.

When the reached Conrad Berg's fence the two bulls moved forward and examined it, standing shoulder to shoulder as though in consultation, fanning their great grey ears, and every few minutes picking up a large pinch of sand in their trunks to throw over their own backs against the worrisome attention of the stinging flies.

In forty years they had travelled, and knew exactly all the boundaries of their reserve. As they stood there contemplating the game fence, it was as though they were fully aware that its destruction would be a criminal act, and injurious to their reputations and good standing.

Conrad Berg was deadly serious when he discussed 'his' elephants sense of right and wrong with David. He spoke of them like schoolboys who had to be placed on good behaviour, and disciplined when they transgressed. Discipline might take the form of driving, darting with drugs, or formal execution with a heavy rifle. This ultimate punishment was reserved for the incorrigibles who raided cultivated crops, chased motor-cars or otherwise endangered human life.

Sorely tempted, the two old bulls left the fence and ambled back to the breeding herd that waited patiently for their decision amongst the thorn trees. For three days the herd drifted back and forth along the fence, feeding and resting and waiting–then suddenly the wind turned westerly and it came to them laden with the thick, cloyingly sweet smell of the marula berries.

David parked the Land-Rover on the firebreak road and laughed with delight.

'So much for Connie's fence!'

For reasons of pachyderm prestige, or perhaps merely for the mischievous delight of destruction, no adult elephant would accept the breach made by another.

Each of them had selected his own fence pole, hard wood uprights embedded in concrete, and had effortlessly snapped it off level with the ground. Over a length of a mile the fence was flattened, and the wire mesh lay across the firebreak.

Each elephant had used his broken pole like a tightrope, to avoid treading on the sharp points of the barbed wire. Then once across the fence they had streamed in a tight bunch down to the pools to spend a night in feasting, an elephantine gorge on the yellow berries, which ended at dawn when they had bunched up into closer order and dashed back across the ruined fence into the safety of the Park–perhaps pursued by guilt and remorse and hoping that Conrad Berg would lay the blame on some other herd.

However, the downed fence provided ready access for many others who had long hankered after the sweet untouched grazing and deep water holes.

Ugly little blue wildebeest with monstrous heads, absurdly warlike manes and curved horns in imitation of the mighty buffalo. Clowns of the bush, they capered with glee and chased each other in circles. Their companions the zebra were more dignified, ignoring their antics, and trotted in businesslike fashion down to the pools. Their rumps were striped and glossy and plump, their heads up and ears pricked.

Conrad Berg met David at the remains of his fence, climbing out of his own truck and picking his way carefully over the wire. Sam, the African ranger, followed him.

Conrad shook his head as he surveyed the destruction, chuckling ruefully.

'It's old Mahommed and his pal One-Eye, I'd know that spoor anywhere. They just couldn't help themselves–the bastards–' He glanced quickly at Debra in the Land-Rover.

'That's perfectly all right, Mr Berg,' she forestalled his apology.

Sam had been casting back and forth along the soft break road and now he came to where they stood.

'Hello, Sam,' David greeted him. It had taken a lot of persuasion to get Sam to accept that this terribly disfigured face belonged to the young *nkosi* David who he had taught to track, and shoot and rob a wild beehive without destroying the bees.

Sam saluted David with a flourish. He took his uniform very seriously and conducted himself like a guardsman now. It was difficult to tell his age, for he had the broad smooth moonface of the Nguni–the aristocratic warrior tribes of Africa–but there was a frosting of purest white on the close-curled hair of his temples under the slouch hat, and David knew he had worked at Jabulani for forty years before leaving. The man must be approaching sixty years of age.

Quickly he made his report to Conrad, describing the animals and the numbers which had crossed into Jabulani.

'There is also a herd of buffalo, forty-three of them,' Sam spoke in simple Zulu that David could still follow. 'They are the ones who drank before at Ripape Dam near Hlangulene.'

'That will bring Akkers running–the sirloin of a young buffalo makes the finest biltong there is,' Conrad observed dryly.

'How long will it be before he knows the fence is down?' David asked, and Conrad fell into a long rapid-fire discussion with Sam that lost David after the first few sentences. However, Conrad translated at the end.

'Sam says he knows already, all your servants and their wives buy at his store and he pays them for that sort of information. It turns out that there is bad blood between Sam and Akkers. Sam suspects him of arranging to have him beaten, on a lonely road on a dark night. Sam was in hospital three months–he also accused Akkers of having his hut fired to drive him off Jabulani.'

'It adds up, doesn't it?' David agreed.

'Old Sam is dead keen to help us grab Akkers–and he has a plan of action all worked out.'

'Let's hear it.'

'Well, as long as you are in residence at Jabulani Akkers is going to restrict his activities to night poaching with a killing lamp. He knows every trick there is and we will never get him.'

'So?'

'You must tell your servants that you are leaving for two weeks, going to Cape Town on business. Akkers will know as soon as you leave and he will believe he has the whole of Jabulani to himself–' For an hour more they discussed the details of the plan, then they shook hands and parted.

As they drove back to the homestead they emerged from the open forest into one of the glades of tall grass, and David saw the brilliant white egrets floating like snow flakes over the swaying tops of golden grass.

'Something in there,' he said and cut the engine. They waited quietly until David saw the movement in the grass, the opening and closing at the passage of heavy bodies. Then three egrets, sitting in a row, moved slowly towards him, borne on the back of a concealed beast as it grazed steadily forward.

'Ah, the buffalo!' David exclaimed as the first of them appeared, a great black bovine shape. It stopped as it saw the Land-Rover on the edge of the trees and it regarded them intently from beneath the wide spread of its horns, with its muzzle lifted high. It showed no alarm for these were Park animals, almost as tame as domestic cattle.

Gradually the rest of the herd emerged from the tall grass. Each in turn scrutinized the vehicle and then resumed feeding once more. There were forty-three of them, as Sam had predicted, and amongst them were some fine old bulls standing five and a half feet tall at the shoulder and weighing little less than 2000 lb. Their horns were massively bossed, meeting in the centre of the head and curving downwards and up to blunt points, with a rugged surface that became polished black at the tips.

Crawling over their heavy trunks and thick short legs were numbers of ox-peckers, dull-plumaged birds with scarlet beaks and bright beady eyes. Sometimes head down they scavenged for the ticks and other blood-sucking body vermin in the folds of skin between the limbs. Occasionally one of the huge beasts would snort and leap, shaking and swishing its tail, as a sharp beak pried into a delicate portion of its anatomy, under the tail or around the heavy dangling black scrotum. The birds fluttered up with hissing cries, waited for the buffalo to calm down and then settled again to their scurrying and searching.

David photographed the herd until the light failed, and they drove home in the dark.

Before dinner David opened a bottle of wine and they drank it together on the stoop, sitting close and listening to the night sounds of the bush–the cries of the night birds, the tap of flying insects against the wire screen and the other secret scurrying and rustling of small animals.

'Do you remember once I told you that you were spoiled, and not very good marriage material?' Debra asked softly, nestling her dark head against his shoulder.

'I'll never forget it.'

'I'd like to withdraw that remark formally,' she went on, and he moved her gently away so that he could study her face. Sensing his eyes upon her she smiled, that shy little smile of hers. 'I fell in love with a little boy, a spoiled little boy, who thought only of fast cars and the nearest skirt–' she said, '–but now I have a man, a grown man,' she smiled again, 'and I like it better this way.'

He drew her back to him and kissed her, their lips melded in a lingering embrace before she sighed happily and laid her head back upon his shoulder. They were silent for a while before Debra spoke again.

'These wild animals–that mean so much to you–'

'Yes?' he encouraged her.

'I am beginning to understand. Although I have never seen them, they are becoming important to me also.'

'I'm glad.'

'David, this place of ours–it's so peaceful, so perfect. It's a little Eden before the fall.'

'We will make it so,' he promised, but in the night the gunfire woke him. He rose quickly, leaving her lying warm and quietly sleeping, and he went out on the stoop.

It came again, faintly on the still night, distance muting it to a small unwarlike popping. He felt his anger stirring again, as he imagined the long white shaft of the killing lamp, questing relentlessly through the forest until it settled suddenly upon the puzzled animal, holding it mesmerized in the beam, the blinded eyes glowing like jewels, making a perfect aiming point in the field of the telescopic rifle sight.

Then suddenly the rifle blast, shocking in the silence, and the long licking flame of the muzzle flash. The beautiful head snapping back at the punch of the bullet and the soft thump of the falling body on the hard earth, the last spasmodic kicking of hooves and again the silence.

He knew it was useless to attempt pursuit now, the gunman would have an accomplice in the hills above them ready to flash a warning if any of the homestead lights came on, or if an auto engine whirred into life. Then the killing lamp would be doused and the poacher would creep away. David would search the midnight expanse of Jabulani in vain. His quarry was cunning and experienced in his craft of killing, and would only be taken by greater cunning.

David could not sleep again. He lay awake beside Debra, and listened to her soft breathing–and at intervals to the distant rifle fire. The game was tame and easily approached, innocent after the safety of the Park. It would run only a short distance after each shot, and then it would stand again staring without comprehension at the mysterious and dazzling light that floated towards it out of the darkness.

David's anger burned on through the night, and in the dawn the vultures were up. Black specks against the pink dawn sky, they appeared in ever-increasing numbers, sailing high on wide pinions, tracing wide swinging circles before beginning to drop towards the earth.

David telephoned Conrad Berg at Skukuza Camp, then he and Debra and the dog climbed into the Land-Rover, warmly dressed against the dawn chill. They followed the descent of the birds to where the poacher had come on the buffalo herd.

As they approached the first carcass, the animal scavengers scattered–slope-backed hyena cantering away into the trees, hideous and cowardly, looking back over their misshapen shoulders, grinning apologetically–little red jackal with silvery backs and alert ears, trotting to a respectful distance before standing and starting back anxiously.

The vultures were less timid, seething like fat brown maggots over the carcass as they squawled and squabbled, fouling everything with their stinking droppings and loose feathers, leaving the kill only when the Land-Rover was very close and then flapping heavily up into the trees to crouch there grotesquely with their bald scaly heads out-thrust.

There were sixteen dead buffalo, lying strung out along the line of the herd's flight. On each carcass the belly had been split open to let the vultures in, and the sirloin and fillet had been expertly removed.

'He killed them just for a few pounds of meat?' Debra asked incredulously.

'That's all,' David confirmed grimly. 'But that's not bad–sometimes they'll kill a wildebeest simply to make a fly whisk of its tail, or they'll shoot a giraffe for the marrow in its bones.'

'I don't understand.' Debra's voice was hopeless. 'What makes a man do it? He can't need the meat that badly.'

'No,' David agreed. 'It's deeper than that. This type of killing is a gut thing. This man kills for the thrill of it, he kills to see an animal fall, to hear the death cry, to smell the reek of fresh blood–' his voice choked off, 'this is one time you can be thankful you cannot see,' he said softly.'

Conrad Berg found them waiting beside the corpses, and he set his rangers to work butchering the carcasses.

'No point in wasting all that meat. Food there for a lot of people.'

Then he put Sam to the spoor. There had been four men in the poaching party, one wearing light rubber-soled shoes and the others bare-footed.

'One white man, big man, long legs. Three black men, carry meat, blood drip here and here.'

They followed Sam slowly through the open forest as he parted the grass with his long thin tracking staff, and moved towards the unsurfaced public road.

'Here they walk backwards,' Sam observed, and Conrad explained grimly.

'Old poacher's trick. They walk backwards when they cross a boundary. If you cut the spoor while patrolling the fence you think they have gone the other way–leaving instead of entering–and you don't bother following them.'

The spoor went through the gap in the fence, crossed the road and entered the tribal land beyond. It ended where a motor vehicle had been parked amongst a screening thicket of wild ebony. The tracks bumped away across the sandy earth and rejoined the public road.

'Plaster casts of the tyre tracks?' David asked.

'Waste of time.' Conrad shook his head. 'You can be sure they are changed before each expedition, he keeps this set especially and hides it when it's not in use.'

'What about spent cartridge shells?' David persisted.

Conrad laughed briefly. 'They are in his pocket, this is a fly bird. He's not going to scatter evidence all over the country. He picks up as he goes along. No–we'll have to sucker him into it.' And his manner became businesslike. 'Right, have you selected a place to stake old Sam out?'

'I thought we would put him up on one of the kopjes, near the String of Pearls. He'll be able to cover the whole estate from there, spot any dust on the road, and the height will give the two-way radio sufficient range.'

After lunch David loaded their bags into the luggage compartment of the Navajo. He paid the servants two weeks' wages in advance.

'Take good care.' He told them. 'I shall return before the end of the month.'

He parked the Land-Rover in the open hangar with the key in the ignition facing the open doorway, ready for a quick start. He took off and kept on a westerly heading, passing directly over Bandolier Hill and the buildings amongst the mango trees. They saw no sign of life, but David held his course until the hill sank from view below the horizon, then he came around on a wide circle to the south and lined up for Skukuza, the main camp of the Kruger National Park.

Conrad Berg was at the airstrip in his truck to meet the Cessna, and Jane had placed fresh flowers in the guest room. Jabulani lay fifty miles away to the north-west.

It was like squadron 'Red' standby again, with the Navajo parked under one of the big shade trees at the end of the Skukuza airstrip, and the radio set switched on, crackling faintly on the frequency tuned to that of Sam's transmitter, as he waited patiently on the hill-top above the pools.

The day was oppressively hot, with the threat of a rainstorm looming up out of the east, great cumulus thunderheads striding like giants across the bushveld.

Debra and David and Conrad Berg sat in the shade of the aircraft's wing, for it was too hot in the cockpit. They chatted in desultory fashion, but always listening to the radio crackle, and they were tense and distracted.

'He is not going to come,' said Debra a little before noon.

'He'll come,' Conrad contradicted her. 'Those buffalo are too much temptation. Perhaps not today–but tomorrow or the next day he'll come.'

David stood up and climbed in through the open door of the cabin. He went forward to the cockpit.

'Sam,' he spoke into the microphone. 'Can you hear me?'

There was a long pause, presumably while Sam struggled with radio procedure, then his voice, faint but clear: 'I hear you, *Nkosi*.'

'Have you seen anything?'

'There is nothing.'

'Keep good watch.'

'*Yebho, Nkosi*.'

Jane brought a cold picnic lunch down to the airstrip, they ate heartily despite the tension, and they were about to start on the milk tart, when suddenly the radio set throbbed and hummed. Sam's voice carried clearly to where they sat.

'He has come!'

'Red standby–Go! Go!' shouted David, and they rushed for the cabin door, Debra treading squarely in the centre of Jane's milk tart before David grabbed her arm and guided her to her seat.

'Bright Lance, airborne and climbing,' David laughed with excitement and then memory stabbed him with a sharp blade. He remembered Joe hanging out there at six o'clock but he shut his mind to it and he banked steeply on to his heading, not wasting time in grabbing for altitude but staying right down at tree-top level.

Conrad Berg was hunched in the seat behind them, and his face was redder than usual–seeming about to burst like an over-ripe tomato.

'Where is the Land-Rover key?' he demanded anxiously.

'It's in the ignition–and the tank is full.'

'Can't you go faster?' Conrad growled.

'Have you got your walkie-talkie?' David checked him.

'Here!' It was gripped in one of his huge paws, and his double-barrelled ·450 magnum was in the other.

David was hopping the taller trees, and sliding over the crests of higher ground with feet to spare. They flashed over the boundary fence and ahead of them lay the hills of Jabulani.

'Get ready,' he told Conrad, and flew the Navajo into the airstrip, taxiing up to the hangar where the Land-Rover waited.

Conrad jumped down at the instant that David braked to a halt, then he slammed the cabin door behind him and raced to the Land-Rover. Immediately David opened the throttle and swung the aircraft around, lining up for his take-off before the Navajo had gathered full momentum.

As he climbed, he saw the Land-Rover racing across the airstrip, dragging a cloak of dust behind it.

'Do you read me, Connie?'

'Loud and clear,' Conrad's voice boomed out of the speaker, and David turned for the grey ribbon of the public road that showed through the trees, beyond the hills.

He followed it, flying five hundred feet above it, and he searched the open parkland.

The green Ford truck had been concealed from observation at ground level, again in a thicket of wild ebony, but it was open from the sky. For Akkers had never thought of discovery coming from there.

'Connie, I've got the truck. He's stashed it in a clump of ebony about half a mile down the bank of the Luzane stream. Your best route is to follow the road to the bridge, then go down into the dry river bed and try and cut him off before he gets to the truck.'

'Okay, David.'

'Move it, man.'

'I'm moving.' David saw the Land-Rover's dust above the trees, Conrad must have his foot down hard.

'I'm going to try and spot the man himself–chase him into your arms.'

'You do that!'

David started a long climbing turn towards the hills, sweeping and searching, up and around. Below him the pools glinted and he opened the throttles slightly, seeking altitude to clear the crests.

From the highest peak, a tiny figure waved frantically.

'Sam,' he grunted. 'Doing a war dance.' He altered course slightly to pass him closely, and Sam stopped his imitation of a windmill and stabbed with an extended arm towards the west. David acknowledged with a wave, and turned again, dropping down the western slopes.

Ahead of him the plain spread, dappled like a leopard's back with dark bush and golden glades of grass. He flew for a minute before he saw a black mass, moving slowly ahead of him, dark and amorphous against the pale grass. The remains of the buffalo herd had bunched up and were running without direction, desperate from the harrying they had received.

'Buffalo,' he told Debra. 'On the run. Something has alarmed them.' She sat still and intent beside him, hands in her lap, staring unseeingly ahead.

'Ah!' David shouted. 'Got him–with blood on his hands!'

In the centre of one of the larger clearings lay the black beetle-body of a dead buffalo, its belly swollen and its legs sticking out stiffly as it lay on its side.

Four men stood around it in a circle, obviously just about to begin butchering the carcass. Three of them were Africans, one with a knife in his hand.

The fourth man was Johan Akkers. There was no mistaking the tall gaunt frame. He wore an old black Fedora hat on his head, strangely formal attire for the work in which he was engaged, and his braces criss-crossed his tan-coloured shirt. He carried a rifle at the trail in his right hand, and at the sound of the aircraft engines he swung round and stared into the sky, frozen with the shock of discovery.

'You swine. Oh, you bloody swine,' whispered David, and his anger was strong and bright against the despoilers.

'Hold on!' he warned Debra, and flew straight at the man, dropping steeply on to him.

The group around the dead buffalo scattered, as the aircraft bore down on them, each man picking his own course and racing away on it, but David selected the lanky galloping frame with the black hat jammed down over the ears and sank down behind him. The tips of his propellers clipped the dry grass, as he swiftly overtook the running Akkers.

He was set to fly into him, driven by the unreasoning anger of the male animal protecting his own, and he lined up to cut him down with the spinning propeller blades.

As David braced himself for the impact Akkers glanced back over his shoulder, and his face was muddy grey with fright, the skull eyes dark and deeply set. He saw the murderous blades merely feet from him, and he threw himself flat into the grass.

The Navajo roared inches over his prone body, and David pulled it round in a steep turn, with the wing-tip brushing the grass. As he came round he saw that Akkers was up and running, and that he was only fifty paces from the edge of the trees.

David levelled out, aimed for the fugitive again but realized that he could not reach him before he was into the trees. Swiftly he sped across the clearing, but the lumbering figure drew slowly closer to the timber line and as he reached the sanctuary of a big leadwood trunk, Akkers whirled and raised the rifle to his shoulder. He aimed at the approaching aircraft; although the rifle was unsteady in his hands the range was short.

'Down,' shouted David, pushing Debra's head below the level of the windshield, and he pulled open the throttles and climbed very steeply away.

Even above the bellow of the engines David heard the heavy bullet clang into the fuselage of the aircraft.

'What's happening, David?' Debra pleaded.

'He fired at us, but we've got him on the run. He'll head back for his truck now, and Conrad should be there waiting for him.'

Akkers kept under cover of the trees, and circling above him David caught glimpses of the tall figure trotting purposefully along his escape route.

'David, can you hear me?' Conrad's voice boomed suddenly in the tense cockpit.

'What is it, Connie?'

'We've got trouble. I've hit a rock in your Land-Rover and knocked out the sump. She's had it, pouring oil all over the place.'

'How the hell did you do that?' David demanded.

'I was trying a short cut.' Conrad's chagrin carried clearly over the ether.

'How far are you from the Luzane stream?'

'About three miles.'

'God, he'll beat you to it,' David swore. 'He's two miles from the truck and going like he's got a tax collector after him.'

'You have not seen old Connie move yet. I'll be there waiting for him,' Berg promised.

'Good luck,' David called, and the transmission went dead.

Below them Akkers was skirting the base of the hills, his black hat bobbing along steadily amongst the trees. David kept his starboard wing pointed at him and the Navajo turned steadily, holding station above him.

Other movement caught David's eye on the open slope of the hill above Akkers. For a moment he thought it was an animal, then with an intake of breath he realized that he was mistaken.

'What is it?' Debra demanded, sensing his concern.

'It's Sam, the damned fool. Connie told him not to leave his post–he's unarmed–but he's haring down the slope to try and cut Akkers off.'

'Can't you stop him?' Debra asked anxiously, and David didn't bother to answer.

He called Conrad four times before there was a reply. Conrad's voice was thick and wheezing with the effort of running.

'Sam is on to Akkers. I think he's going to confront him.'

'Oh God damn him,' groaned Conrad. 'I'll kick his black ass for him.'

'Hold on,' David told him, 'I'm going around for a closer look.'

David saw it all quite plainly, he was only three hundred feet above them when Akkers became aware of the running figure on the slope above him. He stopped dead, and half-lifted the rifle; perhaps he shouted a warning but Sam kept on down, bounding over the rocky ground towards the man who had burned his children to death.

Akkers lifted the rifle to his shoulder and aimed deliberately, the rifle jumped sharply, the barrel kicking upwards at the recoil and Sam's legs kept on running while his upper torso was flung violently backwards by the strike of the heavy soft-nosed bullet.

The tiny brown-clad body bounced and rolled down the slope, before coming to a sprawling halt in a clump of scrub.

David watched Akkers reload the rifle, stooping to pick up the empty cartridge shell. Then he looked up at the circling aircraft above him, David may have been mistaken but it seemed the man was laughing–that obscene tooth-clucking giggle of his–then he started off again at a trot towards the truck.

'Connie,' David spoke hoarsely into his handset, 'he just killed Sam.'

Conrad Berg ran heavily over the broken sandy ground. He had lost his hat and sweat poured down his big red face, stinging his eyes and plastering the lank grey hair down his forehead. The walkie-talkie set bounced on his back, and the butt of the rifle thumped rhythmically against his hip.

He ran with grim concentration, trying to ignore the swollen pounding of his heart and the torture of breath that scalded his lungs. A thorn branch clawed at his upper arms, raking thin bloody lines through his skin, but he did not break the pattern of his run.

He turned his red and streaming face to the sky and saw David's aircraft, circling ahead of him and slightly to his left. That marked for him Akkers' position–and it was clear that Conrad was losing ground in his desperate race to head off the escape.

The radio set on his back buzzed, but he ignored the call, he could not halt now. To break his run would mean he would only slump down exhausted. He was a big heavy man, the air was hot and enervating, and he had run three miles through loose and difficult going–he was almost finished. He was burning the last of his reserves now.

Suddenly the earth seemed to fall away under him, and he pitched forward and half-slid–half-rolled–down the steep bank of the Luzane stream, to finish lying on his back in the white river sand, clean and grainy as sugar. The radio was digging painfully into his flesh and he dragged it out from under him.

Still lying in the sand he panted like a dog, blinded by sweat and he fumbled the transmit button of the set.

'David–' he croaked thickly, 'I am in the bed of the stream–can you see me?'

The aircraft was arcing directly overhead now, and David's answer came back immediately.

'I see you, Connie, you are a hundred yards down-stream from the truck. Akkers is there, Connie, has just reached the truck, he'll be coming back down the river bed at any moment.'

Painfully, gasping, choking for breath, Conrad Berg dragged himself to his knees–and at that moment he heard the whirr and catch and purr of an engine. He unstrapped the heavy radio and laid it aside, then he unslung his rifle, snapped open the breech to check the load, and pulled himself to his feet.

Surprised at the weakness of his own massive body, he staggered into the centre of the river bed.

The dry river bed was eight feet deep with banks cut sheer by flood water, and it was fifteen feet wide at this point, and the floor was of smooth white sand, scattered with small water-rounded stones no bigger than a baseball. It made a good illegal access road into Jabulani, and the tracks of Akkers' truck were clearly etched in the soft sand.

Around a bend in the stream Conrad heard the truck revving and roaring as it came down a low place in the bank into the smooth bed.

Conrad stood squarely in the middle of the river bed with the rifle held across his hip, and he fought to control his breathing. The approaching roar of the truck reached a crescendo as it came skidding wildly around the bend in the stream, and raced down towards him. Showers of loose sand were thrown out from under the spinning rear wheels.

Johan Akkers crouched over the steering wheel, with the black hat pulled down to his eyebrows, and his face was grey and glistening with sweat, and he saw Conrad blocking the river bed.

'Stop!' Conrad shouted, hefting the rifle. 'Stop or I shoot!'

The truck was swaying and sliding, the engine screamed in tortured protest. Akkers began to laugh, Conrad could see the open mouth and the shaking shoulders. There was no slackening in the truck's roaring, rocking charge.

Conrad lifted the rifle and sighted down the stubby double barrels. At that range he could have put a bullet through each of Johan Akkers' deep-set eyes, and the man made no effort to duck or otherwise avoid the menace of the levelled rifle. He was still laughing, and Conrad could clearly see the teeth lying loosely on his gums. He steeled himself with the truck fifty feet away, and racing down upon him.

It takes a peculiar state of mind before one man can deliberately and cold-bloodedly shoot down another. It must either be the conditioned reflex of the soldier or law-enforcement officer, or it must be the terror of the hunted, or again it must be the unbalanced frenzy of the criminal lunatic.

None of these was Conrad Berg. Like most big strong men, he was essentially a gentle person. His whole thinking was centred on protecting and cherishing life–he could not pull the trigger.

With the truck fifteen feet away, he threw himself aside, and Johan Akkers swung the wheel wildly, deliberately driving for him.

He caught Berg a glancing blow with the side of the truck, hurling him into the earthen bank of the stream. The truck went past him, slewing out of control. It hit the bank farther down the stream in a burst of earth and loose pebbles, swaying wildly as Akkers fought the bucking wheel. He got it under control again, jammed his foot down on the accelerator and went roaring on down the river bed, leaving Conrad lying in the soft sand below the bank.

As the truck hit him, Conrad felt the bone in his hip shatter like glass, and the breath driven from his lungs by the heavy blow of metal against his rib cage.

He lay in the sand on his side and felt the blood well slowly into his mouth. It had a bitter salt taste, and he knew that one of the broken ribs had pierced his lung like a lance and that the blood sprang from deep within his body.

He turned his head and saw the radio set lying ten paces away across the river bed. He began to drag himself towards it and his shattered leg slithered after him, twisted at a grotesque angle.

'David,' he whispered into the microphone, 'I couldn't stop him. He got away,' and he spat a mouthful of blood into the white sand.

David picked the truck up as it came charging up the river bank below the concrete bridge of the Luzane, bounced and bumped over the drainage ditch and swung on to the road. It gathered speed swiftly and raced westwards towards Bandolier Hill and the highway. Dust boiled out from behind the green chassis, marking its position clearly for David as he turned two miles ahead of it.

After crossing the Luzane the road turned sharply to avoid a rocky outcrop, and then ran arrow-straight for two miles, hedged in with thick timber and undulating like a switchback, striking across the water shed and the grain of the land.

As David completed his turn he lowered his landing gear, and throttled back. The Navajo sank down, lined up on the dusty road as though it was a landing-strip.

Directly ahead was the dust column of the speeding truck. They were on a head-on course, but David concentrated coldly on bringing the Navajo down into the narrow lane between the high walls of timber. He was speaking quietly to Debra, reassuring her and explaining what he was going to attempt.

He touched down lightly on the narrow road, letting her float in easily, and when she was down he opened the throttles again, taking her along the centre of the road under power but holding her down. He had speed enough to lift the Navajo off, if Akkers chose a collision rather than surrender.

Ahead of them was another hump in the road, and as they rolled swiftly towards it the green truck suddenly burst over the crest, not more than a hundred yards ahead.

Both vehicles were moving fast, coming together at a combined speed of almost two hundred miles an hour, and the shock of it was too much for Johan Akkers.

The appearance of the aircraft dead in the centre of the road, bearing down on him with the terrible spinning discs of the propellers was too much for nerves already run raw and ragged.

He wrenched the wheel hard over, and the truck went into a broadside dry skid. It missed the port wing-tip of the Navajo as it went rocketing off the narrow road.

The front wheels caught the drainage ditch and the truck went over, cartwheeling twice in vicious slamming revolutions that smashed the glass from her windows and burst the doors open. The truck ended on its side against one of the trees.

David shut the throttles and thrust his feet hard down on the wheel brakes, bringing the Navajo up short.

'Wait here,' he shouted at Debra, and jumped down into the road. His face was a frozen mask of scar tissue, but his eyes were ablaze as he sprinted back along the road towards the wreckage of the green truck.

Akkers saw him coming, and he dragged himself shakily to his feet. He had been thrown clear and now he staggered to the truck. He could see his rifle lying in the cab, and he tried to scramble up on to the body to reach down through the open door. Blood from a deep scratch in his forehead was running into his eyes blinding him, he wiped it away with the back of his hand and glanced around.

David was close, hurdling the irrigation ditch and running towards him. Akkers scrambled down from the battered green body, and groped for the hunting knife on his belt. It was eight inches of Sheffield steel with a bone handle, and it had been honed to a razor edge.

He hefted it under-handed, in the classical grip of the knife-fighter and wiped the blood from his face with the palm of his free hand.

He was crouching slightly, facing David, and the haft of the knife was completely covered by the huge bony fist.

David stopped short of him, his eyes fastened on the knife, and Akkers began to laugh again. It was a cracked falsetto giggle, the hysterical laughter of a man driven to the very frontiers of sanity.

The point of the knife weaved in the slow mesmeric movement of an erect cobra, and it caught the sunlight in bright points of light. David watched it, circling and crouching, steeling himself, summoning all the training of paratrooper school, screwing up his nerve to go in against the naked steel.

Akkers feinted swiftly, leaping in, and when David broke away, he let out a fresh burst of high laughter.

Again they circled, Akkers mouthing his teeth loosely, sucking at them, giggling, watching with those muddy green eyes from their deep, close-set sockets. David moved back slowly ahead of him, and Akkers drove him back against the body of the truck, cornering him there.

He came then, flashing like the charge of a wounded leopard. His speed and strength were shocking, and the knife hissed upwards for David's belly.

David caught the knife hand at the wrist, blocking the thrust and trapping the knife low down. They were chest to chest now, face to face, like lovers, and Akkers' breath stank of unwashed teeth.

They strained silently, shifting like dancers to balance each other's heaves and thrusts.

David felt the knife hand twisting in his grip. The man had hands and arms like steel, he could not hold him much longer. In seconds it would be free, and the steel would be probing into his belly.

David braced his legs and twisted sideways. The move caught Akkers off-balance and he could not resist it. David was able to get his other hand on to the knife arm, but even with both hands he was hard put to hold on.

They swayed and shuffled together, panting, grunting, straining, until they fell, still locked together, against the bonnet of the truck. The metal was hot and smelled of oil.

David was concentrating all his strength on the knife, but he felt Akkers' free hand groping for his throat. He ducked his head down on his shoulders, pressing his chin against his chest but the fingers were steel hard and powerful as machinery. They probed mercilessly into his flesh, forcing his chin up, and settling on his throat, beginning to squeeze the life out of him.

Desperately David hauled at the knife arm, and found it more manageable now that Akkers was concentrating his strength on strangling him.

The open windscreen of the truck was beside David's shoulder, the glass had been smashed out of it, but jagged shards of it still stood in the metal rim, forming a crude but ferocious line of saw-teeth.

David felt the fingers digging deep into his throat, crushing the gristle of his larynx and blocking off the arteries that fed his brain. His vision starred and then began to fade darkly, as though he were pulling eight G's in a dogfight.

With one last explosive effort David pulled the knife arm around on to the line of broken glass, and he dragged it down, sawing it desperately across the edge.

Akkers screamed and his strangling grip relaxed, back and forth David sawed the arm, slashing and ripping through skin and fat and flesh, opening a wound like a ragged-petalled rose, hacking down into the nerves and arteries and sinews so that the knife dropped from the lifeless fingers and Akkers screamed like a woman.

David broke from him and shoved him away. Akkers fell to his knees still screaming and David clutched at his own throat massaging the bruised flesh, gasping for breath and feeling the flow of fresh blood to his brain.

'God Jesus, I'm dying. I'm bleeding to death. Oh sweet Jesus, help me!' screamed Akkers, holding the mutilated arm to his belly. 'Help me, oh God, don't let me die. Save me, Jesus, save me!'

Blood was streaming and spurting from the arm, flooding the front of his trousers. As he screamed his teeth fell from his mouth, leaving it a dark and empty cave in the palely glistening face.

'You've killed me. I'll bleed to death!' he screamed at David, thrusting his face towards David. 'You've got to save me–don't let me die.'

David pushed himself away from the truck and took two running steps towards the kneeling man, then he swung his right leg and his whole body into a flying kick that took Akkers cleanly under the chin and snapped his head back.

He went over backwards and lay still and quiet, and David stood over him, sobbing and gasping for breath.

For purposes of sentence Mr Justice Barnard of the Transvaal division of the Supreme Court took into consideration four previous convictions–two under the wildlife conservation act, one for aggravated assault, and the fourth for assault with intent to do grievous bodily harm.

He found Johan Akkers guilty of twelve counts under the Wildlife Conservation Act, but considered these as one when sentencing him to three years at hard labour without option of a fine, and confiscation of firearms and motor vehicles used in commission of these offences.

He found him guilty of one count of aggravated assault, and sentenced him to three years at hard labour without option.

The prosecutor altered one charge from attempted murder to assault with intent to do grievous bodily harm. He was found guilty as charged on this count, and the sentence was five years' imprisonment without option.

On the final charge of murder he was found guilty and Justice Barnard said in open court:

'In considering sentence of death on this charge, I was obliged to take into account the fact that the accused was acting like an animal in a trap, and I am satisfied that there was no element of premeditation–'

The sentence was eighteen years' imprisonment, and all sentences were to run consecutively. They were all confirmed on appeal.

As Conrad Berg said from his hospital bed with one heavily plastered leg in traction, and a glass of Old Buck gin in his hand, 'Well, for the next twenty-eight years we don't have to worry about that bastard–I beg your pardon, Mrs Morgan.'

'Twenty-nine years, dear,' Jane Berg corrected him firmly.

In July the American edition of *A Place of Our Own* was published, and it dropped immediately into that hungry and bottomless pool of indifference wherein so many good books drown. It left not a sign, not a ripple of its passing.

Bobby Dugan, Debra's new literary agent in America, wrote to say how sorry he was–and how disappointed. He had expected at least some sort of critical notice to be taken of the publication.

David took it as a personal and direct insult. He ranted and stormed about the estate for a week, and it seemed that at one stage he might actually journey to America to commit a physical violence upon that country–a sort of one-man Vietnam in reverse.

'They must be stupid,' he protested. 'It's the finest book ever written.'

'Oh, David!' Debra protested modestly.

'It is! And I'd love to go over there and rub their noses in it,' and Debra imagined the doors of editorial offices all over New York being kicked open, and literary reviewers fleeing panic-stricken, jumping out of skyscraper-windows or locking themselves in the women's toilets to evade David's wrath.

'David my darling, you are wonderful for me,' she giggled with delight, but it had hurt. It had hurt very badly. She felt the flame of her urge to write wane and flutter in the chill winds of rejection.

Now when she sat at her desk with the microphone at her lips, the words no longer tumbled and fought to escape, and the ideas no longer jostled each other. Where before she had seen things happening as though she were watching a play, seen her characters laugh and cry and sing, now there was only the dark cloud banks rolling across her eyes–unrelieved by colour or form.

For hours at a time she might sit at her desk and listen to the birds in the garden below the window.

David sensed her despair, and he tried to help her through it. When the hours at the desk proved fruitless he would insist she leave it and come with him along the new fence lines, or to fish the big blue Mozambique bream in the deep water of the pools.

Now that she had completely learned the layout of the house and its immediate environs, David began to teach her to find her way at large. Each day they would walk down to the pools and Debra learned her landmarks along the track; she would grope for them with the carved walking-stick David had given her. Zulu soon realized his role in these expeditions, and it was David's idea to clip a tiny silver bell on to his collar so that Debra could follow him more readily. Soon she could venture out without David, merely calling her destination to Zulu and checking him against her own landmarks.

David was busy at this time with the removal of Conrad's game fence, as he was still laid up with the leg, and with building his own fences to enclose the three vulnerable boundaries of Jabulani. In addition there was a force of African rangers to recruit and train in their duties. David designed uniforms for them, and built outposts for them at all the main access points to the estate. He flew into Nelspruit at regular intervals to consult Conrad Berg on these arrangements, and it was at his suggestion that David began a water survey of the estate. He wanted surface water on the areas of Jabulani that were remote from the pools, and he began studying the feasibility of building catchment dams or sinking boreholes. His days were full and active, and he became hard and lean and sunbrowned. Yet always there were many hours spent in Debra's company.

The 35-mm. colour slides that David had taken of the buffalo herd before Johan Akkers had decimated it, were returned by the processing laboratory and they were hopelessly inadequate. The huge animals seemed to be standing on the horizon, and the ox-peckers on their bodies were tiny grey specks. This failure spurred David, and he returned from one trip to Nelspruit with a 600-mm. telescopic lens.

While Debra was meant to be working, David set up his camera beside her and photographed the birds through her open window. The results were mixed. Out of thirty-six exposures, thirty-five could be thrown away, but one was beautiful, a grey-headed bush shrike at the moment of flight, poised on spread wings with the sunlight catching his vivid plumage and his sparkling eye.

David was hooked by the photography bug, and there were more lenses and cameras and tripods, until Debra protested that it was a hobby which was completely visual, and from which she was excluded.

David had one of his inspirations of genius. He sent away for pressings of June Stannard's bird song recordings–and Debra was enchanted. She listened to them intently, her whole face lighting with pleasure when she recognized a familiar call.

From there it was a natural step for her to attempt to make her own bird recordings, which included the tinkle of Zulu's silver bell, the buzz of David's Land-Rover, the voices of the servants arguing in the kitchen yard–and faintly, very faintly, the chatter of a glossy starling.

'It's no damned good,' Debra complained bitterly. 'I wonder how she got hers so clear and close.'

David did some reading, and built a parabolic reflector for her. It did not look particularly lovely, but it worked. Aimed at a sound source it gathered and directed the sound waves into the microphone.

From the window of Debra's study they became more adventurous and moved out. He built permanent and comfortable hides beside the drinking places at the pools, and when his rangers reported a nesting site of an interesting bird species, they would built temporary blinds of thatch and canvas–sometimes on tall stilts–where David and Debra spent many silent and enjoyable hours together, shooting film and catching sound. Even Zulu learned to lie still and silent with his bell removed on these occasions.

Slowly they had begun to build up a library of photographs and recordings of a professional standard–until at last David plucked up sufficient courage to send to *African Wild Life Magazine* a selection of a dozen of his best slides. Two weeks later, he received a letter of acceptance, with a cheque for a hundred dollars. This payment represented a return of approximately one-twentieth of one per cent of his capital outlay on equipment. David was ecstatic, and Debra's pleasure almost as great as his. They drank two bottles of Veuve Clicquot for dinner, and under the spell of excitement and champagne their love-making that night was particularly inventive.

When David's photographs were published in *Wild Life* accompanied by Debra's text, they reaped an unexpected harvest of letters from persons of similar interest all over the world, and a request from the editors for a full-length, illustrated article on Jabulani, and the Morgans' plans for turning it into a game sanctuary.

Debra made a lovely model for David's photographs that he compiled for the article, and she also worked with care on the text–while David fed her ideas and criticism.

Debra's new book lay abandoned, but her disappointment was forgotten in the pleasure of working together.

Their correspondence with other conservationists provided them with sufficient intellectual stimulus, and the occasional company of Conrad Berg and Jane satisfied their need for human contact. They were still both sensitive about being with other people, and this way they could avoid it.

The *Wild Life* article was almost complete and ready for posting, when a letter arrived from Bobby Dugan in New York. The editor of *Cosmopolitan* magazine had chanced upon one of the few copies of *A Place of Our Own* in circulation. She had liked it, and the magazine was considering serialization of the book–possibly linked with a feature article on Debra. Bobby wanted Debra to let him have a selection of photographs of herself, and four thousand words of autobiographical notes.

The photographs were there, ready to go to *Wild Life,* and Debra ran through the four thousand words in three hours with David making suggestions, some helpful and some bawdy.

They sent off the tape and pictures in the same post as the article to *Wild Life.* For nearly a month they heard nothing more about it and then something happened to drive it from their minds.

They were in the small thatch and daub hide beside the main pool, sitting quietly and companionably during a lull in the evening activity. David had his camera tripod set up in one of the viewing windows and Debra's reflector was raised above the roof of the hide, daubed with camouflage paint and operated by a handle over her head.

The water was still and black, except where a surface-feeding bream was rising near the far reed banks. A flock of laughing doves was lining up with a chittering troop of spotted guinea fowl at the water's edge, sipping water and then pointing their beaks to the sky as they let it run down their throats.

Suddenly David took her wrist as a cautionary signal, and by the intensity of his grip she knew that he had seen something unusual and she leaned close against him so that she could hear his whispered descriptions, and with her right hand she switched on the recorder and then reached up to aim the reflector.

A herd of the rare and shy nyala antelope were approaching the drinking place timidly, clinging until the last possible moment to the security of the forest. Their ears were spread, and their nostrils quivered and sucked at the air, huge dark eyes glowing like lamps in the gloom.

There were nine hornless females, delicate chestnut in colour, striped with white, dainty-stepping and suspicious, as they followed the two herd bulls. These were so dissimilar from their females as though to belong to a different species. Purplish black, and shaggy with a rough mane extending from between the ears to the crupper. Their horns were thick and corkscrewed, tipped with cream, and between their eyes was a vivid white chevron marking.

Advancing only a step at a time, and then pausing to stare with the limitless patience of the wild, searching for a hint of danger, they came slowly down the bank.

They passed the hide so closely that David was afraid to press the trigger of his camera lest the click of the shutter frighten them away.

He and Debra sat frozen as they reached the water; Debra smiled happily as she picked up the soft snort with which the lead bull blew the surface before drinking, and the liquid slurping with which he drew his first mouthful.

Once they were all drinking David aimed and focused with care, but at the click of the shutter the bull nearest him leapt about and uttered a hoarse, throbbing alarm bark. Instantly the entire herd whirled and raced away like pale ghosts through the dark trees.

'I got it! I got it!' exulted Debra. 'Wow! He was so close, he nearly burst my eardrums.'

The excitement on Jabulani was feverish. Nyala antelope had never been seen on the estate before, not even in David's father's time, and all steps were taken to encourage them to remain. The pools were immediately placed out of bounds to all the rangers and servants, lest the human presence frighten the herd off before they had a chance to settle down and stabilize their territory.

Conrad Berg arrived, still using a stick and limping heavily as he would for the rest of his life. From the hide he watched the herd with David and Debra, and then back at the homestead he sat before the log fire, eating prime beef steak and drinking Old Buck while he gave his opinion.

'They aren't from the Park, I shouldn't think. I would have recognized a big old bull like that if I'd ever seen him before–they have probably sneaked in from one of the other estates–you haven't got the south fence up yet, have you?'

'Not yet.'

'Well, that's where they have moved from–probably sick of being stared at by all the tourists. Come up here for a bit of peace.' He took a swallow of his gin. 'You're getting a nice bit of stuff together here, Davey–another few years and it will be a real show-place. Have you got any plans for visitors–you could make a good thing out of this place, like they have at Mala-Mala. Five-star safaris at economy prices–'

'Connie, I'm just too damn selfish to want to share this with anybody else.'

The distractions and the time had given Debra an opportunity to recover from the American failure of *A Place of Our Own*, and one morning she sat down at her desk and began working again on her second novel. That evening she told David:

'One of the blocks I have had is that I hadn't a name for it. It's like a baby–you have to give it a name or it's not really a person.'

'You have got a name for it?' he asked.

'Yes.'

'Would you like to tell me?'

She hesitated, shy at saying it to some other person for the first time. 'I thought I'd call it–*A Bright and Holy Thing*,' she said, and he thought about it for a few moments, repeating it softly.

'You like it?' she asked anxiously.

'It's great,' he said. 'I like it. I really do.'

With Debra once more busy on her novel it seemed each day was too short for the love and laughter and industry which filled it.

The call came through while David and Debra were sitting around the barbecue in the front garden. David ran up to the house when the telephone bell insisted.

'Miss Mordecai?' David was puzzled, the name was vaguely familiar.

'Yes. I have a person-to-person call from New York for Miss Debra Mordecai,' the operator repeated impatiently, and David realized who she was talking about.

'She'll take it,' he said, and yelled for Debra. It was Bobby Dugan, and the first time she had heard his voice.

'Wonder girl,' he shouted over the line. 'Sit down, so you don't fall down. Big Daddy has got news for you that will blow your mind! *Cosmopolitan* ran the article on you two weeks ago. They did you real proud, darling, full-page photograph–God, you looked good enough to eat–'

Debra laughed nervously and signalled David to put his ear against hers to listen.

'–the mag hit the stands Saturday, and Monday morning was a riot at the book stores. They were beating the doors down. You've caught the imagination of everybody here, darling. They sold seventeen thousand hardback in five days, you jumped straight into the number five slot on the *New York Times* bestseller list–it's a freak, a phenomenon, a mad crazy runner–darling, we are going to sell half a million copies of this book standing on our heads. All the big papers and mags are screaming for review copies–they've lost the ones we sent them three months ago. Doubleday are reprinting fifty thousand–and I told them they were crazy–it should have been a hundred thousand–it's only just starting–next week will see the west coast catch fire and they'll be screaming for copies across the whole country–' There was much more, Bobby Dugan riding high, shouting his plans and his hopes, while Debra laughed weakly and kept saying, 'No! I can't believe it!' and 'It's not true!'

They drank three bottles of Veuve Clicquot that night, and a little before midnight Debra fell pregnant to David Morgan.

'Miss Mordecai combines superb use of language and a sure literary touch with the readability of a popular bestseller,' said the *New York Times*.

'Who says good literature has to be dull?' asked *Time*, 'Debra Mordecai's talent burns like a clean white flame.'

'Miss Mordecai takes you by the throat, slams you against the wall, throws you on the floor and kicks you in the guts. She leaves you as shaken and weak as if you had been in a car smash,' added the *Free Press*.

Proudly David presented Conrad Berg with a signed copy of *A Place of Our Own*. Conrad had finally been prevailed upon to drop the 'Mrs Morgan' and call Debra by her given name. He was so impressed with the book that he had an immediate relapse.

'How do you think of those things, Mrs Morgan?' he asked with awe.

'Debra,' Debra prompted him.

'She doesn't think of them,' Jane Berg explained helpfully. 'It just comes to her–it's called *inspiration*.'

Bobby Dugan was correct, they had to reprint another fifty thousand copies.

It seemed as though the fates, ashamed of the cruel pranks they had played upon them, were determined to shower Debra and David with gifts.

As Debra sat at her olive-wood table, growing daily bigger with her child, once again the words flowed as strongly and as crystal clear as the spring waters of the String of Pearls. However, there was still time to help David with the illustrated publication he was compiling on the birds of prey of the bushveld, and to accompany him on the daily expeditions to different areas of Jabulani, and to plan the furnishings and the layout of the empty nursery.

Conrad Berg came to her secretly to enlist her aid in his plan to have David nominated to the Board of the National Parks Committee. They discussed it in length and great detail. A seat on the Board carried prestige and was usually reserved for men of greater age and influence than David. However, Conrad was confident that the dignity of the Morgan name combined with David's wealth, ownership of Jabulani, demonstrated interest in conservation and his ability to devote much time to the affairs of the Board would prevail.

'Yes,' Debra decided. 'It will be good for him to meet people and get out a little more. We are in danger of becoming recluses here.'

'Will he do it?'

'Don't worry,' Debra assured him, 'I'll see to it.'

Debra was right. After the initial uneasiness of the first meeting of the Board, and once the other members became accustomed to that dreadful face and realized that behind it was a warm and forceful person, David gathered increasing confidence with each subsequent journey to Pretoria where the Board met. Debra would fly up with him and while they were at their deliberations she and Jane Berg shopped for the baby and the other items of luxury and necessity that were not readily come by in Nelspruit.

However, by November Debra was carrying low and she felt too big and uncomfortable to make the long flight in the cockpit of the Navajo, especially as the rains were about to break and the air was turbulent with storm cloud and static and heavy thermals. It would be a bumpy trip, and she was deeply involved in the last chapters of the new book.

'I'll be perfectly all right here,' she insisted. 'I've got a telephone and I have also got six game rangers, four servants and a fierce hound to guard me.'

David argued and protested for five days before the meeting and agreed only after he had worked out a timetable.

'If I leave here before dawn I'll be at the meeting by nine, we'll be finished by three and I can be back here by six-thirty at the latest,' he muttered. 'If it wasn't the budget and financial affairs vote, I would cut it–tell them I was sick.'

'It's important, darling. You go.'

'You sure now?'

'I won't even notice you're not here.'

'Don't get too carried away by it,' he told her ruefully. 'I might stay just to punish you.'

In the dawn the thunderheads were the colour of wine and flame and ripe fruit, fuming and magnificent, towering high above the tiny aircraft, high above the utmost ceiling of which it was capable.

David flew the corridors of open sky alone and at peace, wrapped in the euphoria of flight which never failed for him. He altered course at intervals to avoid the mountainous upsurges of cloud; within them lurked death and disaster, great winds that would tear the wings from his machine and send the pieces whirling on high, up into the heights where a man would perish from lack of oxygen.

He landed at Grand Central where a hire car was waiting for him, and spent the journey into Pretoria reading through the morning papers. It was only when he saw the meteorological prediction of a storm front moving in steadily from the Mozambique channel that he felt a little uneasy.

Before he entered the conference-room he asked the receptionist to take a telephone call to Jabulani.

'Two-hour delay, Mr Morgan.'

'Okay, call me when it comes through.'

When they broke for lunch he asked her again.

'What happened to my call?'

'I'm sorry, Mr Morgan. I was going to tell you. The lines are down. They are having very heavy rainfall in the low veld.'

His vague uneasiness became mild alarm.

'Would you call the meteorological office for me, please?'

The weather was down solid. From Barberton to Mpunda Milia and from Lourenço Marques to Machadodorp, the rain was heavy and unrelenting. The cloud ceiling was above twenty thousand feet and it was right down on the ground. The Navajo had no oxygen or electronic navigational equipment.

'How long?' David demanded of the meteorological officer. 'How long until it clears?'

'Hard to tell, sir. Two or three days.'

'Damn! Damn!' said David bitterly, and went down to the canteen on the ground floor of the government building. Conrad Berg was at a corner table with two other members of the Board, but when he saw David he jumped up and limped heavily but urgently across the room.

'David,' he took his arm, and his round red face was deadly serious. 'I've just heard–Johan Akkers broke jail last night. He killed a guard and got clean away. He's been loose for seventeen hours.'

David stared at him, unable to speak with the shock of it.

'Is Debra alone?'

David nodded, his face stiff with scar tissue, but his eyes dark and afraid.

'You'd better fly down right away to be with her.'

'The weather–they've grounded all aircraft in the area.'

'Use my truck!' said Conrad urgently.

'I need something faster than that.'

'Do you want me to come with you?'

'No,' said David. 'If you aren't there this afternoon, they won't approve the new fencing allocations. I'll go on my own.'

Debra was working at her desk when she heard the wind coming. She switched off her tape recorder and went out on to the veranda with the dog following her closely.

She stood listening, not sure of what she was hearing. It was a soughing and sighing, a far-off rushing like that of a wave upon a pebble beach.

The dog pressed against her leg and she squatted beside him, placing one arm around his neck, listening to the gathering rush of the wind, hearing the roar of it building up swiftly, the branches of the marula forest beginning to thrash and rattle.

Zulu whimpered, and she hugged him a little closer.

'There, boy. Gently. Gently,' she whispered and the wind struck in a mighty squalling blast, crashing through the tree-tops, tearing and cracking the upper branches.

It banged into the insect screen of the veranda with a snap like a mainsail filling, and unsecured windows and doors slammed like cannon shots.

Debra sprang up and ran back into her workroom, the window was swinging and slamming, dust and debris boiling in through it. She put her shoulder to it, closing it and securing the latch, then she ran to do the same to the other windows and bumped into one of the house servants.

Between them they battened down all the doors and windows.

'Madam, the rain will come now. Very much rain.'

'Go to your families now,' Debra told them.

'The dinner, madam?'

'Don't worry, I'll make that,' and thankfully they streamed away through the swirling dust to their hutments beyond the kopje.

The wind blew for fifteen minutes, and Debra stood by the wire screen and felt it tugging and whipping her body. Its wildness was infectious, and she laughed aloud, elated and excited.

Then suddenly the wind was passed, as swiftly as it had come, and she heard it tearing and clawing its way over the hills above the pools.

In the utter silence that followed the whole world waited, tensed for the next onslaught of the elements. Debra felt the cold, the sudden fall in temperature as though the door to a great ice-box had opened and she hugged her arms and shivered; she could not see the dense dark cloud banks that rolled across Jabulani, but somehow she sensed their menace and their majesty in the coldness that swamped her.

The first lightning bolt struck with a crackling electric explosion that seemed to singe the air about her, and Debra was taken so unawares that she cried out aloud. The thunder broke, and seemed to shake the sky and rock the earth's very foundations.

Debra turned and groped her way back into the house, locking herself into her room, but walls could not diminish the fury of the rain when it came. It drummed and roared and deafened, battering the window panes, and striking the walls and doors, pouring through the screen to flood the veranda.

As overpowering as was the rainstorm, yet it was the lightning and the thunder that racked Debra's nerves. She could not steel herself for each mighty crack and roar. Each one caught her off balance, and it seemed that they were aimed directly at her.

She crouched on her day bed, clinging to the soft warm body of the dog for a little comfort. She wished she had not allowed the servants to leave, and she thought that her nerve might crack altogether under the bombardment.

Finally she could stand it no longer. She groped her way into the living-room. In her distress she had almost lost her way about her own home, but she found the telephone and lifted it to her ear.

Immediately she knew that it was dead, there was no tone to it but she cranked the handle wildly, calling desperately into the mouthpiece, until finally she let it fall and dangle on its cord.

She began to sob as she stumbled back to her workroom, hugging the child in her big belly, and she fell upon the day bed and covered her ears with both hands.

'Stop it,' she screamed. 'Stop it, oh please God, make it stop.'

The new national highway as far as the coal-mining town of Witbank was broad and smooth, six lanes of traffic, and David eased the hired Pontaic into the fast lane and went flat, keeping his foot pressed down hard. She peaked out at a hundred and thirty miles an hour, and she sat so solid upon the road that he hardly needed to drive her. His mind was free to play with horror stories, and to remember Johan Akkers' face as he stood in the dock glaring across the Court Room at them. The deep-set muddy eyes, and the mouth working as though he were about to spit. As the warders had led him to the stairs down to the cells he had pulled free and shouted back.

'I'm going to get you, Scarface,' he giggled. 'If I have to wait twenty-nine years–I'm going to get you,' and they took him away.

After Witbank the road narrowed. There was heavy traffic and the bends had dangerous camber and deceptive gradients. David was able to concentrate on keeping the big car on the road, and to drive the phantoms from his mind.

He took the Lydenburg turn off, cutting the corner of the triangle, and the traffic thinned out to an occasional truck. He was able to go flat out again, and race along the edge of the high escarpment. Then suddenly the road turned and began its plunge down into the low veld.

When he emerged from the Erasmus tunnel David ran into the rain. It was a solid grey bank of water that filled the air and buffeted the body of the Pontiac. It flooded the road, so David had difficulty following its verge beneath the standing sheets of water, and it swamped the windshield, so that the efforts of the wipers to clear it were defeated.

David switched on his headlights and drove as fast as he dared, craning forward in his seat to peer into the impenetrable blue-grey curtains of rain.

Darkness came early in the rain, beneath the lowering black clouds, and the wet road dazzled him with the reflections of his own headlights, while the fat falling drops seemed as big as hail stones. He was forced to moderate his speed a little more, creeping down the highway towards Bandolier Hill.

In the darkness he almost missed the turning, and he reversed back to it, swinging on to the unmade surface.

It was slushy with mud, puddled and swampy, slippery as grease. Again he was forced to lower his speed. Once he lost it, and slid broadside into the drainage ditch. By packing loose stones under the wheels and racing the engine he pulled the Pontiac out and drove on.

By the time he reached the bridge over the Luzane stream, he had been six hours at the wheel of the Pontiac, and it was a few minutes after eight o'clock in the evening.

As he reached the bridge the rain stopped abruptly, a freak hole in the weather. Directly overhead the stars showed mistily, while around them the cloud banks swirled, turning slowly, as though upon the axis of a great wheel.

David's headlights cut through the darkness, out across the mad brown waters to the far bank a hundred yards away. The bridge was submerged under fifteen feet of flood water, and the water was moving so swiftly that its waves and whirlpools seemed sculptured in polished brown marble, and the trunks of uprooted trees dashed downstream upon the flood.

It seemed impossible that the bed of this raging torrent had been the narrow sandy bed in which Johan Akkers had run down Conrad with the green Ford truck.

David climbed out of the Pontiac and walked down to the edge of the water. As he stood there he saw the level creeping up perceptibly towards his feet. It was still rising.

He looked up at the sky, and judged that the respite in the weather would not last much longer.

He reached his decision and ran back to the Pontiac. He reversed well back on to the highest ground and parked it off the verge with the headlights still directed at the river edge. Then, standing beside the door, he stripped down to his shirt and underpants. He pulled his belt from the loops of his trousers and buckled it about his waist, then he tied his shoes to the belt by their laces.

Barefooted he ran to the edge of the water, and began to feel his way slowly down the bank. It shelved quickly and within a few paces he was knee-deep and the current plucked at him, viciously trying to drag him off-balance.

He poised like that, braced against the current, and waited, staring upstream. He saw the tree trunk coming down fast on the flood, with its roots sticking up like beseeching arms. It was swinging across the current and would pass him closely.

He judged his moment and lunged for it. Half a dozen strong strokes carried him to it and he grasped one of the roots. Instantly he was whisked out of the beams of the headlight into the roaring fury of the river. The tree rolled and bucked, carrying him under and bringing him up coughing and gasping.

Something struck him a glancing blow and he felt his shirt tear and the skin beneath it rip. Then he was under water again, swirling end over end and clinging desperately to his log.

All about him the darkness was filled with the rush and threat of crazy water, and he was buffeted and flogged by its raw strength, grazed and bruised by rocks and driftwood.

Suddenly he felt the log check and bump against an obstruction, turning and swinging out into the current again.

David was blinded with muddy water and he knew there was a limit to how much more of this treatment he could survive. Already he was weakening quickly. He could feel his mind and his movements slowing, like a battered prize fighter in the tenth round.

He gambled it all on the obstruction which the log had encountered being the far bank, and he released his death-grip on the root and struck out sideways across the current with desperate strength.

His overarm stroke ended in the trailing branches of a thorn tree hanging over the storm waters. Thorns tore the flesh of his palm as his grip closed over them, and he cried out at the pain but held on.

Slowly he dragged himself out of the flood and crawled up the bank, hacking and coughing at the water in his lungs. Clear of the river, he fell on his face in the mud and vomited a gush of swallowed water that shot out of his nose and mouth.

He lay exhausted for a long while, until his coughing slowed and he could breathe again. His shoes had been torn from his belt by the current. He dragged himself to his feet and staggered forward into the darkness. As he ran, he held his hand to his face, pulling the broken thorns from the flesh of his palm with his teeth.

Stars were still showing overhead and by their feeble light he made out the road, and he began to run along it, gathering strength with each pace. It was very still now, with only the dripping of the trees and the occasional far-out mutter of thunder to break the silence.

Two miles from the homestead, David made out the dark bulk of something on the side of the road, and it was only when he was a few paces from it that he realized it was an automobile–a late model Chevy. It had been abandoned, bogged down in one of the greasy mudholes that the rains had opened.

The doors were unlocked and David switched on the interior and parking lights. There was dried blood on the seat, a dark smear of it, and on the back seat was a bundle of clothing. David untied it quickly and recognized immediately the coarse canvas suiting as regulation prison garb. He stared at it stupidly for a moment, until the impact of it struck him.

The car was stolen, the blood probably belonging to the unfortunate owner. The prison garb had been exchanged for other clothing, probably taken from the body of the owner of the Chevy.

David knew then beyond all possible doubt that Johan Akkers was at Jabulani, and that he had arrived before the bridge over the Luzane stream had become impassable–probably three or four hours previously.

David threw the prison suiting back into the car, and he began to run.

Johan Akkers drove the Chevy across the Luzane bridge with the rising waters swirling over the guard rail, and with the rain teeming down in blinding white sheets.

The muddy water shoved at the body of the car, making steering difficult, and it seeped in under the doors, flooding the floorboards and swirling about Akkers' feet; but he reached the safety of the far bank and raced the engine as he shot up it. The wheels spun on the soft mud, and the Chevy skidded and swayed drunkenly in the loose footing.

The closer he drew to Jabulani the more reckless he became in his haste.

Before his conviction and imprisonment, Akkers had been a twisted and blighted creature, a man of deep moods and passionate temper. Feeling himself rejected and spurned by his fellow men he had lived in a world of swift defensive violence, but always he had kept within the bounds of reason.

However, during the two years that he had laboured and languished within prison walls, his anger and his lust for vengeance had driven him over that narrow boundary.

Vengeance had become the sole reason for his existence, and he had rehearsed it a hundred times each day. He had planned his prison break to give himself three days of freedom–after that it did not matter. Three days would be enough.

He had infected his own jaw, running a needle poisoned with his excreta deeply into the gum. They had taken him to the dental clinic as he had planned. The guard had been easily handled, and the dentist had co-operated with a scalpel held to his throat.

Once clear of the prison, Akkers had used the scalpel, vaguely surprised by the volume of blood that could issue from a human throat. He had left the dentist slumped over his steering-wheel on a plot of waste ground and, with his white laboratory gown over his prison suit, he had waited at a set of traffic lights.

The shiny new Chevy had pulled up for a red light and Akkers had opened the passenger door and slid in beside the driver.

He had been a smaller man than Akkers, plump and prosperous-looking, with a smooth pale face and soft little hairless hands on the steering-wheel. He had obeyed meekly Akkers' instruction to drive on.

Akkers had rolled his soft white body, clad only in vest and shorts, into a clump of thick grass beside a disused secondary road and pulled the grass closed over him, then he had beaten the first road block out of the city area by forty minutes.

He stayed on the side roads, picking his way slowly eastwards. The infection in his jaw had ached intolerably despite the shot of antibiotics the dentist had given him, and his crippled claw of a hand had been awkward and clumsy on the gear lever–for the severed nerves and sinews had never knitted again. The hand was a dead and insensate thing.

Using the caution of a natural predator and helped by the news flashes on the radio, he had groped his way carefully through the net that was spread for him, and now he was on Jabulani and he could restrain himself no longer.

He hit the mud hole at forty and the Chevy whipped and spun, slewing her back end deep into the mud and high-centring her belly on the soft ooze.

He left her there and went on swiftly through the rain, loping on long legs. Once he giggled and sucked at his teeth, but then he was silent again.

It was dark by the time he climbed the kopje behind Jabulani homestead. He lay there for two hours peering down into the driving rain, waiting for the darkness. Once night fell, he could see no lights, and he began to worry, there should have been lights burning.

He left the kopje and moved cautiously through the darkness down the hill. He avoided the servants' quarters, and went through the trees to the landing-strip.

He ran into the side of the hangar in the dark and followed the wall to the side doorway.

Frantically he spread his arms and felt for the aircraft that should be here–and when he realized that it was not he let out a groan of frustration.

They were gone. He had planned and schemed in vain, all his desperate striving was in vain.

Growling like an animal, he smashed the fist of his good hand against the wall, enjoying the pain of it in his frustration, and his anger and his hatred was so strong that it shook his body like a fever, and he cried out aloud, a formless animal cry without coherence or sense.

Suddenly the rain stopped. The heavy drum of it upon the iron roof of the hangar ceased so abruptly that Akkers was distracted. He went to the opening and looked out.

The stars were swimming mistily above him, and the only sound was the gurgle and chuckle of running water and the dripping of the trees.

There was the glimmering of light now, and he saw the white walls of the homestead shine amongst the trees. He could do damage there, Akkers realized. He could find there some outlet for his terrible frustration. There was furniture to smash, and the thatch would burn–if lit from inside, the thatch would burn even in this weather.

He started towards the homestead through the dark sodden trees.

Debra woke in the silence. She had fallen asleep in the midst of the storm, perhaps as a form of escape.

Now she groped for the warm comforting body of the dog but he was gone. There was a patch of warmth on the bed beside her where he had lain.

She listened intently and there was nothing but the soft sounds of water in the guttering and far-off the growl of thunder. She remembered her earlier panic and she was ashamed.

She stood up from the bed and she was shivering with the cold in her loose, free-flowing dark blue maternity blouse, and the elastic-fronted slacks that were adjustable to her expanding waistline. She felt with her toes and found the light ballet pumps on the stone floor and pushed her feet into them.

She started towards her dressing-room for a sweater, then she would make herself a cup of hot soup, she decided.

Zulu started barking. He was outside in the front garden. Clearly he had left the house through the small hinged doorway that David had built especially for him in the veranda wall.

The dog had many barks, each with a different meaning which Debra understood.

A self-effacing woof, that was the equivalent of the watchman's 'Ten o'clock on a June night–and all's well.'

Or a longer-drawn-out yowl, that meant, 'There is a full moon out tonight, and the wolf's blood in my veins will not allow me to sleep.'

A sharper, meaningful bark, 'Something is moving down near the pumphouse. It may be a lion.'

And then there was an urgent clamouring chorus, 'There is dire danger threatening. Beware! Beware!'

It was the danger bark now, and then growling through closed jaws as though he were worrying something.

Debra went out on to the veranda and she felt the puddled rainwater soaking through her light shoes. Zulu was harrying something in the front garden, she could hear the growling and scuffling, the movement of bodies locked in a struggle. She stood silently, uncertain of what to do, knowing only that she could not go out to Zulu. She was blind and helpless against the unknown adversary. As she hesitated she heard clearly the sound of a heavy blow. It cracked on bone, and she heard the thump of a body falling. Zulu's growls were cut off abruptly, and there was silence. Something had happened to the dog. Now she was completely alone in the silence.

No, not silence. There was the sound of breathing–a heavy panting breath.

Debra shrank back against the veranda wall, listening and waiting.

She heard footsteps, human footsteps coming through the garden towards the front door. The footsteps squelched and splashed in the rain puddles.

She wanted to call out a challenge, but her voice was locked in her constricted throat. She wanted to run, but her legs were paralysed by the sound of the intruder climbing the front steps.

A hand brushed against the wire screening, and then settled on the handle, rattling it softly.

At last Debra found her voice. 'Who is that?' she called, a high panicky cry that ran out into the night silence.

Instantly the soft sounds ceased. The intruder was frozen by her challenge. She could imagine whoever it was standing on the top step, peering through the screening into the darkness of the veranda, trying to make her out in the gloom. Suddenly she was thankful for the dark blouse and black slacks.

She waited motionlessly, listening, and she heard a little wind shake the tree-tops, bringing down a sudden quick patter of droplets. A hunting owl called down near the dam. She heard the thunder murmur bad-temperedly along the hills, and a nightjar screeched harshly from amongst the poinsettia bushes.

The silence went on for a long time, and she knew she could not stand it much longer. She could feel her lips beginning to quiver and the cold and fear and the weight of the child were heavy upon her bladder, she wanted to run–but there was nowhere to run to.

Then suddenly the silence was broken. In the darkness there was the sound of a man giggling. It was shockingly close and clear, and it was a crazy sound. The shock of it seemed to clutch at her heart and crush the air from her lungs.

Her legs went weak under her, beginning to shake, and the pressure on her bladder was intolerable–for she recognized the sound of that laughter, the sick insane sound of it was graven upon her mind.

A hand shook the door handle, jerking and straining at it. Then a shoulder crashed into the narrow frame. It was a screen door–not built to withstand rough treatment. Debra knew it would yield quickly.

She screamed then, a high ringing scream of terror, and it seemed to break the spell which held her. Her legs would move again, and her brain would work.

She whirled and ran back into her workroom, slamming the door and locking it swiftly.

She crouched beside the door, thinking desperately. She knew that as soon as he broke into the house Akkers need only switch on a light. The electricity generator would automatically kick in on demand, and in the light he would have her at his mercy. Her only protection was darkness. In the darkness she would have the advantage, for she was accustomed to it.

She had heard the nightjar and the owl calling so she knew that night had fallen, and it was probable that the rain cloud still blanketed moon and stars. Darkness was out there in the forest. She must get out of the house, and try to reach the servants' quarters.

She hurried through the rooms towards the rear of the house, and as she went she thought of a weapon. The firearms were locked in the steel cabinet in David's office–and the key was with him. She ran through to the kitchen and her heavy walking-stick was in its place by the door. She grasped it thankfully and slipped open the door catch.

At that moment she heard the front door crash open, with the lock kicked in, and she heard Akkers charge heavily into the living-room. She closed the kitchen door behind her and started across the yard. She tried not to run, she counted her steps. She must not lose her way. She must find the track around the kopje to the servants' hutments.

Her first landmark was the gate in the fence that ringed the homestead. Before she reached it she heard the electricity generator throb to life in the power house beyond the garages. Akkers had found a light switch.

She was slightly off in her direction and she ran into the barbed-wire fence. Frantically she began to feel her way along it, trying for the gate. Above her head she heard the buzz and crackle of the element in one of the arc lamps that lined the fence and could flood the gardens with light.

Akkers must have found the switch beside the kitchen door, and Debra realized that she must be bathed in the light of the arcs.

She heard him shout behind her, and knew that he had seen her. At that moment she found the gate, and with a sob of relief she tore it open and began to run.

She must get out of the light of the arcs, she must find the darkness. Light was mortal danger, darkness was sanctuary.

The track forked, left to the pools, right to the hutments. She took the right-hand path and ran along it. Behind her she heard the gate clank shut. He was after her.

She counted as she ran, five hundred paces to the rock on the left side of the path that marked the next fork. She tripped over it, falling heavily and barking her shins.

She rolled to her knees, and she had lost the walking-stick. She could not waste precious seconds in searching for it. She groped for the path and ran on.

Fifty paces and she knew she was on the wrong fork. This path led down to the pumphouse–and she was not familiar with it. It was not one of her regular routes.

She missed a turn and ran into broken ground. She stumbled on until rank grass wrapped about her ankles and brought her down again, falling heavily on her side so that she was winded.

She was completely lost, but she knew she was out of the arc lights now. With luck she was shielded by complete darkness–but her heart was racing and she felt nauseous with terror.

She tried to control her gulping, sobbing breath, and to listen.

She heard him coming then, pounding footsteps that rang clearly, even on the rain-soaked earth. He seemed to be coming directly to where she lay, and she shrank down against the wet earth and she pressed her face into her arms to hide her face and muffle her breathing.

At the last moment his blundering footsteps passed her closely, and ran on. She felt sick with relief, but it was premature for abruptly the footsteps ceased and he was so close she could hear him panting.

He was listening for her, standing close beside where she lay in the grass. They stayed like that during the long slow passage of minutes. For Debra it seemed an eternity of waiting–broken at last by his voice.

'Ah! There you are,' he giggled, 'there you are. I can see you.'

Her heart jumped with shock, he was closer than she had thought. Almost she jumped up and began to run again–but some deeper sense restrained her.

'I can see you hiding there,' he repeated, giggling and snickering. 'I've got a big knife here, I'm going to hold you down and cut–'.

She quailed in the grass, listening to the awful obscenities that poured from his mouth. Then suddenly she realized that she was safe here. She was covered by the night and the thick grass, and he had lost her. He was trying to panic her, make her run again and betray her position. She concentrated all her attention on remaining absolutely still and silent.

Akkers' threats and sadistic droolings ended in silence again. He listened for her with the patience of the hunter, and the long minutes dragged by.

The ache in her bladder was like a red-hot iron, and she wanted to sob out loud. Something loathsome crawled out of the wet grass over her arm. Her skin prickled with fresh horror at the feel of multiple insect feet on her skin, but she steeled herself not to move.

The thing, scorpion or spider, crawled across her neck and she knew her nerves would crack within seconds.

Suddenly Akkers spoke again. 'All right!' he said, 'I'm going back to fetch a flashlight. We'll see how far you get then. I'll be back soon–don't think you'll beat old Akkers. He's forgotten more tricks than you'll ever learn.'

He moved away heavily, noisily, and she wanted to strike the insect from her cheek and run again, but some instinct warned her. She waited five minutes, and then ten. The insect moved up into her hair.

Akkers spoke again out of the darkness near her. 'All right, you clever bitch. We'll get you yet,' and she heard him move away. This time she knew he had gone.

She brushed the insect from her hair, shuddering with horror. Then she stood up and moved quietly into the forest. Her fingers were stiff with cold on the fastenings of her slacks, but she loosened them and squatted to relieve the burning ache in her lower belly.

She stood up again and felt the child move within her body. The feel of it evoked all her maternal instincts of protection. She must find a safe place for her child. She thought of the hide by the pools.

How to reach them? For she was now completely lost. Then she remembered David telling her about the wind, the rain wind out of the west, now reduced to an occasional light air, and she waited for the next breath of it on her cheek. It gave her direction. She turned her back to the next gust and set off steadily through the forest with hands held out ahead to prevent herself running into one of the trunks. If only she could reach the pools, she could follow the bank to the hide.

As the cyclonic winds at the centre of the storm turned upon their axis, so they swung, changing direction constantly and Debra followed them faithfully, beginning a wide aimless circle through the forest.

Akkers raged through the brightly lit homestead of Jabulani, jerking open drawers and kicking in locked cupboard doors.

He found the gun cabinet in David's office, and ransacked the desk drawers for keys. He found none, and giggled and swore with frustration.

He crossed the room to the built-in cupboard unit. There was a sealed-cell electric lantern on the shelf with a dozen packets of shotgun shells. he took down the lantern eagerly and thumbed the switch. The beam was bright white, even in the overhead lights–and he sucked his teeth and chuckled happily.

Once more he ran into the kitchen, pausing to select a long stainless-steel carving knife from the cutlery drawer before hurrying across the yard to the gate and along the path.

In the lantern beam, Debra's footprints showed clearly in the soft earth with his own overlaying them. He followed them to where she had blundered off the path, and found the mark of her body where she had lain.

'Clever bitch, he chuckled again and followed her tracks through the forest. She had laid an easy trail to follow, dragging a passage through the rain-heavy grass and wiping the droplets from the stems. To the hunter's eye it was a clearly blazed trail.

Every few minutes he paused to throw the beam of the lantern ahead of him amongst the trees. He was thrilling now to the hunter's lust, the primeval force which was the mainspring of his existence. His earlier set-back made the chase sweeter for him.

He went on carefully, following the wandering trail, the aimless footprints turning haphazardly in a wide circle.

He stopped again and panned the lantern beam across the rain-laden grass tops, and he saw something move at the extreme range of the lamp, something pale and round.

He held it in the lantern beam, and saw the woman's pale strained face as she moved forward slowly and hesitantly. She went like a sleep-walker, with arms extended ahead of her, and with shuffling uncertain gait.

She was coming directly towards him, oblivious of the light which held her captive in its beam. Once she paused to hug her swollen belly and sob with weariness and fear.

The legs of her trousers were sodden with rain water and her flimsy shoes were already torn, and as she hobbled closer he saw that her arms and her lips were blue and shivering with the cold.

Akkers stood quietly watching her coming towards him, like a chicken drawn to the swaying cobra.

Her long dark hair hung in damp ropes down her shoulders, and dangled in her face. Her thin blouse was wet also with drops fallen from the trees, and it was plastered over the thrusting mound of her belly.

He let her come closer, enjoying the fierce thrill of having her in his power. Drawing out the final consummation of his vengeance–hoarding each moment of it like a miser.

When she was five paces from him he played the beam full in her face, and he giggled.

She screamed, her whole face convulsing, and she whirled like a wild animal and ran blindly. Twenty paces before she ran headlong into the stem of a marula tree.

She fell back, collapsing to her knees and sobbed aloud, clutching at her bruised cheek.

Then she scrambled to her feet and stood shivering, turning her head and cocking it for the next sound.

Silently he moved around her, drawing close and he giggled again, close behind her.

She screamed again and ran blindly, panic-stricken, witless with terror until an ant-bear hold caught her foot and flung her down heavily to the ground, and she lay there sobbing.

Akkers moved leisurely and silently after her, he was enjoying himself for the first time in two years. Like a cat he did not want to end it, he wanted it to last a long time.

He stooped over her and whispered a filthy word, and instantly she rolled to her feet and was up and running again–wildly, sightlessly, through the trees. He followed her, and in his crazed mind she became a symbol of all the thousand animals he had hunted and killed.

David ran barefooted in the soft earth of the road. He ran without feeling his bruised and torn skin, without feeling the pounding of his heart nor the protest of his lungs.

As the road rounded the shoulder of the hill and dipped towards the homestead he stopped abruptly, and stared panting at the lurid glow of the arc lights that floodlit the grounds and garden of Jabulani. It made no sense that the floodlights should be burning, and David felt a fresh flood of alarm. He sprinted on down the hill.

He ran through the empty, ransacked rooms shouting her name–but the echoes mocked him.

When he reached the front veranda he saw something moving in the darkness, beyond the broken screen door.

'Zulu!' He ran forward. 'Here, boy! Here, boy! Where is she?'

The dog staggered up the steps towards him, his tail wagged a perfunctory greeting, but he was obviously hurt. A heavy blow along the side of his head had broken the jaw, or dislocated it, so that it hung lopsided and grotesque. He was still stunned, and David knelt beside him.

'Where is she, Zulu? Where is she?' The dog seemed to make an effort to gather its scattered wits. 'Where is she, boy? She's not in the house. Where is she? Find her, boy, find her.'

He led the labrador out into the yard, and he followed gamely as David circled the house. At the back door Zulu picked up the scent on the fresh damp earth. He started resolutely towards the gate, and David saw the footprints in the floodlights, Debra's and the big masculine prints which ran after them.

As Zulu crossed the yard, David turned back into his office. The lantern was missing from its shelf, but there was a five-cell flashlight near the back. He shoved it into his pocket and grabbed a handful of shotgun shells. Then he went quickly to the gun cabinet and unlocked it. He snatched the Purdey shotgun from the rack and loaded it as he ran.

Zulu was staggering along the path beyond the gates, and David hurried after him.

Johan Akkers was no longer a human being, he had become an animal. The spectacle of the running quarry had roused the predator's single-minded passion to chase and drag down and kill–yet it was seasoned with a feline delight in torment. He was playing with his wounded dragging prey, running it when he could have ended it, drawing it out, postponing the climax, the final consuming thrill of the kill.

The moment came at last, some deep atavistic sense of the ritual of the hunt–for all sport killing has its correct ceremony–and Akkers knew it must end now.

He came up behind the running figure and reached out to take a twist of the thick dark hair in the crippled claw of his hand, wrapping it with a quick movement about his wrist and jerking back her head, laying open the long pale throat for the knife.

She turned upon him with a strength and ferocity he had not anticipated. Her body was hard and strong and supple, and now that she could place him she drove at him with the wild terror of a hunted thing.

He was unprepared, her attack took him off-balance, and he went over backwards with her on top of him, and he dropped the knife and the lantern into the grass to protect his eyes, for she was tearing at them with long sharp nails. He felt them rip into his nose and cheek, and she screeched like a cat–for she was also an animal in this moment.

He freed the stiff claw from the tangle of her hair, and he drew it back, holding her off with his right hand–and he struck her. It was like a wooden club, stiff and hard and without feeling. A single blow with it had stunned the labrador and broken his jaw. It hit her across the temple, a sound like an axe swung at a tree trunk. It knocked all the fight out of her, and he came up on his knees, holding her with his good hand and with the other he clubbed her mercilessly, beat her head back and across with a steady rhythm. In the light of the fallen lantern, the black blood spurted from her nose, and the blows cracked against her skull, steady and unrelenting. Long after she was still and senseless he continued to beat her. Then at last he let her drop, and he stood up. He went to the lantern and played the beam in the grass. The knife glinted up at him.

There is an ancient ceremony with which a hunt should end. The culminating ceremony of the gralloch, when the triumphant huntsman slits open the paunch of his game, and thrusts his hand into the opening to draw out the still-warm viscera.

Johan Akkers picked the knife out of the grass and set down the lantern so the beam fell upon Debra's supine figure.

He went to her and, with his foot, rolled her on to her back. The dark black mane of sodden hair smothered her face.

He knelt beside her and hooked one iron-hard finger into the front of her blouse. With a single jerk he ripped it cleanly open, and her big round belly bulged into the lantern light. It was white and full and ripe with the dark pit of the navel in its centre.

Akkers giggled and wiped the rain and sweat from his face with his arm. Then he changed his grip on the knife, reversing it so the blade would go shallow, opening the paunch neatly from crotch to rib cage without cutting into the intestines, a stroke as skilful as a surgeon's that he had performed ten thousand times before.

Movement in the shadows at the edge of the light caused him to glance up. He saw the black dog rush silently at him, saw its eyes glow in the lantern light.

He threw up his arm to guard his throat and the furry body crashed into him. They rolled together, with Zulu mouthing him, unable to take a grip with his injured jaws.

Akkers changed his grip on the hilt of the carving knife and stabbed up into the dog's rib cage, finding the faithful heart with his first thrust. Zulu yelped once, and collapsed. Akkers pushed the glossy black body aside, pulling out the knife and he crawled back to where Debra lay.

The distraction that Zulu had provided gave David a chance to come up.

David ran to Akkers, and the man looked up with the muddy green eyes glaring in the lantern light. He growled at David with the long blade in his hand dulled by the dog's blood. He started to come to his feet, ducking his head in exactly the same aggressive gesture as the bull baboon.

David thrust the barrels of the shotgun into his face and he pulled both triggers. The shot hit solidly, without spreading, tearing into him in the bright yellow flash and thunder of the muzzle blast, and it took away the whole of Akkers' head above the mouth, blowing it to nothingness. He dropped into the grass with his legs kicking convulsively, and David hurled the shotgun aside and ran to Debra.

He knelt over her and he whispered, 'My darling, oh my darling. Forgive me, please forgive me. I should never have left you.' Gently he picked her up and holding her to his chest, he carried her up to the homestead.

Debra's child was born in the dawn. It was a girl, tiny and wizened and too early for her term. If there had been skilled medical attention available she might have lived, for she fought valiantly. But David was clumsy and ignorant of the succour she needed. He was cut off by the raging river and the telephone was still dead, and Debra was still unconscious.

When it was over he wrapped the tiny little blue body in a clean sheet and laid it tenderly in the cradle that had been prepared for her. He felt overwhelmed by a sense of guilt at having failed the two persons who needed him.

At three o'clock that afternoon, Conrad Berg forced a passage of the Luzane stream with the water boiling above the level of the big wheels of his truck, and three hours later they had Debra in a private ward of the Nelspruit hospital. Two days later she became conscious once more, but her face was grotesquely swollen and purple with bruises.

Near the crest of the kopje that stood above the homestead of Jabulani there was a natural terrace, a platform which overlooked the whole estate. It was a remote and peaceful place and they buried the child there. Out of the rock of the kopje David built a tomb for her with his own hands.

It was best that Debra had never felt the child in her arms, or at her breast. That she had never heard her cry or smelled the puppy smell of her.

Her mourning was therefore not crippling and corrosive, and she and David visited the grave regularly. One Sunday morning as they sat upon the stone bench beside it, Debra talked for the first time about another baby.

'You took so long with the first one, Morgan,' she complained. 'I hope you've mastered the technique.'

They walked down the hill again, put the rods and a picnic basket into the Land-Rover and drove down to the pools.

The Mozambique bream came on the bite for an hour just before noon and they fought over the fat yellow wood grubs that David was baiting. Debra hung five, all around three pounds in weight, and David had a dozen of the big blue fish before it went quiet and they propped the rods and opened the cold box.

They lay together on the rug beneath the outspread branches of the fever trees, and drank white wine cold from the icebox.

The African spring was giving way to full summer, filling the bush with bustle and secret activity. The weaver birds were busy upon their basket nests, tying them to the bending tips of the reeds, fluttering brilliant yellow wings as they worked with black heads bobbing. On the far bank of the pool a tiny bejewelled kingfisher sat his perch on a dead branch above the still water, plunging suddenly, a speck of flashing blue to shatter the surface and emerge with a silver sliver wriggling in his outsize beak. Hosts of yellow and bronze and white butterflies lined the water's edge below where they lay, and the bees flew like golden motes of light to their hive in the cliff, high above the quiet pools.

The water drew all life to it, and a little after noonday David touched Debra's arm.

'The nyala are here–' he whispered.

They came through the grove on the far side of the pool. Timid and easily spooked, they approached a few cautious steps at a time before pausing to stare about them with huge dark eyes, questing muzzles and widespread ears; striped and dainty and beautiful they blended with the shadows of the grove.

'The does are all belly now,' David told her. 'They'll be dropping their lambs within the next few weeks. Everything is fruitful.' He half-turned towards her and she sensed it and moved to meet him. When the nyala had drank and gone, and a white-headed fish eagle circled high above them on dark chestnut wings, chanting its weird and haunting cry, they made love in the shade beside the quiet water.

David studied her face as he loved her. She lay beneath him with her eyes closed, and her dark hair spread in a shiny black sheet upon the rug. The bruise on her temple had faded to soft yellow and palest blue, for it was two months since she had left hospital. The white fleck of the grenade scar stood out clearly against the pale bruising. The colour rose in Debra's cheeks, and the light dew of perspiration bloomed across her forehead and upper lip and she made little cooing sounds, and them whimpered softly like a suckling puppy.

David watched her, his whole being engorged and heavy with the weight of his love. From above them an errant beam of sunlight broke through the canopy of leaves and fell full upon her upturned face, lighting it with a warm golden radiance so that it seemed to be the face of a madonna from some medieval church window. It was too much for David and his love broke like a wave, and she felt it and cried out. Her eyes flew wide, and he looked down into their gold-flecked depths. The pupils were huge black pools but as the sunlight struck full into them they shrank rapidly to black pinpoints.

Even in the extremity of his love, David was startled by the phenomenon, and long afterwards when they lay quietly together she asked, 'What is it, David? Is something wrong?'

'No, my darling. What could possibly be wrong?'

'I feel it, Davey. You send out the strongest signals–I am sure I could pick them up from half-way around the world.'

He laughed, and drew away from her almost guiltily. He had imagined it perhaps, a trick of the light, and he tried to dismiss it from his mind.

In the cool of the evening he packed up the rods and the rug and they strolled back to where he had parked and they took the firebreak road home, for David wanted to check the southern fence line. They had driven for twenty minutes in silence before Debra touched his arm.

'When you are ready to tell me about whatever is bugging you–I'm ready to listen,' and he began talking again to distract both her and himself, but a little too glibly.

In the night he rose and went to the bathroom. When he returned he stood for many seconds beside their bed looking down at her dark sleeping shape. He would have left it then, but at that moment a lion began roaring down near the pools. The sound carried clearly through the still night across the two miles that separated them.

It was the excuse that David needed. He took the five-cell flashlight from his bedside table and shone it into Debra's face. It was serene and lovely, and he felt the urge to stoop and kiss her, but instead he called.

'Debra! Wake up, darling!' and she stirred and opened her eyes. He shone the beam of the flashlight full into them and again, unmistakably, the wide black circles of the pupils contracted.

'What is it, David?' she murmured sleepily, and his voice was husky as he replied.

'There is a lion holding a concert down near the pools. Thought you might want to listen.' She moved her head, averting her face slightly, almost as though the powerful beam of the flashlight was causing discomfort, but her voice was pleased.

'Oh yes. I love that big growly sound. Where do you suppose this one is from?'

David switched out the flashlight and slipped back into bed beside her.

'Probably coming up from the south. I bet he has dug a hole under the fence you could drive a truck through.' He tried to speak naturally as they reached for each other beneath the bedclothes and lay close and warm, listening to the far-away roaring until it faded with distance as the lion moved back towards the reserve. They made love then, but afterwards David could not sleep and he lay with Debra in his arms until the dawn.

Still it was a week before David could bring himself to write the letter:

Dear Dr Edelman,

We agreed that I should write to you if any change occurred in the condition of Debra's eyes, or her health.

Recently Debra was involved in unfortunate circumstances, in which she was struck repeated heavy blows about the head and was rendered unconscious for a period of two and a half days.

She was hospitalized for suspected fracture of the skull, and concussion, but was discharged after ten days.

This occurred about two months ago. However, I have since noticed that her eyes have become sensitive to light. As you are well aware, this was not previously the case, and she has showed no reaction whatsoever until this time. She has also complained of severe headaches.

I have repeatedly tested my observations with sunlight and artificial light, and there can be no doubt that under the stimulus of a strong light source, the pupils of her eyes contract instantly and to the same degree as one would expect in a normal eye.

It now seems possible that your original diagnosis might have to be revised, but–and I would emphasize this most strongly–I feel that we should approach this very carefully. I do not wish to awaken any false or ill-founded hope.

For your advice in this matter I would be most grateful, and I wait to hear from you.

Cordially yours,
David Morgan

David sealed and addressed the letter, but when he returned from the shopping flight to Nelspuit the following week, the envelope was still buttoned in the top pocket of his leather jacket.

The days settled into their calmly contented routine. Debra completed the first draft of her new novel, and received a request from Bobby Dugan to carry out a lecture tour of five major cities in the United States. *A Place of Our Own* had just completed its thirty-second week on the *New York Times* bestseller list–and her agent informed her that she was 'hotter than a pistol'.

David said that as far as he was concerned she was probably a lot hotter than that. Debra told him he was a lecher, and she was not certain what a nice girl like herself was doing shacked up with him. Then she wrote to her agent, and refused the lecture tour.

'Who needs people?' David agreed with her, knowing that she had made the decision for him. He knew also that Debra as a lovely, blind, bestselling authoress would have been a sensation, and a tour would have launched her into the superstar category.

This made his own procrastination even more corrosive. He tried to re-think and rationalize his delay in posting the letter to Dr Edelman. He told himself that the light-sensitivity did not mean that Debra could ever regain her vision; that she was happy now, had adjusted and found her place and that it would be cruel to disrupt all this and offer her false hope and probably brutal surgery.

In all his theorizing he tried to make Debra's need take priority, but it was deception and he knew it. It was special pleading, by David Morgan, for David Morgan–for if Debra ever regained her sight, the delicately balanced structure of his own happiness would collapse in ruin.

One morning he drove the Land-Rover alone to the farthest limits of Jabulani and parked in a hidden place amongst camel thorn trees. He switched off the engine and, still sitting in the driving-seat, he adjusted the driving-mirror and stared at his own face. For nearly an hour he studied the ravaged expanse of inhuman flesh, trying to find some redeeming feature in it–apart from the eyes–and at the end he knew that no sighted woman would ever be able to live close to that, would ever be able to smile at it, kiss and touch it, to reach up and caress it in the critical moments of love.

He drove home slowly, and Debra was waiting for him on the shady cool stoop and she laughed and ran down the steps into the sunlight when she heard the Land-Rover. She wore faded denims and a bright pink blouse, and when he came to her she lifted her face and groped blindly but joyously with her lips for his.

Debra had arranged a barbecue for that evening, and although they sat close about the open fire under the trees and listened to the night sounds, the night was cool. Debra wore a cashmere sweater over her shoulders, and David had thrown on his flying jacket.

The letter lay against his heart, and it seemed to burn into his flesh. He unbottoned the leather flap and took it out. While Debra chatted happily beside him, spreading her hands to the crackling leaping flames, David examined the envelope turning it slowly over and over in his hands.

Then suddenly, as though it were a live scorpion, he threw it from him and watched it blacken and curl and crumple to ash in the flames of the fire.

It was not so easily done, however, and that night as he lay awake, the words of the letter marched in solemn procession through his brain, meticulously preserved and perfectly remembered. They gave him no respite, and though his eyes were gravelly and his head ached with fatigue, he could not sleep.

During the days that followed he was silent and edgy. Debra sensed it, despite all his efforts to conceal it–and she was seriously alarmed, believing that he was angry with her. She was anxiously loving, distracted from all else but the need to find and cure the cause of David's ills.

Her concern only served to make David's guilt deeper.

Almost in an act of desperation they drove one evening down to the String of Pearls, leaving the Land-Rover they walked hand in hand to the water's edge. They found a fallen log screened by reeds and sat quietly together. For once neither of them had anything to say to each other.

As the big red sun sank to the tree-tops and the gloom thickened amongst the trees of the grove, the nyala herd came stepping lightly and fearfully through the shadows.

David nudged Debra, and she turned her head into a listening attitude and moved a little closer to him as he whispered.

'They are really spooky this evening, they look as though they are standing on springs and I can see their muscles trembling from here. The old bulls seem to be on the verge of a nervous breakdown, they are listening so hard their ears have stretched to twice their usual length, I swear. There must be a leopard lurking along the edge of the reed bed–' he broke off, and exclaimed softly, 'oh, so that's it!'

'What is it, David?' Debra tugged at his arm insistently, her curiosity spurring her.

'A new fawn!' David's delight was in his voice. 'One of the does has lambed. Oh God, Debra! His legs are still wobbly and he is the palest creamy beige–' He described the fawn to her as it followed the mother unsteadily into the open. Debra was listening with such intensity, that it was clear the act of birth and the state of maternity had touched some deep chord within her. Perhaps she was remembering her own dead infant. Her grip on his arm tightened, and her blind eyes seemed to glow in the gathering dusk–and suddenly she spoke. Her voice low, but achingly clear, filled with all the longing and sadness which she had suppressed.

'I wish I could see it,' she said. 'Oh God! God! Let me see. Please, let me see!' and suddenly she was weeping; great racking sobs that shook her whole body.

Across the pool the nyala herd took fright, and dashed away among the trees. David took Debra and held her fiercely to his chest, cradling her head, so her tears were wet and cold through the fabric of his shirt–and he felt the icy winds of despair blow across his soul.

He re-wrote the letter that night by the light of a gas lamp while Debra sat across the room knitting a jersey she had promised him for the winter and believing that he was busy with the estate accounts. David found that he could repeat the words of the original letter perfectly and it took him only a few minutes to complete and seal it.

'Are you working on the book tomorrow evening?' he asked casually, and when she told him she was, he went on. 'I have to nip into Nelspruit for an hour or two.'

David flew high as though to divorce himself from the earth. He could not really believe he was going to do it. He could not believe that he was capable of such sacrifice. He wondered whether it was really possible to love somebody so deeply that he would chance destroying that love for the good of the other–and he knew that it was, and as he flew on southwards he found that he could face it at last.

Of all persons, Debra needed her vision, for without it the great wings of her talent were clipped. Unless she could see it, she could not describe it. She had been granted the gift of the writer, and then half of it had been taken from her. He understood her cry, 'Oh God! God! Let me see. Please, let me see,' and he found himself wishing it for her also. Beside her need his seemed trivial and petty, and silently he prayed.

'Please God, let her see again.'

He landed the Navajo at the airstrip and called the taxi and had it drive him directly to the Post Office, and wait while he posted the letter and collected the incoming mail from the box.

'Where now?' the driver asked as he came out of the building, and he was about to tell him to drive back to the airfield when he had inspiration.

'Take me down to the bottle store, please,' he told the driver and he bought a case of Veuve Clicquot champagne.

He flew homewards with a soaring lightness of the spirit. The wheel was spinning and the ball clicking, nothing he could do now would dictate its fall. He was free of doubt, free of guilt–whatever the outcome, he knew he could meet it.

Debra sensed it almost immediately, and she laughed aloud with relief, and hugged him about the neck.

'But what *happened*?' she kept demanding. 'For weeks you were miserable. I was worrying myself sick–and then you go off for an hour or two and you come back humming like a dynamo. What on earth is going on, Morgan?'

'I have just found out how much I love you,' he told her, returning her hug.

'Plenty?' she demanded.

'Plenty!' he agreed.

'That's my baby!' she applauded him.

The Veuve Clicquot came in useful. In the batch of mail that David brought back with him from Nelspruit was a letter from Bobby Dugan. He was very high on the first chapters of the new novel that Debra had airmailed to him, and so were the publishers; he had managed to hit them for an advance of $100,000 dollars.

'You're rich!' David laughed, looking up from the letter.

'The only reason you married me,' agreed Debra. 'Fortune hunter!' but she was laughing with excitement, and David was proud and happy for her.

'They like it, David.' Debra was serious then. 'They *really* like it. I was so worried.' The money was meaningless, except as a measure of the book's value. Big money is the sincerest type of praise.

'They would have to be feeble-minded not to like it,' David told her, and then went on. 'It just so happens that I have a case of French champagne with me, shall I put a bottle or ten on the ice?'

'Morgan, man of vision,' Debra said. 'At times like this, I know why I love you.'

The weeks that followed were as good then as they had ever been. David's appreciation was sharper, edged by the storm shadows on the horizon, the time of plenty made more poignant by the possibility of the drought years coming. He tried to draw it out beyond its natural time. It was five weeks more before he flew to Nelspruit again, and then only because Debra was anxious to learn of any further news from her publishers and agent, and to pick up her typing.

'I would like to have my hair set, and although I know we don't really need them, David, my darling, we should keep in touch with people–like once a month–don't you think?'

'Has it been that long?' David asked innocently, although each day had been carefully weighed and tallied, the actuality savoured and the memory stored for the lean times ahead.

David left Debra at the beauty salon, and as he went out he could hear her pleading with the girl not to 'put it up into those tight little curls and plaster it with lacquer' and even in the anxiety of the moment, David grinned for he had always thought of the hairstyle she was describing as 'Modern Cape Dutch' or 'Randburg Renaissance'.

The postbox was crammed full and David sorted quickly through the junk mail and picked out three letters from Debra's American agent, and two enveloped with Israeli stamps. Of these one was addressed in a doctor's prescription scrawl, and David was surprised that it had found its destination. The writing on the second envelope was unmistakable, it marched in martial ranks, each letter in step with the next, and the high strokes were like the weapons of a company of pike men, spiky and abrupt.

David found a bench in the park under the purple jacaranda trees, and he opened Edelman's letter first. It was in Hebrew, which made deciphering even more difficult.

Dear David,

Your letter came as a surprise, and I have since studied the X-ray plates once more. They seem unequivocal, and upon an interpretation of them I would not hesitate to confirm my original prognosis–

Despite himself, David felt the small stirrings of relief.

–However, if I have learned anything in twenty-five years of practice, it is humility. I can only accept that your observations of light-sensitivity are correct. Having done so, then I must also accept that there is at least partial function of the optic nerves. This presupposes that the nerve was not completely divided, and it seems reasonable to believe now that it was only partially severed, and that now–possibly due to the head blows that Debra received–it has regained some function.

The crucial question is just how great that recovery is, and again I must warn you that it may be as minimal as it is at the present time, when it amounts to nothing more than light sensitivity without any increase to the amount of vision. It may, however, be greater, and it is within the realms of possibility that with treatment some portion of sight may be regained. I do not expect, however, that this will amount to more than a vague definition of light or shape, and a decision would have to be made as to whether any possible benefit might not be outweighed by the undesirability of surgery within such a vulnerable area.

I would, of course, be all too willing to examine Debra myself. However, it will probably be inconvenient for you to journey to Jerusalem, and I have therefore taken the liberty of writing to a colleague of mine in Cape Town who is one of the leading world authorities on optical trauma. He is Dr Reuben Friedman and I enclose a copy of my letter to him. You will see that I have also despatched to him Debra's original X-ray plates and a clinical history of her case.

I would recommend most strongly that you take the first opportunity of presenting Debra to Dr Friedman, and that you place in him your complete confidence. I might add that the optical unit of Groote Schuur Hospital is rightly world-renowned and fully equipped to provide any treatment necessary–they do not restrict their activities to heart transplants!

I have taken the liberty of showing your letter to General Mordecai, and of discussing the case with him–

David folded the letter carefully. 'Why the hell did he have to bring the Brig into it, talk about a war horse in a rose garden–' and he opened the Brig's letter.

Dear David,

Dr Edelman has spoken with me. I have telephoned Friedman in Cape Town, and he has agreed to see Debra.

For some years I have been postponing a lecture tour to South Africa which the S.A. Zionist Council has been urging upon me. I have today written to them and asked them to make the arrangements.

This will give us the excuse to bring Debra to Cape Town. Tell her I have insufficient time to visit you on your farm, but insist upon seeing her.

I will give you my dates later, and expect to see you then–

It was in typical style, brusque and commanding, presupposing acquiescence. It was out of David's hands now. There was no turning back, but there was still the chance that it would not work. He found himself hoping for that–and his own selfishness sickened him a little. He turned over the letter and on the reverse he drafted a dummy letter from the Brig setting out his plans for the forthcoming tour. This was for Debra, and he found faint amusement in aping the Brig's style, so that he might read it aloud to Debra convincingly.

Debra was ecstatic when he read it to her and he experienced a twinge of conscience at this deceit.

'It will be wonderful seeing him again, I wonder if Mother will be coming out with him–?'

'He didn't say, but I doubt it.' David sorted the American mail into chronological order from the post marks, and read them to her. The first two were editorial comment on *Burning Bright* and were set aside for detailed reply–but the third letter was another with hard news.

United Artists want to film *A Place of Our Own* and were talking impressively heavy figures for the twelve-month option against an outright purchase of the property and a small percentage of the profits. However, if Debra would go to California and write the screenplay, Bobby Dugan felt sure he could roll it all into a quarter-million-dollar package. He wanted her to weigh the fact that even established novelists were seldom asked to write their own screenplays–this was an offer not to be lightly spurned, and he urged Debra to accept.

'Who needs people?' Debra laughed it away quickly, too quickly–and David caught the wistful expression before she turned her head away and asked brightly, 'Have you got any of that champagne left, Morgan? I think we can celebrate–don't you?'

'The way you're going, Morgan, I'd best lay in a store of the stuff,' he replied, and went to the gas refrigerator. It foamed to the rim of the glass as he poured the wine, and before it subsided and he had carried the glass to her, he had made his decision.

'Let's take his advice seriously, and think about you going to Hollywood,' he said, and put the glass in her hand.

'What's to think about?' she asked. 'This is where we belong.'

'No, let's wait a while before replying–'

'What do you mean?' She lowered the glass without tasting the wine.

'We will wait until–let's say, until after we have seen the Brig in Cape Town.'

'Why?' She looked puzzled. 'Why should it be different then?'

'No reason. It's just that it is an important decision–the choice of time is arbitrary, however.'

'Beseder!' she agreed readily, and raised the glass to toast him. 'I love you.'

'I love you,' he said, and as he drank he was glad that she had so many roads to choose from.

The Brig's arrangements allowed them three more weeks before the rendezvous in Cape Town, and David drew upon each hour to the full, anticipating his chances of expulsion from their private Eden.

They were happy days and it seemed that nature had conspired to give them of her best. The good rains fell steadily, always beginning in the afternoon after a morning of tall clouds and heavy air filled with static and the feel of thunder. In the sunset the lightning played and flickered across the gilt cloud banks, turned by the angry sun to the colour of burnished bronze and virgins' blushes. Then in the darkness as they lay entwined, the thunder struck like a hammer blow and the lightning etched the window beyond the bed to a square of blinding white light, and the rain came teeming down with the sound of wild fire and running hooves. With David beside her, Debra was unafraid.

In the morning it was bright and cool, the trees washed sparkling clean so that the leaves glinted in the early sun and the earth was dark with water and spangled with standing pools.

The rains brought life and excitement to the wild things, and each day held its small discoveries–unexpected visitations, and strange occurrences.

The fish eagles moved their two chicks from the great shaggy nest in the mhobahoba at the head of the pools and taught them to perch out on the bare limb that supported it. They sat there day after day, seeming to gather their courage. The parent birds were frenetic in their ministrations, grooming their offspring for the great moment of flight.

Then one morning, as he and Debra ate breakfast on the stoop, David heard the swollen chorus of their chanting cries, harsh with triumph, and he took Debra's hand and they went down the steps into the open. David looked up and saw the four dark shapes spread on wide wings against the clear blue of the sky–and his spirit soared with them in their moment of achievement. They flew upwards in great sweeping circles, until they dwindled to specks and vanished, gone to their autumn grounds upon the Zambezi River, two thousand miles to the north.

There was, however, one incident during those last days that saddened and subdued them both. One morning, they walked four miles northwards beyond the line of hills to a narrow wedge-shaped plain on which stood a group of towering leadwood trees.

A pair of martial eagles had chosen the tallest leadwood as their mating ground. The female was a beautiful young bird but the male was past his prime. They had begun constructing their nest on a high fork, but the work was interrupted by the intrusion of a lone male eagle, a big young bird, fierce and proud and acquisitive. David had noticed him lurking about the borders of the territory, carefully avoiding overflying the airspace claimed by the breeding pair, choosing a perch on the hills overlooking the plain and gathering his confidence for the confrontation he was so clearly planning. The impending conflict had its particular fascination for David and his sympathy was with the older bird as he made his warlike show, screeching defiance from his perch upon the high branches of the leadwood or weaving his patrols along his borders, turning on his great wings always within the limits of that which he claimed as his own.

David had decided to walk up to the plain that day, in order to choose a site for the photographic blind he planned to erect overlooking the nest site, and also in curiosity as to the outcome of this primeval clash between the two males.

It seemed more than chance that he had chosen the day when the crisis was reached.

David and Debra came up through the gap in the hills and paused to sit on an outcrop of rock overlooking the plain, while they regained their breath. The battlefield was spread below them.

The old bird was at the nest, a dark hunched shape with white breast and head set low on the powerful shoulders. David looked for the invader, sweeping the crests of the hills with his binoculars, but there was no sign of him. He dropped the binoculars to his chest and he and Debra talked quietly for a while.

Then suddenly David's attention was attracted by the behaviour of the old eagle. He launched suddenly into flight, striking upwards on his great black pinions, and there was an urgency in the way he bored for height.

His climb brought him close over their heads, so that David could clearly see the cruel curve of the beak and the ermine black splashes that decorated the imperial snow of his breast.

He opened the yellow beak and shrieked a harsh challenge, and David turned quickly in the old fighter pilot's sweep of sky and cloud. He saw the cunning of it immediately. The younger bird had chosen his moment and his attack vector with skill beyond his years. He was towering in the sun, high and clear, a flagrant trespasser, daring the old eagle to come up at him and David felt his skin crawl in sympathy as he watched the defender climb slowly on flogging wings.

Quickly, and a little breathlessly, he described it to Debra and she reached for his hand, her sympathy with the old bird also.

'Tell me!' she commanded.

The young bird sailed calmly in waiting circles, cocking his head to watch his adversary's approach.

'There he goes!' David's voice was taut, as the attacker went wing over and began his stoop.

'I can hear him,' Debra whispered, and the sound of his wings carried clearly to them, rustling like a bush fire in dry grass as he dived on the old bird.

'Break left! Go! Go! Go!' David found he was calling to the old eagle as though he were flying wingman for him, and he gripped Debra's hand until she winced. The old eagle seemed almost to hear him, for he closed his wings and flicked out of the path of the strike, tumbling for a single turn so that the attacker hissed by him with talons reaching uselessly through air, his speed plummeting him down into the basin of the plain.

The old bird caught and broke out of his roll with wings half-cocked, and streaked down after the other. In one veteran stroke of skill he had wrested the advantage.

'Get him!' screamed David. 'Get him when he turns! Now!'

The young bird was streaking towards the tree-tops and swift death, he flared his wings to break his fall, turning desperately to avoid the lethal stoop of his enemy. In that moment he was vulnerable and the old eagle reached forward with his terrible spiked talons and without slackening the searing speed of his dive he hit the other bird in the critical moment of his turn.

The thud of the impact carried clearly to the watchers on the hill and there was a puff of feathers like the burst of explosives, black from the wings and white from the breast.

Locked together by the old bird's honed killing claws, they tumbled, wing over tangled wing, feathers streaming from their straining bodies and then drifting away like thistledown on the light breeze.

Still joined in mortal combat, they struck the top branches of one of the leadwood trees, and fell through them to come to rest at last in a high fork as an untidy bundle of ruffled feathers and trailing wings.

Leading Debra over the rough ground David hurried down the hill and through the coarse stands of arrow grass to the tree.

'Can you see them?' Debra asked anxiously, as David focused his binoculars on the struggling pair.

'They are trapped,' David told her. 'The old fellow has his claws buried to the hilt in the other's back. He will never be able to free them and they have fallen across the fork, one on either side of the tree.'

The screams of rage and agony rang from the hills about them, and the female eagle sailed anxiously above the leadwood. She added her querulous screeching to the sound of conflict.

'The young bird is dying.' David studied him through the lens, watching the carmine drops ooze from the gaping yellow beak to fall and glisten upon the snowy breast, like a dying king's rubies.

'And the old bird–' Debra listened to the clamour with face upturned, her eyes dark with concern.

'He will never get those claws loose, they lock automatically as soon as pressure is applied and he will not be able to lift himself. He will die also.'

'Can't you do something?' Debra was tugging at his arm. 'Can't you help him?'

Gently he tried to explain to her that the birds were locked together seventy feet above the earth. The bole of the leadwood was smooth and without branches for the first fifty feet of its height. It would take days of effort to reach the birds, and by then it would be too late.

'Even if one could reach them, darling, they are two wild creatures, fierce and dangerous, those beaks and talons could tear the eyes out of your head or rip you to the bone–nature does not like interference in her designs.'

'Isn't there anything we can do?' she pleaded.

'Yes,' he answered quietly. 'We can come back in the morning to see if he has been able to free himself. But we will bring a gun with us, in case he has not.'

In the dawn they came together to the leadwood tree. The young bird was dead, hanging limp and graceless, but the old bird was still alive, linked by his claws to the carcass of the other, weak and dying but with the furious yellow flames still burning in his eyes. He heard their voices and twisted the shaggy old head and opened his beak in a last defiant cry.

David loaded the shotgun, snapping the barrels closed and staring up at the old eagle. 'Not you alone, old friend,' he thought, and he lifted the gun to his shoulder and hit him with two charges of buckshot. They left him hanging in tatters with trailing wings and the quick patter of blood slowing to a dark steady drip. David felt as though he had destroyed a part of himself in that blast of gunfire, and the shadow of it was cast over the bright days that followed.

These few days sped past too swiftly for David, and when they were almost gone he and Debra spent the last of them wandering together across Jabulani, visiting each of their special places and seeking out the various herds or individual animals almost as if they were taking farewell of old friends. In the evening they came to the place amongst the fever trees beside the pools, and they sat there until the sun had fallen below the earth in a splendour of purples and muted pinks. Then the mosquitoes began whining about their heads, and they strolled back hand in hand and came to the homestead in the dark.

They packed their bags that night and left them on the stoop, ready for an early start. Then they drank champagne beside the barbecue fire. The wine lifted their mood and they laughed together in their little island of firelight in the vast ocean of the African night–but for David there were echoes from the laughter, and he was aware of a sense of finality, of an ending of something and a new beginning.

When they took off from the landing-strip in the early morning, David circled twice over the estate, climbing slowly, and the pools glinted like gunmetal amongst the hills as the low sun touched them. The land was lush with the severe unpromising shade of green, so different from that of the lands of the northern hemisphere, and the servants stood in the yard of the homestead, shading their eyes and waving up at them, their shadows lying long and narrow against the ruddy earth.

David came around and steadied on course.

'Cape Town, here we come,' he said, and Debra smiled and reached across to lay her hand upon his leg in warm and companionable silence.

They had the suite at the Mount Nelson Hotel, preferring its ancient elegance and spacious palmy gardens to the modern slabs of glass and concrete upon the foreshore and the rocks of Sea Point. They stayed in the suite for two days, awaiting the Brig's arrival, for David had grown unaccustomed to humanity in its massed and unlovely multitudes, and found the quick inquisitive glances and murmurs of pity that followed him hard to stomach.

On the second day the Brig arrived. He knocked on the door of the suite and then entered with his aggressive and determined stride. He was lean and hard and brown, as David remembered, and when he and Debra had embraced, he turned to David and his hand was dry and leathery–but it seemed that he looked at David with a new calculation in the fierce warrior eyes.

While Debra bathed and dressed for the evening, he took David to his own suite and poured whisky for him without asking his preference. He gave David the glass and began immediately to discuss the arrangements he had made.

'Friedman will be at the reception. I will introduce him to Debra and let them talk for a while, then he will be seated next to her at the dinner-table. This will give us the opportunity to persuade Debra to undergo an examination later–'

'Before we go any further, sir,' David interrupted, 'I want your assurance that at no time will it ever be suggested to her that there is a possibility of Debra regaining her sight.'

'Very well.'

'I mean, at no time whatsoever. Even if Friedman determines that surgery is necessary, it must be for some other reason than to restore sight–'

'I don't think that is possible,' the Brig snapped angrily. 'If matters go that far, then Debra must be told. It would not be fair–'

It was David's turn for anger, although the frozen mask of his features remained immobile, the lipless slit of mouth turned pale and blue eyes glared.

'Let me determine what is fair. I know her as you never can, I know what she feels and what she is thinking. If you offer her a chance of sight, you will create for her the same dilemma in which I have been trapped since the possibility first arose. I would spare her that.'

'I do not understand you,' the Brig said stiffly. The hostility between them was a tangible essence that seemed to fill the room with the feel of thunder on a summer's day.

'Then let me explain,' David held his eyes, refusing to be brow-beaten by this fierce and thrusting old warrior. 'Your daughter and I have achieved an extraordinary state of happiness.'

The Brig inclined his head, acknowledging. 'Yes, I will accept your word for that–but it is an artificial state. It's a hot-house thing, reared in isolation–it has no relation to the real world. It's a dream state.'

David felt his anger begin to shake the foundations of his reason. He found it offensive that anybody should speak of Debra and his life in those terms–but at the same time he could see the justification.

'You may say so, sir. But for Debra and me, it is very real. It is something of tremendous value.'

The Brig was silent now.

'I will tell you truly that I thought long and hard before I admitted that there was a chance for Debra, and even then I would have hidden it for my own selfish happiness–'

'You still do not make sense. How can Debra regaining her sight affect you?'

'Look at me,' said David softly, and the Brig glared at him ferociously, expecting more, but when nothing further came his expression eased and he did look at David–for the first time truly seeing the terribly ravaged head, the obscene travesty of human shape–and suddenly he thought on it from David's side, whereas before he had considered it only as a father.

His eyes dropped and he turned to replenish his whisky glass.

'If I can give her sight, I will do it. Even though it will be an expensive gift for me, she must take it.' David felt his voice trembling. 'But I believe that she loves me enough to spurn it, if she were ever given the choice. I do not want her ever to be tortured by that choice.'

The Brig lifted his glass and took a deep swallow, half the contents at a gulp.

'As you wish,' he acquiesced, and it may have been the whisky, but his voice sounded husky with an emotion David had never suspected before.

'Thank you, sir.' David set down his own glass, still untasted. 'If you'll excuse me, I think I should go and change now.' He moved to the door.

'David!' the Brig called to him and he turned back. The gold tooth gleamed in the dark bristly patch of moustache, as the Brig smiled a strangely embarrassed but gentle smile.

'You'll do,' he said.

The reception was in the banquet-room at the Heerengracht Hotel, and as David and Debra rode up together in the elevator she seemed to sense his dread, for she squeezed his arm.

'Stay close to me tonight,' she murmured. 'I'll need you,' and he knew it was said to distract him and he was grateful to her. They would be a freak show, and even though he was sure most of the guests had been prepared, yet he knew it would be an ordeal. He leaned to brush her cheek with his.

Her hair was loose and soft, very dark and glossy–and the sun had gilded her face to gold. She wore a plain green sheath that fell in simple lines to the floor, but left her arms and shoulders bare. They were amongst and smooth, with the special lustre of the skin highlighting the smooth flow of her flesh.

She wore little make-up, a light touch on the lips only, and the serene expression of her eyes enhanced the simple grace of her carriage as she moved on his arm, giving David just that courage he needed to face the crowded room.

It was an elegant gathering, women in rich silks and jewellery, the men dark-suited, with the heaviness of body and poise which advertises power and wealth–but the Brig stood out amongst them, even in a civilian suit, lean and hard where they were plump and complacent–like a falcon amongst a flock of pheasants.

He brought Reuben Friedman to them and introduced them casually. He was a short heavily built man, with a big alert head seeming out of proportion to his body. His hair was cropped short and grizzled to the round skull, but David found himself liking the bright bird eyes and the readiness of his smile. His hand was warm, but dry and firm. Debra was drawn to him also, and smiled when she picked up the timbre of his voice and the essential warmth of his personality.

As they went in to dinner, she asked David what he looked like, and laughed with delight when he replied.

'Like a koala bear,' and they were talking easily together before the fish course was served. Friedman's wife, a slim girl with horn-rimmed spectacles, neither beautiful nor plain, but with her husband's forthright friendly manner, leaned across him to join the conversation and David heard her say,

'Won't you come to lunch tomorrow? If you can stand a brood of squalling kids.'

'We don't usually–' Debra replied, but David could hear her wavering, and she turned to him.

'May we–?' and he agreed and then they were laughing like old friends, but David was silent and withdrawn, knowing it was all subterfuge and suddenly oppressed by the surging chorus of human voices and the clatter of cutlery. He found himself longing for the night silence of the bushveld, and the solitude which was not solitude with Debra to share it.

When the master of ceremonies rose to introduce the speaker, David found it an intense relief to know the ordeal was drawing to a close and he could soon hurry away with Debra to hide from the prying, knowing eyes.

The introductory speech was smooth and professional, the jokes raised a chuckle–but it lacked substance, five minutes after you would not remember what had been said.

Then the Brig rose and looked about him with a kind of Olympian scorn, the warrior's contempt for the soft men, and though these rich and powerful men seemed to quail beneath the stare, yet David sensed that they enjoyed it. They derived some strange vicarious pleasure from this man. He was a figure-head–he gave to them a deep confidence, a point on which their spirits could rally. He was one of them, and yet apart. It seemed that he was a storehouse of the race's pride and strength.

Even David was surprised by the power that flowed from the lean old warrior, the compelling presence with which he filled the huge room and dominated his audience. He seemed immortal and invincible, and David's own emotions stirred, his own pulse quickened and he found himself carried along on the flood.

'–but for all of this there is a price to pay. Part of this price is constant vigil, constant readiness. Each of us is ready at any moment to answer the call to the defence of what is ours–and each of us must be ready to make without question whatever sacrifice is demanded. This can be life itself, or something every bit as dear–'

Suddenly David realized that the Brig had singled him out, and that they were staring at each other across the room. The Brig was sending him a message of strength, of courage–but it was misinterpreted by others in the gathering.

They saw the silent exchange between the two men, and many of them knew that David's terrible disfigurement and Debra's blindness were wounds of war. They misunderstood the Brig's reference to sacrifice, and one of them began to applaud.

Immediately it was taken up, a smattering here and there amongst the tables, but quickly the sound rose–became thunder. People were staring at David and Debra as they clapped, other heads turned towards them. Chairs began to scrape as they were pushed back and men and women came to their feet, their faces smiling and their applause pounding, until it filled the hall with sound and they were all standing.

Debra was not sure what it was all about, until she felt David's desperate hand in hers and heard his voice.

'Let's get out of here–quickly. They are all staring. They are staring at us–'

She could feel his hand shaking and the strength of his distress at being the subject of their ghoulish curiosity.

'Come, let's get away.' And she rose at his urging with her heart crying out in pain for him, and followed him while the thunder of applause burst upon his defenceless head like the blows of an enemy and their eyes wantonly raked his ravaged flesh.

Even when they reached the sanctuary of their own suite, he was still shaking like a man in fever.

'The bastard,' he whispered, as he poured whisky in a glass and the neck of the bottle clattered against the crystal rim. 'The cruel bastard–why did he do that to us?'

'David.' She came to him groping for his hand. 'He didn't mean it to hurt. I know he meant it well, I think he was trying to say he was proud of you.'

David felt the urge to flee, to find relief from it all within the sanctuary of Jabulani. The temptation to say to her 'Come' and lead her there, knowing that she would do so instantly, was so strong that he had to wrestle with it, as though it were a physical adversary.

The whisky tasted rank and smoky. It offered no avenue of escape and he left the glass standing upon the counter of the private bar and turned instead to Debra.

'Yes,' she whispered into his mouth. 'Yes, my darling,' and there was a woman's pride, a woman's joy in being the vessel of his ease. As always she was able to fly with him above the storm, using the wild winds of love to drive them both aloft, until they broke through together into the brightness and peace and safety.

David woke in the night while she lay sleeping. There was a silver moon reflecting from the french windows and he could study her sleeping face, but after a while it was not sufficient for his need and he reached across gently and switched on the bedside lamp.

She stirred in her sleep, coming softly awake with small sighs and tumbling black hair brushed from her eyes with a sleep-clumsy hand, and David felt the first chill of impending loss. He knew he had not moved the bed when he lit the lamp, what had disturbed her he knew beyond doubt was the light itself–and this time not even their loving could distract him.

Reuben Friedman's dwelling proclaimed his station in the world. It was built above the sea with lawns that ran down to the beach and big dark green melkhout trees surrounding the swimming-pool, with an elaborate Cabana and barbecue area. Marion Friedman's horde of kids were especially thinned out for the occasion, probably farmed out with friends, but she retained her two youngest. These came to peer in awe at David for a few minutes, but at a sharp word from their mother they went off to the pool and became immersed in water and their own games.

The Brig had another speaking engagement, so the four adults were left alone, and after a while they relaxed. Somehow the fact that Reuben was a doctor seemed to set both David and Debra at their ease. Debra remarked on it, when the conversation turned to their injuries and Reuben asked solicitously,

'You don't mind talking about it?'

'No, not with you. Somehow it's all right to bare yourself in front of a doctor.'

'Don't do it, my dear,' Marion cautioned her. 'Not in front of Ruby anyway–look at me, six kids, already!' And they laughed.

Ruby had been out early that morning and taken half a dozen big crayfish out of the crystal water, from a kelp-filled pool in the rocks which he boasted was his private fishing-ground.

He wrapped them in fresh kelp leaves and steamed them over the coals until they turned bright scarlet and the flesh was milk white and succulent as he broke open the carapaces.

'Now, if that isn't the finest spring chicken you have ever seen–' he crowed as he held up the dismembered shellfish, '–you all bear witness that it's got two legs and feathers.'

David admitted that he had never tasted poultry like it and as he washed it down with a dry Cape Riesling he found it was no terrible hardship to reach for another. Both he and Debra were enjoying themselves, so that it came as a jolt when Reuben at last began on the real purpose of their meeting.

He was leaning across Debra to refill her wine glass, when he paused and asked her.

'How long is it since your eyes were last checked out, my dear?' and gently he placed his hand under her chin and tilted her face to look into her eyes. David's nerves snapped taut, and he moved quickly in his chair, watching intently.

'Not since I left Israel–though they took some X-rays when I was in hospital.'

'Any headaches?' Ruby asked, and she nodded. Ruby grunted and released her chin.

'I suppose they could strike me off, drumming up business, but I do think that you should have periodic checks. Two years is a long time, and you have foreign matter lodged inside your skull.'

'I hadn't even thought about it.' Debra frowned slightly and reached up to touch the scar on her temple. David felt his conscience twinge as he joined actively in the conspiracy.

'It can't do any harm, darling. Why not let Ruby give you a going over while we are here? Heaven knows when we will have another opportunity.'

'Oh, David–' Debra disparaged the idea. 'I know you are itching to head for home–and so am I.'

'Another day or two won't matter, and now that we have thought about it, it's going to worry us.'

Debra turned her head in Ruby's direction. 'How long will it take?'

'A day. I'll give you an examination in the morning, and then we'll shoot some X-ray plates in the afternoon.'

'How soon could you see her?' David asked, his voice unnatural for he knew that the appointment had been arranged five weeks previously.

'Oh, I'm sure we could fit her in right away–tomorrow–even if we have to do a little juggling. Yours is a rather special case.'

David reached across and took Debra's hand. 'Okay, darling?' he asked.

'Okay, David,' she agreed readily.

Ruby's consulting-rooms were in the Medical Centre that towered above the harbour and looked out across Table Bay to where the black south-easter was hacking the tops from the waves in bursts of white, and shrouding the far shores of the bay in banks of cloud as grey as wood smoke.

The rooms were decorated with care and taste: two original landscapes by Pierneef and some good carpets, Samarkand and a gold-washed Abedah–even Ruby's receptionist looked like a hostess from a Playboy Club, without the bunny ears and tail. It was clear that Dr Friedman enjoyed the good things of life.

The receptionist was expecting them, but still could not control the widening of her eyes and the shocked flight of colour from her cheeks as she looked at David's face.

'Dr Friedman is waiting for you, Mr and Mrs Morgan. He wants you both to go through, please.'

Ruby looked different without his prosperous paunch bulging over the waistband of a bathing costume, but his greeting was warm as he took Debra's arm.

'Shall we let David stay with us?' he asked Debra in mock conspiracy.

'Let's,' she answered.

After the usual clinical history which Ruby pursued relentlessly, he seemed satisfied and they went through into his examination-room. The chair looked to David to be identical to a dentist's, and Ruby adjusted it for Debra to lie back comfortably while he made a physical examination, directing light through the pupils deep into the body of each eye.

'Nice healthy eyes,' he gave his opinion at last, 'and very pretty also, what do you say, David?'

'Smashing,' David agreed, and Ruby sat Debra upright while he attached electrodes to her arm and swung forward a complicated-looking piece of electronic equipment.

'ECG,' David guessed, and Ruby chuckled and shook his head.

'No–it's a little invention of my own. I'm quite proud of it, but in reality it's only a variation on the old-fashioned lie-detector.'

'Question time again?' Debra asked.

'No. We are going to flash lights at you, and see just what sort of subconscious reaction you have to them.'

'We know that already,' Debra told him, and they both heard the edge in her voice now.

'Perhaps. It's just an established routine we work to.' Ruby soothed her, and then to David. 'Stand back here, please. The lights are pretty fierce, and you don't want to be looking into them.'

David moved back and Ruby adjusted the machine. A roll of graph paper began running slowly under a moving stylus which settled almost immediately into a steady rhythmic pattern. On a separate glass screen a moving green dot of light began to repeat the same rhythm, leaving a fading trail across the screen like the tail of a comet. It reminded David of the interceptor radar screen on the instrument panel of a Mirage jet. Ruby switched out the top lights, plunging the room into utter darkness, except for the pulsing green dot on the screen.

'Are we ready now, Debra? Look straight ahead, please. Eyes open.'

Soundlessly a brilliant burst of blue light filled the room, and distinctly David saw the green dot on the screen jump out of its established pattern, and for a beat or two it went haywire, then settled again into the old rhythm. Debra had seen the light flash, even though she was unaware of it; the pulse of light had registered on her brain and the machine had recorded her instinctive reaction.

The play with light went on for another twenty minutes while Ruby adjusted the intensity of the light source and varied the transmissions. At last he was satisfied, and turned the top lights up.

'Well?' Debra demanded brightly. 'Do I pass?'

'There's nothing more I want from you,' Ruby told her. 'You did just great, and everything is the way we want it.'

'Can I go now?'

'David can take you to lunch, but this afternoon I want you at the radiologist's. My receptionist arranged it for 2.30, I believe, but you had best check with her.' Neatly Ruby countered any attempt of David's to get him alone.

'I shall let you know as soon as I have the X-ray results. Here, I'll write down the radiologist's address.' Ruby scribbled on his prescription pad and handed it to David.

'See me *alone* tomorrow 10 a.m.'

David nodded and took Debra's arm. He stared at Ruby a moment trying to draw some reaction from him, but he merely shrugged his shoulders and rolled his eyes in a music-hall comedian's gesture of uncertainty.

The Brig joined them for lunch in their suite at the Mount Nelson, for David still could not endure the discomfort of the public rooms. The Brig drew upon some hidden spring of charm, as though sensing that his help was needed, and he had both of them laughing naturally with stories of Debra's childhood and the family's early days after leaving America. David was grateful to him, for the time passed so quickly that he had to hurry Debra to her appointment.

'I am going to use two different techniques on you, my dear–' David wondered what it was about her that made all males over forty refer to Debra as though she were twelve years old. 'First of all we will do five of what we call police mug shots, front, back, sides and top–' The radiologist was a red-faced, grey-haired man with big hands and heavy shoulders like a professional wrestler. 'We aren't even going to make you take your clothes off–' he chuckled, but David thought he detected a faint note of regret. 'Then after that, we are going to be terribly clever and take a continuous moving shot of the inside of your head. It's called tomography. We are going to clamp your head to keep it still and the camera is going to describe a circle around you, focused on the spot where all the trouble is. We are going to find out everything that's going on in that pretty head of yours–'

'I hope it doesn't shock you too much, doctor,' Debra told him, and he looked stunned for a moment, then let out a delighted guffaw, and later David heard him repeating it to the sister with gusto.

It was a long tedious business, and afterwards when they drove back to the hotel, Debra leaned close to him and said, 'Let's go home, David. Soon as we can?'

'Soon as we can,' he agreed.

David did not want it that way, but the Brig insisted on accompanying David on his visit to Ruby Friedman the following morning. For one of the very few times in his life David had lied to Debra, telling her he was meeting with the Morgan Trust accountants, and he had left her in a lime-green bikini lying beside the hotel swimming pool, brown and slim and lovely in the sunlight.

Ruby Friedman was brusque and businesslike. He seated them opposite his desk and came swiftly to the core of the business.

'Gentlemen,' he said. 'We have a problem, a hell of a problem. I am going to show you the X-ray plates first to illustrate what I have to tell you–' Ruby swivelled his chair to the scanner and switched on the book-light to bring the prints into high relief. 'On this side are the plates that Edelman sent me from Jerusalem. You can see the grenade fragment.' It was stark and hard edged, a small triangular shard of steel lying in the cloudy bone structure. 'And here you can see the track though the optic chiasma, the disruption and shattering of the bone is quite evident. Edelman's original diagnosis–based on these plates, and on the complete inability to define light or shape–seems to be confirmed. The optic nerve is severed, and that's the end of it.' Quickly he unclipped the plates, and fitted others to the scanner. 'All right. Now here are the second set of plates, taken yesterday. Immediately notice how the grenade fragment has been consolidated and encysted.' The stark outline was softened by the new growth of bone around it. 'That is good, and expected. But here in the channel of the chiasma we find the growth of some sort that leaves itself open to a number of interpretations. It could be scarring, the growth of bone chips, or some other type of growth either benign or malignant.' Ruby arranged another set of plates upon the scanner. 'Finally, this is the plate exposed by the technique of tomography, to establish the contours of this excrescence. It seems to conform to the shape of the bony channel of the chiasma, except here–' Ruby touched a small half-round notch which was cut into the upper edge of the growth, '–this little spot runs through the main axis of the skull, but is bent upwards in the shape of an inverted U. It is just possible that this may be the most significant discovery of our whole examination.' Ruby switched off the light of the scanner.

'I don't understand any of this,' the Brig's voice was sharp. He did not like being bludgeoned by another man's special knowledge.

'No, of course.' Ruby was smooth. 'I am merely setting the background for the explanations that will follow.' He turned back to the desk, and his manner changed. He was no longer lecturing, but leading with authority.

'Now as to my own conclusions. There can be absolutely no doubt that certain function of the optic nerve remains. It is still conveying impulses to the brain. At least a part of it is still intact. The question arises as to just how much that is, and to what extent that function can be improved. It is possible that the grenade fragment cut through part of the nerve–severing five strands of a six-strand rope, or four or three. We do not know the extent, but what we do know is that damage of that nature is irreversible. What Debra may be left with is what she has now–almost nothing.'

Ruby paused and was silent. The two men opposite him watched his face intently, leaning forward in their seats.

'That is the dark side–if it is true, then Debra is for all practical purposes blind and will remain that way. However, there is another side to the question. It is possible that the optic nerve has suffered little damage, or none at all, please God–'

'Then why is she blind?' David asked angrily. He felt baited, driven by words, goaded like the bull from so long ago. 'You can't have it both ways.'

Ruby looked at him, and for the first time saw beyond that blank mask of scarred flesh and realized the pain he was inflicting, saw the hurt in the dark eyes, blue as rifle steel.

'Forgive me, David. I have been carried away by the intriguing facts of this case, seeing it from my own academic point of view rather than yours, I'm afraid. I will come to it now without further hedging.' He leaned back in his chair and went on speaking. 'You recall the notch in the outline of the chiasma. Well, I believe that is the nerve itself, twisted out of position, kinked and pinched like a garden hose by bone fragments and the pressure of the metal fragment so that it is no longer capable of carrying impulses to the brain.'

'The blows on her temple–?' David asked.

'Yes. Those blows may have been just sufficient to alter the position of the bone fragments, or of the nerve itself, so as to enable the passage of a minimal amount of impulse to the brain–like the garden hose, movement could allow a little water to pass through but still hold back any significant flow, but once the twist is straightened the full volume of flow would be regained.'

They were all silent then, each of them considering the enormity of what they had heard.

'The eyes,' the Brig said at last. 'They are healthy?'

'Perfectly,' Ruby nodded.

'How could you find out–I mean, what steps would you take next?' David asked quietly.

'There is only one way. We would have to go to the site of the trauma.'

'Operate?' David asked again.

'Yes.'

'Open Debra's skull?' The horror of it showed only in his eyes.

'Yes,' Ruby nodded.

'Her head–' David's own flesh quailed in memory of the ruthless knife. He saw the lovely face mutilated and the pain in those blind eyes. 'Her face–' His voice shook now. 'No, I won't let you cut her. I won't let you ruin her, like they have me–'

'David!' The Brig's voice cracked like breaking ice, and David sank back in his chair.

'I understand how you feel,' Ruby spoke gently, his voice in contrast to the Brig's. 'But we will go in from behind the hairline, there will be no disfigurement. The scar will be covered by her hair when it grows out, and the incision will not be very large anyway–'

'I won't have her suffer more.' David was trying to control his voice, but the catch and break were still in it. 'She has suffered enough, can't you see that–'

'We are talking about giving her back her sight,' the Brig broke in again. His voice was hard and cold. 'A little pain is a small price to pay for that.'

'There will be very little pain, David. Less than an appendectomy.' Again they were silent, the two older men watching the younger in the agony of his decision.

'What are the chances?' David looked for help, wanting the decision made for him, wanting it taken out of his hands.

'That is impossible to say.' Ruby shook his head.

'Oh God, how can I judge if I don't know the odds?' David cried out.

'All right. Let me put it this way–there is a possibility, not probability, that she may regain a useful part of her sight.' Ruby chose his words with care. 'And there is a remote possibility that she may regain full vision or almost full vision.'

'That is the best that can happen.' David agreed. 'But what is the worst?'

'The worst that can happen is there will be no change. She will have undergone a deal of discomfort and pain to no avail.'

David jumped out of his chair and crossed to the windows. He stared out at the great sweep of bay where the tankers lay moored and the far hills of the Tygerberg rose smoky blue to the brilliant sky.

'You know what the choice must be, David.' The Brig was ruthless, allowing him no quarter, driving him on to meet his fate.

'All right,' David surrendered at last, and turned back to face them. 'But on one condition. One on which I insist. Debra must not be told that there is a chance of her regaining her sight–'

Ruby Friedman shook his head. 'She must be told.'

The Brig's moustache bristled fiercely. 'Why not? Why don't you want her to know?'

'You know why.' David answered without looking at him.

'How will you get her there–if you don't explain it to her?' Ruby asked.

'She has been having headaches–we'll tell her there is a growth–that you've discovered a growth–that it has to be removed. That's true, isn't it?'

'No.' Ruby shook his head. 'I couldn't tell her that. I can't deceive her.'

'Then I will tell her,' said David, his voice firm and steady now. 'And I will tell her when we discover the result after the operation. Good or bad. I will be the one who tells her–is that understood? Do we agree on that?'

And after a moment the two others nodded and murmured their agreement to the terms David had set.

David had the hotel chef prepare a picnic basket, and the service bar provided a cool bag with two bottles of champagne.

David craved for the feeling of height and space, but he needed also to be able to concentrate all his attention on Debra, so he reluctantly rejected the impulse to fly with her–and instead they took the cableway up the precipitous cliffs of Table Mountain, and from the top station they found a path along the plateau and followed it, hand in hand, to a lonely place upon the cliff's edge where they could sit together high above the city and the measureless spread of ocean.

The sounds of the city came up two thousand feet to them, tiny and disjointed, on freak gusts of the wind or bouncing from the soaring canyons of grey rock–the horn of an automobile, the clang of a locomotive shunting in the train yards, the cry of a muezzin calling the faithful of Islam to pray, and the distant shrilling of children released from the classroom–yet all these faint echoes of humanity seemed to enhance their aloneness and the breeze out of the south east was sweet and clean after the filthy city air.

They drank the wine together, sitting close while David gathered his resolve. He was about to speak when Debra forestalled him.

'It's good to be alive and in love, my darling,' she said. 'We are very lucky, you and I. Do you know that, David?'

He made a sound in his throat that could have been agreement, and his courage failed him.

'If you could, would you change anything?' he asked at last, and she laughed.

'Oh, sure. One is never absolutely content until and unless one is dead. I'd change many small things–but not the one big thing. You and I.'

'What would you change?'

'I would like to write better than I do, for one thing.'

They were silent again, sipping the wine.

'Sun is going down fast now,' he told her.

'Tell me,' she demanded, and he tried to find words for the colours, that flickered over the cloud banks and the way the ocean shimmered and dazzled with the last rays of gold and blood–and he knew he could never tell it to her. He stopped in the middle of a sentence.

'I saw Ruby Friedman today,' he said abruptly, unable to find a gentle approach, and she went still beside him in that special way of hers, frozen like a timid wild thing at the scent of some fearful predator.

'It's bad!' she said at last.

'Why do you say that?' he demanded quickly.

'Because you brought me here to tell me–and because you are afraid.'

'No,' David denied it.

'Yes. I can feel it now, very clearly. You are afraid for me.'

'It's not true,' David tried to reassure her. 'I'm a little worried, that's all.'

'Tell me,' she said.

'There is a small growth. It's not dangerous–yet. But they feel something should be done about it–' He stumbled through the explanation he had so carefully prepared, and when he ended she was silent for a moment.

'It is necessary, absolutely necessary?' she asked.

'Yes,' he told her, and she nodded, trusting him completely–then she smiled and squeezed his arm.

'Don't fret yourself, David, my darling. It will be all right. You'll see, they can't touch us. We live in a private place where they can't touch us.' Now it was she who was striving to comfort him.

'Of course it will be all right.' He hugged her to him roughly, slopping a little wine over the rim of his glass.

'When?' she asked.

'Tomorrow you will go in, and they'll do it the following morning.'

'So soon?'

'I thought it best to have it over with.'

'Yes. You are right.'

She sipped her wine, withdrawn, fearful, despite her brave show.

'They are going to cut my head open?'

'Yes,' he said, and she shuddered against him.

'There is no risk,' he said.

'No. I'm sure there isn't,' she agreed quickly.

He woke in the night with the instant knowledge that he was alone, that she was not curled warm and sleeping beside him.

Quickly he slipped from the bed and crossed to the bathroom. It was empty and he padded to the sitting-room of the suite and switched on the lights.

She heard the click of the switch and turned her head away, but not before he had seen the tears glowing on her cheeks like soft grey pearls. He went to her quickly.

'Darling,' he said.

'I couldn't sleep,' she said.

'That's all right.' He knelt before the couch on which she sat, but he did not touch her.

'I had a dream,' she said. 'There was a pool of clear water and you were swimming in it, looking up at me and calling to me. I saw your dear face clearly, beautiful and laughing–' David realized with a jolt in his guts that she had seen him in her dream as he had been, she had seen the beautiful dream-David, not the monstrous ravaged thing he was now. 'Then suddenly you began to sink, down, down, through the water, your face fading and receding–' Her voice caught and broke, and she was silent for a moment. 'It was a terrible dream, I cried out and tried to follow you, but I could not move and then you were gone down into the depths. The water turned dark and I woke with only the blackness in my head. Nothing but swirling mists of blackness.'

'It was only a dream,' he said.

'David,' she whispered. 'Tomorrow, if anything happens tomorrow–'

'Nothing will happen,' he almost snarled the denial, but she put out a hand to his face, finding his lips and touching them lightly to silence them.

'Whatever happens,' she said, 'remember how it was when we were happy. Remember that I loved you.'

The hospital of Groote Schuur sits on the lower slopes of Devil's Peak, a tall conical peak divided from the massif of Table Mountain by a deep saddle. Its summit is of grey rock and below it lie the dark pine forests and open grassy slopes of the great estate that Cecil John Rhodes left to the nation. Herds of deer and indigenous antelope feed quietly in the open places and the south-east wind feathers the crest with a flying pennant of cloud.

The hospital is a massive complex of brilliant white buildings, substantial and solid-looking blocks, all roofed in burnt red tiles.

Ruby Friedman had used all his pull to secure a private ward for Debra, and the sister in charge of the floor was expecting her. They took her from David and led her away, leaving him feeling bereft and lonely, but when he returned to visit her that evening she was sitting up in the bed in the soft cashmere bedjacket that David had given her and surrounded by banks of flowers which he had ordered.

'They smell wonderful,' she thanked him. 'It's like being in a garden.'

She wore a turban around her head and, with the serene golden eyes seeming focused on a distant vision, it gave her an exotic and mysterious air.

'They have shaved your head.' David felt a slide of dismay, he had not expected that she must also sacrifice that lustrous mane of black silk. It was the ultimate indignity, and she seemed to feel it also, for she did not answer him and instead told him brightly how well they were treating her, and what pains they were taking for her comfort.'You'd think I was some sort of queen,' she laughed.

The Brig was with David, gruff and reserved and patently out of place in these surroundings. His presence cast restraint upon them and it was a relief when Ruby Friedman arrived. Bustling and charming, he complimented Debra on the preparations she had undergone.

'Sister says that you are just fine, all nicely shaved and ready. Sorry, but you aren't allowed anything to eat or drink except the sleeping pill I've prescribed.'

'When do I go to theatre?'

'We've got you down bright and early. Eight o'clock tomorrow. I am tremendously pleased that Billy Cooper is the surgeon, we were very lucky to get him, but he owes me a favour or two. I will be assisting him, of course, and he'll have one of the best surgical teams in the world backing him up.'

'Ruby, you know how some women have their husbands with them when they are confined–'

'Yes.' Ruby looked uncertain, taken aback by the question.

'Well, couldn't David be there with me tomorrow? Couldn't we be together, for both our sakes, while it happens?'

'With all due respects, my dear, but you are not having a baby.'

'Couldn't you arrange for him to be there?' Debra pleaded, with eloquent eyes and an expression to break the hardest heart.

'I'm sorry,' Ruby shook his head. 'It's completely impossible–' then he brightened. 'But I tell you what. I could get him into the students' room. It will be the next best thing, in fact he would have a better view of the proceedings than if he were in theatre. We have closed-circuit television relayed to the students' room and David could watch from there.'

'Oh, please!' Debra accepted immediately. 'I'd like to know he was close, and that we were in contact. We don't like being parted from each other, do we, my darling?' She smiled at where she thought he was, but he had moved aside and the smile missed him. It was a gesture that wrenched something within him.

'You will be there, David, won't you?' she asked, and though the idea of watching the knife at work was repellent to him, he forced himself to reply lightly.

'I'll be there,' and he almost added, 'always', but he cut off the word.

This early in the morning there were only two others in the small lecture-room with its double semi-circular rows of padded chairs about the small television screen, a plump woman student with a pretty face and shaggy-dog hairstyle and a tall young man with a pale complexion and bad teeth. They both wore their stethoscopes dangling with calculated nonchalance from the pockets of their white linen jackets. After the first startled glance they ignored David, and they spoke together in knowing medical jargon.

'The Coop's doing an exploratory through the parietal.'

'That's the one I want to watch–'

The girl affected blue Gauloises cigarettes, rank and stinking in the confined room. David's eyes felt raw and gravelly for he slept little during the night, and the smoke irritated them. He kept looking at his watch, and imagining what was happening to Debra during these last minutes–the undignified purging and cleansing of her body, the robing, and the needles of sedation and antisepsis.

The slow drag of minutes ended at last when the screen began to glow and hum, the image shimmered and strobed then settled down into a high view of the theatre. The set was in colour, and the green theatre gowns of the figures moving around the operating-table blended with the subdued theatre green walls. Height had foreshortened the robed members of the operating team and the muttered and disjointed conversation between the surgeon and his anaesthetist was picked up by the microphones.

'Are we ready there yet, Mike?'

David felt the sick sensation in the pit of his stomach, and he wished he had eaten breakfast. It might have filled the hollow place below his ribs.

'Right,' the surgeon's voice sharpened as he turned towards the microphone. 'Are we on telly?'

'Yes, doctor,' the theatre sister answered him, and there was a note of resignation in the surgeon's voice as he spoke for the unseen audience.

'Very well, then. The patient is a twenty-six-year-old female. The symptoms are total loss of sight in both eyes, and the cause is suspected damage or constriction of the optic nerve in or near the optic chiasma. This is a surgical investigation of the site. The surgeon is Dr William Cooper, assisted by Dr Reuben Friedman.'

As he spoke, the camera moved in on the table and with a start of surprise David realized that he had been looking at Debra without knowing it. Her face and the lower part of her head were obscured by the sterile drapes that covered all but the shaven round ball of her skull. It was inhuman-looking, egglike, painted with Savlon antiseptic that glistened in the bright, overhead lights.

'Scalpel please, sister.'

David leaned forward tensely in his seat, and his hands tightened on the armrests, so the knuckles turned white, as Cooper made the first incision drawing the blade across the smooth skin. The flesh opened and immediately the tiny blood vessels began to dribble and spurt. Hands moved in the screen on the television, clad in rubber so that they were yellow and impersonal, but quick and sure.

An oval flap of skin and flesh was dissected free and was drawn back, exposing the gleaming bone beneath, and again David's flesh crawled as though with living things, as the surgeon took up a drill that resembled exactly a carpenter's brace and bit. His voice continued its impersonal commentary, as he began to drill through the skull, cranking away at the handle as the gleaming steel bit swiftly through the bone. He pierced the skull with four round drill holes, each set at the corners of a square.

'Peri-osteal elevator, please, sister.'

Again David's stomach clenched as the surgeon slid the gleaming steel introducer into one of the drill holes and manœuvred it gently until its tip reappeared through the next hole in line. Using the introducer, a length of sharp steel wire saw was threaded through the two holes and lay along the inside of the skull. Cooper sawed this back and forth and it cut cleanly through the bone. Four times he repeated the procedure, cutting out the sides of the square, and when he at last lifted out the detached piece of bone he had opened a trapdoor into Debra's skull.

As he worked David's gorge had risen until it pressed in his throat, and he had felt the cold glistening sheen of nauseous sweat across his forehead, but now as the camera's eye peered through the opening he felt his wonder surmount his horror, for he could see the pale amorphous mass of matter, enclosed in its tough covering membrane of the dura mater that was Debra's brain. Deftly Cooper incised a flap in the dura.

'We have exposed now the frontal lobe, and it will be necessary to displace this to explore the base of the skull.'

Working swiftly, but with obvious care and skill, Cooper used a stainless steel retractor, shaped like a shoe horn, to slide under the mass of brain and to lift it aside. Debra's brain–staring at it, David seemed to be looking into the core of her being, it was vulnerable and exposed, everything that made her what she was. What part of that soft pale mass contained her writer's genius, he wondered, from which of its many soft folds and coils sprang the fruitful fountain of her imagination, where was her love for him buried, what soft and secret place triggered her laughter and where was the vale of her tears? Its fathomless mystery held him intent as he watched the retractor probe deeper and deeper through the opening, and slowly the camera moved in to peer into the gaping depths of Debra's skull.

Cooper opened the far end of the dura mater and commented on his progress.

'We have here the anterior ridge of the sphenoid sinus, note this as our point for access to the chiasma–'

David was aware of the changed tone of the surgeon's voice, the charging of tension as the disembodied hands moved slowly and expertly towards their goal.

'Now this is interesting, can we see this on the screen, please? Yes! There is very clearly a bone deformation here–'

The voice was pleased, and the two students beside David exclaimed and leaned closer. David could see soft wet tissue and hard bright surfaces deep in the bottom of the wound, and the necks of steel instruments crowding into it, like metallic bees into the stamen of a pink and yellow bloom. Cooper scratched through to the metal of the grenade fragment.

'Now here we have the foreign body, can we have a look at those X-ray plates again, sister–'

The image cut quickly to the X-ray scanner, and again the students exclaimed. The girl puffed busily on her stinking Gauloise.

'Thank you.'

The image cut back to the operating field, and now David saw the dark speck of the grenade fragment lodged in the white bone.

'We will go for this, I think. Do you agree, Dr Friedman?'

'Yes, I think you should take it.'

Delicately the long slender steel insects worried the dark fragment, and at last with a grunt of satisfaction it came free of its niche, and Cooper drew it out carefully. David heard the metallic ping as it was dropped into a waiting dish.

'Good! Good!' Cooper gave himself a little encouragement as he plugged the hole left by the fragment with beeswax to prevent haemorrhage. 'Now we will trace out the optic nerves.'

They were two white worms, David saw them clearly, converging on their separate trails to meet and blend at the opening of the bony canal into which they disappeared.

'We have got extraneous bone-growth here, clearly associated with the foreign body we have just removed. It seems to have blocked off the canal and to have squeezed or severed the nerve. Suggestions, Dr Friedman?'

'I think we should excise that growth and try and ascertain just what damage we have to the nerve in that area.'

'Good. Yes, I agree. Sister, I will use a fine bone-nibbler to get in there.'

The swift selection and handling of the bright steel instruments again, and then Cooper was working on the white bone growth which grew in the shape of coral from a tropical sea. He nibbled at it with the keen steel, and carefully removed each piece from the field as it came away.

'What we have here is a bone splinter that was driven by the steel fragment into the canal. It is a large piece, and it must have been under considerable pressure, and it has consolidated itself here–'

He worked on carefully, and gradually the white worm of the nerve appeared from beneath the growth.

'Now, this is interesting.' Cooper's tone altered. 'Yes, look at this. Can we get a better view here, please?' The camera zoomed in a little closer, and the focus realigned. 'The nerve has been forced upwards, and flattened by pressure. The constriction is quite obvious, it has been pinched off–but it seems to be intact.'

Cooper lifted another large piece of bone aside, and now the nerve lay exposed over its full length.

'This is really remarkable. I expect that it is a one in a thousand chance, or one in a million. There appears to be no damage to the actual nerve, and yet the steel fragment passed so close to it that it must have touched it.'

Delicately, Cooper lifted the nerve with the blunt tip of a probe.

'Completely intact, but flattened with pressure. Yet I don't suspect any degree of atrophy, Dr Friedman?'

'I think we can confidently expect good recovery of function.' Despite the masked features, the triumphant attitude of the two men was easily recognized, and watching them, David felt his own emotions at war. With a weight upon his spirits he watched Cooper close up, replacing the portion of Debra's skull that he had removed, and once the flap of scalp was stitched back into place there was little external evidence of the extent and depth of their penetration. The image on the screen changed to another theatre where a small girl was to receive surgery for a massive hernia, and the fickle interest of the watching students changed with it.

David stood up and left the room. He rode up in the elevator and waited in the visitors' room on Debra's floor until the elevator doors opened again and two white uniformed male nurses trundled Debra's stretcher down the corridor to her room. She was deadly pale, with dark bruised-looking eyes and lips, her head swathed in a turban of white bandages. There was a dull brown smear of blood on the sheets that covered her and a whiff of anaesthetic hung in the corridor after she was gone.

Ruby Friedman came then, changed from theatre garb into an expensive light-weight grey mohair suit and a twenty-guinea Dior silk tie. He looked tanned and healthy, and mightily delighted with his achievement.

'You watched?' he demanded, and when David nodded he went on exuberantly, 'It was extraordinary.' He chuckled, and rubbed his hands together with glee.

'My God, something like this makes you feel good. Makes you feel that if you never do another thing in your life, it was still worthwhile.' He was unable to restrain himself any longer and he threw a playful punch at David's shoulder. 'Extraordinary,' he repeated, drawing it out into two words with relish, rolling the word around his tongue.

'When will you know?' David asked quietly.

'I know already, I'll stake my reputation on it!'

'She will be able to see as soon as she comes around from the anaesthetic?' David asked.

'Good Lord, no!' Ruby chuckled. 'That nerve has been pinched off for years, it's going to take time to recover.'

'How long?'

'It's like a leg that has gone to sleep when you sit wrongly. When the blood flows back in, it's still numb and tingling until the circulation is restored.'

'How long?' David repeated.

'Immediately she wakes, that nerve is going to start going crazy, sending all sorts of wild messages to the brain. She's going to see colours and shapes as though she is on a drug binge, and it's going to take time to settle down–two weeks to a month, I would guess–then it will clear, the nerve will have recovered its full and normal function and she will begin having real effective vision.'

'Two weeks,' David said, and he felt the relief of a condemned man hearing of his reprieve.

'You will tell her the good news, of course.' Ruby gave another buoyant chuckle, shaped up to punch David again and then controlled himself. 'What a wonderful gift you have been able to give her.'

'No,' David answered him. 'I won't tell her yet, I will find the right time later.'

'You will have to explain the initial vision she will experience, the colour and shape hallucinations, they will alarm her.'

'We will just tell her that it's the normal after-effect of the operation. Let her adjust to that before telling her.'

'David, I–' Ruby began seriously, but he was cut off by the savage blaze of blue in the eyes that watched him from the mask of scarred flesh.

'I will tell her!' The voice shook with such fury, that Ruby took a step backwards. 'That was the condition, I will tell her when I judge the time is ripe.'

Out of the darkness a tiny amber light glowed, pale and far off, but she watched it split like a breeding amœba and become two, and each of those split and split again until they filled the universe in a great shimmering field of stars. The light throbbed and pulsed, vibrant and triumphant, and it changed from amber to brightest purest white like the sparkle from a paragon diamond, then it turned to the blue of sunlight on a tropical ocean, to soft forest greens and desert golds–an endless cavalcade of colours, changing, blending, fading, flaring in splendour that held her captive.

Then the colours took shape, they spun like mighty Catherine wheels, and soared and exploded, showered down in rivers of flame that burst again into fresh cascades of light.

She was appalled by the dimensions of shape and colour that engulfed her, bewildered by the beauty of it and at last she could bear it no longer in silence and she cried out.

Instantly there was a hand in hers, a strong hard familiar hand, and his voice, dearly beloved, reassuring and firm.

'David,' she cried with relief.

'Quietly, my darling. You must rest.'

'David. David.' She heard the sob in her own voice as new torrents of colour poured over her, insupportable in their richness and variety, overwhelming in their depth and range.

'I'm here, my darling. I'm here.'

'What's happening to me, David? What's happening?'

'You are all right. The operation was a success. You are just fine.'

'Colours,' she cried. 'Filling my whole head. I've never known it like this.'

'It's the result of the operation. It shows that it was a success. They removed the growth.'

'I'm frightened, David.'

'No, my darling. There is nothing to be afraid of.'

'Hold me, David. Hold me safe.' And in the circle of his arms the fear abated, and slowly she learned to ride the oceanic waves and washes of colour, came gradually to accept and then at last to look upon them with wonder and with intense pleasure.

'It's beautiful, David. I'm not frightened any more, not with you holding me. It's wonderful.'

'Tell me what you see,' he said.

'I couldn't. It's impossible. I couldn't find the words.'

'Try!' he said.

David was alone in the suite, and it was after midnight when the call that he had placed to New York came through.

'This is Robert Dugan, to whom am I speaking?' Bobby's voice was crisp and businesslike.

'It's David Morgan.'

'Who?'

'Debra Mordecai's husband.'

'Well, hello there, David.' The agent's voice changed, becoming expansive. 'It's sure nice to talk to you. How is Debra?' It was obvious that Dugan's interest in David began and ended with his wife.

'That's why I am calling. She's had an operation and she's in hospital at the moment.'

'God! Not serious, is it?'

'She's going to be fine. She'll be up in a few days and ready for work in a couple of weeks.'

'Glad to hear it, David. That's great.'

'Look here, I want you to go ahead and set up that script-writing contract for *A Place of Our Own*.'

'She's going to do it?' Dugan's pleasure carried six thousand miles with no diminution.

'She'll do it now.'

'That's wonderful news, David.'

'Write her a good contract.'

'Depend on it, boyo. That little girl of yours is hot property. Playing hard to get hasn't done her any harm, I tell you!'

'How long will the script job last?'

'They'll want her for six months,' Dugan guessed. 'The producer who will do it is making a movie in Rome right now. He'll probably want Debra to work with him there.'

'Good,' said David. 'She'll like Rome.'

'You coming with her, David?'

'No,' David answered carefully. 'No, she'll be coming on her own.'

'Will she be able to get by on her own?' Dugan sounded worried.

'From now on she'll be able to do everything on her own.'

'Hope you are right,' Dugan was dubious.

'I'm right.' David told him abruptly. 'One other thing. That lecture tour, is it still on?'

'They are beating the door down. Like I said, she's hotter than a pistol.'

'Set it up for after the script job.'

'Hey, David boy. This is the business. Now we are really cooking with gas. We are going to make your little girl into one very big piece of property.'

'Do that,' said David. 'Make her big. Keep her busy, you hear. Don't give her time to think.'

'I'll keep her busy.' Then as though he had detected something in David's voice. 'Is something bugging you, David? You got some little domestic problem going there, boy? You want to talk about it?'

'No, I don't want to talk about it. You just look after her. Look after her well.'

'I'll look after her,' Dugan's tone had sobered. 'And David–'

'What is it?'

'I'm sorry. Whatever it is, I'm sorry.'

'That's okay.' David had to end the conversation then, immediately. His hand was shaking so that he knocked the telephone from the table and the plastic cracked through. He left it lying and went out into the night. He walked alone through the sleeping city, until just before the morning he was weary enough to sleep.

The streams of colour settled to steady runs and calmly moving patterns, no longer the explosive bursts of brightness that had so alarmed her. After the grey shifting banks of blindness that had filled her head like dirty cotton wool for those long years, the new brightness and beauty served to buoy her spirits, and after the main discomfort of her head surgery had passed in the first few days, she was filled with a wondrous sense of well-being, a formless optimistic expectation, such as she had not experienced since she was a child anticipating the approach of a long-awaited holiday.

It was as though in some deep recess of her subconscious she was vaguely aware of the imminent return of her sight. However, the knowledge seemed not to have reached her conscious mind. She knew there was change, she welcomed her release from the dark and sombre dungeons of nothingness into the new brightness, but she did not realize that there was more to come, that after colour and fantasy would follow shape and reality.

Each day David waited for her to say something that might show that she had realized that her sight was on the way back; he hoped for and at the same time dreaded this awareness–but it did not come.

He spent as much of each day with her as hospital routine would allow, and he hoarded each minute of it, doling out time like a miser paying coins for a diminishing hoard. Yet Debra's ebullient mood was infectious, and he could not help but laugh with her and share the warm excitement as she anticipated her release from the hospital and their return together to the sanctuary of Jabulani.

There were no doubts in her mind, no shadows across her happiness, and gradually David began to believe that it would last. That their happiness was immortal and that their love could survive any pressure placed upon it. It was so strong and fine when they were together now, carried along by Debra's bubbling enthusiasm, that surely she could regain her sight and weather the first shock of seeing him.

Yet he was not sure enough to tell her yet, there was plenty of time. Two weeks, Ruby Friedman had told him, two weeks before she would be able to see him and it was vitally important to David that he should extract every grain of happiness that was left to him in that time.

In the lonely nights he lay with the frantic scurryings of his brain keeping him from sleep. He remembered that the plastic surgeon had told him there was more they could do to make him less hideous. He could go back and submit to the knife once more, although his body cringed at the thought. Perhaps they could give Debra something less horrifying to look at.

The following day he braved the massed stares of hundreds of shoppers to visit Stuttafords Departmental Store in Adderley Street. The girl in the wig department, once she had recovered her poise, took him into a curtained-off cubicle and entered into the spirit of finding a wig to cover the domed cicatrice of his scalp.

David regarded the fine curly head of hair over the frozen ruins of his face, and for the first time ever he found himself laughing at it, although the effect of laughter was even more horrifying as the tight lipless mouth writhed like an animal in a trap.

'God!' he laughed. 'Frankenstein in drag!' and for the sales girl who had been fighting to control her emotions this was too much. She broke into hysterical giggles of embarrassment.

He wanted to tell Debra about it, making a joke of it and at the same time prepare her for her first sight of his face, but somehow he could not find the words. Another day passed with nothing accomplished, except a few last hours of warmth and happiness shared.

The following day Debra began to show the first signs of restlessness. 'When are they going to let me out, darling? I feel absolutely wonderful. It's ridiculous to lie in bed here. I want to get back to Jabulani–there is so much to do.' Then she giggled. 'And they've had me locked up here ten days now. I'm not used to convent life, and to be completely honest with you, my big lusty lover, I am climbing the wall–'

'We could lock the door,' David suggested.

'God, I married a genius,' Debra cried out delightedly, and then later. 'That's the first time it ever happened for me in Technicolor. I think I could get hooked on that.'

That evening Ruby Friedman and the Brig were waiting for him when he returned to his suite, and they came swiftly to the reason for their visit.

'You have already left it too long. Debra should have been told days ago,' the Brig told him sternly.

'He is right, David. You are being unfair to her. She must have time to come to terms, latitude for adjustment.'

'I'll tell her when I get the opportunity,' David muttered doggedly.

'When will that be?' the Brig demanded, the gold tooth glowing angrily in its furry nest.

'Soon.'

'David,' Ruby was placatory, 'it could happen at any time now. She has made strong and vigorous progress, it could happen much sooner than I expected.'

'I'll do it,' said David. 'Can't you stop pushing me? I said I'll do it–and I will. Just get off my back, won't you.'

'Right.' The Brig was brisk now. 'You've got until noon tomorrow. If you haven't told her by then, I'm going to do it.'

'You're a hard old bastard, aren't you,' David said bitterly, and anger paled the Brig's lips and they could see the effort he made to force it down.

'I understand your reluctance,' he spoke carefully. 'I sympathize. However, my first and only concern is for Debra. You are indulging yourself, David. You are wallowing in self-pity, but I am not going to allow that to hurt her more. She has had enough. No more delay. Tell her, and have done.'

'Yes,' David nodded, all the fight gone out of him. 'I will tell her.'

'When?' the Brig persisted.

'Tomorrow,' said David. 'I will tell her tomorrow morning.'

It was a bright warm morning, and the garden below his room was gay with colour. David lingered over breakfast in his suite, and he read all of the morning papers from end to end, drawing out the moment to its utmost. He dressed with care afterwards, in a dark suit and a soft lilac shirt, then, when he was ready to leave, he surveyed his image in the full-length mirror of the dressing-room.

'It's been a long time–and I'm still not at ease with you,' he told the figure in the mirror. 'Let's pray that somebody loves you more than I do.'

The doorman had a cab ready for him under the portico, and he settled in the back seat with the leaden feeling in his stomach. The drive seemed much shorter this morning, and when he paid off the cab and climbed the steps to the main entrance of Groote Schuur, he glanced at his wrist-watch. It was a few minutes after eleven o'clock. He was hardly aware of the curious glances as he crossed the lobby to the elevators.

The Brig was waiting for him in the visitors' room on Debra's floor. He came out into the corridor, tall and grim, and unfamiliar in his civilian clothes.

'What are you doing here?' David demanded, it was the ultimate intrusion and he resented it fiercely.

'I thought I might be of help.'

'Good on you!' said David sardonically, making no effort to hide his anger.

The Brig let the anger slide past him, not acknowledging it with either word or expression as he asked mildly, 'Would you like me to be with you?'

'No.' David turned away from him as he spoke. 'I can manage, thank you,' and he set off along the corridor.

'David!' the Brig called softly, and David hesitated and then turned back.

'What is it?' he asked.

For a long moment they stared at each other, then abruptly the Brig shook his head. 'No,' he said. 'It's nothing,' and watched the tall young man with the monstrous head turn and walk swiftly towards Debra's room. His footsteps echoed hollowly along the empty corridor, like the tread of a man upon the gallows steps.

The morning was warm with a light breeze off the sea. Debra sat in her chair by the open window, and the warm air wafted the scent of the pine forests to her. Resinous and clean-smelling, it mingled with the faint whiff of the sea and the kelp beds. She felt quiet and deeply contented, even though David was late this morning. She had spoken to Ruby Friedman when he made his rounds earlier, and he had teased her and hinted that she would be able to leave in a week or so, and the knowledge rounded out her happiness.

The warmth of the morning was drowsy, and she closed her eyes subduing the strong rich flow of colour into a lulling cocoon of soft shades which enfolded her, and she lay on the downy edges of sleep.

David found her like that, sitting in the deep chair with her legs curled sideways under her and her face side-lit by the reflected sunlight from the window. The turban of white bandages that swathed her head was crisp and fresh and her gown was white as a bride's, with cascades of filmy lace.

He stood before her chair studying her with care, her face was pale, but the dark bruises below her eyes had cleared and the set of her full lips were serene and peaceful.

With infinite tenderness he leaned forward and laid his open hand against her cheek. She stirred drowsily, and opened eyes that were honey brown and flecked with bright flakes of gold. They were beautiful, and vague, misty and sightless–then suddenly he saw them change, the look of them was sharp and aware. Her gaze focused, and steadied. She was looking at him–and seeing him.

Debra was roused from the warm edge of sleep by the touch upon her cheek, as light as the fall of an autumn leaf. She opened her eyes to soft golden clouds, then suddenly like the morning wind slashing away the sea mist, the clouds rolled open and she looked beyond to the monster's head that swam towards her, a colossal disembodied head that seemed must arise from the halls of hell itself, a head so riven with livid lines and set with the bestial, crudely worked features of one of the dark hosts, that she flung herself back in her chair, cringing away from the terror of it, and she lifted her hands to her face and she screamed.

David turned and ran from the room, slamming the door behind him, his feet pounded down the passage and the Brig heard him coming and stepped into the corridor.

'David!' He reached out a hand to him, to hold him back, but David struck out at him wildly, a blow that caught him in the chest throwing him back heavily against the wall. When he regained his balance, and staggered from the wall clutching his chest, David was gone. His frantic footsteps clattered up from the well of the stairs.

'David!' he called, his voice croaking. 'Wait!' But he was gone, his footsteps fading, and the Brig let him go. Instead he turned and hurried painfully down the corridor to where the hysterical sobs of his daughter rang from behind the closed door.

She looked up from her cupped hands when she heard the door open, and wonder dawned through the terror in her eyes.

'I can see you,' she whispered, 'I can see.'

He went to her quickly and took her in the protective circle of his arms.

'It's all right,' he told her awkwardly, 'it's going to be all right.'

She clung to him, stifling the last of her sobs.

'I had a dream,' she murmured, 'a terrible dream,' and she shuddered against him. Then suddenly she pulled away.

'David,' she cried, 'where is David? I must see him.'

The Brig stiffened, realizing that she had not recognized reality.

'I must see him,' she repeated, and he replied heavily, 'You have already seen him, my child.'

For many seconds she did not understand, and then slowly it came to her.

'David?' she whispered, her voice catching and breaking. 'That was David?'

The Brig nodded, watching her face for the revulsion and the horror.

'Oh dear God,' Debra's voice was fierce. 'What have I done? I screamed when I saw him. What have I done to him? I've driven him away.'

'So you still want to see him again?' the Brig asked.

'How can you say that?' Debra blazed at him. 'More than anything on this earth. You must know that!'

'Even the way he is now?'

'If you think that would make any difference to me–then you don't know me very well.' Her expression changed again, becoming concerned. 'Find him for me,' she ordered. 'Quickly, before he has a chance to do something stupid.'

'I don't know where he has gone,' the Brig answered, his own concern aroused by the possibility which Debra had hinted at.

'There is only one place he would go when he is hurt like this,' Debra told him. 'He will be in the sky.'

'Yes,' the Brig agreed readily.

'Get down to Air Traffic Control, they'll let you speak to him.' The Brig turned for the door and Debra's voice urged him on.

'Find him for me, Daddy. Please find him for me.'

The Navajo seemed to come around on to a southerly heading under its own volition. It was only when the sleek, rounded nose settled on course, climbing steadily upwards towards the incredibly tall and unsullied blue of the heavens that David knew where he was going.

Behind him, the solid flat-topped mountain with its glistening wreaths of cloud fell away. This was the last of the land, and ahead lay only the great barren wastes of ice and cruel water.

David glanced at his fuel gauges. His vision was still blurred but he saw the needles registering a little over the half-way mark on the dials.

Three hours' flying perhaps, and David felt a chill relief that there was to be a term to his suffering. He saw clearly then how it would end down there in the wilderness below the shipping lanes. He would continue to bore for height, climbing steadily until at last his engines starved and failed. Then he would push the nose down into a vertical dive and go in hard and fast, like the final suicide stoop of a maimed and moribund eagle. It would be over swiftly, and the metal fuselage would carry him down to a grave that could not be as lonely as the desolation in which he now existed.

The radio crackled and hummed into life. He heard Air Traffic snarl his call sign through the static crackle, and he reached for the switch to kill the set–when the well-remembered voice stayed his hand.

'David, this is the Brig.' The words and the tone in which they were spoken transported him back to another cockpit in another land.

'You disobeyed me once before. Don't do it again.'

David's mouth tightened into a thin colourless line and again he reached for the switch. He knew they were watching him on the radar plot, that they knew his course, and that the Brig had guessed what he intended. Well, there was nothing they could do about it.

'David,' the Brig's voice softened, and some sure instinct made him choose the only words to which David would listen. 'I have just spoken to Debra. She wants you. She wants you desperately.'

David's hand hovered over the switch.

'Listen to me, David. She needs you–she will always need you.'

David blinked, for he felt tears scalding his eyes once more. His determination wavered.

'Come back, David. For her sake, come back.'

Out of the darkness of his soul, a light shone, a small light which grew and spread until it seemed to fill him with its shimmering brightness.

'David, this is the Brig.' Again it was the voice of the old warrior, hard and uncompromising. 'Return to base immediately.'

David grinned, and lifted the microphone to his mouth. He thumbed the transmit button, and spoke the old acknowledgement in Hebrew.

'Beseder! This is Bright Lance leader, homeward bound,' and he brought the Navajo around steeply.

The mountain was blue and low on the horizon, and he let the nose sink gradually towards it. He knew that it would not be easy–that it would require all his courage and patience, but he knew that in the end it would be worth it all. Suddenly he needed desperately to be alone with Debra, in the peace of Jabulani.

Gold Mine

GOLD MINE

FOR DEE

I

It began in the time when the world was young, in the time before man, in the time before life itself had evolved upon this planet.

The crust of the earth was still and soft, distorted and riven by the enormous pressures from within.

What is now the flat, compacted shield of the African continent, stable and unchanging, was a series of alps. It was range upon range of mountains, thrown up and tumbled down by the movements of the magma at great depth. These were mountains such as man has never seen, so massive as to dwarf the Himalayas, mountains of steaming rock from whose clefts and gaping wounds the molten magma trickled.

It came up from the earth's centre along the fissures and weak places in the crust, bubbling and boiling, yet cooling steadily as it neared the surface so that the least volatile minerals were deposited deeper down, but those with a lower melting point were carried to the surface.

At one point in the measureless passage of time, another series of these fissures opened upon one of the nameless mountain ranges, but from them gushed rivers of molten gold. Some natural freak of temperature and chemical change had resulted in a crude but effective process of refinement during the journey to the earth's surface. The gold was in high concentration in the matrix, and it cooled and solidified at the surface.

If the mountains of that time were so massive as to challenge the imagination of man, then the storms of wind and rain that blew around them were of equal magnitude.

It was a hellish landscape in which the gold field was conceived, cruel mountains reaching stark and sheer into the clouds. Cloud banks dark with the sulphurous gases of the belching earth, so thick that the rays of the sun never penetrated them.

The atmosphere was laden with all the moisture that was to become the seas, so heavy with it that it rained in one perpetual wind-lashed storm upon the hot rock of the cooling earth, then the moisture rose in steam to condense and fall again.

As the years passed by their millions, so the wind and the rain whittled away at the nameless mountain range with its coating of gold-rich ore, grinding it loose and carrying it down in freshets and rivers and rushes of mud and rock into the valley between this range and the next.

Now as the country rock cooled, so the waters lay longer upon the earth before evaporating, and they accumulated in this valley to form a lake the size of an inland sea.

Into this lake poured the storm waters from the golden mountains, carrying with them tiny particles of the yellow metal which settled with other sand and quartz gravel upon the lake bed, to be compacted into a solid sheet.

In time all the gold was scoured from the mountains, transported and laid down upon the lake beds.

Then, as happened every ten million years or so, the earth entered another period of intense seismic activity. The earth shuddered and heaved as earthquake after mammoth earthquake convulsed it.

One fearsome paroxysm cracked the bed of the lake from end to end draining it and fracturing the sedimentary beds, scattering fragments haphazardly so that great sheets of rock many miles across tilted and reared on end.

Again and again the earthquakes gripped and shook the earth. The mountains tottered and collapsed, filling the valley where the lake had stood, burying some of the sheets of gold-rich rock, pulverizing others.

That cycle of seismic activity passed, and the ages wheeled on in their majesty. The floods and the great droughts came and receded. The miraculous spark of life was struck and burned up brightly, through the time of the monstrous reptiles, on through countless twists and turns of evolution until near the middle of the pleistocene age a man-ape–australopithecus–picked up the thigh bone of a buffalo from inside an outcrop of rock to use it as a weapon, a tool.

Australopithecus stood at the centre of a flat, sun-seared plateau that reached five hundred miles in each direction to the sea, for the mountains and the lake beds had long ago been flattened and buried.

Eight hundred thousand years later, one of australopithecus' distant but direct line stood at the same spot with a tool in his hand. The man's name was Harrison and the tool was more sophisticated than that of his ancestor, it was a prospector's pick of wood and metal.

Harrison stooped and chipped at the outcrop of rock that protruded from the dry brown African earth. He freed a piece of the stone and straightened with it in his hand.

He held it to catch the sun and grunted with disgust. It was a most uninteresting piece of stone, conglomerate, marbled black and grey. Without hope he held it to his mouth and licked it, wetting the surface before again holding it to the sun, an old prospectors' trick to highlight the metal in the ore.

His eyes narrowed in surprise as the tiny golden flecks in the rock sparkled back at him.

History remembers only his name, not his age nor his antecedents, not the colour of his eyes nor how he died, for within a month he sold his claim for £10 and disappeared–in search, perhaps, of a really big strike.

He might have done better to retain his title to those claims.

In the eighty years since then an estimated five hundred million ounces of fine gold have been recovered from the fields of the Transvaal and Orange Free State. This is a fraction of that which remains, and which in time will be taken from the earth. For the men who mine the South African fields are the most patiently persistent, inventive and pig-headed of all Vulcan's brood.

The mass of precious metal is the foundation on which the prosperity of a vigorous young nation of eighteen million souls is based.

Yet the earth yields her treasure reluctantly–men must coax and wrest it from her.

2

Even with the electric fan blowing up a gale from the corner it was stinking hot in Rod Ironsides' office.

He reached for the silver Thermos of iced water at the edge of his desk, and arrested the movement as the jug began to dance before his finger tips touched it. The metal bottle skittered across the polished wooden surface; the desk itself shuddered, rustling the papers upon it. The walls of the room shook, so that the windows rattled in their frames. Four seconds the tremor lasted, and then it was still again.

'Christ!' said Rod, and snatched up one of the three telephones on his desk.

'This is the Underground Manager. Get me the rock mechanic's lab, honey, and snap it up, please.'

He drummed his fingers on the desk impatiently as he waited to be connected. The interleading door of his office opened and Dimitri put his head around the jamb.

'You feel that one, Rod? That was a bad one.'

'I felt it.' Then the telephone spoke into his ear.

'Dr Wessels here.'

'Peter, it's Rod. Did you read that one?'

'I haven't got a fix on it yet–can you hold on a minute?'

'I'll wait.' Rod curbed his impatience. He knew that Peter Wessels was the only person who could read the mass of complicated electronic equipment that filled the instrument room of the rock mechanic's laboratory. The laboratory was a joint research project by four of the major gold-mining companies; between them they had put up a quarter of a million Rand to finance an authoritative investigation of rock and seismic activity under stress. They had selected the Sonder Ditch Gold Mining Company's lease area as the site for the laboratory. Now Peter Wessels had his microphones sited thousands of feet down in the earth, and his tape-recorders and stylus graphs ready to pinpoint any underground disturbance.

Another minute ticked by, and Rod swivelled his chair and stared out of the plate glass window at the monstrous head gear of No. 1 shaft, tall as a ten-storey building.

'Come on, Peter, come on, boy,' he muttered to himself. 'I've got twelve thousand of my boys down there.'

With the telephone still pressed to his ear, he glanced at his watch.

'Two-thirty,' he muttered. 'The worst possible time. They'll still be in the stopes.'

He heard the receiver picked up on the other end, and Peter Wessels' voice was almost apologetic.

'Rod?'

'Yes.'

'I'm sorry, Rod, you've had a force seven pressure burst at 9,500 feet in sector Sugar seven Charlie two.'

'Christ!' said Rod and slammed down the receiver. He was up from his desk in one movement, his face set and angry.

'Dimitri,' he snapped at his assistant still in the doorway. 'We won't wait for them to call us, it's a top-sequence emergency. That was a force seven bump, with its source plumb in the middle of our eastern longwall at 95 level.'

'Sweet Mary Mother,' said Dimitri, and darted back into his own office. He bent his glossy black head of curls over the telephone and Rod heard him start his top-sequence calls.

'Mine hospital . . . emergency team . . . Chief Ventilation Officer . . . General Manager's office.'

Rod turned away, as the outer door of his office opened and Jimmy Paterson, his electric engineer, came in.

'I felt it, Rod. How's it look?'

'Bad,' said Rod, then there were the other line managers crowding into his office talking quietly, lighting cigarettes, coughing and shuffling their feet, but all of them watching the white telephone on Rod's desk. The minutes crawled by like crippled insects.

'Dimitri,' Rod called out to break the tension. 'Have you got a cage held at the shaft head?'

'They're holding the Mary Anne for us.'

'I've got five men checking the high tension cable on 95 level,' said Jimmy Paterson, and they ignored him. They were watching the white phone.

'Have you located the boss yet, Dimitri?' Rod asked again, he was pacing in front of his desk. It was only when he stood close to other men that you saw how tall he was.

'He's underground, Rod. He went down at twelve-thirty.'

'Put in an all-stations call for him to contact me here.'

'I've done that already.'

The white phone rang.

Only once, a shrill note that ripped along Rod's nerve ends. Then he had the receiver up to his ear.

'Underground Manager,' he said. There was a long silence and he could hear the man breathing on the other end.

'Speak, man, what is it?'

'The whole bloody thing has come down,' said the voice. It was husky, rough with fear and dust.

'Where are you speaking from?' Rod asked.

'They're still in there,' said the voice. 'They're screaming in there. Under the rock. They're screaming.'

'What is your station?' Rod made his voice cold, hard, trying to reach the man through his shock.

'The whole stope fell in on them. The whole bloody thing.'

'God damn you! You stupid bastard!' Rod bellowed into the phone. 'Give me your station!'

There was stunned silence for a moment. Then the man's voice came back, steadier now, angry from the insult.

'95 level main haulage. Section 43. Eastern longwall.'

'We're coming.' Rod hung up, picked up his yellow fibre-glass hard helmet and lamp from the desk.

'43 section. The hanging wall has come down,' he said to Dimitri.

'Fatals?' the little Greek asked.

'For sure. They've got squealers under the rock.'

Rod clapped on his hat.

'Take over on surface, Dimitri.'

3

Rod was still buttoning the front of his white overalls as he reached the shaft head. Automatically he read the sign above the entrance.

STAY ALERT. STAY ALIVE.
WITH YOUR COOPERATION THIS MINE HAS WORKED
16 FATALITY FREE DAYS.

'We'll have to change the number again,' Rod thought with grim humour.

The Mary Anne was waiting. Into its heavily wired confines were crowded the first-aid team and emergency squad. The Mary Anne was the small cage used for lowering and hoisting personnel, there were two much larger cages that could carry 120 men at one trip, while the Mary Anne could handle only forty. But that was sufficient for now.

'Let's go,' said Rod as he stepped into the cage, and the onsetter slammed the steel roller doors closed. The bell rang once, twice, and the floor dropped away from under him as the Mary Anne started down. Rod's belly came up to press against his ribs. They went down in one long continuous rush in the darkness. The cage jarring and racketing, the air changing in smell and taste, becoming chemical and processed, the heat building up rapidly.

Rod stood hunch-shouldered, leaning against the metal screen of the cage. The head room was a mere six foot three, and with his helmet on Rod stood taller than that. *So today we get another butcher's bill,* he thought angrily.

He was always angry when the earth took its payment in mangled flesh and snapping bones. All the ingenuity of man and the experience gained in sixty years of deep mining on the Witwatersrand were used in trying to keep the price in blood as low as possible. But when you go down into the ultra-deep levels below eight thousand feet and from those depths you remove a quarter of a million tons of rock each month, mining on an inclined sheet of reef that leaves a vast low-roofed chamber thousands of feet across, then you must pay, for the stress builds up in the rock as the focal points of pressure change until the moment when it reaches breaking point and she bumps. That is when men die.

Rod's knees flexed under him as the cage braked and then yo-yoed to a halt at the brightly lit station on 66 level.

Here they must trans-ship to the sub-main shaft. The door rattled up and Rod left the cage, striding out down the main haulage the size of a railway tunnel; concreted and white-washed, brightly lit by the bulbs that lined the roof, it curved gently away.

The emergency team followed Rod. Not running, but walking with the suppressed nervous energy of men going into danger. Rod led them towards the sub-main shaft.

There is a limit to the depth which you can sink a shaft into the earth and then equip it to carry men suspended on a steel cable in a tiny wire cage. The limit is about 7,000 feet.

At this depth you must start again, blast out a new head-gear chamber from the living rock and below it sink your new shaft, the sub-main.

The sub-main Mary Anne was waiting for them, and Rod led them into it. They stood shoulder to shoulder, and the door rattled shut and again the stomach-swooping rush down into darkness.

Down, down, down.

Rod switched on his head lamp. Now there were tiny motes in the air–air that had been sterilely clean before.

Dust! One of the deadly enemies of the miner. Dust from the burst. As yet the ventilation system had been unable to clear it.

Endlessly they fell in darkness and now it was very hot, the humidity building up so the faces about him, both black and white, were shiny with sweat in the light of his head lamp.

The dust was thicker now, someone coughed. The brightly lit stations flashed past them–76, 77, 78–down, down. The dust was a fine mist now. 85, 86, 87. No one had spoken since entering the cage. 93, 94, 95. The deceleration and stop.

The door rattled up. They were 9,500 feet below the surface of the earth.

'Come on,' said Rod.

4

There were men cluttering the lobby of 95 station, 150, perhaps 200 of them. Still filthy from the work in the stopes, clothing sodden with sweat, they were laughing and chattering with the abandon of men freshly released from frightful danger.

In a clear space in the centre of the lobby lay five stretchers, on two of them the bright red blankets were pulled up to cover the faces of the men upon them. The faces of the other three men looked as though they had been dusted with flour.

'Two'–grunted Rod–'so far.'

The station was a shambles, with men milling aimlessly, each minute more of them came back down the haulages as they were pulled out of the undamaged stopes, which were now suspect.

Quickly Rod looked about him, recognizing the face of one of his mine captains.

'McGee,' he shouted. 'Take over here. Get them sitting down in lines ready to load. We'll start hauling the shift out immediately. Get into the hoist room, tell them I want the stretcher cases out first.'

He paused long enough to watch McGee take control. He glanced at his watch. Two fifty-six. He realized with astonishment that only twenty-six minutes had passed since he felt the pressure burst in his office.

McGee had the station under a semblance of control. He was shouting into the hoist room telephone, on Rod's authority demanding priority to clear 95 station.

'Right,' said Rod. 'Come on.' And he led into the haulage.

The dust was thick. He coughed. The hanging wall was lower here. As he trudged on once more, Rod pondered the unfortunate choice of mining terminology that had named the roof of an excavation 'the hanging wall'. It made one think of a gallows, or at best it emphasized the fact that there were millions of tons of rock *hanging* overhead.

The haulage branched, and unerringly Rod took the right fork. In his head he carried an accurate three-dimensional map of the entire 176 miles of tunnels that comprised the Sonder Ditch's workings. The haulage came to a 'T' junction and the arms were lower and narrower. Right to 42 section, left to 43 section. The dust was so thick that visibility was down to ten feet. The dust hung in the air, sinking almost imperceptibly.

'Ventilations knocked out here,' he called over his shoulder. 'Van den Bergh!'

'Yes, sir.' The leader of the emergency squad came up behind him.

'I want air in this drive. Get it on. Use canvas piping if you have to.'

'Right.'

'Then I want pressure on the water hoses to lay this dust.'

'Right.'

Rod turned into the drive. Here the foot wall–the floor–was rough and the going slower. They came upon a line of steel trolleys filled with gold reef abandoned in the centre of the drive.

'Get these the hell out of the way,' ordered Rod, and went on.

Fifty paces and he stopped abruptly. He felt the hair on his forearms stand on end. He could never accustom himself to the sound, no matter how often he heard it.

In the deliberately callous slang of the miner they called them 'squealers'. It was the sound of a grown man, with his legs crushed under hundreds of tons of rock, perhaps his spine broken, dust suffocating him, his mind unhinged by the mortal horror of the situation in which he was trapped, calling for help, calling to his God, calling for his wife, his children, or his mother.

Rod started forward again, with the sound of it becoming louder, a terrifying sound, hardly human, sobbing and babbling into silence, only to start again with a blood-chilling scream.

Suddenly there were men ahead of Rod in the tunnel, dark shapes looming in the dust mist, their head lamps throwing shafts of yellow light, grotesque, distorted.

'Who is that?' Rod called, and they recognized his voice.

'Thank God. Thank God you've come, Mr Ironsides.'

'Who is that?'

'Barnard.' The 43 section shift boss.

'What's the damage?'

'The whole hanging wall of the slope came down.'

'How many men in the stope?'

'Forty-two.'

'How many still in?'

'So far we've got out sixteen unhurt, twelve slightly hurt, three stretcher cases and two dead 'uns.'

The squealer started again, but his voice was much weaker.

'Him?' asked Rod.

'He's got twenty ton of rock lying across his pelvis. I've hit him with two shots of morphine but it won't stop him.'

'Can you get into the stope?'

'Yes, there is a crawling hole.' Barnard flashed his lamp over the pile of fractured blue quartzite that jammed the drive like a collapsed garden wall. On it was an aperture big enough for a fox terrier to run through. Reflected light showed from the hole, and faintly from within came the grating sounds of movement over loose rock and the muffled voices of men.

'How many men have you got working in there, Barnard?'

'I'–Barnard hesitated, 'I think about ten or twelve.'

And Rod grabbed a handful of his overall front and jerked him almost off his feet.

'You think!' In the head lamps Rod's face was white with fury. 'You've put men in there without recording their numbers? You've put twelve of my boys against the wall to try and save nine?' With a heave Rod lifted the shift boss off his feet and swung him against the side wall of the drive, pinning him there.

'You bastard, you know that most of those nine are chopped already. You know that stope is a bloody killing ground, and you send in *twelve* more to get the chop *and* you don't record their numbers. How the hell would we ever know who to look for if the hanging fell again?' He let the shift boss free, and stood back. 'Get them out of there, clear that stope.'

'But, Mr Ironsides, the General Manager is in there, Mr Lemmer is in there. He was doing an inspection in the stope.'

For a moment Rod was taken aback, then he snarled. 'I don't give a good damn if the State President is in there, clear the stope. We'll start again and this time we'll do it properly.'

Within minutes the rescuers had been recalled, they came squirming out of the aperture, white with dust like maggots wriggling from rotten cheese.

'Right,' said Rod, 'I'll risk four men at a time.'

Quickly he picked four of the floury figures, among them an enormous man on whose right shoulder was the brass badge of a boss boy.

'Big King–you here?' Rod spoke in Fanikalo, the lingua franca of the mines enabled men from a dozen ethnic groups to communicate.

'I am here,' answered Big King.

'You looking for more awards?' A month before, Big King had been lowered on a rope 200 feet down a vertical orepass to retrieve the body of a white miner. The bravery award by the company had been 100 Rand.

'Who speaks of awards when the earth has eaten the flesh of men?' Big King rebuked Rod softly. 'But today is children's play only. Is the Nkosi coming into the stope?' It was a challenge.

Rod's place was not in the stope. He was the organizer, the co-ordinator. Yet, he could not ignore the challenge, no Bantu would believe that he had not stood back in fear and sent other men in to die.

'Yes,' said Rod, 'I'm coming into the stope.'

He led them in. The hole was only just big enough to admit the bulk of Rod's body. He found himself in a chamber, the size of an average room, but the roof was only three and a half feet high. He played his lamp quickly across the hanging wall, and it was wicked. The rock was cracked and ugly, 'a bunch of grapes' was the term.

'Very pretty,' he said, and dropped the beam of his lamp.

The squealer was within an arm's length of Rod. His body from the waist up protruded from under a piece of rock the size of a Cadillac. Someone had wrapped a red blanket around his upper body. He was quiet now, lying still. But as the beam of Rod's lamp fell upon him, he lifted his head. His eyes were crazed, unseeing, his face running with the sweat of terror and insanity. His mouth snapped open, wide and pink in the shiny blackness of his face. He began to scream, but suddenly the sound was drowned by a great red-black gout of blood that came gushing up his throat, and spurted from his mouth.

As Rod watched in horror, the Bantu posed like that, his head thrown back, his mouth gaping as though he were a gargoyle, the life blood pouring from him. Then slowly the head sagged forward, and flopped face downwards. Rod crawled to him, lifted his head and pillowed it on the red blanket.

There was blood on his hands and he wiped it on the front of his overalls.

'Three,' he said, 'so far.' And leaving the dying man he crawled on towards the broken face of the fall.

Big King crawled up beside him with two pinch bars. He handed one to Rod.

Within an hour it had become a contest, a trial of strength between the two men. Behind them the other three men were shoring up and passing back the rock that Rod and Big King loosened from the face. Rod knew he was being childish, he should have been back in the main haulage, not only directing the rescue, but also making all the other decisions and alternative arrangements that were needed now. The company paid him for his brains and his experience, not for his muscle.

'The hell with it,' he thought. 'Even if we miss the blast this evening, I'm staying here.' He glanced at Big King, and reached forward to get his hands onto a bigger piece of rock in the jam. He strained, using his arms first, then bringing the power of his whole body into it, the rock was solid. Big King placed huge black hands on the rock, and they pulled together. In a rush of smaller rock it came away, and they shoved it back between them, grinning at each other.

At seven o'clock Rod and Big King withdrew from the stope to rest and eat sandwiches, and drink Thermos coffee while Rod spoke to Dimitri over the field telephone that had been laid up to the face.

'We've pulled shift on both shafts, Rod, the workings are clear to blast. Except for your lot, there are fifty-eight men in your 43 section.' Dimitri's voice was reedy over the field telephone.

'Hold on.' Rod revolved the situation in his mind. He worked it out slower than usual, for he was tired, emotionally and physically drained. If he stopped the blast on both shafts for fear of bringing down more rock in 43 section, it would cost the Company a day's production, ten thousand tons of gold reef worth sixteen Rand a ton, the formidable sum of R160,000 or £80,000 or $200,000 whichever way you looked at it.

It was highly probable that every man in the stope was already dead, and the original pressure burst had de-stressed the rock above and around the 95 level, so there was little danger of further bumps.

And yet there might be someone alive in there, someone lying pinned in the womb-warm darkness of the stope with a bunch of loose grapes hanging over his unprotected body. When they hit all the blast buttons on the Sonder Ditch Mine, they fired eighteen tons of Dynagel. The kick was considerable, it would bring down those grapes.

'Dimitri,' Rod made his decision, 'burn all longwalls on No. 2 shaft at seven-thirty exactly.' No. 2 shaft was three miles away. That would save the Company R80,000. 'Then at precisely five minute intervals burn south, north and west longwalls here on No. 1 Shaft.' Spreading the blast would reduce the disturbance, and that put another R60,000 in the shareholders' pockets. The total monetary loss inflicted by the disaster was around R20,000. Not too bad really, Rod thought sardonically, blood was cheap. You could buy it at three Rand a pint from the Central Blood Transfusion Service.

'All right,' he stood up, and flexed his aching shoulders, 'I'm pulling everybody back into the safety of the shaft pillar while we blast.'

5

After the successive earth tremors of the blast, Rod put them back into the stope, and at nine o'clock they uncovered the bodies of two machine boys crushed against the metal of their own rock drill. Ten feet further on they found the white miner, his body was unmarked, but his head was flattened.

At eleven o'clock they found two more machine boys. Rod was in the haulage when they dragged them out through the small opening. Neither of them were recognizable as human, they looked more like lumps of raw meat that had been rubbed in dirt.

A little after midnight Rod and Big King went into the stope again to take over from the team at the face, and twenty minutes later they holed through the wall of loose rock into another chamber that had been miraculously left standing.

The air in here was steamy with heat. Rod recoiled instinctively from the filthy moist gush of it against his face. Then he forced himself to crawl forward and peer into the opening.

Ten feet away lay Frank Lemmer, the General Manager of the Sonder Ditch Mine. He lay on his back. His helmet had been knocked from his head, and a deep gash split the skin above his eye. Blood from the gash had run back into his silver hair and clotted black. He opened his eyes and blinked owlishly in the dazzle of Rod's lamp. Quickly Rod averted the beam.

'Mr Lemmer,' he said.

'What the bloody hell are you doing with the rescue team?' growled Frank Lemmer. 'It's not your job. Haven't you learned a single goddamned thing in twenty years of mining?'

'Are you all right, sir?'

'Get a doctor in here,' replied Frank Lemmer. 'You're going to have to cut me loose from this lot.'

Rod wriggled up to where he lay, and then he saw what Frank Lemmer meant. From the elbow his arm was pinned under a solid slab of rock. Rod ran his hands over the slab, feeling it. Only explosive would shift that rock. As always Frank Lemmer was right.

Rod wriggled out of the opening and called over his shoulder.

'Get the telephone up here.'

After a few minutes' delay he had the receiver, and was through to the station at 95 level which had been set up as an advance aid post and rest station for the rescuers.

'This is Ironsides, get me Doctor Stander.'

'Hold on.'

Then moments later, 'Hello, Rod, it's Dan.'

'Dan, we've found the old man.'

'How is he, conscious?'

'Yes, but he's pinned–you'll have to cut.'

'Are you sure?' Dan Stander asked.

'Of course I'm bloody well sure,' snapped Rod.

'Whoa, boy!' admonished Dan.

'Sorry.'

'Okay, where's he caught?'

'Arm. You'll have to cut above the elbow.'

'Charming!' said Dan.

'I'll wait here for you.'

'Right. I'll be up in five minutes.'

6

'It's funny, you see them chopped time and again, but you know it will never happen to you.' Frank Lemmer's voice was steady and even, the arm must be numb, Rod thought as he lay beside him in the stope.

Frank Lemmer rolled his head towards Rod. 'Why don't you go farming, boy?'

'You know why,' said Rod.

'Yes.' Lemmer smiled a little, just a twitching of the lips. With his free hand he wiped his mouth. 'You know, I had just three months more before I went on pension. I nearly made it. You'll end like this, boy, in the dirt with your bones crunched up.'

'It's not the end,' said Rod.

'Isn't it?' asked Frank Lemmer, and this time he chuckled. 'Isn't it?'

'What's the joke?' asked Dan Stander, poking his head into the tiny chamber.

'Christ, it took you long enough to get here,' growled Frank Lemmer.

'Give me a hand, Rod.' Dan passed his bag through, then as he crawled forward he spoke to Frank Lemmer.

'Union Steel closed at 98 cents tonight. I told you to buy.'

'Over-priced, over-capitalized,' snorted Frank Lemmer. Dan lay on his side in the dirt and laid out his instruments, and they argued stocks and shares. When Dan had the syringe full of pentathol and was swabbing Frank Lemmer's stringy old arm, Lemmer rolled his head towards Rod again.

'We made a good dig here, Rodney, you and I. I wish they'd give it to you now, but they won't. You're still too young. But whoever they put in my place, you keep an eye on him, you know the ground–don't let him balls it up.'

And the needle went in.

Dan cut through the arm in four and a half minutes, and twenty-seven minutes later Frank Lemmer died of shock and exposure in the Mary Anne on his way to the surface.

7

Once he had paid Patti's alimony there was not too much of Rod's salary left for extravagances, but one of these was the big cream Maserati. Although it was a 1967 model, and had done nearly thirty thousand miles when he bought it, yet the instalments still took a healthy bite out of his monthly pay cheque.

On mornings like this he reckoned the expense worthwhile. He came twisting down from the Kraalkop ridge, and when the national road flattened and straightened for the final run into Johannesburg he let the Maserati go. The car seemed to flatten against the ground like a running lion, and the exhaust note changed subtly, becoming deeper, more urgent.

Ordinarily, it was an hour's run from the Sonder Ditch Mine into the city of Johannesburg, but Rod could clip twenty minutes off that time.

It was Saturday morning, and Rod's mood was light and expectant.

Since the divorce Rod had lived a Jekyll and Hyde existence. Five days of the week he was the company man in top-line management, but on the last two days of the week he went into Johannesburg with his golf clubs in the boot of the Maserati, the keys to his luxury Hillbrow apartment in his pocket, and a chuckle on his lips.

Today the anticipation was keener than ever for, in addition to the twenty-two-year-old blonde model who was prepared to devote her evening to entertaining Rodney Ironsides, there was the mysterious summons from Dr Manfred Steyner to answer.

The summons had been delivered by a nameless female caller describing herself as 'Dr Steyner's Secretary'. It had come the day after Frank Lemmer's funeral, and was for Saturday at 11 a.m.

Rod had never met Manfred Steyner, but he had, of course, heard of him. Anyone who worked for any of the fifty or sixty companies that comprised the Central Rand Consolidated Group must have heard of Manfred Steyner, and the Sonder Ditch Gold Company was just one of the Group.

Manfred Steyner had a bachelor's degree in Economics from Berlin University, and a Doctor's degree in Business Administration from Cornell. He had joined C.R.C. a mere twelve years previously at the age of thirty, and now he was the front runner, Hurry Hirschfeld could not live for ever, although he gave indications of doing so, and when he went down to make a takeover bid on Hades, the word was that Manfred Steyner would succeed him as Chairman of C.R.C.

Chairmanship of C.R.C. was an enviable position, the incumbent automatically became one of the five most powerful men in Africa, and that included heads of state.

The betting favoured Dr Steyner for a number of good reasons. He had a brain that had earned him the nickname of 'The Computer'; no one had yet been able to detect in him the slightest evidence of a human weakness, and more than this he had taken the trouble ten years previously to catch Hurry Hirschfeld's only granddaughter as she emerged from Cape Town University and marry her.

Dr Steyner was in a strong position, and Rod was intrigued with the prospect of meeting him.

The Maserati was registering 125 miles an hour as he went under the overpass of the Kloof Gold Mining Company property.

'Johannesburg, here I come!' Rod laughed aloud.

It was ten minutes before eleven o'clock when Rod found the brass plaque reading 'Dr M. K. Steyner' in a secluded lane of the lush Johannesburg suburb of Sandown. The house was not visible from the road, and Rod let the Maserati roll gently in through the tall white gates, with their imitation Cape Dutch gables.

The gates, he decided, were a display of shocking taste but the gardens beyond them were paradise. Rod knew rock, but flowers were his weak suit. He recognized the massed banks of red and yellow against the green lawns as cannas, but after that he had no names for the blazing beauty spread about him.

'Wow!' he muttered in awe. 'Someone has done a hell of a lot of work around here.'

Around a curve in the macadamized drive lay the house. It also was Cape Dutch and Rod forgave Dr Steyner his gates.

'Wow!' he said again, and involuntarily braked the Maserati to a standstill.

Cape Dutch is one of the most difficult styles to copy effectively, where one line in a hundred out of place could spoil the effect; this particular example worked perfectly. It gave the feel of timelessness, of solidarity, and mixed it subtly with a grace and finesse of line. He guessed that the shutters and beams were genuine yellow wood and the windows hand-leaded.

Rod looked at it, and felt envy prickle and burn within him. He loved fine things, like his Maserati, but this was another concept in material possessions. He was jealous of the man that owned it, knowing that his own entire year's income would not be sufficient for a down payment on the land alone.

'So I've got my flat,' he grinned ruefully, and coasted down to park in front of the line of garages.

It was not clear which was the correct entrance to use, and he chose at random from a number of paved paths that all led in the general direction of the house.

Around a bend in this path he came on another spectacle. Though smaller it had, if anything, a more profound effect on Rod than the house had. It was a feminine posterior of equal grace and finesse of line, clad in Helanka stretch ski-pants, and protruding from a large and exotic bush.

Rod was captivated. He stood and watched as the bush shook and rustled, and the bottom wriggled and heaved.

Suddenly, in ladylike tones there issued from the bush a most unladylike oath and the bottom shot backwards and its owner straightened up with her forefinger in her mouth, sucking noisily.

'It bit me!' she mumbled around the finger. 'Damned stinkbug bit me!'

'Well, you shouldn't tease them,' said Rod.

And she spun round to face him. The first thing Rod noticed were her eyes, they were enormous, completely out of proportion to the rest of her face.

'I wasn't–' she started, and then stopped. The finger came out of her mouth. Instinctively one hand went to her hair, and the other began straightening her blouse and brushing off bits of vegetation that were clinging to her.

'Who are you?' she asked, and those huge eyes swept over him. This was fairly standard reaction for any woman between the ages of sixteen and sixty viewing Rodney Ironsides for the first time, and Rodney accepted it gracefully.

'My name is Rodney Ironsides. I've an appointment to see Dr Steyner.'

'Oh.' She was hurriedly tucking her shirt-tails into her slacks. 'My husband will be in his study.'

He had known who she was. He had seen her photographs fifty times in the Group newspaper; but in them she was usually in full-length evening dress and diamonds, not in a blouse with a tear in one sleeve nor pig-tails that were coming down. In the pictures her make-up was immaculate, now she had none at all and her face was flushed and dewed with perspiration.

'I must look a mess. I've been gardening,' said Theresa Steyner unnecessarily.

'Did you do this garden yourself?'

'Only a very little of the muscle work, but I planned it,' she answered. She decided he was big and ugly–no, not really ugly, but battered-looking.

'It's beautiful,' said Rod.

'Thank you.' No, not battered-looking, she changed her mind, tough-looking, and the chest hair curled out of the vee of his open neck shirt.

'This is a protea, isn't it?' He indicated the bush from which she had recently emerged. He was guessing.

'Nutans,' she said; he must be in his late thirties, there was greying at his temples.

'Oh, I thought it was a protea.'

'It is. "Nutans" is its proper name. There are over two hundred different varieties of proteas,' she answered seriously. His voice didn't fit his appearance at all, she decided. He looked like a prize fighter but spoke like a lawyer, probably was one. It was usually lawyers or business consultants who came calling on Manfred.

'Is that so? It's very pretty.' Rod touched one of the blooms.

'Yes, isn't it? I've got over fifty varieties growing here.'

And suddenly they were smiling at each other.

'I'll take you up to the house,' said Theresa Steyner.

8

'Mr Ironsides is here, Manfred.'

'Thank you.' He sat at the stinkwood desk in a room that smelled of wax polish. He made no effort to rise from his seat.

'Would you like a cup of coffee?' Theresa asked from the doorway. 'Or tea?'

'No, thank you,' answered Manfred Steyner without consulting Rod who stood beside her.

'I'll leave you to it, then,' she said.

'Thank you, Theresa.' And she turned away. Rod went on standing where he was, he was studying this man of whom he had heard so much.

Manfred Steyner appeared younger than his forty-two years. His hair was light brown, almost blond, and brushed straight back. He wore spectacles with heavy black frames, and his face was smooth and silky-looking, soft as a girl's with no beard shadow on his chin. His hands that lay on the polished desk top were hairless, smooth, so that Rod wondered if he had used a depilatory on them.

'Come in,' he said, and Rod moved to the desk. Steyner wore a white silk shirt in which the ironing creases still showed, the cloth was snowy white and over it he wore a Royal Johannesburg Golf Club tie, with onyx cuff links. Suddenly Rod realized that neither shirt nor tie had ever been worn before, that much was true of what he had heard then. Steyner ordered his shirts hand-made by the gross and wore each once only.

'Sit down, Ironsides.' Steyner slurred his vowels slightly, just a trace of a Teutonic accent.

'Dr Steyner,' said Rod softly, 'you have a choice. You may call me Rodney or *Mr* Ironsides.'

There was no change in Steyner's voice nor expression.

'I would like to go over your background, please, Mr Ironsides, as a preliminary to our discussion. You have no objection?'

'No, Dr Steyner.'

'You were born October 16th, 1931, at Butterworth in the Transkei. Your father was a native trader, your mother died January 1939. Your father was commissioned Captain in the Durban Light Infantry and died of wounds on the Po River in Italy during the winter of 1944. You were raised by your maternal uncle in East London. Matriculating from Queen's College, Grahamstown, in 1947, you were unsuccessful in obtaining a Chamber of Mines scholarship to Witwatersrand University for a B.Sc (Mining Engineering) degree. You enrolled in the G.M.T.S. (Government Mining Training School) and obtained your blasting ticket during 1949. At which time you joined the Blyvooruitzicht Gold Mining Company Ltd as a learner miner.'

Dr Steyner stood up from his desk and crossing to the panelled wall he pressed a concealed switch and a portion of the panelling slid back to reveal a wash basin and towel rack. As he went on talking he began very meticulously to soap and wash his hands.

'In the same year you were promoted to miner and in 1952 to shift boss, 1954 to mine captain. You successfully completed the examination for the Mine Manager's ticket in 1959, and in 1962 you came to us as an Assistant Section Manager; in 1963, Section Manager, 1965, Assistant Underground Manager, and in 1968 you achieved your present position as Underground Manager.'

Dr Steyner began drying his hands on a snowy white towel.

'You've memorized my company record pretty thoroughly,' Rod admitted.

Dr Steyner crumpled the towel and dropped it into a bin below the wash basin. He pressed the button and the panelling slid closed, then he came back to the desk stepping precisely over the glossy polished wooden floor, and Rod realized that he was a small man, not more than five and a half feet tall, about the same height as his wife.

'This is something of an achievement,' Steyner went on. 'The next youngest Underground Manager in the entire Group is forty-six years of age, whereas you are not yet thirty-nine.'

Rod inclined his head in acknowledgement.

'Now,' said Dr Steyner as he reseated himself and laid his freshly washed hands on the desk top. 'I would like briefly to touch on your private life–you have no objections?'

Again Rod inclined his head.

'The reason that your application for the Chamber of Mines scholarship was refused, despite your straight A matriculation was the recommendation of your headmaster to the selection board in effect that you were of unstable and violent disposition.'

'How the hell did you know that?' ejaculated Rod.

'I have access to the Board's records. It seems that once you had received your matric you immediately assaulted your former headmaster.'

'I beat the hell out of the bastard,' Rod agreed happily.

'An expensive indulgence, Mr Ironsides. It cost you a university degree.'

And Rod was silent.

'To continue: In 1959 you married Patricia Anne Harvey. Of the union was born a girl child in the same year, to be precise, seven and a half months after the wedding.'

Rod squirmed slightly in his chair, and Dr Steyner went on quietly.

'This marriage terminated in divorce in 1964. Your wife suing you on the grounds of adultery, and receiving custody of the child, alimony and maintenance in the sum of R450.00 monthly.'

'What's all this about?' demanded Rod.

'I am attempting to establish an accurate picture of your present circumstances. It is necessary, I assure you.' Dr Steyner removed his spectacles and began polishing the lens on a clean white handkerchief. There were the marks of the frames on the bridge of his nose.

'Go on, then.' Despite himself, Rod was fascinated to learn just how much Steyner knew about him.

'In 1968 there was a paternity suit brought against you by a Miss Diane Johnson and judgement for R150.00 per month.'

Rod blinked and was silent.

'I should mention two further actions against you for assault, both unsuccessful on the grounds of justification or self-defence.'

'Is that all?' asked Rod sarcastically.

'Almost,' admitted Dr Steyner. 'It is only necessary to note further recurrent expenditure in the form of a monthly payment of R150.00 on a continental sports car, and a further R100.00 per month rental on the premises 596 Glen Alpine Heights, Corner Lane, Hillbrow.'

Rod was furious, he had believed that no one in C.R.C. knew about the flat.

'Damn you! You've been prying into my affairs!'

'Yes,' agreed Dr Steyner levelly. 'I am guilty, but in good cause. If you bear with me, you'll see why.'

Suddenly Dr Steyner stood up from the desk, crossed the room to the concealed wash basin, and again began to wash his hands. As he dried them, he spoke again.

'Your monthly commitments are R850. Your salary, after deduction of tax, is less than one thousand Rand. You have no mining degree, and the chances of your taking the next step upwards to General Manager without it are remote. You are at your ceiling, Mr Ironsides. On your own ability you can go no further. In thirty years' time you will not be the youngest Underground Manager in the C.R.C. Group, but the oldest.' Dr Steyner paused. 'That is, provided that your rather expensive tastes have not landed you in a debtors' prison, and that neither the quickness and heat of your temper, nor the matching speed and temperature of your genitalia have gotten you into really serious trouble.'

Steyner dropped the towel in the bin and returned to his seat. They sat in absolute silence, regarding each other for a full minute.

'You got me all the way up here to tell me this?' asked Rod, his whole body was tense, his voice slightly husky, it needed only one ounce more of provocation to launch him across the desk at Steyner's throat.

'No.' Steyner shook his head. 'I got you up here to tell you that I will use all my influence, which I flatter myself is considerable, to secure your appointment–and I mean immediate appointment–to the position of General Manager of the Sonder Ditch Gold Mining Company Ltd.'

Rod recoiled in his chair as though Steyner had spat in his face. He stared at him aghast.

'Why?' he asked at last. 'What do you want in exchange?'

'Neither your friendship, nor your gratitude,' Dr Steyner told him. 'But your unquestioning obedience to my instructions. You will be my man–completely.'

Rod went on staring at him while his mind raced. Without Steyner's intervention he would wait at the very least ten years for his promotion, if it ever came. He wanted it, my God, how he wanted it. The achievement, the increase in income, the power that went with the job. His own mine! His own mine at the age of thirty-eight–and an additional ten thousand Rand per annum.

Yet Rod was not gullible enough to believe that Manfred Steyner's price would be cheap. When the instruction came that he was to follow with unquestioning obedience, he knew it would stink like a ten-day corpse. But once he had the job he could refuse the instruction. Get the job first, then decide once he received the instruction whether to follow it or not.

'I accept,' he said.

Manfred Steyner stood up from the desk.

'You will hear from me,' he said. 'Now you may go.'

9

Rod crossed the wide-flagged stoep without seeing or hearing, vaguely he wandered down across the lawns towards his car. His mind was harrying the recent conversation, tearing it to pieces like a pack of wild dogs on a carcass. He almost bumped into Theresa Steyner before he saw her, and abruptly his mind dropped the subject of the General Managership.

Theresa had changed her clothing, made up her face and eyes, and the pigtails were concealed under a lime-coloured silk scarf, all this in the half hour since their last meeting. She was hovering over a flower bed with a flower basket on one arm, as bright and pleasing as a hummingbird.

Rod was amused and flattered, vain enough to realize that the change was in his honour, and connoisseur enough to appreciate the improvement.

'Hello.' She looked up, contriving successfully to look both surprised and artless. Her eyes were really enormous, and the make-up was designed to enhance their size.

'You are a busy little bee.' Rod ran a knowledgeable appraisal over the floral slack suit she wore, and saw the colour start in her cheeks as she felt his eyes.

'Did you have a successful meeting?'

'Very.'

'Are you a lawyer?'

'No. I work for your grandfather.'

'Doing what?'

'Mining his gold.'

'Which mine?'

'Sonder Ditch.'

'What's your position?'

'Well, if your husband is as good as his word, I'm the new General Manager.'

'You're too young,' she said.

'That's what I thought.'

'Pops will have something to say on the subject.'

'Pops?' he asked.

'My grandfather,' and Rod laughed before he could stop himself.

'What's so funny?'

'The Chairman of C.R.C. being called "Pops".'

'I'm the only one who calls him that.'

'I bet you are.' Rod laughed again. 'In fact I'd bet you'd get away with a lot of things no one else would dare.'

Suddenly the underlying sexuality of his last remark occurred to them both and they fell silent. Theresa looked down and carefully snipped the head off a flower.

'I didn't mean it that way,' apologized Rod.

'What way, Mr Ironsides?' She looked up and inquired with mischievous innocence, and they laughed together with the awkwardness gone again.

She walked beside him to the car, making it seem a completely natural thing to do, and as he slipped behind the steering-wheel she remarked.

'Manfred and I will be coming out to the Sonder Ditch next week. Manfred is to present long service and bravery awards to some of your men.' She had already refused the invitation to accompany Manfred, she must now see to it that she was re-invited. 'I shall probably see you then.'

'I look forward to it,' said Rod, and let in the clutch.

Rod glanced in the rear view mirror. She was a remarkably provocative and attractive woman. A careless man could drown in those eyes.

'Dr Manfred Steyner has got himself a big fat problem there,' he decided. 'Our Manfred is probably so busy soaping and scrubbing his equipment, that he never gets round to using it.'

10

Through the leaded windows Dr Steyner caught a glimpse of the Maserati as it disappeared around the curve in the driveway, and he listened as the throb of the engine dwindled into silence.

He lifted the receiver of the telephone and wiped it with the white handkerchief before putting it to his ear. He dialled and while it rang he inspected the nails of his free hand minutely.

'Steyner,' he said into the mouthpiece. 'Yes–yes.' He listened.

'Yes . . . He has just left . . . Yes, it is arranged . . . No, there will be no difficulty there, I am sure.' As he spoke he was looking at the palm of his hand, he saw the tiny beads of perspiration appear on his skin and an expression of disgust tightened his lips.

'I am fully aware of the consequences. I tell you, I know.'

He closed his eyes and listened for another minute without moving as the receiver squawked and clacked, then he opened his eyes.

'It will be done in good time, I assure you. Goodbye.'

He hung up and went to wash his hands. Now, he thought, as he worked up lather, to get it past the old man.

11

He was old now, seventy-eight long hard years old. His hair and his eyebrows were creamy white. His skin was folded and creased, freckled and spotted, hanging in unexpected little pouches under his chin and eyes.

His body had dried out, so he stood gaunt and stooped like a tree that has taken a set before the prevailing winds; but there was still the underlying urgency in the way he held himself, the same urgency that had earned him the name of 'Hurry' Hirschfeld when first he bustled into the gold fields sixty years ago.

On this Monday morning he was standing before the full length windows of his penthouse office, looking down on the city of Johannesburg. Reef House stood shoulder to massive shoulder with the Schlesinger Building on the Braamfontein ridge above the city proper. From this height it seemed that Johannesburg cowered at Hurry Hirschfeld's feet, as well it should.

Long ago, even before the great depression of the thirties, he had ceased to measure his wealth in terms of money. He owned outright a little over a quarter of the issued share capital of Central Rand Consolidated. At the present market price of R120 per share, this was a staggering sum. In addition, through a complicated arrangement of trusts, proxy rights and interlocking directorates, he had control of a further massive block of twenty per cent of the company's voting rights.

The overhead intercom pinged softly into this room of soft fabrics and muted colours, and Hurry started slightly.

'Yes,' he said, without turning away from the window.

'Dr Steyner is here, Mr Hirschfeld,' his secretary's voice whispered, ghostly and disembodied into the luscious room.

'Send him in,' snapped Hurry. That goddamned intercom always gave him the creeps. The whole goddamned room gave him the creeps. It was, as Hurry had said often and loudly, like a fairy brothel.

For fifty-five years he had worked in a bleak uncarpeted office with a few yellowing photographs of men and machinery on its walls. Then they had moved him in here–he glanced around the room with the distaste that five years had not lulled. What did they think he was, a bloody ladies' hairdresser?

The panelling door slid noiselessly aside and Dr Manfred Steyner stepped neatly into the room.

'Good morning, Grandfather,' he said. For ten years, ever since Terry had been bird-brained enough to marry him, Manfred Steyner had called Hurry Hirschfeld that, and Hurry hated it. He remembered now that Manfred Steyner was also responsible for the design and decor of Reef House, and therefore the author of his recent irritation.

'What ever it is you want–No!' he said, and he moved across to the air-conditioning controls. The thermostat was already set at 'high', now Hurry turned it to 'highest'. Within minutes the room would be at the correct temperature for growing orchids.

'How are you this morning, Grandfather?' Manfred seemed not to have heard, his expression was bland and neutral as he moved to the desk and laid out his papers.

'Bloody awful,' said Hurry. It was impossible to disconcert the little prig, he thought, you might as well shout insults at an efficiently functioning piece of machinery.

'I am sorry to hear that.' Manfred took out his handkerchief and touched his chin and forehead. 'I have the weekly reports.'

Hurry capitulated and went across to the desk. This was business. He sat down and read quickly. His questions were abrupt, cutting and instantly answered, but Manfred's handkerchief was busy now, swabbing and dabbing. Twice he removed his spectacles and wiped steam from the lens.

'Can I turn the air-conditioning down a little, Grandfather?'

'You touch it and I'll kick your arse,' said Hurry without looking up.

Another five minutes and Manfred Steyner stood up suddenly.

'Excuse me, Grandfather.' And he shot across the office and disappeared into the adjoining bathroom suite. Hurry cocked his head to listen, and when he heard the taps hiss he grinned happily. The air-conditioning was the only method he had discovered of disconcerting Manfred Steyner, and for ten years he had been experimenting with various techniques.

'Don't use all the soap,' he shouted gleefully. 'You are the one always on about office expenses!'

It did not seem ludicrous to Hurry that one of the richest and most influential men in Africa should devote so much time and energy to baiting his personal assistant.

At eleven o'clock Manfred Steyner gathered his papers and began packing them carefully in his monogrammed pigskin briefcase.

'About the appointment of a new General Manager for the Sonder Ditch to replace Mr Lemmer. You will recall my memo regarding the appointment of younger men to key positions–'

'Never read the bloody thing,' lied Hurry Hirschfeld. They both knew he read everything, and remembered it.

'Well–' Manfred went on to enlarge his thesis for a minute, then ended, 'In view of this, my department, myself concurring entirely, urges the appointment of Rodney Barry Ironsides, the present Underground Manager, to the position. I hoped that you would initial the recommendation and we can put it through at Friday's meeting.'

Dextrously Manfred slid the yellow memo in front of Hurry Hirschfeld, unscrewed the cap of his pen and offered it to him. Hurry picked the memo up between thumb and forefinger as though it were someone's dirty handkerchief and dropped it into the waste-paper bin.

'Do you wish me to tell you in detail what you and your planning department can do?' he asked.

'Grandfather,' Manfred admonished him mildly, 'you cannot run the company as though you were a robber baron. You cannot ignore the team of highly trained men who are your advisers.'

'I've run it that way for fifty years. You show me who's going to change that.' Hurry leaned back in his chair with vast satisfaction and fished a powerful-looking cigar out of his inner pocket.

'Grandfather, that cigar! The doctor said–'

'And I said Fred Plummer gets the job as Manager of the Sonder Ditch.'

'He goes on pension next year,' protested Manfred Steyner.

'Yes,' Hurry nodded. 'But how does that alter the position?'

'He's an old dodderer,' Manfred tried again, there was a desperate edge to his voice. He had not anticipated one of the old man's whims cutting across his plans.

'He's twelve years younger than I am,' growled Hurry ominously. 'How's that make him an old dodderer?'

12

Now that the weekend was over, Rod found the apartment oppressive, and he longed to get out of it.

He shaved, standing naked before the mirror, and he caught a whiff of the reeking ashtrays and half-empty glasses in the lounge. The char would have her customary Monday-morning greeting when she came in later today. From Louis Botha Avenue the traffic noise was starting to build up and he glanced at his watch–six o'clock in the morning. A good time to examine your soul, he decided, and leaned forward to watch his own eyes in the mirror.

'You're too old for this type of living,' he told himself seriously. 'You've had four years of it now, four years since the divorce, and that's about enough. It would be nice now to go to bed with the same woman on two consecutive nights.'

He rinsed his razor, and turned on the taps in the shower cabinet.

'Might even be able to afford it, if our boy Manfred delivers the goods.' Rod had not allowed himself to believe too implicitly in Manfred Steyner's promise; but during the whole of these last two days the excitement had been there beneath the cynicism.

He stepped into the shower and soaped himself, then turned the cold tap full on. Gasping he shut it off and reached for his towel. Still drying himself, he went through and stood at the foot of the bed; as he towelled himself he examined the girl who lay among the tousled sheets.

She was tanned dark toffee brown so she appeared to be dressed in white transparent bra and panties where the skin was untouched by the sun. Her hair was a blonde-gold flurry across her face and the pillow, at odds with the jet black triangle of body hair. Her lips in sleep were fixed in a soft pink pout, and she looked disquietingly young. Rod had to make a conscious effort to remember her name, she was not the companion with whom he had begun the week-end.

'Lucille,' he said, sitting down beside her. 'Wake up. Time to roll.'

She opened her eyes.

'Good morning,' he said and kissed her gently.

'Mmm.' She blinked. 'What time is it? I don't want to get fired.'

'Six,' he told her.

'Oh, good. Plenty of time.' And she rolled over and snuggled down into the sheets.

'Like hell.' He slapped her bottom lightly. 'Move, girl, can you cook?'

'No–' She lifted her head. 'What's your name again?' she asked.

'Rod,' he told her.

'That's right–Piston Rod,' she giggled. 'What a way to die! Are you sure you aren't powered by steam?'

'How old are you?' he asked.

'Nineteen. How old are you?'

'Thirty-eight.'

'Daddy, you're vintage!' she told him vehemently.

'Yes, sometimes I feel that way.' He stood up. 'Let's go.'

'You go. I'll lock up when I leave.'

'No sale,' he said, the last one he had left in the flat had cleaned it out–groceries, liquor, glasses, towels, even the ashtrays. 'Five minutes to dress.'

Fortunately she lived on his way. She directed him to a run-down block of flats under the mine dumps at Booysens.

'I'm putting three blind sisters through school. You want to help?' she asked as he parked the Maserati.

'Sure.' He eased a five-Rand note out of his wallet and handed it to her.

'Ta muchly.' And she slipped out of the red leather seat, closed the door and walked away. She did not look back before she disappeared into the block, and Rod felt an unaccountable wave of loneliness wash over him. It was so intense that he sat quiescent for a full minute before he could throw it off, then he hit the gears and screeched away from the kerb.

'My little five-Rand friend,' he said. 'She really cares!'

He drove fast, so that as he topped the Kraalkop ridge the shadows were still long, and the dew lay silver on the grass. He pulled the Maserati into a layby and climbed out. Leaning against the bonnet he lit a cigarette, grimacing at the taste, and looked down at the valley.

There was no natural surface indication of the immense treasure house that lay below. It was like any of the other countless grassy plains of the Transvaal. In the centre stood the town of Kitchenerville, which for half a century had rejoiced in the fact that Lord Kitchener had camped one night there in pursuit of the wily Boer: a collection of three dozen buildings which had expanded miraculously into three thousand, around a magnificent town hall and shopping complex. Dressed in public lawns and gardens, wide streets and bright new houses, all of it paid for by the mining houses whose lease areas converged on the town.

Out of the bleak veld surrounding the town their headgears stood like colossal monuments to the gold hunger of man. Around the headgears clustered the plants and work-shops. There were fourteen headgears in the valley. The field was divided into five lease areas, following the original farm titles, and was mined by five separate companies. Thornfontein Gold Mining, Blaauberg Gold Mining, West Tweefontein Mining, Deep Gold Levels, and the Sonder Ditch Gold Mining Company.

It was to this last that Rod naturally directed his attention.

'You beauty,' he whispered, for in his eyes the mountainous dumps of blue rock beside the shafts were truly beautiful. The complex but carefully thought out pattern of the works buildings, even the sulphur-yellow acres of the slimes dam, had a functional beauty.

'Get it for me, Manfred,' he spoke aloud. 'I want it. I want it badly.'

On the twenty-eight square miles of the Sonder Ditch's property lived fourteen thousand human beings, twelve thousand of them were Bantu who had been recruited from all over Southern Africa. They lived in the multi-storied hostels near the shaft heads, and each day they went down through two small holes in the ground to depths that were scarcely credible, and came up again out of those same two holes. Twelve thousand men down, twelve thousand up. That was not all: out of those two same holes came ten thousand tons of rock daily, and down them went timber and tools and piping and explosive, ton upon ton of material and equipment. It was an undertaking that must evoke pride in the men who accomplished it.

Rod glanced at his watch, 7.35 a.m. They were down already, all twelve thousand of them. They had started going down at three-thirty that morning and now it was accomplished. The shift was in. The Sonder Ditch was breaking rock, and bringing the stuff out.

Rod grinned happily. His loneliness and depression of an hour ago were gone, swallowed up in the immensity of his involvement. He watched the massive wheels of the headgears spinning, stopping briefly, and then spinning again.

Each of those shafts had cost fifty million Rand, the surface plant and works another fifty million. The Sonder Ditch represented an investment of one hundred and fifty million Rand, two hundred and twenty million dollars. It was big, and it would be his.

Rod flicked away the butt of his cigarette. As he drove down the ridge, his eyes moved eastward down the valley. All mining activity ceased abruptly along an imaginary north-south line, drawn arbitrarily across the open grassland. There was no surface indication why this should be so, but the reason was deep down.

On that line ran a geological freak, a dyke, a wall of hard serpentine rock that had been named 'the Big Dipper'. It cut through the field like an axe stroke, and beyond it was bad ground. The gold reef existed in the bad ground, they knew this; but not one of the five companies had gone after it. They had prospected it tentatively and then shied away from it, for the boreholes that they sank were frightening in their inconsistency.

A big percentage of the Sonder Ditch lease area lay on the far side of the Dipper, and there was a diamond-drilling team working there now. They had already completed five holes.

Rod could remember accurately the results:

Borehole	S.D. No. 1.	Abandoned in water at 4,000 ft.
	S.D. No. 2.	Abandoned in dry hole at 5,250 ft.
	S.D. No. 3.	Intersected carbon leader reef at 6,600 ft.
	Assay valve	27,323 inch penny-weights.
	First deflection	6,212 inch penny-weights.
	Second deflection	2,114 inch penny-weights.
	S.D. No. 4.	Abandoned in artesian water at 3,500 ft.
	S.D. No. 5.	Intersected carbon leader at 8,116 ft.
	Assay valve	562 inch penny-weights.

And they were drilling the deflections on that one now.

The problem was to build up a picture from the results like that. It looked like a mess of faulted and water-logged ground with the gold reef fragmented and fluky, showing unbelievably high values at one spot, and then more than likely pinching out fifty feet away.

They may mine it one day, thought Rod, but I hope to hell I'm on pension by the time they do.

In the distance beyond the slimes dam he could just make out the spidery triangle of the drilling rig against the grown grass.

'Go to it, boys,' he muttered. 'Whatever you find there won't make much difference to me.'

And he went in through the imposing gates at the entrance to the mine property, halting carefully at the stop sign where the railway line crossed the road and he forked two fingers at the traffic policeman lurking behind the gates.

The traffic cop grinned and waved, he had caught Rod the previous week, so he was still one up.

Rod drove down to his office.

13

That Monday morning Allen 'Popeye' Worth was preparing to drill his first deflection on the S.D. No. 5 borehole. Allen was a Texan–not a typical Texan. He stood five feet four inches tall, but was as tough as the steel drill with which he worked. Thirty years before he had started learning his trade on the oilfields around Odessa and he had learned it well.

Now he could start at the surface and drill a four-inch hole down thirteen thousand feet through the earth's crust, keeping the hole straight all the way, an almost impossible task if you took into account the whippiness and torque in a jointed rod of steel that long.

If, as happened occasionally, the steel snapped and broke off thousands of feet down, Allen could fit a fishing tool on the end of his rig, and patiently grope for the stump, find it, grapple it and pull it out of the borehole. When he hit the reef down there, he could purposely kick his drill off the line and pierce the reef again and again to sample it over an area of hundreds of feet. This was what was meant by deflecting.

Allen was one of the best. He could command his own salary and behave like a prima donna, and his bosses would still fawn on him, for the things he could do with a diamond drill were almost magical.

Now he was assessing the angle of his first deflection. The previous day he had lowered a long brass bottle to the end of his borehole and left it overnight. The bottle was half filled with concentrated sulphuric acid, and it had etched the brass of the bottle. By measuring the angle of the etching he knew just how his drill was branching off from his original hole.

In the tiny wood and iron building beside the drilling rig he finished his measurements and stood back from the work bench, grunting with satisfaction.

From his hip pocket he drew a corncob pipe and pouch. Once he had stuffed tobacco into the pipe and lit it, it became very clear as to why his nickname was 'Popeye'. He was a dead ringer for the cartoon character, aggressive jaw, button eyes, battered maritime cap and all.

He puffed contentedly, watching through the single window of the shack as his gang went about the tedious business of lowering the drilling bit down into the earth. Then he took the pipe from his mouth and spat accurately through the window, replaced the pipe and stooped to minutely check his measurements.

His foreman driller interrupted him from the doorway.

'On bottom, and ready to turn, boss.'

'Huh!' Popeye checked his watch. 'Two hours forty to get down, you don't reckon to rupture a gut do you?'

'That's not bad,' protested the foreman.

'And it sure as hell isn't good either! Okay, okay, cut the cackle and let's get her turning.' He bounced out of the shed and set off for the rig, darting quick beady little glances about him. The rig was a fifty-foot high tower of steel girders and within it the drill rod hung down until it disappeared into the collar. The twin two hundred-horsepower diesel engines throbbed expectantly, waiting to provide the power, their exhausts smoking blue in the early morning sunlight. Beside the rig lay a mountainous heap of drilling rods, beyond them the ten thousand-gallon puddling reservoir to provide water for the hole. Water was pumped into the hole continuously to cool and lubricate the tool as it cut into the rock.

'Stand by to turn her,' Popeye called to his gang, and they moved to their stations. Dressed in blue overalls, coloured fibreglass helmets, and leather gloves, they stood ready and tensed. This was an anxious moment for the whole team, power had to be applied with a lover's touch to the mile and a half length of rod, or it would buckle and snap.

Popeye climbed nimbly up onto the collar, and glanced about him to make sure all was in readiness. The foreman driller was at his controls, watching Popeye with complete absorption, his hands resting on the levers.

'Power up!' shouted Popeye and made the circular motion with his right hand. The diesels bellowed harshly, and Popeye reached out to lay his left hand on the drilling rod. This was how he did it, feeling the rod with his bare hand as he brought in the power, judging the tension by ear and eye and touch.

His right hand gestured and the foreman delicately let in the clutch, the rod moved under Popeye's hand, he gestured again and it revolved slowly. He could feel it was near breaking point and he cut down the power instantly, then let it in again. His right hand moved eloquently, expressively as an orchestral conductor, and the foreman followed it, the junior member of a highly skilled team.

Slowly the tension of the gang relaxed as the revolutions of the drill built up steadily, until Popeye gave the clenched fist 'okay' and jumped down from the collar. They scattered casually to their other duties, while Popeye and the foreman strolled back to the shed, leaving the drill to grind away at a steady four hundred revolutions a minute.

'Got something for you,' said the foreman, as they entered the shed.

'What?' demanded Popeye.

'The latest *Playboy*.'

'You're kidding!' Popeye accused him delightedly, but the foreman fished the rolled magazine out of his lunch box.

'Hey, there!' Popeye snatched it from him and turned immediately to the coloured foldout.

'Isn't that something!' He whistled. 'This dolly could get a job in a stockyard beating the oxen to death with her boo-boos!'

The foreman joined the discussion of the young lady's anatomy, and so neither of them noticed the change in the sound of the drill until two minutes had passed. Then Popeye heard it through the erotic haze. He flung the magazine from him, and went through the door of the shed white-faced.

It was fifty yards from the shed to the rig, but even at that distance Popeye could see the vibration in the drilling rod. He could hear the labouring note of the diesels as they carried increased load, and he ran like a fox terrier, trying to reach the controls and shut off the engines before it happened.

He knew what it was. His drill had cut into one of the many fissures with which this badly faulted ground was criss-crossed. The puddling water from his borehole had drained away leaving the bit to run dry against dry rock. The friction head had built up, the dust from the cut was not being washed away–and in consequence the rod had jammed. It was being held tightly at one end while at the other the two big diesels were straining to turn it. The whole rig was seconds away from a twist off.

There should have been an operator at the controls to meet just such an emergency, but he was a hundred yards away, just emerging from the wood and iron latrine beyond the puddling dam. He was desperately trying to hoist his pants, clinch the buckle of his belt and run all at the same time.

'You whore's chamberpot!' roared Popeye, as he ran. 'What the hell you goofing off–'

The words choked off in his throat, for as he reached the door of the engine room there was a report like a cannon shot as the rod snapped, and immediately the diesels screamed into over-rev as they were relieved of the load. Just too late, Popeye punched the earth buttons on the magnetos, and the engines spluttered into silence.

In that silence Popeye was sobbing with exertion and frustration and anger.

'A twist-off,' he sobbed. 'A deep one. Oh no! God, no!' It might take two weeks to fish out the broken rod, pump cement into the fissure to seal it, and then start again.

He removed the cap from his head, and with all his strength hurled it on the engine room floor. He then proceeded to jump on it with both feet. This was standard procedure. Popeye jumped on his cap at least once a week, and the foreman knew that when he had finished doing that he would then assault anybody within range.

Quietly the foreman slipped behind the wheel of the Ford truck, and the rest of the gang scrambled aboard. They all bumped away down the rutted track. There was a roadhouse on the main road where they went for coffee at times like this. When the mists of rage had dispersed sufficiently from his mind for Popeye to start seeking a human sacrifice, he looked about to find the drilling area strangely still and deserted.

'Stupid bunch of yellow-bellied baboons!' he bellowed in frustration after the retreating truck, and, as the next best thing, went to the shed to phone his Managing Director.

This gentleman sitting in the air-conditioned offices of 'Hart Drilling and Cementation' high above Rissik Street in Johannesburg was a little taken aback to learn from Popeye Worth that he, the Managing Director, was directly responsible for the twist-off of an expensive diamond drill at the Sonder Ditch No. 5 hole.

'If you used that sack of custard that passes for a brain, you'd fight shy of trying to sink holes into this bunch of knitting.' Popeye yelled into the mouthpiece. 'I'd prefer to stick my old man into a meat grinder, than put a drill into this ground. It stinks, I tell you! It's really ugly down there. God help the poor son of a bitch who tries to mine it!'

He slammed down the phone and stuffed his pipe with trembling fingers. Ten minutes later his breathing had returned to normal and his hands were steady. He picked up the phone again and dialled the number of the roadhouse. The proprietor answered.

'José, tell my boys it's okay, they can come home now,' said Popeye.

14

For Rod Ironsides there was more excitement than usual in meeting and solving the dozen paper problems that lay on his desk to welcome him back to the office. As he worked he kept remembering that Manfred Steyner might be able to do it, might just be able to do it.

The Sonder Ditch might really belong to him soon. He dispatched the last problem and lay back in his swivel chair. His mind was clear of the last cobwebs of dissipation and, as always, he felt purged and cleansed.

If I get her, I'll make her the star performer in the whole field, he thought greedily, they'll talk about the Sonder Ditch from Wall Street to the Bourse, and about the man who is running her. I know how to do it too. I'll cut the costs to the bone, I'll tighten her up solid. Frank Lemmer was a good man, he could get the stuff out of the ground, but he let it creep up on him. It cost him almost nine Rand a ton to mill it.

Well, I'll get it out as well as he did *and* I'll get it out cheaper. An operation takes its temperament from the man at the head. Frank Lemmer would talk about costs every now and then, but he didn't mean it and we knew he didn't mean it. We have become a wasteful operation because we are on a rich reef, we have become big spenders. Well, I'm going to talk costs, and I'll skin the arse of anybody who thinks I'm joking.

Last year Hamilton at Western Holdings kept his working costs per ton milled down to just a touch over six Rand. I could do the same here! I could jump our profits twelve million Rand in one year, if only they give me the job I'll shout the Sonder Ditch's name across the financial markets of the world.

The problem that Rod was pondering was the nightmare of the gold mining industry. Since the 1930's the price of gold had been fixed at $35 a fine ounce. Each year since then the cost of mining had crept up steadily. In those days they reckoned four penny-weights of gold in a ton of ore was payable value. Now around eight penny-weights was the marginal value.

So in the interim all those millions of tons of ore whose values fell between four and eight penny-weights had been placed beyond the reach of man until such time as they increased the price of gold.

There were many mines with vast reserves of gold-bearing ore, millions in bullion, whose values lay just below the magical number eight. Those mines stood deserted and forlorn, rust reddening their headgears, and the corrugated iron roofs of the buildings collapsing wearily. Rising costs had shot the guts out of them, they were condemned by the single word 'UNPAY'.

The Sonder Dam was running twenty to twenty-five penny-weights per ton. She was fat, but she could be fatter, Rod decided.

There was a knock at the door.

'Come in!' called Rod, and looked at his watch. It was nine o'clock already. Time for the Monday meeting of his mine captains.

They came in singly and in pairs, twelve of them. These were Rod's front-line men, his combat officers. They went down there each day, each to his own section and directed the actual assault on the rock.

While they chatted idly, waiting for the meeting to begin, Rod looked them over surreptitiously and was reminded of a remark that Herman Koch of

Anglo American had made to him once.

'Mining is a hard game, and it attracts a hard breed of men.'

These were men of the hard breed, physically and mentally tough, and Rod realized with a start that he was one of them. No, more than one of them. He was their leader, and with a fierce affection and pride he opened the meeting.

'Right, let's hear your gripes. Who is going to be first to break my heart?'

There are some men with a talent for controlling, and getting the very best results out of other men. Rod was one of them. It was more than his physical size, his compelling voice and hearty chuckle. It was a special magnetism, a personal charm and unerring sense of timing. Under his Chairmanship the meeting would erupt, voices crackle and snap, then subside into chuckles and nods as Rod spoke.

They knew he was as tough as they were, and they respected that. They knew that when he spoke it made sense, so they listened. They knew that when he promised, he delivered, so they were placated. And they knew that when he made a decision or judgement, he acted upon it, so every man knew exactly where he stood.

If asked, any one of these mine captains would have admitted grudgingly that 'there was no bulldust in Ironsides'. This was the equivalent of a presidential citation.

'Very well then.' Rod terminated the meeting. 'You have spent a good two hours of the company's time beating your gums. Now, will you kindly haul arse, go down there and start sending the stuff out.'

15

As these men planned the week's operation, so their men were at work in the earth below them.

On 87 level, Kowalski moved like a great bear down the dimly-lit drive. He had switched off the lamp on his helmet, and he moved without sound, lightly for a man of such bulk. He heard their voices ahead of him in the dimly-lit tunnel, and he paused, listening intently. There was no sound of shovel crunching into loose rock, and Kowalski's Neanderthal features convulsed into a fearsome scowl.

'Bastards!' he muttered softly. 'They think I am in stopes, hey? They think it all right if they sit on fat black bum, no move da bloody rock, hey?'

He started forward again, a bear on cat's feet.

'They find plenty different from what they bloody think, soon!' he threatened.

He stepped around the angle of the drive and flashed his lamp. There were three men Kowalski had put on lashing, shovelling the loose stuff from the footwall into waiting cocopans. Two of them sat against the cocopan, smoking contentedly while the third regaled them with an account of a beer drink he had attended the previous Christmas. Their shovels and sledge hammers leaned unemployed against the side wall of the drive.

All three of them froze into rigidity as the beam of Kowalski's lamp played over them.

'So!' The word burst explosively from Kowalski, and he snatched up a fourteen-pound hammer in one massive fist, reversed it and struck the butt of the handle against the foot wall. The steel head of the hammer fell off and Kowalski was left with a four foot length of selected hickory in his hand.

'You, boss boy!' he bellowed, and his free hand shot out and fastened on the throat of the nearest Bantu. With one heave he jerked him off his feet onto his knees and began dragging him away up the drive. Even in his rage, Kowalski was making sure there were no witnesses. The other two men sat where they were, too horrified to move, while their companion's wails and cries receded into the darkness.

Then the first blow reverberated in the confined space of the drive, followed immediately by a shriek of pain.

The next blow, and another shriek.

The crack, thud, crack, thud, went on repeatedly, but the accompanying shrieks dwindled into moans and soft whimperings, then into complete silence.

Kowalski came back down the drive alone, he was sweating heavily in the lamp light, and the handle of the hammer in his hand was black and glistening with wet blood.

He threw it at their feet.

'Work!' he growled, and was gone, big and bearlike, into the shadows.

16

On 100 level, Joseph M'Kati was hosing down and sweeping the spillings from under the giant conveyor belt. Joseph had been on this job for five years, and he was a contented and happy man.

Joseph was a Shangaan approaching sixty years of age, the first frost was touching his hair. There were laughter lines around his eyes and at the corner of his mouth. He wore his helmet pushed to the back of his head, his overalls were hand-embroidered and ornamentally patched in blue and red, and he moved with a jaunty bounce and strut.

The conveyor was many hundreds of yards long. From all the levels above the shattered gold reef was scraped from the stopes and trammed back down the haulages in the cocopans. Then from the cocopans it was tipped into the mouths of the ore-passes. These were vertical shafts that dropped down to 100 level, hundreds of feet through the living rock to spew the reef out onto the conveyor belt. A system of steel doors regulated the flow of rock onto the conveyor, and the moving belt carried it down to the shaft and dumped it into the enormous storage bins. From there it was fed automatically into the ore cage in fifteen-ton loads and carried at four-minute intervals to the surface.

Joseph worked on happily beneath the whining conveyor. The spillings were small, but important. Gold is strange in its behaviour, it moves downwards. Carried by its own high specific gravity it works its way down through almost any other material. It would find any crack or irregularity in the floor and work its way into it. It would disappear into the solid earth itself if left long enough.

It was this behaviour of gold that accounted in some measure for Joseph M'Kati's contentment. He had worked his way to the end of the conveyor, washing and sweeping, and now he straightened, laid his bast broom aside and rubbed his kidneys with both hands, looking quickly around to make certain that there was no one else in the conveyor tunnel. Beside him was the ore storage bin into which the conveyor was emptying its load. The bin could hold many thousands of tons.

Satisfied that he was alone, Joseph dropped onto his hands and knees and crawled under the storage bin, ignoring the continuous roar of rock into the bin above him, working his way in until he reached the holes.

It had taken Joseph many months to chisel the heads off four of the rivets that held the seam in the bottom of the bin, but once he had done it, he had succeeded in constructing a simple but highly effective heavy media separator.

Free gold in the ore that was dumped into the storage bin immediately and rapidly worked its way down through the underlying rock, its journey accelerated by the vibration of the conveyor and bin as more reef was dropped. When the gold reached the floor of the bin, it sought an avenue through which to continue its downward journey, and it found Joseph's four rivet holes, beneath which he had spread a square polythene sheet.

The gold-rich fines made four conical piles on the sheet of polythene, looking exactly like powdered black soot.

Crouched beneath the bin, Joseph carefully transferred the black powder to his tobacco pouch, replaced the polythene to catch the next filtering, stuffed the pouch into his hip pocket, and scrambled out from under the bin. Whistling a tribal planting tune Joseph picked up his broom and returned to the endless job of sweeping and hosing.

17

Johnny Delange was marking his shot holes. Lying on his side in the low stope of 27 section he was calculating by eye the angle and depth of a side cutter blast to straighten a slight bulge in his longwall.

In the Sonder Ditch they were on a single blast. One daily, centrally fired, blast. Johnny was paid on *fathomage,* the cubic measure of rock broken and taken out of his stope. He must, therefore, position his shot holes to achieve the maximum disruption and blow-out from the face.

'So,' he grunted, and marked the position of the hole in red paint. 'And so.' With one bold stroke of the paint brush he set the angle on which his machine boy was to drill.

'Shaya, madoda!' Johnny clapped the shoulder of the black man beside him. 'Hit it, man.'

Machine boys were selected for stamina and physique, this one was a Greek sculpture in glistening ebony.

'Nkosi!' The machine boy grinned an acknowledgement, and with his assistant lugged his rock drill into position. The drill looked like a gargantuan version of a heavy calibre machine gun.

The noise as the big Bantu opened the drill was shattering in the low-roofed, constricted space of the stope. The compressed air roared and fluttered into the drill, buffeting the eardrums. Johnny made the clenched-fist gesture of approval, and for a second they smiled at each other in the companionship of shared labour. Then Johnny crawled on up the stope to mark the next shot hole.

Johnny Delange was twenty-seven years old, and he was top rock breaker on the Sonder Ditch. His gang of forty-eight men were a tightly-knit team of specialists. Men fought each other for a place on 27 section, for that's where the money was. Johnny could pick and choose, so each month when the surveyors came in and measured up, Johnny Delange was way out ahead in fathomage.

Here was the remarkable position where the man at the lowest point of authority earned more than the man at the top. Johnny Delange earned more than the General Manager of the Sonder Ditch. Last year he had paid super-tax on an income of twenty-two thousand Rand. Even a miner like Kowalski, who brutalized and bullied his gang until he was left with the dregs of the mine, would earn eight or nine thousand Rand a year, about the same salary as an official of Rod Ironsides' rank.

Johnny reached the top of his longwall and painted in the last shot holes. Down the inclined floor of the stope below him all his drills were roaring, his machine boys lying or crouching behind them. He lay there on one elbow, removed his helmet and wiped his face, resting a moment.

Johnny was an extraordinary-looking young man. His long jet black hair was swept back and tied with a leather thong at the back of his head in a curlicue. His features were those of an American Indian, gaunt and bony. He had cut the sleeves out of his overalls to expose his arms–arms as muscular and sinuous as pythons, tattooed below the elbows, immensely powerful and supple. His body was the same, long and sinewy and powerful.

On his right hand he wore eight rings, two on each finger, and it was clear from the design of the rings that they were not merely ornamental. They were heavy gold rings with skull and cross-bones, wolves' heads and other irregularities worked into them, a mass of metal that formed a permanent knuckle-duster. Of the big eyes in the one skull's head Rod Ironsides had once asked: 'Are those real rubies, Johnny?' And Johnny had replied seriously:

'If they aren't, then I've sure as hell been gypped out of three Rand fifty, Mr Ironsides.'

Johnny Delange had been a really wild youngster, until eight months ago. It was then he had met and married Hettie. Courtship and marriage occupying the space of one week. Now he was settling down very well. It was all of ten days since he had last fought anybody.

Lying in the stope he allowed himself five minutes to think about Hettie. She was almost as tall as he was, with a wondrously buxom body and chestnut red hair. Johnny adored her. He was not the best speechmaker in Kitchenerville when it came to expressing his affection, so he bought her things.

He bought her dresses and jewellery, he bought her a deep-freezer *and* a fifteen cubic foot Frigidaire, he bought her a Chrysler Monaco with leopard-skin upholstery and a Kenwood Chef. In fact, it was becoming difficult to enter the Delange household without tripping over at least one of Johnny's gifts to Hettie. The congestion was made more acute by the fact that living with them was Johnny's brother, Davy.

'Hell, man!' Happily Johnny shook his head. 'She's a bit of all-right, hey!'

There was an eye-level oven he had spotted in a furniture store in Kitchenerville the previous Saturday.

'She'll love that, man,' he muttered, 'and it's only four hundred Rand. I'll get it for her on pay day.'

The decision made, he clapped his helmet onto his head and began crawling out of the stope. It was time now to go up to the station and collect the explosives for the day's blast.

His boss boy should have been waiting for him in the drive, and Johnny was furious to find no sign of him nor the piccanin who was his assistant.

'Bastard!' he grunted, playing the beam of his lamp up and down the drive. 'He's been acting up like hell.'

The boss boy was a pock-marked Swazi, not a big man, but powerful for his size and highly intelligent. He was also a man of mean disposition, Johnny had never seen him smile, and for an extrovert Johnny it was galling to work with someone so sullen and taciturn. He tolerated the Swazi because of his drive and reliability, but he was the only man in the gang that Johnny disliked.

'Bastard!' The drive was deserted, the roar of the rock drills was muted.

'Where the hell is he?' Johnny scowled impatiently. 'I'll skin him when I find him.'

Then he remembered the latrine.

'That's where he is!' Johnny set off down the drive. The latrine was a rock chamber cut into the side of the drive, a flap of canvas served as a door; beyond was a regular four-holer over sanitary buckets.

Johnny pulled the canvas aside and stepped into the cubicle. The boss boy and his assistant were there. Johnny stared in surprise, for a moment not understanding what they were doing. They were so absorbed they were unaware of Johnny's presence.

Suddenly realization dawned, and Johnny's face tightened with revulsion and disgust.

'You filthy–' Johnny snarled, and catching the boss boy by the shoulders pulled him backwards and pinned him against the wall. He lifted his heavily metalled fist and drew it back ready to hurl it into the boss boy's face.

'Strike me and you know what happens,' said the boss boy softly, his expression flat and neutral, looking steadily into Johnny's eyes. Johnny hesitated. He knew the Company rules, he knew the Government labour officers' attitude, he knew what the police would do. If he hit him, they would crucify him.

'You are a pig!' Johnny hissed at him.

'You have a wife,' said the boss boy. 'My wife is in Swaziland. Two years I have not seen her.'

Johnny lowered his fist. Twelve thousand men, and no women. It was a fact. The actuality sickened him, but he understood why it happened.

'Get dressed.' He stepped back, releasing the boss boy. 'Get dressed both of you. Come to the station, I will meet you there.'

18

For a week now, since the fall of hanging in 43 section, Big King had been out of the stopes.

Rod had ordered it that way. The excuse was that Big King's white miner had been killed in the fall and now he must await an allocation to another section. In reality Rod wanted to rest him. He had seen the strain both physical and emotional that Big King had undergone during the rescue. When together they had unearthed the miner's corpse, the man with whom Big King had worked and laughed, Rod had seen the tears roll unashamedly down Big

King's cheeks as he picked up the body and held it easily against his chest.

'Hamba gahle, madoda,' Big King had muttered. 'Go in peace, man.'

Big King was a legend on the Sonda Ditch. They boasted about him; how much Bantu beer he could drink in a sitting, how much rock he could lash single-handed in a shift, how he could dance any other man off his feet. He had been awarded a total of over a thousand Rand in bravery awards. Big King set the pace, others tried to equal him.

Rod had put him in charge of a transport team. For the first few days Big King had enjoyed the opportunity of showing off his strength and socializing, for the transport team moved about the workings allowing Big King to visit most of his numerous friends during a shift. But now Big King was becoming bored. He wanted to get back into the stopes.

'This,' he told his transport team contemptuously, 'is work for old men and young women.' And with one snatch and lift he picked up a forty-four gallon drum of dieseline and unaided placed it on the platform of the loco.

A forty-four gallon drum of dieseline weighs a little over eight hundred pounds avoirdupois.

19

All this fuss for that, Davy Delange paused in his labour of tamping the Dynagel into the shot holes. He leaned forward to inspect the reef. In the face of the stope it was a black line, drawn against the blue quartz rock.

The Carbon Leader Reef, it was called. A thin layer of carbon never more than a few inches thick, more often half an inch. Black soot, that's what it was. Davy shook his head thoughtfully. You could not even see the gold in it.

Davy was two years older than his brother Johnny, and there was no physical or mental resemblance between the two of them. Davy's sandy hair was cropped into a conventional 'short back and sides'. He wore no personal jewellery, and his manner was quiet and reserved.

Johnny was tall and lean, David squat and muscular. Johnny was extravagant, Davy careful beyond the point of meannness. Their only common trait was that they were both first-class miners. If Johnny broke more rock than Davy, it was only because Davy was more careful than Johnny; he did not take the same chances, he observed all the safety procedures which Johnny frequently flouted.

Davy earned less money than Johnny, but saved every penny he could. It was for his farm, Davy was going to buy a farm one day. Already he had saved a little over R49,000 towards it. In five more years he would have enough. Then he could get himself a farm and a wife to help run it. Johnny, on the other hand, spent every penny he earned. He was usually in debt to Davy by the end of each month.

'Lend us a hundred 'till pay day, Davy.' Disapprovingly, Davy lent him the money. Davy disapproved of Johnny, his appearance, attire and habits.

Abandoning his microscopic inspection of the Carbon Leader Reef, Davy resumed tamping in the explosive, working carefully and precisely on this highly dangerous procedure. The sticks of explosive were charged with detonators and ready to burn. By law, nobody but the miner-in-charge could perform this operation, but Davy did it automatically while he thought about

Johnny's latest trespass. He had raised Davy's rent.

'A hundred Rand a month!' Davy protested aloud. 'I've got a good mind to move out and find my own digs.'

But he knew he would do no such thing. Hettie's cooking was too good, and her presence too feminine and alluring. Davy would stay on with them.

20

'Rod.' Dan Stander's voice was serious and low. 'I've got a nasty one for you.'

'Thanks for nothing.' Rod made his own voice weary and resigned as he spoke into the telephone. 'I'm just going on my underground tour. Can't it wait?'

'No,' Dan assured him. 'Anyway, it's on your way. I'm speaking from the first-aid station at the shaft head. Come across.'

'What is it?'

'Assault. White on Bantu.'

'Christ.' Rod jerked upright in his chair. 'Bad?'

'Ugly. Worked him over with the handle of a fourteen pound hammer. I've put in forty-seven stitches, but I am worried about a fracture of the skull.'

'Who did it?'

'Miner by the name of Kowalski.'

' Him!' Rod was breathing heavily. 'All right, Dan. Can he make a statement?'

'No. Not for a day or two.'

'I'll be there in a few minutes.'

Rod hung up the phone and crossed the office.

'Dimitri.'

'Boss?'

'Pull Kowalski out of the stopes. I want him in my office soonest. Put someone in to finish his shift.'

'Okay, Rod, what's the trouble?'

'He beat up one of his boys.'

Dimitri whistled softly, and Rod went on.

'Call personnel, get them onto the police.'

'Okay, Rod.'

'Have Kowalski here when I get back from my tour.'

Dan was waiting for him in the first-aid room.

'Take a look.' He indicated the figure on the stretcher. Rod knelt beside him, his mouth tightening into a thin pale line.

The catgut stitches lay neatly across the dark swollen gashes in the man's flesh. His one ear had been torn off, and Dan had sewn it back on. There was a black gap where teeth had been behind the swollen purple lips.

'You will be all right now.' Rod spoke gently, and the Bantu's eyes swivelled towards him. 'The man who did this will be punished.'

Rod stood up. 'Let me have a written report on his injuries, Dan.'

'I'll fix it. See you for a drink at the Club after work?'

'Sure,' said Rod, but underneath he was seething with anger, and it stayed with him during the whole of his underground tour.

21

Rod dropped straight down to 100 level. His first duty was to get the stuff out, and he wanted to check the reserve in the ore storage bins. He came into the long brightly-lit tunnel beneath the ore passes, and paused. The loaded conveyor belt whined monotonously, speeding the broken reef towards the bins.

The tunnel was deserted, except for the lonely figure of the sweeper at the far end. It was one of the phenomena of a well-run gold mine that in a tour through the workings you encountered so few human beings. Mile after mile of haulage and drive were silent and devoid of life, and yet there were twelve thousand men down here.

Rod set off towards the bins at the shaft end of the tunnel.

'Joseph,' he greeted the old sweeper with a smile.

'Nkosi.' Joseph ducked and bobbed with shy pleasure.

'All is well?' Rod asked. Joseph was one of Rod's favourites, he was always so cheerful, so uncomplaining, so patently honest and without guile. Rod always made a point of stopping to chat to him.

'It is well with me, Nkosi. Is it well with you?'

Rod's smile died suddenly, he had noticed the fine white powdering of dust on Joseph's upper lip.

'You old rogue!' he scolded him. 'How often must I tell you to hose down before you sweep? Water! You must use water!'

This was part of the ceaseless battle of the miner to keep down the dust.

'The dust will eat your lungs!'

Phthisis, the dread incurable occupational disease of the miner, caused by silica particles being drawn into the lungs and there solidifying.

Joseph grinned shamefaced, shifting from one foot to the other. He was always embarrassed by Rod's childish obsession with dust. In Joseph's opinion this was one of the few flaws in Rod Ironsides' character. Apart from this weird delusion that dust could hurt a man, he was a good boss.

'It is much harder to sweep wet dirt than dry dirt,' Joseph explained patiently. Rod never seemed to understand this self-evident fact, Joseph had to point it out to him every time they had this particular discussion.

'Listen to me, old man, without water the dust will enter your body.' Rod was exasperated. 'The dust will kill you!'

Joseph bobbed again, grinning at Rod to placate him.

'Very well, I will use plenty water.'

To prove it he picked up the hose and began spraying the floor with enthusiasm.

'That is good!' Rod encouraged him. 'Use plenty of water.' And Rod went on down to the storage bins.

When Rod was out of sight, Joseph turned off the hose and leaned on his broom.

'The dust will kill you!' he mimicked Rod, and chuckled merrily, shaking his head in wonder at the childishness of it.

'The dust will kill you!' he repeated, and burst into delighted laughter, slapping his thigh.

He did a few shuffling dance steps, it was so funny.

The dance steps were awkward, for under his trousers, strapped to the calves of both legs, were heavy polythene bags filled with gold fines from under the bins.

22

Rod stepped out of the Mary Anne at 85 level, and paused to watch Big King loading a baulk of timber onto the loco while his transport team stood back respectfully and watched him. Turning from his task Big King saw Rod standing on the station landing and marched up to him.

'I see you,' he greeted Rod. Big King was not one to make hasty judgements, it was only after the rescue operations in 43 section that he had decided Rod was a man. He was now ready to accept him as an equal.

'I see you also, King Nkulu.' Rod returned the greeting.

'Find me work with men. I sicken of this.'

'You will be back in the stopes before the week is ended,' Rod promised.

'You are my father,' Big King thanked him and went back to the transport team.

23

Johnny Delange saw the Underground Manager coming up the haulage towards him. There was no mistaking that tall wide-shouldered silhouette, nor the man's free swinging stride.

'Whee!' Johnny whistled with relief, grateful for the premonition that had warned him to pack the fifty-pound cardboard cartons of Dynagel into the explosives locker of the railway truck, rather than, as he usually did, pile them haphazard onto the platform in defiance of safety standards.

'Stop!' Johnny commanded the boss boy and his assistant who were pushing the truck, and it trundled to a halt beside Rod.

'Morning, Johnny.'

'Hello, Mr Ironsides.'

'How's it going?'

Johnny hesitated before replying, and immediately Rod was aware of the tension between the three men. He glanced at the two Swazis, they were sullen and apprehensive.

'There's been trouble,' he thought. 'Not like Johnny, he's too clever to let tension cut down his fathomage.'

'Well–' Johnny paused again. 'Look, Mr Ironsides, get rid of this bastard for me.' He jerked his thumb at the boss boy. 'Give me someone else.'

'What's the trouble?'

'No trouble, I just can't work with him.'

Rod raised an eyebrow in disbelief, but turned to the boss boy.

'Are you happy in this section, or do you want transfer?'

'I want transfer!' growled the boss boy.

'Right.' Rod was relieved, sometimes in a case like this the Swazi would refuse transfer. 'Tomorrow you will be told your new section.'

'Nkosi!' The boss boy glanced sideways at his assistant. 'It is the wish of my friend that he transfers with me.'

So that's it, Rod thought, the ever-present spectre which we must ignore because we can find no way to lay it. Johnny had probably caught them at it.

'Your friend shall go with you,' Rod nodded, telling himself that this was not condonation, but merely practical politics. If he separated them, the boss boy would pick on someone else who might not be receptive. Then there would be more trouble, stabbings, faction fighting.

'I'll get you a replacement,' he told Johnny, and then suddenly a thought occurred to him. My God, yes! What a team they would make!

'Johnny, how would you like Big King?'

'Big King!' Johnny's gaunt bony features split into a wide smile. 'Now you're talking, boss!'

24

At three o'clock Rod had finished his tour and was in the cage on the way to the surface. The cage was crowded, men pressed shoulder to shoulder, the stench of sweat almost overpowering. They were hauling shift now, the day's work was over, the stopes were scraped and washed down, the shot drilled and charged, the fuses connected into the electrical circuit.

The men were out of the stopes now, falling back in orderly companies and battalions along the haulages to the stations. There to wait patiently for their turn to enter the cages and be whisked to the surface.

Rod was mulling over the myriad problems he had encountered during the day, and the solutions he had dreamed up. He had opened a new section in the back pages of his notebook and headed it simply 'COSTS'.

Already there were two entries there. Let them give me the job, he thought fervently, just let me have it one month and I'll move the world.

'Mr Ironsides.' The man beside him spoke. Rod glanced down at him recognizing him.

'Hello, Davy.' It was remarkable how dissimilar the two brothers were.

'Mr Ironsides, my boss boy has worked his ticket. He's going home at the end of the month. Can you see that I get a good man to replace him?'

'Your brother's boss boy has asked for transfer. Will you take him?'

'Ja!' Davy Delange nodded. 'I know him, he's a good boy.'

And that takes care of one more detail, thought Rod, as he stepped out of the cage into a bright summer's afternoon and tasted the fresh sweet air with pleasure. Now there are only the butt ends of the day's work to tidy up. Then I can go and fetch the drink that Dan promised me.

Dimitri met him in the passage outside the office.

'I've got Kowalski in my office.'

'Good,' said Rod grimly. He went into his own office and sat on the edge of his desk.

'Send him in,' he called through to Dimitri.

Kowalski came through the door and stopped. He stood very still, his long arms hanging slackly at his side, his belly bulging out over his belt.

'You call me,' he muttered thickly, his English hardly intelligible. It was a peasant's face, coarse-featured, dull-eyed. He had not shaved, dirt from the stopes clung in the thick black stubble of beard.

'You beat a man today?' Rod asked softly.

'He no work,' Kowalski nodded. 'I beat him. Maybe next time his brothers they work. No bloody nonsense!'

'You're fired,' said Rod. 'Pull your time and get the hell off this property.'

'You fire?' Kowalski blinked in surprise.

'There will be criminal charges pressed against you by the company.' Rod went on. 'But in the meantime I want you off this property.'

'Police?' Kowalski growled. There was expression on his face now.

'Yes,' said Rod, 'police.'

The spade-sized hands at the end of Kowalski's arms balled slowly into massive fists.

'You call da bloody police!' He took a step towards the desk, big, menacing.

'Dimitri,' Rod called sharply, 'close the door,'

Dimitri had been listening intently, now he jumped up from his desk and closed the interleading door. He stood with his ear pressed to the panelling. For thirty seconds more there was the growl and mutter of voices, then suddenly a thud, a bellow, another thud and a shattering crash.

Dimitri winced theatrically.

'Dimitri!' Rod's voice, and he pushed the door open.

Rod sat on the edge of his desk, swinging one leg casually, he was sucking the knuckle of his right hand.

'Dimitri, tell them not to put so much polish on the floor. Our friend slipped and hit his jaw on the desk.'

Dimitri clucked sympathetically as he stood over the reclining bulk of the big Pole. Kowalski was snoring loudly through his mouth.

'Gave himself a nasty bump,' said Dimitri. 'Shame!'

25

Dr Steyner worked on quietly for the remainder of Monday morning. He favoured the use of a tape recorder, for this cut out human contact which Manfred found vaguely repellent. He disliked having to speak his thoughts to a female who sat opposite him with skirts up around her thighs, squirming her bottom and touching her hair. However, what he really could not abide was the odour. Manfred was very sensitive to smells, even his own body smell of perspiration disgusted him. Women, he found, had a peculiar cloying odour that he could detect beneath their perfume and cosmetics. It nauseated him. This was why he had insisted on separate bedrooms for Theresa and himself. Naturally he had not told her the reason, but had insisted instead that he was such a light sleeper that he could not share a room with another person.

His office was in white and ice-blue, the air clean and cold from the air-conditioning unit, his voice was crisp and impersonal, the whirr of the recorder subdued, and with the conscious portion of his mind Manfred was happily absorbed in his conjuring tricks with figures and money, past performance and future estimates, a three-dimensional structure of variables and contingencies which only a super-normal brain could visualize. But beneath it was a sense of disquiet, he was waiting, hanging in time, and the outward sign of his agitation was the way the fingers of his right hand ran up and down his thigh as he worked, a caressing narcissistic gesture.

A few minutes before noon the unlisted direct telephone on his desk rang, and the movement of his hand stilled. Only one caller could reach him here, only one caller had that number. For a few seconds he sat unmoving, delaying the moment, then deliberately he switched off the recorder and lifted the telephone.

'Dr Manfred Steyner.' He identified himself.

'You have got our man in?' the voice inquired.

'Not yet, Andrew.'

There was silence from the other end, a dangerous crackling silence.

'But there is no cause for alarm. It is nothing. A delay merely, not a setback.'

'How long?'

'Two days–at the latest by the end of the week.'

'You will be in Paris next week?'

'Yes.' Manfred was an adviser to the Government team which was to meet the French for gold price talks.

'He will meet you there. It would be best for you that your side of the bargain were completed by then. You understand?'

'I understand, Andrew.'

The discussion was ended, but Manfred interjected to prevent the caller from hanging up.

'Andrew!'

'Yes.'

'Will you ask him if–' Manfred's tone had changed almost imperceptibly, there was an obsequious edge in it. 'Ask him if I may play tonight, please, Andrew.'

'Wait.'

The minutes drifted by, and then the voice came back on the line.

'Yes, you may play. Simon will inform you of your limits.'

'Thank you. Tell him, thank you.'

Manfred made no effort to conceal his relief as he cradled the receiver. He sat beaming at the ice-blue paper on the far wall of his office, even his spectacles seemed to sparkle.

26

There were five men in the opulently furnished room. One of the men was subservient to the others, he was younger than they, attentive to their moods and wishes. Clearly he was a servant. Of the remaining four, one was just as obviously the host. He was seated at the focus of all their attention. He was fat, but not excessively so, the fat of good living not of gluttony. He was speaking, addressing himself to his three guests.

'You have expressed doubts as to reliability of the tool I intend using in the coming venture. I have arranged a demonstration which I hope will convince you that your concern is groundless. That is the reason for the invitation that Andrew here conveyed to you this afternoon.'

The host turned to the younger man. 'Andrew, would you be good enough to go through and wait for Dr Steyner to arrive, as soon as that happens, please let Simon seat him while you come through and inform us.' He gave his orders with dignity and courtesy, a man accustomed to command.

'Now, gentlemen, while we wait may I offer you a drink?'

The conversation that sprang up between the four of them as they sipped their drinks was knowledgeable, and extraordinarily well informed. At its roots was one subject: wealth. Mineral wealth, industrial wealth, the harvest of the land and the sea. Oil, steel, coal, fish, wheat and–gold.

There were clues to the stature of these men in the cut and quality of the cloth they wore, the sparkle of a stone on a finger, the tone of authority in a voice, the casual unaffected use of a high name.

'He is here, sir,' Andrew interrupted them from the doorway.

'Oh! Thank you, my boy.' The host stood up. 'Would you mind stepping this way, please, gentlemen?'

He crossed the room and drew aside one of the gold and maroon drapes. Behind it was a window.

The four men clustered about the window and looked through into the room beyond. It was a gaming room of an expensive gambling establishment. There were men and women sitting about a baccarat table, and none of them so much as glanced up at the window overlooking them.

'This is a one-way glass, gentlemen,' the host explained. 'So you need not worry about being seen in such a den of iniquity.'

They chuckled politely.

'What kind of profit does this place show you?' one of them asked.

'My dear Robert!' The host feigned shock. 'You don't for a moment believe that I would be in any way associated with an illegal undertaking?'

This time they chuckled with genuine amusement.

'Ha!' explained the host. 'Here he is.'

Across the gaming room Dr Manfred Steyner was being ushered to a seat at the table by a tall sallow-faced young man, who in his evening dress looked like an undertaker.

'I have asked Simon to place him so that you may watch his face as he plays.'

They were intent now, leaning forward slightly scrutinizing the man as he arranged the plaques that Simon had stacked at his elbow.

Dr Manfred Steyner began to play. His face was completely devoid of expression, but the pallor was startling. Every few seconds the pink tip of his tongue slipped out between his lips, then disappeared again. In the intervals between each coup, there was a reptilian stillness about him, the stillness of a lizard or an iguana. Only a pulse beat steadily in his throat and his spectacles glittered like a snake's eyes.

'May I direct your attention to his right hand during the play of this coup,' the host murmured, and all their eyes flicked downwards.

Manfred's right hand lay open beside the pile of his chips, but as his card was laid before him so his fingers closed.

'*Carte.*' Soundlessly he mouthed the word, and now his hand was a fist, the knuckles whitened, the tension was so fierce that his fist trembled. Yet, still his face was neutral.

The banker flipped his card.

'*Sept!*' The croupier's mouth formed the number. He faced Manfred's card, then he swept Manfred's stake away. Manfred's hand flopped open and lay soft and hairless as a dead fish on the green baize.

'Let us leave him to his pleasures,' suggested the host and drew the curtains across the window. They returned to their chairs, and they were strangely subdued.

'Jesus,' muttered one of the guests. 'That was ugly. I felt like a peeping tom, like watching someone, you know, pulling his pudding.'

The host glanced at him quickly, surprised at his perception.

'In effect, that is exactly what you were watching,' he told him. 'You will excuse me playing the role of lecturer, but I know a little about this man. It cost me nearly four hundred Rand for an analytical report on him by one of our leading psychiatrists.'

The host paused, assuring himself of their complete attention.

'The reasons are obscure, probably arising from an event or series of events during the period in which Dr Steyner was an orphan wandering through the smoking ruins of war-torn Europe.' The host coughed, deprecating his own flight of oratory. 'Be that as it may. The results are there for all to see. Dr Manfred Kurt Steyner's intelligence quotient is a genius rating of 158. He neither smokes nor drinks. He has no hobbies, plays no sport, has never made so much as an improper remark to any woman other than his wife, and there is some doubt as to just how often or to what extent she is favoured by his attentions.' The host sipped his drink conscious of their intense interest. 'Mechanically, if that is the correct term, Dr Steyner is neither impotent nor deficient in his manhood. However, he finds all bodily contact, and especially the secretions that may arise from such contact, to be utterly loathsome. For arousal he relies on the baccarat cards, for release he might endure a brief contact with a member of the opposite sex, but more likely he would–oh, what was the expression you used, Robert?'

They absorbed this in silence.

'He is, to be precise, a compulsive gambler. He is also a compulsive loser.'

They stirred with disbelief.

'You mean he tries to lose?' demanded Robert incredulously.

'No,' The host shook his head. 'Not on the conscious level. He believes he is trying to win, but he lays bets against odds that, with his magnificent brain, he must realize are suicidal. It is a deep-seated sub-conscious need to lose, to be humiliated. A form of masochism.'

The host opened a black leather notebook and checked its contents.

'During the period from 1958 to 1963 Dr Steyner lost the total sum of R227,000 at this table. In 1964 he was able to arrive at an arrangement with his sole creditor to discharge the debt plus the accumulated interest.'

You could see the faces change as they rapidly searched their memories for a set of circumstances which would fit the dates and principals. Robert reached the correct deduction first. In 1964 their host has sold his majority holdings in the North Maun Copper Co. to C.R.C. at a price that could only be considered advantageous. Just prior to this Dr Steyner had been made head of finance and planning at C.R.C.

'North Maun Copper,' said Robert with admiration. That is how he had done it, the cunning old fox! He had forced Steyner to buy well above market value.

The host smiled softly, deferentially, neither confirming nor denying.

'Since 1964 to the present Dr Steyner has continued to patronize this establishment. His gambling losses for this further period amount to—' he consulted his notebook again, pretending surprise at the figure, 'to a touch over R300,000.'

They sighed and moved restlessly. Even to these men it was a very large sum of money.

'I think we can rely on him.' The host closed his notebook with a snap, and smiled around at them.

27

Theresa lay in the dark. The night was warm, the stillness spoiled only by the klonking of a frog down at the fishpond. The moonlight came in through the window, playing shadow pictures through the branches of the Pride of India tree onto the wall of her bedroom.

She threw back the single sheet, and swung her legs off the bed. She could not sleep, it was too warm, her nightdress kept binding under her armpits. She stood up and on a sudden reckless impulse she drew the nightdress off over her head and tossed it through the open door of her dressing-room, then, naked, she walked out onto the wide veranda. Into the moonlight, with the cool stone flags under her bare feet, and the warm night air moving like the touch of fairy hands on her skin.

She felt suddenly devilish and daring, she wanted to run down across the lawns and to have someone catch her doing it. She giggled, uncertain of this mood. It was so far removed from Manfred's conception of a good German Hausfrau's behaviour.

'He'd be furious,' she whispered with wicked delight, and then she heard the motor of the car.

She froze with horror, the headlights flicked through the trees as the car came up the driveway and she darted back into her room; in panic she dropped to her knees and searched for her nightgown, found it and ran to the bed as she dragged it on over her head.

She lay in the darkness and listened to the car door slam. There was silence until she heard him pass her door. His heels clacked on the yellow wood floor, he was almost running. Theresa knew the symptoms, the late night return, the suppressed urgency, and she lay rigid in her bed, waiting.

The minutes passed slowly, and then the interleading door from Manfred's suite swung open silently.

'Manfred, is that you?' She sat up and reached for the switch of the bedside lamp.

'Don't put the light on.' His voice was breathless, slurred as though he had been drinking but there was no trace of liquor on his breath as he stooped over her and kissed her. His lips were dry and tightly closed, as he slipped off his dressing-gown.

Two and a half minutes later he stood up from the bed, turning his back to Theresa as he quickly shrugged into the silk dressing-gown.

'Excuse me a minute, Theresa.' The breathlessness was gone from his voice. He went through the door of his own suite, and seconds later she heard the hiss of the shower and the tinkling splash of water.

She lay on her back and her fingernails cut into the palms of her hands. Her body was trembling with a mixture of revulsion and desire, it had been so fleeting a contact–enough to stir her, but so swift as to leave her with a feeling of having been used and sullied. She knew that the rest of the night would pass infinitely slowly, with restless burning tension, remorse and self-pity alternating with wild elation and half-crazed erotic fantasy.

'Damn him,' she screamed silently within her skull. 'Damn him! Damn him!'

She heard the shower stop, and then Manfred returned to her room. He smelt of 4711 Eau de Cologne, and he sat down carefully on the end of the bed.

'You may turn on the light, Theresa.'

It required a conscious effort for her to unclench her hand and reach out for the lamp switch. Manfred blinked behind his spectacles at the flood of light. His hair was damp and freshly combed, his cheeks shone like ripe apples.

'I hope you had an enjoyable day?' he asked, and listened seriously to her reply. Despite her tension, Theresa found herself falling under the almost hypnotic influence he wielded over her. His voice precise, almost monotonous. The glitter of his spectacles, the reptilian stillness of his body and features.

As she had so many times before, she thought of herself as a warm fluffy rabbit sitting tense and fascinated before the cobra.

'It is late,' he said at last and he stood up.

Looking down at her as she lay cuddled into the white silk sheets, he asked with as little emphasis as if he were requesting her to pass the sugar: 'Theresa, could you raise three hundred thousand Rand without your grandfather knowing?'

'Three hundred thousand!' She sat up startled.

'Yes. Could you?'

'Good Lord. Manfred, that's a small fortune.' She truly saw nothing unusual in her choice of adjective. 'You know it's all in the Trust Fund, well, most of it. There is the farm and the–no, I couldn't find half of that without Pops knowing.'

'Pity,' murmured Manfred.

'Manfred, you aren't in–difficulties?'

'No. Good Lord, no. It was just a thought. Forget that I asked. Good night, Theresa, I hope you sleep well.'

Involuntarily she lifted her hands towards him in invitation.

'Good night, Manfred.'

He turned and left the room, she let her hands fall to her sides. For Theresa Steyner the long night had begun.

28

'Ladies and Gentlemen, it is customary for the General Manager to introduce the distinguished guest who presents our special service awards. Last week, in tragic circumstances our General Manager, Mr Frank Lemmer, was killed in the Company's service, a loss which we all bitterly regret, and I am sure you all join me in sincere condolence to Mrs Eileen Lemmer.' Rod paused for the acknowledging murmur from his audience. There were two hundred of them packed into the mine club hall. 'It falls upon me, therefore, as Acting General Manager, to introduce to you Dr Manfred Steyner who is a senior Director of Central Rand Consolidated, our parent company. He is also head of the Departments of Finance and Planning.'

Sitting beside her husband, Theresa Steyner had noticed Manfred's irritation at Rod's mention of Frank Lemmer. It was company policy not to draw public attention to accidental death or injury inflicted on employees by the Company's operation. She liked Rod the better for this small tribute to Frank Lemmer.

Theresa was wearing sunglasses, for her eyes were swollen and red. In the dawning, after a sleepless night, she had succumbed suddenly to a fit of bitter weeping. The tears were without cause, or reason, and had left her feeling strangely lightheaded and with a brittle sense of well-being. However, her enormous eyes always showed up badly for hours after she had wept.

She sat with her legs demurely crossed, immaculate in a suit of cream shantung, a black silk scarf catching her hair and then letting it fall in a dark glossy brown cascade onto her shoulders. She leaned forward in polite attention to the speaker, one elbow on her knee, her chin cupped in her palm, one long tapered finger lying against her cheek. A lady with diamonds on her fingers and pearls at her throat, smiling an acknowledgement at Rod's reference to 'the lovely granddaughter of our Chairman'.

Except for the slight incongruity of the sunglasses, she was the perfect image of the young matron. Polished, poised, cosseted, secure in her unassailable virtue and duty.

However, the thoughts that were running through Theresa Steyner's head, and the flutterings and sensations that were prickling and tickling her, had they been known, would have broken up the assembly in disorder. All the formless fantasy and emotional disturbance of the previous night were now directed at one target–Rodney Ironsides. Suddenly, with a start of amusement and alarm, she was aware of a phenomenon that she had last experienced many years ago. She moved quickly, shifting her seat for the cream shantung marked so easily with any moisture.

'Terry Steyner!' she thought, deliciously shocked at herself, and found with relief that Rod had finished speaking and Manfred was standing up to reply. She joined in the applause enthusiastically to distract her errant fancy.

Manfred briefly mentioned the six gentlemen sitting in the front row of seats whose courage and devotion to duty they had come to honour, he then went on into an exploration of the prospects of an increase in the price of gold. In measured, carefully considered terms, he set out the advantages and benefits that would accrue to the industry, the nation and the world at large. It was an erudite and convincing dissertation, and there was a large contingent of newspaper men to record it. The press had been alerted by the public relations department of C.R.C. to the text of Dr Steyner's speech and all the leading dailies, weeklies, financial gazettes and journals were represented.

At intervals a photographer would come to crouch below the platform and pop a flash bulb up at Dr Steyner. On the eve of the gold price talks with France this would make good copy, for Steyner was the boy genius in the South African team.

The six heroes sat uncomfortably, forlorn in their best suits, scrubbed like schoolboys at a prize-giving ceremony, staring up at the speaker, not understanding a single word of the foreign language, but maintaining expressions of grave dignity.

Rod caught Big King's eye and winked at him. Solemnly Big King's right eyelid drooped and rose in reply, and quickly Rod averted his gaze to prevent himself laughing out loud.

He looked straight into Theresa Steyner's face, taking her completely off her guard. Not even the dark glasses could conceal her thoughts, they were as clear as if she had spoken them aloud. Before she could drop her eyes to examine the hem of her skirt, Rod knew with a stomach swoop of excitement how it could be if he chose.

With a new awareness he examined her from the corner of his eye, seeing her for the first time as an accessible woman, a highly desirable woman, but nevertheless still the granddaughter of Hurry Hirschfeld and the wife of Manfred Steyner. This made her as dangerous as a force ten pressure burst, he knew, but the desire and temptation was hard to deny, inflamed perhaps rather than dampened by the danger.

He saw that she was blushing now, her fingers picking nervously at the hem of her skirt. She was as agitated as a school-girl, she knew he was watching her. Rod Ironsides, who until five minutes before had been thinking of nothing but his speech, now found himself impelled into a completely new and exciting dimension.

After the awards had been made, tea had been drunk, biscuits consumed and the crowd had dispersed, Rod escorted the Steyners down across the vivid green lawns of Kikuyu grass to where the chauffeur was holding the Daimler.

'What a magnificent physique that Shangaan has, what was his name–King?' Terry was walking between the two men.

'King Nkulu. Big King, we call him.'

Rod found his speech unsteady, he had stuttered slightly. This thing between the two of them was suddenly overpowering, it hummed like a turbine, making the space between them crackle with tension. Unless he were deaf, Manfred Steyner must be aware of it.

'He is pretty special. There is nothing he can't do, and do it far and away better than his nearest rival. My God, you should see him dance.'

'Dance?' inquired Terry with interest.

'Tribal dancing, you know.'

'Of course.' Terry hoped the relief in her voice was not obvious, she had been racking her badly flustered brains for an excuse to visit the Sonder Ditch again or have Rod Ironsides come to Johannesburg. 'I have a friend who is absolutely mad keen on seeing the dances. She pesters me every time I see her.'

Quickly she selected a name from her list of friends, she must have one ready should Manfred ask.

'They dance every Saturday afternoon, bring her out any time.' Rod fielded the ball neatly.

'What about this Saturday?' Terry turned to her husband, 'Would that be all right, Manfred?'

'What's that?' Manfred looked at her vaguely, he had not been following the conversation. Manfred Steyner was a worried man, he was pondering his obligation to gain control of the management of the Sonder Ditch within two days.

'May we come out here on Saturday afternoon to watch the tribal dancing?' Terry repeated her request.

'Have you forgotten that I fly to Paris on Saturday morning, Theresa?'

'Oh, dear.' Terry bit her lip thoughtfully. 'It *had* slipped my mind. What a pity, I would have enjoyed it.'

Manfred frowned slightly, irritated.

'My dear Theresa, there is no reason why you shouldn't come out to the

Sonder Ditch without me. I am sure you will be safe enough in Mr Ironsides' hands.'

His choice of words brought the colour to Terry's cheeks again.

29

After the award ceremony, Big King's first stop was the Recruiting Agency Office at the entrance to the No. 1 shaft hostel. There were men clustered about the counter, but they stood aside for Big King and he acknowledged the courtesy by slapping their backs indiscriminately and greeting them with:

'Kunjane, madoda. How is it, men?'

The clerk behind the counter hurried to serve him. Up at the Mine Club Big King might be a little out of his depth, but here he was treated like a reigning monarch.

In two neat bundles Big King placed the award money on the counter.

'Twenty-five Rand you will send to my senior wife.' He instructed the clerk. 'And twenty-five Rand you will put to my book.'

Big King was scrupulously fair. Half of all his earnings was remitted to the senior of his four wives, and half was added to the substantial sum already credited in his savings bank passbook.

The Agency was the procurer of labour for the insatiably man-hungry gold mines of the Witwatersrand and Orange Free State. Its representatives operated across the southern half of the continent. From the swamps and fever lagoons along the great Zambezi, from among the palm groves fringing the Indian Ocean, out of those simmering plains that the bushmen called 'the big dry', down from the mountains of Basutoland and the grasslands of Swaziland and Zululand they gathered the Bantu, the men themselves completing the first fifty or sixty miles of the journey on foot. Individuals meeting on a footpath to become pairs, arriving at a little general dealer's store in the bleak scrub desert to find three or four others already waiting, the arrival of the recruiting truck with a dozen men and their luggage aboard, the long bumping grinding progress through the bush. The stops at which more men scrambled aboard, until a full truck load of fifty or sixty disembarked at a railway siding in the wilderness.

Here the tiny trickle of humanity joined a stream, and at the first major centre they trans-shipped and became part of the great flood that washed towards 'Goldi'.

However, once they had reached Johannesburg and been allocated to one of the sixty major gold mines, the Agency's obligations towards its recruits were not yet discharged. Between them the employing mine and the Agency must provide each man with employment, training, advice and comfort, maintain contact between him and his family, for very few of them could write, reassure him when he worried that his goats were sick or his wife unfaithful. They must provide a banking and savings service with a personal involvement unknown to any commercial banking institute. They had, in short, to make certain that a man taken from an environment that had not changed in a thousand years and deposited into the midst of a sophisticated and technological society would retain his health, happiness and sanity, so that at the end of his contract he would return to the place from which he had come and tell them all how wonderful it was at 'Goldi'. He would show them his hard helmet, and his new suitcase crammed with clothes, his transistor radio and the little blue book with its printed figures, inflaming them also with the desire to make the pilgrimage, and keep the flood washing towards 'Goldi'.

Big King completed his business transactions and went in through the gates of the hostel, he was going to take advantage of the fact that he had missed the shift and would be among the first at the ablutions and dining-hall.

He went down across the lawns to his block. Despite the size of an establishment that housed six thousand men, the Company had tried to make it as attractive as possible. The result was an unusual design, half-way between a motel and an advanced penitentiary.

As a senior boss boy, Big King rated a room of his own. An ordinary labourer would share with five others.

Carefully Big King brushed down his suit and hung it in the built-in cupboard, wiped down his glossy shoes and racked them, then with a towel around his waist he set off for the ablution block and was irritated to find it already filled with new recruits up from the acclimatization centre.

Big King ran an appraising eye over their naked bodies and judged that this batch must be nearing the completion of their eight-day acclimatization. They were sleek and shiny, the muscle definition showing clearly through the skin.

You could not take a man straight out of his village, probably suffering from malnutrition, and put him down a gold mine to lash and bar and drill in a dry bulb heat of 91 Fahrenheit and 84% relative humidity, without running a serious risk of killing him with heat stroke or exhaustion.

Every recruit judged medically fit to work underground went into acclimatization. For eight days, eight hours a day, he and hundreds of others stood with only a loin cloth about his middle in a vast barn-like hall stepping up onto and down from a platform. The height of the platform was carefully matched to the man's height and body weight, the speed of his movements was regulated by a flashing panel of lights, the temperature and humidity were controlled at 91 and 84%, every ten minutes he was given water and his body temperature was registered by the half dozen trained medical assistants in charge of the room.

At the end of the eighth day he emerged as fit as an olympic athlete, and quite able to perform heavy physical labour in conditions of high temperature and humidity without discomfort or danger.

'Gwedeni!' growled Big King, and the nearest recruit, still white with soap suds, hurriedly vacated his shower with a respectful 'Keshle!' in deference to Big King's rank and standing. Big King removed his towel and stepped under the shower, revelling as always in the rush of hot water over his skin, flexing the great muscles of his arms and chest.

The messenger found him there.

'King Nkulu, I have word for thee.' The man used Shangaan, not the bastard Fanikalo.

'Speak,' Big King invited, soaping his belly and buttocks.

'The Induna bids you call at his house after you have eaten the evening meal.'

'Tell him I will attend his wishes,' said Big King and held his face up into the rush of steaming water.

Dressed in a white open-neck shirt and blue slacks, Big King sauntered down to the kitchens. Again the recruits were ahead of him, queuing with bowls in hand outside the serving hatches. Big King walked past them through the door marked 'No Admittance–Staff only'.

The kitchens were cavernous, glistening with white porcelain tile and stainless steel cookers and bins that could serve eighteen thousand hot meals a day.

When Big King entered a room, even one as large as this, no one was unaware of his presence. One of the assistant cooks snatched up a bowl not much smaller than a baby's bath, and hurried across to the nearest stainless steel bin. He opened the lid and looked expectantly at Big King. Big King nodded and the cook ladled about two litres of steaming sugar beans into the bowl, before passing on to the next bin where he again looked for and obtained Big King's approval. He added an equal quantity of mixed vegetables to the bowl, slammed down the lid and scampered across to where a second assistant waited with a spade beside yet another bin.

The spade was the same as those used for lashing gold reef underground, but the blade of this one had been polished to gleaming cleanliness. The second cook dug into the bin and came up with a spadeful of white maize porridge, cooked stiff as a cake, the smell of it as saliva-making as the smell of new bread. This was the staple of Bantu diet. He deposited the spadeful in the bowl.

'I am hungry.' Big King spoke for the first time, and the second cook dug out another spadeful and added it to the bowl. They passed on to the end of the kitchens, and at their approach another cook lifted the lid on a pressure cooker the size of a washing machine. From it rose a cloud of fragrant steam.

Apologetically the cook held out his hand and Big King produced his meat ticket. Meat was the only food that was rationed. Each man was limited to one pound of meat a day; the Company had long ago discovered to its astonishment and cost that a Bantu, offered unlimited supplies of fresh meat, was quite capable of eating his own weight of it monthly.

Having ascertained that Big King was entitled to his daily pound, the cook proceeded to ladle at least five pounds of it into the bowl.

'You are my brother,' Big King thanked him, and the little procession moved on to where yet another cook was filling a half-gallon jug of thick, gruel-like, mildly alcoholic Bantu beer from one of the multiple spiggots beneath the thousand-gallon tank.

The bowl and jug were ceremonially handed to Big King and he went out onto the covered terraces where benches and tables were set out for alfresco dining in mild weather.

While he ate, the terrace began to fill, for the shift was out of the mine now. Every man who passed his table greeted Big King, but only a few privileged persons took the liberty of seating themselves at the same table. One of them was Joseph M'Kati, the little old sweeper from 100 level.

'It has been a good week, King Nkulu.'

'You say so.' Big King was non-committal. 'I go now to a meeting with the Old One. Then we shall see.'

The Old One, the Shangaan Induna, lived in a Company house. A self-contained residence with lounge and dining-room, kitchen and bathroom. He was handsomely paid by the Company, provided with servants, food, furniture and all the other appurtenances of his rank and station.

He was the head of the Shangaan community on the Sonder Ditch. A chief of the blood, a greybeard and member of the tribal councils. In similar houses and with the same privileges and in equal style lived the Indunas of the other tribal groups that made up the labour force of the Sonder Ditch. They were the paternal figureheads, the tribal jurists, ruling and judging within the framework of law and custom. The Company could not hope to maintain harmony and order without the assistance of these men.

'Baba!' Big King greeted his Induna from the doorway of his house, touching the forehead in respect not only for the man but also for what he represented.

'My son.' The Induna smiled his greeting. 'Come and sit by me.' He gestured for his servants to leave the room, and Big King went to squat at the feet of the old man. 'It is true you go now to work with the mad one?' That was Johnny Delange's nickname.

They talked, the Induna questioning him on fifty matters that affected the welfare of his people. For Big King this was a comforting and nostalgic experience, for the Induna stood in the place of his father.

At last, satisfied, the Induna went on to other matters.

'There is a parcel ready tonight. Crooked Leg waits for you.'

'I shall go for it.'

'Go in peace then, my son.'

On his way through the gates of the hostel Big King stopped to chat with the guards. These men had the right of search over any person entering or leaving the hostel. Particularly they were concerned with preventing either women disguised as men or bottles of spirits entering the premises, both of which tended to have a disruptive effect on the community. As an after-thought they were also instructed to look out for stolen property entering or leaving. Big King had to ensure that none of them would ever, under any circumstances, take it into his head to search Big King.

While he stood at the gates, the last glow of the sunset faded and the lights began to come on across the valley. The clusters of red aerial warning lights atop the headgears, the massed yellow squares of the hotels, the strings of street lamps and the isolated pinpricks of the residential areas up on the ridge.

When it was truly dark, Big King left the guards and sauntered down the main road, until a bend in the road took him out of their sight. Then Big King left the road and started up the slope. He moved like a night animal, swiftly and with certainty of the path he followed.

He passed the ranch-type split-levels of the line management officials with their wide lawns and swimming-pools, pausing only once when a dog yapped nearby, then moving on again until he was into the broken rock and rank grass of the upper ridge; he crossed the skyline and started down the far side until he made out the grass-covered mound of rubble in the moonlight. He slowed and moved cautiously forward until he found the rusty barbed wire fence that guarded the entrance. He vaulted it easily and went on into the black mouth of the tunnel.

Fifty years before, a long-defunct mining company had suspected the existence of a gold reef in this area and had driven prospecting adits into the side of the ridge, exhausting its funds in the process, and finally abandoning the network of tunnels in despair.

Big King paused long enough to draw an electric torch from his pocket before going on into the tunnel, flashing the beam ahead of him. Soon the air stank of bats and their wings swished about his head. Unperturbed, Big King went on deeper and deeper into the side of the hill, taking a turning and fork in the tunnel without hesitation. At last there was a faint glow of yellow light ahead and Big King switched off his torch.

'Crooked Leg!' he called, his voice bounced and boomed along the tunnel. There was no reply.

'It is I, Big King!' he shouted again, and immediately a shadow detached itself from the sidewall and limped towards him, sheathing a wicked-looking knife as it came.

'All is ready.' The little cripple came to meet him. 'Come, I have it here.'

Crooked Leg had earned his limp and his nickname in a rock-fall a dozen years ago. Now he owned and operated the concession photographic studio on the mine property, a flourishing enterprise, for dearly the Bantu love their own image on film. Not, however, as profitable as his nocturnal activities in the abandoned workings beyond the ridge.

He led Big King into a small rock chamber lit by a suspended hurricane lantern. Mingled with the bat stench was the acrid reek of sulphuric acid in high concentration.

On a wooden trestle table that occupied most of the chamber were earthenware jars, heavy glass bowls, polythene bags, and a variety of shoddy and very obviously second-hand laboratory equipment. In a clear space amongst all this clutter stood a large screw-topped bottle. The bottle was filled with a dirty yellow powder.

'Ha!' Big King exclaimed his pleasure. 'Plenty!'

'Yes. It has been a good week,' Crooked Leg agreed.

Big King picked up the bottle, marvelling once again at the unbelievable weight of it. This was not pure gold, for Crooked Leg's acid reduction methods were crude, but it was at least sixteen carats fine.

The bottle represented the week's collection of fines and concentrates by men like Joseph M'Kati from a dozen vulnerable points along the line of production; in some cases carried out from the company reduction works itself under the noses of the heavily armed guards.

All the men involved in this surreptitious milking off of the company's gold were Shangaans, there was only one man in whom was vested sufficient authority and prestige to prevent the greed and hostility which gold breeds from destroying the whole operation. That was the Shangaan Induna. There was only one man with the physical presence and necessary command of the Portuguese language to negotiate the disposal of the gold. That was Big King.

Big King placed the bottle in his pocket. The weight pulled his clothing out of shape.

'Run like a gazelle, Crooked Leg.' He turned back into the dark tunnel.

'Hunt like a leopard, King Nkulu,' chuckled the little cripple, as he disappeared into the moving shadows.

30

'A packet of Boxer tobacco,' said Big King. The eyes of José Almeida, the Portuguese owner of the mine concession store and the local roadhouse, narrowed slightly. He took down the yellow four-ounce packet from the shelves and handed it across the counter, accepted Big King's payment and counted the change into his palm.

He watched as the giant Bantu wandered down between the loaded shelves and racks of merchandise to disappear through the front door of the store into the night.

'Take charge,' he muttered in Portuguese to his plump little wife with her silky dark moustache, and she nodded in understanding, moving into José's place in front of the cash register. José went through into his storerooms and living quarters behind the store.

Big King was waiting in the shadows. When the back door opened he slipped through and José closed the door behind him. José led him through into a cubicle of an office, and from a cupboard he took down a jeweller's balance. Under Big King's watchful eye he began to weigh the gold.

José Almeida purchased the gold from the unofficial outlets of each of the five major mines on the Kitchenerville field, paying five Rands an ounce and selling again for sixteen. He justified the large profit margin he allowed himself by the fact that mere possession of unregistered gold was a criminal offence in South Africa, punishable by up to five years' imprisonment.

Almeida was a man in his middle thirties with lank black hair that he continually pushed back from his forehead, bright brown inquisitive eyes and dirty fingernails. Despite his grubby and well-worn clothing and unkempt hair style, he was a man of substance.

He had been able to pay in cash the forty thousand Rand demanded by the Company for the monopoly concession to trade on the mine property. He had, therefore, an exclusive clientele of twelve thousand well-paid Bantu, and had recovered his forty thousand during the first year of trading. He did not really need to run the risk of illicit gold buying, but gold is strange material. It infects most men who touch it with a reckless greed.

'Two hundred and sixteen ounces,' said José. His scale was set to record a twenty per cent error–in José's favour.

'One thousand and eighty Rand,' agreed big King in Portuguese, and José went to the big green safe in the corner.

31

Terry Steyner entered the 'Grape and Gable' bar of the President Hotel at 1.14 p.m. precisely, and as Hurry Hirschfeld stood to greet her he reflected that fourteen minutes was hardly late at all for a beautiful woman. Terry's grandmother would have considered herself to be early if she was only that late.

'You're late,' growled Hurry. No sense in letting her get away with it unscathed.

'And you are a big, cuddly, growly, lovable old bear,' said Terry and kissed him on the tip of his nose before he could duck. Hurry sat down quickly scowling thunderously with pleasure. He decided he didn't give a good damn if Marais and Hardy, who further down the bar were listening and trying to cover their grins, repeated the incident to the entire membership of the Rand Club.

'Good day, Mrs Steyner.' The scarlet-jacketed barman smiled his greeting. 'Can I mix you a Manhattan?'

'Don't tempt me, Thomas. I'm on a diet. I'll just have a glass of soda water.'

'Diet,' snorted Hurry. 'You're skinny enough as it is. Give her a Manhattan,

Thomas, and put a cherry in it. Never was a Hirschfeld woman that looked like a boy, and you'll not be the first of them.' As an afterthought, he added; 'I've ordered your lunch also, you'll not starve yourself in my company.'

'You are a shocker, Pops,' said Terry fondly.

'Now, young lady, let's hear what you've been up to since I last saw you.'

They talked together as friends, very dear and trusted friends. The affection they felt for each other went beyond the natural duty of their blood tie. There was a kinship of the spirit as well as the flesh. They sat close, heads together, watching each other's face as they talked, completely lost in the pleasure of each other's company, the murmur of their voices interrupted by a tinkling burst of laughter or a deep chuckle.

They were so absorbed that Peter, the headwaiter, came through from the Transvaal Room to find them.

'Mr Hirschfeld, the chef is in tears.'

'Good Lord.' Hurry looked at the antique clock above the bar. 'It's almost two o'clock. Why didn't someone tell me?'

The oysters had been flown up from Mossel Bay that morning, and Terry sighed with pleasure after each of them.

'I was out at the Sonder Ditch with Manfred on Wednesday.'

'Yes, I saw the photograph in the paper,' Hurry engulfed his twelfth and final oyster.'

'I must say I like your new General Manager.'

Hurry laid down his fork and a little flush of anger started in his withered old cheeks.

'You mean Fred Plummer?'

'Don't be silly, Pops, I mean Rodney Ironsides.'

'Has that cold fish of yours been briefing you?' Hurry demanded.

'Manfred?' She was genuinely puzzled by the question, Hurry could see that. 'What's he got to do with it?'

'All right, forget it.' Hurry dismissed Manfred with a shake of his head. 'Why do you like Ironsides?'

'Have you heard him speak?'

'No.'

'He's very good. I'm sure he must be a first-class mining man.'

'He is.' Hurry nodded, watchful and non-committal.

Peter whisked Terry's plate away, giving her the respite she needed to gather her resources. In the previous few seconds she had realized that Rodney Ironsides was not, as she had believed, a certainty for the job. In fact, Pops had already chosen old plum-faced Plummer for the General Managership. It took another moment for her to decide that she would use even the dirtiest in-fighting to see that Rod was not overlooked.

Peter laid plates of cold rock lobster in front of them, and when he had withdrawn Terry looked up at Hurry. She had perfected the trick of enlarging her already enormous eyes. By holding them open like this she could flood them with tears. The effect was devastating.

'Do you know, Pops, he reminds me so much of the photographs of Daddy.'

Colonel Bernard Hirschfeld, Terry's father, had burned to death in his tank at Sidi Rezegh. She saw Hurry Hirschfeld's expression crack with pain, and Terry felt a sick little flutter of guilt. Had it been necessary to use such a vicious weapon to achieve her ends?

Hurry pushed at the rock lobster with his fork, his head was bowed so she could not see his face. She reached out to touch his hand.

'Pops–' she whispered, and he looked up. There was a restrained excitement in Hurry's manner.

'You know, you're bloody well right! He does look a bit like Bernie. Did I ever tell you about the time when your father and I–'

Terry felt dizzy with relief. I didn't hurt him, she told herself, he likes the idea, he really does. With a woman's instinct she had chosen the only form of persuasion that could have moved Hurry Hirschfeld from his decision.

32

Manfred Steyner fastened his safety belt and lay back in the seat of the Boeing 707, feeling slightly nauseated with relief.

Ironsides was in, and he was safe. Hurry Hirschfeld had sent for him two hours before to wish him farewell and good luck with the talks. Manfred had stood before him, trying desperately to think of some way in which he could bring up the subject naturally. Hurry saved him the trouble.

'By the way, I'm giving Ironsides the Sonder Ditch. Reckon it's about time we had some young blood in top management.'

It was as easy as that. Manfred had difficulty in persuading himself that those threats which had kept him lying awake during the past four nights were no longer of consequence. Ironsides was in. He could go to Paris and tell them. *Ironsides is in. We are ready to go.*

The note of the jets changed, and the Boeing began to roll forward. Manfred twisted his head against the neck rest and peered through the perspex porthole. He could not distinguish Terry's figure amongst the crowd on the observation balcony of Jan Smuts Airport. They taxied past a Pan Am Boeing which cut off his view and Manfred looked straight ahead. Instantly his nostrils flared, he looked around quickly.

The passenger in the seat beside him had stripped to his shirt-sleeves. He was a big beefy individual who very obviously did not use deodorant. Almost in desperation Manfred looked about. The aircraft was full, there would be little chance of changing seats and beside him the beefy individual produced a pack of cigarettes.

'You can't smoke,' cried Manfred. 'The light's on.' The combination of body odour and cigarette smoke would be unbearable.

'I'm not smoking,' said the man, 'yet.' And placed a cigarette between his lips, his lighter ready in the other hand.

Nearly two thousand miles to Nairobi, thought Manfred, with his stomach starting to heave.

33

'Terry darling, why on earth should I go all the way out to Kitchenerville to watch a lot of savages prancing around?'

'As a favour to me, Joy,' Terry pleaded into the telephone.

'It means mucking up my whole weekend. I've got rid of the kids to their grandmother, I've got a copy of *A Small Town in Germany* and I was going to have a lovely time reading and–'

'Please, Joy, you're my last hope.'

'What time will we be home?' Joy was weakening. Terry sensed her advantage and pressed forward ruthlessly.

'You might meet a lovely man out at the mine, and he'll sweep you–'

'No, thanks.' Joy had been divorced a little over a year ago, some people took longer than others to recover. 'I've had lovely men in big fat chunks.'

'Oh, Joy, you can't sit around moping for ever. Come on, I'll pick you up in half an hour.'

Joy sighed with resignation. 'Damn you, Terry Steyner.'

'Half an hour,' said Terry and hung up before she could change her mind.

'I'm playing golf. It's Saturday, and I'm playing golf.' said Doctor Daniel Stander stubbornly.

'You remember when I drove all the way to Bloemfontein to–' Rod began, and Dan interrupted quickly.

'All right, all right, I remember. You don't have to bring that up again.'

'You owe me plenty, Stander,' Rod reminded him. 'All I am asking is one of your lousy Saturday afternoons. Is that so much?'

'I can't let the boys down. It's a long-standing date.' Dan wriggled to escape.

'I've already phoned Ben. It will be a pleasure for him to take your place.'

There was a long gloomy silence, then Dan asked, 'What's this bird like?'

'She's a beautiful, rich nymphomaniac, and she owns a brewery.'

'Yeah! Yeah!' said Dan sarcastically. 'All right, I'll do it. But I hereby declare all my obligation and debts to you fully discharged.'

'I'll give you a written receipt,' Rod agreed.

Dan was still sulking when the Daimler came up the drive and parked at the front of the Mine Club. He and Rod were standing at the Ladies' Bar, watching for the arrival of their guests.

Dan had just ordered his third beer.

'Here they come,' said Rod.

'Is that them?' Dan's depression lifted magically as he peered through the coloured-glass windows. The chauffeur was letting the two ladies out of the Daimler. They were both in floral slack suits and dark glasses.

'That's them.'

'Jesus!' said Dan with rare approval. 'Which one is mine?'

'The blonde.'

'Ha!' Dan grinned for the first time since their meeting. 'Why the hell are we standing here?'

'Why indeed?' asked Rod, his stomach was tied up in knots that twisted tighter as he went down the front steps toward Terry.

'Mrs Steyner. I'm so glad you could come.' With a wild lift of elation he saw it was still there, he had not imagined it, it was there in her eyes and her smile.

'Thank you, Mr Ironsides.' She was like a schoolgirl again, uncertain of herself, flustered.

'I'd like you to meet Mrs Albright. Joy, this is Rodney Ironsides.'

'Hello.' He smiled at her as he clasped her hand. 'It's gin time, I think.'

Dan was waiting at the bar for them, and Rod made the introductions.

'Joy is so excited at the chance of watching the dancing,' said Terry as they sat down on the bar stools. 'She's been looking forward to it for days.' And for an instant Joy looked stunned.

'You'll love it,' agreed Dan moving in to take up a position at Joy's elbow. 'I wouldn't miss it for anything.'

Joy was a tall slim girl with long straight golden hair that hung to her shoulders, her eyes were cool green but her mouth when she smiled was soft and warm. She smiled now full into Dan's eyes.

'Nor would I,' she said, and with relief Rod knew he could devote all his attention to Terry Steyner. Joy Albright would be more than adequately looked after. He ordered drinks, and all four of them promptly lost further interest in tribal dancing.

At one stage Rod told Terry Steyner, 'I am going up to Johannesburg this evening. There is no point in having your unfortunate chauffeur sit around all afternoon. Let him go, and I'll take you home.'

'Good,' Terry agreed immediately. 'Would you tell him, please?'

The next time Rod looked at his watch it was half past three.

'Good Lord!' he exclaimed. 'If we don't hurry, it will be all over.' Reluctantly Joy and Dan, who had their heads close together, drew apart.

The overflow from the amphitheatre pressed about them, a merry jostling throng, all inhibitions long since evaporated in the primeval excitement of the dance, much like the crowd at a bull ring.

Rod and Dan ran interference for the girls, ploughing a path through the main gateway and down to their reserved seats in the front row. All four of them were laughing and flushed by the time they were seated, the excitement about them was infectious and the liquor had heightened their sensibilities.

An expectant hum of voices.

'The Shangaans!' And the audience craned towards the entrance from which pranced a dozen drummers, their long wooden drums hung on rawhide straps about their necks, they took up stations around the circular earthen stage.

Tap, tap. Tap, tap–from one of the drummers, and silence gripped the amphitheatre.

Tap, tap. Tap, tap. Naked, except for their brief loin cloths, stooped over the drums that they clasped between their knees, they began to lay down the rhythm of the dance. It was a broken, disturbing beat, that jerked and twitched like a severed nerve. A compelling, demanding sound, the pulse of a continent and a people.

Then came the dancers, shuffling, row upon row, headdresses dipping and rustling, the animal tail kilts, swirling, war rattles at the wrists and ankles, black muscles already oiled with the sweat of excitement, coming in slowly, rank upon majestic rank, moving as though the drums were pumping life into them.

A shrill blast on a duiker horn and the ranks whirled like dry leaves in a wind, they fell again into a new pattern, and through the opening in their midst came a single gigantic figure.

'Big King!' The name blew a sigh through the audience, and immediately the drums changed their rhythm. Faster, demanding, and the dancers hissed in their throats a sound like storm surf rushing up a stony beach.

Big King flung his arms wide, braced on legs like black marble columns, his head thrown back. He sang a single word of command, shrilling it, and in instantaneous response every right knee was brought up to the level of the chest. Half a second's pause and then two hundred horny bare feet stamped down simultaneously with a crash that shook the amphitheatre to its foundations. The Shangaans began to dance, and reality was gone in the moving, charging, swirling, retreating ranks.

Once Rod tore his eyes from the spectacle. Terry Steyner was sitting forward on the bench, eyes sparkling, lips slightly parted, completely lost in the erotic turmoil and barbaric splendour of it.

Joy and Dan had a firm hold of each other's hands, their shoulders and the outside of their thighs were pressed tightly together, and Rod was stabbed by a painful thrust of envy.

Afterwards, back in the Ladies' Bar of the Club, there was very little conversation but they were all of them tensed up, restless, moved by strange undercurrents and interplays of primitive desires and social restraints.

'Well,' said Rod at last, 'if I am to get you two ladies back to Johannesburg at a decent hour–'

Dan and Joy spoke together.

'Don't worry, Rod, I'll–'

'Dan says he will–' Then they stopped and grinned at each other sheepishly.

'I take it that Dan has suddenly remembered that he has to go to Johannesburg this evening also, and he has offered to give you a lift?' asked Rod dryly, and they laughed in confirmation.

'It looks as though we are on our own, Mrs Steyner.' Rod turned to Terry.

'I'll trust you,' said Terry.

'If you do that, you're crazy,' said Dan.

Outside the Maserati, darkness was falling swiftly. The horizon blending into the black sky, isolated lights winking at them out of the surrounding veld.

Rod switched on the headlights, and the instrument panel glowed softly, turning the interior into a warm secluded place, isolating them from the world. The wind whispered, and the tyres and the engine hummed a gentle intimate refrain.

Terry Steyner sat with her legs curled up under her, cuddled into the soft maroon leather of the bucket seat. She was staring ahead down the path of the headlights, and she seemed withdrawn and yet very close. Every few minutes Rod would take his eyes from the road and study her profile briefly. He did so again, and this time she met his gaze frankly.

'You realize what is happening?' she asked.

'Yes,' he answered as frankly.

'You know how dangerous it could be for you?'

'And you.'

'No, not me. I am invulnerable. I am a Hirschfeld–but you, it could destroy you.'

Rod shrugged.

'If we counted the consequences before every action, nobody would do anything.'

'Have you thought that I might be a spoiled little rich girl amusing myself? I might do this all the time.'

'You might,' Rod agreed. They were silent for a long while, then Terry spoke again.

'Rod?' she used his given name for the first time.

'Yes?'

'I don't, you know. I really don't.'

'I guessed that.'

'Thank you.' She opened her bag. 'I need a cigarette. I feel as though I'm standing poised on the edge of a cliff and I've got this terrible compulsion to hurl myself over the edge.'

'Light me one, Terry.'

'You need one also?'

'Badly.'

They smoked in silence again, both of them staring ahead, then Terry rolled down the window and flicked the cigarette butt away.

'You've got the job, you know.' All day she had wanted to tell him, it had been bubbling inside her. Watching his face, she saw his lips stiffen, his eyes creased into slits.

'Did you hear me?' she asked at last, and he braked the Maserati, swinging it off onto the shoulder of the road. He pulled on the hand brake and turned to face her.

'Terry, what did you say?'

'I said, you've got the job.'

'What job?' he demanded harshly.

'Pops signed the instruction this morning. You'll receive it on Monday. You're the new General Manager of the Sonder Ditch.' She wanted to go on and say–*and I got it for you. I made Pops give it to you.*

I never will, she promised, I will never spoil it for him. He must believe he won it fairly, not as my gift.

34

It was Saturday night, the big night in Dump City.

The Blaauberg Mine was the oldest producer on the Kitchenerville field. There were sections of its property which had been worked out completely, and the old waste dumps were now abandoned and overgrown. Among the scrub and head-high weed in the valleys between these man-made hills had grown up a shanty town. Dump City, the inhabitants had named it. The buildings were made of discarded galvanized iron sheets and flattened oil drums, there was no sanitation or running water.

Remote from the main roads, the residential communities of the neighbouring mines or the town of Kitchenerville, hidden among the dumps, accessible only to a man on foot, never visited by members of the South African Constabulary, it was ideally suited to the purposes for which its three hundred permanent inhabitants had chosen it.

Every one of the shacks was a shebeen, a clip joint where watered liquor was sold at inflated prices, where dagga* was freely obtainable and where men from the surrounding mines gathered to carouse.

They came not so much for the liquor. Each of the mine hostels had a bar where a full range of liquor was on sale at club prices. Very few of them came for the dagga. There was little addiction amongst these well-fed, hard-worked and contented men. What they came for were the women.

*Marijuana.

Five mines in the area, each employing ten or twelve thousand men. Here at Dump City were two hundred women, the only available women within twenty miles. It was not necessary for the young ladies of Dump City to solicit custom, even the fat, the withered, the toothless, could behave like queens.

Big King came down the path that skirted the mine dump. With him were two dozen of his fellow tribesmen, big Shangaans wearing their regalia, carrying their fighting sticks and still tensed up from the dancing. They came at a trot, Big King leading them. They were singing, not the gentle planting or courting melodies, not the work chant nor the song of welcome.

They were singing the fighting songs, those their forefathers had sung when they carried the spear in search of cattle and slaves. The driving inflammatory rhythm, the fiercely patriotic words wrought so mightily on the delicate susceptibilities of the average Shangaan that the company had found it necessary to ban the singing of these songs.

Like a Scot hearing the pipes, when a Shangaan began singing these warlike chants, he was ready for violence.

The song ended as Big King led them down to the nearest shanty, and pushed aside the sacking that acted as a door. He stooped through the opening, and his comrades crowded in behind him.

A brittle electric silence fell on the large room. The air was so thick with smoke, and the light from the suspended hurricane lamps so feeble, that it was impossible to see the far wall. The room was filled with men, forty or fifty of them, the smell of humanity and bad liquor was solid. Among this press of men were half a dozen bright spots of the girls' dresses, but with their curiosity aroused by the singing more girls were coming through from the interleading doorways at the back, some of them had men with them and were still shrugging into their clothing. When they saw Big King and his warriors in full war kit, they fell silent and watchful.

At Big King's shoulder one of the Shangaans whispered:

'Basutos! They are all Basutos!' He was right, Big King saw that they were all men of that mountainous little independent state.

Big King started forward, swaggering just enough to make his leopard tail kilt swing and swirl and the heron feathers of his headdress rustle. He reached the primitive bar counter.

'Flying Bird,' he told the crone who owned the house, and she placed a bottle of Eagle Brandy on the counter.

Big King half filled a tumbler, conscious that every eye was on him, and drained it.

Slowly he turned and surveyed the room.

'What is it,' he asked in a voice that carried to every corner, 'that sits on top of a mountain and scratches its fleas. Is it a baboon, or a Basuto?'

A roar of delight went up from his Shangaans.

'A Basuto!' they shouted, crowding forward to the bar, while a growl and mutter went up from the rest of the room.

'What is it,' shouted a Basuto jumping to his feet, 'that has feathers on its head and crows from a dungheap? Is it a rooster, or a Shangaan?'

Without seeming to move, Big King picked up the bottle of Eagle Brandy and hurled it. With a crack it burst against the Basuto's forehead and he went over backwards taking two of his companions with him.

The old drone snatched up her cash register and ran as the room exploded into violent movement.

There was not enough space in which to use the fighting sticks, Big King realized, so he lifted a section of the bar counter off its trestles and holding it in front of him like the blade of a bulldozer, he charged across the room, flattening all and everything before him.

The crash of breaking furniture and the yelp and squeal of men being struck down drove Big King beyond the frontiers of sanity into the red atavistic fury of the berserker.

Basuto is also one of the fighting tribes of the N'guni group. These wiry mountaineers rushed into the conflict with the same savage joy as the Shangaans, a conflict that raged and roared out of the single room to engulf the entire population of Dump City.

One of the girls, her dress ripped from her back so she was left with only a tattered pair of bloomers, had climbed on top of the remains of the bar counter from where, with her big melon breasts swinging in the lamp light, she shrilled that peculiar ululation that Bantu women used to goad their menfolk into battle frenzy. A dozen of the other girls joined in, trilling, squealing, and the sound was too much for Big King.

With the bar top held ahead of him he charged straight through the flimsy wall of the shack, bursting it open like a paper bag, the roof sagged down wearily, and Big King raged on unchecked down the narrow dirt street, striking down any man who crossed his path, scattering chickens and yelping dogs, roaring like a bull gorilla.

He turned at the end of the encampment and came back, his frustration mounting as he found the street deserted except for a few prostrate bodies, through the gaping hole in the wall he entered the shebeen once more to find that here also the fighting had died down. A few of the participants were crawling, or moaning as they lay on a carpet of broken glass.

Big King glared about him, seeking a further outlet for his wrath.

'King Nkulu!' The girl was still on the trestle table, her eyes bright with excitement, her legs trembling with it.

Big King let out another roar, and hurled the bar top from him. It clattered against the far wall and Big King started towards her.

'You are a lion!' She shrieked encouragement at him, and she took one of her big black velvety breasts in each hand and pointed them at him, squeezing them together, shaking with excitement.

'Eat me!' she screamed, as Big King swept her off the table and lifting her high, ran with her out into the night. Carrying her into the scrub below the mine dumps, holding her easily with one arm, ripping the leopard-tail kilt from his own waist as he ran.

35

It was Saturday night in Paris also, but there were men who were still working, for there were lights burning in the upstairs rooms of one of the big Embassies in the rue Royale.

The fat man who had been the host in the gambling establishment in Johannesburg was now the guest. He sat at ease in a leather club easy, his corpulence and the steel-grey hair at his temples giving him dignity. His face heavy, tanned, intelligent. His eyes glittery and hard as the diamond on his finger.

He was listening intently to a man of about the same age as himself who stood before a projected image on a screen that covered one wall of the room. There was that in the man's bearing and manner that marked him as a scholar, he was speaking now, addressing himself directly to the listener in the easy chair, pointing with a marker to the screen beside him.

'You see here a plan of the working of the five producing gold mines of the Kitchenerville fields in relation to each other.' He touched the screen with a marker. 'Thornfontein, Blaauberg, Tweefontein, Deep Gold Levels and Sonder Ditch.'

The man in the chair nodded. 'I have seen and studied this diagram before.'

'Good, then you will know that the Sonder Ditch property sits in the centre of the field. It has common boundaries with the other four mines and here,' he tapped the screen again, 'it is intersected by the massive serpentine dyke which they call the Big Dipper.'

Again the fat man nodded.

'It is for these reasons we have selected the Sonder Ditch as the trigger point.' The lecturer touched a button on the wall panel and the image on the screen changed.

'Now, here is something you have not seen before.'

The man in the chair crouched forward.

'What is it?'

'It is an underground map based on the borehole results of the five companies who have been exploring the ground to the east of the Big Dipper. These results have been pooled and interpreted by some of the finest brains in the fields of geology and hydrophysics. You have here a carefully considered representation of exactly what lies on the far side of the Big Dipper fault.'

The big man moved uncomfortably in his chair.

'It's a monster!'

'Yes, a monster. Lying just beyond the fault is an underground lake, no, that is not the correct word. Let us call it an underground sea, the size of, say, Lake Eyrie. The water is held in a vast sponge of porous dolomite rock.'

'My God.' For the first time the fat man had lost his poise. 'If this is right, why don't the mining companies arrive at the same conclusion and keep well away from it?'

'Because,' the lecturer switched off the image and the overhead lights came on, 'because in their highly competitive attitudes none of them has access to the findings of the others. It is only when all the results are studied that the picture becomes clear.'

'How did your Government come to be in possession of *all* the results?' demanded the fat man.

'That is not important.' The lecturer was brusque, impatient of the interruption. 'We are also in possession of the findings of a certain Dr Peter Wessels who is at present head of a research team in Rock Mechanics based on the Sonder Ditch mine property. It is Company classified information and consists of a paper that Dr Wessels has written on the shatter patterns and stresses of rock. His researches are directly related to the Ventersdorp quartzites which comprise the country rock of the Sonder Ditch workings.'

The lecturer picked up a pamphlet from his desk.

'I will not weary you by asking you to wade through its highly technical findings. Instead I will give it to you in capsule form. Dr Wessels arrives at the conclusion that a column of Ventersdorp quartzite 120 feet thick would shatter under a side pressure of 4000 pounds per square inch.'

The lecturer dropped the pamphlet back on the desk.

'As you know, by law, the gold mining companies are bound to leave a barrier of solid rock 120 feet thick along their boundaries. That is all that separates one mine's workings from another, just that wall of rock. You understand?'

'Of course. It is very simple.'

Simple? Yes, it is simple! This Dr Steyner, over whom you have control, will instruct the new General Manager of the Sonder Ditch to drive a tunnel through the Big Dipper dyke. The drive will puncture the vast underground reservoir and the water will run back and flood the entire Sonder Ditch workings. Once they are flooded, the pressure delivered by a 6000-foot head of water at the lower levels will be in excess of 4000 pounds per square inch. That is sufficient to burst the rock walls, and flood the Thornfontein, the Blaauberg, Deep Gold Levels and Tweefontein gold mines.

'The entire Kitchenerville gold fields would be effectively and permanently put out of production. The consequences for the economy of the Republic of South Africa would be catastrophic.'

The fat man was visibly shaken.

'Why do you want to do it?' he asked, shaking his head in awe.

'My colleague here,' the lecturer indicated a man who was sitting quietly in one corner, 'will explain that to you presently.'

'But–people!' the fat man protested. 'There will be people down there when it bursts, thousands of them.'

The lecturer smiled, raising one eyebrow. 'If I were to tell you that six thousand men would drown, would you refuse to proceed, and forfeit the million-dollar payment my Government has offered you?'

The fat man looked down, embarrassed, and muttered barely audibly. 'No.'

The lecturer chuckled. 'Good! Good! However, you may salve your aching conscience by assuring yourself that we do not expect more than forty or fifty fatalities from the flooding. Naturally, those men actually working on the face will be killed. But that tremendous volume of water under immense pressure should make it a merciful death. For the rest of them, the mine can be evacuated swiftly enough to allow them excellent chances of survival. The surrounding mines will have days to evacuate before the water pressure builds up sufficiently to burst through the boundary walls.'

There was silence then in the room for nearly a minute.

'Have you any questions?'

The fat man shook his head.

'Very well, in that case I will leave it to my colleague to complete the briefing. He will explain the necessity for this operation, will arrange the terms of payment and conditions upon which you will proceed.' The lecturer gathered up the pamphlet and other papers from the desk. 'It remains only for me to wish you good luck.' He chuckled again and left the room quickly.

The little man who up until then had remained silent, suddenly bounced out of his chair and began pacing up and down the wall-to-wall carpeting. He spoke rapidly, shooting occasional sideways glances at his audience, his bald head shining in the fluorescent lighting, wriggling his moustache like rabbit whiskers, puffing nervously at his cigarette.

'Reasons first. I'll make it short and sweet, right? The South Africans and the Frogs have got together. They're here in Paris now cooking up mischief. We know what they're up to, they're going to launch an all-out attack on my Government's currency. Gold price increase, you know. Very complicated and very nasty for us, right? They might just be able to do it, South Africa is the world's biggest gold producer. With the Frogs helping her, they might just be able to force an increase.'

He stopped in front of the fat man and thrust out an accusing finger.

'Are we going to sit back and let them have a free run? No, sir! We are going to throw down our own curve ball! In three months time the Syndicate will be ready to attack. At that precise moment we will kick the chair out from under the South Africans by cutting their gold production in half. We will flood the Kitchenerville goldfields and the attack will fizzle out like a damp squib, right?'

'As simple as that?' asked the fat man.

'As simple as that!' The bald head nodded vigorously. 'Now, my next duty is to make clear to you that the agreed million dollars is *all* the reward you receive. Neither you nor your agents may indulge in any financial transactions that might, in retrospect, show that this was a planned operation, right?'

'Right.' The fat man nodded.

'You give your assurance that you will not deal in any of the shares of the companies involved?'

'You have my solemn word.' The fat man told him earnestly, and not for the first time in his life reflected how easily and painlessly a promise could be given.

With the assistance of the three men who had watched Manfred Steyner that night at the gambling club in Johannesburg, he intended launching a bear offensive on the stock exchanges of the world.

On the day that they drilled into the Big Dipper dyke he and his partners would sell millions of the shares of the five mining companies for one of the biggest financial killings in the history of money.

'We are agreed then.' The bald head bobbed. 'Now, as for this Dr Steyner, we have had a screening and personality analysis and we believe that, despite the secure hold you have on his loyalties, he would jib at giving the order to drive on the Big Dipper if he were aware of the consequences. Therefore we have prepared a second geological report,' he produced from his brief case a thick manila folder, 'incorporating those figures which he will recognize. In other words the drilling results of the CRC exploration teams, but the other figures are fictitious. This report purports to prove the existence of a fabulously rich gold reef beyond the fault.' He crossed to the fat man and handed him the folder. 'Take it. It will help you convince Dr Steyner, and he in turn to convince the new General Manager of the Sonder Ditch gold mine.'

'You have been thorough,' said the fat man.

'We try to give a satisfactory service to our customers,' said the bald man.

36

The game was five card stud poker, and there were two big winners at the table, Manfred Steyner and the Algerian.

Manfred had timed his arrival in Paris to ensure himself an uninterrupted weekend before the rest of the delegates came in on the Monday morning flight.

He had checked in at the Hotel George Cinq on Saturday afternoon, bathed and rested for three hours until eight in the evening, then he had set out for the Club Chat Noir by taxi.

He had been playing now for five hours, and a steady succession of strong cards had pushed his winnings up to a formidable sum. It lay piled in front of him, a fruit salad of garish French bank notes. Across the table sat the Algerian, a slim dark-skinned Arab with toffee eyes and a silky black moustache. His teeth were very white against the creamy brown skin. He wore a turtle-neck shirt in pink silk, and a linen jacket of baby blue. With long brown fingers he kept smoothing and stacking his own pile of bank notes.

A girl sat on the arm of his chair, an Arab girl in a skin-tight gold trouser suit. Her hair was shiny black and hung onto her shoulders, her eyes were disconcertingly level as she watched Manfred.

'Ten thousand.' Manfred's voice was explosive, like that of a teutonic drillmaster. He was betting on his fourth card which had just been dealt to him. He and the Algerian were the remaining players in the game. The others had folded their hands and were sitting back watching with the casual interest of men no longer involved.

The Algerian's eyes narrowed slightly and the girl leaned down to whisper softly in his ear. He shook his head, annoyed, and drew on his cigarette. He had a pair of queens and a six showing and he leaned forward to study Manfred's cards.

The dealer's voice prodded. 'The bet is ten thousand francs, from four, five, seven of clubs. Possible straight flush.'

'Bet or drop,' said one of the uncommitted players. 'You're wasting time.'

The Algerian flashed him a venomous glance.

'Bet,' he said, and counted out ten thousand-franc notes into the pool.

'*Carte.*' The dealer slid a card face down in front of each of them. Quickly the Algerian lifted one corner of his card with his thumb, glanced at it and then closed the face.

Manfred sat very still, the card lying inches from his right hand. His face was pale, calm, but he was seething internally. Far from a possible straight flush, Manfred was holding four, five, seven of clubs and the eight of hearts. A six was the only card that could improve his hand and one six was already showing among the Algerian's cards. His chances were remote.

His lower belly and loins were tight and hot with excitement, his chest constricted. He drew out the sensation, wanting it to last for ever.

'Pair of queens still to bet,' murmured the dealer.

'Ten thousand.' The Algerian pushed the notes forward.

'He has found another queen,' thought Manfred, 'but he is uncertain of my flush or straight.'

Manfred placed his smooth white hand over his fifth card, cupping it. He lifted it.

'Table,' said Manfred calmly, and there was a gasp and rustle from the watchers. The girl's hand tightened on the Algerian's sleeve, she stared with hatred into Manfred's face.

'The gentleman has made a table bet,' intoned the croupier. 'House rules. Any player may bet the entire stake he has upon the table.' He reached across and began to count the notes in front of Manfred.

Minutes later he announced the total. 'Two hundred and twelve thousand francs.' He looked across at the Algerian. 'It is now up to you to bet against the possible straight flush.'

The girl whispered urgently into the Arab's ear, but he snapped a single word at her and she recoiled. He looked about the room, as if seeking guidance, then he lifted and examined his hole cards again.

Suddenly his face hardened, and he looked steadily across at Manfred.

'Call!' he blurted, and Manfred's clenched right fist fell open upon the table.

The Arab faced his hand. Three queens. The whole room looked expectantly at Manfred.

He flicked over his last card. Two of diamonds. His hand was worthless.

With a birdlike cry of triumph the Algerian leaped from his seat and reaching across the table began raking Manfred's stake with both arms towards him.

Manfred stood up from the table, and the Arab girl grinned maliciously at him, taunting him in Arabic. He turned quickly away and almost ran down the steps that led to the cloakrooms. Twenty minutes later, feeling weak and slightly dizzy, Manfred slipped into the back seat of a Citroen taxi cab.

'George Cinq,' he told the driver. As he entered the lobby of the hotel he saw a tall figure rise from one of the leather armchairs and follow him across to the lifts. Shoulder to shoulder they stepped into the lift and as the doors slid closed the tall man spoke.

'Welcome to Paris, Dr Steyner.'

'Thank you, Andrew. I presume you have come to give me my instructions?'

'That is correct. He wishes to see you tomorrow at ten o'clock. I will call for you.'

37

It was Saturday night in Kitchenerville and in the men's bar of the Lord Kitchener Hotel the daily-paid men from the five gold mines were bellying up to the counter three deep.

The public dance had been in progress for three hours. At tables along the veranda the women-folk sat primly sipping their port and lemonade. Although they all were admirably ignoring the absence of the men, yet a constant and merciless vigil was kept on the door to the men's bar. Most of the wives already had the automobile keys safely in their handbags.

In the dining-hall, cleared of its furniture and sprinkled liberally with french chalk, the local four-piece band who played under the unlikely name of the 'Wind Dogs' launched without preliminaries into a lively rendition of 'Die Ou Kraal Liedjie', and from the men's bar, in various stages of inebriation, answering the call to arms came the troops.

Many of them had shed their jackets, the knots of their ties had slipped, their voices were boisterous and legs were a little unsteady as they led their women onto the dance floor and immediately showed to which school of the dance they belonged.

There was the cavalry squadron which tucked partner under one arm, very much like a lance, and charged. At the other end of the scale were those who plodded grimly around the perimeter, looking neither left nor right, speaking to no one, not even their partners. Then there were the sociables who reeled about the floor, red in the face, their movements completely unrelated to the music, shouting to their friends and attempting to pinch any feminine posterior that came within range. Their unpredictable progress interfered with the evolutions of the dedicated.

The dedicated took up their positions in the centre of the floor and twisted. A half dozen years previously the twist had swept like an Asian 'flu epidemic through the world and then faded out. Gone, forgotten, except in places like Kitchenerville. Here it had been taken and firmly entrenched into the social culture of the community.

Even in this stronghold of the twist, there was one master. 'Johnny Delange? Gott man, but he can twist, hey!' they murmured with awe.

With the sinuous erotic movements of an erect cobra, Johnny was twisting with Hettie. His shiny rayon suit caught the light and the lace ruffles of his shirt fluttered at his throat. There was a fierce grin of pleasure on his hawk features, and the jewelled buckles of his pointed Italian shoes twinkled as he danced.

A big girl with copper hair and creamy skin, Hettie was light on her feet. She had a tiny waist and swelling regal bottom under the emerald-green skirt. She laughed as she danced, a full healthy laugh to match her body.

The two of them moved with the expertise of a couple who have danced together often. Hettie anticipated each of Johnny's movements, and he grinned his approval at her.

From the veranda Davy Delange watched them. He stood in the shadows, clutching a tankard of beer, a squat, lonely figure. When another dancing couple cut off his view of Hettie's luscious revolving buttocks he would exclaim with irritation and move restlessly.

The music ended and the dancers spilled out onto the veranda, laughing and breathless, mopping streaming faces; girls squealing and giggling as the men led them to their seats, deposited them and then headed for the bar.

'See you.' Johnny left Hettie reluctantly, he would have liked to stay with her, but he was sensitive about what the boys would say if he spent the whole evening with his wife.

He was absorbed into the masculine crowd, to join their banter of loud laughter. He was deeply involved in a discussion of the merits of the new Ford Mustang, which he was considering buying, when Davy nudged him.

'It's Constantine!' he whispered, and Johnny looked up quickly. Constantine was a Greek immigrant, a stoper on the Blaauberg Mine. He was a big strong black-haired individual with a broken nose. Johnny had broken his nose for him about ten months previously. As a bachelor Johnny would fight him on the average of once a month, nothing serious, just a semi-friendly punch-up.

However, Constantine could not understand that nowadays Johnny was forbidden by his brand new wife from indulging in casual exchanges of fisticuffs. He had developed the erroneous theory that Johnny Delange was afraid of him.

He was coming down the bar room now, holding his glass in his massive hairy right hand with the little finger extended genteelly. On his hip rested his other hand and he minced along with a simpering smile on his blue-jowled granite-textured features. Stopping in front of the mirror to pat his hair into place, he winked at his cronies and then came on down to where Johnny stood. He paused and ogled Johnny heavily, fluttering his eyelids and wriggling his hips. His colleagues from the Blaauberg Mine were weak with laughter, gurgling merrily, hanging onto each other's shoulders.

Then with a bump and grind that raised another howl of laughter Constantine disappeared into the lavatories, to emerge minutes later and blow Johnny a kiss as he went back to join his friends. They plied liquor on the Greek in appreciation of his act. Johnny's smile was a little strained as he resumed the discussion on the Mustang's virtues.

Twenty minutes and half a dozen brandies later, Constantine repeated his little act again on the way to the latrine. His repertoire was limited.

'Hold it, Johnny,' whispered Davy. 'Let's go and sit on the veranda.'

'He's asking for it. I'm telling you!' Johnny's smile had disappeared.

'Come on, Johnny, man.'

'No, hell, they'll think I'm running. I can't go now.'

'You know what Hettie will say,' Davy warned him. For a moment longer Johnny hesitated.

'The hell with what Hettie says.' Johnny bunched his right fist with its array of gold rings as he moved down to Constantine and leaned beside him on the counter.

'Herby,' he called the barman, and when he had his attention he indicated the Greek. 'Please give the lady a port and lemonade.'

And the bystanders scattered for cover. Davy shot out of the door onto the veranda to report to Hettie.

'Johnny!' he gasped. 'He's fighting again.'

'Is he!' Hettie came to her feet like a red-headed Valkyrie. But her progress to the men's bar was delayed by the crowd of spectators that jammed the doorway and all the windows. The crowd was tiptoeing and climbing onto the chairs and tables for a better view, every thud or crash of breaking furniture was greeted with a roar of delight.

Hettie had her handbag clutched in her right hand, and like a jungle explorer hacking his way through the undergrowth with a machete, she opened a path for herself to the bar room door.

At the door she paused. The conflict had reached a critical stage. Among a litter of broken glass and shattered stools, Johnny and the Greek were circling each other warily, weaving and feinting, all their wits concentrated upon each other. Both of them were marked. The Greek was bleeding from his lip, a thin red ribbon of blood down his chin that dripped onto his shirt. Johnny had a shiny red swelling closing one eye. The crowd were silent, waiting.

'Johnny Delange!' Hettie's voice cracked like a mauser rifle fired from ambush. Johnny started guiltily, dropping his hands, half turning towards her as the Greek's fist crashed into the side of his head. Johnny spun from the blow, hit the wall and slid down quietly.

With a roar of triumph Constantine rushed forward to put the boots into Johnny's prostrate form, but he pitched forward to sprawl unconscious beside

Johnny. Hettie had hit him with the water bottle snatched up from one of the table tops.

'Please help me get my husband to the car,' she appealed to the men around her, suddenly helpless and little-girlish.

She sat beside Davy in the front of the Monaco, fuming with anger.

Johnny lay at ease upon the back seat. He was snoring softly.

'Don't be angry, Hettie.' Davy was driving sedately.

'I've told him, not once, a hundred times.' Hettie's voice crackled with static. 'I told him I wouldn't put up with it.'

'It wasn't his fault. The Greek started it,' Davy explained softly and placed his hand on her leg.

'You stick up for him, just because he is your brother.'

'That's not true,' Davy soothed her, stroking her leg. 'You know how I feel about you, Hettie.'

'I don't believe you.' His hand was moving higher. 'You men are all the same. You all stick together.

Her anger was fast solidifying into a burning resentment of Johnny Delange, one in which she was willing to take a calculated revenge. She knew that Davy's hand was no longer trying to comfort her and quench her anger. Before she married Johnny Delange, Hettie had had every opportunity to learn about men, and she had been an enthusiastic and receptive pupil. She placed no special importance on an act of the flesh, dispensing her favours as casually as someone might offer a cigarette-case around.

'Why not?' she thought. 'That will fix Mr Johnny Delange! Not all the way, of course, but just enough to get my own back on him.'

'No, Hettie. It's true–I tell you.' Davy's voice was husky, as he felt her knees fall apart under his hand. He touched the silky-smooth skin above her stocking top.

The Monaco slowed to almost walking pace, and it was ten minutes before they reached the company-owned house on the outskirts of Kitchenerville.

In the back seat Johnny groaned. Immediately Davy's hand jerked back to the steering-wheel, and Hettie sat up in the seat, straightening her skirt.

'Help me get him inside,' she said, and her voice was shaky and her cheeks flushed. She was no longer angry.

38

They were both a little tipsy. They had stopped to celebrate Rod's promotion at the Sunnyside Hotel. They had sat side by side in one of the booths, drinking quickly, excitedly, laughing together, sitting close but not touching.

Terry Steyner could not remember when she had last behaved this way. It must have been all of ten years ago, her last term at Cape Town varsity, swigging draught beer in the 'Pig and Whistle' at Randall's Hotel and talking the most inane rubbish. All the matronly dignity that Manfred insisted she maintain was gone, she felt like a freshette on a first date with the captain of the rugby team.

'Let's get out of here,' Rod said suddenly, and she stood up unquestioningly. He took her arm down the stairs, and the light touch of his fingers tingled on her bare skin.

In the Maserati again she experienced the feeling of isolation from reality.

'How often do you see your daughter, Rod?' she asked as he settled into the seat beside her, and he glanced at her, surprised.

'Every Sunday.'

'Tomorrow?'

'Yes.'

'How old is she?'

'Nine next birthday.'

'What do you do with her?'

Rod pressed the starter.

'How do you mean?'

'Where do you take her, what do you do together?'

'We go rowing on Zoo Lake, or eat ice cream sundaes. If it's cold or raining we sit in the apartment and we play mahjong.' He let in the clutch, and as they pulled away he added, 'She cheats.'

'The apartment?'

'I keep a hideaway in town.'

'Where?'

'I'll show you,' said Rod quietly.

She sat on the studio couch and looked about her with interest. She had not expected the obvious care that he had taken in furnishing the apartment. It was in wheatfield gold, chocolate brown and copper. There was a glorious glowing autumn landscape on the far wall that she recognized as a Dino Paravano.

She noticed a little ruefully how Rod stage-managed the lighting for full romantic effect, and then moved automatically to the liquor cabinet.

'Where is the bathroom?' Terry asked.

'Second left, down the passage.'

She lingered in the bathroom, opening the medicine cabinet like a thief. There were three toothbrushes hanging in the slots, and below them an aerosol can of 'Bidex'. Quickly she shut the cabinet. Feeling disturbed, not sure if it was jealousy or guilt at her own prying.

The bedroom door was open and so she could not help seeing the double bed as she went back to the lounge. She stood in front of the painting.

'I love his work,' she said.

'Not too photographic for your taste?'

'No. I love it.'

He gave her the drink and stood beside her, studying the painting. She tinkled the ice in her glass, and he turned towards her. The feeling of unreality was still holding Terry as she felt him take the glass from her hand.

She was conscious of his hands only, they were strong and very practised. They touched her shoulders, and then moved on to her back calmly. She felt a voluptuous shudder shake her whole body, and then his mouth came down over hers and the sense of unreality was complete. It was all warm and misty, and she let him take control.

She never knew how long afterwards she jerked back to complete, chilling reality. They were on the couch. She lay in his arms. The front of her slack suit was open to the waist and her bra was unhooked. His head was bowed over her and with a handful of his thick springy hair she was directing his lips in their quest. His mouth was warm and sucky on her breast.

'I must be mad!' she gasped, and struggled violently from his arms. She was trembling with fright, horrified with herself. Nothing like this had ever happened to her before.

'This is madness!' Her eyes were great dark pools in her pale face, and her fingers were frantic as she buttoned her blouse. As the last button slipped into its hole, anger replaced her fright.

'How many women have you seduced on that couch, Rodney Ironsides?'

Rod stood up, reaching out a hand to reassure her.

'Don't touch me!' She stepped back. 'I want to go home!'

'I'll take you home, Terry. Just calm down. Nothing happened.'

'That's not your fault,' she blazed.

'No, it's not,' he agreed.

'If you had your way, you'd have–' she bit it off.

'Yes, I would have.' Rod nodded. 'But only if you wanted the same thing.'

She stared at him, starting to recover her temper and her control.

'I shouldn't have come up here, I know. It was asking for trouble, but please take me home now.'

39

The telephone woke Rod. He checked his wrist watch as he tottered naked and half asleep through to the lounge. Eight o'clock.

'Ironsides!' He yawned into the mouthpiece, and then came fully awake as he recognized her voice.

'Good morning, Rodney. How's your hangover?'

He had not expected to hear from her again.

'Just bearable.'

'I called to thank you for an amusing and–instructive evening.'

'Hark at the girl!' He grinned and scratched his chest. 'She changes with the wind. Last night I expected a bullet between the eyes.'

'Last night I got one big fright,' she admitted. 'It comes as a bit of a shock to discover suddenly that you are quite capable of acting the wanton. Not all the names I called you were meant.'

'I am sorry for my contribution to your distress,' Rod said.

'Don't be, you were very impressive.' Then quickly, changing the subject, 'You are picking up your daughter today?'

'Yes.'

'I'd like to meet her.'

'That could be arranged.' Rod was cautious.

'Does she like horses?'

'She's crazy about them.'

'Would you like to take her and me out to my stud farm on the Vaal river?'

Rod hesitated. 'Is it safe? I mean, being seen together?'

'It's my reputation, I'll look after it.'

'Fine!' Rod agreed. 'We'd love to visit your farm.'

'I'll meet you at your apartment. When?'

'Half past nine!'

Patti was still in her dressing-gown and she offered Rod her cheek casually to be pecked. There were curlers in her hair and from her eyes he could tell she'd had a late night.

'Hello, you're getting thin. Melly is dressing. Do you want some coffee? Your maintenance cheque was late again this month.' And she took a swipe at the spaniel pup as it squatted on the carpet. 'Damn dog pees all over the place. *Melanie.*' She raised her voice. 'Hurry up! Your Papa is here.'

'Hello, Daddy!' Melanie's voice shrieked delightedly from the interior of the apartment.

'Hello, baby.'

'You can't come in, Daddy, I haven't got any clothes on.'

'Well hurry up! I've come a million miles to see you.'

'Not a *million*!' You couldn't fool Melanie Ironsides.

'Did you say you wanted coffee? It's no trouble, it's made already.' Patti led him through into the sitting-room.

'Thanks.'

'How are things?' she asked as she filled a cup and gave it to him.

'They've made me General Manager of the Sonder Ditch.' He could not prevent himself, it was too good. He had to boast.

Pattie looked at him, startled.

'You're joking!' she accused, and then he saw her mind beginning to work like a cash register.

He almost laughed out loud. 'No. It's true.'

'God!' She sat down limply. 'It will nearly *double* your salary.'

He looked at her dispassionately, and not for the first time felt a great wash of relief as he realized he was no longer shackled to her.

'It's usual to offer congratulations,' he prompted her.

'You don't deserve it.' She was angry now. 'You are a selfish, philandering bastard, Rodney Ironsides, you don't deserve the good things that keep happening to you.' He had cheated her. She could have been the General Manager's wife, first lady of the goldfields. Now she was a divorcée, stuck with a miserable four fifty a month. It had seemed good before, but not now.

'I hope you will have enough conscience to make a suitable adjustment for Melanie and me. We are entitled to a share.'

The door burst open and Melanie Ironsides arrived at a gallop to wrap herself around Rod's neck. She had long blonde hair and green eyes.

'I got nine out of ten for spelling!'

'You're not clever, you're a genius. Also you're beautiful.'

'Will you carry me down to the car, Daddy?'

'What's wrong? Your legs in plaster?'

'Please, please, pretty please times three.'

Patti interrupted the love feast.

'Have you got your jersey, young lady?' And Melanie flew.

'I'll have her back before seven,' said Rod.

'You haven't answered my question.' Patti was surly. 'Do we get a share?'

'Yes, of course,' said Rod. 'The same big juicy four fifty you've had all along.'

They had been in Rod's apartment ten minutes when the doorbell announced Terry's arrival. She was in jeans and a checked shirt with her hair in a plait, and she greeted Rod self-consciously. When he introduced her to Melanie, she did not look much older than his daughter.

The two girls summed each other up solemnly. Melanie suddenly very demure and refined, and Rod was relieved to see that Terry had the good sense not to gush over the child.

They were in the Maserati and half way to the village of Parys on the Vaal River before Melanie had completed her microscopic scrutiny of Terry.

'Can I come up front and sit on your lap?' she asked at last.

'Yes, of course.' Terry was hard put to conceal her relief and pleasure. Melanie scrambled over the seat and settled on Terry's lap.

'You are pretty,' Melanie gave her considered opinion.

'Thank you. So are you.'

'Are you Daddy's girl friend?' Melanie demanded. Terry glanced at Rod, then burst out laughing.

'Almost,' she gurgled, and then all three of them were laughing.

They laughed often that day. It was a day of sunshine and laughter.

Terry and Rod walked together with fingers almost touching through the green paddocks along the willow-lined bank of the Vaal. Melanie ran ahead of them shrieking with glee at the antics of the foals.

They went up to the stables where Melanie fed sugar lumps to a winner of the Cape Metropolitan Handicap and then kissed his velvety muzzle.

They swam in the pool beside the elegant white-washed homestead, laughter mingling with the splashes, and when they drove back to Johannesburg in the evening Melanie curled in exhausted slumber on Terry's lap, her head cushioned on Terry's bosom.

Terry waited in the Maserati while Rod carried the sleeping child up to her mother, and when he returned and slipped into the driver's seat, Terry murmured, 'My car is at your apartment. You'll have to take me with you.'

Neither of them spoke until they were back in Rod's sitting-room. Then he said, 'Thank you for a wonderful day.' And he took her to his chest and kissed her.

In the darkness she lay pressed to his sleeping body, clinging to him, as though he might be taken from her. She had never felt such intensity of emotion before, it was a compound of awed wonder and gratitude. She had just been admitted to a new level of human experience she had never suspected existed.

The sheets were still damp. She felt bruised internally, aching, a slow voluptuous pulse of pain that she cherished.

Lightly she touched his body, not wanting to wake him, running her fingertips through the coarse curls that covered his chest, marvelling still at the infinity that separated this from what she had known before.

She shuddered with almost unbearable pleasure as she remembered his voice describing her body to her, making her proud of it for the first time in her life. She remembered the words he had used to tell her exactly what they were doing together, and the feel of his hands, so gentle, sure, so lovingly possessive upon her.

He was so unashamed, taking such obvious joy in her, that the reserves which the barren years of her marriage had placed in her mind were swept away and she was able to go with Rodney Ironsides beyond the storm into that tranquil state where mind and body are completely at peace.

She became aware of him awakening beside her, and she touched his face, his lips and his eyes with her fingertips.

'Thank you,' she whispered, and he seemed to understand, for he took her head and drew it gently down into the hollow of his shoulder.

'Sleep now,' he told her softly, and she closed her eyes and lay very still and quiet beside him, but she did not sleep. She would not miss one moment of this experience.

40

Rod's letter of appointment lay on his desk when he arrived at his office at seven-thirty on the Monday morning.

He sat down and lit a cigarette. Then he began to read it slowly, savouring each word.

'Duly instructed by the Board of Directors,' it began, and ended, 'it remains only to tender the congratulations of the Board, and to voice their confidence in your ability.'

Dimitri came through his office, distracted.

'Hey! Rod! Christ what a start to the week! We've got a fault in the main high voltage cable on 90 level, and–'

'Don't come squealing to me,' Rod cut him short. 'I'm not the Underground Manager.'

Dimitri gaped at him, taken by surprise.

'What the hell, have they fired you?'

'Next best thing,' said Rod and flipped the letter across the desk. 'Look what the bastards have done to me.'

Dimitri read and then whooped.

'My God, Rod! My God!' He shot down the passage to carry the news to the other line managers. Then they were all in his office, shaking his hand. He judged most of their reactions as favourable, though occasionally he detected a false note. A twinge of envy here, one there who had recently had his ears burned by the Ironsides tongue, and an incompetent who knew his job was now in danger. The phone rang. Rod answered it, his expression changed and he cleared his office with a peremptory wave.

'Hirschfeld here.'

'Morning, Mr Hirschfeld.'

'Well, you've got your chance, Ironsides.'

'I'm grateful for it.'

'I want to see you. I'll give you today to sort yourself out. Tomorrow morning at nine o'clock, my office at Reef Buildings.'

'I'll be there.'

'Good.'

Rod hung up, and the day dissolved into a welter of activity and reorganization, constantly interrupted by a stream of well-wishers. He was still running the Underground Manager's job in addition to the General Manager's. It would be some considerable time before a new Underground Manager was transferred in from one of the other group mines. He was trying to arrange his move to the big office in the main Administrative Block up on the ridge, when he had another visitor, Frank Lemmer's secretary, Miss Lily Jordan, in a severe grey flannel suit looking like a wardress from Ravensbruck.

'Mr Ironsides, you and I have not seen eye to eye in the past.' This was the understatement of the year. 'It is unlikely that we will in the future. Therefore, I have come to tender my resignation. I have made arrangements.'

The phone rang. Dan Stander's voice, breezy and carefree. 'Rod, I'm in love.'

'Oh Christ, no!' Rod groaned. 'Not this morning.'

'I've got to thank you for introducing me to her. She's the most wonderful–'

'Yeah, yeah!' Rod cut him short. 'Look, Dan, I'm rather busy. Some other time, all right?'

'Oh yes, I forgot. You are the new General Manager they tell me. Congratulations. You can buy me a drink at the Club. Six o'clock.'

'Right. By then I'll need one.' Rod hung up, and faced the hanging-judge expression of Miss Lily Jordan.

'Miss Jordan, in the past our interests have conflicted. In future they will not. You are the best private secretary within a hundred miles of the Sonder Ditch. I need you, the Company needs you.'

That was the magic word. Miss Jordan had twenty-five years' service with the Company. She wavered visibly.

'Please, Miss Jordan, give me a chance.' Shamelessly Rod switched on his most engaging smile. Miss Jordan's femininity was not so completely atrophied that she could resist that smile.

'Very well, then, Mr Ironsides. I'll stay on initially until the end of the month. We'll see after that.' She stood up. 'Now, I'll get your things moved up to the new office.'

'Thank you, Miss Jordan.' With relief he let her take over, and tackled the problems that were piling up on his desk. One man, two jobs. Now he was responsible for surface operation as well as underground. The phone rang, men queued up in the passage, memos kept coming through from Dimitri's office. There was no lunch hour, and by the time she rang he was exhausted.

'Hello,' she said. 'Do I see you tonight?' Her voice was as refreshing as a wet cloth on the brow of a prizefighter between rounds.

'Terry.' He simply spoke her name in reply.

'Yes or no. If it's *no,* I intend jumping off the top of Reef Building.'

'Yes,' he said. 'Pops has summoned me to a meeting at nine tomorrow morning, so I'll be staying overnight at the apartment. I'll call you as soon as I get in.'

'Goody! Goody!' said she.

At five-thirty Dimitri stuck his head around the door.

'I'm going down to No. 1 shaft to supervise the shoot, Rod.'

'My God, what time is it?' Rod checked his watch. 'So late already.'

'It gets late early around here,' Dimitri agreed. 'I'm off.'

'Wait!' Rod stopped him. 'I'll shoot her.'

'No trouble.' Dimitri demurred. Company standard procedure laid down that each day's blast must be supervised by either the Underground Manager or his Assistant.

'I'll do it,' Rod repeated. Dimitri opened his mouth to protest further, then he saw that expression on Rod's face and changed his mind quickly.

'Okay then. See you tomorrow.' And he was gone.

Rod grinned at his own sentimentality. The Sonder Ditch was his now and, by God, he was going to shoot his own first blast on her.

They were waiting for him at the steel door of the blast control room at the shaft head. It was a small concrete room like a wartime pillbox, and there were only two keys to the door. Dimitri had one, Rod the other.

The duty mine captain and the foreman electrician added their congratulations to the hundreds he had received during the day, and Rod opened the door and they went into the tiny room.

'Check her out,' Rod instructed, and the mine captain began his calls to the shaft overseers at both No. 1 and No. 2 for their confirmation that the workings of the Sonder Ditch were deserted, that every human being who had gone down that morning had come out again this evening.

Meanwhile, the foreman electrician was busy at the electrical control board. He looked up at Rod.

'Ready to close the circuits, Mr Ironsides.'

'Go ahead,' Rod nodded and the man touched a switch. A green light showed up on the board.

'No. 1 north longwall closed and green.'

'Lock her in,' Rod instructed and the electrician touched another switch.

'No. 1 east longwall closed and green.'

'Lock her in.'

The green light showed that the firing circuit was intact. A red light would indicate a fault and the faulty circuit would not be locked into the blast pattern.

Circuit after circuit was readied until finally the foreman stood back from the control board.

'All green and locked in.'

Rod glanced at the mine captain.

'All levels clear, Mr Ironsides. She's ready to burn.'

'Cheesa!' said Rod, the traditional command that had come down from the days when each fuse had been individually lit by a hand-held igniter stick.

'Cheesa' was the Bantu word for 'burn'.

The mine captain crossed to the control board and opened the cage that guarded a large red button.

'Cheesa!' echoed the mine captain and hit the button with the heel of his hand.

Immediately the row of green lights on the control board were extinguished, and in their place showed a row of red lights. Every circuit had been broken by the explosions.

The ground under their feet began to tremble. Throughout the workings the shots were firing. In the stopes the head charges fired at the top of the inclines, then in succession the other shots went off behind them. Each charge taking a ten-ton bite of rock and reef out of the face.

At the end of the development drives, a more complicated pattern was shooting. First a row of *cutters* went off down the middle of the oval face. Then the *shoulder charges* at the top corners, followed by the *knee charges* at the bottom corners. A moment's respite with the dust and nitrous fumes swirling back down the drive, then a roar as the *easers* on each side shaped the hole. Another respite and then the *lifters* along the bottom picked up the heap of broken rock and threw it back from the face.

Rod could imagine it clearly. Though no human eye had ever witnessed the blast, he knew exactly what was taking place down there.

The last tremor died away.

'That's it. A full blast,' said the mine captain.

'Thank you.' Rod felt tired suddenly. He wanted that drink, even though their brief exchange that morning had warned him that Dan would probably be insufferable. He could guess the conversation would revolve around Dan's new-found love.

Then he smiled as he thought about what waited for him in Johannesburg later that night, and suddenly he wasn't all that tired.

41

They sat facing each other.

'Only three things worry me,' Terry told Rod.

'What are they?' Rod rubbed soap into the face flannel.

'Firstly, your legs are too long for this bath.'

Rod rearranged his limbs, and Terry shot half out of the water with a squeak.

'Rodney Ironsides, would you be good enough to take a bit more care where you put your toes!'

'Forgive me.' He leaned forward to kiss her. 'Tell me what else worries you.'

'Well, the second thing that worries me is that I'm not worried.'

'What part of Ireland did you say you were from?' Rod asked. 'County Cork?'

'I mean, it's terrible but I'm not even a little conscience-stricken. Once I believed that if it ever happened to me I would never be able to look another human being in the eyes, I'd be so ashamed.' She took the flannel from his hands and began soaping his chest and shoulders. 'But, far from being ashamed, I'd like to stand in the middle of Eloff Street at rush hour and shout "Rodney Ironsides is my lover".'

'Let's drink to that.' Rodney rinsed the soap from his hands and reached over the side of the bath to pick up the two wine glasses from the floor. He gave one to Terry and they clinked them together, the sparkling Cape Burgundy glowed ruby red.

'Rodney Ironsides is my lover!' she toasted him.

'Rodney Ironsides is your lover,' he agreed and they drank.

'Now, I give *you* a toast,' he said.

'What is it?' She held her glass ready, and Rod leaned forward and poured the red wine from the crystal glass between her breasts. It ran like blood down her white skin and he intoned solemnly:

'Bless this ship and all who sail in her!'

Terry gurgled with delight.

'To her Captain. May he keep a firm hand on the rudder!'

'May her bottom never hit the reef!'

'May she be torpedoed regularly!'

'Terry Steyner, you are terrible.'

'Yes, aren't I?' And they drained their glasses.

'Now,' Rod asked, 'what is your third worry?'

'Manfred will be home on Saturday.'

They stopped laughing, Rod reached down for the Burgundy bottle and refilled the glasses.

'We still have five days,' he said.

42

It had been a week of personal triumph for Manfred Steyner. His address to the conference had been the foundation of the entire talks, all discussion had revolved upon it. He had been called upon to speak at the closing banquet which General de Gaulle had attended in person, and afterwards the General had asked Manfred to take coffee and brandy with him in one of the ante-rooms. The General had been gracious, had asked questions and listened attentively to the answers. Twice he had called his finance minister's attention to Manfred's replies.

Their farewells had been cordial, with a hint of state recognition for Manfred, a decoration. In common with most Germans, Manfred had a weakness for uniforms and decorations. He imagined how a star and ribbon might look on the snowy front of his dress shirt.

There had been a wonderful press both in France and at home. Even a bad-tempered quarter column in *Time* Magazine, with a picture, De Gaulle stooping over the diminutive Manfred solicitously, one hand on his shoulder. The caption read:

'The huntsman and the hawk. To catch a dollar?'

Now standing in the tiny cloakroom in the tail of the South Africa Airways Boeing, Manfred was whistling softly as he stripped his shirt and vest, crumpled them into a ball and dropped them into the waste bin.

Naked to the waist, he wiped his upper body with a wet cloth and then rubbed 4711 Eau de Cologne into his skin. From the briefcase he took an electric razor. The whistling stopped as he contorted his face for the razor.

Through his mind ran page after page of the report that Andrew had delivered that morning to his hotel room. Manfred had total recall when it came to written material. Although the report was in the briefcase beside him, in his mind's eye he could review it word for word, figure for figure.

It was a stupendous piece of work. How the authors had gained access to the drilling and exploration reports of the five Kitchenerville field companies he could not even guess, for the gold mining companies' security was as tight as that of any national intelligence agency. But the figures were genuine. He had checked those purporting to be from C.R.C. carefully. They were correct. So therefore the other four must also be genuine.

The names of the authors of the report were legend. They were the top men in the field. Their opinions were the best in Harley Street. The conclusion that they reached was completely convincing. In effect it was this:

If a haulage was driven from 66 level of the Sonder Ditch No. 1 shaft through the Big Dipper dyke, it would pass *under* the limestone water-bearing formations, and just beyond the fault it would intersect a reef of almost unbelievable value.

It had not needed the lecture that Manfred had received from his corpulent creditor to show him the possibilities. The man who gave the order to drive through the Big Dipper would receive the credit. He would certainly be elected to the Chairmanship of the Group when that office fell vacant.

There was another possibility. A person who purchased a big packet of Sonder Ditch shares immediately before the reef was intersected would be a very rich man when he came to sell those shares later. He would be so rich that he would no longer be dependent on his wife for the means to live the kind of life he wanted, and indulge his own special tastes.

Manfred blew the hairs from his razor and returned it to his brief case. Then as he took out a fresh shirt and vest, he began to sing the words to the tune:

Heute ist der schönste Tag
In meinem Leben.

He would telephone Ironsides from Jan Smuts Airport as soon as he had passed through customs. Ironsides would come up to the house on Sunday morning and receive his orders.

As he knotted the silk of his tie Manfred knew that he stood at the threshold of a whole new world, the events of the next few months would lift him high above the level of ordinary men.

It was the chance for which he had worked and waited all these years.

43

Circumstances had changed completely since his last visit, Rod reflected, as he took the Maserati up the drive towards the Dutch gabled house.

He parked the car and switched off the ignition, sitting a while, reluctant to face the man who had sponsored his career and whom Rod in turn had presented with a fine pair of horns.

'Courage, Ironsides!' he muttered and climbed out of the Maserati and went up the path across the lawns.

Terry was on the veranda in a gay print dress, with her hair loose, sprawled in a canvas chair with the Sunday papers scattered about her.

'Good morning, Mr Ironsides,' she greeted him as he came up the steps. 'My husband is in his study. You know the way, don't you?'

'Thank you, Mrs Steyner.' Rod kept his voice friendly but disinterested, then as he passed her chair he growled softly, 'I could eat you without salt.'

'Don't waste it, you gorgeous beast,' Terry murmured and ran the tip of her tongue over her lips.

Fifteen minutes later, Rod sat stony-faced and internally chilled before Manfred Steyner's desk. When at last he forced himself to speak, it felt as though the skin on his lips would tear with the effort.

'You want me to drive through the Big Dipper,' he croaked.

'More than that, Mr Ironsides. I want you to complete the drive within three months, and I want a complete security blanket on the development,' Manfred told him primly. Despite the fact that it was Sunday he was formally dressed, white shirt and dark suit. 'You will commence the drive from No. 1 shaft 66 level and make an intersect on reef at 6,600 feet with the S.D. No. 3 borehole 250 feet beyond the calculated extremity of the serpentine intrusion of the Big Dipper.'

'No,' Rod shook his head. 'You can't go through that. No one can take the chance. God alone knows what is on the other side, we only know that it is bad ground. Stinking rotten ground.'

'How do you know that?' Manfred asked softly.

'Everyone on the Kitchenerville field knows it.'

'How?'

'Little things.' Rod found it hard to put into words. 'You get a feeling, the signs are there and when you've been in the game long enough you have a sixth sense that warns you when–'

'Nonsense,' Manfred interrupted brusquely. 'We no longer live in the days of witchcraft.'

'Not witchcraft, experience,' Rod snapped angrily. 'You've seen the drilling results from the other side of the fault?'

'Of course,' Manfred nodded. 'S.D. No. 3 found values of thousands of penny-weights.'

'And the other holes went dry and twisted off, or had water squirting out of them like a pissing horse!'

Manfred flushed fiercely. 'You will be good enough not to employ bar-room terminology in this house.'

Rod was taken off balance, and before he could answer Manfred went on.

'Would you put the considered opinions of,' Manfred named three men, 'before your own vague intuitions?'

'They are the best in the business,' Rod conceded reluctantly.

'Read that,' snapped Manfred. He tossed a manila folder onto the desk top, then stood up and went to wash his hands at the concealed basin.

Rod picked up the folder, opened it and was immediately engrossed. Ten minutes later, without looking up from the report, he fumbled a pack of cigarettes from his pocket.

'Please do not smoke!' Manfred stopped him sharply.

Three-quarters of an hour later, Rod closed the folder. During that time Manfred Steyner had sat with reptilian stillness behind his desk, with the glitter of his eyes the only signs of life.

'How the hell did you get hold of those figures and reports?' Rod asked with wonder.

'That does not concern you.' Manfred retrieved the folder from him, his first movement in forty-five minutes.

'So that's it!' muttered Rod. 'The water is in the limestone near the surface. We go in under it!' He stood up from the chair abruptly and began to pace up and down in front of Manfred's desk.

'Are you convinced?' Manfred asked, and Rod did not answer.

'I have promoted you above older and more experienced men,' said Manfred softly. 'If I tear you down again, and tell the world you were not man enough for the job, then, Rodney Ironsides, you are finished. No one else would take a chance on you again, ever!'

It was true. Rod knew it.

'However, if you were to follow my instructions and we intersected this highly enriched reef, then part of the glory would rub off on you.'

That was also true. Rod stopped pacing, he stood with shoulders hunched, in an agony of indecision. Could he trust that report beyond his own deep intuition? When he thought about that ground beyond the dyke, his skin tickled with gooseflesh. He almost had the stink of it in his nostrils. Yet he could be wrong, and the weight of the opposition was heavy. The eminent names on the report, the threats which he knew Manfred would not hesitate to put into effect.

'Will you give me a written instruction?' Rod demanded harshly.

'What effect would that have?' Manfred asked mildly. 'As General Manager, the decision to work certain ground or not to work it is technically yours. In the very unlikely event that you encountered trouble beyond the fault, it would be no defence to produce a written instruction from me. Just as if you murdered my wife you could not defend yourself by producing a written instruction from me to do so.'

This again was true. Rod knew he was trapped. He could refuse, and wreck his career. Or he could comply and take the consequences whatever they may be.

'No,' said Manfred, 'I will not give you a written instruction.'

'You bastard,' Rod said softly.

Manfred answered as gently. 'I warned you that you would not be able to refuse to obey me.'

And the last twinge of remorse that Rod felt for his association with Terry Steyner faded and was gone.

'You've given me three months to hit the Big Dipper. All right, Steyner. You've got it!'

Rod turned on his heel and walked out of the room.

Terry was waiting for him among the protea plants on the bottom lawn. She saw his face and dropped all pretence. She went to meet him.

'Rod, what is it?' Her hand on his arm, looking up into his eyes.

'Careful!' he warned her, and she dropped her hand and stood back.

'What is it?'

'That bloody Gestapo bastard,' Rod snarled, and then, 'I'm sorry, Terry, he's your husband.'

'What has he done?'

'I can't tell you here. When can I see you?'

'I'll find an excuse to get away later today. Wait for me at your apartment.'

Later she sat on the couch below the Paravano painting and listened while he told her about it. All of it, the report, the threat and the order to pierce the Big Dipper.

She listened but expressed neither approval nor disapproval of his decision.

Manfred turned away from the window and went back to his desk. Even at that distance there had been no doubt about his wife's gesture. The hand outstretched, the face turned up, the lips parted in anxious inquiry, and then the guilty start and withdrawal.

He sat down at his desk, and laid his hands neatly in front of him. For the first time he was thinking of Rodney Ironsides as a man and not a tool.

He thought how big he was, tall and as wide across the shoulders as a gallows. Any reprisal on Ironsides could not be physical, and it could not be immediate. It must be after the drive to the Big Dipper.

I can wait, he thought coldly, there is time for everything in this life.

44

Johnny and Davy Delange sat in the two chairs before Rod's desk. They were both awkward and uncomfortable up here in the big office with picture windows looking out over the Kitchenerville valley.

I don't blame them, Rod thought, even I am not accustomed to it yet. Wall-to-wall carpeting, air-conditioning, original paintings on the wood-panelled walls.

'I have sent for you because you two are the best rock breakers on the Sonder Ditch,' Rod began.

'Tin ribs wants something,' thought Davy, with all the suspicion of the union man for management.'

'We will now have a few words from our sponsor,' Johnny grinned to himself. 'Before we start the programme.'

Rod looked at their faces and knew exactly what they were thinking. He had been on daily pay himself once. Cut out the compliments, Ironsides–he advised himself–these are two tough cookies and they are not impressed.

'I am pulling you out of the stopes and putting you onto a special development end. You will take it in turns to work day and night shift. You will be directly responsible to me and there will be a security blanket on your activity.'

They watched him without reaction, their expressions guarded. Johnny broke the short silence.

'One end, one blast a day?' He was thinking of his pay. Calculated on the amount of rock broken, he would earn little more than basic salary with a blast on one small face daily.

'No.' Rod shook his head. 'Ultra-fast, multi-blast, and shaft sinkers' rates.'

And both the Delange brothers sat forward in their chairs.

'Multi-blast?' Davy asked. That meant that they could shoot just as soon as they were ready. A good team could blast three–maybe four times a shift.

'Ultra-fast?' Johnny demanded. That was language Johnny understood. It was a term employed only in emergency, as when driving in to rescue trapped men after a fall. It was tacit approval from management to waive standard safety procedure in favour of speed. Christ, Johnny exulted, I can shoot her four–maybe five times a shift.

'Shaft sinkers' rates?' they asked together. That was a 20 per cent bonus on stopers' rates. It was a fortune they were being offered.

Rod nodded affirmative to their questions, and waited for the reaction which he knew would follow. It came immediately.

The Delange brothers now began to look for the catch. They sat stolidly turning the deal over in their minds, like two cautious housewives examining a tomato for blemishes because the price was too cheap.

'How long is this drive?' Johnny asked. If the drive was short, a few hundred feet, then it was worth nothing. They would hardly get into their stride before it was completed.

'Close on six thousand feet,' Rod assured him. They looked relieved.

'Where is it headed?' Davy discovered the rub.

'We are going to drive through the Big Dipper to intersect on reef at 6,000 feet.'

'Jesus!' said Johnny. 'The Big Dipper!' He was awed but unafraid. It excited him, the danger, the challenge. Had he been born earlier, Johnny Delange would have made a fine Spitfire pilot.

'The Big Dipper,' Davy murmured, his mind was racing. Nothing in this world or beyond would entice Davy Delange to drive through the Big Dipper. He had an almost religious fear of it. The name alone conjured up all sorts of hidden menace and unspeakable horror. Water. Gas. Friable ground faults. Mudrushes. All a miner's nightmare.

There was no question of him doing it, yet the money was too good to pass up. He could net ten or eleven thousand Rand on those terms.

'All right, Mr Ironsides,' he said. 'I'll take the first night shifts. Johnny can start the day shifts.'

Davy Delange had made his decision. He would work until his drills hit the greenish-black serpentine rock of the dyke. He would then walk out of the drive and quit. He would go up to, but not beyond the dyke.

Afterwards, any of the other mines would snap him up, he had an impeccable record and he would force Johnny to follow him.

'Hey, Davy!' Johnny was delighted, he had expected Davy to turn the deal down flat.

Now he would be able to buy the Mustang for certain–perhaps an M.G.B. G.T. for Hettie–and take a holiday to Durban over Christmas, and . . .

Rod was puzzled by Davy's easy agreement. He studied him a moment and decided that he had ferrety eyes. He's a sneaky little bastard, Rod decided, I'll have to watch him.

45

It took one shift only to prepare for the development. Rod selected the starting point. The main haulage curved away from the shaft on 66 level. Three hundred feet along this tunnel there was a chamber that had been cut out as a loco repair station but which was now out of use. Two large batwing ventilation doors were fitted to the opening of the chamber to provide privacy and behind them the chief underground surveyor set up his instruments and marked out the head of the tunnel that would fly arrow straight a mile and more through the living rock to strike through the Big Dipper into the unknown.

The area surrounding the head chamber was roped off and sign-posted with warnings.

DANGER
INDEPENDENT BLASTING

The mine captains were instructed to keep their men well away, and all loco traffic was rerouted through a secondary haulage.

On the doors of the chamber another notice was fixed.

FIERY MINE PROCEDURE IN FORCE
NO NAKED LIGHTS BEYOND THIS POINT

Owing to small deposits of coal and other organic substance in the upper strata of rock, the Sonder Ditch was classed as a fiery mine and subject to the Government legislation covering this subject. No matches, lighters or other spark-generating devices were allowed into a new development end, because the presence of methane gas was always suspected.

Colourless, odourless, tasteless, detectable only by test with a safety lamp, it was a real and terrifying danger. A nine per cent concentration in air was highly explosive. Stringent precautions were taken against accidental triggering of methane that may have oozed out of a fissure or cavity in the rock.

From the main compressed air-pipes running down the corners of the shaft were taken leads to air tanks in the haulage, ensuring that sixty pounds per square inch of pressure was available for the rock drills. Then drills, pinch-bars, hammers, shovels, and the other tools were unloaded from the cage at 66 level and stored at the shaft head.

Lastly, explosive was placed in the red lockers at the head of the development, and on the evening of October 23rd 1968, thirty minutes after the main blast, Davy Delange and his gang disembarked from the cage and went to the disused loco shop.

Davy, with the surly little Swazi boss boy beside him, stood before the rock wall on which the surveyor had marked the outline of the tunnel. Behind him his gang had fallen unbidden to their labour, each man knowing exactly what was expected of him.

Already the machine boys and their assistants were lugging their ungainly tools forward.

'You! You! You! You!' Davy indicated to each of them the hole on which he was to begin and then stepped back.

'Shaya!' he commanded. 'Hit it!' And with a fluttering bellow that buffeted the eardrums the drive began.

The drilling ceased and Davy charged the holes. The fuses hung like the tails of white mice from their holes. Each length carefully cut to ensure correct firing sequence.

'Clear the drive!' The boss boy's whistle shrilled, the tramp of heavy boots receded until silence hung heavy in the chemically cleaned air.

'Cheesa!' Davy and the boss boy, with the igniters burning like children's fireworks in their right hands, touched them to the hanging tails until the chamber was lit by the fierce blue light of the burning fuses. The shadows of the two men flickered gigantic and distorted upon the walls.

'All burning. Let's go!' And the two men walked quickly back to where the gang waited along the haulage.

The detonations sucked at their ears, and thrust against their lungs, so that afterwards the silence was stunning.

Davy checked his wristwatch. By law there was a mandatory thirty minutes' wait before anyone could go back to the face. There may be a hang-fire waiting to blow the eyes out of someone's head. Even if there were not, there was still the cloud of poisonous nitrous fumes that would destroy the hair follicles in a man's nostrils and render him still more vulnerable to the fine particles of rock dust that would seek to enter his lungs.

Davy waited those thirty minutes, by which time the ventilation had sucked away the fumes and dust.

Then, alone, he went up the haulage. With him he carried his safety lamp, its tiny blue flame burning behind the screen of fine brass wire mesh. That mesh was flash proof and insulated the flame from any methane in the air.

Standing before the raw circular wound in the rock wall, Davy tested for methane gas. Watching the blue flame for the tell-tale cap. There was no sign of it, and satisfied he extinguished the lamp.

'Boss boy!' he yelled, and the Swazi came up uncoiling the hose behind him. 'Water down!'

Only when the rock face and all the loose rubble below it was glistening and dripping with water was Davy satisfied that the dust was laid sufficiently to bring up his gang.

'Bar boys!' he yelled, and they came up, carrying the twelve-foot long pinchbars, a tool like a giant crowbar.

'Bar down. Make safe!' And the bar boys attacked the bunches of loose rock that were flaking and crumbling from the hanging wall. Two of them manipulating one bar between them, with the steel point striking sparks from the rock. The dislodged fragments rained down, heavily at first and then less and less until the rock above their heads was solid and clean.

Only then did Davy scramble over the pile of rubble to reach the face and begin marking in the shot holes.

Behind him his gang were lashing the stuff into the waiting coco pans, and his machine boys were dragging the drills up to the face.

Davy's gang made three blasts that first night. As he rode up in the cage into a pink, sweet-smelling dawn, Davy was satisfied.

'Perhaps tonight we will get in four blasts,' he thought

In the Company change house he showered, running the water steaming hot so his skin turned dull angry red, and he worked up a fat white lather of soap suds over his head and at his armpits and crotch.

He rubbed down with a rough thick towel and dressed quickly. Crossing the parking lot to his battered old Ford Anglia he felt happy and good-tired; hungry and ready for bed.

He drove into Kitchenerville at a steady forty miles an hour, and by this time the sun was just showing over the Kraalkop ridge. The dawn was misty rose, with long shadows against the earth, and he thought that this was how it would be in the early mornings on the farm.

On the outskirts of the town Johnny's Monaco roared past him going in the opposite direction. Johnny waved and blew the horn, shouting something that was lost in the howl of wind and motor.

'They'll catch him yet.' Davy shook his head in disapproval. 'The speed limit is forty-five along here.'

He parked the Anglia in the garage and let himself in through the kitchen door. The Bantu maid was busy over the stove.

'Three eggs,' he told her and went through to his bedroom. He shrugged off his jacket and threw it on the bed. Then he returned to the door and glanced quickly up and down the passage. It was deserted, and there was no sound besides the clatter of the maid in the kitchen.

Davy sidled into the passage. The door to Johnny's bedroom was ajar, and Davy moved quietly down to it. His heart was pounding in his throat, his breathing was stifled by his guilt and excitement.

He peered around the edge of the door and gasped aloud. This morning it was better than usual.

Hettie was a sound sleeper. Johnny always maintained it would take a shot of Dynagel to wake her. She never wore night clothes and she never rose before ten-thirty in the morning. She lay on her stomach, hugging a pillow to her chest, her hair was a joyous tangle of flaming red against the green sheets. The morning was warm and her blankets had been kicked aside.

Davy stood in the passage. A nerve in his eyelid began to twitch, and under his shirt a drop of perspiration slid from his armpit down along his flank.

On the bed Hettie mumbled unintelligibly in her sleep, drew her knees up and rolled slowly on to her back. One arm came up and flopped limply over her face, her eyes were covered by the crook of her elbow.

She sighed deeply. The twin mounds of her bosom were pulled out of shape by their own weight and the angle of her arm. The hair in her armpit and at the base of her belly was bright shiny red-gold. She was long and smooth and silky white, crowned and tipped with flame.

She moved her body languorously, voluptuously, and then settled once more into slumber.

'Breakfast ready, master,' the maid called from the kitchen. Davy started guiltily, then retreated down the passage.

He found with surprise that he was panting, as though he had run a long way.

46

Johnny Delange leaned against the sidewall of the haulage, his hard helmet tilted at a jaunty angle and a cigarette dangling from his lips.

Down at the face the shots began to fire. Johnny recognized each detonation, and when the last dull jar disrupted the air about them, he pushed himself away from the wall with his shoulder.

'That was the *lifters*,' he announced. 'Come on Big King!'

Not for Johnny Delange a thirty-minute waste of time. As he and Big King set off down the haulage together they were binding scarves over their noses and mouths. Ahead of them a bluey-white fog of dust and fumes filled the tunnel, and Big King had the hose going, using a fine mist spray to absorb the fumes and particles.

They pushed on up to the face, Johnny stooping over the safety lamp. Even he had a healthy respect for methane gas.

'Bar boys!' he bellowed, not waiting for Big King to finish watering down. They came up like ghosts in the fog. Hard behind them the machine boys hovered with their drills.

Taking calculated risks Johnny had his drills roaring forty-five minutes sooner than Davy Delange would have in the same circumstances.

When he came back to the face from cutting fuses and priming his explosives, he found his lashing gang struggling with a massive slab of rock that had been blown intact from the face. Five of them were beating on it with fourteen-pound hammers in an attempt to crack it into manageable pieces. As Johnny reached them, Big King was berating them mercilessly.

'You look like a bunch of virgins grinding millet.'

The hammers clanged and struck sparks from the slab. Sweat oozed from every pore of the hammer boys' skin, greasing their bodies, flying from their heads in sparkling droplets with each blow.

'Shaya!' Big King goaded them on. 'Between you all you wouldn't crack the shell of an egg. Hit it, man! Hit it!'

One by one the men fell back exhausted, their chests heaving, gulping air through gaping mouths, blinded by their own sweat.

'All right,' Johnny intervened. The rock was holding up the whole blast. It warranted drastic measures to break it up.

'I'll pop her,' he said, and any government inspector or mine safety officer would have paled at those words.

'Stand far back and turn your faces away,' Big King instructed his gang. From the forehead of one of his men he took a pair of wire mesh goggles, designed to shield the eyes from flying splinters and rock fragments. He handed them to Johnny who placed them over his eyes.

From the canvas carrying bag he took out a stick of Dynagel. It looked like a candle wrapped in yellow greased paper.

'Give me your knife.' Big King opened a large clasp knife and handed it to Johnny.

Carefully Johnny cut a coin-shaped sliver of explosive from one end of the stick, a piece twice as thick as a penny. He returned the remains of the stick to the bag and handed it to Big King.

'Get back,' he said and Big King moved away.

Johnny eyed the slab of rock thoughtfully and then placed the fragment of Dynagel in the centre of it. He adjusted the goggles over his eyes, and picked up one of the fourteen pound hammers.

'Turn your eyes away,' he warned and took deliberate aim. Then with a smooth overhead two-handed swing he brought the hammer down on the Dynagel.

The explosion was painful in the confined space of the drive, and afterwards Johnny's ears hummed with it. A tiny drop of blood ran down his cheek from the scratch inflicted by a flying splinter. His wrists ached from the jolt of the hammer in his hands.

'Gwenyama!' grunted Big King in admiration. 'The man is a lion.'

The explosion had cracked the slab into three wedge-shaped segments. Johnny pushed the goggles on to his forehead and wiped the blood from his cheek with the back of his hand.

'Get it the hell out of here,' he grinned, then he turned to Big King.

'Come.' He jerked his head towards the end of the tunnel. 'Help me charge the holes.'

The two of them worked quickly, sliding the sticks of Dynagel into the shot holes and tamping them home with the charging sticks.

For anyone who was not in possession of a blasting licence, to charge up was an offence punishable by a fine of one hundred Rand or two months' imprisonment, or both. Big King had no licence, but his assistance saved fifteen minutes on the operation.

Johnny and his gang blew the face five times that day, but as they rode up in the cage into the cool evening air he was not satisfied.

'Tomorrow we'll shoot her six times,' he told Big King.

'Maybe seven,' said Big King.

Hettie was waiting for him in the lounge when he got home. She flew to him and threw her arms about his neck.

'Did you bring me a present?' she asked with her lips against his ear, and Johnny laughed tantalizingly. It was very seldom that he did not have a gift for her.

'You did!' she exclaimed, and began to run her hands over his pockets.

'There!' She thrust her hand into the inside pocket of his jacket, and brought out the little white jeweller's box.

'Oh!' She opened it, and then her expression changed slightly.

'You don't like them?' Johnny asked anxiously.

'How much did they cost?' she inquired as she examined the porcelain and lacquer earrings, representing two vividly coloured parrots.

'Well,' Johnny looked shamefaced, 'you see, Hettie, it's the end of the month, you see, and well, like I'm a bit short till pay day, you see, so I couldn't–'

'How much?'

'Well, you see,' he took a breath, 'two Rand fifty.'

'Oh,' said Hettie, 'they're nice.' And she promptly lost interest in them. She tossed the box carelessly on to the crowded mantelpiece and set off for the kitchen.

'Hey, Hettie,' Johnny called after her. 'How about we go across to Fochville? There's a dance there tonight. We go and twist, hey?'

Hettie turned her back, her expression alive again.

'Gee, yes, man!' she enthused. 'Let's do that. I'll go and change, hey!' And she ran up the passage.

Davy came out of his bedroom, on his way to work.

'Hey, Davy.' Johnny stopped him. 'You got any money on you?'

'Are you broke again?'

'Just 'till pay day.'

'Hell, man, Johnny, you got a cheque for eleven hundred the beginning of the month. You spent it all?'

'Next month,' Johnny winked, 'I'm going to get a cheque for two or three thousand. Then watch me go! Come, Davy, lend me fifty. I'm taking Hettie dancing.'

47

For Rod the days flicked past like telegraph poles viewed from a speeding automobile. Each day he gained confidence in his own ability. He had never doubted that he could handle the underground operation and now he found that he had a firm grasp on the surface as well. He knew that his campaign to reduce working costs was having effect, but its full harvest would only be apparent when the quarterly reports were drafted.

Yet he lay awake in the big Manager's residence on the ridge in which he and his few sticks of furniture seemed lost and lonely, and he worried. There were always myriad nagging little problems, but there were others more serious.

This morning Lily Jordan had come through into his office.

'Mr Innes is coming up to see you at nine.'

'What's he want?' Herbert Innes was the Manager of the Sonder Ditch Reduction works.

'He wouldn't tell me,' Lily answered. The end of the month had come and gone and Lily was still with him. Rod presumed that he had been approved.

Herby Innes, burly and red-faced, sat down and drank the cup of tea that Lily provided, while he regaled Rod with a stroke by stroke account of his Sunday afternoon golf round. Rod interrupted him after he had hit a nine-iron short at the third, and shanked his chip.

'Okay, Herby. What's the problem?'

'We've got a leak, Rod.'

'Bad?'

'Bad enough,' Herby grunted. To him the loss of a single ounce of gold during the process of recovery and refinement was catastrophic.

'What do you reckon?'

'Between the wash and the pour we are losing a couple hundred ounces a week.'

'Yes,' Rod agreed. 'That is bad enough.'

Twenty thousand Rand a month, one hundred twenty thousand a year.

'Have you any ideas?'

'It's been going on for some time, even in Frank Lemmer's day. We have tried everything.'

Rod was a little hazy about the workings of the reduction plant, not that he would admit that, but he was. He knew that the ore was weighed and sampled when it reached the surface, from this a fairly accurate estimate of gold content was made and compared with actual recovery. Any discrepancy had to be investigated and traced.

'What is your recovery rate for the last quarter?'

'Ninety-six point seven-three.'

'That's pretty good,' Rod admitted. It was impossible to recover all the gold in the ore that was surfaced but Herby was getting most of it out. 96.73 per cent of it, to be precise. Which meant that very little of the missing two hundred ounces was being lost into the dumps and the slimes dam.

'I tell you what, Herby,' Rod decided. 'I'll come down to the plant this afternoon. We'll go over it together, perhaps a fresh eye may be able to spot the trouble.'

'May do.' Herby was sceptical. 'We've tried everything else. We are pouring this afternoon. What time shall I expect you?'

'Two o'clock.'

They started at the shaft head, where the ore cage, the copie, arrived at the surface every four minutes with its cargo of rock which it dumped into a concrete shute. Each load was classified as either 'reef' or 'waste'.

The reef was dropped into the massive storage bins, while the waste was carried off on a conveyor to the wash house to be sluiced down before going to the dump. Tiny particles of gold sticking to the waste rock were gathered in this way.

Herby put his lips close to Rod's ear to make himself heard above the rumbling roar of rock rolling down the chute.

'I'm not worried about this end. It's all bulk here and very little shine.' Herby used the reduction plant slang for gold 'The closer we get to the end, the more dangerous it is.'

Rod nodded and followed Herby down the steel ladder until they reached a door below the storage bins. They went through into a long underground tunnel very similar to the ore tunnel on 100 level.

Again there was a massive conveyor belt moving steadily along the tunnel while ore from the bins above was fed onto it. Rod and Herby walked along beside the belt until it passed under a massive electro magnet. Here they paused for a while. The magnet was extracting from the ore all those pieces of metal which had found their way into the ore passes and bins.

'How much you picking up?' Rod asked.

'Last week fourteen tons,' Herby answered, and taking Rod's arm led him through the door beside them. They were in an open yard that looked like a scrap-metal merchant's premises. A mountain of pinch bars, jumper bits, shovels, steel wire rope, snatch blocks, chain, spanners, fourteen-pound hammers, and other twisted and unrecognizable pieces of metal filled the yard. All of it was rusted, much of it unusable. It had been separated from the ore by the magnet.

Rod's mouth tightened. Here he was presented with indisputable evidence of the carelessness and it-belongs-to-the-company attitude of his men. This pile of scrap represented a waste that would total hundreds of thousands of Rand annually.

'We will see about that!' he muttered.

'If one of those hammers got into my jaw mills it would smash it to pieces,' Herby told him dolefully and led him back into the conveyor tunnel.

The belt angled upwards sharply and they followed the catwalk beside it. They climbed steadily for five minutes and Herby was puffing like a steam engine. Through the holes in the honeycomb steel plate under his feet, Rod could see that they were now a few hundred feet above ground level.

The conveyor reached the head of a tall tower and dumped its load of ore into the gaping mouths of the screeners. As the rock fell down the tower to ground level again it was sorted for size, and the larger pieces diverted to the jaw crushers which chewed it into fist-size bites.

'See anything?' Herby asked, barely concealing the sarcasm.

Rod grinned at him.

They climbed down the steel ladders that seemed endless. The screeners rattling and the crushers hammering, until Rod's eardrums pleaded for mercy.

At last they reached ground level and went through into the mill room. This was a cavernous galvanized-iron shed the size of a large aircraft hangar. At least one hundred yards long and fifty feet high, it was filled with long rows of the cylindrical tube mills.

Forty of them in all, they were as thick as the boiler of a steam locomotive and about twice as long. Into one end of them was fed the ore which had been reduced in size by the jaw crushers. The tube mills revolved and the loose steel balls within them pounded the rock to powder.

If the noise before had been bad, it was hideous in the mill room. Rod and Herby made no effort to speak to each other until they had walked through into the comparative quiet of the first heavy-media separator room.

'Now,' Herby explained. 'This is where we start worrying.' He indicated the rows of pale blue six-inch piping that came through the wall from the mill room.

'In there is the powdered rock mixed with water to a smooth flowing paste. About forty per cent of the gold is free.'

'No one can get into those pipes and you've checked for any possible leak?' Rod asked. Herby nodded.

'But,' he said 'have a look here!'

Along the far wall was a series of cages. They were made of heavy steel mesh, the perforations would not allow a man's finger through. The heavy steel doors were barred and locked. Outside each battery of cages stood a Bantu attendant in clean white overalls. They were all concentrating on the manipulation of the turncock that obviously regulated the flow of the powdered ore through the pipes.

Herby stopped at one of the cages.

'Shine!' he pointed. Beyond the heavy guard screen the grey paste of rock powder was flowing from a series of nozzles over an inclined black rubber sheet. The surface of the rubber sheet was deeply corrugated, and in each corrugation the free gold was collecting, held there by its own weight. The gold was thick as butter in a Dagwood sandwich, greasy yellow-looking in the folds of rubber.

Rod laid hold of the steel screen and shook it.

'No,' Herby laughed. 'No one will get in that way.'

'How do you clean the gold off that sheet? Does someone have access to the separator?' Rod asked.

'The separator cleans itself automatically,' Herby answered. 'Look!'

Rod noticed for the first time that the rubber sheet was moving very slowly, it was also an endless belt running round two rollers. As the belt inverted, so fine jets of water washed the gold from the corrugations into a collection tank.

'I'm the only one who has access. We change the collection tanks daily,' said Herby.

It looked foolproof, Rod had to admit.

Rod turned and glanced down the row of four Bantu attendants. They were all intent on their duties, and Rod knew that each of them had a high security rating. They had been carefully selected and screened before being allowed into the reduction works.

'Satisfied?' Herby asked.

'Okay,' Rod nodded, and the two of them went out through the door in the far wall. Locking it behind them.

Immediately they had gone the four Bantu attendants reacted. They straightened up, the scowls of concentration smoothed out to be replaced by grins of relief. One made a remark and they all laughed, and opened the waist bands of their tunics. From inside each trouser leg they drew a length of quarter-inch copper wire and began probing them through the steel screen.

It had taken Crooked Leg, the photographer, almost a year to work out a means of milking gold from the heavily screened and guarded separators. The method which he had discovered was, like all workable plans, extremely simple.

Mercury, quicksilver, absorbs gold the way blotting paper sucks up moisture. It will suck in any speck of gold that comes in contact with it. Mercury has a further property, it can be made to spread on copper like butter on bread. This layer of mercury on copper retains its powers of absorbing gold.

Crooked Leg had devised the idea of coating lengths of copper wire with mercury. The wire could be inserted through the apertures in the steel mesh and the wire laid across the corrugated rubber sheet, where it set about mopping up every speck of gold that flowed over it. The lengths of wire could be quickly slipped down the trouser leg at the approach of an official, and they could be smuggled in and out of the reduction works the same way.

Every evening Crooked Leg retrieved the gold-thickened wire, and issued his four accomplices with newly coated lengths. Every night in the abandoned workings beyond the ridge he boiled the mercury to make it release its gold.

'Now,' Herby could speak normally in the blessed quiet of the cyanide plant, 'we have skimmed off the free gold–and we are left with the sulphide gold.' He offered Rod a cigarette as they made their way between the massive steel tanks that spread over many acres. 'We pump this into the tanks and add cyanide. The cyanide dissolves the gold and takes it into solution. We tap it off and run it through zinc powder. The gold is deposited on the zinc, we burn away the zinc and we are left with the gold.'

Rod lit his cigarette. He knew all this but Herby was giving him a Cooks' tour for visiting V.I.P.s. He flicked his lighter for Herby. 'There is no way anyone could swipe it when it's in solution.'

Herby shook his head, exhaling smoke. 'Apart from anything else, cyanide is a deadly poison.' He glanced at his watch. 'Three-twenty, they'll be pouring now. Shall we go across to the smelt house?'

The smelt house was the only brick building among all the galvanized iron. It stood a little isolated. Its windows were high up and heavily barred.

At the steel door Herby buzzed, and a peephole opened in the door. He and Rod were immediately recognized and the door swung open. They were in a cage of bars which could only be opened once the door was closed behind them.

'Afternoon, Mr Ironsides, Mr Innes.' The guard was apologetic. 'Would you sign, please?' He was a retired policeman with a paunch and a holstered revolver on his hip.

They signed and the guard signalled to his mate on the steel catwalk high above the smelt room floor. This guard tucked his pump action shotgun under one arm, and threw the switch on the walk beside him.

The cage door opened and they went through.

Along the far wall the electric furnaces were set into the brickwork. They resembled the doors of the bread ovens in a bakery.

The concrete floor of the room was uncluttered, except for the mechanical loader that carried the gold crucible in its steel arms, and the moulds before it. The half dozen personnel of the smelt house barely looked up as Rod and Herby approached.

The pour was well advanced, the arms of the loader tilted and a thin stream of molten gold issued from the spout of the crucible, and fell into the mould. The gold hissed and smoked and crackled, and tiny red and blue sparks twinkled on its surface as it cooled.

Already forty or fifty bars were laid out on the rubber-wheeled trolley beside the mould. Each bar was a little smaller than a cigar box. It had the knobby bumpy look of roughly cast metal.

Rod stopped and touched one of the bars. It was still hot and it had the slightly greasy feeling that new gold always has.

'How much?' he asked Herby, and Herby shrugged.

'About a million Rands' worth, perhaps a little more.'

So that's what a million Rand looks like, Rod mused, it's not very impressive.

'What's the procedure now?' Rod asked.

'We weigh it, and stamp the weight and batch number into each bar.' He pointed to a massive circular safe deposit door in the near wall. 'It's stored there over-night, and tomorrow a refinery armoured car will come out from Johannesburg and pick it up.' Herby led the way out of the smelt house. 'Anyway, that's not the trouble. Our leak is sucking off the shine before it ever reaches the smelt house.'

'Let me think about it for a few days,' Rod said. 'Then we'll get together again, try and find the solution.'

He was still thinking about it now. Lying in the darkness and smoking cigarette after cigarette.

There seemed to be only one solution. They would have to plant Bantu police in the reduction works.

It was an endless game involving all the mining companies and their reduction plant personnel. An inventive mind would devise a new system of sucking off the shine. The Company would become aware of the activity by comparison of estimated and actual recovery and they would work on the leak for a week, a month, sometimes a year. Then they would break the system. There would be prosecutions, stiff gaol sentences, and the Company would circularize its neighbours, and they would all settle back and wait for the next customer to appear.

Gold has many remarkable properties, its weight, its non-corruptibility and, not least, the greed and lust it conjures up in the hearts of men.

Rod stubbed his cigarette, rolled onto his side and pulled the bed-clothes up over his shoulders. His last thought before sleep was for the major problem that, these days, was never very far from the surface of his mind.

The Delange brothers had driven almost fifteen hundred feet in two weeks. At this rate they would hit the Big Dipper seven weeks from now, then even the theft of gold would pale into insignificance.

48

At the time that Rod Ironsides was composing himself for sleep, Big King was taking a little wine with his business associate and tribal brother Philemon N'gabai, alias Crooked Leg.

They sat facing each other in a pair of dilapidated cane chairs with a lantern and a gallon jug of Jeripigo set between them. The bat stench of the abandoned workings did little to bring out the bouquet of the wine, which was of small concern to either man, for they were drinking not for taste but for effect.

Crooked Leg refilled the cheap glass tumbler that Big King proffered, and as the wine glug-glugged from the jar he continued his attack on the character and moral fibre of José Almeida, the Portuguese.

'For many months now I have had it in my heart to speak to you of these matters,' he told Big King, 'but I have waited until I could set a deadfall for the man. He is like a lion that preys upon our herds, we hear him roar in the night and in the dawn we see his spoor in the earth about the carcases of our animals, but we cannot meet him face to face.'

Big King enjoyed listening to the oratory of Crooked Leg and while he listened he drank the Jeripigo as though it were water, and Crooked Leg kept refilling the tumbler for him.

'In counsel with myself I spoke thus: "Philemon N'gabai, it is not enough that thou should suspect this white man. It is necessary also that you see with your own eyes that he is eating your substance".'

'How, Crooked Leg?' Big King's voice was thickening, the level of the jug had fallen steadily and now showed less than half. 'Tell me how we shall take this man.' Big King showed a fist the size of a bunch of bananas. 'I will . . .'

'No, Big King.' Crooked Leg was scandalized. 'You must not hurt the man. How then would we sell our gold? We must prove he is cheating us and show him we know it. Then we will proceed as ever, but he will give us full measure in the future.'

Big King thought about that for some time, then at last he sighed regretfully. 'You are right, Crooked Leg. Still, I would have liked to . . .' He showed that fist again, and Crooked Leg went on hurriedly.

'Therefore, I have sent to my brother who drives a delivery van for S.A. Scale Company in Johannesburg, and he has taken from his Company a carefully measured weight of eight ounces.' Crooked Leg produced the cylindrical metal weight from his pocket and handed it to Big King who examined it with interest. 'Tonight, after the Portuguese has weighed the gold you take to him, you will say. "Now, my friend, please weigh this for me on your scale," and you will watch to see that his scale reads the correct number. Each time in the future he will weigh this on his scale before we sell our gold.'

'Hau!' Big King chuckled. 'You are a crafty one, Crooked Leg.'

Big King's eyes were smoky and blood-shot. The Jeripigo was a raw rough fortified wine, and he had drunk very nearly a gallon of it. He sat opposite the Portuguese store-keeper in the back room behind the concession store, and watched while he poured the gold dust into the pan of the jeweller's scale. It made a yellow pyramid that shone dully in the light from the single bare bulb above their heads.

'One hundred and twenty-three ounces.' Almeida looked up at Big King for confirmation, a strand of greasy black hair hung onto his forehead. His face was pale from lack of sun so that the blue stubble of beard was in heavy contrast.

'That is right,' Big King nodded. He could taste the liquor fumes in the back of his throat, and they were as strong as his distaste for the man who sat opposite him. He belched.

Almeida removed the pan from the scale and carefully poured the dust back into the screw top bottle.

'I will get the money.' He half rose from his chair.

'Wait!' said Big King, and the Portuguese looked at him in mild surprise.

Big King took the weight from the pocket of his jacket. He placed it on the desk.

'Weigh that on your scale,' he said in Portuguese.

Almeida's eyes flicked down to the weight, and then back to Big King's face. He sank back into his seat, and pushed the strand of hair off his forehead. He began to speak, but his voice cracked and he cleared his throat.

'Why? Is there something wrong?' Suddenly he was aware of the size of the man opposite him. He could smell the liquor on his breath.

'Weigh it!' Big King's voice was flat, without rancour. His face was expressionless, but the smoky red glare of his eyes was murderous.

Suddenly Almeida was afraid, deadly, coldly afraid. He could guess what would happen once the error in his balance was disclosed.

'Very well,' he said, and his voice was forced and off key. The pistol was in the drawer beside his right knee. It was loaded, with a cartridge under the hammer. The safety-catch was on, but that would only delay him an instant. He knew it would not be necessary to fire, once he had the weapon in his hand he would have control of the situation again.

If he did have to fire, the calibre was .45 and the heavy slug would stop even a giant like this Bantu. *Self defence*, he was working it out feverishly. *A burglar*, I surprised him and he attacked. *Self defence*. It would work. They'd believe it.

But how to get the pistol? Try and sneak it out of the drawer, or make a grab for it?

There was a desk between them, it would take a few seconds for the Bantu to realize what he was doing, a few more for him to get around the desk. He would have plenty of time.

He snatched the handle of the drawer, and it flew open. His fingernails scrabbled against the wood work as he clawed for the big black U.S. Navy automatic, and with a surge of triumph his hand closed over the butt.

Big King came over the top of the desk like a black avalanche. The scale and the jar of gold dust was swept aside to clatter and shatter against the floor.

Still seated in his chair, with the pistol in his hand, Almeida was borne over backwards with Big King on top of him. Many years before, Big King had worked with a safari outfit in Portuguese East Africa, and he had seen the effect of gunshot wounds in the flesh of dead animals.

In the instant that he had recognized the weapon in Almeida's hand, he had been as afraid as the Portuguese. Fear had triggered the speed of his reaction, it was responsible for the savagery of his attack as he lay over the struggling body of the Portuguese.

He had Almeida's pistol hand held by the wrist and he was shaking it to force him to drop the firearm. With his right hand he had the Portuguese by the throat, and instinctively he was applying the full strength of his arms to both grips. He felt something break under his right hand, cracking like the kernel of a nut, and his fingers locked deeper into the quivering flesh. The pistol flew from fingers that were suddenly without strength, and skittered across the floor to come up against the far wall with a thump.

Only then did Big King begin to regain the sanity that fear had scattered. Suddenly he realized that the Portuguese was lying quietly under him. He released his grip and scrambled to his knees. The Portuguese was dead. His neck was twisted away from his shoulders at an impossible angle. His eyes were wide and surprised, and a smear of blood issued from one nostril over his upper lip.

Big King backed away towards the door, his gaze fixed in horror on the sprawling corpse. When he reached the door, he hesitated, fighting down the urge to run. He subdued it, and went back to kneel beside the desk. First he picked up the controversial cylindrical weight and placed it in his pocket, then he began sweeping up the scattered gold dust and the shattered fragments of the screw-topped container. He placed them into separate envelopes that he found among the papers on the desk. Ten minutes later he slipped out through the back door of the concession store, into the night.

49

At the time Big King was hurrying back towards the mine hostel, Rod Ironsides thrashed restlessly in a bed in which the sheets were already bunched and damp with sweat. He was imprisoned in his own fantasy, locked in a nightmare from which he could not break away. The nightmare was infinite and green, quivering, unearthly, translucent. He knew it was held back only by a transparent barrier of glass. He cowered before it, and he knew it was icy cold, he could see light shining through it, and he was deadly afraid.

Suddenly there was a crack in the glass wall, a hairline crack, and through it oozed a single drop. A large, pearshaped drop, as perfect as though it had been painted by Tretchikoff. It glittered like a gemstone.

It was the most terrifying thing that Rod had ever seen in his life. He cried out in his sleep, trying to warn them, but the crack starred further, and the drop slid down the glass, to be followed by another and another. Suddenly a jagged slab of glass exploded out of the wall, and Rod screamed as the water burst through, in a frothing jet.

With a roar the entire glass wall collapsed, and a mountain high wave of green water hissed down upon him, carrying a white plume of spray at its crest.

He awoke sitting upright in his bed, a cry of horror on his lips and his body bathed in sweat. It took minutes for him to steady the wild racing of his heart. Then he went through to the bathroom. He ran a glass of water and held it up to the light. 'Water. It's there!' he muttered. 'I know it's there!' He drank from the tumbler.

Standing naked, with his sweat drying cold on his body, the tumbler held to his lips, the idea came to him. He had never heard of anyone trying it before, but then nobody he knew would be crazy enough to dive into a death trap like the Big Dipper.

'I'll drill and charge a matt of explosive into the hanging wall of the drive. I'll get the Delange boys on to it right away. Then at any time I choose I can blast the whole bloody roof in and seal off the tunnel.'

Rod was surprised at the strength of the relief that flooded over him. He knew then how it had been worrying him. He went back to the bedroom and straightened out his bedclothes. However, sleep would not come easily to him. His imagination was overheated, and a series of events and ideas kept playing through his mind, until abruptly he was presented with the image of Terry Steyner.

He had not seen her for almost two weeks, not since Manfred Steyner's return from Europe. He had spoken to her twice on the telephone, hasty, confused conversations that left him feeling dissatisfied. He was increasingly aware that he was missing her. His one attempt to find solace elsewhere had been a miserable failure. He had lost interest half way through the approach manœuvres and had returned the young lady to the bosom of her family at the unheard of hour of eleven o'clock on a Saturday night.

Only the unremitting demands of his new job had prevented him from slipping away to Johannesburg and taking a risk.

'You know, Ironsides, you'd better start bracing up a little, don't lose your head over this woman. Remember our vow–*Never Again*!'

He punched the pillow into shape and settled into it.

Terry lay quiet, waiting for it. It was after one o'clock in the morning. It was one of those nights. He would come soon now. As never before she was filled with dread. A cold slimy feeling in the pit of her stomach. Yet she had been fortunate. He had not been near her since his return from Paris. Over two weeks, but it could not last. Tonight.

She heard the sound of the car coming up the drive and she felt physically ill. I can't do it, she decided, not any more, not ever again. It wasn't meant to be like this, I know that now. It's not dirty and furtive and horrible, it's like . . . like . . . it's the way Rod makes it.

She heard him in his bedroom, suddenly she sat up in bed. She felt desperate, hunted.

The door of her room opened softly.

'Manfred?' she asked sharply.

'It's me. Don't worry.' He came briskly towards her bed, a dark impersonal shape and he was undoing the cord of his dressing-gown.

'Manfred,' Terry blurted, 'I'm early this month, I'm sorry.'

He stopped. She saw his hands fall back to his sides, and he stood completely still.

'Oh!' he said at last, and she heard him shuffle his feet into the thick pile of the carpet. 'I just came to tell you,' he hesitated, seeking an excuse for his visit, 'that . . . that I'll be going away for five days. Leaving on Friday. I have to go to Durban and Cape Town.'

'I'll pack for you,' she said.

'What? Oh, yes–thank you.' He shuffled his feet again. 'Well, then.' He hesitated, then stooped quickly and brushed her cheek with his lips. 'Good night, Theresa.'

'Good night, Manfred.'

Five days, she lay alone in the darkness and gloated. *Five whole days alone with Rod.*

50

Detective Inspector Hannes Grobbelaar of the South African Criminal Investigation Department sat on the edge of the office chair with his hat tipped onto the back of his head and spoke into the telephone, which he held in a handkerchief-covered hand. He was a tall man with a long sad face and a mournful looking moustache that was streaked with grey.

'Gold buying,' he said into the receiver, and then in reply to the obvious question, 'There's gold dust spilled all over the place and a jeweller's scale, and a .45 automatic with a full magazine and the safety-catch still on, dead man's prints on it.' He listened. 'Ja. Ja. All right, ja. Broken neck, looks like.' Inspector Grobbelaar swivelled his chair and looked down at the corpse that lay on the floor beside him. 'Bit of blood on his lip, but nothing else.'

One of the finger print men came to the desk and Grobbelaar stood up to give him room to work, the receiver still held to his ear.

'Prints? he asked in disgust. 'There are finger prints on everything, we have isolated at least forty separate sets so far.' He listened a few seconds. 'No, we will get him, all right. It must be a Bantu mine worker and we have got all the finger prints of the men from outside the Republic. It's just a matter of checking them all out and then questioning. Ja, we'll have him within a month, that's for sure? I'll be back at John Vorster Square about five o'clock, just as soon as we finish up here.' He hung up the receiver, and stood looking down at the murdered man.

'Ugly bastard,' said Sergeant Hugo beside him. 'Asked for it, buying gold. It's as bad as diamonds.' He drew attention to the large envelope he carried in his hand. 'I've got a whole lot of glass fragments. Looks like the container the gold was in. The murderer tried to clean up, but he didn't make a very good job. These were under the desk.'

'Prints?'

'Only one piece big enough. It's got a smeary print on it. Might be of use.'

'Good,' Grobbelaar nodded. 'Get cracking on that, then.'

There was a feminine wail from somewhere in the interior of the building, and Hugo grimaced.

'There she starts again. Hell, I thought she'd exhausted herself. Bloody Portuguese women are the end.'

'You should hear them having a baby,' grunted Grobbelaar.

'Where did you hear one?'

'There was one in the ward next door to my old girl at the maternity home. She nearly brought the bloody roof down.'

Grobbelaar's moustache took on a more melancholy droop as he thought about the work that lay ahead. Hours, days, weeks of questioning and checking and cross-checking, with a succession of sullen and unco-operative suspects.

He sighed and jerked a thumb at the corpse. 'All right, we've finished with him. Tell the butcher boys to come and fetch him.'

51

It had taken Rod almost two days to design his drop-blast matt. The angle and depth of the shot holes were carefully placed to achieve maximum disruption of the hanging wall. In addition he had decided to drill and charge the side walls of the drive with charges timed to explode *after* the hanging wall had collapsed. This would kick in on the rubble filling the tunnel and jam it solid.

Rod was fully aware of the power of water under pressures of 2,000 pounds per square inch and more and he had decided it was necessary to block at least three hundred feet of the tunnel. His matt blast was designed to do so, and yet he knew that this would not seal off the water completely. It would, however, reduce the flow sufficiently to allow cementation crews to get in and plug the drive solid.

The Delange brothers did not share Rod's enthusiasm for the project.

'Hey man, that's going to take three or four days to drill and charge,' Johnny protested when Rod showed him his carefully drawn plan.

'Like hell it will,' Rod growled at him. 'I want it done properly. It will take at least a week.'

'You said ultra fast. You didn't say nothing about drilling the hanging wall with more holes than a cheese!'

'Well, I'm saying it now,' Rod told him grimly. 'And I'm also saying that you will drill, but you won't charge the holes until I come down and make sure that you've gone in as deep as I want them.'

He didn't trust either Johnny or Davy to spend time drilling in twenty feet, when he could go in six feet, charge up and nobody would know the difference. Not until it was too late.

Davy Delange spoke for the first time.

'Will you credit us bonus fathomage while we fiddle around with this?' he asked.

'Four fathoms a shift.' Rod agreed to pay them for the removal of fictitious rock.

'Eight?' said Davy.

'Hell, no!' Rod exclaimed. That was robbery.

'I don't know,' Davy murmured, watching Rod with sly ferrety little eyes. 'Maybe I should talk to Brother Duivenhage, you know, ask his advice.'

Duivenhage was No. 1 shaft shop steward for the Mine Workers' Union. He had driven Frank Lemmer to the edge of a nervous breakdown and was now starting on Rodney Ironsides. Rod was pleading with Head Office to offer Duivenhage a fat job in management to get him out of the way. The last thing in the world that Rod wanted was Brother Duivenhage snooping around his drive on the Big Dipper.

'Six,' he said.

'Well . . .' Davy hesitated.

'Six is fair, Davy,' Johnny interrupted, and Davy glared at him. Johnny had snatched complete victory from his grasp.

'Good, that's agreed.' Quickly Rod closed the negotiations. 'You'll start drilling the matt right away.'

Rod's design demanded nearly twelve hundred shot holes to be filled with two and a half tons of explosive. It was a thousand feet down the drive from the main haulage on 66 level to where the matt began.

The drive now was a spacious, well lit and freshly ventilated tunnel, with the vent piping, the compressed air pipe, and the electrical cable bolted into the hanging wall, and a set of steel railway tracks laid along the floor.

All work on the face ceased while the Delange brothers set about drilling the matt. It was light work that demanded little from the men. As each hole was drilled, Davy would insert his charging rod to check the depth and then plug the entrance with a wad of paper. There was much time for drinking Thermos coffee and for thinking.

There were three subjects that endlessly occupied Davy's mind as he sat at ease, waiting for the completion of the next shot hole. Sometimes for half an hour at a time Davy would hold the image of that fifty thousand Rand in his mind. It was his, tax paid, painstakingly accumulated over the years and lovingly deposited with the local branch of the Johannesburg Building Society. He imagined it bundled and stacked in neat green piles in the Society's vault. Each bundle was labelled 'David Delange'.

Then his imagination would pass automatically on to the farm that the money would buy. He saw how it would be in the evenings when he sat on the wide stoep, with the setting sun striking the peaks of the Swart Berg across the valley, and the cattle coming in from the paddocks towards the homestead.

Always there was a woman sitting beside him on the stoep. The woman had red hair.

On the fifth morning Davy drove home in the dawn, he was not tired. The night's labours had been easy and unexacting.

The door of Johnny and Hettie's bedroom was closed. Davy read the newspapers with his breakfast, as always the cartoon strip adventures of Modesty Blaise and Willie Garvin intrigued him completely. This morning Modesty was depicted in a bikini and Davy studied her comparing her to the big healthy body of his brother's wife. The thought of her stayed with him as he rolled into his bed, and he lay unsleeping, daydreaming an adventure in which Modesty Blaise had become Hettie, and Willie Garvin was Davy.

An hour later he was still awake. He sat up and reached for the towel which lay across the foot of his bed. He wrapped the towel around his waist as he went down the passage to the bathroom. As he reached for the handle of the bathroom door, it opened under his hand and he was face to face with Hettie Delange.

She wore a white lace dressing-gown with ostrich-feather mules on her feet. Her face was innocent of make-up and she had brushed her hair and tied it with a ribbon.

'Oh!' she gasped with surprise. 'You gave me a fright, man.'

'I'm sorry, hey.' Davy grinned at her, holding the towel with one hand. Hettie let her eyes run quickly over his naked upper body.

Davy was muscled like a prize fighter. His chest hair was crisp and curly. On both arms the tattoos drew attention to the thickness and weight of muscle.

'Gee, you *are* built,' Hettie murmured in admiration, and Davy sucked in his belly reflexively.

'You think so?' His grin was self-conscious now.

'Yes.' Hettie leaned forward and touched his arm. 'It's hard too!'

The movement had allowed the front of her dressing-gown to gape open. Davy's face flushed as he looked down into the opening. He started to say something, but his voice had dried up on him. Hettie's fingers stroked down his arm, and she was watching the direction of his eyes. Slowly she moved closer to him.

'Do you like me, Davy?' she asked, her voice throaty and low, and with an animal cry Davy attacked her.

His hands ripping at the opening of her gown, pinning her to the wall of the bathroom with his mouth frantically hunting hers. His body pressing hard and urgent, his eyes wild, his breathing ragged.

Hettie was laughing, a breathless gasping laugh.

This was what she loved. When they lost their heads, when they went mad for her.

'Davy,' she said, jerking loose his towel. 'Davy.'

She kept wriggling away from his thrusting hips, knowing that it would inflame him further. His hands were tearing at her body, his eyes were maniacal.

'Yes!' she hissed into his mouth. He threw her off balance and she slid down the wall onto the floor.

'Wait,' she panted. 'Not here–the bedroom.'

But it was too late.

Davy had spent the afternoon locked in his bedroom, lying on his bed in an agony of black all-pervading remorse and guilt.

'My brother,' he kept repeating. 'Johnny is my brother.'

Once he wept, each sob tearing something in his chest. The tears squeezed out between burning eyelids, leaving him feeling exhausted and weak.

'My *own* brother,' he shook his head slowly in horrified disbelief. 'I cannot stay here,' he decided miserably. 'I'll have to go.'

He went to the washbasin and washed his eyes. Stooping over the basin, water still dripping from his face, he decided.

'I will have to tell him.' The burden of guilt was too heavy. 'I'll write to Johnny. I'll write it all, and then I'll go away.'

Frantically he searched for pen and paper, it was almost as though he could wipe away the deed by writing it down. He sat at the table by the window and wrote slowly and laboriously. When he had finished it was three o'clock. He felt better.

He sealed the four closely written pages into an envelope and slipped it into the inside pocket of his jacket. He dressed quickly, and crept out of the house, fearful of meeting Hettie, but she was nowhere about. Her big white Monaco was not in the garage, and with relief he turned out of the driveway and took the road out to the Sonder Ditch. He wanted to reach the mine before Johnny came off shift.

Davy listened to his brother's voice, as he kidded and laughed with the other off-duty miners in the company change house. He had locked himself in one of the lavatory closets to avoid meeting his brother, and he sat disconsolately on the toilet seat. The sound of Johnny's voice brought his guilt flooding back in its full strength. His letter of confession was buttoned into the top pocket of his overalls, and he took it out, broke open the flap and reread the contents.

'So long, then.' Johnny's voice sang out gaily from the change room. 'See you bastards tomorrow.'

There was an answering chorus from the other miners, then the door slammed.

Davy went on sitting alone for another twenty minutes in the stench of stale bodies and urine, dirty socks and rank disinfections from the foot baths. At last he tucked the letter away in his pocket and opened the closet door.

Davy's gang were at their waiting place at the head of the drive. They were sitting along the bench laughing and chatting. There was a holiday spirit amongst them for they knew it would be another shift of easy going.

They greeted Davy cheerfully, as he came down the haulage. Both the Delange brothers were popular with their gangs and it was unusual that Davy did not reply to the chorused greeting. He did not even smile.

The Swazi boss boy handed him the safety lamp, and Davy grunted an acknowledgement. He set off alone down the tunnel, trudging heavily, not conscious of his surroundings, his mind encased in a padding of guilt and self-pity.

A thousand feet along the drive he reached the day's work area. Johnny's shift had left the rock drills in place, still connected to the compressed air system, ready for use. Davy came to a halt in the centre of the work area, and without a conscious command from his brain his hands began the routine process of striking the wick of the safety lamp

The little blue flame came alight behind the protective screen of wire mesh, and Davy held the lamp at eye level before him and walked slowly along the drive. His eyes were watching the flame without seeing it.

The air in the tunnel was cool and refrigerated, scrubbed and filtered, there was no odour nor taste to it. Davy walked on somnambulantly. He was wallowing in self-pity now. He saw himself in a semi-heroic role, one of the great lovers of history caught up in tragic circumstances. His brain was fully occupied with the picture. His eyes were unseeing. Blindly he performed the ritual that a thousand times before had begun the day's shift.

Slowly in its wire mesh cage the blue flame of the safety lamp changed shape. Its crest flattened, and there formed above it a ghostly pale line. Davy's eyes saw it, but his brain refused to accept the message. He walked on in a stupor of guilt and self-pity.

That light above the flame was called 'the cap', it signified that there was at least a five per cent concentration of methane gas in the air. The last shot hole that Johnny Delange's gang had drilled before going off shift, had bored into a methane-filled fissure. For the previous three hours gas had been blowing out of that hole. The ventilation system was unable to wash the air fast enough and now the gas had spread slowly down the drive. The air surrounding Davy's body was heavy with gas, he had breathed it into his lungs. It needed just one spark to ignite it.

Davy reached the end of the drive and snapped the snuffer over the wick, extinguishing the flame in the lamp.

'All safe,' he muttered, not realizing that he had spoken. He went back to his waiting men.

'All safe,' he repeated, and with the Swazi boss boy leading them the forty men of Davy Delange's gang trooped gaily into the mouth of the drive.

Moodily Davy followed them. As he walked he reached into his hip pocket and took out a pack of Lexington filter tips. He put one between his lips, returned the pack and began patting his pockets to locate his lighter.

Davy went from team to team of his machine boys, directing them in the line and spot to be drilled. Every time he spoke, the unlit cigarette waggled between his lips. He gesticulated with the hand that held his cigarette-lighter.

It took twenty minutes for him to set all his drills to work. And he stood and looked back along the tunnel. Each machine boy and his assistant formed a separate sculpture. Most of them were stripped to the waist. Their bodies appeared to be carved and polished in oiled ebony, as they braced themselves behind the massive rock drills.

Davy lifted his cupped hands, holding the cigarette-lighter near his face and he flicked the cog wheel.

The air in the tunnel turned to flame. In a flash explosion, the flame reached the temperature of a welding torch. It seared the skin from the faces and exposed bodies of the machine boys, it burned the hair from their scalps. It turned their ears to charred stumps. It roasted their eyeballs in their sockets. It scorched their clothing, so as they fell the cloth smouldered and burned against their flesh.

In that instant, as the skin was licked from his face and hands, Davy Delange opened his mouth in a great gasp of agony. The flame shot down his throat into his gas-drenched lungs. Within the confines of his body the gas exploded and his chest popped like a paper bag, his ribs fanning outward about the massive wound like the petals of a sunflower.

Forty-one men died at the same moment. In the silence after that whooshing, sucking detonation, they lay like scorched insects along the floor of the drive. One or two of them were moving still, an arched spine relaxing, a leg straightening, charred fingers unclenching, but within a minute all was absolutely still.

Half an hour later Doctor Dan Stander and Rodney Ironsides were the first men into the drive. The smell of burned flesh was overpowering. Both of them had to swallow down their nausea as they went forward.

52

Dan Stander sat at his desk and looked out over the car park in front of the mine hospital. He appeared to have aged ten years since the previous evening. Dan envied his colleagues that detachment they could bring to their work. He had never been able to perfect the trick. He had just completed forty-one examinations for issue of death certificates.

For fifteen years he had been a mine doctor, so he was accustomed to dealing with death in its more hideous forms. This, however, was the worst he had ever encountered. Forty-one of them, all victims of severe burning and massive explosion trauma.

He felt washed out, exhausted with ugliness. He massaged his temples as he examined the tray of pathetic possessions that lay on the desk before him. This was the contents of the pocket of the man Delange. Extracting them from the scorched clothing had been a filthy business in itself. Cloth had burned into the flesh, the man had been wearing a cheap nylon shirt under his overalls. The fabric had melted in the heat and had become part of his blistered skin.

There was a bunch of keys on a brass ring, a Joseph Rogers pen-knife with a bone handle, a Ronson cigarette-lighter which had been clutched in the man's clawed and charred right hand, a springbok skin wallet, and a loose envelope with one corner burned away.

Dan had already passed on the effects of the Bantu victims to the agent of the Bantu Recruiting Agency, who would send them on to the men's families. Now he sighed with distaste and picked up the wallet. He opened it.

In one compartment there were half a dozen postage stamps, and five Rands in notes. The other flap bulged with paper. Dan glanced through salesman's cards, dry-cleaning receipts, newspaper cuttings offering farms for sale, a folded page from the *Farmer's Weekly* on the planning of a dairy herd, a J.B.S. Savings Book.

Dan opened the Savings Book and whistled when he saw the total. He fanned the remaining pages.

There was a much-fingered envelope, unsealed and tucked behind the cardboard cover of the Savings Book. Dan opened it, and pulled a face. It contained a selection of photographs of the type which one found offered for sale in the dock area of the Mozambique port of Lourenço Marques. It was for this type of material that Dan was searching.

When the man's possessions were returned to his grieving relatives, Dan wanted to spare them this evidence of human frailty. He burned the photographs and the envelope in his ashtray and then crushed the blackened sheets to powder before spilling it into his waste-paper bin.

He went across to the window and opened it to let the smell of smoke escape. He stood at the window and searched the car park for Joy's Alfa Romeo. She had not arrived as yet and Dan returned to his desk.

The remaining envelope caught his eye and he picked it up. There was a smear of blood upon it, and the corner was burned away. Dan removed the four sheets of paper and spread them on the desk:

Dear Johnny,

When Pa died you were still little–and I always reckoned you were more like my son, you know, than my brother.

Well, Johnny, I reckon now I've got to tell you something . . .

Dan read slowly, and he did not hear Joy come into the room. She stood at the door watching him. Her expression fond, a small smile on her lips, shiny blonde hair hanging straight to her shoulders. Then she moved up quietly behind his chair and kissed his ear. Dan started and turned to face her.

'Darling,' Joy said and kissed him on the mouth. 'What is so interesting that you ignore my arrival?'

Dan hesitated a moment before telling her.

'There was a man killed last night in a ghastly accident. This was in his pocket.'

He handed her the letter and she read it slowly.

'He was going to send this to his brother?' she asked, and Dan nodded.

'The bitch,' Joy whispered, and Dan looked surprised.

'Who?'

'The girl–it's her fault, you know.' Joy opened her purse and took out a tissue to dab her eyes. 'Damn it, now I'm messing my make-up.' She sniffed and then went on. 'It would serve her right if you gave that letter to her husband.'

'You mean I shouldn't give it to him?' Dan asked. 'We have no right to play God.'

'Haven't we?' asked Joy, and Dan watched quietly as she tore the letter to tiny shreds, screwed them into a ball, then dropped them into the waste bin.

'You are wonderful,' he said. 'Will you marry me?'

'I've already answered that question, Dr Stander.' And she kissed him again.

53

Hettie Delange was in a turmoil.

It had started with the phone call that had roused Johnny from their bed. He had said nothing about trouble at the shaft as he pulled on his clothes, but she had come only briefly awake and then drifted off again as Johnny hurried out into the night.

He had come in hours later and sat on the edge of the bed, his hands clasped between his knees and his head bowed.

'What's wrong, man,' she had snapped at him. 'Come to bed. Don't just sit there.'

'Davy's dead.' His voice had been listless.

There was a moment's shock that had convulsed the muscles of her belly, and brought her fully awake. Then, immediately she had felt a swift cleansing rush of relief.

He was dead. It was as easy as that! All day she had worried. She had been stupid to let it happen. Just that moment of weakness, that self-indulgent slip and she had been dreading the consequences all that day. She had imagined Davy trailing after her with puppy eyes, trying to touch her, making it so obvious that even Johnny would see it. She had enjoyed it but just the once was enough. She wanted no repeat performance and certainly no complications to follow the original deed.

Now it was all taken care of. He was dead.

'Are you sure?' she had asked anxiously, and Johnny heard the tone as concern.

'I saw him!' Johnny had shuddered, and wiped the back of his hand across his mouth.

'Gee, that's terrible.' Hettie had remembered her role, and sat up to put her arms about Johnny. 'That's terrible for you.'

She had not slept again that night. Somehow the thought of Davy going directly from her to his violent death was exciting. It was like in the movies, or a book, or something. Like he was an airman and he had been shot down, and she was his girl. Perhaps she was pregnant and all alone in the world, and she would have to go to Buckingham Palace to get his medal for him. And the Queen would say . . .

The fantasies had played out in her mind until the dawn, with Johnny tossing and muttering beside her.

She woke him when it was first light in the room.

'How was he?' she asked softly. 'What did he look like, Johnny?'

Johnny shuddered again, and then he started to tell her. His voice was husky, and the sentences broken and disconnected. When he stumbled into silence, Hettie found herself trembling with excitement.

'How terrible,' she kept repeating. 'Oh, how awful!' And she pressed against him. After a while Johnny made love to her, and for Hettie it was better than she had ever known it to be.

All that morning there were phone calls, and four of her friends came over to drink coffee with her. A reporter and photographer from the *Johannesburg Star* called and asked questions. Hettie was the centre of attraction, and again and again she repeated the story with all its grisly details.

After lunch Johnny came home with a little dark-haired man in a charcoal suit and black Italian shoes, with a matching black briefcase.

'Hettie, this is Mr Boart. He was Davy's lawyer. He's got something to tell you.'

'Mrs Delange. May I convey to you my sincere condolences in the tragic bereavement you and your husband have suffered.'

'Yes, it's terrible, isn't it?' Hettie was apprehensive. Had Davy told this lawyer about them? Had this man come to make trouble?

'Your brother-in-law made a will of which I am the executor. Your brother-in-law was a wealthy man. His estate is in excess of fifty thousand Rand.' Boart paused portentously. 'And you and your husband are the sole beneficiaries.'

Hettie looked dubiously from Boart to Johnny.

'I don't–what's that mean? Beneficiary?'

'It means that you and your husband share the estate between you.'

'I get half of fifty thousand Rand?' Hettie asked in delighted disbelief.

'That's right.'

'Gee,' exulted Hettie. 'That's fabulous!' She could hardly wait for Johnny and the lawyer to go before she phoned her friends again. All four of them returned to drink more coffee, to thrill again and to envy Hettie the glamour and excitement of it.

'Twenty-five thousand,' they kept repeating the sum with relish.

'Hell, man, he must really have liked you a lot, Hettie,' one of the girls commented with heavy emphasis, and Hettie lowered her eyes and contrived to look bereft and mysterious.

Johnny came home after six, unsteady on his feet and reeking of liquor. Reluctantly Hettie's four friends left to rejoin their waiting families, and almost immediately after that a big white sports car pulled up in the driveway and Hettie's day of triumph was complete. Not one of her friends had ever had the General Manager of the Sonder Ditch Gold Mining Company call at their home.

She had the front door open the instant the doorbell rang. Her greeting had been shamelessly plagiarized from a period movie that had recently played at the local cinema.

'Mr Ironside, how good of you to come.'

When she led Rod through into the over-furnished lounge, Johnny looked up but did not get to his feet.

'Hello, Johnny,' said Rod. 'I have come to tell you that I'm sorry about Davy, and to . . .'

'Don't give me that bull dust, Tin ribs,' said Johnny Delange.

'Johnny,' gasped Hettie, 'you can't talk to Mr Ironsides like that.' And she turned to Rod, laying a hand on his sleeve. 'He doesn't mean it, Mr Ironsides. He has been drinking.'

'Get out of here,' said Johnny. 'Get into the bloody kitchen where you belong.'

'Johnny!'

'Get out!' roared Johnny, rising from his chair, and Hettie fled from the room.

Johnny lurched across to the chrome and glass liquor cabinet that filled one corner. He sloshed whisky into two glasses and handed one to Rod.

'God speed to my brother,' he said.

'To Davy Delange, one of the best rock hounds on the Kitchenerville field,' said Rod, and tossed the drink back in one gulp.

'The best!' Johnny corrected him, and emptied his own glass. He gasped at the sting of the whisky, then leaned forward to speak into Rod's face.

'You've come to find out if I'm game to finish your bloody drive for you, or if I'm going to quit. Davy didn't mean nothing to you and I don't mean nothing to you. Only one thing worrying you–you want to know about your bloody drive.' Johnny refilled his glass. 'Well, hear this, friend, and hear it well. Johnny Delange don't quit. That drive ate my brother but I'll beat the bastard, so you got nothing to worry about. You go home and get a good night's sleep, 'cos Johnny Delange will be on shift and breaking rock tomorrow morning first thing.'

54

A Silver Cloud Rolls Royce was parked amongst the trees in the misty morning. Ahead was the practice track with the white-painted railings curving away towards the willow-lined river. The mist was heavier along the river and the grass was very green against it.

The uniformed chauffeur stood away from the Rolls, leaving its two occupants in privacy. They sat on the back seat with an angora wool travelling rug spread over their knees. On the folding table in front of them was a silver Thermos of coffee, shell-thin porcelain cups, and a plate of ham sandwiches.

The fat man was eating steadily, washing each mouthful down with coffee. The little bald-headed man was not eating, instead he puffed quickly and nervously at his cigarette and looked out of the window at the horses. The grooms were walking the horses in circles, nostrils steaming in the morning chill, blankets flapping. The jockeys stood looking up at the trainer. They wore hard caps and polo-necked jerseys. All of them carried whips. The trainer was speaking urgently, his hands thrust deep into the pockets of his overcoat.

'It's a very fine service,' said the little man. 'I particularly enjoyed the stop in Rio. My first visit there.'

The fat man grunted. He was annoyed. They shouldn't have sent this agent out. It was a mark of suspicion, distrust, and it would seriously hamper his market operation.

The conference between trainer and jockeys had ended. The diminutive riders scattered to their mounts, and the trainer came towards the Rolls.

'Good morning, sir.' He spoke through the open window, and the fat man grunted again.

'I'm giving him a full run,' the trainer went on. 'Emerald Isle will make pace for him to the five, Pater Noster will take over and push him to the mile, I've Tiger Shark to pace him for the run in.'

'Very well.'

'Perhaps you'd like to keep time, sir.' The trainer proffered a stop-watch, and the fat man seemed to recover his urbanity and charm.

'Thank you, Henry.' He smiled. 'He looks good, I'll say that.'

The trainer was pleased by the condescension.

'Oh! He's red hot! By Saturday I'll have him sharpened down to razor edge.' He stood back from the window. 'I'll get them off, then.' He walked away.

'You have a message for me?' asked the fat man.

'Of course.' The other wriggled his moustache like a rabbit's whiskers. It was an annoying habit. 'I didn't fly all this way out here to watch a couple of mokes trotting around a race-track.'

'Would you like to give me the message?' The fat man hid his affront. What the agent had called a moke was some of the finest horseflesh in Africa.

'They want to know about this gas explosion.'

'Nothing.' The fat man dismissed the question with a wave of his hand. 'A flash explosion. Killed a few men. No damage to the workings. Negligence on the part of the miner in charge.'

'Will it affect our plans?'

'Not one iota.'

The two horses had jumped away from the start, shoulder to shoulder, with the wreaths of mists swirling in their wake. The glossy bay horse on the rails ran with an easy floating action while the grey plunged along beside it.

'My principals are very concerned.'

'Well, they have no need to be,' snapped the fat man. 'I tell you it makes no difference.'

'Was the explosion due to an error of judgement on the part of this man Ironsides?'

'No.' The fat man shook his head. 'It was negligence of the miner in charge. He should have detected the gas.'

'Pity.' The bald man shook his head regretfully. 'We had hoped it was a flaw in the Ironsides character.'

The grey horse was tiring, while the bay ran on smoothly, drawing away from him. From the side rail a third horse came in to replace the grey, and ran shoulder to shoulder with the bay.

'Why should the character Ironsides concern you?'

'We have heard disturbing reports. This is no pawn to be moved at will. He is taking the job of general manager by the throat. Already our sources indicate that he has reduced running costs on the Sonder Ditch by a scarcely believable two per cent. He seems to be tireless, inventive–a man, in short, to reckon with.'

'Well and good,' the fat man conceded. 'But I still fail to see why your–ah, principals–are alarmed. Do they expect that this man will hold back the flood water by the sheer force of his personality?'

The second pacemaker was faltering, but still the big bay ran on alone. A far figure in the mist, passing the mile post, joined at last by the third pacemaker.

'I know nothing about horses,' said the bald man watching the two flying forms. 'But I've just seen that one,' he pointed with his cigarette at the far-off bay. 'I've just seen him run the guts out of the other two. One after the other he has broken their hearts and left them staggering along behind him. We would call him an imponderable, one who cannot be judged by normal standards.' He puffed at his cigarette before going on. 'There are men like that also, imponderable. It seems to us that Ironsides is one of them, and we don't like it. We don't like them on the opposing team. It is just possible that he could upset the entire operation, not, as you put it, by sheer force of personality, but by suddenly doing the unexpected, by behaving in a manner for which we have not allowed.'

Both men fell silent watching the galloping horses come round the last bend and hit the straight.

'Watch this.' The fat man spoke softly, and as though in response to his words the big bay lengthened his stride, reaching out, driving strongly away from the other horse. His head was going like a hammer, twin jets of steam shot from wide flaring nostrils, and thrown turf and dirt flew from his hooves. Five lengths clear of the following horse he went slashing past the finish line and the fat man clicked his stop watch.

He scrutinized the dial of the watch anxiously and then chuckled like a healthy baby.

'And he wasn't really being extended!'

He rapped on the window beside him, and immediately the uniformed chauffeur opened the driving door and slid in behind the wheel.

'To my office,' instructed the fat man, 'and close the partition.'

When the sound-proof glass panel had slid closed between driver and passengers, the fat man turned to his guest.

'And so, my friend, you consider Ironsides to be an imponderable. What do you want me to do about him?'

'Get rid of him.'

'Do you mean what I think you mean?' The fat man lifted an eyebrow.

'No. Nothing that drastic.' The bald head bobbed agitatedly. 'You have been reading too much James Bond. Simply arrange it that Ironsides is far away and well occupied when the drive holes through the Big Dipper Dyke, otherwise there is an excellent chance that he will do something to frustrate our good intentions.'

'I think we can arrange that,' said the fat man and helped himself to another ham sandwich.

55

As he had promised, Manfred caught the Friday evening flight for Cape Town. On the Saturday night Rod and Terry took a wild chance on not being recognized and spent the evening at the Kyalami Ranch Hotel. They danced and dined in the Africa Room, but they were on their way back to the apartment before midnight.

In the dawn a playful slap with the rolled-up Sunday papers which Rod delivered to Terry's naked posterior as she slept triggered off a noisy brawl in which a picture was knocked off the wall by a flying pillow, a coffee table overturned and the shrieking and laughter reached such a pitch that it called down a storm of indignant thumping from the apartment above them.

Terry made a defiant gesture at the ceiling, but they both subsided gasping with laughter back onto the bed to indulge in activity every bit as strenuous if not nearly so noisy.

Later, much later, they collected Melanie and once again spent the Sunday at the stud farm on the Vaal. Melanie actually *rode* a horse, a traumatic experience which bade fair to alter her whole existence. After lunch they launched the speedboat from the boat house on the bank of the river and waterskied down as far as the barrage, Terry and Rod taking turns at the wheel and on the skis. It occurred to Rod that Terry Steyner looked good in a white bikini. It was dark before Rod delivered his sleeping daughter to her mother.

'Who is this *Terry* that Melanie talks about all the time?' demanded Patti, she was still sulking about Rod's promotion. Patti had a memory like a tax collector.

'Terry?' Rod feigned surprise. 'I thought you knew.' And he left Patti glaring after him as he went back down the stairs.

Terry was curled up in the leather bucket seat of the Maserati, just the tip of her nose protruding from the voluminous fur coat she wore.

'I love your daughter, Mr Ironsides,' she murmured.

'It would appear that the feeling is reciprocated.'

Rod drove slowly towards the hillbrow ridge, and Terry's hand came out of the wide fur sleeve and lay on his knee.

'Wouldn't it be nice if we had a daughter of our own one day?'

'Wouldn't it,' Rod agreed dutifully, and then found to his intense amazement that he really meant it.

He was still investigating this remarkable phenomenon as he parked the Maserati in the basement garage of his apartment and went round to open Terry's door.

Manfred Steyner watched Terry climb out of the Maserati and lift her face towards Rodney Ironsides. Ironsides stooped over her and kissed her, then he slammed and locked the door of the Maserati, and arm in arm the two of them crossed to the elevator.

'Peterson Investigations always delivers the goods,' said the man at the wheel of the black Ford parked in the shadows of the garage. 'We will give them half an hour to get settled in comfortably, then we will go up and knock on the door of his apartment.'

Manfred Steyner sat very still and unblinking on the seat beside the private detective. He had arrived back in Johannesburg three hours previously in answer to the summons from the investigation bureau.

'You will leave me here. Drive the Ford out and park at the corner of Clarendon Circle. Wait for me there,' said Manfred.

'Hey? Aren't you going to . . .?' The detective was taken aback.

'Do as I tell you.' Manfred's voice stung like thrown vitriol, but the detective persisted.

'You will need evidence for the court, you need me as a witness . . .'

'Get out,' Manfred snapped, and opening the door of the Ford he climbed out and closed the door behind him. The detective hesitated a moment longer, then started the engine and drove out of the garage leaving Manfred alone.

Manfred moved slowly towards the big shiny sports car. From his pocket he took a gold-plated pen-knife and opened the large blade.

He had recognized that the car was of special significance to the man. It was the only form of retaliation he could make at the moment. Until Rodney Ironsides completed the drive on the Big Dipper Dyke, he could not confront him nor Theresa Steyner. He could not let them know he even suspected them.

Such human emotions as love and hate and jealousy Manfred Steyner seldom experienced, except in their mildest manifestations. Theresa Hirschfeld he had never loved, as he had loved any woman. He had married her for her wealth and station in life. The emotion that gripped him was neither hatred nor jealousy. It was affront. He was affronted that these two insignificant persons should conspire to cheat him.

He would not rush in blindly now with threats of physical violence and divorce. No, he would administer an anonymous punishment that would hurt the man deeply. This would be part payment. Later, when he had served his purpose, Manfred would crush him as coldly as though he were stepping on an ant.

As for the woman, he was aware of a mild relief. Her irresponsible behaviour had placed her completely at his mercy, both legally and morally. As soon as the strike beyond the Big Dipper had made him financially secure and independent, he could throw her aside. She would have served her purpose admirably.

The journey which he had interrupted by this hurried return to Johannesburg was connected with the purchase of Sonder Ditch shares. He was touring the major centres arranging with various firms of stock brokers that on a given date they would commence to purchase every available scrap of Sonder Ditch script.

As soon as he had completed this business he would tell the private detective to drive him out to Jan Smuts Airport where he had a reservation on the night plane to Durban where he would continue his preparations.

It had all worked out very well, he thought, as he slipped the knife blade through the rubber buffer of the triangular side window of the Maserati. With a quick twist he lifted the window catch, and pushed the window open. He reached through and turned the door handle. The door clicked open and Manfred climbed into the driver's seat.

The blade of the pen-knife was razor sharp. He started on the passenger seat and then the driver's seat, ripping the leather upholstery to shreds before moving to the back seat and repeating the process there. He slid the panel that concealed the tray of tools each in their separate foam rubber padded compartment, and selected a tyre lever.

With this he smashed all the dials on the dashboard, broken glass tinkling and falling to the carpeted floor. With the point of the tyre lever he dug into the rosewood panelling and tore out a section, splintering and cracking the woodwork into complete ruin.

He climbed out of the Maserati and struck the windshield with the tyre lever. The glass starred. He rained blows on it, unable to shatter it but reducing it to a sagging opaque sheet.

Then he dropped the tyre lever and groped for his pen-knife again. On his knees he slashed at the front offside tyre. The rubber was tougher than he had allowed. Annoyed, he slashed again. The knife turned in his hand, the blade folded against the blow. It sliced the ball of his thumb, a deep stinging cut. Manfred came to his feet with a cry, clutching his injured thumb. Blood spurted from the wound.

'Mein Gott! Mein Gott!' Manfred gasped, horrified by his own blood. As he staggered wildly from the basement garage, he was wrapping a handkerchief around his thumb.

He reached the waiting Ford, hauled the door open and fell into the front seat beside the detective.

'A doctor! For God's sake, get me to a Doctor. I'm badly hurt. Quickly! Drive quickly!'

56

Terry's husband is due back in town today, Rod thought, as he sat down at his desk. It was not a thought that gave him strength to work through a day he knew would be filled with hectic activity.

The quarterly reports were due at Head Office tomorrow morning. In consequence the entire administration was in its usual last-minute panic. Already there was a mob in the waiting-room outside his office that Lily Jordan would soon need a stock whip to control. At three o'clock he was due at a consultants' meeting at Head Office, but before that he wanted to go underground to check the drop-blast matt that Johnny Delange had now completed and charged up.

The phone went as Lily led in his first visitor, a tall, thin, sorrowful-looking man with a droopy moustache.

'Mr Ironsides?' said the voice on the phone.

'Yes.'

'Porters Motors here. I've got an estimate on the repairs to your Maserati.'

'How much?' Rod crossed his fingers.

'Twelve hundred Rand.'

'Wow!' Rod gasped.

'Do you want us to go ahead?'

'No, I'll have to contact my insurance company first. I'll call you.' He hung up. That act of unaccountable vandalism still irked him terribly. He realized that he would be reduced to the Company Volkswagen for a further indefinite period.

He turned his attention to his visitor.

'Detective Inspector Grobbelaar,' the tall man introduced himself. 'I am investigating officer in the murder of José Almeida, the concession store proprietor on this mine.'

They shook hands.

'Have you any ideas on who did it?' Rod asked.

'We have always got ideas,' said the Inspector, so sadly that for a moment Rod had the impression that his name was on the list of suspects. 'We believe that the murderer is employed by one of the mines in the district, probably the Sonder Ditch. I have called on you to ask for your co-operation in the investigation.'

'Of course.'

'I will be conducting a great number of interrogations amongst your Bantu employees. I hoped you might find a room for me to use on the premises.'

Rod lifted his phone and while he dialled he told Grobbelaar, 'I'm calling our Compound Manager.' Then he transferred his attention to the mouthpiece. 'Ironsides here. I am sending an Inspector Grobbelaar down to see you. Please see that an office is placed at his disposal and that he receives full co-operation.'

Grobbelaar stood up and extended his hand.

'I won't take up more of your time. Thank you, Mr Ironsides.'

His next visitor was Van der Bergh, his Personnel Officer, brandishing his departmental reports as though they were a winning lottery ticket.

'All finished,' he announced triumphantly. 'All we need is your signature.'

As Rod uncapped his pen, the telephone squealed again.

'My God,' he muttered with pen in one hand and telephone in the other. 'Is it worth it?'

It was well after one o'clock when Rod fled his office, leaving Lily Jordan to hold back the tide. He went directly to No. 1 shaft where he was welcomed like the prodigal son by Dimitri and his old Line Managers. They were all anxious to know who would be replacing him as Underground Manager. Rod promised to find out that afternoon when he visited Head Office, and changed into his overalls and helmet.

At the spot where Davy Delange had died, Rod found a gang fixing a screen of wire mesh over the hanging wall to protect the fuses of his drop-blast. The electric cable that carried the blasting circuit to the surface was covered with a distinctive green plastic coating and securely pegged to the roof of the drive.

In the concrete blast room at the shaft head, his electrician had already set up a separate control for this circuit. It would be in readiness at all times. He could fire it within minutes. Rod felt as though a great weight had been lifted from his shoulders as he passed through the swinging ventilation doors and tramped on up the drive to speak to Johnny Delange.

Half-way to the face he met the gigantic figure of Big King coming back towards him with a small gang of lashing boys under his command. Rod greeted him, and Big King stopped and let his gang go on out of earshot before he spoke.

'I wish to speak.'

'Speak then.' Rod noticed suddenly that Big King's face was gaunt, his eyes appeared sunken and his skin had the dusty greyish look of sickness so evident in an ailing Bantu.

'I wish to return to my wives in Portuguese Mozambique,' said Big King.

'Why?' Rod was dismayed at the prospect of losing such a valuable boss boy.

'My blood is thin.' This was as non-committal an answer as any man has ever received. In essence it meant, 'My reasons are my own, and I have no intention of disclosing them.'

'When your blood is thick again, will you return to work here?' Rod asked.

'That is with the gods.' An answer signifying no more than the one preceding it.

'I cannot stop you if you wish to go, Big King, you know that,' Rod told him. 'Report to the Compound Manager and he will mark your notice.'

'I have told the Compound Manager. He wants me to work out my ticket, thirty-three more days.'

'Of course,' Rod nodded. 'You know that it is a contract. You must work it out.'

'I wish to leave at once,' Big King replied stubbornly.

'Then you must give me your reason. I cannot let you break contract except if there is some good reason.' Rod knew better than to set a dangerous precedent like that.

'There is no reason.' Big King admitted defeat. 'I will work out the ticket.'

He left Rod and followed his gang down the drive. Since the night he killed the Portuguese, Big King had slept little and eaten less. Worry had kept his stomach in a turmoil of dysentery, he had neither danced nor sung. Nothing that Crooked Leg nor the Shangaan Induna could say comforted him. He waited for the police to come. As the days passed, so the flesh melted from his body, he knew that they would come before the thirty-three days of his contract expired.

His approach to Rod had been a last despairing effort. Now he was resigned. He knew that the police were inexorable. One day soon they would come. They would lock the silver chains on his wrists and lead him to the closed van. He had seen many men led away like that and he had heard what happened to them after that. The white man's law was the same as the tribal law of the Shangaans. The taking of life must be paid for with life.

They would break his neck with the rope. His ancestors would have crushed his skull with a war club, it was the same in the end.

Rod found Johnny Delange drinking cold tea from his canteen while his gang barred down the face.

'How's it going?' he asked.

'Now we have finished messing about, it has started moving again.' Johnny wiped cold tea from his lips and recorked the canteen. 'We have broken almost fifteen hundred feet since Davy died.'

'That's good going.' Rod ignored the reference to the methane explosion and the drop-blast matt.

'Would have been better if Davy were still alive.' Johnny disliked Campbell, the miner who had replaced Davy on the night shift. 'The night shift aren't breaking their fair ground.'

'I'll chase them up,' Rod promised.

'You do that.' Johnny turned away to shout an order at his gang.

Rod stood and stared at the end of the drive. Less than a thousand feet ahead lay the dark hard rock of the Big Dipper–and beyond it . . .? Rod felt his skin creep as he remembered his nightmare. That cold green translucent thing waiting for them beyond the dyke.

'All right, Johnny, you are getting close now.' Rod tore his imagination away from that green horror. 'As soon as you hit the Serpentine rock you are to stop work immediately and report to me. Is that understood?'

'You'd better tell that to Campbell also,' said Johnny. 'The night shift may hit the Big Dipper.'

'I'll tell him,' Rod agreed. 'But you make sure you remember. I want to be down here when we hole through the dyke.'

Rod glanced at his watch. It was almost two o'clock. He had an hour to get to the consultants' meeting at Head Office.

'You are late, Mr Ironsides.' Dr Manfred Steyner looked up from the head of the board-room table.

'My apologies, gentlemen.' Rod took his seat at the long oak table. 'Just one of those days.'

The men about the table murmured sympathetic acknowledgement, and Dr Steyner studied him for a moment without expression before remarking.

'I would be obliged for a few minutes of your time after this meeting, Mr Ironsides.'

'Of course, Dr Steyner.'

'Good.' Manfred nodded. 'Now that Mr Ironsides has graced the table with his presence, the meeting can come to order.' It was the closest any of them had ever heard Dr Steyner come to making a joke.

It was dark outside when the meeting ended. The participants shrugged on their coats, made their farewells and left Manfred and Rod sitting at the table with its overflowing ash trays and littered pencils and note pads.

Manfred Steyner waited for fully three minutes after the door had closed on the last person to leave. Rod was accustomed to these long intent silences, yet he was uneasy. He sensed a new hostility in the man's attitude. He covered his awkwardness by lighting another cigarette and blowing a series of smoke rings at the portrait of Norman Hradsky, the original chairman of the company. Flanking Hradsky's portrait were two others. One of a slim blond man, with ravaged good looks and laughing blue eyes. The caption read; 'Dufford Charleywood. Director of C.R.C. from 1867-1872.' The other portrait in its heavy gilt frame depicted an impressively built man with mutton-chop whiskers and black Irish features. 'Sean Courtney' said the caption, and the dates were the same as Charleywood's.

These three had founded the Company, and Rod knew a little of their story. They had been as pretty a bunch of rogues as would be found in any convict settlement. Hradsky had ruined the other two in an ingenious bear raid on the stock exchange, and had virtually stolen their shares in the Company.

We have become a lot more sophisticated since then, thought Rod. He looked instinctively towards the head of the long table and met Dr Steyner's level, unblinking stare. *Or have we?* he wondered. Just what devilment has our friend in mind?

Manfred Steyner was examining Rod with detached curiosity. So remote from any emotional rancour was Manfred, that he intended using the relationship that had developed between this man and his wife to further the instructions he had received that morning.

'How far is the end of the drive from the dyke?' he asked suddenly.

'Less than a thousand feet.'

'How much longer before you reach it?'

'Ten days. No more, possibly less.'

'As soon as the dyke is reached, all work on it must cease immediately. The timing of this is important, do you understand?'

'I have already instructed my miners not to hole through without my specific orders.'

'Good.' Manfred lapsed into silence for another full minute. Andrew had called him that morning with instructions from the man. Ironsides was to be well away from the Sonder Ditch when they pierced the dyke. It was left to Manfred to engineer his absence.

'I must inform you, Mr Ironsides, that it will be at least three weeks before I give the order to drill through. When you reach the dyke, it will be necessary for me to proceed to Europe to make certain arrangements there. I will be away for at least ten days during which time no work of any type must be allowed in the drive to the Big Dipper.'

'You will be away over Christmas?' Rod asked with surprise.

'Yes,' Manfred nodded, and could read Rod's mind.

Terry will be alone, Rod thought quickly, she will be alone over Christmas. The Sonder Ditch goes onto *essential services only* for a full seven days over Christmas. Just a skeleton crew to keep her going. I could get away for a week, a whole week away together.

Manfred waited until he knew that Rod had reached the decision to which he had been steered, then he asked: 'You understand? You will await my order to hole through. You need not expect that order until the middle of January.'

'I understand.'

'You may go.' Manfred dismissed him.

'Thanks,' Rod acknowledged drily.

There was a coffee bar in the ground-floor shopping centre of Reef Building. Rod beat a bearded hippie to the telephone booth, and dialed the Sandown number. It was safe enough, he had just left Manfred upstairs.

'Theresa Steyner,' she answered his call.

'We've got a week to ourselves,' he told her. 'One whole glorious week.'

'When?' she demanded joyously.

And he told her.

'Where shall we go?' she asked.

'We'll think of somewhere.'

57

At 11.26 a.m. on December 16th, Johnny Delange blasted the face of the drive, and went forward in the fumes and dust.

In the beam of his lantern, the new rock blown from the face was completely different from the bluish Ventersdorp quartzite. It was a glassy, blackish green, veined with tiny white lines, more like marble than country rock.

'We are on the dyke.' He spoke to Big King, and stopped to pick up a lump of the Serpentine rock. He weighed it in his hand.

'We've done it, we've beaten the bastard!'

Big King stood silently beside him. He did not share Johnny's elation.

'Right!' Johnny tossed the lump of rock back onto the pile. 'Bar down, and make safe. Then pull them out of the drive. We are finished here until further orders.'

'Well done, Johnny,' applauded Rod. 'Clean her up and pull out of the drive. I don't know how much longer it will be till we get the order to hole through the dyke. But take a holiday in the meantime. I'll pay you four fathoms of bonus a day while you are waiting.' He broke the connection with his finger, keeping the receiver to his ear. He dialled and spoke to the switchboard girl at Head Office. 'Get me Dr Steyner, please. This is Rodney Ironsides.' He waited a few seconds and then Manfred came on the line.

'We've hit the Big Dipper,' Rod told him.

'I will leave for Europe on tomorrow morning's Boeing,' said Manfred. 'You are to do nothing until I return.' Manfred cradled the receiver and depressed the button on his intercom

'Cancel all my appointments,' he told his secretary. 'I am unavailable.'

'Very well, Dr Steyner.'

Manfred picked up the receiver of his unlisted, direct-line telephone. He dialled.

'Hello, Andrew. Will you tell him that I am ready to discharge my obligations. We have intersected the Big Dipper.' He listened for a few seconds, then spoke again. 'Very well, I will wait for your reply.'

Andrew replaced the telephone and went out through the sliding glass doors onto the terrace. It was a lazy summer's day, hushed with heat, and the sun sparkled on the crystal clear waters of the swimming-pool. Insects murmured languidly in the massed banks of blooms that surrounded the terrace.

The fat man stood before an artist's easel. He wore a blue beret and a white smock that hung like a maternity dress over his jutting stomach.

His model lay face down on an air mattress by the edge of the pool. She was a dainty, dark-haired girl with a pixy face and a doll-like body. Her discarded bikini lay in a damp bundle on the flags of the terrace. Drops of water caught the sun and bejewelled her creamy buttocks, giving her a paradoxical air of innocence and oriental eroticism.

'That was Steyner,' said Andrew. 'He reports that they have hit the Big Dipper.'

The fat man did not look up. He went on laying paint upon the canvas with complete concentration.

'Please lift your right shoulder, my dear, you are covering that utterly delightful bosom of yours,' he instructed, and the girl obeyed him immediately.

Finally he stepped back and regarded his own work critically.

'You may have a break now.' He wiped his brushes while the naked girl stood up, stretched like a cat and then dived into the pool. She surfaced with the water slicking her short dark hair against her head like the pelt of an otter, and swam slowly to the far end of the pool.

'Cable New York, Paris, London, Tokyo and Berlin the code word "Gothic",' he instructed Andrew. This was the word which would unleash the bear offensive on the financial markets of the world. On the receipt of those cables, agents in the major cities would begin to sell the shares of the companies mining the Kitchenerville field, sell them by the millions.

'Then instruct Steyner to get Ironsides out of the way, and hole through the dyke.'

Manfred answered Andrew's return call on the unlisted line. He listened to, and acknowledged, his instructions. Afterwards he sat still as a lizard, running over his preparations. Reviewing them minutely, examining them for flaws. There were none.

It was time to begin the purchase of Sonder Ditch shares. He called his secretary on the intercom and instructed her to place calls to numbers in Cape Town, Durban and Johannesburg itself. He wanted the purchase orders to come through a number of different brokers, so that it would not be obvious that there was only one buyer in the market. There was also the question of credit; he was not covering his purchase orders with Banker's guarantees. The stock brokers were buying for him simply on his name and reputation and position with C.R.C. Manfred could not place too large a buying order with any one firm lest they ask him to provide surety. Dr Manfred Steyner had no surety to offer.

So instead, he placed moderate orders with dozens of different firms. By three o'clock that afternoon Manfred had ordered the purchase of three quarters of a million Rands' worth of shares. He had no means of paying for those shares but he knew he would never be called upon to do so. When he sold them again in a few weeks' time they would have doubled in value.

A few minutes after his final conversation with the firm of Swerling and Wright in Cape Town, his secretary came through on the intercom.

'S.A.A. have confirmed your reservation on the Boeing to Salisbury. Flight 126 at nine a.m. tomorrow morning. You are booked to return to Johannesburg on the Rhodesian Airways Viking at 6 p.m. tomorrow evening.'

'Thank you.' Manfred grudged this wasted day but it was imperative that Theresa believed he had left for Europe. She must see him depart on the S.A.A. flight. 'Please get my wife on the phone for me.'

'Theresa,' he told her, 'something important has come up. I have to fly to London tomorrow morning. I am afraid I will be away over Christmas.'

Her display of surprise and regret was unconvincing. She and Ironsides had made their own arrangements for the time he was away, Manfred was convinced of this.

It was all working out very well, he thought, as he cradled the receiver, very well indeed.

58

The Daimler drew up under the portico of Jan Smuts Airport and the chauffeur opened the door for Terry and then for Manfred.

While the porter removed his luggage from the boot of the Daimler, Manfred swept the car park with a quick scrutiny. So early in the morning it was less than half filled. There was a cream Volkswagen with a Kitchenerville number plate parked near the far end. All the line and senior managers of the Sonder Ditch had cream Volkswagens as their official vehicles.

'The bee has come to the honeypot,' thought Manfred, and smiled bleakly. He took Terry's elbow and they followed the porter with the crocodile-skin luggage into the main concourse of the airport.

Terry waited while Manfred went through his ticket and immigration formalities. On the outside she was a demure and dutiful wife, but she also had seen the Volkswagen and inside she was itching and bubbling with excitement. Darting surreptitious glances from behind her sunglasses, looking for that broad-shouldered figure among the crowds.

It seemed a lifetime until she stood alone on the observation balcony with the wind whipping her piebald calf-skin coat around her legs, and blowing her hair into a snapping, dancing tangle. The long shark-like shape of the Boeing jet crouched at the far end of the runway and as it started forward Terry turned from the balcony rail and ran back into the main building.

Rod was waiting for her just inside the doors, and he swung her off her feet.

'Gottcha!'

With her feet dangling, she put her arms around his neck and kissed him.

The watchers paused and smiled, and there was a minor traffic jam at the head of the stairs.

'Come on,' she entreated, 'let's not waste a minute of it.' He put her on her feet, and they ran down the staircase hand in hand. Terry paused only to dismiss the chauffeur, and then they ran through the car park like children let out of school, and clambered into the Volkswagen. Their luggage was on the back seat.

'Go,' she said, 'go as fast as you can!'

Twenty minutes later Rod pulled the Volkswagen to a tyre-squealing halt in front of the hangars at the private airfield.

The twin-engined Cessna stood on the tarmac. Both engines were ticking over in readiness, and the mechanic climbed down from the cockpit when he recognized Terry.

'Hello, Terry, right on time,' he greeted her.

'Hello Hank. You've got her warmed up already. You are a sweety!'

'Filed your flight plan also. Nothing too good for my most favourite customer.' The mechanic was a chunky grizzled little man, and he looked at Rod curiously.

'Give you a hand with the bags,' he said.

By the time they had the luggage stowed away in its compartment, Terry was in the cockpit speaking to the control tower.

Rod climbed up into the passenger seat beside her.

Terry switched off her radio and leaned over Rod's lap to speak to Hank.

'Thanks, Hank.' She paused delicately, and then went on with a rush. 'Hank, if anyone asks you, I was on my own today, okay?'

'Okay.' Hank grinned at her. 'Happy landings.' And he closed the cockpit door, and Terry taxied out onto the runway.

'Is this yours?' Rod asked. It was a hundred thousand Rands' worth of aircraft.

'Pops gave it to me for my birthday,' Terry replied. 'Do you like it?'

'Not bad,' Rod admitted.

Terry turned upwind and applied the wheel brakes while she ran the engines up to peak revs, testing their response.

Suddenly Rod realized that he was in the hands of a woman pilot. He fell silent and his nerves began to tighten up.

'Let's go,' said Terry and kicked off the brakes. The Cessna surged forward, and Rod gripped the arm rests and froze with his gaze fixed dead ahead.

'Relax, Ironsides,' Terry advised him without taking her eyes off the runway, 'I've been flying since I was sixteen.'

At three thousand feet she levelled out and banked gently onto an easterly heading.

'Now that didn't hurt too much did it?' She smiled sideways at him.

'You are quite a girl,' he told her. 'You can do all sorts of tricks.'

'You just wait,' she warned him. 'You ain't seen nothing yet!'

They flew in silence until the Highveld had fallen away behind them, and they were over the dense green mattress of the Buchveld.

'I'm going to divorce him.' She broke the silence, and Rod was not surprised that they were experiencing the mental telepathy of closely attuned minds. He had been thinking about her husband also.

'Good,' he said.

'You think I'd have a chance with you if I did?'

'If you played your cards right, you might get that lucky.'

'Conceited swine,' she said. 'I don't know why I love you.'

'Do you?' he said.

'Yes.'

'And I you.'

They relapsed into a contented silence, until Terry put the Cessna into a shallow dive.

'What's wrong?' Rod asked with alarm.

'Going down to have a look for game.'

They flew low over thick olive-green bush broken by vleis of golden brown grass.

'There,' said Rod, pointing ahead. A line of fat black bugs moving across one of the open places. 'Buffalo!'

'And over there.' Terry pointed left.

'Zebra and wildebeeste,' Rod identified them. 'And there is a giraffe.' Its long stalk of a neck stuck up like a periscope. It broke into an awkward stiff-legged run as the aircraft roared overhead.

'We have arrived.' Terry indicated a pair of round granite koppies on the horizon ahead. They were as symmetrical as a young girl's breasts, and as they drew nearer Rod made out the thatched roof of a large building standing in the hollow between the koppies. Beyond it a long straight landing-strip had been cut from the trees, and the fat white sausage of a wind sock flew from its pole.

Terry throttled back and circled the homestead. On the lawns half a dozen tiny figures waved up at the Cessna, and as they watched, two of the figures climbed into a toy Landrover and set off for the landing-strip. A ribbon of white dust blew out from behind it.

'That's Hans,' Terry explained. 'We can go down now.'

She lined the Cessna up for its approach, and then let it sink down with the motors bumbling softly. The ground came up and jarred the undercarriage, then they were taxiing to meet the racing Landrover.

The man who piled out of the Landrover was white-haired, and sunburned like old leather.

'Mrs Steyner!' He was making no attempt to conceal his pleasure. 'It's been much too long. Where have you been?'

'I've been busy, Hans.'

'New York? What the hell for?' said Hans surprisingly.

'This is Mr Ironsides.' Terry introduced them. 'Rod, this is Hans Kruger.'

'Van Breda?' asked Hans as they shook hands. 'You related to the van Bredas from Caledon?'

'I don't think so,' Rod muttered weakly and looked at Terry appealingly.

'He is stone deaf,' Terry explained. 'Both his ear drums blown out by a hangfire in the 1930's. He won't admit it though.'

'I'm glad to hear it,' Hans nodded, happily. 'You always were a healthy girl. I remember when you were a little piccanin.'

'He is an absolute darling though, so is his wife. They look after the shooting for Pops,' Terry told Rod.

'Good idea!' Hans agreed heartily. 'Let's get your bags into the Landrover and go up to the house. I bet Mr van Breda could use a drink also.' And he winked at Rod.

The lodge had thatch and rough-hewn timber roofing, stone-flagged floors covered with cured animal skins and Kelim rugs. There was a walk-in fireplace flanked by gun racks on which were displayed fifty fine examples of the gunsmith's art. The furniture was massive and masculine, leather-cushioned and low. The Spanish plaster walls were hung with trophies, horned heads and native weapons.

A vast wooden staircase led up to the bedrooms that opened off the gallery above the main room. The bedrooms were air-conditioned and after they had got rid of Hans and his fat wife, Rod and Terry tested the bed to see if it was suitable.

An hour and a half later the bed had been judged eminently satisfactory, and as they went down to pass further judgement on the gargantuan lunch that fat Mrs Hans had spread for them, Terry remarked, 'Has it ever occurred to you, Mr Ironsides, that there are parts of your anatomy other than your flanks which are ferrous in character?' Then she giggled and added softly, 'And thank the Lord for that!'

Lunch was an exhausting experience and Terry pointed out that there was little sense in going out before four o'clock as the game would still be in thick cover avoiding the midday heat, so they went back upstairs.

After four o'clock Rod selected a .375 magnum Holland and Holland rifle from the rack, filled a cartridge belt with ammunition from one of the drawers, and they went out to the Landrover.

'How big is this place?' Rod asked as he turned the Landrover away from the gardens and took the track out into the virgin bush.

'You can drive for twenty miles in any direction and it's all ours. Over there our boundary runs against the Kruger National Park,' Terry answered.

They drove along the banks of the river, skirting sandbanks on which grew fluffy-headed reeds. The water ran fast between glistening black rocks, then spread into slow lazy pools.

They saw a dozen varieties of big game, stopping every few hundred yards to watch some lovely animal.

'Pops obviously doesn't allow shooting here,' Rod remarked, as a kudu bull with long spiral horns and trumpet-shaped ears studied them with big wet eyes from a range of thirty feet. 'The game is as tame as domestic cattle.'

'Only family are allowed to shoot,' Terry agreed. 'You qualify as family, however.'

Rod shook his head. 'It would be murder.' Rod indicated the kudu. 'That old fellow would eat out of your hand.'

'I'm glad you feel like that,' Terry said, and they drove on slowly.

The evening was not cool enough to warrant a log fire in the cavernous fireplace of the lodge. They lit one anyway because Rod decided it would be pleasant to sit in front of a big, leaping fire, drink whisky and hold the girl you love.

59

When Inspector Grobbelaar lowered his teacup, there was a white scum of cream on the tips of his moustache. He licked it off carefully, and looked across at Sergeant Hugo.

'Who have we got next?' he asked.

Hugo consulted his notebook.

'Philemon N'gabai.' He read out the name, and Grobbelaar sighed.

'Number forty-eight, only sixteen more.' The single smeary fingerprint on the fragment of glass from the gold container had been examined by the fingerprint department. They had provided a list of sixty-four names anyone of which might be the owner of that print. Each of them had to be interrogated, it was a lengthy and so far unrewarding labour.

'What do we know about friend Philemon?' Grobbelaar asked.

'He is approximately forty years old. A Shangaan from Mozambique. Height 5′ 7½″, weight 146 lb. Crippled right leg. Two previous convictions. 1956: 60 days for bicycle theft. 1962: 90 days for stealing a camera from a parked car,' Hugo read from the file.

'At one hundred forty-six pounds I don't see him breaking many necks. But send him in, let's talk to him,' Grobbelaar suggested and dunked his moustache in the tea cup again. Hugo nodded to the African Sergeant and he opened the door to admit Crooked Leg and his escort of an African constable.

They advanced to the desk at which the two detectives sat in their shirt sleeves. No one spoke. The two interrogators subjected him to a calculated and silent scrutiny to set him at as great a disadvantage as possible.

Grobbelaar prided himself on being able to sniff out a guilty conscience at fifty paces, and Philemon N'gabai reeked of guilt. He could not stand still, he was sweating heavily, and his eyes darted from floor to ceiling. He was guilty as hell, but not necessarily of murder. Grobbelaar did not feel the slightest confidence as he shook his head sorrowfully and asked, 'Why did you do it, Philemon? We have found the marks of your hand on the gold bottle.'

The effect on Crooked Leg was instantaneous and dramatic. His lips parted and began to tremble, saliva dribbled onto his chin. His eyes for the first time fixed on Grobbelaar's face, wide and staring.

'Hello! Hello!' Grobbelaar thought, straightening in his chair, coming completely alert. He sensed Hugo's quickening interest beside him.

'You know what they do to people who kill, Philemon? They take them away to . . .' Grobbelaar did not have an opportunity to finish.

With a howl Crooked Leg darted for the door. His crippled gait was deceptive, he was fast as a ferret. He had the door open before the Bantu Sergeant collared him and dragged him gibbering and struggling back into the room.

'The gold, but not the man! I did not kill the Portuguese,' he babbled, and Grobbelaar and Hugo exchanged glances.

'Pay dirt!' Hugo exclaimed with deep satisfaction.

'Bull's eye!' agreed Grobbelaar, and smiled, a rare and fleeting occurrence.

60

'You see it has a little light that comes on to show you where the keyhole is,' said the salesman pointing to the ignition switch on the dashboard.

'Ooh! Johnny, see that!' Hettie gushed, but Johnny Delange had his head under the bonnet of the big glossy Ford Mustang.

'Why don't you sit in her?' the salesman suggested. He was very cute really, Hettie decided, with dreamy eyes and the most *fabulous* side burns.

'Ooh! Yes, I'd love to.' She manœuvred her bottom into the leather bucket seat of the sports car. Her skirt pulled up, and the salesman's dreamy eyes followed the hem all the way.

'Can you adjust the seat?' Hettie asked innocently looking up at him.

'Here, I'll show you.' He leaned into the interior of the Mustang and reached across Hettie's lap. His hand brushed over her thigh, and Hettie pretended not to notice his touch. He smelled of Old Spice after-shave lotion.

'That's better!' Hettie murmured, and wriggled into a more comfortable position, contriving to make the movement provocative and revealing.

The salesman was encouraged, he lingered with his wrist just touching a sleek thigh.

'What's the compression ratio on this model?' Johnny Delange demanded as he emerged from the engine, and the salesman straightened up quickly and hurried to join him.

An hour later Johnny signed the purchase contract, and both he and Hettie shook the salesman's hand.

'Let me give you my card,' the salesman insisted, but Johnny had returned to his new toy, and Hettie took the cardboard business card.

'Call me if you need anything, anything at all,' said the salesman with heavy significance.

'Dennis Langley. Sales Manager,' Hettie read out aloud. 'My! You're very young to be Sales Manager.'

'Not all that young!'

'I'll bet,' Hettie murmured, and her eyes were suddenly bold. She ran the tip of a pink tongue over her lips. 'I won't lose it,' she promised, and placing the card in her handbag, walked to the Mustang, leaving him with a tantalizing promise and a memory of swaying hips and clicking heels.

They raced the new Mustang as far as Potchefstroom; Hettie encouraging Johnny to overtake slower vehicles with inches to spare for oncoming traffic. With horn blaring he tore over blind rises, forking ringed fingers at the protesting toots of other drivers. They had the speedometer registering 120 m.p.h. on the return run, and it was dark as they pulled into the driveway and Johnny hit the brakes hard to avoid running into the back of a big black Daimler that was parked outside their front door.

'Jesus,' gasped Johnny. 'that's Dr Steyner's bus!'

'Who is Dr Steyner?' Hettie demanded.

'Hell, he's one of the big shots from Head Office.'

'You're kidding!' Hettie challenged him.

'Truth!' Johnny affirmed. 'One of the real big shots.'

'Bigger than Mr Ironsides?' The General Manager of the Sonder Ditch was as high up the social ladder as Hettie had ever looked.

'Tin Ribs is chicken feed compared to this joker. Just look at his bus, it's five times better that Tin Rib's clapped-out old Maserati.'

'Gee!' Hettie could follow the logic of this line of argument. 'What's he want with us?'

'I don't know,' Johnny admitted with a twinge of anxiety. 'Let's go and find out.'

The lounge of the Delange home was not the setting which showed Dr Manfred Steyner to best advantage.

He sat on the edge of a scarlet and gold plastic-covered armchair as stiff and awkward as the packs of china dogs that stood on every table and shelf of the show cabinet, or the porcelain wild ducks which flew in diminishing perspective along the pale pink painted wall. In contrast to the tinsel Christmas decorations that festooned the ceiling and the gay greeting cards that Hettie had pinned to strips of green ribbon, Manfred's black homburg and Astrakhan-collared overcoat were unnecessarily severe.

'You will forgive my presumption,' he greeted them without rising. 'You were not at home and your maid let me in.'

'You're welcome, I'm sure,' Hettie simpered.

'Of course you are, Dr Steyner,' Johnny supported her.

'Ah! So you know who I am?' Manfred asked with satisfaction. This would make his task much easier.

'Of course we do.' Hettie went to him and offered her hand. 'I am Hettie Delange, how do you do?'

With horror Manfred saw that her armpit was unshaven, filled with damp ginger curls. Hettie had not bathed since the previous evening. Manfred's nostrils twitched and he fought down a queasy wave of nausea.

'Delange, I want to speak to you alone.' He cowered away from Hettie's overwhelming physical presence.

'Sure.' Johnny was eager to please. 'How about you making us some coffee, honey,' he asked Hettie.

Ten minutes later Manfred sank with relief into the lush upholstery of the Daimler's seat. He ignored the two Delanges waving their farewells, and closed his eyes. It was done. Tomorrow morning Johnny Delange would be on shift and drilling into the glassy green rock of the Big Dipper.

By noon Manfred would own quarter of a million shares in the Sonder Ditch.

In a week he would be a rich man.

In a month he would be divorced from Theresa Steyner. He would sue with all possible notoriety on the grounds of adultery. He no longer needed her.

The chauffeur drove back to Johannesburg.

61

It began on the floor of the Johannesburg Stock Exchange.

For some months nearly all the activity had been in the industrial counters, centring about the Alex Sagov group of companies and their merger negotiations.

The only spark of life in the mining and mining financials had been the Anglo American Corporation and De Beers Deferred rights issues, but this was now old news and the prices had settled at their new levels. So it was that nobody was expecting fireworks when the call over the gold mining counters began. The brokers' clerks crowding the floor were quietly spoken and behaved, when the first squib popped.

'Buy Sonder Ditch,' from one end of the hall.

'Buy Sonder Ditch,' a voice raised.

'Buy!' The throng stirred, heads turned.

'Buy.' The brokers suddenly agitated swirled in little knots, broke and reformed as transactions were completed. The price jumped fifty cents, and a broker ran from the floor to confer with his principal.

Here a broker thumped another on the back to gain his attention, and his urgency was infectious.

'Buy! Buy!'

'What the hell's happening?'

'Where is the buying coming from?'

'It's local!'

The price hit ten Rand a share, and then the panic began in earnest.

'It's overseas buying.'

'Eleven Rand!'

Brokers rushed to telephone warnings to favoured clients that a bull ring was developing.

'Twelve fifty. It's only local buying.'

'Buy at best. Buy five thousand.'

Clerks raced back onto the floor carrying the hastily telephoned instructions, and plunged into the hysterical trading.

'Jesus Christ! Thirteen Rand, sell now. Take your profit! It can't go much higher.'

'Thirteen seventy five, it's overseas buying. Buy at best.'

In fifty brokers' offices around the country, the professionals who spent their lives hovering over the tickers regained their balance and, cursing themselves for having been taken unawares, they scrambled onto the bull wagon. Others, the more canny ones, recognized the makings of a sick run and off-loaded their holdings, selling industrial shares as well as mining shares. Prices ran amok.

At ten-fifteen there was a priority call from the offices of the Minister of Finance in Pretoria to the office of the President of the Johannesburg Stock Exchange.

'What are you going to do?'

'We haven't decided. We won't close the floor if we can possibly help it.'

'Don't let it go too far. Keep me informed.'

Sixteen Rand and still spiralling when at eleven o'clock South African time, the London Stock Exchange came in. For the first fifteen wild minutes the price of Sonder Ditch gold mining rocketed in sympathy with the Johannesburg market.

Then suddenly and unexpectedly the Sonder Ditch shares ran head-on into massive selling pressure. Not only the Sonder Ditch, but all the Kitchenerville gold mining companies staggered as the pressure increased. The prices wavered, rallied a few shillings and then fell back, wavered again, and then crashed downwards, plummeting far below their opening prices.

'Sell!' was the cry. 'Sell at best!' Within minutes freshly-made paper fortunes were wiped away.

When the price of the Sonder Ditch gold mining shares fell to five Rand seventy-five cents, the committee of the Johannesburg Stock Exchange closed the floor in the interests of the national welfare, preventing further trade.

But in New York, Paris and London the investing public continued to beat South African gold mining shares to death.

In the air-conditioned office of a skyscraper building, the little bald-headed man was smashing his balled fist onto the desk top of his superior officer.

'I told you not to trust him,' he was almost sobbing with anger. 'The fat greedy slug. One million dollars wasn't enough for him! No, he had to blow the whole deal!'

'Please, Colonel,' his chief intervened. 'Control yourself. Let us make a fair objective appraisal of this financial activity.'

The bald-headed man sank back into his chair, and tried to light a cigarette with hands that trembled so violently as to extinguish the flame of his lighter.

'It sticks out a mile.' He flicked the lighter again, and puffed quickly. 'The first activity on the Johannesburg Exchange was Dr Steyner being clever. Buying up shares on the strength of our dummy report. That was quite natural and we expected it, in fact we wanted that to happen. It took suspicion away from us.' His cigarette had gone out, the tip was wet with spit. He threw it away and lit another.

'Fine! Everything was fine up to then. Doctor Steyner had committed financial suicide, and we were on the pig's back.' He sucked at his new cigarette. 'Then! Then our fat friend pulls the big double-cross and starts selling the Kitchenerville shares short. He must have gone into the market for millions.'

'Can we abort the operation at this late date?' his chief asked.

'Not a chance.' The bald head shook vigorously. 'I have sent a cable to our fat friend, ordering him to freeze the work on the tunnel but can you imagine him obeying that order? He is financially committed for millions of dollars and he will protect that investment with every means at his disposal.'

'Could we not warn the management of the Sonder Ditch company?'

'That would put the finger squarely on us, would it not?'

'Hmm!' the chief nodded. 'We could send them an anonymous warning.'

'Who would put any credence on that?'

'You're right,' the chief sighed. 'We will just have to batten down our hatches and ride out the storm. Sit tight and deny everything.'

'That is all we can do.' The cigarette had gone out again, and there were bits of wet tobacco in his moustache. The little man flicked his lighter.

'The bastard, the fat, greedy bastard!' he muttered.

62

Johnny and Big King rode up shoulder to shoulder in the cage. It had been a good shift. Despite the hardness of the Serpentine rock that cut down the drilling rate by fifty per cent, they had been able to get in five blasts that day. Johnny reckoned they had driven more than half-way through the Big Dipper. There was no night shift working now. Campbell had gone back to the stopes, so the honour of holing through would be Johnny's. He was excited at the prospect. Tomorrow he would be through into the unknown.

'Until tomorrow, Big King,' he said as they reached the surface and stepped out of the cage.

They separated, Big King heading for the Bantu hostel, Johnny to the glistening new Mustang in the car park.

Big King went straight to the Shangaan Induna's cottage without changing from his working clothes. He stood in the doorway and the Induna looked up from the letter he was writing.

'What news, my father?' Big King asked.

'The worst,' the Induna told him softly. 'The police have taken Crooked Leg.'

'Crooked Leg would not betray me,' Big King declared, but without conviction.

'Would you expect him to die in your place?' asked the Induna. 'He must protect himself.'

'I did not mean to kill him,' Big King explained miserably. 'I did not mean to kill the Portuguese, it was the gun.'

'I know, my son.' The Induna's voice was husky with helpless pity.

Big King turned from the doorway and walked down across the lawns to the ablution block. The spring and swagger had gone from his step. He walked listlessly, slouching, dragging his feet.

63

Manfred Steyner sat at his desk. His hands lay on the blotter before him, one thumb wearing a turban of crisp white bandage. His only movement was the steady beat of a pulse in his throat and a nerve that fluttered in one eyelid. He was deathly pale, and a light sheen of perspiration gave his features the look of having been sculptured from washed marble.

The volume of the radio was turned high, so the voice of the announcer boomed and reverberated from the panelled walls.

'The climax of the drama was reached at eleven forty-five South African time when the President of the Johannesburg Stock Exchange declared the floor closed and all further trading suspended.

'Latest reports from the Tokyo Stock Exchange are that Sonder Ditch gold mining shares were being traded at the equivalent of four Rand forty cents. This compares with the morning's opening price of the same share on the Johannesburg Stock Exchange of nine Rand forty-five cents.

'A spokesman for the South African Government stated that although no reason for these extraordinary price fluctuations was apparent, the Minister of Mines, Doctor Carel De Wet, had ordered a full-scale commission of enquiry.'

Manfred Steyner stood up from his desk and went through into the bathroom. With his flair for figures he did not need pen and paper to compute that the shares he had purchased that morning had depreciated in value by well over one million Rand at the close of business that evening.

He knelt on the tiled floor in front of the toilet bowl and vomited.

64

The sky was darkening rapidly, for the sun had long ago sunk below a blazing horizon.

Rod heard the whisper of wings, and strained his eyes upward into the gloom. They came in fast, in vee-formation, slanting down towards the pool of the river. He stood up from the blind and swung the shotgun on them, leading well ahead of the line of flight.

He squeezed off both barrels, Wham! Wham! And the duck broke formation and rocketed upwards, whirring aloft on noisy wings.

'Damn it!' said Rod.

'What's wrong, dead-eye Dick, did you miss?' asked Terry.

'The light's too bad.'

'Excuses! Excuses!' Terry stood up beside him, and Rod pushed a balled fist lightly against her cheek.

'That's enough from you, woman. Let's go home.'

Carrying the shotguns and bunches of dead duck, they trudged along the bank in the dusk to the waiting Landrover.

It was completely dark as they drove back to the lodge.

'What a wonderful day it's been,' Terry murmured dreamily. 'If for nothing else, I will always be grateful to you for teaching me how to enjoy my life.'

Back at the lodge, they bathed and changed into fresh clothes. For dinner they had wild duck and pineapple, with salads from Mrs Fat Hans' vegetable garden. Afterwards, they sprawled on the leopard-skin rugs in front of the fire-place and watched the log fire without talking, relaxed and happy and tired.

'My God, it's almost nine o'clock,' Terry checked her wrist-watch. 'I fancy a bit of bed myself, how about you, Mr Ironsides?'

'Let's hear the nine o'clock news first.'

'Oh Rod! Nobody ever listens to the news here. This is fairyland!'

Rod switched on the radio and the word froze them both. It was '*Sonder Ditch*'.

In horrified silence they listened to the full report. Rod's expression was granite hard, his mouth a tight grim line. When the news report ended, Rod switched off the radio set and lit a cigarette.

'There is trouble,' he said. 'Big trouble. I'm sorry, Terry, we must go back. As soon as possible. I have to get back to the mine.'

'I know,' Terry agreed immediately. 'But Rod, I can't take off from this landing-strip in the dark. There is no flare path.'

'We'll leave at first light.'

Rod slept very little that night. Whenever she woke, Terry sensed him lying unsleeping, worrying. Twice she heard him get up and go to the bathroom.

In the very early hours of the morning she woke from her own troubled sleep and saw him silhouetted against the starlit window. He was smoking a cigarette and staring out into the darkness. It was the first night they had spent together without making love. In the dawn Rod was haggard and puffy-eyed.

They were airborne at eight o'clock and they landed in Johannesburg a little after ten.

Rod went straight to the telephone in Hank's office and Lily Jordan answered his call.

'Miss Jordan, what the hell is happening? Is everything all right?'

'Is that you, Mr Ironsides. Oh! Thank God! Thank God you've come, something terrible has happened!'

65

Johnny Delange blew the face of the drive twice before nine o'clock, cutting thirty feet further into the glassy green dyke.

He had found that by drilling his cutter blast holes an additional three feet deeper, he could achieve a shatter effect on the serpentine rock which more than compensated for the additional drilling time. This next blast he was going to flout standard regulations and experiment with double charging his cutter holes. He would need additional explosives.

'Big King,' he shouted to make himself heard above the roar of drills. 'Take a gang back to the shaft station. Pick up six cases of Dynagel.'

He watched Big King and his gang retreat back down the drive, and then he lit a cigarette and turned his attention to his machine boys. They were poised before the rock face, sweating behind their drills. The dark rock of the dyke absorbed the light from the overhead electric bulbs. It made the end of the drive a gloomy place, filled with a sense of foreboding.

Johnny began to think about Davy. He was aware suddenly of a sense of disquiet, and he moved restlessly. He felt the hair on his forearms come slowly erect, each on a separate goose pimple. *Davy is here.* He knew it suddenly, and surely. His flesh crawled and he went cold with dread. He turned quickly and looked over his shoulder. The tunnel behind him was deserted, and Johnny gave a sickly grin.

'Shaya, madoda,' he called loudly and unnecessarily to his gang. They could not hear him above the roar of the drills, but the sound of his own voice helped reassure him.

Yet the creepy sensation was still with him. He felt that Davy was still there, trying to tell him something.

Johnny fought the sensation. He walked quickly forward, standing close to his machine boys, as though to draw comfort from their physical presence. It did not help. His nerves were shrieking now, and he felt himself beginning to sweat.

Suddenly the machine boy who was drilling the cutter hole in the centre of the face staggered backwards.

'Hey!' Johnny shouted at him, then he saw that water was spurting in fine needle jets from around the drill steel. Something was squeezing the drill steel out of its hole, like toothpaste out of a tube. It was pushing the machine boy backwards.

'Hey!' Johnny started forward and at that instant the heavy metal drill was fired out of the rock with the force of a cannon ball. It decapitated the machine boy, tearing his head from his body with such savagery that his carcass was thrown far back down the drive, his blood spraying the dark rock walls.

From the drill hole shot a solid jet of water. It came out under such pressure that when it caught the machine boy's assistant in the chest it stove in his ribs as though he had been hit by a speeding automobile.

'Out!' yelled Johnny. 'Get out!' And the rock face exploded. It blew outwards with greater force than if it had been blasted with Dynagel. It killed Johnny Delange instantly He was smashed to a bloody pulp by the flying rock. It killed every man in his gang with him, and immediately afterwards the monstrous burst of water that poured from the face picked up their mutilated remains and swept them down the drive.

Big King was at the shaft station when they heard the water coming. It sounded like an express train in a tunnel, a dull bellow of irresistible power. The water was pushing the air from the drive ahead of it, so that a hurricane of wind came roaring from the mouth of the drive, blowing out a cloud of dust and loose rubbish.

Big King and his gang stood and stared in uncomprehending terror until the head of the column of water shot from the drive, frothing solid, carrying with it a plug of debris and human remains.

Bursting into the T-junction of the main 66 level haulage, the strength of the flood was reduced, yet still it swept down towards the lift station in a waist deep wall.

'This way!' Big King was the first to move. He leapt for the steel emergency ladder that led up to the level above. The rest of his gang were not fast enough, the water picked them up and crushed them against the steel-mesh barrier that guarded the shaft. The crest of the wave burst around Big King's legs, sucking at him, but he tore himself from its grip and climbed to safety.

Beneath him the water poured into the shaft like bath water into a plug hole, forming a spinning whirlpool about the collar as it roared down to flood the workings below 66 level.

66

Leaving Terry at the airfield to solicit transport from Hank the mechanic, Rod drove directly to the head of No. 1 shaft of the Sonder Ditch. He jumped from the Volkswagen into the clamouring crowd clustered above the shaft head.

Dimitri was wide-eyed and distracted, beside him Big King towered like a black colossus.

'What happened?' Rod demanded.

'Tell him.' Dimitri instructed Big King.

'I was at the shaft with my gang. A river leaped from the mouth of the drive, a great river of water running faster than the Zambesi in flood; roaring like a lion the water ate all the men with me. I alone climbed above it.'

'We've hit a big one, Rod,' Dimitri interrupted. 'It's pouring in fast. We calculate it will flood the entire workings up to 66 level in four hours from now.'

'Have you cleared the mine?' Rod demanded.

'All the men are out except Delange and his gang. They were in the drive. They've been chopped, I'm afraid,' Dimitri answered.

'Have you warned the other mines we could have a burst through into their workings.'

'Yes, they are pulling all their shifts out.'

'Right.' Rod set off for the blast control room with Dimitri trotting to keep up with him. 'Give me your keys, and find the foreman electrician.'

Within minutes the three of them were crowded into the tiny concrete control room.

'Check in the special circuit,' Rod instructed. 'I'm going to shoot the drop-blast matt and seal off the drive.'

The foreman electrician worked quickly at the control panel. He looked up at Rod.

'Ready!' he said.

'Check her in,' Rod nodded.

The foreman threw the switch. The three of them caught their breath together.

Dimitri said it for them: 'Red!'

On the control panel of the special circuit the red bulb glared balefully at them, the Cyclops eye of the god of despair.

'Christ!' swore the foreman. 'The circuit is shot. The water must have torn the wires out.'

'It may be a fault in the board.'

'No.' The foreman shook his head with certainty.

'We've had it,' whispered Dimitri. 'Goodbye the Sonder Ditch!'

Rod burst out of the blast control room into the expectant crowd outside.

'Johnson!' He singled out one of his mine captains. 'Go down to the Yacht Club at the dam, get me the rubber rescue dinghy. Quick as you can, man.'

The man scurried away, and Rod turned on the electrician foreman as he emerged from the control room.

'Get me a battery hand-operator blaster, a reel of wire, pliers, gloves, two coils of nylon rope. Hurry!'

The foreman went.

'Rod.' Dimitri caught his arm. 'What are you going to do?'

'I'm going down there. I'm going to find the break in the circuit and I'm going to blast her by hand.'

'Jesus!' Dimitri gasped. 'You are crazy, Rod. You'll kill yourself for sure!'

Rod completely ignored his protest.

'I want one man with me. A strong man. The strongest there is, we will have to drag the dinghy against the flood.' Rod looked about him. Big King was standing by the banksman's office. The two of them were tall enough to face each other over the heads of the men between them.

'Will you come with me, Big King?' Rod asked.

'Yes,' said Big King.

67

In less than twenty minutes they were ready. Rod and Big King were stripped down to singlets and bathing-trunks. They wore canvas tennis shoes to protect their feet, and the hard helmets on their heads were incongruous against the rest of their attire.

The rubber dinghy was ex-naval disposal. A nine-foot air-filled mattress, so light that a man could lift it with one hand. Into it was packed the equipment they would need for the task ahead. A water-proof bag contained the battery blaster, the reel of insulated wire, the pliers, gloves and a spare lantern. Lashed to the eyelets along the sides of the dinghy were two coils of light nylon rope, a small crowbar, an axe and a razor-sharp machete in a leather sheath. To the bows of the dinghy were fastened a pair of looped nylon towing lines.

'What else will you need, Rod?' Dimitri asked.

Rod shook his head thoughtfully. 'That's it, Dimitri. That should do it.'

'Right!' Dimitri beckoned and four men came forward and carried the dinghy into the waiting cage.

'Let's go,' said Dimitri and followed the dinghy into the cage. Big King went next and Rod paused a second to look up at the sky. It was very blue and bright.

Before the onsetter could close the shutter door, a Silver Cloud Rolls Royce came gliding onto the bank. From the rear door emerged first Hurry Hirschfeld and then Terry Steyner.

'Ironsides!' roared Hurry. 'What the hell is going on?'

'We've hit water,' Rod answered him from the cage.

'Water? Where did it come from?'

'Beyond the Big Dipper.'

'You drove through the Big Dipper?'

'Yes.'

'You bastard, you've drowned the Sonder Ditch,' roared Hurry, advancing on the cage.

'Not yet, I haven't,' Rod contradicted.

'Rod.' Terry was white-faced beside her grandfather. 'You can't go down there.' She started forward.

Rod pushed the onsetter aside and pulled down the steel shutter door of the cage. Terry threw herself against the steel mesh of the guard barrier, but the cage was gone into the earth.

'Rod,' she whispered, and Hurry Hirschfeld put his arm around her shoulders and led her to the Rolls Royce.

From the back seat of the Rolls, Hurry Hirschfeld was conducting a Kangaroo Court Trial of Rodney Ironsides. One by one he called for the line managers of the Sonder Ditch and questioned them. Even those who were loyal to Rod could say little in his defence, and there were others who took the opportunity to level old scores with Rodney Ironsides.

Sitting beside her grandfather, Terry heard such a condemnation of the man she loved as to chill her to the depths of her soul. There was no doubt that Rodney Ironsides, without Head Office sanction, had instituted a new development so risky and contrary to company policy as to be criminal in concept.

'Why did he do it?' muttered Hurry Hirschfeld. He seemed bewildered. 'What could he possibly achieve by driving through the Big Dipper. It looks like a deliberate attempt to sabotage the Sonder Ditch.' Hurry's anger began to seethe within him. 'The bastard! He has drowned the Sonder Ditch and killed dozens of men.' He punched his fist into the palm of his hand. 'I'll make him pay for this. I'll break him, so help me God, I'll smash him! I'll bring criminal charges against him. Malicious damage to property. Manslaughter. Culpable homicide! By Jesus, I'll have his guts for this.'

Listening to Hurry ranting and threatening, Terry could keep silent no longer.

'It wasn't his fault, Pops. Truly it wasn't. He was forced to do it.'

'Ha!' snorted Hurry. 'I heard you at the pithead a few minutes ago. Just what is this man to you, Missy, that you spring to his defence so nobly?'

'Pops, please believe me.' Her eyes were enormous in her pale face.

'Why should I believe you? The two of you are obviously up to mischief together. Naturally you will try and protect him.'

'Listen to me at least,' she pleaded, and Hurry checked the run of his tongue and breathing heavily he turned to face her.

'This better be good, young lady,' he warned her.

In her agitation she told it badly, and half-way through she realized that she wasn't even convincing herself. Hurry's expression became more and more bleak, until he interrupted her impatiently.

'Good God, Theresa, this isn't like you. To try to put the blame for this onto your own husband! That's despicable! To try and switch the blame for this . . .'

'It's true! As God is my witness.' Terry was almost in tears, she was tugging at Hurry's sleeve in her agitation. 'Rod was forced to do it. He had no option.'

'You have proof of this?' Hurry asked drily, and Terry fell silent, staring at him dumbly. What proof was there?

68

The cage checked and slowed as it approached 65 level. The lights were still burning, but the workings were deserted. They lugged the dinghy out onto the station.

They could hear the dull waterfall roar of the flood on the level below them. The displacement of huge volumes of water disturbed the air so that a strong cool breeze was blowing up the shaft.

'Big King and I will go down the emergency ladder. You will lower the dinghy to us afterwards,' Rod told Dimitri. 'Make sure all the equipment is tied into it.'

'Right.' Dimitri nodded.

All was in readiness. The men who had come down with them in the cage were waiting expectantly. Rod could find no reason for further delay. He felt something cold and heavy settle in his guts.

'Come on, Big King.' And he went to the steel ladder.

'Good luck, Rod.' Dimitri's voice floated down to him, but Rod saved his breath for that cold dark climb downwards.

All the lights had fused on 66 level, and in the beam of his lamp the water below him was black and agitated. It poured into the mouth of the shaft, bending the mesh barrier inwards. The mesh acted as a gigantic sieve, straining the floating rubbish from the flood. Amongst the timber and planking, the sodden sacking and unrecognizable objects, Rod made out the waterlogged corpses of the dead pressed against the wire.

He climbed down and gingerly lowered himself into the water. Instantly it dragged at his lower body, shocking in its power. It was waist deep here, but he found that by bracing his body against the steel ladder he could maintain his footing.

Big King climbed down beside him, and Rod had to raise his voice above the hissing thunder of water.

'All right?'

'Yes. Let them send down the boat.'

Rod flashed his lamp up the shaft, and within minutes the dinghy was swaying slowly down to them. They reached up and guided it right side up to the surface of the water, before untying the rope.

The dinghy was sucked firmly against the wire mesh, and Rod checked its contents quickly. All was secure.

'Right.' Rod tied a bight of the nylon rope around his waist, and climbed up the wire mesh barrier until he could reach the roof of the tunnel. Behind him Big King was paying out the nylon line.

Rod leaned out until he could get his hands on the compressed air pipes that ran along the roof of the tunnel. The pipes were as thick as a man's wrist, bolted securely into the hanging wall of the drive they would support a man's weight with ease. Rod settled his grip firmly on the piping and then kicked his feet free from the barrier. He hung above the rushing waters, his feet just brushing the surface.

Hand over hand, swinging forward with his feet dangling, he started up the tunnel. The nylon rope hung down behind him like a long white tail. It was three hundred feet to where the water boiled from the drive into the main haulage, and Rod's shoulder muscles were shrieking in protest before he reached it. It seemed that his arms were being wrenched from their sockets, for the weight of the nylon rope that was dragging in the water was fast becoming intolerable.

There was a back eddy in the angle formed by the drive and the haulage. Here the flood swirled in a vortex, and Rod lowered himself slowly into it. The water buffeted him, but again he was able to cower against the side wall of the haulage and hold his footing. Quickly he began tying the rope onto the rawlbolts that were driven into the sidewall to consolidate the rock. Within minutes he had established a secure base from which to operate, and when he flashed his lamp back down the haulage he saw Big King following him along the compressed air piping.

Big King dropped into the waist deep water beside Rod, and they gripped the nylon rope and rested their burning arm muscles.

'Ready?' asked Rod at last, and Big King nodded.

They laid hold of the rope that led back to the dinghy and hauled upon it. For a moment nothing happened, the other end might just as well have been anchored to a mountain.

'Together!' grunted Rod, and they recovered a foot of rope.

'Again!' And they drew the dinghy inch by inch up the haulage against the rush of water.

Their hands were bleeding when they at last pulled the laden dinghy up to their own position and anchored it to the rawlbolts beside them. It bounced and bobbed with the water drumming against its underside.

Neither Rod nor Big King could talk. They hung exhausted on the body lines with the water ripping at their skin and gasped for breath.

At last Rod looked up at Big King, and in the lamp light he saw his own doubts reflected in Big King's eyes. The drop-blast matt was a thousand feet up the drive. The strength and speed of the water in the drive was almost double what it was in the haulage. Could they ever fight their way against such primeval forces as these that were now unleashed about them?

'I will go next,' Big King said and Rod nodded his agreement.

The huge Bantu drew himself up the rope until he could reach the compressed air pipe. His skin in the lamp light glistened like that of a porpoise. Hand over hand he disappeared into the gaping black maw of the drive. His lamp threw deformed and monstrous shadows upon the walls of rock.

When Big King's lamp flashed the signal to him, Rod climbed up to the pipe and followed him into the drive. Three hundred feet later he found that Big King had established another base. But here they were exposed to the full force of the flood, and they were pulled so violently against the body lines that the harsh nylon smeared the skin from their bodies. Together they dragged the dinghy up to them and anchored it.

Rod was sobbing softly as he held his torn hands to his chest and wondered if he could do it again.

'Ready?' Big King asked beside him, and Rod nodded. He reached up and placed the raw flesh of his palms onto the metal piping, and felt the tears of pain flood his eyes. He blinked them back and dragged himself forward.

Vaguely he realized that should he fall, he was a dead man. The flood would sweep him away, dragging him along the jagged side walls of the drive, ripping his flesh from the bone, and finally hurling him against the mesh surrounding the shaft to crush the life from his body.

He went on until he knew he could go no farther. Then he selected a rawlbolt in the side wall and looped the rope through it. And they repeated the whole heart-breaking procedure. Twice as he strained against the dinghy rope Rod saw his vision explode into stars and pinwheels. Each time he dragged himself back from the brink of unconsciousness by sheer force of will.

The example that Big King was setting was the inspiration which kept Rod from failing. Big King worked without change of expression, but his eyes were bloodshot with exertion. Only once Rod heard him grunt like a gut-shot lion, and there was bright blood on the rope where he touched it.

Rod knew he could not give in while Big King held on.

Reality dissolved slowly into a dark roaring nightmare of pain, wherein muscles and bone were loaded beyond all endurance, and yet continued to function. It seemed that for all time Rod had hung on arms that were leadened and slow with exhaustion. He was inching his way along the compressed air pipe for yet another advance up the drive. Sweat running into his eyes was blurring his vision, so at first he did not credit what he saw ahead of him in the darkness.

He shook his head to clear his eyes, and then squinted along the beam of his lamp. A heavy timber structure was hanging drunkenly from the roof of the drive. The bolts that held it were resisting the efforts of the water to tear it loose.

Rod realized abruptly that this was what remained of the frame which had held the ventilation doors. The doors were gone, ripped away, but the frame was still in position. He knew that just beyond the ventilation doors the drop-blast matt began. They had reached it!

New strength flowed into his body and he swung forward along the pipe. The timber frame made a fine anchor point and Rod secured the rope to it, and flashed back the signal to Big King. He hung in the loop of rope and rested awhile, then he forced himself to take an interest in his surroundings. He played the beam over the distorted timber frame and saw instantly why the blasting circuit had been broken.

In the lamp light the distinctive green plastic-coated blasting cable hung in festoons from the roof of the drive, clearly it had become entangled in the ventilation doors and been severed when they were ripped away. The loose end of the cable dangled to the surface of the racing water. Rod fastened his eyes on it, drawing comfort and strength from the knowledge that they would not have to continue their agonizing journey down the drive.

When Big King came up out of the gloom, Rod indicated the dangling cable.

'There!' he gasped, and Big King narrowed his eyes in acknowledgement; he was unable to speak.

It was five minutes before they could commence the excruciating business of hauling the dinghy up and securing it to the door frame.

Again they rested. Their movements were slowing up drastically. Neither of them had much strength left to draw upon.

'Get hold of the end of the cable,' Rod instructed Big King, and he dragged himself over the side of the dinghy and lay sprawled full-length on the floor boards.

His weight forced the dinghy deeper, increasing its resistance to the racing water, and the rope strained against the wooden frame. Rod began clumsily to unpack the battery blaster. Big King stood waist deep clinging with one arm to the wooden frame, reaching forward with the other towards the end of the green-coated cable. It danced just beyond his finger tips, and he edged forward against the current, steadying himself against the timber frame, placing a greater strain on the retaining bolts.

His fingers closed on the cable and with a grunt of satisfaction he passed it back to Rod.

Working with painstaking deliberation, Rod connected the crocodile clips from the reel of wire to the loose end of the green cable. Rod's plan was for both he and Big King to climb aboard the dinghy and, paying out the nylon rope, let themselves be carried back down the drive. At the same time they would be letting the wire run from its reel. At a safe distance they would fire the drop-blast matt.

Rod's fingers were swollen and numbed. The minutes passed as he completed his preparations and all that while the strain on the wooden frame was heavy and consistent.

Rod looked up from his task, and crawled to his knees.

'All right, Big King,' he wheezed as he knelt in the bows of the dinghy and gripped the wooden frame to steady the dinghy. 'Come aboard. We are ready.'

Big King waded forward and at that instant the retaining bolts on the side of the heavy timber frame gave way. With a rending, tearing sound the frame slewed across the tunnel. The beams of timber crossed each other like the blades of a pair of gigantic scissors. Both Rod's arms were between the beams. The bones in his forearms snapped with the loud crackle of breaking sticks.

With a scream of pain Rod collapsed onto the floorboards of the dinghy, his arms useless, sticking out at absurd angles from their shattered bones. Three feet away Big King was still in the water. His mouth was wide open, but no sound issued from his throat. He stood still as a black statue and his eyes bulged from their sockets. Even through his own suffering Rod was horrified by the expression on Big King's contorted features.

Below the surface of the water the bottom timber beams had performed the same scissor movement, but this time they had caught Big King's lower body between them. They had closed across his pelvis and crushed it. Now they held him in a vicelike grip from which it was not possible to shake them.

The white face and the black face were but a few feet apart. The two stricken companions in disaster, looked into each other's eyes and knew that there was no escape. They were doomed.

'My arms,' whispered Rod huskily. 'I cannot use them.' Big King's bulging eyes held Rod's gaze.

'Can you reach the blaster?' Rod whispered urgently. 'Take it and turn the handle. Burn it, Big King, burn it!'

Slow comprehension showed in Big King's pain-glazed eyes.

'We are finished, Big King. Let us go like men. Burn it, bring down the rock!'

Above them the rock was sown with explosive. The blaster was connected. In his agitation Rod tried to reach out for the blaster. His forearm swing loosely, the fingers hanging open like the petals of a dead flower, and the pain checked him.

'Get it, Big King,' Rod urged him, and Big King picked up the blaster and held it against his chest with one arm.

'The handle!' Rod encouraged him. 'Turn the handle!'

But instead Big King reached into the dinghy once more and drew the machete from its sheath.

'What are you doing?' Rod demanded, and in reply Big King swung the blade back over his shoulder and then brought it forward in a gleaming arc aimed at the nylon rope that held the dinghy anchored to the wooden frame. Clunk! The blade bit into the wood, severing the rope that was bound around it.

Freed by the stroke of the machete, the dinghy was whisked away by the current. Lying in the dancing rubber dinghy, Rod heard a bull voice bellow above the rush of the water.

'Go in peace, my friend.'

Then Rod was careening back along the drive, a hell ride during which the dinghy spun like a top and in the beam of his lamp the roof and walls melted into a dark racing blur as Rod lay maimed on the floor of the dinghy.

Then suddenly the air jarred against his ear drums, a long rolling concussion in the confines of the drive and he knew that Big King had fired the drop-blast matt. Rodney Ironsides slipped over the edge of consciousness into a soft warm dark place from which he hoped never to return.

69

Dimitri squatted on his haunches above the shaft at 65 level. He was smoking his tenth cigarette. The rest of his men waited impatiently as he did, every few minutes Dimitri would cross to the shaft and flash his lamp down the hundred foot hole to 66 level.

'How long have they been gone,' he asked, and they all glanced at their watches.

'An hour and ten minutes.'

'No, an hour and fourteen minutes.'

'Christ, call me a liar for four minutes!'

And they lapsed into silence once more. Suddenly the station telephone shrilled, and Dimitri jumped up and ran to it.

'No, Mr Hirschfeld, nothing yet!'

He listened a moment.

'All right, send him down then.'

He hung up the telephone, and his men looked at him enquiringly.

'They are sending down a policeman,' he explained.

'What the hell for?'

'They want Big King.'

'Why?'

'Warrant of arrest for murder.'

'Murder?'

'Ja, they reckon he murdered that Portuguese store-keeper.'

'Jeez!'

'Big King, is that so!' Delighted to have found something to pass the time, they fell into an animated debate.

The police inspector arrived in the cage at 65 level, but he was disappointing. He looked like a down-at-heel undertaker, and he replied to their eager questions with a sorrowful stare that left them stuttering.

For the fifteenth time Dimitri went to the shaft and peered down into it. The blast shook the earth around them, a long rumbling that persisted for many seconds.

'They've done it!' yelled Dimitri, and began to caper wildly. His men leapt to their feet and began beating each other on the back, shouting and laughing. The police inspector alone took no part in the celebrations.

'Wait,' yelled Dimitri at last. 'Shut up all of you! Shut up! Damn it! Listen!'

They fell silent.

'What is it?' someone asked. 'I can't hear anything.'

'That's just it!' exulted Dimitri. 'The water! It has stopped!'

Only then did they become aware that the dull roar of water to which their ears had become resigned was now ended. It was quiet; a cathedral hush lay upon the workings. They began to cheer, their voices thin in the silence, and Dimitri ran to the steel ladder and swarmed down it like a monkey.

From thirty feet up Dimitri saw the dinghy marooned amongst the filth and debris around the shaft. He recognized the crumpled figure lying in the bottom of it.

'Rod!' he was shouting before he reached the station at 66 level. 'Rod, are you all right?'

The floor of the haulage was wet, and here and there a trickle of water still snaked towards the shaft. Dimitri ran to the stranded dinghy and started to turn Rod onto his back. Then he saw his arms.

'Oh, Christ!' he gasped in horror, then he was yelling up the ladder. 'Get a stretcher down here.'

Rod regained consciousness to find himself covered with blankets and strapped securely into a mine stretcher. His arms were splinted and bandaged, and from the familiar rattle and rush of air he knew he was in the cage on the way to the surface.

He recognized Dimitri's voice raised argumentatively.

'Damn it! The man is unconscious and badly injured, can't you leave him alone?'

'I have my duty to perform,' a strange voice answered.

'What's he want, Dimitri?' Rod croaked.

'Rod, how are you?' At the sound of his voice Dimitri was kneeling beside the stretcher anxiously.

'Bloody awful,' Rod whispered. 'What does this joker want?'

'He's a police officer. He wants to arrest Big King for murder,' Dimitri explained.

'Well, he's a bit bloody late,' whispered Rod, and even through his pain this seemed to Rod to be terribly funny. He began to laugh. He sobbed with laughter, each convulsion sending bright bursts of pain along his arms. He was shaking uncontrollably with shock, sweat pouring from his face, and he was laughing wildly.

'He's a bit bloody late,' he repeated through his hysterical laughter as Dr Dan Stander pushed the hypodermic needle into his arm and shot him full of morphine

70

Hurry Hirschfeld stood in the main haulage on 66 level. There was bustle all around him. Already the crews from the cementation company were manhandling their equipment up towards the blocked drive.

These were specialists from an independent contracting company. They were about to begin pumping thousands of tons of liquid cement into the rock jam that sealed the drive. They would pump it in at pressures in excess of 3000 pounds per square inch, and when that concrete set it would form a plug that would effectively seal off the drive for all time. It would also form a burial vault for the body of Big King, thought Hurry, a fitting monument to the man who had saved the Sonder Ditch.

He would arrange to have a commemorative plaque placed on the outer wall of the cement plug with a suitable inscription describing the man and the deed.

The man's dependants must be properly taken care of, perhaps they could be flown down for the unveiling of the plaque. Anyway he could leave that to Public Relations and Personnel.

The haulage stank of wetness and mud. It was dank and clammy cool, and it would not improve his lumbago. Hurry had seen enough; he started back towards the shaft. Faintly he was aware of the muted clangour of the mighty pumps which in a few days would free the Sonder Ditch of the water that filled her lower levels.

The laden stretchers with their grisly blanket-covered burdens stood in a row under the hastily rigged electric lights along one wall of the tunnel. Hurry's expression hardened as he passed them.

'I'll have the guts of the man responsible for this,' he vowed silently as he waited for the cage.

Terry Steyner rode in the rear of the ambulance with Rod. She wiped the mud from his face.

'How bad is it, Dan?' she asked.

'Hell, Terry, he'll be up and about in a few days. The arms of course are not very pretty, that's why I'm taking him directly to Johannesburg. I want a specialist orthopaedic surgeon to set them. Apart from that he is suffering from shock pretty badly and his hands are superficially lacerated. But he will be fine.'

Dan watched curiously as Terry fussed ineffectually with the damp hair of the drugged man.

'You want a smoke?' he asked.

'Light me one, please Dan.'

He passed her a cigarette.

'I didn't know that you and Rod were so friendly,' he ventured.

Terry looked up at him quickly.

'How very delicate you are, Dr Stander,' she mocked him.

'None of my business, of course.' Hurriedly Dan withdrew.

'Don't be silly Dan. You're a good friend of Rod's and Joy is mine. You two are entitled to know. I am desperately, crazily in love with this big hunk. I intend divorcing Manfred just as soon as possible.'

'Is Rod going to marry you?'

'He hasn't said anything about marriage but I'll sure as hell start working on him,' Terry grinned, and Dan laughed.

'Good luck to you both, then. I'm sure Rod will be able to get another job.'

'What do you mean?' Terry demanded.

'They say your grandfather is threatening to fire him so high he'll be the first man on the moon.'

Terry relapsed into silence. Proof was what Pops had asked for, but what proof was there?

'They'll be waiting on the X-Ray reports.' Joy Allbright gave her opinion. Since her engagement to Dan, Joy had suddenly become something of a medical expert. She had rushed down to the Johannesburg Central Hospital at Dan's hurried telephone request. Dan wanted her to keep Terry company while she waited for Rod to come out of emergency. They sat together in the waiting-room.

'I expect so,' Terry agreed. Something Joy had just said had jolted in her mind, something she must remember.

'It takes them twenty minutes or so to expose the plates and develop them. Then the radiologist has to examine the plates and make his report to the surgeon.'

There, Joy had said it again. Terry sat up straight and concentrated on what Joy had said. Which word had disturbed her?

Suddenly she had it.

'The report!' she exclaimed. 'That's it! The report, that's the proof.'

She leapt out of her chair.

'Joy! Give me the keys of your car,' she demanded.

'What on earth?' Joy looked startled.

'I can't explain now. I have to get home to Sandown urgently, give me your keys. I'll explain later.'

Joy fished in her handbag and produced a leather key folder. Terry snatched it from her.

'Where are you parked?' Terry demanded.

'In the car park, near the main gate.'

'Thanks, Joy.' Terry dashed from the waiting-room, her high heels clattered down the passage.

'Crazy woman.' Joy looked after her bewildered.

Ten minutes later Dan looked into the waiting-room.

'Rod's fine now. Where's Terry?'

'She went mad–' And Joy explained about her abrupt departure. Dan looked grave.

'I think we'd better follow her, Joy.'

'I think you're right, darling.'

'I'll just grab my coat,' said Dan.

There was only one place where Manfred would keep the geological report on the Big Dipper that Rod had told her about. That was in the safe deposit behind the panelling in his study. Because her jewellery was kept in the same safe, Terry had a key and the combination to the lock.

Even in Joy's Alfa Romeo, taking liberties with the traffic regulations, it was a thirty-five minute drive out to Sandown. It was after five in the evening when Terry coasted down the long driveway and parked before the garages.

The extensive grounds were deserted, for the gardeners finished at five, and there was no sign of life from the house. This was as it should be, for she knew Manfred was still in Europe. He was not due back for at least another four days.

Leaving the ignition keys in the Alfa, Terry ran up the pathway and onto the stoep. She fumbled in her handbag and found the keys to the front door. She let herself in, and went directly to Manfred's study. She slid the concealing panel aside and set about the lengthy business of opening the steel safe. It required both key and combination to activate the mechanism, and Terry had never developed much expertise at tumbling the combination.

Finally, however, the door swung open and she was confronted by the voluminous contents. Terry began removing the various documents and files, examining each one and then stacking them neatly on the floor beside her.

She had no idea of the shape, size nor colour of the report for which she was searching, it was ten minutes before she selected an unmarked folder and flicked open the cover.

'Confidential Report on the geological formations of the Kitchenerville gold fields, with special reference to those areas lying to the east of the Big Dipper Dyke.'

Terry felt a wonderful lift of relief as she read the titling for she had begun doubting that the report was here. Quickly she thumbed through the pages and began reading at random. There was no doubt.

'This is it!' she exclaimed aloud.

'*I'll take that, thank you.*' The dreaded familiar voice cut into her preoccupation, and Terry spun around and came to her feet in one movement, clutching the file protectively to her breast. She backed away from the man who stood in the doorway.

She hardly recognized her own husband. She had never seen him like this. Manfred was coatless, and his shirt was without collar or stud. He appeared to have slept in his trousers, for they were rumpled and baggy. There was a yellow stain down the front of his white shirt.

His scanty brown hair was dishevelled, hanging forward wispily onto his forehead. He had not shaved, and the skin around his eyes was discoloured and puffy.

'Give that to me.' He came towards her with hand out-stretched.

'Manfred.' She kept moving away from him. 'What are you doing here? When did you get back?'

'Give it to me, you slut.'

'Why do you call me that?' She asked, trying for time.

'Slut!' he repeated, and lunged towards her. Terry whirled away from him lightly.

She ran for the study door, with Manfred close behind her. She beat him into the passage and raced for the front door. Her heel caught in one of the persian carpets that covered the floor of the passage, and she staggered and fell against the wall.

'Whore!' He was on her instantly trying to wrestle the report out of her hands, but she clung to it with all her strength. Face to face they were almost of a height, and she saw the madness in his eyes.

Suddenly Manfred released her. He stepped back, bunched his fist and swung it round-armed into her cheek. Her head jerked back and cracked against the wall. He drew back his fist and hit her again. She felt the quick warm burst of blood spurt from her nose, and staggered through the door beside her into the dining-room. She was dizzy from the blows and she fell against the heavy stinkwood table.

Manfred was close behind her. He charged her, sending her sprawling backwards onto the table. He was on top of her, both his hands at her throat.

'I'm going to kill you, you whore,' he wheezed. His thumbs hooked and pressed deep into the flesh of her throat. With the frenzied strength of despair, Terry clawed at his eyes with both hands. Her nails scored his face, raking long red lines into his flesh. With a cry Manfred released her, and backed away holding both hands to his injured face, leaving Terry lying gasping across the table.

He stood for a moment, then uncovered his face and inspected the blood on his hands.

'I'll kill you for that!'

But as he advanced towards her, Terry rolled over the table.

'Whore! Slut! Bitch!' he screamed at her, following her around the table. Terry kept ahead of him.

There were a matched pair of heavy Stuart crystal decanters on the sideboard, one containing port, the other sherry. Terry snatched up one of them and turned to face Manfred. She hurled the decanter with all her remaining strength at his head.

Manfred did not have time to duck. The decanter cracked against his forehead, and he fell backwards, stunned. Terry snatched up the report and ran out of the dining-room, down the passage, out of the front door and into the garden. She was running weakly, following the driveway towards the main road.

Then behind her she heard the engine of an automobile roar into life. Panting wildly, holding the report, she stopped and looked back. Manfred had followed her out of the house. He was behind the steering wheel of Joy's Alfa Romeo. As she watched he threw the car into gear and howled towards her, blue smoke burning from the rear tyres with the speed of the acceleration. His face behind the windscreen was white and streaked with the marks of her nails, his eyes were staring, insane, and she knew he was going to ride her down.

She kicked off her shoes and ran off the driveway onto the lawns.

Crouched forward in the driver's seat of the Alfa, Manfred watched the fleeing figure ahead of him.

Terry ran with the full-hipped sway of the mature woman, her long legs were tanned and her hair flew out loosely behind her.

Manfred was not concerned with the return of the geological report, its existence was no longer of significance to him. What he wanted was to completely destroy this woman. In his crazed state, she had become the symbol and the figurehead of all his woes. His humiliation and fall were all linked to her, he could exact his vengeance by destroying her, crushing that revolting warm and clinging body, bruising it, ripping it with the steel of the Alfa Romeo's chassis.

He hit second gear and spun the steering-wheel. The Alfa swerved from the driveway, and as its rear wheels left the tarmac, they skidded on the thick grass. Deftly Manfred checked the skid and lined up on Terry's running back.

Already she was among the protea bushes on the lower terrace. The Alfa buck-jumped the slope, flying bird-free before crashing down heavily on its suspension. Wheels spun and bit, and the sleek vehicle shot forward again.

Terry looked back over her shoulder, her face was white and her eyes very big and fear-filled. Manfred giggled. He was aware of a sense of power, the ability to dispense life or death. He steered for her, reckless of all consequences, intent on destroying her.

There was a six-foot tall protea bush ahead of him, and Manfred roared through it, bursting it asunder. Scattering branches and leaves, giggling again, he saw Terry directly ahead of him. She was still looking back at him, and at that moment she stumbled and fell onto her knees.

She was helpless. Her face streaked with tears and blood, her hair falling forward in wild disorder, kneeling as though for the headsman's stroke. Manfred felt a flood of disappointment. He did not want it to end so soon, he wanted to savour this sadistic elation, this sense of power.

At the last possible moment he yanked the wheel over and the car slewed violently. It shot past Terry with six inches to spare, and its rear wheels pelted her with clods of turf and thrown dirt.

Laughing aloud, wild-eyed, Manfred held the wheel hard over, bringing the Alfa around in a tight skidding circle, crackling sideways through another protea bush.

Terry was up and running again. He saw immediately that she was heading for the change rooms of the swimming-pool among the trees on the bottom lawn and she was far enough ahead to elude him, perhaps.

'Bitch!' he snarled, and crash-changed into third gear, with engine revs peaking. The Alfa howled in pursuit of the running girl.

Had Terry thrown the bulky report aside, she might have reached the brick changing rooms ahead of the racing sports car, but the report hampered and slowed her. She still had twenty yards to cover, she was running along the paved edge of the swimming-pool, and she sensed that the car was right on top of her.

Terry dived sideways, hitting the water flat on her side, and the Alfa roared past. Manfred trod heavily on the brakes, the Michelin metallic tyres screeched against the paving stones, and Manfred was out of the driver's seat the moment the Alfa stopped.

He ran back to the pool side. Terry was floundering towards the far steps. She was exhausted, weak with exertion and terror. Her sodden hair streamed down over her face, and she was gasping open-mouthed for air.

Manfred laughed again, a high-pitched, almost girlish giggle, and he dived after her, landing squarely between Terry's shoulder blades with his full weight. She went under, sucking water agonizingly into already aching lungs, and when she surfaced she was coughing and gagging, blinded with water and her own wet hair.

Almost immediately she felt herself seized from behind and forced face down into the water. For half a minute she struggled fiercely, then her movements slowed and became weaker.

Manfred stood over her, chest deep in the clear water, gripping her around the waist and by a handful of her sodden hair, forcing her face deep below the surface. He had lost his spectacles, and he blinked owlishly. The wet silk of his shirt clung to his upper body, and the water had slicked his hair down.

As he felt the life going out of her, and her movements becoming sluggish and slow, he began to laugh again. The broken, incoherent laughter of a madman.

'Dan!' Joy pointed off through the trees. 'That's my car down there, parked by the swimming-pool!'

'What the hell is it doing there?'

'There's something wrong, Terry wouldn't drive through her beloved garden, unless there was!'

Dan braked sharply and pulled his Jaguar to the side of the driveway.

'I'm going to take a look.' He slid out of the car and started off across the lawns. Joy opened her own door and trotted after him.

Dan saw the man in the water, fully dressed, intent on what he was doing. He recognized Manfred Steyner.

'What the hell is he up to?' Dan started running. He reached the edge of the pool, and suddenly realized what was happening.

'Christ! He's drowning her,' he shouted aloud, and he sprang into the water.

He did not waste time struggling with Manfred. He hit him a great open-handed, round-armed blow, that cracked against the side of Manfred's head like a pistol shot and sent him lurching sideways, releasing his grip on Terry.

Ignoring Manfred, Dan picked Terry from the water like a drowned kitten and waded to the steps. He carried her out and laid her face down on the paving. He knelt over her and began applying artificial respiration. He felt Terry stir under his hands, then cough and retch weakly.

Joy came up at the run and dropped on her knees beside him.

'My God, Dan, what happened?'

'That little bastard was trying to drown her.'

Dan looked up from his labours without interrupting the rhythm of his movement over Terry. She spluttered and retched again.

On the far side of the pool Manfred Steyner had dragged himself from the pool. He was sitting on the edge with his feet still dangling into the water, his head was hanging and he was fingering the side of his face where Dan had hit him. On his lap he held a wet pulpy mess that had been the geological report.

'Joy, can you take over here? Terry's not too far gone, and I want to get my hands on that little Hun.'

Joy took Dan's place over Terry's prostrate form, and Dan stood up.

'What are you going to do to him?' Joy asked.

'I'm going to beat him to a pulp.'

'Good show!' Joy encouraged him. 'Give him one for me.'

Manfred heard the exchange and as Dan ran around the edge of the pool he scrambled to his feet, and staggered to the parked Alfa. He slammed the door and whirred the engine to life. Dan was just too late to stop him. The car shot forward across the lawns, leaving Dan running, futile, behind it.

'Look after her, Joy!' Dan shouted back.

By the time Dan had run up the terrace to his Jaguar and reversed it to point in the opposite direction, the Alfa had disappeared through the white gates with a musical flutter of its exhaust.

'Come on, girly,' Dan spoke to his Jaguar. 'Let's go get him.'

The rear wheels spun as he pulled away.

Without his spectacles Manfred Steyner's vision was blurred and milky. The outlines of all objects on which he looked were softened and indistinct.

He instinctively checked the Alfa at the stop street at the bottom of the lane. He sat undecided, water still streaming from his clothing, squelching in his shoes. Beside him on the passenger seat lay the sodden report, its pages beginning to disintegrate from its soaking and the rough handling it had received.

He had to get rid of it. It was the shred of incriminating evidence. That was the only clear thought Manfred had. For the first time in his life the crystalline clarity of his thought processes was interrupted. He was confused, his mind jerking abruptly from one subject to another, the intense pleasure of inflicting hurt on Terry mingled with the sting and smart of his own injuries. He could not concentrate on either sensation for overlying it all was a sense of fear, of uncertainty. He felt vulnerable, hunted, hurt and shaken. His brain flickered and wavered as though a computer had developed an electrical fault. The answers it produced were nonsensical.

He looked in the rear view mirror, saw the Jaguar glide out between the white gates and turn towards him.

'Christ!' he panicked. He rammed his foot down on the accelerator and engaged the clutch. The Alfa screeched out into the main highway, swerved into the path of a heavy truck, bounded over the far kerb and swung back into the road.

Dan watched it tear away towards Kyalami.

He let the truck pass and then swung into the traffic behind it. He had to wait until the road was clear ahead before he could overtake the truck, and by that time the Alfa was a dwindling cream speck ahead of him.

Dan settled back in the leather bucket seat, and gave the Jaguar its head. He was furious, outraged by the treatment he had seen Manfred meting out to Terry. Her swollen and bruised face had shocked him and his feet were firmly set upon the path of vengeance.

His hands gripped the steering-wheel fiercely, he was muttering threats of violence as the speedometer moved up over the hundred mile per hour mark and he began relentlessly overhauling the cream sports car.

Steadily he moved up behind the Alfa until he was driving almost on its rear bumper. The Alfa was held up by a green school bus. Dan could not pass, however, for there was a steady stream of traffic coming in the opposite direction.

He fastened his attention on the back of Manfred's head still fuming with anger.

Dan dropped down a gear, ready to pull out and overtake the Alfa when the opportunity arose. At that moment Manfred looked up into his rear view mirror. Dan saw the reflection of his white face with disordered damp hair hanging onto the forehead, saw his expression change immediately he recognized Dan and the Alfa shot out into the face of the approaching traffic.

There was the howl and blare of horns, vehicles swerved to make way for Manfred's wild rush. Dan glimpsed frightened faces flicking past, but the Alfa had squeezed around the green bus and was speeding away.

Dan dropped back, then sent the Jaguar like a thrown javelin through the gap between bus and kerb, overtaking on the wrong side and ignoring the bus driver's yell of protest.

The Jaguar had a higher top speed, and on the long straight Pretoria highway Dan crept up steadily on the cream Alfa.

He could see Manfred glancing repeatedly into his driving-mirror, and he grinned mirthlessly.

Ahead of them the highway rose and then dipped over a low rounded ridge. A double avenue of tall blue gum trees flanked each side of the road.

Travelling in the same direction as the two high performance sports cars was a mini of a good vintage year. Its elderly driver was triumphantly about to overtake an overloaded vegetable truck. Neck and neck they approached the blind rise at twenty-five miles per hour, between them they effectively blocked half the road.

The horn of the Alfa wailed a high-pitched warning, and Manfred pulled out to overtake both slower vehicles. He was level with them, well out over the white dividing line, when a cement truck popped up over the blind rise.

Dan stood on his brake pedal with all the strength of his right leg, and watched it happen.

The cement truck and the Alfa came head on towards each other at a combined speed of well over a hundred miles per hour. At the last moment the Alfa began to turn away but it was too late by many seconds.

It caught the heavy cement truck a glancing blow and was hurled across the path of the two slower vehicles, miraculously touching neither of them; it skidded sideways leaving reeking black smears of rubber on the tarmac, and hurdled the low bank. It struck one of the blue gums full on, with a force that shivered the giant tree trunk and brought down a rain of leaves.

Dan pulled the Jaguar into the side of the road, parked it and walked back.

He knew there was no hurry. The drivers of the mini and the vegetable truck were there before him. They were attempting to talk each other down, both of them excited and relieved by their own escapes.

'I'm a doctor,' said Dan, and they fell back respectfully.

'He doesn't need a doctor,' said one of them. 'He needs an undertaker.'

One look was sufficient. Dr Manfred Steyner was as dead as Dan had ever seen anybody. His crushed head was thrust through the windscreen. Dan picked up the sodden bundle of paper from the seat beside the huddled body. He was aware that some particular importance was attached to it.

Dan's anger had evaporated entirely, and he felt a twinge of pity as he looked into the wreckage at the corpse. It appeared frail and small–of such little consequence.

71

The sunlight was sparkling bright, broken into a myriad eyestinging fragments by the rippling surface of the bay.

The breeze was strong enough for the Arrow class yachts to fly their spinnakers as they came down on the wind. The sails bulged out blue and yellow and bright scarlet against the sombre green of the great whale-back bluff above Durban Bay.

Under the awning on the afterdeck of the motor yacht it was cool, but the fat man wore only a pair of white linen slacks with his feet thrust into dark blue cloth espadrilles.

Sprawled in a deck-chair, his belly bulged smooth and hard over the waistband of his slacks; he was tanned a dark mahogany colour and his body-hair grew thick and curly from chest to navel.

'Thank you, Andrew.' He extended his empty glass, and the younger man carried it to the open-air bar. The fat man watched him as he mixed another Pimms No. 1 cup.

A white-clad crew member clambered down the companion way from the bridge. He touched his cap respectfully to the fat man.

'Captain's respects, sir, and we are ready to sail when you give the order.'

'Thank you. Please tell the captain we will sail as soon as Miss du Maine comes aboard.' And the crew man ran back to the bridge.

'Ah!' The fat man sighed happily as Andrew placed the Pimms in his outstretched hand. 'I have really earned this break. The last few weeks have been nerve-racking, to say the least.'

'Yes, sir,' Andrew agreed dutifully. 'But, as usual, you snatched victory from the ashes.'

'It was close,' the fat man agreed. 'Young Ironsides gave us all a nasty fright with his drop-blast matt. I was only just able to make good my personal commitments before the price shot up again. The profit was not as high as I had anticipated, but then I have never made a habit of peering into the mouths of gift-horses.'

'It was a pity that our associates lost all that money,' Andrew ventured.

'Yes, yes. A great pity. But rather them than us, Andrew.'

'Indeed, sir.'

'In a way I am glad it worked out as it did. I am a patriotic man, at heart. I am relieved that it was not necessary to disrupt the economy of the country to make our little profit.'

He stood up suddenly, his interest quickening as a taxi cab came down onto the Yacht Club jetty. The cabby opened a rear door and from it emerged a very beautiful young lady.

'Ah, Andrew! Our guest has arrived. You may warn the captain that we will be sailing within minutes; and send a man to fetch her luggage.'

He went to the entry port to welcome the young lady.

72

In mid-summer in the Zambesi Valley the heat is a solid white shimmering thing. In the noon day nothing moves in the merciless sunlight.

At the centre of the native village grew a baobab tree. A monstrous bloated trunk with malformed branches like the limbs of a polio victim. The carrion crows sat in it, black and shiny as cockroaches. A score of grass huts ringed the tree, and beyond them lay the tilled fields. The millet stood tall and green in the sun.

Along the rude track towards the village came a Landrover. It came slowly, lurching and jolting over the rough ground, its motor growling in low gear. Printed in black on its sides were the letters A.R.C., African Recruiting Corporation.

The children heard it first, and crawled from the grass huts. Naked black bodies, and shrill excited voices in the sunlight.

They ran to meet the Landrover and danced beside it, shrieking and laughing. The Landrover came to a halt in the meagre shade under the baobab tree. An elderly white man climbed from the cab. He wore khaki safari clothes and a wide-brimmed hat. Complete silence fell, and one of the oldest boys fetched a carved stool and placed it in the shade.

The white man sat on the stool. A girl came forward, knelt before him and offered a gourd of millet beer. The white man drank from the gourd. No one spoke, none would disturb an honoured guest until he had taken refreshment, but from the grass huts the adult members of the village came. Blinking into the sunlight, winding their loin clothes about their waists. They came and squatted in a semi-circle before the white man on his stool.

He lowered the gourd and set it aside. He looked at them.

'I see you, my friends,' he greeted them, and the response was warm.

'We see you, old one,' they chorused, but the expression of their visitor remained grave.

'Let the wives of King Nkulu come forward,' he called. 'Let them bring their first-born son with them.'

Four women and four adolescent boys left the crowd and came shyly into the open. For a moment the white man studied them compassionately, then he stood and stepped forward. He placed a hand on the shoulder of each of the two eldest lads.

'Your father has gone to *his* fathers,' he told them. There was a stirring, an intake of breath, a startled cry, and then, as was proper, the eldest wife let out the first sobbing wail of mourning.

One by one each wife sank down onto the dry dusty earth and covered her head with her shawl.

'He is dead,' the white man repeated against the background of their keening lament. 'But he died in such honour as to let his name live on forever. So great was his dying that for all their lives money will each month be paid to his wives, and for each of his sons there is already set aside a place at the University that each may grow as strong in learning as his father was in body. Of Big King there will be raised up an image in stone.

'The wives of Big King and his sons will travel in a flying machine to I'Goldi, that their eyes also may look upon the stone image of the man who was their husband and their father.' The white man paused for breath, it was a lengthy speech in the midday heat of the valley. He wiped his face and then tucked the handkerchief into his pocket.

'He was a lion!'

'Ngwenyama!' whispered the sturdy twelve-year-old boy standing beside the white man. The tears started from his eyes and greased down his cheeks. He turned away and ran alone into the millet fields.

73

Dennis Langley, the Sales Manager of Kitchenerville Motors who were the local Ford agents, stretched his arms over his head luxuriously. He sighed with deep contentment. What a lovely way to spend a working day morning.

'Happy?' asked Hettie Delange beside him in the double bed. In reply Dennis grinned and sighed again.

Hettie sat up and let the sheet fall to her waist. Her breasts were big and white, and damp with perspiration. She looked down on his naked chest and arm muscles approvingly.

'Gee, you're built nicely.'

'So are you,' Dennis smiled up at her.

'You're different from the other chaps I've gone out with,' Hettie told him. 'You speak so nicely–like a gentleman, you know.'

Before Dennis Langley could decide on a suitable reply, the front door bell shrilled, the sound of it echoing through the house. Dennis shot into an upright position with a fearful expression on his face.

'Who's that?' he demanded.

'It's probably the butcher delivering the meat.'

'It may be my wife!' Dennis cautioned her. 'Don't answer it.'

'Of course I've got to answer it, silly.' Hettie threw back the sheet, and rose in her white and golden glory to find her dressing-gown. The sight was enough to momentarily quiet Dennis Langley's misgivings, but as she belted her gown and hid it from view he urged her again.

'Be careful! Make sure it's not her before you open the door.'

Hettie opened the front door, and immediately drew her gown more closely around her with one hand, while with the other she tried to pat her hair into a semblance of order.

'Hello,' she breathed.

The tall young man in the doorway was really rather dreamy. He wore a dark business suit and carried an expensive leather briefcase.

'Mrs Delange?' he inquired. He had a nice soft dreamy voice.

'Yes, I'm Mrs Delange.' Hettie fluttered her eyelashes. 'Won't you come in?'

She led him through to the lounge, and she was pleasantly aware of his eyes on the opening of her gown.

'What can I do for you?' she asked archly.

'I am your local representative of the Sanlam Insurance Company, Mrs Delange. I have come to express my company's condolences on your recent sad bereavement. I would have called sooner, but I did not wish to intrude on your sorrow.'

'Oh!' Hettie dropped her eyes, immediately adopting the role of the widow.

'However, we hope we can bring a little light to disperse the darkness that surrounds you. You may know that your husband was a policy-holder with our Company?'

Hettie shook her head, but watched with interest while the visitor opened his briefcase.

'Yes, he was. Two months ago he took out a straight life policy with double indemnity. The policy was ceded to you.' The Insurance man extracted a sheaf of papers from his case. 'I have here my company's cheque in full settlement of all claims under the policy. If you will just sign for it, please.'

'How much?' Hettie abandoned the role of the bereaved.

'With the double indemnity, the cheque is for forty-eight thousand Rand.'

Hettie's eyes flew wide with delight.

'Gee!' she gasped. 'That's *fabulous*!'

74

Hurry's original intentions had expanded considerably. Instead of a plaque on the cement plug at 66 level, the monument to Big King had become a life-sized statue in bronze. He sited it on the lawns in front of the Administrative offices of the Sonder Ditch on a base of black marble.

It was effective. The artist had captured a sense of urgency, of vibrant power. The inscription was simple, just the name of the man–'King Nkulu'–and the date of his death.

Hurry attended the unveiling in person, even though he hated ceremonies and avoided them whenever possible. In the front row of the guests facing him his granddaughter sat beside Doctor Stander and his very new blonde wife. She winked at him and Hurry frowned lovingly back at her.

From the seat beside Hurry, young Ironsides stood up to introduce the Chairman. Hurry noted the expression on his granddaughter's face as she transferred all her attention to the tall young man with both his arms encased in plaster of Paris and supported by slings.

'Perhaps I should have fired him, after all,' thought Hurry. 'He is going to cut one out of my herd.'

Hurry glanced sideways at his General Manager, and decided with resignation, 'Too late'. Then went on to cheer himself. 'Anyway he looks like good breeding stock.'

His line of thought switched again. 'Better start making arrangements to transfer him up to Head Office. He will need a lot of grooming and polishing.'

Without thinking he fished a powerful-looking cigar from his breast pocket. He had it half-way to his mouth when he caught Terry's scandalized glare. Silently her lips formed the words: 'Your doctor!'

Guiltily Hurry Hirschfeld stuffed the cigar back into his pocket.

Shout at the Devil

Wilbur Smith

FOREWORD

I will not deny that this story was suggested to me by the action in World War I, when the German mercantile raider *Königsberg* was sunk in the Kikunya channel of the Rufiji delta by ships of the Royal Navy.

However, I will most emphatically deny that the rogues and scoundrels depicted in my tale bear the slightest resemblance to any members of the company of men that operated to the destruction of *Königsberg*. In particular, I would strongly resist the suggestion that Flynn Patrick O'Flynn is based on the character of the gallant Colonel 'Jungle Man' Pretorius, who actually went aboard *Königsberg*, disguised as a native bearer, and paced out the ranges for the guns of His Majesty's warships *Severn* and *Mersey.*

I would like to express my thanks to Lieutenant-Commander Mathers (R.N. retired) for his assistance in my researches.

PART I

I

Flynn Patrick O'Flynn was an ivory poacher by profession, and modestly he admitted that he was the best on the east coast of Africa.

Rachid El Keb was an exporter of precious stones, of women for the harems and great houses of Arabia and India, and of illicit ivory. This he admitted only to his trusted clients; to the rest he was a rich and respectable owner of coastal shipping.

In an afternoon during the monsoon of 1912, drawn together by their mutual interest in pachyderms, Flynn and Rachid sat in the back room of El Keb's shop in the Arab quarter of Zanzibar, and drank tea from tiny brass thimbles. The hot tea made Flynn O'Flynn perspire even more than usual. It was so humid hot in the room that the flies sat in languid stupor upon the low ceiling.

'Listen, Kebby, you lend me just one of those stinking little ships of yours and I'll fill her so high with tusks, she'll damn nigh sink.'

'Ah!' replied El Keb carefully, and went on waving the palm-leaf fan in his own face–a face that resembled that of a suspicious parrot with a straggly, goatee beard.

'Have I ever let you down yet?' Flynn demanded aggressively, and a drop of sweat fell from the tip of his nose on to his already damp shirt.

'Ah!' El Keb repeated.

'This scheme has a flair. It has the touch of greatness to it. This scheme . . .' Flynn paused to find a suitable adjective, '. . . this scheme is Napoleonic. It is Caesarian!'

'Ah!' El Keb said again, and refilled his tea cup. Lifting it delicately between thumb and forefinger, he sipped before speaking. 'It is necessary only that I should risk the total destruction of a sixty-foot dhow worth . . .' prudently he inflated the figure, '. . . two thousand English pounds?'

'Against an almost certain recovery of twenty thousand,' Flynn cut in quickly, and El Keb smiled a little, almost dreamily.

'You'd put the profits so high?' he asked.

'That's the lowest figure. Good God, Kebby! There hasn't been a shot fired in the Rufiji basin for twenty years. You know damn well it's the Kaiser's private hunting reserve. The Jumbo are so thick in there I could round them up and drive them in like sheep.' Involuntarily Flynn's right forefinger crooked and twitched as though it were already curled around a trigger.

'Madness,' whispered El Keb, with the gold gloat softening the shape of his lips. 'You'd sail into the Rufiji river from the sea, hoist the Union Jack on one of the islands in the delta, and fill the dhow with German ivory. Madness.'

'The Germans have formally annexed none of those islands. I'd be in and out again before Berlin had sent their first cable to London. With ten of my gun-boys hunting, we'd fill the dhow in two weeks.'

'The Germans would have a gunboat there in a week. They've got the *Blücher* lying at Dar es Salaam under steam, heavy cruiser with nine-inch guns.'

'We'd be under protection of the British flag. They couldn't dare touch us–not on the high seas–not with things the way they are now between England and Germany.'

'Mr O'Flynn, I was led to believe you were a citizen of the United States of America.'

'You damn right I am.' Flynn sat up a little straighter, a little more proudly.

'You'd need a British captain for the dhow,' El Keb mused, and stroked his beard thoughtfully.

'Jesus, Kebby, you didn't think I was fool enough to sail that cow in myself?' Flynn looked pained. 'I'll find someone else to do that, and to sail her out again through the Imperial German Navy. Me, I'm going to walk in from my base camp in Portuguese Mozambique and go out the same way.'

'Forgive me.' El Keb smiled again. 'I underestimated you.' He stood up quickly. The splendour of the great jewelled dagger at his waist was somewhat spoiled by the unwashed white of his ankle-length robe. 'Mr O'Flynn, I think I have just the man to captain your dhow for you. But first it is necessary to alter his financial circumstances so that he might be willing to accept employment.'

2

The leather purse of gold sovereigns had been the pivot on which the gentle confusion of Sebastian Oldsmith's life turned. It had been presented to him by his father when Sebastian had announced to the family his intention of sailing to Australia to make his fortune in the wool trade. It had comforted him during the voyage from Liverpool to the Cape of Good Hope, where the captain had unceremoniously deposited him after Sebastian's misalliance with the daughter of the gentleman who was proceeding to Sydney to take up his appointment as Governor of New South Wales.

In gradually dwindling quantity the sovereigns had remained with him through the series of misfortunes that ended in Zanzibar, when he awoke from heat-drugged sleep in a shoddy room to find that the leather purse and its contents were gone, and with them were gone the letters of introduction from his father to certain prominent wool-brokers of Sydney.

It occurred to Sebastian as he sat on the edge of his bed that the letters had little real value in Zanzibar, and with increasing bewilderment, he reviewed the events that had blown him so far off his intended course. Slowly his forehead creased in the effort of thought. It was the high, intelligent forehead of a philosopher crowned by a splendid mass of shiny black curls; his eyes were dark brown, his nose long and straight, his jaw firm, and his mouth sensitive. In his twenty-second year, Sebastian had the face of a young Oxford don;

which proves, perhaps, how misleading looks can be. Those who knew him well would have been surprised that Sebastian, in setting out for Australia, had come as close to it as Zanzibar.

Abandoning the mental exercise that was already giving him a slight headache, Sebastian stood up from the bed and, with the skirt of his nightshirt flapping around his calves, began his third minute search of the hotel room. Although the purse had been under his mattress when he went to sleep the preceding evening, this time Sebastian emptied the water jug and peered into it hopefully. He unpacked his valise and shook out each shirt. He crawled under the bed, lifted the coconut matting, and probed every hole in the rotten flooring before giving way to despair.

Shaved, the bedbug bites on his person anointed with saliva, and dressed in the grey three-piece suit which was showing signs of travel fatigue, he brushed his derby hat and placed it carefully over his curls, picked up his cane in one hand, and lugging his valise in the other, he went down the stairs into the hot noisy lobby of the Hotel Royal.

'I say,' he greeted the little Arab at the desk with the most cheerful smile he could muster. 'I say, I seem to have lost my money.'

A silence fell upon the room. The waiters carrying trays out to the hotel veranda slowed and stopped, heads turned towards Sebastian with the same hostile curiosity as if he had announced that he was suffering from a mild attack of leprosy.

'Stolen, I should imagine,' Sebastian went on, grinning. 'Nasty bit of luck, really.'

The silence exploded as the bead curtains from the office were thrown open and the Hindu proprietor erupted into the room with a loud cry of, 'Mr Oldsmith, what about your bill?'

'Oh, the bill. Yes, well, let's not get excited. I mean, it won't help, now, will it?'

And the proprietor proceeded to become very excited indeed. His cries of anguish and indignation carried to the veranda, where a dozen persons were already beginning the daily fight against heat and thirst. They crowded into the lobby to watch with interest.

'Ten days you owe. Nearly one hundred rupees.'

'Yes, it's jolly unfortunate, I know.' Sebastian was grinning desperately, when a new voice added itself to the uproar.

'Now just hold on a shake.' Together Sebastian and the Hindu turned to the big red-faced, middle-aged man with the pleasantly mixed American and Irish accent. 'Did I hear you called Mr Oldsmith?'

'That is correct, sir.' Sebastian knew instinctively that here was an ally.

'An unusual name. You wouldn't be related to Mister Francis Oldsmith, wool merchant of Liverpool, England?' Flynn O'Flynn inquired politely. He had perused Sebastian's letters of introduction passed on to him by Rachid El Keb.

'Good Lord!' Sebastian cried with joy. 'Do you know my pater?'

'Do I know Francis Oldsmith?' Flynn laughed easily, and then checked himself. His acquaintance was limited to the letterheads. 'Well, I don't exactly know him person to person, you understand, but I think I can say I know *of* him. Used to be in the wool business myself once.' Flynn turned genially to the hotel proprietor and breathed on him a mixture of gin fumes and good-fellowship. 'One hundred rupees was the sum you mentioned.'

'That's the sum, Mr O'Flynn.' The proprietor was easily soothed.

'Mr Oldsmith and I will be having a drink on the veranda. You can bring the receipt to us there.' Flynn placed two sovereigns on the counter; sovereigns that had so recently reposed beneath Sebastian's mattress.

With his boots propped on the low veranda wall, Sebastian regarded the harbour over the rim of his glass. Sebastian was not a drinking man, but in view of Flynn O'Flynn's guardianship he could not be churlish and refuse hospitality. The number of craft in the bay suddenly multiplied miraculously before his eyes. Where a moment before one stubby little dhow had been tacking in through the entrance, there were now three identical boats sailing in formation. Sebastian closed one eye and by focusing determinedly, he reduced the three back to one. Mildly elated with his success, he turned his attention to his new friend and business partner who had pressed such large quantities of gin upon him.

'Mr O'Flynn,' he said with deliberation, slurring the words slightly.

'Forget that mister, Bassie, call me Flynn. Just plain Flynn, the same as in gin.'

'Flynn,' said Sebastian. 'There isn't anything–well, there isn't anything funny about this?'

'How do you mean *funny*, boy?'

'I mean'–and Sebastian blushed slightly. 'There isn't anything illegal, is there?'

'Bassie.' Flynn shook his head sorrowfully. 'What do you take me for, Bassie? You think I'm a crook or something, boy?'

'Oh, no, of course not, Flynn,' and Sebastian blushed a shade deeper. 'I just thought–well, all these elephants we're going to shoot. They must belong to somebody. Aren't they German elephants?'

'Bassie, I want to show you something.' Flynn set down his glass and groping in the inside pocket of his wilted tropical suit, he produced an envelope. 'Read that, boy!'

The address at the head of the sheet of cheap notepaper was 'The Kaiserhof. Berlin. Dated June 10th, 1912', and the body of the letter read:

Dear Mr Flynn O'Flynn,

I am worried about all those elephants down in the Rufiji basin eating up all the grass and smashing up all the trees and things, so if you've got time, would you go down there and shoot some of them as they're eating up all the grass and smashing up all the trees and things.

Yours sincerely,
Kaiser Willem III,
Emperor of Germany

A vague uneasiness formed through the clouds of gin in Sebastian's skull. 'Why did he write to you?'

'Because he knows I'm the best goddamned elephant hunter in the world.'

'You'd expect him to use better English, wouldn't you?' Sebastian murmured.

'What's wrong with his English?' Flynn demanded truculently. He had spent some time in composing the letter.

'Well, I mean that bit about eating up all the grass–he said that twice.'

'Well, you've got to remember he's a German. They don't write English too good.'

'Of course! I hadn't thought of that.' Sebastian looked relieved and lifted his glass. 'Well, good hunting!'

'I'll drink to that,' and Flynn emptied his glass.

3

Sebastian stood with both hands gripping the wooden rail of the dhow and stared out across a dozen miles of water at the loom of the African mainland. The monsoon wind had ruffled the sea to a dark indigo and it flipped spray from the white-caps into Sebastian's face. Overlaying the clean salt of the ocean was the taint of the mangrove swamps, an evil smell as though an animal had died in its own cage. Sebastian sniffed it with distaste as he searched the low green line of the coast for the entrance to the maze of the Rufiji delta.

Frowning, he tried to reconstruct the admiralty chart in his mind. The Rufiji river came to the sea through a dozen channels spread over forty miles, and in doing so, it carved fifty, maybe a hundred, islands out of the mainland.

Tidal water washed fifteen miles upstream, past the mangroves to where the vast grass swampland began. It was there in the swampland that the elephant herds had taken shelter from the guns and arrows of the ivory hunters, protected by Imperial decree and by a formidable terrain.

The murderous-looking ruffian who captained the dhow uttered a string of singsong orders, and Sebastian turned to watch the complicated manœuvre of tacking the ungainly craft. Half-naked seamen dropped out of the rigging like over-ripe brown fruit and swarmed around the sixty-foot teak boom. Bare feet padding on the filthy deck, they ran the boom back and forward again. The dhow creaked like an old man with arthritis, came round wearily on to the wind, and butted its nose in towards the land. The new motion, combined with the swamp smell and the smell of freshly stirred bilges, moved something deep within Sebastian. His grip upon the rail increased, and new sweat popped out like little blisters on his brow. He leaned forward, and, to shouts of encouragement from the crew, made another sacrifice to the sea gods. He was still draped worshipfully across the rail as the dhow wallowed and slid in the turbulent waters of the entrance, and then passed into the calm of the southernmost channel of the Rufiji basin.

Four days later, Sebastian sat cross-legged with the dhow captain on a thick Bokhara carpet spread upon the deck, and they explained to each other in sign language that neither of them had the vaguest idea where they were. The dhow was anchored in a narrow waterway hemmed in by the twisted and deformed trunks of the mangroves. The sensation of being lost was not new to Sebastian, and he accepted it with resignation, but the dhow captain, who could run from Aden to Calcutta and back to Zanzibar with the certainty of a man visiting his own outhouse, was not so stoical. He lifted his eyes to the heavens and called upon Allah to intercede with the djinn who guarded this stinking labyrinth, who made the waters flow in strange, unnatural ways, who changed the shape of each island, and thrust mud banks in their path. Driven on by his own eloquence, he leapt to the rail and screamed defiance into the brooding mangroves until flocks of ibis rose and milled in the heat mists above the dhow. Then he flung himself down on the carpet and fixed Sebastian with a stare of sullen malevolence.

'It's not really my fault, you know.' Sebastian wriggled with embarrassment under the stare. Then once again he produced his admiralty chart, spread it on the deck, and placed his finger on the island which Flynn O'Flynn had ringed in blue pencil as the rendezvous. 'I mean, it *is* rather your cup of tea, finding the place. After all, you *are* the navigator, aren't you?'

The captain spat fiercely on his deck, and Sebastian flushed.

'Now that sort of thing isn't going to get us anywhere. Let's try and behave like gentlemen.'

This time the captain hawked it up from deep down in his throat and spat a lump of yellow phlegm into the blue pencil circle on Sebastian's map, then he rose to his feet and stalked away to where his crewmen squatted in a group under the poop.

In the short dusk, while the mosquitoes whined in a thin mist about Sebastian's head, he listened to the Arabic muttering and saw the glances that were directed at him down the length of the dhow. So when the night closed over the ship like a bank of black steam, he took up a defensive position on the foredeck and waited for them to come. As a weapon he had his cane of solid ebony. He laid it across his lap and sat against the rail until the darkness was complete, then, silently, he changed his position and crouched beside one of the water barrels that was lashed to the base of the mast.

They were a long time coming. Half the night had wasted away before he heard the stealthy scuff of bare feet on the planking. The absolute blackness of the night was filled with the din of the swamp; the boom and tonk of frogs, the muted buzz of insects, and the occasional snort and splash of a hippo, so that Sebastian had difficulty in deciding how many they had sent against him. Crouching by the water barrel he strained his eyes unavailingly into the utter blackness and tuned his hearing to filter out the swamp noises and catch only those soft little sounds that death made as it came down the deck towards him.

Although Sebastian had never scaled any academic heights, he had boxed light heavyweight for Rugby, and fast-bowled for Sussex the previous cricket season when he had led the county bowling averages. So, although he was afraid now, Sebastian had a sublime confidence in his own physical prowess and it was not the kind of fear that filled his belly with oily warmth, nor turned his ego to jelly, but rather, it keyed him to a point where every muscle in his body quivered on the edge of exploding. Crouching in the night he groped for the cane that he had laid on the deck beside him. His hand fell on the bulky sackful of green coconuts that made up part of the dhow's deck cargo. They were carried to supplement, with their milk, the meagre supply of fresh water on board. Quickly Sebastian tore open the fastenings of the sack and hefted one of the hard round fruits.

'Not quite as handy as a cricket ball, but–' murmured Sebastian and came to his feet. Using the short run up, he delivered the fast ball with which he had shattered the Yorkshire first innings the previous year. It had the same effect on the Arab first innings. The coconut whirred and cracked against the skull of one of the approaching assassins and the rest retired in confusion.

'Now send the men,' roared Sebastian and bowled a short lifter that hastened the retreat.

He selected another coconut and was about to deliver that also when there was a flash and a report from aft, and something howled over Sebastian's head. Hastily he ducked behind the sack of coconuts.

'My God, they've got a gun up there!' Sebastian remembered then the ancient muzzle-loading Jezail he had seen the captain polishing lovingly on their first day out from Zanzibar, and he felt his anger rising in earnest.

He jumped to his feet and hurled his next coconut with fury.

'Fight fair, you dirty swine!' he yelled.

There was a delay while the dhow captain went through the complicated process of loading his piece. Then a cannon report, a burst of flame, and another potleg howled over Sebastian's head.

Through the dark hours before dawn the lively exchange of jeers and curses, of coconuts and potlegs continued. Sebastian more than held his own, for he scored four howls of pain and a yelp, while the dhow captain succeeded only in shooting a great deal of his own standing rigging. But as the light of the new day increased, so Sebastian's advantage waned. The Arab captain's shooting improved to such an extent that Sebastian spent most of his time crouching behind the sack of coconuts. Sebastian was nearly exhausted. His right arm and shoulder ached unmercifully, and he could hear the first stealthy advance of the Arab crew as they crept down the deck towards his hide. In daylight they could surround him and use their numbers to drag him down.

While he rested for the final effort, Sebastian looked out at the morning. It was a red dawn, angry and beautiful through the swamp mists so the water glowed with a pink sheen and the mangroves stood very dark around the ship.

Something splashed farther up the channel, a water bird perhaps. Sebastian looked for it without interest, and heard it splash again and then again. He stirred and sat up a little straighter. The sound was too regular for that of a bird or a fish.

Then around the bend in the channel, from behind the wall of mangroves, driven on by urgent paddles, shot a dug-out canoe. Standing in the bow with a double-barrelled elephant gun under his arm and a clay pipe sticking out of his red face, was Flynn O'Flynn.

'What the hell's going on here?' he roared. 'Are you fighting a goddamned war? I've been waiting a week for you lot!'

'Look out, Flynn!' Sebastian yelled a warning. 'That swine has got a gun!'

The Arab captain had jumped to his feet and was looking around uncertainly. Long ago he had regretted his impulse to rid himself of the Englishman and escape from this evil swamp, and now his misgivings were truly justified. Having committed himself, however, there was only one course open to him. He lifted the Jezail to his shoulder and aimed at O'Flynn in the canoe. The discharge blew a long grey spurt of powder smoke from the muzzle, and the potleg lifted a burst of spray from the surface of the water beyond the canoe. The echoes of the shot were drowned by the bellow of O'Flynn's rifle. He fired without removing the pipe from his mouth and the narrow dug-out rocked dangerously with the recoil.

The heavy bullet picked up the Arab captain's scrawny body, his robe fluttered like a piece of old paper, and his turban flew from his head and unwound in mid-air as he was flung clear of the rail to drop with a tall splash alongside. He floated face down, trapped air ballooning his robe about him, and then he drifted away slowly on the sluggish current. His crew, stunned and silent, stood by the rail and watched him depart.

Dismissing the neat execution as though it had never happened, O'Flynn glared up at Sebastian and roared, 'You're a week late. I haven't been able to do a goddamned thing until you got here. Now let's get the flag up and start doing some work!'

4

The formal annexation of Flynn O'Flynn's island took place in the relative cool of the following morning. It had taken some hours for Flynn to convince Sebastian of the necessity of occupying the island for the British Crown, and he succeeded only by casting Sebastian in the role of empire builder. He made some flattering comparisons between Clive of India and Sebastian Oldsmith of Liverpool.

The next problem was the choice of a name. This stirred up a little Anglo-American enmity, with Flynn O'Flynn campaigning aggressively for 'New Boston'. Sebastian was horrified, his patriotic ardour burned brightly.

'Now hold on a jiffy, old chap,' he protested.

'What's wrong with it? You just tell me what's wrong with it!'

'Well, first of all this is going to be one of His Britannic Majesty's possessions, you know.'

'New Boston,' O'Flynn repeated. 'That sounds good. That sounds real good.'

Sebastian shuddered. 'I think it would be–well, not quite suitable. I mean, Boston was the place where they had that tea thing, you know.'

The argument raged more savagely as Flynn lowered the level in the gin bottle, until finally Sebastian stood up from the carpet on the floor of the dhow cabin, his eyes blazing with patriotic outrage. 'If you would care to step outside, sir,' he enunciated with care as he stood over the older man, 'we can settle this matter.' The dignity of the challenge was spoiled by the low roof of the cabin which made it necessary for Sebastian to stoop.

'Man, I'd eat you without spitting the bones.'

'That, sir, is your opinion. But I must warn you I was highly thought of in the light heavyweight division.'

'Oh, goddamn it,' Flynn shook his head wearily and capitulated. 'What difference does it make what we call the mother-loving place. Sit down, for God's sake. Here! Let's drink to whatever you want to call it.'

Sebastian sat on the carpet, and accepted the mug that Flynn handed him. 'We shall call it–' he paused dramatically, 'we shall call it New Liverpool,' and he lifted the mug.

'You know,' said Flynn, 'for a limey, you aren't a bad guy,' and the rest of that night was devoted to celebrating the birth of the new colony.

In the dawn the empire builders were paddled ashore in the dug-out by two of Flynn's gun-bearers.

The canoe ran aground on the narrow muddy beach of New Liverpool, and the sudden halt threw both of them off-balance. They collapsed gently together on to the floor of the dug-out, and had to be assisted ashore by the paddlers.

Sebastian was formally dressed for the occasion, but had buttoned his waistcoat awry and he kept tugging at it as he peered about him.

Now at high tide New Liverpool was about a thousand yards long and half as broad. At the highest point it rose not more than ten feet above the level of the Rufiji river. Fifteen miles from the mouth the water was only slightly tainted with salt and the mangrove trees had thinned out and given way to tall matted elephant grass and slender bottle palms.

Flynn's gun-bearers and porters had cleared a small opening above the beach, and had erected a dozen grass huts around one of the palm trees. It was a dead palm, its crown leaves long gone, and Flynn pointed an unsteady finger at it.

'Flag pole,' he said indistinctly, took Sebastian's elbow, and led him towards it.

Tugging at his waistcoat with one hand and clutching the bundled Union Jack that Flynn had provided in the other, Sebastian felt a surge of emotion within him as he looked up at the slender column of the palm tree.

'Leave me,' he mumbled and shook off Flynn's guiding hand. 'We got to do this right. Solemn occasion–very solemn.'

'Have a drink.' Flynn offered him the gin bottle, and when Sebastian waved it away, he lifted it to his own lips.

'Shouldn't drink on parade.' Sebastian frowned at him. 'Bad form.'

Flynn coughed at the vicious sting of the liquor and smote himself on the chest with his free hand.

'Should draw the men up in a hollow square,' Sebastian went on. 'Ready to salute the flag.'

'Jesus, man, get on with it,' grumbled Flynn.

'Got to do it right.'

'Oh, hell,' Flynn shrugged with resignation, then issued a string of orders in Swahili.

Puzzled and amused, Flynn's fifteen retainers gathered in a ragged circle about the flag pole. They were a curious band, gathered from half a dozen tribes, dressed in an assortment of cast-off western clothing, half of them armed with ancient double-barrelled elephant rifles from which Flynn had carefully filed the serial numbers so they could never be traced back to him.

'Fine body of men.' Sebastian beamed at them in alcoholic goodwill, unconsciously using the words of a Brigadier who had inspected Sebastian's cadet parade at Rugby.

'Let's get this show on the road,' Flynn suggested.

'My friends,' Sebastian obliged, 'we are gathered here today . . .' It was a longish speech, but Flynn weathered it by nipping away quietly at the gin bottle, and at last Sebastian ended with his voice ringing and tears of great emotion pricking his eyelids, '. . . In the sight of God and man, I hereby declare this island part of the glorious Empire of His Majesty, George V, King of England, Emperor of India, Protector of the Faith . . .' His voice wavered as he tried to remember the correct form, and he ended lamely, '. . . and all that sort of thing.'

A silence fell on the assembly and Sebastian fidgeted with embarrassment. 'What do I do now?' he inquired of Flynn O'Flynn in a stage whisper.

'Get that goddamn flag up.'

'Ah, the flag!' Sebastian exclaimed with relief, and then uncertainly, 'How?'

Flynn considered this at length. 'I guess you have to climb up the palm tree.'

With shrill cries of encouragement from the gun-bearers, and with Flynn shoving and cursing from below, the Governor of New Liverpool managed to scale the flag pole to a height of about fifteen feet. There he secured the flag and descended again so swiftly he tore the buttons off the front of his waistcoast, and twisted his ankle. He was borne away to one of the grass huts singing 'God save our Gracious King' in a voice broken with gin, pain, and patriotism.

For the rest of their stay on the island the Union Jack flew at half mast above the encampment.

Carried initially by two Wakamba fishermen, it took fully ten days for the word of the annexation to reach the outpost of the German Empire one hundred miles away at Mahenge.

5

Mahenge was in the bush country above the coastal lowlands. It consisted, in its entirety, of four trading posts owned by Indian shopkeepers–and the German boma.

The German boma was a large stone building, thatched, set about with wide verandas over which purple bougainvillaea climbed in profusion. Behind it stood the barracks and parade ground of the African Askari, and before it a lonely flag pole from which streamed the black, red, and yellow of the empire. A speck in the vastness of the African bush, seat of government for an area the size of France. An area that spread south to the Rovuma river and the border of Portuguese Mozambique, east to the Indian Ocean, and west to the uplands of Sao Hill and Mbeya.

From this stronghold the German Commissioner (Southern Province) wielded the limitless powers of a medieval robber baron. One of the Kaiser's arms, or, more realistically, one of his little fingers, he was answerable only to Governor Schee in Dar es Salaam. But Dar es Salaam was many tortuous miles away, and Governor Schee was a busy man not to be troubled with trivialities. Just as long as the Herr Commissioner Herman Fleischer collected the taxes, he was free to collect them in his own sweet way; though very few of the indigenous inhabitants of the southern province would have described Herman Fleischer's ways as sweet.

At the time that the messenger, carrying the news of the British annexation of New Liverpool, trotted up over the last skyline and saw through the acacia thorn trees ahead of him the tiny clustered buildings of Mahenge, Herr Fleischer was finishing his midday meal.

A man of large appetite, his luncheon consisted of approximately two pounds of *Eisbein,* as much pickled cabbage, and a dozen potatoes, all swimming in thick gravy. Having aroused his taste-buds, he then went on to the sausage. The sausage came by weekly fast-runner from Dodoma in the north, and was manufactured by a man of genius, a Westphalian immigrant who made sausage with the taste of the Black Forest in them. The sausage, and the Hansa beer cooling in its earthenware jug, aroused in Herr Fleischer a delicious nostalgia. He ate not quietly but steadily, and, these quantities of food confined within the thick grey corduroy of his tunic and breeches, built up a pressure that squeezed the perspiration from his face and neck, forcing him to pause and mop up at regular intervals.

When he sighed at last and sagged back in his chair, the leather thongs squeaked a little under him. A bubble of trapped gas found its way up through the sausage and passed in genteel eruption between his lips. Tasting it, he sighed again in happiness, and squinted out from the deep shade of the veranda into the flat shimmering glare of the sunlight.

Then he saw the messenger coming. The man reached the steps of the veranda and squatted down in the sun with his loincloth drawn up modestly between his legs. His body was washed shiny black with sweat, but his legs were powdered with fine dust to the knees, and his chest swelled and subsided as he drank the thin hot air. His eyes were downcast, he could not look directly at the Bwana Mkuba until his presence was formally acknowledged.

Herman Fleischer watched him broodingly, his mood evaporating, for he had been looking forward to his afternoon siesta–and the messenger had spoiled that. He looked away at the low cloud above the hills in the south and sipped his beer. Then he selected a cheroot from the box before him and lit it. The cheroot burned slowly and evenly, restoring a little of his good humour. He smoked it short before flicking the stub over the veranda wall.

'Speak,' he grunted, and the messenger lifted his eyes, and gasped with wonder and awe at the beauty and dignity of the Commissioner's person. Although this was ritual admiration, it never failed to stir a faint pleasure in Herr Fleischer.

'I see you, Bwana Mkuba–Great Lord,' and Fleischer inclined his head slightly. 'I bring you greetings from Kalani, headman of Batja, on the Rufiji. You are his father, and he crawls on his belly before you. Your hair of yellow, and the great fatness of your body, blind him with beauty.'

Herr Fleischer stirred restlessly in his chair. References to his corpulence, however well-intentioned, always annoyed him. 'Speak' he repeated.

'Kalani says thus: "Ten suns ago, a ship came into the delta of the Rufiji, and stopped by the Island of the Dogs, Inja. On the island, the men of this ship have built houses, and above the houses, they have placed on a dead palm tree the cloth of the Insingeese which is of blue and white and red, having many crosses within crosses."'

Herr Fleischer struggled upright in his chair and stared at the messenger. The pink of his complexion slowly became cross-veined with red and purple.

'Kalani also says: "Since their coming the voices of their guns have never ceased to speak along the Rufiji river, and there has been a great killing of elephants, so that in the noon-day the sky is dark with the birds that come for the meat."'

Herr Fleischer was thrashing around in his chair, speech was locked in his throat, and his face had swollen so it threatened to burst like an over-ripe fruit.

'Kalani says further: "Two white men are on the island. One is a man who is very thin and young and is therefore of no account. The other white man Kalani has seen only at a great distance, but by the redness of this man's face, and by his bulk, he knows in his heart it is Fini."'

At the name Herr Fleischer became articulate, if not coherent–he bellowed like a bull in rut. The messenger winced, such a bellow from the Bwana Mkuba usually preceded a multiple hanging.

'Sergeant!' The next bellow had form, and Herr Fleischer was on his feet, struggling to clinch the buckle of his belt.

'Rasch!' he roared again. O'Flynn was in German territory again; O'Flynn was stealing German ivory once more–and compounding the insult by flying the Union Jack over the Kaiser's domain.

'Sergeant, where the thunder of God are you?' With incredible speed for a fat man Herr Fleischer raced down the long length of the veranda. For three years now, ever since his arrival in Mahenge, the name of Flynn O'Flynn had been enough to ruin his appetite, and produce in him a condition very close to epilepsy.

Around the corner of the veranda appeared the sergeant of the Askari, and Herr Fleischer braked just in time to avert collision.

'A storm patrol,' bellowed the Commissioner, blowing a cloud of spittle in his agitation. 'Twenty men. Full field packs, and one hundred pounds of ammunition. We leave in an hour.'

The sergeant saluted and doubled away across the parade ground. A minute later a bugle began singing with desperate urgency.

Slowly, through the black mists of rage, reason returned to Herman Fleischer. He stood with shoulders hunched, breathing heavily through his mouth, and mentally digested the full import of Kalani's message.

This was not just another of O'Flynn's will-o'-the-wisp forays across the Rovuma from Mozambique. This time he had sailed brazenly into the Rufiji delta, with a full-scale expedition, and hoisted the British flag. A queasy sensation, not attributable to the pickled pork, settled on Herr Fleischer's stomach. He knew the makings of an international incident when he saw one.

This, perhaps, was the goad that would launch the fatherland on the road of its true destiny. He gulped with excitement. They had flapped that hated flag in the Kaiser's face just once too often. This was history being made, and Herman Fleischer stood in the centre of it.

Trembling a little, he hurried into his office, and began drafting the report to Governor Schee that might plunge the world into a holocaust from which the German people would rise as the rulers of creation.

An hour later, he rode out of the boma on a white donkey with his slouch uniform hat set well forward on his head to shield his eyes from the glare. Behind him his black Askari marched with their rifles at the slope. Smart in their pillbox kepis with the backflaps hanging to the shoulder, khaki uniforms freshly pressed, and putteed legs rising and falling in unison, they made as gallant a show as any commander could wish.

A day and a half march would bring them to the confluence of the Kilombero and Rufiji rivers where the Commissioner's steam launch was moored.

As the buildings of Mahenge vanished behind him, Herr Fleischer relaxed and let his ample backside conform to the shape of the saddle.

6

'Now, have you got it straight?' Flynn asked without conviction. The past eight days of hunting together had given him no confidence in Sebastian's ability to carry out a simple set of instructions without introducing some remarkable variation of his own. 'You go down the river to the island, and you load the ivory on to the dhow. Then you come back here with all the canoes to pick up the next batch.' Flynn paused to allow his words to absorb into the spongy tissue of Sebastian's head before he went on. 'And for Chrissake don't forget the gin.'

'Right you are, old chap.' With eight days' growth of black beard, and the skin peeling from the tip of his sunburned nose, Sebastian was beginning to fit the role of ivory poacher. The wide-brimmed terai hat that Flynn had loaned him came down to his ears, and the razor edges of the elephant grass had shredded his trouser legs and stripped the polish from his boots. His wrists and the soft skin behind his ears were puffy and speckled with spots of angry red where the mosquitoes had drunk deep, but he had lost a little weight in the heat and the ceaseless walking, so now he was lean and hard-looking.

They stood together under a monkey-bean tree on the bank of the Rufiji, while at the water's edge the bearers were loading the last tusks into the canoes. There was a purple-greenish smell hanging over them in the steamy heat, a smell which Sebastian hardly noticed now–for the last eight days had seen a great killing of elephant, and the stink of green ivory was as familiar to him as the smell of the sea to a mariner.

'By the time you get back tomorrow morning the boys will have brought in the last of the ivory. We'll have a full dhow-load and you can set off for Zanzibar.'

'What about you? Are you staying on here?'

'Not bloody likely. I'll light out for my base camp in Mozambique.'

'Wouldn't it be easier for you to come along on the dhow? It's nearly two hundred miles to walk.' Sebastian was solicitous; in these last days he had conceived a burning admiration for Flynn.

'Well, you see, it's like this . . .' Flynn hesitated. This was no time to trouble Sebastian with talk of German gunboats waiting off the mouth of the Rufiji. 'I have to get back to my camp, because . . .' Suddenly inspiration came to Flynn O'Flynn. 'Because my poor little daughter is there all alone.'

'You've got a daughter?' Sebastian was taken by surprise.

'You damn right I have.' Flynn experienced a sudden rush of paternal affection and duty. 'And the poor little thing is there all alone.'

'Well, when will I see you again?' The thought of parting from Flynn, of being left to try and find his own way to Australia, saddened Sebastian.

'Well,' Flynn was tactful. 'I hadn't really given that much thought.' This was a lie. Flynn had thought about it ceaselessly for the last eight days. He was eagerly anticipating waving farewell to Sebastian Oldsmith for all time.

'Couldn't we . . .' Sebastian blushed a little under his sun-reddened cheeks. 'Couldn't we sort of team up together. I could work for you, sort of as an apprentice?'

The idea made Flynn wince. He almost panicked at the thought of Sebastian permanently trailing along behind him and discharging his rifle at random intervals. 'Well now, Bassie boy,' he clasped a thick arm around Sebastian's shoulders, 'first you sail that old dhow back to Zanzibar and old Kebby El Keb will pay you out your share. Then you write to me, hey? How about that? You write me, and we'll work something out.'

Sebastian grinned happily. 'I'd like that, Flynn. I'd truly like that.'

'All right, then, off you go. And don't forget the gin.'

With Sebastian standing in the bows of the lead canoe, the double-barrelled rifle clutched in his hands, and the terai hat pulled down firmly over his ears, the little flotilla of heavily laden canoes pulled out from the bank and caught the current. Paddles dipped and gleamed in the evening sunlight as they arrowed away towards the first bend downstream.

Still standing unsteadily in the frail craft, Sebastian looked back and waved his rifle at Flynn on the bank.

'For Chrissake, be careful with that goddamn piece,' Flynn bellowed too late. The rifle fired, and the recoil toppled Sebastian sprawling on to the pile of ivory behind him. The canoe rocked dangerously while the paddlers struggled to keep it from capsizing, and then disappeared around the bend.

Twelve hours later, the canoes reappeared around the same bend, and headed towards the lone monkey-bean tree on the bank. The canoes rode lightly, empty of ivory, and the paddlers were singing one of the old river chants.

Freshly shaved, wearing a clean shirt, and his other pair of boots, a case of Flynn's liquor between his knees, Sebastian peered eagerly ahead for the first glimpse of the big American.

A fine blue tendril of camp-fire smoke smeared out across the river, but there were no figures waving a welcome from the bank. Suddenly Sebastian frowned as he realized that the silhouette of the monkey-bean tree had altered. He wrinkled his eyes, peering ahead uncertainly.

Behind him rang the first cry of alarm from his boatmen. 'Allemand!' And the canoe swerved under him.

He glanced back and saw the other canoes wheel away in tight circles aimed downstream, the boatmen jabbering in terror as they leaned forward to thrust against the paddles.

His own canoe was in swift pursuit of the others as they darted beyond the bend.

'Hey!' Sebastian shouted at the sweat-shiny backs of his paddlers. 'What do you think you're doing?'

They gave him no answer, but the muscles beneath their black skins bunched and rippled in their frantic efforts to drive the canoe faster.

'Stop that immediately!' Sebastian yelled at them. 'Take me back, dash it all. Take me to the camp.'

In desperation Sebastian lifted the rifle and aimed at the nearest man. 'I'm not joking,' he yelled again. The native glanced over his shoulder into the gaping twin muzzles and his face, already twisted with fear, now convulsed into a mask of terror. They had all developed a healthy reverence for the way Sebastian handled that rifle.

The man stopped paddling, and one by one the others followed his example. Sitting frozen under the hypnotic eyes of Sebastian's rifle.

'Back!' said Sebastian and gestured eloquently upstream. Reluctantly the man nearest him dipped his paddle and the canoe turned broadside across the current. 'Back!' Sebastian repeated and the men dipped again.

Slowly, warily, the single canoe crept upstream towards the monkey-bean tree and the grotesque new fruit that hung from its branches.

The hull slid in on to the firm mud and Sebastian stepped ashore.

'Out!' he ordered the boatmen and gestured again. He wanted them well away from the canoe, for he knew that, otherwise, the moment his back was turned they would set off downstream again with renewed enthusiasm. 'Out!' and he herded them up the steep bank into Flynn O'Flynn's camp.

The two bearers who had died of gunshot wounds lay beside the smouldering fire. But the four men in the monkey-bean tree had been less fortunate. The ropes had cut deeply into the flesh of their necks and their faces were swollen, mouths wide in the last breath that had never been taken. On the lolling tongues the flies crawled like metallic green bees.

'Cut them down!' Sebastian roused himself from the nausea that was bubbling queasily up from his stomach. The boatmen stood paralysed and Sebastian felt anger now mixed with his revulsion. Roughly he shoved one of the men towards the tree. 'Cut them down,' he repeated, and thrust the handle of his hunting knife into the man's hand. Sebastian turned away as the native shinned up into the fork of the tree with the knife blade clamped between his teeth. Behind him he heard the heavy meaty thuds as the dead men dropped from the tree. Again his stomach heaved, and he concentrated on his search of the trampled grass around the camp.

'Flynn!' he called softly. 'Flynn. I say, Flynn! Where are you?' There were the prints of hobnailed boots in the soft earth, and at one place he stooped and picked up the shiny brass cylinder of an empty cartridge case. Stamped into the metal of the base around the detonator cap were the words *Mauser Fabriken. 7 mm.*

'Flynn!' more urgently now as the horror of it came home to him. 'Flynn!' and he heard the grass rustle near him. He swung towards it, half raising the rifle.

'Master!' and Sebastian felt disappointment swoop in his chest.

'Mohammed. Is that you, Mohammed?' and he recognized the wizened little figure with the eternal fez perched on the woolly head as it emerged. Flynn's chief gun-boy, the only one with a little English.

'Mohammed,' with relief, and then quickly, 'Fini? Where is Fini?'

'They shot him, master. The Askari came in the early morning before the sun. Fini was washing. They shot him and he fell into the water.'

'Where? Show me where.'

Below the camp, a few yards from where the canoe was drawn up, they found the pathetic little bundle of Flynn's clothing. Beside it was a half-consumed cake of cheap soap and a metal hand-mirror. There were the deep imprints of naked feet in the mud, and Mohammed stooped and broke off one of the green reeds at the water's edge. Wordlessly he handed it to Sebastian. A drop of blood had dried black on the leaf, and it crumbled as Sebastian touched it with his thumbnail.

'We must find him. He might still be alive. Call the others. We'll search the banks downstream.'

In an agony of loss Sebastian picked up Flynn's soiled shirt and crumpled it in his fist.

7

Flynn shucked off his pants and the filthy bush-shirt. Shivering briefly in the chill of dawn, he hugged himself and massaged his upper arms while he peered into the shallow water, searching the bottom for the telltale chicken-wire pattern that would mean a crocodile was buried in the mud waiting for him.

His body was porcelain-white where clothing had protected it from the sun, but his arms were chocolate-brown, and a deep vee of the same brown dipped down from his throat on to his chest. Above it the battered red face was creased and puffy with sleep, and his long, greying hair was tangled and matted. He belched thunderously, and grimaced at the taste of old gin and pipe tobacco, then, satisfied that no reptile lay in ambush, he stepped into the water and lowered his massive hams to sit waist-deep. Snorting, he scooped water with his cupped hands over his head, then lumbered out on to the bank again. Sixty seconds is a long time to stay in a river like the Rufiji, for the crocodiles come quickly to the sound of splashing.

Naked, dripping, hair plastered down across his face, Flynn began to soap himself, working up a thick lather at his crotch and tenderly massaging his abundant genitalia, he washed away the sloth of sleep and his appetite stirred. He called up at the camp, 'Mohammed, beloved of Allah and son of his prophet, shake your black arse out of the sack and get the coffee brewing.' Then as an afterthought, he added, 'And put a little gin in it.'

Soapsuds filled Flynn's armpits, and coated the melancholy sag of his belly when Mohammed came down the bank to him. Mohammed was balancing a large enamel mug from which curled little wisps of aromatic steam, and Flynn grinned at him, and spoke in Swahili. 'Thou art kind and merciful; this charity will be writ against your name in the Book of Paradise.'

He reached for the mug, but before his fingers touched it, there was a fusillade of gunfire above them and a bullet hit Flynn high up in the thigh. It spun him sideways so he sprawled half in mud and half in water.

Lying stunned with the shock, he heard the rush of Askari into the camp, heard their shouted triumph as they clubbed with the gun-butt those who had survived the first volley. Flynn wriggled into a sitting position.

Mohammed was coming to him anxiously.

'Run,' grunted Flynn. 'Run, damn you.'

'Lord . . .'

'Get out of here,' savagely Flynn lashed out at him, and Mohammed recoiled. 'The rope, you fool. They'll give you the rope and wrap you in a pigskin.'

A second longer Mohammed hesitated, then he ducked and scampered into the reeds.

'Find Fini,' roared a bull voice in German. 'Find the white man.'

Flynn realized then that it was a stray bullet that had hit him–perhaps even a ricochet. His leg was numb from the hip down, but he dragged himself into the water. He could not run, so he must swim.

'Where is he? Find him!' raged the voice, and suddenly the grass on the bank burst open and Flynn looked up.

For the first time they confronted each other. These two who had played murderous hide-and-seek for three long years across ten thousand square miles of bush.

'Ja!' Fleischer's jubilant bellow as he swung and sighted the pistol at the man in the water below him. 'This time!' aiming carefully, steadying the Luger with both hands.

The brittle snapping sound of the shot, and the slap of the bullet into the water a foot from Flynn's head was followed by Fleischer's snarl of disappointment.

Filling his lungs, Flynn ducked below the surface. Frog-kicking with his good leg, trailing the wounded one, he turned with the current and swam. He swam until his trapped breath threatened to explode in his chest, and coloured lights flashed and twinkled behind his clenched eyelids. Then he clawed to the surface. On the bank Fleischer was waiting for him with half a dozen of his Askari. 'There he is!' as Flynn blew like a whale thirty yards downstream. Gunfire crackled and the water whipped and leaped and creamed around Flynn's head.

'Shoot straight!' Howling in frustration and blazing wildly with the Luger, Fleischer watched the head disappear and Flynn's fat white buttocks break the surface for an instant as he dived. Sobbing with anger and exertion, Fleischer turned his fury on the Askari around him. 'Pigs! Stupid black pig dogs!' And he swung the empty pistol against the nearest head, knocking the man to his knees. Intent on avoiding the flailing pistol, none of them were ready when Flynn surfaced for the second time. A desultory volley kicked fountains no closer than ten feet to Flynn's bobbing head, and he dived again.

'Come on! Chase him!' Herding his Askari ahead of him, Fleischer trotted along the bank in pursuit. Twenty yards of good going, then they came to the first swamp hole and waded through it to be confronted by a solid barrier of elephant grass. They plunged into it and were swallowed so they no longer had sight of the river.

'Schnell! Schnell! He'll get away,' gasped Fleischer and the thick stems wrapped his ankles so that he fell headlong in the mud. Two of his Askari dragged him up and they staggered on until the thicket of tall grass ended, and they stood on the elbow of the river bend with a clear view a thousand yards downstream.

Disturbed by the gunfire, the birds were up, milling in confused flight above the reed-beds. Their alarm cries blended into a harsh chorus that spoiled the peace of the brooding dawn. They were the only living things in sight. From bank to far bank, the curved expanse of water was broken only by a few floating islands of papyrus grass; rafts of matted vegetation cut loose by the current and floating unhurriedly down towards the sea.

Panting, Herman Fleischer shook off the supporting hands of his two Askari and searched desperately for a glimpse of Flynn's bobbing head. 'Where did he go?' His fingers trembled as he fitted a new clip of ammunition into the Luger. 'Where did he go?' he demanded again, but none of his Askari drew attention to himself by venturing a reply.

'He must be on this side!' The Rufiji was half a mile wide here, Flynn could not have crossed it in the few minutes since they had last seen him. 'Search the bank!' Fleischer ordered. 'Find him!'

With relief the sergeant of his Askari turned on his men, quickly splitting them into two parties and sending them up and downstream to scour the water's edge.

Slowly Fleischer returned the pistol to its holster and fastened the flap, then he took a handkerchief from his pocket and mopped at his face and neck.

'Come on!' he snapped at his sergeant, and set off back towards the camp.

When he reached it his men had already set out the folding table and chair. New life had been stirred into Flynn's camp-fire, and the Askari cook was preparing breakfast.

Sitting at the table with the front of his tunic open, spooning up oatmeal porridge and wild honey, Fleischer was soothed into a better humour by the food, and by the thorough manner in which the execution of the four captives was conducted.

When the last of them had stopped twitching and kicking and hung quietly with his comrades in the monkey-bean tree, Herman wiped up the bacon grease in his plate with a hunk of black bread and popped it into his mouth. The cook removed the plate and replaced it with a mug of steaming coffee at the exact moment when the two parties of searchers straggled into the clearing to report that a few drops of blood at the water's edge was the only sign they had found of Flynn O'Flynn.

'Ja,' Herman nodded, 'the crocodiles have eaten him.' He sipped appreciatively at his coffee mug before he gave his next orders. 'Sergeant, take this up to the launch.' He pointed at the stack of ivory on the edge of the clearing. 'Then we will go down to the Island of the Dogs and find this other white man with his English flag.'

8

There was only the entry wound, a dark red hole from which watery blood still oozed slowly. Flynn could have thrust his thumb into it, but instead he groped gently around the back of his leg and located the lump in his flesh where the spent slug had come to rest just below the skin.

'God damn it, God damn it to hell,' he whispered in pain, and in anger, at the unlikely chance which had deflected the ricochet downwards to where he had stood below the bank, deflecting it with just sufficient velocity to lodge the bullet in his thigh instead of delivering a clean in-and-out wound.

Slowly he straightened the leg, testing it for broken bone. At the movement, the matt of drifting papyrus on which he lay rocked slightly.

'Might have touched the bone, but it's still in one piece,' he grunted with relief, and felt the first giddy swing of weakness in his head. In his ears was the faint rushing sound of a waterfall heard far off. 'Lost a bit of the old juice,' and from the wound a fresh trickle of bright blood broke and mingled with the water-drops to snake down his leg and drip into the dry matted papyrus. 'Got to stop that,' he whispered.

He was naked, his body still wet from the river. No belt or cloth to use as a tourniquet, but he must staunch the bleeding. His fingers clumsy with the weakness of the wound, he tore a bunch of the long sword-blade leaves from the reeds around him and began twisting them into a rope. Binding it around his leg above the wound, he pulled it tight, and knotted it. The dribble of blood slowed and almost stopped before Flynn sank back and closed his eyes.

Beneath him the island swung and undulated with the eddy of the current and the wavelets pushed up by the rising morning wind. It was a soothing motion, and he was tired–terribly, achingly, tired. He slept.

The pain and the cessation of motion woke him at last. The pain was a dull persistent throb, a pulse that beat through his leg and groin and his lower belly. Groggily he pulled himself on to his elbows and looked down on his own body. The leg was swollen, bluish-looking from the constriction of the grass rope. He stared at it dully, without comprehension, for a full minute before memory flooded back.

'Gangrene!' he spoke aloud, and tore at the knot. The rope fell away and he gasped at the agony of new blood flowing into the leg, clenching his fists and grinding his teeth against it. The pain slowed and settled into a steady beat, and he breathed again, wheezy as a man with asthma.

Then the change of his circumstances came through to the conscious level of his mind and he peered around shortsightedly. The river had carried him down into the mangrove swamps again, down into the maze of little islands and water-ways of the delta. His raft of papyrus had been washed in and stranded against a mud bank by the falling tide. The mud stank of rotting vegetation and sulphur. Near him a gathering of big green river crabs were clicking and bubbling over the body of a dead fish, their little eye-stalks raised in perpetual surprise. At Flynn's movement they sidled away towards the water with their red-tipped claws raised defensively.

Water! Instantly Flynn was aware of the gummy saliva that glued his tongue to the roof of his mouth. Reddened by the harsh sunlight, heated by the first fever of his wound, his body was a furnace that craved moisture.

Flynn moved and instantly cried out in pain. His leg had stiffened while he slept. It was now a heavy anchor, shackling him helplessly to the papyrus raft. He tried again, easing himself backwards on his hands and his buttocks, dragging the leg after him. Each breath was a sob in his dry throat, each movement a white-hot lance into his thigh. But he must drink, he had to drink. Inch by inch, he worked his way to the edge of the raft and slid from it on to the mud bank.

The water had receded with the tide, and he was still fifty paces from the edge. With the motion of a man swimming on his back, he moved across the slimy evil-smelling mud, and his leg slithered after him. It was beginning to bleed again, not copiously but a bright wine-drop at a time.

He reached the water at last, and rolled on to his side with the bad leg uppermost in an attempt to keep the wound out of the mud. On one elbow he buried his face in the water, drinking greedily. The water was warm, tainted with sea salt, and musky with rotted mangroves so it tasted like animal urine. But he gulped it noisily with his mouth and his nostrils and his eyes below the surface. At last he must breathe, and he lifted his head, panting for breath, coughing so the water shot up his throat, out through his nose, and dimmed his vision with tears. Gradually his breathing steadied and his eyes cleared. Before he bowed his head to drink again, he glanced out across the channel and saw it coming.

It was on the surface, still a hundred yards away but swimming fast, driving towards him with the great tail churning the water. A big one–at least fifteen feet of it–showing like the rough bark of a pine log, leaving a wide wake across the surface as it came.

And Flynn screamed, just once, but shrill and high and achingly clear. Forgetting the wound in his panic, he tried to get to his feet, pushing himself up with his hands–but the leg pinned him. He screamed again, in panic and in fear.

Belly down, he wriggled in frantic haste from the shallow water back on to the mud bank, dragging himself across the glutinous slime, clawing and threshing towards the papyrus raft where it lay stranded among the mangrove roots fifty yards away. Expecting each moment to hear the slithering rush of the huge reptile across the mud behind him, he reached the first of the mangroves and rolled on his side, looking back, coated with black mud, his face working in his terror and the sound of it spilling in an incoherent babble through his lips.

The crocodile was at the edge of the mud bank, still in the river. Only its head showed above the surface and the little piggy bright eyes watched him unwinkingly, each set on its knot of horny scale.

Desperately Flynn looked about him. The mud bank was a tiny island with this grove of a dozen mangroves set in the centre of it. The trunks of the mangroves were twice as thick as a man's chest, but without branches for the first ten feet of their height; smooth bark slimy with mud and encrusted with little colonies of freshwater mussels. Unwounded, Flynn would not have been able to climb any of them–with his leg those branches above him were doubly inaccessible.

Wildly now he searched for a weapon–anything, no matter how puny–to defend himself. But there was nothing. Not a branch of driftwood, not a rock–only the slick black sheet of mud around him.

He looked back at the crocodile. It had not moved. His first feeble hope that it might not come out on to the mud bank withered almost before it was born. It would come. Cowardly, loathsome creature it was–but in time it would gather its courage. It had smelled his blood; it knew him to be wounded, helpless. It would come.

Painfully Flynn leaned his back against the roots of the mangrove, and his terror settled down to a steady, pulsing fear–as steady as the pain in his leg. During the frantic flight across the bank, stiff mud had plugged the bullet hole and stopped the bleeding. But it does not matter now, Flynn thought, nothing matters. Only the creature out there, waiting while its appetite overcomes its timidity, swamps its reluctance to leave its natural element. It might take five minutes, or half a day–but, inevitably, it will come.

There was a tiny ripple around its snout, the first sign of its movement, and the long scaly head inched in towards the edge. Flynn stiffened.

The back showed, its scales like the patterned teeth of a file, and beyond it, the tail with the coxcomb double crest. Cautiously, on its short bowed legs, it waddled through the shallows. Wet and shiny, as broad across the back as a percheron stallion, more than a ton of cold, armoured flesh, it emerged from the water. Sinking elbow-deep into the soft mud, so its belly left a slide mark behind it. Grinning savagely, but with the jagged, irregular teeth lying yellow and long on its lips, and the small eyes watching him.

It came so slowly that Flynn lay passively against the tree, mesmerized by the deliberate waddling approach.

When it was half-way across the bank, it stopped–crouching, grinning–and he smelled it. The heavy odour of stale fish and musk on the warm air.

'Get away!' Flynn yelled at it, and it stood unmoving, unblinking. 'Get away!' He snatched up a handful of mud and hurled it. It crouched a little lower on its stubby legs and the fat crested tail stiffened, arching slightly.

Sobbing now, Flynn threw another handful of mud. The long grinning jaws opened an inch, then shut again. He heard the click as its teeth met, and it charged. Incredibly fast through the mud, grinning still, it slithered towards him.

This time Flynn's voice was a lunatic babble of horror and he writhed helplessly against the mangrove roots.

The deep booming note of the gun seemed not part of reality, but the crocodile reared up on its tail, drowning the echoes of the shot with its own hissing bellow, and above the next boom of the gun, Flynn heard the bullet strike the scaly body with a thump.

Mud sprayed as the reptile rolled in convulsions, and then, lifting itself high on its legs, it lumbered in ungainly flight towards the water. Again and again the heavy rifle fired, but the crocodile never faltered in its rush, and the surface of the water exploded like blown glass, as it launched itself from the bank and was gone in the spreading ripples.

Standing in the bows of the canoe with the smoking rifle in his hands, while the paddlers drove in towards the bank, Sebastian Oldsmith shouted anxiously, 'Flynn, Flynn–did it get you? Are you all right?'

Flynn's reply was a croak. 'Bassie. Oh, Bassie boy, for the first time in my life I'm real pleased to see you,' and he sagged only half conscious against the mangrove roots.

9

The sun burned down on the dhow where it lay at anchor off the Island of the Dogs, yet a steady breeze came down the narrow waterway between the mangroves and plucked at the furled sail on the boom.

With a rope sling under his armpits, they lifted Flynn from the canoe and swung him, legs dangling, over the bulwark. Sebastian was ready to receive him and lower him gently to the deck.

'Get that goddamn sail up, and let's get the hell out of the river,' gasped Flynn.

'I must tend to your leg.'

'That can wait. We've got to get out into the open sea. The Germans have got a steam launch. They'll be looking for us. We can expect them to drop in on us at any minute.'

'They can't touch us–we're under the protection of the flag,' Sebastian protested.

'Listen, you stupid, bloody limey,' Flynn's voice was a squawk of pain and impatience. 'That murdering Hun will give us a rope dance with or without the flag. Don't argue, get that sail up!'

They laid him on a blanket in the shadow of the high poop before Sebastian hurried forward to release the Arab crew from the hold. They came up shiny with sweat and blinking in the dazzle of the sun. It took perhaps fifteen seconds for Mohammed to explain to them the urgency of the situation, and this invoked a few seconds of paralysed horror before they scattered to their stations. Four of them were hauling ineffectively at the anchor rope, but the great lump of coral was buried in the gluey mud of the bottom. Sebastian pushed them aside impatiently and with one knife stroke, severed the rope.

The crew, with the enthusiastic assistance of Flynn's bearers and gun-boys, ran up the faded and patched old sail. The wind caught it and bellied it. The deck canted slightly and two Arabs ran back to the tiller. From under the bows came the faint giggle of water, and from the stern spread a wide oily wake. With a cluster of the Arabs and bearers calling directions in the bows to the steersmen at the rudder, the ancient dhow pointed downstream and ambled towards the sea.

When Sebastian went back to Flynn, he found old Mohammed squatting anxiously beside him and watching, as Flynn drank from the square bottle. Already a quarter of its contents had disappeared.

Flynn lowered the gin bottle, and breathed heavily through his mouth. 'Tastes like honey,' he gasped.

'Let's look at that leg.' Sebastian stooped over Flynn's naked, mud-besmeared body. 'My God, what a mess! Mohammed, get a basin of water and try and find some clean cloth.'

10

With the coming of evening, the breeze gathered strength, kicking up a chop on the widening waterways of the delta. All afternoon the little dhow had butted against the run of the tide, but now began the ebb and it helped push her down towards the sea.

'With any luck we'll reach the mouth before sunset.' Sebastian was sitting beside Flynn's blanket-wrapped form under the poop. Flynn grunted. He was weak with pain, and groggy with gin. 'If we don't, we'll have to moor somewhere for the night. Can't risk the channel in the dark.' He received no reply from Flynn and himself fell silent.

Except for the gurgle of the bow-wave and the singsong chant of the pilot, a lazy silence blanketed the dhow. Most of the crew and the bearers were strewn in sleep about the deck, although two of them worked quietly over the open galley as they prepared the evening meal.

The heavy miasma of the swamps blended poorly with the stench of the bilges and the cargo of green ivory in the holds. It seemed to act as a drug, increasing Sebastian's fatigue. His head sagged forward on his chest and his hands slipped from the rifle in his lap. He slept.

The magpie chatter of the crew, and Mohammed's urgent hands on his shoulder, shook him awake. He came to his feet and gazed blearily around him. 'What is it? What is the trouble, Mohammed?'

For answer, Mohammed shouted the crew into silence, and turned back to Sebastian. 'Listen, master.'

Sebastian shook the remnants of sleep from his head, then cocked it slightly. 'I can't hear . . .' He stopped, an expression of uncertainty on his face.

Very faintly in the still of the evening he heard it, a faint huffing rhythm, as though a train passed in the distance. 'Yes,' he said, still uncertain. 'What is it?'

'The toot-toot boat, she comes.'

Sebastian stared at him without comprehension.

'The Allemand. The Germans.' Mohammed's hands fluttered with agitation. 'They follow us. They chase. They catch. They . . .' He clutched his own throat with both hands and rolled his eyes. His tongue protruded from the corner of his mouth.

Flynn's entire retinue was gathered in a mob around Sebastian, and at Mohammed's graphic little charade, they burst once more into a frightened chorus. Every eye was on Sebastian, waiting for his lead, and he felt confused, uncertain. Instinctively he turned to Flynn. Flynn lay on his back, his mouth open, snoring. Quickly Sebastian knelt beside him. 'Flynn! Flynn!' Flynn opened his eyes but they were focused beyond Sebastian's face. 'The Germans are coming.'

'The Campbells are coming. Hurrah! Hurrah!' muttered Flynn and closed his eyes again. His usually red face was flushed hot-scarlet with fever.

'What must I do?' pleaded Sebastian.

'Drink it!' advised Flynn. 'Never hesitate. Drink it!' his eyes still closed, his voice slurred.

'Please, Flynn. Please tell me.'

'Tell you?' muttered Flynn in delirium. 'Sure! Have you heard the one about the camel and the missionary?'

Sebastian jumped to his feet and looked wildly about him. The sun was low, perhaps another two hours to nightfall. *If only we can hold them off until then.* 'Mohammed. Get the gun-boys up into the stern,' he snapped, and Mohammed, recognizing the new crispness in his voice, turned on the mob about him to relay the order.

The ten gun-boys scattered to gather their weapons and then crowded up on to the poop. Sebastian followed them, gazing anxiously back along the channel. He could see two thousand yards to the bend behind them and the channel was empty, but he was sure the sound of the steam engine was louder.

'Spread them along the rail,' he ordered Mohammed. He was thinking hard now; always a difficult task for Sebastian. Stubborn as a mule, his mind began to sulk as soon as he flogged it. He wrinkled his high scholar's forehead and his next thought emerged slowly. 'A barricade,' he said. The thin planking of the bulwark would offer little protection against the high-powered Mausers. 'Mohammed, get the others to carry up everything they can find, and pile it here to shield the steersmen and the gun-boys. Bring everything–water barrels, the sacks of coconuts, those old fishing-nets.'

While they hurried to obey the order, Sebastian stood in frowning concentration, prodding the mass within his skull and finding it as responsive as a lump of freshly kneaded dough. He tried to estimate the relative speeds of the dhow and a modern steam launch. Perhaps they were moving at half the speed of their pursuers. With a sliding sensation, he decided that even in this wind, sail could not hope to out-run a propeller-driven craft.

The word *propeller,* and the chance that at that moment he was forced to move aside to allow four of the men to drag an untidy bundle of old fishing-nets past, eased the next idea to the surface of his mind.

Humbled by the brilliance of his idea, he clung to it desperately, lest it somehow sink once more below the surface to be lost. 'Mohammed . . .' he stammered in his excitement. 'Mohammed. Those nets . . .' He looked back again along the wide channel, and saw it still empty. He looked ahead and saw the next bend coming towards them; already the helmsman was chanting the orders preparatory to tacking the dhow. 'Those nets. I want to lay them across the channel.'

Mohammed stared at him aghast, his wizened face crinkling deeper in disbelief.

'Cut off the corks. Leave every fourth one.' Sebastian grabbed his shoulders and shook him in agitation. 'I want the net to sag. I don't want them to spot it too soon.'

They were almost up to the bend now, and Sebastian pointed ahead. 'We'll lay it just around the corner.'

'Why, master?' pleaded Mohammed. 'We must run. They are close now.'

'The propeller,' Sebastian shouted in his face. He made a churning motion with his hands. 'I want to snag the propeller.'

A moment longer Mohammed stared at him, then he began to grin, exposing his bald gums.

While they worked in frantic haste the muffled engine beat from upstream grew steadily louder, more insistent.

The dhow wallowed and balked at the efforts of the helmsman to work her across the channel. Her head kept falling away before the wind, threatening to snarl the net in her own rudder, but slowly the line of bobbing corks spread from the mangroves on one side towards the far bank, while in grim concentration Sebastian and a group led by Mohammed paid the net out over the stern. Every few minutes they lifted their faces to glance at the bend upstream, expecting to see the German launch appear and hear the crackle of Mauser fire.

Gradually the dhow edged in towards the north bank, sowing the row of corks behind her, and abruptly Sebastian realized that the net was too short–too short by fifty yards. There would be a gap in their defence. If the launch cut the bend fine, hugging the bank as it came, then they were lost. Already the note of its engine was so close that he could hear the metallic whine of the drive shaft.

Now also there was a new problem. How to anchor the loose end of the net? To let it float free would allow the current to wash it away, and open the gap still further.

'Mohammed. Fetch one of the tusks. The biggest one you can find. Quickly. Go quickly.'

Mohammed scampered away and returned immediately, the two bearers with him staggering under the weight of the long curved shaft of ivory.

His hands clumsy with haste, Sebastian lashed the end rope of the net to the tusk. Then grunting with the effort, he and Mohammed hoisted it to the side rail, and pushed it overboard. As it splashed, Sebastian shouted to the helmsman, 'Go!' and pointed downstream. Thankfully the Arab wrenched the tiller across. The dhow spun on her heel and pointed once again towards the sea.

Silently, anxiously, Sebastian and his gun-boys lined the stern and gazed back at the bend of the channel. In the fists of each of them were clutched the short-barrelled elephant rifles, and their faces were set intently.

The chug of the steam engine rose louder and still louder.

'Shoot as soon as it shows,' Sebastian ordered. 'Shoot as fast as you can. Keep them looking at us, so they don't see the net.'

And the launch came around the bend; flying a ribbon of grey smoke from its single stack and the bold red, yellow, and black flag of the Empire at its bows. A neat little craft, forty-footer, low in the waist, small deck-house aft, gleaming white in the sunlight, and the white moustache of the bow wave curled about her bows.

'Shoot!' bellowed Sebastian as he saw the Askari clustered on the foredeck. 'Shoot!' and his voice was lost in the concerted blast of the heavy calibre rifles around him. One of the Askari was flung backwards against the deck-house, his arms spread wide as he hung there a moment in the attitude of crucifixion before subsiding gently on to the deck. His comrades scattered and dropped into cover behind the steel bulwark. A single figure was left alone on the deck; a massive figure in the light grey uniform of the German colonial service, with his wide-brimmed slouch hat, and gold gleaming at the shoulders of his tunic.

Sebastian took him in the notch of his rear sight, held the bead on his chest, and jerked the trigger. The rifle jumped joyously against his shoulder, and he saw a fountain of spray leap from the surface of the river a hundred yards beyond the launch. Sebastian fired again, closing his eyes in anticipation of the savage recoil of the rifle. When he opened them, the German officer was still on his feet, shooting back at Sebastian with a pistol in his outstretched right hand. He was making better practice than Sebastian. The fluting hum of his fire whipped about Sebastian's head, or smacked into the planking of the dhow.

Hastily Sebastian ducked behind the water barrel and clawed a pair of cartridges from his belt. Sharper, higher than the dull booming of the elephant rifles, climbed the brittle crackle of the Mauser fire as the Askari joined in.

Cautiously Sebastian lifted his eyes above the water barrel. The launch was cutting the bend fine, and with a sudden swoop of dismay, he knew it was going to clear the fish-net by twenty feet. He dropped his rifle on to the deck and jumped to his feet. A Mauser bullet missed his ear by so little that it nearly burst his eardrum. Instinctively he ducked, then checked the movement and instead ran to the helmsman. 'Get out of the way!' he yelled in his excitement and his fear. Roughly he shoved the man aside and, grasping the tiller, pushed it across. Perilously close the jibe, the dhow veered across the channel, opening the angle between it and the launch. Looking back Sebastian saw the fat German officer turn and shout an order towards the wheel-house. Almost immediately the bows of the launch swung, following the dhow's manœuvre, and Sebastian felt triumph flare in his chest. Now directly in the path of the launch lay the line of tiny black dots that marked the net.

His deep-drawn breath trapped in his lungs, Sebastian watched the launch sweep over the net. His grip on the tiller tightened until his knuckles threatened to push out through the skin, and then he expelled his breath in a howl of joy and relief.

For the line of corks was suddenly plucked below the surface, leaving the small disturbance of ripples where each had stood. For ten seconds the launch sped on, then abruptly the even sound of her passage altered, a harsh clattering intruded, and her bows swung suddenly as she slowed.

The gap between the two craft widened. Sebastian saw the German officer drag a frightened Askari from the wheel-house and club him unmercifully about the head, but the squeals of Teutonic fury were muted by the swiftly increasing distance, and then drowned by the tumultuous clamour of his own crew, as they pranced and danced about the deck.

The Arab helmsman hopped up on to the water barrel and hoisted the skirts of his dirty grey robe to expose his naked posterior at the launch in calculated mockery.

11

Long after the dhow had sailed sedately first out of rifle range, and then out of sight, Herman Fleischer gave himself over completely to the epilepsy of frustrated anger. He raved about the tiny deck, lashing out with ham-sized fists while his Askari skittled around him trying to keep out of range. Repeatedly he returned to the unconscious form of his helmsman to kick him as he lay. At last his fury burned itself down to the level where it allowed him to trundle aft and hang over the stern rail peering down at the sodden bundle of netting which was wrapped around the propeller.

'Sergeant!' His voice was hoarse with strain. 'Get two men with knives over the side to cut that away!'

And a stillness fell upon them all. Every man tried to shrink himself down into insignificance, so that the choice might not fall on him. Two volunteers were selected, divested of their uniforms, and hustled to the stern, despite their terrified entreaties.

'Tell them to hurry,' grunted Herman, and went to his folding chair. His personal boy placed the evening meal with its attendant pitcher of beer on the table before him and Herman fell to.

Once from the stern there was a squeak and a splash, followed by a furious burst of rifle fire. Herman frowned and looked up from his plate.

'A crocodile has taken one of the men,' his sergeant reported in agitation.

'Well, put another one over,' said Herman and returned with unabated relish to his meal. This last batch of sausage was particularly tasty.

The netting had wound so tightly about the blades and shaft of the propeller, that it was an hour after midnight when the last of it was hacked away by lantern light.

The drive shaft had twisted slightly and run one of its bearings, so even at quarter speed there was a fearsome clattering and threshing sound from the stern as the launch limped slowly down the channel towards the sea.

In the grey and pallid pink of dawn they crept past the last island of mangroves and the launch lifted her head to the sluggish thrust of the Indian Ocean. It was a windless morning of flat calm, and Herman peered without hope into the misty half light that obscured the ocean's far horizon. He had come this far only on the slight chance that the dhow might have gone aground on a mud bank during her night run down the river.

'Stop!' he shouted at his battered helmsman. Immediately the agonized clatter of the propeller ceased, and the launch rose and fell uneasily on the long oil swells.

So they had got clear away then. He could not risk his damaged launch on the open sea. He must go back, and leave the dhow and its ivory and its many candidates for the rope, to head unmolested for that pest-hole of rogues and pirates of Zanzibar island.

Moodily he looked out across the sea and mourned that cargo of ivory. There had been perhaps a million Reichsmarks of it aboard, of which his unofficial handling fee would have been considerable.

Also he mourned the departure of the Englishman. He had never hanged one before.

He sighed and tried to comfort himself with the thought of that damned American, now well digested in the maw of a crocodile, but truly it would have been more satisfying to see him kick and spin on the rope.

He sighed again. Ah, well! At least he would no longer have the perpetual worry of Flynn O'Flynn's presence on his border, nor would he have to suffer the nagging of Governor Schee and his endless demands for O'Flynn's head.

Now it was breakfast time. He was about to turn away when something out there in the lightening dawn caught his attention.

A long low shape, its outline becoming crisper as he watched. There were cries from his Askari as they saw it also, huge in the dawn. The stark square turrets with their slim gun-barrels, the tall triple stacks and neat geometrical patterns of its rigging.

'The *Blücher*!' roared Herman in savage elation. 'The *Blücher*, by God!' He recognized the cruiser, for he had seen her not six months before, lying in Dar es Salaam harbour. 'Sergeant, bring the signal pistol!' He was capering with excitement. In reply to Herman's hasty message, Governor Schee must have sent the *Blücher* racing southwards to blockade the Rufiji mouth. 'Start the engine. Schnell! Run out to her,' he shouted at the helmsman as he slid one of the fat Very cartridges into the gaping breech of the pistol, snapped it closed, and pointed the muzzle to the sky.

Beside the tall bulk of the cruiser the launch was as tiny as a floating leaf, and Herman looked up with apprehension at the frail rope ladder he was expected to climb. His Askari assisted him across the narrow strip of water between the two vessels and he hung for a desperate minute until his feet found the rungs and he began his ponderous ascent. Sweating profusely he was helped on to the deck by two seamen and faced an honour guard of a dozen or more. Heading them was a young lieutenant in crisp, smart tropical whites.

Herman shrugged off the helping hands, drew himself to attention with a click of heels. 'Commissioner Fleischer.' His voice shaky with exertion.

'Lieutenant Kyller.' The officer clicked and saluted.

'I must see your captain immediately. A matter of extreme urgency.'

12

Kapitän zur See Count Otto von Kleine inclined his head gravely as he greeted Herman. He was a tall, thin man, who wore a neat, pointed blond beard with just a few threads of grey to give it dignity. 'The English have landed a full-scale expeditionary force in the Rufiji delta, supported by capital ships? This is correct?' he asked immediately.

'The report was exaggerated.' Herman regretted bitterly the impetuous wording of his message to the Governor; he had been fired with patriotic ardour at the time. 'In fact, it was only . . . ah,' he hesitated, 'one vessel.'

'Of what strength? What is her armament?' demanded von Kleine.

'Well, it was an unarmed vessel.'

And von Kleine frowned. 'Of what type?'

Herman flushed with embarrassment. 'An Arab dhow. Of about twenty-two metres.'

'But this is impossible. Ridiculous. The Kaiser has delivered an ultimatum to the British Consul in Berlin. He has issued mobilization orders to five divisions.' The captain spun on his heel and began to pace restlessly about his bridge, clapping his hands together in agitation. 'What was the purpose of this British invasion? Where is this . . . this dhow? What explanation must I send to Berlin?'

'I have since learned that the expedition was led by a notorious ivory poacher named O'Flynn. He was shot resisting arrest by my Askari, but his accessory, an unknown Englishman, escaped down the river last night in the dhow.'

'Where will they be headed?' The Captain stopped pacing and glared at Herman.

'Zanzibar.'

'This is stupidity, utter stupidity. We will be a laughing stock! A battle cruiser to catch a pair of common criminals!'

'But, Captain, you must pursue them.'

'To what purpose?'

'If they escape to tell their story, the dignity of the Emperor will be lowered throughout the length of Africa. Think if the British Press were to hear of this! Also, these men are dangerous criminals.'

'But I cannot board a foreign ship on the high seas. Especially if she flies the Union Jack. It would be an act of war–an act of piracy.'

'But, Captain, if she were to sink with all hands, sink without a trace?'

And Captain von Kleine nodded thoughtfully. Then abruptly he snapped his fingers and turned to his pilot. 'Plot me a course for Zanzibar Island.'

13

They lay becalmed below a sky of brazen cobalt, and every hour of the calm allowed the Mozambique current to push the little dhow another three miles off its course. Aimlessly she swung her head to meet each of the long swells, and then let it fall away into the troughs.

For the twentieth time since dawn, Sebastian climbed up on to the poop-deck and surveyed the endless waters, searching for a ruffle on the glassy surface that would herald the wind. But there was never any sign of it. He looked towards the west, but the blue line of the coast had long since sunk below the horizon.

'I'm an old dog, *Fisi*,' bellowed Flynn from the lower deck. 'Hear me laugh,' and he imitated faithfully the yammering cry of an hyena. All day Flynn had regaled the company with snatches of song and animal imitations. Yet his delirium was interspaced with periods of lucidity. 'I reckon this time old Fleischer got me good, Bassie. There's a sack of poison forming round that bullet. I can feel it there. A fat, hot sack of it. Reckon we've got to dig for it pretty soon. Reckon if we can't make it back to Zanzibar pretty soon, we're going to have to dig for it.' Then his mind escaped once more into the hot land of delirium.

'My little girl, I'll bring you a pretty ribbon. There, don't cry. A pretty ribbon for a pretty girl.' His voice syrupy, then suddenly harsh. 'You cheeky little bitch. You're just like that goddamned mother of yours. Don't know why I don't chase you out,' this last followed immediately by the hyena imitation again.

Now Sebastian turned away from the poop rail and looked down on Flynn. Beside him the faithful Mohammed was dipping strips of cloth in a bucket of seawater, wringing them out and then laying them on Flynn's flushed forehead in a futile attempt to reduce the fever.

Sebastian sighed. His responsibilities lay heavily. The command of the expedition had devolved squarely upon him. And yet, there was a sneaky sensation of pleasure, of pride in his execution of that command to be present. He went back and replayed in his mind the episode of the fish-net, remembering the quick decision that had altered the launch's course and lured it into the trap. He smiled at the memory, and the smile was not his usual self-effacing grin, but something harder. When he turned away to pace the narrow deck there was more spring in his step, and he set his shoulders square.

Again he stopped by the rail and looked towards the west. There was a cloud on the horizon, a tiny dark finger of it. And he watched it with hope that it might herald the start of the afternoon sea breeze. Yet it seemed unnatural. As he watched, it moved. He could swear it moved. Now his whole attention was fastened upon it. Realization began to flicker in him, building up until it was certainty.

A ship. By God, a ship!

He ran to the poop ladder, and slid down into the waist, across it to the mast.

The crew and the bearers watched him with awakening interest. Some of them got to their feet.

Sebastian jumped on to the boom, balancing there a moment before he started to shin up the mast. Using the mainsail hoops like the rungs of a ladder, he reached the masthead and clung there, peering eagerly into the west.

There she was–no doubt about it. He could see the tips of the triple stacks, each with its feather of dark smoke, and he began to cheer.

Below him the rail was lined with his men, all peering out in the direction they took from him. Sebastian slid down the mast, the friction burning his hands in his haste. His feet hit the deck and he ran to Flynn. 'A ship. A big ship coming up fast.' Flynn rolled his head and looked at him vaguely. 'Listen to me, Flynn. There'll be a doctor aboard. We'll get you to a port in no time.'

'That's good, Bassie.' Flynn's brain clicked back into focus. 'You've done real good.'

She came up over the horizon with astonishing rapidity, and her silhouette changed as she altered course towards them. But not before Sebastian had seen the gun turrets.

'A warship!' he shouted. To his mind this proved her British–only one nation ruled the waves. 'They've seen us!' He waved his hands above his head.

Bows on, each second growing in size, grey and big, she bore down upon the little dhow.

Gradually the cheering of the crew faltered and subsided into an uneasy silence. Magnified by the still, hot air, huge on the velvety gloss of the ocean, lifting a bow wave of pearling white, the warship came on. No check in her speed, the ensign of her masthead streaming away from them so they could not see the colours.

'What are they going to do?' Sebastian asked aloud, and was answered by Flynn's voice. Sebastian glanced around. Balancing on his good leg with one arm draped around Mohammed's neck, Flynn was hopping across the deck towards him.

'I'll tell you what they're going to do! They're going to hit us smack-bang up the arse!' Flynn roared. 'That's the *Blücher*! That's a German cruiser!'

'They can't do that!' Sebastian protested.

'You'd like to bet? She's coming straight from the Rufiji delta–and my guess is she's had a chat with Fleischer. He's probably aboard her.' Flynn swayed against Mohammed, gasping with the pain of his leg before he went on. 'They're going to ram us, and then machine-gun anyone still floating.'

'We've got to make a life raft.'

'No time, Bassie. Look at her come!'

Less than five miles away, but swiftly narrowing the distance, the *Blücher*'s tall bows knifed towards them. Wildly Sebastian looked around the crowded deck, and he saw the pile of cork floats they had cut from the fish-nets.

Drawing his knife, he ran to one of the sacks of coconuts and cut the twine that closed the mouth. He slipped the knife back into its sheath, stooped, and up-ended the sack, spilling coconuts on to the deck. Then with the empty sack in his hand he ran to the pile of floats and dropped on his knees. In frantic haste he shovelled them into the sack, half filling it before he looked up again. The *Blücher* was two miles away, a tall tower of murderous grey steel.

With a length of rope Sebastian tied the sack closed and dragged it to where

Flynn stood supported by Mohammed.

'What are you doing?' Flynn demanded.

'Fixing you up! Lift your arms!' Flynn obeyed and Sebastian tied the free end of the rope around his chest at the level of his armpits. He paused to unlace and kick off his boots before speaking again. 'Mohammed, you stay with him. Hang on to the sack and don't let go.' He left them, trotting on bare feet to find his rifle propped against the poop. Buckling on his cartridge belt, he hurried back to the rail.

Sebastian Oldsmith was about to engage a nine-inch battle cruiser with a double-barrelled Gibbs ·500.

She was close now, hanging over them like a high cliff of steel. Even Sebastian could not miss a battle cruiser at two hundred yards, and the heavy bullets clanged against the armoured hull, ringing loudly above the hissing rush of the bow wave.

While he reloaded, Sebastian looked up at the line of heads in the bows of the *Blücher*; grinning faces below the white caps with their little swallow-tailed black ribbons. 'You bloody swines,' he shouted at them. Hatred stronger than he had ever dreamed possible, choked his voice. 'You filthy, bloody swine.' He lifted the rifle and fired without effect, and the *Blücher* hit the dhow.

It struck with a crash and the crackling roar of rending timber. It crushed her side and cut through in the screaming of dying men and the squeal of planking against steel.

It trod the dhow under, breaking her back, forcing her far below the surface. At the initial shock, Sebastian was hurled overboard, the rifle thrown from his hands. He struck the armoured plate of the cruiser a glancing blow and then dropped into the sea beside her. The thrust of the bow wave tumbled him aside, else he would have been dragged along the hull and his body shredded against the steel plate.

He surfaced just in time to suck a lungful of air before the turbulence of the great screws caught him and plucked him under again, driving him deep so the pressure stabbed like red-hot needles in his eardrums. He felt himself swirled end over end, buffeted, shaken vigorously as the water tore at his body.

Colour flashed and zigzagged behind his closed eyelids. There was a suffocating pain in his chest and his lungs pumped, urgently craving air, but he sealed his lips and kicked out with his legs, clawing at the water with his hands.

The churning wake of the cruiser released its grip upon him, and he was shot to the surface with such force that he broke clear to the waist before dropping back to drink air greedily. He unbuckled the heavy cartridge belt and let it sink before he looked about him.

The surface of the sea was scattered with floating debris, and a few bobbing wooden heads. Near him a section of torn planking rose in a burst of trapped air bubbles. Sebastian struck out for it and clung there, his legs hanging in the clear green water.

'Flynn,' he gasped. 'Flynn, where are you?'

A quarter of a mile away, the *Blücher* was circling slowly, long and menacing and shark-like, and he stared at it in hatred and in fear.

'Master!' Mohammed's voice behind him.

Sebastian turned quickly and saw the black face and the red face beside the floating sack of corks a hundred yards away. 'Flynn!'

'Goodbye, Bassie,' Flynn called. 'The old Hun is coming back to finish us off. Look! They've got machine guns set up on the bridge. See you on the other side, boy.'

Quickly Sebastian looked back at the cruiser and saw the clusters of white uniforms on the angle of her bridge.

'Ja, there are still some of them alive.' Through borrowed binoculars, Fleischer scanned the littered area of the wreck. 'You will use the Maxims, of course, Captain? It will be quicker than picking them off with rifles.'

Captain von Kleine did not answer. He stood tall on his bridge, slightly round-shouldered, staring out at the wreckage with his hands clasped behind him. 'There is something sad in the death of a ship,' he murmured. 'Even such a dirty little one as this.' Suddenly he straightened his shoulders and turned to Fleischer. 'Your launch is waiting for you at the mouth of the Rufiji. I will take you there, Commissioner.'

'But first the business of the survivors.'

Von Kleine's expression hardened. 'Commissioner, I sank that dhow in what I believed to be my duty. But now I am not sure that my judgement was not clouded by anger. I will not trespass further on my conscience by machine-gunning swimming civilians.'

'You will then pick them up. I must arrest them and give them trial.'

'I am not a policeman,' he paused and his expression softened a little. 'That one who fired the rifle at us. I think he must be a brave man. He is a criminal, perhaps, but I am not so old in the ways of the world that I do not love courage merely for its own sake. I would not like to know I have saved this man from the noose. Let the sea be the judge and the executioner.' He turned to his lieutenant. 'Kyller, prepare to drop one of the life rafts.' The lieutenant stared at him in disbelief. 'You heard me?'

'Yes, my Captain.'

'Then do it.' Ignoring Fleischer's squawks of protest, von Kleine crossed to the pilot. 'Alter course to pass the survivors at a distance of fifty metres.'

'Here she comes,' Flynn grinned tightly, without humour, and watched the cruiser swing ponderously towards them.

The cries of the swimmers around them, pleading mercy, were plaintive as the voices of sea birds–tiny on the immensity of the ocean.

'Flynn. Look at the bridge!' Sebastian's voice floated across to him. 'See him there. The grey uniform.'

Tears from the sting of sea salt in his wound, and the distortion of fever had blurred Flynn's vision, yet he could make out the spot of grey among the speckling of white uniforms on the bridge of the cruiser.

'Who is it?'

'You were right. It's Fleischer,' Sebastian shouted back, and Flynn began to curse.

'Hey, you filthy, fat butcher,' he bellowed, trying to drag himself up on to the floating sack of corks. 'Hey, you whore's chamber pot.' His voice carried above the murmur of the cruiser's engines running at dead-slow. 'Come on, you blood-smeared little pig.'

The tall hull of the cruiser was close now, so close he could see the bulky figure in grey turn to the tall white-uniformed officer beside him, gesticulating in what was clearly entreaty.

The officer turned away and moved to the rail of the bridge. He leaned out and waved to a group of seamen on the deck below him.

'That's right. Tell them to shoot. Let's get it over with. Tell them . . .'

A large square object was lifted over the rail by the gang below the bridge. It dropped and fell with a splash alongside.

Flynn's voice dried up, and he watched in disbelief as the white-clad officer lifted his right arm in a gesture that might have been a salute. The beat of the cruiser's engines mounted as it increased speed, and she swung away towards the west.

Flynn O'Flynn began to laugh, the cackling hysteria of relief and delirium. He rolled off the sack of corks and his head dropped forward, so the warm green water smothered his laughter. Mohammed took a handful of the grey hair and lifted his face to prevent him drowning.

14

Sebastian reached the raft, and grasped the rope that hung in loops around its sides. He paused to regain his breath before hauling himself up to lie gasping, the blood-warm seawater streaming from his sodden clothing, and watched the shape of the battle cruiser recede into the west.

'Master! Help me!'

The voice roused him and he sat up. Mohammed was struggling, dragging Flynn and the sack through the water. Among the floating wreckage a dozen others of the crew and the bearers were flapping their way towards the raft; the weaker swimmers were already failing, their cries becoming more pitiful, and their splashing more frenzied.

There were oars roped to the slatted deck of the raft. Quickly Sebastian cut one loose with his hunting knife and began rowing towards the pair. His progress was slow, for the raft was an ungainly bitch that balked and swung away from the thrust of the oar.

An Arab crewman reached the raft and scrambled aboard, then another, and another. Each of them freed an oar and helped with the rowing. They passed the body of one of the bearers floating just below the surface, both its legs cut off above the knees and the bone sticking out of the ragged meat of the stumps. This was not the only one–there was other human flotsam among the scattered wreckage, and the pinky-brown stains that drifted away on the current attracted the sharks.

The Arab beside Sebastian saw the first one and called out, pointing with the oar.

It came hunting, its fin waggling from side to side as it tacked up against the current, so that they could sense its excitation, the cold, unthinking excitement of Euselachii hunger. Below the surface, distorted and dark, showed the tapering length of its body. Not a big one. Perhaps nine feet in length and four hundred pound in weight, but big enough to chop a leg with one bite. No longer guided by the drift of blood-taste, picking up the vibrations of the swimmers, it straightened and came in on its first run.

'Shark!' Sebastian yelled at Flynn and Mohammed where they floundered ten yards away. And both of them panicked; no longer making for the raft, they tried to clamber on to the sack of corks. Terror has no logic. Their only concern was to lift their dangling legs from the water, but the sack was too small, too unstable and their panic attracted the shark's attention. It veered towards them, showing the full height of its curved triangular fin, each sweep of its tail breaking the surface as it drove in.

'This way,' shouted Sebastian. 'Come to the raft!' He was hacking at the water with the oar, while beside him the Arabs worked in equal dedication. 'This way, Flynn. For God's sake, this way.'

His voice penetrated their panic, and once more they struck out for the raft. But the shark was closing fast, long and dappled by sunlight through the surface ripple.

The sack was still tied to Flynn's body, and its resistance to the water slowed them as it dragged behind. The shark swerved and made its first pass; it seemed to hump up out of the water, and its mouth opened. The upper jaw bulged out, the lower jaw gaped, and the multiple rows of teeth came erect like the quills of a porcupine, *and it hit the sack*. Locking its jaws into the coarse jute material, worrying it, still humped out of the water, shaking its blunt head clumsily, scattering a spray of water drops that flew like shattered glass in the sun.

'Grab here!' commanded Sebastian, leaning out to offer the blade of the oar to the pair in the water. They clutched at it with the strength of fear, and Sebastian drew them in.

But the sack and the shark were still attached to Flynn, its threshing threatening to break Flynn's hold on the life-line around the raft.

Dropping to his knees, Sebastian fumbled the knife from its sheath and sawed at the rope. It parted. The shark, still worrying the sack, worked away from the raft and Sebastian helped the Arabs to drag first Flynn, and then Mohammed, over the side.

They were not finished yet. There were still half a dozen men in the water.

Realizing its error at last, the shark relinquished its hold on the sacking. It backed away. For a moment it hung motionless, puzzled, then it circled out towards the nearest sounds of splashing. One of the gun-boys, clawing at the water in exhausted dog-paddle. The shark hit him in the side, and pulled him under. Moments later he reappeared, his mouth an open pink cave as he screamed, the water about him clouded dark red-brown by his own blood. Again he was pulled under as the shark hit his legs, but again he floated. This time face down, wriggling feebly, and the shark circled him, dashing in to chop off a mouthful of his flesh, backing away to gulp it down before coming in again.

Then there was another shark, two more, ten, so many that Sebastian could not count them, as they circled and wove in ecstatic greed, until the sea around the raft trembled and swirled in agitation.

Sebastian and his Arabs managed to drag two more of the crew into the raft and they had a third half out of the water when a six-foot white-pointer shot up from the depths, and fastened on his thigh with such violence that it almost jerked all of them overboard. But they steadied themselves and held on to the man's arms, frozen in this gruesome tug-of-war, while the shark worried the leg, so dog-like in its determination that Sebastian expected it to growl.

Little Mohammed staggered to his feet, snatched up an oar and swung it against the pointed snout with all his strength. They had dragged the shark's head from the water, and the oar fell on it with a series of rubbery thumps, but the shark held on. Fresh, bright blood squirted and trickled from the leg in its jaws, running down the shark's glistening snake-like head into the open slits of its gill covers.

'Hold him!' gasped Sebastian, and drew his knife. The raft rocking crazily under him, he leaned over the man's outstretched body and drove the knife blade into the shark's expressionless little eye. It popped in a burst of clear fluid, and the shark stiffened and trembled. Sebastian withdrew the blade, and stabbed into the other eye. With a convulsive gulp the shark opened its jaws and slid back into the sea to meander blindly away.

There were no more swimmers. The little group on the raft huddled together and watched the shark pack milling hungrily, seeming to sniff at the tainted water as they gathered the last morsels of meat.

The shark victim hosed the deck with his severed femoral artery and died before any of them could arouse themselves to apply a tourniquet.

'Push him over,' grunted Flynn.

'No,' Sebastian shook his head.

'Chrissake, we're crowded enough as it is. Chuck the poor bastard over.'

'Later on, not now.' Sebastian could not stand to watch the sharks squabble over the corpse.

'Mohammed, get a couple of your lads on the oars. I want to pick up as many of those coconuts as we can.'

By the time darkness stopped them, they had retrieved fifty-two of the floating coconuts, sufficient to keep the seven of them thirst-free for a week.

It was cold that night. They crowded together for warmth and watched the underwater pyrotechnics, as the shark pack circled the raft in phosphorescent splendour.

15

'You've got to cut for it,' Flynn whispered, and he shivered with cold in the burning heat of the midday sun.

'I don't know anything about it,' Sebastian protested, yet he could see that Flynn was dying.

'No more do I. But this is certain–you've got to do it soon . . .' Flynn's eyes had sunk into plum-coloured cavities and the smell of his breath was that of something long dead.

Staring at the leg, Sebastian had difficulty controlling his nausea. It was swollen fat and purple. The bullet hole was covered with crusty black scab, but Sebastian caught a whiff of the putrefaction under it–and this time his nausea came up acid-sweet into the back of his throat. He swallowed it.

'You've got to do it, Bassie boy.'

Sebastian nodded, and tentatively laid his hand on the leg. Immediately he jerked his fingers away, surprised by the heat of the skin.

'You've got to do it,' urged Flynn. 'Feel for the slug. It's not deep. Just under the skin.'

He felt the lump. It moved under his fingers, the size of a green acorn in the taut hot flesh.

'It's going to hurt like Billy-o.' Sebastian's voice was hoarse.

The rowers were resting on their oars, watching with frank curiosity, while the raft eddied and swung in the drift of the Mozambique current. Above them the sail that Sebastian had rigged from salvaged planking and canvas, flapped wearily, throwing a shadow across the leg.

'Mohammed, you and one other to hold the master's shoulders. Two others to keep his legs still.'

Flynn lay quiescent, pinioned beneath them on the slats of the deck.

Sebastian knelt over him, gathering his resolve. The knife he had sharpened against the metal edge of the raft, and then scrubbed clean with coconut fibre and seawater. He had sluiced the leg also, and washed his hands until the skin tingled. Beside him on the deck stood half a coconut shell containing perhaps an ounce of evaporated salt scraped from the deck and the sail, ready to pack into the open wound. 'Ready?' he whispered.

'Ready,' grunted Flynn, and Sebastian located the lump of the bullet and drew the edge of the blade across it timidly. Flynn gasped, but human skin was tougher than Sebastian allowed. It did not part.

'Goddamn you!' Flynn was sweating already. 'Don't play with it. Cut, man, cut!'

This time Sebastian slashed, and the flesh split open under the blade. He dropped the knife and drew back in horror as the infection bubbled up through the lips of the knife wound. It looked like yellow custard mixed with prune juice–and the smell of it filled his nostrils and his throat.

'Go for the slug. Go for it with your fingers.' Flynn writhed beneath the men who held him. 'Hurry. Hurry. I can't take much more.'

Steeling himself, closing his throat against the vomit that threatened to vent at any moment, Sebastian slipped his little finger into the slit. Hooking with it for the bullet, finding it, easing it up although tissue clung to it reluctantly, until it popped from the wound and dropped on to the deck. A fresh gush of warm poison followed it out, flowing over Sebastian's hand, and he crawled to the edge of the raft, choking and gagging.

16

'If only we had some red cloth.' Flynn sat against the rickety mast. He was still very weak but four days ago the fever had broken with the release of the poison.

'What would you do with it?' Sebastian asked.

'Catch me one of those dolphins. Man, I'm so goddamned hungry I'd eat it raw.'

A four-day diet of coconut pulp and milk had left all their bellies grumbling.

'Why red?'

'They go for red. Make a lure.'

'You haven't any hooks or line.'

'Tie it to a bit of twine from the sack and tease them up to the surface–then harpoon one with your knife tied to an oar.'

Sebastian was silent, peering thoughtfully over the side at the deep flashes of gold where the shoal of dolphin played under the raft. 'It's got to be red, hey?' he asked, and Flynn looked at him sharply.

'Yeah. It's got to be red.'

'Well . . .' Sebastian hesitated, and then flushed with embarrassment under his tropical sunburn.

'What's wrong with you?'

Still blushing, Sebastian stood up and loosened his belt–then, shyly as a bride on her wedding night, he drew down his pants.

'My God,' breathed Flynn in shock, as he held up his hand to shield his eyes.

'Hau! Hau!' was the chorus of admiration from the crew.

'Got them at Harrods,' said Sebastian with becoming modesty.

Red, Flynn had asked for–but Sebastian's underpants were the brightest, most beautiful red; the most vivid sunset and roses red, he could have imagined. They hung in oriental splendour to Sebastian's knees.

'Pure silk,' said Sebastian, fingering the cloth. 'Ten shillings a pair.'

'Whoa now! Come on, little fishy. Come on here,' Flynn whispered as he lay on his belly, head and shoulders over the edge of the raft. On its thread of twine, the scrap of red danced deep in the green water. A long, slithering flash of gold shot towards it, and Flynn jerked the twine away at the last instant. The dolphin swirled and darted back. Again Flynn jerked the twine. Chameleon lines and dots of excitement showed against the gold of the dolphin's body. 'That's it, fishy. Chase it.' The other fish of the shoal joined hunt, forming a sparkling planetary system of movement around the lure. 'Get ready!'

'I'm ready.' Sebastian stood over him, poised like a javelin thrower. In the excitement he had forgotten to don his pants and his shirt-tails flapped around his thighs in a most undignified manner. But his legs were long and finely muscled, the legs of an athlete. 'Get back!' he snapped at the crew who were crowded around him so that the raft was listing dangerously. 'Get back–give me room,' and he hefted the oar with the long hunting knife lashed to the tip.

'Here they come.' Flynn's voice trembled with excitement as he worked the scrap of red cloth upwards, and the shoal followed it. 'Now!' he shouted as a single fish broke the surface–four feet of flashing gold, and Sebastian lunged. The steady hand and eye that had once clean-bowled the great Frank Woolley directed the oar. Sebastian hit the dolphin an inch behind the eye, and the blade slipped through to lacerate the gills.

For a few seconds the oar came alive in his hands as the dolphin twitched and fought on the blade, but there were no barbs to hold in the flesh, and the fish slipped from the knife.

'God damn it to hell!' bellowed Flynn.

'Dash it all!' echoed Sebastian.

But ten feet down the dolphin was mortally wounded; it jigged and whipped like a golden kite in a high wind while the rest of the shoal scattered.

Sebastian dropped the oar and began stripping his shirt.

'What are you doing?' demanded Flynn.

'Going after it.'

'You're mad. Sharks!'

'I'm so hungry, I'll eat a shark also,' and he dived over the side. Thirty seconds later he surfaced, blowing like a grampus but grinning triumphantly, with the dead dolphin clasped lovingly to his bosom.

They ate strips of raw fish seasoned with evaporated salt, squatting around the mutilated carcass of the dolphin.

'Well, I've paid a guinea for worse meals than this,' said Sebastian, and belched softly. 'Oh, I beg your pardon.'

'Granted,' Flynn grunted with his mouth full of fish; and they eyeing Sebastian's nudity with a world-weary eye, 'Stop boasting and put your pants on before you trip over it.'

Flynn O'Flynn was slowly, very slowly, revising his estimate of Sebastian Oldsmith.

17

The rowers had long since lost any enthusiasm they might have had for the task. They kept at it only in response to offers of bodily violence by Flynn–and the example set by Sebastian, who worked tirelessly. The thin layer of fat that had sheathed Sebastian's muscles was long since consumed, and his sun-baked body was a Michelangelo sculpture, as he leaned and dug and pulled the oar.

Six days they had dragged the raft across the southward push of the current. Six days of sun-blazing calm, with the sea flattening, until now in the late afternoon, it looked like an endless sheet of smooth green velvet.

'No,' said Mohammed. 'That means, *The two porcupines make love under the blanket.*'

'Oh!' Sebastian repeated the phrase without interrupting the rhythm of his rowing. Sebastian was a dogged pupil of Swahili, making up in determination what he lacked in brilliance. Mohammed was proud of him, and opposed any attempt by the other members of the crew to usurp his position as chief tutor.

'That's all right about the porcupines shagging themselves to a standstill,' grunted Flynn. 'But what does this mean . . .?' and he spoke in Swahili.

'It means, *Big winds will blow across the sea,*' interpreted Sebastian, and glowed with achievement.

'And I'm not joking either.' Flynn stood up, crouching to favour his bad leg, and shaded his eyes to peer into the east. 'You see that line of cloud?'

Laying aside the oar, Sebastian stood beside him and flexed the aching muscles of his back and shoulders. Immediately all activity ceased among the other rowers.

'Keep going, me beauties!' growled Flynn, and reluctantly they obeyed. Flynn turned back to Sebastian. 'You see it?'

'Yes.' It was drawn like a kohl line across the eyelid of a Hindu woman, smeared black along the horizon.

'Well, Bassie, there's the wind you've been griping about. But, my friend, I think it's a little more than you bargained for.'

In the darkness they heard it coming from far away, a muted sibilance in the night. One by one, the fat stars were blotted out in the east as dark cloud spread out to fill half the midnight sky.

A single gust hit the raft, and flogged the makeshift sail with a clap like a shotgun, and the sleepers woke and sat up.

'Hang on to those fancy underpants,' muttered Flynn, 'or you'll get them blown right up your backside.'

Another gust, another lull, but already there was the boisterous slapping of small waves against the sides of the raft.

'I'd better get that sail down.'

'You had, and all,' agreed Flynn, 'and while you're at it, use the rope to fix life-lines for us.' In haste, spurred on by the rising hiss of the wind, they lashed themselves to the slats of the deck.

The main force of the wind spun the raft like a top, splattering them with spray; the spray was icy cold in the warm rush of the wind. The wind was steady now and the raft moved uneasily–the jerky motion of an animal restless at the prick of spurs.

'At least it will push us towards the land,' Sebastian shouted across at Flynn.

'Bassie, boy, you think of the cutest things,' and the first wave came aboard, smothering Flynn's voice, breaking over their prostrate bodies, and then streaming out through the slatted deck. The raft wallowed in dismay, then gathered itself to meet the next rush of the sea.

Under the steady fury of the wind, the sea came up more swiftly than Sebastian believed was possible. Within minutes the waves were breaking over the raft with such weight as to squeeze the breath from their lungs, submerging them completely, driving the raft under before its buoyancy reasserted itself and lifted it, canting crazily, and they could gasp for air in the smother of spray.

Waiting for the lulls, Sebastian inched his way across the deck until he reached Flynn. 'How are you bearing up?' he bellowed.

'Great, just great,' and another wave drove them under.

'Your leg?' spluttered Sebastian as they came up.

'For Chrissake, stop yapping,' and they went under again.

It was completely dark, no star, no silver of moon, but each line of breaking water glowed in dull, phosphorescent malevolence as it dashed down upon them, warning them to suck air and cling with cramped fingers hooked into the slats.

For all eternity Sebastian lived in darkness, battered by the wind and the wild, flying water. The aching chill of his body dulled out into numbness. Slowly his mind emptied of conscious thought, so when a bigger wave scoured them, he heard the tearing sound of deck slats pulling loose, and the lost wail as one of the Arabs was washed away into the night sea–but the sound had no meaning to him.

Twice he vomited seawater that he had swallowed, but it had no taste in his mouth, and he let it run heedlessly down his chin and warm on to his chest, to be washed away by the next torrential wave.

His eyes burned without pain from the harsh rake of wind-flung spray, and he blinked them owlishly at each advancing wave. It seemed, in time, that he could see more clearly, and he turned his head slowly. Beside him, Flynn's face was a leprous blotch in the darkness. This puzzled him, and he lay and thought about it but no solution came, until he looked beyond the next wave, and saw the faint promise of a new day show pale through the black massed cloud-banks.

He tried to speak, but no sound came for his throat was swollen closed with the salt, and his tongue was tingling numb. Again he tried. 'Dawn coming,' he croaked, but beside him Flynn lay like a corpse frozen in rigor mortis.

Slowly the light grew over that mad, grey sea but the scudding black cloud-banks tried desperately to oppose its coming.

Now the seas were more awesome in their raging insanity. Each mountain of glassy grey rose high above the raft, shielding it for a few seconds from the whip of the wind, its crest blowing off like the plume of an Etruscan helmet, before it slid down, collapsing upon itself in the tumbling roar of breaking water.

Each time, the men on the raft shrank flat on the deck, and waited in bovine acceptance to be smothered again beneath the white deluge.

Once, the raft rode high and clear in a freak flat of the storm, and Sebastian looked about him. The canvas and rope, the coconuts and the other pathetic accumulation of their possessions were all gone. The sea had ripped away many of the deck slats so that the metal floats of the raft were exposed; it had torn the very clothing from them so they were clad in sodden tatters. Of the seven men who had ridden the raft the previous day, only he and Flynn, Mohammed and one more, were left–the other three were gone, gobbled up by the hungry sea.

Then the storm struck again, so that the raft reeled and reared to the point of capsizing.

Sebastian sensed it first in the altered action of the waves; they were steeper, marching closer together. Then, through the clamour of the storm, a new sound, like that of a cannon fired at irregular intervals with varying charges of gunpowder. He realized suddenly that he had been hearing this sound for some time, but only now had it penetrated the stupor of his fatigue.

He lifted his head, and every nerve of his being shrieked in protest at the effort. He looked about, but the sea stood up around him like a series of grey walls that limited his vision to a circle of fifty yards. Yet that discordant boom, boom, boom, was louder now and more insistent.

In the short, choppy waves, a side-break caught the raft and tossed it high–lifting him so he could see the land; so close that the palm trees showed sharply, bending their stems to the wind and threshing their long fronds in panic. He saw the beach, grey-white in the gloom and, beyond it, far beyond it, rose the watery blue of the high ground.

These things had small comfort for him when he saw the reef. It bared its black teeth at him, snarling through the white water that burst like cannon-fire upon it before cascading on into the comparative quiet of the lagoon. The raft was riding down towards it.

'Flynn,' he croaked. 'Flynn, listen to me!' but the older man did not move. His eyes were fixed open and only the movement of his chest, as he breathed, proved him still alive. 'Flynn.' Sebastian released one of his clawed hands from its grip on the wooden slatting. 'Flynn!' he said, and struck him across the cheek.

'Flynn!' The head turned towards Sebastian, the eyes blinked, the mouth opened, but no voice spoke.

Another wave broke over the raft. This time the cold, malicious rush of it stirred Sebastian, roused a little of his failing strength. He shook the water from his head. 'Land,' he whispered. 'Land,' and Flynn stared at him dully.

Two lines of surf away, the reef showed its ragged back again. Clinging with only one hand to the slatting, Sebastian fumbled the knife from its sheath and hacked clumsily at the life-line that bound him to the deck. It parted. He reached over and cut Flynn's line, sawing frantically at the wet hemp. That done, he slid back on his belly until he reached Mohammed and freed him also. The little African stared at him with bloodshot eyes from his wrinkled monkey face.

'Swim,' whispered Sebastian. 'Must swim,' and re-sheathing the knife, he tried to crawl over Mohammed to reach the Arab but the next wave caught the raft, rearing up under it as it felt the push of the land, rearing so steeply that this time the raft was overturned and they were thrown from it into the seething turmoil of the reef.

Sebastian hit the water flat, and was hardly under, before he had surfaced again. Beside him, close enough to touch, Flynn emerged. In the strength born of the fear of death, Flynn caught at Sebastian, locking both arms around his chest. The same wave that had capsized them, had poured over the reef and covered it completely, so that where the coral fangs had been was now only a frothy area of disturbed water. In it bobbed the debris of the raft, shattered into pieces against the reef. The mutilated corpse of the Arab was still roped to a piece of the wreckage. Flynn and Sebastian were locked like lovers in each other's arms and the next wave, following close upon the first, lifted them, and shot them forward over the submerged reef.

In one great swoop that left their guts behind them, they were carried over the coral which could have minced them into jelly, and tumbled into the quiet lagoon. With them went little Mohammed, and what remained of the raft.

The lagoon was covered by a thick scum of wind spume, creamy as the head of a good beer. So when the three of them staggered waist-deep towards the beach, supporting each other with arms around shoulders, they were coated with white froth. It made them look like a party of drunken snowmen returning home after a long night out.

18

Mohammed squatted with a pile of madafu, the shiny green coconuts, beside him. The beach was littered with them, for the storm had stripped the trees. He worked in feverish haste with Sebastian's hunting knife, his face frosted with dried salt, mumbling to himself through cracked and swollen lips, shaving down through the white, fibrous material of the shell, until he exposed the hollow centre filled with its white custard and effervescent milk. At this point the madafu was snatched from his hands by either Flynn or Sebastian. His despair growing deeper, he watched for a second the two white men drinking with heads thrown back, throats pulsing as they swallowed, spilled milk trickling from the corners of their mouths, eyes closed tight in their intense pleasure; then he picked up another nut and got to work on it. He opened a dozen before he was able to satiate the other two, and he held the next nut to his own mouth and whimpered with eagerness.

Then they slept. Bellies filled with the sweet, rich milk, they sagged backwards on the sand and slept the rest of that day and that night, and when they woke, the wind had dropped, although the sea still burst like an artillery bombardment on the reef.

'Now,' said Flynn, 'where, in the name of the devil and all his angels, are we?' Neither Sebastian nor Mohammed answered him. 'We were six days on the raft. We could have drifted hundreds of miles south before the storm pushed us in.' He frowned as he considered the problem. 'We might even have reached Portuguese Mozambique. We could be as far as the Zambesi river.'

Flynn focused his attention on Mohammed. 'Go!' he said. 'Search for a river, or a mountain that you know. Better still, find a village where we can get food–and bearers.'

'I'll go also,' Sebastian volunteered.

'You wouldn't know the difference between the Zambesi and the

Mississippi,' Flynn grunted impatiently. 'You'd be lost after the first hundred yards.'

Mohammed was gone for two days and a half, but Sebastian and Flynn ate well in his absence.

Under a sun shelter of palm fronds they feasted three times a day on crab and sand-clams, and big green rock-lobster which Sebastian fished from the lagoon, baking them in their shells over the fire that Flynn coaxed from two dry sticks.

On the first night the entertainment was provided by Flynn. For some years now, Flynn's intake of gin had averaged a daily two bottles. The abrupt cessation of supply resulted in a delayed but classic visitation of *delirium tremens*. He spent half the night hobbling up and down the beach brandishing a branch of driftwood, and hurling obscenities at the phantoms that had come to plague him. There was one purple cobra in particular which pursued him doggedly, and it was only after Flynn had beaten it noisily to death behind a palm tree, that he allowed Sebastian to lead him back to the shelter and seat him beside the camp-fire. Then he got the shakes. He shook like a man on a jack-hammer. His teeth rattled together with such violence that Sebastian was sure they must shatter. Gradually, however, the shakes subsided and by the following noon he was able to eat three large rock-lobsters and then collapse into a death-like sleep.

He woke in the late evening, looking as well as Sebastian had ever seen him, to greet the returning Mohammed and the dozen tall Angoni tribesmen who accompanied him. They returned Flynn's greeting with respect. From Beira to Dar es Salaam, the name 'Fini' was held in universal awe by the indigenous peoples. Legend credited him with the powers far above the natural order. His exploits, his skill with the rifle, his volcanic temper, and his seeming immunity from death and retribution, had formed the foundation of a belief that Flynn had carefully fostered. They said in whispers around the night fires when the women and the children were not listening that 'Fini' was in truth a reincarnation of the Monomatapa. They said further that in the intervening period between his death as the Great King and his latest birth as 'Fini', he had been first a monstrous crocodile, and then *Mowana Lisa*, the most notorious man-eating lion in the history of East Africa, a predator responsible for at least three hundred human killings. The day, twenty-five years previously, that Flynn had stepped ashore at Port Amelia was the exact day that *Mowana Lisa* had been shot dead by the Portuguese Chef D'Post at Sofala. All men knew these things–and only an idiot would take chances with 'Fini'–hence the respect with which they greeted him now.

Flynn recognized one of the men. 'Luti,' he roared, 'you scab on an hyena's backside!'

Luti smiled broadly, and bobbed his head in pleasure at being singled out by Flynn.

'Mohammed,' Flynn turned to his man. 'Where did you find him? Are we near his village?'

'We are a day's march away.'

'In which direction?'

'North.'

'Then we are in Portuguese territory!' exalted Flynn. 'We must have drifted down past the Rovuma river.'

The Rovuma river was the frontier between Portuguese Mozambique and

German East Africa. Once in Portuguese territory, Flynn was immune from the wrath of the Germans. All their efforts at extraditing him from the Portuguese had proved unsuccessful, for Flynn had a working agreement with the Chef D'Post, Mozambique, and through him with the Governor in Lourenço Marques. In a manner of speaking, these two officials were sleeping partners in Flynn's business, and were entitled to a quarterly financial statement of Flynn's activities, and an agreed percentage of the profits.

'You can relax, Bassie boy. Old Fleischer can't touch us now. And in three or four days we'll be home.'

The first leg of the journey took them to Luti's village. Lolling in their maschilles, hammock-like litters slung beneath a long pole and carried by four of Luti's men at a synchronized jog trot, Flynn and Sebastian were borne smoothly out of the coastal lowland into the hills and bush country.

The litter-bearers sang as they ran, and their deep melodious voices, coupled with the swinging motion of the maschille, lulled Sebastian into a mood of deep contentment. Occasionally he dozed. Where the path was wide enough to allow the maschilles to travel side by side, he lay and chatted with Flynn, at other times he watched the changing country with the animal life along the way. It was better than London Zoo.

Each time Sebastian saw something new, he called across for Flynn to identify it.

In every glade and clearing were herds of the golden brown impala; delicate little creatures that watched them in wide-eyed curiosity as they passed.

Troops of guinea-fowl, like a dark cloud shadow on the earth, scratched and chittered on the banks of every stream.

Heavy, yellow eland, with their stubby horns and swinging dewlaps, trotting in Indian file, formed a regal frieze along the edge of the bush.

Sable and roan antelope; purple-brown waterbuck, with a perfect circle of white branded on their rumps; buffalo, big and black and ugly; giraffe; dainty little klipspringer, standing like chamois on the tumbled granite boulders of a kopje. The whole land seethed and skittered with life.

There were trees so strange in shape and size and foliage that Sebastian could hardly credit them as existing. Swollen baobabs, fifty feet in circumference, standing awkwardly as prehistoric monsters, fat pods filled with cream of tartar hanging from their deformed branches. There were forests of msasa trees, leaves not green as leaves should be, but rose and chocolate and red. Fever trees sixty feet high, with bright yellow trunks, shedding their bark like the brittle parchment of a snake's skin. Groves of mopani, whose massed foliage glittered a shiny, metallic green in the sun; and in the jungle growth along the river banks, the lianas climbed up like long, grey worms and hung in loops and festoons among the wild fig and the buffalo-bean vines and the tree ferns.

'Why haven't we seen any sign of elephant?' Sebastian asked.

'Me and my boys worked this territory over about six months ago,' Flynn explained. 'I guess they just moved on a little–probably up north across the Rovuma.'

In the late afternoon they descended a stony path into a valley, and for the first time Sebastian saw the permanent habitations of man. In irregular shaped plots, the bottom land of the valley was cultivated, and the rich black soil threw up lush green stands of millet, while on the banks of the little stream stood Luti's village; shaggy grass huts, shaped like beehives, each with a circular mud-walled granary standing on stilts beside it. The huts were arranged in a rough circle around an open space where the earth was packed hard by the passage of bare feet.

The entire population turned out to welcome Flynn: three hundred souls, from hobbling old white heads with grinning toothless gums, down to infants held on mothers' naked hip, who did not interrupt their feeding but clung like fat black limpets with hands and mouth to the breast.

Through the crowd that ululated and clapped hands in welcome, Flynn and Sebastian were carried to the chief's hut and there they descended from the maschilles.

Flynn and the old chief greeted each other affectionately; Flynn because of favours received and because of future favours yet to be asked for, and the chief because of Flynn's reputation and the fact that wherever Flynn travelled, he usually left behind him large quantities of good, red meat.

'You come to hunt elephants?' the chief asked, looking hopefully for Flynn's rifle.

'No.' Flynn shook his head. 'I return from a journey to a far place.'

'From where?'

In answer, Flynn looked significantly at the sky and repeated, 'From a far place.'

There was an awed murmur from the crowd and the chief nodded sagely. It was clear to all of them that 'Fini' must have been to visit and commune with his *alter ego*, Monomatapa.

'Will you stay long at our village?' again hopefully.

'I will stay tonight only. I leave again in the dawn.'

'Ah!' Disappointment. 'We had hoped to welcome you with a dance. Since we heard of your coming, we have prepared.'

'No,' Flynn repeated. He knew a dance could last three or four days.

'There is a great brewing of palm wine which is only now ready for drinking,' the chief tried again, and this time his argument hit Flynn like a charging rhinoceros. Flynn had been many days without liquor.

'My friend,' said Flynn, and he could feel the saliva spurting out from under his tongue in anticipation. 'I cannot stay to dance with you but I will drink a small gourd of palm wine to show my love for you and your village.' Then turning to Sebastian he warned, 'I wouldn't touch this stuff, Bassie, if I were you–it's real poison.'

'Right,' agreed Sebastian. 'I'm going down to the river to wash.'

'You do that,' and Flynn lifted the first gourd of palm wine lovingly to his lips.

Sebastian's progress to the river resembled a Roman triumph. The entire village lined the bank to watch his necessarily limited ablutions with avid interest, and a buzz of awe went up when he disrobed to his underpants.

'Bwana Manali,' they chorused. 'Lord of the Red Cloth,' and the name stuck.

As a farewell gift the headman presented Flynn with four gourds of palm wine, and begged him to return soon–bringing his rifle with him.

They marched hard all that day and when they camped at nightfall, Flynn was semi-paralysed with palm wine, while Sebastian shivered and his teeth chattered uncontrollably.

From the swamps of the Rufiji delta, Sebastian had brought with him a souvenir of his visit–his first full go of malaria.

They reached Lalapanzi the following day, a few hours before the crisis of Sebastian's fever. Lalapanzi was Flynn's base camp and the name meant 'Lie Down', or more accurately, 'The Place of Rest'.

It was in the hills of a tiny tributary of the great Rovuma river, a hundred miles from the Indian Ocean, but only ten miles from German territory across the river. Flynn believed in living close to his principal place of business.

Had Sebastian been in full possession of his senses, and not wandering in the hot shadow land of malaria, he would have been surprised by the camp at Lalapanzi. It was not what anybody who knew Flynn O'Flynn would have expected.

Behind a palisade of split bamboo to protect the lawns and gardens from the attentions of the duiker and steenbok and kudu, it glowed like a green jewel in the sombre brown of the hills. Much hard work and patience must have gone into damming the stream, and digging the irrigation furrows, which suckled the lawns and flower-beds and the vegetable garden. Three indigenous fig trees dwarfed the buildings, crimson frangipani burst like fireworks against the green kikuyu grass, beds of bright barberton daisies ringed the gentle terraces that fell away to the stream, and a bougainvillaea creeper smothered the main building in a profusion of dark green and purple.

Behind the long bungalow, with its wide, open veranda, stood half a dozen circular rondavels, all neatly capped with golden thatch and gleaming painfully white, with burned limestone paint, in the sunlight.

The whole had about it an air of feminine order and neatness. Only a woman, and a determined one at that, could have devoted so much time and pain to building up such a speck of prettiness in the midst of brown rock and harsh thorn veld.

She stood on the veranda in the shade like a valkyrie, tall and sun-browned and angry. The full-length dress of faded blue was crisp with new ironing, and the neat mends in the fabric invisible except at close range. Gathered close about her waist, her skirt ballooned out over her woman's hips and fell to her ankles, slyly concealing the long straight legs beneath. Folded across her stomach, her arms were an amber brown frame for the proud double bulge of her bosom, and the thick braid of black hair that hung to her waist twitched like the tail of an angry lioness. A face too young for the marks of hardship and loneliness that were chiselled into it, was harder now by the expression of distaste it wore as she watched Flynn and Sebastian arriving.

They lolled in their maschilles, unshaven, dressed in filthy rags, hair matted with sweat and dust; Flynn full of palm wine, and Sebastian full of fever–although it was impossible to distinguish the symptoms of their separate disorders.

'May I ask where you've been these last two months, Flynn Patrick O'Flynn?' Although she tried to speak like a man, yet her voice had a lift and a ring to it.

'You may not ask, daughter!' Flynn shouted back defiantly.

'You're drunk again!'

'And if I am?' roared Flynn. 'You're as bad as that mother of yours (may her soul rest in peace), always going on and on. Never a civil word of welcome for your old Daddy, who's been away trying to earn an honest crust.'

The girl's eyes switched to the maschille that carried Sebastian, and narrowed in mounting outrage. 'Sweet merciful heavens, and what's this you've brought home with you now?'

Sebastian grinned inanely, and tried valiantly to sit up as Flynn introduced him. 'That is Sebastian Oldsmith. My very dear friend, Sebastian Oldsmith.'

'He's also drunk!'

'Listen, Rosa. You show some respect.' Flynn struggled to climb from his maschille.

'He's drunk,' Rosa repeated grimly. 'Drunk as a pig. You can take him straight back and leave him where you found him. He's not coming in this house.' She turned away, pausing only a moment at the front door to add, 'That goes for you also, Flynn O'Flynn. I'll be waiting with the shotgun. You just put one foot on the veranda before you're sober–and I'll blow it clean off.'

'Rosa–wait–he isn't drunk, please,' wailed Flynn, but the fly-screen door had slammed closed behind her.

Flynn teetered uncertainly at the foot of the veranda stairs, for a moment it looked as though he might be foolhardy enough to put his daughter's threat to the test, but he was not that drunk.

'Women,' he mourned. 'The good Lord protect us,' and he led his little caravan around the back of the bungalow to the farthest of the rondavel huts. This room was sparsely furnished in anticipation of Flynn's regular periods of exile from the main building.

19

Rosa O'Flynn closed the front door behind her and leaned back against it wearily. Slowly her chin sagged down to her chest, and she closed her eyes to imprison the itchy tears beneath the lids, but one of them squeezed through and quivered like a fat, glistening grape on her lashes, before falling to splash on the stone floor.

'Oh, Daddy, Daddy,' she whispered. It was an expression of those months of aching loneliness. The long, slow slide of days when she had searched desperately for work to fill her hands and her mind. The nights when, locked alone in her room with a loaded shotgun beside her bed, she had lain and listened to the sounds of the African bush beyond the window, afraid then of everything, even the four devoted African servants sleeping soundly with their families in their little compound behind the bungalow.

Waiting, waiting for Flynn to return. Lifting her head in the noonday and standing listening, hoping to hear the singing of his bearers as they came down the valley. And each hour the fear and the resentment building up within her. Fear that he might not come, and resentment that he left her for so long.

Now he had come. He had come drunk and filthy, with some oafish ruffian as a companion, and all her loneliness and fear had vented itself in that shrewish outburst. She straightened and pushed herself away from the door, Listlessly she walked through the shady cool rooms of the bungalow, spread with a rich profusion of animal skins and rough native-made furniture, until she reached her own room and sank down on the bed.

Beneath her unhappiness was a restlessness, a formless, undirected longing for something she did not understand. It was a new thing; only in these last few years had she become aware of it. Before she had gloried in the companionship of her father, never having experienced and, therefore, never missing the society of others. She had taken it as the natural order of things that much of her time must be spent completely alone with only the wife of old Mohammed to replace her natural mother–the young Portuguese girl who had died in the struggle to give life to Rosa.

She knew the land as a slum child knows the city. It was her land and she loved it.

Now all of it was changing, she was uncertain, without bearings in this sea of new emotion. Lonely, irritable–and afraid.

A timid knocking on the back door of the bungalow roused her, and she felt a leap of hope within her. Her anger at Flynn had long ago abated–now he had made the first overture she could welcome him to the bungalow without sacrifice of pride.

Quickly she bathed her face in the china wash-basin beside her bed, and patted her hair into order before the mirror, before going through to answer the knock.

Old Mohammed stood outside, shuffling his feet and grinning ingratiatingly. He stood in almost as great an awe of Rosa's temper as that of Flynn himself. It was with relief, therefore, that he saw her smile.

'Mohammed, you old rascal,' and he bobbed his head with pleasure.

'You are well, Little Long Hair?'

'I am well, Mohammed–and I can see you are also.'

'The Lord Fini asks that you send blankets and quinine.'

'Why?' Rosa frowned quickly. 'Is the fever on him?'

'Not on him, but on Manali, his friend.'

'Is he bad?'

'He is very bad.'

The rich hostility that her first glimpse of Sebastian had invoked in Rosa, wavered a little. She felt the woman in her irresistibly drawn towards anything wounded or sick, even such an uncouth and filthy specimen as she had seen Sebastian to be.

'I will come,' she decided aloud, while silently qualifying her surrender by deciding that under no circumstances would she let him in the house. Sick or healthy, he would stay out there in the rondavel.

Armed with a pitcher of boiled drinking water, and a bottle of quinine tablets, closely attended by Mohammed carrying an armful of cheap trade blankets, she crossed to the rondavel and entered.

She entered it at an unpropitious moment. For Flynn had spent the last ten minutes exhuming the bottle he had so carefully buried some months before beneath the earthen floor of the rondavel. Being a man of foresight, he had caches of gin scattered in unlikely places around the camp, and now, in delicious anticipation, he was carefully wiping damp earth from the neck of the bottle with the tail of his shirt. So engrossed with this labour he was not aware of Rosa's presence until the bottle was snatched from his hands, and thrown through the open side window to pop and tinkle as it burst.

'Now what did you do that for?' Flynn was hurt as deeply as a mother deprived of her infant.

'For the good of your soul.' Icily Rosa turned from him to the inert figure on the bed, and her nose wrinkled as she caught a whiff of unwashed body and fever. 'Where did you find this one?' she asked without expecting an answer.

20

Five grains of quinine washed down Sebastian's throat with scalding tea, heated stones were packed around his body, and half a dozen blankets swaddled him to begin the sweat.

The malarial parasite has a thirty-six-hour life cycle, and now at the crisis, Rosa was attempting to raise his body temperature sufficiently to interrupt the cycle and break the fever. Heat radiated from the bed, filling the single room of the rondavel as though it were a kitchen. Only Sebastian's head showed from the pile of blankets, and his face was flushed a dusky brick colour. Although sweat spurted from every pore of his skin and ran back in heavy drops to soak his hair and his pillow, yet his teeth rattled together and he shivered so that the camp-bed shook.

Rosa sat beside his bed and watched him. Occasionally she leaned forward with a cloth in her hand and wiped the perspiration from his eyes and upper lip. Her expression had softened and become almost broody. One of Sebastian's curls had plastered itself wetly across his forehead, and, with her finger-tips, Rosa combed it back. She repeated the gesture, and then did it again, stroking her fingers through his damp hair, instinctively gentling and soothing him.

He opened his eyes, and Rosa snatched her hand away guiltily. His eyes were misty grey, unfocused as a new-born puppy's, and Rosa felt something squirm in her stomach.

'Please don't stop.' His voice was slurred with the fever, but even so Rosa was surprised at the timbre and inflection. it was the first time she had heard him speak and it was not the voice of a ruffian. Hesitating a moment, she glanced at the door of the hut to make sure they were alone before she reached forward to touch his face.

'You are kind–good and kind.'

'Sshh!' she admonished him.

'Thank you.'

'Sshh! Close your eyes.'

His eyes flickered down and he sighed, a gusty, broken sound.

The crisis came like a big wind and shook him as though he were a tree in its path. His body temperature rocketed, and he tossed and writhed in the camp-bed, trying to throw off the weight of blankets upon him, so that Rosa called for Mohammed's wife to help her restrain him. His perspiration soaked through the thin mattress and dripped to form a puddle on the earth floor beneath the bed, and he cried out in the fantasy of his fever.

Then, miraculously, the crisis was past, and he slumped into relaxation. He lay still and exhausted so that only the shallow flutter of his breathing showed there was life in him. Rosa could feel his skin cooling under her hand, and she saw the yellowish tinge with which the fever had coloured it.

'The first time it is always bad.' Mohammed's wife released her grip on the blanket-wrapped legs.

'Yes,' said Rosa. 'Now bring the basin. We must wash him and change his blankets, Nanny.'

She had worked many times with men who were sick or badly hurt; the servants and the bearers and the gun-boys, and, of course, with her father. But now, as Nanny peeled back the blankets and Rosa swabbed Sebastian's unconscious body with the moist cloth, she felt an inexplicable tension within her–a sense of dread mingled with tight excitement. She could feel new blood warming her cheeks, and she leaned forward, so that Nanny could not see her face as she worked.

The skin of his chest and upper arms was creamy-smooth as polished alabaster, where the sun had not stained it. Beneath her fingers it had an elastic hardness, a rubbery sensuality and warmth that disturbed her. When she realized suddenly that she was no longer wiping with the flannel but using it to caress the shape of hard muscle beneath the pale skin, she checked herself and made her actions brusque and businesslike.

They dried his upper body, and Nanny reached to jerk the blankets down below Sebastian's waist.

'Wait!' It came out of Rosa as a cry, and Nanny paused with her hand on the bedclothes and her head held at an angle, quizzical, birdlike. Her wizened old features crinkling in sly amusement.

'Wait,' Rosa repeated in confusion. 'First help me get the night-shirt on him,' and she snatched up one of Flynn's freshly ironed but threadbare old night-shirts from the chair beside the bed.

'It cannot bite you, Little Long Hair,' the old woman teased her gently. 'It has no teeth.'

'You just stop that kind of talk,' snapped Rosa with unnecessary violence. 'Help me sit him up.'

Between them they lifted Sebastian and slipped the night-shirt down over his head, before lowering him to the pillow again.

'And now?' Nanny asked innocently. For answer, Rosa handed her the flannel, and turned to stare fixedly out of the rondavel window. Behind her she heard the rustle of blankets and then Nanny's voice.

'Hau! Hau!' The age-old expression of deep admiration, followed by a cackle of delighted laughter, as Nanny saw the back of Rosa's neck turning bright pink with embarrassment.

Nanny had smuggled Flynn's cut-throat razor out of the bungalow, and was supervising critically as Rosa stroked it gingerly over Sebastian's soapy cheeks. There was no sound medical reason why a malaria patient should be shaved immediately after emerging from the crisis, but Rosa had advanced the theory that it would make him feel more comfortable and Nanny had agreed enthusiastically. Both of them were enjoying themselves with all the sober delight of two small girls playing with a doll.

Despite Nanny's cautionary clucks and sharp hisses of indrawn breath, Rosa succeeded in removing the hair that covered Sebastian's face like the black pelt of an otter without inflicting any serious wounds. There was a nick on the chin and another below the left nostril, but neither of these bled more than a drop or two.

Rose rinsed the razor and then narrowed her eyes thoughtfully as she surveyed her handiwork, and that thing squirmed in her stomach again. 'I think,' she muttered, 'we should move him into the main bungalow. It will be more comfortable.'

'I will call the servants to carry him,' said Nanny.

21

Flynn O'Flynn was a busy man during the period of Sebastian's convalescence. His band of followers had been seriously depleted during the recent exchange with Herman Fleischer on the Rufiji, so to replace his losses, he press-ganged all the maschille-bearers who had carried them home from Luti's village. These he put through a preliminary course of training and at the end of four days selected a dozen of the most promising, to become gun-boys. The remainder he dispatched homeward despite their protests; they would dearly have loved to stay for the glamour and reward that they were certain would be heaped upon their more fortunate fellows.

Thereafter the chosen few were entered upon the second part of their training. Securely locked in one of the rondavels behind the bungalow, Flynn kept the tools of his trade. It was an impressive arsenal.

Rack upon rack of cheap Martini Henry ·450 rifles, a score of W.D. Lee-Metfords that had survived the Anglo-Boer war, a lesser number of German Mausers salvaged from his encounters with Askari across the Rovuma, and a very few of the expensive hand-made doubles by Gibbs and Messrs Greener of London. Not a single weapon had a serial number on it. Above these, neatly stacked on the wooden shelves, were bulk packages of cartridges, wrapped and soldered in lead foil–enough of them to fight a small battle.

The room reeked with the slick, mineral smell of gun oil.

Flynn issued his recruits with Mausers, and set about instructing them in the art of handling a rifle. Again he weeded out those who showed no aptitude and he was left finally with eight men who could hit an elephant at fifty paces. This group passed into the third and last period of training.

Many years previously, Mohammed had been recruited into the German Askari. He had even won a medal during the Salito rebellion of 1904, and from there had risen to the rank of sergeant and overseer of the officers' mess. During a visit by the army auditor to Mbeya, where Mohammed was at that time stationed, there had been discovered a stock discrepancy of some twenty dozen bottles of schnapps, and a hole in the mess funds amounting to a little over a thousand Reichsmarks. This was a hanging matter, and Mohammed had resigned without ceremony from the Imperial army and reached the Portuguese border by a series of forced marches. In Portuguese territory he had met Flynn, and solicited and received employment from him. However, he was still an authority on German army drill procedure and retained a command of the language.

The recruits were handed over to him, for it was part of Flynn's plans that they be able to masquerade as a squad of German Askari. For days thereafter the camp at Lalapanzi reverberated to Mohammed's Teutonic cries, as he goose-stepped about the lawns at the head of his band of nearly naked troopers, with his fez set squarely on the grey wool of his head.

This left Flynn free to make further preparations. Seated on the stoep of the bungalow, he pored sweatily over his correspondence for many days. First there was a letter to:

His Excellency, The Governor,
German Administration of East Africa,
Dar es Salaam.
Sir,
I enclose my account for damages, as follows, herewith:

1 Dhow (Market value)	£1,500 – –
10 Rifles	£200 – –
Various stores and provisions etcetera (too numerous to list)	£100 – –
Injury, suffering and hardships (estimated)	£200 – –
TOTAL	£2,000 – –

This claim arises from the sinking of the above-said dhow off the mouth of the Rufiji, July 10th, 1912, which was an act of piracy by your gunboat, the *Blücher*.

I would appreciate payment in gold, on or before September 25th, 1912, otherwise I will take the necessary steps to collect same personally.

Yours sincerely,
Flynn Patrick O'Flynn, Esq.
(Citizen of The United States of America)

After much heavy thought, Flynn had decided not to include a claim for the ivory as he was not too certain of its legality. Best not to mention it.

He had considered signing himself 'United States Ambassador to Africa', but had discarded the idea on the grounds that Governor Schee knew damned well that he was no such thing. However, there was no harm in reminding him of Flynn's nationality–it might make the old rogue hesitate before hanging Flynn out of hand if ever he got his hooks into him.

Satisfied that the only response to his demands would be a significant increase in Governor Schee's blood pressure, Flynn proceeded with his preparations to make good his threat of collecting the debt *personally*.

Flynn used this word lightly–he had long ago selected a representative debt collector in the form of Sebastian Oldsmith. It now remained to have him suitably outfitted for the occasion, and, armed with a tape-measure from Rosa's work-basket, Flynn visited Sebastian's sick bed. These days, visiting Sebastian was much like trying to arrange an interview with the Pope. Sebastian was securely under the maternal protection of Rosa O'Flynn.

Flynn knocked discreetly on the door of the guest bedroom, paused for a count of five, and entered.

'What do you want?' Rosa greeted him affectionately. She was sitting on the foot of Sebastian's bed.

'Hello, hello,' said Flynn, and then again lamely, 'Hello.'

'I suppose you're looking for a drinking companion,' accused Rosa.

'Good Lord, no!' Flynn was genuinely horrified by the accusation. What with Rosa's depredations his stock of gin was running perilously low, and he had no intention of sharing it with anyone. 'I just called in to see how he was doing.' Flynn transferred his attention to Sebastian. 'How you feeling, old Bassie boy?'

'Much better, thank you.' In fact, Sebastian was looking very chirpy indeed. Freshly shaved, dressed in one of Flynn's best night-shirts, he lay like a Roman emperor on clean sheets. On the low table beside his bed stood a vase of frangipani blooms, and there were other floral tributes standing about the room–all of them cut and carefully arranged by Rosa O'Flynn.

He was steadily putting on weight again as Rosa and Nanny stuffed food into him and colour was starting to drive the yellowish fever stains from his skin. Flynn felt a prickle of irritation in the way Sebastian was being pampered like a stud stallion, while Flynn himself was barely tolerated in his own home.

The metaphor which had come naturally into Flynn's mind, now sparked a further train of thought, and a sharper prickle of irritation. *Stud stallion!* Flynn looked at Rosa with attention, and noticed that the dress she wore was the white one with gauzy sleeves, that had belonged to her mother–a garment that Rosa usually kept securely locked away, a garment she had worn perhaps twice in her life. Furthermore, her feet, which were usually bare about the house, were now neatly clad in store-bought patent leather, and, by Jesus, she was wearing a sprig of bougainvillaea tucked into the shiny black slick of her hair. The tip of her long braid, which was usually tied carelessly with a thong of leather, flaunted a silk ribbon.

Now, Flynn O'Flynn was not a sentimental man but suddenly he recognized in his daughter a strange new glow, and a demure air that had never been there before, and within himself he became aware of an unusual sensation, so unfamiliar that he did not recognize it as paternal jealousy. He did, however, recognize that the sooner he sent Sebastian on his way, the safer it would be.

'Well, that's fine, Bassie,' he boomed genially. 'That's just fine. Now, I'm sending bearers down to Beira to pick up supplies, and I just thought they might as well get some clothes for you while they were there.'

'Well, thank you very much, Flynn.' Sebastian was touched by the kindness of his friend.

'Might as well do it properly.' Flynn produced his tape-measure with a flourish. 'We'll send your measurements down to old Parbhoo and he can tailor-make some stuff for you.'

'I say, that *is* jolly decent of you.'

And completely out of character, thought Rosa O'Flynn as she watched her father carefully noting the length of Sebastian's legs and arms, and the girth of his neck, chest, and waist.

'The boots and the hat will be a problem,' Flynn mused aloud when he had finished. 'But I'll find something.'

'And what do you mean by that, Flynn O'Flynn?' Rosa demanded suspiciously.

'Nothing, just nothing at all.' Hurriedly Flynn gathered his notes and his tape, and fled from further interrogation.

Some time later, Mohammed and the bearers returned from the shopping expedition to Beira, and he and Flynn immediately closeted themselves in secret conclave in the arsenal.

'Did you get it!' demanded Flynn eagerly.

'Five boxes of gin I left in the cave behind the waterfall at the top of the valley,' whispered Mohammed, and Flynn sighed with relief. 'But one bottle I brought with me.' Mohammed produced it from under his tunic. Flynn took it from him and drew the cork with his teeth, before spilling a little into the enamel mug that was standing ready.

'And the other purchases?'

'It was difficult–especially the hat.'

'But did you get it?' Flynn demanded.

'It was a direct intervention of Allah.' Mohammed refused to be hurried. 'In the harbour was a German ship, stopped at Beira on its way north to Dar es

Salaam. On the boat were three German officers. I saw them walking upon the deck.' Mohammed paused and cleared his throat portentously. 'That night a man who is my friend rowed me out to the ship, and I visited the cabin of one of the soldiers.'

'Where is it?' Flynn could not hold his patience. Mohammed stood up, went to the door of the rondavel, and called to one of the bearers. He returned and set a bundle on the table in front of Flynn. Grinning proudly, he waited while Flynn unwrapped the bundle.

'Good God Almighty,' breathed Flynn.

'Is it not beautiful?'

'Call Manali. Tell him to come here immediately.'

Ten minutes later Sebastian, whom Rosa had at last reluctantly placed on the list of walking wounded, entered the rondavel, to be greeted effusively by Flynn. 'Sit down, Bassie boy. I've got a present for you.'

Reluctantly, Sebastian obeyed, eyeing the covered object on the table. Flynn stood over it and whisked away the cloth. Then, with the same ceremony as the Archbishop of Canterbury placing the crown, he lifted the helmet above Sebastian's head and lowered it reverently.

On the summit a golden eagle cocked its wings on the point of flight and opened its beak in a silent squawk of menace, the black enamel of the helmet shone with a polished gloss, and the golden chain drooped heavily under Sebastian's chin.

It was indeed a thing of beauty. A thing of such presence that it completely overwhelmed Sebastian, enveloping his head to the bridge of his nose so that his eyes were just visible below the jutting brim.

'A few sizes too large,' Flynn conceded. 'But we can stuff some cloth into the crown to keep it up.' He backed away a few paces and cocked his head on one side as he examined the effect. 'Bassie boy, you'll slay them.'

'What's this for?' Sebastian asked in concern from under the steel helmet.

'You'll see. Just hold on a shake.' Flynn turned to Mohammed who was cooing with admiration in the doorway. 'The clothes?' he asked, and Mohammed beckoned imperiously to the bearers to bring in the boxes they had carried all the way from Beira.

Parbhoo, the Indian tailor, had obviously laboured with dedication and enthusiasm. The task set him by Flynn had touched the soul of the creative artist in him.

Ten minutes later, Sebastian stood self-consciously in the centre of the rondavel while Flynn and Mohammed circled him slowly, exclaiming with delight and self-congratulation.

Below the massive helmet, which was now propped high with a wad of cloth between steel and scalp, Sebastian was dressed in the sky-blue tunic and riding breeches. The cuffs of the jacket were ringed with yellow silk–a stripe of the same material ran down the outside of his breeches–and the high collar was covered with embroidered metal thread. Complete with spurs, the tall black boots pinched his toes so painfully that Sebastian stood pigeon-toed and blushed with bewilderment. 'I say, Flynn,' he pleaded, 'what's all this about?'

'Bassie boy.' Flynn laid a hand fondly on his shoulder. 'You're going to go in there and collect hut tax for . . .' he almost said *me*, but altered it quickly to '. . . us.'

'What is hut tax?'

'Hut tax is the annual sum of five shillings, paid by the headmen to the

German Governor for each hut in his village.' Flynn led Sebastian to the chair and seated him as gently as though he were pregnant. He lifted a hand to still Sebastian's further inquiries and protests. 'Yes, I know you don't understand. But I'll explain it to you carefully. Just keep your mouth shut and listen.' He sat down opposite Sebastian and leaned forward earnestly. 'Now! The Germans owe us for the dhow and that, like we agreed–right?'

Sebastian nodded, and the helmet slid forward over his eyes. He pushed it back.

'Well, you are going to go across the river with the gun-bearers dressed as Askari. You are going to visit each of the villages before the real tax-collector gets there and picks up the money that they owe us. Do you follow me so far?'

'Are you coming with me?'

'Now, how can I do that?' Me with my leg not properly healed yet?' Flynn protested impatiently. 'Besides that, every headman on the other side knows who I am. Not one of them has ever laid eyes on you before. You just tell them you're a new officer–straight out from Germany. One look at that uniform, and they'll pay up sharpish.'

'What happens if the real tax-collector has already been?'

'They don't start collecting until September usually–and then they start in the north and work down this way. You'll have plenty of time.'

Frowning below the rim of the helmet, Sebastian brought forward a series of objections–each one progressively weaker than its predecessor, and, one by one, Flynn annihilated them. Finally there was a long silence while Sebastian's brain ground to a standstill.

'Well?' Flynn asked. 'Are you going to do it?'

And the question was answered from an unexpected quarter in feminine, but not dulcet, tones. 'He is certainly *not* going to do it!'

Guiltily as small boys caught smoking in the school latrines, Flynn and Sebastian wheeled to face the door which had carelessly been left ajar.

Rosa's suspicions had been aroused by all the surreptitious activity around the rondavel, and when she had seen Sebastian join in, she had not the slightest qualms about listening outside the window. Her active intervention was not on ethical grounds. Rosa O'Flynn had acquired a rather elastic definition of honesty from her father. Like him, she believed that German property belonged to anybody who could get their hands on it. The fact that Sebastian was involved in a scheme based on dubious moral foundations in no way lowered her opinion of him–rather, in a sneaking sort of way, it heightened her estimate of him as a potential breadwinner. To date, this was the only area in which she had held misgivings about Sebastian Oldsmith.

From experience she knew that those of her father's business enterprises in which Flynn was not eager to participate personally always involved a great deal of risk. The thought of Sebastian Oldsmith dressed in a sky-blue uniform, marching across the Rovuma, and never coming back–roused in her the same instincts as those of a lioness shortly to be deprived of her cubs.

'He is certainly *not* going to do it,' she repeated, and then to Sebastian. 'Do you hear me? I forbid it. I forbid it absolutely.'

This was the wrong approach.

Sebastian had, in turn, acquired from his father very Victorian views on the rights and privileges of women. Mr Oldsmith, the senior, was a courteous domestic tyrant, a man whose infallibility had never been challenged by his wife. A man who regarded sex deviates, Bolsheviks, trade union organizers, and suffragettes, in that descending order of repugnance.

Sebastian's mother, a meek little lady with a perpetually harassed expression, would no more have contemplated *absolutely forbidding* Mr Oldsmith a course of action, than she would have contemplated denying the existence of God. Her belief in the divine rights of man had extended to her sons. From a very tender age Sebastian had grown accustomed to worshipful obedience, not only from his mother, but also from his large flock of sisters.

Rosa's present attitude and manner of speech came as a shock. It took him but a few seconds to recover and then he rose to his feet and adjusted the helmet. 'I beg your pardon?' he asked coldly.

'You heard me,' snapped Rosa. 'I'm not going to allow this.'

Sebastian nodded thoughtfully, and then hastily grabbed at the helmet as it threatened to spoil his dignity by blind-folding him again. Ignoring Rosa he turned to Flynn. 'I will leave as soon as possible–tomorrow?'

'It will take a couple more days to get organized,' Flynn demurred.

'Very well then.' Sebastian stalked from the room, and the sunlight lit his uniform with dazzling splendour.

With a triumphant guffaw, Flynn reached for the enamel mug at his elbow. 'You made a mess of that one,' he gloated, and then his expression changed to unease.

Standing in the doorway, Rosa O'Flynn's shoulders had sagged, the angry line of her lips drooped.

'Oh, come on now!' gruffed Flynn.

'He won't come back. You know what you are doing to him. You're sending him in there to die.'

'Don't talk silly. He's a big boy, he can look after himself.'

'Oh, I hate you. Both of you–I hate you both!' and she was gone, running across the yard to the bungalow.

22

In a red dawn Flynn and Sebastian stood together on the stoep of the bungalow, talking together quietly.

'Now listen, Bassie. I reckon the best thing you can do is send back the collection from each village, as you make it. No sense in carrying all that money round with you.' Tactfully Flynn refrained from pointing out that by following this procedure, in the event of Sebastian running into trouble half-way through the expedition, the profits to that time would be safe-guarded.

Sebastian was not really listening–he was more preoccupied with the whereabouts of Rosa O'Flynn. He had seen very little of her in the last few days.

'Now you listen to old Mohammed. He knows which are the biggest villages. Let him do the talking–those headmen are the biggest bunch of rogues you'll ever meet. They'll all plead poverty and famine, so you've got to be tough. Do you hear me? Tough, Bassie, tough!'

'Tough,' agreed Sebastian absent-mindedly, glancing surreptitiously into the windows of the bungalow for a glimpse of Rosa.

'Now another thing,' Flynn went on. 'Remember to keep moving fast. March until nightfall. Make your cooking fire, eat, and then march again in the dark before you camp. Never sleep at your first camp, that's asking for trouble. Then get away again before first light in the morning.' There were many other instructions, and Sebastian listened to them without attention. 'Remember the sound of gunfire carries for miles. Don't use your rifle except in emergency, and if you do fire a shot, then don't hang about afterwards. Now the route I've planned for you will never take you more than twenty miles beyond the Rovuma. At the first sign of trouble, you run for the river. If any of your men get hurt, leave them. Don't play hero, leave them and run like hell for the river.'

'Very well,' muttered Sebastian unhappily. The prospect of leaving Lalapanzi was becoming less attractive each minute. Where on earth was she?

'Now remember, don't let those headmen talk you out of anything. You might even have to . . .' Here Flynn paused to find the least offensive phraseology, '. . . you might even have to hang one or two of them.'

'Good God, Flynn. You're not serious.' Sebastian's full attention jerked back to Flynn.

'Ha! Ha!' Flynn laughed away the suggestion. 'I was joking, of course. But . . .' he went on wistfully, 'the Germans do it, and it gets results, you know.'

'Well, I'd better be on my way.' Sebastian changed the subject ostentatiously and picked up his helmet. He placed it upon his head and descended the steps to where his Askari, with rifles at the slope, were drawn up on the lawn. All of them, including Mohammed, were dressed in authentic uniform, complete with puttees and the little pillbox kepis. Sebastian had prudently refrained from asking Flynn how he had obtained these uniforms. The answer was evident in the neatly patched circular punctures in most of the tunics, and the faint brownish stain around each mend.

In single file, the blazing eagle on Sebastian's head-piece leading like a beacon, they marched past the massive solitary figure of Flynn O'Flynn on the veranda. Mohammed called for a salute and the response was enthusiastic, but ragged. Sebastian tripped on his spurs and with an effort, regained his equilibrium and plodded on gamely.

Shading his eyes against the glare, Flynn watched the gallant little column wind away down the valley towards the Rovuma river. Flynn's voice was without conviction as he spoke aloud, 'I hope to God he doesn't mess this one up.'

23

Once out of sight of the bungalow, Sebastian halted the column. Sitting beside the footpath, he sighed with relief as he removed the weight of the metal helmet from his head and replaced it with a sombrero of plaited grass, then he eased the spurred boots from his already aching feet, and slipped on a pair of rawhide sandals. He handed the discarded equipment to his personal bearer, stood up, and in his best Swahili ordered the march to continue.

Three miles down the valley the footpath crossed the stream above a tiny waterfall. It was a piece of shade where great trees reached out towards each other across the narrow watercourse. Clear water trickled and gurgled between a tumble of lichen-covered boulders, before jumping like white lace in the sunlight down the slippery black slope of the falls.

Sebastian paused on the bank and allowed his men to proceed. He watched them hop from boulder to boulder, the bearers balancing their loads without effort, and then scramble up the far bank and disappear into the dense river bush. He listened to their voices becoming fainter with distance, and suddenly he was sad and alone.

Instinctively he turned and looked back up the valley towards Lalapanzi, and the sense of loss was a great emptiness inside him. The urge to return burned up so strongly, that he took a step back along the bath before he could check himself.

He stood irresolute. The voices of his men were very faint now, muted by the dense vegetation, overlaid by the drowsy droning of insects, the wind murmur on the top branches of the trees, and the purl of falling water.

Then the soft rustle beside him, and he turned to it quickly. She stood near him and the sunlight through the leaves threw a golden dapple on her giving a sense of unreality, a fairy quality, to her presence.

'I wanted to give you something to take with you, a farewell present for you to remember,' she said softly. 'But there was nothing I could think of,' and she came forward, reached up to him with her arms and her mouth, and she kissed him.

24

Sebastian Oldsmith crossed the Rovuma river in a mood of dreamy goodwill towards all men.

Mohammed was worried about him. He suspected that Sebastian had suffered a malarial relapse and he watched him carefully for evidence of further symptoms.

Mohammed at the head of the column of Askari and bearers had reached the crossing place on the Rovuma, before he realized that Sebastian was missing. In wild concern he had taken two armed Askari with him and hurried back along the path through the thorn scrub and broken rock–expecting at any moment to find a pride of lions growling over Sebastian's dismembered corpse. They had almost reached the waterfall when they met Sebastian ambling benignly along the path towards them, an expression of ethereal contentment lighting his classic features. His magnificent uniform was now a little rumpled; there were fresh grass stains on the knees and elbows, and dead leaves and bits of dried grass clung to the expensive material. From this Mohammed deduced that Sebastian had either fallen, or in sickness had lain down to rest.

'Manali,' Mohammed cried in concern. 'Are you well?'

'Never better–never in all my life,' Sebastian assured him.

'You have been lying down,' Mohammed accused.

'Son of a gun,' Sebastian borrowed from the vocabulary of Flynn O'Flynn. 'Son of a gun, you can say that again–and then repeat it!' and he clapped Mohammed between the shoulder blades with such well-intentioned violence that it almost floored him. Since then, Sebastian had not spoken again, but every few minutes he would smile and shake his head in wonder. Mohammed was truly worried.

They crossed the Rovuma in hired canoes and camped that night on the far bank. Twice during the night Mohammed awoke, slipped out of his blanket, and crept across to Sebastian to check his condition. Each time Sebastian was sleeping easily and the silver moonlight showed just a suggestion of a smile on his lips.

In the middle of the next morning, Mohammed halted the column in thick cover and came back from the head to confer with Sebastian. 'The village of M'topo lies just beyond,' he pointed ahead. 'You can see the smoke from the fires.'

There was a greyish smear of it above the trees, and faintly a dog began yapping.

'Good. Let's go.' Sebastian had donned his eagle helmet and was struggling into his boots.

'First I will send the Askari to surround the village.'

'Why?' Sebastian looked up in surprise.

'Otherwise there will be nobody there when we arrive.' During his service with the German Imperial Army, Mohammed had been on tax expeditions before.

'Well–if you think it necessary,' Sebastian agreed dubiously.

Half an hour later Sebastian swaggered in burlesque of a German officer into the village of M'topo, and was dismayed by the reception he received. The lamentations of two hundred human beings made a hideous chorus for his entry. Some of them were on their knees and all of them were wringing their hands, smiting their breasts, or showing other signs of deep distress. At the far end of the village M'topo, the headman, waited under guard by Mohammed and two of his Askari.

M'topo was an old man, with a cap of pure white wool, and an emaciated body covered with a parchment of dry skin. One eye was glazed over with tropical ophthalmia, and he was clearly very agitated. 'I crawl on my belly before you, Splendid and Merciful Lord,' he greeted Sebastian, and prostrated himself in the dust.

'I say, that isn't necessary, you know,' murmured Sebastian.

'My poor village welcomes you,' whimpered M'topo. Bitterly he recriminated himself for thus being taken unawares. He had not expected the tax expedition for another two months, and had taken no pains with the disposal of his wealth. Buried under the earthen floor of his hut was nearly a thousand silver Portuguese escudos and half again as many golden Deutsche Marks. The traffic of his villagers in dried fish, netted in the Rovuma river, was highly organized and lucrative.

Now he dragged himself pitifully to his old knees and signalled two of his wives to bring forward stools and gourds of palm wine.

'It has been a year of great pestilence, disease, and famine,' M'topo began his prepared speech, when Sebastian was seated and refreshed. The rest of it took fifteen minutes to deliver, and Sebastian's Swahili was now strong enough for him to follow the argument. He was deeply touched. Under the spell of palm wine and his new rosy outlook on life, he felt his heart going out to the old man.

While M'topo spoke, the other villagers had dispersed quietly and barricaded themselves in their huts. It was best not to draw attention to oneself when candidates for the rope were being selected. Now a mournful silence hung over the village, broken only by the mewling of an infant and the squabbling of a pair of mangy mongrels, contesting the ownership of a piece of offal.

'Manali,' impatiently Mohammed interrupted the old man's catalogue of misfortune. 'Let me search his hut.'

'Wait,' Sebastian stopped him. He had been looking about, and beneath the single baobab tree in the centre of the village he had noticed a dozen or so crude litters. Now he stood up and walked across to them.

When he saw what they contained, his throat contracted with horror. In each litter lay a human skeleton, the bones still covered with a thin layer of living flesh and skin. Naked men and women mixed indiscriminately, but their bodies so wasted that it was almost impossible to tell their sex. The pelvic girdles were gaunt basins of bone, elbows and knees great deformed knobs distorting the stick-like limbs, each rib standing out in clear definition, the faces were skulls whose lips had shrunk to expose the teeth in a perpetual sardonic grin. But the real horror was contained in the sunken eye cavities; the lids were fixed wide open–and the eyeballs glared like red marbles. There was no pupil nor iris, just those polished orbs the colour of blood.

Sebastian stepped back hurriedly, feeling his belly heave and the taste of it in his throat. Not trusting himself to speak, he beckoned for M'topo to come to him, and pointed at the bodies in the litters.

M'topo glanced at them without interest. They were so much part of the ordinary scene that for many days he had not consciously been aware of their existence. The village was situated on the edge of a tsetse fly belt, and since his childhood there had always been the sleeping sickness cases lying under the baobab tree, deep in the coma which always precedes death. He could not understand Sebastian's concern.

'When . . .?' Sebastian's voice faltered, and he swallowed before going on. 'When did these people last eat?' he asked.

'Not for a long time.' M'topo was puzzled by the question. Everybody knew that once the sleeping time came they never ate again.

Sebastian had heard of people dying of starvation. It happened in places like India, but here he was confronted with the actual fact. A revulsion of feeling swept over him. This was irrefutable proof that all M'topo had told him was true. This was famine as he had not believed really could exist–and he had been trying to extort money from these people!

Sebastian walked slowly back to his stool and sank down upon it. He removed the heavy helmet from his head, held it in his lap, and sat staring at his own feet. He was helpless with guilt and compassion.

Flynn O'Flynn had reluctantly provided Sebastian with one hundred escudos as travelling expenses to meet any emergency that might arise before he could make his first collection. Some of this had been expended on the hire of canoes to cross the Rovuma, but there was still eighty escudos left.

From his hip-pocket, Sebastian produced the tobacco pouch containing the money and counted out half of it. 'M'topo,' his voice was subdued. 'Take this money. Buy food for them.'

'Manali,' screeched Mohammed in protest. 'Manali. Do not do it.'

'Shut up!' Sebastian snapped at him, and prodded the handful of coins towards M'topo. 'Take it!'

M'topo stared at him as though he offered a live scorpion. It was as unnatural as though a man-eating lion had walked up and rubbed itself against his leg.

'Take it,' Sebastian insisted impatiently, and in disbelief, M'topo extended his cupped hands.

'Mohammed,' Sebastian stood up and replaced his helmet, 'we'll move on immediately to the next village.'

Long after Sebastian's column had disappeared into the bush again, old M'topo squatted alone, clutching the coins, too stunned to move. At last he roused himself and shouted for one of his sons.

'Go quickly to the village of Saali, who is my brother. Tell him that a madman comes to him. A German lord who comes to collect the hut tax and stays to offer gifts. Tell him . . .' here his voice broke as though he could not believe what he was about to say, '. . . tell him that this lord should be shown the ones who sleep, and that the madness will then come upon him, and he will give you forty escudos of the Portuguese. And, furthermore, there will be no hangings.'

'Saali, my uncle, will not believe these things.'

'No,' M'topo admitted. 'It is true that he will not believe. But tell him anyway.

25

Saali received the message from his elder brother, and it induced in him a state of terror bordering on paralysis. M'topo, he knew, had a vicious sense of humour–and there was between them that matter of the woman Gita, a luscious little fourteen-year-old who had deserted the village of M'topo within two days of taking up her duties as M'topo's junior wife, on the grounds that he was impotent and smelled like an hyena. She was now a notable addition to Saali's household. Saali was convinced that the true interpretation of his brother's message was that the new German commissioner was a rampaging lion who would not be content with merely hanging a few of the old men but who might extend his attentions to Saali himself. Even should he escape the noose, he would be left destitute; his carefully accumulated hoard of silver, his six fine tusks of ivory, his goat herd, his dozen bags of white salt, the bar of copper, his two European-made axes, the bolts of trade cloth–all of his treasures gone! It required an heroic effort to rouse himself from the stupor of despair and make his few futile preparations for flight.

Mohammed's Askari caught him as he was heading for the bush at a trot, and when they led him back to meet Sebastian Oldsmith, the tears that coursed freely down his cheeks and dripped on to his chest were genuine.

Sebastian was very susceptible to tears. Despite the protests of Mohammed, Sebastian pressed upon Saali twenty silver escudos. It took Saali about twenty minutes to recover from the shock, at the end of which time he, in turn, shocked Sebastian profoundly by offering him on a temporary basis the unrestricted services of the girl, Gita. This young lady was witness to the offer made by her husband, and was obviously wholeheartedly in favour of it.

Sebastian set off again hurriedly, with his retinue straggling along behind him in a state of deep depression. Mohammed now had a bad case of the mutters.

Drums tap-tap-tapped, runners scurried along the network of footpaths that crossed and criss-crossed the bush; from hilltop to hilltop men called one to the other in the high-pitched wail that carries for miles. The news spread. Village after village buzzed with incredulous excitement, and then the inhabitants flocked out to meet the mad German commissioner.

By this time Sebastian was thoroughly enjoying himself. He was carried away with the pleasure of giving, delighted with these simple lovable people who welcomed him sincerely and pressed humble little gifts upon him. Here a scrawny fowl, there a dozen half-incubated eggs, a basin of sweet potatoes, a gourd of palm wine.

But Santa Claus's bag, or, more accurately, his tobacco pouch, was soon empty–and Sebastian was at a loss for some way to help alleviate the misery and poverty he saw in each village. He considered issuing indulgences from future tax . . . *the bearer is hereby excused from the payment of hut tax for five years* . . . but realized that this was a lethal gift. He shuddered at what Herman Fleischer might do to anybody he caught in possession of one of these.

Finally he struck on the solution. These people were starving. He would give them food. He would give them meat.

In fact, this was one of the most desirable commodities Sebastian could have offered. Despite the abundance of wild life, the great herds of game that spread across the plains and hills, these people were starved for protein. The primitive hunting methods they employed were so ineffectual, that the killing of a single animal was an event that happened infrequently, and then almost by accident. When the carcass was shared out among two or three hundred hungry mouths, there was only a few ounces of meat for each. Men and women would risk their lives in attempting to drive a pride of lions from their kill, for just a few mouthfuls of this precious stuff.

Sebastian's Askari joined in the sport with delight. Even old Mohammed perked up a little. Unfortunately, their marksmanship was about the same standard as Sebastian's own, and a day's hunting usually resulted in the expenditure of thirty or forty rounds of Mauser ammunition, and a bag of sometimes as little as one half-grown zebra. But there were good days also, like the memorable occasion when a herd of buffalo virtually committed suicide by running down the line of Askari. In the resulting chaos one of Sebastian's men was shot dead by his comrades, but eight full-grown buffalo followed him to the happy hunting grounds.

So Sebastian's tax tour proceeded triumphantly, leaving behind a trail of empty cartridge cases, racks of meat drying in the sun, full bellies, and smiling faces.

26

Three months after crossing the Rovuma river, Sebastian found himself back at the village of his good friend, M'topo. He had bypassed Saali's in order to avoid the offended Gita.

Sitting alone in the night within the hut that M'topo placed at his disposal, Sebastian was having his first misgivings. On the morrow, he would begin the return to Lalapanzi, where Flynn O'Flynn was waiting for him. Sebastian was acutely aware that from Flynn's point of view the expedition had not been a success–and Flynn would have a great deal to say on the subject. Once more Sebastian puzzled on the fates which took his best intentions, and manipulated them in such a manner that they became completely unrecognizable from the original.

Then his thoughts kicked off at a tangent. Soon, the day after tomorrow, if all went well, he would be back with Rosa. The deep yearning that had been his constant companion these last three months throbbed through Sebastian's whole body. Staring into the wood-fire on the hearth of the hut, it seemed as though the embers formed a picture of her face, and in his memory he heard her voice again.

'Come back, Sebastian. Come back soon.'

And he whispered the words aloud, watching her face in the fire. Gloating on each detail of it. He saw her smile, and her nose wrinkled a little, the dark eyes slanted upwards at the corners.

'Come back, Sebastian.'

The need of her was a physical pain so intense that he could hardly breathe, and his imagination reconstructed every detail of their parting beside the waterfall. Each subtle change and inflection of her voice, the very sound of her breathing, and the bitter salt taste of her tears upon his lips. He felt again the touch of her hands, her mouth–and through the woodsmoke that filled the hut, his nostrils flared at the warm woman smell of her body.

'I'm coming, Rosa. I'm coming back,' he whispered, and stood up restlessly from beside the fire. At that moment his attention was jerked back to the present by a soft scratching at the door of the hut.

'Lord. Lord.' He recognized M'topo's hoarse croaking.

'What is it?'

'We seek your protection.'

'What is the trouble?' Sebastian crossed to the door and lifted the cross-bar. 'What is it?'

In the moonlight M'topo stood with a skin blanket draped around his frail shoulders. Behind him a dozen of the villagers huddled in trepidation.

'The elephant are in our gardens. They will destroy them before morning. There will be nothing, not a single stalk of millet left standing.' He swung away and stood with his head cocked. 'Listen, you may hear them now.'

It was an eerie sound in the night, the high-pitched elephant squeal, and Sebastian's skin crawled. He could feel the hair on his forearms become erect.

'There are two of them.' M'topo's voice was a scratchy whisper. 'Two old bulls. We know them well. They came last season and laid waste our corn. They killed one of my sons who tried to drive them off.' In entreaty, the old man clawed hold of Sebastian's arm and hugged at it. 'Avenge my son, lord. Avenge my son for me, and save our millet that the children will not go hungry again this year.'

Sebastian responded to the appeal in the same manner that St George would have done.

In haste he buttoned his tunic and went to fetch his rifle. On his return he found his entire command armed to the teeth, and as eager for the hunt as a pack of foxhounds. Mohammed waited at their head.

'Lord Manali, we are ready.'

'Now, steady on, old chap.' Sebastian had no intention of sharing the glory. 'This is my shauri. Too many cooks, what?'

M'topo stood by, wringing his hands with impatience, listening alternately first to the distant sounds of the garden raiders feeding contentedly in his lands, and then to the undignified wrangling between Sebastian and his Askari, until at last he could bear it no longer. 'Lord, already half the millet is eaten. In an hour it will all be gone.'

'You're right,' Sebastian agreed, and turned angrily on his men. 'Shut up, all of you, shut up!'

They were unaccustomed to this tone of command from Sebastian, and it surprised them into silence.

'Only Mohammed shall accompany me. The rest of you go to your huts and stay there.'

It was a working compromise, Sebastian now had Mohammed as an ally. Mohammed turned on his comrades and scattered them before falling in beside Sebastian.

'Let us go.'

At the head of the main gardens, high on its stilts of poles, stood a rickety platform. This was the watch-tower from which, night and day, a guard was kept over the ripening millet. It was now deserted, the two young guards had left hurriedly at the first sight of the garden raiders. Kudu or waterbuck were one thing, a pair of bad-tempered old elephant bulls were another matter entirely.

Sebastian and Mohammed reached the watch-tower and paused beneath it. Quite clearly now they could hear the rustling and ripping sound of the millet stalks being torn up and trampled.

'Wait here,' whispered Sebastian, slinging his rifle over his shoulder, as he turned to the ladder beside him. He climbed slowly and silently to the platform, and from it, looked out over the gardens.

The moon was so brilliant as to throw sharply defined shadows below the tower and the trees. Its light was a soft silver that distorted distance and size, reducing all things to a cold homogeneous grey.

Beyond the clearing the forest rose like frozen smoke clouds, while the field of standing millet moved in the small night wind, rippling like the surface of a lake.

Humped big and darker grey, standing high above the millet, two great islands in the soft sea of vegetation, the old bulls grazed slowly. Although the nearest elephant was two hundred paces from the tower, the moon was so bright that Sebastian could see clearly as he reached forward with his trunk, coiled it about a clump of the leafy stalks and plucked them easily. Then swaying gently, rocking his massive bulk lazily from side to side, he beat the millet against his lifted foreleg to shake the clinging earth from the roots before lifting it and stuffing it into his mouth. The tattered banners of his ears flapping gently, an untidy tangle of millet leaves hanging from his lips between the long curved shafts of ivory, he moved on, feeding and trampling so that behind him he left a wide path of devastation.

On the open platform of the tower, Sebastian felt his stomach contracting, convulsing itself into a hard ball, and his hands on the rifle were unsteady; his breathing whistled softly in his own ears as the elephant thrill came upon him. Watching those two huge beasts, he found himself held motionless with an almost mystic sense of awe; a realization of his own insignificance, his presumption in going out against them, armed with this puny weapon of steel and wood. But beneath his reluctance was the tingle of tight nerves–that strange blend of fear and eagerness–the age-old lust of the hunter. He roused himself and climbed down to where Mohammed waited.

Through the standing corn that reached above their heads, stepping with care between the rows so that they disturb not a single leaf, they moved in towards the centre of the garden. Ears and eyes tuned to their finest limit, breathing controlled so that it did not match the wild pump of his heart, Sebastian homed in on the crackle and rustle made by the nearest bull.

Even though the millet screened him, he could feel the weak wash of the wind move his hair softly, and the first whiff of elephant smell hit him like an open-handed blow in the face. He stopped so suddenly that Mohammed almost bumped into him from behind. They stood crouching, peering ahead into the moving wall of vegetation. Sebastian felt Mohammed lean forward beside him, and heard his whisper breathed softer than the sound of the wind. 'Very close now.'

Sebastian nodded, and then swallowed jerkily. He could hear clearly the soft slithering scrape of leaves brushing against the rough hide of the old bull. It was feeding down towards them. They were standing directly in the path of its leisurely approach, at any moment now–at any moment!

Standing with the rifle lifted protectively, sweat starting to prickle his forehead and upper lip in the cool of the night, his eyes watering with the intensity of his gaze, Sebastian was suddenly aware of massive movement ahead of him. A solid shape through the bank of dancing leaves, and he looked up. High above him it loomed, black and big so that the night sky was blotted out by the spread of its ears, so near that he stood beneath the forward thrust of its tusks, and could see the trunk uncoil like a fat python and grope forward blindly towards him; and beneath it the mouth gaped a little, spilling leaves at the corners.

He lifted the rifle, pointed it upwards without aiming, almost touching the elephant's hanging lower lip with the muzzle, and he fired. The shot was a blunt burst of sound in the night.

The bullet angled up through the pink palate of the animal's mouth, up through the spongy bone of the skull; mushrooming and exploding, it tore into the fist-sized cell that contained the brain, and burst it into a grey jelly.

Had it passed four inches to either side, had it been deflected by one of the larger bones, Sebastian would have died before he had time to work the bolt of the Mauser, for he stood directly below the outstretched tusks and trunk. But the old bull reeled backwards from the shot, his trunk falling flabbily against his chest, his forelegs spreading, and his head unbalanced by long tusks sagged forwards, knees collapsed suddenly under him, and he fell so heavily that they heard the thump in the village half a mile away.

'Son of a gun!' gasped Sebastian, staring in disbelief at the dead mountain of flesh. 'I did it. Son of a gun, I did it!' Jubilation, a delirious release from fear and tension, mounted giddily within him. He lifted an arm to hit Mohammed across the back, but he froze in that attitude.

Like the shriek of steam escaping from a burst boiler, the other bull squealed in the moonlight nearby. And they heard the crackling rush of his run in the corn.

'He's coming!' Sebastian looked frantically about him for the sound had no direction.

'No,' squawked Mohammed. 'He turns against the wind. First he seeks for the smell of us, and then he will come.' He grabbed Sebastian's arm and clung to him, while they listened to the elephant circling to get down-wind of them.

'Perhaps he will run,' whispered Sebastian.

'Not this one. He is old and evil-tempered, and he has killed men before. Now he will hunt us.' Mohammed pulled at Sebastian's arm. 'We must get into the open. In this stuff we will have no chance, he will be on top of us before we see him.'

They started to run. There is no more piquant sauce for fear than flying feet. Once he starts to run, even a brave man becomes a coward. Within twenty paces, both of them were in headlong flight towards the village. They ran without regard for stealth, fighting their way through the tangle of leaves and stalks, panting wildly. The noise of their flight blanketed the sounds made by the elephant, so they lost all idea of his whereabouts. This sharpened the spurs of terror that drove them, for at any moment he might loom over them.

At last they stumbled out into the open, and paused, panting, sweating heavily, heads swinging from side to side as they tried to place the second bull.

'There!' shouted Mohammed. 'He comes,' and they heard the shrill pig-squealing, the noisy rush of his charge through the millet.

'Run!' yelled Sebastian, still in the grip of panic, and they ran.

Around a freshly lit bonfire at the edge of the village, waited the rejected Askari and a hundred of M'topo's men. They waited in anxiety for they had heard the shot and the fall of the first bull–but since then, the squealing and shouting and crashing had left them in some doubt as to what was happening in the gardens.

This doubt was quickly dispelled as Mohammed, closely followed by Sebastian, came down the path towards them, giving a fair imitation of two dogs whose backsides had been dipped in turpentine. A hundred yards behind them the bank of standing millet burst open, and the second bull came out in full charge.

Immense in the great light, hump-backed, shambling in the deceptive speed of his run, streaming his huge ears, each squeal of rage enough to burst the eardrums–he bore down on the village.

'Get out! Run!' Sebastian's shouted warning was as wheezy as it was unnecessary. The waiting crowd was no longer waiting, it scattered like a shoal of sardines at the approach of a barracuda.

Men threw aside their blankets and ran naked; they fell over each other and ran headlong into trees. Two of them ran straight through the middle of the bonfire and emerged on the other side trailing sparks with live coals sticking to their feet. In a wailing hubbub they swept back through the village, and from each hut women with infants bundled under their arms, or slung over their backs, scurried out to join the terrified torrent of humanity.

Still making good time, Sebastian and Mohammed were passing the weaker runners among the villagers, while from behind, the elephant was gaining rapidly on all of them.

With the force and velocity of a great boulder rolling down a steep hillside, the bull reached the first hut of the village and ran into it. The flimsy structure of grass and light poles exploded, bursting asunder without diminishing the fury of the animal's charge. A second hut disintegrated, then a third, before the elephant caught the first human struggler.

She was an old woman, tottering on thin legs, the empty pouches of her breasts flopping against her wrinkled belly, a long monotonous wail of fear keening from the toothless pit of her mouth as she ran.

The bull uncoiled his trunk from his chest, lifted it high above the woman and struck her across the shoulder. The force of the blow crumpled her, bones snapped in her chest like old dry sticks, and she died before she hit the ground.

The next was a girl. Groggy with sleep, yet her naked body was silver-smooth and graceful in the moonlight, as she emerged from a hut into the path of the bull's charge. Lightly the thick trunk enfolded her, and then with an effortless flick threw her forty feet into the air.

She screamed, and the sound of the scream knifed through Sebastian's panic. He glanced over his shoulder in time to see the girl thrown high into the night sky. Her limbs were spread-eagled and she spun in the air like a cartwheel before she dropped back to earth–falling heavily so that the scream was cut off abruptly. Sebastian stopped running.

Deliberately the elephant knelt over the girl's feebly squirming body, and driving down with his tusks, impaled her through the chest. She hung from the shaft of ivory, squashed and broken, no longer recognizable as human, until the elephant shook his head irritably and threw her off.

It needed a sight as horrible as this to rally Sebastian's shattered nerves–to summon the reserves of his manhood from the far places that fear had scattered them. The rifle was still in his hands, he was shaking with fear and exertion; sweat had drenched his tunic and plastered his curly hair on to his forehead, and his breath sawed hoarsely in his throat. He stood irresolute, fighting the driving urge to run again.

The bull came on, and now his one tusk was painted glistening black with the girl's blood, and gouts of the same stuff were splattered across the bulging forehead and the bridge of his trunk. It was this that changed Sebastian's fear first to disgust, and then to anger.

He lifted the rifle and it weaved unsteadily in his hands. He sighted along the barrel and suddenly his vision snapped into sharp focus and his nerves stilled their clamour. He was a man again.

Coldly he moved the blob of the foresight on to the bull's head, holding it on the deep lateral crease at the root of the trunk, and he squeezed the trigger. The butt jumped solidly into his shoulder, the report stung his eardrums, but he saw the bullet strike exactly where he had aimed it–a spurt of dust from the crust of dried mud that caked the animal's head and the skin around it, twitched, the eyelids quivered shut for an instant, then blinked open again.

Without lowering the rifle Sebastian jerked the bolt open, and the empty case ejected crisply, pinging away into the dust. He levered another cartridge into the breech and held his aim into the massive head. Again he fired and the elephant staggered drunkenly. The ears which had been cocked half back, now fanned open and the head swung vaguely in his direction.

He fired again, and the bull winced as the bullet lanced into the bone and gristle of his head, then he turned and came for Sebastian–but there was a slackness, a lack of determination in his charge. Aiming now for the chest, handling the rifle with cold method, Sebastian fired again and again, leaning forward against the recoil of the rifle, sighting every shot with care, knowing that each of them was raking the chest cavity, tearing through lung and heart and liver.

And the bull broke his run into a shuffling, uncertain walk, losing direction, turning away from Sebastian to stand broadside, the barrel of his chest heaving against the agony of his torn vitals.

Sebastian lowered the rifle and with steady fingers pressed fresh cartridges down into the empty magazine. The bull groaned softly and from the tip of his trunk blood hosed up from the haemorrhaging lungs.

Without pity, cold in his anger, Sebastian lifted the reloaded rifle, and aimed for the dark cavity that nestled in the centre of the huge ear. The bullet struck with the sharp thwack of an axe swung against a tree trunk, and the elephant sagged and fell forward to the brain shot. His weight drove his tusks into the earth, burying them to the lip.

27

Four tons of meat delivered fresh to the very centre of the village was good value. The price paid was not exorbitant, M'topo decided. Three huts could be rebuilt in two days, and only four acres of millet had been destroyed. Furthermore, of the women who had died, one was very old and the other, although she was almost eighteen years old, had never conceived. There was a good reason, therefore, to believe she was barren and not a great loss to the community.

Warmed by the early sun, M'topo was a satisfied man. With Sebastian beside him, he sat on his carved wooden stool and grinned widely as he watched the fun.

Two dozen of his men, armed with short-handled, long-bladed spears, and divested of all clothing, were to act as butchers. They were gathered beside the mountainous carcass arguing good-naturedly as they waited for Mohammed and his four assistants to remove the tusks. Around them, in a wider circle, waited the rest of the villagers, and while they waited, they sang. A drum hammered out the rhythm for them, and the clap of hands and the stamp of feet confirmed it. The masculine bass was a foundation from which the clear, sweet soprano of the women soared, and sank, and soared again.

Beneath Mohammed's patiently chipping axe, first the one tusk and then the other were freed from the bone that held them, and, with two Askari staggering under the weight, they were carried to where Sebastian sat; and laid with ceremony at his feet.

It occurred to Sebastian that four big tusks carried home to Lalapanzi might in some measure mollify Flynn O'Flynn. They would at least cover the costs of the expedition. The thought cheered him up considerably, and he turned to M'topo. 'Old one, you may take the meat.'

'Lord.' In gratitude, M'topo clapped his hands at the level of his chest, and then turned to squawk an order at the waiting butchers.

A roar of excitement and meat hunger went up from the crowd as one of them scrambled up on to the carcass, and drove his spear through the thick grey hide behind the last rib. Then walking backwards, he drew it down towards the haunch and the razor steel sliced deep. Two others made the lateral incisions, opening a square flap–a trapdoor into the belly cavity from which the fat coils of the viscera bulged, pink and blue and glossy wet in the early morning sunlight. In mounting eagerness, four others dragged from the square hole the contents of the belly, and then, while Sebastian stared in disbelief, they wriggled into the opening and disappeared. He could hear their muffled shouts reverberating within the carcass as they competed for the prize of the liver. Within minutes one of them reappeared, clutching against his chest a slippery lump of tattered purple liver. Like a maggot, he came squirming out of the wound, painted over-all with a thick coating of dark red blood. It had matted in the woolly cap of his hair, and turned his face into a gruesome mask from which only his teeth and his eyes gleamed white. Carrying the mutilated liver, laughing in triumph, he ran through the crowd to where Sebastian sat.

The offering embarrassed Sebastian. More than that, it made his gorge rise, and he felt his stomach heave as it was thrust almost into his lap.

'Eat,' M'topo encouraged him. 'It will make you strong. It will sharpen the spear of your manhood. Ten, twenty women will not tire you.'

It was M'topo's opinion that Sebastian needed this type of tonic. He had heard from his brother Saali, and from the chiefs along the river, about Sebastian's lack of initiative.

'Like this.' M'topo cut a hunk of the liver and popped it into his mouth. He chewed heartily, and the juice wet his lips as he grinned in appreciation. 'Very good.' He thrust a piece into Sebastian's face. 'Eat.'

'No.' Sebastian's gorge pressed heavily on the back of his throat, and he stood up hurriedly. M'topo shrugged, and ate it himself. Then he shouted to the butchers to continue their work.

In a miraculously short space of time the huge carcass disintegrated under the blades of the spears and machetes. It was a labour in which the entire village joined. With a dozen strokes of the knife, a butcher would free a large hunk of flesh and throw it down to one of the women. She, in turn, would hack it into smaller pieces and pass these on to the children. Squealing with excitement, they would run with them to the hastily erected drying racks, deposit them, and come scampering back for more.

Sebastian had recovered from his initial revulsion and now he laughed to see how every mouth was busy, chewing as they worked and yet at the same time managing to emit a surprising volume of noise.

Among the milling feet the dogs snarled and yipped, and gulped the scraps. Without interrupting their feeding, they dodged the casual kicks and blows that were aimed at them.

Into the midst of this cosy, domestic scene entered Commissioner Herman Fleischer with ten armed Askari.

28

Herman Fleischer was tired and there were blisters on his feet from the series of forced marches that had brought him to M'topo's village.

A month before he had left his headquarters at Mahenge to begin the annual tax tour of his area. As was his custom, he had started in the northern province, and it had been an unusually successful expedition. The wooden chest with the rampant black eagle painted on its lid had grown heavier with each day's journey. Herman had amused himself by calculating how many more years' service in Africa would be necessary before he could resign and return home to Plaven and settle down on the estate he planned to buy. Three more years as fruitful as this, he decided, would be sufficient. It was a bitter shame that he had not been able to capture O'Flynn's dhow on the Rufiji thirteen months previously–that would have advanced his departure by a full twelve months. Thinking about it stirred his residual anger at that episode, and he placated it by doubling the hut tax on the next village he visited. This raised such a howl of protest from the village headman that Herman nodded at his sergeant of Askari, who began ostentatiously to unpack the rope from his saddlebag.

'O fat and beautiful bull elephant,' the headman changed his mind hastily. 'If you will wait but a little while, I will bring the money to you. There is a new hut, without lice or fleas, in which you may rest your lovely body, and I will send a young girl to you with beer for your thirst.'

'Good,' agreed Herman. 'While I rest, my Askari will stay with you.' He nodded to the sergeant to bind the chief, then waddled away to the hut.

The headman sent two of his sons to dig beneath a certain tree in the forest, and they returned an hour later with mournful faces, carrying a heavy skin bag.

Contentedly Herman Fleischer signed an official receipt for ninety per cent of the contents of the bag–Fleischer allowed himself a ten per cent handling fee–and the headman, who could not read a word of German, accepted it with relief.

'I will stay tonight in your village,' Herman announced. 'Send the same girl to cook my food.'

The runner from the south arrived in the night, and disturbed Herman Fleischer at a most inopportune moment. The news he carried was even more disturbing. From his description of the new German commissioner who was doing Herman's job for him in the southern province, and shooting up the countryside in the process, Herman immediately recognized the young Englishman whom he had last seen on the deck of a dhow in the Rufiji delta.

Leaving the bulk of his retinue, including the bearers of the tax chest, to follow him at their best speed, Herman mounted at midnight on his white donkey and, taking ten Askari with him, he rode southwards on a storm patrol.

Five nights later, in those still dark hours that precede the dawn, Herman was camped near the Rovuma river when he was awakend by his sergeant.

'What is it?' Grumpy with fatigue, Herman sat up and lifted the side of his mosquito net.

'We heard the sound of gunfire. A single shot.'

'Where?' He was instantly awake, and reaching for his boots.

'From the south, towards the village of M'topo on the Rovuma.'

Fully dressed now, Herman waited anxiously, straining his ears against the small sounds of the African night. 'Are you sure . . . ?' he began as he turned to his sergeant, but he did not finish. Faintly, but unmistakable in the darkness, they heard the pop, pop, pop, of a distant rifle–a pause and then another shot.

'Break camp,' bellowed Herman. 'Rasch! You black heathen. Rasch!'

The sun was well up by the time they reached M'topo's village. They came upon it suddenly through the gardens of tall millet that screened their approach. Herman Fleischer paused to throw out his Askari in a line of skirmishers before closing in on the cluster of huts, but when he reached the fringe, he stopped once more in surprise at the extraordinary spectacle which was being enacted in the open square of the village.

The dense knot of half-naked black people that swarmed over the remains of the elephant was perfectly oblivious of Herman's presence until at last he filled his lungs, and then emptied them again in a roar that carried over the hubbub of shouts and laughter. Instantly a vast silence fell upon the gathering, every head turned towards Herman, and from each head eyes bulged in horrified disbelief.

'Bwana Intambu,' a small voice broke the silence at last. 'Lord of the rope.' They knew him well.

'What . . . ?' Herman began, and then gasped in outrage as he noticed in the crowd a black man he had never seen before, dressed in the full uniform of German Askari. 'You!' he shouted, pointing an accusing finger, but the man whirled and ducked away behind the screen of blood-smeared black bodies. 'Stop him!' Herman fumbled with the flap of his holster.

Movement caught his eye and he turned to see another pseudo-Askari running away between the huts. 'There's another one! Stop him! Sergeant, Sergeant, get your men here!'

The initial shock that had held them frozen was now past, and the crowd broke and scattered. Once again, Herman Fleischer gasped in outrage as he saw, for the first time, a figure sitting on a carved native stool on the far side of the square. A figure in an outlandish uniform of bright but travel-stained blue, frogged with gold, his legs clad in high jackboots, and on his head the dress helmet of an illustrious Prussian regiment.

'Englishman!' Despite the disguise, Herman recognized him. He had finally succeeded in unbuttoning the flap of his holster, and now he withdrew his Luger. 'Englishman!' He repeated the insult and lifted the pistol.

With the quickness of mind for which he was noted, Sebastian sat bewildered by this unforeseen turn of events, but when Herman showed him the working end of the Luger, he realized that it was time to take his leave, and he attempted to leap nimbly to his feet. However, the spurs on his boots became entangled once more and he went backwards over the stool. The bullet hissed harmlessly through the empty space where he would have been standing.

'God damn!' Herman fired again, and the bullet kicked a burst of splinters out of the heavy wooden stool behind which Sebastian was lying. This second failure aroused in Herman Fleischer the blinding rage which spoiled his aim for the next two shots he fired, as Sebastian went on hands and knees around the corner of the nearest hut.

Behind the hut, Sebastian jumped to his feet and set off at a run. His main concern was to get out of the village and into the bush. In his ears echoed Flynn O'Flynn's advice.

'Make for the river. Go straight for the river.'

And he was so occupied with it that, when he charged around the side of the next hut, he could not check himself in time to avoid collision with one of Herman Fleischer's Askari, who was coming in the opposite direction. Both of them went down together in an untidy heap, and the steel helmet fell forward over Sebastian's eyes. As he struggled into a sitting position, he removed the helmet and found the man's woolly black head in front of him. It was ideally placed and Sebastian was holding the heavy helmet above it. With the strength of both his arms, he brought the helmet down again, and it clanged loudly against the Askari's skull. With a grunt the Askari sagged backwards and lay quietly in the dust. Sebastian placed the helmet over his sleeping face, picked up the man's rifle from beside him and got to his feet once more.

He stood crouching in the shelter of the hut while he tried to make sense of the chaos around him. Through the pandemonium set up by the panic-stricken villagers, who were milling about with all the purpose of a flock of sheep attacked by wolves, Sebastian could hear the bellowed commands of Herman Fleischer, and the answering shots of the German Askari. Rifle-fire cracked and whined, to be answered by renewed outbursts of screaming.

Sebastian's first impulse was to hide in one of the huts but he realized this would be futile. At the best it would only delay his capture.

No, he must get out of the village. But the thought of covering the hundred yards of open ground to the shelter of the nearest trees, while a dozen Askari shot at him, was most unattractive.

At this moment Sebastian became aware of an unpleasant warmth in his feet, and he looked down to find that he was standing in the live ashes of a cooking fire. The leather of his jackboots was already beginning to char and smoke. He stepped back hurriedly, and the smell of burning leather acted as a laxative for the constipation of his brain.

From the hut beside him he snatched a handful of thatch and stooped to thrust it into the fire. The dry grass burst into flame, and Sebastian held the torch to the wall of the hut. Instantly fire bloomed and shot upwards. With the torch in his hand, Sebastian ducked across the narrow opening to the next hut and set fire to that also.

'Son of a gun!' exulted Sebastian as great oily billows of smoke obscured the sun and limited his field of vision to ten paces.

Slowly he moved forward in the rolling cloud of smoke, setting fire to each hut he passed, and delighting in the frustrated bellows of Germanic rage he heard about him. Occasionally ghostly figures scampered past him in the acrid half-darkness but none of them paid him the slightest attention, and each time Sebastian relaxed the pressure of his forefinger on the trigger of the Mauser, and moved on.

He reached the last hut and paused there to gather himself for the final sprint across open ground to the edge of the millet garden. Through the eddying bank of smoke, the mass of dark green vegetation from which he had fled in terror not many hours before, now seemed as welcoming as the arms of his mother.

Movement near him in the smoke, and he swung the Mauser to cover it; he saw the square outline of a kepi and the sparkle of metal buttons, and his finger tightened on the trigger.

'Manali!'

'Mohammed! Good God, I nearly killed you.' Sebastian threw up the rifle barrel as he recognized him.

'Quickly! They are close behind me.' Mohammed snatched at his arm and dragged him forward. The jackboots pinched his toes and thumped like the hooves of a galloping buffalo as Sebastian ran. From the huts behind them a voice shouted urgently and, immediately afterwards, came the vicious crack of a Mauser and the shrill whinny of the ricochet.

Sebastian had a lead of ten paces on Mohammed as he plunged into the bank of leaves and millet stalks.

29

'What should we do now, Manali?' Mohammed asked, and the expression on the faces of the two other men echoed the question with pathetic trust. A benevolent chance had reunited Sebastian with the remnants of his command. During the flight through the millet gardens, with random rifle-fire clipping the leaves about their heads, Sebastian had literally fallen over these two. At the time they were engaged in pressing their bellies and their faces hard against the earth, and it had taken a number of lusty kicks with the jackboot to get them up and moving.

Since then Sebastian, mindful of Flynn's advice, had cautiously and circuitously led them down to the landing-place on the bank of the Rovuma. He arrived to find that Fleischer's Askari, by using the direct route and without the necessity of concealing themselves, had arrived before him. From the cover of the reed-banks Sebastian watched dejectedly, as they used an axe to knock the bottoms out of the dug-out canoes that were drawn up on the little white beach.

'Can we swim across?' he asked Mohammed in a whisper, and Mohammed's face crumpled with horror, as he considered the suggestion. Both of them peered out through the reeds across a quarter of a mile of deep water that flowed so fast, its surface was dimpled with tiny whirlpools.

'No,' said Mohammed with finality.

'Too far?' asked Sebastian hopelessly.

'Too far. Too fast. Too deep. Too many crocodiles,' agreed Mohammed, and in an unspoken, but mutual desire to get away from the river and the Askari, they crawled out of the reed-bank and crept away inland.

In the late afternoon they were lying up in a bushy gully about two miles from the river and an equal distance from M'topo's village.

'What should we do now, Manali?' Mohammed repeated his question, and Sebastian cleared his throat before answering.

'Well . . .' he said, and paused while his wide brow wrinkled in the agony of creative thought. Then it came to him with all the splendour of a sunrise. 'We'll just jolly well have to find some other way of getting across the river.' He said it with the air of a man well pleased with his own perspicacity. 'What do you suggest, Mohammed.'

A little surprised to find the ball returned so neatly into his own court, Mohammed remained silent.

'A raft?' hazarded Sebastian. The lack of tools, materials, and opportunity to build one was so obvious, that Mohammed did not deign to reply. He shook his head.

'No,' agreed Sebastian. 'Perhaps you are right.' Again the classic beauty of his features was marred by a scowl of concentration. At last he demanded, 'There are other villages along the river?'

'Yes,' Mohammed conceded. 'But the Askari will visit each of them and destroy the canoes. Also they will tell the headmen who we are, and threaten them with the rope.'

'But they cannot cover the whole river. It has a frontier of five or six hundred miles. We'll just keep walking until we find a canoe. It may take us a long time but we'll find one eventually.'

'If the Askari don't catch us first.'

'They'll expect us to stay close to the border. We'll make a detour well inland, and march for five or six days before we come back to the river again. We'll rest now and move tonight.'

Heading on a diagonal line of march away from the Rovuma and deeper into German territory, moving north-west along a well defined footpath, the four of them kept walking all that night. As the slow hours passed the pace flagged and twice Sebastian noticed one or other of his men wander off the path at an angle until suddenly they started and looked about in surprise, before hurrying back to join the others. It puzzled him and he meant to ask them what they were doing, but he was tired and the effort of speech was too great. An hour later he found the reason for their behaviour.

Plodding along with the movement of his legs become completely automatic, Sebastian was slowly overcome by a state of gentle well-being. He surrendered to it and let the warm, dark mists of oblivion wash over his mind.

The sting of a thorn branch across his cheek jerked him back to consciousness and he looked about in bewilderment. Ten yards away on his flank, Mohammed and the two gun-boys walked along the path in single file, their faces turned towards him with expressions of mild interest in the moonlight. It took some moments for Sebastian to realize that he had fallen asleep on his feet. Feeling a complete ass, he trotted back to take his place at the head of the line.

When the fat silver moon sank below the trees, they kept going by the faint glow of reflected light, but slowly that waned until the footpath hardly showed at their feet. Sebastian decided that dawn could be only an hour away and it was time to halt. He stopped and was about to speak when Mohammed's clutching hand on his shoulder prevented him.

'Manali!' There was a tone in Mohammed's whisper that cautioned him, and Sebastian felt his nerves jerk taut.

'What is it?' he breathed, protectively unslinging the Mauser.

'Look. There–ahead of us.'

Screwing up his eyes Sebastian searched the blackness ahead, and it was a long time before the faint ruddiness in the solid blanket of darkness registered itself upon the exhausted retinas of his eyes. 'Yes!' he whispered. 'What is it?'

'A fire,' breathed Mohammed. 'There is someone camped across the path in front of us.'

'Askari?' asked Sebastian.

'Perhaps.'

Peering at the ruby puddle of dying coals, Sebastian felt the hair on the back of his neck stir and come erect with alarm. He was fully awake now. 'We must go around them.'

'No. They will see our spoor in the dust of the path and they will follow us,' Mohammed demurred.

'What then?'

'First let me see how many there are.'

Without waiting for Sebastian's permission, Mohammed slipped away and disappeared into the night like a leopard. Five anxious minutes Sebastian waited. Once he thought he heard a scuffling sound but he was not certain. Mohammed's shape materialized again beside him. 'Ten of them,' he reported. 'Two Askari and eight bearers. One of the Askari sat guard by the fire. He saw me, so I killed him.'

'Good God!' Sebastian's voice rose higher. 'You did what?'

'I killed him. But do not speak so loud.'

'How?'

'With my knife.'

'Why?'

'Lest he kill me first.'

'And the other?'

'Him also.'

'You killed both of them?' Sebastian was appalled.

'Yes, and took their rifles. Now it is safe to go on. But the bearers have with them many cases. It comes to me that this party follows after Bwana Intambu, the German commissioner, and that they carry with them all his goods.'

'But you shouldn't have killed them,' protested Sebastian. 'You could have just tied them up or something.'

'Manali, you argue like a woman,' Mohammed snapped impatiently, and then went on with his original line of thought. 'Among the cases is one that by its size I think is the box for the tax money. The one Askari slept with his back against it as though to give it special care.'

'The tax money?'

'Yes.'

'Well, son of a gun!' Sebastian's scruples dissolved and in the darkness his expression was suddenly transformed into that of a small boy on Christmas morning.

They woke the German bearers by standing over them and prodding them with the rifle barrels. Then they hustled them out of their blankets and herded them into a small group, bewildered and shivering miserably in the chill of dawn. Wood was heaped on the fire; it burned up brightly, and by its light Sebastian examined the booty.

The one Askari had bled profusely from the throat on to the small wooden chest. Mohammed took him by the heels and dragged him out of the way, then used his blanket to wipe the chest clean.

'Manali,' he said with reverence. 'See the big lock. See the bird of the Kaiser painted on the lid . . .' He stooped over the chest and took a grip of the handles, '. . . but most of all, feel the weight of it!'

Among the other equipment around the fire, Mohammed found a thick coil of one-inch manila rope. A commodity which was essential equipment on any of Herman Fleischer's safaris. With it, Mohammed roped the bearers together, at waist level, allowing enough line between each of them to make concerted movement possible but preventing individual flight.

'Why are you doing that?' Sebastian asked with interest, through a mouthful of blood sausage and black bread. Most of the other boxes were filled with food, and Sebastian was breakfasting well and heartily.

'So they cannot escape.'

'We're not taking them with us–are we?'

'Who else will carry all this?' Mohammed asked patiently.

Five days later Sebastian was seated in the bows of a long dug-out canoe, with the charred soles of his boots set firmly on the chest that lay in the bilges. He was eating with relish a thick sandwich of polony and pickled onions, wearing a change of clean underwear and socks that were a few sizes too large, and there was clutched in his left hand an open bottle of Hansa beer–all these with the courtesy of Commissioner Fleischer.

The paddlers were singing with unforced gaiety, for the hiring fee that Sebastian had paid them would buy each of them a new wife at least.

Hugging the bank of the Rovuma on the Portuguese side, driven on by willing paddles and the eager current, in twelve hours they covered the distance that had taken Sebastian and his heavily-laden bearers five days on foot.

The canoe deposited Sebastian's party at the landing opposite M'topo's village, only ten miles from Lalapanzi. They walked that distance without resting and arrived after nightfall.

30

The windows of the bungalow were darkened, and the whole camp slept. After cautioning them to silence, Sebastian drew his depleted band up on the front lawn with the tax chest set prominently in front of them. He was proud of his success and wanted to achieve the appropriate mood for his home-coming. Having set the stage, he went up on to the stoep of the bungalow and tip-toed towards the front door with the intention of awakening the household by hammering upon it dramatically.

However, there was a chair on the stoep, and Sebastian tripped over it. He fell heavily. The chair clattered and the rifle slipped from his shoulder and rang on the stone flags.

Before Sebastian could recover his feet, the door was flung open and through it appeared Flynn O'Flynn in his night-shirt and armed with a double-barrelled shotgun. 'Caught you, you bastard!' he roared and lifted the shotgun.

Sebastian heard the click of the safety-catch and scrambled to his knees.

'Don't shoot! Flynn, it's me.'

The shotgun wavered a little. 'Who are you–and what do you want?'

'It's me–Sebastian.'

'Bassie?' Flynn lowered the shotgun uncertainly. 'It can't be. Stand up, let's have a look at you.'

Sebastian obeyed with alacrity.

'Good God,' Flynn swore in amazement. 'It *is* you. Good God! We heard that Fleischer caught you at M'topo's village a week ago. We heard he'd nobbled you for keeps!' He came forward with his right hand extended in welcome. 'You made it, did you? Well done, Bassie boy.'

Before Bassie could accept Flynn's hand, Rosa came through the doorway, brushed past Flynn, and almost knocked Sebastian down again. With her arms locked around his chest and her cheek pressed to his unshaven cheek, she kept repeating, 'You're safe! Oh Sebastian, you're safe.'

Acutely aware of the fact that Rosa wore nothing under the thin night-gown, and that everywhere he put his hands they came in contact with thinly-veiled warm flesh, Sebastian grinned sheepishly at Flynn over his shoulder.

'Excuse me,' he said.

His first two kisses were off target for she was moving around a lot. One caught her on the ear, the next on her eyebrow, but the third was right between the lips.

When at last they were forced to separate or suffocate, Rosa gasped, 'I thought you were dead.'

'All right, missie,' growled Flynn. 'You can go and put some clothes on now.'

Breakfast at Lalapanzi that morning was a festive affair. Flynn took advantage of his daughter's weakened condition and brought a bottle of gin to the table. Her protests were half-hearted, and later with her own hands she poured a little into Sebastian's tea to brace it.

They ate on the stoep in golden sunshine that filtered through the bougainvillaea creeper. A flock of glossy starlings hopped and chirruped on the lawns, and an oriel sang from the wild fig trees. All nature conspired to make Sebastian's victory feast a success, while Rosa and Nanny did their best from the kitchen–drawing upon the remains of Herman Fleischer's supplies that Sebastian had brought home with him.

Flynn O'Flynn's eyes were bloodshot and underhung with plum-coloured pouches, for he had been up all night counting the contents of the German tax chest and working out his accounts by the light of a hurricane lamp. Nevertheless, he was in a merry mood made merrier by the cups of fortified tea on which he was breakfasting. He joined warmly in the chorus of praise and felicitation to Sebastian Oldsmith that was being sung by Rosa O'Flynn.

'You turned up one for the book, so help me, Bassie,' he chortled at the end of the meal. 'I'd just love to hear how Fleischer is going to explain this one to Governor Schee. Oh, I'd love to be there when he tells him about the tax money–son of a gun, it'll nigh kill them both.'

'While you're on the subject of the money,' Rosa smiled at Flynn, 'have you worked out how much Sebastian's share comes to, Daddy?' Rosa only used Flynn's paternal title when she was extremely well-disposed towards him.

'That I have,' admitted Flynn, and the sudden shiftiness of his eyes aroused Rosa's suspicions. Her lips pursed a little.

'And how much is it?' she asked in the syrupy tone which Flynn recognized as the equivalent of the blood roar of a wounded lioness.

'Sure now, and who wants to be spoiling a lovely day with the talking of business?' Under pressure, Flynn exaggerated the brogue in his voice in the hope that Rosa would find it beguiling. A forlorn hope.

'How much?' demanded Rosa, and he told her.

There was a sickly silence. Sebastian paled under his sunburn and opened his mouth to protest. On the strength of his half share, he had the previous night made to Rosa O'Flynn a serious proposal, which she had accepted.

'Leave this to me, Sebastian,' she whispered and laid a restraining hand on his knees as she turned back to her father. 'You'll let us have a look at the accounts, won't you?' Still syrupy sweet.

'Sure and I will. They're all straight and square.'

The document that Flynn O'Flynn produced under the main heading, 'Joint Venture Between F. O'Flynn, Esq., S. Oldsmith, Esq., and Others. German East Africa. Period May 15th, 1913, to August 21st, 1913', showed that he belonged to an unorthodox school of accountancy.

The contents of the tax chest had been converted to English sterling at the rates laid down by Pear's Almanac for 1893. Flynn set great store by this particular publication.

From the gross proceeds of £4,652 18*s* 6*d*, Flynn had deducted his own fifty per cent share and the ten per cent of the other partners–the Portuguese Chef D'Post and the Governor of Mozambique. From the balance he had then deducted the losses incurred on the Rufiji expedition (for which see separate account addressed to German East African Administration). From there he had gone on to charge the expenses of the second expedition, not forgetting such items as:

To L. Parbhoo (Tailor)	£15 10 –
To One German Dress Helmet (say)	£5 10 –
To Five Uniforms (Askari) at £2 10–each	£12 10 –
To Five Mauser Rifles at £10––each	£50 – –
To Six Hundred and Twenty-Five Rounds 7mm Ammunition	£22 10 –
To Advance re travelling expenses, One Hundred Escudos made to S. Oldsmith, Esq.	£1 5 –

Finally, Sebastian's half share of the net losses amounted to a little under twenty pounds.

'Don't worry,' Flynn assured him magnanimously. 'I don't expect you to pay it now–we'll just deduct it from your share of the profits of the next expedition.'

'But, Flynn, I thought you said–well, I mean, you told me I had a half share.'

'And so you have, Bassie, and so you have.'

'You said we were equal partners.'

'You must have misunderstood me, boy. I said a half share–and that means after expenses. It's just a great pity there was such a large accumulated loss to bring forward.'

While they discussed this, Rosa was busy with a stub of indelible pencil on the reverse side of Flynn's account. Two minutes later she thrust the result across the breakfast table at Flynn. She said, 'And that's the way I work it out.'

Rosa O'Flynn was a student of the 'One-for-you-one-for-me' school, and her reckonings were much simpler than those of her father.

With a cry of anguish, Flynn O'Flynn lodged objection. 'You don't understand business.'

'But I recognize crookery when I see it,' Rosa flashed back.

'You'd call your old father a crook?'

'Yes.'

'I've a damn good mind to take the kiboko to you. You're not too big and uppity that I can't warm your tail up good.'

'You just try it!' said Rosa, and Flynn backpedalled.

'Anyway, what would Bassie do with all that money? It's not good for a youngster. It would spoil him.'

'He'd marry me with it. That's what he'd do with it.'

Flynn made a noise as though there was a fish-bone stuck in his throat, his face mottled over with emotion, and he swung ominously in Sebastian's direction. 'So!' he rasped. 'I thought so!'

'Now steady on, old chap,' Sebastian tried to soothe him.

'You come into my home and act like the king of bloody England. You try to fraudulently embezzle my money–but that's not enough! Oh no! That's not a bloody 'nough. You've also got to start tampering with my daughter just to round things off.'

'Don't be coarse,' said Rosa.

'That's rich–*don't be coarse,* she says, and just what exactly have you two been up to behind my back?'

Sebastian stood up from the breakfast table with dignity. 'I will not have you speak so of a lady in my presence, sir. Especially of the lady who has done me the great honour of consenting to become my wife.' He began unbuttoning his jacket. 'Will you step into the garden with me, and give me satisfaction?'

'Come along, then.' As Flynn lumbered out of his chair he made as if to pass Sebastian, but at the moment Sebastian's arms were behind him, still bound by the sleeves of his jacket as he attempted to shrug it off. Flynn side-stepped swiftly, paused a moment as he took his aim, and then drove his left fist into Sebastian's stomach.

'Oof!' said Sebastian, and leaned forward involuntarily to meet Flynn's other fist as it came up from the level of his knees. It took Sebastian between the eyes, and he changed direction abruptly and ran backwards across the veranda. The low wooden railing caught him behind the knees and he toppled slowly into the flower-beds below the stoep.

'You've killed him,' wailed Rosa, and picked up the heavy china tea-pot.

'I hope so,' said Flynn, and ducked as the pot flew towards his head, passed over it, and burst against the wall of the stoep, spraying tea and steam.

There was an ominous stirring among Rosa's flowers, and presently Sebastian's head emerged with blue hydrangea petals festively strewn in his hair and the skin around both eyes fast swelling and chameleoning to a creditable match with the petals. 'I say, Flynn. That wasn't fair,' he announced.

'He wasn't looking,' Rosa accused. 'You hit him before he was ready.'

'Well, he's looking now,' roared Flynn and went down the veranda stairs like a charging hippopotamus. From the hydrangeas, Sebastian rose to meet him and took up the classic stance of the ring fighter. 'Marquis of Queensberry rules?' he cautioned as Flynn closed in.

Flynn signified his rejection of the Marquis' code by kicking Sebastian on the shin. Sebastian yelped and hopped one-legged out of the flower-bed, while Flynn pursued him with a further series of lusty kicks. Placing his boot twice in succession into Sebastian's posterior, the third kick, however, missed and the force behind it was sufficient to throw Flynn on to his back. He sprawled on the lawn, and the pause while he scrambled to his knees, gave Sebastian respite to ready himself for the next round.

Both his eyes had puffed and he was experiencing discomfort from his rear end; nevertheless, he stood once again with his left arm extended and the right crossed over his chest. Glancing beyond Flynn, Sebastian saw his fiancée descending from the veranda. She was armed with a bread-knife.

'Rosa!' Sebastian was alarmed. It was clear that Rosa would not stop at patricide to protect her love. 'Rosa! What are you doing with that knife?'

'I'm going to stick him with it!'

'You'll do no such thing,' said Sebastian, but Flynn did not have the same faith in his daughter's restraint. Very hurriedly, he moved into a defensive position behind Sebastian. From there he listened with attention to the argument between Sebastian and Rosa. It took a full minute for Sebastian to persuade Rosa that her assistance was not necessary and that he was capable of handling the situation on his own. Reluctantly, Rosa retreated to the veranda.

'Thanks, Bassie,' said Flynn, and kicked him in his already bruised behind. It was extremely painful.

Very few people had ever seen Sebastian Oldsmith lose his temper. The last time it had happened was eight years previously; the two sixth-formers who had invoked it by forcing Sebastian's head into a toilet bowl and flushing the cistern, were both hospitalized for a short period.

This time there were more witnesses. Attracted by the cries and crash of breaking crockery, Flynn's entire following, including Mohammed and his Askari, had arrived from the compound and were assembled at the top of the lawn. They watched in breathless wonder.

From the grandstand of the veranda, Rosa, her eyes sparkling with that strange feminine ferocity that arises in even the mildest women when their man fights for them, exhorted Sebastian to even greater violence.

Like all great storms, it did not last long, and when it was over the silence was appalling. Flynn lay stretched full-length on the lawn. His eyes closed and his breathing snoring softly in his throat, and bursting from his nose in a froth of red bubbles.

Mohammed and five of his men carried him towards the bungalow. He lay massive on their shoulders with the bulge of his belly rising and falling softly, and an expression of unusual peace on his bloody face.

Standing alone on the lawn, Sebastian's features were contorted with savagery and his whole body shook as though he was in high fever. Then, watching them carry the huge, inert body, suddenly Sebastian's mood was past. His expression changed first to concern and then to gentle dismay. 'I say . . .' his voice was husky and he took a pace after them. 'You shouldn't have kicked me.' His hands opened helplessly, and he lifted them in a gesture of appeal. 'You shouldn't have done it.'

Rosa came down from the veranda and walked slowly towards him. She stopped and looked up at him, half in awe, half in glowing pride. 'You were magnificent,' she whispered. 'Like a lion.' She reached up with both arms around his neck, and before she kissed him she spoke again. 'I love you,' she said.

Sebastian had very little luggage to take with him. He was wearing everything he possessed. Rosa on the other hand, had boxes of it, enough to give full employment to the dozen bearers that were assembled on the lawn in front of the bungalow.

'Well,' murmured Sebastian, 'I suppose we should start moving.'

'Yes,' whispered Rosa, and looked at the gardens of Lalapanzi. Although she had suggested this departure, now that the time had come she was uncertain. This place had been her home since childhood. Here she had spun a cocoon that had shielded and protected her, and now that the time had come to emerge from it, she was afraid. She took Sebastian's arm, drawing strength from him.

'Don't you want to say goodbye to your father?' Sebastian looked down at her with the tender protectiveness that was such a new and delightful sensation for him.

Rosa hesitated a moment, and then realized that it would take very little to weaken her resolve. Her dutiful affection for Flynn, which at the moment was submerged beneath the tide of anger and resentment, could easily re-emerge should Flynn employ a little of his celebrated blarney. 'No,' she said.

'I suppose it's best,' Sebastian agreed. He glanced guiltily towards the bungalow where Flynn was, presumably, still lying in state–attended by the faithful Mohammed. 'But do you think he'll be all right? I mean, I did hit him rather hard, you know.'

'He'll be all right,' Rosa said without conviction, and tugged at his sleeve. Together they moved to take their places at the head of the little column of bearers.

Kneeling on the floor of the bedroom, below the window sill, peering with one swollen eye through a slit in the curtain, Flynn saw this decisive move. 'My God,' he whispered in concern. 'The young idiots are really leaving.'

Rosa O'Flynn was his last link with that frail little Portuguese girl. The one person in his life that Flynn had truly loved. Now that he was about to lose her also, Flynn was suddenly aware of his feelings for his daughter. The prospect of never seeing her again filled him with dismay.

As for Sebastian Oldsmith, here no sentiment clouded his reasoning. Sebastian was a valuable business asset. Through him, Flynn could put into operation a number of schemes that he had shelved as involving disproportionate personal risk. In these last few years Flynn had become increasingly aware of the depreciation that time and large quantities of raw spirit had wrought in his eyes and legs and nerves. Sebastian Oldsmith had eyes like a fish eagle, legs like a prize fighter, and no nerves at all that Flynn could discern. Flynn needed him.

Flynn opened his mouth and groaned. It was the throaty death rattle of an old bull buffalo. Peering through the curtain, Flynn grinned as he saw the young couple freeze, and stand tense and still in the sunlight. Their faces were turned towards the bungalow, and in spite of himself, Flynn had to admit they made a handsome pair; Sebastian tall above her with the body of a gladiator and the face of a poet; Rosa small beside him but with the full bosom and wide hips of womanhood. The slippery black cascade of her hair glowed in the sun, and her dark eyes were big with concern.

Flynn groaned again but softly this time. A breathless, husky sound, the last breath of a dying man, and instantly Rosa and Sebastian were running towards the bungalow. Her skirts gathered up above her knees, long legs flying, Rosa led Sebastian up on to the veranda.

Flynn had just sufficient time to return to his bed and compose his limbs and his face into the attitude of one fast sinking towards the abyss.

'Daddy!' Rosa leaned over him, and Flynn opened his eyes uncertainly. For a moment he did not seem to recognize her, then he whispered, 'My little girl,' so faintly she hardly caught the words.

'Oh, Daddy, what is it?' She knelt beside him.

'My heart.' His hand crawled up like a hairy spider across his belly and clutched weakly at his hairy chest. 'Like a knife. A hot knife.'

There was a terrible silence in the room, and then Flynn spoke again. 'I wanted to . . . give you my . . . blessing. I wish happiness for you . . . wherever you go.' The effort of speech was too much, and for a while he lay gasping. 'Think of your old Daddy sometimes. Say a prayer for him.'

A fat, shiny tear broke from the corner of Rosa's eye and slid down her cheek.

'Bassie, my boy.' Slowly Flynn's eyes sought him, found him, and focused with difficulty. 'Don't blame yourself for this. I was an old man anyway–I've had my life.' He panted a little and then went on painfully. 'Look after her. Look after my little Rosa. You are my son now. I've never had a son.'

'I didn't know . . . I had no idea that your heart . . . Flynn, I'm dreadfully sorry. Forgive me.'

Flynn smiled, a brave little smile that just touched his lips. He lifted his hand weakly and held it out towards Sebastian. While Sebastian clasped his hand, Flynn considered offering him the money that had been the cause of the dispute as a dying man's gift but he manfully restrained himself from such extravagance. Instead he whispered, 'I would like to have seen my grandson, but no matter. Goodbye, my boy.'

'You'll see him, Flynn. I promise you that. We'll stay, won't we, Rosa? We'll stay with him.'

'Yes, we'll stay,' said Rosa. 'We won't leave you, Daddy.'

'My children.' Flynn sank back and closed his eyes. Thank God, he hadn't offered the money. A peaceful little smile hovered around his mouth. 'You've made an old man very happy.'

31

Flynn made a strong come-back from the edge of death, so strong, in fact, that it aroused Rosa's suspicions. However, she let it pass for she was happy to have avoided the necessity of leaving Lalapanzi. In addition, there was another matter which was taking up a lot of her attention.

Since she had said goodbye to Sebastian at the start of his tax tour, Rosa had been aware of the cessation of certain womanly functions of her body. She consulted Nanny who, in turn, consulted the local nangane who, in his turn, opened the belly of a chicken, and consulted its entrails. His findings were conclusive, and Nanny reported back to Rosa, without disclosing the source of her information, for Little Long Hair had an almost blasphemous lack of faith in the occult.

Delighted, Rosa took Sebastian for a walk down the valley, and they reached the waterfall where it had all began, she stood on tip-toe, put both arms around his neck, and whispered in his ear. She had to repeat herself for her voice was muffled with breathless laughter.

'You're joking,' gasped Sebastian, and then blushed bright crimson.

'I'm not, you know.'

'Good grief,' said Sebastian; and then, groping for something more expressive, 'Son of a gun!'

'Aren't you pleased?' Rosa pouted playfully. 'I did it for you.'

'But we aren't even married.'

'That can be arranged.'

'And quickly, too,' agreed Sebastian. He grabbed her wrist. 'Come on!'

'Sebastian, remember my condition.'

'Good grief, I'm sorry.'

He took her back to Lalapanzi, handing her over the rough ground with as much care as though she was a case of sweating gelignite.

'What's the big hurry?' asked Flynn jovially at dinner that evening. 'I've got a little job for Bassie first. I want him to slip across the river . . .'

'No, you don't,' said Rosa. 'We're going to see the priest at Beira.'

'It would only take Bassie a couple of weeks. Then we could talk about it when he gets back.'

'We are going to Beira–tomorrow!'

'What's the rush?' Flynn asked again.

'Well, the truth is, Flynn, old boy . . .' Wriggling in his chair, colouring up vividly, Sebastian relapsed into silence.

'The truth is I'm going to have a baby,' Rosa finished for him.

'You're *what*?!' Flynn stared at her in horror.

'You said that you wanted to see your grandchild,' Rosa pointed out.

'But I didn't mean you to start work on it right away,' roared Flynn, and he rounded on Sebastian. 'You dirty young bugger!'

'Father, your heart!' Rosa restrained him. 'Anyway, don't pick on Sebastian, I did my share as well.'

'You shameless . . . You brazen little . . .'

Rosa reached behind the seat cushion where Flynn had hidden the gin bottle. 'Have a little of this–it will help calm you.'

They left for Beira the following morning. Rosa was carried in a maschille with Sebastian trotting beside it in anxious attendance, ready to help ease the litter over the fords and rough places, and to curse any of the bearers who stumbled.

When they left Lalapanzi, Flynn O'Flynn brought up the rear of the column, lying in his maschille with a square-faced bottle for company, scowling and muttering darkly about 'fornication' and 'sin'.

But both Rosa and Sebastian ignored him, and when they camped that night the two of them sat across the camp-fire from him, and whispered and laughed secretly together. They pitched their voices at such a tantalizing level that even by straining his ears, Flynn could not overhear their conversation. It infuriated him to such an extent that finally he made a loud remark about '. . . beating the hell out of the person who had repaid his hospitality by violating his daughter'.

Rosa said that she would give anything to see him try it *again*. In her opinion it would be better than a visit to the circus. And Flynn gathered his dignity and his gin bottle and stalked away to where Mohammed had laid out his bedding under a lean-to of thorn bushes.

During the dark hours before dawn they were visited by an old lion. He came with a rush from the darkness beyond the fire-light, grunting like an angry boar, the great black bush of his mane erect, snaking with incredible speed towards the huddle of blanket-wrapped figures about the fire.

Flynn was the only one not asleep. He had waited all night, watching Sebastian's reclining figure; just waiting for him to move across to the temporary thorn-bush shelter that gave Rosa privacy. Lying beside Flynn was his shotgun, double-loaded with big loopers, lion shot, and he had every intention of using it.

When the lion charged into the camp, Flynn sat up quickly and fired both barrels of the shotgun at point-blank range into the man-eater's head and chest, killing it instantly. But the momentum of its rush bowled it forward, sent it sliding full into Sebastian, and both of them rolled into the camp-fire.

Sebastian awoke to lion noises, and gunfire, and the violent collision of a big body into his, and red-hot coals sticking to various parts of his anatomy. With a single bound, and a wild cry, he threw off his blanket, came to his feet, and went into a such a lively song and dance routine, yodelling and high-kicking, and striking out at his imaginary assailants that Flynn was reduced to a jelly of helpless laughter.

The laughter, and the praise and thanks showered on him by Sebastian, Rosa, and the bearers, cleared the air.

'You saved my life,' said Sebastian soulfully.

'Oh Daddy, you're wonderful,' said Rosa. 'Thank you. Thank you,' and she hugged him.

The mantle of the hero felt snug and comfortable on Flynn's shoulders. He became almost human–and the improvement continued as each day's march brought him closer to the little Portuguese port of Beira, for Flynn greatly enjoyed his rare visits to civilization.

The last night they camped a mile from the outskirts of the town, and after a private conference with Flynn, old Mohammed went ahead armed with a small purse of escudos to make the arrangements for Flynn's formal entry on the morrow.

Flynn was up with the dawn, and while he shaved with care, and dressed in clean moleskin jacket and trousers, one of the bearers polished his boots with hippo fat, and two others scaled the tall bottle palm tree near the camp and cut fronds from its head.

All things being ready, Flynn ascended his maschille and lay back elegantly on the leopard-skin rugs. On each side of Flynn a bearer took his position, armed with a palm-frond, and began to fan him gently. Behind Flynn, in single file, followed other servants bearing tusks in ivory and the still-green lion skin. Behind this, with instructions from Flynn not to draw undue attention to themselves, followed Sebastian and Rosa, and the baggage bearers.

With a languid gesture such as might have been used by Nero to signal the start of a Roman circus, Flynn gave the order to move.

Along the rough road through the thick coastal bush, they came at last to Beira and entered the main street in procession.

'Good Lord,' Sebastian expressed his surprise when he saw the reception that awaited them, 'where did they all come from?'

Both sides of the street were lined with cheering crowds, mainly natives, but with here and there a Portuguese or an Indian trader come out of his shop to find the cause of the disturbance.

'Fini!' chanted the crowd, clapping their hands in unison. 'Bwana Mkuba! Great Lord! Slayer of elephant. Killer of lions!'

'I didn't realize that Flynn was so well regarded.' Sebastian was impressed.

'Most of them have never heard of him,' Rosa disillusioned him. 'He sent Mohammed in last night to gather a claque of about a hundred or so. Pays them one escudo each to come and cheer–they make so much noise that the entire population turns out to see what is going on. They fall for it every time.'

'What on earth does he go to so much trouble for?'

'Because he enjoys it. Just look at him!'

Lying in his maschille, graciously acknowledging the applause. Flynn was very obviously loving every minute of it.

The head of the procession reached the only hotel in Beira and halted. Madame da Souza, the portly, well-moustached widow who was the proprietress of the hotel, rushed down to welcome Flynn with a smacking kiss and usher him ceremoniously through the shabby portals. Flynn was the kind of customer she had always dreamed about.

When Rosa and Sebastian at last fought their way through the crowd into the hotel, Flynn was already seated at the bar counter and half-way through a tall glass of Laurentia beer. The man sitting on the stool beside his was the Governor of Mozambique's aide-de-camp, who had come to deliver His Excellency's invitation for Flynn O'Flynn to dine at Government House that evening. It was settlement day in the partnership of 'Flynn O'Flynn and Others'. His Excellency José De Clare Don Felezardo da Silva Marques had received from Governor Schee, in Dar es Salaam, an agitated report, in the form of an official protest and an extradition demand, of the success of the partnership's operations during the last few months–and His Excellency was delighted to see Flynn.

In fact, so pleased was His Excellency with the progress of the partnership's affairs, that he exercised his authority to waive the formalities required by law to precede a marriage under Portuguese jurisdiction. This saved a week, and the afternoon after their arrival in Beira, Rosa and Sebastian stood before the altar in the stucco and thatch cathedral, while Sebastian tried with little success to remember enough of his schoolroom Latin to understand just what he was getting himself into.

The wedding veil, that had belonged to Rosa's mother, was yellowed by many years of storage under tropical conditions, but it served well enough to keep off the flies which were always bad during the hot season in Beira.

Towards the end of the long ceremony, Flynn was so overcome by the heat, the gin he had taken at lunch, and an unusually fine flood of Irish feeling, that he began snuffling loudly. While he mopped at his eyes and nose with a grubby handkerchief, the Governor's aide-de-camp patted his shoulder soothingly and murmured encouragement.

The priest declared them husband and wife, and the congregation launched into a faltering rendition of the *Te Deum*. His voice quivering with emotion and alcohol, Flynn kept repeating, 'My little girl, my poor little girl.' Rosa lifted her veil and turned to Sebastian who immediately forgot his misgivings as to the form of the ceremony, and enfolded her enthusiastically in his arms.

Still maintaining his chorus of 'My little girl', Flynn was led away by the aide-de-camp to the hotel where the proprietress had prepared the wedding feast. In deference to Flynn O'Flynn's mood this started on a sombre note but as the champagne, which Madame da Souza had specially bottled the previous evening, started to do its work, so the tempo changed. Among his other actions, Flynn gave Sebastian a wedding present of ten pounds and poured a full glass of beer over the aide-de-camp's head.

When, later that evening, Rosa and Sebastian slipped away to the bridal suite above the bar, Flynn was giving lusty tongue in the chorus of 'They are jolly good fellows', Madame da Souza was seated on his lap, and over-flowing it in all directions. Every time Flynn pinched her posterior, great gusts of laughter made her shake like a stranded jellyfish.

Later the pleasure of Rosa and Sebastian's wedding-bed was disturbed by the fact that, in the bar-room directly below them, Flynn O'Flynn was shooting the bottles off the shelves with a double-barrelled elephant rifle. Every direct hit was greeted by thunderous applause from the other guests. Madame da Souza, still palpitating with laughter, sat in a corner of the bar-room dutifully making such entries in her notebook as, 'One bottle of Grandino London Dry Gin 14.50 escudos; one bottle Grandino French Cognac Five Star 14.50 escudos; one bottle Grandino Scotch whisky 30.00 escudos; 1 magnum Grandino French Champagne 75.90 escudos.' 'Grandino' was the brand-name of the house, and signified that the liquor each bottle contained had been brewed and bottled on the premises under the personal supervision of Madame da Souza.

Once the newly-wed couple realized that the uproar from the room below was sufficient to mask the protests of their rickety brass bedstead, they no longer grudged Flynn his amusements.

For everyone involved it was a night of great pleasure, a night to be looked back upon with nostalgia and wistful smiles.

32

Even at Flynn's prodigious rate of expenditure, his share of the profits from Sebastian's tax expedition lasted another two weeks.

During this period Rosa and Sebastian spent a little of their time wandering hand in hand through the streets and bazaars of Beira, or sitting, still hand in hand, on the beach and watching the sea. Their happiness radiated from them so strongly that it affected anyone who came within fifty feet of them. A worried stranger hurrying towards them along the narrow little street with his face creased in a frown would come under the spell; his pace would slacken, his step losing its urgency, the frown would smooth away to be replaced by an indulgent grin as he passed them. But mostly they remained closeted in the bridal suite above the bar–entering it in the early afternoon and not reappearing until early noon the following day.

Neither Rosa nor Sebastian had imagined such happiness could exist.

At the expiry of the two weeks Flynn was waiting for them in the bar-room as they came down to lunch. He hurried out to join them as they passed the door. 'Greetings! Greetings!' He threw an arm around each of their shoulders. 'And how are you this fine morning?' He listened without attention as Sebastian replied at length on how well he felt, how well Rosa was, and how well both of them had slept. 'Sure! Sure!' Flynn interrupted his rhapsodizing. 'Listen, Bassie, my boy, you remember that £10 I gave you?'

'Yes.' Sebastian was immediately wary.

'Let me have it back, will you?'

'I've spent it, Flynn.'

'You've *what*?' bellowed Flynn.

'I've spent it.'

'Good God Almighty! All of it? You've squandered ten pounds in as many days?' Flynn was horrified by his son-in-law's extravagance and Sebastian, who had honestly believed the money was his to do with as he wished, was very apologetic.

They left for Lalapanzi that afternoon. Madame da Souza had accepted Flynn's note of hand for the balance outstanding on his bill.

At the head of the column Flynn, broke to the wide, and nursing a burning hangover, was in evil temper. The line of bearers behind him, bedraggled and billious from two weeks spent in the flesh-pots, were in similar straits. At the rear of the doleful little caravan, Rosa and Sebastian chirruped and cooed together–an island of sunshine in the sea of gloom.

The months passed quickly at Lalapanzi during the monsoon of 1913. Gradually, as its girth increased, Rosa's belly became the centre of Lalapanzi. The pivot upon which the whole community turned. The debates in the servants' quarters, led by Nanny, the accepted authority, dealt almost exclusively with the contents thereof. All of them were hot for a man-child, although secretly Nanny cherished a treacherous hope that it might be another Little Long Hair.

Even Flynn, during the long months of enforced inactivity while the driving monsoon rains turned the land into a quagmire and the rivers into seething brown torrents, felt his grand-parental instincts stirred. Unlike Nanny, he had no doubts as to the unborn child's sex, and he decided to name it Patrick Flynn O'Flynn Oldsmith.

He conveyed his decision to Sebastian while the two of them were hunting for the pot in the kopjes above the homestead.

By dint of diligent application and practice, Sebastian's marksmanship had improved beyond all reasonable expectation. He had just demonstrated it. They were jump-shooting in thick cat-bush among the broken rock and twisted ravines of the kopjes. Constant rain had softened the ground and enabled them to move silently down-wind along one of the ravines. Flynn was fifty yards out on Sebastian's right, moving heavily but deceptively fast through the sodden grass and undergrowth.

The kudu were lying in dense cover below the lip of the ravine. Two young bulls, bluish-gold in colour, striped with thin chalk lines across the body, pendulant dewlaps heavily fringed with yellow hair, two and a half twists in each of the corkscrew horns–big as polo ponies but heavier. They broke left across the ravine when Flynn jumped them from their hide, and the intervening bush denied him a shot.

'Breaking your way, Bassie,' Flynn shouted and Sebastian took two swift paces around the bush in front of him, shook the clinging raindrops from his lashes, and slipped the safety-catch. He heard the tap of big horn against a branch, and the first bull came out of the ravine at full run across his front. Yet it seemed to float, unreal, intangible, through the blue-grey rain mist. It blended ghostlike into the background of dark rain-soaked vegetation, and the clumps of bush and the tree trunks between them made it an almost impossible shot. In the instant that the bull flashed across a gap between two clumps of buffalo thorn, Sebastian's bullet broke its neck a hand's width in front of the shoulder.

At the sound of the shot, the second bull swerved in dead run, gathered its forelegs beneath its chest, and went up in a high, driving leap over the thorn bush that stood in its path. Sebastian traversed his rifle smoothly without taking the butt from his shoulder, his right hand flicked the bolt open and closed, and he fired as a continuation of the movement.

The heavy bullet caught the kudu in mid-air and threw it sideways. Kicking and thrashing, it struck the ground and rolled down the bank of the ravine.

Whooping like a Red Indian, Mohammed galloped past Sebastian, brandishing a long knife, racing to reach the second bull and cut its throat before it died so that the dictates of the Koran might be observed.

Flynn ambled across to Sebastian. 'Nice shooting, Bassie boy. Salted and dried and pickled, there's meat there for a month.'

And Sebastian grinned in modest recognition of the compliment. Together they walked across to watch Mohammed and his gang begin paunching and quartering the big animals.

With the skill of a master tactician, Flynn chose this moment to inform Sebastian of the name he had selected for his grandson. He was not prepared for the fierce opposition he encountered from Sebastian. It seemed that Sebastian had expected to name the child Francis Sebastian Oldsmith. Flynn laughed easily, and then in his most reasonable and persuasive brogue he started pointing out to Sebastian just how cruel it would be to saddle the child with a name like that.

It was a lance in the pride of the Oldsmiths, and Sebastian rose to the defence. By the time they returned to Lalapanzi, the discussion needed about six hot words to reach the stage of single combat.

Rosa heard them coming. Flynn's bellow carried across the lawns. 'I'll no have my grandson called a pewling, milksop name like that!'

'Francis is the name of kings and warriors and gentlemen!' cried Sebastian.

'My aching buttocks, it is!'

Rosa came out on to the wide veranda and stood there with her arms folded over the beautiful bulge that housed the cause of the controversy.

They saw her and started an undignified race across the lawns, each trying to reach her first to enlist her support for their respective causes.

She listened to the pleadings, a small and secret smile upon her lips, and then said with finality, 'Her name will be Maria Rosa Oldsmith.'

Some time later Flynn and Sebastian were together on the veranda.

Ten days before the last rains of the season had come roaring in from the Indian Ocean and broken upon the unyielding shield of the continent. Now the land was drying out; the rivers regained their sanity and returned, chastened to the confines of their banks. New grass lifted from the red earth to welcome the return of the sun. For this brief period the whole land was alive and green; even the gnarled and crabbed thorn trees wore a pale fuzz of tender leaves. Behind each pair of guinea-fowl that clinked and scratched on the bottom lawns of Lalapanzi, there paraded a file of dappled chicks. Early that morning a herd of eland had moved along the skyline across the valley, and beside each cow had trotted a calf. Everywhere was new life, or the expectation of new life.

'Now, stop worrying!' said Flynn, as his impatient pacing brought him level with Sebastian's chair.

'I'm not worrying,' Sebastian said mildly. 'Everything will be all right.'

'How do you know that?' challenged Flynn.

'Well . . .'

'You know the child could be stillborn, or something.' Flynn shook his finger in Sebastian's face. 'It could have six fingers on each hand–how about that? I heard about one that was born with . . .'

While Flynn related a long list of horrors, Sebastian's expression of proud and eager anticipation crumbled slowly. He rose from his chair and fell into step beside Flynn. 'Have you got any gin left?' he asked hoarsely, glancing at the shuttered windows of Rosa's bedroom. Flynn produced the bottle from the inside pocket of his jacket.

An hour later, Sebastian was hunched forward in his chair, clutching a half-full tumbler of gin with both hands. He stared into it miserably. 'I don't know what I'd do if it was born with . . .' He could not go on. He shuddered and lifted the tumbler to his lips. At that instant a long, petulant wail issued from the closed bedroom. Sebastian leapt as though he had been bayoneted from behind, and spilled the gin down his shirt. His next leap was in the direction of the bedroom, a direction which Flynn had also chosen. They collided heavily and then set off together at a gallop along the veranda. They reached the locked door and hammered upon it for admission. But Nanny, who had evicted them in the first instance, still adamantly refused to lift the locking bar or to give them any information as to the progress of the birthing. Her decision was endorsed by Rosa.

'Don't you dare let them in until everything is ready,' she whispered huskily, and roused herself from the stupor of exhaustion, to help Nanny with washing and wrapping the infant.

When at last everything was ready, she lay propped on the pillows with her child held against her chest, and nodded to Nanny. 'Open the door,' she said.

The delay had confirmed Flynn's worst suspicions. The door flew open, and he and Sebastian fell into the room, wild with anxiety.

'Oh, thank God, Rosa. You're still alive!' Sebastian reached the bed and fell on his knees beside it.

'You check his feet,' instructed Flynn. 'I'll do his hands and head,' and before Rosa could prevent him, he had lifted the infant out of her arms.

'His fingers are all right. Two arms, one head,' Flynn muttered above Rosa's protests and the infant's muffled squawls of indignation.

'This end is fine. Just fine!' Sebastian spoke in rising relief and delight. 'He's beautiful, Flynn!' And he lifted the shawl that swaddled the child's body. His expression cracked and his voice choked. 'Oh, my God!'

'What's wrong?' Flynn asked sharply.

'You were right, Flynn. He's deformed.'

'What? Where?'

'There!' Sebastian pointed. 'He hasn't got a what-ye-ma-call-it,' and they both stared in horror.

It was many long seconds before they realized simultaneously that the tiny cleft was no deformity but very much as nature had intended it.

'It's a girl!' said Flynn in dismay.

'A girl!' echoed Sebastian, and quickly pulled down the shawl to preserve his daughter's modesty.

'It's a girl,' Rosa smiled, wan and happy.

'It's a girl,' cackled Nanny in triumph.

Maria Rosa Oldsmith had arrived without fuss and with the minimum of inconvenience to her mother, so that Rosa was on her feet again within twenty-four hours. All her other activities were conducted with the same consideration and dispatch. She cried once every four hours; a single angry howl which was cut off the instant the breast was thrust into her mouth. Her bowel movements were equally regular and of the correct volume and consistency, and the rest of her days and nights were devoted almost entirely to sleeping.

She was beautiful; without the parboiled, purple look of most new-borns; without the squashed-in pug features or the vague, squinty eyes.

From the curly cap of silk hair to the tips of her pink toes, she was perfection.

It took Flynn two days to recover from the disappointment of having been cheated out of a grandson. He sulked in the arsenal or sat solitary at the end of the veranda. On the second evening Rosa pitched her voice just high enough to carry the length of the veranda.

'Don't you think Maria looks just like Daddy–the same mouth and nose? Look at her eyes.'

Sebastian opened his mouth to deny the resemblance emphatically but closed it again, as Rosa kicked him painfully on the ankle.

'She is the image of him. There's no doubting who her grandfather is.'

'Well, I suppose . . . If you look closely,' Sebastian agreed unhappily.

At the end of the veranda, Flynn sat with his head cocked in an attitude of attention. Half an hour later Flynn had sidled up to the cradle and was studying the contents thoughtfully. By the following evening he had moved his chair alongside and was leading the discussion with such remarks as, 'There is quite a strong family resemblance. Look at those eyes–no doubt who her Granddaddy is!'

Interspersing his observations with warnings and instructions, 'Don't get so close, Bassie. You're breathing germs all over her.' 'Rosa, this child needs another blanket. When did she have her last feed?'

It was not long before he started bringing pressure to bear on Sebastian.

'You've got responsibilities now. Have you thought about that?'

'How do you mean, Flynn?'

'Just answer me this. What have you got in this world?'

'Rosa and Maria,' Sebastian answered promptly.

'Fine. That's just great! And how are you going to feed them and clothe them and . . . and look after them?'

Sebastian expressed himself well satisfied with the existing arrangements.

'I bet you are! It isn't costing you a thing. But I reckon it's about time you got up off your bum and did something.'

'Like what?'

'Like going and shooting some ivory.'

Three days later, armed and equipped for a full-scale poaching expedition, Sebastian led a column of gun-boys and bearers down the valley towards the Rovuma river.

Fourteen hours later, in the dusk of evening, he led them back.

'What in the name of all that's holy, are you doing back here?' Flynn demanded.

'I had this premonition.' Sebastian was sheepish.

'What premonition?'

'That I should come back,' muttered Sebastian.

He left again two days later. This time he actually crossed the Rovuma before the premonition over-powered him once more, and he came back to Rosa and Maria.

'Well,' Flynn sighed with resignation. 'I reckon I'll just have to go along with you and make sure you do it.' He shook his head. 'You've been a big disappointment to me, Bassie.' The biggest disappointment being the fact that he had hoped to have his granddaughter to himself for a few weeks.

'Mohammed,' he bellowed. 'Get my gear packed.'

33

Flynn sent his scouts across the river and when they reported back that the far bank was clear of German patrols, Flynn made the crossing.

This expedition was a far cry from Sebastian's amiable and aimless wandering in German territory. Flynn was a professional. They crossed in the night. They crossed in strictest silence and landed two miles downstream from M'topo's village. There was no lingering on the beach, but an urgent night march that began immediately and went on in grim silence until an hour before dawn; a march that took them fifteen miles inland from the river, and ended in a grove of elephant thorn, carefully chosen for the kopjes and ravines around it that afforded multiple avenues of escape in each direction.

Sebastian was impressed by the elaborate precautions that Flynn took before going into camp; the jinking and counter-marching, the careful sweeping of their spoor with brushes of dry grass, and the placing of sentries on the kopje above the camp.

During the ten days they waited there, not a single branch was broken from a tree, not a single axe-stroke swung to leave a tell-tale white blaze on the dark bush. The tiny night fire fed with dry trash and dead wood was carefully screened, and before dawn was smothered with sand so that not a wisp of smoke was left to mark them in the day.

Voices were never raised above conversational tones, and even the clatter of a bucket brought such a swift and ferocious reprimand from Flynn, that on all of them was a nervous awareness, an expectancy of danger, a tuning of the minds and bodies to action.

On the eighth night the scouts that Flynn had thrown out began drifting back to the camp. They came in with all the stealth and secrecy of night animals and huddled over the fire to tell what they had seen.

'. . . Last night three old bulls drank at the water-hole of the sick hyena. They carried teeth so, and so, and so . . .' showing the arm to measure the length of ivory, '. . . apart from them, ten cows left their feet in the mud, six of them young with calves. Yesterday, at the place where the hill of Inhosana breaks and turns its arms, I saw where another herd had crossed, moving towards the dawn; five young bulls, twenty-three cows, and . . .'

The reports were jumbled, unintelligible to Sebastian who did not carry a map of the land in his head. But Flynn, sitting beside the fire listening, fitted the fragments together and built them into an exact picture of how the game was moving. He saw that the big bulls were still separated from the breeding herds–that they lingered on the high ground while the cows had started moving back towards the swamps from which the floods had driven them, anxious to take their young away from the dangers that the savannah forests would offer once the dry season set in.

He noted the estimates of thickness and length of tusk. Immature ivory was hardly worth carrying home, good only for carving into billiard balls and piano keys. The market was glutted with it.

But on the other hand, a prime tusk, over one hundred pounds in weight, seven foot long, and twice the thickness of a fat woman's thigh, would fetch fifty shillings a pound avoirdupois.

An animal carrying such a tusk on each side of his face was worth four or five hundred pounds in good, gold sovereigns.

One by one Flynn discarded the possible areas in which he would hunt. This year there were no elephant in the M'bahora hills. There was good reason for this; thirty piles of great sun-bleached bones lay scattered along the ridge, marking the path that Flynn's rifles had followed two years before. The memory of gunfire was too fresh and the herds shunned that place.

There were no elephant on the Tabora escarpment. A blight had struck the groves of mapundu trees, and withered the fruit before it could ripen. Dearly the elephant loved mapundu berries and they had gone elsewhere to find them.

They had gone up to the Sania Heights, to Kilombera, and to the Salito hills.

Salito was an easy day's march from the German boma at Mahenge. Flynn struck it from his mental list.

As each of the scouts finished his report, Flynn asked the question which would influence his final decision.

'What of *Plough the Earth*?'

And they said, 'We saw nothing. We heard nothing.'

The last scout came in two days after the others. He looked sheepish and more than a little guilty.

'Where the hell have you been?' Flynn demanded, and the gun-boy had his excuse ready.

'Knowing that the great Lord Fini would ask of certain matters, I turned aside in my journey to the village of Yetu, who is my uncle. My uncle is a fundi. No wild thing walks, no lion kills, no elephant breaks a branch from a tree but my uncle knows of it. Thus I went to ask him of these matters.'

'Thy uncle is a famous fundi, he is also a famous breeder of daughters,' Flynn remarked drily. 'He breeds daughters the way the moon breeds stars.'

'Indeed, my uncle Yetu is a man of fame.' Hurriedly the scout went on to turn Flynn aside from his line of discussion. 'My uncle sends his greetings to the Lord Fini and bids me speak thus: "This season there are many fine elephants on the Sania Heights. They walk by twos and threes. With my own eyes I have seen twelve which show ivory as long as the shaft of a throwing spear, and I have seen signs of as many more." My uncle bids me speak further. "There is one among them of which the Lord Fini knows for he has asked of him many times. This one is a bull among great bulls. One who moves in such majesty that men have named him *Plough the Earth*."'

'You do not bring a story from the honey-bird to cool my anger against you?' Flynn demanded harshly. 'Did you dream of *Plough the Earth* while you were ploughing the bellies of your uncle's many daughters?' His eagerness was soured by scepticism. Too many times he had followed wild stories in his pursuit of the great bull. He leaned forward across the fire to watch the gun-bearer's eyes as he replied, 'It is true, lord.' Flynn watched him carefully but found no hint of guilt in his face. Flynn grunted, rocked back on his hams, and lowered his gaze to the small flames of the camp-fire.

For his first ten years in Africa, Flynn had heard the legend of the elephant whose tusks were of such length that their points touched the ground and left a double furrow along his spoor. He had smiled at this story as he had at the story of the rhinoceros who fifty years before had killed an Arab slaver, and now wore around his horn a massive gold bangle studded with precious stones. They said the bangle had lodged there as he gored the Arab. There were a thousand other romantic tales come out of Africa; from Solomon's treasure to the legend of the elephants' graveyard, and Flynn believed none of them.

Then he saw a myth come alive. One evening, camped near the Zambesi in Portuguese territory, he had taken a bird-gun and walked along the bank hoping for a brace of sand-grouse. Two miles from the camp he had seen a flight of birds coming in to the water, fly fast as racing pigeons, whistling in on back-swept wings, and he had ducked into a thick bank of reeds and watched them come.

As they banked steeply overhead, dropping towards the sandbanks of the river, Flynn jumped to his feet and fired left and right, folding the lead bird and the second, so they crumpled in mid-air and tumbled, leaving a pale flurry of feathers to mark their fall.

But Flynn never saw the birds hit the ground. For, while the double blast of the shotgun still echoed along the river, the reed-bed below where he stood swayed and crashed and burst open, then an elephant came out into the open.

It was a bull elephant that stood fourteen feet high at the shoulder. An elephant so old that his ears were shredded to half their original size. The hide that covered his body hung in folds and deep wrinkles, baggy at the knees and the throat. The tuft of his tail long ago worn bald. The rheumy tears of great age staining his seared and dusty cheeks.

He came out of the reed-bed in a shambling, hump-backed run, and his head was tilted at an awkward, unnatural angle.

Flynn could hardly credit his vision when he saw the reason why the old bull cocked his head back in that fashion. From each side of the head extended two identical shafts of ivory, perfectly matched, straight as the columns of a Greek temple, with not an inch of taper from lip to bluntly rounded tip. They were stained to the colour of tobacco juice, fourteen long feet of ivory that would have touched the ground, if the elephant had carried his head relaxed.

As Flynn stood frozen in disbelief, the bull passed him by a mere fifty yards and lumbered on into the forest.

It took Flynn thirty minutes to get back to camp and exchange the bird-gun for the double-barrelled Gibbs, snatch up a water bottle, shout for his gun-boys, and return to the river.

He put Mohammed to the spoor. At first there were only the round pad marks in the dusty earth, smooth pad marks the size of a dustbin lid; the graining on the old bull's hooves had long been worn away. Then after five miles of flight there were other marks to follow. One each side of the spoor a double line scuffed through dead leaves and grass and soft earth where the tips of the tusks touched, and Flynn learned why the old bull was called *Plough the Earth*.

They lost the spoor on the third day in the rain, but a dozen times in the years since then, Flynn had followed and lost those double furrows, and once, through his binoculars, he had seen the old bull again, standing dozing beneath a grove of marula trees at a distance of three miles, his eroded old head propped up by the mythical tusks. When Flynn reached the spot on which he had seen the bull, it was deserted.

In all his life Flynn had never wanted anything with such obsessive passion as he wanted those tusks.

Now he sat silently staring into the camp-fire, remembering all these things, and the lust within him was tighter and more compelling than he had ever felt for a woman.

At last he looked up at the scout and said huskily, 'Tomorrow, with the first light, we will go to the village of Yetu, at Sania.'

A fly settled on Herman Fleischer's cheek and rubbed its front feet together in delight, as it savoured the prospect of drinking from the droplet of sweat that quivered precariously at the level of his ear lobe.

The Askari standing behind Herman's chair flicked the zebra tail switch with such skill, that not one of the long black hairs touched the Commissioner's face, and the fly darted away to take its place in the circuit that orbited around Herman's head.

Herman hardly noticed the interruption. He was sunk down in the chair; glowering at the two old men who squatted on the dusty parade ground below the veranda. The silence was a blanket that lay on them all in the stupefying heat. The two headmen waited patiently. They had spoken, and now they waited for the Bwana Mkuba to reply.

'How many have been killed?' Herman asked at last, and the senior of the two headmen answered.

'Lord, as many as the fingers of both your hands. But these are the ones of which we are certain, there may be others.'

Herman's concern was not for the dead, but their numbers would be a measure of the seriousness of the situation. Ritual murder was the first stage on the road to rebellion. It started with a dozen men meeting in the moonlight, dressed in cloaks of leopard skin, with designs of white clay painted on their faces. With the crude iron claws strapped to their hands, they would ceremoniously mutilate a young girl, and then devour certain parts of her body. This was harmless entertainment in Herman's view, but when it happened more frequently, it generated in the district a mood of abject terror. This was the climate of revolt. Then the leopard priests would walk through the villages in the night, walk openly in procession with the torches burning, and the men who lay shivering within the barricaded huts would listen to the chanted instructions from the macabre little procession–and they would obey.

It had happened ten years earlier at Salito. The priests had ordered them to resist the tax expedition that year. They had slaughtered the visiting Commissioner and twenty of his Askari, and they cut the bodies into small pieces with which they festooned the thorn trees.

Three months later a battalion of German infantry had disembarked at Dar es Salaam and marched to Salito. They burned the villages and they shot everything–men, women, children, chickens, dogs, and goats. The final casualty list could only be estimated, but the officer commanding the battalion boasted that they had killed two thousand human beings. He was probably exaggerating. Nevertheless, the Salito hills were still devoid of human life and habitation to this day. The whole episode was irritating and costly–and Herman Fleischer wanted no repetition of it during his term of office.

On the principle that prevention was better than cure, he decided to go down and conduct a few ritual sacrifices of his own. He humped himself forward in his chair, and spoke to his sergeant of Askari.

'Twenty men. We will leave for the village of Yetu, at Salito, tomorrow before dawn. Do not forget the ropes.'

34

On the Sania Heights, in the heat of the day, an elephant stood under the wide branches of a wild fig-tree. He was asleep on his feet but his head was propped up by two long columns of stained ivory. He slept as an old man sleeps, fitfully, never sinking very deep below the level of consciousness. Occasionally the tattered grey ears flapped, and each time a fine haze of flies rose around his head. They hung in the hot air and then settled again. The rims of the elephant's ears were raw where the flies had eaten down through the thick skin. The flies were everywhere. The humid green shade beneath the wild fig was murmurous with the sound of their wings.

Across the divide of the Sania Heights, four miles from the spot where the old bull slept, three men were moving up one of the bush-choked gulleys towards the ridge.

Mohammed was leading. He moved fast, half-crouched to peer at the ground, glancing up occasionally to anticipate the run of the spoor he was following. He stopped at a place where a grove of mapundu trees had carpeted the ground beneath them with a stinking, jellified mass of rotten berries. He looked back at the two white men and indicated the marks in the earth, and the pyramid of bright yellow dung that lay upon it. 'He stopped here for the first time in the heat, but it was not to his liking, and he has gone on.'

Flynn was sweating. It ran down his flushed jowls and dripped on to his already sodden shirt. 'Yes,' he nodded and a small cloudburst of sweat scattered from his head at the movement. 'He will have crossed the ridge.'

'What makes you so certain?' Sebastian spoke in the same sepulchral whisper as the others.

'The cool evening breeze will come from the east–he will cross to the other side of the ridge to wait for it.' Flynn spoke with irritation and wiped his face on the short sleeve of his shirt. 'Now, you just remember, Bassie. This is my elephant, you understand that? You try for it and, so help me God, I'll shoot you dead.'

Flynn nodded to Mohammed and they moved on up the slope, following the spoor that meandered between outcrops of grey granite and scrub.

The crest of the ridge was well defined, sharp as the spine of a starving ox. They paused below it, squatting to rest in the coarse brown grass. Flynn opened the binocular case that hung on his chest, lifted out the instrument, and began to polish the lens with a scrap of cloth.

'Stay here!' Flynn ordered the other two, then on his belly he wriggled up towards the skyline. Using the cover of a tree stump, he lifted his head cautiously and peered over.

Below him the Sania Heights fell away to a gentle slope, fifteen hundred feet and ten miles to the plain below. The slope was broken and crenellated, riven into a thousand gulleys and ravines, covered over-all with a mantle of coarse brown scrub and dotted with clumps of bigger trees.

Flynn settled himself comfortably on his elbows and lifted the binoculars to his eyes. Systematically he began to examine each of the groves below him.

'Yes!' he whispered aloud, wriggling a little on his belly, staring at the picture puzzle beneath the spread branches of the tree, a mile away. In the shade there were shapes that made no sense, a mass too diffuse to be the trunk of the tree.

He lowered the glasses and wiped away the sweat that clung in his eyebrows. He closed his eyes to rest them from the glare, then he opened them again, and lifted the glasses.

For two long minutes he stared before suddenly the puzzle made sense. The bull was standing half away from him, merging with the trunk of the wild fig, the head and half the body obscured by the lower branches of the tree–and what he had taken to be the stem of a lesser tree was, in fact, a tusk of ivory.

A spasm of excitement closed on his chest.

'Yes!' he said. 'Yes!'

Flynn planned his stalk with care, taking every precaution against the intervention of fate that twenty years of elephant hunting had taught him.

He had gone back to where Sebastian and Mohammed waited.

'He's there,' he told them.

'Can I come with you?' Sebastian pleaded.

'In a barrel you can,' snarled Flynn as he sat and pulled off his heavy boots to replace them with the light sandals that Mohammed produced from the pack.

'You stay here until you hear my shot. You so much as stick your nose over the ridge before that–and, so help me God, I'll shoot it off.'

While Mohammed knelt in front of Flynn and strapped the leather pads to his knees to protect them as he crawled over rock and thorn, Flynn fortified himself from the gin bottle. As he recorked it, he glowered at Sebastian again. 'That's a promise!' he said.

At the top of the ridge Flynn paused again with only his eyes lifted over the skyline, while he plotted his stalk, fixing in his memory a procession of landmarks–an ant-hill, an outcrop of white quartz, a tree festooned with weaver birds' nests–so that as he reached each of these he would know his exact position in relation to that of the elephant.

Then with the rifle cradled across the crook of his elbows he slid on his belly to begin the stalk.

Now, an hour after he had left the ridge, he saw before him through the grass a slab of granite like a headstone in an ancient cemetery. It stood square and weathered brown, and it was the end of the stalk.

He had marked it from the ridge as the point from which he would fire. It stood fifty yards from the wild fig tree, at a right angle from the old bull's position. It would give him cover as he rose to his knees to make the shot.

Anxious now, suddenly overcome with a premonition of disaster–sensing that somehow the cup would be dashed from his lips, the maid plucked from under him before the moment of fulfillment, Flynn started forward. Slithering towards the granite headstone, his face set hard in nervous anticipation, he reached the rock.

He rolled carefully on to his side and, holding the heavy rifle against his chest, he slipped the catch across and eased the rifle open, so that the click of the mechanism was muted. From the belt around his waist he selected two fat cartridges and examined the brass casings for tarnish or denting; with relief he saw the fingers that held them were steadier. He slipped the cartridges into the blank eyes of the breeches, and they slid home against the seatings with a soft metallic plong. And now his breathing was faintly ragged at the end of each inhalation. He closed the rifle, and with his thumb pushed the safety-catch forward into the 'fire' position.

His shoulder against the rough, sun-heated granite, he drew up his legs against his belly and rolled gently on to his knees. With his head bowed low and the rifle in his lap, he knelt behind the rock, and for the first time in an hour he lifted his head. He brought it up with inching deliberation. Slowly the crystalline texture of the granite passed before his eyes, then suddenly he looked across fifty yards of open ground at his elephant.

It stood broadside to him but the head was hidden by the leaves and branches of the wild fig. The brain shot was impossible from here. His eyes moved down on to the shoulder and he saw the outline of the bone beneath the thick grey skin. He picked out the point of the elbow and his eyes moved back into the barrel of the chest. He could visualize the heart pulsing softly there beneath the ribs, pink and soft and vital, throbbing like a giant sea anemone.

He lifted the rifle, and laid it across the rock in front of him. He looked along the barrels, and saw the blade of dry grass that was wound around the head of the foresight, obscuring it. He lowered the rifle and with his thumbnail picked away the shred of grass. Again he lifted and sighted.

The black blob of the foresight lay snugly in the deep, wide vee of the backsight, he moved the gun, riding the bead down across the old bull's shoulder then back on to the chest. It lay there ready to kill, and he took up the slack in the trigger, gently, lovingly, with his forefinger.

The shout was faint, a tiny sound in the drowsy immensity of the hot African air. It came from the high ground above him.

'Flynn!' and again, 'Flynn!'

In an explosive burst of movement under the wild fig tree, the old bull swung his body with unbelievable speed, his great tusks riding high, he went away from Flynn at an awkward shambling run, his flight covered by the trunk of the fig tree.

For stunned seconds, Flynn crouched behind the boulder, and with each second the chances of a shot dwindled. Flynn jumped to his feet and ran out to one side of the fig tree, opening his field of fire for a snap shot at the bull as he fled, a try for the spine where it curved down between the massive haunches to the tuftless tail.

Spiked agony stabbed up through the ball of his lightly shod foot, as he trod squarely on a three-inch buffalo thorn. Red-tipped, wickedly barbed, it buried its full length in his flesh, and he stumbled to his knees crying a protest at the pain.

Two hundred yards away, the old bull disappeared into one of the wooded ravines, and was gone.

'Flynn! Flynn!'

Sobbing in pain and frustration, his injured foot twisted up into his lap, Flynn sat in the grass and waited for Sebastian Oldsmith to come down to him.

'I'll let him get real close,' Flynn told himself. Sebastian was approaching with the long awkward strides of a man running downhill. He had lost his hat and the black tangled curls danced on his head at each stride. He was still shouting.

'I'll give it to him in the belly,' Flynn decided. 'Both barrels!' and he groped for the rifle that lay beside him.

Sebastian saw him and swerved in his run.

Flynn hefted the rifle. 'I warned him. I said I'd do it,' and his right hand settled around the pistol grip of the rifle, his forefinger instinctively hooking forward for the trigger.

'Flynn! Germans! A whole army of them, Just over the hill. Coming this way.'

'Christ!' said Flynn, immediately abandoning his homicidal intentions.

35

Lifting himself in the stirrups, Herman Fleischer reached behind to massage himself. His buttocks were of a plump, almost feminine, quantity and quality. After five hours in the saddle Herman longed to rest them. He had just crossed the ridge of the Sania Heights on his donkey, and it was cool here beneath the outspread branches of the wild fig tree. He flirted with the temptation, decided to indulge himself, and turned to give the order to the troop of twenty Askari who stood behind him. All of them were watching him avidly, anticipating the order that would allow them to throw themselves down and relax.

'Lazy dogs!' thought Herman as he scowled at them. He turned away from them, settled his aching posterior gently on to the saddle, and growled.

'Akwende! Let us go!' His heels thumped against the flanks of his donkey and it started forward at a trot.

From a crotch in the trunk of the fig tree ten feet above Herman's head, Flynn O'Flynn viewed his departure over the double barrels of his rifle. He watched the patrol wind away down the slope and drop from sight over a fold in the ground before he put up his gun.

'Phew! That was close.' Sebastian's voice came from the leafy mass above Flynn.

'If he'd touched one foot on the ground, I'd have blown his bloody head off,' said Flynn. He sounded as though he regretted missing the opportunity. 'All right, Bassie, get me down out of this frigging tree.'

Fully-dressed, except for his boots, Flynn sat against the base of the fig tree and proffered his right foot to Sebastian. '. . . I had him right there in my sights.'

'Who?' asked Sebastian.

'The elephant, you idiot. For the first time I had him cold. And then . . . Yeow! What the hell are you doing?'

'I'm trying to get the thorn out, Flynn.'

'Feels like you're trying to knock it in with a hammer.'

'I can't get a grip on it.'

'Use your teeth. That's the only way.' Flynn instructed, and Sebastian paled a little at the thought. He considered Flynn's foot. It was a large foot; corns on the toes, flakes of loose skin and other darker matter between them. Sebastian could smell it at a range of three feet. 'Couldn't you reach it with your own teeth, Flynn?' he hedged.

'You think I'm a goddamned contortionist?'

'Mohammed?' Sebastian's eyes lit up with relief as he turned on the little gun-bearer. In answer to the question Mohammed drew back his lips in a death's head grin, exposing his smooth, pink toothless gums. 'Yes,' agreed Sebastian. 'I see what you mean.' He returned his gaze to the foot, and studied it with sickened fascination. His Adam's apple bobbed as he swallowed.

'Get on with it,' said Flynn, and Sebastian stooped. There was a howl from Flynn, and Sebastian straightened up with the wet thorn gripped in his teeth. He spat it out explosively, and Mohammed handed him the gin bottle. Sebastian gargled from it loudly but when he lifted the bottle to his lips again, Flynn laid a restraining hand on his forearm. 'Now don't overdo it, Bassie boy,' he remonstrated mildly, retrieved the bottle, and placed it to his own mouth. It seemed to refuel Flynn's anger, for when he removed the bottle his voice had fire in it. 'That goddamn sneaking, sausage-eating slug. He spoiled the only chance I've ever had at that elephant.' He paused to breathe heavily. 'I'd like to do something really nasty to him, like . . . like. . .' he searched for some atrocity to commit upon Herman Fleischer, and suddenly he found one. 'My God!' he said, and his scowl changed to a lovely smile. 'That's it!'

'What?' Sebastian was alarmed. He was certain that he would be selected as the vehicle of Flynn's revenge. 'What?' he repeated.

'We will go . . .' said Flynn, '. . . to Mahenge!'

'Good Lord, that's the German headquarters!'

'Yes,' said Flynn. 'With no Commissioner and no Askari to guard it! They've just passed us, heading in the opposite direction.'

36

They hit Mahenge two hours before dawn, in that time of utter darkness when mankind's vitality is at its lowest ebb. The defence put up by the corporal and five Askari whom Fleischer had left to guard his headquarters was hardly heroic. In fact, they were only half awakened by the lusty and indiscriminate use of Flynn's boot, and by the time they were fully conscious, they found themselves securely locked behind the bars of the jail-house. There was only one casualty. It was, of course, Sebastian Oldsmith, who, in the excitement, ran into a half-open door. It was fortunate, as Flynn pointed out, that he struck the door with his head, otherwise he may have done himself an injury. But as it was, he had recovered sufficiently by sunrise to watch the orgy of looting and vandalism in which Flynn and his gun-bearers indulged themselves.

They began in the office of the Commissioner. Built into the thick adobe wall of the room was an enormous iron safe.

'We will open that first,' decreed Flynn as he eyed it greedily. 'See if you can find some tools.'

Sebastian remembered the blacksmith shop at the end of the parade ground. He returned from there laden with sledge-hammers and crow-bars.

Two hours later they were sweating and swearing in an atmosphere heavy with plaster dust. They had torn the safe from the wall, and it lay in the centre of the floor. Three of Flynn's gun-boys were beating on it with sledge-hammers in a steadily diminishing display of enthusiasm, while Sebastian worked with a crow-bar at the hinge joints. He had succeeded in inflicting a few bright scratches upon the metal. Flynn was seated on the Commissioner's desk, steadily working himself into a fury of frustration; for the last hour his contribution to the assault on the safe had been limited to consuming half a bottle of schnapps that he had found in a drawer of the desk.

'It's no use, Flynn.' Sebastian's curls were slick with perspiration, and he licked at the blisters on the palms of his hands. 'We will just have to forget about it.'

'Stand back!' roared Flynn. 'I'll shoot the goddamned thing open.' He rose from the desk wild-eyed, his double-barrelled Gibbs clutched in his hands.

'Wait!' shouted Sebastian and he and the gun-bearers scattered for cover.

The detonations of the heavy rifle were thunderous in the confined space of the office; gun-smoke mingled with the plaster dust, and the bullets ricochetted off the metal of the safe, leaving long smears of lead upon it, before whining away to embed themselves in the floor, wall, and furniture.

This act of violence seemed to placate Flynn. He lost interest in the safe. 'Let's go and find something to eat,' he said mildly, and they trooped through to the kitchens.

Once Flynn had shot away the lock, Herman Fleischer's larder proved to be an Aladdin's cave of delight. The roof was hung with hams and polonies and sausages, there were barrels of pickled meats, stacks of fat round cheeses, cases of Hansa beer, cases of cognac, pyramids of canned truffles, asparagus tips, pâté, shrimps, mushrooms, olives in oil, and other rarities.

They stared at this profusion in awe, and then moved forward together. Each man to his own particular tastes, they fell upon Herman Fleischer's treasure house. The gun-boys rolled out a cask of pickled pork, Sebastian started with his hunting knife on the cans, while Flynn devoted himself to the case of Steinhager in the corner.

It took two hours of dedicated eating and drinking for them to reach saturation point.

'We'd better get ready to move on now.' Sebastian belched softly, and Flynn nodded owlish agreement, the movement spilling a little Steinhager down his bush jacket. He wiped at it with his hand and then licked his fingers.

'Yep! Best we are gone before Fleischer gets home.' He looked at Mohammed. 'Make up full loads of food for each of the bearers. What you can't carry away we'll dump in the latrine buckets.' He stood up carefully. 'I'll just have a look round, and make sure we haven't missed anything important,' and he went out through the door with unsteady dignity.

In Fleischer's office he stood for a minute regarding the invulnerable safe balefully. It was certainly much too heavy to carry away, and abandoning the notion with regret, he looked around for some outlet for his frustration.

There was a portrait of the Kaiser on the entrance wall, a colour print showing the Emperor in full dress, mounted on a magnificent cavalry charger. Flynn picked up an indelible pencil from the desk and walked across to the picture. With a dozen strokes of the pencil he drastically altered the relationship between horse and rider. Then, beginning to chuckle, he printed on the whitewashed wall below the picture, 'The Kaiser loves horses.'

This struck him as being such a pearl of wit, that he had to summon Sebastian and show it to him. 'That's what you call being subtle Bassie, boy. All good jokes are subtle.'

It seemed to Sebastian that Flynn's graffiti were as subtle as the charge of an enraged rhinoceros but he laughed dutifully. This encouraged Flynn to a further essay in humour. He had two of his gun-bearers carry in a bucket from the latrines, and under his supervision, they propped it above the half-open door of Herman Fleischer's bedroom.

An hour later, heavily laden with booty, the raiding party left Mahenge and began the first of a series of forced marches aimed at the Rovuma river.

37

In a state of mental confusion induced by a superfluity of adrenalin in the bloodstream, Herman Fleischer wandered through his ransacked boma. As he discovered each new outrage he regarded it with slitted eyes and laboured breathing. But first it was necessary to effect a jail-break in reverse in order to free his own captive Askari. When they emerged through the hole in the prison wall, Herman curtly ordered his sergeant to administer twenty strokes of the kiboko to each of them, as a token rebuke for their inefficiency. He stood by and drew a little comfort from the solid slap of the kiboko on bare flesh and the shrieks of the recipient.

However, the calming effect of the floggings evaporated when Herman entered the kitchen area of his establishment, and found that his larder of painstakingly accumulated foodstuffs was now empty. This nearly broke his spirit. His jowls quivered with self-pity, and from under his tongue saliva oozed in melancholic nostalgia. It would take a month to replace the sausages alone, heaven knew how long to replace the cheeses imported from the fatherland.

From the larder he went through to his office and found Flynn's subtleties. Herman's sense of humour was not equal to the occasion.

'Pig-swine, English bastard,' he muttered dejectedly, and a dark wave of despair and fatigue washed over him as he realized the futility of setting out in pursuit of the raiders. With two days start he could never hope to catch them before they reached the Rovuma. If only Governor Schee, who was so forthcoming with criticism, would allow him to cross the river one night with his Askari and visit the community at Lalapanzi. There would be no one left the following morning to make complaint to the Portuguese Government about breach of sovereignty.

Herman sighed. He was tired and depressed. He would go to his bed now and rest a while before supervising the tidying up of his headquarters. He left the office and plodded heavily along the stoep to his private quarters, and pushed open the door of his bedroom.

His bedroom temporarily uninhabitable. Herman reposed that night on the open stoep. But his sleep was disturbed by a dream in which he pursued Flynn O'Flynn across an endless plain without ever narrowing the gap between them, while above him circled two huge birds–one with the austere face of Governor Schee, and the other with the face of the young English bandit–at regular intervals these two voided their bowels on him. After the previous afternoon's experience the olfactory hallucinations which formed part of the dream were horribly realistic.

He was tactfully awakened by one of his household servants, and struggled up in bed with an ache behind his eyes and a foul taste in his mouth.

'What is it?' he growled.

'There is a bearer from Dodoma who brings a book with the red mark of the Bwana Mkuba upon it.'

Herman groaned. An envelope with Governor Schee's seal affixed to it usually meant trouble. Surely he could not so speedily have learnt about Flynn O'Flynn's latest escapade.

'Bring coffee!'

'Lord, there is no coffee. It was all stolen,' and Herman groaned again.

'Very well. Bring the messenger.' He would have to endure the ordeal of Governor Schee's rebukes without the fortifying therapy of a cup of coffee. He broke the seal and began to read:

August 4th, 1914
The Residency,
Dar es Salaam

To: The Commissioner (Southern Province).
At: Mahenge.
Sir,

It is my duty to inform you that a state of war now exists between the Empire and the Governments of England, France, Russia, and Portugal.

You are hereby appointed temporary Military Commander of the Southern Province of German East Africa, with orders to take whatever steps you deem necessary for the protection of our borders, and the confusion of the enemy.

In due course a military force, now being assembled at Dar es Salaam, will be dispatched to your area. But I fear that there will be a delay before this can be achieved.

In the meantime, you must operate with the force presently at your disposal.

There was more, much more, but Herman Fleischer read the detailed instructions with perfunctory attention. His headache was forgotten, the taste in his mouth unnoticed in the fierce surge of warrior passions that arose within him.

His chubby features puckered with smiles, he looked up from the letter, and spoke aloud. 'Ja, O'Flynn, now I will pay you for the bucket.'

He turned back to the first page of the letter, and his mouth formed the words as he read '. . . whatever steps you deem necessary for the protection of our borders, and the confusion of the enemy.'

At last. At last he had the order for which he had pleaded so many times. He shouted for his sergeant.

38

'Perhaps they will come home tonight.' Rosa Oldsmith looked up from the child's smock she was embroidering.

'Tonight or tomorrow, or the next day,' Nanny replied philosophically. 'There is no profit in guessing at the coming or going of men. They all have worms in their heads,' and she began again to rock the cradle, squatting beside it on the leopard-skin rugs like an animated mummy. The child snuffled a little in its sleep.

'I'm sure it will be tonight. I can feel it–something good is going to happen.' Rosa laid aside her sewing and crossed to the door that led out on to the stoep. In the last few minutes the sun had gone down below the trees, and the land was ghostly quiet in the brief African dusk.

Rosa went out on to the stoep, and hugging her arms across her chest at the chill of evening, she stared out down the darkening length of the valley. She stood there, waiting restlessly, and as the day passed swiftly into darkness, so her mood changed from anticipation to a formless foreboding.

Quietly, but with an edge to her voice, she called back into the room, 'Light the lamps please, Nanny.'

Behind her she heard the sounds of metal on glass, then the flare of a sulphur match, and a feeble yellow square of light was thrown out on to the veranda to fall around her feet.

The first puff of the night wind was cold on her bare arms. She felt the prickle of goose-flesh and she shivered unexpectedly.

But Rosa lingered, straining her eyes into the darkness until she could no longer see the shape of the fig trees at the bottom of the lawn. Then abruptly she turned away and went into the bungalow. She closed the door and slid the bolt across.

Later she woke. There was no moon outside and the room was dark. Beside her bed she could hear the soft, piglet sounds that little Maria made in her sleep.

Again the disquieting mood of the early evening returned to her and she lay in her bed, waiting and listening in the utter blackness, and the darkness bore down upon her so that she felt herself shrinking, receding, becoming remote from reality, small and lonely in the night.

In fear then she lifted the mosquito netting and groped for the cradle. The baby whimpered as she lifted her and brought her into the bed beside her, but

Rosa's arms quietened her and soon she slept against the breast, and the warmth of the tiny body stilled Rosa's own agitation.

The shouting woke her, and she opened her eyes with a surge of joy, for the shouts would be Sebastian's bearers. Before she was fully awake she had thrown aside the bedclothes, struggled out from under the mosquito netting, and was standing in her night-dress with the baby clasped to her chest.

It was then that she realized that the room was no longer in darkness. From the window into the yard it was lit by a red-gold glow that flared, and flickered, and faded.

The last tarnish of sleep was cleaned from her brain, so she could hear that the shouts from outside were not those of welcome, and on a lower key, there were other sounds–a whispering, rustling, and popping, that she could not identify.

She crossed to the window, moving slowly, with dread for what she might find, but before she reached it a scream froze her. It came from the kitchen yard, a scream that quivered on the air long after it had ended, a scream of terror and of pain.

'Merciful God!' she whispered, and forced herself to peer out.

The servants' quarters and the outhouses were on fire. From the thatch of each the flames stood up in writhing yellow columns, lighting the darkness.

There were men in the yard, many men, and all of them wore the khaki uniform of German Askari. Each of them carried a rifle, and the bayonet blades glittered in the glare of the flames.

'They have crossed the river–No, oh please God, no!' and Rosa hugged the baby to her, crouching down below the window sill.

The scream rang out again, but weaker now, and she saw a knot of four Askari crowded around something that squirmed in the dust of the yard. She heard their laughter, that excited laughter of men who kill for fun, as they stabbed down on the squirming thing with their bayonets.

At that moment another of the servants broke from the burning outbuildings and ran for the darkness beyond the circle of the flames. Shouting again, the Askari left the dying man and chased the other. They turned him like a pack of trained greyhounds coursing a gazelle, laughing and shouting in their excitation, and drove him back into the daylight glare of the flames.

Bewildered, surrounded, the servant stopped and looked wildly about him, his face with terror. Then the Askari swarmed over him, clubbing and hacking with their rifles.

'Oh, oh God, no,' Rosa's whisper sobbed in her throat, but she could not drag her eyes away.

Suddenly in the uproar she heard a new noise, a bull-bellow of authority. She could not understand the words for they were shouted in German but from around the angle of the bungalow appeared a white man, a massive man in the blue corduroy uniform of the German Colonial Service, with a slouch hat pulled low down on his head, and a pistol brandished in one hand. From the description that Sebastian had given her, she recognized the German Commissioner.

'Stop them!' Rosa did not speak aloud, the appeal was in her mind only. 'Please, stop them burning and killing.'

The white man was railing at his Askari, his face turned towards where Rosa crouched and she saw it was round and pink like that of an overweight baby. In the fire-light it glistened with a fine sheen of sweat.

'Stop them. Please stop them,' Rosa pleaded silently, but under the Commissioner's direction three of the Askari ran to where, in the excitement of the chase, they had dropped their torches of dry grass. While they lit them from the flaming out-buildings, the other Askari left the corpses of the two servants and spread out in a circle around the bungalow, facing inwards, with their rifles held at high port. Most of the bayonets were dulled with blood.

'I want Fini and the Singese–not bearers and gun-boys–I want the white men! Burn them out!' shouted Fleischer, but Rosa recognized only her father's name. She wanted to cry out that he was not here, that it was only her and the child.

The three Askari were running in towards the bungalow now, sparks and fire smeared back from the torches they carried. In turn each man checked his run, poised himself like a javelin thrower, then hurled his torch in a high, smoking arc towards the bungalow. Rosa heard them thump, thump, thump, on to the thatched roof above her.

'I must get my baby away, before the fire catches,' and she hurried across the room, out into the passage. It was dark here and she groped along the wall until she found the entrance to the main room. At the front door she fumbled with the bolts, and opened it a crack. Peering through to the fire-lit lawns beyond the stoep, she saw the dark forms of Askari waiting there also, and she drew back.

'The side windows of the kitchen,' she told herself. 'They're closest to the bush. That's the best chance,' and she stumbled back into the passage.

Above her now there was a sound like high wind and wàter, a rushing sound blending with the crackle of burning thatch, and the first taint of smoke stung her nostrils.

'If only I can reach the bush,' she whispered desperately, and the child in her arms began to cry.

'Hush, my darling, hush now,' but her voice was scratchy with fear. Maria seemed to sense it; her petulant whimperings changed to lusty, high-pitched yells and she struggled in Rosa's grasp.

From the side windows of the kitchen Rosa saw the familiar waiting figures of the Askari hovering at the edge of the fire-light. She felt despair catch her stomach in a cold grip and squeeze the resolve from her. Suddenly her legs were weak under her and her whole body was shaking.

From within the bungalow behind her there came a thunderous roar as part of the burning roof collasped. A blast of scalding air blew through the kitchen and the tall column of sparks and flames thrown up by the collapse lit the surroundings even more vividly. It showed another figure beyond the line of Askari, scampering in from the edge of the bush like a little black monkey, and Rosa heard Nanny's voice.

'Little Long Hair! Little Long Hair.' A plaintive, ancient wail.

Nanny had escaped into the bush during the first minutes of the attack. She had lain there watching until the roof of the bungalow fell in–then she could no longer contain herself. Insensible of her own danger, caring for nothing except her precious charges, she was coming back.

The Askari saw her also. Their rigid, well-spaced line crumpled as all of them ran to head her off. Suddenly the ground between Rosa and the edge of the bush was clear. Now there was a chance–just the smallest chance that she could get the child away. She flung the window open and dropped through it to the earth.

One moment she hesitated and glanced towards the confusion of running men away to her right hand. In that moment she saw one of the Askari catch up with the old woman and lunge forward with his bayonet. Nanny reeled from the force of the blow in her back. Involuntarily her arms were flung wide open, and for a fleeting second Rosa saw the point of the bayonet appear miraculously from the centre of her chest, as it impaled her.

Then Rosa was running towards the wall of bush and scrub fifty yards ahead of her, while Maria howled in her arms. The sound attracted the attention of the Askari. One of them shouted a warning, and then the whole pack was after her in full tongue.

Rosa's senses were overwrought by her terror, so finely tuned that it seemed the passage of time was lagging. Weighed down by the child, each pace she took dragged on for ever, as though she waded through waist-deep water. The long night-dress around her legs hampered her, and there was rough stone and thorn beneath her bare feet. The wall of bush ahead of her seemed to come no closer, and she ran with the cold hand of fear squeezing her chest and cramping her breathing.

Then into her line of vision from the side came a man, an Askari, a big man bounding towards her with the long loping gallop of a bull baboon, cutting across her line of flight, his open mouth an obscene pink pit in the shiny black of his face.

Rosa screamed and swung away from him. How she was running parallel to the edge of the bush and behind her she heard the slap of feet upon the earth, closing fast, and the babbling chorus of the pursuit.

A hand snatched at her shoulder, and she twisted away from it, feeling the stuff of her night-gown tear beneath the clutching fingers.

Blind with terror she stumbled a dozen paces back towards the burning homestead. She felt the vast waves of heat from it in her face and through her thin clothing–and then a rifle butt struck her in the small of the back, and a bright burst of agony paralysed her legs. She dropped to her knees, still holding Maria.

They ringed her, in a palisade of human bodies and gloating, blood-crazed faces.

The big one who had felled her with the rifle butt stooped over her and before she recognized his intention, he had snatched Maria from her arms and stepped back again.

He stood laughing, holding the child by the ankles, letting her swing head downwards, so her tiny face was suffused with blood, scarlet in the light of the flames.

'No, please, no!' Rosa crawled painfully towards the man. 'Give her back to me. My baby. Please give her back,' and she lifted her arms towards him.

The Askari dangled the child tantalizingly in front of her, retreating slowly as she crawled towards him. The others were laughing, hoarse sensual laughter, crowding around her, faces contorted with enjoyment, and polished ebony black with the sweat of excitement, as they jostled each other for a better view of the sport.

Then with a wild yell, the Askari swung Maria high, whirled her twice above his head as he pivoted to face the bungalow–and threw Maria up towards the burning roof.

The tiny body flew with the looseness of a rag doll through the air, her night-dress fluttered as she dropped and struck the roof, rolled awkwardly down the slope of it with her clothing blooming into instant flame, until she reached a weak spot in the burning thatch. It sucked Maria in like a fiery mouth and blew a belch of sparks as it swallowed her. At that instant Rosa heard the voice of her child for the last time. It was a sound she was never to forget.

For a moment the men about her were hushed, and then as though wind blew through trees, they moved a little with a sound that was half sigh, half moan.

Still kneeling, facing the burning building which was now a pyre, Rosa slumped forward and lifted her hands to cover her face as though in prayer.

The Askari who had thrown the child snatched up his rifle from where it lay at his feet and stood over her. He lifted it above his head the way a harpooner holds his steel with the point of the bayonet aimed at the base of Rosa's neck where her hair had fallen open to expose the pale skin.

In the moment that the Askari paused to take his aim, Herman Fleischer shot him in the back of the head with the Luger.

'Mad dog!' the Commissioner shouted at the Askari's corpse. 'I told you to take them alive.'

Then, breathing like an asthma case from the exertion of his run to intervene, he turned to Rosa.

'Fräulein, my apologies,' he doffed his slouch hat with ponderous courtesy, and spoke in German that Rosa did not understand. 'We do not make war on women and babies.'

She did not look up at him. She was crying quietly into her cupped hands.

39

'Early in the year for a bush fire,' Flynn muttered. He sat with an enamel mug cupped in his hands and blew steam from the hot coffee. His blanket had slid down to his waist.

Across the camp-fire from him Sebastian was also sitting in a muddle of bedding, and cooling his own pre-dawn mug of coffee. At Flynn's words he looked up from his labour, and out into the dark south.

False dawn had paled the sky just enough to define the hills below it as an undulating mass that seemed much closer than it was. That way lay Lalapanzi–and Rosa and Maria.

Without real interest Sebastian saw the radiated glow at one point along the spine of the ridge; a fan of pink light no larger than a thumbnail.

'Not a very big one,' he said.

'No,' agreed Flynn. 'Hope she doesn't spread though,' and he gulped noisily at his mug.

As Sebastian watched it idly, the glow diminished, shrinking into insignificance at the coming of the sun, and above it the stars paled also.

'We'd best get moving. It's a long day's march and we've wasted enough time on this trip already.'

'You're a regular bloody fire-eater when it comes to getting your home comforts.' Flynn feigned disinterest, yet secretly the thought of returning to his granddaughter had strong appeal. He hurried the coffee a little and scalded his tongue.

Sebastian was right. They had wasted a lot of time on the return trip from the Mahenge raid.

First, there was a detour to avoid a party of German Askari that one of the native headmen had warned them was at M'topo's village. They had trekked upstream for three days before finding a safe crossing, and a village willing to hire canoes.

Then there was the brush with the hippo which had cost them almost a week. As was usual practice, the four hired canoes, loaded to within a few inches of free-board with Flynn, Sebastian, their retinue, and loot, had slipped across the Rovuma and were hugging the Portuguese bank as they headed downstream towards the landing opposite M'topo's village when the hippo had disputed their passage.

She was an old cow hippo who a few hours earlier had given birth to her calf in a tiny island of reeds, separated from the south bank by twenty feet of lily-padded water. When the four canoes entered this channel in line astern with the paddlers chanting happily, she took it as a direct threat to her offspring and she threw a tantrum.

Two tons of hippo in a tantrum has the destructive force of a localized hurricane. Surfacing violently from under the leading canoe, she had thrown Sebastian, two gun-boys, four paddlers, and all their equipment, ten feet in the air. The canoe, rotted with beetle, had snapped in half and sunk immediately.

The mother hippo had then treated the three following canoes with the same consideration, and within the space of a few minutes, the canal was clogged with floating debris, and struggling, panic-stricken men. Fortunately they were no more than ten feet from the bank. Sebastian was first ashore. None of them, however, was very far behind him, and they all took off like the start of a cross-country race over the veld, when the hippo emerged from the river and signified that, not satisified with wrecking the flotilla, she intended chopping a few of them in half with her guillotine jaws.

A hundred yards later she abandoned the pursuit, and trotted back to the water, wiggling her little ears and snorting in triumph. Half a mile farther on the survivors had stopped running.

They camped there that night without food, bedding, or weapons, and the following morning, after a heated council of war, Sebastian was elected to return to the river and ascertain whether the hippo was still in control of the channel. He came back at high speed to report that she was.

Three more days they waited for the hippo and her calf to move away. During this time they suffered the miseries of cold nights and hungry days, but the greatest misery was inflicted on Flynn O'Flynn whose case of gin was under eight feet of water–and by the third morning he was threatening *delirium tremens* again. Just before Sebastian set off for his morning reconnaissance of the channel, Flynn informed him agitatedly that there were three blue scorpions sitting on his head. After the initial alarm, Sebastian went through the motions of removing the imaginary scorpions and stamping them to death, and Flynn was satisfied.

Sebastian returned from the river with the news that the hippo and her calf had evacuated the island, and it was now possible to begin salvage operations.

Protesting mildly and talking about crocodiles, Sebastian was stripped naked and coaxed into the water. On his first dive, he retrieved the precious case of gin.

'Bless you, my boy,' Flynn murmured fervently as he eased the cork out of a bottle.

By the following morning Sebastian had recovered nearly all their equipment and booty, without being eaten by crocodiles, and they set off for Lalapanzi on foot.

Now they were in their last camp before Lalapanzi, and Sebastian felt his impatience rising. He wanted to get home to Rosa and baby Maria. He should be home by evening.

'Come on, Flynn. Let's go.' He flicked the coffee grounds from his mug, threw aside his blanket, and shouted to Mohammed and the bearers who were huddled around the other fire.

'Safari! Let us march.'

Nine hours later, with the daylight around him, he breasted the last rise and paused at the top.

All that day eagerness had lengthened his stride, and he had left Flynn and the column of heavily laden bearers far behind.

Now he stood alone, and stared without comprehension at the smoke-blackened ruins of Lalapanzi from which a few thin tendrils of smoke still drifted.

'Rosa!' Her name was a harsh bellow of fear, and he ran wildly.

'Rosa!' he shouted as he crossed the scorched and trampled lawns.

'Rosa! Rosa! Rosa!' the echo from the kopje above the homestead shouted back.

'Rosa!' He saw something among the bushes at the edge of the lawn, and he ran to it. Old Nanny lying dead with the blood dried black on the floral stuff of her night-gown.

'Rosa!' He ran back towards the bungalow. The ash swirled in a warm mist around his legs as he crossed the stoep.

'Rosa!' His voice rang hollowly through the roofless shell of the house, as he stumbled over the fallen beams that littered the main room. The reek of burned cloth and hair and wood almost choked him, so that his voice was husky as he called again.

'Rosa!'

He found her in the burnt-out kitchen block and he thought she was dead. She was slumped against the cracked and blackened wall. Her night-gown was torn and scorched, and the snarled skeins of hair, that hid her face, were powdered with white wood ash.

'My darling. Oh, my darling.' He knelt beside her, and timidly touched her shoulder. Her flesh was warm and alive beneath his fingers, and he felt relief leap up into his throat, blocking it so he could not speak again. Instead, he brushed the tangle of hair from her face and looked at it.

Beneath the charcoal smears of dirt her skin was pale as grey marble. Her eyes, tight closed, were heavily underscored with blue, and rimmed with crusty red.

He touched her lips with the tips of his fingers, and she opened her eyes. But they looked beyond him; unseeing, dead eyes. They frightened him. He did not want to look into them, and he drew her head towards his shoulder.

There was no resistance in her. She lay against him quietly, and he pressed his face into her hair. Her hair was impregnated with the smell of smoke.

'Are you hurt?' he asked her in a whisper, not wanting to hear her answer. But she made no answer, lying inert in his arms.

'Tell me, Rosa. Speak to me. Where is Maria?'

At the mention of the child's name, she reacted for the first time. She began to tremble.

'Where is she?' more urgency in his voice now.

She rolled her head against his shoulder and looked across the floor of the room. He followed the direction of her gaze.

Near the far wall an area of the floor had been swept clear of debris and ash. Rosa had done it with her bare hands while the ash was still hot. Her fingers were blistered and burned raw in places, and her arms were black to the elbows. Lying in the centre of this cleared space was a small, charred thing.

'Maria?' Sebastian whispered, and Rosa shuddered against him.

'Oh, God,' he said, and lifted Rosa. Carrying her against his chest, he staggered from the ruins of the bungalow out into the cool, sweet evening air, but in his nostrils lingered the smell of smoke and burned flesh. He wanted to escape from it. He ran blindly along the path and Rosa lay unresisting in his arms.

40

The following day Flynn buried their dead on the kopje above Lalapanzi. He placed a thick slab of granite over the small grave that stood apart from the others, and when it was done he sent a bearer to the camp to fetch Rosa and Sebastian.

When they came, they found him standing alone by Maria's grave under the marula trees. His face was puffy and purply red. The thinning grey hair hung limply over his ears and forehead, like the wet feathers of an old rooster. His body looked as though it was melting. It sagged at the shoulders and the belly. Sweat had soaked through his clothing across the shoulders, and at the armpits and crotch. He was sick with drink and sorrow.

Sebastian stood beside Rosa, and the three of them took their silent farewell of the child.

'There is nothing else to do now.' Sebastian spoke huskily.

'Yes,' said Flynn. He stooped slowly and took a handful of the new earth from the grave. 'Yes, there is.' He crumbled the earth between his fingers. 'We still have to find the man who did this–and kill him.'

Beside Sebastian, Rosa straightened up. She turned to Sebastian, lifted her chin, and spoke for the first time since he had come home.

'Kill him!' she repeated softly.

PART II

41

With his hands clasped behind his back, and his chin thrust forward aggressively Rear-Admiral Sir Percy Howe sucked in his lower lip and nibbled it reflectively. 'What was our last substantiated sighting on *Blücher*?' he asked at last.

'A month ago, sir. Two days before the outbreak of war. Sighting reported by S.S. *Tygerberg*. Latitude 0° 27′ N. Longitude 52° 16′ E. Headed south-west; estimated speed, eighteen knots.

'And a hell of a lot of good that does us,' Sir Percy interrupted his flag-captain and glared at the vast Admiralty plot of the Indian Ocean. 'She could be back in Bremerhaven by now.'

'She could be, sir,' the flag-captain nodded, and Sir Percy glanced at him and permitted himself a wintry smile.

'But you don't believe that, do you, Henry?'

'No, sir, I don't. During the last thirty days, eight merchantmen had disappeared between Aden and Lourenço Marques. Nearly a quarter of a million tons of shipping. That's the *Blücher*'s work.'

'Yes, it's the *Blücher*, all right,' agreed the Admiral, and reached across the plot to pick up the black counter labelled '*Blücher*', that lay on the wide green expanse of the Indian Ocean.

A respectful silence held the personnel of the plotting room South Atlantic and Indian Oceans while they waited for the great man to reach his decision. It was a long time coming. He stood bouncing the '*Blücher*' in the palm of his right hand, his grey eyebrows erect like the spines of a hedgehog's back, as his forehead creased in thought. A full minute they waited.

'Refresh my memory of her class and commission.' Like most successful men Sir Percy would not hurry a decision when there was time to think, and the duty lieutenant who had anticipated his request, stepped forward with the German Imperial Navy list open at the correct page.

'"*Blücher*. Commissioned August 16th, 1905. 'B' Class heavy cruiser. Main armament, eight nine-inch guns. Secondary armament, six six-inch guns."'

The lieutenant finished his reading and waited quietly.

'Who is her captain?' Sir Percy asked, and the lieutenant consulted an addendum to the list.

'"Otto von Kleine (Count). Previously commanded the light cruiser *Sturm Vogel*."'

'Yes,' said Sir Percy. 'I've heard of him,' and he replaced the counter on the plot, keeping his hand on it. 'A dangerous man to have here, south of Suez,' and he pushed the counter up towards the Red Sea and the entrance to the canal, where the tiny red shipping lanes amalgamated into a thick artery, '–or here,' and he pushed it down towards the Cape of Good Hope, around which were curved the same red threads that joined London to Australia and India. Sir Percy lifted his hand from the black counter and left it sitting menacingly upon the shipping lanes.

'What force have we deployed against him so far?' and in answer the flag-captain picked up a wooden pointer and touched in turn the red counters that were scattered about the Indian Ocean.

'*Pegasus* and *Renounce* in the north. *Eagle* and *Plunder* sweeping the southern waters, sir.'

'What further force can we spare, Henry?'

'Well, sir, *Orion* and *Bloodhound* are at Simonstown,' and he touched the nose of the African continent with the pointer.

'*Orion*–that's Manderson, isn't it?'

'Yes, sir.'

'And who has *Bloodhound*?'

'Little, sir.'

'Good,' Sir Percy nodded with satisfaction. 'A six-inch cruiser and a destroyer should be able to deal with *Blücher*,' and he smiled again. 'Especially with a hellion like Charles Little handling the *Bloodhound*. I played golf with him last summer–he damn nigh drove the sixteenth green at St Andrews!'

The flag-captain glanced at the Admiral and, on the strength of the destroyer captain's reputation, decided to permit himself an inanity. 'The young ladies of Cape Town will mourn his departure, sir.'

'We must hope that Kapitän zur See Otto von Kleine will mourn his arrival,' chuckled Sir Percy.

'Daddy likes you very much.'

'Your father is a man of exquisite good taste,' Commander the Honourable Charles Little conceded gallantly, and rolled his head to smile at the young lady who lay beside him on a rug, in the dappled shade beneath the pine trees.

'Can't you ever be serious?'

'Helen, my sweet, at times I can be deadly serious.'

'Oh, you!' and his companion blushed prettily as she remembered certain of Charles' recent actions, which would make her father hastily revise his judgement.

'I value your father's good opinion, but my chief concern is that you endorse it.'

The girl sat up slowly and while she stared at him her hands were busy, brushing the pine needles from the glorious tangle of her hair, readjusting the fastenings of her blouse, spreading the skirts of her riding-habit to cover sweet legs clad in dark, tall polished leather boots.

She stared at Charles Little and ached with the strength of her want. It was not a sensual need she felt, but an overpowering obsession to have this man as her very own. To own him in the same way as she already owned diamonds, and furs, and silk, and horses, and peacocks, and other beautiful things.

His body sprawled out on the rug with all the unconscious grace of a reclining leopard. A secret little smile tugged at the corners of his lips and his eyelids drooped to mask the sparkle of his eyes. His recent exertions had dampened the hair that flopped forward on to his forehead.

There was something satanical about him, an air of wickedness, and Helen decided it was the slant of the eyebrows and the way his ears lay flat against his temples, but were pointed like those of a satyr, yet they were pink and smooth as those of an infant.

'I think you have devil's ears,' she said, and then she blushed again, and scrambled to her feet avoiding Charles' arm that reached out for her. 'Enough of that!' she giggled and ran to the thoroughbred hunter that was tied near them in the forest. 'Come on,' she called as she mounted.

Charles stood up lazily and stretched. He tucked the tail of his shirt into his breeches, folded the rug on which they had lain, and went to his own horse.

At the edge of the pine forest, they checked their mounts and sat looking down over the Constania valley.

'Isn't it beautiful?' she said.

'It is indeed,' he agreed.

'I meant the view.'

'And so did I.' Twice in the six days he had known her, she had led him up this mountain and subjected him to the temptation. Below them lay six thousand acres of the richest land in all of Africa.

'When my brother Hubert was killed there was no one left to carry it on. Just my sister and I–and we are only girls. Poor Daddy isn't so well any more–he finds it such a strain.'

Charles let his eye move lazily from the great squat buttress of Table Mountain on their left, across the lush basin of vineyards below them, and then on to where the glittering wedge of False Bay drove into the mountains.

'Doesn't the homestead look lovely from here?' Helen drew his attention to the massive Dutch-gabled residence with its attendant outbuildings, grouped in servility behind it.

'I am truly impressed by the magnificence of the stud fee,' Charles murmured, purposely slurring the last two words, and the girl glanced at him in surprise, beginning to bridle.

'I beg your pardon?'

'It is truly magnificent scenery,' he amended. Her persistent efforts at ensnaring him were beginning to bore Charles. He had teased and avoided more artful huntresses.

'Charles,' she whispered. 'How would you like to live here. I mean, for ever?'

And Charles was shocked. This little provincial had no understanding whatsoever of the rules governing the game of flirtation. He was so shocked that he threw back his head and laughed.

When Charles laughed it sent shivers of delight through every woman within a hundred yards. It was a merry sound with underlying tones of sensuality. His teeth were very white against the sea-tan of his face, and the muscles of his chest and upper arms tensed into bold relief beneath the silk shirt he wore.

Helen was the only witness of this particular performance, and she was helpless as a sparrow in a hurricane. Eagerly she leaned across the space between their horses and touched his arm. 'You would like it, Charles. Wouldn't you?'

She did not know that Charles Little had a private income of twenty thousand pounds a year, that when his father died he would inherit the title

Viscount Sutherton and the estates that went with it. She did not know that one of those estates would swallow her father's own three times over; nor did she know that Charles had passed by willing young ladies with twice her looks, ten times her fortune, and a hundred times her breeding.

'You would, Charles. I know you would!'

So young, so vulnerable, that he stopped the flippant reply before it reached his lips.

'Helen,' he took her hand. 'I am a sea creature. We move with the wind and the waves,' and he lifted her hand to his lips.

A while she sat, feeling the warm pressure of his lips upon her flesh, and the burn of tears behind her eyes. Then she snatched her hand away, and wheeled her horse. She lifted the leather riding-crop and slashed the glossy black shoulder between her knees. Startled, the stallion jumped forward into a dead run back along the road towards the Constania valley.

Charles shook his head and grimaced with regret. He had not meant to hurt her. It had been an escapade, something to fill the waiting days while *Bloodhound* went through the final stages of her refit. But Charles had learned to harden himself to the ending of his adventures–to the tears and tragedy.

'Shame on you, you heartless cad,' he said aloud, and touching his mount with his heels ambled in pursuit of the galloping stallion.

He caught up with the stallion in the stable yards. A groom was walking it, and there were darker sweat patches on its coat, and the barrel of its chest still heaved with laboured breathing.

Helen was nowhere in sight, but her father stood at the stable gates–a big man, with a square-cut black beard picked out with grey.

'Enjoy your ride?'

'Thank you, Mr Uys.' Charles was noncommittal, and the older man glanced significantly at the blown stallion before going on.

'There's one of your sailors been waiting for you for an hour.'

'Where is he?' Charles' manner altered abruptly, became instantly businesslike.

'Here, sir.' From the deep shade of the stable doorway, a young seaman stepped out into the bright sunlight.

'What is it, man?' Impatiently Charles acknowledged his salute.

'Captain Manderson's compliments, sir, and you're to report aboard H.M.S. *Orion* with all possible speed. There's a motor car waiting to take you to the base, sir.'

'An untimely summons, Commander,' Uys gave his opinion lounging against the worked stone gateway. 'I fear we will see no more of you for a long time.'

But Charles was not listening. His body seemed to quiver with suppressed excitement, the way a good gun-dog reacts to the scent of the bird. 'Sailing orders,' he whispered, '–at last. At last!'

There was a heavy south-east swell battering Cape Point, so the sea spray wreathed the beam of the lighthouse on the cliffs above. A flight of malgas came in so high towards the land that they caught the last of the sun, and glowed pink above the dark water.

Bloodhound cleared Cape Hangklip and took the press of the South Atlantic on her shoulder, staggered from it with a welter of white water running waist-deep past her foredeck gun-turrets. Then in retaliation she hurled herself at the next swell, and Charles Little on her bridge exulted at the vital movement of the deck beneath his feet.

'Bring her round to oh-five-oh.'

'Oh-five-oh, sir,' repeated his navigating lieutenant.

'Revolutions for seventeen knots, pilot.'

Almost immediately the beat of the engines changed, and her action through the water became more abandoned.

Charles crossed to the angle of the flimsy little bridge and looked back into the dark, mountain-lined maw of False Bay. Two miles astern the shape of H.M.S. *Orion* melted into the dying light.

'Come along, old girl. Do try and keep up,' murmured Charles Little with the scorn that a destroyer man feels for any vessel that cannot cruise at twenty knots. Then he looked beyond *Orion* at the land. Below the massif of Table Mountain, near the head of the Constantia valley a single pink prick of light showed.

'There'll be fog tonight, sir,' the pilot spoke at Charles' elbow, and Charles turned without regret to peer over the bows into the gathering night.

'Yes, a good night for pirates.'

42

The fog condensed on the grey metal of the bridge, so the footplates were slippery underfoot. It soaked into the overcoats of the men huddled against the rail, and it dewed in minute pearls on the eyebrows and the beard of Kapitän zur See Otto von Kleine. It gave him an air of derring-do, the reckless look of a scholarly pirate.

Every few seconds Lieutenant Kyller glanced anxiously at his captain, wondering when the order to turn would come. He hated this business of creeping inshore in the fog, with a flood tide pushing them towards a hostile coast.

'Stop all engines,' said von Kleine, and Kyller repeated the order to the helm with alacrity. The muted throbbing died beneath their feet, and afterwards the fog-blanketed air was heavy with a sepulchral hush.

'Ask masthead what he makes of the land.' Von Kleine spoke without turning his head, and after a pause Kyller reported back.

'Masthead is in the fog. No visibility,' he paused. 'Foredeck reports fifty fathoms shoaling rapidly.'

And von Kleine nodded. The sounding tended to confirm his estimate that they were sitting five miles off the breakwater of Durban harbour. When the morning wind swept the fog aside he hoped to see the low coastal hills of Natal ahead of him, terraced with gardens and whitewashed buildings–but most of all he hoped to see at least six British merchantmen anchored off the beach waiting their turn to enter the congested harbour, plump and sleepy under the protection of the shore batteries; unaware just how feeble was the protection afforded by half a dozen obsolete ten-pounders manned by old men and boys of the militia.

German naval intelligence had submitted a very detailed report of the defences and conditions prevailing in Durban. After careful perusal of this report, von Kleine had decided that he could trade certain betrayal of his exact position to the English for such a rich prize. There was little actual risk involved. One pass across the entrance of the harbour at high speed, a single broadside for each of the anchored merchantmen, and he could be over the horizon again before the shore gunners had loaded their weapons.

The risk, of course, was in showing *Blücher* to the entire population of Durban city and thereby supplying the Royal Navy with its first accurate sighting since the declaration of war. Within minutes of his first broadside, the British squadrons, which were hunting him, would be racing in from all directions to block each of his escape routes. He hoped to counter this by swinging away towards the south, down into that watery wildnerness of wind and ice below latitude 40°, to the rendezvous with *Esther,* his supply ship. Then on to Australia or South America, as the opportunity arose.

He turned to glance at the chronometer above the ship's compass. Sunrise in three minutes, then they could expect the morning wind.

'Masthead reports the fog dispersing, sir.'

Von Kleine aroused himself, and looked out into the fog banks. They were moving now, twisting upon themselves in agitation at the warmth of the sun. 'All engines slow ahead together,' he said.

'Masthead,' warbled one of the voice-pipes in the battery in front of Kyller. 'Land bearing green four-oh. Range, ten thousand metres. A big headland.'

That would be the bluff above Durban, the massive whale-backed mountain that sheltered the harbour. But in the fog von Kleine had misjudged his approach; he was twice as far from the shore as he had intended.

'All engines full ahead together. New course. Oh-oh-six.' He waited for the order to be relayed to the helm before strolling across to the voice-pipes. 'Guns. Captain.'

'Guns,' the voice from far away acknowledged.

'I will be opening fire with high explosives in about ten minutes. The target will be massed merchant shipping on an approximate mark of three hundred degrees. Range, five thousand metres. You may fire as soon as you bear.'

'Mark three hundred degrees. Range, five thousand metres, sir,' repeated the pipe, and von Kleine snapped the voice-tube cover shut and returned to his original position, facing forward with his hands clasped loosely behind his back.

Below him the gun-turrets revolved ponderously and the long barrels lifted slightly, pointing out into the mist with impassive menace.

A burst of dazzling sunshine struck the bridge so fiercely that Kyller lifted his hand to shield his eyes, but it was gone instantly as the *Blücher* dashed into another clammy cold bank of fog. Then as though they had passed through a curtain on to a brilliantly lit stage, they came out into a gay summer's morning.

Behind them the fog rolled away in a sodden grey wall from horizon to horizon. Ahead rose the green hills of Africa, rimmed with white beach and surf and speckled with thousands of white flecks that were the buildings of Durban town. The scaffolding of the cranes along the harbour wall looked like derelict sets of gallows.

Humped on the smooth green mirror of water between them and the shore, lay four ungainly shapes looking like a troop of basking hippo. The British merchantmen.

'Four only,' muttered von Kleine in chagrin. 'I had hoped for more.'

The forty-foot barrels of the nine-inch guns moved restlessly, seeming to sniff for their prey, and the *Blücher* raced on, lifting a hissing white wave at her bows, vibrating and shuddering to the thrust of her engines as they built up to full speed.

'Masthead,' the voice-tube beside Kyller squawked urgently.

'Bridge,' said Kyller but the reply was lost in the deafening detonation of the first broadside, the long thunderous roll of heavy gunfire. He jumped involuntarily, taken unawares, and then quickly lifted the binoculars from his chest to train them on the British merchantmen.

All attention, every eye on the bridge was concentrated ahead, waiting for the fall of shot upon the doomed vessels.

In the comparative silence that followed the bellow of the broadside, a shriek from the masthead voice-pipe carried clearly.

'Warships! Enemy warships dead astern!'

'Starboard ten.' Von Kleine raised his voice a little louder than was his wont, and still under full power, *Blücher* swerved away from the land, leaning out from the turn, with her wake curved like an ostrich plume on the surface of the sea behind her, and ran for the shelter of the fog banks, leaving the rich prize of cargo shipping unscathed. On her bridge von Kleine and his officers were staring aft, the merchantmen forgotten as they search for this new threat.

'Two warships.' The masthead look-out was elaborating his sighting report. 'A destroyer and a cruiser. Bearing ninety degrees. Range, five-oh-seven-oh. Destroyer leading.'

In the spherical field of von Kleine's binoculars the neat little triangle of the leading destroyer's superstructure popped up above the horizon. The cruiser was not yet in sight from the bridge.

'If they'd been an hour later,' lamented Kyller, 'we'd have finished the business and . . .'

'What does masthead see of the cruiser?' von Kleine interrupted him impatiently. He had no time to mourn this chance of fate–his only concern was to evaluate the force that was pursuing him, and then make the decision whether to run, or to turn back and engage them immediately.

'Cruiser is a medium, six- or nine-inch. Either "O" class, or an "R". She's four miles behind her escort. Both ships still out of range.'

The destroyer was of no consequence; he could run down on her and blast her into a burning wreck, before her feeble little 4·7-inch guns were able to drop a shell within a mile of *Blücher*, but the cruiser was another matter entirely. To tackle her, *Blücher* would be engaging with her own class; victory would only be won after a severe mauling, and she was six thousand miles from the nearest friendly port where she could effect major repairs.

There was a further consideration. These two British ships might be the vanguard of a battle squadron. If he turned now and challenged action, engaged the cruiser in a single ship action, he might suddenly find himself pitted against imponderable odds. There could very well be another cruiser, or two, or three–even a battleship, below the southern horizon.

His duty and his orders dictated instant flight, avoiding action, and so prolonging *Blücher*'s fighting life.

'Enemy are streaming their colours, sir,' Kyller reported.

Von Kleine lifted his binoculars again. At the destroyer's masthead flew the tiny spots of white and red. This time he must leave the challenge to combat unanswered. 'Very well,' he said, and turned away to his stool in the corner of the bridge. He slumped into it and hunched his shoulders in thought. There were many interesting problems to occupy him, not least of them was how long he could run at full speed towards the north while his boilers devoured coal ravenously, and each minute widened the gap between *Blücher* and *Esther*.

He swivelled his stool and looked back over his stern. The destroyer was visible to the unaided eye now, and von Kleine frowned at it in irritation. She would yap at his heels like a terrier, clinging to him and shouting his course and speed across the ether to the hungry British squadrons, that must even now be closing with him from every direction. For days now he could expect to see her sitting in his wake.

43

'Come on! Come on!' Charles Little slapped his hand impatiently against the padded arm of his stool as he watched *Orion*.

For a night and a day he had watched her gaining on *Blücher* but so infinitesimally slowly that it required his range finder to confirm the gain every thirty minutes.

Orion's bows were unnaturally high, and the waves she lifted with the passage of her hull through the water were the white wings of a seagull in the tropical sunlight; for Manderson, her captain, had pumped out her forward fresh-water tanks and fired away half the shell and explosive propellent from her forward magazines. Every man whose presence in the front half of the ship was not essential to her operation had been ordered aft to stand on the open deck as human ballast–all this in an effort to lift *Orion*'s bows and to coax another inch of speed from the cruiser.

Now she faced the most dangerous hour of her life, for she was creeping within extreme range of *Blücher*'s terrible nine-inch armament, and, taking into account the discrepancy in their speeds, it would be another hour before she could bring her own six-inch guns to bear. During that time she would be under fire from *Blücher*'s after turrets and would have no answer to them.

It was heart-breaking for Charles to watch the chase, for *Bloodhound* had not once been asked to extend herself. Below there was a reserve of speed that would allow her to close with *Blücher* in fifty minutes of steaming–always provided she was not smashed into a fiery shambles long before.

Thus the three vessels fled towards the ever-receding northern horizon. The two long shapes of the cruisers flying arrow straight, solid columns of reeking smoke pouring from their triple funnels to besmear the gay, glittering surface of the sea with a long double bank of black that dispersed only slowly on the easterly breeze; while, like a water beetle, the diminutive *Bloodhound* circled out to the side of *Blücher* from where, when the time came, she could spot the fall of *Orion*'s shells more accurately and signal the corrections to her. But always *Bloodhound* tactfully kept outside the fifteen mile radius which marked the length of *Blücher*'s talons.

'We can expect *Blücher* to open fire at any moment now, sir,' the navigating lieutenant commented as he straightened up from the sextant, over which he had been measuring the angle subtended by the two cruisers.

Charles nodded in agreement. 'Yes. Von Kleine must try for a few lucky hits, even at that range.'

'This isn't going to be very pretty to watch.'

'We'll just have to sit tight, keep our fingers crossed, and hope old *Orion* can–' He stopped abruptly, and then jumped up from his stool. 'Hello! *Blücher*'s up to something!'

The silhouette of the German cruiser had altered drastically in the last few seconds. The gap between her funnels widened and now Charles could see the humped menace of her forward turrets.

'By God, she's altering course! The bloody bastard is bringing all his turrets to bear!'

Lieutenant Kyller studied his captain's face. In sleep there was an air of serenity about the man. It reminded Kyller of a painting he had seen in the cathedral at Nürnberg, a portrait of Saint Luke by Holbein. The same fine bone structure, the golden blond beard and moustache that framed the mobile and sensitive lips. He pushed the idea aside and leaned forward. Gently he touched von Kleine's shoulder.

'Captain. My Captain,' and von Kleine opened his eyes. They were smoky blue with sleep but his voice was crisp.

'What is it, Kyller?'

'The gunnery officer reports the enemy will be within range in fifteen minutes.

Von Kleine swivelled his stool and looked quickly about his ship. Above him the smoke poured from every funnel, and from the mouth of each stack a volcano of sparks and shimmering heat blew steadily. The paint had blistered and peeled from the metal of the funnels and they glowed red hot, even in the sunlight. *Blücher* was straining herself far beyond the limits her makers had set. God alone knew what injury this constant running at full speed was doing her, and von Kleine winced as he felt her tremble in protest beneath him.

He turned his eyes astern. The British cruiser was hull up on the horizon now. The difference in their speeds must be a small fraction of a knot, but *Blücher*'s superiority in fire power was enormous.

For a moment he allowed himself to ponder the arrogance of a nation that constantly, almost by choice, matched their men and ships against unnatural odds. Always they sent terriers to fight against wolfhounds. Then he smiled, you had to be English or mad, to understand the English.

He glanced out to starboard. The British destroyer had worked out on to his flank. It could do little harm from there.

'Very well, Kyller . . .' He stood as he spoke.

'Bridge–Engine Room,' the voice-tube squealed.

'Engine Room–Bridge.' Kyller turned to it,

'Our port main bearing is running red hot. I must shut down our port engine!'

The words struck von Kleine like a bucket of iced water thrown down his back. He leaped to the voice-tube.

'This is the Captain. I must have full power for another hour!'

'I can't do it, sir. Another fifteen minutes and the main drive shaft will seize up. God knows what damage it will do.'

For five seconds von Kleine hunched silently over the voice-tube. His mind raced. On one engine *Blücher* would lose ten knots on her speed. The enemy would be able to manœuvre about him freely–possibly hold off until nightfall and then . . . He must attack immediately; turn on them and press his attack home with all his armament.

'Give me full power for as long as you can,' he snapped, and then turning to the gunnery officer's tube, 'This is the Captain. I am turning four points to starboard, and will keep the enemy directly on our starboard beam for the next fifteen minutes. After that I will be forced to reduce speed. Open fire when you bear.' Von Kleine snapped the cover closed and turned to his yeoman of signals. 'Hoist the battle ensign!'

He spoke softly, without heat, but there were lights in his eyes like those in a blue sapphire.

44

'There she goes!' whispered Charles Little without lowering his glasses. Upon the black turrets of *Blücher* the gunfire gleamed and sparkled without sound. Quickly he traversed his glasses across the surface of the sea until he found *Orion*. She was plunging in eagerly, narrowing the gap very rapidly between herself and *Blücher*. In another seven minutes she would be able to return the German's fire.

Suddenly, a quarter of a mile ahead of her, there rose from the sea a series of tall columns, stately as the columns of a Greek temple, slender and beautiful, shining like white marble in the sun. Then slowly they dropped back.

'Short,' grunted the navigating lieutenant.

'Her guns are still cold,' Charles commented. 'Please God let old *Orion* get within range.'

Again *Blücher*'s shells fell short, and short again, but each time they were closer to the low bulk of *Orion*, and the next broadside dropped all around her, partially screening her with spray, and *Orion* started to zigzag.

'Another three minutes,' the navigating lieutenant spoke with tension making his voice husky.

At regular intervals of fifteen seconds the German salvoes fell around *Orion*–once within fifty feet of her bows so that as she tore into the standing columns of spray, they blew back over her and mingled with the black smoke of her funnels.

'Come on, old girl! Go in and get her. Go on! Go on!' Charles was gripping the rail in front of him and cheering like a maniac, all the dignity of his rank and his thirty-five years gone in the tense excitement of the battle. It had infected all of them on the bridge of the destroyer, and they capered and shouted with him.

'There she blows!' howled the lieutenant.

'She's opened fire!'

'Go it, *Orion*, go it!'

On *Orion*'s forward turrets gunfire sparkled, then again and again. The harsh roll of the broadsides carried to them against the light wind.

'Short,' groaned Charles 'She's still out of range.'

'Short again!'

'Still short.'

Each time the call of shot was signalled by the chief yeoman at the Aldis lamp, and briefly acknowledged from *Orion*'s bridgeworks.

'Oh my God,' moaned Charles.

'She's hit!' echoed his lieutenant.

A flat yellow glare, like sheet lightning on a summer's day, lit *Orion*'s afterdeck, and almost immediately a ball of yellowish grey smoke enveloped her. Through it Charles saw her after-funnel sag drunkenly and hang back at an unnatural angle.

'She's holding on!'

Orion emerged from the shell smoke and dragged it after her like a funeral cloak, but her speed seemed unabated, and the regular salvoes burned briefly and brightly on her forward turrets.

'Now she's hitting,' exulted the lieutenant, and Charles turned quickly to see shell-fire burst on *Blücher*, and his wide grin split his face.

'Kill her! Kill her!' he roared, knowing that though *Blücher* was better armed yet she was as vulnerable as *Orion*. Her plating was egg-shell thin and the six-inch shells that crashed through it would be doing her terrible damage.

Now the two cruisers were pounding each other. The range was closing so rapidly that soon they must hit with every broadside. This was a contest from which only one ship, or neither of them, would emerge.

Charles was trying to estimate the damage that had been inflicted upon *Blücher* during the last few minutes. She was on fire forward. Sulphur-yellow flames poured from her, her upperworks were riven into a grotesque sculpture of destruction, and a pall of smoke enveloped her, so her profile was shadowy and vague, yet every fifteen seconds her turrets lit with those deadly little flashes.

Charles turned to assess the relative damage that *Orion* had suffered. He found and held her with his binoculars–and at that moment *Orion* ceased to exist.

Her boilers, pierced by high explosive shell, burst and tore her in half. A cloud of white steam spurted five hundred feet into the air, completely blanketing her. The steam hung for thirty seconds then sagged wearily, and rolled aside. *Orion* was gone. A wide circle of oil slick and floating debris marked her grave. The speed of her charge had run her clean under.

On the bridge of *Bloodhound*, the cheering strangled into deathly silence. The silence was not spoiled but rather accentuated by the mournful note of the wind in her rigging and the muted throb of her engines.

45

For eight long hours Charles Little had ridden his anger and his hatred, using the curb to hold it on the right side of madness, resisting the consuming and suicidal urge to hurl his ship at the German cruiser and die as *Orion* had died.

Immediately after the sinking of *Orion*, the *Blücher* had reduced speed sharply and turned due south. With her fires still raging, she had limped along like a gun-shot lion. The battle ensigns at her masthead were tattered by shrapnel and blackened by smoke.

As soon as she had passed, *Bloodhound* altered course and cruised slowly over the area of water that was still rainbowed by floating oil and speckled with wreckage. There were no survivors from *Orion*; all of them had died with her.

Bloodhound turned and and trailed after the crippled German cruiser, and hatred that emanated from the destroyer was of such strength that it should have reached out across the sea as a physical force and destroyed *Blücher*.

But as Charles Little stood at the rail of his bridge, he saw the smoke and flame upon *Blücher*'s decks reduce perceptibly every minute as her damage control teams fought it to a stand-still. The last wisp of smoke from her shrivelled.

'Fire's out,' said the pilot, and Charles made no answer. He had hoped that the flames would eat their way into one of *Blücher*'s magazines and blow her into the same oblivion into which she had sent *Orion*.

'But she isn't making more than six knots. *Orion* must have hit her in the engine room.' Hopefully the navigating lieutenant went on, 'My bet is that she's got major damage below. At this speed we can expect *Pegasus* and *Renounce* to catch up with us by midday tomorrow. Then *Blücher* will stand no chance!'

'Yes,' agreed Charles softly.

Summoned by *Bloodhound*'s frantic radio transmissions, *Pegasus* and *Renounce*, the two heavy cruisers of the northern squadron, were racing down the East African coast, cutting through the five hundred miles of water that separated them.

46

'Kyller. Ask the chief how he's making out.' Von Kleine was fretting beneath the calm set of his features. Night was closing, and in the darkness, even the frail little English destroyer was a danger to him. There was danger all around, danger must each minute be approaching from every quarter of the sea. He must have power on his port side engine before nightfall; it was a matter of survival; he must have speed to carry him south through the hunting packs of the British–south to where *Esther* waited to give him succour, to replace the shell he had fired away, to replenish his coal bunkers which were now dangerously depleted. Then once more *Blücher* would be a force to reckon with. But first he must have speed.

'Captain.' Kyller was beside him again. 'Commander Lochtkamper reports they have cleared the oil line to the main bearing. They have stripped the bearing and there is no damage to the shaft. He is fitting new half shells. The work is well advanced, sir.'

The words conjured up for von Kleine a picture of half-naked men, smeared to the elbows with black grease, sweating in the confined heat of the drive shaft tunnel as they worked. 'How much longer?' he asked.

'He promised full power on both engines within two hours, sir.'

Von Kleine sighed with relief, and glanced over his stern at the British destroyer that was shadowing him. He began to smile.

'I hope, my friend, that you are a brave man. I hope that when you see me increase speed, you will not be able to control your disappointment. I hope tonight you will try with your torpedoes, so that I can crush you, for your eyes always on me are a dangerous embarrassment.' He spoke so softly that his lips barely moved, then he turned back to Kyller. 'I want all the battle lights checked and reported.'

'Aye, aye, sir.'

Von Kleine crossed to the voice-tubes. 'Gunnery officer,' he said. 'I want "X" turret guns loaded with star shell and trained to maximum elevation . . .' He went on listing his preparations for night action and then he ended,

'. . . stand all your gun crews down. Let them eat and rest. From dusk action stations onwards they will be held in the first degree of readiness.'

'Commander, sir!'

The urgent call startled Commander Charles Little, and he spilled his mug of cocoa. This was the first period of rest he had allowed himself all day, and now it was interrupted within ten minutes. 'What is it?' He flung open the door of the chart room, and ran out on to the bridge.

'*Blücher* is increasing speed rapidly.'

'No!' It was too cruel a blow, and the exclamation of protest was wrung from Charles. He darted to the voice-pipe.

'Gunnery officer. Report your target.'

A moment's delay, and then the reply. 'Bearing mark, green oh-oh. Range, one-five-oh-five-oh. Speed, seventeen knots.'

It was true. *Blücher* was under full power again, with all her guns still operable. *Orion* had died in vain.

Charles wiped his mouth with the open palm of his hand, and felt the brittle stubble of his new beard rasp under his fingers. Beneath the tan, his face was sickly pale with strain and fatigue. There were smears of dark blue beneath his eyes, and in their corners were tiny lumps of yellow mucus. His eyes were bloodshot, and the wisp of hair that escaped from under the brim of his cap was matted on to his forehead by the salt spray, as he peered into the gathering dusk.

The fighting madness which had threatened all that day to overwhelm him, rose slowly from the depth of his belly and his loins. He no longer struggled to suppress it.

'Turn two points to starboard, pilot. All engines full ahead together.' The engine telegraph clanged, and *Bloodhound* pivoted like a polo pony. It would take her thirty minutes to work up to full speed, and by that time it would be dark.

'Sound action stations.' Charles wanted to attack in the hour of darkness before the moon came up. Through the ship the alarm bells thrilled, and without taking his eyes from the dark dot on the darkening horizon, Charles listened to the reports coming into the bridge, until the one for which he waited, 'Torpedo party closed up, sir!'

Now he turned and went to the voice-tube. 'Torps,' he said, 'I hope to give you a chance at *Blücher* with both port and starboard tubes. I am going to take you in as close as possible.'

The men grouped around Charles on the bridge listened to him say 'as close as possible', and knew that he had pronounced sentence of death upon them.

Henry Sergent, the navigating lieutenant, was afraid. Stealthily he groped in the pocket of his overcoat until he found the little silver crucifix that Lynette had given him. It was warm from his own body heat. He held it tightly.

He remembered it hanging between her breasts on its silver chain, and the way she had lifted both hands to the back of her neck as she unclasped it. The chain had caught in the shiny cascade of hair as she had tried to free it, kneeling on the bed facing him. He had leaned forward to help her, and she had clung to him, pressing the warm smooth bulge of her pregnant stomach against him.

'God protect you, my darling husband,' she had whispered. 'Please God bring you back safely to us.'

And now he was afraid for her and the daughter he had never seen.

'Hold your course, damn you!' he snapped at Herbert Cryer, the helmsman.

'Aye, aye, sir,' Herbert Cryer replied with just a trace of injured innocence in his tone. No man could hold *Bloodhound* true when she hurled herself from swell to swell with such abandoned violence; she must yaw and throw her head that fraction before the helm could correct her. The reprimand was unjustified, uttered in fear and tension. 'Give it a flipping break, mate,' Herbert retorted silently. 'You're not the only one who is going to catch it. Tighten up the old arsehole like a bloody officer and a ruddy gentleman.'

In these wordless exchanges of repartee with his officers, Herbert Cryer was never bested. They were wonderful release for resentments and pent-up emotion, and now because he was also afraid, he became silently lyrical.

'Climb-aboard-Romeo's one way express to flipping glory.' Commander Little's reputation with the ladies had resulted in him being irreverently but affectionately baptized by his crew. 'Come along with us. We're off to shout at the devil, while Charlie kisses his daughter.'

Herbert glanced sideways at his commander and grinned. Fear made the grin wolfish, and Charles Little saw it and misinterpreted it. He read it as a mark of the same berserk fury that possessed him. The two of them grinned at each other for an instant in complete misunderstanding, before Herbert refocused his attention on *Bloodhound*'s next wild crabbing lunge.

Charles was afraid as well. He was afraid of finding a weakness in himself–but this was the fear that had walked at his right hand all his life, close beside him, whispering to him, 'Harder, try harder. You must do better, you must do it quicker, or bigger than they do, or they'll laugh at you. You mustn't fail–not in one thing, not for one moment, you mustn't fail. You mustn't fail!' This fear was the eternal companion and partner in every venture on which he embarked.

It had stood beside the thirteen-year-old Charles in a duck blind, while he fired a twelve gauge shotgun, and wept slowly fat tears of agony every time the recoil smashed into his bruised bicep and shoulder.

It had stooped over him as he lay in the mud hugging a broken collar bone. 'Get up!' it hissed at him. 'Get up!' It had forced him to his feet and led him back to the unbroken colt to mount again, and again, and again.

So conditioned was he to respond to its voice that when it crouched beside him now, twisted and misshapen on the footplates of the bridge, its presence almost tangible, and croaked so Charles alone could hear it, 'Prove it! Prove it!' there was only one course open to Charles Little; a peregrine stooping at a golden eagle, he took his ship in against the *Blücher*.

47

'The turn to starboard was a feint.' Otto von Kleine spoke with certainty, staring out to where the dusk had obliterated the frail silhouette of the English destroyer. 'Even now he is turning again to cross our stern. He will attack on our port side.'

'Captain, it could be the double bluff,' Kyller answered dubiously.

'No.' Von Kleine shook his golden beard. 'He must try to outline us against the last of the light from the sunset. He will attack from the east.' A moment longer he frowned in thought, as he anticipated his opponent's moves across the chessboard of the ocean. 'Kyller, plot me his course, assuming a speed of twenty-five knots, a turn four points to port three minutes after our last sighting, a run of fifteen miles across our stern, and then a turn of four points to starboard. If we hold our present course and speed, where will he be in relation to us, in ninety minutes' time?'

Working quickly, Kyller completed the problem. Von Kleine had been mentally checking every step of the calculation. 'Yes,' he agreed with Kyller's solution, and already he had formulated the orders for change of course and speed to place *Bloodhound* in ambush.

48

Under full power, *Bloodhound* threw a bow-wave ten feet high, and a wake that boiled out for a quarter of a mile behind her, a long faintly phosphorescent smear in the darkness.

Aboard *Blücher* a hundred pairs of eyes were straining out into the night, watching for that phosphorescence. Behind the battle lights on her upperworks men waited, in the dimly-lit turrets men waited, on the open bridge, at the masthead, deep in her belly, the crew of *Blücher* waited.

Von Kleine had reduced speed to lessen his own wake, and turned away from the land at an angle of forty-five degrees. He wanted to catch the Englishman on his starboard beam, out of torpedo range.

He stood peering out across the dark sea, with the fur-lined collar of his overcoat drawn up to his ears. The night was cool. The sea was a black immensity, vast as the sky that was lined in glowing ivory by the whorls and smears of the star patterns.

A dozen men saw it at the same instant; pale, ethereal, seeming to float upon the darkness of the sea like a plume of iridescent mist–the wake of the Englishman.

'Star shell!' Von Kleine snapped the order to the waiting guns. He was alarmed by the English destroyer's proximity. He had hoped to spot her at greater range.

High above the ocean, the star shells burst blue-white, so intensely bright as to sear the retina of the eye that looked directly at them. Beneath them the surface of the sea was polished ebony, sculptured and scooped with the pattern of the swells. The two ships were starkly and crisply lit, steaming on converging courses, already so close to each other that the mile-long, solid white beams of their battle lights jumped out to join, fumbling together like the hands of hesitant lovers.

In almost the same second both ships opened fire, but the banging of *Bloodhound*'s little 4·7-inch guns were lost in the bellow of the cruiser's broadside.

Blücher was firing over open sights with her guns depressed until the long barrels were horizontal to the surface of the sea. Her first salvo was aimed a fraction high, and the huge shells howled over *Bloodhound*'s open bridge.

The wind of their passage, the fierce draught of distrupted air they threw out, caught Charles Little and sent him reeling against the compass pinnacle. He felt the ribs below his armpit crack.

The command he shouted at the helm was hoarse with pain.

'Turn four points to port! Steer for the enemy!' and *Bloodhound* spun like a ballet dancer, and charged straight at *Blücher*.

The cruiser's next broadside was high again but now her secondary armament had joined in, and a four-pound shell from one of the quick-firing pom-poms burst on the director tower above *Bloodhound*'s bridge. It swept the exposed area with a buzzing hailstorm of shrapnel.

It killed the navigating lieutenant instantly, cutting away the top of his head as though it were the shell of a soft-boiled egg. He fell on the deck and splattered the footplates with the warm custard of his brains.

A piece of the red hot shell casing the size of a thumbnail entered the point of Herbert Cryer's right elbow and shattered the bone to splinters. He grasped at the shock and sprawled against the wheel.

'Hold her. Hold her true!' The order from Commander Little was blurred as the speech of a spastic. Herbert Cryer pulled himself up with his left hand spun the wheel to meet *Bloodhound*'s wild swing, but with his right arm hanging useless, his steering was clumsy and awkward.

'Steady her, man. Hold her steady!' Again that thick slurring voice, and Cryer was aware of Charles Little beside him, his hands on the helm, helping to hold *Bloodhound*'s frantic head.

'Aye, aye, sir.' Cryer glanced at his commander and gasped again. This time in horror. Razor-sharp steel had sliced off Charles Little's ear, then gone on to cut his cheek away, and expose the bone of his jaw and the white teeth that lined it. A flap of tattered flesh hung down on to his chest, and from a dozen severed blood vessels dark blood dripped and spurted and dribbled.

The two of them crouched wounded over the wheel, with the dead men at their feet, and aimed *Bloodhound* at the long low bulk of the German cruiser.

Now in the daylight glare of the star shells, the sea around them was thrashed and whipped into seething life by the cacophony of *Blücher*'s guns. Tall towers of white water rose briefly and majestically about them, then dropped back to leave the surface troubled and restless with foam.

And *Bloodhound* drove on until suddenly it seemed she had run into a cliff of solid granite. Beneath their feet, she jarred and bucked violently. A nine-inch shell had taken her full in the bows.

'Port full rudder.' Charles Little's voice was sloshy sounding, wet with the blood that filled his mouth, and together they spun the wheel to full left lock.

But *Bloodhound* was dying. The shell had split her bows wide open, torn her plating and fanned it open like the petals of a macabre orchid. The black night sea rushed through her. Already her bows were sinking, slumping wearily, lifting her stern so the rudder no longer had full purchase. But even in death she was trying desperately to obey. Slowly she swung, inchingly, achingly, she swung.

Charles Little left the helm and tottered towards the starboard rail. His legs were numb and heavy under him, and the weakness of his lost blood drummed in his ears. He reached the rail and clung there, peering down on the torpedo tubes that stood on the deck below him.

The tubes looked like a rack of fat cigars, and with weary jubilation Charles saw that there were men still tending them, crouching behind the sheet of armour plate, waiting for *Bloodhound* to turn and bring *Blücher* on to her starboard beam.

'Turn, old girl. Come on! That's it! Turn!' Charles croaked through the blood.

Another shell struck *Bloodhound*, and she heaved in mortal agony. Perhaps this movement, combined with a chance push of the sea swell, was enough to swing her those last few degrees.

There, full in the track of the torpedo tubes, lit by her own star shells and the gunfire from her turrets, a scant thousand yards across the black water, lay the German cruiser.

Charles heard the whoosh, whoosh, whoosh, whoosh, of the tubes as they fired. He saw the long sharklike shapes of the torpedoes leap out from the deck and strike the water, saw the four white wakes arrowing away in formation, and behind him he heard the torpedo officer's triumphant shout, distorted by the voice-pipe.

'All four fired, and running true!'

Charles never saw his torpedoes strike, for one of *Blücher*'s nine-inch shells hit the bridgework three feet below him. For one brief unholy instant, he stood in the centre of a furnace as hot as the flames of the sun.

49

Otto von Kleine watched the English destroyer explode. Towering orange flames erupted from her, and a solid ball of black smoke spun upon itself, blooming on the dark ocean like a flower from the gardens of hell. The surface of the sea around her was dimpled by the fall of thrown debris and the cruiser's shells–for all of *Blücher*'s guns were still blazing.

'Cease fire,' he said, without taking his eyes from the awesome pageant of destruction that he had created.

Another salvo of star shell burst above, and von Kleine lifted his hand to his eyes and pressed his thumb and forefinger into the closed lids, shielding them from the stabbing brilliance of the light. It was finished, and he was tired.

He was tired, drained of nervous and physical energy, overwhelmed by the backwash of fatigue that followed these last two days and nights of ceaseless strain. And he was sad–sad for the brave men he had killed, and the terrible destruction he had wrought.

Still holding his eyes, he opened his mouth to give the order that would send *Blücher* once more thrashing southward, but before the words reached his lips, a wild shout from the lookout interrupted him.

'Torpedoes! Close on the starboard beam!'

Long seconds von Kleine hesitated. He had let his brain relax, let the numbness wash over it. The battle was over, and he had dropped back from the high pinnacle of alertness on which he had balanced these last desperate hours. It needed a conscious physical effort to call up his reserves, and during those seconds, the torpedoes fired by *Bloodhound* in her death throes were knifing in to revenge her.

At last von Kleine snapped the bonds of inertia that bound his mind. He leaped to the starboard rail of the bridge, and saw in the light of the star shells the pale phosphorescent trails of the four torpedoes. Against the dark water they looked like the tails of meteors on a night sky.

'Full port rudder. All engines full astern together!' he shouted, his voice pitched high with consternation.

He felt his ship swerve beneath him, thrown violently over as the great propellers clawed at the sea to hold her from crossing the path of the torpedoes.

Hopelessly he stood and reviled himself. *I should have anticipated this. I should have known the destroyer had fired.*

Helplessly he stood and watched the four white lines drawn swiftly across the surface towards him.

In the last moments he felt a fierce upward surge of hope. Three of the English torpedoes would miss. That was certain. They would cross *Blücher*'s bows as she side-stepped. And the fourth torpedo it was just possible would miss also.

His fingers upon the bridge rail clenched, until it felt as though they must press into the metal. His breath jammed in his throat and choked him.

Ponderously, *Blücher* swung her bows away. If he had given the order for the turn only five seconds earlier . . .

The torpedo struck *Blücher* five feet below the surface, on the very tip of her curved keel.

The explosion shot a mountain of white water one hundred and fifty feet into the air. It slammed *Blücher* back on to her haunches with such violence that Otto von Kleine and his officers were thrown heavily to the steel deck.

Von Kleine scrabbled to his knees and looked forward. A fine veil of spray, like pearl dust in the light of the star shells, hung over *Blücher*. As he watched, it subsided slowly.

All that night they struggled to keep *Blücher* afloat.

They sealed off her bows with the five-inch steel doors in the watertight bulkhead, and behind those doors they locked thirty German seamen whose battle stations were in the bows. At intervals during the frenzied activity of the night, von Kleine had visions of those men floating face-down in the flooded compartments.

While the pumps clanged throughout the ship to free her of the hundreds of tons of sea-water that washed through her, von Kleine left the bridge and, with his engineer commander and damage control officer, they listed the injuries that *Blücher* had received.

In the dawn they assembled grimly in the chart-room behind the bridge, and assessed their plight.

'What power can you give me, Lochtkamper?' von Kleine demanded of his engineer.

'I can give you as much as you ask.' A reddish-purple bruise covered half the engineer's face where he had been thrown against a steam cock-valve when the torpedo struck. 'But anything over five knots will carry away the watertight bulkheads forward. They will take the full brunt of the sea.'

Von Kleine swivelled his stool, and looked at the damage control officer. 'What repairs can you effect at sea?'

'None, sir. We have braced and propped the watertight bulkhead. We have patched and jammed the holes made by the British cruiser's guns. But I can do nothing about the underwater damage without a dry dock–or calm water where I can put divers over the side. We must enter a port.'

Von Kleine leaned back in his stool and closed his eyes to think.

The only friendly port within six thousand miles was Dar es Salaam, the capital of German East Africa, but he knew the British were blockading it. He discarded it from his list of possible refuges.

An island? Zanzibar?–The Seychelles?–Mauritius?–All hostile territories with no anchorage safe from bombardment by a British squadron.

A river mouth? The Zambezi? No, that was in Portuguese territory, navigable for only the first few miles of its length.

Suddenly he opened his eyes. There was one ideal haven situated in German territory, navigable even by a ship of *Blücher*'s tonnage for twenty miles. It was guarded from overland approach by formidable terrain, yet he could call upon the German Commissioner for stores and labour and protection.

'Kyller,' he said. 'Plot me a course for the Kikunya mouth of the Rufiji delta.'

Five days later the *Blücher* crawled painfully as a crippled centipede into the northernmost channel of the Rufiji delta. She was blackened with battle smoke, her riggings hung in tatters, and at a thousand places shell splinters had pierced her upperworks. Her bows were swollen and distorted, and the sea washed through her forward compartments and then boiled and spilled out of the ghastly rents in her plating.

As she passed between the forests of mangroves that lined the channel, they seemed to enfold her like welcoming arms.

Overside she lowered two picket boats and these darted ahead of her like busy little water beetles as they sounded the channel, and searched for a secure anchorage. Gradually *Blücher* wriggled and twisted her way deeper and deeper into the wilderness of the delta. At a place where the flood waters of the Rufiji had cut a deep bay between two islands, and formed a natural jetty on both sides, the *Blücher* came to rest.

50

Herman Fleischer wiped his face and neck with a hand towel and then looked at the sodden material. God, how he hated the Rufiji basin. As soon as he entered its humid and malodorous heat, a thousand tiny taps opened under his skin and out gushed the juices of his body.

The prospect of an extended stay aroused in him a dark resentment to all things, but especially to this young snob who stood beside him on the foredeck of the steam launch. Herman darted a glance at him now. Cool he looked, as though he were sauntering down Unter den Linden in June. The shimmering white of his tropical uniform was unwrinkled and dry, not like the thick corduroy that bunched damply at Herman's armpits and crotch. Mother of a dog, it would start the rash again; he could feel it beginning to itch and he scratched at it moodily, then checked his hand as he saw the lieutenant smile.

'How far are we from *Blücher*?' and then as an afterthought he used the lieutenant's surname without rank, 'How far, Kyller?' It was as well to keep reminding the man that as the equivalent of a full colonel, he far outranked him.

'Around the next bend, Commissioner.' Kyller's voice carried the lazy inflection that made Fleischer think of champagne and opera houses, of skiing parties and boar hunts.

'I hope that Captain von Kleine has made adequate preparation to defend her against enemy attack?'

'She is safe.' For the first time there was a brittle undertone to Kyller's reply, and Fleischer pounced on it. He sensed an advantage. For the last two days, ever since Kyller had met him at the confluence of the Ruhaha river, Herman had been needling him to find a weakness.

'Tell me, Kyller,' he dropped his voice to an intimate, confidential level. 'This is in strict confidence, of course, but do you really feel that Captain von Kleine is able to handle this situation? I mean, do you feel that someone else may have been able to reach a more satisfactory result?' Ah! Yes! That was it! Look at him flush, look at the anger stain those cool brown cheeks. For the first time the advantage was with Herman Fleischer.

'Commander Fleischer,' Kyller spoke softly but Herman exulted to hear his tone. 'Captain von Kleine is the most skilful, efficient, and courageous officer under whom I have had the honour to serve. He is, furthermore, a gentleman.'

'So?' Herman grunted. 'Then why is this paragon hiding in the Rufiji basin with his buttocks shot full of holes?' Then he threw back his head and guffawed in triumph.

'At another time, sir, and in different circumstances, I would ask you to withdraw those words.' Kyller turned from him and walked to the forward rail. He stood there staring ahead, while the launch chugged around another bend in the river, opening the same dreary vista of dark water and mangrove forest. Kyller spoke without turning his head. 'There is the *Blücher*,' he said.

There was nothing but the sweep of water and the massed fuzzy heads of the mangroves below a hump of higher ground upon the bank. The laughter faded from Herman's chubby face as he searched, then a small scowl replaced it as he realized that the lieutenant was baiting him. There was certainly no battle cruiser anchored in the waterway. 'Lieutenant . . .' he began angrily, then checked himself. The high ground was divided by a narrow channel, not more than a hundred yards wide, fenced in by the mangrove forest, but the channel was blocked by a shapeless and ungainly mound of vegetation. He stared at it uncomprehendingly until suddenly beneath the netting that was festooned with branches of mangroves, he saw the blurred outline of turrets and superstructure.

The camouflage had been laid with fascinating ingenuity. From a distance of three hundred yards the *Blücher* was invisible.

51

The bubbles came up slowly through the dark water as though it had the same viscosity as warm honey. They burst on the surface in a boiling white rash.

Captain von Kleine leaned across the foredeck rail of the *Blücher* and peered at the disturbance below him, with the absorption of a man attempting to read his own future in the murky mirror of the Rufiji waters. For almost two hours he had waited like this, drawing quietly on a succession of little black cheroots, occasionally easing his body into a more comfortable position.

Although his body was at rest, his brain was busy, endlessly reviewing his preparations and his plans. His preparations were complete, he had mentally listed them and found no omissions.

A party of six seamen had been dispatched fifteen miles downstream by picket boat to the entrance of the delta. They were encamped on a hummock of high ground above the channel to watch the sea for the British blockade squadron.

As *Blücher* crept up the channel she had sown the last of her globular multi-horned mines behind her. No British ship could follow her.

Remote as the chances of overload attack seemed, yet von Kleine had set up a system of defence around the *Blücher*. Half his seamen were ashore now, spread in a network to guard each of the possible approaches. Fields of fire had been cut through the mangroves for his Maxim guns. Crude fortifications of log and earth had been built and manned, communication lines set up, and he was ready.

After long discussions with his medical officer, von Kleine had issued orders to protect the health of his men. Orders for the purification of water, the disposal of sanitation and waste, for the issue of five grains of quinine daily to each man, and fifty other safeguards to health and morale.

He had ordered an inventory made of stocks of food and supplies, and he was satisfied that with care he could subsist for a further four months. Thereafter he would be reduced to fishing and hunting, and foraging.

He had dispatched Kyller upstream to make contact with the German Commissioner, and solicit his full co-operation.

Four days had been spent in hiding the *Blücher* under her camouflage, in setting up a complete workshop on the foredeck under sun awnings, so that the engineers could work in comparative comfort.

Now at last they had begun a full underwater appraisal of *Blücher*'s wounds.

Behind him he heard the petty officer pass an order to the team at the winch. 'Bring him up–slowly.'

The donkey engine spluttered into life, and the winch clattered and whined shrilly. Von Kleine stirred against the rail and focused his full attention on the water below him.

The heavy line and airpipe reeled in smoothly, then suddenly the surface bulged and the body of the diver was lifted dangling on the line. Black in shiny wet rubber, the three brass-bound cyclopean eyes of his helmet glaring, grotesque as a sea monster, he was swung inboard and lowered to the deck.

Two seamen hurried forward and unscrewed the bolts at the neck, lifted off the heavy helmet, and exposed the head of the engineering commander, Lochtkamper. The heavy face, flat and lined as that of a mastiff, was made heavier than usual by the thoughtful frown it now wore. He looked across at his captain and shook his head slightly.

'Come to my cabin when you are ready, Commander,' said von Kleine, and walked away.

'A small glass of cognac?' von Kleine suggested.

'I'd like that, sir.' Commander Lochtkamper looked out of place in the elegance of the cabin. The hands that accepted the glass were big, knuckles scarred and enlarged by constant violent contact with metal, the skin etched deeply with oil and engine filth. When he sank into the chair at his captain's invitation, his legs seemed to have too many knees.

'Well?' asked von Kleine, and Lochtkamper launched into his report. He spoke for ten minutes and von Kleine followed him slowly through the maze of technicalities where strange and irrelevant obscenities grew along the way. In moments of deep concentration such as these Lochtkamper fell back on the gutter idiom of his native Hamburg, and von Kleine was unable to suppress a smile when he learned that the copulator torpedo had committed a perversion on one of the main frames, springing the plating whose morals were definitely suspect. The damage sounded like that suffered in a brothel during a Saturday night brawl.

'Can you repair it?' von Kleine asked at last.

'It will mean cutting away all the obscenely damaged plating, lifting it to the deck, recutting it, welding and shaping it. But we will still be short of at least eight hundred obscene square feet of plate, sir.'

'A commodity not readily obtainable in the delta of the Rufiji river,' von Kleine mused.

'No, sir.'

'How long will it take you–if I can get the plating for you?'

'Two months, perhaps.'

'When can you start?'

'Now, sir.'

'Do it then,' said von Kleine, and Lochtkamper drained his glass, smacked his lips, and stood up. 'Very good cognac, sir,' he complimented his captain, and shambled out of the cabin.

52

Staring upward at the massive warship, Herman Fleischer surveyed the battle damage with the uncomprehending curiosity of a landsman. He saw the gaping ulcers where *Orion*'s shells had struck, the black blight where the flames had raged through her, the irregular rash with which the splinters had pierced and peppered her upperworks, and then he dropped his eyes to the bows. Work cradles were suspended a few feet above the water, and upon them clutters of seamen were illuminated by the crackling blue glare of the welding torches.

'God in heaven, what a beating!' He spoke with sadistic relish.

Kyller ignored the remark. He was directing the native helmsman of the launch to the landing ladder that had been rigged down the side of *Blücher*. Not even the presence of this sweaty peasant, Fleischer, could spoil his pleasure in this moment of homecoming. To Ernst Kyller, the *Blücher* was home in the deep sense of the word; it contained all that he valued in life, including the man for whom he bore a devotion surpassing the natural duty of a son to his father. He was savouring the anticipation of von Kleine's smile and words of commendation for another task well done.

'Ah, Kyller!' Von Kleine rose from behind his desk and moved around it to greet his lieutenant.

'Back so soon? Did you find Fleischer?'

'He is waiting outside, sir.'

'Good, good. Bring him in.'

Herman Fleischer paused in the companion-way and blinked suspiciously around the cabin. His mind was automatically converting the furnishings into Reichsmarks, the rugs were silk Teheran in blue and gold and red, the chairs were in dark buttoned leather, all the heavy furniture, including the panelling, was polished mahogany. The light fittings were worked in brass, the glasses in the liquor cabinet were sparkling diamond crystal flanked by a platoon of bottles that wore the uniforms of the great houses of Champagne and Alsace and the Rhine. There was a portrait in oils opposite the desk of two women, both beautiful golden women, clearly mother and daughter. The portholes were curtained with forest green velvet, corded and tasselled in gold.

Herman decided that the Count must be a rich man. He had a proper respect for wealth, and it showed in the way he stepped forward, drew himself up, brought his heels together sharply, and then creased his bulging belly in a bow.

'Captain. I came as soon as I received your message.'

'I am grateful, Commissioner.' Von Kleine returned the salutation. 'You will take refreshment?'

'A glass of beer, and . . .' Herman hesitated, he was certain that somewhere aboard *Blücher* there must be a treasure trove of rare foods, '. . . a bite to eat. I have not eaten since noon.'

It was now the middle of the afternoon. Von Kleine saw nothing unusual in a two-hour period of abstinence, yet he passed the word for his steward while he opened a bottle of beer for his guest.

'I must congratulate you on your victory over the two English warships, Captain. Magnificent, truly magnificent!'

Lying back in one of the leather chairs Fleischer was engaged in mopping his face and neck, and Kyller grinned cynically as he listened to this new tune.

'A victory that was dearly bought,' murmured von Kleine, bringing the glass to Fleischer's chair. 'And now I need your help.'

'Of course! You need only ask.'

Von Kleine went to his desk, sat down, and drew towards him a sheaf of notes. From their chamois leather case, he produced a pair of gold-rimmed spectacles and placed them on his nose.

'Commissioner . . .' he started, but at that moment he completely lost Fleischer's attention. For with a discreet knock the Captain's steward returned with a large, heavily laden carving-plate. He placed it on the table beside Fleischer's chair.

'Sweet Mother of God!' whispered Herman, his eyes glittering, and a fresh sweat of excitement breaking out on his upper lip.

'Smoked salmon!'

Neither von Kleine nor Kyller had ever been privileged to watch Herman eat before. They did so now in awed silence. This was a specialist working with skill and dedication. After a while von Kleine made another effort to attract Herman's attention by coughing and rustling his sheaf of notes, but the Commissioner's snufflings and small moans of sensual pleasure continued. Von Kleine glanced at his lieutenant and lifted a golden eyebrow, Kyller half smiled in embarrassment. It was like watching a man in orgasm, so intimate that von Kleine was obliged to light a cheroot and concentrate his attention on the portrait of his wife and daughter across the cabin.

A gusty sigh signalled Herman's climax, and von Kleine looked at him again. He sagged back in the chair, a vague and dreamy smile playing over the ruddy curves of his face. The plate was empty, and with the sweet sorrow of a man remembering a lost love, Herman dabbed a forefinger on to the last shred of pink flesh and lifted it to his mouth.

'That was the best salmon I have ever tasted.'

'I am pleased that you found it so.' Von Kleine's voice crackled a little. He felt nauseated by the exhibition.

'I wonder if I might trouble you for another glass of beer, Captain.'

Von Kleine nodded at Kyller, and the lieutenant went to refill Fleischer's glass.

'Commissioner. I need at least eight hundred square feet of $1\frac{1}{2}$-inch steel plate delivered to me here. I want it within six weeks,' von Kleine said, and Herman Fleischer laughed. He laughed the way a man laughs at a children's tale of fairies and witches, then suddenly he noticed von Kleine's eyes . . . and he stopped abruptly.

'Lying in Dar es Salaam harbour under British blockade is the steamer *Rheinlander*.' Von Kleine went on speaking softly and clearly. 'You will proceed there as fast as you can. I will send one of my engineers with you. He will beach the *Rheinlander* and dismantle her hull. You will then arrange to convey the plating to me here.'

'Dar es Salaam is one hundred kilometres away.' Herman was aghast.

'According to the Admiralty chart it is seventy-five kilometres,' von Kleine corrected him.

'The plating will weigh many tons!' he cried.

'In German East Africa there are many hundreds of thousands of indigents. I doubt not that you will be able to persuade them to serve as porters.'

'The route is impossible . . . and what is more, there is a band of enemy guerrillas operating in the area north of here. Guerrillas led by those same bandits that you allowed to escape from the dhow, off the mouth of this river.' In agitation Fleischer had risen from his chair and now he pointed a fat accusing forefinger at von Kleine. 'You allowed them to escape. Now they are ravaging the whole province. If I try to bring a heavily laden, slow moving caravan of porters down from Dar es Salaam, word will reach them before I have marched five kilometres. It's madness–I won't do it!'

'It seems then, that you have a choice.' Von Kleine smiled with his mouth only. 'The English marauders, or a firing party on the afterdeck of this ship.'

'What do you mean?' howled Fleischer.

'I mean that my request is no longer a request, it is now an order. If you defy it, I will immediately convene a court martial.'

Von Kleine drew his gold watch and checked the time.

'We should be able to dispose of the formalities and shoot you before dark. What do you think, Kyller?'

'It will be cutting things fine, sir. But I think we could manage it.'

53

When the Governor of Mozambique had offered Flynn a captaincy in the army of Portugal, there had been an ugly scene. Flynn felt strongly that he deserved at least the rank of colonel. He had suggested terminating their business relationship. The Governor had countered with an offer of major–and signalled to his aide-de-camp to refill Flynn's glass. Flynn had accepted both offers, but the one under protest. That was seven months ago, a few short weeks after the massacre at Lalapanzi.

Since then Flynn's army, a mixed bag of a hundred native troops, officered by himself, Sebastian, and Rosa Oldsmith, had been operating almost continually in German territory.

There had been a raid on the Songa railway siding where Flynn had burned five hundred tons of sugar, and nearly a thousand of millet that was in the warehouses awaiting shipment to Dar es Salaam, supplies badly needed by Governor Schee and Colonel Lettow von Vorbeck who were assembling an army in the coastal area.

There had been another brilliant success when they had ambushed and wiped out a band of thirty Askari at a river crossing. Flynn released the three hundred native recruits that the Askari were escorting, and advised them to get the hell back to their villages and forsake any ambitions of military glory–using the corpses of the Askari that littered the banks of the ford as tangible argument.

Apart from cutting every telegraph line, and blowing up the railway tracks they came across, three other raids had met with mixed results. Twice they had captured supply columns of bearers carrying in provisions to the massing German forces. Each time they had been forced to run as German reinforcements came up to drive them off. The third effort had been an abject failure, the ignominy of it being compounded by the fact that they had almost had the person of Commissioner Fleischer in their grasp.

Carried on the swift feet of the runners who were part of Flynn's intelligence system came the news that Herman Fleischer and a party of Askari had left Mahenge boma and marched to the confluence of the Ruhaha and Rufiji rivers. There they had gone aboard the steam launch and disappeared into the fastness of the Rufiji delta on a mysterious errand.

'What goes up must come down,' Flynn pointed out to Sebastian. 'And what goes down the Rufiji must come up again. We will go to the Ruhaha and wait for Herr Fleischer to return.'

For once there was no argument from either Sebastian or Rosa. Between the three of them it was understood without discussion that Flynn's army existed chiefly to act as the vehicle of retribution. They had made a vow over the grave of the child, and now they fought not so much from a sense of duty or patriotism, but from a burning desire for revenge. They wanted the life of Herman Fleischer in part payment for that of Maria Oldsmith.

They set out for the Ruhaha river. As happened so often these days, Rosa marched at the head of the column. There was only the long braid of dark hair hanging down her back to show she was a woman, for she was dressed in bush jacket and long khaki cotton trousers that concealed the feminine fullness of her hips. She stepped out long-legged, and from her shoulder the loaded Mauser hung on its strap and bumped lightly against her flank at each pace.

The change in her was so startling as to leave Sebastian bewildered. The new hard line of her mouth, her eyes that gave off the dark hot glow of a fanatic, the voice that had lost the underlying ripple of laughter. She spoke seldom, but when she did, Flynn and Sebastian were forced to hear her with respect. Sometimes listening to that flat deadly tone Sebastian could feel a prickle of horror under his skin.

They reached the landing-place and the jetty on the Ruhaha river and waited for the launch to return. It came three days later, heralding its approach by the soft chugging of its engine. When it came around the river bend, pushing briskly against the current, headed for the wooden jetty, they were lying in wait for it.

'There he is!' Sebastian's voice was thick with emotion as he recognized the plump grey-clad figure in the bows.

'The swine, oh, the bloody swine!' and he jerked the bolt of his rifle open then snapped it shut.

'Wait!' Rosa's hand closed on his wrist before he could lift the butt to his shoulder.

'I can get him from here!' protested Sebastian.

'No. I want him to see us. I want to tell him first. I want him to know why he must die.'

The launch swung in broadside to the current, losing its way, until it came in gently to nudge the jetty. Two of the Askari jumped ashore, laying back on the lines to hold her while the Commissioner disembarked.

Fleischer stood on the jetty for a minute, looking back down the river. This action should have warned Flynn, but he did not see its significance. Then the Commissioner shrugged slightly and trudged up the jetty towards the boat-house.

'Tell your men to drop their weapons into the river,' said Flynn in his best German as he stood up from the patch of reeds beside the jetty.

Herman Fleischer froze in mid-stride, but his belly quivered and his head turned slowly towards Flynn. His blue eyes seemed to spread until they filled his face, and he made a clucking noise in his throat.

'Tell them quickly, or I will shoot you through the stomach,' said Flynn, and Fleischer found his voice. He relayed Flynn's order to the Askari, and there were a series of splashes around the launch as it was obeyed.

Movement in the corner of his eye made Fleischer swing his head, and he was face to face with Rosa Oldsmith. Beyond her in a half circle stood Sebastian and a dozen armed Africans, but some instinct warned Fleischer that the woman was the danger. There was a merciless quality about her, some undefinable air of deadly purpose. It was to her he addressed his question.

'What do you want?' His voice was husky with apprehension.

'What did he say?' Rosa asked her father.

'He wants to know what you want.'

'Ask him if he remembers me.'

As he heard the question, Fleischer remembered her in her night-dress, kneeling in the fire-light, and with the memory came real fear.

'It was a mistake,' he whispered. 'The child! I did not order it.'

'Tell him . . .' said Rosa, 'tell him that I am going to kill him.' And her hands moved deliberately on the Mauser, slipping the safety-catch across, but her eyes never left his face.

'It was a mistake,' Herman repeated and he stepped backwards, lifting his hands to ward off the bullet that he knew must come.

At that moment Sebastian shouted behind Rosa, just one word.

'Look!'

Around the bend of the Ruhaha river, only two hundred yards from where they stood, another launch swept into view. It came silently, swiftly, and at its stubby masthead flew the ensign of the German Navy. There were men in crisp white uniforms clustered around the Maxim machine gun in its bows.

Flynn's party stared at it in complete disbelief. Its presence was as unbelievable as that of the Loch Ness monster in the Serpentine or a man-eating lion in St Paul's Cathedral, and in the long seconds they stood paralysed the launch closed in quickly on the jetty.

Herman Fleischer broke the spell. He opened his mouth and from the barrel of his chest issued a bellow that rang clearly across the water.

'Kyller, they are Englishmen!'

Then he moved, with three light steps he danced sideways, incredibly quickly he moved his gross body from under the threatening muzzle of Rosa's rifle and dived from the jetty into the dark green swirl of water below the boards.

The splash of his dive was immediately followed by the tack, tack, tack of the launch's machine gun–and the air was filled with the swishing crack of a hundred whips. The launch drove straight in towards them with the Maxim blazing on its prow. Around Flynn and Rosa and Sebastian the earth erupted in a rapid series of dust fountains, a ricochet howled dementedly, one of the gun-boys spun on his heels in a brief dervish dance and then sprawled down the bank, with his rifle clattering on the wooden boards of the jetty, and the frozen party on the bank exploded into violent movement. Flynn and his black troopers ducked and dodged away up the bank, but Rosa ran forward. She reached the edge of the jetty unscathed through the hailstorm of Maxim fire, there she checked and aimed the Mauser at the wallowing body of Herman Fleischer in the water below her.

'You killed my baby!' Rosa shrieked, and Fleischer looked up at her and knew he was about to die. A Maxim bullet struck the metal of the rifle, tearing it from Rosa's hands, and she staggered off balance, her arms windmilling as she tottered on the edge of the jetty.

Sebastian reached her as she fell. He caught her and swung her up on his shoulder, whirled with her and bounded away up the bank, running with all the reserves of his strength unlocked by the key of his terror.

With ten of the gun-boys Sebastian took the rearguard; for that day and the next they skirmished back along the line of the retreat, briefly holding each natural defensive point until the Germans brought up the Maxim gun. Then they dropped back, retreating slowly while Flynn and Rosa made a straight run of it. In the second night Sebastian broke contact with the pursuers and fled north towards the rendezvous at the stream below the ruins of Lalapanzi.

Forty-eight hours later he reached it. In the moonlight he staggered into the camp, and Rosa threw off her blankets and came running to him with a low joyous cry of greeting. She knelt before him, unlaced and gently drew off each of his boots. While Sebastian gulped the mug of coffee and hot gin that Flynn brewed for him, Rosa bathed and tended the blisters that had burst on his feet. Then she dried her hands, stood, and picked up her blankets.

'Come,' she said, and together they walked away along the bank of the stream. Behind a curtain of hanging creepers, on a nest of dry grass and blankets, while the jewelled night sky glowed above them, they gave each other the comfort of their bodies for the first time since the death of the child. Afterwards they slept entwined until the low sun woke them. Then they rose and went down the bank together naked into the stream. The water was cold when she splashed him, and she giggled like a little girl and ran through the shallows across the sandbank with the water bursting in a sparkling spray around her legs, drops of it glittering like sequins on her skin, her waist was the neck of a Venetian vase flaring down into full double rounds of her lower body.

He chased and caught her and they fell together and knelt facing each other, spluttering and laughing, and with each gust of laughter her bosom jumped and bounced. Sebastian leaned forward with the laughter drying in his throat and cupped them in his hands.

Instantly her own laughter ceased, she looked at him a moment, then suddenly her faced hardened and she struck his hands away.

'No!' she hissed at him, and jumping to her feet she waded to where her clothing lay on the bank. Swiftly she covered her femininity, and as she strapped the heavy bandolier of ammunition around her body the last soft memory of their loving was gone from her face.

54

It was that stinking Rufiji water, Herman Fleischer decided, and moved painfully in his maschille as another cramp took him.

The hot hand of dysentery that closed on his stomach added to his mood of dark resentment. His present discomfort was directly linked to the arrival of *Blücher* in his territory, the indignities he had experienced at the hands of her captain, the danger he had run into in his brush with the English bandits at the start of this expedition, and since then the constant gruelling work and ever-present fear of another attack, the nagging of the engineer whom von Kleine had placed over him–he hated everything to do with that cursed warship, he hated every man aboard her.

The jogging motion of the maschille bearers stirred the contents of his belly, making it gurgle and squeal. He would have to stop again, and he looked ahead for a suitable place in which to find privacy.

Ahead of him the caravan of porters was toiling along the shallow bottom of a valley between two sparsely wooded ridges of shale and broken rock.

The column was spread out in an untidy straggle half a mile long, for it comprised just under a thousand men.

In the van a hundred of them, stripped to loin-cloths and shiny with sweat, were wielding their long pangas on the scrub. The blades glinting as they rose and fell, the thudding of the blows muted in the lazy heat of afternoon. Working under the supervision of Gunther Raube, the young engineering officer from *Blücher*, they were cutting out the narrow track, widening it for the passage of the bulky objects that followed.

Dwarfing the men that swarmed around them, these four objects rolled slowly along, rocking and swaying over patches of uneven ground. Now and then halting as they came up against a tree stump or an outcrop of rock, before the animal exertions of two hundred black men could get them rolling again.

Three weeks previously they had beached the freighter *Rheinlander* in Dar es Salaam harbour and dismantled eight slabs of her plating. Then from the metal frames of her hull, Raube had shaped eight enormous wheel rims, fourteen feet in diameter, into each of these he had welded a sheet of 1½-inch plating ten foot square. Using the freighter's bollards as axles, he had linked these eight discs in four pairs. Thus each of these contraptions looked like the wheel and axle assembly of a gigantic Roman chariot.

Herman Fleischer had made a swift recruitment tour, and secured nine hundred able-bodied volunteers from the town of Dar es Salaam and its outlying villages. These nine hundred were now engaged in trundling the four sets of wheels southward towards the Rufiji delta. While they worked, Herman's Askari stood by with loaded Mausers to discourage any of the volunteers from succumbing to an attack of homesickness; a malady which was fast reaching epidemic proportions, aggravated as it was by shoulders rubbed raw by contact with harsh sun-heated metal, and by palms whose outer layers of skin had been smeared away on the rough hemp ropes. They had been two weeks at their labours and they were still thirty torturous miles from the river.

Herman Fleischer squirmed again in his maschille as the amoebic dysentery gnawed at his guts.

'Mother of a pig!' he moaned, and then shouted at the bearers, 'Quickly, take me to those trees.' He pointed to a clump of wild ebony that smothered one of the side draws of the valley.

With alacrity, the maschille bearers swung off the path and trotted up the draw. Within the screen of wild ebony they paused while the Commissioner alighted from the hammock and hurried into the deepest recess of the bush to be alone. Then they threw themselves down with a communal sigh and gave themselves up to a session of African callisthenics.

When the Commissioner came out of retreat he was hungry. It was cool and restful in the shade, an ideal place to take his mid-afternoon snack. Raube would have to fend for himself for an hour or so. Herman nodded to his personal servant to set up the camp table and open the food box. His mouth was full of sausage when the first rifle shot clapped dully in the dusty dry air.

55

'Where is he? He must be here. The scouts said he was here. Can you see him?' Rosa Oldsmith spoke through lips that were chapped dry by sun and wind, white flakes of skin had come loose from the raw red patches of sunburn on her nose, and her eyes were bloodshot from the dust and the glare.

She lay on her stomach behind a bank of shale and coarse grass with the Mauser probing out in front of her.

'Can you see him?' she demanded again impatiently, turning her head towards her father.

Flynn grunted noncommittally, holding the binoculars to his eyes, panning them slowly down the length of the valley then back again to the head of the strange caravan.

'There is a white man there,' he said.

'Is it Fleischer, is it?'

'No,' doubtfully Flynn gave the negative.

'No, I don't think so.'

'Look for him. He must be there somewhere.'

'I wonder what the hell those things are.'

Flynn concentrated on the four huge sets of wheels. The lens of the binoculars magnified the heat distortion through the still air, making them change shape and size so that one second they were insignificant and the next they were monstrous.

'Look for Fleischer. Damn those things, look for Fleischer,' Rosa snapped at him.

'He's not with them.'

'He must be. He must be there.' Rosa rolled on her side and reached out to snatch the binoculars from Flynn's hands. Eagerly she scanned the long column that moved slowly towards them up the valley.

'He must be there. Please God, he must be there,' she whispered her hatred through cracked dry lips.

'We will have to attack soon. They are nearly in position now.'

'We must find Fleischer.' Desperately Rosa searched, her knuckles showing white through sun-brown skin as she clutched the binoculars.

'We can't let it go much longer. Sebastian is in position, he will be expecting my signal.'

'Wait! You must wait.'

'No. We can't let them get closer.' Flynn half lifted his body, and called softly.

'Mohammed! Are you ready?'

'We are ready.' The reply came from farther down the slope where the line of riflemen lay.

'Remember my words, oh, thou chosen of Allah. Kill the Askari first and the others will run.'

'Your words ring in my ears with the brightness and the beauty of golden bells,' Mohammed replied.

'Up yours!' said Flynn and unbuttoned the pocket flap of his tunic. He fumbled out the hand-mirror and held it slanted to catch the sun, deflecting a bright splinter of light towards the far slope of the valley. From the jumble of rock and bush there was an immediate answering flash as Sebastian acknowledged the signal.

'Ah!' Flynn breathed theatrical relief, 'I was afraid our Bassie might have fallen asleep over there.' And he picked up the Mauser from the rock in front of him.

'Wait,' pleaded Rosa. 'Please wait.'

'We can't. You know we can't–if Fleischer is down there then we'll get him. If he isn't, then waiting any longer isn't going to help us.'

'You don't care,' she accused. 'You have forgotten about Maria already.'

'No,' said Flynn. 'No, I haven't forgotten,' and he cuddled the Mauser into his shoulder. There was an Askari he had been watching. A big man who moved ahead of the column. Even at this range Flynn sensed that this man was dangerous. He moved with a leopard's slouching awareness, head cocked and alert.

Flynn picked him up in the notch of the rear sight and rode the pip down his body, aiming low to compensate for the downhill shot, taking him in the belly. He gathered the slack in the trigger, squeezing it up gently. The Mauser cracked viciously and the recoil jumped back into his shoulder.

Incredulously Flynn saw the bullet throw a jump of dust from the slope below the Askari. A clean miss at four hundred yards. from a carefully aimed shot–by Christ, he was getting old.

Frantically he worked the bolt of the rifle, but already the Askari had ducked for cover, unslinging his rifle as he disappeared into a bank of grey thorn bush, and Flynn's next shot ripped ineffectively into the coarse dry vegetation.

'Damn it to hell!' howled Flynn, and his voice was small in the storm of gunfire that blew around him. From both slopes all his riflemen were shooting down into the solid pack of humanity that clogged the valley floor.

For startled seconds the mass of native bearers stood quiescent under the lash of the Mausers, each man frozen in the attitude in which the attack had caught him; bent to the giant wheels, leaning forward against the ropes, panga raised to strike at a branch, or merely standing watching while others worked. Every head lifted to stare up at the slopes from which Flynn's hidden rifles menaced them, then with a sound like a rising wind a single voice climbed in a wail of terror, to be lost almost instantly in the babble from a thousand throats.

Without regard for Flynn's orders to single out only the armed Askari, his men were firing blindly into the mass of men around the wheels, bullets striking with a meaty thump, thump, thump, or whining from rock to inflict the ghastly secondary wounds of a ricochet.

Then the bearers broke. Flowing back like flood water along the valley, carrying the Askari whose khaki uniforms bobbed with them like driftwood in the torrent.

Beside Flynn in the donga, Rosa was firing also. Her hands on the rifle incongruously feminine, fingers long and sensitive working the bolt as though it were the shuttle of a loom, weaving death, her eyes slitted behind the gunsight, her lips barely moving as they formed the name which had become her battle hymn.

'Maria! Maria!' With each shot she said it softly.

As he fumbled a fresh clip of cartridges from his bandolier, Flynn glanced sideways at her. Even in this moment of hot excitement Flynn felt the prickle of disquiet as he saw his daughter's face. There was madness in her eyes, the madness of grief too long sustained, the madness of hatred too carefully nourished.

His rifle was loaded and he switched his attention back to the valley. The scene had changed. From the rush of fear-crazed bearers, the German, whom Flynn had earlier watched through the binoculars, was rallying a defence. With him was the big Askari, the one that Flynn had missed with his first shot. These two stood to hold the guards who were being carried away on the rush of panic-stricken bearers, stopping them, turning them back, pushing and shoving them into defensive cover around the four huge wheels. Now they were returning the fire of Flynn's men.

'Mohammed! Get that man! The white man–get him!' roared Flynn, and fired twice, missing with each shot. But his bullets passed so close that the German dodged back behind the metal shield of the nearest wheel.

'That's done it,' lamented Flynn, as his hopes of quick success faded. 'They're getting settled in down there. We are going to have to prise them loose.'

The prospect was unattractive. Flynn had found from experience that while every man in his motley band was a hero when firing from ambush, and a master in the art of strategic retreat, yet their weak suit was frontal assault, or any other manœuvre that involved exposure to the enemy. Of the hundred under his command, there were a dozen whom he could rely on to obey an order to attack. Flynn was understandably reluctant to issue such an order, for there are few situations more humiliating than bellowing, 'Charge!'–then having everybody look at you with a 'Who me? You must be joking!' expression.

Now he steeled himself to do it, aware that with every second the battle madness of his men was cooling and being replaced by sanity and caution. He filled his lungs and opened his mouth, but Rosa saved him.

She rolled and lifted her knees, coming on to her feet with one fluid motion whose continuation was a catlike leap that carried her over the shale bank and into the open. Boyish, big hipped, but graceful–the rifle across her hip, firing. Long hair streaming, long legs flying, she went down the slope.

'Rosa!' roared Flynn in consternation, and jumped up to chase her in an ungainly lumbering run like the charge of an old bull buffalo.

'Fini!' shouted Mohammed, and scampered after his master.

'My goodness!' Sebastian gasped where he lay on the opposite side of the valley. 'It's Rosa!' and in a completely reflex response he found himself on his feet and bounding down the rocky slope.

'Akwende!' yelled the man beside him, carried away in his excitement, and before any of them had time to think, fifty of them were up and following. After the first half-dozen paces they were committed, for once they had started to run down the steep incline they could not stop without falling flat on their faces, they could only accelerate.

Down both slopes of the valley, scrambling, sliding on loose stone, pell-mell through thorn bush, screaming, shouting, they poured down on the cluster of Askari around the wheels.

From opposite sides, Rosa and Sebastian were first to reach the perimeter of the German position. Their momentum carried them unscathed through the first line of the defenders, and then with the empty rifle in her hands Rosa ran chest to chest against the big Askari who rose from behind a boulder to meet her. She shrieked as he caught her, and the sound exploded with Sebastian's brain in a red burst of fury.

Twenty yards away Rosa struggled with the man, but she was helpless as a baby in his arms. He lifted her, changing his grip on her body, snatching her up above his head, steadying himself to hurl her down on to the pointed rock behind which he had hidden. There was such animal power in the bunched muscles of his arms, in the sweat-slimy neck, in the muscular straddled legs, that Sebastian knew that when he dashed Rosa against the rock he would kill her. Her spine, her ribs must shatter with the force of it; the soft vital organs within her trunk must bruise or burst.

Sebastian went for him. Brushing from his path two lesser men of the bewildered defenders, clubbing the Mauser in his hands because he could not fire for fear of hitting Rosa, silently saving his breath for physical effort, he crossed the distance that separated them and reached them in the moment that the Askari began the first downward movement of his arms.

'Aah!' A gusty grunt was forced up Sebastian's throat by the force with which he swung the rifle, he used it like an axe, swinging it low with the full weight of his body behind it. The blade of the butt hit the Askari across the small of his back, and within his body cavity the kidneys popped like overripe satsuma plums. He was dying as he toppled backwards. As he hit the ground Rosa fell on top of him, his body cushioning her fall.

Sebastian dropped the rifle and stooped to gather her in his arms, crouching over her protectively.

Around them Flynn led his men boiling over the defenders, swamping them, knocking the rifles from their hands and dragging them to their feet, laughing in awe of their own courageous assault, chattering in excitement and relief.

Sebastian was on the point of straightening up and lifting Rosa to her feet, he glanced around quickly to assure himself that all danger was past–and his breathing jammed in his throat.

Ten paces away, kneeling in the shadow of one of the huge steel wheels was the white officer. He was a young man, swarthy for a German, but with pale green eyes. The tropical white of his uniform was patchy with damp sweat stains, and smeared with dust; his cap was pushed back, the gold braid on its peak sparkling with incongruous gaiety, for beneath it the face was taut and angry, the mouth pulled tight by the clenched jaws.

There was a Luger pistol clutched in his right hand. He lifted it and aimed.

'No!' croaked Sebastian, clumsily trying to shield Rosa with his own body, but he knew the German was going to fire.

'Mädchen!' cried Sebastian in his schoolboy German. 'Nein shutzen dis ein Mädchen!' and he saw the change in the young officer's expression, the pale green glitter of his eyes softening as he responded automatically to the appeal to his chivalry. Yet still the Luger was levelled, and over it Sebastian and the officer stared at each other. All this in seconds, but the delay was enough. While the officer still hesitated, suddenly it was too late, for Flynn stood over him and pressed the muzzle of his rifle into the back of the German's neck.

'Drop it, me beauty. Else I'll shoot your tonsils clean out through your Adam's apple.'

56

Strewn along the floor of the valley were the loads dropped by the native bearers, in their anxiety to leave for far places and fairer climes. Many of the packs had burst open and all had been trampled in the rush, so the contents littered the ground and discarded clothing flapped in the lower branches of the thorn trees.

Flynn's men were looting, a pastime in which they demonstrated a marked aptitude and industry. Busy as jackals around a lion's kill they gleaned the spoils and bickered over them.

The German officer sat quietly against the metal wheel. In front of him stood Rosa; she had in her hand the Luger pistol. The two of them watched each other steadily and expressionlessly. To one side Flynn squatted and pored over the contents of the German's pocket. Beside him Sebastian was ready to give his assistance.

'He's a naval officer,' said Sebastian, looking at the German with interest. 'He's got an anchor on his cap badge.'

'Do me a favour, Bassie,' pleaded Flynn.

'Of course.' Sebastian was ever anxious to please.

'Shut up!' said Flynn, without looking up from the contents of the officer's wallet which he had piled on the ground in front of him. In his dealings with Flynn, Sebastian had built up a thick layer of scar tissue around his sensitivity. He went on without a change of tone or expression.

'I wonder what on earth a naval officer is doing in the middle of the bush–pushing these funny contraptions around.' Sebastian examined the wheel with interest, before addressing himself to the German. 'Bitte, was is das?' He pointed at the wheel. The young officer did not even glance at him. He was watching Rosa with almost hypnotic concentration.

Sebastian repeated his question and when he found that he was again ignored he shrugged slightly, and leaned across to lift a sheet of paper from the small pile in front of Flynn.

'Leave it,' Flynn slapped his hand away. 'I'm reading.'

'Can I look at this, then?' He touched a photograph.

'Don't lose it,' cautioned Flynn, and Sebastian held it in his lap and examined it. It showed three young men in white overalls and naval peaked caps. They were smiling broadly into the camera with their arms linked together. In the background loomed the superstructure of a warship, the gun-turrets showed clearly. One of the men in the photograph was their prisoner who now sat against the wheel.

Sebastian reversed the square of heavy cardboard and read the inscription on the back of it.

' "Bremerhaven. August 6th, 1911." '

Both Flynn and Sebastian were absorbed in their studies, and Rosa and the German were alone. Completely alone, isolated by an intimate relationship.

Gunther Raube was fascinated. Staring into the girl's face, he had never known this sensation of mingled dread and elation which she invoked within him. Though her expression was flat and neutral, he could sense in her a hunger and a promise. He knew that they were bound together by something he did not understand, between them there was something very important to happen. It excited him, he felt it crawling like a living thing in his loins, ghost-walking along his spine, and his breathing was cramped and painful. Yet there was fear with it, fear that was as cloying as warm olive oil in his belly.

'What is it?' he whispered huskily as a lover. 'I do not understand. Tell me.'

And he sensed that she could not understand his language, but his tone made something move in her eyes. They darkened like a cloud shadow on a green sea, and he saw she was beautiful. With a pang he thought how close he had been to firing the Luger she now held in her hand.

I might have killed her, and he wanted to reach out and touch her. Slowly he leaned forward, and Rosa shot him in the centre of his chest. The impact of the bullet threw him back against the metal frame of the wheel. He lay there looking at her.

Deliberately, each shot spaced, she emptied the magazine of the pistol. The Luger jumped and steadied and jumped again in her hand. Each blurt of gunfire shockingly loud, and the wounds appeared like magic on the white front of his shirt, beginning to weep blood as he slumped sideways, and he lay with his eyes still fastened on her face as he died.

The pistol clicked empty and she let it drop from her hand.

57

Sir Percy held the square of cardboard at arm's length to read the inscription on the back of it.

' "Bremerhaven. August 6th, 1911," ' he said. Across the desk from him his flag-captain sat uncomfortably on the edge of the hard-backed H.M. issue chair. His right hand reached for his pocket, checked, then withdrew guiltily.

'For God's sake, Henry. Smoke that damned thing if you must,' grunted Sir Percy.

'Thank you, sir.' Gratefully Captain Henry Green completed the reach for his pocket, brought out a gnarled briar, and began stuffing it with tobacco.

Laying aside the photograph, Sir Percy took up the bedraggled sheet of paper and studied the crude hand-drawn circles upon it, reading the descriptions that were linked by arrows to the circles. This sample of primitive art had been laboriously drawn by Flynn Patrick O'Flynn as an addendum to his report.

'You say this lot came in the diplomatic bag from the Embassy in Lourenço Marques?'

'That's right, sir.'

'Who is this fellow . . .' Sir Percy checked the name, 'Flynn Patrick O'Flynn?'

'It seems that he is a major in the Portuguese army, sir.'

'With a name like that?'

'You find these Irishmen everywhere, sir.' The captain smiled. 'He commands a group of scouts who raid across the border into German territory. They have built up something of a reputation for derring-do.'

Sir Percy grunted again, dropped the paper, clasped his hands behind his head, and stared across the room at the portrait of Lord Nelson.

'All right, Henry. Let's hear what you make of it.'

The captain held a flaring match to the bowl of his pipe and sucked noisily, waved the match to extinguish it, and spoke through wreaths of smoke.

'The photograph first. It showed three German engineering officers on the foredeck of a cruiser. The one in the centre was the man killed by the scouts.' He puffed again. 'Intelligence reports that the cruiser is a "B" class. Nine-inch guns in raked turrets.'

' "B" class?' asked Sir Percy. 'They only launched two vessels of that class.'

'*Battenburg* and *Blücher*, sir.'

'*Blücher!*' said Sir Percy softly.

'*Blücher!*' agreed Henry Green. 'Presumed destroyed in a surface action with His Majesty's ships *Bloodhound* and *Orion* off the east coast of Africa between 16th and 20th September.'

'Go on.'

'Well, this officer could have been a survivor from *Blücher* who was lucky enough to come ashore in German East Africa–and is now serving with von Vorbeck's army.'

'Still dressed in full naval uniform, trundling strange round objects about the continent?' asked Sir Percy sceptically.

'An unusual duty, I agree, sir.'

'Now what do you make of these things?' With one finger Sir Percy prodded Flynn's diagram in front of him.

'Wheels,' said Green.

'For what?'

'Transporting material.'

'What material?'

'Steel plate.'

'Now who would want steel plate on the east coast of Africa?' mused Sir Percy.

'Perhaps the captain of a damaged battle cruiser.'

'Let's go down into the plotting room.' Sir Percy heaved his bulk out of the chair, and headed for the door.

His shoulders hunched, massive jaw jutting, Admiral Howe brooded over the plot of the Indian Ocean.

'Where was this column intercepted?' he asked.

'Here, sir.' Green touched the vast map with the pointer. 'About fifteen miles south-east of Kibiti. It was moving southwards towards . . .' He did not finish the statement but let the tip of the marker slide down on to the complexity of islands that clustered about the mouth of the long black snake that was the Rufiji river.

'Admiralty plot for East Africa, please.' Sir Percy turned to the lieutenant in charge of the plot, and the lieutenant selected Volume II of the blue-jacketed books that lined the shelf on the far wall.

'What are the sailing directions for the Rufiji mouth?' demanded the Admiral, and the lieutenant began to read.

'*Ras Pombwe to Kikunya mouth, including Mto Rufiji and Rufiji delta* (*Latitude 8° 17′ S, Longitude 39° 20′ E*). For fifty miles the coast is a maze of low, swampy, mangrove-covered islands, intersected by creeks comprising the delta of Mto Rufiji. During the rainy season the whole area of the delta is frequently inundated.

'The coast of the delta is broken by ten large mouths, eight of which are connected at all times with Mto Rufiji.'

Sir Percy interrupted peevishly, 'What is all this *Mto* business?'

'Arabic word for "river", sir.'

'Well, why don't they say so? Carry on.'

'With the exception of *Simba Yranga mouth* and *Kikunya mouth*, all the other entrances are heavily shoaled and navigable only by craft drawing one metre or less.'

'Concentrate on those two then,' grunted Sir Percy, and the lieutenant turned the page.

'*Simba Uranga mouth*. Used by coasting vessels engaged in the timber trade. There is no defined bar and, in 1911, the channel was reported by the German Admiralty as having a low river level mean of ten fathoms.

'The channel is bifurcated by a wedge-shaped island, *Rufiji-yawake*, and both arms afford secure anchorage to vessels of large burden. However, holding ground is bad and securing to trees on the bank is more satisfactory. Floating islands of grass and weed are common.'

'All right!' Sir Percy halted the recitation, and every person in the plotting room looked expectantly at him. Sir Percy was glowering at the plot, breathing heavily through his nose. 'Where is *Blücher*'s plaque?' he demanded harshly.

The lieutenant went to the locker behind him, and came back with the black wooden disc he had removed from the plot two months previously. Sir Percy took it from him, and rubbed it slowly between thumb and forefinger. There was complete silence in the room.

Slowly Sir Percy leaned forward across the map and placed the disc with a click upon the glass top. They all stared at it. It sat sinister as a black cancer where the green land met the blue ocean.

'Communications!' grunted Sir Percy and the yeoman of signals stepped forward with his pad ready.

'Dispatch to Commodore Commanding Indian Ocean. Captain Joyce. H.M.S. *Renounce*. Maximum Priority. Message reads: Intelligence reports indicate high probability . . .'

58

'You know something, Captain Joyce, this is bloody good gin.' Flynn O'Flynn pointed the base of the glass at the ceiling, and in his eagerness to engulf the liquid, he did the same for the slice of lemon that the steward had placed in the glass. He gurgled like an air-locked geyser, his face changed swiftly to a deeper shade of red, then he expelled the lemon and with it a fine spray of gin and Indian tonic in a burst of explosive coughing.

'Are you all right?' Anxiously Captain Joyce leapt across the cabin and begun pounding Flynn between the shoulder-blades. He had visions of his key tool in the coming operation being asphyxiated before they had started.

'Pips!' gasped Flynn. 'Goddamned lemon pips.'

'Steward!' Captain Joyce called over his shoulder without interrupting the tattoo he was playing on Flynn's back. 'Bring the major a glass of water. Hurry!'

'Water?' wheezed Flynn in horror and the shock was sufficient to diminish the strength of his paroxysm.

The steward, who from experience could recognize a drinking man when he saw one, rose nobly to the occasion. He hurried across the cabin with a glass in his hand. A mouthful of raw spirit effected a near miraculous cure, Flynn lay back in his chair his face still bright purple but his breathing easing, and Joyce withdrew to the far side of the cabin to inhale with relief the moist warm tropical air that oozed sluggishly through the open porthole. After a close range whiff of Flynn's body smell, it was as sweet as a bunch of tulips.

Flynn had been in the field for six weeks, and during that time it had not occurred to him to change his clothing. He smelled like a Roquefort cheese.

There was a pause while everybody recovered their breath, then Joyce picked up where he had left off.

'I was saying, Major, how good it was of you to return so promptly to meet me here.'

'I came the moment I received your message. The runner was waiting for us in M'topo's village. I left my command camped south of the Rovuma, and pushed through in forced marches. A hundred and fifty miles in three days! Not bad going, hey?'

'Damn good show!' agreed Joyce, and looked across at the other two men in the cabin for confirmation. With the Portuguese Governor's aide-de-camp was a young army lieutenant. Neither of them could understand a word of English. The aide-de-camp was wearing a politely non-committal expression, and the lieutenant had loosened the top button of his tunic and was lolling on the cabin's day couch with a little black cigarette drooping from his lips. Yet he contrived to look as gracefully insolent as a matador.

'The English captain asks that you recommend me to the Governor for the Star of St Peter.' Flynn translated Captain Joyce's speech to the aide-de-camp. Flynn wanted a medal. He had been hounding the Governor for one these last six months.

'Will you please tell the English captain that I would be delighted to convey his written citation to the Governor.' The aide-de-camp smiled blandly. Through their business association he knew better than to take Flynn's translation literally. Flynn scowled at him, and Joyce sensed the strain in the cabin. He went on quickly.

'I asked you to meet me here to discuss a matter of very great importance.' He paused. 'Two months ago your scouts attacked a German supply column near the village of Kibiti.'

'That's right.' Flynn sat up in his chair. 'A hell of a fight. We fought like madmen. Hand-to-hand stuff.'

'Quite,' Joyce agreed quickly. 'Quite so. With this column was a German naval officer . . .'

'I didn't do it,' interjected Flynn with alarm. 'It wasn't me. He was trying to escape. You can't pin that one on me.'

Joyce looked startled.

'I beg your pardon.'

'He was shot trying to escape–and you try to prove different,' Flynn challenged him hotly.

'Yes, I know. I have a copy of your report. A pity. A great pity. We would dearly have liked to interrogate the man.'

'You calling me a liar?'

'Good Lord, Major O'Flynn. Nothing is further from my mind.' Joyce was finding that conversation with Flynn O'Flynn was similar to feeling your way blindfolded through a hawthorn bush. 'Your glass is empty, may I offer you a drink?'

Flynn's mouth was open to emit further truculent denials, but the offer of hospitality took him unawares and he subsided.

'Thank you. It's damn good gin, haven't tasted anything like it in years. I don't suppose you could spare a case or two?'

Again Joyce was startled.

'I'm sure the wardroom secretary will be able to arrange something for you.'

'Bloody good stuff,' said Flynn, and sipped at his recharged glass. Joyce decided on a different approach.

'Major O'Flynn, have you heard of a German warship, a cruiser, named *Blücher*?'

'Have I, hell!' bellowed Flynn with such vehemence that Joyce was left in no doubt that he had struck another jarring note. 'The bastard sank me!'

These words conjured up in the eye of Captain Joyce's mind a brief but macabre picture of a Flynn floating on his back, while a battle cruiser fired on him with nine-inch guns.

'Sank you?' asked Joyce.

'Rammed me! There I was sailing along in this dhow peaceful as anything, when up she comes and–bang, right up the arse.'

'I see,' murmured Joyce. 'Was it intentional?'

'You bloody tooting it was.'

'Why?'

'Well . . .' started Flynn, and then changed his mind. 'It's a long story.'

'Where did this happen?'

'About fifty miles off the mouth of the Rufiji river.'

'The Rufiji?' Joyce leaned forward eagerly. 'Do you know it? Do you know the Rufiji delta?'

'Do I know the Rufiji delta?' chuckled Flynn. 'I know it like you know the way to your own Thunder Box. I used to do a lot of business there before the war.'

'Excellent! Wonderful!' Joyce could not restrain himself from pursing his lips and whistling the first two bars of 'Tipperary'. From him this .was expression of unadulterated joy.

'Yeah? What's so wonderful about that?' Flynn was immediately suspicious.

'Major O'Flynn. On the basis of your report, Naval Intelligence considers it highly probable that the *Blücher* is anchored somewhere in the Rufiji delta.'

'Who are you kidding? The *Blücher* was sunk months ago–everybody knows that.'

'Presumed sunk. She, and the two British warships that pursued her, disappeared off the face of the earth–or more correctly the ocean. Certain pieces of floating wreckage were recovered that indicated that a battle had been fought by the three ships. It was thought that all three had gone down.' Joyce paused and smoothed the grey wings of hair along his temples. 'But now it seems certain that *Blücher* was badly damaged during the engagement, and that she was holed up in the delta.'

'Those wheels! Steel plating for repairs!'

'Precisely, Major, precisely. But . . .' Joyce smiled at Flynn, '. . . thanks to you, they did not get the plating through.'

'Yes, they did.' Flynn growled a denial.

'They did?' demanded Joyce harshly.

'Yeah. We left them lying in the veld. My spies told me that after we had gone the Germans sent another party of bearers up and took them away.'

'Why didn't you prevent it?'

'What the hell for. They've got no value,' Flynn retorted.

'The enemy's insistence must have demonstrated their value.'

'Yeah. The enemy were so insistent they sent up a couple of Maxim guns with the second party. In my book the more Maxims there are guarding something, the less value it is.'

'Well, why didn't you destroy them while you had the chance?'

'Listen, friend, how do you reckon to destroy twenty tons of steel–swallow it perhaps?'

'Do you realize just what a threat this ship will be once it is seaworthy?' Joyce hesitated. 'I tell you now in strict confidence that there will be an invasion of German East Africa in the very near future. Can you imagine the havoc if *Blücher* were to slip out of the Rufiji and get among the troop convoys.'

'Yeah–all of us have got troubles.'

'Major.' The captain's voice was hoarse with the effect of checking his temper. 'Major. I want you to do a reconnaissance and locate the *Blücher* for us.'

'Is that so?' boomed Flynn. 'You want me to go galloping round in the delta when there's a Maxim behind every mangrove tree. It might take a year to search that delta, you've got no idea what it's like in there.'

'That won't be necessary.' Joyce swivelled his chair, he nodded at the Portuguese lieutenant. 'This officer is an aviator.'

'What's that mean?'

'He is a flyer.'

'Yeah? Is that so good? I did a bit of sleeping around when I was young–still get it up now and then.'

Joyce coughed.

'He flies an aircraft. A flying-machine.'

'Oh!' said Flynn. He was impressed. 'Jeez! is that so?' He looked at the Portuguese lieutenant with respect.

'With the co-operation of the Portuguese army I intend conducting an aerial reconnaissance of the Rufiji delta.'

'You mean flying over it in a flying-machine?'

'Precisely.'

'That's a bloody good idea.' Flynn was enthusiastic.

'When can you be ready?'

'What for?'

'For the reconnaissance.'

'Now hold on a shake, friend!' Flynn was aghast. 'You not getting me into one of those flying things.'

Two hours later they were still arguing on the bridge of H.M.S. *Renounce*, as Joyce conned her back towards the land to deposit Flynn and the two Portuguese on the beach from which his launch had picked them up that morning. The British cruiser steamed over a sea that was oil-slick calm and purple blue, and the land lay as a dark irregular line on the horizon.

'It is essential that someone who knows the delta flies with the pilot. He has just arrived from Portugal, besides which he will be fully occupied in piloting the machine. He must have an observer.' Joyce was trying again.

Flynn had lost all interest in the discussion, he was now occupied with weightier matters.

'Captain,' he started, and Joyce recognized the new tone of his voice and turned to him hopefully.

'Captain, that other business. What about it?'

'I'm sorry–I don't follow you.'

'That gin you promised me, what about it?'

Captain Arthur Joyce, R.N., was a man of gentle mien. His face was smooth and unlined, his mouth full but grave, his eyes thoughtful, the streaks of silver grey at his temples gave him dignity. There was only one pointer to his true temperament, his eyebrows grew in one solid continuous line across his face; they were as thick and furry across the bridge of his nose as they were above his eyes. Despite his appearance he was a man of dark and violent temper. Ten years on his own bridge, wielding the limitless power and authority of a Royal Naval Captain had not mellowed him, but had taught him how to use the curb on his temper. Since early that morning when he had first shaken Flynn O'Flynn's large hairy paw, Arthur Joyce had been exercising every bit of restraint he possessed–now he had exhausted it all.

Flynn found himself standing speechless beneath the full blaze of Captain Joyce's anger. In a staccato, low-pitched speech, Arthur Joyce told him his opinion of Flynn's courage, character, reliability, drinking habits, and sense of personal hygiene.

Flynn was shocked and deeply hurt.

'Listen . . .' he said.

'*YOU* listen,' said Joyce. 'Nothing will give me more pleasure that to see you leave this ship. And when you do so you can rest content in the knowledge that a full report of your conduct will go to my superiors–with copies to the Governor of Mozambique, and the Portuguese War Office.'

'Hold on!' cried Flynn. Not only was he going to leave the cruiser without the gin, but he could imagine that the wording of Joyce's report would ensure that he never got that medal. They might even withdraw his commission. In this moment of terrible stress the solution came to him.

'There is one man. *Only* one man who knows the delta better than I do. He's young, plenty of guts–and he's got eyes like a hawk.'

Joyce glared at him, breathing hard as he fought to check the headlong run of his rage.

'Who?' he demanded.

'My own son,' intoned Flynn, it sounded better than son-in-law.

'Will he do it?'

'He'll do it. I'll see to that,' Flynn assured him.

59

'It's as safe as a horse and cart,' boomed Flynn, he liked the simile, and repeated it.

'How safe is a horse and cart when it's up in the clouds?' asked Sebastian, without lowering his eyes from the sky.

'I'm disappointed in you, Bassie. Most young fellows would jump at this chance.' Flynn was literally in excellent spirits. Joyce had come through with three cases of best Beefeater gin. He sat on one of the gasoline drums that lay beneath the shade of the palm tree above the beach, around him in various attitudes of relaxation lay twenty of his scouts, for it was a drowsy, warm, and windless morning. A bright sun burned down from a clear sky, and the white sand was dazzling against the dark green of the sea. The low surf sighed softly against the beach, and half a mile out, a cloud of seabirds were milling and diving on a shoal of bait-fish. Their cries blending with the sound of the sea.

Even though they were a hundred miles north of the Rovuma mouth, deep in German territory, a holiday atmosphere prevailed. Heightened by anticipation of the imminent arrival of the flying-machine they were enjoying themselves–all of them except Sebastian and Rosa. They were holding each other's hands and looking into the southern sky.

'You must find it for us.' Rosa's voice was low, but not low enough to cover her intensity. For the last ten days, since Flynn had returned from his meeting with Joyce on board the *Renounce*, she had spoken of little else but the German warship. It had become another cup to catch the hatred that overflowed from her.

'I'll try,' said Sebastian.

'You must,' she said. 'You must.'

'Should be able to get a good view from up there. Like standing on a mountain–only with no mountain under you,' said Sebastian and he felt his skin crawl at the thought.

'Listen!' said Rosa.

'What?'

'Ssh!'

And he heard it, an insect drone that swelled and sank and swelled again. They heard it under the trees also, and some of them came out into the sun and stood peering towards the south.

Suddenly in the sky there was a flash of reflected sunlight off metal or glass, and a shout went up from the watchers.

It came in towards them, low on wobbly wings, the clatter of its engine rising to a crescendo, its shadow racing ahead of it along the white beach. The group of native scouts exploded in panic-stricken retreat, Sebastian dropped on his face in the sand, only Rosa stood unmoving as it roared a few feet over her head, and then rose and banked away in a curve out over the sea.

Sebastian stood up and sheepishly brushed sand from his bush-jacket, as the aircraft levelled in the sand down on to the hard-packed sand near the water's edge. The beat of its engine faded to a spluttering burble, and it waddled slowly towards them, the backwash of the propeller sending a misty plume of sand scudding out behind. The wings looked as though they were about to fall off.

'All right,' bellowed Flynn at his men who were standing well back in the palm grove. 'Get these drums down there.'

The pilot switched off the motor, and the silence was stunning. He climbed stiffly out of the cockpit on to the lower wing, dumpy and awkward in his thick leather jacket, helmet, and goggles. He jumped down on to the beach and shrugged out of the jacket, pulled off the helmet, and was revealed as the suave young Portuguese lieutenant.

'Da Silva,' he said offering his right hand as Sebastian ran forward to greet him. 'Hernandez da Silva.'

While Flynn and Sebastian supervised the refuelling of the aircraft, Rosa sat with the pilot under the palms, while he breakfasted on garlic polony and a bottle of white wine that he had brought with him–suitably exotic food for a dashing knight of the air.

Although his mouth was busy, the pilot's eyes were free and he used them on Rosa. Even at a distance of fifty yards Sebastian became aware with mounting disquiet that Rosa was suddenly a woman again. Where before there had been a lifted chin and the straightforward masculine gaze; now there were downcast eyes broken with quick bright glances and secret smiles, now there were soft rose colours that glowed and faded beneath the sunbrowned skin of her cheeks and neck. She touched her hair with a finger, pushing a strand back behind her ear. She tugged at the front of her bush-jacket to straighten it, then drew her long khaki-clad legs up sideways beneath her as she sat in the sand. The pilot's eyes followed the movement. He wiped the neck of the wine bottle on his sleeve, and then with a flourish offered it to Rosa.

Rosa murmured her thanks and accepted the bottle to sip at it delicately. With the freckles across her cheeks and the skin peeling from her nose she looked as fresh and as innocent as a little girl, Sebastian thought.

The Portuguese lieutenant on the other hand looked neither fresh nor innocent. He was handsome, if you liked the slimy continental type with that slightly jaded tom cat look. Sebastian decided that there was something obscenely erotic about that little black moustache, that lay upon his upper lip and accentuated the cherry-pink lips beneath.

Watching him take the bottle back from Rosa and lift it towards her in salutation before drinking, Sebastian was overcome with two strong desires. One was to take the wine bottle and thrust it down the lieutenant's throat, the other was to get him into the flying-machine and away from Rosa just as quickly as was possible.

'Paci. Paci,' he growled at Mohammed's gang who were slopping gasoline into the funnel on the upper wing. 'Get a move on, for cat's sake!'

'Get your clobber into this thing, Bassie, and stop giving orders–you know it just confuses everybody.'

'I don't know where to put it–you'd better tell that greaser to come and show me. I can't speak his language.'

'Put it in the front cockpit–the observer's cockpit.'

'Tell that damned Portuguese to come here.' Sebastian dug in stubbornly. 'Tell him to leave Rosa alone and come here.'

Rosa followed the pilot to the aircraft and the expression of awed respect on her face, as she listened to him throwing out orders in Portuguese, infuriated Sebastian. The ritual of starting the aircraft completed, it stood clattering and quivering on the beach, and the pilot waved imperiously at Sebastian from the cockpit to come aboard.

Instead he went to Rosa and took her possessively in his arms.

'Do you love me?' he asked.

'What?' she shouted above the bellow of the engine.

'Do you love me?' he roared.

'Of course I do, you fool,' she shouted back and smiled up into his face before going up on tip-toe to kiss him while the slipstream of the propeller howled around them. Her embrace had passion in it that had not been there these many months, and Sebastian wondered sickly how much of it had been engendered by an outside agency.

'You can do that when you get back.' Flynn prised him loose from Rosa's grip, and boosted him up into the cockpit. The machine jerked forward and Sebastian clutched desperately to retain his balance, then glanced back. Rosa was waving and smiling, he was not certain if the smile was directed at him or at the helmeted head in the cockpit behind him, but his jealousy was swamped by the primeval instinct of survival.

Clutching with both hands at the sides of the cockpit, even his toes curling in their boots as though to grip the floor-boards of the cockpit, Sebastian stared ahead.

The beach disappeared beneath the fuselage in a solid white blur; the palm trees whipped past on one side, the sea on the other; the wind tore at his face and the tears streamed back along his cheeks, the machine bumped and bucked and bounced, and then leaped upwards under him, dropped back to bounce once more and then was airborne. The earth fell away gently beneath them as they soared, and Sebastian's spirits soared with them. His misgivings melted away.

Sebastian remembered at last to pull the goggles down over his eyes to protect them from the stinging wind, and godlike he looked down through them at a world that was small and tranquil.

When at last he looked back over his shoulder at the pilot, this strange and wonderful shared experience of immortality had lifted him above the petty passions of mere men, and they smiled at each other.

The pilot pointed out over the right wing tip, and Sebastian followed the direction of his arm.

Far, far out on the crenellated blue blanket of the sea, tiny beneath vast fluffy piles of thunderhead cloud, he saw the grey shape of the British cruiser *Renounce* with the pale white feather of its wake fanning on the surface of the ocean behind it.

He nodded and smiled at his companion. Again the pilot pointed, this time ahead.

Still misty in the blue haze of distance, haphazard as the unfitted pieces of a jigsaw puzzle, the islands of the Rufiji delta were spilled and scattered between ocean and mainland.

In the rackety little cockpit, Sebastian squatted over his pack and took from it binoculars, pencil, and map-case.

60

It was hot. Moist itchy hot. Even in the shade beneath the festooned camouflage-nets the decks of *Blücher* were smothered with hot sticky waves of swamp air. The sweat that oozed and trickled down the glistening bodies of the half-naked men who slaved on her foredeck gave them no relief, for the air was too humid to evaporate the moisture. They moved like sleep-walkers, with slow mechanical determination, manhandling the thick sheet of steel plate into its slings beneath the high arm of the crane.

Even the flow of obscenity from the lips of Lochtkamper, the engineering commander, had dried up like a spring in drought season. He worked with his men, like them stripped to the waist, and the tattoos on his upper arms and across his chest heaved and bulged as they rode on an undulating sea of muscles.

'Rest,' he grunted; and they straightened up from their labour, mouths gaping as they sucked in the stale air, massaging aching backs, glowering at the sheet of steel with true hatred.

'Captain.' Lochtkamper became aware of von Kleine for the first time. He stood against the forward gun-turret, tall in full whites, the blond beard half concealing the cross of black enamel and silver that hung at his throat. Lochtkamper crossed to him.

'It goes well?' von Kleine asked, and the engineer shook his head.

'Not as well as I had hoped.' He wiped one huge hand across his forehead, leaving a smudge of grease and rust scale on his own face. 'Slow,' he said. 'Too slow.'

'You have encountered difficulties?'

'Everywhere,' growled the engineer, and he looked around at the heat mist and the mangroves, at the sluggish black waters and the mud banks. 'Nothing works here–the welding equipment, the winch engines, even the men–everything sickens in this obscene heat.'

'How much longer?'

'I do not know, Captain. I truly do not know.'

Von Kleine would not press him. If any man could get *Blücher* seaworthy, it would be this man. When Lochtkamper slept at all, it was here on the foredeck, curled like a dog on a mattress thrown on the planking. He slept a few exhausted hours amid the whine and groan of the winches, the blue hissing glare of the welding torches, and the drum splitting hammering of the riveters, then he was up again bullying, leading, coaxing, and threatening.

'Another three weeks,' Lochtkamper estimated reluctantly. 'A month at the most–if all goes as it does now.'

They were both silent, standing together, two men from different worlds drawn together by a common goal, united by respect for each other's ability.

A mile up the channel, movement caught their attention. It was one of the launches returning to the cruiser, yet it looked like a hayrick under its bulky cargo. It came slowly against the sluggish current, sitting so low in the water that only a few inches of freeboard showed, while its load was a great shaggy hump on which sat a dozen black men.

Von Kleine and Lochtkamper watched it approaching.

'I still do not know about that obscene wood, Captain.' Lochtkamper shook his big untidy head again. 'It is so soft, so much ash, it could clog the furnace.'

'There is nothing else we can do,' von Kleine reminded him.

When *Blüther* entered the Rufiji, her coal-bunkers were almost empty. There was enough fuel for perhaps four thousand miles of steaming. Hardly enough to carry her in a straight run down into latitude 45° south, where her mother ship, *Esther*, waited to refuel her, and fill her magazines with shell.

There was not the faintest chance of obtaining coal. Instead von Klein had set Commissioner Fleischer and his thousand native porters to cutting cordwood from the forests, that grew at the apex of the delta. It was a duty that Commissioner Fleischer had opposed with every argument and excuse he could muster. He felt that in delivering safety to Captain von Kleine the steel plating from Dar es Salaam, he had discharged any obligation that he might have towards the *Blücher*. His eloquence availed him not at all–Lochtkamper had fashioned two hundred primitive axe heads from the steel plate, and von Kleine had sent Lieutenant Kyller up-river with Fleischer to help him keep his enthusiasm for wood-cutting burning brightly.

For three weeks now, the *Blücher*'s launches had been plying steadily back and forth. Up to the present they had delivered some five hundred tons of timber. The problem was finding storage for this unwieldy cargo once the coal-bunkers were filled.

'We will have to begin deck loading the cordwood soon,' von Kleine muttered, and Lochtkamper opened his mouth to reply when the alarm bells began to clamour an emergency, and the loudhailer boomed.

'Captain to the bridge. Captain to the bridge.'

Von Kleine turned and ran.

On the companion ladder he collided with one of his lieutenants. They caught at each other for balance and the lieutenant shouted into von Kleine's face.

'Captain–an aircraft. Flying low. Coming this way. Portuguese markings.'

'Damn it to hell!' Von Kleine pushed past him, and bounded up the ladder. He burst on to the bridge, panting.

'Where is it?' he shouted.

The officer of the watch dropped his binoculars and turned to von Kleine with relief.

'There it is, sir!' He pointed through a hole in the tangled screen of camouflage that hung like a veranda roof over the bridge.

Von Kleine snatched the binoculars from him, as he trained them on the distant winged shape in the mist haze above the mangroves, he issued his orders.

'Warn the men ashore. Everybody under cover,' he barked. 'All guns trained to maximum elevation. Pom-poms loaded with shrapnel. Machine gun crews closed up–but no firing until my orders.'

He held the aircraft in the round field of the field glasses.

'Portuguese, all right,' he grunted; the green and red insignia showed clearly against the brown body of the aircraft.

'She's searching . . .' The aircraft was sweeping back and forth, banking over and turning back at the end of each leg of her search pattern, like a farmer ploughing a field. Von Kleine could make out the head and shoulders of a man crouched forward in the squat round nose of the aircraft. '. . . Now we'll find out how effective is our camouflage.'

So the enemy have guessed at last. They must have reported the convoy of steel plate–or perhaps the chopping of the cordwood has alerted them, he thought, watching the aircraft tacking slowly towards him. *We could not hope to go undetected for ever–but I did not expect them to send an aircraft.*

Then suddenly the thought struck him so hard that he gasped with the danger of it. He whirled and ran to the forward rail of the bridge and peered out through the camouflage net.

Still half a mile distant, trundling slowly down the centre of the channel with the wide rippling V of her wake spread on the current behind her, clumsy as a pregnant hippo with her load of cordwood, the launch was aimed straight at *Blücher*. From the air she would be as conspicuous as a fat tick on a white sheet.

'The launch . . .' shouted von Kleine, '. . . hail her. Order her to run for the bank–get her under cover!'

But he knew it was useless. By the time she was within hail, it would be too late. He thought of ordering his forward turrets to fire on the launch and sink her–but discarded the idea immediately, the fall of shell would immediately draw the enemy's attention.

Impatiently he stood gripping the rail of the bridge, and mouthing his anger and his frustration at the approaching launch.

61

Sebastian hung over the edge of the cockpit. The wind buffeted him, flapping his jacket wildly about his body, whipping his hair into a black tangle. With his usual dexterity Sebastian had managed to drop the binoculars overboard. They were the property of Flynn Patrick O'Flynn, and Sebastian knew that he would be expected to pay for them. This spoiled Sebastian's enjoyment of the flight to some extent, he already owed Flynn a little over three hundred pounds. Rosa would have something to say also. However, the loss of the binoculars was no handicap, the aircraft was flying too low and was so unstable that the unaided eye was much more effective.

From a height of five hundred feet the mangrove forest looked like a fluffy overstuffed mattress, a sickly fever green in colour, with the channels and the waterways between them dark gunmetal veins that flashed the sunlight back like a heliograph. The clouds of white egrets that rose in alarm as the aircraft approached looked like drifts of torn paper scraps. A fish eagle hung suspended in silent flight ahead of them, the wide span of its wings flared at the tips like the fingers of a hand, It dipped away, sliding past the aircraft's wing tip so close, that Sebastian saw the fierce yellow eyes in its white hooded head.

Sebastian laughed with delight, and then grabbed at the side of the cockpit to steady himself, as the machine rocked violently under him. This was the pilot's method of attracting Sebastian's attention, and Sebastian wished he would think up some other way of doing it.

He looked back angrily shouting in the howl of wind and engine.

'Watch it! You stupid dago.'

Da Silva was gesticulating wildly, his pink mouth working under the black moustache, his eyes wild behind the panes of his goggles, his right hand stabbing urgently out over the starboard wing.

Sebastian saw it immediately on the wide waterway, the launch was so glaringly conspicuous that he wondered why he had not seen it before, then he recalled that his attention had been concentrated on the terrain directly beneath the aircraft–and he excused himself.

Yet there was little to justify da Silva's excitement, he thought. This was no battle cruiser, it was a tiny vessel of perhaps twenty-five feet. Quickly he ran his eyes down the channel, following it to the open sea in the blue distance. It was empty.

He glanced back at the pilot and shook his head. But da Silva's excitement had, if anything, increased. He was making another frenzied hand-signal that Sebastian could not understand. To save argument Sebastian nodded in agreement, and instantly the machine dropped away under him so that Sebastian's belly was left behind and he clutched desperately at the side of the cockpit once more.

In a shallow turning dive, da Silva took the machine down and then levelled out with the landing-wheels almost brushing the tops of the mangroves. They rushed towards the channel, and as the last mangroves whipped away under them da Silva eased the nose down still farther and they dropped to within a few feet of the surface of the water. It was a display of fine flying that was completely wasted on Sebastian. He was cursing da Silva quietly, his eyes starting from their sockets.

A mile ahead of them across the open water bobbed the over-laden launch. It was only a few feet below their own level, and they raced towards it with the wash of the propeller blowing a squall of ripples across the surface behind them.

'My God!' The blasphemy was wrung from Sebastian in his distress. 'He's going to fly right into it!'

It was an opinion that seemed to be shared by the crew of the launch. As the machine roared in on them, they began to abandon ship. Sebastian saw two men leap from the high piled load of timber and hit the water with small white splashes.

At the last second da Silva lifted the plane and they hopped over the launch. For a fleeting instant Sebastian stared at a range of fifteen feet into the face of the German naval officer who crouched down over the tiller bar at the stern of the launch. They were then past and climbing sharply, banking and turning back.

Sebastian saw the launch had rounded to, and that her crew were clambering aboard and splashing around her sides. Once more the aircraft dropped towards the channel, but da Silva had throttled back and the engine was burbling under half power. He levelled out fifty feet above the water, and flew sedately, keeping away from the launch and well towards the northern side of the channel.

'What are you doing?' Sebastian mouthed the question at da Silva. In reply the pilot made a sweeping gesture with his right hand at the thick bank of mangroves alongside.

Puzzled, Sebastian stared into the mangroves. What was the fool doing, surely he didn't think that . . .

There was a hump of high ground on the bank, a hump that rose perhaps one hundred and fifty feet above the level of the river. They came up to it.

Like a hunter following a wounded buffalo, moving carelessly through thin scattered bush which could not possibly give cover to such a large animal, and then suddenly coming face to face with it–so close, that he sees the minute detail of crenellation on the massive bosses of the horns, sees the blood dripping from moist black nostrils, and the dull furnace glare of the piggy little eyes–in the same fashion Sebastian found the *Blücher*.

She was so close he could see the pattern of rivets on her plating, the joints in the planking of her foredeck, the individual strands of the canopy of camouflage netting spread over her. He saw the men on her bridge, and the gun-crews behind the pom-poms and the Maxim machine guns on the balconies of her upperworks. From her squatting turrets her big guns gaped at him with hungry mouths, revolving to follow the flight of the machine.

She was monstrous, grey, and sinister among the mangroves, crouching in her lair, and Sebastian cried aloud in surprise and alarm, a sound without shape or coherence, and at the same moment the engine of the aeroplane bellowed in full power as da Silva thrust the throttle wide and hauled the joystick back into his crotch.

As the aircraft rocketed upwards, the deck of the *Blücher* erupted in a thunderous volcano of flame. Flame flew in great bell-shaped ejaculations from the muzzles of her nine-inch guns. Flame spat viciously from the multi-barrelled pom-poms and the machine guns on her upperworks.

Around the little aircraft the air boiled and hissed, disrupted, churned into violent turbulence by the passage of the big shells.

Something struck the plane, and she was whirled upwards like a burning leaf from a garden bonfire. Wing over wing she rolled, her engine surging wildly, her rigging groaning and creaking at the strain.

Sebastian was flung forward, the bridge of his nose cracked against the edge of the cockpit and instantly twin jets of blood spurted from his nostrils to douse the front of his jacket.

The machine stood on her tail, propeller clawing ineffectively at the air, engine wailing in over rev. Then she dropped away on one wing and one side swooped sickeningly downwards.

Da Silva fought her, feeling the sloppiness of the stall in her controls come alive again as she regained air-speed. The fluffy tops of the mangroves rushed up to meet him, and desperately he tried to ease her off. She was trying to respond, the fabric wrinkling along her wings as they flexed to the enormous pressure. He felt her lurch again as she touched the top branches, heard above the howl of the engine the faint crackling brush of the vegetation against her belly. Then suddenly, miraculously, she was clear; flying straight and level, climbing slowly up and away from the hungry swamp.

She was sluggish and heavy, and there was something loose under her. It banged and thumped and slapped in the slip-stream, jarring the whole fuselage. Da Silva could not dare to manœuvre her. He held her on the course she had chosen, easing her nose slightly upwards, slowly gaining precious altitude.

At a thousand feet he brought her round in a wide gentle turn to the south, and banging and thumping, one wing heavy, she staggered drunkenly through the sky towards her rendezvous with Flynn O'Flynn.

62

Flynn stood up with slow dignity from where he had been leaning against the bole of the palm tree.

'Where are you going?' Rosa opened her eyes and looked up at him.

'To do something you can't do for me.'

'That's the third time in an hour!' Rosa was suspicious.

'That's why they call it the East African quickstep,' said Flynn, and moved off ponderously into the undergrowth. He reached the lantana bush, and looked around carefully. He couldn't trust Rosa not to follow him. Satisfied, he dropped to his knees and dug with his hands in the loose sand.

With the air of an old-time pirate unearthing a chest of doubloons, he lifted the bottle from its grave, and withdrew the cork.

The neck of the bottle was in his mouth, when he heard the muted beat of the returning aircraft. The bottle stayed there a while longer, Flynn's Adam's apple pulsing up and down his throat as he swallowed, but his eyes swivelled upwards and creased in concentration.

With a sigh of intense pleasure he recorked, and laid the bottle once more to rest, kicked sand over it, and set course for the beach.

'Can you see them?' he shouted the question at Rosa as he came down through the palms. She was standing out in the open. Her head was thrown back so that the long braid of her hair hung down to her waist behind. She did not answer him, but the set of her expression was hard and strained with anxiety. The men standing about her were silent also, held by an expectant dread.

Flynn looked up and saw it coming in like a wounded bird, the engine stuttering and surging irregularly, streaming a long bluish streak of oily smoke from the exhaust manifold, the wings rocking crazily, and a loose tangle of wreckage hanging and swinging under the belly where one of the landing-wheels had been shot away.

It sagged wearily towards the beach, the broken beat of the engine fading so they could hear the whisper of the wind in her rigging.

The single landing-wheel touched down on the hard sand and for fifty yards she ran true, then with a jerk she toppled sideways. The port wing bit into the sand, slewing her towards the edge of the sea, the tail came up and over. There was a crackling, ripping, tearing sound; and in a dust storm of flying sand she cartwheeled, stern over stem.

The propeller tore into the beach, disintegrating in a blur of flying splinters, and from the forward cockpit a human body was flung clear, spinning in the air so that the outflung limbs were the spokes of a wheel. It fell with a splash in the shallow water at the edge of the beach, while the aircraft careened onwards, tearing herself to pieces. A lower wing broke off–the guy wires snapping with a sound like a volley of musketry. The body of the machine slowed as it hit the water, skidding to a standstill on its back, with the surf washing around it. Da Silva hung motionless in the cockpit, suspended upside down by his safety-straps, his arms dangling.

The next few seconds of silence were appalling.

'Help the pilot! I'll get Sebastian.' Rosa broke it at last. Mohammed and the two Askari ran with her towards where Sebastian was lying awash, a piece of flotsam at the water's edge.

'Come on!' Flynn shouted at the men near him, and lumbered through the soft fluffy sand towards the wreck. They never reached it.

There was a concussion, a vast disturbance in the air that sucked at their eardrums, as the gasoline ignited in explosive combustion. The machine and the surface of the sea about it were instantly transformed into a roaring, raging sheet of flame.

They backed away from the heat. The flames were dark red laced with satanic black smoke, and they ate the canvas skin from the body of the aircraft, exposing the wooden framework beneath.

In the heart of the flames da Silva still hung in his cockpit, a blackened monkey-like shape as his clothing burned. Then the fire ate through the straps of his harness and he dropped heavily into the shallow water, hissing and sizzling as the flames were quenched.

The fire was still smouldering by the time Sebastian regained consciousness, and was able to lift himself on one elbow. Muzzily he stared down the beach at the smoking wreckage. The shadows of the palms lay like the stripes of a tiger on the sand that the low evening sun had softened to a dull gold.

'Da Silva?' Sebastian's voice was thick and slurred. His nose was broken and squashed across his face. Although Rosa had wiped most of the blood away, there were still little black crusts of it in his nostrils and at the corners of his mouth. Both his eyes were slits in the swollen plum-coloured bruises that bulged from the sockets.

'No!' Flynn shook his head. 'He didn't make it.'

'Dead?' whispered Sebastian.

'We buried him back in the bush.'

'What happened?' asked Rosa. 'What on earth happened out there?' She sat close beside him, protective as a mother over her child. Slowly Sebastian turned his head to look at her.

'We found the *Blücher*,' he said.

63

Captain Arthur Joyce, R.N., was a happy man. He stooped over his cabin desk, his hands placed open and flat on either side of the spread Admiralty chart. He glowed with satisfaction as he looked down at the hand-drawn circle in crude blue pencil as though it were the signature of the President of the Bank of England on a cheque for a million sterling.

'Good!' he said. 'Oh, very good,' and he pursed his lips as though he were about to whistle 'Tipperary'. Instead he made a sucking sound, and smiled across at Sebastian. Behind his flattened nose and blue-ringed eyes, Sebastian smiled back at him.

'A damn good show, Oldsmith!' Joyce's expression changed, the little lights of recognition sparkled suddenly in his eyes. 'Oldsmith?' he repeated. 'I say, didn't you open the bowling for Sussex in the 1911 cricket season?'

'That's right, sir.'

'Good Lord!' Joyce beamed at him. 'I'll never forget your opening over to Yorkshire in the first match of the season. You dismissed Graham and

Penridge for two runs–two for two, hey?'

'Two for two, it was.' Sebastian liked this man.

'Fiery stuff! And then you made fifty-five runs?'

'Sixty-five,' Sebastian corrected him. 'A record ninth wicket partnership with Clifford Dumont of–one hundred and eighty-six!'

'Yes! Yes! I remember it well. Fiery stuff! You were damned unlucky not to play for England.'

'Oh, I don't know about that,' said Sebastian in modest agreement.

'Yes, you were.' Joyce pursed his lips again. '*Damned* unlucky.'

Flynn O'Flynn had not understood a word of this. He was thrashing around in his chair like an old buffalo in a trap, bored to the point of pain. Rosa Oldsmith had understood no more than he had, but she was fascinated. It was clear that Captain Joyce knew of some outstanding accomplishment of Sebastian's, and if a man like Joyce knew of it–then Sebastian was famous. She felt pride swell in her chest and she smiled on Sebastian also.

'I didn't know, Sebastian. Why didn't you tell me?' She glowed warmly at him.

'Some other time,' Joyce interrupted quickly. 'Now we must get on with this other business.' And he returned his attention to the chart on the desk.

'Now I want you to cast your mind back. Shut your eyes and try to see it again. Every detail you can remember, every little detail–it might be important. Did you see any signs of damage?'

Obediently Sebastian closed his eyes, and was surprised at how vividly the acid of fear had engraved the picture of *Blücher* on his mind.

'Yes,' he said. 'There were holes in her. Hundreds of holes, little black ones. And at the front end–the bows–there were trapezes hanging down on ropes, near the water. You know the kind that they use when they paint a high building . . .'

Joyce nodded at his secretary to record every word of it.

64

The single fan suspended over the table in the wardroom hummed quietly, the blades stirred the air that was moist and warm as the bedding of a malarial patient.

Except for the soft clink of cutlery on china, the only other sound was that of Commissioner Fleischer drinking his soup. It was thick, green pea soup, scalding hot, so that Fleischer found it necessary to blow heavily on each spoonful before ingesting it with a noise, not of the same volume as, but with the delicate tonal quality of, a flushing water closet. During the pause while he crumbled a slice of black bread into his soup, Fleischer looked across the board at Lieutenant Kyller.

'So you did not find the enemy flying-machine, then?'

'No.' Kyller went on fiddling with his wine glass without looking up. For forty-eight hours he and his patrols had searched the swamps and channels and mangrove forests for the wreckage of the aircraft. He was exhausted and covered with insect bites.

'Ja,' Fleischer nodded solemnly. 'It fell only a short way but it did not hit the trees. I was sure of that. I have seen sand-grouse do the same thing sometimes when you shoot them with a shotgun. Pow! They come tumbling down like this . . .' He fluttered his hand in the air, letting it fall towards his soup, '. . . then suddenly they do this.' The hand took flight again in the direction of the Commander (Engineering) Lochtkamper's rugged Neanderthal face. They all watched it.

'The little bird flies away home. It was bad shooting from so close,' said Fleischer, and ended the demonstration by picking up his spoon, and the moist warm silence once more gripped the wardroom.

Commander Lochtkamper stoked his mouth as though it were one of his furnaces. The knuckles of both his hands were knocked raw by contact with steel plate and wire rope. Even when Fleischer's hand had flown into his face, he had not been distracted from his thoughts. His mind was wholly occupied with steel and machinery, weights and points of balance. He wanted to achieve twenty degrees of starboard list on *Blücher*, so that a greater area of her bottom would be exposed to his welders. This meant displacing one thousand tons of dead weight. It seemed an impossibility–unless we flood the port magazines, he thought, and take the guns from their turrets and move them. Then we could rig camels under her . . .

'It was not bad shooting,' said the gunnery lieutenant. 'She was flying too close, the rate of track was . . .' He broke off, wiped the side of his long pointed nose with his forefinger, and regarded balefully the sweat that came away on it. This fat peasant would not understand, he would not waste energy in explaining the technicalities. He contented himself with repeating, 'It was not bad shooting.'

'I think we must accept that the enemy machine has returned safely to her base,' said Lieutenant Kyller. 'Therefore we can expect the enemy to mount some form of offensive action against us in the very near future.' Kyller enjoyed a position of privilege in the wardroom. No other of the junior officers would have dared to express his opinions so freely. Yet none of them would have made as much sense as Kyller. When he spoke his senior officers listened, if not respectfully, at least attentively. Kyller had passed out sword of honour cadet from Bremerhaven Naval Academy in 1910. His father was a Baron, a personal friend of the Kaiser's, and an Admiral of the Imperial Fleet. Kyller was wardroom favourite, not only because of his dark good looks and courteous manners–but also because of his appetite for hard work, his meticulous attention to detail, and his ready mind. He was a good officer to have aboard–a credit to the ship.

'What can the enemy do?' Fleischer asked with scorn. He did not share the general opinion of Ernst Kyller. 'We are safe here–what can he do?'

'A superficial study of naval history will reveal, sir, that the English can be expected to do what you least expect them to do. And that they will do it, quickly, efficiently, and with iron purpose.' Kyller scratched the lumpy red insect bites behind his left ear.

'Bah!' said Fleischer, and sprayed a little pea soup with the violence of his disgust. 'The English are fools and cowards–at the worst, they will skulk off the mouth of the river. They would not dare come in here after us.'

'I have no doubt that time will prove you correct, sir.' This was Kyller's phrase of violent disagreement with a senior officer, and from experience Captain von Kleine and his commanders recognized it. They smiled a little.

'This soup is bitter,' said Fleischer, satisfied that he had carried the argument. 'The cook has used seawater in it.'

The accusation was so outrageous, that even von Kleine looked up from his plate.

'Please do not let our humble hospitality delay you, Herr Commissioner. You must be anxious to return up-river to your wood-cutting duties.'

And Fleischer subsided quickly, hunching over his food. Von Kleine transferred his gaze to Kyller.

'Kyller, you will not be returning with the Herr Commissioner. I am sending Ensign Proust with him this trip. You will be in command of the first line of defence that I plan to place at the mouth of the delta, in readiness for the English attack. You will attend the conference in my cabin after this meal, please.'

'Thank you, sir.' His voice was husky with gratitude for the honour his captain was conferring upon him. Von Kleine looked from him to his gunnery lieutenant.

'You also, please, Guns. I want to relieve you of your beloved upper deck pom-poms.'

'You mean to take them off their mountings, sir?' the gunnery lieutenant asked, looking at von Kleine dolefully over his long doleful nose.

'I regret the necessity,' von Kleine told him sympathetically.

65

'Well, Henry. We were right. *Blücher*'s there.'

'Unfortunately, sir.'

'Two heavy cruisers tied up indefinitely on blockade service.' Admiral Sir Percy thrust out his lower lip lugubriously as he regarded the plaques of *Renounce* and *Pegasus* on the Indian Ocean plot. 'There is work for them elsewhere.'

'There is, at that,' agreed Henry Green.

'That request of Joyce's for two motor torpedo-boats . . .'

'Yes, sir?'

'We must suppose he intends mounting a torpedo attack into the delta.'

'It looks like it, sir.'

'It might work–worth a try anyway. What can we scratch together for him?'

'There is a full squadron at Bombay, and another at Aden, sir.'

For five seconds, Sir Percy Howe reviewed the meagre forces with which he was expected to guard two oceans. With this new submarine menace, he could not detach a single ship from the approaches to the Suez Canal–it would have to be Bombay. 'Send him an MTB from the Bombay squadron.'

'He asked for two, sir.'

'Joyce knows full well that I only let him have half of anything he requests. He always doubles up.'

'What about this recommendation for a decoration, sir?'

'The fellow who spotted the *Blücher*?'

'Yes, sir.'

'A bit tricky–Portuguese irregular and all that sort of thing.'

'He's a British subject, sir.'

'Then he shouldn't be with the dagos,' said Sir Percy. 'Leave it over until the operation is completed. We'll think about it after we've sunk the *Blücher*.'

66

The sunset was blood and roses, nude pink and tarnished gold as the British blockade squadron stood in towards the land.

Renounce led with the commodore's pennant flying at her masthead. In the smooth wide road of her wake, *Pegasus* slid over the water. Their silhouettes were crisp and black against the garish colours of the sunset. There was something prim and old-maidish about the lines of a heavy cruiser–none of the solid majesty of a battleship, nor the jaunty devil-may-care rake of a destroyer.

Close in under *Pegasus*'s beam, screened by her hull from the land, like a cygnet swimming beside the swan, rode the motor torpedo-boat.

Even in this light surface chop she was taking in water. Each wave puffed up over her bows and then streamed back greenish and cream along the decks. The spray rattled against the thin canvas that screened the open bridge.

Flynn O'Flynn crouched behind the screen and cursed the vaunting ambition that had led him to volunteer as pilot for this expedition. He glanced across at Sebastian who stood in the open wing of the bridge, behind the canvas-shrouded batteries of Lewis guns. Sebastian was grinning as the warm spray flew back into his face and trickled down his cheeks.

Joyce had recommended Sebastian for a Distinguished Service Order. This was almost more than Flynn could bear. He wanted one also. He had decided to go along now for that reason alone. Therefore Sebastian was directly to blame for Flynn's present discomfort, and Flynn felt a small warmth of satisfaction as he looked at the flattened, almost negroid contours of Sebastian's new nose. The young bastard deserved it, and he found himself wishing further punishment on his son-in-law.

'Distinguished Service Order and all . . .' he grunted. 'A half-trained chimpanzee could have done what he did. Yet who was it who found the wheels in the first place? No, Flynn Patrick, there just ain't no justice in this world, but we'll show the sons of bitches this time . . .'

His thoughts were interrupted by the small bustle of activity on the bridge around him. An Aldis lamp was winking from the high dark bulk of *Renounce* ahead of them.

The lieutenant commanding the torpedo-boat spelled the message aloud.

'Flag to YN2. D . . . P departure point. Good luck.' He was a dumpy amorphous figure in his duffle coat with the collar turned up. 'Thanks a lot, old chap–and one up your pipe also. No, Signaller, don't make that.' He went on quickly, 'YN2 to flag. Acknowledged!' Then turning to the engine voice-pipe. 'Both engines stop,' he said.

The beat of her engines faded away, and she wallowed in the trough of the next wave. *Renounce* and *Pegasus* sailed on sedately, leaving the tiny vessel rolling crazily in the turbulence of their wakes. A lonely speck five miles off the mouth of the Rufiji delta, too far off for the shorewatchers to see her in the fading evening light.

67

Lieutenant Ernst Kyller watched through his binoculars as the two British cruisers turned in succession away from the land, and coalesced with the darkness that fell so swiftly over the ocean and the land. They were gone.

'Every day it is the same.' Kyller let the binoculars fall against his chest and pulled his watch from the pocket of his tunic. 'Fifteen minutes before sunset, and again fifteen minutes before sun-up they sail past to show us that they are still waiting.'

'Yes, sir,' agreed the seaman who was squeezed into the crow's nest beside Kyller.

'I will go down now. Moon comes up at 11.44 tonight–keep awake.'

'Yes, sir.'

Kyller swung his legs over the side and groped with his feet for the rungs of the rope ladder. Then he climbed down the palm tree to the beach fifty feet below. By the time he reached it the light had gone, and the beach was a vague white blur down to the green lights of phosphorus in the surf.

The sand crunched like sugar under his boots as he set off to where the launch was moored. As he walked, his mind was wholly absorbed with the details of his defence system.

There were only two of the many mouths of the Rufiji, up which the English could attack. They were separated by a low wedge-shaped island of sand and mud and mangrove. It was on the seaward side of this island that Kyller had sited the four-pounder pom-poms taken from their mountings on *Blücher*'s upper deck.

He had sunk a raft of logs into the soft mud to give them a firm foundation on which to stand, and he had cut out the mangroves so they commanded an arc of fire across both channels. His searchlights he sited with equal care–so they could sweep left or right without blinding his gunners.

From Commander Lochtkamper he had solicited a length of four-inch steel hawser. This was rather like an unrehabilitated insolvent raising an unsecured loan from a money-lender, for Commander Lochtkamper was not easily parted from his stores. Far up river Ensign Proust had diverted some of his axemen to felling fifty giant African mahogany trees. They had floated the trunks down on the tide; logs the size of the columns of a Greek temple. With these and the cable Kyller had fashioned a boom that stretched across both channels, an obstacle so formidable that it would rip the belly out of even a heavy cruiser coming down on it at speed.

Not satisfied with this, for Kyller had highly developed the Teutonic capacity for taking infinite pains, he lifted the fat globular mines with their sinister horns that *Blücher* had sown haphazardly behind her on her journey up-river. These he rearranged into neat geometrical ranks behind his log boom, a labour that left his men almost prostrated with nervous exhaustion.

This work had taken ten days to complete, and immediately Kyller had begun building observation posts. He placed them on every hump of high ground that commanded a view of thc ocean, he built them in the tops of the palm trees, and on the smaller islands that stood out at sea. He arranged a system of signals with his observers–flags and heliographs for the day, skyrockets for the night.

During the hours of darkness, two whale boats rowed steadily back and forth along the log boom, manned by seamen who slapped steadily and sulkily at the light cloud of mosquitoes that haloed their heads, and made occasional brief but vitriolic statements about Lieutenant Kyller's ancestry, present worth, and future prospects.

At 2200 hours on the night of June 16th, 1915, the British motor torpedo-boat YN2 crept with both engines running dead slow into the centre of Lieutenant Kyller's elaborate reception arrangements.

68

After the clean cool air on the open sea, the smell was like entering the monkey-house of London Zoo. The land masked the breeze, and the frolic of the surface chop died away. As the torpedo-boat groped its way into the delta, the miasma of the swamps spread out to meet her.

'My God, that smell.' Sebastian twitched his flattened nose. 'It brings back pleasant memories.'

'Lovely, isn't it?' agreed Flynn.

'We must be almost into the channel.' Sebastian peered into the night, sensing rather than seeing the loom of the mangroves ahead and on either hand.

'I don't know what the hell I'm doing on this barge,' grunted Flynn. 'This is raving bloody madness. We've got more chance of catching a clap than finding our way up to where *Blücher* is anchored.'

'Faith! Major O'Flynn, and shame on ye!' The commander of the torpedo-boat exclaimed in his best music-hall brogue. 'We put our trust in you and the Lord.' His tone changed and he spoke crisply to the helmsman beside him. 'Lay her off a point to starboard.'

The long nose of the boat, with the torpedo tubes lying like a rack of gigantic champagne bottles on her foredeck, swung fractionally. The commander cocked his head to listen to the whispered soundings relayed from the leadsman in the bows.

'Twelve fathoms,' he repeated thoughtfully. 'So far so good.' Then he turned back to Flynn.

'Now, Major, I heard you shooting the blarney to Captain Joyce about how well you know this river, I think your exact words were, "Like you know the way to your own Thunder Box." You don't seem so certain about it any longer. Why is that?'

'It's dark,' said Flynn sulkily.

'My, so it is. But that shouldn't fluster an old river pilot like you.'

'Well, it sure as hell does.'

'If we get into the channel and lay up until the moon rises, would that help?'

'It wouldn't do any harm.'

That exchange seemed to exhaust the subject and for a further fifteen minutes the tense silence on the bridge was spoiled only by the commander's quiet orders to the helm, as he kept his ship within the ten fathom line of the channel.

Then Sebastian made a contribution.

'I say, there's something dead ahead of us.'

A patch of deeper darkness in the night; a low blurred shape that showed against the faint sheen of the star reflections on the surface. A reef perhaps? No, there was a splash alongside it as an oar dipped and pulled.

'Guard boat!' said the commander, and stooped to the voice-pipe. 'Both engines full ahead together.'

The deck canted sharply under their feet as the bows lifted, the whisper of the engines rose to a dull bellow and the torpedo-boat plunged forward like a bull at the cape.

'Hold on! I'm going to ram it.' The commander's voice was pitched at conversational level, and a hubbub of shouts broke out ahead, oars splashed frantically as the guard boat tried to pull out of their line of charge.

'Steer for them,' said the commander pleasantly, and the helmsman put her over a little.

Flash and crack, flash and crack, someone in the guard boat fired a rifle just as the torpedo-boat struck her. It was a glancing blow, taken on her shoulder, that spun the little whale boat aside, shearing off the protruding oars with a crackling popping sound.

She scraped down the gunwhale of the torpedo-boat, and then she was left astern and rocking wildly as the larger vessel surged ahead.

Then abruptly it was no longer dark. From all around them sparkling trails of fire shot into the sky and burst in balls of blue, that lit it all with an eerie flickering glow.

'Sky rockets, be Jesus. Guy Fawkes, Guy,' said the commander.

They could see the banks of mangrove massed on either hand, and ahead of them the double mouths of the two channels.

'Steer for the southern channel.' This time the commander lifted his voice a little, and the ship plunged onward, throwing out white wings of water from under her bows, bucking and jarring as she leapt over the low swells pushed up by the outflowing tide, so the men on the bridge hung on to the hand rail to steady themselves.

Then all of them gasped together in the pain of seared eye-balls as a solid shaft of dazzling white light struck them. It leapt out from the dark wedge of land that divided the two channels, and almost immediately two other searchlights on the outer banks of the channels joined in the hunt. Their beams fastened on the ship like the tentacles of a squid on the carcass of a flying fish.

'Get those lights!' this time the commander shouted the order at the gunners behind the Lewis guns at the corners of the bridge. The tracer that hosed out in a gentle arc towards the base of the searchlight beams was anaemic and pinkly pale, in contrast to the brilliance they were trying to quench.

The torpedo-boat roared on into the channel.

Then there was another sound. A regular thump, thump, thump like the working of a distant water pump. Lieutenant Kyller had opened up with his quick firing pom-pom.

The four-pound tracer emanated from the dark blob of the island. Seeming to float slowly towards the torpedo-boat, but gaining speed as it approached, until it flashed past with the whirr of a rocketing pheasant.

'Jesus!' said Flynn as though he meant it. He sat down hurriedly on the deck and began to unlace his boots.

Still held in the cold white grip of the searchlights, the torpedo-boat roared on with four-pounder shell streaking around her, and bursting in flurries of spray on the surface near her. The long dotted tendrils of tracer from her own Lewis guns still arched out in delicate lines towards the shore, and suddenly they had effect.

The beam of one of the searchlights snapped off as a bullet shattered the glass, for a few seconds the filaments continued to glow dull red as they burned themselves out.

In the relief from the blinding glare, Sebastian could see ahead, and he saw a sea serpent. It lay across the channel, undulating in the swells, bellied from bank to bank by the push of the tide, showing its back at the top of the swells and then ducking into the troughs; long and sinuous and menacing, Lieutenant Kyller's log boom waited to welcome them.

'Good God, what's that?'

'Full port rudder!' the commander bellowed. 'Both engines full astern together.'

And before the ship could answer her helm or the drag of her propellers, she ran into a log four feet thick and a hundred feet long. A log as unyielding as a reef of solid granite that stopped her dead in the water and crunched in her bows.

The men in the well of her bridge were thrown into a heap of tangled bodies on the deck. A heap from which the bull figure of Flynn Patrick O'Flynn was the first to emerge. On stockinged feet he made for the side of the ship.

'Flynn, where are you going?' Sebastian shouted after him

'Home,' said Flynn.

'Wait for me.' Sebastian scrambled to his knees.

The engines roaring in reverse pulled the torpedo-boat back off the log boom, her plywood hull crackling and squeaking, but she was mortally wounded. She was sinking with a rapidity that amazed Sebastian. Already her cockpit was flooding.

'Abandon ship,' shouted the commander.

'You damned tooting,' said Flynn O'Flynn and leaped in an untidy tangle of arms and legs into the water.

Like a playful seal the torpedo-boat rolled over on its side, and Sebastian jumped. Drawing his breath while he was in the air, steeling himself against the cold of the water.

He was surprised at how warm it was.

69

From the bridge of H.M.S. *Renounce*, the survivors looked like a cluster of bedraggled water rats. In the dawn they floundered and splashed around the edge of the balloon of stained and filthy water where the Rufiji had washed them out, like the effluent from the sewer outlet of a city. *Renounce* found them before the sharks did, for there was no blood. There was one broken leg, a fractured collar bone, and a few cracked ribs–but miraculously there was no blood. So from a crew of fourteen, *Renounce* recovered every man–including the two pilots.

They came aboard with their hair matted, their faces streaked, and their eyes swollen and inflamed with engine oil. With a man on either hand to guide them, leaving a trail of malodorous Rufiji water across the deck, they shuffled down to the sick-bay, a sodden and sorrowful-looking assembly of humanity.

'Well,' said Flynn O'Flynn, 'if we don't get a medal for *that*, then I'm going back to my old job–and the hell with them.'

'That,' said Captain Arthur Joyce, sitting hunched behind his desk, 'was not a roaring success.' He showed no inclination to whistle 'Tipperary.'

'It wasn't even a good try, sir,' agreed the torpedo-boat commander. 'The Boche had everything ready to throw at our heads.'

'A log boom'–Joyce shook his head–'good Lord, they went out with the Napoleonic War!' He said it in a tone that implied that he was a victim of unfair play.

'It was extraordinarily effective, sir.'

'Yes, it must have been.' Joyce sighed. 'Well, at the very least we have established that an attack up the channel is not practical.'

'During the few minutes before the tide swept us away from the boom I looked beyond it, and I saw what I took to be a mine. I think it certain that the Boche have laid a minefield beyond the boom, sir.'

'Thank you, Commander,' Joyce nodded. 'I will see to it that their Lordships receive a full account of your conduct. I consider it excellent.' Then he went on. 'I would value your opinion of Major O'Flynn and his son–do you think they are reliable men?'

'Well . . .' the commander hesitated, he did not want to be unfair, '–they can both swim and the young one seems to have good eyesight. Apart from that I am not really in a position to give a judgement.'

'No, I don't suppose you are. Still I wish I knew more about them. For the next phase in this operation I am going to rely quite heavily on them.' He stood up. 'I think I will talk to them now.'

You mean you actually want someone to go on board *Blücher*!' Flynn was appalled.

'I have explained to you, Major, how important it is for me to know exactly what state she is in. I must be able to estimate when she is likely to break out of the delta. I must know how much time I have.'

'Madness,' whispered Flynn. 'Stark raving bloody madness.' He stared at Joyce in disbelief.

'You have told me how well organized is your intelligence system ashore, of the reliable men who work for you. Indeed it is through you that we know that the Germans are cutting cordwood and taking it aboard. We know that they have recruited an army of native labourers and are using them not only for wood-cutting, but also for heavy work aboard the *Blücher*.'

'So?' Into that single word Flynn put a wealth of caution.

'One of your men could infiltrate the labour gangs and get aboard *Blücher*.'

And Flynn perked up immediately; he had anticipated that Joyce would suggest that Flynn Patrick O'Flynn should personally conduct a survey of *Blücher*'s damage.

'It might be done.' There was a lengthy pause while Flynn considered every aspect of the business. 'Of course, Captain, my men aren't fighting patriots like you and I. They work for money. They are . . .' Flynn searched for the word. 'They are . . .'

'Mercenaries?'

'Yes,' said Flynn. 'That's exactly what they are.'

'Hmmm,' said Joyce. 'You mean they would want payment?'

'They'd want a big dollop of lolly–and you can't blame them, can you?'

'The person you send would have to be a first-class man.'

'He would be,' Flynn assured him.

'On behalf of His Majesty's Government, I could undertake to purchase a complete and competent report on the disposition of the German cruiser *Blücher*, for the sum of . . .' he thought about it a moment, '. . . one thousand pounds.'

'Gold?'

'Gold,' agreed Joyce.

'That would cover it nicely.' Flynn nodded, then allowed his eyes to move across the cabin to where Sebastian and Rosa sat side by side on the day couch. They were holding hands, and showing more interest in each other than in the bargainings of Flynn and Captain Joyce.

It was a good thing, Flynn decided, that the Wakamba tribe from which Commissioner Fleischer had recruited the majority of his labour force, effected clean-shaven pates. It would be impossible for a person of European descent to dress his straight hair to resemble the woollen cap of an African.

It was also a good thing about the M'senga tree. From the bark of the M'senga tree the fishermen of Central Africa decocted a liquid in which they soaked their nets. It toughened the fibres of the netting, and it also stained the skin. Once Flynn had dipped his finger into a basin of the stuff, and despite constant scrubbing, it was fifteen days before the black stain faded.

It was finally a good thing about Sebastian's nose. Its new contours were decidedly negroid.

70

'A thousand pounds!' said Flynn O'Flynn as though it were a benediction, and he scooped another mugful of the black liquid and poured it over Sebastian Oldsmith's clean-shaven scalp. 'Think of it, Bassie, me lad, a thousand pounds! Your half share of that is five hundred. Why! You'll be in a position to pay me back every penny you owe me. You'll be out of debt at last.'

They were camped on the Abati river, one of the tributaries of the Rufiji. Six miles downstream was Commissioner Fleischer's wood-cutting camp.

'It's money for jam,' opined Flynn. He was sitting comfortably in a riempie chair beside the galvanized iron tub, in which Sebastian Oldsmith squatted with his knees drawn up under his chin. Sebastian had the dejected look of a spaniel taking a bath in flea shampoo. The liquid in which he sat was the colour and viscosity of strong Turkish coffee and already his face and body were a dark purply chocolate colour.

'Sebastian isn't interested in the money,' said Rosa Oldsmith. She knelt beside the tub and, tenderly as a mother bathing her infant, she was ladling the M'senga juice over Sebastian's shoulders and back.

'I know, I know!' Flynn agreed quickly. 'We are all doing our duty. We all remember little Maria–may the Lord bless and keep her tiny soul. But the money won't hurt us either.'

Sebastian closed his eyes as another mugful cascaded over his head.

'Rub it into the creases round your eyes–and under your chin,' said Flynn, and Sebastian obeyed. 'Now, let's go over it again, Bassie, so you don't get it all balled up. One of Mohammed's cousins is boss-boy of the gang loading the timber into the launches. They are camped on the bank of the Rufiji. Mohammed will slip you in tonight, and tomorrow his cousin will get you on to one of the launches going down with a load for *Blücher*. All you've got to do is keep your eyes open. Joyce just wants to know what work they are doing to repair her; whether or not they've got the boilers fired; things like that. You understand?'

Sebastian nodded glumly.

'You'll come back up-river tomorrow evening, slip out of camp soon as it's dark, and meet us here. Simple as a pimple, right?'

'Right,' murmured Sebastian.

'Right then. Out you get and dry off.'

As the wind from the uplands blew over his naked body, the purply tint of the dye faded into a matt chocolate. Rosa had modestly moved away into the grove of Marula trees behind the camp. Every few minutes Flynn came across to Sebastian and touched his skin.

'Coming along nicely,' he said, and, 'Nearly done,' and, 'Jeez, you look better than real.' Then finally in Swahili, 'Right, Mohammed, mark his face.'

Mohammed squatted in front of Sebastian with a tiny gourd of cosmetics; a mixture of animal fat and ash and ochre. With his fingers he daubed Sebastian's cheeks and nose and forehead with the tribal patterns. His head held on one side in artistic concentration, making soft clucking sounds of concentration as he worked, until at last Mohammed was satisfied.

'He is ready.'

'Get the clothes,' said Flynn. This was an exaggeration. Sebastian's attire could hardly be called clothing.

A string of bark around his neck from which was suspended a plugged duiker horn filled with snuff, a cloak of animal skin that smelled of woodsmoke and man-sweat, draped over his shoulders.

'It stinks!' said Sebastian cringing from contact with the garment. 'And it's probably got lice.'

'The real thing,' agreed Flynn jovially. 'All right, Mohammed, show him how to fit the istopo–the hat.'

'I don't have to wear that also,' Sebastian protested, staring in horror as Mohammed came towards him, grinning.

'Of course you've got to wear it.' Impatiently Flynn brushed aside his protest.

The hat was a hollow six-inch length cut from the neck of a calabash gourd. An anthropologist would have called it a penis-sheath. It had two purposes; firstly to protect the wearer from the scratches of thorns and the bites of insect pests, and secondly as a boost to his masculinity.

Once in position it looked impressive, enhancing Sebastian's already considerable muscular development.

Rosa said nothing when she returned. She took one long startled look at the hat and then quickly averted her gaze, but her cheeks and neck flared bright scarlet.

'For God's sake, Bassie. Act like you proud of it. Stand up straight and take your hands away.' Flynn coached his son-in-law.

Mohammed knelt to slip the rawhide sandals on to Sebastian's feet, and then hand him the small blanket roll tied with a bark string. Sebastian slung it over one shoulder then picked up the long-handled throwing-spear.

Automatically he grounded the butt and leaned his weight on the shaft; lifting his left leg and placing the sole of his foot against the calf of his right leg, he stood in the stork posture of rest.

In every detail he was a Wakamba tribesman.

'You'll do,' said Flynn.

71

In the dawn little wisps of river mist swirled around Commissioner Fleischer's legs as he came down the bank and on to the improvised jetty of logs.

He ran his eyes over the two launches, checking the ropes that held down the cargoes of timber. The launches sat low in the water, their exhausts puttering and blowing pale blue smoke that drifted away across the slick surface of the river.

'Are you ready?' he called to his sergeant of Askari.

'The men are eating, Bwana Mkuba.'

'Tell them to hurry,' growled Fleischer. It was a futile order and he stepped to the edge of the jetty, unbuttoning his trousers. He urinated noisily into the river, and the circle of men who squatted around the three-legged pot on the jetty watched him with interest, but without interrupting their breakfast.

With leather cloaks folded around their shoulders against the chill air off the water, they reached in turn into the pot and took a handful of the thick white maize porridge, moulding it into a mouth-size ball and then with the thumb forming a cup in the ball, dipping the ball into the smaller enamel dish and filling the depression with the creamy yellow gravy it contained, a tantalizing mixture of stewed catfish and tree caterpillars.

It was the first time that Sebastian had tasted this delicacy. He sat with the others and imitated their eating routine, forcing himself to place a lump of the spiced maize meal in his mouth. His gorge rose and gagged him, it tasted like fish oil and new-mown grass, not really offensive–it was just the thought of those fat yellow caterpillars. But had he been eating ham sandwiches, his appetite would not have been hearty.

His stomach was cramped with apprehension. He was a spy. A word from one of his companions, and Commissioner Fleischer would shout for the hanging ropes. Sebastian remembered the men he had seen in the monkey-bean tree on the bank of this same river, he remembered the flies clustered on their swollen, lolling tongues. It was not a mental picture conducive to enjoyment of breakfast.

Now, pretending to eat, he watched Commissioner Fleischer instead. It was the first time he had done so at leisure. The bulky figure in grey corduroy uniform, the pink-boiled face with pale golden eyelashes, the full petulant lips, the big freckled hands, all these revolted him. He felt his uneasiness swamped by a revival of the emotions that had possessed him as he stood beside the newly filled grave of his daughter on the heights above Lalapanzi.

'Black pig-animals,' shouted Herman Fleischer in Swahili, as he rebuttoned his clothing. 'That is enough! You do nothing but eat and sleep. It is time now for work.' He waddled across the logs of the jetty, into the little circle of porters. His first kick sent the three-legged pot clattering, his second kick caught Sebastian in the back and threw him forward on to his knees.

'Rasch!' He aimed another kick at one of them, but it was dodged, and the porters scattered to the launches.

Sebastian scrambled up. He had been kicked only once before in his life, and Flynn O'Flynn had learned not to do it again. For Sebastian there was nothing so humiliating as the contact of another man's foot against his person, also it had hurt.

Herman Fleischer had turned away to chivvy the others, so he did not see the hatred nor the way that Sebastian snarled at him, crouching like a leopard. Another second and he would have been on him. He might have killed Fleischer before the Askari shot him down–but he never made the attempt.

A hand on his arm. Mohammed's cousin beside him, his voice very low.

'Come! Let it pass. They will kill us also.'

And when Fleischer turned back the two of them had gone to the launch.

On the run down-river, Sebastian huddled with the others. Like them, drawing his cloak over his head to keep off the sun, but unlike them, he did not sleep. Through half-hooded eyes he was still watching Herman Fleischer, and his thoughts were hate-ugly.

Even with the current, the run in the deep-laden launches took almost four hours, and it was noon before they chugged around the last bend in the channel and turned in towards the mangrove forests.

Sebastian saw Herman Fleischer swallow the last bite of sausage and carefully repack the remainder into his haversack. He stood up and spoke to the man at the rudder, and both of them peered ahead.

'We have arrived,' said Mohammed's cousin, and removed his cloak from over his head. The little huddle of porters stirred into wakefulness and Sebastian stood up with them.

This time he knew what to look for, and he saw the muzzy silhouette of the *Blücher* skulking under her camouflage. From low down on the water she looked mountainous, and Sebastian's spine tingled as he remembered when last he had seen her from this angle, driving down to ram them with those axe-sharp bows. But now she floated awry, listing heavily.

'The boat leans over to one side.'

'Yes,' agreed Mohammed's cousin. 'The allemand wanted it so. There had been a great carrying of goods within her, they have moved everything to make the boat lean over.'

'Why?'

The man shrugged and pointed with his chin. 'They have lifted her belly from the water, see how they work with fire on the holes in her skin.'

Tiny as beetles, men swarmed on the exposed hull, and even in the bright glare of midday, the welding torches flared and sparkled with blue-white flame. The new plating was conspicuous in its coat of dull brown oxide paint, against the battleship-grey of the original hull.

As the launch approached, Sebastian studied the work carefully. He could see that it was nearing completion, the welders were running closed the last seams in the new plating. Already there were painters covering the oxide red with the matt grey final coat.

The pock marks of the shell splinters in her upperworks had been closed, and here again men hung on the flimsy trapezes of rope and planks, their arms lifting and falling as they plied the paint brushes.

An air of bustle and intent activity gripped the *Blücher*. Everywhere men moved about fifty different tasks, while the uniforms of the officers were restless white spots roving about her decks.

'They have closed all the holes in her belly?' Sebastian asked.

'All of them,' Mohammed's cousin confirmed. 'See how she spits out the water that was in her womb.' And he pointed again with his chin. From a dozen outlet vents, *Blücher*'s pumps were expelling solid streams of brown water as she emptied the flooded compartments.

'There is smoke from her chimneys,' Sebastian exclaimed, as he noticed for the first time the faint shimmer of heat at the mouths of her stacks.

'Yes. They have built fires in the iron boxes deep inside her. My brother Walaka works there now. He is helping to tend the fires. At first the fires were small, but each day they feed them higher.'

Sebastian nodded thoughtfully, he knew it took time to heat cold furnaces without cracking the linings of fireclay.

The launch nosed in and bumped against the cliff-high side of the cruiser.

'Come,' said Mohammed's cousin. 'We will climb up and work with the gangs carrying the wood down into her. You will see more up there.'

A new wave of dread flooded over Sebastian. He didn't want to go up there among the enemy. But already his guide was scrambling up the catwalk that hung down *Blücher*'s flank.

Sebastian adjusted his penis-sheath, hitched up his cloak, took a deep breath, and followed him.

72

'Sometimes it goes like that. In the beginning everything is an obscene shambles; nothing but snags and accidents and delays. Then suddenly everything drops into place and the job is finished.' Standing under the awning on the foredeck, Commander (Engineering) Lochtkamper was a satisfied man, as he looked around the ship. 'Two weeks ago it looked as though we would still be messing around when the war was over–but now!'

'You have done well,' von Kleine understated the facts. 'Again you have justified my confidence. But now I have another task to add to your burdens.'

'What is it, Captain?' Lochtkamper kept his voice noncommittal, but there was a wariness in his eyes.

'I want to alter the ship's profile–change it to resemble that of a British heavy cruiser.'

'How?'

'A dummy stack abaft the radio office. Canvas on a wooden frame. Then mask "X" turret, and block in the dip of our waist. It we run into the British blockade squadron in the night, it may give us the few extra minutes that will make the difference between success or failure.' Von Kleine spoke again as he turned away, 'Come, I will show you what I mean.'

Lochtkamper fell in beside him and they started aft, an incongruous pair; the engineer swaddled in soiled overalls, long arms dangling, shambling along beside his captain like a trained ape. Von Kleine tall over him, his tropical whites crisp and sterile, hands clasped behind his back and golden beard bowed forward on to his chest, leaning slightly against the steeply canted angle of the deck.

He spoke carefully. 'When can I sail, Commander? I must know precisely.

Is the work so far advanced that you can say with certainty?'

Lochtkamper was silent, considering his reply as they picked their way side by side through the milling jostle of seamen and native porters.

'I will have full pressure on my boilers by tomorrow night, another day after that to complete the work on the hull, two more days to adjust the trim of the ship and to make the alterations to the superstructure,' he mused aloud. Then he looked up. Von Kleine was watching him. 'Four days,' he said. 'I will be ready in four days.'

'Four days. You are certain of that?'

'Yes.'

'Four days,' repeated von Kleine, and he stopped in mid-stride to think. This morning he had received a message from Governor Schee in Dar es Salaam, a message relayed from the Admiralty in Berlin. Naval Intelligence reported that three days ago a convoy of twelve troopships, carrying Indian and South African infantry, had left Durban harbour. Their destination was not known, but it was an educated guess that the British were about to open a new theatre of war. The campaign in German West Africa had been brought to a swift and decisive conclusion by the South Africans. Botha and Smuts had launched a double-pronged offensive, driving in along the railroads to the German capital of Windhoek. The capitulation of the German West African army had released the South African forces for work elsewhere. It was almost certain that those troopships were trundling up the east coast at this very moment, intent on a landing at one of the little harbours that dotted the coast of East Africa. Tanga perhaps, or Kilwa Kvinje–possibly even Dar es Salaam itself.

He must have his ship seaworthy and battle-ready to break out through the blockade squadron, and destroy that convoy.

'The big job will be readjusting the ship's trim. There is much to be done. Stores to be manhandled, shell from the magazines, the guns remounted . . .' Lochtkamper interrupted his thoughts, 'We will need labour.'

'I will order Fleischer to bring all his forced labour down to assist with the work,' von Kleine muttered. 'But we must sail in four days. The moon will be right on the night of the thirtieth, we must break out then.' The saintly face was ruffled by the force of his concentration, he paced slowly, the golden beard sunk on his chest as he formulated his plans, speaking aloud. 'Kyller has buoyed the channel. He must start clearing the minefield at the entrance. We can cut the boom at the last moment–and the current will sweep it aside.'

They had reached the waist of the cruiser. Von Kleine was so deep in his thoughts that it took Lochtkamper's restraining hand on his arm, to return him to reality.

'Careful, sir.'

With a start von Kleine looked up. They had walked into a knot of African porters. Wild tribesmen, naked beneath their filthy leather cloaks, faces daubed with yellow ochre. They were manhandling the faggots of cordwood that were coming aboard from the launch that lay alongside *Blücher*. One of the heavy bundles was suspended from the boom of the derrick, it was swaying twenty feet above the deck and von Kleine had been about to walk under it. Lochtkamper's warning stopped him.

While he waited for them to clear away the faggot, von Kleine idly watched the native gang of workers.

One of the porters caught his attention. He was taller than his companions, his body sleeker, lacking the bunched and knotty muscles. His legs also were sturdier and finely moulded. The man lifted his head from his labours, and von Kleine looked into his face. The features were delicate; the lips not as full as, the forehead broader and deeper than, the typical African.

But it was the eyes that jerked von Kleine's attention back from the troop convoy. They were brown, dark brown and shifty. Von Kleine had learned to recognize guilt in the faces of his subordinates, it showed in the eyes. This man was guilty. It was only an instant that von Kleine saw it, then the porter dropped his gaze and stooped to take a grip on the bundle of timber. The man worried him, left him feeling vaguely uneasy, he wanted to speak to him–question him. He started towards him.

'Captain! Captain!' Commissioner Fleischer had come puffing up the catwalk from the launch, plump and sweaty he was pawing von Kleine's arm.

'I must speak with you, Captain.'

'Ah, Commissioner,' von Kleine greeted him coolly, trying to avoid the damp paw. 'One moment, please. I wish to . . .'

'It is a matter of the utmost importance. Ensign Proust . . .'

'In a moment, Commissioner.' Von Kleine pulled away, but Fleischer was determined. He stepped in front of von Kleine, blocking his path.

'Ensign Proust, the cowardly little prig . . .' and von Kleine found himself embroiled in a long report about Ensign Proust's lack of respect for the dignity of the Commissioner. He had been insubordinate, he had argued with Herr Fleischer, and further he had told Herr Fleischer that he considered him 'fat'.

'I will speak to Proust,' said von Kleine. It was a trivial matter and he wanted no part of it. The Commander Lochtkamper was beside them. Would the Captain speak to the Herr Commissioner about the labour for the landing of ballast? They fell into a long discussion and while they talked, the gang of porters lugged the bundle of timber aft and were absorbed by the bustling hordes of workmen.

Sebastian was sweating with fright; trembling, giddy with fright. Clearly he had sensed the German officer's suspicions. Those cold blue eyes had burned like dry ice. Now he stooped under his load, trying to shrink himself into insignificance, trying to overcome the grey clammy sense of dread that threatened to crush him.

'He saw you,' wheezed Mohammed's cousin, shuffling along beside Sebastian.

'Yes.' Sebastian bent lower. 'Is he still watching?'

The old man glanced back over his shoulder.

'No. He speaks with the Mafuta, the fat one.'

'Good.' Sebastian felt a lift of relief. 'We must get back on the launch.'

'The loading is almost finished, but we must first speak with my brother. He waits for us.'

They turned the corner of the aft gun-turrets. On the deck was a mountain of cordwood. Stacked neatly and lashed down with rope. Black men swarmed over it, between them spreading a huge green tarpaulin over the wood pile.

They reached the wood pile and added the faggots they carried to the stack. Then, in the custom of Africa, they paused to rest and talk. A man clambered down from the wood pile to join them, a sprightly old gentleman with woolly grey hair, impeccably turned out in cloak and penis-sheath. Mohammed's cousin greeted him with courteous affection, and they took snuff together.

'This man is my brother,' he told Sebastian. 'His name is Walaka. When he was a young man he killed a lion with a spear. It was a big lion with a black mane.' To Sebastian this information seemed to be slightly irrelevant, his fear of discovery was making him nervously impatient. There were Germans all around them, big blond Germans bellowing orders as they chivvied on the labour gangs, Germans looking down on them from the tall superstructure above them, Germans elbowing them aside as they passed. Sebastian found it difficult to concentrate.

His two accomplices were involved in a family discussion. It seemed that Walaka's youngest daughter had given birth to a fine son, but that during his absence a leopard had raided Walaka's village and killed three of his goats. The new grandson did not seem to compensate Walaka for the loss of his goats. He was distressed.

'Leopards are the excrement of dead lepers,' he said, and would have enlarged on the subject but Sebastian interrupted him.

'Tell me of the things you have seen on this canoe. Say swiftly, there is little time. I must go before the Allemand comes for all of us with the ropes.'

Mention of the ropes brought the meeting to order, and Walaka launched into his report.

There were fires burning in the iron boxes in the belly of the canoe. Fires of such heat that they pained the eye when the door of the box was opened, fires with a breath like that of a hundred bush fires, fires that consumed . . .

'Yes, yes.' Sebastian cut short the lyrical description. 'What else?'

There had been a great carrying of goods, moving of them to one side of the canoe to make it lean in the water. They had carried boxes and bales, unbolted machinery and guns. See how they had been moved. They had taken from the rooms under her roof a great quantity of the huge bullets, also the white bags of powder for the guns and placed them in other rooms on the far side.

'What else?'

There was more, much more to tell. Walaka enthused about meat which came out of little tins, of lanterns that burned without wick, flame, or oil, of great wheels that spun, and boxes of steel that screamed and hummed, of clean fresh water that gushed from the mouths of long rubber snakes, sometimes cold and at other times hot as though it had been boiled over a fire. There were marvels so numerous that it confused a man.

'These things I know. Is there nothing else that you have seen?'

Indeed there was. The Allemand had shot three native porters, lining them up and covering their eyes with strips of white cloth. The men had jumped and wriggled and fallen in a most comical fashion, and afterwards the Germans had washed the blood from the deck with water from the long snakes. Since then none of the other porters had helped themselves to blankets and buckets and other small movables–the price was exorbitant.

Walaka's description of the execution had a chilling effect on Sebastian. He had done what he had come to do and now his urge to leave *Blücher* became overpowering. It was helped on by a German petty officer who joined the group uninvited.

'You lazy black baboons,' he bellowed. 'This is not a bloody Sunday-school outing–move, you swine, move!' And his boots flew. Led by Mohammed's cousin they left Walaka without farewell and scampered back along the deck. Just before they reached the entry port, Sebastian checked. The two German officers stood where he had left them, but now they were looking up at the high smoke stacks. The tall officer with the golden beard was describing sweeping motions with his outstretched hand, talking while the stocky one listened intently.

Mohammed's cousin scurried past them and disappeared over the side into the launch, leaving Sebastian hesitant and reluctant to run the gauntlet of those pale blue eyes.

'Manali, come quickly. The boat swims, you will be left!' Mohammed's cousin called from down below, his voice faint but urgent above the chug of the launch's engine.

Sebastian started forward again, his stomach a cold lump under his ribs. A dozen paces and he had reached the entry port.

The German officer turned and saw him. He challenged with raised voice, and came towards Sebastian, one arm outstretched as though to hold him.

Sebastian whirled and dived down the catwalk. Below him the launch was casting off her lines, water churning back from her propeller.

Sebastian reached the grating at the bottom of the catwalk. There was a gap of ten feet between him and the launch. He jumped, hung for a moment in the air, then hit the gunwhale of the launch. His clutching fingers found a grip while his legs dangled in the warm water.

Mohammed's cousin caught his shoulder and dragged him aboard. They tumbled together in a heap on the deck of the launch.

'Bloody kaffir,' said Herman Fleischer and stooped to cuff them both heavily around the ears. Then he went back to his seat in the stern, and Sebastian smiled at him with something close to affection. After those deadly blue eyes, Herman Fleischer seemed as dangerous as a teddy-bear.

Then he looked back at *Blücher*. The German officer stood at the top of the catwalk, watching them as they drew away, and set a course upstream. Then he turned away from the rail and disappeared.

73

Sebastian sat on the day couch in the master cabin of H.M.S. *Renounce*, he sagged against the arm-rest and fought off the grey waves of exhaustion that washed over his mind.

He had not slept in thirty hours. After his escape from *Blücher* there had been the long launch journey up-river during which he had remained awake and jittery with the after-effects of tension.

After disembarking he had sneaked out of Fleischer's camp, avoiding the Askari guards, and trotted through the moonlight to meet Flynn and Rosa.

A hurried meal, and then all three of them had mounted on bicycles supplied with the compliments of the Royal Navy, and ridden all night along a rough elephant path to where they had left a canoe hidden among the reeds on the bank of one of the Rufiji tributaries.

In the dawn they had paddled out of one of the unguarded channels of the delta and made their rendezvous with the little whaler from H.M.S. *Renounce*.

Two long days of activity without rest, and Sebastian was groggy. Rosa sat beside him on the couch. She leaned across and touched his arm, her eyes dark with concern. Neither of them were taking any part in the conference in which the other persons in the crowded cabin were deeply involved.

Joyce sat as chairman, and beside him an older heavier man with bushy grey eyebrows and a truculent jaw, hair brushed in streaks across his pate in an ineffectual attempt to conceal his baldness. This was Armstrong, Captain of H.M.S. *Pegasus*, the other cruiser of the blockade squadron.

'Well, it looks as though *Blücher* has made good her damage, then. If she has fired her boilers, we can expect her to break out any day now–von Kleine would not burn up good fuel to keep his stokers warm.' He said it with relish, a fighting man anticipating a good hard fight. 'There's a message I'd like to give her from *Bloodhound* and *Orion*–an old account to settle.'

But Joyce also had a message, one that had its origin at the desk of Admiral Sir Percy Howe, Commander-in-Chief, South Atlantic and Indian Oceans. In part this message read:

'The safety of your squadron considered secondary to containing *Blücher*. Risk involved in delaying until *Blücher* leaves the delta before engaging her is too high. Absolutely imperative that she be either destroyed or blocked at her present anchorage. Consequences of *Blücher* running blockade and attacking the troop convoy conveying landing forces to invasion of Tanga will be catastrophic. Efforts being made to send you two tramp steamers to act as block ships, but failing their arrival, and failing also effective offensive action against *Blücher* before July 30th, 1915, you are hereby ordered to scuttle *Renounce* and *Pegasus* in the channel of the Rufiji to block *Blücher*'s exit.'

It was a command that left Captain Arthur Joyce sick with dread. To scuttle his splendid ships–a thought as repulsive and loathsome as that of incest, of patricide, of human sacrifice. Today was July 26th, he had four days in which to find an alternative before the order became effective.

'She'll come out at night, of course, bound to!' Armstrong's voice was thick with battle lust. 'This time she'll not have an old girl and a baby like *Orion* and *Bloodhound* to deal with.' His tone changed slightly. 'We'll have to look lively. New moon in three days so *Blücher* will have dark nights. There could be a change in the weather ' Armstrong was looking a little worried now, '. . . we'll have to tighten up . . .'

'Read this,' said Joyce, and passed the flimsy to Armstrong. He read it.

'My God!' he gasped. 'Scuttle. Oh, my God!'

'There are two channels that *Blücher* could use.' Joyce spoke softly. 'We would have to block both of them–*Renounce* and *Pegasus*!'

'Jesus God!' swore Armstrong in horror. 'There must be another way.'

'I think there is,' said Joyce, and looked across at Sebastian. 'Mr Oldsmith,' he spoke gently, 'would it be possible for you to get on board the German cruiser once again?'

There were tiny lumps of yellow mucus in the corner of Sebastian's bloodshot eyes, but the stain that darkened his skin concealed the rings of fatigue under them.

'I'd rather not, old chap.' He ran his hand thoughtfully over his shaven scalp and the stubble of new hair rasped under his fingers. 'It was one of the most unpleasant hours of my life.'

'Quite,' said Captain Joyce. 'Quite so! I wouldn't have asked you, had I not considered it to be of prime importance.' Joyce paused and pursed his lips to whistle softly the first bar of Chopin's 'Funeral March', then he sighed and shook his head. 'If I were to tell you that you alone have it in your power to save both the cruisers of this squadron from destruction and to protect the lives of fifteen thousand British soldiers and seamen–how would you answer then?'

Glumly, Sebastian sagged back against the couch and closed his eyes. 'Can I have a few hours sleep first?'

74

It was exactly the size of a box of twenty-five Monte Cristo Havana Cigars, for that had been its contents before *Renounce's* chief engine room artificer and the gunnery lieutenant had set to work on it.

It lay on the centre of Captain Joyce's desk, while the artificer explained its purpose to the respectful audience that stood around him.

'It's verra simple,' started the artificer in an accent that was as bracing as the fragrance of heather and highland whisky.

'It would have to be . . .' commented Flynn O'Flynn, '. . . for Bassie to understand it.'

'All you do is lift the lid.' The artificer suited action to the words, and even Flynn craned forward to examine the contents of the cigar box. Packed neatly into it were six yellow sticks of gelignite, looking like candles wrapped in grease-proof paper. There was also the flat dry cell battery from a bull's eye lantern, and a travelling-clock in a pigskin case. All of these were connected by loops and twists of fine copper wire. Engraved into the metal of the clock base were the words:

To my dear husband Arthur,
With love,
Iris.
Christmas 1914

Captain Arthur Joyce stilled a sentimental pang of regret with the thought that Iris would understand.

'Then . . .' said the artificer, clearly enjoying the hold he had on his audience, '. . . you wind the knob on the clock.' He touched it with his forefinger, '. . . close the lid,' he closed it, '. . . wait twelve hours, and–Boom!' The enthusiasm with which the Scotsman simulated an explosion blew a fine spray of spittle across the desk, and Flynn withdrew hurriedly out of range.

'Wait twelve hours?' asked Flynn, dabbing at the droplets on his cheeks. 'Why so long?'

'I ordered a twelve-hour delay on the fusing of the charge.' Joyce answered the question. 'If Mr Oldsmith is to gain access to the *Blücher*'s magazines, he will have to infiltrate the native labour gangs engaged in transferring the explosives. Once he is a member of the gang he might find difficulty in extricating himself and getting away from the ship after he had placed the charge. I am sure that Mr Oldsmith would be reluctant to make this attempt unless we could ensure that there is time for him to escape from *Blücher*, when his efforts . . . ah,' he sought the correct phraseology, ' . . . ah . . . come to fruition.' Joyce was pleased with this speech, and he turned to Sebastian for endorsement. 'Am I correct in my assumption, Mr Oldsmith?'

Not to be outdone in verbosity, Sebastian pondered his reply for a second. Five hours of deathlike sleep curled in Rosa's arms had refreshed his body and sharpened his wit to the edge of a Toledo steel blade.

'Indubitably,' he replied, and beamed in triumph.

75

They sat together in the time when the sun was dying and bleeding on the clouds. They sat together on a kaross of monkey skin in a thicket of wild ebony, at the head of one of the draws that wrinkled down into the valley of the Rufiji. They sat in silence. Rosa bent forward over her needlework, as she stitched a concealed pocket into the filthy cloak of leather that lay across her lap. The pocket would hold the cigar box. Sebastian watched her, and his eyes upon her were a caress. She pulled the last stitch tight, knotted it, then leaned forward to bite the thread.

'There!' she said. 'It's finished.' And looked up into his eyes.

'Thank you,' said Sebastian. They sat together quietly and Rosa reached out to touch his shoulder. The muscle under the black stained skin was rubber hard, and warm.

'Come,' she said and drew his head down to her so that their cheeks touched, and they held each other while the last light faded. The African dusk thickened the shadows in the wild ebony, and down the draw a jackal yipped plaintively.

'Are you ready?' Flynn stood near them, a dark bulky figure, with Mohammed beside him.

'Yes.' Sebastian looked up at him.

'Kiss me,' whispered Rosa, 'and come back safely.'

Gently Sebastian broke from her embrace. He stood tall above her, and draped the cloak over his naked body. The cigar box hung heavily between his shoulder blades.

'Wait for me,' he said, and walked away.

Flynn Patrick O'Flynn moved restlessly under his single blanket and belched. Heartburn moved acid sour in his throat, and he was cold. The earth under him had long since lost the warmth it had sucked from yesterday's sun. A small slice of the old moon gave a little silver light to the night.

Unsleeping he lay and listened to the soft sound of Rosa sleeping near him. The sound irritated him, he lacked only an excuse to waken her and make her talk to him. Instead he reached into the haversack that served as his pillow and his fingers closed round the cold smooth glass of the bottle.

A night-bird hooted softly down the draw, and Flynn released the bottle and sat up quickly. He placed two fingers between his lips and repeated the night-bird's cry.

Minutes later Mohammed drifted like a small black ghost into camp and came to squat beside Flynn's bed.

'I see you, Fini.'

'You I see also, Mohammed. It went well?'

'It went well.'

'Manali has entered the camp of the Allemand?'

'He sleeps now beside the man who is my cousin, and in the dawn they will go down the Rufiji, to the big boat of the Allemand once again.'

'Good!' grunted Flynn. 'You have done well.'

Mohammed coughed softly to signify that there was more to tell.

'What is it?' Flynn demanded.

'When I had seen Manali safely into the care of my cousin, I came back along the valley and . . .' he hesitated, '. . . perhaps it is not fitting to speak of such matters at a time when our Lord Manali goes unarmed and alone into the camp of the Allemand.'

'Speak,' said Flynn.

'As I walked without sound, I came to a place where this valley falls down to the river called Abati. You know the place?'

'Yes, about a mile down the draw from here.'

'That is the place.' Mohammed nodded. 'It was here that I saw something move in the night. It was as though a mountain walked.'

A sliver of ice was thrust down Flynn's spine, and his breathing snagged painfully in his throat.

'Yes?' he breathed.

'It was a mountain armed with teeth of ivory that grew from its face to touch the ground as it walked.'

'*Plough the Earth.*' Flynn whispered the name, and his hand fell on to the rifle that lay loaded beside his bed.

'It was that one.' Mohammed nodded again. 'He feeds quietly, moving towards the Rufiji. But the voice of a rifle would carry down to the ears of the Allemand.'

'I won't fire,' whispered Flynn. 'I just want to have a look at him. I just want to see him again.' And the hand on the rifle shook like that of a man in high fever.

76

The sun pushed up and sat fat and fiery as molten gold, on the hills of the Rufiji basin. Its warmth lifted streamers of mist from the swamps and reed-beds that bounded the Abati river, and they smoked like the ashes of a dying fire.

Under the fever trees the air was still cool with the memory of the night, but the sun sent long yellow shafts of light probing through the branches to disperse and warm it.

Three old eland bulls came up from the river, bigger than domestic cattle, light bluey-brown in colour with faint chalk stripes across the barrel of their bodies, they walked in single file, heavy dewlaps swinging, thick stubby horns held erect, and the tuft of darker hair on their foreheads standing out clearly. They reached the grove of fever trees and the lead bull stopped, suddenly alert. For long seconds they stood absolutely still, staring into the open palisade of fever tree trunks where the light was still vague beneath the canopy of interlaced leaves and branches.

The lead bull blew softly through his nostrils, and swung off the game path that led into the grove. Stepping lightly for such large animals, the three eland skirted the grove and moved away to blend into the dry thorn scrub higher up the slope.

'He is in there,' whispered Mohammed. 'The eland saw him, and turned aside.'

'Yes,' agreed Flynn. 'It is such a place as he would choose to lie up for the day.' He sat in the crotch of a M'banga tree, wedged securely ten feet above the ground, and peered across three hundred yards of open grassland at the dense stand of fever trees. The hands that held the binoculars to his eyes were unsteady with gin and excitement, and he was sweating, a droplet broke from his hair-line and slid down his cheek, tickling like an insect. He brushed it away.

'A wise man would leave him, and walk away even as the eland did.' Mohammed gave his opinion. He leaned against the base of the tree, holding Flynn's rifle across his chest. Flynn did not reply. He peered through the binoculars, swinging them slowly in an arc as he searched.

'He must be deep among the trees, I cannot see him from here.' And he loosened his leg grip from the crotch and clambered down to where Mohammed waited. He took his rifle and checked the load.

'Leave him, Fini,' Mohammed urged softly. 'There is no profit in it. We cannot carry the teeth away.'

'Stay here,' said Flynn.

'Fini, the Allemand will hear you. They are close–very close.'

'I will not shoot,' said Flynn. 'I must see him again–that is all. I will not shoot.'

Mohammed took the gin bottle from the haversack and handed it to him. Flynn drank.

'Stay here,' he repeated, his voice husky from the burn of the raw spirit.

'Be careful, Fini. He is an old one of evil temper–be careful.' Mohammed watched Flynn start out across the clearing. He walked with slow deliberation of a man who goes in good time to a meeting that has long been prearranged. He reached the grove of fever trees and walked on into them without checking.

Plough the Earth was sleeping on his feet. His little eyes closed tightly in their wrinkled pouches. Tears had oozed in a long dark stain down his cheeks, and a fine haze of midges hovered about them. Tattered as battle-riven banners on a windless day, his ears lay back against his shoulders. His tusks were crutches that propped up the gnarled old head, and his trunk hung down between them, grey and slack and heavy.

Flynn saw him, and picked his way towards him between the trunks of the fever trees. The setting had an unreal quality, for the light effect of the low sun through the branches was golden beams reflected in shimmering misty green from the leaves of the fever trees. The grove was resonant with the whine of cicada beetles.

Flynn circled out until he was head on to the sleeping elephant, and then he moved in again. Twenty paces from him Flynn stopped. He stood with his feet set apart, the rifle held ready across one hip, and his head thrown back as he looked up at the unbelievable bulk of the old bull.

Up to this moment Flynn still believed that he would not shoot. He had come only to look at him once more, but it was as futile as an alcoholic who promised himself just one taste. He felt the madness begin at the base of his spine, hot and hard it poured into his body, filling him as though he were a container. The level rose to his throat and he tried to check it there, but the rifle was coming up. He felt the butt in his shoulder. Then he heard with surprise a voice, a voice that rang clearly through the grove and instantly stilled the whine of the cicadas. It was his own voice, crying out in defiance of his conscious resolve.

'Come on, then,' he shouted. And the old elephant burst from massive quiescence into full charge. It came down on him like a dynamited cliff of black rock. He saw it over the open rear sight of his rifle, saw it beyond the minute pip of the foresight that rode unwaveringly in the centre of the old bull's bulging brow–between the eyes, where the crease of skin at the base of its trunk was a deep lateral line.

The shot was thunderous, shattering into a thousand echoes against the boles of the fever trees. The elephant died in the fullness of his run. Legs buckled, and he came toppling forward, carried by his own momentum, a loose avalanche of flesh and bone and long ivory.

Flynn turned aside like a matador from the run of the bull, three quick dancing steps and then one of the tusks hit him. It took him across the hip with a force that hurled him twenty feet, the rifle spinning from his hands so that as he fell and rolled in the soft bed of loose trash and leaf mould, his lower body twisted away from his trunk at an impossible angle. His brittle old bones had broken like china; the ball of the femur snapping off in its socket, his pelvis fracturing clean through.

Lying face down, Flynn was mildly surprised that there was no pain. He could feel the jagged edges of bone rasping together deep in his flesh at his slightest movement, but there was no pain.

Slowly, pulling himself forward on his elbows so that his legs slithered uselessly after him, he crawled towards the carcass of the old bull.

He reached it, and with one hand stroked the yellow shaft of ivory that had crippled him.

'Now,' he whispered, fondling the smoothly polished tusk the way a man might touch his firstborn son. 'Now, at last you are mine.'

And then the pain started, and he closed his eyes and cowered down, huddled beneath the hillock of dead and cooling flesh that had been *Plough the Earth*. The pain buzzed in his ears like cicada beetles, but through it he heard Mohammed's voice.

'Fini. It was not wise.'

He opened his eyes and saw Mohammed's monkey face puckered with concern.

'Call Rosa,' he croaked. 'Call Little Long Hair. Tell her to come.'

Then he closed his eyes again, and rode the pain. The tempo of the pain changed constantly–first it was drums, tom-toms that throbbed and beat within him. Then it was the sea, long undulating swells of agony. Then again it was night, cold black night that chilled him so he shivered and moaned–and the night gave way to the sun. A great fiery ball of pain that burned and shot out lances of blinding light that burst against his clenched eyelids. Then the drums began again.

Time was of no significance. He rode the pain for a minute and a million years, then through the beat of the drums of agony he heard movement near him. The shuffle of feet through the dead leaves, the murmur of voices that were not part of his consuming anguish.

'Rosa,' Flynn whispered, 'you have come!'

He rolled his head and forced his eyelids open.

Herman Fleischer stood over him. He was grinning. His face flushed as a rose petal, fresh sweat clinging in his pale eyebrows, breathing quickly and heavily with exertion as though he had been running, but he was grinning.

'So!' he wheezed. 'So!'

The shock of his presence was muted for Flynn by the haze of pain in which he lay. There were smears of dust dulling the gloss of Fleischer's jackboots, and dark patches of sweat had soaked through the thick grey corduroy tunic at the armpits. He held a Luger pistol in his right hand and with his left hand he pushed the slouch hat to the back of his head.

'Herr Flynn!' he said and chuckled. It was the fat infectious chuckle of a healthy baby.

Mildly Flynn wondered how Fleischer had found him so quickly in the broken terrain and thick bush. The shot would have alerted him, but what had led him directly to the grove of fever trees?

Then he heard a rustling fluting rush in the air above him, and he looked upwards. Through the lacework of branches he saw the vultures spiralling against the aching blue of the sky. They turned and dipped on spread black wings, cocking their heads sideways in flight to look down with bright beady eyes on the elephant carcass.

'Ja! The birds. We followed the birds.'

'Jackals always follow the birds,' whispered Flynn, and Fleischer laughed. He threw back his head and laughed with genuine delight.

'Good. Oh, ja. That is good.' And he kicked Flynn. He swung the jackboot lazily into Flynn's body, and Flynn shrieked. The laughter died instantly in Fleischer's throat, and he bent quickly to examine Flynn.

He noticed for the first time how his lower body was grotesquely twisted and distorted. And he dropped to his knees beside him. Gently he touched Flynn's forehead, and deep concern flashed across his chubby features at the clammy cold feeling of the skin.

'Sergeant!' There was a desperate edge to his voice now. 'This man is badly injured. He will not last long. Be quick! Get the rope! We must hang him before he loses consciousness.'

77

Rosa awoke in the dawn and found that she was alone. Beside Flynn's personal pack, his discarded blanket had been carelessly flung aside. His rifle was gone.

She was not alarmed, not at first. She guessed that he had gone into the bush on one of his regular excursions to be alone while he drank his breakfast. But an hour later when he had not returned she grew anxious. She sat with her rifle across her lap, and every bird noise or animal scuffle in the ebony thicket jarred her nerves.

Another hour and she was fretting. Every few minutes she stood up and walked to the edge of the clearing to listen. Then she went back to sit and worry.

Where on earth was Flynn? Why had Mohammed not returned? What had happened to Sebastian? Was he safe, or had he been discovered? Had Flynn gone to assist him? Should she wait here, or follow them down the draw?

Her eyes haunted, her mouth hard set with doubts, she sat and twisted the braid of her hair around one finger in a nervously restless gesture.

Then Mohammed came. Suddenly he appeared out of the thicket beside her, and Rosa jumped up with a low cry of relief. The cry died in her throat as she saw his face.

'Fini!' he said. 'He is hurt. The great elephant has broken his bones and he lies in pain. He asks for you.'

Rosa stared at him, appalled, not understanding.

'An elephant?'

'He followed *Plough the Earth*, the great elephant, and killed him. But in dying the elephant struck him, breaking him.'

'The fool. Oh, the fool!' Rosa whispered. 'Now of all times. With Sebastian in danger, he must . . .' And then she caught herself and broke off her futile lament. 'Where is he, Mohammed? Take me to him.'

Mohammed led along one of the game paths. Rosa ran behind him. There was no time for caution, no thought of it as they hurried to find Flynn. They came to the stream of the Abati, and swung off the path, staying on the near bank. They plunged through a field of arrow grass, skirted around a tiny swamp and ran on into a stand of buffalo thorn. As they emerged on the far side Mohammed stopped abruptly and looked at the sky.

The vultures turned in a high wheel against the blue, like debris in a lazy whirlwind. The spot above which they circled lay half a mile ahead.

'Daddy!' Rosa choked on the word. In an instant all the hardness accumulated since that night at Lalapanzi disappeared from her face.

'Daddy!' she said again, and then she ran in earnest. Brushing past Mohammed, throwing her rifle aside so it clattered on the earth, she darted out of the buffalo thorn and into the open.

'Wait, Little Long Hair. Be careful.' Mohammed started after her. In his agitation he stepped carelessly, fully on to a fallen twig from the buffalo thorn. There was a worn spot on the sole of his sandal, and three inches of cruel red-tipped thorn drove up through it and buried in his foot.

For a dozen paces he struggled on after Rosa, hopping on one leg, flapping his arms to maintain his balance and calling, but not too loudly.

'Wait! Be careful, Little Long Hair.'

But she took not the least heed, and went away from him, leaving him at last to sink down and tend to his wounded foot.

She crossed the open ground before the fever tree grove with the slack, blundering steps of exhaustion. Running silently, saving her breath for the effort of reaching her father. She ran into the grove, and a drop of perspiration fell into her eye, blurring her vision so she staggered against one of the trunks. She recovered her balance and ran on into the midst of them.

She recognized Herman Fleischer instantly. She had run almost against his chest, and his huge body towered over her. She screamed with shock and twisted away from the bear-like arms outspread to clutch her.

Two of the native Askari who were working over the crude litter on which lay Flynn O'Flynn, jumped up. As she ran they closed on her from either side, the way a pair of trained greyhounds will course a hare. They caught her between them, and dragged her struggling and screaming to where Herman Fleischer waited.

'Ah, so!' Fleischer nodded pleasantly in greeting. 'You have come in time for the fun.' Then he turned to his sergeant. 'Have them tie the woman.'

Rosa's screams penetrated the light mists of insensibility that screened Flynn's brain. He stirred on the litter, muttering incoherently, rolling his head from side to side, then he opened his eyes and focused them with difficulty. He saw her struggling between the Askari and he snapped back into full consciousness.

'Leave her!' he roared. 'Call those bloody animals off. Leave her, you murderous bloody German bastard.'

'Good!' said Herman Fleischer. 'You are awake now.' Then he lifted his voice above Flynn's bellows. 'Hurry, Sergeant, tie the woman–and get the rope up.'

While they secured Rosa, one of the Askari shinned up the smooth yellow trunk of a fever tree. With his bayonet he hacked the twigs from the thick horizontal branch above their heads. The sergeant threw the end of the rope up to him, and at the second attempt the Askari caught it and passed it over the branch. Then he dropped back to earth.

There was a hangman's knot fixed in the rope, ready for use.

'Set the knot,' said Fleischer, and the sergeant went to where Flynn lay. With poles cut from a small tree they had rigged a combination litter and splints. The poles had been laid down Flynn's flanks from ankle to armpit, with bark strips they had bound them firmly so that Flynn's body was held rigidly as that of an Egyptian mummy, only his head and neck were free.

The sergeant stooped over him, and Flynn fell silent, watching him venomously. As his hands came down with the noose to loop it over Flynn's head, Flynn moved suddenly. He darted his head forward like a striking adder and fastened his teeth in the man's wrist. With a howl the sergeant tried to pull away, but Flynn held on, his head jerking and wrenching as the man struggled.

'Fool,' grunted Fleischer, and strode over to the litter. He lifted his foot and placed it on Flynn's lower body. As he brought his weight down on it Flynn stiffened and gasped with pain, releasing the Askari's wrist.

'Do it this way.' Fleischer lunged forward and took a handful of Flynn's hair, roughly he yanked Flynn's head forward. 'Now, the rope quickly.'

The Askari dropped the noose over Flynn's head and drew the slip-knot tight until it lay snugly under Flynn's ear.

'Good.' Fleischer stepped back. 'Four men on the rope,' he ordered. 'Gently. Do not jerk the rope. Walk away with it slowly. I don't want to break his neck.'

Rosa's hysteria had stilled into cold horror as she watched the preparations for the execution, and now she found her voice again.

'Please,' she whispered. 'He's my father. Please don't. Oh no, please don't.'

'Hush, girl,' roared Flynn. 'You'd not shame me now by pleading with this fat bag of pus.' He swivelled his head, his eyes rolled towards the four Askari who stood ready with the rope end. 'Pull! You black sons of bitches. Pull! And damn you. I'll beat you to hell, and speak to the devil so he'll have you castrated and smeared with pig's fat.'

'You heard what Fini told you,' smiled Fleischer at his Askari. 'Pull!'

And they walked backwards in single file, shuffling through the dead leaves, leaning against the rope.

The litter lifted slowly at one end, came upright and then left the ground.

Rosa turned away and clenched her eyelids tight closed, but her hands were bound so she could not stop her ears, she could not keep out the sounds that Flynn Patrick O'Flynn made as he died.

When at last there was silence, Rosa was shivering. Hard spasms that shuddered through her whole body.

'All right,' said Herman Fleischer. 'That's it. Bring the woman. We can get back to camp in time for lunch if we hurry.'

When they were gone, the litter and its contents still hung in the fever tree. Swinging a little and turning slowly on the end of the rope. Near it lay the carcass of the elephant, and a vulture planed down slowly and made a flapping ungainly landing in the top branches of the fever tree. It sat hunched and suspicious, then suddenly squawked and launched again into noisy flight, for it had seen the man coming.

The little old man limped slowly into the grove. He stopped beside the dead elephant and looked up at the man who had been his master and his friend.

'Go in peace, Fini!' said Mohammed.

78

The alleyway was a narrow low-roofed corridor, the bulkheads were painted a pale grey that glistened in the harsh light of the electric globes set in small wire cages at regular intervals along the roof.

At the end of the corridor, a guard stood outside the heavy watertight door in the bulkhead that led through into the handling room of the forward magazine. The guard wore only a thin white singlet and white flannel trousers, but his waist was belted in a blancoed webbing from which hung a sheathed bayonet, and there was a Mauser rifle slung from his shoulder.

From his position he could look into the handling room, and he could keep the full length of the alleyway under surveillance.

A double file of Wakamba tribesmen filled the alleyway, living chains along one of which passed the cordite charges; along the other the nine-inch shells.

The Africans worked with the stoical indifference of draught animals, turning to grip the ugly cylindro-conical shells, hugging a hundred and twenty pounds' weight of steel and explosive to their chests while they moved it on to the next man in the chain.

The cordite charges, each wrapped in thick paper, were not so weighty and moved more swiftly along their line. Each man bobbed and swung as he handled his load, so it seemed that the two ranks were sets in a complicated dance pattern.

From this mass of moving humanity rose clouds of warm body odour, that filled the alleyway and defeated the efforts of the air-conditioning fans.

Sebastian felt sweat trickling down his chest and back under the leather cloak, he felt also the tug of weight within the folds of the cloak each time he swung to receive a fresh cordite charge from his neighbour.

He stood just outside the door of the handling room, and each time he passed a charge through, he looked into the interior of the magazine where another gang was at work, packing the charges into the shelves that lined the bulkheads, and easing the nine-inch shells into their steel racks. Here there was another armed guard.

The work had been in progress since early that morning, with a half-hour's break at noon, so the German guards had relaxed their vigilance. They were restless in anticipation of relief. The one in the magazine was a fat middle-aged man who at intervals during the day had broken the monotony by releasing sudden ear-splitting posterior discharges of gas. With each salvo he had clapped the nearest African porter on the back and shouted happily.

'Have a bite at that one!' or, 'Cheer up–it doesn't smell.'

But at last he also was deflated. He slouched across the handling room, and leaned against the angle of the door to address his colleague in the alleyway.

'It's hot as hell, and smells like a zoo. These savages stink.'

'You've been doing your share.'

'I'll be glad when it's finished.'

'It's cooler in the magazine with the fans running–you are all right.'

'Jesus, I'd like to sit down for a few minutes.'

'Better not, Lieutenant Kyller is on the prowl.'

This exchange was taking place within a few feet of Sebastian. He followed the German conversation with more ease now that he had been able to exercise his rusty vocabulary, but he kept his head down in a renewed burst of energy. He was worried. In a short while the day's shift would end and the African porters would be herded on deck and into the launches to be transported to their camp on one of the islands. None of the native labour force were allowed to spend the night aboard *Blücher*.

He had waited since noon for an opportunity to enter the magazine and place the time charge. But he had been frustrated by the activities of the two German guards. It must be nearly seven o'clock in the evening now. It would have to be soon, very soon. He glanced once more into the magazine, and he caught the eye of Walaka, Mohammed's cousin. Walaka stood by the cordite shelves, supervising the packing, and now he shrugged at Sebastian in eloquent helplessness.

Suddenly there was a thud of a heavy object being dropped to the deck, and a commotion of shouts in the alleyway behind Sebastian. He glanced round quickly. One of the bearers had fainted in the heat and fallen with a shell in his arms, the shell had rolled and knocked down another man. Now there was a milling confusion clogging the alleyway. The two guards moved forward, forcing their way into the press of black bodies, shouting hoarsely and clubbing with the rifle butts. It was the opportunity for which Sebastian had waited.

He stepped over the threshold of the magazine, and went to Walaka beside the cordite shelves.

'Send one of your men to take my place,' he whispered, and reaching up into the folds of his cloak he brought out the cigar box.

With his back towards the door of the magazine, using the cloak as a screen to hide his movements, he slipped the catch of the box and opened the lid.

His hands trembled with haste and nervous agitation as he fumbled with the winder of the travelling-clock. It clicked, and he saw the second hand begin its endless circuit of the dial. Even over the shouts and scuffling in the alleyway, the muted ticking of its mechanism seemed offensively loud to Sebastian. Hastily he shut the lid and glanced guiltily over his shoulder at the doorway. Walaka stood there, and his face was sickly grey with the tension of imminent discovery, but he nodded to Sebastian, a signal that the guards were still occupied without.

Reaching up to the nearest shelf, Sebastian wedged the cigar box between two of the paper-wrapped cylinders of cordite. Then he packed others over it, covering it completely.

He stood back and found with surprise that he was panting, his breathing whistling in his throat, and his legs felt as though they would collapse under him. He could feel the little drops of sweat prickling on his shaven head. In the white electric light they shone like glass beads on his velvety, black-stained skin.

'Is it done?' Walaka croaked beside him.

'It is done,' Sebastian croaked back at him, and suddenly he was overcome with a driving compulsion to be out of this steel room, out of this box-packed room with the ingredients of violent death and destruction; out of the stifling press of bodies that had surrounded him all day. A dreadful thought seized his imagination, suppose the artificer had erred in his assembly of the time charge, suppose that even now the battery was heating the wires of the detonator and bringing them to explosion point. He felt panic as he looked around wildly at the tons of cordite and shell around him. He wanted to run, to fight his way out and up into the open air. He made the first move, and then froze.

The commotion in the alleyway had subsided miraculously, and now only one voice was raised. It came from just outside the doorway, using the curt inflection of authority. Sebastian had heard that voice repeatedly during that long day, and he had come to dread it. It heralded danger.

'Get them back to work immediately,' snapped Lieutenant Kyller as he stepped over the threshold into the magazine. He drew a gold watch from the pocket of his tunic and read the time. 'It is five minutes after seven. There is still almost half an hour before you knock off.' He tucked the watch away, and swept the magazine with a gaze that missed no detail. He was a tall young man, immaculate in his tropical whites. Behind him the two guards were hurriedly straightening their dishevelled uniforms and trying to look efficient and intelligent.

'Yes, sir,' they said in unison.

For a moment Kyller's eyes rested on Sebastian. It was probably because Sebastian was the finest physical specimen among the bearers, he stood taller than the rest of them–as tall as Kyller himself. But Sebastian felt his interest was deeper. He felt that Kyller was searching beneath the stain on his skin, that he was naked of disguise beneath those eyes. He felt that Kyller would remember him, had marked him down in his memory.

'That shelf.' Kyller turned away from Sebastian and crossed the magazine. He went directly to the shelf on which Sebastian had placed his time charge, and he patted the cordite cylinders that Sebastian had handled. They were slightly awry. 'Have it repacked immediately,' said Kyller.

'Right away, sir,' said the fat guard.

Again Kyller's eyes rested on Sebastian. It seemed that he was about to speak, then he changed his mind. He stooped through the doorway and disappeared.

Sebastian stood stony still, appalled by the order that Kyller had given. The fat guard grimaced sulkily.

'Christ, that one is a busy bastard.' And he glared at the cordite shelf. 'There's nothing wrong there.' He crossed to it and fiddled ineffectually. After a moment he asked the guard at the door. 'Has Kyller gone yet?'

'Yes. He's gone down the companion-way into the sick-bay.'

'Good!' grunted the fat one. 'I'm damned if I'm going to waste half an hour repacking this whole batch.' He hunched his shoulders, and screwed up his face with effort. There was a bagpipe squeal, and the guard relaxed and grinned. 'That one was for Lieutenant Kyller, God Bless him!'

79

Darkness was falling, and with it the temperature dropped a few degrees into the high eighties and created an illusion that the faint evening breeze was chilly. Sebastian hugged his cloak around his body, and shuffled along in the slow column of native labourers that dribbled over the side of the German battle cruiser into the waiting launches.

He was exhausted both in body and in mind from the strain of the day's labour in the magazine, so that he went down the catwalk and took his place in the whaler, moving in a state of stupor. When the boat shoved off and puttered up the channel towards the labour camp on the nearest island, Sebastian looked back at *Blücher* with the same dumb stare as the men who squatted beside him on the floorboards of the whaler. Mechanically he registered the fact that Commissioner Fleischer's steam launch was tied up alongside the cruiser.

'Perhaps the fat swine will be aboard when the whole lot blows to hell,' he thought wearily. 'I can at least hope for that.'

He had no way of knowing who else Herman Fleischer had taken aboard the cruiser with him. Sebastian had been below decks toiling in the handling room of the magazine when the launch arrived from up-river, and Rosa Oldsmith had been ushered up the catwalk by the Commissioner in person.

'Come along, Mädchen. We will take you to see the gallant captain of this fine ship.' Fleischer puffed jovially as he mounted the steps behind her. 'I am sure there are many interesting things that you can tell him.'

Bedraggled and exhausted with grief, pale with the horror of her father's death, and with cold hatred for the man who had engineered it, Rosa stumbled as she stepped from the catwalk on to the deck. Her hands were still bound in front of her so she could not check herself. She fell forward, letting herself fall uncaring, and with mild surprise felt hands hold and steady her.

She looked up at the man who had caught her, and in her confusion of mind she thought it was Sebastian. He was tall and dark and his hands were strong. Then she saw the peaked uniform cap with its golden insignia, and she jerked away from him in revulsion.

'Ah! Lieutenant Kyller.' Commissioner Fleischer spoke behind her. 'I have brought you a visitor–a lovely lady.'

'Who is she?' Kyller was appraising Rosa. Rosa could not understand a word that was spoken. She stood in quiet acceptance, her whole body drooping.

'This . . .' answered Fleischer proudly, '. . . is the most dangerous young lady in the whole of Africa. She is one of the leaders of the gang of English bandits that raided the column bringing down the steel plate from Dar es Salaam. It was she who shot and killed your engineer. I captured her and her father this morning. Her father was the notorious O'Flynn.'

'Where is he?' Kyller snapped.

'I hanged him.'

'You hanged him?' demanded Kyller. 'Without trial?'

'No trial was necessary.'

'Without interrogating him?'

'I brought in the woman for interrogation.'

Kyller was angry now, his voice crackled with it.

'I will leave it to Captain von Kleine to judge the wisdom of your actions,' and he turned to Rosa; his eyes dropped to her hands, and, with an exclamation of concern, he took her by the wrist.

'Commissioner Fleischer, how long has this woman been bound?'

Fleischer shrugged. 'I could take no chances on her escaping.'

'Look at this!' Kyller indicated Rosa's hands. They were swollen, the fingers puffy and blue, sticking out stiffly, dead-looking and useless.

'I could take no chances.' Fleischer bridled at the implied criticism.

'Give me your knife,' Kyller snapped at the petty officer in charge of the gangway, and the man produced a large clasp knife. He opened it and handed it to the lieutenant.

Carefully Kyller ran the blade between Rosa's wrists and sawed at the rope. As he bonds dropped away Rosa cried out in pain of fresh blood flowing into her hands.

'You will be lucky if you have not done her permanent damage,' Kyller muttered furiously as he massaged Rosa's bloated hands.

'She is a criminal. A dangerous criminal,' growled Fleischer.

'She is a woman, and therefore deserving of your consideration. Not of this barbarous treatment.'

'She will hang.'

'Her crimes she will answer for, in due course–but until she has stood trial she will be treated as a woman.'

Rosa did not understand the harsh German argument that raged around her. She stood quietly and her eyes were fastened on the knife in Lieutenant Kyller's hand. The hilt brushed her fingers as he worked to restore the circulation of her blood. The blade was long and silver bright, she had seen how keen was its edge by the way in which it had cut through the rope. As she stared at it, it seemed to her fevered fancy that there were two names engraved in the steel of the blade. The names of the two persons she had loved. The names of her father and her child.

With an effort she tore her gaze from the knife and looked at the man she hated. Fleischer had come close up to her, as though to take her away from Lieutenant Kyller's attention. His face was flushed with anger and the fold of flesh under his chin wobbled flabbily as he argued.

Rosa flexed her fingers. They were still numb and stiff, but she could feel the strength flowing back into them. She let her gaze drop down to Fleischer's belly.

It jutted out round and full, soft-looking under the grey corduroy tunic, and again her fevered imagination formed a picture of the blade going into that belly. Slipping in silently, smoothly, burying itself to the hilt, and then drawing upwards to open the flesh like a pouch. The picture was so vivid that Rosa shuddered with the intense sensual pleasure of it.

Kyller was completely occupied with Fleischer. He felt the girl's fingers slide into the cupped palm of his right hand, but before he could pull away she had scooped the knife deftly from his grip. He lunged at her, but she pirouetted lightly away from him. Her knife hand dropped and then darted forward, driven by the full weight of her body at the bulging belly of Herman Fleischer.

Rosa thought that because he was fat he would be slow. She expected him to be stunned by the unexpected attack, to stand and take the knife in his vitals.

Herman Fleischer was fully alert before she even started her thrust. He was fast as a striking mamba, and strong beyond credibility. He did not make the mistake of intercepting the knife with his bare hands. Instead he struck her right shoulder with a clenched fist the size of a carpenter's mallet. The force of the blow knocked her sideways, deflecting the blade from its target. Her arm from the shoulder downwards was paralysed, and the knife flew from her hand and slithered away across the deck.

'Ja!' roared Fleischer triumphantly. 'Ja! So! Now you see how I was right to tie the bitch. She is vicious, dangerous.'

And he lifted the huge fist to smash it into Rosa's face as she crouched, hugging her hurt shoulder, and sobbing with pain and disappointment.

'Enough!' Kyller stepped between them. 'Leave her.'

'She must be tied up like an animal–she is dangerous,' bellowed Fleischer, but Kyller put a protective arm around Rosa's bowed shoulders.

'Petty Officer,' he said. 'Take this woman to the sick-bay. Have Surgeon Commander Buchholz see to her. Guard her carefully, but be gentle with her. Do you hear me?' And they took her away below.

'I must see Captain von Kleine,' Fleischer demanded. 'I must make a full report to him.'

'Come,' said Kyller, 'I will take you to him.'

80

Sebastian lay on his side beside the smoky little fire with his cloak draped over him. Outside he heard the night sounds of the swamp, the faint splash of a fish or a crocodile in the channel, the clink and boom of the tree frogs, the singing of insects, and the lap and sigh of wavelets on the mud bank below the hut.

The hut was one of twenty crude open-sided shelters that housed the native labour force. The earth floor was thickly strewn with sleeping bodies. The sound of their breathing was a restless murmur, broken by the cough and stir of dreamers.

Despite his fatigue, Sebastian was not sleeping, he could not relax from the state of tension in which he had been held all that day. He thought of the little travelling-clock ticking away in its nest of high explosive, measuring out the minutes and the hours, and then his mind side-stepped and went to Rosa. The muscles of his arms tightened with longing. Tomorrow, he thought, tomorrow I will see her and we will go away from this stinking river. Up into the sweet air of the highlands. Again his mind jumped. Seven o'clock, seven o'clock tomorrow morning and it will be over. He remembered Lieutenant Kyller's voice as he stood in the doorway of the magazine with the gold watch in his hand. '. . . The time is five minutes past seven . . .' he had said. So that Sebastian knew to within a few minutes when the time fuse would explode.

He must stop the porters going aboard *Blücher* in the morning. He had impressed on old Walaka that they must refuse to turn out for the next day's shift. They must . . .

'Manali! Manali!' his name was whispered close by in the gloom, and Sebastian lifted himself on one elbow. In the flickering light from the fire there was a shadowy figure, crawling on hands and knees across the earthen floor, and searching the faces of the sleeping men.

'Manali, where are you?'

'Who is it?' Sebastian answered softly, and the man jumped up and scurried to where he lay.

'It is I, Mohammed.'

'Mohammed?' Sebastian was startled. 'Why are you here? You should be with Fini at the camp on the Abati.'

'Fini is dead.' Mohammed's whisper was low with sorrow, so low that Sebastian thought he had misunderstood.

'What? What did you say?'

'Fini is dead. The Allemand came with the ropes. They hung him in the fever trees beside the Abati, and when he was dead they left him for the birds.'

'What talk is this?' Sebastian demanded.

'It is true,' mourned Mohammed. 'I saw it, and when the Allemand had gone, I cut the rope and brought him down. I wrapped him in my own blanket and buried him in an ant-bear hole.'

'Dead? Flynn dead? It isn't true!'

'It is true, Manali.' In the red glow of the camp-fire Mohammed's face was old and raddled and gaunt. He licked his lips. 'There is more, Manali. There is more to tell.'

But Sebastian was not listening. He was trying to force his mind to accept the reality of Flynn's death, but it baulked. It would not accept the picture of Flynn swinging at the rope's end, Flynn with the rope burns at his throat and his face swollen and empurpled, Flynn wrapped in a dirty blanket and crammed into an ant-bear hole. Flynn dead? No! Flynn was too big, too vital–they could not kill Flynn.

'Manali, hear me.'

Sebastian shook his head, bemused, denying it. It could not be true.

'Manali, the Allemand, they have taken Little Long Hair. They have bound her with ropes and taken her.'

Sebastian winced, and jerked away as though he had been struck open-handed across the face.

'No!' He tried to close his mind against the words.

'They caught her this morning early as she went to Fini. They took her down-river in the small boat, and she is now on the great ship of the Allemand.'

'*Blücher?* Rosa is aboard *Blücher*?'

'Yes. She is there.'

'No. Oh, God, *no*!'

In five hours *Blücher* would blow up. In five hours Rosa would die. Sebastian swung his head and looked out into the night, he looked through the open side of the hut, down the channel to where *Blücher* lay at her moorings half a mile away. There was a dim glow of light across the water from the hooded lanterns on *Blücher*'s main deck. But her form was indistinguishable against the dark mass of the mangroves. Between her and the island, the channel was a smooth expanse of velvety blackness on which the reflections of the stars were scattered sequins of light.

'I must go to her,' said Sebastian. 'I cannot let her die there alone.' His voice gathered strength and resolve. 'I cannot let her die. I'll tell the Germans where to find the charge–I'll tell them . . .' Then he faltered. 'I can't. No, I can't. I'd be a traitor then, but, but . . .'

He threw aside his cloak.

'Mohammed, how did you come here? Did you bring the canoe? Where is it?'

Mohammed shook his head. 'No. I swam. My cousin brought me close to the island in the canoe, but he has gone away. We could not leave the canoe here, lest the Askari find it. They would have seen the canoe.'

'There isn't a boat on the island–nothing,' muttered Sebastian. The Germans were careful to guard against deserters. Each night the labour force was marooned on the island–and the Askari patrolled the mud banks.

'Mohammed, hear me now,' Sebastian reached across and laid his hand on the man's shoulders. 'You are my friend. I thank you that you have come to tell me these things.'

'You are going to Little Long Hair?'

'Yes.'

'Go in peace, Manali.'

'Take my place here, Mohammed. When the guards count tomorrow morning, you will stand for me.' Sebastian tightened his grip on the bony shoulder. 'Stay in peace, Mohammed.'

His blackened body blending into the darkness, Sebastian crouched beneath the spread branches of a clump of pampa scrub, and the Askari guard almost brushed against him as he passed. The Askari slouched along with his rifle slung so that the barrel stood up behind his shoulder. The constant patrolling had beaten a path around the circumference of the island, the guard followed it mechanically. Half asleep on his feet, completely unaware of Sebastian's presence. He stumbled in the darkness and swore sleepily, and moved on.

Sebastian crossed the path on his hands and knees, then stretched out on his belly into a reptilian slither as he reached the mud bank. Had he tried to walk across it, the glutinous mud would have sucked so loudly around his feet that every guard within a hundred yards would have heard him.

The mud coated his chest and belly and legs with its coldly loathsome, clinging oiliness, and the reek of it filled his nostrils so he gagged. Then he was into the water. The water was blood warm, he felt the tug of the current and the bottom dropped away beneath him. He swam to the side, careful that neither legs nor arms should break the surface. His head alone showed, like the head of a swimming otter, and he felt the mud washing off his body.

He swam across the current, guided by the distant glimmer of *Blücher*'s deck lights. He swam slowly, husbanding his strength, for he knew he would need all of it later.

His mind was filled with layers of awareness. The lowest layer was a lurking undirected terror of the dark water in which he swam, his dangling legs were vulnerable to the scaly predators which infested the Rufiji river. The current must be carrying his scent down to them. Soon they would come hunting up to find him. But he kept up the easy stroke of arms and legs. It was a chance, one chance of the many he was taking and he tried to ignore it and grapple with the practical problems of his attempt. When he reached *Blücher*, how was he to get aboard her? Her sides were fifty feet high, and the catwalks were the only means of access. These were both heavily guarded. It was a problem without solution, and yet he harried it.

Over this was a thick layer of hopeless sorrow. Sorrow for Flynn.

But the uppermost layer was thickest, strongest. Rosa, Rosa, and Rosa.

He found with surprise that he was saying it aloud.

'Rosa!' with each forward thrust of his body through the water.

'Rosa!' each time he drew breath.

'Rosa!' as his legs kicked out and pushed him towards the *Blücher*.

He did not know what he would do if he reached her. Perhaps there was some half-formed idea of escaping with her, of fighting his way out of *Blücher* with his woman. Getting her away before that moment when the ship would vanish in a holocaust of flame. He did not know, but he swam on quietly.

Then he was under *Blücher*'s side. The towering mass of steel blotted out the starry night sky, and he stopped swimming and hung in the warm water looking up at her.

There were small sounds. The hum of machinery within her, the faint clang of metal struck against metal, the low guttural murmur of voices at her gangway, the thump of a rifle butt against the wooden deck, the soft wash of water around the hull–and then a closer, clearer sound, a regular creak and tap, creak and tap.

He swam in towards the hull, searching for the source of this new sound. It came from near the bows, creak and tap. The creak of rope, and the tap of wood against the steel hull. He saw it then, just above his head. He almost cried out with joy.

The cradles! The platforms still suspended above the water on which the welders and the painters had worked.

He reached up and gripped the wooden edge and drew himself on to the platform. He rested a few seconds and then began to climb the rope. Hand over hand, gripping the rope between the insides of his bare feet, he went up.

His head came level with the deck and he hung there, searching carefully. Fifty yards away he saw two seamen at the gangway. Neither was looking his way.

At intervals the hooded lanterns threw puddles of yellow light upon the deck, but there were concealing shadows beyond them. It was dark around the base of the forward gun-turrets, and there were piles of material, abandoned welding equipment, heaps of rope and canvas in the shadows which would hide him when he had crossed the deck.

Once more he checked the two guards at the gangway, their backs were turned to him.

Sebastian filled his lungs and steeled himself to act. Then with one fluid movement he drew himself up and rolled over the side. He landed lightly on his feet and darted across the exposed deck into the shadows. He ducked down behind a pile of canvas and rope netting, and struggled to control his breathing. He could feel his legs trembling violently under him, so he sat down on the planking and huddled against the protecting pile of canvas. River water trickled from his shaven pate over his forehead and into his eyes. He wiped it away.

'Now what?' He was aboard *Blücher*, but what should he do next?

Where would they hold Rosa? Was there some sort of guard-room for prisoners? Would they put her in one of the officer's cabins? The sick-bay?

He knew roughly where the sick-bay was located. While he was working in the magazine he had heard the one German guard say, 'He has gone down the companion-way to the sick-bay.'

It must be somewhere just below the forward magazine–oh, God! If they had her there she would be almost at the centre of the explosion.

He came up on his knees, and peered over the pile of canvas. It was lighter now. Through the screen of camouflage netting, he could see the night sky had paled a little in the east. Dawn was not far off. The night had passed so swiftly, morning was on its way, and there were but a few scant hours before the hands of the travelling-clock completed their journey, and made the electrical connection that would seal the *Blücher*'s fate, and the fate of all those aboard her.

He must move. He rose slowly and then froze. The guards at the gangway had come to attention. They stood stiffly with their rifles at the slope, and into the light stepped a tall, white-clad figure.

There was no mistaking him. It was the officer that Sebastian had last seen in the forward magazine. Kyller, they had called him, Lieutenant Kyller.

Kyller acknowledged the salutes of the two guards, and he spoke with them a while. Their voices were low and indistinct. Kyller saluted again, and then left them. He came down the deck towards the bows; he walked briskly, and his face below the peak of his cap was in darkness.

Sebastian crouched down again, only his eyes lifted above the piled canvas. He watched the officer and he was afraid.

Kyller stopped in mid-stride. He half stooped to look at the deck at his feet, and then in the same movement, straightened with his right hand dropping to the holstered pistol on his belt.

'Guard!' he bellowed. 'Here! At the double!'

On the holystoned white planking, the wet footprints that Sebastian had left behind him glittered in the lantern light. Kyller started in the direction that they led, coming directly towards Sebastian's hiding-place.

The boots of the two guards pounded heavily along the deck. They had unslung their rifles as they ran to join Kyller.

'Someone has come aboard here. Spread out and search . . .' Kyller shouted at them, as he closed in on Sebastian.

Sebastian panicked. He jumped up and ran, trying to reach the corner of the gun-turret.

'There he is!' Kyller's voice. 'Stop! Stop or I'll fire.'

Sebastian ran. His legs driving powerfully, his elbows pumping, head down, bare feet slapping on the planking, he raced through shadow.

'Stop!' Kyller was balanced on the balls of his feet, legs braced, right shoulder thrust forward and right arm outflung in the classic stance of the pistol marksman. The arm dropped slowly and then kicked up violently, as the shot spouted from the Luger in a ball of yellow flame. The bullet spanged against the plating of the turret and then glanced off in whining ricochet.

Sebastian felt the wind of the bullet pass his head and he jinked his run. The corner of the turret was very close, and he dodged towards it.

Then Kyller's next shot blurted loudly in the night, and simultaneously something struck Sebastian a heavy blow under his left shoulder-blade. It threw him forward off balance and he reeled against the turret, his hands scrabbled at the smooth steel without finding purchase. His body flattened against the side of the turret, so that the blood from the exit hole that the bullet had torn in his breast sprayed on to the pale grey, painted turret.

His legs buckled and he slid down, slowly, still trying to find purchase with the hooked claws of his fingers, so that as his knees touched the deck he was in the attitude of devout prayer. Forehead pressed against the turret, kneeling, arms spread high and wide.

Then the arms sank down, and he slid sideways, collapsed on to the deck, and rolled on to his back.

Kyller came and stood over him. The pistol hanging slackly in the hand at his side.

'Oh, my God,' there was genuine regret in Kyller's voice. 'It's only one of the porters. Why did the fool run! I wouldn't have fired if he had stood.'

Sebastian wanted to ask him where Rosa was. He wanted to explain that Rosa was his wife, that he loved her, and that he had come to find her.

He concentrated his vision on Kyller's face as it hung over him, and he summoned his school-boy German, marshalling the sentences in his mind.

But as he opened his mouth the blood welled up in his throat and choked him. He coughed, racking, and the blood bubbled through his lips in a pink froth.

'Lung shot!' said Kyller, and then to the guards as they came up, 'Get a stretcher. Hurry. We must take him down to the sick-bay.'

81

There were twelve bunks in *Blücher*'s sick-bay, six down each side of the narrow cabin. In eight of them lay German seamen; five malaria cases and three men injured in the work of repairing her bows.

Rosa Oldsmith was in the bunk farthest from the door. She lay behind a movable screen, and a guard sat outside the screen. He wore a pistol at his belt and was wholly absorbed in a year-old variety magazine, the cover of which depicted a buxom blonde woman in a black corset and high boots, with a horse whip in her one hand.

The cabin was brightly lit and smelled of antiseptic. One of the malarial cases was in delirium, and he laughed and shouted. The medical orderly moved along the rows of bunks carrying a metal tray from which he administered the morning dosages of quinine. The time was 5 a.m.

Rosa had slept only intermittently during the night. She lay on top of the blankets and she wore a striped towelling dressing-gown over the blue flannel night-gown. The gown was many sizes too large and she had rolled back the cuffs of the sleeves. Her hair was loose on the pillows, and damp at the temples with sweat. Her face was pale and drawn, with bluish smudges of fatigue under her eyes, and her shoulder ached dully where Fleischer had struck her.

She was awake now. She lay staring up at the low roof of the cabin, playing over in her mind fragments from the happenings of the last twenty-four hours.

She recalled the interrogation with Captain von Kleine. He had sat opposite her in his luxuriously furnished cabin, and his manner had been kindly, his voice gentle, pronouncing the English words with blurring of the consonants and a hardening of the vowel sounds. His English was good.

'When did you last eat?' he asked her.

'I am not hungry,' she replied, making no attempt to conceal her hatred. Hating them all–this handsome, gentle man, the tall lieutenant who stood beside him, and Herman Fleischer who sat across the cabin from her, with his knees spread apart to accommodate the full hang of his belly.

'I will send for food.' Von Kleine ignored her protest and rang for his steward. When the food came, she could not deny the demands of her body and she ate, trying to show no enjoyment. The sausage and pickles were delicious, for she had not eaten since the previous noon.

Courteously von Kleine turned his attention to a discussion with Lieutenant Kyller until she had finished, but when the steward removed the empty tray he came back to her.

'Herr Fleischer tells me you are the daughter of Major O'Flynn, the commander of the Portuguese irregulars operating in German territory?'

'I was until he was hanged, murdered! He was injured and helpless. They tied him to a stretcher . . .' Rosa flared at him, tears starting in her eyes.

'Yes,' von Kleine stopped her, 'I know. I am not pleased. That is now a matter between myself and Commissioner Fleischer. I can only say that I am sorry. I offer you my condolence.' He paused and glanced at Herman Fleischer. Rosa could see by the angry blue of his eyes that he meant what he said.

'But now there are some questions I must ask you . . .'

Rosa had planned her replies, for she knew what he would ask. She replied frankly and truthfully to anything that did not jeopardize Sebastian's attempt to place the time fuse aboard *Blücher*.

What were she and Flynn doing when they were captured? Keeping the *Blücher* under surveillance. Waiting to signal her departure to the blockading cruisers.

How did the British know that Blücher was in the Rufiji? The steel plate, of course. Then confirmation by aerial reconnaissance.

Were they contemplating offensive action against Blücher? No, they would wait until she sailed.

What was the strength of the blockade squadron? Two cruisers that she had seen, she did not know if there were other warships waiting over the horizon.

Von Kleine phrased his questions carefully, and listened attentively to her replies. For an hour the interrogation continued, until Rosa was yawning openly, and her voice was slurred with exhaustion. Von Kleine realized that there was nothing to be learned from her, all she had told him he already knew or had guessed.

'Thank you,' he finished. 'I am keeping you aboard my ship. There will be danger here, for soon I will be going out to meet the British warships. But I believe that it will be better for you than if I handed you over to the German administration ashore.' He hesitated a moment and glanced at Commissioner Fleischer. 'In every nation there are evil men, fools and barbarians. Do not judge us all by one man.'

With distaste at her own treachery, Rosa found that she could not hate this man. A weary smile tugged her mouth and she answered him.

'You are kind.'

'Lieutenant Kyller will see you to the hospital. I am sorry I can offer you no better quarters, but this is a crowded vessel.'

When she had gone, von Kleine lit a cheroot and while he tasted its comforting fragrance, he allowed his eyes to rest on the portrait of the two golden women across the cabin. Then he sat up in his chair and his voice had lost its gentleness as he spoke to the man who lolled on the couch.

'Herr Fleischer, I find it difficult to express fully my extreme displeasure at your handling of this affair . . .'

After a night of fitful sleep, Rosa lay on her hospital bunk behind the screen and she thought of her husband. If things had gone well Sebastian must by now have placed the time charge and escaped from *Blücher*. Perhaps he was already on his way to the rendezvous on the Abati river. If this were so, then she would not see him again. It was her one regret. She imagined him in his ludicrous disguise, and she smiled a little. Dear lovable Sebastian. Would he ever know what had happened to her? Would he know that she had died with those whom she hated? She hoped that he would never know–that he would never torture himself with the knowledge that he had placed the instrument of her death with his own hands.

I wish I could see him just once more to tell him that my death is unimportant beside the death of Herman Fleischer, beside the destruction of this German warship. I wish only that when the time comes, I could see it. I wish there were some way I could know the exact time of the explosion so I could tell Herman Fleischer a minute before, when it is too late for him to escape, and watch him. Perhaps he would blubber, perhaps he would scream with fear. I would like that. I would like that very much.

The strength of her hatred was such that she could no longer lie still. She sat up and tied the belt of her gown around her waist. She was filled with a restless itchy exhilaration. It would be today–she felt sure–sometime today she would slake this burning thirst for vengeance that had tormented her for so long.

She threw her legs over the side of the bunk and pulled open the screen. The guard dropped his magazine and started up from his chair, his hand dropping to the pistol at his hip.

'I will not harm you . . .' Rosa smiled at him, '. . . not yet!'

She pointed to the door which led into the tiny shower cabinet and toilet. The guard relaxed and nodded acquiescence. He followed her as she crossed the cabin.

Rosa walked slowly between the bunks, looking at the sick men that lay in them.

'All of you,' she thought happily. 'All of you!'

She slid the tongue of the lock across, and was alone in the bathroom. She undressed, and leaned across the wash-basin to the small mirror set above it. She could see the reflection of her head and shoulders. There was a purple and red bruise spreading down from her neck and staining the white swell of her right breast. She touched it tenderly with her finger-tips.

'Herman Fleischer,' she said the name gloatingly, 'it will be today–I promise you that. Today you will die.'

And then suddenly she was crying.

'I only wish you could burn as my baby burned–I wish you could choke and swing on the rope as my father did.' And the tears fell fat and slow, sliding down her cheeks to drop into the basin. She started to sob, dry convulsive gasps of grief and hatred. She turned blindly to the shower cabinet, and turned both taps full on so that the rush of the water would cover the sound of her weeping. She did not want them to hear it.

Later, when she had bathed her face and body and combed her hair and dressed again, she unlocked the door and stepped through it. She stopped abruptly and through puffy reddened eyes tried to make sense of what was happening in the sick-bay.

It was crowded. The surgeon was there, two orderlies, four German seamen, and the young lieutenant. All of them hovered about the stretcher that was being manœuvred between the bunks. There was a man on the stretcher, she could see his form under the single grey blanket that covered him, but Lieutenant Kyller's back obscured her view of the man's face. There was blood on the blanket, and a brown smear of blood on the sleeve of Kyller's white tunic.

She moved along the bulkhead of the cabin and craned her head to see around Kyller, but at that moment one of the orderlies leaned across to swab the mouth of the man on the stretcher with a white cloth. The cloth obscured the wounded man's face. Bright frothy blood soaked through the material, and the sight of it nauseated Rosa. She averted her gaze and slipped away towards her own bunk at the end of the cabin. She reached the screen, and behind her somebody groaned. It was a low delirious groan, but the sound of it stopped Rosa instantly. She felt as though something within her chest was swelling to stifle her. Slowly, fearfully, she turned back.

They were lifting the man from the stretcher to lay him on an empty bunk. The head lolled sideways, and beneath its stain of bark juice Rosa saw that dear, well loved face.

'Sebastian!' she cried, and she ran to him, pushing past Kyller, throwing herself on to the blanket-draped body, trying to get her arms around him to hug him.

'Sebastian! What have they done to you!'

82

'Sebastian! Sebastian!' Rosa leaned across him and held her mouth to his ear.

'Sebastian!' She called his name quietly but urgently, then brushed his forehead with her lips. The skin was cold and damp.

He lay on his back with the bed clothes turned back to his waist. His chest was swathed in bandages, and his breathing sawed and gurgled.

'Sebastian. It's Rosa. It's Rosa. Wake up, Sebastian. Wake up, it's Rosa.'

'Rosa?' At last her name had reached him. He whispered it painfully, wetly, and fresh blood stained his lips.

Rosa had been on the edge of despair. Two hours she had been sitting beside him. Since the surgeon had finished dressing the wound, she had sat with him–touching him, calling to him. This was the first sign of recognition he had given her.

'Yes! Yes! It's Rosa. Wake up, Sebastian.' Her voice lifted with relief.

'Rosa?' His eyelashes trembled.

'Wake up.' She pinched his cold cheek and he winced. His eyelids fluttered open.

'Rosa?' on a shallow, sawing breath.

'Here, Sebastian. I'm here.' His eyes rolled in their sockets, searching, trying desperately to focus.

'Here,' she said, leaning over him and taking his face between her hands. She looked into his eyes.

'Here, my darling, here!'

'Rosa!' His lips convulsed into a dreadful parody of a smile.

'Sebastian, did you set the bomb?'

His breathing changed, hoarser, and his mouth twitched with the effort.

'Tell them,' he whispered.

'Tell them what?'

'Seven. Must stop it.'

'Seven o'clock?'

'Don't–want–you–'

'Will it explode at seven o'clock?'

'You–' It was too much and he coughed.

'Seven o'clock? Is that it, Sebastian?'

'You will . . .' He squeezed his eyes closed, putting all his strength into the effort of speaking. 'Please. Don't die. Stop it.'

'Did you set it for seven o'clock?' In her impatience she tugged his head towards her. 'Tell me, for God's sake, tell me!'

'Seven o'clock. Tell them–tell them.'

Still holding him, she looked at the clock set high up on the bulkhead of the sick-bay.

On the white dial, the ornate black hands stood at fifteen minutes before the hour.

'Don't die, please don't die,' mumbled Sebastian.

She hardly heard the pain-muted pleading. A fierce surge of triumph lifted her–she knew the hour. The exact minute. Now she could send for Herman Fleischer, and have him with her.

Gently she laid Sebastian's head back on the pillow. On the table below the clock she had seen a pad and pencil among the bottles and jars, and trays of instruments. She went to it, and while the guard watched her suspiciously she scribbled a note.

Captain,

My husband is conscious. He has a message of vital importance for Commissioner Fleischer. He will speak to no one but Commissioner Fleischer. The message could save your ship.

Rosa Oldsmith

She folded the sheet of paper and pushed it into the guard's hand.

'For the Captain. Captain.'

'Kapitan,' repeated the guard. 'Jawohl.' And he went to the door of the sick-bay. She saw him speak with the second guard outside the door, and then pass him the note.

Rosa sank down on the edge of Sebastian's bunk. She ran her hand tenderly over his shaven head. The new hair was stiff and bristly under her fingers.

'Wait for me. I'm coming with you, my darling. Wait for me.'

But he had lapsed back into unconsciousness. Crooning softly, she gentled him. Smiling to herself, happily, she waited for the minute hand of the clock to creep up to the zenith of the dial.

83

Captain Arthur Joyce had personally supervised the placing of the scuttling charges. Perhaps, long ago, another man had felt the way he did–hearing the command spoken from the burning bush, and knowing he must obey.

The charges were small, but laid in twenty places against the bare plating, they would rip *Renounce*'s belly out of her cleanly. The watertight bulkhead had been opened to let the water rush through her. The magazines had all of them been flooded to minimize the danger of explosion. The furnaces had been damped down, and he had blown the pressure on his boilers–retaining a head of steam, just sufficient to take *Renounce* in on her last run into the channel of the Rufiji.

The cruiser had been stripped of her crew. Twenty men left aboard her to handle the ship. The rest of them transhipped aboard *Pegasus*.

Joyce was going to attempt to force the log boom, take *Renounce* through the minefield, and sink her higher up, where the double mouth of the channel merged into a single thoroughfare.

If he succeeded he would effectively have blocked *Blücher*, and sacrificed a single ship.

If he failed, if *Renounce* sank in the minefield before she reached the confluence of the two channels, then Armstrong would have to take *Pegasus* in and scuttle her also. On his bridge Joyce sat hunched in his canvas deck chair, looking out at the land; the green line of Africa which the morning sun lit in harsh golden brilliance.

Renounce was running parallel to the coast, five miles off shore. Behind her *Pegasus* trailed like a mourner at a funeral.

'06.45 hours, sir.' The officer of the watch saluted.

'Very well.' Joyce roused himself. Until this moment he had hoped. Now the time had come and *Renounce* must die.

'Yeoman of Signals,' he spoke quietly, 'make this signal with *Pegasus* number "Plan A Effective".' This was the code that *Renounce* was to stand in for the channel. 'Stand by to pick up survivors.'

'*Pegasus* acknowledges, sir.'

Joyce was glad that Armstrong has not sent some inane message such as 'Good luck'. A curt acknowledgement, that was as it should be.

'All right, Pilot,' he said, 'take us in, please.'

84

It was a beautiful morning and a flat sea. The captain of the escort destroyer wished it were not, he would have forfeited a year's seniority for a week of fog and rain.

As his ship tore down the line of transports to administer a rebuke to the steamer at the end of the column for not keeping proper station, he looked out at the western horizon. Visibility was perfect, a German masthead would be able to pick out this convoy of fat sluggish transports at a distance of thirty miles.

Twelve ships, fifteen thousand men–and *Blücher* could be out. At any moment she could come hurtling up over the horizon, with those long nine-inch guns blazing. The thought gave him the creeps. He jumped up from his stool, and crossed to the port rail of his bridge to glower at the convoy.

Close alongside wallowed one of the transports. They were playing cricket on her afterdeck. As he watched, a sun-bronzed giant of a South African clad only in short khaki pants swung the bat and cleanly he heard the crack as it struck the ball. The ball soared up and dropped into the sea with a tiny splash.

'Oh, good shot, sir!' applauded the lieutenant who stood beside the captain.

'This is not the members' enclosure at Lords, Mr Parkinson,' snarled the destroyer captain. 'If you have nothing to occupy you, I can find duties for you.'

The lieutenant retired hurt, and the captain glanced along the line of troopships.

'Oh, no!' he groaned. Number Three was making smoke again. Ever since leaving Durban harbour Number Three had been giving periodic impersonations of Mount Vesuvius. It would be a give-away to the look-out at *Blücher*'s masthead.

He reached for his megaphone, ready to hurl the most scathing reprimand he could master at Number Three as he passed her.

'This is worse than being a teacher in a kindergarten. They'll break me yet.' And he lifted the megaphone to his lips as Number Three came abreast.

The infantry men that lined the troopships' rail cheered his eloquence to the echo.

'The fools. Let them cheer *Blücher* when she comes,' growled the captain and crossed the bridge to gaze apprehensively into the west where Africa lay just below the horizon.

'Strength to *Renounce* and *Pegasus*.' He made the wish fervently. 'God grant they hold *Blücher*. If she gets through . . .'

85

'It's no use, Bwana. They won't move,' the sergeant of Askari reported to Ensign Proust.

'What is the trouble?' demanded Proust.

'They say there is a bad magic on the ship. They will not go to her today.'

Proust looked over the mass of black humanity. They squatted sullenly among the huts and palm trees, rank upon rank of them, huddled in their cloaks, faces closed and secretive.

Drawn up on the mud beaches of the island were two motor launches, ready to ferry the bearers downstream to the day's labour aboard *Blücher*. The German seamen tending the launches were watching with interest this charade of dumb rebellion, and Ensign Proust was very conscious of their attention.

Proust was at the age where he had an iron-clad faith in his own sagacity, the dignity of a patriarch, and pimples.

He was, in other words, nineteen years of age.

It was clear to him that these native tribesmen had embarked on their present course of action for no other reason than to embarrass Ensign Proust. It was a direct and personal attack on his standing and authority.

He lifted his right hand to his mouth and began to feed thoughtfully on his fingernails. His rather prominent Adam's apple moved in sympathy with the working of his jaws. Suddenly he realized what he was doing. It was a habit he was trying to cure, and he jerked his hand away and linked it with its mate behind his back, in a faithful imitation of Captain Otto von Kleine, a man whom he held in high admiration. It had hurt him deeply when Lieutenant Kyller had greeted his request for permission to grow a beard like Captain von Kleine's with ribald laughter.

Now he sank his bare chin on to his chest and began to pace solemnly up and down the small clearing above the mud bank. The sergeant of Askari waited respectfully with his men drawn up behind him for Ensign Proust to reach a decision.

He could send one of the launches back to *Blücher*, to fetch Commissioner Fleischer. After all, this was really the Herr Commissioner's shauri (Proust had taken to using odd Swahili words like an old African hand). Yet he realized that to call for Fleischer would be an admission that he was unable to handle the situation. Commissioner Fleischer would jeer at him, Commissioner Fleischer had shown an increasing tendency to jeer at Ensign Proust.

'No,' he thought, flushing so that the red spots on his skin were less noticeable, 'I will not send for that fat peasant.' He stopped pacing and addressed himself to the sergeant of Askari.

'Tell them . . .' he started, and his voice squeaked alarmingly. He adjusted the timbre to a deep throaty rumble, 'Tell them I take a very serious view of this matter.'

The sergeant saluted, did a showy about-face with much feet stamping, and passed on Ensign Proust's message in loud Swahili. From the dark ranks of bearers there was no reaction whatosever, not so much as a raised eyebrow. The crews of the launches were more responsive. One of them laughed.

Ensign Proust's Adam's apple bobbed, and his ears chameleoned to the colour of a good burgundy.

'Tell them that it is *mutiny*!' The last word squeaked again, and the sergeant hesitated while he groped for the Swahili equivalent. Finally he settled for:

'Bwana Heron is very angry.' Proust had been nicknamed for his pointed nose and long thin legs. The tribesmen bore up valiantly under this intelligence.

'Tell them I will take drastic steps.'

Now, thought the sergeant, he is making sense. He allowed himself literary licence in his translation.

'Bwana Heron says that there are trees on this island for all of you–and he has sufficient rope.'

A sigh blew through them, soft and restless as a small wind in a field of wheat. Heads turned slowly until they were all looking at Walaka.

Reluctantly Walaka stood up to reply. He realized that it was foolhardy to draw attention to himself when there was talk of ropes in the air, but the damage had already been done. The hundreds of eyes upon him had singled him out to the Allemand. Bwana Intanbu always hanged the man that everyone looked at.

Walaka began to speak. His voice had the soothing quality of a rusty gate squeaking in the wind. It went on and on, as Walaka attempted a one-man filibust.

'What is he talking about?' demanded Ensign Proust.

'He is talking about leopards,' the sergeant told him.

'What is he saying about them?'

'He says, among other things, that they are the excrement of dead lepers.'

Proust looked stunned, he had expected Walaka's speech to have at least some bearing on the business in hand. He rallied gamely.

'Tell him that he is a wise old man, and that I look to him to lead the others to their duties.'

And the sergeant gazed upon Walaka sternly.

'Bwana Heron says that you, Walaka, are the son of a diseased porcupine and that you feed on offal with the vultures. He says further that you he has chosen to lead the others in the dance of the rope.'

Walaka stopped talking. He sighed in resignation and started down towards the waiting launch. Five hundred men stood up and followed him.

The two vessels chugged sedately down to *Blücher*'s moorings. Standing in the bows of the leading launch with his hands on his hips, Ensign Proust had the proud bearing of a Viking returning from a successful raid.

'I understand these people,' he would tell Lieutenant Kyller. 'You must pick out their leader and appeal to his sense of duty.'

He took his watch from his breast pocket.

'Fifteen minutes to seven,' he murmured. 'I'll have them aboard on the hour.' He turned and smiled fondly at Walaka who squatted miserably beside the wheel-house.

'Good man, that! I'll bring his conduct to Lieutenant Kyller's attention.'

86

Lieutenant Ernst Kyller shrugged out of his tunic and sat down on his bunk. He held the tunic in his lap and fingered the sleeve. The smear of blood had dried, and as he rubbed the material between his thumb and forefinger, the blood crumbled and flaked.

'He should not have run. I had to shoot.'

He stood up and hung the tunic in the little cupboard at the head of his bunk. Then he took his watch from the pocket and sat down again to wind it.

'Fifteen minutes to seven.' He noted the time mechanically, and laid the gold hunter on the flap table beside the bunk. Then he lay back and arranged the pillows under his head, he crossed his still-booted feet and regarded them dispassionately.

'He came aboard to try and rescue his wife. It was the natural thing to do. But that disguise–the shaven head, and stained skin–that must have been carefully thought out. It must have taken time to arrange.'

Kyller closed his eyes. He was tired. It had been a long and eventful watch. Yet there was something nagging him, a feeling that there was an important detail that he had overlooked, a detail of vital–no, of deadly importance.

Within two minutes of the girl's recognition of the wounded man, Kyller and the surgeon commander had established that he was not a native, but a white man disguised as one.

Kyller's English was sketchy, but he had understood the girl's cries of love and concern and accusation.

'You've killed him also. You've killed them all. My baby, my father–and now my husband. You murderers, you filthy murdering swines!'

Kyller grimaced and pressed his knuckles into his aching eyes. Yes, he had understood her.

When he had reported to Captain von Kleine, the captain had placed little importance on the incident.

'Is the man conscious?'

'No, sir.'

'What does the surgeon say his chances are?'

'He will die. Probably before midday.'

'You did the right thing, Kyller.' Von Kleine touched his shoulder in a show of understanding. 'Do not reproach yourself. It was your duty.'

'Thank you, sir.'

'You are off watch now. Go to your cabin and rest–that is an order. I want you fresh and alert by nightfall.'

'Is it tonight then, sir?'

'Yes. Tonight we sail. The minefield has been cleared and I have given the order for the boom to be destroyed. The new moon sets at 11.47. We will sail at midnight.'

But Kyller could not rest. The girl's face, pale, smeared with her tears, haunted him. The strangled breathing of the dying man echoed in his ears, and that nagging doubt scratched against his nerves.

There was something he must remember. He flogged his tired brain, and it balked.

Why was the man disguised? If he came as soon as he had heard that his wife was a prisoner he would not have had time to effect the disguise.

Where had the man been when Fleischer had captured his wife? He had not been there to protect her. Where had he been? It must have been somewhere near at hand.

Kyller rolled on to his stomach and pressed his face into the pillow. He must rest. He must sleep now for tonight they would go out to break through the blockading English warships.

A single ship against a squadron. Their chances of slipping through unchallenged were small. There would be a night action. His imagination was heightened by fatigue, and behind his closed eyelids he saw the English cruisers, lit by the flashes of their own broadsides as they closed with *Blücher*. The enemy intent on vengeance. The enemy in overwhelming strength. The enemy strong and freshly provisioned, their coal-bunkers glutted, their magazines crammed with shell, their crews uncontaminated by the fever miasma of the Rufiji.

Against them a single ship with her battle damage hastily patched, half her men sick with malaria, burning green cord-wood in her furnaces, her fire-power hampered by the desperate shortage of shell.

He remembered the tiers of empty shell racks, the depleted cordite shelves in the forward magazine.

The magazine? That was it? The magazine! It was something about the magazine that he must remember. That was the thing that had been nagging him. The magazine!

'Oh, my God!' he shouted in horror. In one abrupt movement he had leapt from his prone position on the bunk to stand in the centre of his cabin.

The skin on his bare upper arms prickled with goose-flesh.

That was where he had seen the Englishman before. He had been with the labour party–in the forward magazine.

He would have been there for one reason only–sabotage.

Kyller burst from his cabin, and raced, half dressed, along the corridor.

'I must get hold of Commander Lochtkamper. We'll need a dozen men–strong men–stokers. There are tons of explosive to move, we'll have to handle it all to find whatever the Englishman placed there. Please, God, give us time. Give us time!'

87

Captain Otto von Kleine bit the tip from the end of his cheroot, and removed a flake of tobacco from the tip of his tongue with thunb and forefinger. His steward held a match for him and von Kleine lit the cheroot. At the wardroom table, the chairs of Lochtkamper, Kyller, Proust, and one other were empty.

'Thank you, Schmidt,' he said through the smoke. He pushed his chair back and stretched out his legs, crossing his ankles and laying his shoulders against the padded back-rest. The breakfast had not been of gourmet standard; bread without butter, fish taken from the river and strong with the taste of the mud, washed down with black unsweetened coffee. Nevertheless, Herr Fleischer seemed to be enjoying it. He was beginning his third plateful.

Von Kleine found his appreciative snuffling distracting. This would be the last period of relaxation that von Kleine could anticipate in the next many days. He wanted to savour it along with his cheroot, the wardroom was not the place to do so. Apart from the gusto with which the Herr Commissioner was demolishing his breakfast, and the smell of fish–there was a mood among his officers that was almost tangible. This was the last day and it was heavy with the prospect of what the night might bring. They were all of them edgy and tense. They ate in silence, keeping their attention on their plates, and it was obvious that most of them had slept badly. Von Kleine decided to finish his cheroot alone in his cabin. He stood up.

'Excuse me please, gentlemen.'

A polite murmur, and von Kleine turned to leave.

'Yes, Schmidt. What is it?' His steward was standing deferentially in his path.

'For you, sir.'

Von Kleine clamped the cheroot between his teeth and took the note in both hands, screwing up his eyes against the blue spiral of tobacco smoke. He frowned.

This woman, and the man she claimed was her husband, worried him. They were a drain on the attention which he should be devoting entirely to the problem of getting *Blücher* ready for tonight. Now this message–what could she mean by 'could save your ship'? He felt a prickle of apprehension.

He swung around.

'Herr Commissioner, a moment of your time, please.'

Fleischer looked up from his food with a smear of grease on his chin.

'Ja?'

'Come with me.'

'I will just finish . . .'

'Immediately, please.' And to avert argument von Kleine stomped out of the wardroom, leaving Herman Fleischer in terrible indecision, but he was a man for the occasion, he took the remaining piece of fish on his plate and put it in his mouth. It was a tight fit, but he still found space for the half cup of coffee as well. Then he scooped up a slice of bread and wiped his plate hurriedly. With the bread in his hand he lumbered after von Kleine.

He was still masticating as he entered the sick-bay behind von Kleine. He stopped in surprise.

The woman sat on one of the bunks. She had a cloth in her hand and with it she wiped the mouth of a black man who lay there. There was blood on the cloth. She looked up at Fleischer. Her expression was soft with compassion and sorrow, but it changed the moment she saw Fleischer. She stood up quickly.

'Oh, thank God, you've come,' she cried with joy as though she were greeting a dear friend. Then incongruously she looked up at the clock.

Keeping warily away from her, Fleischer worked his way around to the opposite side of the bunk by which she stood. He leaned over and studied the face of the dying man. There was something very familiar about it. He chewed stolidly as he puzzled over it. It was the association with the woman that triggered his memory.

He made a choking sound, and bits of half chewed bread flew from his mouth.

'Captain!' he shouted, 'this is one of them–one of the English bandits.'

'I know,' said von Kleine.

'Why wasn't I told? This man must be executed immediately. Even now it might be too late. Justice will be cheated.'

'Please, Herr Commissioner. The woman has an important message for you.'

'This is monstrous. I should have been told . . .'

'Be still,' snapped von Kleine. Then to Rosa, 'You sent for me? What is it you have to tell us?'

With one hand Rosa was stroking Sebastian's head, but she was looking up at the clock.

'You must tell Herr Fleischer that the time is one minute before seven.'

'I beg your pardon?'

'Tell him exactly as I say it.'

'Is this a joke?'

'Tell him, quickly. There is very little time.'

'She says the time is one minute to seven' von Kleine rattled out the translation. Then in English, 'I have told him.'

'Tell him that at seven o'clock he will die.'

'What is the meaning of that?'

'Tell him first. Tell him!' insisted Rosa.

'She says that you will die at seven o'clock.' And Fleischer interrupted his impatient gobbling over the prone form of Sebastian. He stared at the woman for a moment, then he giggled uncertainly.

'Tell her I feel very well,' he said, and laughed again, 'better than this one here.' He prodded Sebastian. 'Ja, much better.' And his laughter came full and strong, booming in the confined space of the sick-bay.

'Tell him my husband has placed a bomb in this ship, and it will explode at seven o'clock.'

'Where?' demanded von Kleine.

'Tell him first.'

'If this is true you are in danger also–where is it?'

'Tell Fleischer what I said.'

'There is a bomb in the ship.' And Fleischer stopped laughing.

'She is lying,' he spluttered. 'English lies.'

'Where is the bomb?' von Kleine had grasped Rosa's arm.

'It is too late,' Rosa smiled complacently. 'Look at the clock.'

'Where is it?' Von Kleine shook her wildly in his agitation.

'In the *magazine*! The forward magazine.'

'In the *magazine*! Sweet merciful Jesus!' von Kleine swore in German, and turned for the door.

'The magazine?' shouted Fleischer and started after him. 'It is impossible–it can't be.' But he was running, wildly, desperately, and behind him he heard Rosa Oldsmith's triumphant laughter.

'You are dead. Like my baby–dead, like my father. It is too late to run, much too late!'

88

Von Kleine went up the companion-way steps three at a time. He came out into the alleyway that led to the magazine, and stopped abruptly.

The alleyway was almost blocked by a mountain of cordite charges thrown haphazard from the magazine by a knot of frantically busy stokers.

'What are you doing?' he shouted.

'Lieutenant Kyller is looking for a bomb.'

'Has he found it?' Von Kleine demanded as he brushed past them.

'Not yet, sir.'

Von Kleine paused again in the entrance to the magazine. It was a shambles. Led by Kyller, men were tearing at the stacks of cordite, sweeping them from the shelves, ransacking the magazine.

Von Kleine jumped forward to help.

'Why didn't you send for me?' he asked as he reached up to the racks above his head.

'No time, sir,' grunted Kyller beside him.

'How did you know about the bomb?'

'It's a guess–I could be wrong, sir.'

'You're right! The woman told us. It's set for seven o'clock.'

'Help us God! Help us!' pleaded Kyller, and hurled himself at the next shelf.

'It could be anywhere–anywhere!' Captain von Kleine worked like a stevedore, knee-deep in spilled cylinders of cordite.

'We should clear the ship. Get the men off.' Kyller attacked the next rack.

'No time. We've got to find it.'

Then in the uproar there was a small sound, a muffled tinny buzz. The alarm bell of a travelling-clock.

'There!' shouted Kyller. 'That's it!' And he dived across the magazine at the same moment as von Kleine did. They collided and fell, but Kyller was up instantly, dragging himself on to his feet with hands clawing at the orderly rack of cordite cylinders.

The buzz of the clock seemed to roar in his ears. He reached out and his hands fell on the smoothly paper wrapped parcel of death, and at that instant the two copper terminals within the leather case of the clock that had been creeping infinitesimally slowly towards each other for the past twelve hours, made contact.

Electricity stored in the dry cell battery flowed through the circuit, reached the hair-thin filament in the detonator cap, and heated it white-hot. The detonator fired, transferring its energy into the sticks of gelignite that were packed into the cigar box. The wave of explosion leapt from molecule to molecule with the speed of light so that the entire contents of *Blücher*'s magazine were consumed in one hundredth part of a second. With it were consumed Lieutenant Kyller and Captain von Kleine and the men about them.

In the centre of that fiery holocaust they burned to vapour.

The blast swept through *Blücher*. Downwards through two decks with a force that blew the belly out of her as easily as popping a paper bag, down through ten fathoms of water to strike the bottom of the river and the shock wave bounced up to raise fifteen-foot waves along the surface.

It blew sideways through *Blücher*'s watertight bulkheads, crumpling and tearing them like silver paper.

It caught Rosa Oldsmith as she lay across Sebastian's chest, hugging him. She did not even hear it come.

It caught Herman Fleischer just as he reached the deck, and shredded him to nothingness.

It swept through the engine room and burst the great boilers, releasing millions of cubic feet of scalding steam to race through the ship.

It blew upwards through the deck, lifting the forward gun-turret off its seating, tossing the hundreds of tons of steel high in a cloud of steam and smoke and debris.

It killed every single human being aboard. It did more that merely kill them, it reduced them to gas and minute particles of flesh or bone. Then still unsatisfied, its fury unabated, it blew outwards from *Blücher*'s shattered hulk, a mighty wind that tore the branches from the mangrove forest and stripped it of leaves.

It lifted a column of smoke and flame writhing and twisting into the bright morning sky above the Rufiji delta, and the waves swept across the river as though from the eye of a hurricane.

They overwhelmed the two launches that were approaching *Blücher*, pouring over them and capsizing them, swirling them over and over and spilling their human cargo into the frightened frothing water.

And the shock waves rolled on across the delta to burst thunderously against the far hills, or to dissipate out on the vastness of the Indian Ocean.

They passed over the British cruiser *Renounce* as she entered the channel between the mangroves. They rolled overhead like giant cannon-balls across the roof of the sky.

Captain Arthur Joyce leapt to the rail of his bridge, and he saw the column of agonized smoke rise from the swamps ahead of him. A grotesque living thing, unbelievable in its size, black and silver and shot through with flame.

'They've done it!' shouted Arthur Joyce. 'By Jove, they've done it!'

He was shaking; his whole body juddering, his face white as ice, and his eyes which he could not drag from that spinning column of destruction that rose into the sky, filled slowly with tears. He let them overflow his eyelids and run unashamedly down his cheeks.

89

Two old men walked into a grove of fever trees that stood on the south bank of the Abati river. They stopped beside a pile of gargantuan bones from which the scavengers had picked the flesh, leaving them scattered and white.

'The tusks are gone,' said Walaka.

'Yes,' agreed Mohammed, 'the Askari came back and stole them.'

Together they walked on through the fever trees and then they stopped again. There was a low mound of earth at the edge of the grove. Already it had settled and new grass was growing upon it.

'He was a man,' said Walaka.

'Leave me, my cousin. I will stay here a while.'

'Stay in peace, then,' said Walaka, and settled the string of his blanket roll more comfortably over his shoulder before he walked on.

Mohammed squatted down beside the grave. He sat there unmoving all that day. Then in the evening Mohammed stood up and walked away towards the south.

ITH WILBUR SMIT
R SMITH WILBUR
ITH WILBUR SMIT
R SMITH WILBUR
ITH WILBUR SMIT
R SMITH WILBUR
ITH WILBUR SMIT
R SMITH WILBUR
ITH WILBUR SMIT
R SMITH WILBUR
ITH WILBUR SMIT
R SMITH WILBUR